Wilbur Smith

The World's Greatest and Most Popular Writer of Epic Adventure

'Wilbur Smith rarely misses a trick'
Sunday Times

'The world's leading adventure writer'
Daily Express

'Action is the name of Wilbur Smith's game and he is a master'
Washington Post

'The pace would do credit to a Porsche, and the invention is as bright and explosive as a firework display'
Sunday Telegraph

'A violent saga set in Boer War South Africa, told with vigour and enthusiasm . . . Wilbur Smith spins a fine tale'
Evening Standard

'A bonanza of excitement'
New York Times

' . . . a natural storyteller who moves confidently and often splendidly in his period and sustains a flow of convincing incident'
The Scotsman

'Raw experience, grim realism, history and romance welded with mystery and the bewilderment of life itself'
Library Journal

'A thundering good read'
Irish Times

'Extrovert and vigorous . . . constantly changing incidents and memorable portraits'
Liverpool Daily Post

'An immensely powerful book, disturbing and compulsive, harsh yet compassionate'
She

'An epic novel . . . it would be hard to think of a theme that was more appropriate today . . . Smith writes with a great passion for the soul of Africa'
Today

'I read on to the last page, hooked by its frenzied inventiveness piling up incident upon incident . . . mighty entertainment'
Yorkshire Post

'There is a streak of genuine poetry, all the more attractive for being unfeigned'
Sunday Telegraph

' . . . action follows action . . . mystery is piled on mystery . . . tales to delight the millions of addicts of the gutsy adventure story'
Sunday Express

'Action-crammed'
Sunday Times

'Rattling good adventure'
Evening Standard

The novels of Wilbur Smith

The Courtney novels

When the Lion Feeds
The Sound of Thunder
A Sparrow Falls
The Burning Shore
Power of the Sword
Rage
A Time to Die

The Ballantyne novels:

A Falcon Flies
Men of Men
The Angels Weep
The Leopard Hunts in Darkness

Also:

The Dark of the Sun
Shout at the Devil
Gold Mine
The Diamond Hunters
The Sunbird
Eagle in the Sky
The Eye of the Tiger
Cry Wolf
Hungry as the Sea
Wild Justice
Golden Fox
Elephant Song

A Falcon Flies
Men of Men

Wilbur Smith was born in Central Africa in 1933. He was educated at Michaelhouse and Rhodes University.

He became a full-time writer in 1964 after the successful publication of *When the Lion Feeds*, and has since written twenty-three novels, meticulously researched on his numerous expeditions worldwide.

He normally travels from November to February, often spending a month skiing in Switzerland, and visiting Australia and New Zealand for sea fishing. During his summer break, he visits environments as diverse as Alaska and the dwindling wilderness of the African interior. He has an abiding concern for the peoples and wildlife of his native continent, an interest strongly reflected in his novels.

He is married to Danielle, to whom his last nineteen books have been dedicated.

A [illegible]
[illegible] of [illegible]

Wilbur Smith [illegible] [illegible] [illegible] [illegible] [illegible] Rhodes University.

[illegible] successful publication of When the [illegible] [illegible] [illegible] [illegible] [illegible]

He normally travels from November to [illegible] [illegible] and the [illegible] [illegible] [illegible] vanishing wilderness of the African [illegible] [illegible] [illegible] [illegible] [illegible]

He is married to Danielle, to whom [illegible] his books have been dedicated.

WILBUR SMITH

A Falcon Flies

Men of Men

Mandarin

A Mandarin Paperback
A FALCON FLIES
MEN OF MEN

A Falcon Flies first published in Great Britain 1980
by William Heinemann Ltd
Mandarin paperback edition published 1992
Men of Men first published in Great Britain 1981
by William Heinemann Ltd
Mandarin paperback edition published 1991
First published together in this omnibus edition 1993
by Mandarin Paperbacks
an imprint of Reed Consumer Books Ltd
Michelin House, 81 Fulham Road, London SW3 6RB
and Auckland, Melbourne, Singapore and Toronto

A CIP catalogue record for this title
is available from the British Library
ISBN 0 7493 1475 3

Printed and bound in Great Britain
by Cox & Wyman Ltd, Reading

A Falcon Flies

Once again this book
is for my wife
Danielle Antoinette

1860

Africa crouched low on the horizon, like a lion in ambush, tawny and gold in the early sunlight, seared by the cold of the Benguela Current.

Robyn Ballantyne stood by the ship's rail and stared towards it. She had been standing like that since an hour before dawn, long before the land could be seen. She had known it was there, sensed its vast enigmatic presence in the darkness, detected its breath, warm and spicy dry, over the clammy cold exhalations of the current on which the great ship rode.

It was her cry, not that of the masthead, which brought Captain Mungo St John charging up the companionway from his stern quarters, and the rest of the ship's company crowding to the ship's side to stare and jabber. For seconds only, Mungo St John gripped the teak rail, staring at the land, before whirling to call his orders in the low but piercing tone which seemed to carry to every corner of the ship.

'Stand by to go about!'

Tippoo the mate scattered the crew to their duties with knotted rope-end and clubbed fists. For two weeks, furious winds and low, sullen skies had denied them a glimpse of sun or moon, or of any other heavenly body on which to establish a position. On dead reckoning the tall clipper should have been one hundred nautical miles further west, well clear of this treacherous coast with its uncharted hazards and wild deserted shores.

The Captain was freshly awakened, the thick dark mane of his hair tangled, rippling now in the wind, his cheeks lightly flushed with sleep, and also with anger and alarm beneath the smooth darkly tanned skin. Yet his eyes were clear, the whites contrasting starkly against the golden-flecked yellow of the iris. Once again, even in this moment of distraction and confusion, Robyn wondered at the sheer physical presence of the man – a dangerous, disturbing quality that at the same time both repelled and attracted her intensely.

His white linen shirt had been stuffed hastily into his breeches, and the front was unfastened. The skin of his chest was dark and smooth also, as if it had been oiled, and the hair upon it was crisp and black, tight whorls of it that made her blush, reminding her too clearly of that morning early in the voyage – the first morning that they had run into the warm blue waters of the Atlantic Ocean below latitude 35° north, the morning which for her had been the subject of much torment and troubled prayer since.

That morning, she had heard the splash and drum of water on the deck above her, and the clank of the ship's pump. She had left the makeshift desk in her tiny cabin on which she was working at her journal, slipped a shawl over her shoulders and gone up on to the maindeck, stepping unsuspectingly into the bright white sunlight and then stopping aghast.

There were two seamen working the pump lustily, and the clear sea water hissed from its throat in a solid jet. Naked, Mungo St John stood beneath it, lifting his face and his arms towards it, the water sleeking his black hair down over his face and neck, flattening his body hair over his chest and the muscled plane of his belly. She had stood and stared, completely frozen, unable to tear her eyes away. The two seamen had turned their heads and grinned lewdly at her while they kept the handles pumping the hissing water.

Of course she had seen a man's naked body before, laid out on the dissection table, soft white flesh collapsing over bone, and with belly pouch slit open and the internal organs spilling out of it like butchers' offal, or between the grubby blankets of the fever hospital, sweating and stinking and racked with the convulsions of onrushing death – but never like this, not healthy and vital and overwhelming like this.

This was a marvellous symmetry and balance of trunk to long powerful legs, of broad shoulders to narrow waist. There was a lustre to the skin, even where the sun had not gilded it. This was not an untidy tangle of masculine organs, half-hidden by a bush of coarse hair, shameful and vaguely revolting. This was vibrant manhood, and she had been struck with sudden insight as to the original sin of Eve, the serpent and the apples, here offered again, and she had gasped aloud. He had heard her and stepped from under the thundering jet of water, and flicked the hair from his eyes. He saw her standing near, unable to move or tear her eyes away, and he smiled that lazy, taunting smile, making no move to cover himself, the water still streaming down his body, and sparkling like diamond chips on his skin.

'Good morning, Doctor Ballantyne,' he had murmured. 'Perhaps I am to be the subject of one of your scientific studies?'

Only then had she been able to break the spell, to whirl and rush back to her smelly little cabin. She expected to be greatly disturbed, as she threw herself on the narrow planks of her bunk, waiting to be overwhelmed by a sense of sin and shame, but it did not come. Instead, she was confused by a contraction of her chest and lungs that left her breathless, and a remarkable warmth of her cheeks and the skin of her throat, a prickling of the fine dark hairs at the nape of her neck, and the same warmth of other parts of her body which had so alarmed her that she flung herself hurriedly off the bunk and on to her knees to plead for a proper sense of her own unworthiness and a true understanding of her essential baseness and irretrievable wickedness. It was an exercise she had undertaken a thousand times in her twenty-three years, but seldom with so little success.

For the thirty-eight days of the voyage since then, she had tried to avoid those flecked yellow eyes and that lazy taunting smile, and had taken to eating most of her meals in her cabin, even in the daunting heat of the equator, when the taint of the bucket behind the canvas screen in the corner of the cabin had done little to pique her appetite. Only when she knew that heavy weather would keep him on deck did she join her brother and the others in the ship's small saloon.

Watching him now as he conned his ship off the hostile coast, she felt that disturbing prickle once again, and she turned away quickly to the land that was now swinging across the bows. The tackle roared through the blocks and the yards creaked and crackled, the canvas flogged and then filled again with a crash like cannon.

At the sight of the land she almost overcame those earlier memories and was instead filled with such a sense of awe, that she wondered if it were possible that the land of birth could call so clearly and so undeniably to the blood of its children.

It did not seem possible that nineteen years had passed since as a four-year-old waif, clinging to her mother's long skirts she had last seen that great flat-topped mountain that guarded the southernmost tip of the continent sink slowly beneath the horizon. It was one of the only clear memories of this land that she retained. She could still almost feel the coarse cheap stuff that a missionary's wife must wear and hear the sobs that her mother tried to stifle and feel them shake her mother's legs beneath the skirts, as she clung closer. Vividly she recalled the fear and confusion of the little girl at her mother's distress, understanding with childlike intuition that their lives were in upheaval, but knowing only that the tall figure that had been up to that time the centre of her small existence was now missing.

'Don't cry, baby,' her mother had whispered. 'We will see Papa again soon. Don't cry, my little one.' But those words had made her doubt that she would ever see her father again, and she had pushed her face into the coarse skirt, too proud even at that age to let the others hear her wail.

As always it had been her brother Morris who had comforted her, three years her senior, a man of seven years, born like her in Africa, on the banks of a far wild river with a strange exotic name, Zouga, which had given him his middle name. Morris Zouga Ballantyne – she liked the Zouga best and always used it, it reminded her of Africa.

She turned her head back towards the quarterdeck, and there he was now, tall but not as tall as Mungo St John, to whom he was speaking excitedly, pointing at the lion-coloured land, his face animated. The features he had inherited from their father were heavy but strong, the nose bony and beaked and the line of the mouth determined, harsh perhaps.

He lifted the glass to his eye again and studied the low coastline, scanning it with the care that he took with any project from the smallest to the greatest, before lowering it and turning back to Mungo St John. They spoke together quietly. An unlikely relationship had developed between the two men, a mutual, though guarded respect each for the other's strengths and accomplishments. But if the truth be told, it was Zouga who pursued the relationship most assiduously. Always one to profit by any opportunity, he had milked Mungo St John of his knowledge and experience. He had done it with an exercise of charm, but since leaving Bristol harbour he had drawn from the Captain most of what he had learned in many years of trading and voyaging along the coasts of this vast savage continent, and Zouga had written all of it down in one of his calf-bound ledgers, storing knowledge against the day.

In addition to this, the Captain had genially undertaken to instruct Zouga in the mystery and art of astronomical navigation. Each day local apparent noon would find the two of them huddled on the sunny side of the quarterdeck with brass sextants poised, waiting for a glimpse of the fiery orb through the layers of cloud, or, when the sky was clear, eagerly sighting it, swaying to the ship's motion, to hold the sun in the field of the lens as they brought it down to the horizon.

At other times they cut the monotony of a long tack with a contest of arms, taking turns at an empty corked brandy bottle thrown over the stern by a crewman, using a magnificent pair of percussion duelling pistols that Mungo St John brought up from his cabin still in their velvet-lined case, and loaded with care on the chart table.

They shouted with laughter, and congratulated each other as the bottles burst in mid-air in an explosion of shards bright as diamond chips in the sunlight.

At other times Zouga brought up the new Sharps breechloading rifle, a gift from one of the sponsors of the expedition, 'the Ballantyne Africa Expedition', as the *Standard*, that great daily newspaper, had named it.

The Sharps was a magnificent weapon, accurate up to the incredible range of 800 yards, with the power to knock down a bull bison at a thousand. The men who were wiping out the great herds of buffalo from the American prairie at this very time had earned the title 'Sharpshooters' with this weapon.

Mungo St John towed a barrel at the end of an 800-yard length of cable to act as a target, and they shot for a wager of a shilling a bout. Zouga was an accomplished marksman, the best in his regiment, but he had already lost over five guineas to Mungo St John.

Not only were the Americans manufacturing the finest firearms in the world (already John Browning had patented a breechloading repeating rifle that Winchester was evolving into the most formidable weapon known to man), but the Americans were also far and away the finest marksmen. This pointed up the difference between the tradition of the frontiersman with his long rifle, and that of massed British infantry firing smoothbore muskets in strictly commanded volleys. Mungo St John, an

American, handled both the long-barrelled duelling pistol and the Sharps rifle as though they were an extension of his own body.

Now Robyn turned away from the two men, looked back at the land and felt a small dismay to see it already sinking lower into the cold green sea.

She yearned towards it with a quiet desperation, as she had ever since that day of departure so long ago. Her whole life in the intervening years seemed to have been a long preparation for this moment, so many obstacles overcome, obstacles made mountainous by the fact she was a woman; there had been so much struggle against temptation to give in to despair, a struggle that others had read as wilfulness and vaunting pride, as stubbornness and immodesty.

Her education had been gleaned with such toil from the library of her uncle William, despite his active discouragement. 'Too much book learning will only plague you, my dear. It is not a woman's place to trouble herself with certain things. You would do better to assist your mother in the kitchen and learn to sew and knit.'

'I can do both already, Uncle William.'

Later, his reluctant and grumbling assistance changed only slowly into active support when he at last assessed the depth of her intelligence and determination.

Uncle William was her mother's eldest brother, and he had taken in the family when the three of them had returned almost destitute from that far savage land. They had only the father's stipend from the London Missionary Society, a mere £50 per annum, and William Moffat was not a wealthy man, a physician at Kings Lynn with a small practice, hardly sufficient for the ready-made family with which he found himself saddled.

Of course, later – many years later – there had been money, a great deal of money, some said as much as three thousand pounds, the royalties from Robyn's father's books, but it had been Uncle William who had shielded and sustained them through the lean times.

William had somehow found the money to purchase Zouga's commission in his regiment, even selling his two prized hunters and making that humiliating journey to Cheapside and the moneylenders to do so.

With what William could raise, it was perforce not a

fashionable regiment, and not even the regular army, but the 13th Regiment of Madras Native Infantry, a line regiment of the East India Company.

It was Uncle William who had instructed Robyn until she was as advanced in formal education as he was himself, and who had then aided and abetted her in the great deception of which she could never bring herself to be ashamed. In 1854 no hospital medical school in all of England would enrol a woman amongst their student body.

With her uncle's help, and active connivance, she had enrolled, using his sponsorship and the assertion that she was his nephew, at St Matthew's Hospital in the east end of London.

It helped that her name needed only changing from Robyn to Robin, that she was tall and small-breasted, that her voice had a depth and huskiness that she could exaggerate. She had kept her thick, dark hair cropped short, and learned to wear trousers with such panache that ever since, the tangle of petticoats and crinolines around her legs had irritated her.

The hospital governors had only discovered the fact that she was a woman after she had obtained her medical qualification from the Royal College of Surgeons at the age of twenty-one. They had immediately petitioned the Royal College to withdraw the honour, and the ensuing scandal had swept the length and breadth of England, made more fascinating by the fact that she was the daughter of Doctor Fuller Ballantyne, the famous African explorer, traveller, medical missionary and author. In the end, the governors of St Matthew's had been forced to retreat, for Robyn Ballantyne and her Uncle William had found a champion in the small, rotund person of Oliver Wicks, editor of the *Standard*.

With a true journalist's eye, Wicks had recognized good copy, and in a scathing editorial had called upon the British tradition of fair play, ridiculed the dark hints of sexual orgies in the operating rooms and pointed up the considerable achievement of this bright and sensitive young girl against almost insurmountable odds. Yet even when her qualification had been confirmed, it was for her only a short step along the road back to Africa, on which she had determined so long ago.

The venerable directors of the London Missionary Society had been considerably alarmed by the offer of the services of a woman. Missionary wives were one thing, were indeed highly desirable to shield the missionaries themselves against physical blandishments and temptations amongst the unclothed heathen, but a lady missionary was another thing entirely.

There was a further complication which weighed heavily against Doctor Robyn Ballantyne's application. Her father was Fuller Ballantyne, who had resigned from the Society six years previously before disappearing once again into the African hinterland; in their eyes he had completely discredited himself. It was clear to them that the father was more interested in exploration and personal aggrandizement than in leading the benighted heathen into the bosom of Jesus Christ. In fact, so far as they were aware, Fuller Ballantyne had made only one convert in all his thousands of miles of African travel, his personal gunbearer.

He seemed to have made himself a crusader against the African slave trade, rather than an emissary of Christ. He had swiftly changed his first missionary station in Africa into a sanctuary for runaway slaves. The station at Koloberg had been on the southern edge of the great Kalahari Desert, a little oasis in the wilderness where a clear, strong spring of water gushed from the ground, and it had been founded with an enormous expenditure of the Society's funds.

Once Fuller had made it a slave refuge, the inevitable had happened. The Trek Boers from the little independent republics which ringed the mission station to the south were the original owners of the slaves to whom Fuller Ballantyne gave sanctuary. They called 'Commando', the medium through which the Trek Boers dispensed frontier justice. They came riding into Koloberg an hour before dawn, dark swift horsemen, a hundred of them, dressed in coarse homespun, bearded and burned by the sun to the colour of Africa's dark earth. The bright flashes of their muzzle-loaders lit the dawn, and then the burning thatch of the buildings of Fuller Ballantyne's mission station made it bright day.

They roped the recaptured slaves together with the station servants and freedmen into long lines, and drove them away southwards, leaving Fuller Ballantyne standing with his family huddled about him, a few pathetic possessions which they had managed to save from the flames scattered at their feet, and the smoke from the smouldering, roofless buildings drifting in eddies about them.

It had confirmed in Fuller Ballantyne his hatred of the

institution of slavery, and it had given him the excuse for which he had unwittingly been searching, the excuse to rid himself of the encumbrances which had until then prevented him from answering the call of the vast, empty land to the north.

His wife and two small children were packed off back to England for their own good, and with them went a letter to the directors of the London Missionary Society. God had made his will clear to Fuller Ballantyne. He was bidden to journey to the north, to carry God's word across Africa, a missionary at large, no longer tied to one small station, but with the whole of Africa as his parish.

The directors were greatly troubled by the loss of their station, but they were further dismayed by the prospect of having to mount what seemed to be a costly expedition of exploration into an area which all the world knew was merely a vast desert, unpeopled and unwatered except around the littoral, a burning sand desert which stretched to the Mediterranean Sea four thousand miles northward.

They wrote hurriedly to Fuller Ballantyne, uncertain where exactly the letter should be addressed, but feeling the need to deny all responsibility and to express their deep concern; they ended by stating strongly that no further funds other than his stipend of £50 per annum could be voted for Fuller Ballantyne's highly irregular activities. They need not have expended their energy and emotions, for Fuller Ballantyne had departed. With a handful of porters, his Christian gunbearer, a Colt revolver, a percussion rifle, two boxes of medicines, his journals and navigational instruments, Fuller Ballantyne had disappeared.

He emerged eight years later, down the Zambezi river, appearing at the Portuguese settlement near the mouth of that river, to the great chagrin of the settlers there who, after 200 years of occupation, had pushed no further than 100 miles upstream.

Fuller Ballantyne returned to England and his book *A Missionary in Darkest Africa* created a tremendous sensation. Here was a man who had made the 'Transversa', the overland passage of Africa from west to east coast, who had seen, where there should be desert, great rivers and lakes, cool pleasant grassy uplands, great herds of game and strange peoples – but most of all he had seen the terrible depredations of the slave-raiders upon the continent, and his revelations rekindled the anti-slavery zeal of Wilberforce in the hearts of the British people.

The London Missionary Society was embarrassed by the instant fame of their prodigal, and they hurried to make amends. Fuller Ballantyne had chosen the sites for future missionary stations in the interior, and at thc cost of many thousands of pounds they gathered together groups of devoted men and women and sent them out to the selected sites.

Thc British Government, prevailed upon by Fuller Ballantyne's description of the Zambezi river as a wide roadway to the rich interior of Africa, nominated Fuller Ballantyne Her Majesty's Consul, and financed an elaborate expedition to open this artery of trade and civilization to the interior.

Fuller had returned to England to write his book, but during this period of reunion with his family, they saw almost as little of the great man as when he was in the depths of Africa. When he was not locked in Uncle William's study writing the epic of his travels, he was in London hounding the Foreign Office or the directors of the L.M.S. And when he had gained from these sources all that he needed for his return to Africa, then he was travelling about England lecturing in Oxford or preaching the sermon from the pulpit of Canterbury cathedral.

Then abruptly he was gone again, taking their mother with him. Robyn would always remember the feel of his spiky whiskers as he stooped to kiss his daughter farewell for the second time. In her mind her father and God were somehow the same person, all-powerful, all-righteous, and her duty to them was blind, accepting adoration.

Years later, when the missionary sites chosen by Fuller Ballantyne had proved to be death-traps, when the surviving missionaries had stumbled back to civilization, their fellows and spouses dead of fever and famine, killed by wild animals and by the wilder men whom they had gone out to save, then Fuller Ballantyne's star had begun to fade.

The Foreign Office expedition to the Zambezi river, led by Ballantyne, bad faltered and failed upon the terrible rapids and deep falls of the Kaborra-Bassa gorge through which the Zambezi crashed and roared, dropping a thousand feet in twenty miles. Men wondered how Ballantyne, who had claimed to have followed the Zambezi down from its source to the sea, could have not known of such a formidable obstacle to his dreams. They began to question his other claims, while the British Foreign Office, parsimonious as ever, was considerably miffed by the waste of funds on the abortive expedition and withdrew the title of Consul.

The London Missionary Society wrote another of their lengthy letters to Fuller Ballantyne, requesting him in future to confine his activities to the conversion of the heathen and the propagation of God's word.

Fuller Ballantyne had replied by posting them his resignation, thereby saving the society £50 per annum. At the same time he had penned a letter of encouragement to his two children urging them to show fortitude and faith, and sent the manuscript, in which he vindicated his conduct of the expedition, to his publisher. Then he had taken the few guineas that remained from the huge royalties that his other books had earned and had disappeared once more into the interior of Africa. That was eight years previously and no one had heard from him since.

Now here was this man's daughter, already nearly as notorious as the father, demanding admission to the Society as a working missionary.

Once again, Uncle William had come to Robyn's aid, dear mild bumbling Uncle William with his thick pebble spectacles and wild grey bush of untamable hair. With her he had gone before the board of directors and reminded them that Robyn's grandfather, Robert Moffat, was one of the most successful of all African missionaries, with tens of thousands of conversions to his credit. Indeed the old man was still working at Kuruman and had only recently published his dictionary of the Sechuana language. Robyn herself was dedicated and devout, with medical training and a good knowledge of African languages taught her by her now deceased mother, daughter of the same Robert Moffat, and by virtue of the reverence with which the said Robert Moffat was regarded by even the most warlike African king, Mzilikazi of the Ndebele, or as some people called them, the Matabele, the granddaughter would find immediate acceptance amongst the tribes.

The directors had listened stonily.

Then Uncle William had gone on to suggest that Oliver Wicks, the editor of the *Standard* who had championed the girl against the attempt by the governors of St Matthew's Hospital to deprive her of her medical qualification, would be interested in their reasons for refusing her application to the Society.

The directors sat up and listened with great attention,

conferred quietly and accepted Robyn's application. They had then seconded her to another missionary movement who in turn sent her to the industrial slums of northern England.

It was her brother Zouga who had found the way back to Africa for both of them.

He had returned from India on leave, a man of considerable achievement, already a major in the Indian army, promotion that he had won in the field, with the reputation of being a soldier and military administrator of great promise for one so young.

Despite this, Zouga was every bit as dissatisfied with his lot as was Robyn. Like their father, they were both lone wolves, responding badly to authority and regimentation. In spite of the promising start to his military career, Zouga recognized the fact that he had already made powerful enemies in India, and he had begun to doubt that his future lay on that continent. Like Robyn, he was still a searcher, and they had greeted each other after the parting of years with a warmth that they had seldom displayed during their childhood.

Zouga took her to dinner at the Golden Boar. It was such a change from Robyn's daily surroundings that she accepted a second glass of claret and became gay and sparkling.

'By God, Sissy, you really are a pretty thing, you know,' he had told her at last. He had taken to swearing now, and though it had shocked her at first, she had grown accustomed to it quickly enough. She had heard a lot worse in the slums where she worked. 'You are too good to spend your life amongst those ghastly crones.'

It changed the mood between them instantly, and she was able at last to lean close to her brother and pour out all her frustrations. He listened sympathetically, reaching across the table to squeeze her hand so that she went on quietly but with utter determination.

'Zouga, I have to get back to Africa. I'll die if I don't. I just know it. I will shrivel up and die.'

'Good Lord, Sissy, why Africa?'

'Because I was born there, because my destiny is there – and because Papa is there, somewhere.'

'I was born there also.' Zouga smiled, and when he did so it softened the harsh line of his mouth. 'But I don't know about my destiny. I wouldn't mind going back for the hunting, of course, but as for Father – don't you often think that Papa's main concern was always Fuller Ballantyne? I cannot imagine that you still harbour any great filial love for him.'

'He is different from other men, Zouga, you cannot judge him by the usual yardstick.'

'There are many who might agree with that,' Zouga murmured drily. 'At the L.M.S. and at the Foreign Office – but as a father?'

'I love him!' she said defiantly. 'After God, I love him best.'

'He killed mother, you know.' Zouga's mouth hardened into its usual grim line. 'He took her out to the Zambezi in fever season and he killed her as certainly as if he'd put a pistol to her head.'

Robyn conceded after a short, regretful silence, 'He was never a father nor a husband – but as a visionary, a blazer of trails, as a torchbearer . . .'

Zouga laughed and squeezed her hand.

'Really, Sissy!'

'I have read his books, all his letters, every one he ever wrote to mother or to us, and I know that my place is there. In Africa, with Papa.'

Zouga lifted his hand from hers and carefully stroked his thick side whiskers. 'You always had a way of making me feel excited—' Then, seemingly going off at a tangent, 'Did you hear that they have found diamonds on the Orange river?' He lifted his glass and examined the lees in the bottom of it attentively. 'We are so very different, you and I, and yet in some ways so much alike.' He poured fresh wine into his glass and went on casually. 'I am in debt, Sissy.'

The word chilled her. Since her childhood she had been taught a dread of it.

'How much?' she asked at last quietly.

'Two hundred pounds.' He shrugged.

'So much!' she breathed, and then, 'You haven't been gambling, Zouga?'

That was one of the other dread words in Robyn's vocabulary.

'Not gambling?' she repeated.

'As a matter of fact, I have,' Zouga laughed. 'And thank God for that. Without it I would be a thousand guineas under.'

'You mean you gamble – and actually win?' Her horror faded a little, became tinged with fascination.

'Not always, but most of the time.'

She studied him carefully, perhaps for the first time. He was only twenty-six years old, but he had the presence and aplomb of a man ten years older. He was already a hard, professional soldier, tempered in the skirmishes on the border of Afghanistan where his regiment had spent four years. She knew they had been cruel encounters against fierce hill tribes, and that Zouga had distinguished himself. His rapid promotion was proof of that.

'Then how are you in debt, Zouga?' she asked.

'Most of my brother officers, even my juniors, have private fortunes. I am a major now, I have to keep some style. We hunt, we shoot, mess bills, polo ponies –' He shrugged again.

'Will you ever be able to repay it?'

'I could marry a rich wife,' he smiled, 'or find diamonds.'

Zouga sipped his wine, slumped down in his chair, not looking at her, and went on quietly.

'I was reading Cornwallis Harris's book the other day – do you remember the big game we saw when we lived at Koloberg?'

She shook her head.

'No, you were only a baby. But I do. I remember the herds of springbok and wildebeest on the trek down to the Cape. One night there was a lion, I saw it clearly in the light of the campfire. Harris's book described his hunting expeditions up as far as the Limpopo – nobody has been further than that, except Papa, of course. A damned sight better than potting pheasant or black buck. Did you know that Harris made nearly five thousand pounds from his book?'

Zouga pushed his glass away, straightened up in his seat and selected a cigar from his silver case. While he prepared and lit it, he was frowning thoughtfully.

'You want to go to Africa for spiritual reasons. I probably need to go to Africa, for much better reasons, for blood and for money. I make you a proposal. The Ballantyne Expedition!' He lifted his glass to her.

She laughed then, uncertainly, thinking he was joking, but lifted her own glass which was still almost full. 'My word on it. But how? Zouga, how do we get there?'

'What was the name of that newspaper fellow?' Zouga demanded.

'Wicks,' she said, 'Oliver Wicks. But why should he help us?'

'I'll find a good reason why he should.' And Robyn remembered how, even as a child, he had been an eloquent and persuasive pleader of causes.

'You know I rather think you might.'

They drank then, and when she lowered her glass, she had been as happy as she could ever remember being in all her life.

It was another six weeks before she saw Zouga again, striding towards her through the bustle of London Bridge Station as she clambered down from the carriage. He stood tall above the crowd, with the high beaver top hat on his head and the three-quarter length paletot cloak flaring from his shoulders.

'Sissy!' he called, laughing at her, as he lifted her from her feet. 'We are going – we really are going.'

He had a cab waiting for them, and the driver whipped up the horses the moment they were aboard.

'The London Missionary Society were no use at all,' he told her, still with his arm around her shoulders as the cab clattered and lurched over the cobbles. 'I had them down on my list for five hundred iron men, and they nearly had apoplexy. I had the feeling they would rather Papa stayed lost in darkest Africa, and they would pay five hundred to keep him there.'

'You went to the directors?' she demanded.

'Played my losing tricks first,' Zouga smiled. 'The next was Whitehall – actually managed to see the First Secretary. He was damned civil, took me to lunch at the Travellers', and was truly very sorry that they were not able to give financial assistance. They remembered Papa's Zambezi fiasco too clearly, but he did give me letters. A dozen letters, to every conceivable person – to the Governor at the Cape, to Kemp the Admiral at Cape Town, and all the others.'

'Letters won't get us far.'

'Then I went to see your newspaper friend. Extraordinary little man. Smart as a whip. I told him we were going to Africa to find Papa – and he jumped up and clapped his hands like a child at a Punch and Judy show.' Zouga hugged Robyn tighter. 'To tell the truth, I used your name shamelessly – and it did the trick. He will have all the story rights to our diaries and journals, and the publishing rights to both books.'

'Both books?' Robyn pulled away from him and looked into his face.

'Both.' He grinned at her. 'Yours and mine.'

'I am to write a book?'

'You certainly are. A woman's account of the expedition. I have already signed the contract on your behalf.'

She laughed then, but breathlessly. 'You're going too far, much too fast.'

'Little Wicks was in for five hundred, and the next on the list was the Society for the Extinction of the Slave Trade – they were easy. His Royal Highness is the Society's patron, and he had read Papa's books. We are to report on the state of the trade in the interior of the continent north of the Tropic of Capricorn, and they came up with another 500 guineas.'

'Oh Zouga, you are a magician.'

'Then there was the Worshipful Company of London Merchants Trading into Africa. For the last hundred years they have based all their activities on the west coast, I convinced them that they needed a survey of the east coast. I have been appointed the Worshipful Company's Agent, with instructions to examine the market in palm oil, gum-copal, copper and ivory – and they have come up with the third and last 500 guineas – and a presentation Sharps rifle.'

'One thousand five hundred guineas,' Robyn breathed, and Zouga nodded.

'We are going back home in style.'

'When?'

'I have booked passage on an American trading clipper. We sail from Bristol in six weeks, for Good Hope and Quelimane in Mozambique. I have written asking leave from my regiment for two years – you will have to do the same with the L.M.S.'

It had all happened with dreamlike rapidity after that. The directors of the L.M.S., perhaps relieved that they were not to pay for her passage nor the expense of relocating Robyn in the African interior, in a flush of extravagance decided to continue her stipend during the period she was away, and made a guarded promise to review the position at the end of that time. If she proved herself capable – then there would be a permanent post in Africa thereafter. It was more than she had ever expected, and she had thrown herself wholeheartedly into assisting Zouga with the preparations for departure.

There was so much to do that six weeks was barely sufficient, and it seemed only days had passed before the mountain of the expedition's equipment was being swayed down into the holds of the big graceful Baltimore clipper.

The *Huron* proved as swift as she looked, another wise choice by Zouga Ballantyne, and under Mungo St John's skilful navigation she made good her westings before attempting to cross the belt of the doldrums at their narrowest point. They were becalmed not a single day and sped across the line at 29° west and immediately Mungo St John put her on the port tack to stand down across the south east trades. *Huron* clawed her way southwards with the flying fish sailing ahead of her, close on the wind until she broke from their grip at last with Ilha da Trinidade on the horizon. The north-wester came howling at them and *Huron* fled before it, under low, sullen, scudding skies day after day that denied them sight of sun or moon or stars, until she almost hurled herself ashore 200 miles up the west coast of Africa from her destination at the Cape of Good Hope.

'Mr Mate!' Mungo St John called in his clear carrying voice as *Huron* settled down to reach across the wind, pulling swiftly away from the land.

'Captain!' Tippoo bellowed back from the foot of the mainmast, a great blurt of sound from the bull chest.

'Take the name of the masthead watch.'

Tippoo ducked his cannon-ball head on its thick neck like a bare-knuckle fighter taking a punch, and looked up the mast, slitting his eyes in the heavy folds of flesh.

'Twenty minutes more and he would have had us on the beach.' St John's voice was cold, deadly. 'I'll have him on the grating before this day is out, and we will get a peep of his backbone.'

Tippoo licked his thick lips involuntarily, and Robyn, standing near him, felt her stomach heave. There had been three floggings already on this voyage and she knew what to expect. Tippoo was half-Arab, half-African, a honey-coloured giant of a man with a shaven head that was covered with a mesh of tiny pale scars from a thousand violent encounters. He wore a loose embroidered, high-necked tunic over his huge frame, but the forearms that protruded from the wide sleeves were thick as a woman's thighs.

Robyn turned quickly to Zouga as he came down the deck towards her.

'We had a good look at the land, Sissy. Our first definite fix since Ilha da Trinidade. If this wind holds we will be in Table Bay in another five days.'

'Zouga, can't you intercede with the Captain?' she demanded, and Zouga looked startled.

'He is going to flog that poor devil.'

'Damn right too,' Zouga growled. 'The man nearly had us on the rocks.'

'Can't you stop him?'

'I wouldn't dream of interfering with his running of this ship – and nor will I allow you to.'

'Do you have no humanity at all?' she demanded of her brother coldly, but there were bright hot spots of anger on her cheeks, and her eyes snapped clear angry green. 'You call yourself a Christian.'

'When I do, I speak softly though, my dear.' Zouga made the reply he knew would annoy her most. 'And I don't flaunt it at every turn in the conversation.'

Their arguments were always sudden as summer thunderstorms on the African veld, and as spectacular.

Mungo St John sauntered forward to lean his elbow on the railing of his quarterdeck, a long Havana cheroot of coarse black tobacco held between white teeth. He mocked her silently with those flecked yellow eyes, infuriating her further, until she heard her own voice going shrill and she turned from Zouga, and rounded on him.

'The man you had flogged last week could be crippled for life,' she shouted at him.

'Doctor Ballantyne – how would you like Tippoo to carry you down and lock you in your cabin?' Mungo St John asked. 'Until you regain your temper and your manners.'

'You cannot do that,' she flared at him.

'I can, I assure you – that and much more.'

'He's right,' Zouga assured her softly. 'On this ship he can do virtually anything he wants.' He laid his hand on her upper arm. 'Steady now, Sissy. The fellow will be lucky to get away with the loss of a little skin.'

Robyn found she was panting with anger and a sense of helplessness.

'If you are squeamish, Doctor, I will excuse you from witnessing punishment,' Mungo St John mocked her still. 'We must make allowance for the fact that you are a woman.'

'I have never asked for consideration on that score, not once in all my life.' She tried to get her anger back under control, and she shook off her brother's hand and turned away from them.

She walked with stiff back and squared shoulders up into the bows, trying to maintain an aloof dignity, but the ship's motion was awkward and her damned skirts fluttered around her legs. She realized she had thought the word, and she would ask forgiveness later – but not now, and suddenly she said it aloud.

'Damn you, Captain Mungo St John, damn you to hell!'

She stood in the bows, and the wind pulled her hair out of the neat chignon at the nape of her neck and flicked it in her face. It was her mother's thick silken dark hair, shot with tones of russet and chestnut, and as a pale ray of greenish sunlight at last broke through the cloud cover, it turned to a glowing halo around her small neat head.

She stared ahead angrily, hardly noticing the hellish beauty of the scene about her. The cold, green waters, smoked with mist banks, opened and closed about the ship like pearly curtains. Wisps of mist trailed from the sails and yards as though she was on fire.

In patches, the surface of the sea simmered and darkened, for these waters were rich in microscopic sea life, which supported vast shoals of sardine that rose to the surface to feed, to be fed on in turn by flocks of shrieking seabirds that plunged upon them from high above, hitting the water in little cotton puffs of spray.

A thicker bank of mist took the tall ship in its damp cold grip so that when Robyn glanced back she could only just make out the ghostly figures of the Captain and her brother on the quarterdeck.

Then just as suddenly they plunged out again into open sea, and sunny skies. The clouds which had covered them for all these weeks rolled away towards the south while the wind itself increased in strength and veered swiftly into the east, whipping the tops from the waves in graceful ostrich plumes of curling spray.

At the same moment Robyn saw the other ship. It was startlingly close, and she opened her mouth to shout – but a dozen other voices forestalled her.

'Sail oh!'

'Sail fine on the port quarter.'

She was close enough to make out the thin, tall smoke stack between the main and mizzenmasts. Her hull was painted black with a red line below her gunports; five guns each side.

The black hull had a sinister air to it, and the pile of her canvas was not shimmering white as that of *Huron*, but was sullied dirty grey by the belchings from her smoke stack.

Mungo St John played the field of his telescope swiftly over her. Her boilers were unlit, there was not even a tremble of heat from the mouth of her stack. She was under easy canvas only.

'Tippoo!' he called softly, and it seemed that the mate's bulk appeared beside him with the magical speed of a genie.

'Have you seen her before?'

Tippoo grunted and turned his head to spit over the lee rail.

'Lime-juicer,' he said. 'I seen her last in Table Bay eight years back. She called *Black Joke*.'

'Cape Squadron?'

Tippoo grunted, and at that moment the gunboat bore up sharply and at the same time her colours broke out at the masthead. The crisp white and bright scarlet of her ensign shrieked a challenge, a challenge that all the world had learned to heed, and heed swiftly. Only the ships of one nation on earth need not heave to the instant that challenge was flown. The *Huron* was immune, she had only to hoist the Stars and Stripes, and even this importunate representative of the Royal Navy would be forced to respect it.

But Mungo St John was thinking swiftly. Six days before he sailed from Baltimore Harbour, in May, 1860, Abraham Lincoln had been nominated presidential candidate for the United States of America. If elected, as seemed highly likely, he would be invested early in the New Year, and then one of his first actions would surely be to grant to Great Britain the privileges agreed by the Treaty of Brussels, including the right of search of American ships upon the high seas which previous American presidents had so steadfastly denied.

Soon, perhaps sooner than he expected, Mungo St John might have to run his clipper in deadly earnest against one of these ships of the Cape Squadron. It was a heaven-sent opportunity to match his ship, and to observe the capabilities of the other.

He swept one last glance about him, that took in the sea, the wind-driven lines of foam upon it, the piled white pyramids of canvas above him and the evil black hull to leeward – and then his decision was made easier. On the wind came the thud of a gun, and a long feather of gunsmoke spurted from one of the gunboat's bowchasers, demanding instant obedience.

Mungo St John smiled. 'The insolent bastard!' To Tippoo he said, 'We'll try him on a few points of sailing,' to the helmsman beside him, softly, 'Put the helm down.' And as *Huron* paid off swiftly before the wind, beginning to point directly away from the threatening black ship, 'Shake out all reefs, Mr Mate. Set fore and maintop, hoist studding sails and skysails, crack on the main royal – yes, and flying jib too. By God, we'll show that grubby little coal-guzzling lime-juicer how they build them down Baltimore way!'

Even in her anger, Robyn was thrilled by the manner in which the American worked his ship. With his crew swarming out across the yards to the reefing points, the mainsails swelled out to their full extent, dazzling white in the sunshine, and then high above, seemingly at the very base of the aching blue heaven itself, new unfamiliar-shaped sails popped open like over-ripe cotton pods and the long, graceful hull reacted instantly to the pressures thrust upon her.

'By God, she sails like a witch,' Zouga shouted, laughing with excitement, as she knifed into the crests of the Atlantic rollers and he hustled his sister back from the bows before the first green sheets of water came aboard and swept *Huron*'s decks.

More and still more canvas burst open, and the thick trees of her masts began to arch like drawn longbows under the unbearable pressures of thousands of square feet of spread sails. Now *Huron* seemed to fly, taking off from the crest of each roller and smashing into the face of the next with a crash that shocked her timbers and jarred the teeth of her crew in their skulls.

'A cast of the log, Mr Mate,' Mungo St John called, and when Tippoo bellowed back, 'A touch better than sixteen knots, Cap'n!' the Captain laughed aloud, and strode to the stern rail.

The gunboat was falling astern as though she was standing still, although every inch of her grey canvas was spread. Already she was at extreme cannon range.

Again powder-smoke bloomed briefly on her black bows, and this time it seemed that it was more than merely a warning, for Mungo St John saw the fall of shot. It struck the crest of a roller two cable lengths astern and skipped across the green torn waters, before plunging beneath the surface almost alongside *Huron*'s tall side.

'Captain, you are endangering the lives of your crew and passengers.' The voice arrested him and St John turned to the tall young woman who stood beside him, and he raised one thick black eyebrow in polite enquiry.

'That is a British man-of-war, sir, and we are acting like criminals. They are firing live shot now. You have only to heave to, or at the very least show your colours.'

'I think my sister is right, Captain St John.' Zouga stood beside her. 'I do not understand your behaviour either.'

Huron staggered violently to a larger crest, driven wild by the mountainous press of sail, Robyn lost her balance and fell against the Captain's chest, but instantly pulled away, colouring fiercely at the contact.

'This is the coast of Africa, Major Ballantyne. Nothing is what it appears to be. Here only a fool would accept a strange armed vessel at its face value. Now if you and the good doctor will excuse me, I must attend to my duties.'

He strode forward to gaze down at the maindeck, judging the mood of his crew and the wild abandon of his ship. He unhooked the keyring from his belt and tossed it to Tippoo. 'The arms chest, Mr Mate, a pair of pistols to you and the second mate. Shoot any hand who attempts to interfere with the setting of the sails.' He had recognized the fear which gripped the crew. Most of them had never seen a ship driven like this, there might easily be an attempt to shorten sail rather than have her run herself under.

At that moment *Huron* put her shoulder into the Atlantic and took it aboard in a solid roaring green wall. One of the topmast men was not quick enough on to the rat-lines. The water plucked him up and flung him down the length of the deck, until he crashed into the side, and lay huddled against the bulwark like a clump of uprooted kelp on a storm-driven beach.

Two of his fellows tried to reach him, but the next wave drove them back as it came pouring aboard waist-deep and then cascading in a roaring white torrent over the side, and when it was gone the fallen topmast man was gone with it and the deck was empty.

'Mr Tippoo, look you to those skysails, they are not drawing as they should.'

Mungo St John turned back to the stern rail, ignoring Robyn Ballantyne's horrified and accusing glare.

Already the British gunboat was hull down and her sails were barely discernible among the grey beards of the breaking Atlantic rollers, but suddenly Mungo St John saw something change, and he reached quickly for the telescope in its slot under the chart table. There was a fine black line, as though drawn in Indian ink, extending from the tiny cone of the Englishman's sails for a short way across the bumpy horizon.

'Smoke! She has her boiler fired at last,' he grunted, as Tippoo appeared at his shoulder, with the pistols thrust into his belt.

'One screw. She no catch us.' Tippoo nodded his round shaven head.

'No, not downwind in a full gale,' Mungo St John agreed. 'But I'd like to try her on the wind. We'll harden up now, Mr Mate, on the port tack again. I want to see if I can run up to windward of her and pass her out of cannon shot.'

The unexpected manoeuvre caught the gunboat commander completely off-guard, and he was a few minutes slow in altering course to cut the shorter leg of the triangle and prevent the *Huron* wresting the weather gage from him.

Huron went streaming past him at extreme cannon-shot hard on the wind, her yards sheeted around as close-hauled as she would sail. He tried a shot across her dipping, plunging bows with no visible fall of shot, and then he came around to follow her into the wind, and immediately the flaws in the design and construction of his ship were pointed up as clearly as they had been while both ships were running before the wind.

In order to accommodate the heavy boiler and machinery to drive the big bronze screw under her counter, serious compromise had been made with the design of her masts and the amount of canvas she could carry.

Within five miles it became clear that with all sail set and the boilers belching a solid greasy slug of coal smoke over the stern the *Black Joke* could not point as high into the wind as the beautiful tall ship ahead of her. She was drifting steadily away to leeward, and although the difference in their speeds was not as dramatic as when running before the wind, yet *Huron* was headreaching on her steadily.

The gunboat's commander pointed her higher and higher, trying desperately to hold the bigger ship directly over his bows, but all his sails were shaking and luffing before he could do so.

In a fury of frustration, he took in all his canvas, stripping his poles bare and relying only on the drive of his steam boiler pointed up directly into the very eye of the wind, much much higher than *Huron* could sail. But the gunboat's speed bled away when her screw received no help from her sails. Even though her mast and rigging were bare, the storm whistled and howled head-on through them, acting as a great drogue that slowed her further and *Huron* forged ahead more swiftly.

'A bastard contraption.' Mungo St John watched her battle with all his attention, judging her performance at every point of the wind. 'We are toying with her. As long as there is a breath of wind we'll romp away from her.'

Astern, the gunboat's commander had abandoned his attempt to run the clipper down with steam power alone, and had come back on to a fine reach with all his canvas set, plugging along stubbornly in *Huron*'s streaming wake – until abruptly, with no warning at all, *Huron* sailed into a deep hole in the wind.

The line of the gale was drawn clearly across the surface of the sea. On one side, the water was darkened and furrowed by the talons of the wind, on the other, the humped backs of the rollers in the calm had a polished velvety gloss to them.

As *Huron* crossed that line of demarcation, the clamour of the wind which for week after week had battered their ears, fell to an eerie unnatural silence, and the ship's motion changed from the vital charge of a living, straining sea creature, to the patternless rolling and wallowing of a dead log.

Overhead her canvas volleyed and flapped in the directionless eddies created by her own rolling and pitching, and her tackle crashed and clattered so that it seemed that she might roll her masts clean out of her hull.

Far astern, the black-painted gunboat scrambled on eagerly, swiftly beginning to narrow the distance between them, the black column of coal smoke now rising straight up into the stillness of air, giving her a jubilant and menacing air.

Mungo St John ran to the forward rail of the quarterdeck, and stared over his bows. He could see the wind two or three miles ahead clawing at the sea and ruffling it to a sombre shade of indigo, but between them was the oily undulating surface of the calm.

He swung back and the gunboat was closer, sending her smoke spurting high against the bright windswept blue of the sky, so certain of herself now that her gunports were swinging open and the stubby barrels of her 32-pounder cannon protruding from the black sides of her hull, the churning wash of her screw tumbling out from under her counter and sparkling whitely in the sunlight.

With no way upon *Huron*, the helmsman could not hold any course, and the clipper drifted around broadside to the on-rushing man-of-war putting her bows directly into the rollers.

They could make out the individual figures of the three officers on the gunboat's bridge now. Again the bow-chaser fired, and the shell lifted a tall column of water so high and close under the *Huron*'s bows that it collapsed upon the deck and streamed out through the scuppers.

Mungo St John took one last despairing sweep of the horizon, hoping even now for a resurgence of the wind, and then he capitulated.

'Hoist the colours, Mr Tippoo,' he called, and as the gaudy scrap of cloth drooped from the mainyard in the windless air, he watched through the lens of his telescope the consternation it caused upon the gunboat's bridge. That was the last flag they had hoped to see.

They were now close enough to discern the individual expressions of chagrin and alarm and indecision of the naval officers.

'There'll be no prize money for you – not this time around,' Mungo St John murmured with grim satisfaction, and snapped the telescope shut.

The gunboat came on and then rounded up to *Huron*, within

easy hail, showing her full broadside, the long 32-pounder cannon gaping menacingly.

The tallest officer on her bridge seemed also the oldest, for his hair was white in the sunlight. He came to the gunboat's near rail and lifted the voice trumpet to his mouth.

'What ship?'

'*Huron*, out of Baltimore and Bristol,' Mungo St John hailed back. 'With a cargo of trade goods for Good Hope and Quelimane.'

'Why did you not answer my challenge, sir?'

'Because, sir, I do not acknowledge your right to challenge ships of the United States of America on the high seas.'

Both captains knew just what a thorny and controversial question that reply posed, but the Englishman hesitated only a second.

'Do you, sir, accede to my right to satisfy myself as to your nationality and your ship's port of registry?'

'As soon as you run in your guns you may come aboard for that purpose, Captain. But do not send one of your junior officers.'

Mungo St John was making a fine point of humiliating the commander of the *Black Joke*. But inwardly he was still seething at the fluke of wind and weather which had allowed the gunboat to come up with him.

The *Black Joke* launched a longboat on the heavy swell with an immaculate show of seamanship, and it pulled swiftly to *Huron*'s side. While the Captain scrambled up the rope ladder, the boat's crew backed off and rested on their oars.

The naval officer came in through the entry port, so lithe and agile that Mungo St John realized his error in thinking him an elderly man. It was the white-blond hair that had misled him – he was evidently less than thirty years of age. He did not wear a uniform coat, for his ship had been cleared for action, and he was dressed in a plain white linen shirt, breeches and soft boots. There were a pair of pistols in his belt and a naval cutlass in its scabbard on his hip.

'Captain Codrington of Her Majesty's auxiliary cruiser *Black Joke*,' he introduced himself stiffly. His hair was bleached in silver white splashes from the salt and the sun, with darker streaks beneath and it was tied with a leather thong in a short queue at the nape of his neck. His face was weathered to honey-golden brown by the same sun, so that the faded blue of his eyes was in pale contrast.

'Captain St John, owner and master of this vessel.'

Neither man made any move to shake hands, and they seemed to bristle like two dog wolves meeting for the first time.

'I hope you do not intend to detain me longer than is necessary. You can assure yourself that my government will be fully apprised of this incident.'

'May I inspect your papers, Captain?' The young naval officer ignored the threat, and followed St John on to the quarterdeck. There he hesitated for the first time when he caught sight of Robyn and her brother standing together at the far rail, but he recovered immediately, bowed slightly and then turned his full attention to the packet of documents that Mungo St John had ready for his inspection on the chart table.

He stooped over the table, working swiftly through the pile until with a shock of discovery he straightened.

'Damn me – Mungo St John – your reputation precedes you, sir.' The Englishman's expression was strained with strong emotion. 'And what a noble one it is, too.' There was a bitter sting in his voice. 'The first trader ever to carry more than three thousand souls across the middle passage in a single, twelve-month period – small wonder you can afford such a magnificent vessel.'

'You are on dangerous ground, sir,' Mungo St John warned him with that lazy, taunting grin. 'I am fully aware of the lengths to which the officers of your service will go for a few guineas of prize money.'

'Where are you going to pick up your next cargo of human misery, Captain St John?' the Englishman cut in brusquely. 'On such a fine ship you should be able to pack in two thousand.' He had gone pale with unfeigned anger, actually trembling slightly with the force of it.

'If you have finished your investigation—' St John's smile did not slip, but the naval officer went on speaking.

'We have made the west coast a little too hot for you now, have we? Even when you hide behind that pretty piece of silk,' the naval officer glanced up at the flag on the mainyard, 'so you are going to work the east coast now, are you, sir? They tell me you can get a prime slave for two dollars – two for a 10-shilling musket.'

'I must ask you to leave now.' St John took the document from his hand, and when their fingers touched, the Englishman wiped his hand on his own thigh as though to cleanse it of the contact.

'I'd give five years' pay to have the hatches off your holds,' he said bitterly, leaning forward to stare at Mungo St John with those pale fierce eyes.

'Captain Codrington!' Zouga Ballantyne stepped towards the group. 'I am a British subject and an officer in Her Majesty's army. I can assure you that there are no slaves aboard this vessel.' He spoke sharply.

'If you are an Englishman, then you should be ashamed to travel in such company.' Codrington glanced beyond Zouga. 'And that applies equally to you, madam!'

'You overreach yourself, sir,' Zouga told him grimly. 'I have already given you my assurance.'

Codrington's gaze had flicked back to Robyn Ballantyne's face. Her distress was evident, unfeigned. The accusation had shattered her, that she, the daughter of Fuller Ballantyne, the great champion of freedom and sworn adversary of slavery – she, the accredited agent of the Society for the Extinction of the Slave Trade should be travelling aboard a notorious slaver.

She was pale, the green eyes huge and liquid with the shock of it.

'Captain Codrington,' her voice was husky and low, 'my brother is right – I also assure you that there are no slaves aboard this ship.'

The Englishman's expression softened, she was not a beautiful woman, but there was a freshness and wholesomeness about her which was difficult to resist.

'I will accept your word, madam.' He inclined his head. 'Indeed, only a madman would carry black ivory towards Africa, but,' and his voice hardened again, 'if only I were able to enter her holds, I'd find enough down there to run her into Table Bay under a prize crew and have her condemned out of hand at the next session of the Court of Mixed Commission.'

Codrington swung on his heel to face Mungo St John again.

'Oh yes, I know that your slave decks will be struck to make way for your trade cargo, but the spare planks are aboard and it won't take you a day to set them up again,' Codrington almost snarled, 'and I'll wager there are open gratings under those hatch covers,' he pointed down at the maindeck, but without taking his eyes from Mungo St John's face, 'that there are shackles in the lower decks to take the chains and leg irons—'

'Captain Codrington, I find your company wearying,' Mungo St John drawled softly. 'You have sixty seconds to leave this ship, before I have my mate assist you over the side.'

Tippoo stepped forward, hairless as an enormous toad, and stood a foot behind Codrington's left shoulder.

With a visible effort, the English captain retained his temper, as he inclined his head towards Mungo St John.

'May God grant we meet again, sir.' He turned back to Robyn and saluted her briefly.

'May I wish you a pleasant continuation of your voyage, madam.'

'Captain Codrington, I think you are mistaken,' she almost pleaded with him. He did not reply but stared at her for a moment longer, the pale eyes were direct and disturbing – the eyes of a prophet or a fanatic – then he turned and went with a gangling boyish stride to *Huron*'s entry port.

Tippoo had stripped off the high-necked tunic and oiled his upper body so it gleamed in the sunlight with the metallic lustre of the skin of some exotic reptile.

He stood stolidly on flat bare feet, balancing effortlessly to the *Huron*'s roll, his thick arms hanging at his side and the lash of the whip coiled on the deck at his feet.

There was a grating fixed at the ship's side and the sailor who had been at the masthead lookout when they had raised the African coast, was spread-eagled upon it like a stranded starfish on a rock exposed at low tide. He twisted his head awkwardly to look back over his shoulder at the mate, and his face was white with terror.

'You were excused witnessing punishment, Doctor Ballantyne,' Mungo St John told her quietly.

'I feel it my duty to suffer this barbaric–'

'As you wish,' he cut her short with a nod, and turned away. 'Twenty, Mr Tippoo.'

'Twenty it is, Cap'n.'

With no expression at all Tippoo stepped up behind the man,

hooked his finger into the back of his collar and ripped the shirt down to the belt. The man's back was pale as suet pudding, but studded with fat purple carbuncles, the sailor's affliction, caused by salty, wet clothing and the unhealthy diet.

Tippoo stepped back and flicked out the lash so that it extended to its full length along the seamed oak planking.

'Ship's company!' Mungo St John called. 'The charge is inattention to duty, and endangering the ship's safety.' They shuffled their bare feet, but not one of them looked up at him. 'The sentence is twenty lashes.'

On the grating the man turned his face away and closed his eyes tightly, hunching his shoulders.

'Lay on, Mr Tippoo,' Mungo St John said, and Tippoo squinted carefully at the bare, white skin, through which the knuckles of the spine showed clearly. He reared back, one thickly muscled arm thrown high above his head, and the lash snaked higher, hissing like an angry cobra, then he stepped forward into the stroke, pivoting the full weight and force of his shoulders into it.

The man on the grating shrieked, and his body convulsed in a spasm that smeared the skin from his wrists against the coarse hemp bonds.

The white skin opened in a thin bright scarlet line, from one side of his ribs to the other, and one of the angry purple carbuncles between his shoulder blades erupted in a spurt of yellow matter that ran down the pale skin and soaked into the waistband of his breeches.

'One,' said Mungo St John, and the man on the grating began to sob quietly.

Tippoo stepped back, shook out the lash carefully, squinted at the bloody line across the white shuddering flesh, reared back and grunted as he stepped forward into the next stroke.

'Two,' said Mungo St John. Robyn felt her gorge rise to choke her. She fought it down, and forced herself to watch. She could not allow him to see her weakness.

On the tenth stroke the body on the grating relaxed suddenly, the head lolled sideways and the fists unclenched slowly so that she could see the little bloody half-moon wounds where the nails had been driven into the palms. There was no further sign of life during the rest of the leisurely ritual of punishment.

At the twentieth stroke, she almost flung herself down the

ladder to the maindeck and was feeling for the pulse before they could cut the body down from the grating.

'Praise be to God,' she whispered as she felt it fluttering under her fingers, and then to the seamen who were lifting the man down, 'Gently now!' She saw that Mungo St John had got his wish, for the white porcelain crests of the spinal column were jutting up through the sliced meat of the back muscles.

She had a cotton dressing ready and she placed it across the ruined back as they laid him on to an oak plank and hustled him towards the forecastle.

In the narrow, crowded forecastle, thick with the fumes of cheap pipe tobacco and the almost solid reek of bilges and wet clothing, of unwashed men and mouldering food, they laid the man on the mess table and she worked as best she could in the guttering light of the oil-lamp in its gimbals overhead. She stitched back the flaps and ribbons of mushy, torn flesh with horsehair sutures and then bound up the whole in weak phenol solution, treatment which Joseph Lister had recently pioneered with much success against mortification.

The man was conscious again and whimpering with pain. She gave him five drops of laudanum, and promised to visit him the following day to change the bindings.

As she packed away her instruments and closed her black valise, one of the crew, a little pockmarked bosun, named Nathaniel, picked it up and when she nodded her thanks, he muttered with embarrassment, 'We are beholden, missus.'

It had taken all of them time to accept her ministrations. First it had been only the lancing of carbuncles and sea-boils, calomel for the flux and the grippe, but later, after a dozen successful treatments, which included a fractured humerus, an ulcerated and ruptured eardrum and the banishing of a venereal chancre with mercury, she had become a firm favourite amongst the crew, and her sick-call a regular feature of shipboard life.

The bosun climbed the companionway behind her, carrying the valise, but before they reached the deck, an idea struck her and she stooped to him, placing a hand on his shoulder.

'Nathaniel,' she asked urgently, but in a low voice, 'is there a way of entering the ship's hold without lifting the maindeck hatches?'

The man looked startled, and she shook his shoulder roughly. 'Is there?' she demanded.

'Aye, ma'am, there is.'

'Where? How?'

'Through the lazaretto, below the officers' saloon – there is a hatchway through the forward bulkhead.'

'Is it locked?'

'Aye, ma'am, it is – and Captain St John keeps the keys on his belt.'

'Tell nobody that I asked,' she ordered him, and hastened up on the maindeck.

At the foot of the mainmast, Tippoo was washing down the lash in a bucket of seawater that was already tinged pale pink; he looked up at her, still stripping the water off the leather between thick hairless fingers – and he grinned at Robyn as she passed, squatting down on thick, brown haunches with his loin cloth drawn up into his crotch, swinging his round bald head on its bull neck to follow her.

She found herself panting a little with fear and revulsion, and she swept her skirts aside as she passed him. At the door of her cabin she took the valise from Nathaniel with a word of thanks, and then slumped down upon her bunk.

Her thoughts and her emotions were in uproar, for she had still not recovered from the sudden avalanche of events that had interrupted the leisurely pattern of the voyage.

The boarding by Captain Codrington of the Royal Navy overshadowed even her anger at the flogging or her joy at her first view of Africa in nearly two decades – and now his accusations rankled and disturbed her.

After a few minutes' rest she lifted the lid of her travelling-chest that filled most of the clear space in the tiny cabin, and had to unpack much of it before she found the pamphlets from the anti-slavery society with which she had been armed in London before departure.

She sat down to study them once again, a history of the struggle against the trade up to the present time. As she read, her anger and frustration reawakened at the tale of unenforceable international agreements, all with built-in escape clauses: laws that made it an act of piracy to indulge in the trade north of the equator, but allowed it to flourish unchecked in the southern hemisphere; treaties and agreements signed by all nations, except those most actively engaged in the trade, Portugal, Brazil, Spain. Other great nations – France – using the trade to goad their traditional enemy, Great Britain, shamelessly exploiting Britain's commitment to its extinction, trading political advantage for vague promises of support.

Then there was America, a signatory to the Treaty of Brussels which Britain had engineered, agreeing to the abolition of the trade, but not to the abolition of the institution of slavery itself. America agreed that the transport of human souls into captivity was tantamount to active piracy, and that vessels so engaged were liable to seizure under prize and condemnation by courts of Admiralty or Mixed Commission, agreed also to the equipment clause, that ships equipped for transport of slaves, although not actually with a cargo of slaves on board at the time of seizure, could be taken as prize.

There was America agreeing to all of this – and then denying to the warships of the Royal Navy the right of search. The most America would allow was that British officers could assure themselves of the legality of the claim to American ownership, and if that was proven, they could not search, not even though the stink of slaves rose from her holds to offend the very heavens, or the clank of chains and the half-human cries from her 'tween decks came near to deafening them – still they could not search.

Robyn dropped one pamphlet back into her chest, and selected another publication from the society.

ITEM, in the previous year, 1859, estimated 169,000 slaves had been transported from the coasts of Africa to the mines of Brazil, and the plantations of Cuba, and to those of the Southern States of America.

ITEM, the trade in slaves by the Omani Arabs of Zanzibar could not be estimated except by observation of the numbers passing through the markets of that island. Despite the British Treaty with the Sultan as early as 1822, the British Consul at Zanzibar had counted almost 200,000 slaves landed during the previous twelve-month period. The corpses were not landed, nor were the sick and dying, for the Zanzibar customs dues were payable to the Sultan per capita, live or dead.

The dead and those so enfeebled or diseased as to have little hope of survival were thrown overboard, at the edge of the deep water beyond the coral reef. Here a permanent colony of huge man-eating sharks cruised the area by day and by night. Within minutes of the first body, dead or still living, striking the water, the surface around the dhow was torn into a seething white boil by the great fish. The British Consul estimated a forty-per-cent mortality rate amongst slaves making the short passage from the mainland to the island.

Robyn dropped that pamphlet and before picking up the next, she reflected a moment on the sheer multitudes involved in the whole grisly business.

'Five million since the turn of the century,' she whispered, 'five million souls. No wonder that they call it the greatest crime against humanity in the history of the world.'

She opened the next pamphlet and skimmed quickly over an examination of the profits that accrued to a successful trader.

In the interior of Africa, up near the lake country where few white men had ever reached, Fuller Ballantyne had discovered – her father's name in print gave her a prickle of pride and of melancholy – Fuller had discovered that a prime slave changed hands for a cupful of porcelain beads, two slaves for an obsolete Tower musket that cost thirteen shillings in London, or a Brown Bess musket that cost two dollars in New York.

At the coast the same slave cost ten dollars, while on the slave market in Brazil he would sell for five hundred dollars. But once he was taken north of the equator, the risks to the trader increased and the price rose dramatically – a thousand dollars in Cuba, fifteen hundred in Louisiana.

Robyn lowered the text, and thought swiftly. The English Captain had challenged that *Huron* could carry 2,000 slaves at a time. Landed in America, they would be worth an unbelievable three million dollars, an amount which would buy fifteen ships like *Huron*. A single voyage would make a man rich beyond mundane dreams of greed, all risks were acceptable to the traders to win such vast wealth.

But had Captain Codrington been justified in his accusations? Robyn knew the counter-accusations that were made against the officers of the Royal Navy, that their zeal arose from the promise of prize money rather than a hatred of the trade and a love of humanity. That every sail they raised was considered a slaver, and that they were swift to apply the Equipment Clause in the widest possible interpretation.

Robyn was searching for the pamphlet that dealt in detail with this Equipment Clause and she found it next on the pile before her.

To enable a ship to be seized as a slaver under the clause, she need only satisfy one of the stipulated conditions. She could he taken if her hatches were equipped with open gratings to ventilate her holds; if there were dividing bulkheads in her holds to facilitate the installation of slave decks; if there were spare planks aboard for laying as slave decks; if she carried shackles and bolts, or leg irons and cuffs; if she carried too many water casks for the number of her crew and passengers; if she had disproportionally large numbers of mess tubs, or her rice boilers were too big, or if she carried unreasonable quantities of rice or farina.

Even if she carried native matting that might be used as bedding for slaves, she could be seized and run in under a prize crew. These were wide powers given to men who could profit financially by seizure.

Was Captain Codrington one of these, were those pale fanatical eyes merely a mask for avarice and a desire for personal gain?

Robyn found herself hoping they were, or at least that in the case of *Huron* he had been mistaken. But then why had Captain St John put down his helm, and run for it the moment he sighted the British cruiser?

Robyn was confused and miserable, haunted with guilt. She needed comfort and she slipped a lace Stuart cap over her head and shoulders before venturing out on to the deck again, for the wind had risen to an icy gale and *Huron* was always a tender ship, she heeled heavily as she beat southwards, flinging spray high into the falling night.

Zouga was in his cabin, dressed in shirt-sleeves and smoking a cigar as he worked over the lists of the expedition's equipment that would still have to be obtained once they reached Good Hope.

He called to her to enter when she knocked, and rose to greet her with a smile.

'Sissy, are you well? It was a most unpleasant business, even though unavoidable. I hope it has not unsettled you.'

'The man will recover,' she said, and Zouga changed the subject as he settled her on his bunk, the only other seating in the cabin.

'I sometimes think we would have been better off with less money to spend on this expedition. There is always such a temptation to accumulate too much equipment. Papa made the

Transversa with only five porter loads, while we will need a hundred porters at the least, each carrying eighty pounds.'

'Zouga, I must speak to you. This is the first opportunity I have had.'

An expression of distaste flickered across the strong, harsh features as though he sensed what she was about to say. But before he could deny her she blurted out, 'Is this ship a slaver, Zouga?'

Zouga removed the cigar from his mouth and inspected the tip minutely before he replied.

'Sissy, a slaver stinks so you can smell it for fifty leagues downwind, and even after the slaves are removed there is no amount of lye that will get rid of the smell. *Huron does* not have the stench of a slaver.'

'This ship is on her first voyage under this ownership,' Robyn reminded him quietly. 'Codrington accused Captain St John of using his profits from previous voyages to purchase her. She is still clean.'

'Mungo St John is a gentleman.' Zouga's tone had an edge of impatience to it now. 'I am convinced of that.'

'The plantation owners of Cuba and Louisiana are amongst the most elegant gentlemen that you could find outside the court of St James,' she reminded him.

'I am prepared to accept his word as a gentleman,' Zouga snapped.

'Are you not a little eager, Zouga?' she asked with a deceptive sweetness, but his tone had kindled sparks in her eyes like the green lights in an emerald. 'Would it not seriously impede your plans to find ourselves shipped on board a slaver?'

'Damn me, woman, I have his word.' Zouga was getting truly angry now. 'St John is engaged in legitimate trade. He hopes for a cargo of ivory and palm oil.'

'Have you asked to inspect the ship's hold?'

'He has given his word.'

'Will you ask him to open the holds?'

Zouga hesitated, his gaze wavered a moment, and then he made his decision.

'No, I will not,' he said flatly. 'That would be an insult to him and quite rightly, he would resent it.'

'And if we found what you are afraid to find, it would discredit the purpose of our expedition,' she agreed.

'As the leader of this mission. I have made the decision—'

'Papa would never let anything stand in his way either, not even Mama or the family—'

'Sissy, if you still feel that way when we reach the Cape, I will arrange for passage on another vessel to Quelimane. Will that satisfy you?'

She did not reply but continued to stare at him with a flat accusing gaze.

'If we did find evidence,' he waved his hands with agitation, 'what could we do about it?'

'We could make a sworn deposition to the Admiralty at Cape Town.'

'Sissy,' he sighed wearily at her intransigence, 'don't you understand? If I were to challenge St John, we could gain nothing. If the accusation is unwarranted we would place ourselves in a damned awkward position, and if in the very unlikely event that this ship is equipped for the trade, we would then be in considerable danger. Do not underestimate that danger. Robyn. St John is a determined man.' He stopped and shook his head decisively, the fashionable curls dangling over his ears. 'I am not going to endanger you, myself or the whole expedition. That is my decision, and I will insist that you abide by it.'

Alter a long pause, Robyn slowly dropped her gaze to her hands, and inter-meshed her fingers.

'Very well, Zouga.'

His relief was obvious. 'I am grateful for your compliance, my dear.' He stooped over her and kissed her forehead. 'Let me escort you to dinner.'

She was about to refuse, to tell him she was tired and that, once again, she would dine alone in her cabin, and then an idea struck her, and she nodded.

'Thank you, Zouga,' she told him, and then looked up with one of those sudden smiles so brilliant. so warm and so rare as to disarm him completely. 'I am fortunate to have such a handsome dinner companion.'

She sat between Mungo St John and her brother, and had her brother not known better, he might have suspected her of flirting outrageously with the Captain. She was all smiles and sparkles, leaning forward attentively to listen whenever he spoke, recharging his glass whenever it was less than half filled with wine and laughing delightedly at his dry sallies.

Zouga was amazed and a little alarmed by the transformation, while St John had never seen her like this. He had covered his original surprise with an amused half-smile. However, in this mood Robyn Ballantyne was an attractive companion. Her stubborn, rather sharp face softened to the edge of prettiness, while her best features, her hair, her perfect skin, her eyes and fine white teeth, gleamed and flashed in the lamplight. Mungo St John's own mood became expansive, he laughed more readily and his interest was clearly piqued. With Robyn plying his glass, he drank more than on any other night of the voyage, and when his steward served a good plum duff he called for a bottle of brandy to wash it down.

Zouga had also been infected by the strangely festive air of the dinner, and he protested as vigorously as St John when suddenly Robyn declared herself to be exhausted and stood up from the board, but she was adamant.

In her cabin she could still hear the occasional shouts of laughter from the saloon, as she went quietly about her preparations. She slid the locking bar into place to assure her privacy. Then she knelt beside her chest and wormed her way down to the bottom layers, from which she retrieved a pair of man's moleskin breeches, a flannel shirt and cravat, with a high-buttoned monkey jacket to go over them, and well-worn half boots.

This had been her uniform and her disguise as a medical student at St Matthew's Hospital. Now she stripped herself naked, and for a moment enjoyed the wicked freedom of the feeling, even indulging herself to the extent of gazing down at her nudity. She was not too certain if it was a sin to enjoy one's own body, but she suspected that it was. Nevertheless she persisted.

Her legs were straight and strong, her hips flared with a graceful curve and then narrowed abruptly into her waist, her belly was almost flat with just an interesting little bulge below the navel. Now here was definitely sinful ground – of this there was no doubt. But still she could not deny the temptation to let her gaze linger a moment. She understood fully the technical purpose and the physical workings of all her body's highly complicated machinery, both visible and concealed. It was only the feelings and emotions which sprang from this source which both confused and worried her, for they had taught her none of this at St Matthew's. She passed on hurriedly to safer ground, lifting her arms to pile the tresses of her hair on to the top of her head and hold them in place with a soft cloth cap.

Her breasts were round and neat as ripening apples, so firm as hardly to change their shape as she moved her arms. Their resemblance to fruit pleased her and she spent a few moments longer than was necessary in adjusting the cloth cap upon her head looking down at them. But there was a limit to self-indulgence, and she swept the flannel shirt over her head, pulled the tails down around her waist, stepped into the breeches – how good they felt again after so long in those hobbling skirts – and then, sitting upon the bunk, she pulled on the half-boots and buckled the ankle straps of the breeches under the arch of her foot, before standing to clinch the belt at her waist.

She opened her black valise, took out the roll of surgical instruments and selected one of the sturdier scalpels, folded out the blade and tested it with her thumb. It was stingingly sharp. She closed the blade and slipped it into her hip pocket. It was the only weapon available to her.

She was ready now, and she closed the shutter on the bull's-eye lantern, darkening the cabin completely before climbing, fully dressed, into her bunk, pulling the rough woollen blanket to her chin and settling down to wait. The laughter from the saloon became more abandoned, and she imagined that the brandy bottle was being cruelly punished by the men. A long while later she heard her brother's heavy, uneven footsteps on the companion way past her cabin and then there was only the creak and pop of the ship's timbers as she heeled to the wind, and far away the regular tapping of some loose piece of equipment.

She was so keyed, with both fear and anticipation, that there was never any danger of her falling asleep. However, the time passed with wearying slowness. Each time that she opened the shutter of the lantern to check her pocket-watch, the hands seemed hardly to have moved. Then, somehow, it was two o'clock in the morning, the hour when the human body and spirit are at their lowest ebb.

She rose quietly from her bunk, picked up the darkened lantern and went to the door of her cabin. The locking bolt clattered like a volley of musketry, but then it was open and she slipped through.

In the saloon a single oil-lamp still burned smokily, throwing agitated shadows against the wooden bulkheads, while the empty brandy bottle had fallen to the deck, and rolled back and forth with the ship's motion. Robyn squatted to pull off her boots and, leaving them at the entrance, she went forward on bare feet, crossed the saloon and stepped into the passageway that led to the stern quarters.

Her breath was short, as though she had run far, and she paused to lift the shutter of the bull's-eye lantern and flash a narrow beam of light into the darkness ahead. The door to Mungo St John's cabin was closed.

She crept towards it, guiding herself with one hand on the bulkhead and at last her fingers closed over the brass door-handle.

'Please God,' she whispered, and achingly slowly twisted the handle. It turned easily, and then the door slid open an inch along its track, enough for her to peep through into the cabin beyond.

There was just light to see, for the deck above was pierced for a repeating compass so that even while in his bunk the master could at a glance tell his ship's heading. The compass was lit by the dull yellow glow of the helmsman's lantern and the reflection allowed Robyn to make out the cabin's central features.

The bunk was screened off by a dark curtain and the rest of the furnishings were simple. The locked doors of the arms chest to the left, with a row of hooks beyond from which hung a boat cloak and the clothing that St John had been wearing at dinner. Facing the door was a solid teak desk with racks to hold the brass navigational instruments, sextant, straight edge, dividers, and on the bulkhead above it were affixed the barometer and the ship's chronometer.

The Captain had evidently emptied his pockets on to the desk top before undressing. Scattered amongst the charts and ship's papers were a clasp knife, a silver cigar case, a tiny gold inlaid pocket pistol of the type favoured by professional gamblers, a pair of chunky ivory dice – Zouga and St John must have fallen to gaming again after she left them – and then most important, what she had hoped to find, the bunch of ship's keys, that St

John usually wore on a chain from his belt, lay in the centre of the desk.

An inch at a time Robyn slid the door further open, watching the dark alcove to the right of the cabin. The curtains billowed slightly with each roll of the ship, and she screwed her nerves tighter as she imagined the movement to be that of a man about to leap out at her.

When the door was open enough to allow her to pass through, it required a huge effort of will to take the first step.

Half-way across the cabin she froze; now she was only inches from the bunk. She peered into the narrow gap in the curtaining and saw the gleam of naked flesh, and beard the deep regular breathing of the sleeping man. It reassured her and she went on swiftly to the desk.

She had no way of learning which keys fitted the lazaretto and the hatch to the main hold. She had to take the whole heavy bunch, and realized that it would mean returning to the cabin later. She did not know if she would have the courage to do that, and as she lifted the bunch her hand shook so it jangled sharply. Startled, she clutched it to her bosom and stared fearfully at the alcove. There was no movement beyond the curtains, and she glided back towards the door on silent bare feet.

It was only when the door closed again that the curtains of the alcove were jerked open, and Mungo St John lifted himself on one elbow. He paused only a moment and then swung his legs out of the bunk and stood up. He reached the desk in two quick strides and checked the top.

'The keys!' he hissed, and reached out for his breeches hanging on the rack beside him, pulling them on swiftly and then stooping to open one of the drawers in his desk.

He lifted the lid of the rosewood case and took out the pair of long-barrelled duelling pistols, thrust them into his waistband, and started for the door of the cabin.

Robyn found the correct key to the lazaretto on the third attempt and the door gave reluctantly, dragging on the hinge with a squeal that sounded to her like a bugle call commanding a charge of heavy cavalry.

She locked the door behind her again, feeling a rush of relief to know that nobody could follow her now and she opened the shutter of the lantern and looked about her swiftly.

The lazaretto was no more than a large cupboard used as a pantry for the officers' personal stores. Sides of smoked ham and dried polonies hung from hooks in the deck above, there were fat rounds of cheese in the racks, boxes of tinned goods, racks of black bottles with waxed stoppers, bags of flour and rice, and, facing Robyn, another hatch with the locking bar chained in place by a padlock the size of her doubled fists.

The key, when she found it, was equally massive, as thick as her middle finger, and the hatch so heavy that it took all of her strength to drag it aside. Then she had to double over to get through the low opening.

Behind her, Mungo St John heard the scrape of wood on wood and dropped silently down the steps to the door of the lazaretto. With a cocked pistol in one hand, he laid his ear to the oak planking to listen for a moment before trying the handle.

'God's breath!' he muttered angrily as he found it locked, and then turned away and raced on bare feet up the companionway to the cabin of his first mate.

At the first touch on his thickly muscled shoulder, Tippoo was fully awake, his eyes glistening in the gloom like those of a wild animal.

'Someone has broken into the hold,' St John hissed at him, and Tippoo reared up out of his bunk, a huge dark figure.

'We find him,' he grunted, as he bound the loin cloth around his waist. 'Then we feed fish with him.'

The main hold seemed vast as a cathedral. The beam of the lantern could not reach into its deepest recesses, and a great mass of cargo was piled high, in some places as high as the maindeck fifteen feet above her.

She saw at once that the cargo had been loaded in such a way that it could be unloaded piecemeal, that any single item could be identified and swung up through the hatches without the necessity of unloading the whole. This, of course, must be essential in a ship trading from port to port. She saw also that the goods were carefully packaged and clearly labelled. Flashing the lantern around her she saw that the cases of equipment for their own expedition were packed here, 'Ballantyne Africa Expedition' stencilled in black on the raw, white wood.

She clambered up the rampart of cases and bales and balanced on the peak, turning the lantern upwards towards the square opening of the hatch, trying to see if there was an open grating, and immediately she was frustrated for the white canvas cover had been stretched around the lower surface also. She stood at full stretch to try and touch the hatch, to feel for the shape of a grating under the canvas, but her fingertips were inches short of the hatch and a sudden wild plunge of the ship under her sent her flying backwards into the deep aisle between the piles of cargo. She managed to keep her grip on the lantern, but hot oil from its reservoir splashed over her hand, threatening to blister the skin.

Once again she crawled up and over the mountains of cargo, searching for the evidence that she hoped not to find. There was no dividing bulkhead in the hold, but the main mast pierced the deck above and came through the hold to rest its foot on the keel, and there were stepped wedges fixed to the thick column of Norwegian pine.

Perhaps they were there to hold the slave decks. Robyn knelt beside the mast and sighted across the hold to the outward curved side of the ship. In line with the wedges on the mast were heavy wooden ledges, like shallow shelves, and she thought that these might be supports for the outer edges of the slave decks. She guessed that they were between two and a half and three feet apart, which she had read was the average height of the between decks in a slaver.

She tried to imagine what this hold might look like with those decks in place, tiers of low galleries just high enough for a man to crawl into doubled over. She counted the shelves and there were five of them – five piles of decks, each with its layer of naked black humanity laid out sardine fashion, each one in physical contact with his neighbour on either side, lying there in his own filth and that of the slaves above him which leaked through the seams of the deck. She tried to imagine the heat of the middle passage when the ship lay becalmed in the baking doldrums, she tried to imagine 2,000 of them vomiting and purging with seasickness as the ship reared and plunged in the wild seas where the Mozambique current scoured the Agulhas bank. She tried to imagine an epidemic of cholera or smallpox taking hold of that mass of misery, but her imagination could not rise to the task, and she pushed the hideous images aside and crawled on over the heaving cargo, flashing her lantern into each corner, searching for more solid evidence than the narrow ledges.

If there was planking on board it would be laid flat upon the deck, below this cargo, and there was no way in which Robyn could reach it.

Ahead of her she saw a dozen huge casks bolted to the forward bulkhead. They could be water barrels, or they could be filled with trade rum, or the rum could be replaced with water when the slaves were taken on board. There was no means of checking the contents, but she knocked on the oak with the hilt of her scalpel and the dull tone assured her that the casks contained something.

She squatted down on one of the bales and slit the stitching with the scalpel, thrusting her hand into the opening she grasped a handful and pulled it out to examine it in the lamp light.

Trade beads, ropes of them strung on cotton threads, a *bitil* of beads was as long as the interval between fingertip and wrist, four bitil made a *khete*. These beads were made of scarlet porcelain, they were the most valued variety called *sam sam*. An African of the more primitive tribes would sell his sister for a *khete* of these, his brother for two *khete*.

Robyn crawled on, examining crates and bales – bolts of cotton cloth from the mills of Salem, called *merkani* in Africa, a corruption of the word 'American' and the chequered cloth from Manchester known as *kaniki*. Then there were long wooden crates marked simply 'Five Pieces', and she could guess that they contained muskets. However, firearms were common trade goods to the coast, and no proof of the intention to buy slaves – they could just as readily be used to purchase ivory or gum-copal.

She was tired now with the effort of climbing and blundering around over the heaving slopes and peaks of cargo, and with the nervous tension of the search.

She paused to rest a moment, leaning back against one of the bales of *merkani* cloth, and as she did so something dug painfully into her back, forcing her to change her position. Then she realized that cloth should not have hard lumps in it. She shuffled around and once again slit the sacking cover of the bale.

Protruding from between the folded layers of cloth, there was something black and cold to the touch. She pulled it out and it was heavy iron, looped and linked, and she recognized it instantly. In Africa they were called 'the bracelets of death'. Here, at last, was proof, positive and irrefutable, for these steel slave cuffs with the light marching chains were the unmistakable stigmata of the trade.

Robyn tore the bale wider open, there were hundreds of the iron cuffs concealed between layers of cloth. Even if it had been possible, a perfunctory search by a naval boarding party was highly unlikely to have uncovered this sinister hoard.

She selected one set of cuffs with which to confront her brother and she started aft towards the lazaretto, filled suddenly with desire to be out of this dark cavern with its menacing shadows, and back once more in the safety of her own cabin.

She had almost reached the entrance to the lazaretto when suddenly there was a loud scraping sound from the deck above, and she froze with alarm. When the sound was repeated, she had enough of her wits still about her to douse the snuffer of her lantern, and then immediately regretted having done so for the darkness seemed to crush down upon her with a suffocating weight and she felt panic rising up to take possession of her.

With a crash like a cannon shot the main hatch flew open, and as she swung back towards it she saw the white pin-pricks of the stars outlined by the square opening. Then a huge, dark shape dropped through, landing lightly on the piled bales beneath, and at almost the same instant the hatch thudded closed again, blotting out the starlight.

Now Robyn's terror came bubbling to the surface. There was somebody locked in the hold with her, and the knowledge held her riveted for long, precious seconds, before she plunged back towards the lazaretto hatch, suppressing the scream that choked up into her throat.

The shape she had glimpsed for a moment was unmistakable. She knew that it was Tippoo in the hold with her, and it spurred her terror. She could imagine the great hairless toadlike figure, moving towards her in the darkness, with repulsive reptilian swiftness, could almost see the pink tongue flickering out over thick cruel lips, and her haste became uncontrolled. She lost her footing in the darkness and fell heavily, tumbling backwards into one of the deep gullies between banks of cargo, cracking the back of her skull on a wooden case, half-stunning herself so that she lost her grip on the extinguished lantern and could not find it when she groped for it. When she scrambled to her knees again, she had lost all sense of direction in the total blackness of the hold.

She knew that her best defence was to remain still and silent until she could place the man who was hunting her, and she crouched down in a crack between two crates. Her pulse beat in her ears like a drum, deafening her – and her heart seemed to have crammed up into her throat so that she must fight for each breath.

It took many minutes and all her determination to bring herself under control, to be able to think again.

She tried to decide in which direction lay the lazaretto hatch, her only means of escape, but she knew that the only way she would be able to find it would be to grope her way to the ship's wooden side and follow it around. The prospect of doing this, with that grotesque creature hunting her in the darkness, was appalling. She shrank down as far as she could into the narrow space and listened.

The hold was filled with small sounds that she had not noticed before, the heave and creak of the ship's timbers, the shifts of the cargo against its retaining ropes and netting – but then she heard the movement of a living thing close behind her and she caught the shriek of terror before it reached her lips, as she lifted her arm to protect her head. Frozen like that, she waited for a blow which never came.

Instead she heard another movement pass behind her turned shoulder, a whisper of sound, yet so chilling that she felt all power of movement drained from her legs. He was here, very close in the blackness, toying with her, cruel as a cat. He had smelt her out. With some sort of animal sense, Tippoo had found her unerringly in the darkness, and now he crouched over her ready to strike and she could only wait.

Something touched her shoulder, and before she could jerk away it swarmed up over her neck, brushed her face. She flung herself backwards and screamed, striking out wildly with the steel chain and handcuffs which she still held in her right hand.

The thing was furry and quick, and it squealed sharply, like an angry piglet as she struck again and again. Then it was gone, and she heard the scamper of small feet across the rough wood of the crate and she realized that it had been one of the ship's rats, big as a tom cat.

Robyn shuddered, revolted, but with a lift of relief that was short-lived.

There was a flash of light, so unexpected that it almost blinded her, and a lantern beam was thrown in a single swift sweep about the hold, and then extinguished, so that the darkness seemed even more crushing than before.

The hunter had heard her scream, and had flashed his lantern in her direction, had probably seen her, for she had clambered out of her niche between the crates. Now at least she knew in which direction to move, the brief flash of light had orientated her once again, she knew where to find the hatch.

She threw herself over a pile of soft bales, clawing herself towards the hatch, then checking her flight to think a moment. Tippoo must have known how she had entered the hold and would know that she would try to escape in the same direction. She must move with care, with stealth, ready for the moment when he flashed the lantern again, taking care not to rush headlong into the trap he was certainly setting for her.

She changed her grip on the iron chain, only then realizing its potential as a weapon, much more effective than the short-bladed scalpel in her pocket. A weapon! For the first time she was thinking of defending herself, not merely crouching like a chicken before the stoop of the hawk. 'Robbie was always the plucky one.' She could almost hear her mother's voice, troubled but touched with pride, when she had defended herself effectively against the village ruffians, or joined her brother on some of his more hair-raising escapades, and she realized she needed all of that pluck now.

With the chain gripped in her right hand, she started stealthily back towards the hatch, crawling, slithering forward on her belly, pausing to listen every few seconds. It seemed like a complete round of eternity before her outreaching fingers touched the solid planking of the after bulkhead. She was within feet of the hatch now and that was where he would be waiting for her.

She crouched down, with her back firmly against the planking and waited for the flutter of her heart to abate enough to allow her to hear, but any noise her hunter made was covered by the creak and pop and groan of the working wooden hull, and the thud and hiss of the sea as *Huron* beat up hard to the wind.

Then she wrinkled her nose at a new smell that overlaid the pervading reek of the bilges. It was the hot oil smell of a shuttered lantern burning very close by, and now when she listened for it, she thought she could hear the pinkle and tick of the heated metal of the lantern. He must be close, very close, guarding the hatchway, ready to flash the lantern at the moment he could place her whereabouts accurately.

With the slowness of spreading oil she rose to face into the darkness where he was, she slipped the scalpel into the palm of her left hand, and she drew back her right arm with the chain and iron cuff dangling from her fist, ready to strike.

Then she pitched the scalpel with a short underhanded throw, judging the distance to drop it close enough to force him to move again, but far enough to make him move away from her.

The tiny missile struck something soft, the sound muted, almost lost in other small sounds, but then it slithered softly along the deck, like a hesitant footfall and instantly light flooded the hold.

Tippoo's monstrous shape sprang out of the darkness, huge, menacing, unbelievably close. He held the unhooded lantern high in his left hand, and the yellow light glistened on the bare round dome of his yellow skull, and on the broad plain of his back, the muscle rippling and tensing into valleys and ridges as he swung back the heavy club in his right hand, his head hunched down on the thick corded neck. He was facing away from her, but only for an instant. As he realized that there was nobody in front of him, he reacted with animal swiftness, ducking the great round head on to his chest, beginning to swing away.

She moved entirely by instinct. She swung the heavy iron manacle on the length of chain. It hummed in a glittering circle in the lamp-light, and it caught Tippoo high on the temple with a crack like a branch breaking in a high wind, and the thin layer of yellow scalp opened like the mouth of a purse with a crimson velvet lining. Tippoo swayed drunkenly on straddled legs that started to buckle under him. She pulled back the chain and swung again with all the weight of her body and the strength of her fear behind the stroke. Again a deep red wound bloomed on the polished yellow dome of his skull and he went down slowly on to his knees, an attitude she had seen him adopt so often as he prayed on the quarterdeck, making the Moslem obeisance towards Mecca. Now again, his forehead touched the deck, but this time with his blood dribbling into a puddle under it.

The lantern clattered on to the deck, still burning, and in its light Tippoo rolled heavily on to his side with his breath snoring in his throat and his eyes rolled up into his head, glaring ghastly white and unseeing, his thick legs kicking out convulsively.

Robyn stared at the prostrate giant, aghast at the damage she had done, already feeling the need to administer to any hurt or crippled being – but it lasted for only seconds, as Tippoo's eyes rolled back into their deep sockets, and she saw the pupils beginning to focus. The yellow gleaming body heaved, the movement of limbs was no longer spasmodic but more co-ordinated and determined, the head lifted, still lolling, but swinging questingly from side to side.

Unbelievably, the man was no longer crippled by those two cutting blows, had been stunned for seconds only, in seconds more he would be fully conscious and in his fury more dangerous than ever. With a sob Robyn flew at the open hatch of the lazaretto. As she passed him, cruel fingers hooked at her ankle, pulling her off balance so she almost fell before she could kick herself free and dive through the opening.

Tippoo was on hands and knees in the light of the fallen lantern, creeping towards her as she threw all her weight against the hatch. As it thudded into its jamb, she dropped the locking bar into its seating, and at that moment Tippoo's shoulder crashed into the far side of the hatch with a force that shook it in its frame.

Her frantic fingers were so clumsy that it took three attempts to secure the padlock and chain, and only then could she sink to the deck and sob away her fear until her relief came to buoy her up and give her renewed strength.

When she dragged herself to her feet, she was light-headed, intoxicated with the strange fierce jubilation that she had never felt before. She knew it sprang from having fought herself out of danger, from the unfamiliar experience of inflicting punishment on a hated adversary – and she knew she would feel guilt for it later, but not now.

The keys were still in the door between the lazaretto and saloon where she had left them. She pushed the door open quickly and paused in the opening an instant, feeling the quick flare of alarm overtake her feeling of elation.

She had only an instant of time to realize that somebody had trimmed the saloon lamp, and then fingers seized her wrist from behind and swung her off balance, bearing her down heavily to the deck and holding her there with one arm twisted up between her shoulderblades.

'Keep still, damn you – or I'll twist your head off your shoulders.' Mungo St John's voice was low and fierce in her ear.

Her arm holding the chain was trapped under her, and now her captor shifted his weight over her, placing his knee in the small of her back and bearing down so painfully that she wanted to cry out with the agony that flared up her curved spine.

'Tippoo flushed you out quickly enough,' St John murmured with grim satisfaction. 'Now let's have a look at you – before we stretch you out on the grating.'

He reached forward and pulled off the cloth cap that covered her head, and she heard his little grunt of surprise as her hair tumbled loose in a slippery shining mass in the lamplight. His grasp slackened and the pressure of his knee into the base of her spine eased. Roughly he grasped her shoulder to turn her on to her back so he could see her face.

She rolled easily towards him and then as her trapped arm came free, she hurled the chain at his face. He threw up both hands to catch the blow. As slippery as an eel she wormed out from under him and flew at the door to the saloon.

He was quick, quicker than she was, and his fingers were steely, they caught in the thin worn flannel of her shirt and it ripped from collar to hem. She turned and lashed at him with the chain again, but now he was ready for her, and he caught her wrist, trapping it.

She kicked wildly at his shins, and succeeded in hooking an ankle behind his heel and they went down together in a tangle on to the wooden deck, and Robyn found herself carried along by a fierce uncaring madness. She was hissing and snarling like a cat as she raked at his eyes with her nails, raising a bloody line down his neck. The tatters of her shirt flapped around her waist and the coarse dark hair of his chest rasped against the tender points of her naked breasts so that dimly in her madness she realized that he wore only breeches, and the man smell of his body filled her nostrils as he tried to smother her wild struggles with his body.

She reached up towards him with her open mouth, trying to sink her teeth into that flushed handsome face, but he caught a handful of her hair at the back of her head and twisted it. The pain seemed to flow down through her body and explode at the base of her belly in a warm soft spasm that took her breath and crammed it down into her lungs.

He held her helplessly and she felt the strength going out of her, to be replaced by spreading languor, and she stared up into his face with a kind of wonder as though she had never seen it before. She saw his teeth were very white, his lips drawn back into a rictus of emotion, and fierce yellow eyes unfocused and smoky with a kind of madness that matched her own.

She made one last feeble effort to repel him, driving her knee upwards, aimed at the fork of his lower body, but he trapped it between his thighs and then holding her thus he reared up over her and looked down at her bared bosom.

'Sweet Mother of God!' he croaked, and she saw the cords strain tight in his throat, saw the hot yellow fire in his eyes and she could not move, not even when he freed his hooked fingers from the twisted tresses of her hair and ran them slowly down her body, cupping first one tight small breast and then the other in the palm of his hand.

She felt his touch had gone, though the memory lingered on her skin like butterflies' wings. Then his fingers were back, tugging demandingly at the fastenings of her breeches. She closed her eyes and refused to let her mind consider what was about to happen. She knew that there was nothing she could do to escape, and cried out softly with the strange elation of the martyr.

But her cry seemed to touch something deep in him, the smoky yellow eyes focused for a moment, the predatory expression of the face became uncertain and then tinged with horror as he looked down at her spread white body. Swiftly he rolled away from her.

'Cover yourself!' he said harshly, and she was overwhelmed with a cold avalanche of loss, followed immediately by as great a rush of shame and of guilt.

She scrambled to her knees, clutching her clothing around her, suddenly shivering, but not with cold.

'You should not have struggled,' he said and though he was obviously fighting to control it his voice shook as hers did.

'I hate you,' she whispered foolishly, and then it became true. She hated him for what he had aroused in her, for the sickness and the guilt that followed it, and for the sense of loss and bereavement with which he had left her.

'I should kill you,' he muttered, not looking at her. 'I should have Tippoo do it.'

She felt no fear at the threat. She had rearranged her clothing as best she could, but still she knelt opposite him.

'Go!' he almost shouted at her. 'Get back to your cabin.'

She rose slowly, hesitated a moment and then turned to the companionway.

'Doctor Ballantyne!' he stopped her, and she turned back. He had risen and now he stood beside the door to the lazaretto, the keys in his one hand, the slave cuff and chain in the other. 'It would be best not to tell your brother of what you discovered tonight.' His voice was controlled now, cold and low. 'I would not have the same scruples with him. We will be at Cape Town in four days,' he went on. 'After that you may do as you will. Until then you will not provoke me again. One chance is already too many.'

She stared at him mutely, feeling small and helpless.

'Goodnight, Doctor Ballantyne.'

She hardly had time to pack her breeches and torn shirt away in the bottom of her chest, inspect and rub a salve on her bruises, pull on her nightdress and climb into her narrow bunk before someone pounded on the cabin door.

'Who is it?' she called huskily and breathless, not yet fully recovered from the night's stresses.

'Sissy, it's me.' Zouga's voice. 'Someone has beaten Tippoo's skull in. He's bleeding all over the deck – can you come?'

Robyn glowed with a fierce spark of pagan glee, which she tried immediately to suppress with less than complete success.

'I'm coming.'

There were three men in the saloon, Zouga, the second mate and Tippoo. Mungo St John was not there. Tippoo sat stolidly on a stool under the oil lamp, naked except for his cotton loin cloth, and his neck and shoulders ran with sheets of dark slick blood.

The second mate held a wad of grubby cotton to his skull and when Robyn lifted it away the wounds began spurting merrily.

'Brandy,' she demanded, and rinsed her hands and her instruments in the spirit – she was an admirer and believer in the teachings of Jenner and Lister – before she probed the points of her forceps into the open wound. She gripped the vessels and twisted them closed. Tippoo made no move, his expression never changed – and she was still carried along on the pagan mood, in direct defiance to the oath of Hippocrates which she had sworn.

'I must clean the wounds,' she told him, and quickly, before her conscience could prevent it, she tipped the raw brandy into the wounds and swabbed them out.

Tippoo sat still as a temple carving of a Hindu devil, making no acknowledgement of the harsh spirit burning open tissue.

Robyn tied off the vessels with silk thread, leaving an end hanging from the wounds, and then she sutured the lips closed, laying precise neat stitches and pulling them up tightly so that the smooth bald scalp came up in a sharp little peak of flesh with each tug.

'I will pull the thread when the vessels mortify,' she told him. 'The stitches will be ready to come out in a week.' She would not deplete her stock of laudanum, she decided, the man obviously was impervious to pain, and she was still in the throes of unchristian spite.

Tippoo lifted the round head. 'You good doctor,' he told her solemnly, and she learned then a lesson that would last her throughout her life – the stronger the purge, the more astringent or foul-tasting the medicine, and the more radical the surgery, then the more impressed with the surgeon's skill was the African patient.

'Yes,' Tippoo nodded gravely, 'you one bloody fine doctor.' And he opened one huge paw. In his palm lay the scalpel that Robyn had lost in *Huron*'s hold. Without expression he placed it in Robyn's own unresisting hand, and with that eerie swiftness was gone from the saloon, leaving her staring after him.

Huron flew southwards, meeting the long South Atlantic rollers and spurning them carelessly, brushing them aside with her shoulder and letting them cream over her rail and then tumble away astern in a long smooth wake.

There were seabirds in company with them now, beautiful gannets with yellow throats and black diamonds painted around their eyes, coming in from the east and soaring above their wake, shrieking and diving for the galley scraps when they were thrown overboard. There were seals too, lifting their whiskered heads high above the surface to stare curiously after the towering clipper as she burst the sea open with her sharp bows in her flight into the south.

Smeared across the brilliant blue water were long serpentine trails of sea-bamboo, torn from the rocky shoreline by the gales and storms of this uneasy and troubled sea.

All these were indications of the land which was always just below the eastern horizon, and Robyn spent many hours of each day alone at the port rail staring towards it, longing for another glimpse of it, smelling the dryness and the spiced aroma of its grass and herbs on the wind, seeing its blown dust in the marvellous reds and glowing gold of the sunsets, but denied sight of it by the offing that St John was making before coming back on to the starboard tack for the final run into Table Bay.

However, as soon as Mungo St John appeared on his quarterdeck Robyn would hurry below without another glance in his direction and she locked herself in her cabin, brooding there alone so that even her brother sensed that something troubled her. He tried a dozen times to draw her out. She sent him away each time, refusing to open the cabin to him.

'I'm all right, Zouga. I just want to be alone.'

And when he tried to join her in her solitary vigils at the ship's rail, she was short and unbending, exasperating him so that he stamped away and let her be.

She was afraid to talk to him, afraid that she would blurt out her discovery of slaving equipment in *Huron*'s hold and put him in deadly danger. She knew her brother well enough not to trust his temper and not to doubt his courage. Neither did she doubt Mungo St John's warning. He would kill Zouga to protect himself – he could do it himself, she had seen him handle a pistol, or he could send Tippoo to do the work in the night. She had to protect Zouga, until they reached Cape Town, or until she did what she had to do.

'Vengeance is mine, saith the Lord.' She had found the passage in her Bible and studied it carefully, and then she had prayed for guidance which had not been given – and she had ended more confused and troubled than she had begun.

She prayed again kneeling on the bare deck beside her bunk until her knees ached, and slowly her duty became clear to her.

Three thousand souls sold into slavery in a single year – that was what the Royal Naval Captain had accused him of. How many thousands before that, how many thousands more in the years to come if *Huron* and her captain were allowed to continue their depredations, if nobody could prevent them ravaging the east coast of Africa, her land, her people, those peoples whom she was sworn to protect and minister to and to lead into the fold of the Saviour.

Her father, Fuller Ballantyne, was one of the great champions of freedom, the unrelenting adversary of this abominable trade. He had called it 'the running sore on the conscience of the civilized world that must be rooted out with all the means at our disposal'. She was her father's daughter, had made her oath in the sight of God.

This man, this monster, epitomized the sickening evil and monstrous cruelty of the whole filthy business.

'Please show me my duty, oh Lord,' she prayed, and always there was her own guilt and shame. Shame that his eyes had probed her half-naked body, that his hands had touched and fondled her, shame that he had debased her further, by stripping bare his own body. Hastily she thrust the image aside, it was too clear, too over-powering. 'Help me to be strong,' she prayed quickly.

There was shame and there was guilt, a terrible corrosive guilt in the fact that his gaze, his touch, his body, had not revolted and disgusted her, but had filled her instead with a sinful delight. He had tempted her to sin. For the first time in all her twenty-three years she had encountered real sin, and she had not been strong enough. She hated him for that,

'Show me my duty, oh Lord,' she prayed aloud and rose stiffly from her knees to sit on the edge of the bunk. She held her well-worn leather-bound Bible in her lap and whispered again.

'Please give unto your faithful servant guidance.' And she let the book fall open, and with her eyes closed placed her forefinger on the text. When she opened her eyes again she gave a start of surprise, guidance obtained by this little ritual of hers was usually not so unequivocal, for she had chosen Numbers 35: 19. 'The revenger of blood himself shall slay the murderer: when he meeteth him, he shall slay him.'

Robyn had no illusions as to the difficulty she would have in performing the heavy duty placed upon her by God's direct injunction, or how easily roles might be reversed and she become herself the victim rather than the avenger.

The man was as dangerous as he was wicked and time was against her. The accurate observation of the sun that Zouga had made at noon that day placed the ship within a hundred and fifty miles of Table Bay, and the wind stood fair and boisterous. Dawn the next day would reveal that great flat-topped mountain rising out of the sea. She had no time for elaborate planning. Whatever she did must be direct and swift.

There were half a dozen bottles in her medicine chest whose contents would serve – but no, poison was the most disgusting of deaths to inflict. She had seen a man die of strychnine poison when she was at St Matthew's. She would never forget the arching spine as his back muscles convulsed until the man stood on the top of his head and on his heels like a drawn bow.

It must be some other means, there was the big naval colt revolver which Zouga kept in his cabin. He had instructed her in its loading and discharge, or there was the Sharps rifle, but both of those belonged to her brother. She did not want to see him swinging from the gallows on the parade ground below the castle at Cape Town. The more uncomplicated and direct the plan, the greater was its chance of success, she realized, and at the thought she knew just how it must be done.

There was a polite knock on her cabin door, and she started.

'Who is it?'

'Jackson, Doctor.' He was the Captain's steward. 'Dinner is served in the saloon.'

She had not realized how late it had grown.

'I will not be dining tonight.'

'You must keep your strength up, ma'am,' Jackson entreated through the closed door.

'Are you the doctor, then?' she asked tartly, and he went shuffling off down the companionway.

She had not eaten since breakfast but she was not hungry, her stomach muscles were rigid with tension. She lay a while on her bunk, gathering her resolve and then she stood up, selected one of her oldest dresses, in a dark heavy wool. It would be the least loss to her wardrobe, and the dark colour would make it less conspicuous in the shadows.

She left her cabin and went quietly up to the maindeck. There was no one but the helmsman on the quarterdeck, his weathered brown face lit faintly by the binnacle lamp.

She moved quietly across to the skylight of the saloon and looked down.

Mungo St John sat at the head of the table, with a joint of steaming salt beef in front of him. He was carving thin slices of meat, laughing across the board at one of Zouga's sallies. One quick glance was enough. Unless there was a call from the lookout or a need to change sail, Mungo St John would not move for another half hour at the least.

Robyn went back down the ladder, past her own cabin and down the companionway to the after quarters. She reached Mungo St John's quarters and tried the door. Once again it slid open easily, she stepped through and closed it behind her again.

It took her only a few minutes to find the case of pistols in the drawer of the teak desk. She opened it on the desk top and took out one of the beautiful weapons. The mottled Damascus steel barrels were inlaid with bright gold, a hunting scene with horses and hounds and huntsmen.

Robyn sat down on the edge of the bunk, held the weapon muzzle-up between her knees while she unscrewed the silver powder flask and measured the fine powder into the cup. It was a familiar chore, for Zouga had spent hours in her instruction. She rammed the charge down into the long, elegant barrel under the felt wad, and then selected a perfect sphere of lead from the ball compartment of the case, wrapped that in an oiled patch of felt to give it a close fit in the rifled barrel and then rammed it down on top of the powder charge.

Then she reversed the pistol, pointing it down at the deck while she fitted one of the copper percussion caps over the nipple of the breech, drew back the hammer until it clicked at full cock, and laid it on the bunk beside her. She did the same with the other pistol, and when they were both loaded and cocked, she placed them on the edge of the desk, butts towards her, ready for immediate use.

Then she stood and, in the centre of the cabin, lifted her skirts around her waist and loosened the draw string of her drawers. She let them fall to the deck, and the air was cool on her naked buttocks so that she felt the little goose pimples rise on her skin. She dropped her skirts and picked up the cotton undergarment. Holding it across her chest she tore it half through and threw it across the cabin, then she took the fastenings of her bodice in both hands and ripped them down almost to her waist, the hooks and eyes hung on the torn threads of cotton.

She looked at herself in the polished metal mirror on the bulkhead beside the door. There was a lustre in her green eyes and her cheeks were flushed.

For the first time in her life, she thought her image beautiful – not beautiful, she corrected herself, but proud and wild and strong as an avenger should be. She was glad he would see her like this before he died, and she lifted her hand and rearranged one of the thick tresses of hair that had broken free of its retaining ribbon.

She sat back on the bunk and picked up a loaded pistol in each hand, she aimed first the one and then the other at the brass handle of the door, and then laid them in her lap and settled down to wait.

She had left her watch in her own cabin so she could not tell how long she waited. The voices and laughter from the officers' saloon were completely muffled by the closed door, but every time a plank creaked or some part of the ship's gear clattered, her nerves sprang tight and she lifted the pistols to cover the doorway.

Then suddenly she heard his footsteps, there was no mistaking them for any other man aboard. They reminded her somehow of a caged leopard pacing its bars, quick, light and alert. He was on the deck above her, but the footsteps were so close that it seemed he was in the cabin with her. She looked up at the deck, swinging her head slightly to follow his turns from one side of the quarterdeck to the other.

She knew what he was doing, she had watched him on a dozen

other nights. First he would talk quietly with the helmsman, checking the slate on which the ship's course was chalked before going back to inspect the log trailing astern. Then he would light one of his thin black Havana cigars and begin pacing the deck, with his hands clasped in the small of his back as he walked, darting quick glances up at the trim of his sails, studying the stars and the clouds for signs of change in the weather, pausing to feel the scend of the sea and the run of the ship under him before pacing on again.

Suddenly the footsteps stopped and Robyn froze, the moment had come. He had paused to flip the stub of his cigar over the rail and watch it fizzle into darkness as it hit the surface of the sea.

There was still time for her to escape, and she felt her resolve weaken. She half rose. She could still reach her own cabin if she moved now, but her legs would not carry her across the cabin. Then she heard his footsteps cross the deck above her with a different tread. He was coming down. It was too late.

Almost choking on her own breath, she sank back on to the bunk and lifted both pistols. They wavered uncertainly and she realized that her hands were shaking. With a tremendous effort she stilled them. The door slammed open and Mungo St John stooped into the cabin, and then stopped as he saw the dark figure and the twin barrels that menaced him.

'They are loaded and cocked,' she said huskily. 'And I will not hesitate.'

'I see.' He straightened slowly, so the dark head just brushed the deck overhead.

'Close the door,' she said, and he pushed it closed with his foot, his arms folded on his chest, and that mocking half-smile on his lips. It made her forget her carefully rehearsed speech, and she stuttered slightly, and was immediately furious with herself.

'You are a slaver,' she blurted, and he inclined his head, still smiling. 'And I have to stop you.'

'How do you propose doing that?' he asked with polite interest.

'I am going to kill you.'

'That should do it,' he admitted, and now he smiled, a flash of white teeth in the gloom. 'Unfortunately they would probably hang you for it, if my crew didn't tear you to pieces before that.'

'You assaulted me,' she said. She glanced at her torn drawers lying near his feet and then with the butt of one pistol touched her torn bodice.

'A rape, by God!' Now he chuckled aloud, and she felt herself blushing vividly at the word.

'It's no laughing matter, Captain St John. You have sold thousands of human souls into the most vile bondage.'

He took one slow pace towards her and she half rose, panic in her voice.

'Don't move! I warn you.'

He took another pace and she thrust both pistols towards him – at the full stretch of her arms.

'I shall fire.'

The smile never wavered on his lips and the yellow flecked eyes held hers steadily as he took another lazy pace closer.

'You have the most beautiful green eyes I have ever seen,' he said, and the pistols shook in her hands.

'Here,' he said gently. 'Give them to me.'

He took the two gold-worked barrels in one hand and turned their muzzles upwards, pointing them at the deck above them. With the other hand he gently began to open her fingers, untangling them from trigger and butt.

'This is not why you came here,' he said, and her fingers went slack. He took the pistols out of her hands and uncocked them before laying them back in their velvet-lined nests within the rosewood case.

His smile was no longer mocking, and his voice was soft, almost tender as he lifted her to her feet.

'I am glad you came.'

She tried to turn her face away, but he took her chin between his fingers and lifted it. As he brought his mouth down to hers, she saw his lips opening, and the warm wet touch was a physical shock.

His mouth tasted slightly salty, perfumed with cigar smoke. She tried to keep her lips closed, but the pressure of his own lips forced them gently open and then his tongue was invading her. His fingers were still on her face, stroking her cheek, smoothing her hair back from her temples, touching lightly her closed eyelids – and she lifted her face higher to his touch.

Even when he slowly unfastened the last hooks of her bodice and eased it down off her shoulders, her only response was to feel the strength go out of her thighs so she had to lean against his hard chest for support.

Then he lifted his mouth from hers, leaving it empty, cooling after the warmth and she opened her eyes. With a sense of disbelief, she saw that his head was bowing to her breast, and she was looking down on the thick dark curls that covered the back of his neck. She knew it must stop now, before he did what she could hardly believe he was about to do.

When she tried to protest, it was only a whimper in her throat. When she tried to seize his head and thrust it away from her, her fingers merely curled into the springing crisp curls the way a cat claws a velvet cushion, and instead of thrusting him away, she drew his head down and arched her back slightly so that her breasts rose to meet him.

Yet she was unprepared for the feel of his mouth. It seemed as though he were about to suck her very soul out through the swollen, aching tips. It was too strong, she tried not to cry out, remembering that the last time she had done so, it had broken the spell – but it was too strong.

It was a sobbing choked-up little cry, and now her legs gave way under her. Still holding his head she sagged backwards on to the low bunk, and he knelt beside the bunk without lifting his mouth from her body. She arched her back and raised her buttocks off the bunk at his touch and allowed him to draw out her billowing skirts from under her and drop them to the deck.

Suddenly, he pulled abruptly away and she almost screamed to him not to go away again – but he had crossed to the door and locked it. Then, as he came back to where she lay, his own clothing seemed to fall away from his body like morning mist from mountain peak, and she came up on one elbow to stare at him openly. She had never seen anything so beautiful, she thought.

'The devil is beautiful also.' A tiny inner voice tried to warn her, but it was far away and so small that she could ignore it. Besides it was too late, far too late to listen to warnings now – for already he was coming over her.

She expected pain, but not the deep splitting incursion that racked her. Her head was flung back and her eyes flooded with the tears of it. Yet even in the stinging agony of it there was never a thought to reject this stretching, tearing invasion and she clung to him with both her arms about his neck. It seemed that he suffered with her, for except for that single swift deep stroke, he had not moved, trying to alleviate her agony by his utter stillness, his body was rigid as hers, she could feel the muscles taut to the point of tearing, and he cradled her in his arms.

Then suddenly she could breathe again, and she took in air with a great rushing sob, and immediately the pain began to change its shape, becoming something she could not describe to herself. It started as a spark of heat, deep within her, and flared slowly so she was forced to meet it with a slow voluptuous movement of her hips. She seemed to break free of earth and rise up through flames, that flickered redly through her clenched eyelids. There was only one reality – and that was the hard body that rocked and plunged above her. The heat seemed to fill her until she could not bear it any longer. Then at the last moment when she thought she might die of it, it burst within her and she felt herself falling, like a tumbling leaf, down, down, at last, to the hard narrow bunk in a half-dark cabin in a tall ship on a wind-driven sea.

When next she could open her eyes his face was very close to hers. He was staring at her with a thoughtful, solemn expression.

She tried to smile, it was a shaky unconvincing effort.

'Please don't look at me like that.' Her voice was even deeper, more husky than it usually was.

'I don't think I ever saw you before,' he whispered and traced the line of her lips with his fingertip. 'You are so different.'

'Different from what?'

'Different from other women.' His reply gave her a pang.

He made the first movement of withdrawing from her, but she tightened her grip on him panic-stricken at the thought of losing him yet.

'We will only have this one night,' she told him, and he did not reply. He lifted one eyebrow, and waited for her to speak again.

'You don't dispute it,' she challenged. There was that mocking little smile beginning to curl his lip again, and it annoyed her.

'No, I was wrong, you are like all other women,' he smiled. 'You have to talk, always you have to talk.'

She let him go, as punishment for those words. But as he slithered free of her she felt a terrible emptiness and she regretted his going fiercely, beginning to hate him for it.

'You have no God,' she accused him.

'Isn't it strange,' he chided her gently, 'that most of the worst crimes in history have been committed by men with God's name upon their lips.'

The truth of it deflated her momentarily, and she struggled into a sitting position.

'You are a slaver.'

'I don't really want to argue with you, you know.' But she would not accept that.

'You buy and sell human beings.'

'What are you trying to prove to me?' He chuckled now, further angering her.

'I'm telling you that there is a void between us that can never be bridged.'

'We have just done so, convincingly,' and she flushed bright scarlet down her neck on to her bosom.

'I have sworn to devote my life to destroy all you stand for,' she said fiercely, pushing her face close to his.

'Woman, you talk too much,' he told her lazily, and covered her mouth with his own, holding her like that while she struggled, gagging her with his lips so her protests were muffled and incomprehensible. Then when her struggles had subsided he pushed her easily backwards on to the bunk and came over her again.

In the morning when she woke, he was gone, but the bolster beside her was indented by his head. She pressed her face into it and the smell of his hair and of his skin still lingered, though the heat of his blood had dissipated and the linen was cool against her cheeks.

The ship was in the grip of intense excitement. She could hear the voices from the deck above as she scurried down the empty passageway to her own cabin, dreading meeting a member of the crew, or more especially meeting her brother. What excuse could she have for being abroad in the dawn, with her cabin unslept in and her clothing torn and rumpled?

Her escape was a matter of seconds only, for as she locked

and leaned thankfully against the door of her cabin, Zouga beat upon it with his fist from the far side.

'Robyn, wake up! Get dressed. Land is in sight. Come and see!'

Swiftly she bathed her body with a square of flannel dipped into the enamelled jug of cold sea water. She was tender, swollen and sensitive and there was a trace of blood on the cloth.

'The trace of shame,' she told herself severely, but it was difficult to sustain the emotion. Instead she felt a soaring sense of physical well-being and a hearty appetite for her breakfast.

Her step was light, almost skipping as she went up on to the maindeck and the wind tugged playfully at her skirts.

Her first concern was for the man. He stood at the weather rail, in shirt-sleeves only, and immediately a storm of conflicting feelings and thoughts assailed her, the chief of which was that he was so lean and dark and devil-may-care that he should be kept behind bars as a menace to all womankind.

Then he lowered the telescope, turned and saw her by the companionway and bowed slightly, and she inclined her head an inch in reply, very cool and very dignified. Then Zouga hurried to meet her, laughing and excited, and took her arm as he led her to the rail.

The mountain towered out of the steely green Atlantic, a great grey buttress of solid rock, riven and rent by deep ravines and gullies choked with dark green growth. She had not remembered it so huge, seeming to fill the whole eastern horizon and reaching up into the heavens, for its summit was covered in a thick shimmering white mattress of cloud. The cloud rolled endlessly over the edge of the mountain like a froth of boiling milk pouring over the rim of the pot, but as it sank so it was sucked into nothingness, disappearing miraculously to leave the lower slopes of the mountain clear and close, each detail of the rock-face finely etched and the tiny buildings at its foot as startling white as the wing feathers of the gulls that milled the air about the clipper.

'We'll dine tonight in Cape Town,' Zouga shouted over the wind, and the thought of food flooded Robyn's mouth with saliva.

Jackson, the steward, had the hands spread a tarpaulin to break the wind and they breakfasted under its lee, in the sunshine. It was a festive meal, for Mungo St John called for champagne and they toasted the successful voyage and the good landfall in the bubbling yellow wine.

Then Mungo St John ended it. 'The wind comes through there, funnelled down that break in the mountain.' He pointed ahead, and they saw the surface at the mouth of the bay seething with the rush of it. 'Many a ship has been dismasted by that treacherous blast. We'll be shortening sail in a few minutes.' And he signalled to Jackon to clear away the trestles that carried the remains of their breakfast, excused himself with a bow and went back to his quarterdeck.

Robyn watched him strip the canvas off the upper yards, taking in two reefs in the main and setting a storm jib so that *Huron* met the freak wind readily and ran in for Table Bay, giving Robben Island a good berth to port. When the ship had settled on to its new heading, Robyn went up on to the quarter-deck.

'I must speak with you,' she told him, and St John cocked his eyebrow at her.

'You could not have chosen a better time—' and with the eloquent spread of his hands indicated wind and current and the dangerous shore close under their bows.

'This will be the last opportunity,' she told him quickly. 'My brother and I will be leaving this ship immediately you drop anchor in Table Bay.'

The mocking grin slid slowly from his lips.

'If you are determined, then it seems that we have nothing more to say to each other.'

'I want you to know why.'

'I know why,' he said, 'but I doubt that you do.'

She stared at him, but he turned away to call a change of heading to the helmsman and then to the figure at the foot of the mainmast.

'Mr Tippoo, I'll have another reef on her, if you please.'

He came back to her side, but not looking at her, his head tilted back to watch the miniature figures of his crew on the mainyards high above them.

'Have you ever seen sixteen thousand acres of cotton with the pods ready for plucking?' he asked quietly. 'Have you ever seen the bales going down river on the barges to the mills?'

She did not answer, and he went on without waiting. 'I have

seen both, Doctor Ballantyne, and no man dare tell me that the men who work my fields are treated like cattle.'

'You are a cotton-planter?'

'I am, and after this voyage I will have a sugar plantation on the island of Cuba – half my cargo to pay for the land and half of it to work the cane.'

'You are worse than I thought,' she whispered. 'I thought you were merely one of the devil's minions. Now I know you are the devil himself.'

'You are going into the interior.' St John looked down at her now. 'When you get there, if you ever do, you will see true human misery. You will see cruelties that no American slave-owner would dream of. You will see the slaughter of human beings by war and disease and wild beast that will baulk your belief in heaven. Beside this savagery, the barracoons and the slave quarters are an earthly paradise.'

'Do you dare suggest that by catching and chaining these poor creatures you do them favour?' Robyn demanded, aghast at his effrontery.

'Have you ever visited a Louisiana plantation, Doctor?' Then answering his own question, 'No, of course, you have not. I invite you to do so. Come down to Bannerfield as my guest one day and then compare the state of my slaves to the savage blacks you will see in Africa, or even to those damned souls that inhabit the slums and workhouses of your own lovely little green island.'

She remembered those raddled and hopeless human creatures with whom she had worked in the mission hospital. She was speechless. Then suddenly his grin was wicked again. 'Think of it only as forced enlightenment of the heathen. I lead them out of the darkness into the ways of God and civilization – just as you are determined to do – but my methods are more effective.'

'You are incorrigible, sir.'

'No, ma'am. I am a sea-captain and a planter. I am also a trader in, and an owner of, slaves – and I will fight to the death to defend my right to be all of those things.'

'What *right* is that you speak of?' she demanded.

'The right of the cat over the mouse, of the strong over the weak, Doctor Ballantyne The natural law of existence.'

'Then I can only repeat, Captain St John, that I will leave this ship at the very first opportunity.'

'I am sorry that is your decision.' The hard fierce look in the yellow eyes softened a little. 'I wish it were otherwise.'

'I shall devote my life to fighting you and men like you.'

'And what a waste that will be of a lovely woman.' He shook his head regretfully. 'But then your resolve may give us reason to meet again – I must hope that is so.'

'One final word Captain St John – I shall never forgive last night.'

'And I, Doctor Ballantyne, will never forget it.'

Zouga Ballantyne checked his horse at the side of the road, just before it crossed the narrow neck between the crags of Table Mountain and Signal Hill, one of its satellite promontories.

He swung down out of the saddle to rest his mount, for it had been a hard pull up the steep slope from the town, and he tossed the reins to the Hottentot groom who accompanied him on the second horse. Zouga was sweating lightly and there was a residual pulse of dullness behind his eyes from the wine he had drunk the night before, the magnificent rich sweet wine of Constantia, one of the most highly prized vintages in the world, but capable of delivering as thick a head as any of the cheap and common grogs they sold in the waterfront bars.

In the five days since they had disembarked, the friendliness of the Cape Colony citizens had almost overwhelmed them. They had slept only the first night at a public inn in Buitengracht Street, then Zouga had called upon one of the Cape Colony's more prominent merchants, a Mr Cartwright. He had presented his letters of introduction from the directors of the Worshipful Company of London Merchants Trading into Africa, and Cartwright had immediately placed at their disposal the guest bungalow set in the gardens of his large and gracious home on the mountain slope above the old East India Company's gardens.

Every evening since then had been a gay whirl of dinners and dances. Had Robyn and Zouga not insisted otherwise, the days would have been filled with equivalent frivolity – picnics, sailing and fishing expeditions, riding in the forest, long leisurely lunches on the lawns under spreading oak trees that reminded him so vividly of England.

However, Zouga had avoided these diversions and had

managed to accomplish much of the work of the expedition. Firstly there had been the supervising of the unloading of equipment from *Huron* – in itself a major undertaking as the crates had to be swayed up from the hold and lowered into lighters alongside before making the perilous return through the surf to land on the beach at Rogger Bay.

Then he had to arrange temporary warehousing for the cargo. Here again Mr Cartwright had been of assistance. Still Zouga found himself fiercely resenting his sister's insistence that had made all this heavy work necessary.

'Damn me, Sissy, even Papa used to travel in the company of Arab slave-traders when he had to. If this fellow St John *is* a trader, we would do well to learn all we can from him – his methods and sources of supply. No one could give us better information for our report to the society.'

None of his arguments had prevailed, and only when Robyn had threatened to write home to the Society's directors in London, and to follow that up with a frank talk to the editor to the *Cape Times*, had Zouga acceded, with the worst grace possible, to her demands.

Now he looked down longingly at *Huron*, lying well out from the beach, snubbing around on her anchor cable to point into the rumbustious south-easterly wind. Even under bare poles she seemed on the point of flight.

Zouga guessed that St John would be sailing within days, leaving them to await the next ship that might be bound for the Arab and Portuguese coasts.

Zouga had already presented his letter of introduction from the Foreign Secretary to the Admiral of the Cape Squadron of the Royal Navy, and been promised all consideration. Nevertheless, he spent many hours of each morning visiting the shipping agents and owners in the port in hope of an earlier passage.

'Damn the silly wench,' he muttered aloud, thinking bitterly of his sister and her foibles. 'She could cost us weeks, even months.'

Time was, of course, of the very essence. They had to be clear of the fever-ridden coast before the monsoon struck and risk of malaria became suicidal.

At that moment there was the crack of cannon shot from the slopes of the hill above him, and as he glanced up he saw the feather of gunsmoke drifting away from the lookout station on Signal Hill.

The gunshot was to alert the townsfolk that a ship was entering Table Bay, and Zouga shaded his eyes with his cap as the vessel came into view beyond the point of land. He was not a seaman but he recognized instantly the ugly silhouette and single smoke stack of the Royal Naval gunboat that had pursued *Huron* so doggedly. Was it really two weeks ago, he wondered, the days had passed so swiftly. *Black Joke*, the gunboat, had her boilers fired and a thin banner of dark smoke drifted away downwind as she rounded up into the bay, her yards training around as she pointed through the wind and she passed within half a mile of where *Huron* was already at anchor. The proximity of the two ships raised interesting possibilities of the feud between the two captains being revived, Zouga realized, but his immediate feeling was of intense disappointment. He had hoped that the vessel might have been a trader that could have offered the expedition further passage up the east coast – and he turned away abruptly, took the reins from the groom and swung up easily into the saddle.

'Which way?' he asked the servant, and the little yellow-skinned lad in Cartwright's plum-coloured livery indicated the left branch of the road that forked over the neck and dropped down across the dragon's-back of the Cape peninsula to the ocean shore on the far side.

It was another two hours' ride, the last twenty minutes along a rutted cart track, before they reached the sprawling thatched building hidden away in one of the ravines of the mountain slope behind a grove of milkwood trees. The slopes behind the building were thick with protea bushes in full flower and the long-tailed sugar-birds haggled noisily over the blazing blooms. To one side a waterfall smoked with spray as it fell from the sheer rock face and then formed a deep green pool on which a flotilla of ducks cruised.

The building had a dilapidated air to it, the walls needed white-washing and the thatch hung in untidy clumps from the eaves. Under the milkwood trees were scattered items of ancient equipment, a wagon with one wheel missing and the woodwork almost entirely eaten away by worm, a rusty hand forge in which a red hen was sitting upon a clutch of eggs, and mouldering saddlery and ropes hung from the branches of the trees.

As Zouga swung down from the saddle, a pack of half a dozen dogs came storming out of the front porch, snarling and barking around Zouga's legs so that he lashed out at them with his riding whip and with his boots, changing the snarls to startled yelps and howls.

'Who the hell are you and what do you want?' A voice carried through the uproar, and Zouga took one more cut at a great shaggy Boerhound with a ridge of coarse hair fully erect between his shoulders, catching him fairly on the snout and forcing him to circle out of range, with fangs still bared and murderous growls rumbling up his throat.

Then he looked up at the man on the stoep of the building. He carried a double-barrelled shotgun in the crook of his arm, and both hammers were at full cock. He was so tall that he had to stoop beneath the angle of the roof, but he was thin as a blue-gum tree, as though the flesh and fat had been burned off his bones by ten thousand tropical suns.

'Do I have the honour of addressing Mr Thomas Harkness?' Zouga called over the clamour of the dog pack.

'I ask the questions here,' the lean giant bellowed back. His beard was as white as the thunderhead clouds of a summer's day on the highveld and it hung to his belt buckle. Hair of the same silver covered his head and flowed down to the collar of his leather jerkin.

His face and his arms were burned to the colour of plug tobacco, and were speckled by the raised blemishes like little moles and freckles, where years of the fierce African sun had destroyed the upper layers of his skin. The pupils of his eyes were black and bright as drops of fresh tar, but the whites were smoky yellow, the colour of the malarial fevers and the pestilences of Africa.

'What is your name, boy?' His voice was strong and deep. Without the beard he might have been fifty years of age, but Zouga knew with certainty that he was seventy-three. He carried his one shoulder higher than the other and the arm on that side hung at an awkward angle to the joint. Zouga knew that a lion had chewed through the shoulder and through the bone of the upper arm, before Harkness had been able to reach his hunting knife on his belt with the other hand and stab it between the forelegs, up into the heart. That had been forty years before and the injury had become the Harkness hallmark.

'Ballantyne, sir.' Zouga shouted to make himself heard above the dogs. 'Morris Zouga Ballantyne.'

The old man whistled once, a fluting double note that stilled the dogs and brought them back around his legs. He had not lowered the shotgun and a frown puckered his sharp features.

'Fuller Ballantyne's pup, is it?'

'That's right, sir.'

'By God, any son of Fuller Ballantyne's is good enough for a charge of my buckshot in the rump. Don't cock your butt when you get back on that horse, boy, for I'm a man who tempts very easily.'

'I've ridden a long way to see you, Mr Harkness.' Zouga smiled that frank and wining smile of his, standing his ground. 'I'm one of your greatest admirers. I've read everything that has ever been written about you and everything you have written yourself.'

'I doubt that,' Harkness growled, 'they burned most of mine. Too strong for their lily livers.' But the hostile glint in his eyes turned to a twinkle and he cocked his head as he studied the young man before him.

'I have no doubt that you're as ignorant and arrogant as your Daddy, but you've got a fairer turn of speech.' And he stared again at the toes of Zouga's boots, and let his gaze move up slowly.

'Priest,' he asked, 'like your Daddy?'

'No, sir, soldier.'

'Regiment?'

'13th Madras Foot.'

'Rank?'

'Major.'

Harkness' expression eased with each reply until his gaze once more locked with Zouga's.

'Teetotal? Like your Daddy?'

'Perish the thought!' Zouga assured him vehemently and Harkness smiled for the first time as he let the muzzles of the shotgun droop until they pointed at the ground. He tugged at the long spikes of his beard for a moment, then reached a decision.

'Come.' He jerked his head and led the way into the house. There was one huge central room, the high ceiling of dried reed stems kept it cool and the narrow windows kept it gloomy. The floor was of peach-pip shells set into a plaster of mud and cowdung and the walls were three-foot thick.

Zouga paused in the threshold and blinked with surprise at the collection of strange articles that covered the walls, were piled on every table and chair, and packed to the rafters in the dark corners.

There were books, thousands of books, cloth and leatherbound books, pamphlets and journals, atlases and encyclopaedias. There were weapons, assegai of Zulu, shield of Matabele, bow of Bushman with its quiver of poisoned arrows and, of course, guns – dozens of them in racks or merely propped against the walls. There were hunting trophies, the beautiful zigzag-striped hide of zebra, the dark bush of the lion's mane, the elegant curved horn of harris-buck, teeth of hippopotamus and warthog, and then the long, yellow arcs of ivory thicker than a woman's thigh and taller than a man's head. There were rocks, piles of rocks that glittered and sparkled, crystal rocks of purple and green, metallic nodules, native copper redder than gold, hairy strands of raw asbestos – all of it covered with a fine layer of dust and piled untidily wherever it had fallen.

The room smelled of skins and dogs and damp, of stale brandy and fresh turpentine, and there were stacks of new canvases already stretched in their wooden frames, while other canvases stood on their easels with the subjects sketched in charcoal outline, or partly blocked in with bright oil paint. On the walls were hung some finished pictures.

Zouga crossed to examine one of them while the old man blew into a pair of glass tumblers and polished them on his shirt-tail.

'What do you think of my lions?' he asked, as Zouga studied a huge canvas entitled 'Lion Hunt on the Gariep River. Feb. 1846'.

Zouga made an appreciative sound in the back of his throat. Zouga was himself a dauber and scribbler, but he considered that the meticulous reproduction of the subject was the painter's duty, while these paintings had a guileless, almost childlike joy in every primitive line. The colours also were gay and made no pretence to imitate nature, while the perspectives were wildly improbable. The mounted figure with the flowing beard in the background dominated the pride of lions in the foreground. Yet Zouga knew that these strange creations had remarkable value. Cartwright had paid ten guineas for a fanciful landscape. Zouga could only believe it was a fad amongst the colony's fashionable set.

'They say my lions look like English sheepdogs.' Harkness glowered at them. 'What do you think, Ballantyne?'

'Perhaps,' Zouga started, then saw the old man's expression change. 'But tremendously ferocious sheep dogs!' he added swiftly, and Harkness laughed out loud for the first time.

'By God, you'll do!' He shook his head as he half-filled the tumblers with the dark brown local brandy, the fearsome 'Cape Smoke', and brought one glass to Zouga.

'I like a man who speaks his mind. Rot all hypocrites.' He raised his own glass in a toast. 'Especially hypocritical preachers who don't give a damn for God, for truth or for their fellow men.'

Zouga fancied that he recognized the description, but raised his glass. 'Rot them!' he agreed, and managed to suppress a gasp as the liquor exploded in his throat and sizzled behind his eyes.

'Good,' he said hoarsely, and Harkness wiped his silver moustache, left and right, with his thumb before he demanded,

'Why have you come?'

'I want to find my father, and I think you may be able to tell me where to search.'

'Find him?' fulminated the old man. 'We should all be extremely grateful he is lost, and pray each day that he remains that way.'

'I understand how you feel, sir,' Zouga nodded. 'I read the book that was published after the Zambezi expedition.'

Harkness had accompanied Fuller Ballantyne on that ill-fated venture, acting as second-in-command, expedition manager and recording artist. He had been caught up in the squabbling and blame-fixing that had marred the enterprise from the beginning. Fuller Ballantyne had dismissed him, accusing him of theft of the expedition stores, trading on his own account, artistic incompetence, neglecting his duties to hunt for ivory, and total ignorance of the countryside and its trails, of the tribes and their customs and had included these accusations in his account of the expedition, implying that the blame for the expedition's failure could be laid on Thomas Harkness' uneven shoulders.

Now even mention of that book brought the colour to the sun-raddled face and made the white whiskers twitch.

'I crossed the Limpopo for the first time in the year that Fuller

Ballantyne was born. I drew the map that he used to reach Lake Ngami.' Harkness stopped and made a dismissive gesture. 'I might as well try and reason with the baboons barking from the tops of the kopjes.' Then he peered more closely at Zouga.

'What do you know about Fuller? Since he sent you home to the old country, how often have you seen him? How much time have you spent in his company?'

'He came home once.'

'How much time did he spend with you and your mother?'

'Some months – but he was always in Uncle William's study writing, or he was up at London, Oxford or Birmingham to lecture.'

'But you, nevertheless, conceived a burning filial love and duty for the sainted and celebrated father?'

Zouga shook his head. 'I hated him,' he said quietly. 'I could hardly bear the days until he went away again.'

Harkness tilted his head on one side, surprised, speechless for a moment, and Zouga drank the last few drops of liquor in the glass.

'I never told anybody that before.' He seemed puzzled himself. 'I hardly even admitted it to myself. I hated him for what he did to us, to me and my sister, but especially to my mother.'

Harkness took the empty tumbler from his fingers, refilled it and handed it back. He spoke quietly.

'I also will tell you something that I have never told another man. I met your mother at Kuruman, my God, so long ago. She was sixteen or seventeen and I was nearly forty. She was so pretty, so shy and yet so filled with a special quality of joy. I asked her to marry me. The only woman I ever asked.' Harkness stopped himself, turned away to his painting, and peered at it. 'Damned sheep dogs!' he snapped, and then without turning back to face Zouga, 'So why do you want to find your father? Why have you come out to Africa?'

'Two reasons,' Zouga told him. 'Both good. To make my own reputation and my own fortune.'

Harkness swivelled to face him. 'Damn me, but you can be direct.' There was a tinge of respect in his expression now. 'How do you plan to achieve those very desirable ends?'

Zouga explained swiftly – the newspaper sponsorship, that of the Society for the Extinction of the Slave Trade.

'You'll find much grist for your mill,' Harkness interjected.

'The coast is still rife with the trade, despite what you'll hear in London town.'

'I am also an agent for the Worshipful Company of London Merchants Trading into Africa, but I have my own goods to trade, and 5,000 cartridges for my Sharps rifle.'

Harkness wandered across the dim room and stopped before one of the gigantic elephant tusks propped against the far wall. It was so old and heavy that there was very little taper from root to tip, the point worn blunt and rounded. One third of its length was smooth and a clear lovely butter yellow colour, where it had been buried in the jaw of the beast, the rest of it was stained dark with vegetable juices and scarred from the battles and foragings of sixty years.

'This one weighs one hundred and sixty pounds – its value in London is six shillings a pound.' He slapped it with his open palm. 'There are still bulls like that out there, thousands of them. But take a tip from an old dog – forget your fancy Sharps, and use one of the ten-bore elephant guns. They throw a ball that weighs a quarter of a pound, and though they kick like the devil himself, they drive better than any of these new-fangled rifles.' There was a lightness in the worn old features, a sparkle in the dark eyes. 'Another tip – get in close. Forty paces at the outside, and go for the heart. Forget what you'll hear about the brain shot, go for the heart –' He broke off suddenly and waggled his head, grinning ruefully. 'By God, but it's enough to make a man want to be young again!'

He came back and studied Zouga directly, and a thought occurred to him with a suddenness that struck him like a physical blow, taking him so by surprise that he almost spoke it aloud.

'If Helen had given me a different answer, you could be my son.' But he held back the words, and asked instead:

'How can I help you, then?'

'You can tell me where I can start to search for Fuller Ballantyne.'

Harkness threw up his hands, palms uppermost. 'It's a vast land – so big that you could travel across it for a lifetime.'

'That's why I have come to you.'

Harkness went to the long table of yellow Cape deal that ran nearly the full length of the room and with the twisted arm swept a clear space amongst the books and papers and paint pots.

'Bring a chair,' he instructed, and when they sat facing each other across the cleared space, he recharged both their glasses and placed what remained in the bottle between them.

'Where did Fuller Ballantyne go?' Harkness asked, and took a silver tress from the thick beard and began to twist it around his forefinger. The finger was long and bony and covered with the thick ridges of ancient scar tissue where the recoil of overheated or overcharged firearms had driven the trigger guard to the bone.

'Where did Fuller Ballantyne go?' he repeated, but Zouga realized the question was rhetorical, and he said nothing.

'After the Zambezi expedition, his fortune was exhausted, his reputation all but destroyed – and to a man like Fuller Ballantyne that was unbearable. His entire life had been an endless hunt for glory. No risk, no sacrifice was too great, his own or others. He would steal and lie – aye, even kill for it.'

Zouga looked up sharply, challenging.

'Kill,' Harkness nodded. 'Anybody who stood in his way. I have seen him, but that is another tale. Now we want to know where he went.'

Harkness stretched out and selected a roll of parchment from the cluttered table-top, checked it quickly and grunted with approval, as he spread it between them.

It was a map of Central Africa, east to west coast, south to the Limpopo, north to the lakes, drawn in India ink and the borders were illuminated by Harkness' characteristic figures and animals.

Instantly Zouga coveted it with his very soul. All that Harkness had accused his father of he felt in his own heart. He had to have this, even if it was necessary to steal – or, by God, kill. He had to have it.

The map was huge – at least five feet square – hand-drawn on the finest quality linen-backed paper. It was unique, the detail enormous; the notations were profuse but succinct, the observations first hand, the details precise, written in a tiny elegant script that needed a reading glass to be deciphered with ease.

'Here heavy concentrations of elephant herds during June to September.'

'Here I sampled gold reef in ancient workings at two ounces to the ton.'

'Here rich copper is worked by Gutus people.'

'Here slave convoys depart for the coast in June.'

There were literally hundreds of these notations, each in a neatly numbered box, that corresponded to the exact location on the map.

Harkness watched Zouga's face, with a sly half-smile on his face, and then handed him a reading-glass to continue his examination.

It took Zouga a few minutes to realize that the pink shaded areas indicated the 'fly corridors' of the high African plateau. The safe areas through which domestic animals could be moved to avoid the tsetse fly belts. The terrible Ngana disease which the fly carried could decimate the herds. Knowledge of these corridors had been gathered by the African tribes over hundreds of years, and here it was faithfully recorded by Thomas Harkness. The value of this knowledge was incalculable.

'Here Mzilikazi's border impis kill all travellers.'

'Here there is no water between May and October.'

'Here dangerous malarial vapours during October to December.'

The areas of greatest hazard were signposted, while the known routes to the interior were clearly marked, though there were few enough of these.

The cities of the African kings were marked, as was the location of their military kraals, the areas of influence of each were defined and the names of the subservient chiefs noted.

'Here concession to hunt elephant must be obtained from Chief Mafa. He is treacherous.'

Harkness watched the young man eagerly poring over the priceless document. His expression was almost fond, and he nodded his head once as a memory passed like a shadow behind his eyes. He spoke at last.

'Your father would be trying to restore his reputation at a single stroke,' Harkness mused. 'He would have to feed that monstrous ego. There are two areas that come immediately to mind. Here!'

He placed his open hand across an enormous area to the north and west of the defined shape of Lake Marawi. In this area the copious and authoritative notations were replaced by meagre, hesitant observations obtained from hearsay or native legend, and by speculation followed by a question mark.

'Sheikh Assab of the Omani Arabs reports River Lualaba runs north and west. Possible flow into Lake Tanganyika.' The dotted outlines of rivers, instead of crisp detail. 'Pemba, the Chief of the Marakan, reports huge lake shaped like butterfly twenty-five days march from Khoto Khota. Called Lomani. Possible source of Luapula and of Herodotus fountain.' The lake was sketched in. 'Question. Is Lake Tanganyika connected to Lake Albert? Question. Is Lake Tanganyika connected to Lake Lomani? If so, Lomani is ultimate source of Nile river?'

Harkness touched the two question marks with his gnarled and bony finger.

'Here,' said Harkness. 'The big question marks. The Nile river. That would attract Fuller. He spoke of it often.' Harkness chuckled. 'Always with the same introductory words, *"of course, the fame matters not at all to me"*.' The old man shook his silver head. 'It mattered not less than the air he breathed. Yes, the source of the Nile river and the fame that it would bring its discoverer – that would fascinate him.'

Harkness stared for a long time at the empty spaces, dreaming perhaps, visions awakening behind the bright black eyes. He aroused himself at last, shaking his shaggy head as if to clear it.

'There would be only one other feat that would attract as much attention, would be greeted with as much acclaim.' Harkness ran his spread hand southwards down the parchment to cover another vast void in the web of mountains and rivers. 'Here,' he said softly. 'The forbidden kingdom of the Monomatapas.'

The name itself had an eerie quality. *Monomatapa*. The sound of it raised the fine hair on the back of Zouga's neck.

'You have heard of it?' Harkness asked.

'Yes,' Zouga nodded. 'They say it is the Ophir of the Bible, where Sheba mined her gold. Have you travelled there?'

Harkness shook his head. 'Twice I started out,' he shrugged. 'No white man has travelled there. Even Mzilikazi's impis have not raided that far east. The Portuguese made one attempt to reach the Emperor Monomatapa. That was in 1569. The party was wiped out, and there were no survivors.' Harkness made a sound of disgust. 'As you could expect of the Ports, they abandoned any further attempt to reach Monomatapa. For the 200 years since then they have been content to sit in their seraglios at Tete and Quelimane, breeding half-castes, and picking up the slaves and ivory that filter down out of the interior.'

'But still there are the legends of the Monomatapa. I heard them from my father. Gold and great walled cities.'

Harkness stood up from the table with the grace of a man half his age and crossed to an iron-bound chest against the wall behind his chair. The chest was not locked but the lid required both the old man's skinny arms to lift it.

He came back with a draw-string bag made of softly tanned leather. It was obviously weighty for he carried it in both hands. He pulled the mouth open, and upended the contents on to the linen map.

There was no mistaking the lovely yellow metal, it had the deep glowing lustre which has bewitched mankind for thousands of years. Zouga could not resist the urge to reach out and touch it. It had a marvellous soapy feeling against his fingertips. The precious metal had been beaten into heavy round beads, each the size of the top joint of Zouga's little finger and the beads had been strung on to animal sinew to form a necklace.

'Fifty-eight ounces,' Harkness told him, 'and the metal is of unusual purity, I have had it assayed.'

The old man lifted the necklace over his own head and let it lie against the snowy fall of his beard. It was only then that Zouga realized that there was a pendant on the string of golden beads.

It was in the shape of a bird, a stylized falcon-like shape with folded wings. It was seated upon a rounded plinth that was decorated with a triangular design, like a row of sharks' teeth. The figure was the size of a man's thumb. The gold metal was polished by the touch of human skin over the ages so that some of the detail had been lost. The eyes of the bird were glassy green chips.

'It was a gift from Mzilikazi. He has no use for gold, nor for emeralds – yes, the stones are emeralds,' Harkness nodded. 'One of Mzilikazi's warriors killed an old woman in the Burnt Land. They found the leather pouch on her body.'

'Where is the Burnt Land?' Zouga asked.

'I'm sorry.' Harkness fiddled with the little golden bird. 'I should have explained. King Mzilikazi's impis have laid waste to the land along his borders, in some places to a depth of a hundred miles and more. They have killed all who lived there and they maintain it as a buffer strip against any hostile force. The Boer commandos from the south particularly, but from any other hostile invader also. Mzilikazi calls it the Burnt Land, and it was here, to the east of his kingdom, that his border guards killed this solitary old woman. They described her as a very strange old woman, not of any known tribe, speaking a language they did not understand.'

Harkness lifted the necklace from his neck and dropped it carelessly back into the bag, and Zouga felt bereft. He would have liked to feel the full weight and the texture of the metal in his hands for a little longer. Harkness went on quietly:

'Of course you have heard the talk of gold and walled cities, like everybody else. But that is the closest I have ever come to corroboration.'

'Did my father know about the necklace?' Zouga asked, and Harkness nodded. 'Fuller wanted to purchase it, he offered me almost twice its gold value.'

They were both silent for a long while, each brooding on his own thoughts until Zouga stirred.

'How would a man like my father try to reach the Monomatapa?'

'Not from the south nor from the west. Mzilikazi, the Matabele king, will let no man pass through the Burnt Land. I feel that Mzilikazi has some deep superstition attached to the land beyond his eastern border. He does not venture there himself, nor does he allow others to do so.' Harkness shook his head. 'No, Fuller would have to try from the east, from the Portuguese coast, from one of their settlements.' Harkness began to trace out the possible approach marches on the linen chart. 'Here there are high mountains. I have seen them at a distance and they seemed a formidable barrier.' Outside, night had already fallen, and Harkness interrupted himself to order Zouga, 'Tell your groom to off-saddle the horses and take them to the stables. It is too late to return. You will have to stay overnight.'

When Zouga returned a Malay servant had drawn the curtains, lit the lanterns and laid a meal of yellow rice and chicken cooked in a fiery curry – and Harkness had opened another bottle of the Cape brandy. He went on talking as though there had been no interruption. They ate the meal and pushed the enamelled tin plates away to return to the map, and the hours passed unnoticed by either of them.

In the intimate lantern light, the sense of drama and excitement that gripped them both was heightened by the brandy they drank. Once in a while Harkness would rise to fetch some souvenir of his travels to reinforce a point, a sample of quartz rock in which the seams of native gold were clearly visible in the lamplight.

'If there is visible gold, it's rich,' Harkness told Zouga.

'Why did you never mine the reefs you found?'

'I could never stay long enough in one place,' Harkness grinned ruefully. 'There was always another river to cross, a range of mountain or a lake that I had to reach – or I was following a herd of elephant. There was never time to sink a shaft, or build a house, or raise a herd.'

When the dawn was rising, peeping into the huge gloomy room around the curtains, Zouga exclaimed suddenly, 'Come with me. Come with me to find Monomatapa!' And Harkness laughed.

'I thought it was your father you were intent on finding.'

'You know better!' Zouga laughed with him. Somehow he felt at home with the old man, as if he had known him all his life. 'But can you imagine my father's face when you come to rescue him?'

'It would be worth it,' Harkness admitted, and then the laughter faded, and gave way to an expression of such deep regret, of such consuming sorrow that Zouga felt a compulsion to reach out across the table and touch the misshapen shoulder.

Harkness pulled away from his touch. He had lived alone too long. He would never again be able to take comfort from a fellow man.

'Come with me,' Zouga repeated, letting his hand drop to the table-top between them.

'I have made my last journey into the interior,' Harkness said tonelessly. 'Now all I have are my paint pots and my memories.' He lifted his eyes to the ranks of framed canvas with their brilliant joyous images.

'You are still strong, vital,' Zouga insisted. 'Your mind is so clear.'

'Enough!' Harkness' voice was harsh, bitter. 'I am tired now. You must go. Now, immediately.'

Zouga felt his anger rise hotly to his cheeks at the abrupt rejection, this sudden change of mood, and he stood quickly. For a few seconds he stood looking down at the old man.

'Go!' said Harkness again.

Zouga nodded abruptly. 'Very well.' His eyes slid down to the map. He knew he must have it at any price, though he sensed that there was no price that Harkness would accept. He must plan and scheme for it, but he would have it.

He turned and strode to the front door, and the dogs that had slept around their feet rose and followed him.

'Garniet!' Zouga shouted angrily. 'Bring the horses.' And he stood in the doorway rocking impatiently on his toes and heels, hands clasped behind his back, his shoulders stiff, not looking around at the thin stooped figure who still sat at the table in the lamp-light.

The groom brought the horses at last, and still without turning Zouga called roughly, 'Good day to you, Mr Harkness.'

The reply was in a frail old man's quaver that he hardly recognized.

'Come again. We have more to discuss. Come back – in two days.'

The stiffness went out of Zouga's stance. He started to turn back, but the old man waved him away with a brusque gesture and Zouga stamped down the front steps, vaulted into the saddle and whipped his mount into a gallop along the narrow rutted track.

Harkness sat at the table until long after the hoof beats had faded. Strange that the pain had receded to the very back of his consciousness during the hours that he had sat with the youngster. He had felt young and strong, as though he had suckled upon the vigour and the youth of the other.

Then it had come back with a savage rush at Zouga Ballantyne's invitation, almost as if to remind him that his life was no longer his, that it was already forfeit to the hyena that lived deep in his belly, each day growing stronger, bigger, as it fed upon his vitals. When he closed his eyes he could imagine it, the way that he had seen it so often in the light of a thousand camp fires – up there in the wonderful land that he would never visit again. The thing within him had the same furtive slinking presence and he could taste the fetid breath of it in his throat.

Now he gasped as the full strength of the pain returned, as the beast buried its fangs deeper into his gut.

He knocked over the chair in his haste to reach the precious bottle in the back of the cabinet and he gulped a mouthful of the clear pungent liquid without measuring it into the spoon. It was too much, he knew that, but each day he needed more to keep the hyena at bay, and each day the relief took longer to come.

He clung to the corner of the cabinet and waited for it. 'Please,' he whispered, 'please let it end soon.'

There were half a dozen messages and invitations awaiting Zouga on his return to the Cartwright estate that morning, but the one which gave him most excitement was on official Admiralty paper, a polite request to call upon the Hon. Ernest Kemp, Rear-Admiral of the Blue, Officer Commanding the Cape Squadron.

Zouga shaved and changed his clothing, selecting his best jacket for the occasion although it was a long dusty ride to Admiralty House. Despite missing a night's sleep, he felt vital and alert.

The Admiral's Secretary kept him waiting only a few minutes before showing him through, and Admiral Kemp came around from behind his desk to greet Zouga amiably, for the young man came highly recommended and Fuller Ballantyne's name still commanded respect in Africa.

'I have some news which I hope will please you, Major Ballantyne. But first, a glass of Madeira?'

Zouga had to curb his impatience while the Admiral poured the syrupy wine. The Admiral's study was decorated richly, with velvet furnishings and a fashionable profusion of ornaments, small statues, bric-a-brac, stuffed birds in glass showcases, family portraits in ornate frames and pretty ceramics, potted plants and the kind of paintings which Zouga admired.

The Admiral was tall but stooped, as though to accommodate his long frame to the limited headroom between the decks of one of Her Majesty's ships. He seemed old for the responsible appointment he held, guarding the Empire's lifeline to India and the East, but the ageing may have been caused by ill-health rather than years. There were dark-toned pouches of skin below his eyes and other marks of sickness carved around his mouth and evident in the distended blue veins on the back of his hands as he handed a glass of Madeira to Zouga

'Your good health, Major Ballantyne.' And then after he had tasted his own wine, 'I think I have a berth for you. A ship of my squadron anchored in Table Bay yesterday, and as soon as she has replenished her coal bunkers and revictualled I shall detach her for independent duty in the Mozambique channel.'

Zouga knew from his meetings with the directors of the Society for the Extinction of the Slave Trade, that one part of the Admiral's standing orders read:

'You are requested and required to dispose the ships of your squadron in such manner as most expediently to prevent vessels of whatever Christian nation from engaging in the slave trade on the coast of the African continent south of the equator.'

Clearly Kemp intended a sweep of the eastern seaboard with elements of his squadron, and Zouga felt awakening delight as the Admiral went on genially, 'It will not need much of a diversion for my ship to call at Quelimane, and to land you and your party.'

'I cannot thank you sufficiently, Admiral.' His pleasure was transparent, and Admiral Kemp smiled in sympathy. He had put himself out more than his usual wont, for the youngster was attractive and likeable, deserving of encouragement, but now there were other matters awaiting his attention and as he pulled out his gold hunter and consulted it pointedly he went on,

'You should be ready to sail in five days' time.' He returned the watch to the fob of his uniform coat. 'I hope we will see you on Friday? My Secretary did send you an invitation, did he not? Your sister will be with you, I hope.'

'Indeed, sir.' Zouga stood in obedience to his dismissal. 'And my sister and I are honoured.'

In fact Robyn had said, 'I do not waste my evenings, Zouga, and I have no intention of enduring the company of a fleet of tipsy sailors nor of suffering the wagging tongues of their wives.'

The Cape wives were agog with the presence in their midst of the notorious Robyn Ballantyne who had impersonated a man and invaded, successfully, an exclusive masculine preserve. Half of them were deliciously scandalized, and the rest were awed and admiring. However, Zouga was certain that she would pay this price for their passage to Quelimane.

'Very well then.' Admiral Kemp nodded. 'Thank you for calling on me.' And then, as Zouga started for the door, 'Oh, by the way, Ballantyne. The ship is the *Black Joke*, Captain Codrington commanding. My Secretary will give you a letter for him, and I suggest you call upon him to introduce yourself and to learn the date of sailing.'

The name came as a shock, and Zouga checked his stride as he thought quickly of the complication which the choice of ship might bring.

Zouga was sensitive to any threat to the expedition, and Codrington had struck him as being a hot-headed, almost fanatical character. He could not afford any slur to his leadership, and Codrington had seen him sailing in company with a suspected slaver. He could not be sure what Codrington would do.

It was a delicate decision: accept the berth and risk Codrington's denunciation, or refuse the offer of passage and perhaps wait for months in Cape Town before another vessel offered them another.

If they were delayed that long, it would mean missing the cooler and dryer period between the monsoons, they would have to cross the pestilential and fever-ridden coastal lowlands in the most dangerous season.

Zouga made his decision. 'Thank you, Admiral Kemp. I will call on Captain Codrington as soon as possible.'

Thomas Harkness had asked Zouga to return on the second day, and the map was more important even than swift passage to Quelimane.

Zouga sent Garniet, the Cartwrights' groom, down to the beach with a sealed letter addressed to Captain Codrington and with instructions to take one of the water boats out to *Black Joke* and deliver it personally to Codrington. It was a warning, couched in the most polite terms, that Zouga and Robyn would call on the Captain the following morning. Zouga had become aware that his sister had an effect on men quite out of proportion to her physical appearance – even Admiral Kemp had asked for her personally – and he had no compunction in using her to take the edge off Codrington's temper. He would have to warn her to exert her charm, but now there was more important business.

He had mounted on Cartwright's big bay gelding and ridden halfway down the gravelled drive between the oaks, when a thought struck him and he swung the horse's head and cantered back to the guest bungalow again. The Naval Colt revolver was on the top layer of his chest, already fully loaded and with caps on the nipples. He carried it under the tail of his coat while he went back out to the tethered gelding, and then slipped the revolver surreptitiously into the saddlebag as he swung up into the saddle.

He knew he had to have the Harkness map at any price, but he deliberately refused to think what that price might be.

He pushed his mount hard up the steep road to the neck between the peaks, and gave him only a few minutes to blow before starting down the far slope.

The air of dilapidation which hung over the thatched building in the milkwood grove seemed to have deepened. It seemed totally deserted, silent and desolate. He dismounted and threw his reins over a milkwood branch and stooped to ease the girth. Then he quietly unfastened the buckle of the saddlebag and slipped the Colt into his waistband and pulled his coat over it.

As he started towards the stoep, the big ridge-backed Boerhound rose from where it had lain in the shadows and came to meet him. In contrast to its previous ferocity, the animal was subdued, its tail and ears drooping and it whined softly when it recognized Zouga.

He went up on to the stoep and hammered on the front door with his fist, and heard the blows reverberate through the room beyond. Beside him, the Boerhound cocked its head and watched him expectantly, but silence settled again over the old building.

Twice more Zouga beat upon the door, before he tried the handle. It was locked. He rattled the brass lock and put his shoulder to the door; but it was heavy teak in a solid frame. Zouga jumped down off the stoep and circled the house, squinting his eyes at the fierce reflected sunlight from the whitewashed walls. The windows were shuttered.

Beyond the farmyard stood the old slave quarters, now used by Harkness' servant, and Zouga called loudly for him, but his room was deserted and the ashes cold in the cooking place.

Zouga went back to the main house and stood by the locked kitchen door.

He knew that he should go back to his horse and ride away, but he needed the map, even if just for long enough to make a copy. Harkness was not here, and in three days, perhaps less, he would be sailing out of Table Bay.

There was a pile of broken rusted garden tools in the corner of the stoep. Zouga selected a hand scythe, and carefully probed the metal point of the blade into the crack between jamb and door. The lock was old and worn, the tongue slipped back easily under the blade and he jerked the door open with his free hand.

It was still not too late. He paused in the doorway for many seconds, and then he took a deep breath and stepped quietly into the gloom of the interior.

There was a long passage leading past closed doors towards the front room. Zouga went down it, opening doors quietly as he passed. In one room was a huge four-poster bedstead with the curtains opened and the bed clothes in disorder.

Quickly Zouga passed on to the main room. It was in semi-darkness and he stopped to let his eyes adjust, and immediately was aware of a low sound. The hive-murmur of insects seemed to fill the high room. It was a disturbing, almost menacing sound, and Zouga felt the skin prickle on his forearms.

'Mr Harkness!' he called hoarsely, and the hum rose to a loud buzzing. Something alighted on his cheek and crawled across his skin. He struck it away with a shudder of revulsion and stumbled across to the nearest window. His fingers were clumsy on the fastening of the shutters. A shaft of white sunlight burned into the room as the shutter swung open.

Thomas Harkness sat in one of the carved wingback chairs across the cluttered table, and stared at Zouga impassively.

The flies crawled over him, big metallic blue and green flies that glittered in the sunlight. They swarmed with evident glee upon the deep dark wound in the centre of his chest. The snowy beard was black with clotted blood, and blood had formed a congealed pool beneath his chair.

Zouga was rooted by the shock for many seconds, and then reluctantly he took a step forward. The old man had propped one of his big-bored elephant guns against the table leg, reversing the weapon so the muzzle pressed into his own chest and his hands were still locked around the barrel.

'What did you do that for?' Zouga demanded stupidly, speaking aloud, and Harkness stared back at him.

Harkness had removed the boot from his right foot, and depressed the trigger with his bare toe. The massive impact of the heavy lead ball had driven the chair and the man in it back against the wall, but he had retained his death grip on the barrel.

'That was a stupid thing to do.' Zouga took a cheroot from his case and lit it with a Swan Vesta. The smell of death was in the room, coating the back of his throat and the roof of his mouth. Zouga drew deeply on the tobacco smoke.

There was no reason at all to feel grief. He had known the old man for a single day and night. He had come here for one reason only – to get the map the best way he was able. It was ridiculous now to have the deep ache of sorrow turning his legs leaden and stinging the backs of his eyes. Was he mourning the passing of an era perhaps, rather than the man himself? Harkness and the legends of Africa were interwoven. The man had been history itself.

Slowly Zouga approached the figure in the chair, and then reaching out drew his palm slowly down over the old face, ruined by the elements and by pain, closing the lids down over the staring black eyes.

The old man looked more peaceful that way.

Zouga hooked one leg over the corner of the cluttered table, and smoked the cheroot slowly, in almost companionable silence with Thomas Harkness. Then he dropped the stub in the big copper spittoon beside the chair and went through to the bedroom.

He took one of the blankets off the bed and brought it back.

He brushed the flies away into an angry buzzing circle, and threw the blanket over the seated figure. As he drew it up over the head, he murmured softly, 'Get in close, old man, and go for the heart,' the advice that Harkness had given him as a farewell. Then he turned away briskly to the laden table, and began shuffling through the jumbled pieces of canvas and paper, and slowly his impatience turned to alarm – and then to panic as he hunted through pile after pile without finding the map.

He was panting when at last he straightened up and glared at the blanket-covered figure.

'You knew I was coming for it, didn't you!'

He left the table and went to the chest, lifted the lid against groaning hinges and the leather bag with its golden contents was gone also. He ransacked the chest down to its floorboards, but it was not there. Then he started to search in earnest, going carefully through any possible hiding-place in the crowded room. An hour later he went back and perched on the edge of the table once more.

'Damn you, for a cunning old bastard,' he said quietly. He took one more slow look about the room, making certain that he overlooked nothing. The painting of the lion hunt was no longer on the easel, he noticed.

Suddenly the humour of the situation struck him, and his scowl lightened, he began to chuckle ruefully to himself.

'You had the last joke on the Ballantynes, didn't you? By God, but you always did things your way, Tom Harkness, I'll grant you that.'

He stood up slowly, and placed his hand on the blanket-covered shoulder. 'You win, old man. Take your secrets with you then.' He could feel the twisted old bones through the cloth and he shook him gently and then he went out quickly to his horse for there was much to do. It took him the rest of the day to cross the neck again and reach the magistrate's court, then to get back with the coroner and his assistants.

They buried Thomas Harkness that evening, wrapped in the blanket, under the milkwood grove, for the heat was oppressive in the valley and they could not wait for a coffin to be carted out from the city.

Zouga left the coroner to take charge of the estate, to list the equipment and livestock in the yard and put his seals on the doors of the old house until the contents could be taken in.

Zouga rode home in the golden Cape dusk, his boots dusty and his shirt sticky with sweat. He was exhausted from the day's exertions, and low in spirits, still oppressed by grief for the old man, and angry with him for the last trick he had played.

The groom took his horse in front of the bungalow.

'Did you deliver the letter to Captain Codrington?' Zouga demanded, and hardly waited for the reply as he went up into the house. He needed a drink now, and while he poured whisky into a cut crystal glass, his sister came into the room, and reached up casually to kiss his cheek, wrinkling her nose at the tickle of his whiskers and the smell of his sweat.

'You had best change. We are dining with the Cartwrights

tonight,' Robyn told him. 'I could not avoid it.' And then as an afterthought, 'Oh, Zouga, a coloured servant delivered something for you this morning. Just after you had left. I had it put in the study.'

'Who is it from?'

Robyn shrugged. 'The servant spoke only kitchen Dutch and he seemed terrified. He fled before I could find someone to question him.'

With the whisky glass in his hand Zouga crossed to the door of the study, and stopped there abruptly. His expression changed, and he strode through the doorway.

Minutes later Robyn heard his shout of triumphant laughter, and curiously she crossed to the open door. Zouga stood beside the heavy carved stinkwood desk.

On the desk-top lay a draw-string bag of tanned and stained leather from which spilled a heavy necklace of gleaming gold; beside the bag was spread a magnificently illustrated map on a backing of linen parchment, and Zouga stood with his back to her. He held at arm's length a flamboyant picture in oils in a large frame, a figure on horseback with a band of ferocious wild animals in the foreground, and as she watched, Zouga reversed the picture. There was a message freshly carved into the wood of the frame.

For Zouga Ballantyne. May you find the road to all your Monomatapas – would only that I could have gone with you.

Tom Harkness.

Zouga was laughing still, but there was a strange quality to the laughter and when he turned towards her she realized with a shock that her brother's eyes were bright with tears.

Zouga brushed the crumbs from his lips with the damask table napkin and chuckled as he picked up the sheet of newsprint and shook it open again at the second page.

'Damn me, Sissy, I should have known better than to leave

you alone.' He read further and laughed outright. 'Did you really say that to him? Did you really?'

'I cannot remember my exact words,' Robyn told him primly, 'you must remember it was in the heat of battle.'

They sat on the terrace of the bungalow under the pergola of vines, through which the early sun flicked golden coins of light upon the breakfast table.

The previous day the editor of the *Cape Times*, with a speculator's eye to making a profit on Dr Robyn Ballantyne's notoriety, had invited her on a tour of the military hospital at Observatory, and in innocence, Robyn had believed that the visit was at the invitation of the Colony's administration and she had welcomed the opportunity to widen her professional experience.

The visit had succeeded beyond the editor's most extravagant expectations, for the surgeon-general of the Colony had scheduled a tour for the same day and he had walked into the hospital's main operating room, followed by his staff, at the moment that Robyn was expressing herself on the subject of sponges to the hospital matron.

The surgeon's sponges were kept in pails of water, clean water from the galvanized rainwater tanks at the rear of the building. The pails were under the operating table, where the surgeon could reach them readily, and after swabbing away blood and pus and other matter the sponge was dropped into a collection tray, later to be washed out and returned to the original pail of fresh water.

'I assure you, doctor, that my nurses wash the swabs out most thoroughly.' The matron was a formidable figure with the flattened features of a bulldog bitch and the same aggressive thrust to her jaw. She stooped, plunged her hand into the pail, and selected one of the sponges and proffered it to Robyn.

'You can see for yourself bow soft and white they are.'

'Just like the soft white germs that swarm in them.' Robyn was angry, with red spots of colour in her cheeks. 'Have none of you here ever heard of Joseph Lister?'

The surgeon-general answered her question from the doorway.

'The answer to that question, Doctor Ballantyne, is NO we have never heard of that person, whoever he may be. We do not have time to concern ourselves with the opinions of every crank or, for that matter, with male impersonators.'

The surgeon-general had a very good idea of the identity of

the young woman before him. He had followed the gossip which was the Colony's main recreation, and he did not approve of Robyn.

On the other hand, Robyn had no idea as to the identity of the elderly gentleman with the bushy grey whiskers and beetling brows, though by the dried blood stains on the front of his frock coat she guessed that he was a surgeon of the old school, one who operated in his street clothes and let the stains advertise his profession. Here was a much more worthy adversary than the hospital matron, and she rounded on him with the battle light bright in her eyes.

'Then, sir, I am amazed that you admit so readily your ignorance and your bigotry.'

The surgeon-general spluttered for breath and a ready answer.

'By God, madam, you do not truly expect me to look for dangerous poisons in each speck of dust, in each drop of water, on my own hands even.' He held them up for her inspection, shaking them in Robyn's face. There were dark rinds of dried blood under the nails, for he had operated that morning. He pushed his face close to hers, and she drew back a little as his spittle flew angrily.

'Yes, sir,' she told him loudly. 'Look for them there, and on each breath you exhale, on those filthy clothes.'

The editor scribbled delightedly in his shorthand notebook, as the exchanges became more violent, more loaded with personal insult. He had not bargained for anything so spectacular, but the climax came when Robyn had goaded her adversary until he used an oath as potent as his rage.

'Your choice of words is as foul as these lowly little white sponges of yours,' she told him, and let him have the sponge full in the face, hurling it with all her strength so that water flew and dripped from his whiskers on to the front of his frock coat as Robyn marched from the operating room.

'You hit him?' Zouga lowered the newspaper, and stared across the table at his sister. 'Really, Sissy, sometimes you are no lady.'

'True,' Robyn agreed unrepentantly. 'But that is not the first time you have made that observation. Besides I had no idea that he was the surgeon-general.'

Zouga shook his head in mock disapproval and read to her. 'His considered opinion of you, as expressed to the editor, is that you are a fledgling doctor of dubious qualification very recently obtained from an obscure school of medicine, by even more dubious means.'

'Oh, rich!' Robyn clapped her hands. 'He's a better orator than a surgeon.'

'He goes on to say that he is considering going to law to obtain redress.'

'For assault with a sponge.' Robyn laughed lightly as she stood up from the breakfast table. 'A fig for him, but we must hurry if we are to keep our appointment with Captain Codrington.'

Her mood was still gay as she stood beside Zouga in the stern of the water lighter when they came alongside the steel side of the gunboat.

The south-east wind had raked the surface of Table Bay into a cottonfield of white caps, and had spread a thick white tablecloth of cloud upon the flat-topped mountain. The people of the Colony called this wind 'The Cape Doctor', for without it the summers would have been oppressive and enervating. However, it provided a constant hazard to shipping and the bottom of the bay was littered with wrecks. *Black Joke* had two men on her anchor watch as she lunged and fretted against her cable.

As the lighter came alongside, the thick canvas hoses were passed down and a dozen men on the pumps began to transfer the cargo into the gunboat's boiler room tanks, before any attempt was made to take visitors aboard.

As Robyn came up through the entry port to the maindeck she looked immediately to the quarterdeck. Codrington was in shirt sleeves, he was a head taller than the group of warrant officers around him, and his sun-bleached blond hair shone in the sunlight like a beacon.

The group was giving its attention to the coal lighter which was secured against the port side of the ship.

'Have the hands secure a tarpaulin over the buckets.' Codrington shouted down to his boatswain in the lighter. 'Else you'll have us looking like a party of chimneysweeps.'

The deck was alive with the purposeful pandemonium of revictualling, bunkering and watering, and with Zouga beside her, Robyn picked her way through the litter. Codrington turned away from the rail and saw them.

He seemed younger than Robyn remembered, for his expression was relaxed and his manner easy. He had an almost boyish air when contrasted to the grizzled and weatherbeaten sailors about him, but the illusion was dispelled the moment he recognized his visitors. Suddenly his features were stern and the line of his mouth altered, the eyes chilled to the hardness of pale sapphires.

'Captain Codrington,' Zouga greeted him with his most studied charm. 'I am Major Ballantyne.'

'We have met before, sir,' Codrington acknowledged, making no effort to return the smile.

Zouga went on unruffled, 'May I present my sister, Doctor Ballantyne?'

Codrington glanced back at Robyn. 'Your servant, ma'am.' It was more a nod than a bow. 'I have read something of your further exploits since our last meeting in this morning's newssheet.' For a moment the stern expression cracked, and there was a mischievous spark in the blue eyes. 'You have strong views, ma'am, and an even stronger right hand.'

Then he turned back to Zouga. 'I have orders from Admiral Kemp to convey you and your party to Quelimane. No doubt you will find our company dull, after your previous travelling companions.' Deliberately Codrington turned and looked across a half mile of wind.creamed green water to where *Huron* still lay at her anchor, and for the first time Zouga fidgeted uncomfortably as he followed the direction of the Captain's eyes. Codrington went on. 'Be that as it may, I would be grateful if you could present yourselves aboard this ship before noon on the day after tomorrow when I expect a fair tide to leave the bay. Now you must excuse me. I must attend to the management of my ship.' With a nod, not offering to shake hands or make any other civility, Codrington turned away to his waiting warrant officers, and Zouga's charm deserted him. His face darkened and seemed to swell with anger at the abrupt dismissal.

'The fellow has a damnable cheek,' he growled fiercely to Robyn. For a moment he hesitated and then with a curt, 'Come, let us leave,' he turned, crossed the deck, and clambered down into the water lighter, but Robyn made no move.

She waited quietly until Codrington had finished the discussion with his boatswain, and looked up again, feigning surprise to see her still there.

'Captain Codrington, we left *Huron* on my insistence. That is why we are now seeking other passage.' She spoke in a low husky voice, but her manner was so intense that his expression wavered.

'You were correct. That ship is a slaver and St John is a slave-master. I proved it.'

'How?' he demanded, his manner altering instantly.

'I cannot speak now. My brother—' She glanced back at the entry port, expecting her brother to reappear at any moment. He had given her strict instructions as to how he expected her to act towards Codrington.

'I will be at the landing-place at Rogger Bay this afternoon,' she went on quickly.

'What time?'

'Three o'clock,' she said, and turned away, lifted her skirts above her ankles and hurried to the ship's side.

Admiral Kemp sat impatiently in the immense carved abbot's chair which his junior officers referred to as the 'throne'. The size of it emphasized the thinness of the old man's body. It seemed his shoulders were too narrow to support the mass of gold lace which decorated his blue uniform. He clasped the arms of the chair to keep from fidgeting, for this young officer always made him uneasy.

Clinton Codrington leaned forward towards him and spoke quickly, persuasively, using the finely shaped hands to emphasize each point. The Admiral found this much energy and enthusiasm wearying. He preferred men with less mercurial temperament, who could be relied on to carry out orders to the letter without introducing startling improvisations.

Officers with a reputation for brilliance he viewed with deep suspicion. He had never had that reputation as a young man, in fact his nickname had been 'Slogger' Kemp, and he believed that the word brilliance was a pseudonym for instability.

The nature of duty on this station made it necessary for young men like Codrington to be detached for months at a time on independent service, instead of being kept with the battle fleet under the strict eye of a senior officer, ready with a signal of rebuke to check any hot-headedness.

Kemp had an uneasy conviction that he was going to be seriously embarrassed by this particular officer before his appointment of Commander to the Cape Squadron terminated, and allowed him to collect his knighthood and retire to the peace and beloved seclusion of his Surrey home. That his future plans had not already been prejudiced by young Codrington was only a matter of the utmost good fortune, and Kemp had difficulty keeping his expression neutral when he remembered the Calabash affair.

Codrington had run down on the slave barracoons at Calabash on a clear June morning so that the five Argentinian slave ships had spotted his topsails while he was thirty miles out, and had immediately begun frantically re-landing their cargoes of slaves on the beach.

By the time *Black Joke* reached them, the five captains were grinning smugly, their holds empty, and nearly two thousand miserable slaves in clear view squatting in long lines on the shore. To add to the slavers' complacency they were a good twenty nautical miles south of the equator, and therefore at that time beyond the jurisdiction of the Royal Navy. The barracoons had been sited at Calabash to take full advantage of this provision in the international agreements.

The slavers' complacency turned to indignation when the *Black Joke* ran out her guns, and under their menace sent boats with armed seamen on board them.

The Spanish masters, under their Argentinian flags of convenience, protested vigorously and volubly the presence of armed boarding parties.

'We are not a boarding party,' Codrington explained reasonably to the senior captain. 'We are armed advisors, and our advice is that you begin taking aboard your cargo again – and swiftly.'

The Spaniard continued his protests until the crack of a gun from the *Black Joke* drew his attention to the five nooses already dangling from the gunboat's yardarm. The Spaniard was certain that the nooses could not be put to the use for which they were very obviously intended – then he looked once more into the chilled sapphire eyes of the very young silver-haired English officer and decided not to make any bets on it.

Once the slaves were re-embarked the Englishman, their self-appointed armed advisor, gave them his next piece of unsolicited advice. That was that the slave fleet up-anchor and set a course which five hours later intercepted the equatorial line.

Here Captain Codrington made a very precise observation of

the sun's altitude, consulted his almanac and invited the Spanish captain to check his workings and confirm his finding that they were now in 0°05′ North latitude. Then the Englishman immediately arrested him and seized the five vessels; the armed advisors changing their status, without visible pain or discomfort, to that of prize crews.

When Codrington sailed his five prizes into Table Bay, Admiral Kemp listened aghast to the Spaniard's account of his capture, and then immediately retired to his bed with bowel spasms and migraine headache. From his darkened bedroom he dictated first the order confining Codrington to his ship and the ship to its anchorage, and then his horrified report to the First Lord of the Admiralty.

This episode, which might so easily have ended with Codrington court-martialled and beached for life and with the abrupt termination of Admiral Kemp's dogged advance towards his knighthood and retirement, had in fact brought both men riches and advancement.

The sloop carrying Kemp's despatch to the First Lord passed another southbound in mid-ocean, which in its turn bore despatches for the Admiral Commanding the Cape Squadron from not only the First Lord but the Foreign Secretary as well.

Kemp was requested and required in the future to apply the 'equipment clause' to the ships of all Christian nations – with the glaring exception of the United States of America – in all latitudes, both north and south of the equatorial line.

The despatches were dated four days previous to Codrington's raid upon the Calabash barracoons, making his actions not only legal but highly meritorious.

From the very brink of professional disaster, Admiral Kemp had been snatched back, with his knighthood assured and a large sum of prize money paid into his account at Messrs Coutts of the Strand. The five Spaniards were condemned at the next session of the Court of Mixed Commission at Cape Town. Kemp's own share of the prize money had amounted to several thousand pounds, that of his junior captain to nearly twice that amount, and both officers had received personal letters of commendation from the First Lord.

None of this had done anything to increase Kemp's trust or liking for his junior, and now he listened with mounting horror to the suggestion that he sanction the boarding and search of the American trading clipper, which was at present enjoying the hospitality of the port.

For some sickening moments Kemp contemplated his place in history as the officer who had precipitated the second war with the former American colonies. There was nothing equivocal about the view of the American Government as to the sanctity of their shipping, and there were specific sections of Kemp's Admiralty orders covering the subject.

'Admiral Kemp,' Codrington was clearly burning with enthusiasm for the enterprise, 'it is absolutely beyond question that the *Huron* is a slaver, and is equipped for the trade in terms of the act. She is no longer upon the high seas, but lying at anchor within British territorial waters. I can be aboard her within two hours, with impartial witnesses, a Supreme Court judge even.'

Kemp cleared his throat noisily. He had in fact tried to speak, but so appalled was he that the words had not reached his lips. Codrington seemed to take the sound as encouragement.

'This man, St John, is one of the most infamous slavers of modern times. His name is a legend on the coast. They say he carried over 3,000 slaves one year across the middle passage. It's a golden opportunity for us.'

Kemp found his voice at last. 'I dined at Government House on Wednesday. Mr St John was in the company as his Excellency's personal guest. I considered Mr St John to be a gentleman, and I know he is a man of considerable substance and influence in his own country,' he said flatly, no trace of emotion in his voice. His self-control surprised even himself.

'He is a slaver.' Robyn Ballantyne spoke for the first time since she had seated herself at the window of the Admiral's study. The two men had forgotten her existence, but now they both turned to her.

'I have been inside the *Huron*'s main hold and she is fully equipped for the trade,' she said, her voice low but clear, and Kemp felt a sour feeling rising within him. He wondered that he had thought this young woman enchanting at their first meeting. Kemp liked young females and he had personally instructed his Secretary to send the invitations to the Ballantynes, brother and sister, but now he regretted it. He could see, of course, that what he had mistaken for spirit was in fact the mischievousness of the born troublemaker, and that far from being pretty she was in fact downright plain, with a large nose and heavy jaw. He had found her a refreshing change from the simpering and giggling young ladies of the Colony – and realized now that the preference had been unwise. He wondered if he could have his Secretary withdraw the invitation.

'I would think, Admiral Kemp, that it was your duty to send a search party aboard the *Huron*,' Robyn told him – and Kemp leaned back in the big chair and breathed heavily through his mouth. As an Admiral of the Blue it had been some years since anybody had dared point out his duty for him. His grip on his self-control slackened.

He stared at the young person. Did he detect a peculiar venom in her voice? He wondered. She had been a passenger on *Huron*. She had left the ship the instant it reached Table Bay. There was no doubt the woman was 'fast' and that Captain St John was a handsome man.

There was a fine story here, Kemp concluded, as he asked drily, 'Is it true, Miss Ballantyne, that you assaulted the surgeon-general in a fit of ungovernable rage?'

Robyn gaped at him for a moment, the change of direction taking her completely off-balance, and before she could reply he went on,

'You are clearly a highly emotional young lady. I would have to consider very carefully committing a hostile act against an important citizen of a friendly nation on your unsupported testimony.'

He pulled the gold watch from his fob pocket, and consulted it with his full attention.

'Thank you for calling on me, Miss Ballantyne.' Once again he did not use her professional title. 'We look forward to seeing you tomorrow evening. Perhaps you would allow me a private word with Captain Codrington.'

Robyn felt her cheeks burning as she rose from the window seat.

'Thank you, Admiral, you have been very kind and patient,' she said tightly, and swept from the room.

Kemp was not so mild with Codrington. While the young Captain stood to attention before him, he leaned forward in the throne and the veins stood out like twisted blue ropes in the back of his hands as he gripped the arms of the chair.

'You were misguided in bringing that young person here to discuss navy business,' he snapped.

'Sir, I needed to convince you.'

'That's enough, Codrington. I have heard all you have to say. Now you listen to me.'

'Aye, aye, sir.'

'You are naive not to take into account the changed circumstances in the American administration. Are you not aware that Mr Lincoln is likely to be elected to the presidency?'

'I am, sir.'

'Then even you may be dimly aware that very delicate considerations are in the balance. The Foreign Office is confident that the new administration will have a markedly changed attitude to the trade.'

'Sir!' Codrington agreed stiffly.

'Can you imagine what it will mean to us to have full right of search of American shipping on the high seas?'

'Sir.'

'We will have that – once Mr Lincoln takes the oath, and if no junior officers of this service take independent action to prejudice the attitude of the Americans.'

'Sir.' Codrington stood rigid, staring over the Admiral's head at a painting of a lightly veiled Venus on the panelled wall behind him.

'Codrington,' Kemp spoke now with cold menace, 'you have had one very close shave at Calabash. I swear to you, if you let your wild nature get the better of you once more, I will have you hounded from the service.'

'Sir.'

'You are now under the strictest injunction not to approach closer than a cable's length to the trade clipper *Huron*, and if you should encounter her again at sea, you will pay her passing honours and give her a wide berth. Do I make myself sufficiently clear?'

'Sir.' Only Codrington's lips moved, and the Admiral took two long controlled breaths before going on.

'When will you sail for the Mozambique channel?' he asked, his voice more reasonable.

'I have your orders to take the flood on Saturday, sir.'

'Can you advance that sailing?'

'Yes, sir, but it would mean leaving without fully charged magazines – we expect the powder barge alongside at dawn on Saturday.'

Kemp shook his head, and sighed. 'I would feel better with you at sea,' he muttered. 'But, very well then, I will look to see you flying the Blue Peter at first light on Saturday morning.'

Robyn Ballantyne was waiting for him in the borrowed Cartwright carriage, under the portico of Admiralty House.

Codrington came down the steps, with his cocked hat under his arm and climbed stiffly into the buttoned leather seat beside her.

The Hottentot coachman flicked his whip at the shiny rumps, and they swayed in unison as the carriage jerked away down the tree-lined driveway.

Neither of them spoke until they had left the Admiralty grounds, and were whirling down the hill towards the Liesbeeck bridge with the coachman holding them on a light brake.

'What do we do now?' Robyn asked.

'Nothing,' said Clinton Codrington.

Twenty minutes later as they came around the shoulder of the mountain and looked down at the bay where *Huron* rode at anchor, Robyn spoke again.

'Can't you think of anything to stop this monster?'

'Can you?' he asked sharply, and neither of them spoke again until they reached the landing-place.

The fishing-boats were in and beached already, their catch laid out on the sand, a glittering silver and ruby-red pile around which the housewives and their servants bartered and bargained with the brown barelegged fishermen, while the fish horns blared to summon more customers down from the town. The two in the parked carriage watched the commotion with unnatural attention, avoiding each other's eyes.

'You will be at the Admiralty ball tomorrow night? I heard Slogger Kemp say so.'

'No,' Robyn shook her head fiercely. 'I cannot abide the frivolous chatter and silly behaviour of these occasions, and I particularly do not want to be again the guest of that man.'

Codrington turned to her for the first time since they had reached the landing. She was a fine-looking woman, he thought, with that clear lustre to her skin and the thoughtful dark-green eyes under their dark curved brows. He liked a tall strong woman, and he had learned enough of her spirit to accord her respect, a respect that could easily become fascination, he realized.

'Could I prevail upon you to change your mind?' he asked quietly, and she glanced at him, startled. 'I would undertake to provide sober conversation and a dignified dancing partner.'

'I do not dance, Captain.'

'That is a great relief,' he admitted. 'For neither do I, when I have a choice.' He smiled. She could not remember seeing him smile before. It changed him completely. The coldness went from the pale blue eyes and they darkened with merriment while two deep laughter lines formed at the corner of his mouth and arched up to touch the thin straight nose.

'Slogger Kemp keeps a wonderful chef.' He was wheedling now. 'Fine food and serious conversation.'

His teeth were porcelain white and very regular against the deep-water tan. She felt the corners of her own mouth tugging upwards, and he saw the change in her and pressed his advantage.

'I may have further news, some further plan for *Huron* to discuss with you.'

'That makes it irresistible.' She laughed outright at last, with surprisingly unforced gaiety that made some of the nearest bystanders glance around at her and smile in sympathy.

'I will call for you. Where? When?' He had not realized how attractive she truly was until she laughed.

'No.' She laid her hand on his forearm. 'My brother will accompany me, but if you are there I look forward to our momentous conversation.' She felt the devil in her again, and squeezed his arm, finding pleasure in his immediate response, the way the muscles in his forearm corded under her finger-tips.

'Wait,' she told the coachman and watched the slim tall figure go down the beach to where *Black Joke*'s whaler waited for him.

He was wearing his dress uniform for the visit to his commanding Admiral. The gold lace epaulettes emphasized the breadth of his shoulders and his sword belt upped his waist. Abruptly, she wondered whether his body hair was as blond as the queue that was twisted up at the nape of his neck – and then instantly was shocked and agitated at herself. She would never have harboured a thought like that before. Before what? she asked herself, and the answer was clear; before that night on *Huron*. Mungo St John had much to answer for. Comfortably placing blame where it belonged, she pulled her eyes away from the lithe figure of Clinton Codrington and leaned forward to tell the coachman,

'Home, please.'

She would not attend the Admiral's ball, she decided, and then she began to recite silently to herself the Christian articles of faith.

However, Zouga prevailed over her good intentions. The two of them shared the open carriage with the eldest, unmarried Cartwright daughter, for it was one of the balmy nights of a Cape autumn.

Cartwight and his wife followed in the closed carriage, in serious discussion for the entire journey.

'I am sure he is quite taken with Aletta,' Mrs Cartwright had stated.

'My dear, the fellow has no fortune whatsoever.'

'Expectations,' Mrs Cartwright told him benignly. 'I understand he will make thousands from this expedition. He is one of those young men who will get on in life, I am certain of that.'

'I prefer money in the bank, my dear.'

'He has created quite a stir, I assure you – such a serious and sensible young man, and so very attractive. It would be quite a feather in Aletta's cap, and you could make a place for him in the firm.'

Every lamp in Admiralty House was lit and a blaze of golden light welcomed the guests. There were coloured lanterns hung in the trees to illuminate the garden.

The marine band in scarlet and gold had converted the open gazebo into a bandstand, and already there were dancers on the open-air dance floor whirling furiously through the opening waltz, waving and calling greetings to the late-comers in the carriages as they trotted up the curved driveway and took their turn to alight under the portico of the main entrance.

Bewigged footmen in household uniform with silken hose and buckled shoes placed the steps and handed down the ladies on to the welcoming red carpet. At the head of the stairs the major domo announced each group in a low throaty bellow.

'Major and Doctor Ballantyne. Miss Cartwright.'

Robyn had not grown altogether accustomed to the scandalized ripple of feminine interest that followed her entrance to any public gathering here in the Colony. The quick exchange of glances, the nods and murmurs behind covering fans. It still left her with a heightened pulse and a feeling of bitter disdain for all of them.

'Did you bring your sponge, Sissy? They expect you to hit somebody with it,' Zouga murmured, and she shook his arm to silence him, but he went on: 'or to drop your skirts and run up the staircase in your breeches.'

'You are wicked.' She felt the tension go out of her, and she smiled her thanks at him and they were into the throng of uniforms, gold lace on navy blue or dress scarlet, with, here and there, the dead black of evening dress relieved by the high stock and white lace ruffles of silk shirts.

The women's skirts were taffeta and flounced silk over pyramids of petticoats. However, they were at least two years behind the London fashions, for only the most daring ladies had bared their shoulders, and powdered them dead white.

Robyn's own dress made no concession to fashion, for it was years old, the only one that she possessed even vaguely suitable for the occasion. The cloth was wool, the skirt narrow, the bodice adorned with neither seed pearls nor sequins. There were neither ostrich feathers nor diamantines to sparkle in her hair. She should have been dowdy, but instead she was strikingly different.

When she had told Codrington that she did not dance it was because she had never had the occasion, and she regretted it now as she watched Zouga lead Aletta Cartwright on to the floor and swirl away in the graceful dip and turn of the waltz.

She knew that nobody would invite her to dance, and that if they did she would be awkward and untutored. She turned away quickly – seeking a familiar or friendly face. She did not want to be left standing alone in the crowd. She began bitterly to regret that she had not stood by her resolution to stay away.

Her relief came with such a rush that she could have thrown her arms around his neck and embraced him. Instead she said evenly, 'Ah, Captain Codrington. Good evening.'

He really was one of the better-looking men in the room, she thought. She could sense the resentment of some of the younger women, so quite deliberately she took his arm as he offered it, but was surprised that he led her immediately through into the garden.

'He's here!' he said quietly, as soon as they were out of earshot of the others.

She did not have to ask who, and she felt the little jolt of shock that kept her silent for a moment.

'You've seen him?'

'He arrived five minutes before you did – in the Governor's carriage.'

'Where is he now?'

'He went into Slogger's study – with the Governor.' Clinton's face was set and hard. 'The fellow flaunts himself.'

A servant approached them with a silver tray of champagne flutes. Robyn shook her head distractedly but Clinton took a glass and drank it in two gulps.

'The devil of it is that nobody can touch him,' he fumed.

When the evening turned chill, the Marine band moved on to the orchestral balcony above the ballroom floor and punched out the dance tunes with a bouncing martial air that set the dancers spinning and prancing.

One dancer stood out above the others, not merely because of his physical height. When the others hopped and strained with gasping breath and flushed faces, Mungo St John seemed to turn and dip and glide with measured, unhurried grace although he completed a circuit of the ballroom floor more swiftly than any other dancer. Always there was one of the prettiest women in the room swinging in the circle of his arms, laughing up at him, cheeks flushed with excitement, and a dozen others watching him with covert envy over the shoulders of their own partners.

Clinton and Robyn watched him also, from the raised and colonnaded balcony that surrounded the dance floor. They stood in a small circle of Clinton's brother officers and their ladies, making no serious effort to contribute to the light chatter around them.

Robyn found herself hoping that St John would look up at her, would catch her eye so that she could flash her hatred at him; but he never glanced once in her direction.

She even thought of suggesting to Clinton Codrington that they should dance, despite her earlier protestations, but quickly decided against it. She knew that as a dancer, the naval captain would not be able to stand comparison with the elegant American.

When she went in to dinner on Clinton's arm, she saw St John ahead of them. He had a blond woman on his arm, notoriously the Colony's prettiest, richest and most voracious widow. Her coiffure was an elaborate creation of diamanté and ostrich feathers, her shoulders were bared and she showed more of her bosom than she concealed beneath a brocaded bodice stiff with seed pearls.

Mungo St John wore simple black and white evening dress with more panache than any of the most elaborate military uniforms around him.

Robyn watched the woman tap his shoulder with her fan to attract his attention and then reach up on tiptoe to whisper in his ear, while St John stooped gravely to listen.

'The woman's a brazen whore,' Robyn hissed, and beside her Clinton covered his shock at the word, and then nodded.

'And he's the very devil himself.'

It was as though St John heard them, for he glanced up and saw them watching him across the room. He bowed and smiled at Robyn.

It was such an intimate, completely knowing smile that she felt as though he had stripped her naked again, the way he had in the stern cabin of *Huron*, and immediately she felt the same feeling of helplessness overwhelm her.

With a huge effort she managed to turn away, but Clinton had been watching her. She could not meet his eyes, she felt he would be able to read it all if she did.

Two hours after midnight the Marine band was playing the less strenuous airs for the lovers and romantics who still circled the ballroom floor, but most of the company had gone up to the cardrooms on the first floor, if not to play themselves, then to crowd around the tables and watch with hushed attention and the occasional bursts of applause at a particularly audacious or successful coup.

In the largest room the game was whist and the players were Slogger Kemp and the older guests. In the second room the younger set were at the light-hearted chemin-de-fer and Zouga smiled at Robyn as she passed. He and Aletta Cartwright were playing a single hand between them, and the girl squealed with glee as she won a handful of silver shillings.

Robyn and Clinton passed on into the third and smallest salon. Here it was the game that had once been popular only in

America. Recently, however, it had come into sudden vogue at court when the Queen had found it fascinating, and in consequence it was all the rage around the empire despite the odd name – poker.

In spite of Her Majesty's interest in it, it was still not considered a game for ladies to play in mixed company. Only men sat at the green baize, although the ladies fluttered around them like bright butterflies.

Mungo St John sat facing the doorway so that Robyn saw him the instant she stepped into the room. He lazed in his chair, the waves of his dark hair unruffled and sleeked down as if carved from polished ebony, holding a tight fan of cards low against the snowy lace front of his shirt. There was a long black unlit cheroot between his teeth, and as Robyn watched the blond widow leaned across his shoulder displaying the creamy cleavage between her breasts and held a Vesta to the cheroot.

St John sucked flame into the tip of the cheroot, blew a long feather of blue smoke and thanked her with a slant of his eyes before he made his next bid.

He was an obvious winner, a careless pile of gold spilled across the table in front of him, each coin embossed with the Grecian style head of Queen Victoria looking much younger than her forty-one years – and as they watched, he won again.

Excitement seemed to exude from the man like a tangible substance, infecting the women about the table so they exclaimed at every wager he made, and sighed with disappointment if he folded his cards and declined to play a hand. The same excitement spread to the five other men at the table. It was obvious in the glitter of the eyes, in the white knuckles of the fingers that held their cards, in the rash calls and the imprudent urge that made them remain in play long after chance and the odds were evidently against them. It was clear that all of them saw St John as the main adversary, and the tension went out of each hand if he was not in play.

Robyn felt herself held by the same fascination, and unconsciously tightened her grip on Clinton's arm as the suspense mounted in each hand and the gold coins tinkled in the centre of the table, and she heard herself gasp with chagrin or relief at the show of cards that ended each hand.

Unconsciously, she had moved closer to the table drawing Clinton with her, so that when one of the players exclaimed with disgust, 'Fifty guineas is enough for one night. Will you excuse me, gentlemen?' gathered his few remaining coins from the table and pushed back his chair, they had to stand back to allow him to leave.

With surprise Robyn felt Clinton disengage her fingers from his arm, and then he slipped quietly into the vacant chair.

'May I join you, gentlemen?'

There were preoccupied grunts of acknowledgement but only St John looked up and asked civilly,

'Are you aware of the stakes, Captain?'

Clinton did not reply but took a roll of five-pound notes from an inside pocket and placed them beside him. The amount surprised Robyn, it could not have been less than one hundred pounds. Then she remembered that Clinton Codrington had been for many years one of the most successful blockade commanders on the slave coasts. Her brother had repeated to her the rumour that during that period he had won prize money in excess of ten thousand pounds, yet somehow she had never thought of him as a rich man.

Then with sudden intuition Robyn realized that by that gesture Clinton had laid down a silent challenge, and with a little smile Mungo St John had accepted it.

Robyn felt a flare of alarm. She was certain that Clinton Codrington had chosen an opponent too experienced and skilled. She remembered that Zouga who relied on gambling to eke out his regimental pay, had been no match for the man, even with moderate stakes, and in his frustration Clinton had been drinking steadily during the evening. She was sure his judgement would be faulty even if he had any knowledge of the game.

Almost immediately St John subtly altered the style of his play, doubling the stakes before the draw, crowding the game, dominating it, playing from the strength and confidence of his already considerable winnings, and Clinton seemed immediately uncertain of himself, hesitant in accepting the doubled stakes, discarding rather than going at risk for more than a few guineas, lacking the nerve to meet St John head on.

Robyn moved slightly to a position from which she could watch both men. Clinton was pale under the deep-water tan, the rims of his nostril bloodless and his lips compressed into a thin line, and she remembered that he had drunk a dozen glasses of champagne during the evening.

He was nervous, indecisive, every watcher could sense it, and their disappointment was evident. They had hoped for a dramatic confrontation when Clinton had made the flamboyant gesture of placing a hundred pounds on the table, but when the amount was slowly whittled away by unexciting over-cautious play, their interest was transferred to a lively exchange between Mungo St John and one of the Cloete sons, the family that owned half the Constantia valley with its fabled vineyards.

They laughed at the light banter with which the two men made their bets, and admired the grace of the loser and the easy manner of the winner. The other players at the table were almost forgotten, picking up an uncontested ante or falling before the aggression of the leading pair.

Robyn could only pity Clinton, nervous and pale – when he fumbled his cards to expose prematurely one of his few winning hands and suffer the chuckles of the spectators as he picked up odd guineas instead of the fifty that might have been his if he had played it correctly.

Robyn tried to catch his eye, to make him leave before he was further humiliated, but Clinton played on doggedly refusing to look up at her.

Cloete won a hand with four of a kind and as was his right called for a pot to celebrate his good fortune.

'Three of a kind to open the pot and guinea sweeteners,' he announced and grinned across the table at St John. 'To your liking, sir?'

'Very much so,' St John smiled back, and the other players tried to cover their discomfiture. It was a dangerous game – requiring one of the players to be dealt an initial three of a kind to commence the game, but for every unsuccessful deal each player had to contribute a guinea to the pot, and when a lucky player achieved the minimum requirement, he could advance the stakes by as much again as was in the centre of the table. It could amount swiftly to a huge sum, and there was no option of withdrawal – a very dangerous game.

Ten times the deal failed to produce an opening hand, and then with the pot at seventy guineas Mungo St John announced quietly,

'She is open, gentlemen, as wide open as my mother-in-law's mouth.'

Play had stopped at the other tables in the room as St John went on,

'It will cost you another seventy iron men to stay in the game.' He had doubled the pot, and the watchers applauded the bet and then looked eagerly to the other players.

'I am your man,' said Cloete, but at last there was a breathlessness to his voice. He counted out the notes and gold coins and spilled them into the considerable pile in the centre.

Three other players withdrew, dropping their cards with alacrity, clearly relieved to have got out of danger for a mere ten guineas, but Clinton Codrington hunched miserably over his cards and St John had to prod him gently for his decision.

'Please don't hurry, Captain. We have all evening.'

And Clinton looked up at him and nodded jerkily, not trusting his voice, then pushed a sheaf of notes into the centre of the table.

'Three players,' St John said, and swiftly counted the money in the pot. 'Two hundred and ten guineas!'

The next bid could double that amount, and the one after could redouble it. The room was silent now, the players at the other tables in the room had left their seats to watch as the dealer gave two cards to Mungo St John to replace those he tossed into the centre of the table. He was buying honestly, trying to add to the triplets with which he had opened the pot, neither faking a flush nor a full house. Cloete bought three cards, evidently looking for a third to a high pair – and then it was Clinton's turn to request cards.

'One,' he mumbled, and held up a single finger. The finger quivered slightly. The dealer slid the card across to him and he covered it with his hand unable to bring himself to look at it yet. It was all too obvious that he was attempting to find the missing card to a flush or straight.

'The opener to bet,' said the dealer. 'Mr St John.'

There was a pause as St John fanned open his cards, and then he said evenly without a change of expression:

'The bet is doubled.'

'Four hundred and twenty guineas,' said somebody loudly, and this time nobody applauded but every eye swivelled to Cloete as he consulted his cards. Then shook his head abruptly, and let them drop. He had not found another king to go with the original pair.

Now everybody looked to the remaining player. A transformation had come over Clinton Codrington, it was hard to define it exactly. There was just a touch of colour under the tanned cheeks, his lips were slightly parted and for the first time he was looking directly at St John – but somehow confidence and a barely suppressed eagerness shone from him. There was no mistaking it. The man positively glowed.

'Double again,' he said loudly. 'Eight hundred and forty guineas.' He could hardly contain himself, and every man in the room knew he had found the card he needed to transform his hand from worthlessness to a certain winner.

St John did not have to deliberate more than a few seconds.

'Congratulations,' he smiled. 'You found what you were looking for, I must concede this one to you.'

He dropped his cards and pushed them away from him.

'May we see the cards you required to open the pot?' Clinton asked diffidently.

'I beg your pardon.' St John's tone was lightly ironical, and he flipped his hand, face upwards. There were three sevens and two odd cards.

'Thank you,' said Clinton. His manner had changed again. The trembling eagerness, the nervous indecision, both had disappeared. He was calm, almost icy as he began to gather in the piles of scattered gold and bank notes.

'What cards did he have?' demanded one of the women petulantly.

'He does not have to show them,' her partner explained. 'He beat the others out without a showdown.'

'Oh, I'd die to see them,' she squeaked.

Clinton paused in gathering his winnings and looked up at her.

'I beg of you, madam, not to do so,' Clinton smiled. 'I would not wish to have your life on my conscience.'

He turned his cards face upwards on the green baize, and it took the company many seconds to realize what they were looking at. There were cards of every suit, and not one of them matched another.

There were delighted exclamations, for the hand was utterly worthless. It could have been beaten by a single pair of sevens, to say nothing of the triple sevens which St John had discarded.

With this valueless hand the young naval captain had beaten

the American, out-smarting him for almost 900 guineas. It was a spectacular coup. The company gradually realized how carefully it had been engineered, how Clinton had lured his adversary, how he had made a pretence at fumbling uncertainly until exactly the right moment, the moment when he had struck boldly and decisively. They burst into spontaneous applause, the ladies oohing with admiration and the men calling congratulation.

'Oh jolly good play, sir!'

St John held the smile, but his lips drew tighter with the effort, and there was a savage glitter in his eyes as he stared at the cards and realized how he had been duped.

The applause subsided, some of the spectators were beginning to turn away still discussing the hand, and St John began gathering the cards to shuffle when Clinton Codrington spoke. His voice was low but clear, so that nobody about the tables could miss a word of it.

'Even a black-birder's luck can run out at last,' he said. 'I must admit, I would rather have caught you at your dirty slaver's game than beaten you out of a few guineas tonight.'

The company froze, gaping at Clinton with expressions of horror and comical amazement. The silence in the room seemed impenetrable, the only sound was the ripple and click of the cards as Mungo St John began to shuffle them, splitting the pack with a click and then running them into each other under his thumbs in a blur of movement.

He did not look down at his hands as he rippled the cards. He never removed his gaze from Clinton's face, and his smile had still not slipped – only there was a flush of colour under the dark sun-touched skin.

'You like to live dangerously?' St John smiled the question.

'Oh, no.' Clinton shook his head. 'I am in no danger. In my experience, slavers are all cowards.'

Mungo St John's smile disappeared, extinguished instantly, and his expression was coldly murderous, but his fingers never broke the rhythm of cut and ripple, and the cards flowed under his fingers as Clinton went on evenly, 'I was led to believe that so-called Louisiana gentlemen had some exalted code of honour,' he shrugged. 'I suggest, sir, that you are a living contradiction of that notion.'

Every listener was stunned. Not one of them could doubt

what they were hearing; the accusation of slave-dealing. To an Englishman, there could be no worse insult.

The last English duels had been fought in 1840 when Lord Cardigan shot Captain Tuckett, and in 1843 when Munro shot his brother-in-law Colonel Fawcett. In consequence of these encounters, the Queen had made her desire for reform known, and the articles of war were amended in the following year, making duelling an offence. Of course, gentlemen still went abroad, mostly to France, to settle affairs of honour with pistol or sword. But this was Cape Colony, one of the jewels of the Empire and the Naval Captain was one of Her Majesty's commissioned officers. The evening had proved diverting beyond any expectations, and now there was the promise of blood and violent death charging the gaming-room.

'Gentlemen,' an urgent persuasive voice interrupted them. The Admiral's flag-captain had come through from the whist room at the Admiral's orders. 'There has been some misunderstanding.'

But neither of the two men as much as glanced in his direction.

'I don't think there has been any misunderstanding at all,' Mungo St John said coldly, his gaze still locked with Clinton's. 'Captain Codrington's insults cannot possibly be misinterpreted.'

'Mr St John, may I remind you that you are on British soil, subject to Her Majesty's laws.' The flag-captain was becoming desperate.

'Oh, Mr St John sets little store by laws. He sails his slave ship, fully equipped, into a British harbour.' Clinton stared at the American with cold blue eyes. He would have gone on, but St John interrupted him harshly, speaking to the flag-captain but addressing the words to Clinton Codrington. 'I would not dream of abusing Her Majesty's hospitality. In any event I will sail with the tide before noon this day, and in four days I shall be far beyond Her Majesty's territory, in latitude 31° 38′ south. There is a wide river mouth there, between tall bluffs of stone – a good landing and a wide beach. It is unmistakable.' St John stood up. He had recovered his urbane air, and now he adjusted the ruffles of his shirt front and gave the lovely widow his arm. He paused for a moment to look down at Clinton. 'Who knows but that you and I may meet again, when we must certainly discuss the question of honour once more. Until then I give you good morrow, sir.'

He turned away and the spectators fell back ahead of him and seemed to form a guard of honour as St John and his lady sauntered casually from the room.

The flag-captain flung one furious glare at Clinton.

'The Admiral wishes to speak with you, sir,' and then he hurried after the departing couple, followed them down the curve of the staircase and caught up with them at the double doors of carved teak.

'Mr St John, Admiral Kemp asked me to convey his compliments He sets no store by the rash accusations of one of his junior captains. If he did, he would be obliged to send a party aboard your ship.'

'None of us would like that,' St John nodded. 'Nor the consequences.'

'Indeed,' the flag-captain assured him. 'Nevertheless the Admiral feels that, in the circumstances, you should take advantage of the next fair wind and tide to proceed on your passage.'

'Please return my compliments to the Admiral – and convey my assurance that I will clear the Bay before noon.'

At that moment the widow's coach came up, and St John nodded distantly to the flag-captain and handed the lady up the steps.

From the deck of *Black Joke* they watched the clipper raise her anchor, her master skilfully backing and filling his topsails to run up on her cable, and break the anchor flukes out of the mud and sand of the bottom of the bay. As soon as it was free, he piled on his canvas, sail after sail bursting out in quick successive explosions of brilliant white, and *Huron* tore eagerly out of Table Bay on the south-east wind.

She would be out of sight beyond the lighthouse at Mouille Point for almost four hours before *Black Joke* was ready to follow her out of the bay. The Admiralty powder barge was alongside, and all the elaborate precautions for taking on explosives were in force. The red swallow-tail warning flag at the masthead, the boiler fires in the engine room extinguished, the crew barefooted, the decks kept wet with a constant stream from the hoses to prevent a chance spark, and each powder barrel carefully inspected for leakage as it came aboard.

While the engineer refired his boilers the last members of the Ballantyne expedition came aboard. Once again, Zouga's letters of introduction had proved invaluable, and together with his persuasive manner had provided him with the most valuable addition so far to his expedition.

Old Tom Harkness had warned him during the long night discussion, 'Don't try to cross the Chimanimani Mountains without a force of trained men. Beyond the narrow coastal belt there is only one law and it is promulgated from the muzzle of a gun.'

On the strength of the letters, the commander of the Cape Town garrison had allowed Zouga to ask for volunteers from his regiment of Hottentot Infantry. 'They are the only natives of Africa who understand the working of a firearm,' Harkness had told him. 'They are the devil with drink and women, but they can fight and march, and most of them are hardened to fever and famine. Pick them carefully and watch them every moment, night as well as day.'

Zouga's request for volunteers had been most enthusiastically received. By reputation the Hottentots could scent plunder or a willing lady from fifty miles, and the pay and rations that Zouga offered were almost thrice that of the British army. They had volunteered to a man and Zouga's difficulty had been in selecting ten of them.

Zouga had taken an instant liking to these wiry little men, with their almost oriental features, slanted eyes and high cheekbones. Despite appearances, they were more African than almost any other breed. They were the original inhabitants that the first navigators had found on the beach at Table Bay – and they had taken readily to the white man's ways, and more than readily to his vices.

Zouga had solved his problem by making one selection only. This was a man with an ageless face, it might have been forty years or eighty, for the skin was the colour and texture of a papyrus parchment, each wrinkle seemed to have been eroded into it by wind and driven dust, but the little peppercorns of hair that covered his skull were untinged with silver.

'I taught Captain Harris to hunt elephant,' he boasted.

'Where was that?' Zouga demanded, for Cornwallis Harris was one of the most famous of the old African hunters. His book

The Wild Sports of Africa was the great classic of the African chase.

'I took him to the Cashan mountains.' Harris's expedition to the Cashan mountains, which the Boers now called Magaliesberg, was in 1829, thirty-one years previously. That would make the little Hottentot somewhere between fifty and sixty years old, if he were telling the truth.

'Harris did not mention your name,' he said. 'I have read his account carefully.'

'Jan Bloom – that was my name then.' Zouga nodded. Bloom had been one of Harris's most intrepid hunter-retainers.

'Why is your name Jan Cheroot now?' Zouga asked and the dark eyes had twinkled with pixie merriment.

'Sometimes a man gets tired of a name, like he does of a woman, and for his health or his life he changes both.'

The long military-issue Enfield rifle was as tall as Jan Cheroot, but it seemed an extension of his wizened little body.

'Pick nine other men. The best,' Zouga told him, and Sergeant Cheroot brought them aboard while the gunboat was working up a head of steam in her boilers.

Each man carried his Enfield over his shoulder, his worldly possessions in the haversack on his back and fifty rounds in the pouches on his belt

It needed only the 'Rogue's March' to welcome them, Zouga thought wryly, as he watched them come in through the entry port, each one bestowing upon him a beatific grin and a salute so vigorous that it nearly swung the donor off his feet.

Sergeant Cheroot lined them up at the rail. Their original scarlet uniform jackets had suffered strange mutations to ten different shades, ranging from sun-faded pink to dusty puce, and each peppercorn head wore its brimless infantry cap cocked at a different angle from all the others. Thin shanks were bound up with grubby puttees, and brown bare feet slapped the oak planking of the deck in unison as Cheroot brought them to attention, Enfields at the slope and happy grins on each puckish face.

'Very well, Sergeant.' Zouga acknowledged the salute. 'Now let's have the packs open, and the bottles over the side.'

The grins wilted, and they exchanged crestfallen glances – the Major had looked so young and gullible.

'You hear the Major, *julle klomp dom skaape*.' Gleefully Jan

Cheroot likened them to 'a herd of stupid sheep' in the kitchen Dutch of the Cape, and as he turned back to Zouga there was for the first time a gleam of respect in the dark eyes.

There are two passages from which a ship may choose when sailing the south-eastern coast of Africa. The master may stay outside the 100-fathom line which marks the edge of the continental shelf, for here the opposing forces of the Mozambique current and the prevailing winds can generate a sea which seamen call with awe the '100 year wave', a wave over 200 foot from crest to trough, which will overwhelm even the sturdiest vessel as though it were a drifting autumn leaf. The alternative and only slightly less hazardous passage lies close inshore, in the shallows where the rocky reefs await a careless navigator.

For the sake of speed Clinton Codrington chose the inshore passage, so that always the land was in sight as they bustled northwards. Day after day the shimmering white beaches and dark rocky headlands unreeled ahead of *Black Joke*'s bows, sometimes almost lost in the smoky blue sea-fret, and at other times brutally clear under the African sun.

Clinton kept steam in his boilers and the single bronze screw spinning under his counter with every sail set and trained around to glean the smallest puff of the wind, as he drove *Black Joke* on to the rendezvous that Mungo St John had set. His haste was symptom of a compulsion that Robyn Ballantyne only began fully to understand during those days and nights that they drove east and north, for Clinton Codrington sought her company constantly and she spent many hours of each day with him, or all of it that could be spared from the management of the vessel – beginning with the assembly of the ship's company for morning prayers.

Most naval captains went through the motions of divine service once a week, but Captain Codrington held prayers every morning and it did not take Robyn long to realize that his faith and sense of Christian duty was, if anything, greater than her own. He did not seem to experience the terrible doubts and temptations to which she was always such a prey, and if it had not been unchristian to do so she would have felt envy for his sense and secure faith.

'I wanted to go into the church, like my father and my elder brother, Ralph, before me,' he told her.

'Why did you not?'

'The Almighty led me into the path He had chosen for me,' Clinton said simply, and it did not seem pretentious when he said it. 'I know now He meant me to be a shepherd for His flock, here in this land,' and he pointed at the silver beaches and blue mountains. 'I did not realize it at the time, but His ways are wonderful. This is the work He has chosen for me.'

Suddenly she realized how deep was his commitment to the war he was waging against the trade, it was almost a personal crusade. His whole being directed at its destruction, for he truly believed that he was the instrument of God's will.

Yet, like many deeply religious men, he kept his belief closely guarded, never flaunting it in sanctimonious posturing or biblical quotation. The only time he spoke of his God was during the daily prayers and when he was alone with her on his quarter-deck. Quite naturally, he assumed that her belief matched, if not outstripped, his own. She did nothing to disillusion him, for she enjoyed his patent admiration, his deference to the fact that she had been appointed as a missionary, and when she was truthful to herself, which was more and more often these days, she liked the way he looked, the sound of his voice, and even the smell of him. It was a man's smell, like tanned leather or the pelt of an otter she had once had as a pet at Kings Lynn.

He was good to be near, a man, as the pale missionary initiates and medical students she had known, had not been men. He was the Christian warrior. She found a comfort in his presence, not like the wicked excitement of Mungo St John, but something deeper and more satisfying. She looked upon him as her champion, as though the deadly assignation to which he was hurrying was on her behalf, to wipe out the knowledge of sin and to atone for her disgrace.

On the third day they passed the settlement on the shore of Algoa Bay, where the 5,000 British settlers brought out by Governor Somerset forty years before in 1820 had landed and still eked a hard existence from the unforgiving African earth. The white flecks of painted walls looked pitifully insignificant in that wilderness of water and sky and land, and at last Robyn started to come to some small understanding of the vastness of this continent and how puny were the scratches that man had made upon it. For the first time she felt a small cold dread at her own temerity that had brought her so far, so young and so inexperienced, to venture she was not sure what. She hugged her shawl about her shoulders and shivered in the cutting wind that poured in off the green sea. The Africa she had dreamed of so often seemed harsh and unwelcoming now.

As *Black Joke* closed swiftly with the rendezvous that St John had appointed, Clinton Codrington became quieter, and was more often alone in his cabin. He understood clearly the ordeal that faced him. Zouga Ballantyne had discussed it with him on almost every occasion that presented itself. Zouga was unwavering in his opposition to the meeting.

'You have chosen a formidable opponent, sir,' he told Clinton bluntly. 'And I mean no offence when I say I doubt you are a match for him with either pistol or sword – but he'll choose pistols, you can wager on that.'

'He challenged,' Clinton said quietly. 'My weapon is the naval cutlass. We will fight with those.'

'I cannot support you there.' Zouga shook his head. 'If there was a challenge, and I could make a case against that – but if there was one, it came from you, sir. If you fight, it will be with pistols.'

Day after day he tried to persuade Clinton to miss the rendezvous.

'Damn it, man. Nobody fights duels any more, especially against a man who can split the cheroot in your mouth with either hand, at twenty paces.' Or again, 'There was no challenge, Captain Codrington, I was there, and I would stake my honour on it.' At another time, 'You will lose your commission, sir. You have Admiral Kemp's direct order to avoid the meeting, and it is obvious that Kemp is waiting for an opportunity to haul you before a court martial.' Then again, 'By God, sir, you will serve no one – least of all yourself – by being shot to death on some deserted and Godforsaken shore. If St John is a slaver, then your chance to take him at more favourable odds will come later.'

When Zouga's best arguments made no dent on Clinton's resolve Zouga went to Robyn in her cabin.

'You seem to have some influence on the fellow. Can you not persuade him, Sissy?'

'Zouga, why are you so determined to prevent Captain Codrington defending his honour?'

'He's a likable enough chap, and I do not wish to see him pipped.'

'And if he were, you might find it difficult to reach Quelimane. Is that not so?' Robyn asked sweetly. 'Your concern is most Christian.'

'St John can choose which of his eyes he will put a ball into. You have seen him shoot.' Zouga ignored the accusation.

'I believe it is Captain Codrington's duty to destroy that monster. God protects the righteous.'

'In my experience he protects only those who shoot fastest and straightest,' Zouga growled with frustration.

'That is blasphemy,' Robyn told him.

'You deserve to hear some real blasphemy for your stubbornness,' Zouga told her curtly and strode out of the cabin. He had learned through long experience when he was wasting his time.

They passed the mouth of the Kei river – the frontier of British influence and beyond it was the wilderness, unclaimed and untamed, peopled by the tribes which had been driven back inexorably by the white advance, and by scattered bands of renegades and bastards, wandering hunters and hardy travellers and traders.

Even the trekking Boers had by-passed this land, going on into the interior, circling out beyond the mountain massif that divided the littoral from the highland plateau.

Far to the north they had turned back and crossed the mountains again and reached the coast, fighting and shattering the impis of the Zulu nation, beginning to settle the fertile coastal strip until the British ships had sailed into Port Natal, following them up from the Cape Colony, from whence they had trekked so long and so hard to avoid British rule. The Boers had loaded their waggons once more, and driving their herds before them, climbed back over the range that they called the Dragon mountains and abandoned the land they had wrested from the Zulu king Dingaan with the flame and smoke of their muskets.

However, this coast along which *Black Joke* now steamed lay between the English colonies of Cape and Natal, claimed by none, except the wild tribesmen who watched the black-hulled vessel pass almost within arrow shot.

Clinton Codrington had marked the point where latitude 31°

38′ south intersected the coast, and the estuary was shown on the chart with the notation 'St John's river', named, probably, by one of the early Portuguese navigators, but it was ironic that it should bear the same name as the man they were hastening to meet. When *Black Joke* steamed around the last headland the description that St John had given of his namesake was instantly recognizable.

Steep, heavily wooded hills rose almost sheer about a wide lagoon. The forest was very dense dark green, with tall galleries of trees, festooned with lianas. Through the telescope could be made out the troops of little grey vervet monkeys and the brilliant plumage of exotic birds that sported and fluttered through the top branches.

The river came down a deep rocky gorge torn through the barrier of hills, filling the reed-lined lagoon and then flowing out over the bar between the curved white pillows of a sandy beach.

To dispel any doubt that this was the rendezvous, *Huron* lay at anchor a cable's length beyond the first line of breakers, in the deep, where the shoal water turned from pale green to blue.

Clinton Codrington examined her carefully through his telescope, then without a word passed the instrument to Zouga. While he in turn glassed the big clipper, Clinton asked softly, 'Will you act for me?'

Zouga lowered the glass with surprise. 'I expected one of your own officers.'

'I could not ask them.' Clinton shook his head. 'Slogger Kemp would mark their service records if he ever heard of it.'

'You do not have the same qualms about my career,' Zouga pointed out.

'You are on extended absence from your regiment, and you have not been expressly ordered, as I and my officers have been.'

Zouga thought quickly, duelling was not so seriously considered in the army as it was in the Royal Navy, in fact the army manuals still maintained no express prohibitions, and a chance to meet with St John was also a last chance to avert this ridiculous affair that so seriously threatened the continuance of his expedition.

'I accept, then,' Zouga said shortly.

'I am extremely grateful to you, sir,' said Clinton as shortly.

'Let us hope you are as grateful after the business is over,'

Zouga told him drily. 'I had best go across to *Huron* right away. It will be dark in an hour.'

Tippoo caught the line as it was thrown from the gunboat's whaler, and held it while Zouga gathered his cloak and jumped the gap of surging green water to the boarding ladder, clambering up before the next swell could soak his boots.

Mungo St John waited for him at the foot of the mainmast. He held himself unsmiling and aloof, until Zouga hurried to him and offered his right hand, then he relaxed and returned the smile.

'Damn it, Mungo, cannot we make an end to this nonsense?'

'Certainly, Zouga,' Mungo St John agreed. 'An apology from your man would settle it.'

'The man is a fool,' Zouga shook his head. 'Why take the risk?'

'I don't consider there is any risk, but let me remind you he called me a coward.'

'There is no chance then?' The two of them had become good friends during the weeks they had spent together and Zouga felt he could press further. 'I admit the fellow is a prig, but if you kill him, you'll make it damned awkward for me, don't you know?'

Mungo St John threw back his head and laughed delightedly. 'You and I could work together, do you know that, Zouga? You are a pragmatist, like I am. I make a prophecy – you'll go a long way in this world.'

'Not very far, if you kill the man who is taking me.' And Mungo St John chuckled again and clapped a friendly hand upon his shoulder.

'I'm sorry, my friend. Not this time,' and Zouga sighed with resignation.

'You have choice of weapons.'

'Pistols,' said Mungo St John.

'Of course,' Zouga nodded. 'Dawn tomorrow on the beach there.' He pointed to the land with his chin. 'Will that suit you?'

'Admirably. Tippoo here will act for me.'

'Does he understand the conventions?' Zouga asked doubtfully, as he glanced at the half-naked figure that waited near at hand.

'He understands enough to blow Codrington's head off at the shoulders if he levels his pistol a moment before the signal.'

Mungo St John flashed that cruel white smile. 'And that's all he needs to know, as far as I am concerned.'

Robyn Ballantyne slept not a minute during the night and it still lacked two hours of dawn when she bathed and dressed. On an impulse she chose her old moleskin breeches and man's woollen jacket. There would be the need to disembark through the surf from the ship's boat and skirts would hamper her, added to which the morning was damp and chill and her jacket was of good thick Scottish tweed.

She laid out her black leather bag, and checked its contents, making certain she had everything she needed to cleanse and staunch a bullet wound, to bind up torn flesh or hold together shattered bone, and to reduce the agony of either man.

All of them had taken it without question that Robyn would be on the beach that morning. The gunboat did not rate a surgeon, and neither did *Huron*. She was ready with an hour to wait, and she opened her journal and began making the previous day's entry, when there was a light tap on her door.

When she opened it, Clinton Codrington stood in the opening, his face pale and strained in the smoky lamplight and she knew intuitively that he had slept as little as she had. He recovered swiftly from the first shock of seeing her in breeches, dragging his eyes up to her face again.

'I hoped I might speak with you,' he muttered shyly. 'It will be the last opportunity before . . .'

She took his arm and drew him into the cabin. 'You have not breakfasted?' she asked sternly.

'No, ma'am.' He shook his head and his eyes dropped to her trousered legs, and then jerked up guiltily to her face again.

'The medicine worked?' she asked.

He nodded, too embarrassed to reply. She had administered a purge the evening before, for as a surgeon she could dread the effects of a pistol ball through a full bowel or through a belly loaded with breakfast.

She touched his forehead. 'You are warm, you have not taken a chill?' She felt protective towards him, like a mother almost, for he seemed once again so young and untried.

'I wondered if we might pray together.' His voice was so low that she barely caught the words, and she felt a warm, almost suffocating rush of affection for him.

'Come,' she whispered, and she took his hand.

They knelt together on the bare deck of the tiny cabin, still holding hands, and she spoke for both of them, and he made the responses in a soft but firm voice.

When they rose stiffly at last, he kept her hand in his for a while longer.

'Miss Ballantyne – I mean, Doctor Ballantyne – I cannot tell you now what a profound effect meeting you has had on my life.'

She felt herself blushing and tried feebly to disengage her hand, but he clung to it.

'I would like to have your permission to talk to you again in this vein after,' he paused, 'if this morning goes as we hope it will.'

'Oh, it will,' she said fiercely. 'It will – I know it will.' Hardly knowing what she was doing she pressed herself swiftly to him and reaching up kissed him full on the mouth. For a moment he froze, and then clumsily he crushed her to him so that the brass buttons of his coat dug into her bosom and his teeth crushed her lips until she felt them bruising.

'My darling,' he whispered. 'Oh, my darling.'

The strength of his reaction startled her, but almost immediately she found she was enjoying the strength of his embrace, and she tried to free her arms to return it – but he misunderstood her movements and released her hurriedly.

'Forgive me,' he blurted out. 'I don't know what came over me.

Her disappointment was sharp enough to turn instantly to annoyance at his timidity. Buttons and teeth notwithstanding, it had felt very pleasant indeed.

Both boats left the two ships at the same time, and they converged through the thin pearly morning mist as their crews pulled for the low lines of breaking surf and the pale outline of the beach in the dawn.

They landed within a hundred yards of each other, surfing in on the crest of the same low, green wave and the oarsmen leapt out waist-deep to run the boats high up the white sand.

Both parties moved separately over the crest of the sand bar and then down to the edge of the lagoon, screened from the boat crews by the intervening dunes and the stands of tall fluffy-headed reeds. There was a level area of firm damp sand at one edge of the reeds.

Mungo St John and Tippoo halted at one end, and Mungo lit a cheroot and stood with both hands on his hips staring out at the crests of the hills, ignoring the activity about him. He was dressed in black tight-fitting breeches and a white silk shirt with full sleeves, open at the throat to reveal the dark curls of his body hair. The white shirt would give his opponent a fair aiming point, he was observing the conventions scrupulously.

Robyn watched him covertly as she stood beside Clinton Codrington at the further end of the clearing. She tried to capture the hatred she felt for St John, to hold on to her outrage at the way he had abused her, but it was a difficult emotion to sustain. Rather, she was excited and with a strange sense of elation, the satanic presence of this man heightened the feeling. She caught herself staring openly and dragged her eyes off him.

Beside her Clinton stood very erect. He wore his blue uniform jacket with the gold lace of his rank gleaming even in the soft pink light of early dawn. He had scraped the sun-bleached hair back from his forehead and temples and bound it at the nape of his neck, leaving clean the purposeful line of his jaw.

Zouga went forward to meet Tippoo who carried under his arm the rosewood case of pistols. When they met in the centre of the level ground, he opened the case and proffered it, standing straddle-legged and attentive, while Zouga took each weapon from its velvet nest and loaded it with a carefully measured charge of black powder before ramming home the dark-blue leaden ball and setting the cap on the nipple.

The sight of the long-barrelled weapons reminded Robyn forcefully of that night aboard *Huron*, and she bit her lip and shifted uncomfortably.

'Do not fret yourself, Miss Ballantyne.' Clinton mistook her emotion, and whispered soothingly to comfort her while he unbuttoned his jacket and shrugged out of it. Beneath it he also wore a plain white shirt to give St John a fair aim. He handed her the jacket and would have spoken again but Zouga called.

'Will the principals come forward.'

And Clinton gave her another tightly strained smile before he strode out, his heels leaving deep prints in the damp yellow sand.

He faced Mungo St John, holding his gaze steadily, both of them completely expressionless.

'Gentlemen, I appeal to both of you to settle this affair without bloodshed.' Zouga went through the ritual attempt at reconciliation. 'Captain Codrington, as challenger, will you tender an apology?'

Clinton shook his head once, curtly.

'Mr St John, is there any other way in which we can avoid bloodshed?'

'I think not, sir,' St John drawled as he carefully tapped half an inch of grey ash from his cheroot.

'Very well,' Zouga nodded and went on immediately to set the conditions of the meeting. 'At the command "Proceed" each of you gentlemen will take ten paces, which I will count aloud. Immediately after the count of ten I will give the command "Fire" upon which you will be at liberty to turn and discharge your weapon.'

Zouga paused and glanced at Tippoo, there was a long-barrelled muzzle-loading pistol thrust into the waistband of his baggy breeches.

'Both seconds are armed.' Zouga laid his right hand on the butt of the Colt pistol in his own belt. 'If either principal attempts to fire before the command to do so, then he will immediately be shot down by the seconds.'

He paused again looking from one to the other. 'Is that clearly understood, gentlemen?' They both nodded. 'Do either of you have a question?' Zouga waited in silence for a few seconds then went on. 'Very well, we will proceed. Mr St John you have first choice of weapon.'

Mungo St John dropped the cheroot and ground it into the sand with his heel, before stepping forward. Tippoo offered him the rosewood case and after a momentary hesitation St John lifted out one of the beautifully inlaid weapons. He pointed at the sky and cocked the hammer with a sweep of his free hand.

Clinton took the remaining pistol and weighed it experimentally in his hand, settling the butt deeply into the vee formed by thumb and forefinger, turning half away and lifting the pistol at full stretch of his arm to aim it at one of the black and bright yellow bishop birds that chattered in the reeds nearby.

With relief Robyn watched the familiar ease with which her champion handled the weapon, and she felt completely certain of the outcome now. Good must triumph, and she started to pray again, silently, only her lips moving as she recited the twenty-third psalm.

'Though I walk through the valley of the shadow of death.'

'Take your positions, gentlemen.' Zouga stepped back and gestured to Robyn. Still praying, she hurried to where Zouga stood, and fell in a few paces behind him, well out on the flank from the lines of fire of the two principals.

Beside Zouga, Tippoo drew the long, clumsy-looking pistol from the sash around his waist and cocked the big ornate hammer, the bore of the barrel gaped like a cannon as he lifted it into the 'present' position. Zouga drew his own Colt revolver and stood quietly while the two principals walked the last few paces towards each other and then turned back to back.

Beyond them the early sun was gilding the hilltops with bright gold, but leaving the lagoon still in shadow so the still dark waters steamed with wisps of mist. In the silence a ghostly grey heron croaked hoarsely and then launched into flight from the edge of the reedbank with slow wingbeats, its neck drawn back into a snakelike 'S' to balance the long beak.

'Proceed!' called Zouga, so loudly that Robyn started violently.

The two men stepped out, away from each other, with deliberate strides, heeling heavily in the yielding sand, pacing to the count that Zouga called.

'Five.' Mungo St John was smiling softly, as though at some secret joke, and his white silk sleeve fluttered like a moth's wing around the uplifted arm that held the slim steel-blue barrel pointed at the dawn sky.

'Six.' Clinton leaned forward, stepping out with long legs clad in white uniform breeches. His face was set, pale as a mask, his lips drawn into a thin determined line.

'Seven.' Robyn felt the beat of her heart crescendo, thumping painfully against the cage of her ribs so that she could not breathe.

'Eight.' She noticed for the first time the patches of sweat that had soaked through the armpits of Clinton's white shirt, despite the chill of the dawn air.

'Nine.' Suddenly she was deadly afraid for him, all her faith dissolved in a sudden premonition of disaster rushing down upon her.

'Ten!' She wanted to scream to them to stop. She wanted to rush forward and throw herself into the space between the two men. She didn't want them to die, either of them. She tried to fill her lungs but her throat was closed and dry, she tried to drive her legs forward but they were locked rigidly under her, beyond her control.

'Fire!' shouted Zouga, his voice cracking with the tension that gripped all the watchers and out on the damp dark-yellow sand both men turned, like a pair of dancers in a meticulously rehearsed ballet of death.

Their right arms out-flung towards each other in a gesture like that of parted lovers, the left hand on the hip to balance, the classic stance of the expert marksman.

Time seemed suspended, the movements of the two men graceful but measured, without the urgency of onrushing death.

The silence was complete, there was no wind to rustle the reeds, no bird nor animal called from the looming forest across the lagoon, the footfalls of the two men were deadened by the yielding sand – the world seemed to hold its breath.

And then the crash of pistol fire awoke the echoes and sent them bounding and booming across the gorge, leaping from cliff to cliff, startling the birds into raucous flight.

The two shots were within one hundredth of a second of each other, so that they blended into a single blurt of sound. From the levelling blue barrels the dead white powder smoke spurted, and then the barrels were flung upwards in unison with the shock of discharge.

Both men reeled backwards, keeping their feet, but Robyn had seen the smoke fly from the muzzle of Mungo St John's pistol a fraction of a second earlier, and then an instant later Mungo's big dark head flinched as though he had been struck with an open hand across the cheek.

Alter that one staggered pace backwards, he steadied, drawing himself to his full height, the pistol still smoking in his raised hand, staring at his adversary, and Robyn felt a rush of relief. Mungo St John was unscathed. She wanted to run to him, and then suddenly the joy withered, a dark red snake of blood slithered from the thick hair at his temple down the smoothly shaven olive skin of his cheek and dripped with slow sullen drops on to the white silk of his shirt.

She lifted her hand to her mouth to cover the cry that rose within her, and then her attention was distracted by another movement in the corner of her vision and she swung her head with a jerky movement towards Clinton Codrington.

He also had been standing erect, with almost military bearing, but now he began to bow slowly forward at the waist. The right hand holding the pistol hung at his side and now his fingers opened and the ornate weapon dropped into the sand at his feet.

He lifted the empty hand and placed it across his chest with fingers outspread in a gesture that seemed reverential and slowly his body bent forward and now his legs gave way under him and he dropped to his knees, as though in prayer. Kneeling, he lifted his hand away from his chest and examined with an expression of mild surprise the small smear of blood that coated his fingers and then he pitched forward face down on to the sand.

At last Robyn could move. She raced forward and dropped to her knees beside Clinton's fallen body, and with strength of panic rolled him on to his back. The front of the white linen shirt was damp with a little blood around the neat puncture in the cloth six inches to the left of the line of mother of pearl buttons.

He had been half-turned to fire and the ball had taken him low and left, at the level of the lungs, she saw instantly. The lungs! She felt despair overwhelm her. It would mean death, no less certain because it was slow and agonizing. She would have to watch this man drown inexorably in his own blood.

Sand crunched beside her and she looked up.

Mungo St John stood over her, his shirt a mess of wet blood. He was holding a silk kerchief to his temple to staunch the copious flow where the pistol ball had stripped a long ribbon of scalp off his skull above the ear.

His eyes were bleak, his expression forbidding and his voice cold and distant as he told her quietly.

'I trust you will be satisfied at last, madam.' Then he turned abruptly up the white dune towards the beach. She wanted to run after him, to restrain him, to explain – to explain she knew not what, but her duty was here, with the man more gravely stricken. Her fingers shook as she unbuttoned the front of Clinton's shirt and saw the dark blue hole punched into the pale flesh from which a little thick slow blood oozed. So little blood at the mouth of the wound – it was the worst indication – the bleeding would be inside, deep inside the chest cavity.

'Zouga, my bag,' she called sharply.

Zouga came to her, carrying the bag and went down on one knee beside her.

'I am but lightly struck,' murmured Clinton. 'I have no pain. Just a feeling of numbness here.'

Zouga did not reply. He had seen a multitude of gunshot wounds in India, pain was no indication of the severity. A ball through the hand or foot was unbearable agony, another through both lungs was only mildly discomforting.

Only one thing puzzled him and that was why Mungo St John's shot had been so wide. At twenty paces he would surely have taken the head shot, aiming between the eyes with an expectation of the ball deviating less than an inch from the point of aim, yet the shot had taken Clinton low in the chest.

While Robyn pressed a dressing over the wicked little blue mouth of the wound, Zouga picked the pistol out of the sand. The barrel was still warm and there was the peppery whiff of burned powder as he examined it and saw instantly why Mungo's shot had struck wide.

There was a bluish smear of bright new lead on the steel trigger guard.

Mungo St John had indeed aimed at the head, but Clinton had lifted the pistol to his eye at the same instant directly in the line of sight. St John's ball had struck the metal guard and been deflected downwards.

That would account for the fact that Clinton's own ball had been high, for as a less expert marksman he would surely have aimed for St John's chest. The strike of the ball had thrown his weapon upwards at the moment of discharge.

Zouga looked up and handed the pistol to Tippoo who waited impassively close at hand. Without a word, Tippoo took the weapon, turned away and followed his master over the dunes.

By the time four seamen from the gunboat could carry Clinton Codrington down the beach using his boat cloak as a hammock, St John was climbing up from the *Huron*'s whaler on to his maindeck, and before they could rig a block and tackle to lift the prostrate form of her captain into *Black Joke* – *Huron* had broken out her anchor and was spreading sail before the southwesterly breeze and bearing away with the sunrise transforming her into a vessel etched in golden fire.

For twenty-four hours Clinton Codrington surprised Robyn with the strength of his recovery. She looked to see blood on his lips, and she expected him to experience the agony of breathing as the damaged lung collapsed. Every few hours she listened with her sounding trumpet to his chest, stooping over the bunk in his cabin to catch the hiss and saw of his breathing, listening for the bubbling sound of blood, or for the dry rubbing of the lung against the rib cage, and was puzzled when none of these symptoms occurred.

Indeed Clinton was unaccountably resilient for a patient with ball through the chest cavity. He complained only of stiffness reaching up into his left armpit and semi-paralysis of that arm – and he was vociferous in his advice to his surgeon.

'You will bleed me, of course?' he asked.

'I will not,' Robyn told him shortly as she cleaned the area around the wound and then lifted him into a sitting position to bandage his chest.

'You should take at least a pint,' Clinton insisted.

'Have you not bled enough?' Robyn asked witheringly, but he was undaunted.

'There is black rotten blood that must be taken off.' Clinton indicated the massive bruise that was spreading around his chest like some dark parasitic plant around the smooth pale trunk.

'You must bleed me,' Clinton insisted, for all his adult life he had been exposed to the ministrations of naval surgeons. 'If you don't, fever is sure to follow.'

He offered Robyn the inner curve of his elbow where the thin white scars over the blue blood vessels marked where he had been bled before.

'We no longer live in the dark ages,' Robyn told him tartly. 'This is 1860,' and she pushed him down on the bolster and covered him with a grey ship's blanket against the shivering and chilling nausea which she knew must soon accompany such a wound. It did not come, and for the next twenty hours he continued to manage the ship from his bunk, and he chafed at the restraint she placed on him. However, Robyn knew the pistol ball was still in there and that there must be drastic consequences. She wished that there was some technique that could enable a surgeon to locate the whereabouts of a foreign body accurately, and then allow him to enter the rib cage and remove it.

That evening she fell asleep in the rope chair beside his bunk, awakening once to hold the enamel cup of water to his lips when he complained of thirst and noting the dryness and heat of his skin, and in the morning all her fears were confirmed.

He was only semi-conscious, and the pain was fierce. He moaned and cried out at the smallest movement. His eyes were sunken into plum-coloured cavities, his tongue was thickly coated with white and his lips were dried and cracked. He pleaded for drink and his skin was hot, the heat increasing every hour until it seemed to be burning out the core of his being, and he was restless and flushed, tossing in the narrow bunk, fighting off the blankets with which she tried to keep him covered, and whimpering in his delirium at the agony of movement. His breath was sawing painfully in his swollen and bruised chest, his eyes were glittering bright, and when Robyn unwound the bandage to sponge his body with cool water there was only a little pale fluid staining the dressing, but her nostrils flared as she smelled it. It was so horribly familiar, she always thought of that stench as the fetid breath of death itself.

The wound had shrunk, but the crust that had formed over it was so thin that it cracked at one of Clinton's restless movements and through it rose a thick droplet of custard-coloured matter. Immediately the smell was stronger. This was not the benign pus of healing, but the malignant pus that she so dreaded to see in a wound.

She swabbed it away carefully, and then with cold seawater sponged his chest and the hard hot swollen flesh below his armpit. The bruising was extensive and it had changed colour, dark blue as storm clouds, tinged with the yellow of sulphur and the virulent rose of some flower from the gardens of Hell itself.

There was one area just below the point of his shoulder blade particularly sensitive for he screamed when she touched it, and a sparse prickle of sweat broke out across his forehead and amongst the fine golden bristles of his unshaven cheeks.

She replaced the bandage with a fresh dressing and then forced between his dry lips four grams of laudanum mixed with a warm draught of calomel. She watched while he fell into a restless drug-induced sleep.

'Another twenty-four hours,' she whispered aloud, watching him toss and mutter. She had seen it so often. Soon the pus would suffuse his whole body, building up steadily around the ball deep in his chest. She was helpless. No surgeon could enter the rib cage, it had never been done before.

She looked up as Zouga stooped into the cabin. He was grave and quiet, standing beside her chair for a moment and placing a hand on her shoulder comfortingly.

'He improves?' he asked softly.

She shook her head, and he nodded as though he had expected the answer.

'You must eat.' He offered her the pannikin. 'I brought you some pea soup. It has bacon in it, it's very good.'

She had not realized how hungry she was and she ate gratefully, breaking the hard ship's bread into the broth and Zouga went on quietly,

'I loaded the pistols with less than a full charge, as little as I dared.' He shook his head irritably. 'Damned bad luck. After Mungo's ball hit the trigger guard, I'd not have expected it to have entered the chest – it must have lost most of its power.'

She looked up quickly. 'It struck the trigger guard – you did not tell me.'

He shrugged. 'It's not important now. But the ball was deflected.'

She sat very still in her chair for ten minutes after he was gone, and then purposefully she stood over the bunk and stripped back the blanket, unwound the bandage and examined the wound again.

Very carefully she began to sound the ribs beneath it, pressing in with thumb gently to feel for the give of shattered bone. The ribs were all firm, yet that was no proof that the ball had not driven between two of them.

She pressed her thumb into the swelling towards the outside of his chest, and although he thrashed around weakly, she thought she felt the rasp of bone against bone – as though the rib had been chipped or even as if a long splinter had been cracked off it.

She felt a little flutter of excitement, and extended her examination gradually backwards, guided by his delirious cries of pain, until once again she reached the lower point of his shoulder and he came upright in the bunk with another wild yell of agony, breaking out once more into the burning sweat of high fever. But with the tip of her finger she thought she had felt something, something that was neither bone nor knotted muscle.

The excitement quickened her breathing. From the angle at which Clinton had stood, half-turned away from Mungo St John, she now believed that it was possible that the ball had followed a different path from that which she had assumed.

If the pistol had been undercharged with powder, and if the ball had struck the trigger guard, it was just possible that it had not had the velocity to penetrate the rib cage, it had been turned by the bone and ploughed along under the skin, skidding along the groove between two ribs following the track that she had just probed, and lodging at last in the thick bed of the *latissimus dorsi* and *tenes major* muscle.

She stood back from the bunk. She could be very wrong, she realized, but if she was he would die anyway, and that very soon.

'I will cut for it,' she decided, the decision direct and swift. She glanced up at the skylight in the roof of the cabin. There was only an hour or two of good daylight left.

'Zouga!' she called as she raced from the cabin. 'Zouga! Come quickly!'

Robyn administered another five grams of laudanum before they moved Clinton. It was as large a dose as she dared, for he had taken nearly fifteen grams in the preceding thirty-six hours. She waited as long as she could in the failing light for the drug to begin taking effect. Then she passed the word to Lieutenant Denham to shorten sail, reduce engine revolutions and make the ship's motion as easy as possible.

Zouga had chosen two seamen to assist them. One was the boatswain, a burly and greying sailor, the other was the officers' steward who had impressed Robyn with his quiet, controlled manner.

Now as the three of them half-lifted Clinton and rolled him on to his side, the steward spread a sheet of fresh white canvas on the bunk under him to receive the spilled blood, then Zouga swiftly knotted the lengths of soft cotton rope around Clinton's wrists and ankles. He had chosen cotton in preference to the coarse hemp which would tear the skin, and he made the bowline knots that would not slip under pressure.

The boatswain helped him to tie down the ends at the head and foot of the bunk, stretching out the almost naked white body so that for an instant it reminded Robyn of the painting of the crucifixion that stood in Uncle William's study at King's Lynn – the Roman legionaries spread-eagling Christ upon the cross before driving home the nails. She shook her head irritably, driving the memory from her mind, concentrating all her attention on the task ahead.

'Wash your hands!' she ordered Zouga, indicating the bucket of almost boiling water and yellow lye soap the steward had provided.

'Why?'

'Do it,' she snapped, in no mood to argue. Her own hands were pink with the heat of the water and tingled with the harsh soap, as she wiped her instruments with the cloth dipped in a mug of the pungent ship's rum, laying them out on the shelf above the bunk, and then with the same cloth swabbed the hot discoloured flesh at the base of Clinton's shoulder blade. He jerked against his bonds and muttered an incoherent protest, but she ignored it and nodded to the boatswain.

He seized Clinton's head, drawing it back slightly, and thrust a thick pad of felt, a piece of wadding for the maindeck cannon, between his teeth, holding it in place.

'Zouga!'

He took Clinton's shoulders and locked them in his powerful fingers, preventing Clinton from rolling on to his belly.

'Good.'

Robyn took one of the razor-sharp scalpels from the shelf, and then with the forefinger of her other hand probed brutally down to where she had felt that hard foreign body.

Clinton's back arched and he let out a shattering cry that was muffled by the wadding, but Robyn felt it clearly this time, hard and unyielding in the swollen flesh.

She cut swiftly, without hesitation, opening the skin cleanly, following the direction of the muscle fibre beneath, dissecting down through layer after layer of muscle, separating the bluish membrane capsules that covered each of the muscles with the hilt of the scalpel, probing deeper and deeper with her fingers towards that elusive lump in the flesh.

Clinton writhed and heaved at his bonds, his breathing rasping in the back of his throat, his teeth locked into the felt wadding in a fierce rictus so that cords of muscle stood out along his jawline and white spittle frothed upon his lips.

His wild lunges made her task that much more difficult, and her fingers were slippery with blood in his hot flesh, but she found the rubbery pulsing snake of the lateral thoracic artery and worked past it gently, pinching off the smaller spurting blood vessels with the forceps, and tying them with a loop of catgut, torn between the need for speed and the danger of doing greater damage.

Finally she had to use the blade again, and she reversed the scalpel and paused a moment to locate the lump with the tip of her forefinger.

She could feel the sweat sliding down her cheek, and she was aware of the strained tense faces of the men who held Clinton as they watched her work.

She guided the scalpel down into the open wound, and then cut down firmly and a sudden bright yellow fountain spouted up through her fingers, and the cloying stomach-twisting stench of corruption that filled the hot little cabin made her gasp.

That sharp rush of pus lasted only a second, and then there was something black and sodden blocking the wound. She picked it out with the forceps, releasing another lesser welling up of the thick custardy matter.

'The wad,' Zouga grunted with the effort of holding down the struggling naked body. They all stared at the soft rotten object in the teeth of her forceps.

The patch of cloth had been carried deeply into the flesh by the passage of the ball, and Robyn felt a surging lift of relief – she had been right.

Quickly she went back to work, running her finger into the tunnel cut by the ball until she felt it with her fingertip.

'There it is!' She spoke for the first time since she had cut, but the metal pellet was slippery and heavy, she could not prise it loose and she had to cut again and then lock the teeth of the pair of bone forceps over it. It came out with reluctant suck of clinging tissue, and she dropped it impatiently on the shelf. It made a heavy clunk against the wood. There was a temptation to come out immediately, to sew up and bind up – but she resisted it and took an extra ten seconds to probe the wound thoroughly. She was almost immediately justified, there was another rotting and stinking tatter of cloth in the wound track.

'A piece of the shirt.' She identified the white shreds, and Zouga's face mirrored his disgust. 'Now we can come out,' Robyn went on complacently.

She left a bristle in the wound to allow the remaining pus to drain off. It stuck out stiffly between the stitches with which she closed up.

When she stood back at last she was smugly satisfied with her work. There had been nobody at St Matthew's who could lay down stitches so neatly and regularly, not even the senior surgeons could match her.

Clinton had collapsed with the shock of deep surgery. His body was wet and slick with his sweat, and the skin at his wrists and ankles had been smeared away where he had fought against his bonds.

'Let him loose,' she said softly. She felt a vast pride, almost of ownership, in him now, as though he were her special creation, for she had dragged him back almost bodily from the abyss. Pride was sin, she knew, but it did not make the sensation any the less agreeable, and in the circumstances, she decided, she had earned the pleasure of a little sin.

Clinton's recovery was almost miraculous. By the next morning he was fully conscious, and the fever had abated to leave him pale and shaky, with just enough strength to argue bitterly when she had him carried up into the sunshine and laid behind the canvas wind shelter that the carpenter had rigged under the poop.

'Cold air is bad for gunshot wounds, everybody knows that.'

'And I suppose I should bleed you before closing you up in that hot little hell hole you call a cabin,' Robyn asked tartly.

'A navy surgeon would do so,' he muttered.

'Then thank your Maker that I am not one.'

On the second day he was sitting up unaided and eating voraciously, by the third he was managing the ship from his litter, and on the fourth day he was on his quarterdeck once more, although his arm was in a sling and he was still pale and gaunt where the fever had wasted away the flesh from his face, but strong enough to keep on his feet for an hour at a time before resorting to the rope chair the carpenter had rigged at the rail. That day Robyn withdrew the bristle from the wound and was relieved at the tiny quantity of benign pus that followed it out. They watched the little town of Port Natal come up ahead of them, the primitive buildings huddled under the whale-backed mountain they called the Bluff like chickens under the wing of the hen. *Black Joke* did not call, even though this was the furthest outpost of the British Empire on this coast, but steamed on briskly into the north, each day becoming perceptively warmer with the sun standing higher at noon and the sea changing to the darker azure of the tropics beneath *Black Joke*'s bows, and once again the flying fish sported ahead of them on filmy silver wings.

The evening before they reached the Portuguese settlement of Lourenç Marques on the deep bight of Delagoa Bay, Robyn dressed the stitches in Clinton's side, making small cooing and clucking sounds of satisfaction and approval as she saw how cleanly they were healing.

When she helped him into his shirt and then buttoned it for him, like a mother dressing her child, he told her gravely,

'I am aware you have saved my life.'

'Even though you do not approve of my methods?' she asked with a twinkle of a smile.

'I ask your forgiveness for my impertinence.' He dropped his eyes. 'You have proved yourself to be a brilliant physician.'

She made a modest murmur of denial, but when he insisted, 'No, I truly mean that. I think you are gifted,' Robyn protested no further, but moved slightly to make it easier for him to reach her with his good arm, but his declaration of faith in her skills seemed to have exhausted his courage for the moment.

That evening she vented some of her frustration by confiding to her journal that, 'Captain Codrington is clearly a man that can be trusted by a woman, in any circumstances – though a little more boldness would make him a great deal more attractive.'

She was about to close the journal and lock it away in her chest, when another thought occurred to her, and she thumbed back through the preceding pages each crammed with her small neat script, until she reached the single sheet that had become a milestone in her life. The entry for the day before *Huron* reached Cape Town she had left blank. What words were there to describe it? Each moment of it would be engraved forever on her memory. She stared for many minutes at the empty sheet, and then she made a silent calculation, subtracting one date from another. When she had the answer she felt a chill of foreboding, and went over the calculation again, reaching the same answer.

She closed the journal slowly and stared at the lantern flame.

She had missed her lunar courses by almost a week, and with a prickle of dread lilting the fine hair at the nape of her neck she laid her hand upon her own belly as if there was something to feel there like the pistol ball in Clinton's flesh.

Black Joke called at Lourenç Marques for coal bunkers, despite the town's notoriety as a fever port. The swamps and mangroves that half-circled the town to the southwards spread the miasmic airs across the port.

Although Robyn had only very limited first-hand experience of the peculiar fevers of Africa, she had made a close study of all the writings on the subject – the most notable of these being probably those of her own father. Fuller Ballantyne had written a long paper for the British Medical Association, in which he recognized four distinct types of African fever – the recurrent fevers with a definite cycle, he divided into three categories – quotidian, tertian and quartan – by the length of the cycle. These he called the malarial fevers. The fourth type was the black vomit, or the yellow jack.

In his own unmistakable style, Fuller Ballantyne had shown that these diseases were neither contagious nor infectious. He had done so by a horrifying but courageous demonstration to a group of sceptical brother physicians at the military hospital at Algoa Bay.

While the other physicians watched, he had collected a wine glass of fresh vomit from a victim of the yellow jack. Fuller had toasted them with the awful draught and then drunk it down at a single swallow. His colleagues had waited, with a certain keen anticipation for his demise and had some difficulty in hiding their disappointment when he showed no ill effects and set off a week later to walk across Africa. Fuller Ballantyne was a man it was easier to admire than to like. The episode had become part of the legend that surrounded him.

In his writings her father insisted that the disease could only be contracted by breathing the night air of tropical areas, particularly those airs released by swamps or other large bodies of stagnant water. However, some individuals most certainly had a natural resistance to the disease, and this resistance was probably hereditary. He cited the African tribes who lived in known malarial areas, and his own family and that of his wife who had lived and worked in Africa for sixty years with only mild afflictions.

Fuller wrote of the 'seasoning fever' – the first of which either killed or gave partial immunity to the subject. He used the example of the high mortality rate amongst newly arrived Europeans in Africa.

He quoted the case of Nathaniel Isaacs who in 1832 left Port Natal in a party with twenty-one newly arrived white men to hunt hippopotamus in the estuary and swamps of St Lucia river. Within four weeks nineteen had perished while Isaacs and the other survivor were so wracked with the disease that they were invalids for a a year thereafter.

These losses were unnecessary, Fuller Ballantyne pointed out. There was a preventative and a cure that had been known for hundreds of years though under various names, Peruvian bark, or Chinchona bark, more recently called essence of quinine when manufactured in powder form by the Quaker brothers Luke and John Howard. Taken at the dosage of five grains daily it was a highly effective preventative, for even if the disease was subsequently contracted, it was in such mild form as to be no more dangerous than a common cold and responded immediately to a more massive dose of twenty-five grains of quinine.

Of course, Robyn had beard the accusation that her father played down the dangers of the disease to further his grand design. Fuller Ballantyne had a vision of Africa settled by colonists of British stock, bringing to the savage continent the true God, and all the benefits of British justice and ingenuity. His catastrophic expedition to the Zambezi had been in pursuit of this vision, for the great river was to have been his highway to the high and healthy plateau of the interior where his Englishmen would settle, driving out the slavers, bringing the warring and godless tribes to order, and taming and cultivating the savage earth.

Part of his vision had died upon the terrible torrents and rapids of the Kaborra-Bassa gorge.

With a sneaking sensation of disloyalty Robyn admitted to herself that there was probably some shred of justification in the accusation, for she had as a child seen her father in the grip of a malarial fever brought out by the cold of an English winter. It had not seemed as mild as a common cold then. Despite this, there was no one in the medical profession who doubted that Fuller Ballantyne was probably one of the world's leading authorities on the disease and that he had a real talent in diagnosing and treating it. So she followed his dictates faithfully, administering the daily five grains of quinine to herself, to Zouga and under protest to Captain Codrington. She had no success with Zouga's Hottentot musketeers, however. At the first dose Jan Cheroot had begun staggering in circles, clutching his throat and rolling his eyes horribly, crying to all his Hottentot gods that he had been poisoned. Only a tot of ship's rum saved him, but none of the other Hottentots would touch the white powder after that. Not even the thought of a tot of rum would tempt them, which was a measure of their opposition to the cure. Robyn could only hope that they possessed the resistance to the fever that her father spoke of.

Her store of quinine was meant to last for the duration of the expedition, possibly as long as two years, so she had reluctantly to refrain from pressing any of it on *Black Joke*'s seamen. She stilled her conscience with the fact that none of them would be spending a night ashore, therefore they would not be exposed to the dangerous airs. She prevailed upon Clinton Codrington to anchor in the outer roads where the onshore breeze kept the air sweet and, as an added attraction, the distance offshore prevented the swarms of mosquitoes and other flying insects from coming on board during the night.

The first night at anchor, the sound of music, of drunken laughter and the shrill cries of women at play and at work carried across the still waters to the nine Hottentot musketeers in their corner of the forecastle, and the lights of the bordels and bars along the waterfront were as irresistible to the nine as a candle to a hawk moth. Temptation was made unbearable by the weight and heat of the golden sovereign that each of them carried in some secret place upon his person, the princely advance that Major Ballantyne had made against their salaries.

Sergeant Cheroot woke Zouga a little before midnight, his features a mask of outrage.

'They are gone.' He was shaking with anger.

'Where?' Zouga was still more asleep than awake.

'They swim like rats,' stormed Cheroot. 'They all go drinking and a-whoring.' The thought of it was insupportable. 'We must catch them. They will burn their brains out on smoke and pox themselves—' His rage was mixed with an equal portion of raw envy, and once they were ashore his enthusiasm for the chase was almost a frenzy. Cheroot had an unerring instinct that led him directly to the lowest dives on the waterfront.

'You go in, Master,' he told Zouga. 'I'll wait around the back,' and he twitched the short oaken club in his hand with gleeful anticipation.

The tobacco smoke and the fumes of cheap rum and gin were like a solid wall, but the musketeers saw Zouga the moment he stooped through the doorway into the yellow lantern light. There were four of them. They overturned two tables and smashed a dozen bottles in their eagerness to depart, jamming in a solid knot in the doorway to the rear alley before bursting out into the night beyond.

It took Zouga half a minute to push and wrestle his way through the crowd. The women of a dozen rich shades between gold and ebony reached out to pluck shamelessly at the more private areas of his anatomy as he passed, forcing him to defend himself, and the men deliberately blocked his path until he drew the Colt revolver from under his coat tails – only then they sullenly opened a way for him to pass. When he reached the back door Sergeant Cheroot had the four Hottentots laid out in a row in the filth and dust of the alley.

'You haven't killed them?' Zouga asked anxiously.

'*Nee wat!* They got heads of solid bone.' Cheroot tucked the club back in his belt, and stooped to pick up one of the bodies. The strength of his wiry little body was out of all proportion to its size. He carried them down to the beach one at a time as though they were bags of straw, and dumped them head first into the waiting whaler.

'Now we find the others.'

They ferreted them out, singly and in pairs from the fan-tan parlours and the gin hells, tracking down the ninth and last to the embrace of an enormous naked Somali lady in one of the shacks of mud walls and corrugated iron roofs behind the waterfront.

It was almost dawn when Zouga climbed wearily out of the whaler on to *Black Joke*'s deck and booted the ninth Hottentot down the forecastle ladder. He started for his own cabin, red-eyed and irritable, aching with fatigue when it occurred to him that he had not noticed Sergeant Cheroot amongst the dark figures in the whaler, and his penetrating voice and biting sarcasm had been silent on the return from the beach.

Zouga's mood was murderous as he landed once again, and picked his way through the narrow filth-choked alleys to the mud and iron shack. The woman made up four of Jan Cheroot. She was a mountain of polished dark flesh, gleaming with oil, each of her widespread thighs thicker than his waist, her great mammaries each as large as his head, and Jan Cheroot's head was buried between them as though he was drowning himself in exotic and abundant flesh so that his ecstatic cries were almost smothered.

The woman looked down at him fondly, chuckling to herself as she watched Sergeant Cheroot's upended buttocks. They were skinny and a delicate shade of buttercup yellow, but they seemed to blur with the speed of movement, and the shock waves they created were transferred into the mountain of flesh beneath him, creating ripples and waves that undulated through the woman's belly and elephantine haunches, travelling up to agitate the pendulous folds that hung from her upper arms, and at last breaking in a wobbling heaving surf of gleaming black flesh around Sergeant Cheroot's head.

On the final return to the gunboat, Sergeant Cheroot sat, a small dejected figure, in the bows of the whaler. His post coital tristesse considerably enhanced by the buzzing in his ears and the ache in his head. Only Englishmen had the alarming habit of bunching up a hand suddenly, and then hitting with more effect than a man wielding a club or hurling a brick. Sergeant Cheroot found his respect for his new master increasing daily.

'You should be an example to the men,' Zouga growled at him

as he hoisted him up the ladder by the collar of his uniform jacket.

'I know that, Master,' Cheroot agreed miserably. 'But I was in love.'

'Are you still in love?' Zouga demanded harshly.

'No, Master, with me love don't last too long,' Cheroot assured him hurriedly.

'I am a modestly wealthy man,' Clinton Codrington told Robyn seriously. 'Since my days as a midshipman I have saved as much of my pay as I did not need to live by, and of recent years I have been fortunate in the matter of prize money. This, together with the legacy of my mother, would enable me to care very comfortably for a wife.'

They had lunched with the Portuguese Governor at his invitation and the *vinho verde* that had accompanied the meal of succulent seafood and tasteless stringy beef had given Clinton a flush of courage.

Rather than returning immediately to the ship after the meal, he had suggested a tour of the principal city of the Portuguese possessions on the east coast of the African continent.

The Governor's dilapidated carriage rumbled over the rutted roads and splashed through the puddles formed by the overflow from the open sewers. A raucous flock of ragged child-beggars followed them, dancing in their dirty rags to keep pace with the bony, sway-backed mule that drew the carriage, and holding up their tiny pink-palmed hands for alms. The sun was fierce but not as fierce as the smells.

It was not the appropriate setting for what Clinton Codrington had in mind, and with relief he handed Robyn down from the carriage, scattered the beggars by hurling a handful of copper coins down the dusty street, and hurried Robyn into the cool gloom of the Roman Catholic cathedral. The cathedral was the most magnificent building in the city, its towers and spires rising high above the hovels and shacks that surrounded it.

However, Robyn had difficulty in concentrating on Clinton's declaration in these popish surroundings, amongst the gaudy idols, saints and virgins in scarlet and gold leaf. The reek of incense and the flickering of the massed banks of candles distracted her even though what he was saying was what she wanted to hear, she wished he had chosen some other place to say it.

That very morning she had been taken by a sudden spell of vomiting, and a mild nausea persisted even now. As a physician she knew exactly what that heralded.

Before the courtesy visit to the Portuguese Governor's mouldering palace, she had tentatively decided that she would have to take the initiative. That attack of vapours had convinced her of the urgency of the situation, and she had pondered how she could induce Clinton Codrington to stake some sort of claim to the burden she was convinced she was carrying.

When Zouga had still lived at King's Lynn with Uncle William, she had discovered a cheaply printed novel of a most disreputable type concealed amongst the military texts on Zouga's desk. From a furtive study of this publication she had learned that it was possible for a woman to seduce a man, as well as the other way around. Unfortunately, the author had not provided a detailed description of the procedures. She had not even been certain if it were possible in a carriage, or whether anything should be said during the process, but now Clinton was obviating the necessity for experiment by a straightforward declaration. Her relief was tinged with shades of disappointment, after having been forced into the decision to carry out his seduction, she had found herself looking forward to the experience.

Now, however, she forced herself to assume an attentive expression and, when he hesitated, to encourage him with a nod or a gesture.

'Even though I am without powerful friends in the service, yet my record is such that I would never expect half pay appointment, and although it might sound immodest I would confidently look forward to hoisting my own broad pennant before I am fifty years of age.'

It was typical of him that he was already thinking twenty five years ahead. It required an effort to prevent her irritation showing, for Robyn preferred to live in the present, or at least the immediately foreseeable future.

'I should point out that an Admiral's wife enjoys a great deal of social prestige,' he went on comfortably, and her irritation flared higher. Prestige was something she had always intended to win at first hand – crusader against the slave trade, celebrated pioneer in tropical medicine, writer of admired books on African travel.

She could not contain it longer, but her voice was sweet and demure. 'A woman can have a career as well as being a wife.'

Clinton drew himself up stiffly. 'A wife's place is in the home,' he intoned, and she opened her mouth, then slowly closed it again. She knew she was bargaining from weakness, and when she was silent Clinton was encouraged. 'To begin with a comfortable little house, near the harbour in Portsmouth. Of course, once there are children one would have to seek larger premises—'

'You would want many children?' she asked still sweetly, but with colour mounting in her cheeks.

'Oh yes, indeed. One a year,' and Robyn recalled those pale drabs with whom she had worked, women with brats hanging from both breasts and every limb, with another one always in the belly. She shuddered, and he was immediately concerned.

'Are you cold?'

'No. No, please go on.' She felt trapped, and not for the first time resented the role that her sex had forced upon her.

'Miss Ballantyne – Doctor Ballantyne – what I have been trying to say to you – is that I would be greatly honoured if you could find it in yourself to consent to become my wife.'

Now when it came she was not really ready for it, and her confusion was genuine.

'Captain Codrington, this comes as such a surprise—'

'I do not see why. My admiration for you must be apparent, and the other day you led me to believe—' He hesitated, and then with a rush, 'you even allowed me to embrace you.'

Suddenly she was overcome with the urge to burst out laughing, if only he had known her further intentions towards him – but she skittered away from the subject, her expression as solemn as his.

'When would we he able to marry?' she asked instead.

'Well, on my return to—'

'There is a British consul at Zanzibar, and you are bound there, are you not?' she interrupted quickly. 'He could perform the ceremony.'

Clinton's face lit with slow, deep joy. 'Oh Miss Ballantyne, does that mean – can I take it that—' He took a pace towards her, and she had a vivid image of the tiny house in Portsmouth bursting at the seams with little blond replicas of himself, and she took a quick pace backwards and went on hurriedly.

'I need time to think.'

He stopped, joy faded and he said heavily, 'Of course.'

'It means such a change in my life, I would have to abandon all my plans. The expedition – it's such a big decision.'

'I could wait a year, longer if necessary. Until after the expedition, as long as you wished,' he told her earnestly, and she felt a flutter of panic deep in her belly.

'No, I mean I need a few days, that is all,' and she laid her hand on his forearm. 'I will give you an answer before we reach Quelimane. I promise you that.'

Sheikh Yussuf was a worried man. For eight days the big dhow-rigged vessel had lain within sight of land, the single, huge lateen sail drooped from the long yard, the sea about her was velvet smooth during the day and afire with phosphorus during the long moonless, windless nights.

So deep and utter was the calm that not the slightest swell moved the surface. The dhow lay so still that she might have been hard aground.

The Sheikh was a master mariner who owned a fleet of trading vessels and who for forty years had threaded the seaways of the Indian Ocean. He knew intimately each island, each headland and the tricks of the tides that swirled about them. He knew the great roads that the currents cut across the waters the way a post coachman knows each turn and dip of the road between his stages, and he could run them without compass or sextant, steering only by the heavenly bodies a thousand miles and more across open water, making his unerring landfalls on the great horn of Africa, on the coast of India and back again on the island of Zanzibar.

In forty years he had never known the monsoon wind to fail for eight successive days at this season of the year. All his calculations had been based on the wind standing steady out of the south-east, day and night, hour after hour, day after day.

He had taken on his cargo with that expectation, calculating that he could discharge again on Zanzibar Island within six days of loading. Naturally, a man expected losses, they were an integral part of his calculations. Ten per cent losses was the very least, twenty was more likely, thirty was acceptable, forty was always possible and even losses of fifty per cent would still leave the voyage in profit.

But not this. He looked up at the stubby foremast from which drooped the fifteen-foot-long scarlet banner of the Sultan of Zanzibar, beloved of Allah, ruler of all the Omani Arabs and overlord of vast tracts of eastern Africa. The banner was faded and soiled as the lateen sail, both of them veterans of fifty such voyages, of calms and hurricanes, of baking sun and the driving torrential rains of the high monsoon. The golden Arabic script that covered the banner was barely legible now, and he had lost count of the number of times it had been taken down from the masthead and carried at the head of his column of armed men deep into the interior of that brooding land on the horizon.

How many times had that banner wafted out proudly, long and sinuous as a serpent on the breeze, as he brought his vessel up under the fort at Zanzibar Island. Sheikh Yussuf caught himself dreaming again. It was an old man's failing. He straightened up on the pile of cushions and precious rugs of silk and gold thread, and looked down from his command position on the poop deck. His crew lay like dead men in the shade of the sail, their grubby robes folded up over their heads against the heat. Let them lie, he decided, there was nothing mortal man could do now, except wait. It was in the hands of Allah now. 'There is one God,' he murmured. 'And Mohammed is his prophet.' It did not occur to him to question his fate, to rail or pray against it. It was God's will, and God is great.

Yet he could not help feeling regret. It was thirty years since he had taken such a fine cargo as this, and at prices that compared with those of thirty years before.

Three hundred and thirty black pearls, each one perfectly formed, young, by Allah, not one of them over sixteen years of age. They were of a people he had never encountered before, for he had never before traded so far south. It was only in this last season that he had heard of the new source of black pearl from beyond the Djinn Mountains, that forbidden land from which no man returned.

A new people, well favoured and beautifully formed, strong and tall, sturdy limbs, not those stickline legs of the people from beyond the lakes; these had full moon faces and good strong white teeth. Sheikh Yussuf nodded over his pipe, the water bubbled softly in the bowl of the hookah at each inhalation and he let the smoke trickle out softly between his lips. It had stained his white beard pale yellow at the corners of his mouth, and at each lungful he felt the delightful lethargy steal through his old veins, and take the edge off the cold frosts of age which seemed always now to chill his blood.

There was suddenly a higher pitched shriek, that rose above the low hubbub which enveloped the dhow. The sound was part of the ship, day and night it came up from the slave hold below the dhow's maindeck.

Sheikh Yussuf removed the mouthpiece from his lips and cocked his head to listen, combing his fingers through his scraggling white beard – but the shriek was not repeated. It was perhaps the final cry from one of his fine black pearls.

Sheikh Yussuf sighed, the din from below decks had slowly decreased in volume while the dhow lay becalmed, and he was able to judge with great accuracy how high his losses were by that volume. He knew he had already lost half of them. Another quarter at the very least would perish before he could reach Zanzibar, many more would go even after they were landed, only the very hardiest would be fit for the market, and then only after careful convalescence.

Another indication of his losses, though not as accurate, was the smell. Some of them must have gone on the very first day of the calm and without the wind the heat had been blinding. It would be even worse in the holds, the corpses would be swollen to twice life-size. The smell was bad, he could not recall a worse stench in all his forty years. It was a pity that there was no way in which to remove the bodies, but this could only be done in port.

Sheikh Yussuf dealt only in young females. They were smaller and much hardier than males of the same age, and could be loaded more densely. He had been able to reduce the clearance between each deck by six inches, which meant an entire extra deck could be built into the hold.

Females had a remarkable ability to go without water for longer periods than the males, like the camel of the desert they seemed able to exist on the accumulated fat in their thighs, buttocks and bosoms, and to make the Mozambique passage even in the fairest conditions of wind and tide required five days without water.

Another consideration was the loss of males destined for China and the Far East by the necessary surgery. The Chinese buyers insisted that all male slaves be castrated before they would purchase. It was a logical precaution to prevent breeding with local populations, but one that entailed additional losses to the trader who must perform the operation.

The final reason that Sheikh Yussuf dealt only in comely young females was that they commanded a price almost twice that of a young male slave in the Zanzibar market.

Before Sheikh Yussuf loaded his wares, he allowed them to fatten for at least a week in his barracoons, with as much to eat and drink as they could force down their throats. Then they were stripped naked, except for light chains, and at low tide taken out to the dhow where it lay high and dry on the shoaling beach.

The first girls aboard were made to lie on the bare boards of the hull in the bottom of the hold, each on her left side with her knees raised slightly so that the knees of the girl behind her could fit against the back of her legs, the front of her pelvis against buttocks, belly against back, like a row of spoons in a rack.

At intervals the chains were snapped into the ring bolts already set into the deck. This was not only for security but also to prevent the layer of human bodies sliding about in rough weather, piling up in heaps and crushing those beneath.

Once the bottom of the hold was covered with a layer of humanity, the next deck was placed in position over them, so close that they could not attempt to sit upright nor roll over. The next layer of girls was laid over them, and the next deck over them again.

To reach the lower decks meant laboriously unchaining and unloading each layer of humanity, and lifting the intervening decks. It could not even be attempted at sea. However, with the trade wind standing fair, it was a straight run down the channel, and the wind blowing in through the canvas scoops and ports, kept the air below decks breathable, and the heat bearable.

Sheikh Yussuf sighed again and lifted his rheumy eyes to the unbroken blue line of the eastern horizon.

'This will be my last voyage,' he decided, whispering aloud in the way of old men. 'Allah has been good and I am a rich man with many strong sons. Perhaps this is his sign to me. This will indeed be my last voyage.'

It was almost as though he had been overheard, for the scarlet banner moved lazily, like an adder emerging from long hibernation, then slowly reared its head, and Sheikh Yussuf felt the wind on his seared and wrinkled cheek.

He stood up suddenly, quick and supple as a man half his age, and stamped his bare foot on the deck.

'Up', he cried. 'Up, my children. Here is the wind at last.' And while his crew scrambled to their feet, he took the long tiller under his arm and threw back his head to watch the sail bulge outwards, and the thick clumsy pole of the mainmast heel slowly across a horizon suddenly dark with the scurry of the trade wind.

Clinton Codrington caught the first whiff of it during the night. It woke him from a nightmare that he had lived through on many other nights, but when he lay sweating in his narrow wooden bunk the smell persisted and he threw a boat cloak over his bare shoulders and hurried up on deck.

It came in gusts out of the darkness, for minutes at a time the warm sweet rush of the trade wind brought only the iodine and salt smell of the sea, then suddenly there was another curdled whiff of it. It was a smell that Clinton would never forget, like the smell of a cage full of carnivorous beasts that had never been cleaned, the stench of excrement and rotten flesh, and his nightmare came rushing back upon him in full strength.

Ten years before, when Clinton had been a very junior midshipman aboard the old *Widgeon*, one of the very first gunboats of the anti-slavery squadron, they had taken a slaver in northern latitudes. She was a schooner of 300 tons burden, out of Lisbon, but flying a Brazilian flag of convenience, with the unlikely name of *Hirondelle Blanche*, the *White Swallow*. Clinton had been ordered into her as prize-master with orders to run her into the nearest Portuguese port and deliver her to the Courts of Mixed Commission to be condemned as a prize.

They had made the capture a hundred nautical miles off the Brazilian coast, after the *Hirondelle Blanche* and her five hundred black slaves had almost completed the dreaded middle passage. Under orders, Clinton had turned the schooner and sailed her back to the Cape Verde Islands, crossing the equator to do so and lying three days becalmed in the doldrums before breaking from their suffocating grip.

In the harbour of Praia, on the principal island of São Tiago, Clinton had been refused permission to land any of his slaves, and they had lain sixteen days waiting for the Portuguese president of the Court of Mixed Commission to reach a decision. Finally, the president had decided, after strenuous representation by the owners of the *Hirondelle Blanche* that he had no jurisdiction in the case, and ordered Clinton to sail her back to Brazil and submit the vessel to the Brazilian courts.

However, Clinton knew very well what a Brazilian court would decide, and instead set a course for the British naval station on St Helena Island, once more crossing the equator with his burden of human misery.

By the time he dropped anchor in Jamestown roads, the surviving slaves aboard had made three consecutive crossings of the terrible middle passage. There were only twenty-six of them still alive, and the smell of a slaver had become part of the nightmares which still plagued Clinton ten years later.

Now he stood on the darkened deck and flared his nostrils, the same smell coming to him out of the tropical night, horrible and unmistakable. He had to drag himself away with a physical effort to give the orders to fire *Black Joke*'s furnace and work up a head of steam in her boilers, ready for the dawn.

Sheikh Yussuf recognized the dark shape with a sense of utter disbelief, and the dismay of one finally deserted by Allah.

She was still five miles distant, indistinct in the dusty pink light of the dawn, but coming up swiftly, a thick column of black smoke smearing away on her beam, carried low over the green waters of the inshore channel by the boisterous trade wind. The same wind spread out her ensign to full view from the poop of the dhow, and in the field of Sheikh Yussuf's ancient brass and leather-bound telescope it snapped and flickered, the snowy white field crossed by bold bright scarlet.

How he hated that flag, the symbol of an arrogant, bullying

people, tyrants of the oceans, captors of continents. He had seen gunboats like this one in Aden and Calcutta, he had seen that same flag flying in every far corner of every sea he had ever sailed. Very clearly he knew what it all meant.

He put up the helm, in that gesture acknowledging the final end to a disastrous voyage, the dhow came around reluctantly, creaking in every timber, the great sail flogging before it could be trimmed to take the wind over the stern.

There had seemed to be so little risk, he thought with weary resignation. Of course, the treaty that the Sultan had made with the Zanzibar consul of these dangerous infidels allowed his subjects to trade in the black pearls, between any of the Sultan's possessions, with the proviso that only Omani Arabs loyal to the Sultan could indulge in the lucrative traffic. No person of Christian European extraction, not even a converted Moslem, could sail under the Sultan's flag, and not even an Omani Arab might trade beyond the borders of the Sultan's possessions.

The Sultan's African possessions had been very carefully defined in the treaty, and here was he, Sheikh Yussuf, with a cargo of three hundred and thirty living, dying and dead slaves at least one hundred and fifty miles south of the furthest of the Sultan's borders with a British gunboat bearing down upon him. Truly the ways of Allah were wonderful, passing the comprehension of man, Sheikh Yussuf thought with only the slightest taste of bitterness in his throat, as he hung grimly on to the tiller and made his run for the land.

A gun thumped from the gunboat's bows, powder smoke flew bright as a seabird's wing in the first rays of the low sun, and Sheikh Yussuf spat passionately over the lee bulwark and said aloud,

'El Sheetan, the Devil,' using for the first time the name with which, in time, Captain Clinton Codrington would be known throughout the length of the Mozambique channel, and as far north as the great Horn of Africa.

The bronze screw under *Black Joke*'s counter thrashed out a long wide wake behind her. She still had main and jib set, but Codrington would shorten to 'fighting sail' just as soon as he had made the adjustment to counter the dhow's turn away towards the land.

Zouga and Robyn were on the quarterdeck to watch the chase, infected by the restrained businesslike excitement which gripped the vessel so that Zouga laughed aloud and called, 'Gone away! Tally-ho!' as the dhow turned, and Clinton glanced at him with a conspiratory grin.

'She's a slaver. Apart from the stink, that turn-away proves it beyond doubt.'

Robyn strained forward to watch the filthy little vessel, with its discoloured and patched sail, the unpainted timbers of the hull striped with zebra stripes of human excrement and other wastes. It was her first view of a slaver actually carrying on its grisly trade, and she felt herself filled with a new purpose; she had come so far for this moment, and she tried to capture every detail of it all for her journal.

'Mr Denham, give him a gun, if you please,' ordered Clinton.

The bow-chaser thudded, but the dhow held to her new course.

'Be ready to round up and send the boat away on the instant.' Clinton's excitement had given way to obvious anxiety. He turned to look across at his boarding party. They had been issued with cutlass and pistol, and waited now in the waist under the command of a young ensign.

Clinton would dearly have liked to command the boarding-party himself but his arm was still in its sling and the stitches still in the wound. To go aboard a dhow in a rough sea, and fight its crew required both hands and the agility which his wound denied him. Reluctantly he had put Ferris in charge of the boarders.

Now he looked back at the dhow, and his expression was grim.

'He is going to beach.'

They were all silent now, staring ahead, watching the slaver run in towards the land.

'But there is a coral reef.' Robyn spoke for them all, pointing to the black points that broke the surface a quarter of a mile short of the land itself, they looked like a necklace of sharks' teeth, and the surf broke and swirled about them as it was driven in upon the trade wind.

'Yes,' Clinton agreed. 'They will run it up on the coral and escape across the lagoon.'

'But, what about the slaves?' Robyn asked, horrified, and nobody answered her.

Black Joke rushed on purposefully, but with the wind almost dead astern the dhow trained her long boom around to go on to her best point of sailing. The boom was longer than the hull itself, and the huge triangular mainsail bulged far out, almost touching the surface of the water as she hurled down upon the reef.

'We may just cut her off,' Zouga said loudly, but he did not have the seaman's eye for bearing and speed, and Clinton Codrington shook his head angrily.

'Not this time.'

But it was very finely run. Clinton held his course up until the very last moment, and the dhow passed a mere two hundred yards ahead of his bows. So close that they could clearly make out the features of the helmsman on the vessel's poopdeck, a skinny old Arab in long, flowing robe and with the tasselled fez on his head that declared that he had made the pilgrimage to Mecca. On his belt glittered the gold filigree hilt of the short curved dagger of a sheikh, and his long scraggling white beard fluttered in the wind as he leaned on the long tiller and turned his head to watch the high black hull bearing down on him.

'I could put a bullet through the bastard,' Zouga growled.

'It's too late for that,' Clinton told him, for the dhow had passed beneath their bows and the gun boat was as close to the menacing fangs of coral as she dared go. Clinton called to his quartermaster at the gunboat's wheel, 'Heave to! And bring her head to wind.' Then, spinning on his heel, 'Away, the boarding-party!'

There was a squeal of davits as the crowded whaler dropped out of sight towards the choppy green sea alongside, but already the dhow was pitching wildly in the lines of seething white surf that guarded the reef.

It was two days since that dead flat calm had broken, and since then the trades had worked up a goodly swell. It came sweeping in across the inshore channel, in low green humps with dark wind-scarred backs, but as soon as they felt the tilt of the land, they peaked up eagerly, the crests turning opaque as green jelly, shivering and wobbling, and then collapsing on themselves and surging in tumultuous white water up on to the black fangs of the reef.

The dhow caught one of the taller swells, threw up her stern and went racing down upon it like a surf boat, with the skinny old Arab at the tiller prancing like a trained monkey on the stick of the tiller to hold her in the wave, but the dhow was not built for this work, and she dug her shoulder rebelliously into the sliding, roaring chute of green water, breaching so fiercely to the wave that the water poured aboard her in a green wall and she wallowed broadside, half swamped before she took the reef with a force that snapped off her single mast at deck level and sent yard and sail and rigging crashing over the side.

In an instant she was transformed into a broken hulk, and clearly the watchers on *Black Joke*'s deck could hear the crackle and rending of her bottom timbers.

'There they go!' Clinton muttered angrily, as the dhow's crew began to abandon her, leaping over the side and using the swells to carry them over the reef into the quieter waters of the lagoon, thrashing and kicking until the beach shelved up beneath them.

They saw the old Arab steersman amongst the survivors. He waded ashore, beard and robe plastered against his body with seawater, and then lifted his robes to his waist, exposing skinny legs and shrunken buttocks as he scampered up the white beach with the agility of a goat and disappeared amongst the palm groves.

Black Joke's whaler pulled swiftly into the first line of breakers, the Ensign in the stern peering over his shoulder to judge the surf, and then catching his wave taking her in with a rush, swinging sharply into the lee of the dhow's stranded hull where there was calmer water.

They watched the Ensign and four of his men go up over the side, pistols and cutlasses drawn, but by this time the last of the Arab crew were staggering up the beach and into the sanctuary of the palm grove a quarter of a mile away across the lagoon.

The Ensign led his men below decks, and they waited on *Black Joke*'s quarterdeck, watching the abandoned dhow through the telescope. A minute passed before the Ensign appeared on deck again. He crossed quickly to the dhow's rail and leaned against it to vomit over the side, then straightened up and wiped his mouth on the back of his sleeve, before shouting an order down to the oarsmen in the whaler.

Immediately the whaler shot out from the lee of the hull, and pulled lustily back through the surf towards *Black Joke*.

The boatswain came in through the entry port, and knuckled his forehead to his captain.

'Mr Ferris's compliments, sir, and he needs a carpenter to get the slave decks open, and two good men with bolt cutters for the chains.' He had gabbled this out on a single breath, and he paused to refill his lungs. 'Mr Ferris says as how it's fierce bad below decks, and some of them is trapped – and he needs the doctor—'

'I'm ready to go,' Robyn cut in.

'Wait,' Clinton snapped, but Robyn had gathered her skirts and run.

'If my sister goes, I'm going too.'

'Very well, then, Ballantyne, I'm obliged for your assistance,' Clinton nodded. 'Tell Ferris we have an incoming tide, full moon tonight, so it will make springs. There is a twenty-two foot tidal fall on this coast. He will have less than an hour in which to work.'

Robyn appeared on deck again, lugging her black leather valise, and she had exchanged skirts for breeches once more. The seamen on deck gawked at her legs curiously, but she ignored them and hurried to the ship's side. The boatswain gave her a hand and she scrambled down into the whaler with Zouga carrying her valise behind her.

The ride in through the surf was terrifying and exhilarating at the same time; the whaler tilted forward at an alarming angle, the water hissing and creaming alongside, with a belly-swooping rush that ended alongside the dhow's heavily canted side.

The deck was running with water and listed so steeply that Robyn had to crawl up it on her hands and knees, and each time a wave struck the hull, it quivered and shook and more water came streaming down over the deck.

The Ensign and his boarding party had ripped the hatches off the main hold and as she reached them, Robyn gagged and choked with the solid stench that came out of that square opening. She had believed herself hardened to the smell of death and corruption, but never had she experienced anything like this.

'Did you bring the bolt cutters?' the Ensign demanded, white-faced with nausea and horror.

The bolt cutters were heavy duty shears, used for cutting the shrouds and halyards from a dismasted vessel. Two men wielded them now, as they lifted a bunch of small black bodies through the hatch, all of them fastened together at wrist and ankle by the clanking black steel links. It reminded Robyn of the cut-out paper dolls she had amused herself with as a child, fashioning with scissors a single figure from the folded sheet, and then pulling out a chain of identical dolls. The cutters crunched through the light chain and the limp little bodies fell apart.

'They are children,' she cried out aloud, and the men around her worked in grim silence, dragging them out of the hatch, cutting them free and dropping them on to the tilted wet deck.

Robyn seized the first of them, a skeletal stick figure, crusted and streaked with dried filth, vomit and faeces, head lolling as she lifted it into her lap.

'No.' There was no life. The eyeballs had dried already. She let the head drop and a seaman dragged it away.

'No,' and 'No,' and 'No again.' Some of them were already in an advanced state of putrification; at a word from the Ensign, the seamen began dropping the wasted corpses over the side, to make room for those still coming up from below.

Robyn found her first live one, there was feeble pulse and fluttering breath, but it did not need a physician's instinct to tell that the hold on life was tenuous. She worked swiftly, apportioning her time to where the chance of life seemed greater.

Another taller wave struck the dhow, and it tilted sharply, the timbers crackled and snapped deep inside her.

'Tides flooding. Work faster,' shouted the Ensign. They were into the hull now. Robyn could hear the thud of sledge hammers and the rip of irons as they began to tear the slave decks out of her.

Zouga was in there, stripped to the waist, leading the attack on the wooden barricades. He was an officer, with the easy way of command and his natural leadership was swiftly acknowledged by the seamen around him.

The hubbub reminded Robyn of a rookery at sundown, the shrieks of the returning birds and the answering cries from the chicks in the nests. The mass of black girls were aroused from the lethargy of approaching death by the dhow's wild antics, the crash of breaking timbers and the flood of cold salt water into the hold.

Some of those lying in the bilges were already drowning as the hold flooded, and some of them had realized that there was a rescue team aboard, and cried aloud with the last strength of waning hope.

Alongside the slaver, the whaler was moored, and she was almost filled with the wasted bodies in which some life still burned, while on the surface of the lagoon bobbed a hundred or more corpses with gas-swollen bellies like the corks on a fishing-net.

'Take them to the ship,' the Ensign shouted down to his oarsmen in the whaler, 'and come back for more.' As he spoke, another white-crested wave struck the dhow solidly and she heeled, but she was pinned down by the spikes of coral driven through her bottom timbers, otherwise she would have turned turtle.

'Robyn!' Zouga shouted at her from the hatch. 'We need you!'

For a moment she did not even glance at him, but shook her head at the sailor beside her.

'No, she's gone.' Expressionlessly the sailor picked up the frail body and dumped it over the side.

Then Robyn scrambled up to the hatch and dropped through it.

It was a descent into the pit, dark after the brilliant noontide, so that she paused for a moment to let her vision adjust.

The tilting deck beneath her feet was slippery with human waste, so that she had to cling for a handhold.

The air was so thick that for a minute she nearly panicked, as though she were being smothered by a stinking damp pillow. She almost fought her way back into the sweet sunlight, but then she forced herself to take a gulp of it, and though her guts heaved and she tasted the bitter flooding into the back of her throat, she kept it down.

Then her own discomfort was forgotten as she made out the chaos about her.

'That last wave,' Zouga grunted as he steadied her with an arm about her shoulder, 'the decks have collapsed.'

Like a house of cards they had folded in upon each other, raw splinters of timber thrusting up out of the gloom, baulks crossed like the blades of a scissors, with small dark bodies trapped in the jaws, others crushed by the fallen beams, squashed so that they were no longer recognizable as human, others dangling head down on their ankle-chains, suspended in space, writhing weakly as crippled insects, or hanging quietly, swinging to the dhow's movements.

'Oh, sweet Mother of God, where to begin,' Robyn whispered. She let go her handhold, starting forward and her feet shot out from under her on the slick coated deck, and she went plunging down into the hold.

She struck heavily and pain flared in her back and lower body, but she dragged herself on to her knees. Her own pain seemed insignificant in this terrible prison.

'Are you all right?' Zouga asked anxiously, but she shrugged his hands away.

There was one girl screaming. Robyn crawled to her. Her legs were crushed below the knees, trapped under a baulk of hand-hewn timber.

'Can you move that?' she asked Zouga.

'No, she's done for. Come, there are others—'

'No.' Robyn crawled back to where her bag had fallen. The pain was bad, but she forced it below the surface of her consciousness.

She had only seen a leg amputation performed once before. When she started the girl threw off the seamen who held her and attacked Robyn like a tortured wild cat. Her nails raked skin from Robyn's cheek, but by the time Robyn had freed the first leg below the knee, the child was silent and limp. She died before Robyn had reached the bone of the second leg, and Robyn was weeping chokingly to herself as she left the body still hanging in the grip of the timber baulk.

She scrubbed her hands together, they were bloodied to the elbows, her palms sticky against each other. She felt consumed by guilt at her failure, without the strength to move. Dully, she stared about her now.

The hold was more than half flooded, the tide pounded remorselessly at the ship's hull.

'We have to get out,' Zouga called to her urgently, and when she did not turn her head, he seized her shoulder and shook her roughly. 'There's nothing more we can do. It will capsize at any moment.'

Robyn was staring down into the stinking black waters which sloshed from one end of the hold to the other, a single hand broke through the surface directly below her, a child's hand with soft pink palm and pretty tapered fingers spread in a gesture of appeal. The iron cuff seemed too large for the narrow wrist, and weighted it down to the hand sank gently disappearing from her sight. She stared after it with infinite regret, then Zouga hauled her roughly to her feet.

'Come on, damn it!' His face was savage, haunted with the horrors he had experienced in this fetid, half flooded hull.

The next wave hit the swamped hull, and this time it broke the grip of the coral. Timber squealed as it twisted and tore, and the dhow began to roll, the filthy waters rose up out of the darkness into a steep black wave and burst about them, shoulder deep.

The damaged slave decks broke free, sliding down over each other, tumultuous and lethal, releasing a fresh layer of tightly packed black bodies to tumble loosely into the flooded depths.

'Robyn! We'll be trapped.' He dragged her up towards the square of brilliant sunlight, clambering over timbers and bodies.

'We can't leave them,' Robyn resisted.

'They're finished, damn it. The whole thing is going. We have to get out.'

She pulled her arm free, stumbled, collapsed backwards, hit something so that pain flared through her lower body again and she cried out with the strength of it. She was lying on her side, couched on a pile of linked bodies, and there was a face a foot from hers. It was alive, she had never seen such eyes, cat fierce, falcon bright, the colour of boiling honey.

'This one is strong enough!' Robyn thought, and then she shouted. 'Help me Zouga.'

'For God's sake, Robyn.'

She crawled forward and reached the black child, and the deck tilted viciously under her, fresh cold water bursting into the hull.

'Leave her,' shouted Zouga.

The fresh flood swirled up around Robyn's head, and the chained girl disappeared below it.

Robyn lunged for her, groping blindly below the surface, feeling panic rise in her when she could not find the child.

Ducking her head under, choking as the pain in her belly made her gasp and she swallowed water, she at last got a grip on the girl's shoulder, feeling her struggling as desperately as she.

Together they came out above the surface, coughing and gasping weakly, Robyn holding the girl's mouth just clear of the surface, but when she tried to lift her further the chain anchored them both and she screamed.

'Zouga, help me!'

Another surge of water, smelling like raw sewage, filled her mouth and both of them went under once more.

She thought she would never come up again, but stubbornly she held on, sliding one arm under the girl's armpit, and with the other hand gripping her chin, forcing it up so that when they broke out again the girl's face was lifted to take another precious breath of the stinking air, and Zouga was with them.

He took a double turn of the chain around his wrists and threw all his weight on to it. In the gloom of the hull he towered over them, the light from the hatch highlighting the bulging wet muscles in his arms and shoulders as he strained at the chain, his mouth opened in a silent scream of effort, sinewy cords standing out of his throat.

Another wave hissed over them, and this time Robyn was not ready for it, she felt the burn of it in her lungs and knew she was drowning. She need only release her hold on the girl's head and shoulders and she would be free to breathe, but she held on stubbornly, determined suddenly that she would never let this little soul go. She had seen it in the girl's eyes, the fierce will to live. This one she could save, this one out of three hundred or more was the only one she could be certain of saving. She had to have her.

The wave receded and Zouga was still there, his hair streaming with water, slicked down over his face and into his eyes, and now he shifted slightly, jamming his legs against one of the heavy timbers and he reared back once more against the chain, and a low bellow broke from his throat in the agony of effort.

The ring bolt that held the loop of chain to the deck ripped out cleanly, and Zouga dragged both women clear of the water, the chain slithering after them for ten feet or more before coming up hard against the next ring bolt.

Robyn had never suspected Zouga capable of such strength, she had never seen his naked upper body – not since he was a child – had not realized that he had the lean hard muscle of a prizefighter. But even so, he could not repeat the effort, and the girl was still chained. They had won only a temporary respite. Zouga was bellowing now, and the young naval Ensign scrambled down through the open hatch. To re-enter the doomed hull was an act of courage in itself, Robyn realized, as she saw that the Ensign carried the cutting shears, lugging the heavy tool with him as he floundered towards the struggling group in the bottom of the hold.

The hull rolled through another five degrees, the water swirling higher towards them hungrily, it sucked at their bodies. Had not Zouga given them the extra few feet of chain they would be far below the surface now.

Zouga stooped over her and helped her hold the black girl's head above the water, while the Ensign groped for the chain links and fed them into the jaws of the shears. But the blades had been blunted and chipped by the heavy work they had already done, and the Ensign was still only a lad. Zouga pushed him aside.

Again muscle bunched in his shoulders and upper arms and the chain parted with a metallic clunk. Zouga cut twice at ankle and at wrist, then he dropped the shears, picked the frail naked body up against his chest and climbed frantically up towards the hatch.

Robyn tried to follow him, but something tore deep in her belly, she felt it go, tearing like brittle parchment, and the pain was a lance that transfixed her. She doubled over it, clutching herself, unable to move, and the wave hit her, knocking her down, swirling her over the broken timbers into the dark waters, and the darkness began to fill her head. There was temptation to let go now, to let the water and darkness take her, it would be so easy, but she gathered her anger and her obstinacy to her and went on fighting. She was still fighting when Zouga reached her, and dragged her up towards the light.

As they crawled out through the hatch into the sunlight, so the dhow rolled all the way, flinging them as though from a catapult over the side into the shocking cold of the green waters.

As the dhow capsized so the last faint cries from within her were extinguished, and the hull began to break up under the remorseless hammer of the sea. When Robyn and Zouga surfaced, still clinging together, the whaler was hovering over them, the Ensign risking all to come in over the reef for the pick-up.

Strong hands reached down, and the overladen boat heeled dangerously as they were pulled aboard. Then the Ensign swung the bows to meet the next boiling line of surf and they climbed its steep side and crashed over the top, the seamen pulling frantically to hold her bows on.

Robyn crawled to where the black girl lay on a heap of other bodies in the bottom of the boat, her relief at finding her aboard and still alive outweighing the pain of her sodden lungs and the deep ache in her belly.

Robyn rolled the girl on to her back, and lifted her lolling head to cushion it from the pounding of the whaler's hull over the steep swells that threatened to crack her skull against the floorboards.

She saw immediately that the girl was older than she had imagined, although the body was desiccated, dried out and wasted. Yet her pelvis had the breadth of maturity. She would be sixteen years old at least, Robyn thought, and pulled a corner of the tarpaulin over her body to screen her from the men's gaze.

The girl opened her eyes again, and stared at Robyn solemnly. Those eyes were still the colour of dark honey, but the ferocity had dimmed to some other emotion as she looked up into Robyn's face.

'*Ngi ya bonga*,' the girl whispered, and with a shock Robyn realized that she understood the words. She was transported in an instant to another land and another woman, her mother, Helen Ballantyne, teaching her those same words, repeating them to her until Robyn had them perfected.

'*Ngi ya bonga*, I praise you!'

Robyn tried to find a reply, but her mind was as battered as her body, and it had been so long ago that she had learned the language, the circumstances so different that the words came only haltingly.

'*Velapi wena*, who are you and from where do you come?'

The black girl's eyes flew wide with shock.

'You!' she whispered. 'You speak the language of the people.'

They had taken on board twenty-eight living black girls. By the time *Black Joke* got under way again and turned from the land, towards the open sea, the dhow's hull had burst open and the planking and timbers swung and pitched end over end as they sawed across the exposed reef.

A squawking raucous flock of seabirds squabbled over the reef, hovering above the gruesome remnants that were mixed in the floating debris of the wreck, dropping to seize a tidbit and rise again on delicate fans of pearly wings.

In the deeper water along the seaward side of the reef, the shark packs were gathering, lashing themselves into a frenzy, the stubby rounded triangles of their dorsal fins crisscrossing the green sweep of the current, while every few seconds a long torpedo-shaped body would break clear of the surface in an ecstasy of greed, falling back heavily with a boom like distant cannon as it struck the surface.

Twenty-eight from three hundred and more was no great haul, Robyn thought, as she hobbled along the line of barely living bodies, her own bruised limbs protesting every step, and her despair deepened as she realized how far gone they were. It was easy to see which of them had already lost the will to resist. She had read her father's treatise on the sick African, and she knew how important this will to resist was in treating a primitive people. A perfectly healthy man could will himself to die, and once he did so there was nothing that could save him.

That night, despite Robyn's constant attention, twenty-two of the girls died and were carried aft to be dropped over *Black Joke*'s stern. By morning all the others were sinking into the coma and fever of renal failure, their kidneys, shrivelled and atrophied by lack of fluid, were no longer filtering the urinal wastes from the bodies' systems. There was only one treatment and that was to force the patient to drink.

The little Nguni girl resisted strongly. Robyn knew that she belonged to the Nguni group of peoples, although she was uncertain of which tribe, for many of them spoke variations of the original Zulu, and the girl's accent and pronunciation had been strange to Robyn's ear.

Robyn had tried to keep her talking, keep her conscious and keep the will to resist burning in her. She had conceived an almost maternal possessiveness for the child, and though she tried to spread her attention fairly amongst the other survivors, she always returned to where the girl lay under a strip of tarpaulin and held the pannikin of weak sugar solution to her lips.

They shared only a few hundred words in which to converse, as the girl rested between each painful sip of fluid.

'I am called Juba,' the child whispered, in answer to Robyn's question. Even the sound of it brought back to Robyn the memory of the cooing of the plump blue-grey ring-necked doves in the wild fig trees that grew above the mission cottage in which she had been born.

'Little Dove. It is a pretty name.' And the girl smiled shyly, and went on in that dry tortured whisper. Much of it Robyn could not follow, but she listened and nodded, realizing with a pang that the sense of it was going, Juba was sinking into delirium, that she was talking to phantoms from her past. Now she tried to resist when Robyn forced her to drink, muttering and crying out in fear or anger, gagging on the tiny mouthfuls of liquid.

'You must rest yourself,' Zouga told Robyn brusquely. 'You have been with her for almost two days without sleeping. You're killing yourself.'

'I am quite well, thank you,' Robyn told him, but her face was gaunt and white with fatigue and pain.

'At least let me take you down to your cabin.'

By this time Juba was the only black girl still alive, all the others had gone over the stern to feed the following shark pack.

'Very well,' Robyn agreed, and Zouga carried the child down from the makeshift shelter on the aft deck which Robyn had used as a surgery.

The steward brought a canvas pallet filled with straw and laid it on the deck of Robyn's tiny cabin. There was only just room for it, and Zouga laid the naked body upon it.

Robyn was tempted to stretch out on her own narrow bunk to rest for a while, but she knew that if she let go now, even for a moment, she would fall into a death-like sleep, and her patient would die of such neglect.

Alone in the cabin, she sat cross-legged on the straw pallet, wedged her back against the sea-chest, and lifted Juba into her lap. Doggedly she went on with the task of forcing liquid between the girl's lips, drop by drop, hour after hour.

Through the single port, the light turned to a ruby glow at the short tropical sunset and then it swiftly faded. It was almost completely dark in the cabin when suddenly Robyn felt a copious warm flood soak through her skirts into her lap. and she smelt the strong ammoniacal taint of the girl's urine.

'Thank you, God,' she whispered. 'Oh, thank you, God!' The girl's kidneys were functioning again, she was safe. Robyn rocked the girl in her lap, feeling no revulsion from her soaked skirts, welcoming them as the promise of life.

'You did it,' she whispered. 'You did, with sheer pluck, my little dove.'

She had just enough strength left herself to wipe down the child's body with a cloth soaked in sea water, then she stepped out of her soiled dress and collapsed face down on her hard narrow bunk.

Robyn slept for ten hours, and then the cramps woke her groaning. Her knees were drawn up against her chest by the severity of the pain, and her belly muscles were hard as stone and it felt as though she had been clubbed across the back, a deep bruised sensation that alarmed her seriously.

For many minutes after waking she believed herself seriously stricken, and then with a rush of relief and joy that was far stronger than the pain she realized what was happening to her. She dragged herself across the cabin, doubled over with the pain, and bathed in the bucket of cold sea water. Then she knelt beside Juba on the pallet.

The girl's fever had abated. The skin felt cooler to the touch. Her continued recovery added to Robyn's sense of deep pleasure and relief. Now she would have to find the right moment to tell Clinton Codrington that she would not marry him, and the vision of the little house above the Portsmouth harbour receded. Despite the pain, she felt free, light of body, like a bird poised on the point of flight.

She filled the pannikin with water and lifted Juba's head.

'We will be all right now,' she told the girl, and Juba opened her eyes.

'We'll both be all right now,' she repeated, watching the girl drink thirstily, smiling happily to herself.

Juba's recovery was swift. Soon she ate with a robust appetite. Her body filled almost before Robyn's eyes, her skin took on the lustre of health and youth again, her eyes regained the sparkle of high spirits – and Robyn realized with proprietorial approval that she was a pretty girl, no, more than that, she had natural grace and poise, the voluptuous curve of bosom and buttock which ladies of high fashion tried to achieve with bustle and padded bodice. She possessed also a sweet moon-face, the big wide-set eyes and full sculptured lips that were exotic and strangely beautiful.

Juba could not understand Robyn's concern with having her cover her breasts and legs, but Robyn had seen the seamen's eyes when the girl followed her up on to the deck with only a scrap of canvas covering the most vital point of her anatomy and showing no concern at all when the wind lifted the canvas and fluttered it like a beckoning flag. Robyn commandeered one of Zouga's oldest shirts. It hung to Juba's knees and she belted it at the waist with a bright ribbon that had the child cooing with the eternal feminine delight in pretty things.

She followed Robyn about like a puppy, and Robyn's ear tuned to the Nguni language. Her vocabulary expanded swiftly, and the two of them chatted late every night, sitting side by side on the straw pallet.

Clinton Codrington began showing acute signs of jealousy. He had become used to having more of her company, and Robyn was using the girl as an excuse to taper off their relationship, preparing him for the news that she must deliver before they reached Quelimane.

Zouga also disapproved of her growing intimacy with the girl.

'Sissy, you must remember that she is a native. It never pays to let them get too familiar,' Zouga told her gravely. 'I've seen that happen too often in India. One has to keep one's reserve. After all, you are an English woman.'

'And she is a Matabele of Zanzi blood, which makes her an aristocrat, for her family came up with Mzilikazi from the south. Her father was a famous general and she can trace her bloodline back to Senzangakhona, the King of the Zulu, and the father of Chaka himself. We, on the other hand, can trace our family as far as great grandfather, who was a cattle herd.'

Zouga's expression stiffened. He did not enjoy discussing the family origins.

'We are English. The greatest and most civilized people in the world's history.'

'Grandfather Moffat knows Mzilikazi,' Robyn pointed out, 'and thinks him a great gentleman.'

'You are being foolish,' Zouga snapped. 'How can you compare the English race to these blood-thirsty savages.' But he stooped out of the cabin for he did not wish to continue the discussion.

As usual, Robyn had her facts correct and her logic was infuriating.

His own grandfather, Robert Moffat, had first met Mzilikazi back in '29 and over the years the two men had become firm and trusted friends. The King relied on Moffat, whom he called Tshedi, for counsel in his dealings with the world beyond his borders and for medical treatment for the gout which plagued him as he grew older.

The route northwards to the land of the Matabele always passed through Robert Moffat's mission station at Kuruman. A prudent traveller would ask for a safe conduct from the old missionary, and the Matabele impis guarding the Burnt Land along the border would honour that safe conduct.

Indeed, the ease with which Fuller Ballantyne had moved through the wild, untamed tribes along the Zambezi river as far west as Lake Ngami, unmolested and unharmed, was in great part due to his relationship with Robert 'Tshedi' Moffat. The mantle of protection which the Matabele King spread over his old friend extended to his immediate family, and was recognized by all the tribes within range of the Matabele long arm, an arm that wielded the assegai, the terrible stabbing spear which King Chaka of the Zulu had first conceived, and with which he had conquered his known world.

In his pique at Robyn's comparison of the ancestry of his family and that of the pretty half-naked black girl, Zouga at first missed the significance of what she had told him. When it struck him, he hurried back to Robyn's cabin.

'Sissy,' he burst out excitedly. 'If she comes from Mzilikazi country – why! that's almost a thousand miles due west of Quelimane. She must have passed through the land of Monomatapa to reach this coast. Get her to tell us about it.'

He regretted his childhood inattention to the language when his mother had taught them. He concentrated savagely now as the two girls chatted animatedly, and began recognizing some of the words, but it needed Robyn to translate the full sense for him.

Juba's father was a famous Induna, a great warrior who had fought the Boers at Mosega, and a hundred other battles since then, his shield had been thick with the tassels of cow tails, black and white, each of which signified a heroic deed.

He had been granted the headring of the Induna when he was

still a young man of less than thirty summers, and had become one of the highest elders in the council of the nation. He had fifty wives, many of them of pure Zanzi blood like his own, a hundred and twelve sons and uncounted daughters. Although all the cattle of the nation belonged to the King, yet over five thousand were put in the charge of Juba's father, a mark of the King's high favour.

He was a great man – perhaps too great for bis own safety. Somebody whispered the word 'treason' in the King's ear, and the King's executioners had surrounded the kraal in the dawn, and called out Juba's father.

He had stooped out through the low entrance of his thatched beehive hut, naked from the embrace of his favourite wife.

'Who calls?' he cried into the dawn, and then he saw the ring of black figures, tall in their feather headdresses, but standing motionless, silent and menacing.

'In the King's name,' a voice answered him, and out of the ranks stepped a figure he recognized immediately. It was one of the King's Indunas also, a man named Bopa a short powerful man, with a deep-muscled bare chest and a head so heavy that the broad features seemed to have been carved out of a chunk of granite from the kopjes across the Nyati River.

There was no appeal, no escape, not that either consideration even passed briefly through the old Induna's mind.

'In the King's name.' That was sufficient. Slowly he drew himself to his full height. Despite the grey cap of his hair, he was still a finely built warrior with broad rangy shoulders and the ridged battle scars crawled across his chest and flanks like live serpents.

'The Black Elephant,' he began to recite the praise names of his King. 'Bayete! The Thunder of the Heavens. The Shaker of the Earth. Bayete!'

Still calling the King's names he went down on one knee, and the King's executioner stepped up behind him.

The wives and elder children had crawled from their huts now and huddled together in dread, watching from the shadows, their voices blending in a single cry of horror and sorrow as the executioner drove his short thick-bladed assegai between the Induna's shoulder blades, and two hands breadth out of his chest. As he withdrew the blade, there was the crude sucking sound of steel leaving flesh and the old Induna's life blood spurted head high as he fell forward on to his face.

With his smeared red blade the King's executioner commanded his warriors forward, for the sentence of death included the old man's wives, every one of their sons and daughters, the household slaves and their children, every inhabitant of the large village, three hundred or more souls.

The executioners worked swiftly, but there was a change in the ancient ritual of death. The old women, the grey-headed slaves died swiftly, not honoured with the blade but clubbed to death with the heavy knob-kerries that each warrior carried. The infants, and unweaned toddlers were snatched up by the ankles, and their brains were dashed from their skulls against the trunk of a tree, against the heavy poles of the cattle enclosure or against a convenient rock. It was very swift, for the warriors were highly trained and disciplined troops and this was something they had done many times before.

Yet this time there was a difference, the younger women, the adolescent children, even those on the verge of puberty, were hustled forward and the King's executioner glanced at them appraisingly, and with a gesture of the bloody spear sent them left or right.

On the left hand was swift death, while those who were sent right were forced into a trot and led away towards the east, towards the sunrise as the girl Juba explained it to Robyn.

'Many days we travelled,' her voice sinking, the horror of it still in the dark brown eyes. 'I do not know how long it was. Those who fell were left where they lay, and we went on.'

'Ask her what she remembers of the country,' Zouga demanded.

'There were rivers,' the girl replied. 'Many rivers and great mountains.' Her memories were confused, she could make no estimates of distance, they had encountered no other people, no villages nor towns, they had seen no cattle nor standing crops. Juba shook her head to each of Zouga's questions, and when he showed her the Harkness map in a forlorn hope that she might be able to point out features upon it, the child giggled in confusion. Drawn symbols on parchment were beyond her comprehension, she could not begin to relate them to features of landscape.

'Tell her to go on,' he ordered Robyn impatiently.

'At the end we passed through deep gorges in high mountains

where the slopes were covered with tall trees, and the rivers fell with white spray, until at last we came to where the *bunu* – the white men – waited.'

'The white men?' Robyn demanded.

'Men of your people,' the girl nodded. 'With a pale skin and pale eyes. There were many men, some white and others brown or black men, but dressed as the white men were dressed, and armed with the *isibamu*, with guns.' The Matabele people knew well the power and effect of firearms, they had encountered enemies armed with them at least thirty years before. Even some of the Matabele Indunas carried muskets, although they always handed these to a servant to carry when there was serious fighting in the offing.

'These people had built kraals, such as we build for our cattle, but these were filled with people, a great multitude of people and with them we were bound with the *insimbi*, the links of iron.' She rubbed her wrists instinctively at the memory, and the callouses raised by the slave cuffs still blemished the skin of her forearms.

'Each day that we stayed at this place in the mountains, more people came. Sometimes only as many as the fingers on both your hands, on other days there were great numbers so we could hear their lamentations at a distance. And always there were warriors guarding them.

'Then before the sun one morning, at the time of the horns,' Robyn recalled the expression for the time of dawning when the horns of the cattle first show against the morning sky, 'they led us from the kraals, wearing the *insimbi*, and we formed a great snake of people so long that the head was out of sight ahead of me in the forest while the tail was still up in the clouds of the mountains when we came down the Hyena Road.'

'The Hyena Road, *Ndlele umfisi*.' It was the first time that Robyn had heard the name spoken. It conjured up an image of a dark trail through the forests, beaten by tens of thousands of bare feet, with the loathsome eaters of dead flesh slinking along beside it, chuckling and shrieking their inane chorus.

'Those that died, and those that fell and could not rise again were released from their chains and dragged to one side. The *fisi* have grown so bold along the road, that they rushed out of the bushes and devoured the bodies while we passed in full sight. It was worst when the body still lived.'

Juba broke off and stared unseeingly at the bulkhead across the cabin. Slowly her eyes filled with tears, and Robyn took her hand and held it in her lap.

'I know not how long we followed the Hyena Road,' Juba went on, 'for each day became as the one before it, and as the one that followed it, until at last we came to the sea.'

Afterwards Zouga and Robyn discussed the girl's story.

'She must have gone through the kingdom of Monomatapa, and yet she says there were no towns nor signs of occupation.'

'The slavers might have avoided contact with Monomatapa's people.'

'I wish she had seen and remembered more.'

'She was in a slave caravan,' Robyn pointed out. 'Survival was her only concern.'

'If only these damned people could even read a map.'

'It's a different culture, Zouga,' and he saw the spark in her eye, and sensed the drift of the conversation and turned it aside swiftly.

'Perhaps the legend of Monomatapa is only a myth, perhaps there are no gold mines.'

'The important thing about Juba's story is that the Matabele are dealing in slaves, they have never done so before.'

'Nonsense!' grunted Zouga. 'They are the greatest predators since Genghis Khan! They and all the Zulu splinter tribes – the Shangaan, the Angoni and the Matabele. War is their way of life, and plunder is their main crop. Their whole nation was built on a system of slave-taking.'

'But they have never sold them before,' said Robyn mildly. 'At least as far as we know from all that grandfather and Harris and the others have written.'

'The Matabele never found a market before,' Zouga replied reasonably. 'Now they have at last made contact with the slave-masters, and found an opening to the coast. That was all it lacked before.'

'We must witness this, Zouga,' Robyn spoke with quiet determination. 'We have to bear witness to this terrible crime against humanity and carry word back to London.'

'If only the child had seen evidence of the Monomatapa, or the gold mines,' muttered Zouga. 'You must ask her if there were elephant.' He pored over the Harkness map, lamenting the blank spaces. 'I cannot believe that it does not exist. There is too much evidence.' Zouga looked up at his sister. 'One other thing – I seem to have forgotten almost every word of the language that mother taught us, except some of the nursery rhymes and lullabies.

*'Munya, mabili zinthatu, Yolala umdade wethu,'** he recited, and then chuckled and shook his head. 'I shall have to study it again, you and Juba will have to help me.'

The Zambezi comes to the sea through a delta of vast swampland, and a hundred confused shallow channels spread out for thirty miles down the low featureless coastline.

Floating islands of papyrus grass break free from the main pastures which blanket the waters of the delta and are carried out to sea on the dirty brown water. Some of these islands are many acres in extent and the roots of the plants so entangled that they can support the weight of a heavy animal. On occasions small herds of buffalo are trapped and carried twenty miles out to sea before the action of the waves smashes up the islands and plunges the great bovine animals into the water, prey for the big sharks which cruise the tainted estuary waters for just such a prize.

The muddy smell of the swamps carries far from the land when the wind is right, and the same wind carries strange insects with it. There is a tiny spider no bigger than the head of a wax Vesta which lives in the papyrus banks of the delta. It spins a gossamer web on which it launches itself into the breeze in such numbers that the gossamer fills the sky in clouds, like the smoke from a raging bushfire, rising many hundreds of feet and eddying and swirling in misty columns that are touched by the sunset into shades of pink and lovely pale mauve.

The river pours a muddy brown effluent into the sea, silt enriched with the bodies of drowned animals and birds, and the huge Zambezi crocodiles join the shark packs at the feast.

Black Joke found the first of these hideous creatures ten miles from land, wallowing in the low swells like a log, the rough scales glittering wetly in the sunlight until the gunboat

* 'One, two, three,
Go to sleep my little sister,'

approached too closely and the reptile dived with a lash and swirl of its powerful ridged tail.

Black Joke steamed obliquely across the multiple mouths of the river, none of which offered passage for a vessel of her size. She was headed further north for the Congone channel which was the only passage upriver to the town of Quelimane.

Clinton Codrington planned to enter it the following morning, after having lain hove-to during the night off the mouth. Robyn knew that she must remove the stitches from the wound under his armpit, though she would have liked to leave them a few days longer. They must come out before she left the gunboat at Quelimane.

She decided to use the same opportunity to give him the answer for which he had waited so patiently. She knew it was going to be painful for him to hear that she would not marry him, and she felt guilty that she had so encouraged him. It was alien to her nature to inflict suffering on another, and she would try to tell him as gently as possible.

She ordered him to her cabin for the removal of the horsehair stitches, seating him on the narrow bunk naked to the waist, with his arm raised. She was delighted with the way the wound had healed, and proud of the neatness of her work. She cooed over each knot as she snipped it with the pointed scissors, then seized it with the forceps and gently tugged and worried it free of his flesh. The stitches left twin punctures, one on each side of the raised purple welt of the scar and they were clean and dry. Only one of them leaked a single drop of blood which she swabbed away gently.

Robyn was training Juba as her assistant, teaching her to hold the tray of instruments, and receive the discarded and soiled dressings or instruments. Now she stood back and appraised the healed wound, without looking at Juba.

'You may go now,' she said quietly. 'I will call you when I need you.'

Juba smiled like a conspirator, and murmured, 'He is truly beautiful, so white and smooth,' and Robyn blushed pinkly, for that was exactly what she had been thinking. Clinton's body, unlike that of Mungo St John, was hairless as a girl's but finely muscled, and the skin had an almost marble sheen to it.

'His eyes are like two moons when he looks at you, Nomusa,'

Juba went on with relish, and Robyn tried to frown at her but her lips kept puckering into a smile.

'Go swiftly,' she snapped, and Juba giggled.

'There is a time to be alone,' and she rolled her eyes lewdly. 'I shall guard the door, and hardly listen at all, Nomusa.' Robyn found it impossible to be angry when the child used that name, for it meant 'the daughter of mercy', and Robyn found it highly acceptable. She would have had difficulty picking a better name for herself, and she was smiling as she hurried Juba from the cabin with a gentle slap and a push.

Clinton must have had some idea of the exchange, for he was buttoning his shirt as she turned back to him, and looking embarrassed.

She drew a deep breath, folded her arms and began.

'Captain Codrington, I have thought unceasingly of the great honour you have done me by inviting me to be your wife.'

'However,' Clinton forestalled her, and she faltered, the prepared speech forgotten, for her next word would indeed have been, 'However'.

'Miss Ballantyne, I mean Doctor Ballantyne, I would rather you did not say the rest of it.' His face was pale and intense, he really was beautiful now, she thought, with a pang. 'That way I can still cherish hope.'

She shook her head vehemently, but he lifted a hand.

'I have come to realize that you have a duty, to your father and the poor unhappy people of this land. I understand and deeply admire that.'

Robyn felt her heart go out to him, he was so good and so perceptive to have understood that about her.

'However, I feel sure that one day, you and I shall . . .'

She wanted to spare him pain.

'Captain,' she began, shaking her head again.

'No,' he said. 'Nothing you say will ever make me abandon hope. I am a very patient man, and I realize that now is not the time. But I know in the depths of my soul that our destiny binds us together, even if I must wait ten or fifty years.'

A time-span of that magnitude no longer frightened Robyn. She relaxed visibly.

'I love you, my dear Doctor Ballantyne, nothing will ever alter that, and in the meantime I ask only your good opinion, and friendship.'

'You have both,' she said, with truth and relief. It had been a great deal easier than she had expected, yet strange that a shadow of regret lingered.

There was no further opportunity to speak privately, for Clinton was fully occupied with bringing *Black Joke* into the treacherous channel, with its shifting banks and uncharted shoals guarding the mouth. The channel meandered twenty miles through the mangrove forests to the port of Quelimane on the northern bank.

The heat in the delta was rendered scarcely bearable by the humid effluxion of mud and rotting vegetation that rose from the mangrove forests. The weird shapes of the mangroves fascinated Robyn and she stood by the rail and watched them slide past. Each tree stood clear of the slick chocolate-coloured mud on its pyramid of roots, like the multiple legs of a grotesque insect reaching up to join the thick pulpy stem which in turn extended upwards to the roof of poisonous green foliage. Amongst the roots skittered the purple and yellow fiddler crabs, each of them holding aloft a single disproportionably huge claw, and waving it in menace or ponderous greeting at the passing vessel.

Black Joke's wake spread across the channel, flopping wavelets on the mud banks and startling the small green and purple night herons into laborious flight.

Around a bend in the channel the decaying buildings of Quelimane came into view, dominated by the square towers of the stucco church. The plaster was falling away in unsightly chunks and the whitewash was streaked and splotched with grey and green mould, like a ripening cheese.

This port had once been one of the most busy slave ports on the entire African coast. The Zambezi river had acted as a highway to the interior for the slave-masters, and the Shire river, its major tributary, led directly to Lake Marawi and the highlands which had been the mother lode from which hundreds and thousands of black slaves had poured.

When the Portuguese, under British pressure, had signed the Brussels Agreement, the barracoons at Quelimane and Lourenç Marques and Mozambique Island had been closed down. However, the slaving dhow that *Black Joke* had intercepted proved that the abominable trade still flourished covertly along the

Portuguese coast. That was typical of these people, Clinton Codrington thought.

Clinton curled his lip with distaste. In the many hundred years since their great navigators had opened up this coast, the Portuguese had clung to the narrow unhealthy strip of the littoral, making only one half-hearted effort to penetrate the interior and since then, lying here like their disintegrating buildings and crumbling empire, content with the bribes and extortions of petty officialdom and their seraglios of women, tolerant of any crimes or evil as long as there was a little dash or profit in it.

As he worked *Black Joke* in towards the quay, he could see them gathering already, gaudy vultures, in their fool's motley of uniform, tarnished gold braid and ornate swords sported by even the lowliest customs officer.

There would be endless forms and declarations unless he was firm, and always the open palm and the leering wink. Well, this time there would be none of that. This was a ship of the Queen's Navy.

'Mr Denham,' Clinton called sharply, 'issue pistols and cutlasses to the anchor watch, and nobody comes aboard without the express permission of the officer of the watch.'

He turned away to shake hands briefly with Zouga; they had found little in common during the voyage and the parting was cool.

'Never thank you enough, sir,' said Zouga briskly.

'Only my duty, Major.' But already Zouga's eyes were following Sergeant Cheroot as he assembled his men on the foredeck. They were in full marching order, eager to be ashore after the tedious voyage.

'I must see to my men, Captain,' Zouga excused himself and hurried forward.

Clinton turned to Robyn and looked steadily into her green eyes.

'I beg a small token of remembrance,' he said quietly.

In response to his request she reached up and took one of the cheap paste earrings from her lobe. As they shook hands, she slipped the little ornament into his palm, and he touched it briefly to his lips before slipping it into his pocket.

'I will wait,' he repeated, 'ten or even fifty years.'

*

Black Joke had come up-channel on the flood, unloaded the mountainous stores of the Ballantyne Africa Expedition on to the stone quay during slack water, and two hours later thrown off her mooring ropes and swung sharply across the ebb, pointing her high bows down the channel.

From his position on the quarterdeck, Clinton Codrington stared across the widening gap at the slim, tall figure in long skirts standing on the very edge of the quay. Beyond her, her brother did not look up from his lists as he checked the stores and equipment. Sergeant Cheroot stood armed guard with his little pug-featured Hottentots, and the idlers and watchers kept well clear.

The Portuguese officials had treated the red wax seals and ribbons which decorated Zouga's letters of authority from the Portuguese ambassador in London with great respect. However, even more important was the fact that Zouga was an officer of Queen Victoria's army, that he had arrived in a Royal Navy gunboat, and lastly that there was every reason to believe that the same gunboat would remain in the area for the foreseeable future.

The Governor of Portuguese East Africa himself would not have commanded greater respect. Already minor officials were scampering about the squalid little town arranging the best accommodation, securing warehousing for the stores, commandeering river transport for the next leg of the journey up-river to Tete, the last outpost of Portuguese empire on the Zambezi, drafting orders to have bearers and guides meet the expedition at Tete, and doing everything else that the young British officer casually demanded as though it was his God-given right.

In this turmoil of activity Robyn Ballantyne stood alone, staring after the blue-clad figure on *Black Joke*'s quarterdeck. How tall he was, and his hair caught the sunlight in a flash of white gold as he lifted his hand in farewell. She waved until *Black Joke* disappeared behind a palisade of mangrove, though her masts and fuming smokestack stayed in view for a long time after. She watched until they, too, dwindled to nothingness, and only the smear of black smoke lay low over the tops of the green mangrove.

*

Clinton Codrington stood on his deck, hands clasped loosely at the small of his back, and an expression of near rapture in the pale blue eyes. In this temper the knight-errant of old must have ridden out at chance, Clinton thought.

He did not find the notion at all melodramatic. He felt truly ennobled by his love, sensing somehow that be must earn something so precious, and that the opportunity to do so lay ahead of him. The earring that Robyn had given him was suspended by a thread around his neck, lying under his shirt against his skin. He touched it now, peering impatiently ahead down the channel. It seemed to him that for the first time he had a steady direction in his life, constant as the pole star to the navigator.

This gallant mood was still strong five days later when *Black Joke* rounded the headland of Ras Elat and steamed into the anchorage. There were eight large dhows keeled over on the exposed sand bar at low tide. The tidal fall on this coast at full springs was twenty-two feet. These craft were designed to take the ground readily, and it facilitated loading. The long ranks of chained slaves were being goaded out to the stranded vessels, slipping and splashing through the shallow tidal pools, to await patiently their turn to climb the ladder up the side of the dhow.

Black Joke's unannounced arrival caused pandemonium, and the beach was alive with running stumbling figures, the screams and shrieks of the slaves, the pop of the kurbash whips and the frantic cries of the slave-masters carried clearly to *Black Joke*'s deck as she dropped her anchor just beyond the reef and rounded up to the wind.

Clinton Codrington stared longingly at the heeled vessels and the concourse of panicky humanity, the way a slum-child stares at the display in the window of a food shop.

His orders were clear, had been spelled out by Admiral Kemp with painful attention to detail. The Admiral remembered with lingering horror his young Captain's capture of the slaving fleet at Calabash after forcing the masters to load their cargoes and sail north of the equator. He wanted no repetition of this type of risky action on this patrol.

Black Joke's commander was strictly adjured to respect the territorial integrity of the Sultan of the Omani Arabs, and the exact letter of the treaty that the British Consul had negotiated at Zanzibar.

Clinton Codrington was strictly forbidden to interfere with

any subject of the Sultan who was engaged in trade between any of the Sultan's dominions. He was denied even the right of search of any vessel flying the red-and-gold flag of Omani on any of the Sultan's recognized trade routes, and these were carefully defined for Captain Codrington's benefit.

He was to confine his patrol to intercepting only vessels that did not belong to the Sultan, particularly vessels of the European powers. Naturally no American vessel might be searched on the high seas. Within these limits Captain Codrington had powers of independent action.

Far from being allowed to seize or search the Sultan's vessels, Clinton was ordered to use the first opportunity to make a courtesy call on the port of Zanzibar. There he would take counsel from the British Consul as how best to use his influence to reinforce the existing treaties, and especially to remind the Sultan of his own obligations under those treaties.

So now Clinton paced his deck like a caged lion at feeding time, and glowered helplessly, through the pass in the coral reef, at the slaving fleet of Omani engaged in legitimate trade, for the Gulf of Elat was very much part of the Sultan's possessions, and had so been recognized by Her Majesty's Government.

After the first wild panic ashore, the beach and dhows were now deserted, but Clinton was aware of the thousands of watchful eyes upon him from the mud-walled town and the shadows of the coconut groves.

The thought of hauling his anchor and sailing away filled him with bitter chagrin, and he stood bare-headed and stared with cold hungry blue eyes at the prize spread before him.

The palace of the Sheikh of Elat, Mohamed Bin Salim, was an unpainted mud-walled building in the centre of the town. The only opening in the parapeted wall was the gate closed by thick, brass-studded double doors in carved teak, which led through to the dusty central courtyard.

In this courtyard, under the spreading branches of an ancient takamaka tree the Sheikh was in earnest conclave with his senior advisors and the emissaries of bis supreme sovereign – the Sultan of Zanzibar. They were discussing a matter, literally, of life or death.

Sheikh Mohamed Bin Salim had the plump smooth body of the bon vivant, the bright red lips of the sensualist, and the hooded eyes of a falcon.

He was a very worried man, for his ambition had led him into dire danger. His ambition had been quite simply to accumulate the sum of one million gold rupees in his treasury, and he had very nearly satisfied that reasonable goal, when his overlord, the omnipotent Sultan of Zanzibar, had sent his emissaries to call the Sheikh to account.

Sheikh Mohamed had begun to satisfy his ambition ten years previously by very gently mulching the Sultan's tithe, and each year since then he had increased his depredations. Like all greedy men, one successful coup was the signal for the next. The Sultan had known this, for though he was old, he was also exceedingly cunning. He knew that the missing tithes were safely stored for him in the Sheikh's treasure house, to be collected whenever he felt inclined. He need only benignly feign ignorance of the Sheikh's manipulations, until he was so deeply in the trap that no squirming or squealing would get him out again. After ten years that moment had arrived. The Sultan would collect not only his due but the Sheikh's own accumulations.

Further retribution would be a lengthy business. It would begin with a beating on the soles of the Sheikh's bare feet, until all those delicate little bones were cracked or fractured making it extremely painful for the Sheikh to be marched into the Sultan's presence. There, the final judgement would be read, and it would end with the knotted strip of buffalo hide wound up tighter and tighter around the forehead, until first the Sheikh's falcon eyes popped from their sockets and then his skull collapsed like a bursting melon. The Sultan truly enjoyed these spectacles – and had been looking forward to this particular one for ten years.

Both men knew the ritual, and it had begun with the polite visit of the Sultan's emissaries who even now were sitting opposite the Sheikh under the takamaka, sipping thick black coffee from the brass thimbles, munching the yellow and pink coconut sweetmeats, and smiling at the Sheikh with cold passionless eyes.

It was into this chilling atmosphere that the messengers from the harbour came running to fling themselves prostrate and gabble out the news of the British warship, whose great guns threatened the harbour and the town.

The Sheikh listened quietly and then dismissed the messengers, before turning back to his distinguished guests.

'This is a serious business,' he began, relieved to be able to change the subject under discussion. 'It would be wise to view this strange vessel.'

'The Ferengi have a treaty with our master,' pronounced one greybeard, 'and they set great store by these pieces of paper.'

They all nodded, none of them showing the agitation which filled all of their breasts. Although this coast had only received passing attention from these brash northern people, still it had been enough to engender fear and apprehension.

The Sheikh deliberated for a few minutes, stroking his thick curly beard, hooding his eyes as the ideas began to flow. His mind had been almost paralysed with the extent of the disaster which had overtaken him, but now it began to work again.

'I must go out to this warship,' he announced. There was an immediate hubbub of protest, but he held up his hand to silence them. He was still the Sheikh of Elat, and they had, perforce, to hear him out.

'It is my duty to ascertain the intentions of the commander and to send word immediately to our master.'

Clinton Codrington had almost resigned himself to give the order to weigh anchor. There had been no sign of life on the beach for many hours, and there was nothing he could accomplish here. His hope that he might catch a European slaver, actually taking on slaves in the anchorage, had proved forlorn. He should have sailed hours ago, the sun was half way down the sky already and he did not want to run the dangers of the inshore channel in darkness, but some instinct had kept him here.

He kept returning to the starboard rail, and glassing the flat-roofed mud buildings that just showed amongst the palm trees. Each time his junior officers stiffened expectantly, then relaxed as he turned away without a word or change of expression.

This time Clinton saw movement, the flash of white robes in the deserted, single street of the town, and as he watched through the telescope he felt a prickle of excitement and a lift of self-congratulation. A small deputation was emerging from the grove and coming down the beach.

'Pass the word to my steward to lay out my number ones and sword,' he ordered without lowering his glass. The party on the beach was led by a portly figure in blindingly white robes and a full headdress that gleamed with gold. Behind him a bearer carried the long floating banner, scarlet and gold, of the Sultan.

'We'll treat him as a Governor,' Clinton decided. 'And give him four guns.' With that he turned on his heel and went to his cabin to change his uniform.

The Arab climbed out of the little felucca and came in through the entry port puffing for breath, assisted by two house-slaves. As his foot touched the deck, the first gun of the salute crashed out unexpectedly, and the Sheikh let out a whinny like a wild stallion and leapt two feet straight up in the air, the high colour flying from his cheeks leaving them ashen and trembling.

Clinton stepped forward, resplendent in cocked hat, blue and gold jacket, white breeches and sword and took the Sheikh's arm to steady him through the rest of the salute, and to prevent him stampeding back into the crazily rocking felucca where the oarsmen were in equal terror.

'Will you step this way, Your Excellency,' Clinton murmured, and without releasing his iron grip on the Sheikh's pudgy arm, marched him briskly down to his cabin.

Translation was a problem, but one of the Sheikh's entourage had a smattering of French and some English. It was almost dark before Clinton was able to see through the flowery verbiage and the atrocious rendering of his mother tongue. When it came it was like a great light filling the cabin, and Clinton found himself buoyed up with a savage, warlike glee.

The fat Sheikh, Governor of Elat, with his soft, red lips, was asking for the protection of her Britannic Majesty against the injustices and tyrannies of the Sultan of Zanzibar.

'*Dites lui je ne peux pas* – oh, damn it, tell him I can only protect him if he declares Elat free of the Sultan's dominions, *comprenez vous?*'

'*Je m'excuse, je ne comprends pas.*'

It was tedious, especially in view of Clinton's eagerness to remove the province of Elat from under the sway of Zanzibar.

The Foreign Office had provided all commanders of the Atlantic anti-slavery squadrons with blank treaty forms, drawn up with deference to protocol and in correct legal terminology. These were for signature of any indigenous chiefs, warlords, petty princes and native kings who could be induced to place their mark upon them.

These documents started with a declaration of mutual recognition between Her Majesty's government and the signatory, went on in vague terms to promise protection and free trade, and ended in very specific terms with a round condemnation of the slave trade and the granting of rights to Her Majesty's government to search, seize and destroy all ships engaged in such trade within the signatory's territorial waters. Further it granted rights to Her Majesty's Navy to land troops, destroy barracoons, free slaves, arrest slave-masters and do any such other act as should be deemed necessary to the extinction of the trade in all the signatory's lands and possessions.

Admiral Kemp in Cape Town had overlooked the fact that Captain Codrington had a good supply of these documents in his possession. They had been intended for use entirely on the west African coast north of the equator. The good Admiral would have been a very worried man indeed if he had realized that he had detached his most brilliant but mercurial junior on independent patrol armed with anything so explosive.

'He must sign here,' Clinton explained briskly, 'and I will give him an order on the British treasury for a hundred guineas.' The treaty made provision for annual tribute to be paid to the signatory. Clinton considered a hundred guineas sufficient. He was not sure of what authority he had to write treasury orders, but Sheikh Mohamed was delighted. He had negotiated for life alone, and received not only the protection of this fine warship but the promise of good gold as well. He was smiling happily, pursing his red lips as he signed his long signature under his new title 'Prince and Supreme Ruler of the sovereign possessions of Elat and Ras Telfa.'

'Good,' said Clinton briskly, rolling his copy of the treaty and slipping the retaining ribbon over it as he hurried to the door of his cabin.

'Mr Denham,' he bellowed up the companionway. 'I want a landing-party, muskets, pistols, cutlasses and carrying combustibles, forty men ready to go ashore at first light tomorrow!' He was grinning as he turned back and told the Sheikh's translator, 'It would be best if His Excellency remained on board tonight. We will see him safely installed at noon tomorrow.' And for the first time the Sheikh felt a thrill of apprehension. This Ferengi had the cold blue merciless eyes of a devil. 'El Sheetan,' he thought, 'the very devil.' And made the sign against the evil eye.

'Sir, may I speak?' Mr Denham, *Black Joke*'s First Lieutenant looked puzzled in the light of the binnacle. It was an hour short of sunrise and he glanced down at the ranks of armed seamen squatting on the foredeck.

'Speak your heart,' Clinton invited him magnanimously. Lieutenant Denham was not accustomed to this jovial mood from his captain, and he expressed himself cautiously. In essence Lieutenant Denham's views came very close to those of the Admiral in Cape Town.

'If you would like to make a protest against my orders, Lieutenant,' Clinton interrupted him cheerfully, 'I will be pleased to enter it in the ship's log.'

Thus absolved of responsibility for having been party to an act of war on the territory of a foreign ruler, Lieutenant Denham was so relieved that when Clinton told him, 'I am taking command of the landing party. You will command the ship in my absence,' he shook Clinton's hand impulsively.

'Good luck, sir,' he blurted.

They went ashore in two boats, the whaler leading through the pass in the reef and the gig following two lengths astern. The moment the keel touched, Clinton sprang knee-deep into the blood-warm water and the rush of armed men followed him ashore. He drew his cutlass and his shoes squelched as he led his team of five men to the nearest dhow at a dead run.

As he jumped down from the ladder on to the dhow's heavily canted deck, an Arab watchman ducked out of the stern cabin and aimed a long jezail at Clinton's head. The range was point blank and Clinton struck out instinctively in an underhand parry, just as the gun's lock clicked and smoke and spark shot from the pan under the steel and flint.

His blade clashed against the steel barrel, deflecting it upwards as the jezail roared an instant after the snap of the lock, and a blinding billow of smoke and burning powder struck his face and singed his eyebrows, but the chunk of beaten potleg howled inches over his head. When his vision cleared the watchman had thrown his empty weapon aside, leaped over the side of the dhow and was hopping and hobbling across the sand towards the grove of palms.

'Search her, and then put fire into her,' Clinton ordered brusquely.

It was the first chance he had had to look across at the other dhows of the fleet. One of them was already on fire, the flames bright in the early light, rising straight up with little smoke. The furled mainsail was blackening like a dried leaf, and he could hear the crackle of the tinder dry timbers of the hull and stern cabin. His seamen were spilling out of her and straggling across to the next vessel.

'She's aflame, sir,' his boatswain panted, and a hot gust of air struck Clinton's cheek at that moment and a quiver of heat hung over the main hatch.

'We'd best be getting on,' he said mildly, and scrambled down the ladder on to the packed damp sand. Behind him the flames roared like a cageful of wild animals.

The biggest dhow, a two-hundred tonner, lay ahead of them and Clinton reached it fifty paces ahead of his men.

'Make sure there is nobody below,' he ordered, and one of the seamen came back on deck carrying a rolled silk prayer rug under his arm.

'Belay that!' snapped Clinton. 'There'll be no looting.'

Reluctantly the seaman dropped the precious burden back into the hatchway, and the flames sucked up in a hot breath to accept it as though it was an offering to Baal.

By the time they reached the tree-line, all eight of the stranded vessels were burning fiercely, the stubby masts collapsing as they burned through at the base, the furled sails disappearing in bright explosions of flame. In one of the burning hulls a keg of powder went up with a thunderous crash of sound, and a tall column of dark smoke hovered over the beach for a few seconds, shaped like a gigantic grey octopus before it drifted slowly out across the reef, leaving the dhow shattered, its timbers scattered across the sand, the flames extinguished by the shock wave of the explosion.

'Was there anybody aboard her?' Clinton demanded quietly.

'No, sir.' His boatswain was panting beside him, red-faced with excitement, and with a bared cutlass in his hand. 'All accounted for.'

Clinton hid his relief behind a cool nod, and spent a few precious minutes drawing his men into an orderly formation, giving them time to regain their breath, and getting them well in hand again.

'Check your muskets,' he ordered, and there was the click of the locks. 'Fix bayonets.' Metal rattled on metal as the long blades were fitted to the barrels of the Enfield rifles. 'If there is resistance we'll find it in the town, I fancy,' and he ran an eye down the uneven ranks. They were neither marines nor lobster-backs, he thought with quick affection. They might not be perfect in drill, but they were men with spirit and initiative, not parade-ground automatons.

'Come along then.' He waved them forward into the dusty street between the mud-brown flat-roofed buildings. The town smelled of wood smoke and raw sewage, of rice cooked with saffron and of ghee, clarified butter.

'Shall we burn 'em?' His boatswain jerked a thumb at the buildings that flanked the deserted street.

'No, we are here to protect them,' Clinton told him stiffly. 'They belong to our new ally, the Sheikh.'

'I see, sir,' the boatswain grunted, looking mildly perplexed, and Clinton took pity on him.

'We are after the barracoons,' he explained. as they trotted up the street in compact formation. They halted where the road branched left and right.

The heat was oppressive and the silence menacing. There was no wind and the coconut groves had stilled the eternal clatter of their fronds. From the beach far behind them, came the faint popping of burning timbers, and overhead the ubiquitous pied crows of Africa circled and cawed raucously, but the buildings and dense coconut groves were deserted.

'I don't like this,' one of the men croaked behind Clinton. He could understand the man's point of view. A seaman always felt awkward when parted from his ship, and there were a mere forty of them, out of sight of the beach and surrounded by thousands of unseen but none the less savage warriors. Clinton knew he must keep the momentum of surprise rolling through the town, yet he hesitated a moment longer until he realized that the amorphous sacklike shape lying on the edge of the right hand street was a human body, naked and black and very dead. One of the slaves trampled in the previous day's panic and left where he had fallen.

That way must lie the barracoons, he decided. 'Quiet!' he cautioned his men, and cocking his head, listened with all his attention to the faint sussuration on the still air. It might have been the wind except there was no wind, or the flames, except that the flames were behind them. It was the distant sound of human voices, he decided, many voices, thousands of voices.

'This way. Follow me.' They went forward at a full run, taking the right fork and running immediately into the ambush which had been so carefully prepared for them.

The volley of musket fire crashed out from both sides of the narrowing track, and powder smoke rolled out towards them and hung like a thick, pearly curtain amongst the palm boles and the cashew nut trees.

Through the smoke danced the ethereal robed figures of the attackers, brandishing the long-barrelled jezails or swinging the half-moon-bladed scimitars, with wild shrieks of 'Allah Akbar, Allah is great!'

They rushed down on the little band of seamen, caught in enfilade on the narrow track. There were at least a hundred of them, Clinton judged instantly, and they were pressing in determinedly. Those scimitars were glittering – bright bare steel has a particularly chilling effect.

'Close up,' Clinton shouted. 'We'll give them a volley then take the bayonet to them, through the smoke.'

The first rank of racing Arabs were almost on top of the levelled Enfields. Incongruously, Clinton noticed that many of them had tucked up the skirts of their robes, leaving their legs bared to the thighs. Their skins varied from the colour of ivory to tobacco, and there were wrinkled grey beards in the front rank, screaming and howling with rage and battle-lust. They had just seen their livelihood burned to heaps of ash upon the beach. All that remained to them of their wealth was the contents of the barracoons set back amongst the groves of cashew nut and coconut trees.

'Fire!' roared Clinton, and the solid blast of sound deafened him for a moment. The gun-smoke wiped out all vision ahead of him and then hung on the windless morning in an impenetrable fog bank.

'Forward!' howled Clinton and led the charge into the smoke. He stumbled over the body of an Arab. The man's turban had unwound and come down over his eyes, soaked with blood like the sultan's scarlet banner which Clinton could see waving ahead of him above the smoke.

A figure loomed ahead of him. and he heard the fluting whistle of a scimitar blade, like wild goose wings overhead. He ducked.

The sharp breeze puffed a loose strand of hair into his eyes, as the blade passed an inch from his forehead, and Clinton straightened from the knees and put his whole body into the counter-lunge.

The point of his blade went in with a dead, soggy feel, sliding grudgingly through flesh until the point grated on bone. The Arab dropped his scimitar and clutched the cutlass blade with bare hands. Clinton leaned back and jerked the cutlass free of flesh. As the blade slid through the Arab's nerveless fingers the tendons parted with a faint popping sound, and the man went down on his knees, holding his mutilated hands up in front of his eyes with a look of amazement on his face.

Clinton ran on to catch up with his seamen, and found them scattered in little groups amongst the grove, laughing and shouting with excitement.

'They've run like steeplechasers, sir,' the boatswain called. 'Grand National, ten to one the field!' He snatched up the fallen banner of the Sultan and waved it furiously over his head, completely overtaken by excitement.

'Did we lose anybody?' Clinton demanded. He also felt the dizzy euphoria of battle. The killing of the Arab, far from sickening him, had elated him. In that moment he was quite capable of turning back and taking the man's scalp. However, the question sobered them.

'Jedrow caught one in the belly, but he can walk. Wilson got a sword cut in the arm.'

'Send them back to the beach. They can escort each other. The rest of you, come on!'

They found the barracoons a quarter of a mile further on. The guards had fled.

The slave-pens stretched out for a half mile along both banks of a small stream that provided both drinking water and sewage disposal for the inmates.

They were unlike the barracoons that Clinton had captured and sacked on the west coast, for those had been built by European traders with the white man's orderly eye. There was no resemblance in these sprawling compounds built of rough, unbarked forest poles, bound together with rope made from plaited palm fronds. Behind the outer barricades were open godowns with thatched roofs in which the chained slaves could find some shelter from sun and rain. The only thing the same was the smell. An epidemic of tropical dysentery had swept through the barracoons and most of the sheds contained the decomposing bodies of the victims. The crows and buzzards and vultures were waiting patiently in the palms and cashew trees, misshapen, dark silhouettes against the hard bright blue of the morning sky.

Clinton met the new ruler of the state of Elat, Sheikh Mohamed, at the water's edge and escorted him up the beach. The incoming tide was dousing the piles of smouldering ash that marked the last resting-places of eight fine dhows, and the Sheikh tottered uncertainly, like a man in deep shock, relying for support on the sturdy shoulder of one of his house-slaves, looking about him with lugubrious disbelief at the carnage that had overtaken him. The Sheikh owned one third shares in every one of those smoking piles of ash.

He had to rest when they reached the tree-line above the beach. A slave placed a carved wooden stool in the shade, and another waved a fan of plaited palm fronds over his head to keep off the flies and to cool his heated brow that was dewed with the heavy sweat of despair.

His misery was completed by the lecture in broken French and pidgin English which 'El Sheetan', the mad British sea captain with the devil's eyes, was relaying to him through the shocked and incredulous interpreter. Such things could only be repeated in a hoarse whisper, and the Sheikh greeted each new revelation with a soft cry of 'Waai!' and the upturning of his eyes to heaven.

He learned that the village blacksmiths had been dragged out of the bushes and were already knocking the fetters off long rows of perplexed slaves.

'Waai!' wailed the Sheikh. 'Does the devil not realize that those slaves have already been purchased and that the tax has been collected.'

Comfortably Clinton explained that once the slaves were freed, they would be marched back into the interior, and the Sheikh would send guards with them to see them safely home, and to warn any slave caravans that they encountered on the down-route that all the ports of Elat were now closed to the trade.

'Waai!' This time the Sheikh's eyes actually brimmed with tears. 'He will beggar me. My wives and children will starve.'

'El Sheetan counsels you to enlarge the trade in gum-copal and copra,' explained the interpreter in a sepulchral voice. 'And as your closest ally, he promises to call upon you regularly with his great ship of many guns, to make certain that you heed this advice.'

'Waai!' The Sheikh plucked at his beard, so that long curly hairs came out between his fingers. 'This ally makes one long for ordinary enemies.'

Twenty-four hours later *Black Joke* sailed into Telfa bay, forty miles further up the coast. Nobody had thought to warn the slaving fleet that was anchored there of the new policies of the state of Elat to which the territory now belonged.

The five dhows in the outer anchorage managed to cut their anchor cables and slip away into the maze of shallow coral channels and shoals to the north of the bay. where *Black Joke* could not follow.

However, there were another six smaller vessels on the beach and four magnificent double-decked ocean-going dhows lying in the inner anchorage. Clinton Codrington burned two of them and seized the four newest and biggest vessels, put prize crews into them and sent them south to the nearest British base at Port Natal.

Two days later, off the beach at Kilwa, Clinton Codrington exercised his ship at gunnery practice. Running out his thirty-two pounders, and firing them in broadsides which set the surface of the lagoon seething and dancing with foam and white fountains of spray. The thunder of gunfire burst against the far hills and rumbled back across the sky like cannon balls rolled across a wooden deck.

The Sultan's local Governor was reduced to a quivering jelly of terror by this display of might, and had to be carried bodily into *Black Joke*'s whaler to be rowed out to a conclave with the gunboat's Captain. Clinton had the treaty forms already filled out and ready for signature when they carried the Governor aboard to learn that he was heir to a kingdom to which he had never aspired, and a title which he knew was too grandiose not to bring with it certain retribution from somebody whose name he did not dare to breathe aloud.

Admiral Kemp, sitting in his study in the magnificent mansion of Admiralty House, overlooking the wide smoky-blue haze of the Cape flats to the far mountains of the Hottentots Holland, hopefully dismissed the first reports as the wild imaginings of some crazed subordinate who had served too long in the godforsaken outpost of Port Natal, and who was suffering from the bush madness of 'El Cafard' that sometimes affects a person so isolated.

Then the details began to arrive with every despatch from the north, and they were too graphic to be lightly dismissed. An armada of captured prizes was arriving in the bay of Port Natal, twenty-six sizable dhows to date, some of them loaded with slaves.

The Lieutenant-Governor of Port Natal was desperate for the Admiral's advice as to what should be done with the dhows. The slaves had been taken ashore, released and immediately been contracted as indentured labourers to the hardy and hopeful gentlemen who were attempting to raise cotton and sugarcane in the wilderness of the Umgeni valley. The shortage of labour was critical, the local Zulu tribesmen much preferred cattle raiding and beer drinking to agricultural labour, so the Governor would be delighted to receive as many freed slaves as the Royal Navy wished to send him. (The Admiral was not entirely certain of the difference between indentured labourers and slaves.) However, what was the Lieutenant-Governor to do with twenty-six – no, the latest figure was thirty-two captured dhows. A further flotilla of six vessels had arrived as the Governor was dictating his report.

Two weeks later, one of the captured dhows, which had been purchased into the Colonial Service by the Lieutenant-Governor, arrived in Table Bay bearing a further batch of despatches.

One of these was from Sir John Bannerman, H.M. Consul on the island of Zanzibar. Another was from the Sultan of Omani in person, with copies to the Foreign Secretary in London and, quite remarkably, to the Governor-General in Calcutta. The Sultan evidently believed that as the representative of the Queen of England the Governor-General would have some jurisdiction in the Indian Ocean, which was virtually his front garden.

Admiral Kemp split the seals on both packets with a queasy feeling of impending doom.

'Good God!' he groaned, as he began reading, and then, 'Oh

sweet merciful Jesus, no!' And later, 'It's too much, it's like some sort of nightmare!'

Captain Codrington, one of the most junior post-captains on the Admiralty list, seemed to have taken powers unto himself which would have made a Wellington or a Bonaparte pause.

He had annexed to the British Crown vast African territories, which hitherto had formed part of the Sultan's dominions. With a high hand he had negotiated with various local chiefs and dignitaries of dubious title and authority, pledging recognition and good British gold. 'Good God!' the Admiral cried again in real anguish, 'What will that blighter Palmerston have to say.' As a staunch Tory, Kemp had no great opinion of the new Whig prime minister.

Since the troubles in India, the sepoy risings of a few years previously, the British government was very wary of accepting further responsibility for overseas territory and backward peoples. Their orders were specific, and Captain Codrington's recent activity went far from the essence of those orders.

The scramble for Africa was still in the future, and the spirit of the Little Englanders motivated British foreign policy – of this Admiral Kemp was very painfully aware. Daunting as this was, yet it was far from the entire story, Kemp realized, as he read on into the Consul's despatch, his breath rasping hoarsely, his colour rising steadily, and his eyes behind the gold-wire framed reading-glasses swimming with tears of rage and frustration.

'When I get my hands on that puppy—' he promised himself.

Captain Codrington seemed to have declared single-handed war upon the Sultan. Yet even in his outrage the Admiral felt a prickle of professional appreciation for the scope of his subordinate's operations.

There was a formidable list of over thirty separate incidents recited by H.M. Consul. The puppy had stormed fortified castles, raided ashore to burn and destroy barracoons, released tens of thousands of slaves, seized slaving vessels on the high seas, burned others at their moorings, and wreaked the kind of chaos worthy of a marauding Nelson himself.

The Admiral's reluctant admiration for Codrington's technical conduct of the campaign in no way lessened his determination to exact vengeance for the disruption of his life and career that those actions presaged.

'Nothing can save him this time. Nothing!' the Admiral rumbled, as he turned to study the Sultan's protest. This was obviously the work of a professional letter-writer, and every paragraph began and ended with incongruous and flowery enquiries after Kemp's health, between which were sandwiched cries of anguish, screams of outrage, and bitter protest against the broken promises and treaties of Her Majesty's government.

At the very end the letter-writer had not been able to resist adding a prayer for the Admiral and the Queen's prosperity and health in this life, and happiness in the one to follow. This detracted a little from the tone of injury in which the protests and demands had been couched.

The Sultan assessed his losses at over fourteen lakhs of rupees, almost a million of sterling, in plundered shipping and released slaves, and that did not take into account the irreplaceable damage to his prestige, nor the break-down of the entire trade along the coast. The confusion was such that some ports might never again be opened to the trade. The system of gathering slaves in the interior of the continent and the network of routes to the coastal ports had been so sadly disrupted that they might take years to re-open, to say nothing of the gross shortage of shipping resulting from the depredations of 'El Sheetan'. Those ports still open to the trade were swamped with patient slaves, waiting for the dhows which were already scattered wrecks upon the reefs and beaches of the Mozambique channel, or sailing southwards under prize crews.

'Nothing can save him,' repeated Admiral Kemp, and then paused. His own career was finished also. He realized that, and he felt the deep injustice of it. For forty years he had put not a single foot wrong, and his retirement was so close, so very close. He shook off the lethargy of despair, and began to draft his orders.

The first was to all ships of his squadron, to detach immediately and to steam in search of *Black Joke*. In despair he realized that it might take as much as six weeks for his orders to reach his commanders, for they were scattered across two oceans. It might also take as long again for them to search out the errant gunboat in the maze of islands and bays along the Mozambique channel.

However, when they did so, Captain Codrington was to be relieved of his command with immediate effect. Lieutenant

Denham was to take over as temporary commander, with orders to bring *Black Joke* into Table Bay as soon as possible.

Admiral Kemp was confident that he could assemble sufficient senior officers on the Cape Station to convene an immediate court-martial. It might help his own position a little if he could report to the First Lord that a savage sentence had already been handed down to Codrington.

Then there was a despatch to H.M. Consul in Zanzibar, suggesting he keep the Sultan reassured and quiescent until the situation could once more be brought under control – and until instructions could be forwarded from the Foreign Office in London regarding possible redress and compensation, although naturally at this stage, no promises or commitments were to be given the Sultan, beyond expressions of good faith and commiseration.

Then there was the onerous task of making his report to the Admiralty. There were no words to soften the actions of his subordinate, and his own responsibility. Besides he had been a serving officer too long to make any such attempt. Yet when the bare facts were stated, even in the beloved unemotional jargon of the navy, they seemed so magnified that Admiral Kemp was himself utterly appalled, all over again. The packet-boat was delayed five hours while the Admiral completed, sealed and addressed this missive. It would be in London in less than a month.

His last despatch was addressed to the officer commanding Her Majesty's ship *Black Joke* in person. And in it Admiral Kemp allowed himself to give expression to some of his own bitterness, taking a sour sadistic pleasure in weighing the relative effectiveness of such words as 'corsair' and 'pirate' – or 'malicious' and 'irresponsible'. He had his little masterpiece of venom written out in five copies to be disseminated in every direction and by every available means that might most speedily bring the puppy to heel. Yet when they were sent, all he could do was wait – and that was the worst part of the affair. Uncertainty and inaction seemed to corrode his very soul.

He dreaded each new arrival in Table Bay, and whenever the signal gun on the hill above the town boomed its brief feather of gunsmoke, his spirit quailed and that sour ache of dread stabbed him in his guts.

Each new despatch lengthened the toll of destruction and

depredation, until at last there was a report from the culprit himself, sewn up in a package of canvas and addressed to Admiral Kemp, delivered by the prize crew of a particularly valuable dhow over eighty feet long and of a hundred-ton burden.

The tone in which Captain Codrington listed his achievements infuriated the Admiral as much as the deeds themselves. In an almost casual opening paragraph, Captain Codrington recorded the addition of some million square miles of Africa to the Empire.

He had the grace to admit that his action may have exceeded his orders, and he explained away the discrepancy winningly. 'It had been my firm intention to avoid scrupulously, whilst on this service, every act of a political nature. However, I was forced to accept the cession of the kingdoms of Elat and Telfa by the entreaties of the Sheikh and the Imam – together with that of their people, who seek refuge from the inimical and savage acts of the Sultan of Zanzibar.'

This was hard fare to serve their Lordships, especially the First Lord, Lord Somerset, who had always grudged the use of his men and ships to fight against slavery. However, much worse was to follow. Captain Codrington went on to lecture the Admiral and to deliver a few homilies for their Lordships' instruction.

'By God's providence, an Englishman with no other force than the character of his noble nation has brought to these poor people salvation. Their Lordships must pardon me for using an unfashionable argument,' a sneer at the Little Englanders, 'however, it is as clear to me as the African sun that God has prepared this continent for the only nation on earth that has the public virtue sufficient to govern it for its own benefit, and for the only people who take the revealed word for their moral law.'

Admiral Kemp gulped as he read it, swallowed the wrong way, and was prostrated with a coughing fit from which he recovered some minutes later to read on.

'In all the foregoing I have been influenced by no personal motive or interest, by no desire of vainglory, but my endeavours have solely been to use the powers granted me to the honour of my God, my Queen and to the benefit of my country and all mankind.'

The Admiral removed his reading glasses and stared at the glass case of stuffed songbirds on the wall opposite him.

'To write that, he is either the world's greatest fool – or a brave man or both,' he decided at last.

Admiral Kemp was wrong in his estimate. In fact, Clinton Codrington was having an attack of cockiness and self-importance occasioned by the sense of limitless power which this command had given him. He had been wielding this power for many months, and his judgement and good sense had warped. Yet he still truly believed that he was fulfilling, in this order, the will of God, his patriotic duty and the spirit of his orders from the Lords of the Admiralty.

He was also fully aware that he had demonstrated superior professional ability in carrying out a series of land and sea actions, nearly always against superior numbers, without a single reverse and with the loss of only three men killed in action and less than a dozen wounded. There was only one area in which Clinton had any reservations regarding the success of the patrol up to this time.

Huron was still on the coast, he had intelligence of her from a dozen sources. Mungo St John was trading, paying top prices for only the best merchandise, hand-picked by either himself or his mate, the bald yellow giant, Tippoo. They were taking only healthy, mature men and women fit to withstand the long voyage back around Good Hope and across the middle passage, and there was a shortage of this type of merchandise.

For Clinton every dawn brought the hope that *Black Joke* would once again raise that towering pyramid of beautiful white sails, but each day the hope faded slowly with the passage of the fierce tropical sun across the heavens, to be extinguished each night as the huge red orb plunged into the sea, and to be resurrected again with the next dawn.

Once they missed the big American clipper by a single day. She had slipped out of the bay at Lindi twenty-four hours before *Black Joke*'s arrival, after taking on fifty prime slaves. The watchers from the beach could not be certain if she had turned north or south, for she had made her offing below the horizon, and had been lost to sight from the shore before coming around on to her intended course.

Clinton guessed *Huron* would go south, and had steamed in

pursuit for three days, over an empty sea, down a seemingly deserted coast with barren anchorages before admitting that St John had sailed away from him again, and he was forced to abandon the hunt.

At the very least he knew that if *Huron* had turned north, St John was still trading, and there was always a chance of another encounter. He prayed for it every evening. It was all that he needed to make this patrol a clean sweep, so that he could fly a broom from his masthead when he sailed into Table Bay again.

This time he had the sworn and witnessed depositions of the men who had sold St John his slaves as proof positive that *Huron* was trading. He did not have to rely on the equipment clause, or the dubious rights of search. He had his proof and somehow he knew his chance would come.

The tide was running at full flow for Clinton. He was imbued with a new sense of worthiness, a new, iron-clad confidence in himself and his own good fortune. He carried himself differently, chin higher, shoulders squarer, and if his gait was not yet a swagger, it was at least an assured stride. He smiled more often and when he did there was a wicked curl to his upper lip and a devilish twinkle in the pale blue eyes. He had even grown a full moustache, golden and curling that gave him a piratical air, and his crew, who had always respected his cold precise management of the ship, but felt little affection for him, now cheered him when he came back on board from one of his forays ashore.

'Good old Tongs!' It was his new nickname from 'Hammer and Tongs'. They had never had a pet name for him before, but now they were a proud ship, proud of themselves, and proud of their twenty-seven-year-old 'Old Man'.

'Give 'em hell, Tongs!' they cheered behind him, as he led them, naked cutlass in hand, over the outer stockade of a barracoon with musket smoke swirling around his lanky figure.

'At 'em, the Jokers!' they cheered themselves, as they leaped the gap between *Black Joke*'s rail and the deck of a slaving dhow, swinging their cutlasses, pistols popping as they drove the slavers down into their own holds and battened the hatches down on them, or chased them over the side where the sharks were cruising.

They knew they were creating a legend. Tongs and his Jokers sweeping the slavers from the Mozambique channel, a hell of a story to tell the nippers back home, and a good slice of prize money to prove the tale.

It was in this mood that *Black Joke* sailed into Zanzibar harbour, the stronghold of the Omani Sultan, little Daniel into the lion's den. The gunners on the parapets of the fort, though they stood with the slow match burning in their hands, could not bring themselves to touch them to the huge bronze cannon as the ugly little gunboat came fussing up the Zanzibar roads.

Black Joke had her yards manned with neatly uniformed seamen. A spectacular display, geometrical white ranks of men against the backdrop of tropical anvil-headed thunder-clouds.

Her officers were in cocked hats and full ceremonial dress, uniform, swords, white gloves and white breeches, and as she made her turn into the inner harbour, *Black Joke* began firing her courtesy salute – which was a signal for most of the population to head for the hills, jamming the narrow alleyways of the old city with a lamenting torrent of refugees.

The Sultan himself fled his palace, and with most of his court took refuge in the British consulate, overlooking the harbour.

'I am not a coward,' the Sultan explained bitterly to Sir John Bannerman, 'but the Captain of that ship is a madman. Allah himself does not know what he will do next.'

Sir John was a large man, of large appetite. He possessed a noble belly like the glacis of a mediaeval castle and full mutton-chop whiskers around a florid face, but the clear intelligent eyes, and the wide friendly mouth of a man of humanity and humour. He was a noted oriental scholar, and had written books of travel and of religious and political appraisal of the East, as well as a dozen translations of minor Arabic poets.

He was also a confirmed opponent of the slave trade, for the Zanzibar markets were held in the square below the windows of his residence and from his bedroom terrace he could watch on any morning the slaving dhows unloading their pitiful cargoes on the stone wharf they called, with cruel humour, the 'Pearl Gate'.

For seven years he had patiently negotiated a series of treaties with the Sultan, each one nipping a few more twigs off the flourishing growth which he detested, but found almost impossible to prune effectively, let alone root out entirely.

In all the Sultan's territories Sir John had absolute jurisdiction only over the community of Hindu traders on the island, for they were British subjects, and Sir John published a bulletin requiring them to free all their slaves forthwith, against a penalty of £100 for non-compliance.

His bulletin made no mention of compensation, so the most influential of the merchants sent Sir John a defiance which was the Pushtu equivalent of 'The hell with you and your bulletins'.

Sir John, with his one good foot, personally kicked in the merchant's door, dragged him out from under his charpoy bed, dropped him to his knees with a full-blooded round-house punch, chained him around the neck and marched him through the city streets to the consulate and locked him in the wine cellar until the fine was paid and the slaves' manumission papers signed. There had been no further defiance and no takers for the Hindu merchant's subsequent, privately circulated offer to pay another £100 to anybody who would stick a knife between Sir John's ribs during one of his evening promenades through the old city. Thus it was that Sir John was still bluff and hale as he stood on his terrace puffing a cigar – his only indisposition was the gouty foot thrust into a carpet slipper. He watched the little black-hulled gunboat coming up the channel.

'She behaves like a flagship,' he smiled indulgently, and beside him, Said the Sultan of Zanzibar, hissed like a faulty steam valve.

'El Sheetan!' His wrinkled turkey neck turned bright red with impotent anger, his bony nose beaked like that of an unhappy parrot. 'He sails here, into my harbour, and my gunners stand by their cannons like dead men. He who has beggared me, who has plunged my empire into ruins – what does he dare here?'

The answer that Clinton 'Tongs' Codrington would have given him was quite simple. He was carrying out to the letter the orders given him in Cape Town many months previously by Admiral Kemp, the Commander of the South Atlantic and Indian Ocean Squadron.

'You are further requested and required to take advantage of the first opportunity to call into the harbour of Zanzibar, where you will accord to his Royal Highness the Sultan of Omani full honours, while taking the advice of Her Majesty's Consul, Sir John Bannerman, as to reinforcing existing treaties between His Royal Highness and Her Britannic Majesty's Government.'

Which, being translated, was an instruction to show the Union Jack against a background of thirty-two pounder cannons, and by doing so remind the Sultan of his commitments under the various treaties.

'To teach the naughty old beggar to mind his P's and Q's,' as Clinton explained cheerfully to Lieutenant Denham with a twirl of his new golden moustache.

'I would have thought, sir, that the lesson had already been given,' Denham answered darkly.

'Not at all,' Clinton demurred. 'The treaties with the new sultans on the mainland no longer affect the Zanzibar fellow. We still have to ginger this old boy up a little.'

Sir John Bannerman limped up on to *Black Joke*'s deck, favouring his gouty foot and cocked a lively eye at the young naval officer who stepped forward to greet him.

'Well, sir, you have been busy indeed,' he murmured. My God, the fellow was little more than a boy, a fresh-faced youngster, despite the cocked hat and moustache. It was difficult to believe that he had created such havoc with this tiny ship.

They shook hands, and Bannerman found himself liking the boy, despite the turmoil that he brought into the Consul's normally tranquil existence.

'A glass of madeira, sir?' Clinton suggested.

'Damned decent of you, I must say.'

In the small cabin, Bannerman mopped his streaming face, and came directly to business.

'By God, you've put the cat amongst the pigeons,' he wagged his big head.

'I don't see . . .'

'Now, listen to me,' Bannerman snapped, 'and I'll explain to you the facts of life as they apply to eastern Africa in general, and Zanzibar in particular.'

Half an hour later, Clinton had lost much of his new-found bumptiousness.

'What should we do?' he asked.

'Do?' Bannerman asked. 'What we do is take full advantage of the situation which you have precipitated, before these idiots in Whitehall come stumbling in. Thanks to you the Sultan is at last in a mood to sign the treaty I have been after for five years. I'll trade a handful of these utterly illegal, untenable treaties that you have made with non-existent states and mythical princes for one that will truss the old goat up the way I've wanted him for years.'

'Excuse me, Sir John,' Clinton looked slightly perplexed, 'from what you said earlier, I understood that you heartily disapproved of my recent actions.'

'On the contrary,' Sir John grinned at him expansively, 'you have stirred my blood, and made me proud to be an Englishman again. I say, do you have a little more of the madeira?'

He raised the glass to Clinton. 'My hearty congratulations, Captain Codrington. I only wish that I could do something to save you from the fate that so certainly awaits you, once the Admiralty and Lord Palmerston catch up with you.' Sir John drank half the glass, smacked his lips, 'Jolly good stuff,' he nodded, set the glass aside and went on briskly, 'Now, we have to work fast and get the Sultan to sign an iron-clad treaty – before Whitehall rushes in with apologies and protestations of good faith which will put to naught all the fine work you have done to date. Something tells me that won't be very long,' he added lugubriously, and then more brightly, 'You could have your ship's guns run out whilst we are ashore. Do wear your sword. Oh, and one other thing, don't take your eyes off the old goat while I do the talking. There is already talk about your eyes – that extraordinary colour of blue, don't you know – and the Sultan has heard about them already. As you probably know, they now call you "El Sheetan" on this coast, and the Sultan is a man who sets great store by djinns and the occult.'

Sir John's predictions as to the imminent arrival of tidings from higher sources was almost clairvoyant, for as he spoke H.M. sloop *Penguin*, with urgent despatches on board for Sir John Bannerman, for the Sultan, and for Captain Codrington, was on a fair wind, which, if it held, would bring her into Zanzibar harbour within the next two days. Time was shorter than even Sir John believed.

With some trepidation, the Sultan had moved back into his palace. He had only half believed Sir John's assurances, but, on the other hand, the palace was half a mile from the harbour where that evil black ship was displaying its formidable broadside of carronades, while the consulate was on the harbour front – or the front line of fire, depending on how one looked at it.

On Sir John's advice Clinton had come ashore with a

bodyguard of a dozen picked seamen, who could be trusted to resist the temptations of the old city's red-light area, the grog and the women that seamen dream of. It was dusk when the party plunged into the labyrinth of narrow alleys, where the balconies almost met overhead, led by Sir John who despite his game leg set a good pace, picking his way around heaps of noisome garbage and avoiding the puddles in the uneven paving that looked like a cold minestrone soup and smelled a great deal higher.

He chatted affably with Clinton, pointing out the various sites and buildings of interest, relating the island's history and giving a quick perceptive character-sketch of the Sultan and the more important men in his empire, including those unfortunate new princes who had signed Clinton's blank treaty forms.

'That's one thing, Sir John. I wouldn't want anything to happen to them,' Clinton cut in for the first time. 'I hope they won't be victimized for having, well, how can one say, for having seceded from the Sultan's empire—'

'Forlorn hope.' Sir John waggled his head. 'Not one of them will be alive by Ramadan. The old goat has a nasty streak.'

'Couldn't we put a clause in the new treaty to protect them?'

'We could, but it would be a waste of paper and ink.' Sir John clapped his shoulder. 'Your concern is misplaced. The finest collection of ruffians, rogues and assassins south of the equator, or north of it, for that matter. One of the side benefits of the whole business, getting rid of that lot. Old goat will have a lovely time, compensate him for the loss of face when he straps their heads or hands them the cup of datura tea. Ghastly death, datura poisoning. Oh, by the way, you must look at these gates.' They had reached the front of the palace. 'One of the most magnificent examples of craftsmanship on the island.'

The massive teak doors were fifteen feet high, intricately carved, but in accordance with Moslem law the carvings depicted neither human nor animal figures. They were the only impressive feature of the drab square building with its blank walls relieved by the wooden balconies high above street level, shuttered against the night air and the gaze of the curious.

The gates swung open at their approach, and the palace guards armed with ancient jezails were the first living beings they had seen since leaving the harbour. The city was still deserted, and cowering under the menace of *Black Joke*'s guns.

Clinton noticed, since Sir John had mentioned it, that the guards averted their gaze as he passed, one of them actually covering his face with the loose tail of his turban. So the business of the eyes was true. He was not sure whether to feel insulted or amused.

'You must see these.' Sir John stopped him in the cavernous ante-chamber lit with guttering oil lamps suspended in heavy brass chandeliers from a ceiling lost in the gloom. 'The heaviest recorded specimens in the world, one of them over three-hundred-pounds weight.'

They were a pair of African elephant tusks, suspended on the stone wall with retaining bands of copper, two incredible curves of ancient ivory, as thick as a girl's waist, taller than a man could reach, with hardly any taper from hilt to blunt tip, gleaming with the lustre of precious porcelain.

'You have not hunted these beasts?'

Clinton shook his head, he had never even seen one of them, but the huge teeth impressed him none the less.

'Before my foot, I shot them in India and in Africa. No other sport to beat that, incredible animals.' He patted one of the tusks. 'The Sultan killed this one when he was a young man, with a jezail! But there aren't any monsters like that around any more, more's the pity. Come along, mustn't keep the old goat waiting.'

They went on through half a dozen chambers, each of them Aladdin's caves of rare treasures, carved jade, beautifully worked ivory carvings, a palm tree and suspended moon, the symbol of Mohamed, in solid gold, carpets of silk and thread of gold and silver, a collection of fifty priceless Korans in silver and golden containers set with precious and semi-precious stones.

'Look at that shiner.' Sir John stopped again, and pointed out a native cut diamond in the hilt of an Arabian scimitar. The diamond was cushion-shaped and a little out of true, but burning with a weird blue and icy fire even in the semi-dark. 'Legend says the sword was Saladin's, I doubt it, but the stone is one hundred and fifty-five carats. I weighed it myself.' And then as he took Clinton's arm and stumped off again, 'Old goat is rich as Croesus. He has been milking rupees out of the mainland for forty years, and his father for fifty years before that. Ten rupees for every slave, ten for every kilo of ivory, God knows how much for copra and gum-copal concessions.'

Clinton saw instantly why Sir John called him the old goat. The resemblance was startling, from the white, pointed beard and square yellow teeth to the mournful Roman nose and elongated ears.

He took one look at Clinton, catching his eye for a split part of a second, before he looked away hurriedly, blanching visibly, as he waved his two visitors to the piles of velvet and silk cushions.

'Keep the old beady eye on him,' Sir John counselled aside, 'and don't eat anything.' He indicated the display of sweetmeats and sugared cakes on the bronze trays. 'If they aren't poisoned, they'll probably turn your stomach anyway. It's going to be a long night.'

The prediction was accurate, the talk went on hour after tedious hour, in flowing Arabic hyperbole and flowery diplomacy, that concealed the hard bargaining. Clinton understood not a word. He forced himself not to fidget, though his buttocks and legs soon lost all feeling from the unusual position on the cushions, yet he maintained a stern expression and kept his gaze fixed on the Sultan's wrinkled and whiskered visage. Sir John assured him later that it had helped greatly to shorten the negotiations, yet it seemed a full round of eternity before Sir John and the Sultan were exchanging polite fixed smiles and deep bows of agreement.

There was a triumphant gleam in Sir John's eye, as he strode out of the palace, and he took Clinton's arm affectionately.

'Whatever happens to you, my dear fellow, generations unborn will have reason to bless your name. We have done it, you and I. The old goat has agreed. The trade will wither and die out within the next few years now.'

On the walk back through the narrow streets, Sir John was as lively and cheerful as a man returning from a convivial party rather than the bargaining table. His servants were still waiting his coming, and all the lamps in the consulate were burning.

Clinton would have liked immediately to go back aboard his ship, but Sir John restrained him with an arm about his shoulder, as he called for his Hindu butler to bring champagne. On the silver tray with the green bottle and crystal glasses was a small package in stitched and sealed canvas. While the uniformed butler poured the champagne, Sir John handed Clinton the package.

'This came in earlier on a trading dhow. I did not have the opportunity to deliver it to you before we left for the palace.'

Clinton accepted it warily, and read the address : – 'Captain Clinton Codrington, Officer Commanding Her Majesty's Ship *Black Joke*. Please forward to H.M. Consul at Zanzibar to await collection.'

The address was repeated in French, and Clinton felt a quick thrill kindle his blood as he recognized the bold round script in which the package was addressed. It took an effort to restrain himself from ripping the package open immediately.

However, Sir John was handing him a glass of wine, and Clinton suffered through the toasts, the loyal toast to the Queen, and that ironical one to the Sultan and the new treaty, before he blurted out, 'Excuse me, Sir John, I believe this to be a communication of importance,' and the Consul waved him into his study and closed the door after him to give Clinton privacy.

On the leather top of the marquetry desk, Clinton slit the seals and stitching of the package with a silver knife from the Consul's desk set. From it fell a thick sheaf of closely written notepaper, and a woman's earring of paste and silver, the twin to the one that Clinton wore under his shirt against his chest.

Black Joke groped her way out through the dark, unbuoyed channel an hour before the first flush of dawn in the eastern sky. Turning southwards she set all canvas and worked up swiftly to her best speed.

She was making eleven knots when she passed the sloop *Penguin* a little before midnight the following night. *Penguin* bearing her urgent dispatches was hull down on the eastern horizon and her running lights were obscured by a heavy tropical deluge, the first fanfare of the coming monsoon that passed between the two vessels hiding them from each other's lookouts.

By dawn the two ships were fifty nautical miles apart, and rapidly widening the gap, while Clinton Codrington paced his quarterdeck impatiently, stopping at every turn to peer impatiently into the south.

He was hurrying to answer the most poignant appeal, the most pressing duty of a dutiful man, the call for succour from the woman he loved, a woman in terrible and pressing jeopardy.

The flow of the Zambezi had a majesty that Zouga Ballantyne had seen on no other great river, neither the Thames, nor the Rhine, nor the Ganges.

The water was the almost iridescent green of molten slag pouring down the side of a steel-yard dump, and it formed powerful, slowly turning vortices in the angles of the broad bends, while in the shallows it seemed to roll upon itself as though the leviathan of all the world sported below its dark mysterious surface. Here the main channel was more than a mile across, though there were other lesser channels, and other narrower mouths beyond the waving banks of papyrus and cotton-headed reeds.

The small flotilla of boats hardly seemed to move against the current. In the lead was the steam launch *Helen*, named after Zouga's mother.

Fuller Ballantyne had designed the vessel and had it manufactured in Scotland for the disastrous Zambezi expedition which had penetrated only as far as the Kaborra-Bassa gorge. The launch was almost ten years old now, and for most of that time had been the victim of the engineering prowess of the Portuguese trader who had purchased her from Fuller Ballantyne when the expedition was abandoned.

The launch's steam engine creaked and thudded, leaked steam from every pipe and joint, and sprayed sparks and thick black smoke from her wood-burning furnace, exerting herself far beyond the dictates of her age and maker's specifications as she towed the three deeply laden barges against the flow of the mighty river. They were making good a mere fifteen miles a day, and it was more than two hundred up river from Quelimane to Tete.

Zouga had chartered the launch and her barges to carry the expedition upstream to the jump-off point at Tete. He and Robyn rode in the first barge, together with the most valuable and delicate equipment: the medical stores, the navigational equipment, sextants, barometers and chronometers, the ammunition and firearms, and the personal camping gear.

In the third and last barge, under the bright and restless eye of Sergeant Cheroot, were the few porters that had been recruited at Quelimane. Zouga was assured that the additional hundred porters that he needed could be procured at Tete, but it had seemed prudent to sign on these healthy and vigorous men, as they became available. So far there had been no desertions, which was something unusual for the beginning of a long safari, when the proximity of home and hearth could be expected to exert sudden irresistible attractions on the weaker souls.

In the middle barge, on the tow-line directly behind Zouga, were the bulkier stores. In the main these were trade goods, cloth and beads, knives and axes, some cheap muskets and lead bars for ball, bags of black powder and flints. These were essential commodities with which to buy fresh provisions, to bribe local headmen for right to passage, to purchase concessions to hunt and prospect, and generally sustain the expedition's objects.

In charge of this middle barge was Zouga's newest and most dubious acquisition, who had been hired as guide, translator and camp manager. His slight admixture of blood showed in his skin, a smooth dark olive and his hair, thick and lustrous as a woman's. His teeth were very white and he flashed them in a perpetually ready smile. Yet, even when he smiled, his eyes were cold and black as those of an angry mamba.

The Governor in Quelimane had assured Zouga that this man was the most famous elephant hunter and traveller in all the Portuguese territories. He had ventured further into the interior than any other living Portuguese, and he spoke a dozen of the local dialects and understood the customs of the local tribes.

'You cannot travel without him,' the Governor assured Zouga. 'It would be madness to do so. Even your own father, the famous Dr Fuller Ballantyne, made use of his services. It was he who showed your sainted father the way to reach Lake Marawi.'

Zouga had raised an eyebrow. 'My father was the first man to reach Lake Marawi.'

'The first *white* man,' the Governor corrected him delicately, and Zouga smiled as he realized that it was one of the subtle distinctions which Fuller Ballantyne used to protect the value of his discoveries and explorations. Of course, there had been men living on the shores of the lake for at least two thousand years, and the Arabs and Mulattos had traded there for two hundred years, but they were not *white* men. That made an enormous difference.

Zouga had at last acceded to the Governor's suggestions when he had realized that this paragon was also the Governor's nephew, and that the further course of the expedition would be much smoothed by employing somebody so well connected.

He had reason to reconsider this opinion within the first few days. The man was a braggart and a bore. He had an endless fund of tales, of which he was always the hero, and the evident disregard for the truth that these demonstrated made all his facts and information suspect.

Zouga was uncertain just how well the man spoke the tribal dialects. He seemed to prefer to communicate with the toe of his boot or the *sjambok* of cured hippopotamus hide which he always carried. As for his hunting prowess, he certainly expended a great deal of powder and shot.

Zouga was sprawled on the barge's afterdeck, in the shade of the canvas awning, and he was sketching on the board he held on his knees. It was a pastime he had taken up in India, and though he knew that he had no great talent, yet it filled the idle hours of camp life and served as a useful record of places and persons, of events and animals. Zouga intended incorporating some of the sketches and water colours in the book describing the expedition. The book which would make his fortune and reputation.

He was trying to capture on paper the river's immensity, and the tallness of that aching blue sky set with the afternoon's building thunderheads, when there was the sharp crack of a rifle shot, and he looked up frowning with annoyance.

'He is at it again.' Robyn dropped her book into her lap and glanced back at the second barge.

Camacho Nuño Alvares Pereira sat high on the barge's cargo, reloading the rifle, ramrodding the charge down the long barrel. The high beaver hat sat on his head like a chimney stack and the bunch of white ostrich feathers plumed out above the crown like smoke from the furnace. Zouga could not see what he had fired at, but he guessed what would be his next target, for the steamer was being pushed out by the current to the outside of a broad bend in the river, and it was forced to steer between two low sandbanks.

The sand shone in the sunlight with the peculiar brilliance of an alpine snowfield, contrasting with the dark shapes upon it that looked like rounded granite boulders.

As the steamer slowly closed the gap, the shapes resolved into a troop of sprawling somnolent hippopotami. There were a dozen of them, one a huge scarred bull, lying on his side and exposing the expanse of his belly.

Zouga glanced back from the huge sleeping animals to the figure of Camacho Pereira on the second barge. Camacho lifted the plumed beaver and waved it in jovial salute. His teeth flashing like a semaphore even at that distance.

'You chose him,' said Robyn sweetly, following the direction of his gaze.

'That's a great comfort.' Zouga glanced at his sister. 'They told me he was the greatest sportsman and guide on the east coast.'

They both watched Camacho finish loading the rifle and setting the cap on its nipple.

The sleeping hippopotami suddenly became aware of the approaching vessels. They scrambled upright with amazing alacrity for such clumsy-looking animals, and galloped over the white sand, scattering clouds of it under their huge feet and then entered the water in a high crashing cascade of thrown spray, disappearing swiftly, and leaving the water churned and flecked with foam. Standing in the bows of the first barge, Zouga could clearly see the dark shapes below the surface of the water, galloping in comical slow motion, their movements inhibited by the water. They were silhouetted against the lighter-coloured sandbanks, and as he watched them, the ungainly creatures evoked his sympathy and amusement. He remembered a nursery rhyme that his Uncle William had recited to him as a child that began 'A hippo – what – amus?'

Zouga was still smiling as the bull hippo surfaced fifty paces from the barge's side. The bulky grey head broke clear, the flaps of flesh that sealed the nostrils flared open as he breathed and the small round ears fluttered like the wings of a bird as he cleared them of water.

For a moment he stared at the strange vessels through pinkly inflamed, piggy blue eyes. Then he opened the full gape of his jaws, a cavern the colour and the texture of a pink rose. The tusks were yellow and curved to murderous cutting edges, quite capable of biting a bullock cleanly in half, and he no longer seemed fat and comical. Instead he looked exactly what he was, the most dangerous of all African big game.

Zouga knew that the hippopotamus had killed more human beings than all the elephant and lion and buffalo together. With ease they could crunch in the fragile hull of a dugout canoe, the ubiquitous *makoro* of Africa, and then cut in half the terrified swimmers. They would readily leave the water to chase and kill any human who they believed threatened a calf, and in areas where they had been hunted they would attack without provocation. However, the steel hulls of the barges were invulnerable even to the jaws and tusks of the massive creature, and Zouga could afford to watch with complete objectivity.

From the bull's gaping pink jaws came a challenging series of bellows, each mounting in volume and menace as he moved closer to drive off the intruders who threatened his females and their young. Camacho put his hand up behind his head, and tilted the beaver hat at a jaunty angle over one eye. As always, he was smiling as he swung up the rifle and fired.

Zouga saw the strike of the bullet deep in the animal's throat, it severed an artery and instantly bright crimson blood gushed against the roof of the open mouth, discolouring the gleaming tusks, and pouring in a quick flood over the rubbery, bewhiskered lips. The bull's bellow rose into a piercing scream of agony, and he lunged half clear of the surface in a burst of white water.

'I keel heem!' roared Camacho, and his shout of laughter filled the sudden void of silence as the bull dived below the surface, leaving his blood to swirl away down the current.

Robyn had jumped up and was clinging to the barge's rail, a flush overlaying her sunbronzed cheeks and throat.

'That was callous butchery,' she said quietly.

'No point in it,' Zouga agreed. 'The animal will die below the surface and be washed out to sea.'

But he was wrong, for the bull surfaced again, closer to the barge. His jaws still gaping and streaming gouts of blood, he thrashed and lunged in maddened circles, his bellows distorted by blood and water, as his death frenzy rose to a crescendo. Perhaps the bullet had damaged his brain, making it impossible for him to close his jaws or to control his limbs.

'I keel heem!' roared Camacho, dancing with excitement on the foredeck of the second barge, pouring shot after shot into the immense grey body, grabbing a rifle from his black gunbearer or from his second loader as soon as it was primed.

His two black servants worked with the expertise of long practice, so that it seemed that Camacho always had a loaded rifle ready to snatch and waiting hands ready to take the smoking weapon from him the moment he had fired.

Slowly the string of barges drew away upstream, leaving the stricken animal wallowing with increasing feebleness in its own expanding circle of blood-tinged waters, until at last it rolled belly upwards, all four stubby legs sticking up towards the sky for a moment before it sank at last and the blood was diluted and swept away downstream.

'That was sickening,' whispered Robyn.

'Yes, but he has trained those gunbearers of his damned well,' said Zouga thoughtfully. 'If one is going to hunt elephant, that is the way to do it.'

Two hours before sunset the *Helen* edged in towards the south bank. For the first time since leaving Quelimane there was some feature on the shore, beyond the endless reed swamps and sandbanks.

The bank was steeper here, rising ten feet above the river, and game paths had been cut into the grey earth by thousands of sharp hooves, and polished to shiny clay by the sliding wet bellies of the long lizard-like shapes of the big crocodiles that came tobogganing down the almost vertical slope when they were disturbed by *Helen*'s churning propeller. The heavily armoured reptiles with the staring yellow eyes set on a hard horny scale atop the long saurian head repulsed Robyn, the first African animal to do so.

There were trees on the bank now, not just waving stands of papyrus. Chief of these were the graceful palms with stems sculptured like a claret bottle.

'Ivory palms,' Zouga told her. 'The fruit has a kernel like a ball of ivory.'

Then far beyond the palms, low against the ruddy evening sky, they could make out the first silhouette of hills and kopjes. They were leaving the delta at last, and that night the company would camp on firm ground, instead of soft white sand, and burn heavy logs on the camp fires rather than the pulpy papyrus stems.

Zouga checked the sentries that Sergeant Cheroot had placed over the irreplaceable cargoes in the barges on which the whole expedition depended, then he supervised the siting of the tents before taking the Sharps rifle and starting out into the open forest and grassland beyond the camp site.

'I come weeth you,' offered Camacho. 'We keel something.'

'Your job is to make camp,' Zouga told him coolly, and the Portuguese flashed his smile and shrugged.

'I make one damn fine camp – you see.'

But as Zouga disappeared amongst the trees, the smile slid off his face, and he hawked in his throat and spat in the dust. Then he turned back into the turmoil of men raising canvas on poles, or dragging in branches of freshly cut thorns to build the *scherm* against marauding lions or scavenging hyena.

Camacho lashed out at a bare black back. 'Hurry, you one mother, twenty-seven fathers.' The man cried out at the pain of the cured hippo-hide whip, redoubling his efforts as a purple welt, thick as a man's little finger, rose across his sweat-oiled muscles.

Camacho strode on towards the small grove of trees which Zouga had picked as the site for the tents of his sister and himself, and he saw that the tents had already been erected and that the woman was busy with the evening muster when she treated the ailments of the camp.

She had been seated at the collapsible camp table, but as Camacho approached, she rose and stooped to examine the foot of one of the bearers whose axe had slipped and almost severed a toe.

The Portuguese stopped abruptly. and his throat dried out as he watched her. As soon as they had left Quelimane, the woman had taken to wearing men's breeches. Camacho found them more provocative than naked flesh itself. It was the first time he had ever seen a white woman dressed like this, and he found it hard to take his eyes off her. Whenever she was in sight, he would watch her surreptitiously, waiting hungrily for the moment when she stooped or leaned forward and the moleskin stretched over her buttocks, as it was now. It lasted too short a time, for the woman straightened up and began speaking to the little black girl who seemed more of a companion to her than a servant.

Still Camacho leaned against the bole of one of the tall umsivu trees and watched her with those black eyes gone velvet and swimming with desire. He was carefully weighing the consequences of what he had dreamed about every night since they had left Quelimane. He had imagined every detail, every expression, every word, each movement and each sigh or cry.

It was not as improbable as it seemed at first. She was an English woman, of course, daughter of a famous man of God, both facts should have been prohibitive to his intentions. However, Camacho had a canny instinct when it came to women, there was a sensuality about her eye and in the full soft lips, and she moved with animal awareness of her body. Camacho stirred restlessly and thrust his hands into his pockets, kneading and tugging gently at himself.

He was fully aware that he was a magnificent specimen of masculinity – those thick tresses of black hair, the gypsy feyness of eyes, the blazing smile, and powerful and well-proportioned body. He was attractive, perhaps irresistibly so, for more than once he had intercepted a quizzical appraising look from the woman. Often the admixture of his blood was attractive to white women, it was an exoticism, the attraction of the forbidden and dangerous, and he sensed in this woman a rebellious disregard for the rules of society. It was possible, no more than possible, Camacho decided, and there was unlikely to be a better opportunity than now. The cold stiff English brother was out of camp, would be so for another hour or more, and the woman had finished attending the little group of sick bearers. A servant had brought a kettle of boiling water to her tent, and she was closing the fly.

Camacho had watched this little ritual every evening. Once the oil lamp had cast her shadow upon the canvas, and he had watched her silhouette lowering those tantalizing breeches, and then using the sponge to – he shuddered deliciously at the memory, and pushed himself away from the tree trunk.

Robyn mixed the hot water from the kettle into the enamel basin. It was still scalding hot, but she liked it so that it reddened the skin and left her feeling glowing with cleanliness. She began to unbutton the flannel shirt, sighing with pleasant weariness, when something scratched on the fly of the tent.

'Who is it?' she called sharply, and felt a faint stir of alarm as she recognized the low voice. 'What do you want?'

'I want talk you, missus.' Camacho's tone was conspiratorial.

'Not now, I am busy.' The man repelled her, and yet in a contrary manner, fascinated her as well. She had found herself staring at him more than once – as she would at a beautiful but poisonous insect. She was annoyed that he had noticed and was vaguely aware that it was unwise to show even the vaguest interest in a man like that.

'Come back tomorrow.' It suddenly occurred to her that Zouga was not in the camp, and she had sent little Juba on an errand.

'I cannot wait. I am sick.'

That was one appeal she could not deny.

'Oh very well. Wait,' she called, and buttoned her shirt, and then as an excuse perhaps to delay the moment turned her attention to her instruments still spread on the table that had been carried into the tent. It reassured her to touch them, and rearrange the bottles and pots of medicines.

'Enter,' she called at last, and faced the entrance of the tent.

Camacho stooped through the entrance, and for the first time she realized bow tall he was. His presence in the small tent was almost overpowering, and his smile seemed to light up the interior. His teeth were startlingly white and perfect, she found herself staring again, like a chicken at the dancing cobra perhaps. He was beautiful in a decadent, overblown way, he was bare-headed, all dark dancing hair and scalding eyes.

'What is the trouble?' she asked, trying to sound brisk and businesslike.

'I show you.'

'Very well,' she nodded, and he unbuttoned his shirt. His skin had the sheen of wet marble, but was deep olive in colour, and his body hair grew in crisply springing whorls. His belly was moulded like that of a greyhound and his waist narrow as a girl's. She ran her eyes down his body, quite certain that her gaze was level and professional, but there was no denying the fact that he was an extraordinary animal.

'Where is it?' she asked, and with a single movement he had unclinched and lowered the light duck trousers that were all he wore on his lower body.

'Where?' she asked, and realized that her voice croaked, and she could not go on with the question, for suddenly it dawned upon her that she had been the victim of a carefully planned ruse, and she was in a potentially dangerous position.

'Is that where it hurts?' she found her voice was still a husky whisper.

'Yes,' his voice was a whisper also, and he made a slow stroking movement. 'You can fix, maybe.' He took a step towards her.

'I can fix, certainly,' she said softly, and her hand dropped on to the array of surgical instruments. She actually experienced a twinge of real regret, for it was a superior example of nature's art, and afterwards she was relieved that she had selected a needle probe – and not one of the razorlike scalpels that she had reached for.

The instant before she stabbed, he realized what was about to happen and an expression of utter terror blanched his swarthy, handsome face. He tried frantically to return it to whence it had come, but fear had slowed his hand.

He screamed like a teenage girl as the probe plunged into him, and kept on screaming as he spun around on the same spot as though one foot had been nailed to the ground. Now he was using both hands to hold himself, and once again, with cool professional interest, Robyn noticed the quite miraculous change that had taken place.

She advanced the probe once more into the ready position, and Camacho could no longer stand his ground. He snatched up his trousers, and with a last terrified howl, launched himself head-first into the tent pole. The collision checked him only a moment, and then he was gone, and Robyn found herself trembling violently and yet she was strangely elated. It had been an unusual and instructive experience. However, she would have to use her own personal code when describing it in her journal.

From that evening onwards the Portuguese kept well away from Robyn, and she was relieved not to have those hot dark eyes caressing her wherever she turned. She thought of telling Zouga of the incident, but decided that the embarrassment to both of them and the difficulty of finding the correct words was not worth it. Then there would be the extreme reaction which Zouga would almost certainly have, or that she expected he would have. She had learned never to expect the obvious reaction from her brother, behind the cool and reserved exterior she suspected there existed mysterious passions and dark emotions. After all, they were full-blooded brother and sister, and if she was so afflicted, why should he not be also?

On the other hand, she suspected that, like a cornered wild animal, the Portuguese could be a grave danger even to an experienced soldier and man of action like Zouga. She had a horror of forcing her brother into a position which might lead, if not to his death. then at least to serious injury. Besides which, she had effectively taken care of the man herself. He would be no further trouble, she decided comfortably, and she dismissed Camacho from her mind, and concentrated instead on the pleasure of the last few leisurely days of the voyage up-stream.

The river had narrowed, and the flow was swifter, so that the rate of the convoy's advance slowed even further. The banks provided an ever-changing panorama. Sitting under the awning, with Zouga sketching or writing beside her, she was able to call his attention to the new birds and trees and animals and to have the benefit of his knowledge, gathered to be sure mostly from books, but still wide-reaching and interesting.

The hills of the escarpment rose in a series of cockscombs, so two-dimensional that they seemed to be cut out from thin sheets of some opaque material that allowed the colours of the sunrise to glow through with a weird luminosity. As the sun rose higher, the colours washed out to ethereal eggshell blues, and finally faded altogether in the heat haze of midday, to reappear in the late afternoon in a new suit of totally different colours – pale pinks and ash of roses, ripe plum and delicate apricot.

The hills formed a backdrop to the forests that now ran in a narrow belt along the river banks. Tall galleries of trees, with spreading upper branches in which the troops of vervet monkeys frolicked. The trunks of these trees were daubed with multicoloured lichens, sulphurous yellows, burnt oranges and the blues and greens of a summer sea. The tangled ropes of lianas, which as a child Robyn had called 'monkey ropes', dangled down from the upper branches to touch the surface of the river or cascade into the dense dark greens of the undergrowth.

Beyond this narrow strip of vegetation, there were occasional glimpses of a different forest on the higher, drier ground, and Robyn saw again with a sharp nostalgic pang the ugly and bloated baobab tree with its scrubby bare little branches topping the huge swollen stem. The African legends that her mother had repeated to her so often, explained how the Nkulu-kulu, the great great one, had planted the baobab upside down, with its roots in the air.

Nearly every baobab had a nest of one of the big birds of prey in its bare branches, each a shaggy mass of dried twigs and small branches looking like a small, air-borne haystack. Often the birds were at the nest site, sitting on a look-out branch, with that typical raptorial stillness, or soaring above in wide circles, with only an occasional lazy flap of the spread wings, and the stiff tip-feathers feeling the air currents like the fingers of a concert pianist upon the ivory keys.

There was very little game along this part of the river, and the rare antelope rushed back into cover at the first distant approach – a pale blur of movement, with a mere fleeting glimpse of the tall corkscrew horns of a greater kudu, or the flirt of the white, powder-puff underside of a reedbuck's tail.

The game close to the river had been heavily hunted, if not by the Portuguese themselves then by their armed servants, for nearly two hundred years.

When Zouga asked Camacho, 'Do you ever find elephant on this part of the river?' the Portuguese had flashed his smile and declared, 'If I find heem, I keel heem.'

A sentiment that was probably shared by nearly every traveller along this busy waterway, and which accounted for the timidity and scarcity of game in the area.

Camacho was reduced to firing at the roosting fish eagles on their fishing-perches overhanging the water. These handsome birds had the same snowy white head, breast and shoulders of the famous American bald eagle, and a body of lovely dark russet and glistening black. When a shout of Camacho's laughter signalled a hit, a bird would tumble untidily over its disproportionately large wings as it fell into the green water, reduced from imperial dignity to awkward and ungainly death by the strike of the lead bullet.

Within a few days Camacho had recovered from the peculiar, bow-legged and deliberate gait, with which he favoured the injury that Robyn had inflicted on him, and his laughter regained its ringing timbre. But there were other injuries that did not heal so readily, those to his pride and his masculinity. His lust had been changed on the instant to burning hatred, and the more he brooded upon it the more corrosive it became and the deeper his craving for vengeance.

However, his personal considerations would have to wait. There was still much important work for him to do. His uncle, the Governor of Quelimane, had placed great trust in him by assigning him to this task – and his uncle would be unforgiving of any failure. The family fortune was involved, and to a lesser extent the family honour, although this last was a commodity that through constant attrition had lost much of its lustre. However, the family fortunes had suffered considerably since Portugal had been forced to heed the Brussels Treaty. What was left to the family had to be protected. Gold before honour, and honour only when it does not affect the profits – this might have been the family motto.

His uncle had been perceptive, as always, in recognizing in this English expedition a further threat to their interests. It was, after all, headed by the son of a notorious trouble-maker who could be expected to aggravate the enormous damage done by the father. Furthermore, nobody could be sure of the real objects of the expedition.

Major Ballantyne's assertion that it was an expedition to find his missing father was, of course, utterly absurd. That explanation was much too simple and direct, and the English were never simple or direct. This elaborate expedition must have cost many thousands of English pounds, a huge sum of money, far beyond the means of a junior army officer, or the family of a missionary whose futile effort to navigate the Zambezi had ended in disgrace and ridicule, a sick old man who must have perished years ago in the uncharted wilderness.

No, there was another motive for all this activity – and the Governor wanted to know what it was.

It was, of course, possible that this was a clandestine reconnaissance by an officer of the British army ordered by his overbearing government. Who knew what outrageous designs they had upon the sovereign territory of the glorious Portuguese empire? The avarice of this impudent race of shopkeepers and tradesmen was scarcely to be believed. The Governor did not trust them, despite their traditional alliance with Portugal.

On the other hand, it might indeed be a private expedition, but the Governor never lost sight of the fact that it was led by the son of that notorious old busy-body who had possessed the scavenging eye of a vulture. Who knew what the old devil had stumbled upon out there in the unknown land, a mountain of gold or silver, the fabled lost city of Monomatapa with all its treasures intact: anything was possible. Of course, the old missionary would have sent news of the discovery to his own son. If there was a mountain of gold out there, then the Governor would be very pleased to know about it.

Even if there were no new treasures to discover, there were certainly old ones to protect. It would be Camacho Pereira's duty to steer the expedition away from certain areas, to prevent it stumbling on secrets known not even to the Governor's masters in Lisbon.

Camacho's orders were clear: distract the Englishman by accounts of the insurmountable difficulty of travel in certain directions, the swamps, the mountain ranges, the disease, the savage animals and even more savage men, and contrast that with the friendly people in pleasant lands, rich with ivory, that lay in other directions.

If this was unsuccessful – and Major Ballantyne had all the earmarks of arrogance and intractability peculiar to his nation – then Camacho was to use what other means of persuasion came to hand. This was a euphemism perfectly understood by both the Governor and his nephew.

Camacho had almost convinced himself that this was really the only sensible course of action. Beyond Tete there was no law, except that of the knife, and Camacho had always lived by that law. Now he savoured the thought. He had found the Englishman's unconcealed contempt as galling as the woman's rejection had been painful.

He had convinced himself that the reason for the attitude towards him of both brother and sister was his Mulatto blood. This was a sensitive area of Camacho's self-esteem, for even in Portuguese territories where miscegenation was almost universal practice, mixed blood still carried a stigma. He would enjoy the work ahead, for not only would it wipe out the insults he had suffered, but it would bring rich pickings, and even after they had been shared out with his uncle, and others, there would still be much profit in it for himself.

The equipment that the expedition carried represented, in Camacho's view, a vast fortune. There were barge-loads of excellent trade goods. Camacho had taken the first opportunity to check secretly the contents of the packs. There were firearms, and valuable instruments, chronometers and sextants, and there was a forged-steel field-safe that the Englishman kept locked and guarded. The merciful God alone knew how many golden

English sovereigns it contained, and if He did not know – then his good uncle the Governor knew less. It would make the division of spoils more in Camacho's favour. The more he brooded upon it, the more he looked forward to the arrival at Tete, and the jump-off into the unexplored territory beyond.

To Robyn the tiny town of Tete marked her real arrival in Africa, and her return to the world for which she had trained so assiduously and yearned so deeply.

She was secretly glad that Zouga had used the unloading of the barges as an excuse not to accompany her.

'You find the place, Sissy, and we'll go there together tomorrow.'

She had changed back into skirts, for small and isolated as it was, Tete was still a backwater of civilized behaviour and there was no point in giving offence to the local inhabitants. Though she found the heavy folds about her legs annoying, she soon forgot them as she walked the single, dusty street of the village where her father and mother must have walked together for the last time, and peered at the mud-walled trading stores built haphazardly along a rough line with the bank of the river.

She stopped at one of these little *duka's* and found that the storekeeper could understand a mixture of her basic Swahili, English and Nguni language, enough anyway to direct her on to where the village street petered out in a mere footpath that meandered off into the acacia forest.

The forest was hushed in the heat of the noon, even the birds were silent and the mood weighed on Robyn, depressing her and awakening the memories of long-ago mourning.

She saw a flash of white amongst the trees ahead, and stopped, reluctant to go on to what she knew she would find. For a moment she was transported to girlhood again, to a grey November day standing beside her Uncle William waving upwards at the passenger decks of the departing ship, her eyes so dimmed with tears that she could not make out at the crowded rail the beloved face for which she searched, while the distance between ship and quay opened like the gulf between life and death.

Robyn shook the memory away and went on. There were six graves amongst the trees, she had not expected that, but then she recalled that there had been heavy mortality amongst the members of her father's Kaborra-Bassa expedition, four of disease, one drowned and a suicide.

The grave for which she searched stood a little apart from the others. It was demarcated by a square of whitewashed river stones and at the head was a cross built of mortar. It also had been whitewashed. Unlike the other graves, it had been kept cleaned of grass and weed, and the cross and stones freshly painted. There was even a small bunch of wilted wild flowers standing in a cheap blue china vase. They were not more than a few days old. That surprised Robyn.

Standing at the foot of the grave she read the still fully legible lettering on the plaster cross:

In loving memory of
Helen
beloved wife of Fuller Morris Ballantyne.
Born August 4th 1814. Died of fever December 16th 1852.
God's will be done.

Robyn closed her eyes and waited for the tears to come up from deep inside, but there were no tears, they had been shed long ago. Instead there were only the memories.

Little fragments of memory played over and over in her mind – the smell of strawberries as they gathered them together in Uncle William's garden, standing on tiptoe to place one of the lush red fruit between her mother's white teeth and then eating the half that was left especially for her; lying cuddled under her bed-clothes as she listened drowsily to her mother's voice reading aloud to her in the candlelight; the lessons at the kitchen table in winter, under the elm trees in summer and her own eagerness to learn and to please; her first pony ride, her mother's hands holding her in the saddle, her legs too short for the stirrups; the feel of the soapy sponge down her back as her mother stooped over the iron hipbath; the sound of her mother's laughter, and then at night the sound of her weeping beyond the thin partition beside her cot; then the final memory of the smell of violets and lavender as she pressed her face to her mother's bodice.

'Why must you go, Mama?'

'Because your father needs me. Because your father has sent for me, at last.'

And Robyn's own terrible consuming jealousy at the words, mingled with the sense of impending loss.

Robyn knelt in the soft cushion of dust beside the grave, and began to pray, and as she whispered, the memories came crowding back, happy ones and sad ones together, and she had not felt so close to her mother in all the intervening years.

She did not know how long she had knelt there, it seemed an eternity, when a shadow fell across the earth in front of her and she looked up, jerked back to the present with a little gasp of surprise and alarm.

A woman and child stood near her, a black woman, with a pleasant, even pretty, face. Not young, in her middle thirties possibly, though it was always difficult to guess an African's age. She wore European-style clothing, cast-offs probably, for they were so faded that the original pattern was hardly visible, but starched and fastidiously clean. Robyn sensed that they had been donned for the occasion.

Although the child wore the brief leather kilt of the local Shangaan tribe, he was clearly not a full-blooded African. He could not have been more than seven or eight years of age, a sturdy boy, with a head of dusty-coloured curls and oddly pale-coloured eyes. There was something vaguely familiar about him that made Robyn stare.

He carried a small bunch of the yellow acacia flowers in his hands, and smiled shyly at Robyn before hanging his head and shuffling his feet in the dust. The woman said something to him and tugged at his hand, and he came hesitantly to Robyn and handed her the flowers.

'Thank you,' she said automatically, and raised the bouquet to her nose. They were faintly, but sweetly perfumed.

The woman hiked her skirts and squatted beside the grave, removed the wilted flowers and then handed the little blue china vase to the boy. He scampered away towards the river-bank.

While he was gone the woman plucked out the first green sprouts of weeds from the mound of the grave and then rearranged the whitewashed stones carefully. The familiar manner in which she performed the chore left no doubt in Robyn's mind that she was responsible for the upkeep of her mother's grave.

Both women maintained a friendly, comfortable silence, but when their eyes met they smiled and Robyn nodded her thanks. The child came trotting back, muddy to the knees and slopping water from the vase, but puffed up with self-importance. He had clearly performed this task before.

The woman took the vase from him and set it carefully on the grave, then both of them looked expectantly towards Robyn and watched her while she arranged the acacia flowers in the vase.

'Your mother?' said the woman softly, and Robyn was startled to hear her speak English.

'Yes,' she tried to hide her surprise. 'My mother.'

'Good lady.'

'You knew her?'

'Please?'

After the valiant opening, the woman had very little English, and their communication was halting, until Robyn, out of the habit of talking to little Juba, said something in Matabele. The woman's face lit with pleasure and she answered swiftly in a language which was obviously one of the Nguni group, and whose inflection and vocabulary differed very little from that to which Robyn was accustomed.

'You are Matabele?' Robyn demanded.

'I am Angoni,' the woman put in hastily, for there was rivalry and hostility between even the closely related tribes of the Nguni.

Her tribe, the Angoni, had swept northwards from their origins in the grassy hills of Zululand, and crossed the Zambezi river thirty years before, she explained in her lilting musical dialect. They had conquered the land along the northern shores of Lake Marawi. It was from there that the woman had been sold to one of the Omani slave-masters, and had come down the Shire river in chains.

Unable to keep up with the slave caravan, reduced by starvation, and the fevers and hardships of the long journey, she had been freed of her chains and left for the hyenas beside the slave road. It was there that Fuller Ballantyne had found her and taken her into his own small camp.

She had responded to his rough nursing and when she was recovered, Fuller had baptized her with the Christian name of Sarah.

'So my father's detractors are mistaken,' Robyn laughed, and spoke in English. 'He made more than one convert.'

Sarah did not understand but laughed in sympathy. By now it was almost dusk and the two women, followed by the half-naked child, left the little cemetery and started back along the footpath, with Sarah still telling how when Robyn's mother, summoned at last by Fuller Ballantyne, arrived in Tete with other members of the Kaborra-Bassa expedition, Sarah had been presented to her by Fuller as a personal servant.

By now they had stopped at a fork in the path, and after a moment of hesitation Sarah invited Robyn to her village which was only a short way off the path. Robyn glanced up at the sun and shook her head, it would be dark in an hour and Zouga would be certain to turn out the camp to search for her if she had not returned by then.

She had enjoyed the hours spent with the young woman and the bright sweet child, and when she saw Sarah's obvious disappointment, she said quickly, 'Although I must go – I will return tomorrow at the same time. I wish to hear all you can tell me of my mother and my father.'

Sarah sent the little boy with her as far as the buildings of the village. and after the first few yards Robyn quite naturally took the boy's hand, and he skipped along beside her, chattering gay childish nonsense, which helped to lift her sombre mood until Robyn laughed and chattered with him.

Before they reached the outskirts of Tete, Robyn's fears were confirmed. They met Zouga and Sergeant Cheroot. Zouga was armed with the Sharps rifle and angry with relief the moment he saw her.

'Damn me, Sissy, but you have had us all beside ourselves. You've been missing for five hours.'

The child stared at Zouga with wide eyes. He had never seen anything like this tall lordly man with the imperious manner and sharp commanding voice. He must be a great chief, and he slipped his hand out of Robyn's, retreated two paces, then turned and darted away like a sparrow from the circling hawk.

Some of Zouga's anger left him as he watched the child go, and a small smile touched his lips.

'For a moment I thought you'd picked up another stray.'

'Zouga, I found Mama's grave.' Robyn hurried to him and took his arm. 'It's only a mile or so.'

Zouga's expression changed again and he glanced up at the sun that was already on the tops of the acacia trees and turning deep smouldering red.

'We'll come back tomorrow,' he said. 'I don't like to leave the camp after dark, there are too many jackals lurking about – two legged jackals.' Firmly. he led her back towards the village, continuing his explanation as they walked.

'We are still having a great deal of difficulty obtaining porters, despite the fact that the Governor in Quelimane assured me they would be readily available, and the good Lord knows there are any amount of able-bodied men hereabouts. Yet that strutting poppinjay Pereira finds obstacles at every turn.' The frown made him look much older than his years as did the full beard which he had allowed to grow since disembarking from *Black Joke*. 'He says that the porters refuse to contract until they know the direction and duration of the safari.'

'That seems logical,' Robyn agreed. 'I know I wouldn't carry one of those huge packs, unless I knew where I was going.'

'I don't think at all that it's the porters – there is no reason why the destination should worry them. I am offering top wages, and not a single man has come forward.'

'What is it, then?'

'Pereira has been trying to wheedle our intentions out of me, ever since we left the coast. I think this is a form of blackmail, no porters until I tell him.'

'Then why don't you tell him?' Robyn asked, and Zouga shrugged.

'Because he is too damned insistent. It's not a casual interest, and instinct warns me not to trust him with any information which it is not essential for him to know.'

They walked on in silence until they reached the perimeter of the camp. Zouga had laid it out on the lines of a military base, with an outer stockade of acacia thorn branches, a Hottentot guard at the gate and the *boma* for the porters separated from the stores depot by the tent lines.

'It looks like home already,' Robyn congratulated him, and would have left him for her own tent when Camacho Pereira hurried forward.

'Ah! Major, I wait for you with good news.'

'That's a pleasant change,' Zouga murmured drily.

'I find man who has seen your father, not eight months ago.'

Robyn turned back instantly, her excitement matching that of the flamboyant Portuguese and she spoke directly to him for the first time since the incident in her tent.

'Where is he? Oh, this is wonderful news.'

'If it's true,' qualified Zouga, with considerably less enthusiasm.

'I bring the man, damned quick – you see!' Camacho promised, and hurried away towards the porters' *boma*, shouting as he went.

Within ten minutes he returned dragging with him a skinny old man dressed in greasy tatters of animal skins, and with his eyes rolling up into his head with terror.

As soon as Camacho released him, the old man prostrated himself before Zouga who sat in one of the canvas camp chairs under the awning of the dining tent, and gabbled replies to the queries that Camacho shouted at him in hectoring tones.

'What dialect is that he speaks?' Zouga interrupted within the first few seconds.

'Chichewa,' Camacho replied. 'He no speak other.'

Zouga glanced at Robyn, but she shook her head. They had to rely entirely on Camacho's rendition of the old man's replies.

It seemed that the old man had seen 'Manali', the man with the red shirt, at Zimi on the Lualaba river. Manali had been camped there with a dozen porters, and the old man had seen him with his own eyes.

'How does he know it was my father?' Zouga asked.

Everybody knew 'Manali', the old man explained, he was a living legend from the coast to 'Chona langa', the land where the sun sets.

'When did he see Manali?'

One moon before the coming of the last rains, which made it in October of the previous year, as Camacho had said, about eight months previously.

Zouga sat lost in thought, but his gaze fixed with such ferocity on the unfortunate who grovelled before him that the old man suddenly burst out on a plaintive note that made Camacho's handsome face darken with anger and he touched the skeletal ribs with the toe of his boot, a threatening gesture that quieted the old man instantly.

'What did he say?' Robyn demanded.

'He swears he speak the truth only,' Camacho assured her, resurrecting his smile with an effort.

'What else does he know of Manali?' Zouga asked.

'He speak with the porters of Manali, they say they go follow the Lualaba river.'

It made some sense, Zouga thought. If Fuller Ballantyne was indeed seeking the source of the Nile river to recover his lost reputation, then that is where he would have gone. The Lualaba, which was reputed to run directly northward, was one of obvious choices for the source river.

Camacho questioned the old man for another ten minutes, and would have taken the hippo-hide whip to jog his memory, but Zouga stopped him with a gesture of annoyance. It was obvious that there was nothing further to learn from him.

'Give him a bolt of *merkani* cloth and a *khete* of beads – and let him go,' Zouga ordered and the old man's gratitude was pathetic to watch.

Zouga and Robyn sat later than usual beside the camp fire, while it collapsed slowly upon itself in spasmodic torrents of rising sparks and the murmur of sleepy voices from the porters' *boma* died into silence.

'If we go north,' Robyn mused, watching her brother's face, 'we will be going into the stronghold of the slave trade, from Lake Marawi northwards. From that area into which no white man, not even Pater, has ever ventured must come all the slaves for the markets of Zanzibar and the Omani Arabs—'

'What about the evidence of the trade to the south,' Zouga glanced across the clearing at the silent figure of Juba, waiting patiently by the entrance to Robyn's tent. 'That girl is the living proof that a new trade is flourishing south of the Zambezi.'

'Yes, but it seems to be nothing compared to the activity north of here.'

'The northern trade has been fully documented. Father reached Marawi and followed the slave caravans down to the coast fifteen years ago, and Bannerman at Zanzibar has written a dozen reports on the Zanzibar market,' Zouga pointed out, nursing a precious tumbler of his fast-dwindling supply of whisky, and staring into the ashes of the fire. 'Whereas nobody knows anything about the trade with the Monomatapa and the Matabele south of here.'

'Yes, I acknowledge that,' Robyn admitted reluctantly.

'However, in his *Missionary Travels* father wrote that the Lualaba was the source of the Nile and he would one day prove it by following it from its headwaters. Besides which, he has been seen in the north.'

'Has he, though?' Zouga asked mildly.

'That old man . . .'

' . . . Was lying. Somebody put him up to it, and I don't need more than one guess,' Zouga finished.

'How do you know he was lying?' Robyn demanded.

'If you live long enough in India you develop an instinct for the lie,' Zouga smiled at her. 'Besides why would father wait eight years *after* he disappeared to explore the Lualaba river. He would have gone there directly – if he had gone north.'

'My dear brother,' Robyn's voice was stinging, 'it would not be the legend of Monomatapa that makes you so stubbornly determined to go south of the river, would it? Is that gleam in your eye the gleam of gold?'

'That is a mean thought,' Zouga smiled again. 'But what does intrigue me is the determination of that great guide and explorer, Camacho Pereira, to discourage any journey to the south, and instead to lead us northwards.'

Long after Robyn had disappeared into her tent and the lantern within was extinguished Zouga sat on beside the fire, nursing the whisky in the tumbler and staring into the fading coals. When he reached his decision he drained the last drop of precious golden brown spirit in the glass and stood up abruptly. He strode down the lines to where Camacho Pereira's tent stood at the furthest end of the camp.

There was a lantern burning within even at this late hour, and when Zouga called out, a squeak of alarm in feminine tones was quickly hushed with a man's low growl and a few minutes later Camacho Pereira pulled the fly aside and peered out at Zouga warily.

He had thrown a blanket over his shoulders to cover his nudity, but in one hand he carried a pistol and relaxed only slightly as he recognized Zouga.

'I have decided,' Zouga told him brusquely, 'that we'll go north, up the Shire river to Lake Marawi – and then on to the Lualaba river.'

Camacho's face shone like the full moon as he smiled.

'That is very good. Very good – much ivory, we find your father – you see, we find him damn soon.'

Before noon the following day Camacho, with a great deal of shouting and swishing of the kurbash, marched a hundred strong healthy men into the camp. 'I find you porters,' he announced. 'Plenty porters – damn good, hey?'

The Christian girl Sarah was waiting beside the grave again when Robyn came down through the acacia forest the following afternoon.

The child saw her first and ran to greet her, he was laughing with pleasure, and Robyn was struck once again by the familiarity of his face. It was something about his mouth and his eyes. The resemblance to somebody she had known was so forcible that she stopped dead and stared at him, but could not recapture the memory before the boy took her hand and led her to where his mother waited.

They went through the little ritual of changing the flowers on the grave and then settled side by side on a fallen acacia branch. It was cooler in the shade and in the branches above their heads a pair of shrikes hunted little green caterpillars. The birds were black and white across the back and wings, but their breasts were a striking shade of crimson that glowed like the blood of a dying gladiator, and Robyn watched them with rare pleasure while she and Sarah talked quietly.

Sarah was telling her about her mother, how brave and uncomplaining she had been in the terrible heat of the Kaborra-Bassa where the black ironstone cliffs turned the gorge into a furnace.

'It was the bad season,' Sarah explained. 'The hot season before the rains break.' Robyn recalled her father's written account of the expedition in which he had laid the blame for the delays upon his subordinates, old Harkness and Commander Stone, so that they had missed the cool season, and entered the gorge in the suicide month of November.

'Then when the rains came, the fever came with it,' Sarah went on. 'It was very bad. The white men and your mother became sick very quickly.' Perhaps her mother had lost much of her immunity to malaria during the years in England while she waited for her husband's summons. 'Even Manali himself became sick. It was the first time I had seen him sick of the fever. He was filled with the devils for many days,' the expression described vividly the delirium of malarial fever, Robyn thought. 'So he did not know when your mother died.'

They were silent again. The child, bored by the interminable talk of the two women, threw a stone at the birds in the acacia branches above their heads, and with a flash of their marvellous crimson breasts the two shrikes winged away towards the river, and again the child engaged Robyn's attention. It was as if she had known that face all her life.

'My mother?' Robyn asked, still watching the child.

'Her water turned black,' said Sarah simply. The blackwater fever – Robyn felt her skin prickle. When malaria changed its course, attacking the kidneys and transforming them into thin-walled sacks of clotted black blood, that could rupture at the patient's smallest movement. The blackwater fever, when the urine changed to dark mulberry-coloured blood, and few, very few victims, ever recovered.

'She was strong,' Sarah went on quietly. 'She was the last of them to go.' She turned her head towards the other neglected graves. Thc curly pods of the acacia were scattered thickly over the unadorned mounds. 'We buried her here, while Manali was still with his devils. But later, when he could walk he came with the book and said the words for her. He built the cross with his own hands.'

'Then he went away again?' Robyn asked.

'No, he was very sick, and new devils came to him. He wept for your mother.' The thought of her father weeping was something so completely alien that Robyn could not imagine it. 'He spoke often of the river that had destroyed him.'

Through the acacia trees there were glimpses of the wide green river, and both their heads turned towards it naturally.

'He came to hate that river as though it was a living enemy that had denied him a road to his dreams. He was like a man demented, for the fever came and went. At times he would battle with his devils, shouting his defiance the way a warrior *giyas* at the enemy host.' The *giya* was a challenge dance with which the Nguni warrior baits his adversary. 'At other times he would speak wildly of machines that would tame his enemy, of walls that he would build across the waters to carry men and ships up above the gorge.' Sarah broke off, her lovely dark moon face stricken with the memory, and the child sensed her distress and came to her, kneeling on the earth and laying his dusty little head in her lap. She stroked the tight cap of curls with an absentminded caress.

With a sudden little chill of shock Robyn recognized the child. Her expression changed so drastically that Sarah followed the direction of her gaze, looking down with all her attention at the head in her lap, then up again to meet Robyn's eyes. It did not really need words to pass, the question was posed and answered with silent exchange of feminine understanding, and Sarah drew the child towards her with a protective gesture.

'It was only after your mother . . .' Sarah began to explain and then fell silent, and Robyn went on staring at the little boy. It was Zouga at the same age, a dusky miniature Zouga. It was only the colour of his skin which had prevented her from seeing it immediately.

Robyn felt as though the earth had lurched beneath her feet, then it steadied again and she felt a strange sense of release. Fuller Ballantyne was no longer the godlike figure hewn from unforgiving, unbending granite that had overshadowed her entire life.

She held out both her hands to the child and he went to her unhesitatingly, trustingly. Robyn embraced him, and his skin was smooth and warm as she kissed him. He wriggled against her like a puppy, and she felt a deep glow of affection and of gratitude to the child.

'He was very sick,' said Sarah softly, 'and alone. They had all gone or died, and he was sad, so that I feared for his life.'

Robyn nodded understanding. 'And you loved him?'

'There was no sin in it, for he was a God,' said Sarah simply.

'No,' thought Robyn with intense relief. 'He was a man, and I, his daughter, am a woman.'

In that moment she knew that she never need again feel shame and guilt for her body and the demands and desires which sprang from it. She hugged the child who was proof of her father's humanity, and Sarah smiled with relief.

For the first time in her life Robyn was able to face the fact that she loved her father, and she understood part of the compulsion that over the years had grown stronger rather than dwindling.

The longing she had felt for the father had been submerged

completely by the awe and majesty of the legend. Now she knew why she was here, on the banks of this majestic river, on the very frontier of the known world. She had come not to find Fuller Ballantyne, but to discover rather the father and the self that she had never known before.

'Where is he, Sarah, where is my father? Which way did he go?' she demanded eagerly, but the woman dropped her eyes.

'I do not know,' she whispered. 'I woke one morning and he was gone. I do not know where he is, but I will wait for him, until he returns to me and his son.' She looked up quickly. 'He will come back?' she asked pathetically. 'If not to me then for the child?'

'Yes,' Robyn answered with certainty that she did not feel. 'Of course he will come back.'

The selection of porters was a lengthy business, and after Zouga had signalled his choice with a slap on the shoulder, the men were sent to Robyn's tent to be examined for signs of disease or infirmity that might prevent them performing their duties.

Then came the allocation of packs.

Although Zouga had already made up and weighed each pack, making sure that not one of them exceeded the stipulated eighty pounds weight, the newly engaged porters had to watch the loads reweighed publicly, and then there was interminable haggling over the size and balance of the burden that each of them would carry for months, perhaps even years ahead.

Although Zouga brusquely forbade Pereira to hasten the selection process with his kurbash, and entered good-naturedly into the spirit of banter and bargain, he was, in fact, using the occasion to assess the spirit of his men, to pick out the malcontents who would sour that spirit in the hardships ahead, and also to select the natural leaders to whom the others turned instinctively for decision.

The following day when planning the order of march, Zouga used the knowledge he had gained in this way. To begin with, seven of the more obvious trouble-makers were given a *khete* of beads each and ordered out of the camp without explanation or apology. Then Zouga called out five of the brightest and best and made them captains of divisions of twenty porters each.

They would be responsible for maintaining the pace of the march, for preventing pilfering of the loads, making and breaking camp, distributing rations, and acting as the spokesmen of each division, presenting complaints to and transmitting orders from Zouga.

When the roll was complete there were one hundred and twenty-six names upon it, including Sergeant Cheroot's Hottentots, the porters who had come up from Quelimane, Camacho Pereira and the two principals – Robyn and Zouga himself.

It would be a slow and unwieldy caravan unless properly organized, that was bad enough – but on the march it would also be very vulnerable. Zouga gave much thought to defence of the column, and he and Sergeant Cheroot shared the last quarter bottle of whisky as they pooled their experience and planned the order of march.

Zouga, with a small party of local guides and personal bearers, planned to travel independently of the main caravan, reconnoitering the terrain ahead of the march, and making himself free to prospect and hunt as the opportunity arose. He would return most nights to rejoin the caravan, but would be equipped to spend many days out of contact.

Camacho Pereira with five of the Hottentot musketeers would lead the van of the main column, and even when Robyn chaffed him lightly, Zouga saw nothing ludicrous in Camacho marching under the Union Jack.

'It's an English expedition, and we will carry the flag,' Zouga replied stiffly.

'Rule, Britannia,' Robyn laughed irreverently, and Zouga ignored her and went on describing the order of march.

The divisions of porters would remain separate but closed up, and Sergeant Cheroot with the remainder of his musketeers would form the rearguard of the column.

There was a simple system of signals to control the movements of the column, a pre-arranged series of blasts on the kudu-horn trumpets would sound the 'march' or 'halt', the 'close up' or 'form square'.

For four days Zouga exercised the column in these evolutions and though proficiency would only come much later, at last he felt that they were ready to make a start, and he told Robyn so.

'But how are we to cross the river?' she asked looking across at the north bank.

The river was half a mile wide, and the heavy rainfalls over millions of square miles had drained into it. The flow was swift and powerful. If they were going northwards to the Shire river and Lake Marawi they would need a flotilla of dugout canoes and many days to make the crossing to the north bank.

The steam launch *Helen* had long ago departed on the flood of the river, making good at least twenty knots with the current pushing her, so she would already be back in Quelimane.

'All the arrangements have been made,' Zouga told her, and she had to be satisfied with that.

On the last day Robyn allowed Juba to accompany her to the cemetery for the first time, and both of them were laden with gifts. Bolts of trade cloth and a thirty-five-pound bag of ceramic beads, the most sought-after scarlet *sam-sam* variety.

It was as much as she dare ask for from the expedition's stores without arousing Zouga's ire and interest.

She had thought of telling Zouga of Sarah and the child, but had wisely decided against it.

Zouga's reaction to finding a half-brother of mixed blood was too terrible to contemplate. Zouga had acquired his opinions on caste and colour in the hard school of the Indian army, and to find that his own father had trespassed against these iron rules would be too much of a shock. Instead, Robyn had mentioned that she had met one of her father's former servants, who tended their mother's grave over the years. The gift would have to be in proportion to these services.

Sarah and her child were waiting by the grave, and she accepted the gifts with a gracious little curtsy and her palms held together at the level of her eyes.

'We leave tomorrow,' Robyn explained, and saw the immediate regret in Sarah's eyes, followed by acceptance.

'It is God's will,' and Robyn could almost hear her father saying it.

Juba and the child soon became involved in collecting the pods from a kaffir boom tree nearby and stringing together the pretty scarlet lucky beans, each with its little black eye at the end to make necklaces and bracelets. The two of them, girl and boy, made a delightfully uninhibited pair, their laughter and shrill happy voices a pleasant background to the talk under the acacia tree.

Robyn and Sarah had become friends in the short time they had known each other. Her father had written in his *Missionary Travels* that he preferred the company of black people to white, and certainly all the evidence seemed to point that way. It seemed that Fuller Ballantyne had done nothing but squabble with his own kind. Contact with other white men seemed to bring out in him all the pettiness, suspicion and jealousy of his complex nature; while he had spent the greater part of his life with black men, and received from them trust and honour and lasting friendships. His relationship with Sarah was only a natural extension of those feelings, Robyn realized. She contrasted these feelings with those of her brother, and knew that he could never cross the dividing line. A black man could possibly earn Zouga's liking and even his respect, but the gulf was too wide. For Zouga they would always be 'those people', and she guessed that he could never change in that. If he lived on in Africa for another fifty years, he would never learn to understand them, while she, within weeks, had made real friendships. She wondered if, like her father, she would come one day to prefer them to her own kind. It didn't seem possible now, but she recognized in herself the capacity for adjustment and change.

Beside her, Sarah was speaking, so softly, so shyly that Robyn had to make an effort to tear herself away from her own thoughts and ask:

'What was that you said?'

'Your father, Manali, will you tell him about the boy when you find him?'

'He did not know?' Robyn was stunned, and Sarah shook her head.

'Why did you not go with him then?' Robyn demanded.

'He did not wish it. He said the journey would be too hard, but in reality, he is like an old bull elephant who does not like to stay too long with his cows but always must follow the wind.'

Camacho Pereira towered above the wiry little tribesmen, checking off their names against the camp register. This evening he wore a jerkin of kudu skin that was decorated with fancy stitching and trade beads, and unfastened down the front to expose bulging hairy chest and the flat belly with its ridged muscles like the patterns in the sand of a windswept beach.

'We feed them too much,' he told Zouga. 'Fat nigger is lazy nigger.' He chuckled when he saw Zouga's expression, for that word had already been the cause of dissension. Zouga had forbidden him to use it, particularly in front of the expedition's black servants, for some of them it was the only word of English they understood. 'Feed small, kick heavy and they work hard,' Camacho went on with relish.

Zouga ignored these gems of philosophy. He had heard them before, many times. Instead he turned to the captains of divisions, and watched them finish the rationing.

Two of them, their arms floury to the elbows, dipped into the bags of meal and doled it out to the shrinking line of porters. Each man had his calabash or chipped enamel basin to receive the scoop of stone-ground red-brown grain. Then one of the other captains slapped a split and smoked river fish on top of the pile. The fish looked like Scotch kippers, but their odour punched like a prize-fighter. Weevils, maggots and all, they were a delicacy that the porters would miss once they left the river.

Pereira suddenly hauled a man out of the line and hit him a lusty clout across the back of the head with the stock of his kurbash.

'He come twice, try for double,' he explained cheerfully, and took a playful kick at the man as he ran. If it had landed it would have knocked him off his feet, but all the porters had come to anticipate Camacho's flying boots.

Zouga waited until the last porter had been rationed, then he called to the captains.

'*Indaba!* Tell the men, *indaba.*'

It was the call to council, to discuss affairs of consequence, and the whole camp left the cooking fires and came hurrying, agog with excitement.

Zouga paced up and down before the ranks of intent squatting black men, drawing out the moment, for he had come quickly to realize the African love of the theatrical. Most of them could understand the basic Nguni which Zouga now spoke with some fluency, for many of them were Shangaans or Angoni.

Now he spread his arms to his audience, paused for a second and then announced portentously,

'*Kusasa isufari*, tomorrow the march begins!'

There was a hive murmur of comment and excitement, and then one of the captains rose from the front rank.

'*Phi? Phi?* Where? Which way?'

Zouga lowered his arms, and let the suspense build up for a few moments, and then he stabbed out towards the far blue southern hills with a bunched fist.

'*Laphaya!* That way!'

They roared with approval, just as they would have done if Zouga had pointed north or west for that matter. They were ready to go now. The direction was not important. The captains of divisions, the indunas, were shouting out the translation to those who had not understood and the first roar of the crowd settled to a boisterous rumble of comment and speculation, but it died away suddenly, and Zouga turned quickly.

Camacho Pereira had stepped beside Zouga, and his face was swollen and dark with rage. This was the first time he had heard Zouga's intention to go southwards so that when he started to speak, it was so forcefully that droplets of spittle flew from his lips. He was using one of the local dialects, and speaking so swiftly that Zouga understood only a word here and there. The sense was unmistakable, however, and he saw the shock on the faces of the men who squatted before them.

Camacho was warning them of the dangers beyond the southern hills. Zouga heard the word 'Monomatapa' and knew that he was speaking of the terrible armies of the legendary empire, merciless legions whose favourite sport was to cut off a man's genitals and force him to eat them himself. The shock of the listening black faces was changing swiftly to terror and Camacho had been speaking for only a few seconds, a minute more and nothing would induce the caravan to march, two minutes more and most of his porters would have deserted by morning.

There was nothing to be gained by arguing with the Portuguese except an unseemly shouting match, which would be watched with interest by the entire assembled camp. One thing that Zouga had learned was that the Africans, like the Asians he had come to know well in India, were immensely respectful of a victor and impressed by success. He could demonstrate neither qualities by becoming embroiled in an undignified wrangle in a language that none of the spectators could understand.

'Pereira!' he snapped, in a tone that cut through the

Portuguese's torrent of words, and for an instant stilled them. Zouga had the Englishman's peculiar sense of fair play which made him warn an enemy before an attack. As the Portuguese turned to face him, Zouga swung in towards him with two light steps and he flicked his left hand at Camacho's eyes, forcing him to throw up both hands to protect his face. As he did so, Zouga slammed his fist into his belly, just under the ribs, with a force that doubled him in the middle, his breath whooshing out of his gaping mouth in an agonized explosion of sound and his hand dropping to cover his injured belly, leaving his face open for the next blow.

It was a short chopping left-handed shot that took Camacho cleanly under the right ear, on the hinge of the jaw. The plumed beaver hat spun off his head. His eyes rolled up into his skull, leaving the whites glaring madly, and Camacho's knees gave way under him. He pitched forward, making no effort to cushion his fall and dropped face down on to the grey sandy soil.

The silence lasted only a second, and then a shout went up from the watchers. Most of them had felt Camacho's boots or his kurbash, and they hugged one another happily. The trepidation that Camacho's little speech had raised was completely lost in wonder at the swiftness and the effect of those two blows. Most of them had never seen a man strike with a bunched hand, and the novelty of this form of combat impressed and delighted them.

Casually, Zouga turned his back on the prone figure. Not a trace of anger showed on his face, in fact he was smiling slightly as he strolled down the front rank of men and lifted one hand to quieten them.

'There are soldiers who travel with us,' he told them, in a low voice that yet reached clearly to every one of them, 'and you have seen them shoot.' He had made sure they had, and that news of the prowess in weapons of Sergeant Cheroot's men would travel ahead of them.

'You see that flag?' He flung one hand dramatically at the red and white and blue jack floating above the main tent on its improvised flag pole. 'No man, no chief nor warrior dare. . . .'

'Zouga!' shrieked Robyn. To the terrible urgency of her tone Zouga reacted instantly, spinning aside with two dancing paces, and the crowd exploded with a single word, a deep drawn-out 'Jee!'

It is a blood-chilling sound, for it is the cry with which an African warrior encourages himself or another in the fatal moments of a battle to the death.

Camacho's stroke had been aimed at the small of Zouga's back. He was a man who had fought with the knife many times before, and he had not taken the more tempting target between the shoulder blades, where the point could turn against the ribs. He had gone for the soft area above the kidneys, and even with Robyn's warning, Zouga was not quite quick enough. The point raked his hip, slitting the cloth of his breeches in a six-inch rent, beneath which skin and flesh opened cleanly and the bright blood spread swiftly to the knee.

'Jee!' The deep sonorous chant of the watchers as Camacho reversed the stroke of his extended right hand, cutting sideways at Zouga's belly. The blade twinkled and hissed like an angry cobra, ten inches of tempered steel, and Zouga threw up his hands and sucked in his belly muscles as he jumped back. There was a sharp tug as the point caught in his shirt, but it did not touch the skin.

'Jee!' again as Camacho lunged. His face was bloated and mottled with purple and white, the eyes squinting with rage and the after-effects of the blow to his jaw. Zouga felt the sting of the wound on his hip pulling open as he swayed back out of the path of the blade, and the stronger flood of warm blood down his leg.

He paused out of range of the knife for Zouga had heard the snap of a weapon being cocked and from the corner of his eye he saw Sergeant Cheroot levelling the Enfield, waiting for a clear shot at the Portuguese.

'No! Don't shoot!' Zouga called urgently. He did not relish a bullet in his own belly, for he and Camacho were dancing close together, with the weaving point of the knife seeming to bind them to each other.

'Don't shoot, Sergeant!' There was another reason why he could afford no interference. There were a hundred men judging him now, men with whom he would march and work in the months and years ahead. He needed their respect.

'Jee!' sang the watchers, and Camacho was panting with rage. Again the blade in his right hand whispered like the wing of a swallow in flight, and this time Zouga over-reacted, blundering back half a dozen paces, and then losing his balance for a moment he dropped on one knee and put a hand to the ground to steady himself. But as Camacho charged again, he rebounded to his feet and arched his hips aside, the way a matador swings out of the line of the bull's run. In the hand that had touched the ground, Zouga held a handful of the coarse grey sand.

His eyes were locked to those of the Portuguese, it was the eyes not the knife hand that would signal Camacho's intentions. They flickered left, while the hand feigned the other way, and Zouga moved in past the blade, and was ready again when Camacho rounded.

They faced each other, shuffling in a slow cycle that stirred wisps of pale dust around their feet. Camacho kept the knife low, and stirred it gently as though he was conducting a slow passage of music, but Zouga studying his eyes saw the first small nervous flickers of uncertainty.

He jumped in, launching himself off the right foot.

'Jee!' roared the watchers, and for the first time Camacho broke ground, falling back and then turning hurriedly as Zouga checked and feinted to his open side.

Twice more Zouga drove him back with threats, until it needed only a feint with his upper body to make Camacho scramble away. The watchers were laughing now, mocking shouts of glee every time he gave ground, and the rage that had flushed Camacho's face had given way to fear, the angry purple mottling had chilled to white. Zouga was still watching his eyes, as they darted from side to side seeking an escape – but the knife kept weaving between them, bright and razor sharp, broad as three fingers and grooved along its length to break the suction of clinging wet flesh once it was buried.

Camacho's eyes flickered away once more and Zouga moved, pulling the knife hand around as he crossed the man's front, holding out his empty hand for the eyes to follow, keeping the other low and moving in as close to the knife as he dared, then at the moment that Camacho lunged, using the momentum of his avoiding turn, he hurled the handful of coarse sand into Camacho's eyes – blinding him, and still in the same movement reversing his direction, and going straight in on the knife, chancing it all on locking the wrist before the man could see again.

'Jee!' the crowd roared as Camacho's wrist slapped into Zouga's palm, and he locked it down with all his strength.

Tears were already streaming from Camacho's eyes, and his

lids fluttered, grinding the sharp grains across the unseeing eyeballs. He could not judge nor meet Zouga's weight as, still locked grimly to the wrist, he threw him off-balance. As Camacho went over, Zouga reared back, resisting with all his strength, holding the knife arm against the fall. Something went with a loud rubbery popping sound in Camacho's shoulder and he screamed, as he sprawled again, face down, with the arm twisted up behind him.

Once again Zouga jerked viciously, and this time Camacho screeched like a girl and the knife dropped from his fingers. He made a feeble effort to snatch it with the other hand, but Zouga trod down on the blade with a booted foot, then scooped it up, released the damaged arm and stepped back holding the heavy weapon in his right hand.

'*Bulala!*' chanted the watchers. '*Bulala!* Kill him! Kill him!' They wanted to see the blood, for that was the fitting end and they hungered for it.

Zouga stabbed the blade deeply into the trunk of the acacia tree and then wrenched against the steel. It snapped at the hilt with a crack like a pistol shot, and he dropped the hilt contemptuously.

'Sergeant Cheroot,' he said, 'get him out of this camp.'

'I should shoot him,' the little Hottentot told him as he came up, and thrust the muzzle of the Enfield rifle into the fallen man's belly.

'If he tries to enter the camp again, you can shoot him. But now just get him out.'

'Big mistake,' Sergeant Cheroot's pug face took on a theatrically mournful expression. 'Always stamp on the scorpion – before he stings.'

'You are hurt.' Robyn was running towards him.

'It's a scratch.' Zouga unwound the bandanna from around his throat and pressed it to the wound in his hip as he strode away towards his tent, forcing himself not to favour it with a limp. He had to get away quickly for the reaction was on him, he felt dizzy and nauseated, the wound stung abominably, and he did not want anybody to see that his hands were trembling.

'I reset the shoulder,' Robyn told Zouga as she bound up his hip wound. 'I don't think there is anything broken, and it went in again very neatly – but you,' she shook her head, 'you won't be able to march with that. Every step will pull against the stitches.'

She was right, it was four days before the march could begin, and Camacho Pereira put that time to good use. He had left an hour after Robyn reset his dislocated shoulder, four paddlers taking a dugout canoe down the Zambezi with the current. When they would have pulled into the bank to make camp, Camacho snarled at them from the bows where he crouched, hugging the injured arm, that even after being set and strapped into a sling, still ached so fiercely that it lit little white sparks of agony behind his closed eyelids every time he tried to doze.

He also would have liked to rest, but his hatred drove him onwards, and the dugout canoe arrowed down-current under a fat yellow moon that paled slowly at the coming of the new day.

Camacho went ashore on the south bank of the Zambezi at noon at the small native village at Chamba, a hundred miles below Tete.

He paid off the crew of the dugout and he hired two bearers to carry his rifle and blanket roll. Then he set off again immediately along the network of narrow foot paths that crisscross the entire African continent like the blood vessels of a living body, laid down by wandering men and migrating animals over the centuries.

Two days later he reached the Hyena Road that runs from the mountains of Dismay, Inyangaza, to the sea. The Hyena Road was a secret track. Although it paralleled the old road from the coast to Vila Manica, it kept forty miles north of it, following the course of the Pungwe river so that there would be water for the multitudes who unwillingly used the road on their long, last journey from their homeland to other lands, other continents.

Vila Manica was the last outpost of the Portuguese administration in East Africa. A decree by the Governor in council forbade any man, black or white, Portuguese or foreigner, to journey beyond that clay-walled fort towards the haunting range of mountains with the chilling name. It was for this reason that the Hyena Road had been secretly opened by enterprising men, and pushed up through the dense forests of the lower slopes to the bleak and open grasslands atop the mountains.

The march from Chamba to the Pungwe river was a hundred and fifty miles. To make it in three days with the agony of a healing shoulder was good going, and once they reached it, the temptation to rest was almost irresistible. But Camacho kicked his two bearers to their feet and drove them with stinging words and lash along the deserted road towards the mountains.

The road was twice as wide as any of the other footpaths they had followed to reach it, wide enough for a double column rather than the Indian file that was the usual order of African travel. Although the surface had been beaten hard by the passage of thousands of bare feet, it was a source of satisfaction to Camacho that the road had clearly not been used for many months, except by the occasional herd of antelope, and once, perhaps a week before, by an old bull elephant, whose huge piles of dung had long dried out.

'The caravan has not passed yet,' Camacho muttered, as he scanned the trees ahead for the shapes of the vultures and searched without success for the sly skulking shapes of hyena in the undergrowth beside the road.

True there were human bones scattered along the route, here and there the thick knuckle of the thigh bone that had defied even the iron jaws of the scavengers, or other splintered fragments that they had overlooked, but even these were dried out and bleached white. They were the debris of the previous caravan that had passed this way three months before.

He had reached the road in time, and now he hurried along it, pausing now and then to listen or to send one of the bearers up a tree to search ahead.

However, it was two days later that they heard the first faint sound of many voices, and this time Camacho himself climbed to the highest fork of one of the umsisa trees beside the track, and peering ahead he saw the vultures circling, a wide slow wheel of tiny black specks turning against the silver and blue ranges of cloud, as though caught in a hidden vortex of the high heavens.

He sat in the fork thirty feet above the ground, while the sound of voices grew stronger, became the sound of singing. This was no sound of joy, but a terrible mourning dirge, slow and heart-breaking, rising and fading as flukes of the breeze and folds of the ground blanketed the sound, but each time it came back a little stronger, until Camacho could make out far away the head of the column, like the head of a maimed serpent writhing out of the forest into an open glade a mile ahead.

He slid down the trunk of the umsisa, and hurried forward. There was an armed party ahead of the main column, five blacks dressed in the tatters of cast-off European-style clothing and carrying muskets, but at their head was a white man, a little man with a face like a vicious gnome, wrinkled and burned darkly by the sun. The thick drooping black moustache was laced with grey, but he stepped out with a bouncing elastic stride and he recognized Camacho from two hundred paces and snatched his hat off his head and waved it.

He shouted 'Camacho!' and the two men ran to embrace, and then hold each other at arm's length, laughing with pleasure. It was Camacho who sobered first, the laughter changing to a scowl as he said,

'Alphonse, my beloved brother, I have bad tidings – the worst possible.'

'The Englishman?' Alphonse was still smiling, he had a tooth missing from the front of his upper jaw, which made the cold humourless smile seem less dangerous than it really was.

'Yes, the Englishman,' Camacho nodded. 'You know of him?'

'My father sent a message. I know.' Alphonse was the Governor of Quelimane's eldest surviving son, full-blooded Portuguese by the lawfully wedded bride who had come out forty years previously from Lisbon, a pale sickly mail-order bride, who had borne three sons in swift succession, the first two of which had succumbed to malaria and infantile dysentery even before the appearance of the little wizened yellowed mite whom they had named Alphonse Jose Vila y Pereira, and expected to bury with his brothers before the end of the rains. However, it was the mother they had buried in the end, and the child had flourished at the breast of a black wet nurse.

'He did not go north, then?' Alphonse demanded, and Camacho dropped his eyes guiltily, for he was speaking to the eldest, full-blooded and legitimate son.

Camacho himself was a bastard and a half-breed, son of one of the Governor's once beautiful Mulatto concubines, now fat and faded and forgotten in one of the back rooms of the seraglio. He was not even recognized as a son, but had to bear the ignominious title of nephew. This in itself was enough for him to show respect for the other, but added to this Alphonse was as determined as their father had been at the same age, though even crueller and harder. Camacho had seen him sing a plaintive fado as he flogged a man to death, accompanying the traditional love song with the flute and percussion of the lash.

'He did not go north,' Camacho agreed uneasily.

'You were told to see that he did.'

'I could not stop him. He is English,' Camacho's voice croaked a little, 'he is stubborn.'

'We will speak again of that,' Alphonse promised coldly. 'Now, swiftly tell me where he is and what he plans to do.'

Camacho recited the explanation he had prepared, skirting delicately around the most offensive parts of the story, and dwelling on subjects such as the wealth that the Ballantyne expedition carried with it rather than his own brutal beating at the Englishman's hands.

Alphonse had thrown himself down in the shade of a tree beside the track and listened broodingly, chewing at the straggling ends of his moustache, filling in for himself the conspicuous gaps in his half-brother's recital, and speaking again only at the end.

'When will he leave the valley of the Zambezi?'

'Soon,' Camacho hedged, for the unpredictable Englishman might already be half-way to the escarpment. 'Although I cut him deeply, it may be he has had himself carried in a *mushila* (litter).'

'He must not be allowed to enter the Monomatapa,' Alphonse said flatly, and came to his feet with a single lithe movement. 'The best place to do the business would be in the bad ground below the rim of the valley.'

He glanced back along the winding road. The head of the column was a mile away still, across a glade of open golden grass. The shuffling double rank of bowed creatures, yoked at the neck, did not seem human, though the singing was sad and beautiful.

'I can spare fifteen men.'

'It will not be enough,' Camacho cut in swiftly.

'It will be,' said his brother coldly, 'if you do the business in the night.'

'Twenty men,' Camacho pleaded. 'He has soldiers with him, trained soldiers and he is a soldier himself.'

Alphonse was silent, weighing risk and advantage – but the worst part of the Hyena Road already lay behind the column, and each mile nearer the coast, the land was tamer, the risk diminished and the need for guards less pressing.

'Twenty!' he agreed abruptly, and turned to Camacho. 'But not one of the foreigners must escape.' Looking into his brother's cold black eyes, Camacho felt his skin crawl. 'Leave no sign, bury them deep, so the jackal and hyena do not dig them out. Use the porters to carry the expedition's equipment to the place in the hills, and when they have done so, kill them also. We will bring it down with the next caravan to the coast.'

'Si. Si. I understand.'

'Do not fail us again, my beloved cousin-brother.' Alphonse made the endearment a threat, and Camacho swallowed with a nervous little gulp.

'I will leave as soon as I have rested.'

'No,' Alphonse shook his head. 'You will leave immediately. Once that Englishman enters the land beyond the mountains, there will soon be no more slaves. It is bad enough that there has been no gold for twenty years and more, but if the river of slaves were to dry up, both my father and I would be displeased – very displeased.'

At Zouga's order the long mournful blast of the kudu-horn trumpet shattered the silence of the utterly dark hour before the dawn.

The Indunas took up the cry 'Safari! We march!' and they prodded the sleeping porters off their reed sleeping-mats. The camp fires had burned down to dim red mounds of coals smothered in the soft grey powder of their own ash. As fresh logs were thrown upon them they flared up in a false dawn that lit the underside of the umbrella-shaped acacia trees with wavering yellow light.

The smell of roasting *ropoko* cakes rose on tendrils of pale smoke straight into the windless dark sky. The muted voices became louder, more cheerful as the flames drove away the chills and the nightmares.

'Safari!' The cry was taken up, and the divisions assembled, ghostly figures in the gloom, emerging more clearly as the growing dawn light paled the sky and snuffed out the stars.

'Safari!' And the mass of men and equipment resolved itself and order grew out of chaos.

Like those long columns of big shiny black serowe ants that endlessly cross and re-cross the African earth, the stream of porters moved steadily away into the still gloomy forest.

As each of them passed Zouga and Robyn standing together at the gate of the thorn *scherm*, they shouted a greeting and executed a few prancing steps to demonstrate their loyalty and enthusiasm – while Robyn laughed with them and Zouga called encouragement.

'We no longer have a guide, and we don't know where we are going.' She took Zouga's arm. 'What is to become of us?'

'If we knew, it would take all the fun out of it.'

'At least a guide.'

'While you thought I was hunting I went out as far as the escarpment which is further than that swaggering Portuguese ever went, further than any white man, except of course Pater, has ever been. Follow me, Sissy, I am your guide.'

She looked up at him now in the strengthening light of coming dawn.

'I knew you were not hunting,' she told him.

'The escarpment is rugged and very broken, but I have examined two passes through the telescope that I think will go—'

'And beyond that?'

He laughed, 'We will find out.' Then he squeezed her around the waist. 'That is the whole fun of the thing.'

She studied his face with full attention for a few moments. The new full beard emphasized the strong, almost stubborn, lines of his jaw. There was a piratical devil-may-care lift to the corner of his lips, and Robyn realized that no man of conventional mind would have proposed and engineered this expedition. She knew he possessed courage, his exploits in India had proved that beyond doubt, and yet when she looked at his sketches and water colours and read the rough notes he was making for the book, she discovered a sensitivity and an imagination she had never before suspected. He was a difficult person to know and understand.

Perhaps she could have told him about Sarah and the child or even about Mungo St John, and that night in the main cabin of *Huron*, for when he laughed like this, the stern features softened with humour and humanity, and green lights sparkled in his eyes.

'That's what we arc here for, Sissy, the fun of it all.'

'And the gold,' she teased, 'and the ivory.'

'Yes, by God, the gold and ivory as well. Come on, Sissy, this is where it truly begins,' and he limped after the column as its tail disappeared into the acacia forest, favouring his injured leg and using a freshly cut staff to move across the sandy earth. For a moment Robyn hesitated and then she shrugged aside her doubts and ran to catch up with her brother.

That first day the porters were rested and eager, the valley floor flat and the going easy, so Zouga ordered *tirikeza*, the double march, so that even at their slow pace the column left many miles of dusty grey earth behind them that day.

They marched until the heat came up in the middle of the morning and the merciless sun dried the sweat the moment it burst through their pores and left tiny salt crystals on the skin, that sparkled like diamond chips. Then they found shade and lay like dead men through the heat of noon, stirring again only when the lowering sun gave the illusion of cooling the air and the blast of the kudu-horn trumpet forced them to their feet again.

The second stage of the *tirikeza* lasted until sunset when it became too dark to see the ground under their feet.

The fires were dying and the voices of the porters in their thorn bush *scherms* had slowly descended through the occasional mutter and soft murmur to ultimate silence before Zouga left his tent and limped silently as a night creature out of the camp.

He carried the Sharps rifle slung over his shoulder, the staff in one hand and a bull's eye lantern in the other, while the Colt revolver hung in its holster upon his belt. Once clear of the camp, he stepped out as briskly as his leg would allow two miles along the freshly beaten footpath that the column had made that afternoon until he reached the fallen tree trunk that was the agreed rendezvous.

He stopped and whistled softly, and a smaller figure stepped out from the undergrowth into the moonlight, carrying a rifle at high-port. The jaunty step and alert set of head on narrow shoulders was unmistakable.

'All is well, Sergeant.'

'We are ready, Major.'

Zouga inspected the ambush positions that Sergeant Cheroot had chosen for his men astride the path. The little Hottentot had a good eye for ground and Zouga found his trust and liking for him increasing with every such display of competence.

'A puff?' Jan Cheroot asked now, with the clay pipe already in his mouth.

'No smoking,' Zouga shook his head. 'They will smell it.' And Jan Cheroot reluctantly buttoned the pipe into his hip pocket.

Zouga had chosen a position in the centre of the line, where he could make himself comfortable against the trunk of the fallen tree. He settled down with a sigh, his leg thrust out stiffly ahead of him – after the *tirikeza* it was going to be a long wearying night.

The moon was a few days short of full, and it was almost light enough to read the headlines of a newspaper. The bush was alive with the scurry and rustle of small animals, and it kept their nerves tightened and their ears strained to catch the other sounds for which they waited.

Zouga was the first to hear the click of a pebble striking against another. He whistled softly and Jan Cheroot snapped his fingers, imitating the sound of a black scarab beetle to show that he was alert. The moon had dropped low upon the hills, and its light through the forest trees laid silver and black tiger stripes upon the earth and played tricks with the eye.

Something moved in the forest, and then was gone, but Zouga picked up the whisper of bare feet scuffling the sandy disturbed earth of the path, and then suddenly they were there, and very close, man shapes in file, hurrying, silent, furtive. Zouga counted them, eight – no nine. Each of them straight-backed under the bulky burden he carried balanced upon his head. Zouga's anger simmered to the surface and yet at the same time he felt a grim sense of satisfaction that he had not wasted the night.

As the leading figure in the file came level with the fallen tree trunk, Zouga pointed the muzzle of the Sharps rifle straight into the air and pressed the trigger. The crash of the shot broke the night into a hundred echoes that bounced and rebounded through the forest, and the silence magnified it until it seemed like the thunder of all the heaven.

The echoes had not dispersed, and the nine dark figures were still frozen with shock when Jan Cheroot's Hottentots fell upon them from every direction in a shrieking pack.

The sound of their cries was so shrill, so inhuman, that it even startled Zouga, while the effect on the victims was miraculous. They let fall the burdens they carried, and dropped to earth in a paralysis of superstitious awe, adding their wails and screams to the pandemonium. Then the thud and clatter of cudgels against skull and cringing flesh mingled with it all, and the screams and howls rose to a new pitch.

Jan Cheroot's men had spent much time and care on selecting and cutting their clubs and now they wielded them with a lusty glee, making up for a night of discomfort and boredom. Sergeant Cheroot himself was in the thick of it, and in his excitement he had almost lost his voice. He was yipping squeakily like a demented fox terrier with a cat up a tree.

Zouga knew he would have to stop it soon, before they killed or seriously maimed somebody, but the punishment was richly earned, and he gave it a minute more. He even joined in himself when one of the prostrate figures scrambled to its feet and tried to dart away into the undergrowth. Zouga swung his staff and brought him down again with a blow to the back of his knees, and when he sprang up again as though he were on springs, Zouga dropped him in the dust with a short right-handed punch to the side of the head.

Then, stepping back out of the fray, Zouga took one of his few remaining cheroots from his top pocket, and lit it from the chimney of the lantern, inhaling with deep satisfaction, while around him the enthusiasm of his Hottentots flagged a little as they tired and Jan Cheroot regained his voice and became coherent for the first time.

'*Slat hulle, kerels!* Hit them, boys!'

It was time to stop it, Zouga decided and opened the shutter of the lantern.

'That's enough, Sergeant,' he ordered, and the thuds of blows became intermittent and then ceased while the Hottentots rested on the cudgels, panting and streaming with the honest sweat of their exertions.

The deserting porters lay moaning and whimpering in pitiful

heaps, with their loot scattered about them. Some of the packs had burst open, and trade cloth and beads, flasks of gunpowder, knives, mirrors and glass jewellery were strewn about and trodden into the dirt. Zouga's fury returned at full strength when he recognized the tin box which contained his dress uniform and hat. He delivered a last kick at the nearest figure and then growled at Sergeant Cheroot,

'Get them on their feet and clean it up.'

The nine deserters were marched into camp, roped together and bearing not only the heavy burdens which they had stolen – but also an impressive set of contusions, cuts and bruises. Lips were swollen and split, some teeth were missing, a good many eyes were puffed closed and most of their heads were as lumpy as newly-picked Jerusalem artichokes.

More painful than their injuries, however, was the ridicule of the entire camp which turned out to a man to jeer and mock them with laughter.

Zouga lined up the captives, with their booty piled in front of them, and in the presence of their peers made a speech in limping but expressive Swahili in which he likened them to sneaking jackals and lurking hyena and fined them each a month's wages.

The audience was delighted with the show, and hooted at every insult while the culprits tried physically to shrink themselves into insignificance. There was not one of the watching porters who would not have done the same thing. In fact, had the escape succeeded, most of them would have followed the next night, but now that it had been foiled, they could enjoy the vicarious pleasure of having escaped punishment, and the discomfort of their companions who had committed the sin of being caught.

During the noon rest that divided the two stages of the next day's *tirikeza*, the clusters of porters chatting in the shade of the mopani groves agreed that they had found a strong master to follow, one whom it would not be easy to cheat, and it gave them all confidence for the future of the safari. Coming directly after his defeat of the Portuguese, the recapture of the deserting porters added immeasurably to Zouga's standing.

The four indunas of the divisions agreed that it was fitting that such a man have a praise-name. They conferred at length, and after considering many suggestions, finally decided on 'Bakela'.

'Bakela' means 'the one-who-strikes-with-the-fist', for this was still the one of Zouga's many accomplishments which impressed them most.

Where Bakela led, they were now prepared to follow, and though Zouga spread a dragnet of his faithful Hottentots behind the column each of the following nights, no more fish swam into it.

'How many?' Zouga whispered, and Jan Cheroot rocked on his heels, sucking softly on the empty clay pipe and squinting his oriental eyes thoughtfully, before he shrugged, 'Too many to count. Two hundred, three hundred, perhaps even four.'

The ground had been ploughed up into soft fluffy dust by the multitude of huge cloven hooves, and the dark pats of dung were round and shaped in little concentric circles, completely indistinguishable from those of domestic cattle, and the rank smell of cattle was heavy on the heated air of the Zambezi valley.

For an hour they had followed a small herd through the open mopani forest, stooping under the low branches with the thick shiny double leaves, each of them shaped like the cloven spoor that they followed, and now where the spoor emerged from the forest it had been joined by another much larger herd.

'How close?' Zouga asked again, and Jan Cheroot slapped his own neck where one of the buffalo flies had settled. It was the size of a honey bee, but dull black and the long needle of its proboscis stung as though it was white hot.

'We are so close that the flies that follow the herd still linger,' and he pushed his forefinger into the nearest pat of wet dung, 'and the body heat is still in the dung, but,' Jan Cheroot went on as he wiped his finger on a handful of dry grass, 'but they have gone into bad ground—' and he pointed ahead with his chin.

A week before they had reached the escarpment of the valley, but each of the possible passes that Zouga had examined through the telescope had proved on closer inspection to be dead-ends, the gorges pinching out into abrupt rock faces, or falling off into some terrifying abyss.

They had turned westwards, following the edge of the escarpment, Zouga ranging ahead with his small scouting party. Yet day after day those impassable heights loomed at their left hand, rising sheer into the unknown. Even below the main escarpment, the ground was tortured and riven by deep gorges and ravines, by cliffs of dark rock and hills of enormous tumbled boulders. The ravines were choked with the drab grey stands of thorn, so densely interwoven that a man would have to crawl in on hands and knees, and his vision would be limited to a few feet ahead, yet the herd of many hundreds of buffalo that they were following had disappeared into one of these narrow gorges, their thick hides impervious to the cruel red-tipped thorn.

Zouga took the telescope from his haversack carried by his bearer, and carefully scanned the ground ahead. It had a wild and menacing beauty and for the hundredth time in the last few days he wondered if there was a way through this maze to the empire of Monomatapa.

'Did you hear that?' Zouga demanded, lowering the glass suddenly. It had sounded like the distant lowing of the milk herd as it returned to the farmyard.

'Ja!' Sergeant Cheroot nodded, as again the mournful sound echoed against the black ironstone cliffs, and was answered by the bleat of a calf. 'They are lying up in the jessie bush. They won't move again until sunset.'

Zouga glanced up at the sun. It was four hours or so from its zenith. He had over a hundred mouths to feed, and they had rationed out the last of the dried fish two days before.

'We will have to go in after them,' he said, and Jan Cheroot removed the stem of the pipe from between yellow teeth and spat reflectively in the dust.

'I am a very happy man,' he said. 'Why would I want to die now?'

Zouga lifted the glass again, and while he scanned the ridges of higher ground about the choked valley, he imagined what it would be like in there. When the first shot was fired, the jessie bush would be filled with huge, furiously charging black animals.

The fluky breeze coming down the steep narrow valley brought with it another powerful whiff of the herd smell before it faded.

'The wind is down the valley,' he said.

'They have not smelled us,' Cheroot agreed, but that was not what Zouga had meant. Again he examined the nearest ridge of high ground. A man could work his way along the edge of it, up towards the head of the narrow valley.

'Sergeant, we are going to flush them out,' he smiled, 'like spring pheasant.'

Zouga had found the native names of his personal bearers hard to pronounce, and tiresome to remember. There were four of them, he had selected them with care, rejecting half a dozen others in the process, and he had rechristened them Matthew, Mark, Luke and John. They had earned enormous prestige by being so honoured, and had proved keen and willing to learn their duties. In a few days they were already proficient at reloading, though not yet of the same standard as Camacho Pereira's gunbearers – but that would come.

Zouga carried the Sharps rifle, but each of the four bearers had one of the heavy four-to-the-pound elephant guns that Harkness had recommended to Zouga. At any time he had only to reach back over his shoulder and a loaded and primed weapon would be thrust into his hand.

Apart from the elephant guns, his bearers carried his blanket roll, water bottle, canvas food bag, spare ball and powder, and the little clay fire pot from which a smouldering ball of moss and wood pulp could be blown into flame in a few seconds. It was wise to conserve the amenities of civilization, such as Swan Vestas, for the months and years ahead.

Zouga relieved Luke, the quickest and most wiry of the four, of all his equipment except the fire pot, pointed out the path along the cliff, and explained carefully to him what he was to do.

All of them listened with approval, even Sergeant Cheroot nodded sagely at the end. 'My old mother tells me, before she throws me out, "Jan", she says, "remember it's brains what counts." '

In the mouth of the valley, where it debouched out into the mopani forest, was a low outcrop of rock, the black ironstone boulders had been split into strange shapes by sun and erosion, and they formed a natural redoubt, with chest-high walls behind which a man could crouch. A hundred paces directly ahead, the dense palisade of iron-grey thorn blocked the valley, but the ground between was fairly open, with a few stunted second-growth mopani bushes and clumps of coarse dried razor grass as high as a man's shoulder.

Zouga moved his party into the lee of the rocks, and himself scrambled onto the highest point to follow through his glass the progress of the almost naked bearer as he picked his way cautiously along the rim of the cliff. Within half an hour he had worked so far up the escarpment that he had disappeared from Zouga's view.

It was another hour before, from the head of the valley, a thin tendril of pure white smoke rose gently into the heated air, and then bent into the elegant shape of an ostrich plume before the gentle breath of the breeze.

With miraculous suddenness the rising column of white smoke was surrounded by another living cloud, hundreds of tiny black specks that weaved and darted about and around it. The faint but excited bird cries carried down to where Zouga waited, and through the glass he could make out the rainbow, turquoise and sapphire plumage of the blue jay as they rolled and dived for the insects put to flight by the flames. Competing with them for the feast, were the iridescent black drongas with their long, forked tails catching the sunlight with metallic glitter as they swirled above the spreading smoke clouds.

Luke was doing his job well. Zouga grunted with satisfaction, as new columns of smoke rose at intervals, sealing off the valley from side to side as they spread to meet each other. Now there was a solid wall of smoke from one cliff to the other, and as the smoke turned dirty black, billowing upwards, spinning upon itself, carrying flaming fragments of leaves and twigs within it, it began to roll ponderously down the valley.

It reminded Zouga of a snow avalanche he had watched in the high Himalayas, the slow majestic progress gathering weight and momentum, building up its own wind storm as it sucked the valley of air.

He could see the tops of the flames now, leaping above the thorn, and hear the sound of them, like the whispering waters of a distant river. The alarm bellow of a bull buffalo rang like the blast of a war trumpet from the ironstone cliffs, and the whisper of flames rose swiftly to a dull crackling roar.

The smoke clouds rose across the sun, plunging them into an unnatural gloom, and Zouga felt a sharp drop in his spirits at the extinction of the bright morning sun, that infernal swirling pall of dun smoke seemed to hold a world of menace.

From the edge of the jessie bush broke a herd of kudu, led by a magnificent bull with his corkscrew horns laid flat along his back. He saw Zouga standing on the pinnacle of rock, and snorted with alarm, swinging away out of easy shot with his cows flying big-eared and scary behind him, their fluffy white tails flickered away amongst the mopani groves.

Zouga scrambled down from his too obvious position, and propped himself comfortably against the rock, checked the nipple on the cap of the Sharps and then cocked the big hammer.

Ahead of the flames, a pale white dust cloud was rising over the tops of the jessie bush, and another sound was added to the roar of flames. It was a low thunder that made the earth tremble under their feet.

'They are coming,' Jan Cheroot muttered to himself, and his little eyes sparkled.

A single buffalo burst from the palisade of thorn. He was an old bull, almost bald across the shoulders and rump, the dusty grey skin criss-crossed by a thousand ancient scars and scabby with the bites of bush ticks. The big bell-shaped ears were torn and tattered, and one thickly curved horn was broken off at the tip. He came out at a crabbing gallop, dust exploding at each hoof beat like miniature mortar bursts.

He was on a line to pass the rocky redoubt at twenty paces, and Zouga let him come on to twice that distance before he threw up the Sharps rifle.

He aimed for the fold of thick skin under the throat that marked the frontal aiming point for the heart and its complex of arteries and blood vessels. He hardly noticed the recoil nor the blurt of the shot as he watched for the strike of the lead bullet. There was a little spurt of dust off the grey hide precisely on his aiming point, and the sound of the hit was exactly like his headmaster swinging the malacca cane against his own schoolboy backside, sharp and meaty.

The bull took the bullet without a stumble or lurch, instead it swung towards them, and seemed immediately to double in size as it lifted its nose into the high attitude of the charge.

Zouga reached for his second gun, but he groped in vain. Mark, his number two, showed the whites of his eyes in a flash of terror, let out a squawk, hurled the elephant gun aside, and went bounding away towards the mopani grove.

The bull saw him and swerved again, thundering ten feet past Zouga as it went after the fleeing bearer. Waving the empty Sharps, Zouga shouted desperately for another rifle, but the bull was past him in a grey blur and it caught Mark as he reached the tree line.

The great bossed head dropped until the snout almost touched the earth, and then flew up again in a powerful tossing motion that bunched the muscle in the thick black neck. Mark was looking back over his shoulder, his eyes wide and glaring white in the black face, rivulets of sweat pouring down his naked back, his mouth a pink gape as he screamed.

Then he was in the air. Legs and arms tumbling wildly, he went up like a rag doll thrown by a petulant child and disappeared into the thick green canopy of mopani foliage overhead. Without missing a stride, the bull drove on into the forest, but that was all that Zouga saw, for a cry from Sergeant Cheroot made him turn again.

'*Hier kom hulle!* Here they come!'

Across their whole front, the earth seemed to move, as though racked by the convulsions of an earthquake. Shoulder to shoulder, nose to rump, the main herd broke from cover, flattening the thorn bush under the great wave of bodies, filling the valley from side to side.

They lifted behind them a dense curtain of pale dust, from which the front ranks seemed endlessly to emerge, their great bossed heads nodding in unison as they pounded on, long silver strings of saliva dangling from open jaws as they bellowed in alarm and anger, and the roar of their hooves drowned the sound of the flames.

Matthew and John, Zouga's two remaining bearers, had stood their ground, and one of them snatched away the empty Sharps and thrust the thick stock of an elephant gun into Zouga's hand.

The weapon seemed heavy and unbalanced after the Sharps, and the sights were crudely fashioned, a blunt cone for the foresight, and a deep vee for the backsight.

The solid wall of bodies was bearing down upon them with frightening speed. The cows were a dark chocolate colour, and their horns were more delicately curved. The calves that raced at their flanks were sleek russet with crowns of reddish curls between the rudimentary little horn spikes. The herd was so tightly packed that it seemed impossible that they could split open to pass the rock. There was a tall rangy cow in the leading rank, coming straight on to Zouga.

He held half a beat aiming into the centre of her chest, and squeezed off the shot. The firing cap popped with a tiny puff of white smoke, and a heartbeat later the elephant gun vomited a deafening gust of powder smoke and bright flame, the burning patches went spinning away over the heads of the charging buffalo, and Zouga felt as though one of them had kicked in his shoulder. He staggered backwards, the barrel thrown high by the recoil, but the big red cow seemed to run into an invisible barrier. A quarter of a pound of mercury-hardened lead drove into her chest, and brought her down in a rolling sliding tangle of hooves and horns.

'Tom Harkness! That one was yours!' Zouga shouted, offering the kill to the memory of the old white bearded hunter, and he grabbed the next loaded rifle.

There was a prime bull, big and black, a ton of enraged bovine flesh. It had seen Zouga, and was coming in over the rocks in a long scrambling leap – hunting him out, so close that Zouga seemed to touch it with the gaping muzzle of the four-to-the-pound. Again the great clanging burst of sound and flame and smoke, and half the bull's head flew away in a gust of bone chips and bloody fragments. It reared up on its hind legs, striking out with fore hooves, and then crashed over in a cloud of dust.

Impossibly, the herd split, galloping down each side of their rocky hide, a heaving, grunting, forked river of striving muscle and bone. Jan Cheroot was yipping shrilly with the fever of the chase, ducking down behind the rock to reload, biting open the paper cartridge with powder dribbling down his chin, spitting the ball into the muzzle and then plying the ramrod in a frenzy, before bobbing up again to fire into the solid heaving press of gigantic bodies.

It lasted for two minutes, which seemed to take a round of eternity, and then they were left choking and gasping in the swirling clouds of dust, surrounded by half a dozen huge black carcasses, with the drum-beats of the herd fading away into the mopani forest, and a louder more urgent din roaring down on them from in front.

The first tongue of heat licked across them, and Zouga heard the lock of sunbleached hair that hung on his forehead frizzle sharply and smelt the stink of it. At the same instant, the dust cloud fell abruptly aside, and for seconds they stared at a spectacle which deprived them of power of movement.

The jessie bush was not burning, it was exploding into sheets of flame.

'Run!' shouted Zouga. 'Get out of here!'

The sleeve of his shirt charred, and the air he breathed scorched his lungs painfully. As they reached the edge of the mopani forest, the shiny green leaves about their heads shrivelled and yellowed, curling their edges in the heat, and Zouga felt his eyeballs drying out as the dark smoke clouds rolled over them. He knew that they were experiencing only the heat and smoke carried on the wind, but if the flames were able to jump the gap, then they were all doomed. Ahead of him, the Hottentots and the other bearers were shadowy wraiths, staggering forward but weakening and losing direction.

Then, as suddenly as they had been engulfed by them, the billowing smoke clouds lifted. The flames had not been able to jump the open ground, and the heat came only in gusts. A ray of sunshine pierced the thick gloom overhead, and a puff of sweet fresh air came through. They sucked at it gratefully, and huddled in awed silence, beating at their clothing which still smouldered in patches. Zouga's face was blackened and blistered, and his lungs still convulsed in spasms of coughing. As he caught his breath, he grunted hoarsely,

'Well the meat is cooked already,' and he pointed back at the buffalo carcasses.

At that moment something fell limply out of the dense top branches of a mopani tree, and then picked itself up and limped painfully towards them. Zouga let out a husky growl of laughter.

'Oh, thou swift of foot,' he greeted Mark, the bearer, and the others took up the mockery.

'When you fly, the eagles are put to shame,' Jan Cheroot hooted.

'Your true home is in the treetops,' Matthew added with relish, 'with your hairy brethren.'

By evening they had hacked the buffalo carcasses into wet red chunks, and spread these on the smoking racks. The racks were waist high, cross-poles set in forked branches, with a slow smoking fire of wet mopani wood smouldering under it.

Here was meat for the caravan that would last them many weeks.

Camacho Pereira had no doubts that by simply following the line of the escarpment, keeping just below the bad broken ground, he must at last cut the spoor of the caravan. A hundred men, in column, would blaze a track that even a blind man would trip over.

His certainty dwindled with each day's march through the quivering, breathless heat that seemed to rebound from black kopjes and the ironstone cliffs which glittered in the aching sunlight like the scales of some monstrous reptile.

Of the men that his half-brother, Alphonse, had given him, he had already lost two. One had stepped on something that looked like a pile of dried leaves, but which had transformed itself instantly into six feet of infuriated gaboon adder, thick as a man's calf, with a repulsively beautiful diamond-patterned back, and a head the size of a man's fist. The gaping mouth was a lovely shade of salmon pink, and the curved fangs three inches long. It had plunged them into the man's thigh and squirted half a cupful of the most toxic venom in Africa into his bloodstream.

After blowing the serpent to shreds with volleys of rifle fire, Camacho and his companions had wagered all their expectations of loot on exactly how long it would take the victim to die. Camacho, the only one who owned a watch, was elected time-keeper, and they gathered around where the dying man lay, either urging him to give up the useless struggle or pleading with him raucously to hang on a little longer.

When he went into back-arching convulsions, with his eyes rolled up into his skull, his jaws locked into a grinning rictus and he lost control of his sphincter muscle, Camacho knelt beside him, holding a bunch of smouldering tambooti leaves under his nostrils to shock him out of it, and crooning, 'Ten minutes more – hang on for just ten minutes more for your old friend Machito!'

The last convulsion ended with a dreadful gargling expulsion of breath, and when the heart beat faded completely, Camacho stood and kicked the corpse with disgust.

'He always was a dung-eating jackal.'

When they began to strip the corpse of all items of any possible value, five coins, heavy golden mohurs of the East India Company, fell out of the folds of his turban.

There was not one man in all that company who would not have willingly sold his mother into slavery for a single gold mohur, let alone five.

At the first gleam of gold, all their knives came out with a sardonic metallic snickering, and the first man to snatch for the treasure reeled away, trying to push his intestines back into the long clean slice through his stomach wall.

'Leave them lie,' Camacho shouted. 'Don't touch them until the lots are drawn!'

Not one of them trusted another, and the knives stayed out while the lots were cast, and grudgingly the winners were allowed one at a time to claim their prize.

The man with the belly wound could not march without his stomach falling out, and because he could not march, he was as good as dead. The dead, as everybody knows, have no need of personal possessions. The logic was apparent to all. They left him his shirt and breeches, both torn and badly stained anyway, but stripped him of all else as they had stripped the first corpse. Then, with a few ribald pleasantries, they propped him against the base of a marula tree, with the naked corpse of the snake-bite victim beside him for company, and they marched away along the line of the escarpment.

They had gone a hundred yards when Camacho was overcome by a rush of compassion. He and the dying man had fought and marched and whored together for many years. He turned back.

The man gave him a haggard grin, his dry crusted lips cracking with the effort. Camacho answered him with that marvellous flashing smile as he dropped the man's loaded pistol in his lap.

'It would be better to use it *before* the hyena find you tonight,' he told him.

'The thirst is terrible,' the man croaked, a tiny bead of blood appeared on his deeply cracked lower lip, bright as an emperor's ruby in the sunlight. He eyed the two-gallon water bottle on Camacho's hip.

Camacho resettled the water bottle on its strap so it was out of sight behind his back. The contents sloshed seductively.

'Try not to think about it,' he counselled.

There was a point where compassion ended and stupidity

began. Who knew where and when they would find the next water? In this God-blasted desolation, water was an item not to be wasted on a man who was already as good as dead.

He patted the man's shoulder comfortingly, gave him a last lovely smile and then swaggered away amongst the grey iron-thorn scrub, whistling softly under his breath with the plumed beaver cocked over one eye.

'Camachito went back to make sure we had forgotten nothing.' The one-eyed Abyssinian greeted him as he caught up with the column, and they shouted with laughter. Their spirits were still high, the water-bottles more than half filled and the prospects of immense loot danced like a will-o-the-wisp down the valley ahead of them.

That had been ten days ago, the last three of which without water, for you could not count the cupful of mud and elephant piss they had from the last puddled water-hole. Apart from the lack of water, the going had become appalling. Camacho had never marched through such broken and harsh terrain, toiling up one rocky slope and then battling down through tearing thorn to the next dry river course, and then up again.

Also, it now seemed highly probable that either the Englishman had changed his mind and gone north of the Zambezi river after all, in which case they had lost him, or else, and Camacho's skin crawled at the thought, or else they had crossed the spoor of the caravan in the early dawn or late evening when the light was too bad to make it out clearly. It was an easy mistake to make, they had crossed hundreds of game tracks each day, and the spoor could have been wiped by a herd of game, or one of the fierce short-lived little whirlwinds, the dust devils which ravaged the valley at this season of the year.

To cap all Camacho's tribulations, his band of noble warriors was on the point of mutiny. They were talking quite openly about turning back. There never had been an Englishman and a caravan of riches, even if there had, he was now far from here and getting further every day. They were exhausted by these switchback ridges and valleys and the water bottles were nearly all of them dry, which made it hard to maintain enthusiasm for the venture. The ringleaders were reminding the others that in their absence, their share of the profits of the slave caravan were blowing in the wind. Fifty slaves, for certain, were worth a hundred mythical Englishmen. They had many excellent reasons for turning back.

Camacho, on the other hand, had nothing to return for, apart from his half-brother's ire. He also had a score to settle, two scores. He still hoped that they might manage to take the Englishman and his sister alive, especially the woman. Even in the thirst and the heat, his groin swelled at the memory of her in men's breeches. He jerked himself back to reality, and he glanced over his shoulder at the straggling line of ruffians who followed him.

Soon it would be necessary to kill one of his men, he had decided hours ago. Dung-eaters all of them – it was the only language they truly understood. He must make an example to stiffen their backbones, and keep them slogging onwards.

He had already decided which one it would be. The one-eyed Abyssinian was the biggest talker, the most eloquent apostle of the return to the coast, and what made his choice even more attractive was that his left side was blind. The problem was that the job must be done properly. The others would be impressed by the knife but not the gun. However, the Abyssinian allowed no man into that blind spot. Without making it too obvious, Camacho had twice sidled up on his left, but each time the Abyssinian had swung his head with its frizzed-up halo of dense curly hair towards him, and given him a grin with a slow trickle of a tear running down his cheek from that obscenely empty eye-socket.

However, Camacho was a persistent man, and an inventive one, for he noticed that whenever he moved out of the Abyssinian's blind spot, the man relaxed, and immediately became more verbose and arrogant. Twice more Camacho tried an approach from the left, and twice more was met with a single cold beady stare. He was establishing a pattern, teaching the victim that threat came only from the left, and when they halted in the middle of the morning, he ostentatiously squatted on the right. The Abyssinian grinned at him as he wiped the spout of his almost empty water bottle on his sleeve.

'This is the place. I go no further.' The one-eyed man announced in fluent Portuguese. 'I make the oath on Christ's sacred wounds.' And he touched the Coptic gold cross that hung around his neck. 'Not another step forward. I am going back.'

Fanning himself with the beaver hat, Camacho shrugged, and

answered the cold grin with his own sunny smile. 'Let's drink to your going then.' With his free hand, he lifted his own water bottle, and shook it slightly. There was a cupful, no more. All their eyes went instinctively to the bottle. Here water was life, even the Abyssinian's single eye fastened on it.

Then Camacho let it slip from his fingers. It looked like an accident, the bottle rolled to the Abyssinian's feet with clear water glugging out on to the baked earth, and, with an exclamation, the man stooped for it with his right hand, his knife hand.

Nobody really saw Camacho move. He had been holding the knife in the lining of the beaver hat. Suddenly it seemed to reappear behind the Abyssinian's right ear, just the carved bone handle protruding, the blade completely buried. The Abyssinian lifted his hand with a mystified expression and touched the hilt of the knife, blinked his single eye rapidly, opened his mouth and then closed it firmly and fell forward on top of the water bottle.

Camacho was standing over them, a cocked pistol in each hand.

'Who else wishes to make an oath on Christ's sacred wounds?' he smiled at them, his teeth very big and white and square. 'Nobody? Very well then, I will make an oath. I make it on the long-lost maidenheads of your sisters which they sold a hundred times for an escudo the bunch.'

Even they were shocked by such blasphemy,

'I make it on your flaccid and puny manhoods which it will be my great pleasure to shoot off,' he was interrupted, and broke off in mid-sentence.

There was a faint popping sound on the hushed heated morning, so distant, so indistinct, that for a moment none of them recognized it as the sound of gunfire. Camacho recovered first, he thrust the pistols into his waistband. They were no longer needed – and he ran to the crest of the rocky kopje on which they sat.

There was a column of dun-coloured smoke rising into the washed-out blue sky far ahead. In this terrain, it lay a day's march away against the steep and fearsome edge of the escarpment.

Around him his men, once again loyal and filled with fire, were laughing and hugging each other with delight. It was a pity about the Abyssinian, Camacho conceded, like all his people he had been a good fighter, and now they had found the Englishman, he would be missed.

Camacho cupped the cheroot in both hands and inhaled deeply. Holding the smoke in his lungs, he squinted his eyes against the flat glare of rising noon. The sun had bleached all colour from the landscape, only the shadows were cut clearly, very sharp-edged and black below each tree and rock.

Across the narrow valley the long column of men he was watching moved at the pace of the slowest. Camacho doubted if they were making a single mile in an hour.

He removed the beaver hat from his head and blew the smoke into it gently, so that it dispersed into nothingness instead of standing in the still air to draw the eye of a watcher.

Camacho saw nothing odd in that the leading Hottentot musketeer in the column carried an English flag. Even in this barren, forsaken corner of the earth, although its gaudy folds were already dulled with dust and the ends shredded by grasping thorn, it was the promise of protection, a warning to those who might check their passage. All caravans in Africa went under a banner.

Camacho dragged on the black cheroot and considered once again how infallible was the advice of his brother Alphonse. The night was the only time to do the business. Here the column was spread out for more than a mile, there were wide gaps between each of the four divisions – and with himself he had eighteen men left. If he attacked in daylight, he would be forced to concentrate them on the detachments of Hottentot musketeers at the head and tail of the caravan. He imagined vividly what might happen at the first shot. One hundred porters would drop their packs and scatter away into the bush, and when the fighting was over he would have nobody to carry the loot.

It was necessary, furthermore, for him to wait until the Englishman rejoined the caravan. He guessed that Zouga Ballantyne was scouting or hunting, but that he would rejoin the column before nightfall.

The woman was there. He had another glimpse of her at that moment as she stepped up on to a log that lay across the path; for a moment she balanced there, long-legged, in those maddening breeches, and then jumped down off the log. Camacho passed a pleasant few minutes in erotic imaginings. He had been twenty days without a woman and it had put a razor edge to his appetite which even the hot hard trek had not dulled.

He sighed happily, and then squinted his eyes again as he concentrated on the immediate problems. Alphonse was right, they would have to wait until night. And tonight would be a good night for it, three days after the full moon, and yet the moon would rise very late, an hour or so after midnight.

He would let the Englishman come in, let the camp settle down, let the fires die, and let the Hottentot sentries drowse off. Then when the moon rose and the vitality of the camp was at its lowest ebb, he and his men would go in.

Every one of his men was good with the knife, the fact that they had lived so long showed that, Camacho smiled to himself, and they would have an opportunity to prove it again tonight. He personally would mark the position of the sentries while it was stili light. They would start with them, Camacho did not expect more than three or four. Alter the sentries, then the Hottentot musketeers that were sleeping. They were the most dangerous, and after them there would be time for indulgence.

He would go to the woman's tent himself, he squirmed slightly at the thought and adjusted his dressing. It was just a terrible pity that he could not take care of the Englishman as well. He would send two of his best men to do that work. He had dreamed of driving a long wooden spike up between the Englishman's buttocks, and then taking wagers on how long he would take to die, amusing himself and the company while regaining some of his previous losses at the same time.

Then reluctantly, and prudently, he had decided not to chance such pleasures, not with a man like that. Best to cut his throat while he still slept. They could have their fun with the woman instead, Camacho decided firmly.

His single regret was that he would have only a short time with her, before the others demanded their turns, though a few minutes would probably be enough for him. Strange how months of craving could be satiated so swiftly, and after that brief outpouring become indifference and even distaste. That was a very philosophical thought, Camacho realized. Once again he had astonished himself with his own wisdom and sensitivity to things of the mind. He had often thought that if he had ever learned to read and write he could have been a great man, like his father the Governor. After all, the blood in his veins was that of aristocrats and Dons, only slightly diluted.

He sighed, yes, five minutes would suffice and then the others could have her, and when they also had finished they could play the betting game with the long wooden stake – and, of course, there was a more amusing place to put it. He chuckled aloud at the thought and took a last draw on the cheroot, and the stub was so short that the ember scorched his fingers. He dropped it and crushed it under his heel. He moved like a panther, slipping quietly over the skyline and circling out stealthily to get ahead of the creeping caravan.

Zouga had left his bearers tending the smoking-racks, feeding the fire with chips of wet wood, and turning the hunks of red meat so they cured evenly. It was wearisome work, for the racks had to be guarded at all times from the hyena and jackals, the crows and kites which hung about the camp, while there was always wood to cut and the baskets of mopani bark to weave in which the smoked meat would be carried.

Jan Cheroot was happy to escape with Zouga as he marched back to find the main caravan and guide it to the buffalo camp. Even the tsetse fly could not repress his high spirits. They had been in 'fly-country' for a week or more now. Tom Harkness had called these importunate little insects 'the guardians of Africa' and certainly they made it impossible for man to move his domestic animals through vast tracts of country.

Here they were one of the many reasons why the Portuguese colonization had been confined to the low coastal littoral. Their cavalry had never been able to penetrate this deadly screen, nor had their draught animals been able to drag their war trains up from the coast.

They were the reason, also, why Zouga had not attempted to use waggons or beasts of burden to carry his stores. There was not even a dog with the caravan, for only man and wild game were immune to the dreadful consequences of the bite.

In some areas of the 'fly-belt' there were so few of the insects as to cause little annoyance, but in others they swarmed like hiving bees, plaguing and persecuting even during the moonlight periods of the night.

That day on the march back to rejoin the column, Zouga and Jan Cheroot suffered the worst infestation of fly they had yet met with in the valley of the Zambezi. They rose from the ground to sit thickly upon their legs, and clustered on the backs of their necks and between their shoulder blades, so that he and Jan Cheroot took turns to walk behind each other and brush them off with a freshly cut buffalo tail.

As suddenly as they had entered it, they found themselves out of the 'fly-belt' and with blessed relief from the torment they settled down to rest in the shade. Within half an hour they heard distant singing, and as they waited for the caravan to come up, they smoked and chatted in the desultory fashion of the good companions they had become.

During one of the long pauses in their talk Zouga thought he saw vague movement on the far side of the shallow valley in front of them. Probably a herd of kudu or a troop of baboon, both of which were plentiful in the valley, but apart from the buffalo herd the only game they had encountered since leaving Tete.

The approaching caravan would have alarmed whatever it was, Zouga thought, removing his cap and using it to drive away the persistent cloud of tiny black mopani bees which hovered around his head,attracted by the moisture of his eyes and lips and nostrils. The movement in the forest opposite was not repeated. Whatever it was had probably crossed the ridge. Zouga turned back to listen to Jan Cheroot.

'The rains only stopped six weeks ago,' Jan Cheroot was musing aloud. 'The water-holes and rivers up on the high ground will still be full, not here, of course – this ground drains too steeply.' He indicated the dry and rocky water course below them. 'So the herds spread out, and follow their old roads.' He was explaining the complete lack of elephant, or even recent evidence of elephant herds in the valley, and Zouga listened with attention, for here was an expert speaking. 'The old elephant roads, they used to run from the flat mountain of Good Hope to the swamps of the far Sud,' he pointed north. 'But each year they shrink as we, the *jagters* (hunters), and men like us, follow the herds and drive them deeper and deeper into the interior.'

Jan Cheroot was silent again, and his pipe gurgled noisily as he sucked on it.

'My father told me that he killed the last elephants south of the Olifants river – the river of elephants – when he was still a young man. He boasted that he killed twelve elephants that day, he alone with his old *roer* (muzzle-loader) that was too heavy to hold to the shoulder. He had to rest it on the crutch of a forked stick he carried for it. Twelve elephants in one day – by one man. That is a feat.' He gurgled his pipe again, and then spat a little yellow tobacco juice. 'But then my father was even more famous as a liar than he was as a hunter,' Jan Cheroot chuckled and shook his head fondly.

Zouga smiled, and then the smile vanished and his head jerked up. He narrowed his eyes, for a tiny dart of reflected sunlight had struck his eye coming from the same place across the valley. Whatever he had seen was still there, and it was neither kudu nor baboon. It had to be a man, for only metal or glass could have shot that reflection. Jan Cheroot had noticed nothing and he was musing on.

'When I rode with Cornwallis Harris, we found the first elephant on the Cashan mountains, that's a thousand miles further north of where my father killed his herd. There was nothing in between – it had all been hunted bare. Now there are no elephant in the Cashan mountains. My brother Stephan was there two years ago. He tells me that there are no elephant south of the Limpopo river. The Boers graze their herds where we hunted ivory – perhaps we will find no elephant even up there on the high ground, perhaps there are no elephant left in all the world.'

Zouga was not really listening any more. He was thinking about the man on the opposite side of the valley. It was probably somebody from the caravan, a party sent ahead to cut firewood for the night's bivouac, yet it was still early to think of making camp.

The singing of the bearers was louder now. There was a single voice carrying the marching song. Zouga recognized it. The man was a tall Angoni, with a fine tenor voice, and a poet who improvised his own verses, adding to them and altering them on the march. Zouga, cocking his head, could make out the words.

'Have you heard the Fish Eagle cry above Marawi?

Have you seen the setting sun turn the snows of Kilimanjaro
to blood?'

And then the chorus coming in after him, those haunting African voices, so beautiful, so moving,

'Who will lead us to these wonders, my brother?
We will leave the women to weep,
We will let their sleeping mats grow cold,
If a strong man leads, we will follow him, my brother.'

Zouga smiled at the next verse, as he recognized his name.

Bakela will lead us like a father leads his children,
Bakela will give you a *khete* of *sam-sam* beads—
Bakela will feed you upon the fat of the
hippopotamus and meat of the buffalo—'

Zouga closed his mind against the distraction, concentrating on the man across the valley. Here, a hundred miles from the nearest habitations of men, it must have been somebody from the caravan – woodcutter, honey-hunter, deserter, who knew?

Zouga stood up and stretched, and Jan Cheroot knocked out his pipe and stood with him. The head of the column appeared amongst the trees lower down the slope, the red, white and blue banner flapped lazily open and then drooped again dejectedly.

Zouga glanced once more at the opposite slope, it seemed deserted again. He was tired, the soles of his feet felt as though he had marched across burning embers, for they had been going hard since dawn, and the barely healed knife wound in his hip ached dully.

He should really go up that slope to check what he had seen, but it was steep and rocky. It would take another half an hour of scrambling to reach the crest and return. They went down to meet the caravan, and when Zouga saw Robyn striding along with that easy coltish grace of hers behind the standard bearer, he lifted his cap and waved it above his head.

She ran to meet him, laughing like a child with delight. He had been gone three days.

Below a polished face of smooth black rock, that when the river was in spate would be a roaring cascade, there was a bend in the dry water bed filled with pure white sand.

On the banks above it the wild mahogany stood tall and

vigorous, its roots in water and the baboon had been scratching in the sand below the bank.

Robyn and Zouga sat together on the edge of the dry waterfall, watching the men that Zouga had set to digging for water.

'I pray there will be enough.' Robyn watched them with interest. 'I have not used my bath since we left Tete.' Her enamelled hip bath was the expedition's single bulkiest item of equipment.

'I'll be satisfied with enough for a pot of tea,' Zouga replied vaguely, but he was clearly distracted.

'Something is worrying you?' she asked.

'I was thinking of a valley in Kashmir.'

'Was it like this?'

'Not really – it is just that,' he shrugged. In that far away valley, when he had been a young ensign leading a patrol ahead of the battalion, he had seen something as he had today. Something of no account, a stray movement, a glint of light that might have been off a gunbarrel, or the horn of a wild goat. Then, as now, it had been too much trouble to check it. That night he had lost three men, killed while they fought their way out of the valley. The fight had earned praise from his Colonel, but the men remained dead.

He glanced up at the slanting sun, there was an hour of light left. He knew he should have climbed that slope. While Robyn watched him with a puzzled expression, he wavered a few seconds longer and then with an exclamation of exasperation stood up wearily. His feet still ached abominably and he rubbed his hip where the knife-wound throbbed. It was going to be a long walk back down the valley.

Zouga used a deep and narrow ravine to get out of the camp unobtrusively, and once clear he scrambled out and kept to the thicker bush just above the river-bed until he reached a tangled barrier of driftwood carried down during the recent rains which blocked the dry water-course from bank to bank.

He used this to cover his crossing, and started up the far slope. He went very carefully, dodging from one tree to another and watching and listening before each move.

On the crest there was a faint movement of cooler air, the evening breeze coming down the escarpment that cooled the sweat on his neck and almost made the hard climb worth-while. It seemed that was all the reward he would get. The stony ground was too hard to carry sign, and it was deserted of life, animal or human. However, Zouga was determined to make up for his previous sloth. He stayed too long. It would be fully dark before he reached the camp again, moon-rise was late, and he risked a broken leg moving over this sort of terrain in the pitch dark.

He turned to go back, and he smelt it before he saw it, and the hair prickled along his forearms and he felt his belly muscles contract, yet it was such a commonplace smell. He stooped and picked up the small squashed brown object. He had smoked the last of his own cheroots two days before, perhaps that was why his nose was so sensitive to the smell of tobacco.

The cigar had been smoked down to a thin rind, and crushed out so it resembled a scrap of dried bark. Without the smell to guide him, he would never have found it. Zouga shredded it between his fingers, and there was still a little residual dampness of saliva in the chewed end. He lifted his fingers and sniffed them. He knew where he had smelled that particular scented type of Portuguese tobacco before.

Camacho left fifteen of his men well back off the crest, in a tumble of rock that looked like a ruined castle, and whose caves and overhangs gave shade and concealment. They would sleep, he knew, and he grudged it to them. His own eyelids were drooping as he lay belly down in cover, on the other side of the ridge watching the caravan making camp.

He had only two of his men with him to help him mark the sentries and *scherms*, the watch fires and the tent sites. They would be able to lead the others in, even in the complete darkness before the moon, if that should become necessary. Camacho hoped not. In the dark mistakes could be made, and it needed only a shot or a single shout. No, they would wait for the moon, he decided.

The Englishman had come into camp earlier, just before the caravan halted. He had the Hottentot with him, and they both hobbled stiffly like men who had made long, hard marches. Good, he would sleep soundly, was probably doing so already, for Camacho had not seen him in the last hour. He must be in the tent beside the woman's. He had seen a servant carrying a steaming bucket of water to her.

They had watched the Hottentot Sergeant set only two sentries. The Englishman must be feeling very secure, two sentries merely to watch against lions. They would probably both be fast asleep by midnight. They would never wake again. He, personally, would cut one of them. He smiled in anticipation, and he would send a good knife to cut the other.

The remaining Hottentots had built their usual lean-to shelter and thatched it in a rudimentary fashion. There was no chance of rain, not at this season and not with that unblemished egg-shell-blue sky. It was almost two hundred paces from the tents, a groan or a whimper would not carry that far. Good, Camacho nodded again. It was working out better than he had hoped.

As always, the two tents were set close together, almost touching. The gallant Englishman guarding the woman, Camacho smiled again, and felt his drowsiness lifting miraculously as his groin charged once more. He wished the night away, for he had already waited so long.

Night came with the dramatic suddenness of Africa, within minutes the valley was filled with shadows, the sunset made its last theatrical flare of apricot and old gold light and then it was dark.

For an hour more Camacho could see the occasional dark figure silhouetted by the flames of the camp fires. Once the sound of singing carried softly and sweetly to the ridge, and the other camp sounds, the clank of a bucket, the thud of a log thrown on the fire, the drowsy murmur of voices, showed that the routine was unaltered, and the camp completely unaware.

The noises faded and the fires died. The silence and the darkness was disturbed only by the piping lament of a jackal across the valley.

The star patterns turned slowly across the sky marking the passage of the hours, and then gradually paled out before the greater brilliance of the rising moon.

'Fetch the others,' Camacho told the man nearest him, and rose stiffly to his feet, stretching like a cat to relieve numbed muscles. They came silently, and gathered close about Camacho, to listen to his final whispered instructions.

When he finished whispering, he looked from one to the other in turn. Their faces in the bright moonlight had the pale greenish hues of freshly exhumed corpses, but they nodded their agreement to his words, and then followed him down the slope, dark silent shapes like a troop of wolves; they reached the dry water course in the gut of the valley, and split into their prearranged groups.

Camacho moved up the newly beaten path towards the camp. He carried his knife in his right hand and his musket in the other, and his feet made a barely audible brushing sound through the short dry grass. Ahead of him, beneath the outspread branches of a mukusi tree, he could make out the shape of the sentry, where he had been placed six hours before. The man was asleep, curled like a dog on the hard earth. Camacho nodded with satisfaction and crept closer. He saw the man had pulled a dark blanket over his head. The mosquitoes had bothered him also, Camacho grinned and knelt beside him.

With his free hand he felt softly for the man's head through the blanket, then the hand stilled. He gave a little grunt of surprise, and jerked the blanket aside. It had been arranged over the exposed roots of the mukusi tree to look like the shape of a sleeping man, and Camacho swore quietly but with great vehemence.

The sentry had chosen the wrong time to sneak away from his post. He was probably back in the lean-to shelter snoring happily on a mattress of dry grass. They would get him with the others, when they cleaned out the shelter. Camacho went on up the slope into the camp. In the moonlight the canvas of the tents shone ghostly silver, a beacon on which his lust could concentrate. Camacho slipped the sling of the musket over his shoulder as he hurried forward, towards the left-hand tent, and then checked as another dark figure emerged from the shadows, the knife in his right hand instinctively came up and then he recognized his own man, one of those whom he had sent to cut the Englishman's throat.

The man nodded jerkily, all was well so far and they went forward together, separating only as they approached the two tents. Camacho would not use the fly opening of the woman's tent – for he knew it would be laced closed, and if there were any surprises they would be at the entrance. He slipped around the side of the tent, and stooped to one of the hooded ventilator openings. He ran the point of the blade into it and then drew it upwards in a single stroke. Although it was heavy canvas, the blade had been whetted expertly, and the side wall split with only a whisper of sound.

Camacho stepped through the opening, and while he waited for his eyesight to adjust to the deeper darkness of the interior, he fumbled with the fastening of his breeches, grinning happily to himself as he made out the narrow collapsible cot and the little white tent of the muslin mosquito net. He shuffled towards it slowly, careful not to trip over the cases of medical stores that were piled between him and the cot.

Standing over the cot, he ripped the muslin netting aside violently, and lunged full length on to the cot, groping for the woman's head to smother her cries, the loose ends of his belt flapping at his waist, and his breeches sagging around his hips.

For a moment he was paralysed with shock at the fact that the cot was empty. Then he groped frantically over every inch of it, before coming to his feet again and hoisting his breeches with his free hand. He was confused, disconnected, and wild ideas flashed through his mind. Perhaps the woman had left the cot to answer a call of nature, but then why was the fly carefully laced closed. She had heard him and was hiding behind the cases, armed with a scalpel, and he swung round panicking to lash out with the knife, but the tent was empty.

Then the coincidence of the missing sentry and the empty cot struck him with force, and he felt deep and urgent concern. Something was happening that he did not understand. He charged for the rent in the canvas, tripped and sprawled over one of the cases and rolled on to his feet again, nimble as a cat. He ran out, clinching his belt and looking about him wildly, unslinging his musket and only just preventing himself from calling aloud to his men.

He ran to the Englishman's tent, just as his man came running out of the long dark tear in the canvas side, brandishing his knife, his face pale and fearful in the moonlight. He saw Camacho, screamed and struck out at him wildly with the long silver blade.

'Silence, you fool,' Camacho snarled at him.

'He's gone,' the man panted, craning to stare about into the deep shadows that the moon cast under the trees. 'They've gone. They've all gone.'

'Come!' snapped Camacho, and led him at a run down towards the lean-to that the Hottentot musketeers had built.

Before they reached it they met their companions running towards them in a disorderly bunch.

'Machito?' somebody called nervously.

'Shut your mouth,' Camacho growled at them, but the man blurted on.

'The *scherm* is empty, they have gone.'

'The Devil has taken them.'

'There is nobody.'

There was an almost superstitious frenzy of awe on them all, the darkness and the silent empty camp turned them all into cowards. Camacho found himself, for once, without an order to give, uncertain of what to do. His men crowded around him helplessly, seeming to take comfort from each other's physical presence, cocking and fiddling with their muskets and peering nervously into the shadows.

'What do we do now?' A voice asked the question that Camacho had feared, and somebody else threw a log from the pile on to the smouldering watch fire in the centre of the camp.

'Don't do that,' Camacho ordered uncertainly, but instinctively they were all drawn to the warmth and comfort of the orange tongue of flame that soared up brightly, blowing like a dragon's breath.

They turned their backs towards it, forming a half circle and faced outwards into the dark which in contrast to the flames was suddenly impenetrably black.

It was out of this darkness that it came. There was no warning, just the sudden thunderous burst of sound and flame, the long line of spurting muzzle flashes, blooming briefly and murderously, and then the sound of the striking balls in their midst, like a handful of children's marbles hurled into a mud puddle, as the musket balls slogged into human flesh.

Immediately men were hurled lightly about by the heavy lead slugs, and the little band about the watch fire was thrown into struggling, shouting confusion.

One of them flew backwards, at a run, doubled in the middle where a ball had taken him low in the belly. He tripped over the burning log and fell full length into the blazing watch fire. His hair and beard flared like a torch of pine needles and his scream rang wildly through the tree tops.

Camacho himself threw up his musket, aiming blindly into

the night from whence the Englishman's voice was chanting the ritual infantry orders for mass volley fire.

'Section One. Reload. Section Two. Three paces forward. One round volley fire.'

Camacho realized that the devastating blast of close range musketry that had just swept them, would be repeated within seconds. With mild derision Camacho had watched on many a hot afternoon as the Englishman drilled his double line of red-jacketed puppets, the front rank levelling and firing on command, then the second rank taking three paces forward in unison, stepping through the gaps in the first rank and in their turn levelling and firing. The same evolutions which, when magnified ten thousand times, had broken the charge of French cavalry up the slope at Quatre Bras, now filled Camacho with unutterable terror, and he flung up his musket and fired it unsighted into the darkness, in the direction of the cool, precise English voice. He fired at the same instant as one of his own men who had been knocked down by the first volley scrambled to his feet only lightly wounded, directly in front of Camacho's musket muzzle. Camacho shot him cleanly between the shoulder blades at a range of two feet, so close that the powder burn scorched the man's shirt. It smouldered in little red sparks as he sprawled at full length on his face once more, until the glowing sparks were quenched by the quick flow of the man's heart blood.

'Fool!' Camacho howled at the corpse, and turned to run. Behind him the English voice called, 'Fire!'

Camacho threw himself down on to hard earth, howling again as his hands and knees sank into the hot ash of the watch fire and he felt his breeches char and his skin blister.

The second volley swept over his head, and around him more men were falling and screaming, and Camacho rebounded to his feet at a dead run. He had lost both his knife and musket.

'Section One, three paces forward, one round volley fire.'

The night was suddenly filled with running, shouting figures, as the porters burst out of their encampment. There was no direction or purpose in their flight. They ran like Camacho, driven by gunfire and their own terrible panic, scattering away into the surrounding bush, singly and in small groups.

Before the command ordering the next volley of musket fire, Camacho ducked behind the hillock of porters' packs, which had been piled close to the Englishman's tent and covered with waterproof tarpaulin.

Camacho was sobbing with the agony of his scorched hands and knees, and with the humiliation of having walked so guilelessly into the Englishman's trap.

He found his terror giving way to bitter and spiteful hatred. As little groups of terrified porters stumbled towards him out of the darkness, he drew one of the pistols from his belt and shot the leader in the head and then leapt up howling like a demented ghost – they ran and he knew they would not stop until, miles away in the trackless wilderness, they dropped with exhaustion, easy prey for lion or hyena. It gave him a moment's sour satisfaction, and he looked around for some other damage he could wreak.

The pile of stores behind which he crouched and the dying fire in front of the Englishman's deserted tent caught his attention. He snatched a brand from the fire, blew it into flame and tossed it flaring brightly on to the high canvas-covered pile of stores and equipment, then flinched as another volley crashed out of the darkness, and he heard the Englishman's voice.

'As a line of skirmishers, take the bayonet to them now, men.'

Camacho jumped down into the dry river-bed, and blundered through the crunching sugary sand to the far bank, where he scrambled thankfully into the dense riverine bush.

At the re-assembly point on the ridge there were three of his men already waiting, two of them had lost their muskets and all three were as shaken and sweaty and breathless as Camacho himself.

Two more came in while they regained their breath and power of speech. One was badly hit, his shoulders shattered by a musket ball.

'There won't be any others,' he gasped, 'those little yellow bastards caught them with bayonets as they were crossing the river.'

'They'll be here any minute.' Camacho dragged himself to his feet again, looking back down into the valley. He saw with grim satisfaction that the pile of stores was blazing brightly, despite the efforts of half a dozen tiny dark figures to beat out the flames. He had only moments to enjoy the spectacle, for lower down the slope came the thin, but warlike cries of the Hottentot musketeers and the thud and flash of their musket fire.

'Help me,' cried the man with the shattered shoulder. 'Don't leave me here, my friends, my comrades, give me an arm,' he pleaded, trying to struggle back on to his feet, but he was speaking to the empty night, and as the rush of footsteps down the far slope of the hill dwindled, his knees buckled under him and he sank back on to the rock earth sweating with pain and the terror which lasted only until one of the Hottentots drove the point of a bayonet into his chest and out between his shoulder blades.

Zouga strode angrily through the camp in the rising heat and bright sunlight of morning. His face and arms were blackened with soot, his eyes still red and smarting from the smoke of the fires, his beard was scorched and his eyelashes burned half away from fighting the flames. They had lost most of their stores and equipment for the fire had run away through the tents and thatched shelters. Zouga paused to glance at the charred and trodden scraps of canvas that were all that were left of the tents; they would miss them when the rains broke, but that was the very least of their losses.

He tried to make a mental list of the most grievous damage they had suffered. There were firstly only forty-six porters left out of more than one hundred. Of course, he could expect Jan Cheroot and his Hottentots to bring in a few more. They were at this moment scouring the valleys and hills around the camp for scattered survivors. He could still hear the kudu-horn trumpets calling in the stragglers. However, many would have risked the long and dangerous journey back to Tete rather than a recurrence of the night's attack, and they would have seized the opportunity to desert. Others would be lost after their midnight flight and panic. They would fall prey to wild animals or succumb to thirst. Half a dozen had been killed by random musketry fire and by the retreating brigands who had deliberately fired into the masses of unarmed porters. Four others were so badly wounded that they would die before nightfall.

That was the most serious loss, for without porters they were helpless. Without porters to carry them, what remained of the carefully selected equipment and trade goods were as useless to them as if they had left them in London or dumped them overboard from *Huron*'s deck.

Of the equipment itself, it would take them hours to count their losses, to find what had burned and what they could salvage from the stinking, smouldering mass of cloth and canvas, what they could pick out of the trodden and dusty mess scattered down the rock hillside. The scene reminded Zouga forcefully of so many other battlefields, the terrible destruction and waste affronted him, as it had done before.

The few remaining porters were already at work, picking over the field like a line of harvesters, retrieving anything of value from the ash and the dust. Little Juba was with them concentrating on the search for Robyn's medical stores, and books and instruments.

Robyn herself had set up an emergency clinic under the wide green branches of the mukusi tree in the centre of the camp, and when Zouga paused to look at the wounded men who still awaited her attention, and at the dead bodies laid out in a neat row and covered with a blanket or a scrap of charred and dirty canvas, he was angry with himself all over again.

Though what alternative had there been for him, he wondered.

If he had turned the camp into an armed fortress, it would have meant enduring a long drawn-out siege with Camacho's wolves skulking around the perimeter, sniping and harrying them until their opportunity came.

No, he had been right to set the trap and end it at a single stroke. At least now he could be certain that the Portuguese were still in full flight for the coast, but the price had been too high, and Zouga was still angry.

The expedition, so well conceived and lavishly equipped, had ended in disaster before it had achieved a single one of its objectives. The loss of equipment and life had been heavy, but that was not what burned so acidly in Zouga's stomach as he paused at the perimeter of the devastated camp and lifted his eyes longingly towards the high broken ground of the southern escarpment. It was the idea of having to give up, before he had begun, and when he was so close, so very close. Twenty, fifty, not more than a hundred miles ahead of him lay the frontier of the empire of Monomatapa. Behind him, one hundred miles to the north was the dirty little village of Tete, and the wide river which was the beginning of the long ignoble road back to England, back to obscurity, back to a commission in a third-rate regiment, back to conformity and the wearying discipline of the cantonments of the Indian army. Only now that he was doomed to return to that life did he realize how deeply he had hated and resented it, just how much the desire to escape it had brought him here to this wild untouched land. Like a long-term prisoner who has tasted one day of sweet freedom, so the prospect of return to his cage was that much more painful, now. The pain of it cramped his chest, and he had to breathe deeply to control it.

He turned away from the southern vista of ragged peaks and savage black rock cliffs, and he walked slowly to where his sister worked quietly in the shade of the mukusi. She was pale, with dark smudges of fatigue and strain under her green eyes. Her blouse was speckled with spots of her patients' blood, and her forehead appeared blistered with tiny beads of perspiration.

She had started work in the darkness, by the light of a bull's eye lantern and now it was mid-morning.

She looked up wearily as Zouga stood over her.

'We won't be able to go on,' he said quietly. She stared at him a moment without change of expression, and then dropped her eyes and went on smearing salve on the badly burned leg of one of the porters. She had treated the worst cases first, and was now finishing with the burns and abrasions.

'We've lost too much vital equipment,' Zouga explained. 'Stores that we need to survive.' Robyn did not look up this time, 'And we've not enough porters to carry what is left.'

Robyn began bandaging the leg with her full attention.

'Papa made the Transversa with four porters,' she observed mildly.

'Papa was a man,' Zouga pointed out reasonably, and Robyn's hands stilled ominously and her eyes narrowed, but Zouga had not noticed. 'A woman cannot travel or survive without the necessities of civilization,' he went on seriously. 'That is why I am sending you back to Tete. I'm sending Sergeant Cheroot and five of his Hottentots to escort you. You'll have no difficulty, once you reach Tete. I will send with you what remains in cash, a hundred pounds for the launch down river to Quelimane and a passage to Cape Town on a trader. There you can draw on the money I deposited in Cape Town to pay for a passage on the mailship.'

She looked up at him. 'And you?' she asked.

Until then he had not made the decision. 'The important thing is what happens to you,' he told her gravely, and then he knew what he was going to do. 'You will have to go back and I am going on alone.'

'It'll take more than Jan Cheroot and five of his damned Hottentots to carry me,' she told him, and the oath was a measure of her determination.

'Be reasonable, Sissy.'

'Why should I start now?' she asked sweetly.

Zouga opened his mouth to reply angrily, then closed it slowly and stared at her. There was a hard uncompromising line to her lips, and the prominent, almost masculine, jaw was clenched stubbornly.

'I don't want to argue,' he said.

'Good,' she nodded. 'That way you won't waste any more of your precious time.'

'Do you know what you are letting yourself in for?' he asked quietly.

'As well as you do,' she replied.

'We won't have trade goods to buy our way through the tribes.' She nodded. 'That means we'll have to fight our way through if anyone tries to stop us.'

He saw the shadow in her eyes at that, but there was no wavering of her determination.

'No tents for shelter, no canned food, no sugar or tea.' He knew what that meant to her. 'We will live straight off the land, and what we can't scavenge or kill or carry, we go without. We'll have nothing but powder and shot.'

'You'd be a fool to leave the quinine,' she told him quietly, and he hesitated.

'The bare minimum of medicines,' he agreed, 'and remember, it won't be for just a week or a month.'

'We'll probably go a great deal faster than we have so far,' she answered quietly, as she stood up and brushed off the seat of her breeches.

The choice of what to take and what to leave had been nicely balanced, Zouga thought, as he listed and weighed the new loads.

He had chosen paper and writing equipment in place of sugar

and most of the tea. His navigational instruments in place of spare boots, for the boots they wore could be resoled with raw buffalo hide. Quinine and other medicines together with Robyn's instruments in place of the extra clothing and blankets. Powder and shot in place of trade beads and cloth.

The pile of abandoned equipment grew steadily, cases of potted jams, bags of sugar, canned foods, insect nets, folding camp chairs and cots, cooking pots, Robyn's enamel hip bath and her flowered chamber pot, trade goods, *merkani* cloth and beads, hand mirrors and cheap knives. When the pile was complete, Zouga put fire into it, a token of finality and of determination. Yet they watched it burn with trepidation.

There were two small concessions Zouga had made: a single case of Ceylon tea for, as Robyn pointed out, no Englishman could be expected to explore undiscovered territories without that sovereign brew, and the sealed tin which contained Zouga's dress uniform, for their very lives might depend on impressing a savage African potentate. Otherwise they had divested themselves of all but the very essentials.

Chief of these essentials was the ammunition, the sacks of first-grade Curtis and May black powder and the ingots of soft lead, the bullet moulds, the flask of quicksilver to harden the balls and the boxes of copper caps. Out of the remaining forty-six porters, thirty of them carried this powder and shot.

Jan Cheroot's musketeers were horrified when they were informed that their field packs would in future hold two hundred, and not fifty, rounds of Enfield ammunition.

'We are warriors, not porters,' his Corporal told him loftily. Jan Cheroot used the metal scabbard of his long bayonet to reason with him, and Robyn dressed the superficial wounds in the Corporal's scalp.

'They now understand the need for carrying extra ammunition, Major,' Jan Cheroot reported to Zouga cheerfully.

It truly was interesting to realize how much fat they could shed, Zouga mused, as he watched the shorter, more manageable column start out. It was less than a hundred and fifty yards from head to tail, and the pace of its march was almost doubled. The main body nearly matched the speed of Zouga's advance party – falling only a mile or so behind during the first day's march.

That first day they reached the scene of the buffalo hunt before noon, and found more than bark baskets of cured black buffalo meat awaiting there. Zouga's head gunbearer, Matthew, came running to meet him through the forest and he was so excited as to be almost incoherent.

'The father of all elephant,' he gibbered, shaking like a man in fever, 'the grandfather of the father of all elephants!'

Jan Cheroot squatted beside the spoor and grinned like a gnome in a successful piece of sorcery, his slant eyes almost disappearing in the web of wrinkles and folds of yellow skin.

'Our luck has come at last,' he exulted. 'This is indeed an elephant to sing about.'

He took a roll of twine out of the bulging pocket of his tunic and used it to measure the circumference of one of the huge pad marks. It was well over five feet, close to six feet around.

'Double that is how high he stands at the shoulder,' Jan Cheroot explained. 'What an elephant!'

Matthew had at last controlled his excitement enough to explain how he had awoken that dawn, when the light was grey and uncertain, and seen the herd passing close to the camp in deathly silence, three great grey ghostly shapes, moving out of the forest and entering the blackened and barren valley through which the fire had swept. They were gone so swiftly, that it had seemed that they had never existed, but their spoor was impressed so clearly into the soft layer of fire ash that every irregularity in the immense footprints, the whorls and wavy creases of the horny pads, were clearly visible.

'There was one of them, bigger and taller than the others, his teeth were long as a throwing spear and so heavy that he held his head low and moved like an old man, a very old man.'

Now Zouga also shivered with excitement, even in the stultifying heat of the burned-out valley, where it seemed the blackened earth had retained the heat of the flames. Jan Cheroot, mistaking the small movement, grinned wickedly around the stem of his clay pipe.

'My old father used to say that even a brave man is frightened three times when he hunts the elephant, once when he sees its spoor, twice when he hears its voice and the third time when he see the beast – big and black as an ironstone kopje.'

Zouga did not trouble to deny the accusation, he was following the run of the spoor with his eyes. The three huge animals had moved up the centre of the valley, heading directly into the bad ground of the escarpment rim.

'We will follow them,' he said quietly.

'Of course,' Jan Cheroot nodded, 'that is what we came for.'

The spoor led them over the cold grey ash, amongst the blackened and bared branches of the burned-out jessie bush and up the rising funnel of the narrow valley.

Jan Cheroot led. He had discarded his faded tunic for a sleeveless leather jerkin with loops for the Enfield cartridges across the chest. Zouga followed him closely, carrying the Sharps and fifty extra rounds, together with his two-gallon water bottle. His gunbearers, in strict order of seniority backed him, each with his burden of blankets and water bottles, food bag, powder flask and ball pouch, and of course the big smooth-bored elephant guns.

Zouga was anxious to see Jan Cheroot work. The man talked a very good elephant hunt, but Zouga wanted to know if he was as good on the spoor as he was at telling about it around the camp fire. The first test came swiftly when the valley pinched out against another low cliff of impassable rock, and it seemed as though the great beasts they followed had taken wing and soared away above the earth.

'Wait,' said Jan Cheroot and cast swiftly along the base of the cliff. A minute later he whistled softly and Zouga went forward.

There was a smudge of dark ash on a block of ironstone, and another above it, seeming to lead directly into sheer rock face.

Jan Cheroot scrambled up over the loose scree at the foot of the cliff, and disappeared abruptly. Zouga slung his rifle and followed him. The blocks of ironstone had fractured in the shape of a giant's staircase – each step as high as his waist so that he had to use a hand to climb.

Even the elephants would have extended themselves to make each step, rising on their back legs as he had seen them do at the circus, for an elephant is incapable of jumping. They must keep two feet on the earth before they can heave their ungainly bulks upwards.

Zouga reached the spot where Jan Cheroot had disappeared

and stopped short in amazement at the threshold of the stone portals, invisible from below, which marked the beginning of the ancient elephant road.

The portals were symmetrically formed in fractured rock, and had eroded through the softer layers, leaving straight joints so they seemed to have been worked by a mason. The opening was so narrow that it seemed impossible that such a large animal could pass through, and looking above the level of his own head, Zouga saw how over the centuries their rough skin had worn the stone smooth as thousands upon thousands of elephant had squeezed through the gap. He reached up and plucked a coarse black bristle, almost as thick as a Swan Vesta, from a crack in the face. Beyond the natural gateway, the gap in the cliffs widened and rose at a more gentle pitch. Already Jan Cheroot was four hundred yards up the pathway.

'Come!' he called, and they followed him up.

The elephant road might have been surveyed and constructed by the corps of engineers, for never was the gradient steeper than thirty degrees and when there were natural steps they were never higher than a man or an elephant could comfortably negotiate, although it seemed there were always accidents, for within a quarter of a mile they found where one of the big animals had missed his footing and struck the tip of one tusk against the ironstone edge.

The tusk had snapped above the point, and twenty pounds of ivory lay in the path. The fragment was worn and stained, so thick around that Zouga could not span it with both hands, but where it had sheared the fresh ivory was a lovely finely grained porcelain white.

Jan Cheroot whistled again when he saw the girth of the fragment of tusk. 'I have never seen an elephant so big,' he whispered, and instinctively checked the priming of his musket.

They followed the road out of the rocky pass on to forested slopes, where the trees were different, more widely spaced, and here the three old bulls had paused to strip off long slabs of bark from the msasa trunks before moving on. A mile further along the road, they found the chewed balls of bark still wet and smelling of elephant saliva, a rank gamey smell. Zouga held one of the big stringy balls to his nostrils and inhaled the elephant smell. It was the most exciting odour he had ever known.

When they rounded a shoulder of the mountain, there was a

terrifying drop of open blue space before them in which the tiny shapes of vultures soared. Zouga was sure that it was the end of the road.

'Come!' Jan Cheroot whistled and they stepped out on to the narrow secret ledge, with the deep drop close at hand and followed the road that had been smoothed for them by tens of thousands of roughly padded feet over the centuries.

Zouga at last was allowing himself to hope, for the road climbed always, and there seemed to be a definite purpose and direction to it – unlike the meandering game trails of the valley. This road was going somewhere, climbing and bearing determinedly southwards.

Zouga paused a moment and looked back. Far behind and below the sunken plain of the Zambezi shimmered in the blue and smoky haze of heat. The gigantic baobab trees seemed like children's miniatures, the terrible ground over which they had laboured for weeks seemed smooth and inviting, and far away just visible through the haze the serpentine belt of darker, denser vegetation marked the course of the great wide river itself.

Zouga turned his back upon it and followed Jan Cheroot up around the shoulder of the mountain, and a new and majestic vista opened around him as dramatically as though a theatre curtain had been drawn aside.

Another steep slope stretched away above the cliffs, and there were luxuriant forests of marvellously shaped trees, the colours of their foliage was pink and flaming scarlet and iridescent green. These lovely forests reached up to a rampart of rocky peaks that Zouga was certain must mark the highest point of the escarpment.

There was something different with this new scene, and it took Zouga some moments to realize what it was. Then suddenly he drew a deep breath of pleasure. The air fanning down from the crest was sweet and cool as that on a summer's evening on the South Downs, but carrying with it the scent of strange shrubs and flowers and the soft exotic perfume of that beautiful pink and red forest of msasa trees.

That was not all, Zouga realized suddenly. There was something more important still. They had left the tsetse 'fly-belt' behind them. It was many hours and a thousand feet of climbing since he had noticed the last of the deadly little insects. The land ahead of them now was clean, they were entering a land where man could live and rear his animals. They were leaving the killing heat of that harsh and forbidding valley for something softer and cleaner, something good, Zouga was certain of it, at last.

He stared about him with delight and wonder. Below him in the void a pair of vultures came planing in on wide-stretched pinions, so close that he could see every individual feather in their wingtips. and above the shaggy mound of their nest that clung precariously to a fissure in the sheer rock cliff they beat at the air, hovering, before settling upon the nest site. Clearly Zouga heard the impatient cries of the hungry nestlings.

On the rock shelf high above his head a family of hyrax, the plump rabbit-like rock dassie, sat in a row and stared down at him with patent astonishment, fluffy as children's toys, until at last they took fright and disappeared into their rocky warrens with the speed of a conjurer's illusion.

The sun, sinking through the last quadrant of its course, lit it all with richer and mellower light, and turned the cloud ranges to splendour, tall mushroom-shaped thunderheads of silver and brightest gold, touched with fleshy pink tongues and the tinge of wild roses.

Now at last Zouga could not doubt where the elephant road was leading him and he felt his spirits soaring, his body wearied from the climb was suddenly recharged with vigour, with vaulting expectations. For he knew that those rugged peaks above him were the threshold, the very frontiers of the fabled kingdom of Monomatapa.

He wanted to push past Jan Cheroot on the narrow track, and run ahead up the broad beautiful forested slope that led to the crest, but the little yellow Hottentot stopped him with a hand upon his shoulder.

'Look!' he hissed softly. 'There they are!'

Zouga followed his outflung arm and saw instantly. Far ahead amongst those magical red and pink groves something moved, vast and grey and slow, ethereal and insubstantial as a shadow. He stared at it, feeling his heartbeat quicken at this, his first glimpse of an African elephant in its savage habitat, but the slow grey movement was immediately screened by the dense foliage.

'My telescope.' He snapped his fingers urgently behind his back, never taking his eyes from the spot where the huge beast had disappeared, and Matthew thrust the thick cylinder of cool brass into his hand.

With fingers that shook slightly he pulled out the sections of the spy-glass, but before he could lift it to his eye the tree that had screened the elephant's body began to tremble and shake as though it had been struck by a whirlwind, and faintly they heard the rending crackle of tearing timber, the squealing protest of living wood, and slowly the tall tree leaned outwards and then toppled with a crack that echoed off the cliffs like a cannon shot.

Zouga lifted the telescope and rested it on Matthew's patient shoulder. He focused the eye-piece. Abruptly, in the rounded field of the glass, the elephant was very close. His head was framed by the foliage of the tree he had uprooted. The vast ears seemed wide as a clipper's mainsail as they flapped lazily and he could see the puffs of dust that their breeze raised from the massive grey withers.

Clearly he could see the dark wet tear-path from the little eye down the sered and wrinkled cheek, and when the animal raised its head, Zouga drew breath sharply at the unbelievable size of the double arches of stained yellow ivories. One tip was foreshortened, broken off cleanly, and the ivory was brilliant snowy white in the fresh break.

As Zouga watched, the bull used his trunk, with its rubbery fingers of flesh at the tip, to pluck a handful of the delicate new leaves from the fallen tree. He used his trunk with the finesse of an expert surgeon, and then drooped open his triangular lower lip and thrust the leaves far down his own throat, and his rheumy old eyes wept with slow contentment.

An urgent tap on his shoulder disturbed Zouga and irritably he lifted his eye from the telescope. Jan Cheroot was pointing further up the slope.

Two other elephants had drifted into view from out of the forest. Zouga refocused upon them and then gasped. He had thought the first elephant massive, and here was another bull just as big – yet it was the third elephant which daunted his belief.

Beside him Jan Cheroot was whispering with suppressed tension making his voice hoarse and his slanted black eyes shine.

'The younger bulls are his two askari, his indunas. They are his ears and his eyes. For in his great age he is probably almost deaf and more than half blind, but look at him. Is he not still a king?'

The oldest bull was tall and gaunt, taller by almost a head than his protégés, but the flesh seemed to have wasted off the ancient frame. His skin hung in baggy folds and creases from the massive framework of bones. He was thin in the way that some old men are thin; time had eroded him, seeming to leave only skin and stringy sinew and brittle bone. Matthew had been right in his description, the bull moved the way an old man moves, as though each joint protested with rheumatic pangs, and the weight of ivory he had carried for a hundred years was at last too much for him.

The ivory had once been the symbol of his majesty, and it was still perfect, flaring out from the lip and then turning in again so the points almost met. The gracious curves seemed perfectly matched, and the ivory was a lovely, butter yellow, unblemished despite the dominance battles he had fought with them, despite the forest trees that the bull had toppled with them and stripped of their bark or the desert roots he had dug from stony soil with them.

But now, at last, these great tusks were a burden to him, they wearied him and he carried his head low as they ached in his old jaws. It had been many years now since he had used them as fearsome weapons to keep control of the breeding herds. It had been as many years since he had sought the company of the young cows and their noisy squealing calves.

Now the long yellow ivories were a mortal danger to him, as well as a source of discomfort and pain. They made him attractive to man, his only enemy in nature. Always it seemed that the hunters were camped upon his spoor, and the man-smell was associated with the flash and thudding discharge of muzzle-loading firearms, or the rude stinging intrusion of sharpened steel into his tired old flesh.

There were pieces of beaten iron pot-leg and of round hardened lead ball deep in his body, the shot lying against the bone castle of his skull had become encysted with gristle and formed lumps as big as ripe apples beneath the skin, while the scars from arrows and stabbing spears, from the fire-hardened wood spikes of the dead-fall-trap had thickened into shiny grey scars and become part of the rough, folded and creased mantle of his bald grey hide.

Without his two askari he would long ago have fallen to the hunters. It was a strangely intimate relationship that knit the little herd of old bulls, and it had lasted for twenty years or more. Together they had trekked tens of thousands of miles, from the Cashan mountains in the far south, across the burning, waterless wastes of the Kalahari desert, along the dry river beds where they had knelt and with their tusks dug for water in the sand. They had wallowed together in the shallow lake of Ngami while the wings of the water fowl darkened the sky above them, and they had stripped the bark from the forests along Linyati and Chobe, and crossed those wide rivers, walking on the bottom with just the tips of their trunks raised above the surface to give them breath.

Over the seasons they had swung in a great circle through the wild land that lay north of the Zambezi, feasting on the fruits of different forests scattered over a thousand miles, timing their arrival as each crop of berries came into full ripening.

They had crossed lakes and rivers, had stayed long in the hot swamps of the Sud where the midday heat, reaching 120°, soothed the aches in the old bull's bones. But then the wanderlust had driven them on to complete the circle of their migration, south again over mountain ranges and across the low alluvial plains of the great rivers, following secret trails and ancient passes that their ancestors had forged and which they had first trodden as calves at their mother's flank.

In these last dozen seasons, however, there were men where there had never been men before. There were white-robed Arabs in the north around the lakes, with their long-barrelled jezails. There were big bearded men in the south, dressed in dark rough homespun and hunting from tough shaggy little ponies, while everywhere they met the tiny little bushmen with their wicked poisoned arrows, or the Nguni regiments hunting a thousand strong, driving the game into set positions where the plumed spearmen waited.

With each round of the seasons, the elephant ranges were shrinking, new terrors and new dangers waited in the ancient ancestral feeding grounds and the old bull was tired and his bones ached and the ivory in his jaws weighed him down. Still he moved on up the slope to the head of the pass with slow determination and dignity, driven on by his instincts, by the need for space about him, by the memory of the taste of the fruits he knew were already ripening in a distant forest on the shores of a far-away lake.

'We must hurry.' Jan Cheroot's voice roused Zouga, for he had been mesmerized by the sight of the regal old animal, filled with a strange feeling of *déjà-vu*, as though he had lived this moment before, as though this meeting was part of his destiny. The old bull filled him with awe, with a sense of timelessness and grandeur, so he was reluctant to return to the reality of the moment.

'The day dies fast,' Jan Cheroot insisted, and Zouga glanced over his shoulder to where the sun was setting like a mortally wounded warrior bleeding upon the clouds.

'Yes,' he acknowledged, and then frowned as he realized that Jan Cheroot was stripping off his puttees and breeches, folding them and stuffing them together with his blanket and food bag into a crevice in the rock face beside him.

'I run faster like this,' he answered Zouga's silent enquiry with a twinkling grin.

Zouga followed his example, leaving his own pack and pulling off the webbing belt from which hung knife and compass, stripping down to good running order, but he stopped short of removing his breeches. Jan Cheroot's skinny naked yellow buttocks were totally devoid of dignity and his dangling penis played hide-and-seek from under his shirt tails. There were some conventions that an officer of the Queen must observe, Zouga decided firmly, and one was to keep his breeches on in public. He followed Jan Cheroot along the narrow ledge, until they stepped off it on to the forested slope and immediately their forward vision was limited to a dozen yards by the lichen-covered tree trunks. From higher up the slope, however, they could hear the crackle and the ripping sound as the bull with the broken tusk fed on the uprooted tree.

Jan Cheroot worked out swiftly across the slope to avoid the askari, to circle around him and come at the lead bull. Twice he paused to check the wind. It held steadily down the slope into their faces and the colourful leaves above their heads quivered and sighed at its passing.

They had gone a hundred yards when the sounds of the feeding bull ceased abruptly; again Jan Cheroot paused and the little group of hunters froze with him, every man instinctively holding his breath as they listened, but there was only the sound of the wind and the singing whine of a cicada in the branches above.

'He has moved on to join the others,' Jan Cheroot whispered at last. Zouga was also certain that the bull could not yet have suspected their presence. The wind was steady, he could not have scented them. Zouga knew that the eyesight of the elephant was as weak as his hearing and sense of smell were acute, but they had made no sound.

Yet this was a clear demonstration of the benefits that the three old bulls derived from their association. It was always difficult for the hunter to place each of them accurately, especially in thick forest such as this, and the two askaris seemed always to take station on the lead bull to cover and protect him. To come at him, the hunter must penetrate the screen they threw around him.

Standing now, listening and waiting, Zouga wondered if a genuine affection existed between the three animals, whether they derived the pleasure of companionship from each other, and whether the askaris would mourn or pine when the old bull fell at last with the musket ball in his brain or his heart.

'Come!' Silently Jan Cheroot made the open-handed signal to advance and they went on up the slope, stooping under the low trailing branches, Zouga keeping four paces out on the Hottentot's flank to open his field of vision and fire, concentrating his whole being in his eyes and his ears. Far up the slope there was the snap of a breaking twig and it stopped them dead once more, breathing shallowly with the tension, but the sound fastened all their attention ahead so none of them saw the askari.

The elephant waited with the stillness of granite, his sered hide grey and rough as the lichen-covered tree trunks, the shadows thrown by the low sun barred him and broke up the shape of his great body so he blended into the forest, grey and unearthly as mist, and they tiptoed past him at twenty paces without seeing him.

He let the hunters pass him and get up above the wind and when the acrid stench of carnivorous man was borne thickly down to him through the forest, he took it in his trunk and lifted it to his mouth and sprayed the tainted air over the little olfactory organs under his upper lip, and his smell buds flared open like soft wet pink rose buds and the askari bull squealed.

It was a sound that seemed to bounce against the sky, and

ring from the peaks above them, it was an expression of all the hatred and pain, the terrible memories of that acrid man-smell from a hundred other encounters, and the askari bull squealed again and launched his huge body up the slope to destroy the source of that evil odour.

Zouga spun to the piercing din, his shocked eardrums still buzzing with the sound, and the forest shook with the bull's charge. The dense shiny vegetation burst open, like a storm surf running on to rock, and the bull came through.

Zouga was not conscious of his own movements, he was aware only that he was looking at the bull over the open sights of the Sharps rifle, and the blast of shot seemed muted and far off after the ringing squeal that initiated the charge. He saw dust fly from the bull's forehead in a brief little puff, saw the grey skin ripple like that of a stallion stung by a bee, and he reached back and found the stubby wooden stock of one of the big elephant guns in his band. Again, there was no awareness of conscious movement, but over the crude vee of the sight the elephant appeared much closer. Zouga seemed to be leaning back to look up at the gigantic head and the long shafts of yellow ivory reached out over him, blotting out the sky. Clearly he could see the bright white porcelain break in one point of the left-hand tusk.

He heard Jan Cheroot beside him, and heard his excited shrieks.

'*Skiet hom!* Shoot him!'

Then the heavy weapon leapt against his own shoulder, driving him back a pace, and he saw the tiny fountain of bright blood squirting out of the elephant's throat like a lovely scarlet flamingo feather. He reached back for the next loaded gun, although he knew there would be no time to fire again.

He was surprised that he felt no fear, although he knew he was a dead man. The elephant was on him, his life was forfeit, there could be no question, yet he went on with the motions of living, hefting the new gun, thumbing back the clumsy hammer as he swung the barrel up.

The shape of the huge animal above him had altered, it was no longer so close, and he realized with a thrill that the bull was turning, it had been unable to endure the fearful punishment of the heavy-bored guns.

He was turning, passing by them with blood streaming down his head and chest. As he passed, he exposed his neck and flank, and Zouga shot him a hand's span behind the joint of his shoulder on the line of the lungs and the ball slogged into his rib cage.

The bull was going, crashing away up the slope, and with the fourth gun Zouga hit him high in the back, aiming for the bony knuckles of the spine where they showed through the scabby grey hide of the sloping back and the bull whipped his thick tufted tail at the agony of the strike and disappeared into the forest, gone like a wraith in the failing light of the sunset.

Zouga and Jan Cheroot stared at each other speechlessly, each of them holding a smoking weapon at high port across his chest, and they listened to the run of the bull up the slope ahead of them.

Zouga found his voice first, he turned to his gunbearers.

'Load!' he hissed at them, for they also were paralysed by the close passage of violent, thundering death, but his command liberated them and they each snatched a handful of black powder from the bag slung at their sides and poured it into the still-hot muzzles of the guns.

'The lead bull and the other askari will run,' lamented Jan Cheroot, himself frantically busy with the ramrod of his Enfield.

'We can still catch them before the summit,' Zouga told him, grabbing the first loaded gun. An elephant goes on a steep uphill at a very measured pace that a good runner can gain upon, but downhill he goes like a run-away locomotive, nothing can catch him, not even a good horse.

'We must catch them before the crest,' Zouga repeated, and launched himself at the slope. Weeks of hard going over bad terrain had toughened him, and the driving lust of the hunter was the spur. He flew at the slope.

Awareness of his own lack of experience that had resulted in such poor shooting, made Zouga more fiercely determined to close with the lead bull and vindicate himself. He guessed that as a complete novice he had failed to find the vitals with any of the balls he had fired, he had missed brain and heart and lungs by inches, inflicting pain and mutilation, instead of the quick kill for which the true huntsman strives. He wanted desperately to have another chance to end it cleanly, and he pelted up the slope.

Before he had gone two hundred yards, he had evidence that his shooting had not been as wide as he had at first believed.

He checked at a spot where it looked as though someone had thrown a bucket of blood across the stony earth. The blood was a peculiarly bright scarlet, and it frothed with tiny bubbles, lung blood. There was no question, that last ball fired into the bull's back as he went away up the slope must have raked the lungs. It was a killing shot, but a slow killer. The old bull was drowning in his own bright arterial blood, desperately trying to rid himself of it by squirting it out through his trunk as it bubbled up into his throat.

He was dying, but it would take time still, and Zouga raced on after him.

He had not expected the bull to stand again. He expected him to run until he dropped, or until the hunters caught up with him. Zouga knew the folly of attributing human motives and loyalties to wild animals, even so it seemed that the stricken bull had determined to sacrifice himself in order to allow the lead bull and the second askari to escape across the pass at the crest of the mountains.

Up the slope, he was waiting for Zouga, listening for him with those vast grey ears spread wide, his chest with the girth of a Cognac cask of Limousine oak racked and strained to force air into his torn lung.

He charged as soon as he heard the man. His huge ears cocked back and rolled at the tips, trunk curled at his chest, shrilling and squealing, blowing a fine red mist of blood from his trunk, pounding through the forest so the earth trembled with each massive footfall and the branches crackled and broke like a discharge of musketry.

Panting, Zouga stood to meet the charge, ducking his head and weaving for a clean shot through the thick forest. At the last moment the bull broke off the charge, and swerved up the slope again. Each time the hunters began to move forward, he launched another thunderous mock-attack, forcing them to stand to meet him, and then breaking off again.

Minutes passed between each charge, and the hunters were pinned down in the thick forest, fretting with the knowledge that already the lead bull and his surviving protégé must have reached the crest and gone away in a rush like an avalanche down the far side.

Zouga was learning two hard lessons: the first, as old Tom Harkness had tried to teach him, was that only a novice or a fool under-guns an elephant. The light ball of the Sharps might be highly effective on American bison, but the African elephant has ten times the body weight and resistance. Standing in the msasa forests, listening to the squealing and crashing of the wounded monster, Zouga determined never again to use the light American rifle on heavy game.

The second lesson he was learning was that if the first ball does not kill, then it seems to numb and anaesthetize heavy game to further punishment. Kill cleanly, or the subsequent shots into heart and lungs seem to be without effect. It was not only anger and provocation which made a wounded animal so dangerous, it was also this shock-induced immortality.

After standing down half a dozen mock charges, Zouga abandoned caution and patience, and he ran forward shouting to meet the next charge.

'Whoa there!' he called. 'Come on then, old fellow!'

This time he got in close, and crashed another ball through the bull's rib cage as he turned away. He had controlled his first wild excitement, and the ball struck precisely at the point of aim. He knew it was a heart shot, but the bull came again squealing, and Zouga fired a last time before the angry trumpeting and shrilling turned to a long sad bellow, that echoed off the peaks and rang out into the blue void of sky beyond the cliffs.

They heard him go down, the impact of the heavy body against the earth made it shiver under their feet. Cautiously, the little group of hunters went forward through the forest and they found him kneeling, his forelegs folded neatly under his chest, his long, yellow ivories propping up the dusty wrinkled old head, still facing down the slope as though defiant even in death.

'Leave him,' shouted Jan Cheroot. 'Follow the others.' And they ran on past him.

Night caught them before they reached the crest of the slope, the sudden impenetrably black night of central Africa, so they lost the spoor and missed the pass.

'We will have to let them go,' Jan Cheroot lamented in the darkness, his yellow face a pale blob at Zouga's shoulder.

'Yes,' Zouga agreed. 'This time we must let them go.' But somehow he knew there would be another time. The feeling that the old bull was part of his destiny was still strongly with Zouga. Yes, there would be another time, of that he was certain.

That night for the first time Zouga ate the hunter's greatest delicacy: slices of elephant heart threaded on to a green stick with cubes of white fat cut out from the chest cavity, salted and peppered, and roasted over the slow coals of the camp fire, eaten with cold cakes of stone-ground corn and washed down with a mug of tea, steaming hot, bitter, strong and unsweetened. He could not remember a finer meal, and afterwards Zouga lay down on the hard earth, covered by a single blanket and protected from the chill of the wind by the huge carcass of the old bull, and slept as though he also had been struck down, without dreams, without rolling over even once in his sleep.

In the morning, by the time they had chopped out one of the tusks and laid it under the msasa trees, they could already hear the singing of the porters as the main body of the caravan filed along the narrow ledge, rounding the shoulder of the mountain and then came up on to the slope.

Robyn was a hundred paces ahead of the standard-bearer, and when she reached the carcass of the bull she stopped.

'We heard the gunfire last evening,' she said.

'He's a fine old bull,' Zouga told her, indicating the freshly chopped tusk. It was the unbroken right-hand ivory, taller than Zouga, but a third of its length had been buried in the skull. This portion was smooth, unblemished white, whereas the rest of it was stained by vegetable juices.

'It will weigh almost a hundred pounds,' he went on, touching the tusks with the toe of his boot. 'Yes, he's a fine old bull.'

'Not any more, he isn't,' Robyn told him quietly, watching Jan Cheroot and the gunbearers hacking away at the enormous mutilated head. Little chips of white bone flew in the early sunlight, as they whittled away the heavy skull to free the second tusk. Robyn watched the butchery for a few seconds only before going on up the slope towards the crest.

Zouga was irritated and angry with her, for she had detracted from his own vaulting pleasure in his first elephant hunt. So, an hour later when he heard Robyn calling to him from higher up the slope, he ignored her cries. However, she was persistent, as always, and at last with an exclamation of exasperation, he followed her up through the forest. She came running down to meet him, with the unrestrained infectious joy of a child shining on her face.

'Oh Zouga.' She seized his hand, and began to drag him impetuously up the slope. 'Come and see, you must come and see.'

The old elephant road crossed the saddle, through a deep pass, guarded on each hand by grey buttresses of rough grey rock and as they took the last few paces over the highest point a new and beautiful world opened below and ahead of them. Zouga gasped involuntarily, for he had not anticipated anything like this.

Low foothills fell away from beneath their feet, regular as the swells of the ocean, covered with stately trees whose trunks were tall and grey as the oaks of Windsor Park, and then beyond the hills the undulating lightly forested grasslands, golden as fields of ripe wheat, spread to a tall blue horizon. There were streams of clear water meandering through the glades of pale grass, where herds of wild game drank or lazed upon the banks.

There were buffalo everywhere Zouga looked, black bovine shapes, standing shoulder to shoulder in dark masses under the umbrella branches of the acacia trees. Closer at hand a troop of sable antelope, that loveliest of all antelope, jet black above but with snowy bellies, their long symmetrical curve of horn extended backwards almost to touch the haunches, followed the herd bull in long file to the water, pausing unafraid to stare curiously at the interlopers, forming a frieze of stately, almost Grecian, design.

The endless stretch of land was dotted with hills like ruined natural castles of stone, seeming to have been built in past aeons by giants and ogres from mammoth blocks of stone, and tumbled now in fantastic shapes, some with fairy turrets and spires, others again flat topped, geometrically laid out as though by a meticulous architect with plumb-line and theodolite.

This lovely scene was lit by a peculiar pearly luminosity of the morning light, so that even the furthest hills, probably more than a hundred miles distant, were sharply silhouetted through the sweet clear air.

'It's beautiful,' Robyn murmured, still holding Zouga's hand.

'The kingdom of Monomatapa,' Zouga answered her, his own voice husky with emotion.

'No,' Robyn answered softly. 'There is no sign of man here, this is the new Eden.'

Zouga was silent, letting his eyes rove across the scene, searching for, but not finding, any evidence of man. It was a land untouched, unspoiled.

'A new land, there for the taking!' he said, still holding Robyn's hand. They were as close, in that moment, as they had ever been or would ever be again, and the land awaited them, wide, limitless, empty and beautiful.

At last, reluctantly, he left Robyn at the head of the pass and went back through the grey rock portals to bring on the caravan. He found the second tusk removed, and both of them bound up with bark rope on to the carrying-poles of newly cut msasa wood, but the porters had laid aside their packs and were indulging in an orgy of fresh meat, and that most sought-after of African spoils, thick white globs of elephant fat.

They had cut a trapdoor into the belly of the elephant carcass, and pulled out the entrails, and these glistened in the early sunlight, huge rubbery tubes of purple and yellow guts, already swelling and ballooning with the trapped gases they contained.

Half a dozen porters, stripped mother-naked, had crawled into the interior of the elephant's carcass, disappearing completely from view and wading almost waist-deep in the clotting, congealing bath of trapped blood. They crawled out, painted with it from head to foot, eyes and grinning teeth startlingly white in the grisly shining wet red visages, their arms filled with tidbits of liver and fat and spleen.

These delicacies were hacked into pieces with the blade of an assegai and thrown on the glowing coals of one of half a dozen fires, then snatched up again, black on the outside and more than half raw within to be wolfed down with every appearance of ecstatic pleasure.

There would be no moving them until they were satiated, Zouga realized. So he left instructions to Jan Cheroot, himself already pot-bellied with the meat he had gorged, to follow as soon as the carcass had been either eaten or packed up for carrying, and taking the Sharps rifle returned back up the slope to where he had left Robyn.

He called for her, fruitlessly, for almost half an hour, and was really becoming concerned for her safety when her reply echoed off the cliffs, and looking upwards he saw her standing on a ledge a hundred feet above him, waving him to come up to her.

Zouga climbed up swiftly to where she stood on the ledge,

and checked the rebuke that he had ready for her when he saw her expression. She was pale, a sickly greyish colour, under the gilding of the sun, and her eyes were reddened and still swimming with tears.

'What is it, Sissy?' he asked with quick concern, but she seemed unable to reply, the words choking in her throat so she had to swallow thickly, and motion him to follow her.

The ledge on which they stood was narrow, but level – and was cut back under the cliff, forming a low long cavern. The cavern had been used before by other men, for the rocky roof was blackened with the sooty smoke of countless cooking-fires, and the back wall was decorated with the lyrically childlike paintings of the little yellow bushmen who over the centuries must have used this as a regular camp during their endless wanderings.

The paintings lacked both perspective and accurate form, but they captured the essential nature of all they recorded, from the graceful sweep of the giraffe's neck, to the bulky shoulders of the Cape buffalo with the mournful drooping horns framing the lifted nose.

The bushman artist saw himself and his tribe as frail, sticklike figures, with drawn bows, dancing and prancing about the quarry, and again, out of all proportion to the rest of the painting, each little man sported a massively erect penis. Even in the heat of the chase, such was the universal conceit of all male kind, Zouga thought.

Zouga was enchanted by the frozen cavalcade of man and beast which covered the walls of the cave, and he had already determined to camp here so that he could have more time to study and record this treasure house of primitive art, when Robyn was calling him again.

He followed her along the ledge until they reached the point where it ended abruptly, forming a balcony over the dreaming land ahead of them. Zouga's attention was torn between this fresh vista of forest and glade and the cave art at his shoulder, but Robyn summoned him again impatiently.

There were strata of multi-coloured rock running horizontally through the rock face of the cliff. The different layers of rock varied in hardness, and the erosion of a softer layer had formed the long low cavern beyond the ledge.

This layer of rock was a soapy green colour, where it had not been painted over by the bushmen artists or discoloured with the smoke of their fires, and here at the point overlooking the empire of Monomatapa someone had used a metal tool to scrape a smooth square plaque into the green soapstone. The freshly cut surface stood out rawly as though it had been done that very day, but the words gave the lie to that impression.

There was a simple Christian cross chiselled deeply into the stone, and below it the name and the date, the lettering very carefully cut and designed by an expert penman.

'FULLER MORRIS BALLANTYNE'

Zouga exclaimed aloud at seeing his father's name, so clearly rendered by his father's own hand.

Despite the apparent freshness of the cut, the date was seven years previously – 20th July, 1853. After that single exclamation they were both speechless, staring at the inscription, each of them gripped by differing emotion – Robyn by a resurgence of filial love and duty, by a crushing desire to be with her father again after so many years, the vast empty place in her life aching more excruciatingly at the prospect of being soon filled. Her eyes refilled with tears, and they broke from her eyelids and ran down her cheeks.

'Please, God,' she prayed silently, 'lead me to my father. Dear God, grant me that I am not too late.'

Zouga's emotions were as strong, but different. He felt a corroding resentment that any other man, father or not, should have preceded him through these rocky gates into the kingdom of Monomatapa. This was his land, and he did not want to share it with another. Especially, he did not want to share it with that monster of cruelty and conceit that was his father.

He stared coldly at the inscription that followed the name and date, but inwardly he seethed with anger and resentment.

'In God's Holy name.' The words were carved below his father's name.

It was typical of Fuller Ballantyne that he should carve his own name here with cross and credentials as the Lord's ambassador, as he had on trees and rocks at a hundred other places across the continent which he regarded as a personal gift from his God.

'You were right, Zouga dear. You are leading us to him, as you promised. I should never have doubted you.'

If he had been alone Zouga realized that he might have defaced that inscription, scraped the rock bare with his hunting knife, but as he had the thought, he realized how futile it would be, for such an action would not wipe out the ghostly presence of the man himself.

Zouga turned away from the rock wall and its taunting plaque. He stared out over the new land – but somehow his heady pleasure in it had been dimmed by the knowledge that another man had passed this way ahead of him. He sat down with his feet dangling over the sheer drop to wait for Robyn to tire of staring at her father's name.

However, the caravan of porters came before she did that. Zouga heard the singing from the forested slope behind the pass long before the head of the line crossed the saddle. The porters had voluntarily doubled their own loads, and they struggled up the slope under the enormous weight of elephant meat and fat and marrow bones, bound up in baskets of green msasa leaves and bark rope.

If Zouga had asked them to carry that weight of trade cloth or beads, or even gunpowder, he would have had an immediate mutiny to deal with, he thought grimly, but at least they were carrying the tusks. He could see them near the head of the line. Each tusk slung on a long pole, a man at either end, but even here they had hung extra baskets of meat on the same pole as the tusk. The total weight must have been well over three hundred pounds, and they struggled up the slope uncomplainingly, even cheerfully.

Slowly, the caravan wound out of the forest and entered the gut of the pass, beginning to move directly under where Zouga sat, the figures of the porters and of Jan Cheroot's Hottentot musketeers foreshortened by the angle. Zouga rose to his feet, he wanted to order Jan Cheroot to camp just beyond the point where the pass debouched on to the foothills. From where Zouga stood, he could see a patch of green grass against the foot of the cliffs far below him, and a pair of pale grey herons hunting frogs in this verdant marshy area. There was certainly a spring, and with the meat upon which they had gorged, his servants would be burning with thirst by nightfall.

The spring would be a good place to camp, and it would allow him the following morning to copy and record the Bushman paintings in the cavern. He cupped his hands to his mouth to hail Jan Cheroot – when a crash like the broadside from a ship-of-the-line filled the pass with thunder that echoed and bounced back and forth between the cliffs.

For many seconds Zouga could not understand what was happening for the thunderous bursts of sound were repeated, almost drowning the thin screams of his porters. They were throwing down their burdens and scattering like a flight of doves under the stoop of the falcon.

Then another movement caught his attention, a large round shape went bounding down the scree slope below the cliffs, charging straight at his panic-stricken caravan. For a moment Zouga believed it was some sort of living predator that was attacking his servants, and, running along the lip of the ledge, he unslung the Sharps rifle, ready to fire down into the pass as soon as he could get a sight on one of the dark bounding shapes.

Then he realized that at each leap the thing struck sparks and fine grey smoke from the scree slope, and he could smell the faint smell, like burnt salt-petre that the sparks left in the air. He realized abruptly that they were giant rounded boulders rolling down upon his caravan, not one but a dozen or more, each weighing many tons, an onslaught which seemed to spring from the very air itself, and he looked wildly about for its source, goaded by the screams of his men and the sight of the rolling boulders smashing open packs of his precious irreplaceable provisions and scattering them across the rocky ground of the saddle.

Far below him, he heard the thudding report of an Enfield rifle, and glancing back he saw the tiny figure of Jan Cheroot aiming almost directly upwards at the sky, and following the direction of his rifle Zouga saw movement, just a flicker of movement on the edge of the cliff, outlined against the blue soaring vault of the heavens.

The deluge of huge boulders was coming from the very top of the cliff, and as Zouga stared, another and then another came raining down into the pass. Zouga squinted his eyes, head thrown back, as he studied the cliff rim. There was some animal up there. Zouga did not at first think of man, for he had already convinced himself that this new land was devoid of human presence.

He felt an almost superstitious chill of horror that some pack of giant apes was on top of the cliff, bombarding his men with huge rocks, then he shook himself free of the feeling, and looked quickly for some way to get higher up his side of the pass, to reach a position from where he could fire across the rocky gateway at the attackers on the opposite cliff and give some protection to his servants.

Almost immediately he discovered another ledge rising at a steep angle from the one on which he stood. Only a soldier's eye would have picked it out. The tiny feet of the little rock hyrax that used it had put a light sheen on the rock and it was this that had drawn Zouga's attention to the narrow pathway.

'Stay here!' he shouted at Robyn, but she stepped in front of him.

'Zouga, what are you going to do?' she demanded, and then before he could answer. 'Those are men up there! You cannot fire upon them!' Her cheeks were still smeared with tears, but her pale face was set and determined.

'Get out of the way,' he snapped at her.

'Zouga, it will be murder.'

'That's what they are trying to do to my men.'

'We must bargain with them.' Robyn caught at his arm as he pushed past her, but he shook her off and ran to the higher ledge.

'It will be murder!' Robyn's cry followed him, and as he climbed, Zouga was reminded of the words of old Tom Harkness. The accusation that his father would not stop at killing anybody who stood in his way. This was what he had meant, Zouga was suddenly sure of it. He wondered if his father had fought his way through this pass, just as Zouga himself was about to do.

'If the champion of the Almighty can do it, then what a fine example to follow,' he muttered to himself as he went up the steep ledge.

Below him the Enfield rifle thudded again, the sound muted by distance, almost lost in the roar of a new avalanche of murderous rock. Jan Cheroot could only hope to discourage his attackers with rifle fire from that angle; only if one of them actually leaned far out over the edge of the cliff would he be vulnerable to fire from the gut of the pass.

Zouga climbed in cold anger, stepping unhesitatingly over dangerous spots in the narrow ledge where small pieces of rock crumbled under his boots and went rattling down into the pass hundreds of feet below.

Abruptly he came out on to a broader ledge, formed by the strata of rock, which rose at a gentler pitch so that now Zouga could run along it without fear of losing his footing. He climbed swiftly, it was less than ten minutes since that first boulder had come crashing down into the pass; the attackers were continuing the bombardment, the hills reverberated with the crash and rumble of flying boulders.

Ahead of Zouga on the ledge, a pair of tiny grey klipspringer went bouncing up over broken rock, seeming to flit on the tips of their elongated hooves, terrified by the men and the rumble of falling rock. They reached the corner of the ledge and one after another they made what seemed suicidal leaps out into space, phenomenal leaps that carried them forty feet to the next sheer wall of rock, rock which seemed devoid of foothold, but they clung to it like flies and scrambled swiftly up out of sight over the top of the cliff.

Zouga envied them that birdlike agility as he toiled up the steep incline, sweat soaking his shirt and streaming stingingly into his eyes. He could not stop to rest, for far below him a thin wailing scream of agony told him that at least one of the flying boulders had struck down a porter.

He turned another steep corner in the goat track, scrambled over the rim, and was suddenly out upon the flat table-like summit, dotted with little clumps of broom-bush and sparse stiff yellow grass, like hedgehog quills.

Zouga threw himself down on the edge of the plateau, heaving and straining for breath and he struck the sweat from his eyes, peering across the deep void of the pass at the cliffs on the opposite side. He found himself on a level with the heights opposite. It was three or four hundred yards across, easy range for the Sharps – though one of the smooth-bore four-to-the-pounds would have been hopelessly inaccurate at that distance.

While he primed the rifle, he studied the ground opposite him and saw almost immediately why the attackers had chosen that side of the pass in preference to the one on which Zouga lay.

They were on a flat-topped pinnacle of sheer rock, with no visible access to it from any direction, what path there was would be secret and highly defensible. The attackers had an inexhaustible supply of missiles for the rounded boulders were scattered everywhere upon the heights, varying in size from that of a man's head to that of an elephant carcass, and as Zouga watched them they were using heavy raw timber baulks to lever one of these over the edge of the cliff.

Zouga's hands were shaking and he fought to bring them under control, but the Sharps rifle wavered as he tried to take a sight on the little group of men across the open void of space. There were not more than two dozen of them, all of them naked except for a brief kilt of leather, their dark skins polished with a sheen of sweat in the sunlight.

He was regaining his breath swiftly, and now he wriggled forward on his belly and propped the stock of the Sharps rifle on a rock in front of him. It was a dead rest, and as he levelled his gaze over the open sights the group of men succeeded in working the huge boulder over the edge of the cliff.

It went with a brief grating that carried clearly to Zouga, and then it fell with the soft rushing of eagle's wings until it struck again in the pass two hundred feet below – and once again the hills rang and rumbled to the force and weight of it.

The little group of black men had drawn back from the edge of the cliff, resting a moment before they selected another missile. Only one of them wore a headdress. It looked like a cap made from the mane of a male lion, long tawny hair tipped with black. It made the man taller than his companions, and he seemed to be giving orders to them, gesticulating and pushing those nearest to him.

'You'll do, my beauty!' Zouga whispered. He had regained his breath now, and the sweat was cooling his back and his neck. He pushed up the leaf of his backsight to its 300-yard adjustment and then settled down on his elbows to peer over it. The rifle was rock-steady on its rest, while he took a fine bead on the man with the lion headdress.

He touched off the shot, and while the crack of it still stung his eardrums he saw a tiny chip of rock fly from the lip of the cliff across the valley. 'Low, but very nicely on line,' he told himself, opened the breech of the Sharps and forced the paper cartridge into it.

The shot had startled the little group of men. They peered about them, mystified, not certain of what it was or from where it had come. The tall figure in the headdress moved cautiously forward to the edge of the cliff and stooped to examine the fresh chip on the ironstone rim, touching it with one finger.

Zouga set the cap, and thumbed back the hammer. He gave it a full bead, and aimed at the waving yellow headdress, set the hair-trigger and then with a lover's touch stroked the curved trigger.

The bullet told loudly, a meaty slap like a housewife beating a carpet, and the man in the lion headdress spun round sharply, his arms jerking out wide, his legs shuffling in a grotesque little dance, they collapsed under him and he flopped on the very edge of the cliff like a harpooned catfish.

His companions stood frozen, making no effort to help him as he slid towards the edge of the cliff, and a final spasmodic jerk of his legs tumbled him into the void. He fell for a long time, his outspread limbs spinning like the spokes of a wagon wheel, and there was another meaty thump as he landed at last on the broken scree slope far below.

Zouga fired again, into the tight knot of men, not attempting to single out one of them, and he hit two of them with a single bullet, for even at that range the Sharps could drive the hardened lead ball through a man's body with hardly any loss of velocity, and the group was bunched up.

As the ball whacked into them, they split into separate racing figures, their yells of fright carrying clearly to where Zouga lay, and before he could fire again, they had disappeared into a narrow rocky gulley with the miraculous speed of a troop of little furry hyrax.

The silence was sudden and startling after the uproar of falling boulders and heavy gun fire and it lasted for many minutes, broken at last by the shrill voice of Jan Cheroot calling up from the deep gut of the pass. Zouga stood up, and hanging on to the branch of a monkey orange tree, leaned out over the edge of the cliff.

'Take the caravan through, Sergeant.' He pitched his voice to carry, and the echoes mocked him with his own words. 'Sergeant – Sergeant – Sergeant—'

'I will cover you – cover you – cover you,' taunted the echoes.

Zouga called the little Matabele maiden from the fireside where she knelt beside Robyn, helping her treat one of the porters who had been struck by a flying splinter of rock during the attack, and whose shoulder had been laid open to the bone.

'Juba,' he told her, 'I want you to come with me.' And the girl glanced back at Robyn, hesitating to obey him. Zouga's irritation flared again. He and Robyn had not spoken again since Zouga had broken up the attack with rifle fire, and Jan Cheroot had reassembled the caravan and led it out of the deadly trap of the gorge to where it was camped now in the foothills beyond the pass.

'Come,' Zouga repeated, and the child dropped her eyes at his tone and followed him submissively as he started back towards the pass.

Zouga moved back cautiously, pausing every fifty paces or so to survey the clifftops suspiciously, although he was fairly certain that there would be no renewal of the boulder rolling. However, he kept in close under the sheer rock face so that any boulder would fall beyond them.

The going was difficult over the loose scree, and through the thick scrub that covered it. It took them nearly an hour to get back to the spot where Zouga had marked the fall of the body of the warrior in the lion headdress, and then they had to search for nearly as long again before they found the corpse.

He had fallen into a deep crevice between two rocks, and he lay at the bottom of it on his back. The body appeared unmarked except for the small black bullet hole low on the left side of his naked chest.

The eyes were still wide open, but he had lost his headdress.

After a moment Zouga turned to Juba enquiringly. 'Who is he? Of what tribe is he?' he asked, and the child showed no concern at the presence of violent death. She bad seen very much worse in her short life.

'Mashona!' she told Zouga scornfully. Juba was Matabele of Zanzi blood, and there was no more noble breeding outside the kraal of King Mzilikazi himself. She felt nothing but contempt for all the other tribes of Africa, especially for these people.

'Mashona!' she repeated. 'Eaters of dirt.'

It was the ultimate term of denigration that the Matabele applied to all the tribes that they have taken into slavery, or driven to the very point of extinction.

'It is always the way these baboons fight.' She indicated the dead man with a toss of her pretty head. 'They stand on the hilltops and throw down stones.'

Her dark eyes sparkled. 'It becomes more difficult each year for our young men to blood their spears, and until they do so the King will not give them leave to marry.' She broke off, and Zouga smiled ironically. The child's resentment was clearly not so much at the Mashona's alleged lack of sportsmanship, but at the havoc that this wrought on the Matabele marriage markets.

Zouga scrambled down into the rocky crevice, and stooped over the dead warrior. Despite Juba's contempt, the man was well formed, with straight strong limbs, and handsome intelligent features. For the first time Zouga felt a twinge of regret at having fired the ball which had caused that innocuous-looking little wound. It was a good thing that the warrior lay upon his back for the exit would have been ghastly. A soldier should never examine the bodies of the men he kills in the heat of battle. Zouga had made that discovery long ago in India, for afterwards there was always this moment of guilt and remorse. He shrugged it away, for he had not come either to gloat over the kill or to torture himself with it, but to merely identify his enemy.

Why had these warriors attacked the caravan without warning, he wondered? Were they the border guards of the fabled Monomatapa? It seemed the most likely explanation, though, of course, they could be ordinary bandits, like the dacoits of India with whom he had made bitter acquaintance.

Zouga stared moodily down at the corpse. Who had he been? And how much danger did his tribe still present to Zouga's caravan? But there was nothing more to learn and Zouga began to straighten up again when he noticed the necklace around the corpse's throat. He knelt again to examine it.

It was made of cheap trade beads on a thong of gut, a gaudy little trifle except for the pendant that had hung on to his chest but had slipped back under the armpit, half concealed so that Zouga noticed it now for the first time.

He pulled it free, examined it a moment and then slipped the entire necklace off over the man's head. When he put his hand around the back of the dead man's head to lift it he felt the pieces of skull grate together deep in his head like shards of broken pottery under his fingers. He lowered the shattered head and stood up with the necklace twined about his fingers, examining the pendant.

It had been carved from ivory that had yellowed with age, and tiny black cracks formed a fine web across its polished surfaces.

Zouga held it to catch the sunlight, and turned it between his fingers to study it from every angle.

He had seen another figurine that was almost a twin to this one, a golden figurine that was now in a bank vault in Cape Town where he had deposited it before they had sailed on board the gunboat *Black Joke*.

This was the same stylized bird-like shape, perched on a round plinth. The plinth was decorated with the same triangular shark's-teeth pattern, and the bird had the same swelling chest and short, sharply pointed wings folded across its back. It could have been a pigeon or a dove, except for one detail. The beak was the curved and hooked weapon of a raptor.

It was a falcon, he knew it beyond any doubt, and it was certain that the heraldic bird had some deep significance. The golden necklace that Tom Harkness had left him must have belonged to a king or a queen or a high priest. The choice of material, gold, was an indication of that. Now here was the same shape, worn by a man who seemed to be a chieftain, and once again the shape was faithfully copied in a precious material, ivory.

The falcon of Monomatapa, Zouga wondered, studying the ancient pendant, ancient it must be, for the ivory had acquired a deep patina and lustre.

Zouga looked up at the little Matabele girl, standing almost naked above him, and watching him with interest.

'Do you see this?' he asked.

'It is a bird.'

'Have you seen it before?'

Juba shook her head, and her fat little breasts joggled at the movement.

'It is a Mashona thing,' and she shrugged. What would a daughter of the sons of Senzangakhona and Chaka want with such a nonsense?

On an impulse Zouga lifted the necklace and dropped it over his own head, letting the ivory falcon fall inside the vee of his flannel shirt, where it nested against the darkly springing curls of his body hair.

'Come!' he told Juba. 'There is nothing more for us here,' and he led the way back towards the camp beyond the pass.

The land into which the old bull had led them by the secret road through the pass was an elephant kingdom. Perhaps the pressure of the hunters moving up from the far southern tip of the continent had driven them into this unpeopled world. The herds were everywhere. Each day Zouga and Jan Cheroot hunting far ahead of the main caravan came up with the huge grey pachyderms, and they shot them down.

They shot and killed forty-eight elephant the first month and almost sixty the second, and Zouga meticulously recorded each kill in his journal, the circumstances of the hunt, the weight of each tusk, and the exact location of the cache in which they buried them.

His small band of porters could not carry even a small part of such a mass of ivory, and the distance and direction which they must still travel was uncertain. Zouga buried his treasure, always near a readily recognizable landmark, a distinctive tree, or an unusual rock, a hilltop or a confluence of rivers, to enable him to find it again.

He would return one day for it, and when he did, it would have dried off its excess moisture and be easier for the porters to carry.

In the meantime, he spent all his daylight hours in pursuit of the quarry, walking and running great distances until his body was hard and fit as that of a highly trained athlete, and his arms and face a deep mahogany brown, even his full beard and moustache gilded to shades of gold by the bright sunlight.

Every day he learned from Jan Cheroot the tricks of bush-lore, until he could run a difficult spoor over rocky ground without a check. He learned to anticipate the turns and the twists that the driven herds made to get below the wind and take his scent. He learned to anticipate the pattern of their movements so that by cutting across the circuitous spoor he could save many hours of dogged pursuit. He learned to judge the sex and size and age and ivory of a beast by the mark of its rounded pads in the earth.

He found that if the herd was allowed to settle into that swinging gait between a trot and a canter, then they could keep it up for a day and a night without pause – whereas if they were taken in the full heat of noon, he could run them hard for the first five miles, winding them, bringing the tiny calves to a standstill so the cows stopped with them – flapping their huge ears to fan themselves, thrusting their trunk down their own throat to suck the water out of their belly and spray it over their head and neck.

He learned to find the heart and the brain, the lungs and the spine hidden in that amorphous mountain of grey hide and flesh. He learned to break the shoulder when the beast stood broadside, dropping him as though he had been struck by lightning, or to take the hip-shot as he ran choking in the dust cloud behind the herd, shattering the hip joint and pinning the beast for an unhurried coup-de-grâce.

He hunted the herds on the hilltops where they had climbed to catch the soothing evening breeze. At dawn he hunted in the thick forests and the open glades, and at noon he hunted them in the old overgrown gardens of a vanished people. For the land that he had first believed devoid of human presence was not, and had never been so, for unnumbered thousands of years.

Beyond the abandoned gardens where once man had planted his crops, but where now the elephant herds had returned to reclaim their heritage, Zouga found the remains of huge native cities, the long deserted keystones of a once-flourishing civilization, though all that remained were the circular outlines of the thatch-and-daub huts on the bare earth, the blackened hearth stones, and the charred fence poles of the cattle enclosures which must once have penned great herds. Judging by the height of the secondary growth in the ancient gardens, no man had farmed here for many decades.

It seemed strange to find these great grey herds of elephant ranging slowly through the ruined towns and fields. Zouga was reminded of a line from that strange exotic poetry that had been published in London the previous year, and which he had read just before sailing.

They say the Lion and the Lizard keep
The Courts where Jamshyd gloried and drank deep:
And Bahram, that great Hunter – the Wild Ass
Stamps o'er his Head, and he lies fast asleep.

Zouga scratched amongst foundations of the huts and found the deep ash, which must once have been the wooden walls and thatched roofs. In one ancient village Zouga counted a thousand such dwellings, before giving up the count. A numerous people, but where had they gone?

He found a partial answer in an ancient battlefield on the open ground beyond the thousand huts. The bones were white as daisies in the sunlight bleached and dried out, most of them half buried in the rich red soil or covered by the dense fields of waving fluffy-topped grass.

The human remains covered an area of many acres and they lay in clumps and chains like newly-cut wheat awaiting the reavers. Nearly every one of the skulls had been crushed in as if by a fierce blow with a club or mace.

Zouga realized that it was not so much a battlefield as a killing ground, for such slaughter could not be called warfare. If this toll had been repeated at each of the ruined towns he had stumbled upon, then the final total of the dead must have been in the tens or even hundreds of thousands. It was small wonder that what human presence remained was in tiny scattered groups, like the handful of warriors that had tried to prevent them crossing the pass of the elephant road. There were others. Occasionally, Zouga spied the smoke from a cooking fire rising from the highest point of one of the strangely-shaped rock hillocks that dotted the land in all directions. If these were the survivors of the vanished civilization, then they still lived in terror of the fate that had overtaken their forbears.

When Zouga and his hunting party approached any of these tiny elevated settlements, they found the crests were fortified with built up walls of rock, and they were greeted with a hail of boulders rolled down the slope upon them, that forced them to retreat hurriedly. Often there were small cultivated gardens on the level ground below the fortified hill tops.

In the gardens grew millet, ropoko and big sweet yams, but most important for Zouga, dark green native tobacco. The soil was rich, the ropoko grew twice the height of a man and the corn sprays were loaded with red grain.

The tobacco leaves were thick-stemmed, the size of an elephant's ear. Zouga rolled the tip leaves into powerful cigars that had a rich distinction of taste and as he smoked them, he pondered bow the plant had reached this distant land from its far origins. There must once have been an avenue of trade between these people and the coast. The trade beads on the necklace he had taken from the body at the pass, and now these exotic plants proved that, as did the tamarind trees, native of India, which grew amongst the ruins of the ancient villages.

Zouga wondered what a colony of British settlers with their industry and sophisticated agricultural technique, plough and crop rotation, seed selection and fertilization, might make of this lush rich soil, as he moved on slowly through the sparsely populated, well-timbered land that abounded with game and game birds, and was fed by strong clear streams of water.

Whenever he returned to the main body of the caravan, he made his meticulous observations of the sun and worked with chronometer and almanac to compute his exact positions, to add them, and his own succinct descriptions, to the map that old Tom Harkness had bequeathed him. The map increased in value, as new rivers were marked in, new boundaries set to the fly-belts and the 'fly-corridors' extended, as Zouga's observations of the terrain, of soil and vegetation types began to cover the blank portions of the old parchment.

If he was not immersed in his map, then he worked as long as the light was good enough on his journal and the manuscript which was an adjunct to it – and while he did so, Jan Cheroot and the porters brought in the latest harvest of ivory, only just beginning to stink, and buried it.

Totalling the harvest from the lists in his journal, Zouga found that he had over twelve thousand pounds of tusks cached along his route. They were worth six shillings a pound in London, nearly four thousand pounds sterling. The trick was to get it to London. Zouga grinned to himself as he completed the calculation, a dozen wagons, or five hundred porters, and two thousand miles to carry it – that was all it required.

At each river-crossing Zouga took the flat black iron pan, which doubled as laundry tub and cooking pot, and for miles in each direction along the river bed he worked the gravel. He would fill the pan from a likely spot under the bank in the bend of the river, and then set the contents swirling awash, dipping and turning the pan, spilling a little of the lighter gravel at each turn, refilling with water and spinning it again until at last he was left with a smear of the finest and heaviest material lying around the bottom of the pan in a 'tail'. Always the tail was dark and uninteresting, without the golden sparkle for which he longed so ardently.

When he detailed all these activities in his journal, only one thing gave Zouga a pause – and that was what to call this new and beautiful land. So far there was no evidence at all that it was the empire of Monomatapa, or even that Monomatapa existed. The timid, scattered and demoralized people he had so far encountered were certainly not the warriors of a powerful emperor. One other consideration decided him not to use that name. If he did so, it was tacit acknowledgement that the land had already been claimed, and each day that he travelled through the empty wilderness the dreams of himself claiming it for a queen and a nation seemed less far-fetched. Zouga began to use the name 'Zambezia' – the land below the Zambezi river – and that was how he wrote it in his journal and in the thick bundle of pages of his manuscript.

With all this work to impede progress, the pace of the caravan was leisurely, or, as Robyn told Zouga furiously, 'You would make a snail look like a Derby-winner.' For although Zouga might cover two hundred miles in the sweeping circular patterns of the hunt, the caravan camped and waited for his return, and then waited another four or five days as Jan Cheroot and the porters ferried in the loads of wet ivory.

'For all you know, Morris Zouga, your own father might be dying out there somewhere for want of a handful of medicine, while you . . .'

'If he has survived eight years already, the old devil is unlikely to turn up his toes for another few days.' Zouga's light tone covered the irritation he felt. Since he had killed the Mashona at the pass on the elephant road, the feeling between brother and sister had been strained to the point where each of them found it difficult to maintain a civil tone of voice on the few occasions when they spoke together.

Zouga's long and frequent absences from the main body were not entirely on account of his dedication to the chase and exploration of the surrounding countryside. He found it less wearying on the nerves to be away from his sister. That ecstatic mood when they had stood like two children on Christmas morning, hand in hand, upon the heights of the escarpment, was months in the past.

Brooding beside his solitary camp fire, with the hyena giggling and shrieking over the freshly killed elephant carcasses in the nearby forest, Zouga thought how it was really a miracle that two such definite personalities as his and Robyn's whose objects were so widely divergent, should have come this far without serious disagreement. It had been too good to last indefinitely, and now he wondered how it might end. He should have followed his instincts and sent Robyn back to Tete and Cape Town when he had the excuse to do so, for the collision course on which they were so clearly set could only end in disaster for the entire expedition.

When he rejoined the main body the following day he would have it out with her, one way or the other. She would have at last to accept that he was the leader of the expedition and as such, his decisions were final. If she did so, then he could make some concession to her wishes, though the hunt for Fuller Ballantyne was very low on Zouga's list of priorities. It would probably be best for all of them, Fuller Ballantyne not excluded, if he had long ago been laid by his faithful bearers in a hero's grave.

The thought gave Zouga a prick of guilt, and he knew he would never write it, not even in the most private pages of his journal, nor would he voice it to his sister. But the idea persisted, even while he rolled into his blanket, with a small fire at his feet and another at his head to break the thick crunching white frost which would cover the earth and grass at dawn, serenaded by Jan Cheroot's snores which took the basso profundo to the soprano of the hyena packs. Zouga fell asleep at last.

Having made the decision to assert his authority, Zouga rolled out of his blanket in the frosty dawn determined on a forced march that would take them back to where he had left Robyn and the caravan twelve days previously. He reckoned it was forty miles, perhaps a little less, to the main camp site and he set a cruel pace, not even taking the usual noon break, but pushing on remorselessly.

Zouga had deliberately left the main body encamped below a distinctively shaped kopje, whose rocky spires could be clearly seen from many miles around and which Zouga had named 'Mount Hampden' in memory of a childhood visit to that castle.

They were still far out when Zouga had his first misgivings. There was no smoke rising from the base of the hills, and there should have been. He had left almost a ton of elephant meat curing on the smoking-racks, and on the outward march he had been able to look back and see the rising column of smoke long after the crests of the hills had disappeared below the tops of the forest trees.

'There is no smoke!' he told Jan Cheroot, and the little Hottentot nodded.

'I did not want to be the first to say that.'

'Can Camacho have followed us this far?'

'There are other man-eating animals out here beside the Portuguese,' Jan Cheroot said, and cocked his head at an inquisitive bird-like angle as Zouga began swiftly to strip down to light running order. Then, still without another word, Jan Cheroot followed his example, and handed his breeches and other traps to the bearers.

'Follow as fast as you can!' Zouga told them, snatching a spare powder-bag from Matthew and turning away and breaking into a run.

Jan Cheroot fell in at his shoulder and they ran as they had run so often before, at the driving pace which could bring a breeding herd of elephant to a winded standstill within a few miles. All Zouga's feelings of antagonism towards his sister were swept away in the rush of deep concern for her safety. A series of horrific images flashed through his mind, of a sacked camp site, of mutilated bodies lying in the bloody trampled grass, shattered by the balls of the Portuguese muskets, or stabbed to death by the broad-bladed assegais of plumed and kilted warriors.

He found himself praying for her safety, repeating the formulas of his childhood which he had used so seldom since then, and unconsciously he increased the pace, until Jan Cheroot grunted a protest at his shoulder, and then slowly fell back, as Zouga forged powerfully ahead.

He reached the foot of the hill a mile ahead of Jan Cheroot, and turned to face the lowering red orb of the sun as he skirted the rocky base, crested a low rise and stopped there, hunting for breath, his chest swelling and subsiding and the sweat running down into his beard.

He stared down at the shaded dell, under the tall mukusi trees where he had left the caravan and his heart plunged. He felt physically nauseated with horror. The camp site was deserted, the fires were cold black ash and the thatched lean-to shelters had already acquired that dejected air of all deserted habitation. Still fighting for breath, Zouga plunged down the gentle slope into the abandoned camp, and looked about him wildly, for the bodies. There were none, and his first thought was of slavers. They would have taken them all, and he shuddered with horror at the thought of what Robyn must have suffered.

Zouga ran to her hut first. It was totally devoid of any trace of her. He ran to the next hut and the next – all of them were empty, but in the last hut he found a single body. It was curled on the sandy floor of the primitive shelter, and wrapped in a blanket. The blanket was drawn up over the head and wound tightly around the trunk.

Reluctant to discover his sister's horribly mutilated corpse, Zouga knelt beside it. Sweat half-blinded him as he reached out a hand that trembled with dread and exhaustion and gently drew back the fold of a grey blanket that covered the still head.

The corpse came to life with a howl of fright and leapt two feet into the air, gibbering wildly, trying to throw off the blanket and lashing out with feet and fists to defend itself.

'Hellhound!' Zouga had so christened the laziest of his porters, a skinny fellow with a vast appetite for meat and less enthusiasm for anything that involved physical exertion. 'What has happened? Where is Nomusa?'

Hellhound, once he had been quieted and had sufficiently recovered from shock, had a brief note to answer his questions. The single scrap of paper torn from Robyn's journal was double-folded and sealed with a splash of red wax, it read:

Dear Zouga,

I am of the opinion that further delay will seriously prejudice the interests of the sponsors of this expedition.

Accordingly, I have decided to move on at a speed better suited to achieving our objects before the onset of the rainy season.

I leave Hellhound to await your eventual return. Do follow at your own speed.

Your affectionate sister,
Robyn.

The note was dated ten days previously, and it was all she had left him. There was not even a pouch of salt or a bag of tea leaves, both of which commodities Zouga had been without for days.

Zouga's numbing shock lasted until Jan Cheroot reached the

deserted camp, but by the time his exhausted bearers came, black rage had begun to replace all other emotion. He would have made a night march of it in pursuit of the caravan, but though he kicked their ribs as they lay and cursed them coldly, his bearers were so exhausted that they could not rise from where they had thrown themselves down.

Robyn had great difficulty getting the bearers to break camp and take up their packs. Her first efforts to do so were greeted with amusement and light laughter, for none of them believed she was serious. Even Juba could not understand that Nomusa, a woman, was taking command of the caravan.

When all argument failed, Robyn took the hippo-hide kurbash whip to the little yellow Hottentot Corporal, whom Jan Cheroot had left in command of his musketeers. The Corporal shouted frantic orders to his men from the upper branches of the mukusi where Robyn had him treed.

They were on the march within the hour, but the light laughter had given way to scowls and sulks. They were all convinced that the safari was now doomed, for who had ever heard of a woman, a young woman – worst of all a young white woman – leading into the unknown. Within half a mile most of the porters were complaining of thorns in the feet or bad blood behind the eyes, afflictions common only to porters reluctant to advance.

Robyn got them to their feet again by firing a shot from the big naval Colt revolver over their heads, it almost sprained her wrist, but proved an amazingly effective cure for both feet and eyes, and finally they made a fair day's march of it, south and west, ten miles, as Robyn reckoned it as she marked her journal that night.

Despite the brave countenance she put on before the porters and musketeers, Robyn had her own doubts. She had watched closely as Zouga plotted a course with the prismatic compass, and she had mastered the technique of sighting a distant hill or other feature and marching upon it, before again sighting ahead on another feature. It was the only way to maintain a direct line of march in this rolling forested country.

She had studied, whenever she had the opportunity, the Harkness map, and had seen the wisdom of Zouga's choice of direction. He was aiming to traverse this wide unexplored land he had called Zambezia, and eventually to hit the road that their grandfather, Robert Moffat, had pioneered from his mission station at Kuruman to the town of the Matabele king, Mzilikazi, at Thabas Indunas.

However, Zouga's intention had been to cut south of the frontiers of the Matabele kingdom, avoiding the Burnt Land where, according to Tom Harkness, the rapacious border impis of Mzilikazi killed all travellers. Neither she nor Zouga could trust to their relationship to Moffat to protect them.

Once they gained the wagon road to Kuruman, they would be back in the known world, and the road would lead them to the series of waterholes that grandfather Moffat had marked. At Kuruman, after the family reunion, the road to Cape Town was long and wearying, but well travelled and in less than a year they could be back in London. The delicate part was to grope the way south of Matabele land, through the untold hazards still ahead and to reach the road.

Robyn did not truly anticipate that she would be called upon to perform this feat of navigation entirely on her own. It could only be a matter of days before Zouga reached Mount Hampden camp and then hurried to catch up with the main body. There would be an interesting clash of wills then. However, at the end of it, she was certain that Zouga would be convinced that their father's whereabouts and safety were more important than the slaughter of animals, whose teeth could probably never be retrieved from their burial mounds.

This was a gesture of defiance only, soon Zouga would be with her once more. In the meantime, however, she had an unpleasantly hollow and lonely sensation beneath her ribs as she strode along in her tight-fitting breeches, the Hottentot standard-bearer carrying the grubbied and tattered Union Jack a few paces behind her, and a sullen line of porters straggling along behind that again.

They camped the second night on the edge of a river that had been reduced to a string of still green pools in the sugary white sand of the river bed. On the steep bank stood a small grove of strangler figs, the smooth pale trunk and branches had crept up like thick and sinuous pythons to smother the host trees. The parasites were now taller and more robust than the rotting remains that supported them had ever been, and the clusters of ripening figs covered their branches. Fat green pigeons came to feed on the fruits, flicked their wings and whistled their shrill cry, unlike that of any other pigeon, that to Robyn sounded like 'Oh well, oh very well!' and they cocked their heads to peer down through the green leaves at the men camped below.

The porters had cut the *scherms* of thorn branches and lit the cooking fires when they all heard the lion roar. The sound checked the murmur of voices for only a few seconds, for it was very faint and distant, seeming to come from miles downstream, and it was a sound to which they had all long grown accustomed.

There had hardly been a night since they had crossed the pass on the elephant road that they had not heard the lions, and in the morning found the pug marks, sometimes almost the size of a soup plate, in the soft earth around the camp where the big inquisitive cats had circled them during the night.

However, Robyn had never seen one of them for they are almost entirely nocturnal, and her first tremors of trepidation had long turned to indifference. She felt quite secure behind the *scherm* of thornbush, and now at the distant muttering rumble she hardly bothered to look up from her journal in which she was exaggerating only slightly the competent manner in which she had directed the day's march.

'We are making as good a time as we ever did when Z was leading,' she wrote smugly, but did not go on to mention the mood of the porters.

The lion roared only once, and when it was not repeated, the sullen talk around the cooking fires was resumed and Robyn bowed her head once more over her journal.

A few hours after the setting of the sun the camp settled for the night, and lying under her hastily thatched shelter with Juba curled on the mattress of freshly cut grass beside her, Robyn listened to the melodious African voices of her porters fade gradually into silence. She sighed once, deeply, and fell instantly asleep – to wake with a confusion of sound and movement all around her.

She knew that it was late by the frostiness of the air, the utter darkness and her own sleep-drugged stupor. The night rang with the terrified shouts of men and the rush of their feet. Then there was the thudding report of a musket, the crash of heavy logs being thrown on the watch fires and then, heart-stoppingly, the screams of Juba close to her head.

'Nomusa! Nomusa!'

Still groggy with sleep, Robyn struggled up. She was not certain what she was dreaming and what was reality.

'What is it?'

'A devil!' shrieked Juba. 'Devils have come to kill us all.'

Robyn flung off her blanket, and ran out of the shelter barefooted, dressed only in her flannel nightgown with ribbons in her hair.

At that moment the new logs blazed up on the watch fire, and she saw naked yellow and black bodies, and terrified faces, whites of rolling eyes and open shouting mouths.

The little Hottentot Corporal, stark naked, pranced beyond the fire, brandishing his musket, and as Robyn ran towards him he fired it blindly into the darkness.

Robyn caught his arm as he began to reload.

'What is it?' she shouted into his ear.

'*Leeuw!* Lion!' His eyes were glittering with fright and bubbles of spittle ran from the corners of his mouth.

'Where is it?'

'It has taken Sakkie! It pulled him out of his blankets.'

'Quiet!' Robyn shouted. 'Keep quiet all of you!'

Now, at last, they all turned instinctively to her for leadership.

'Quiet!' she repeated, and the gabble of fright and uncertainty died swiftly.

'Sakkie!' she called in the silence, and the missing Hottentot's voice answered her faintly from below the steep bank of the river-bed.

'*Die leeuw het my!* The lion has me! *Die duiwel gaan my dood maak*, the devil is going to kill me,' and he broke off with a shriek of agony.

Above the high-pitched shriek they all clearly heard the crunch of bone, and the muffled growl like that of a dog with food in its jaws. With a rush of horror that raised goose pimples along her arms, Robyn realized that she was listening to the sounds of a man being eaten alive not fifty yards from where she stood.

'*Hy vreet my bene,*' the voice out of the darkness rang with unbearable agony. 'He is eating my legs,' and the gruesome cracking, tearing sounds made Robyn's gorge rise to choke her. Without thinking, she snatched a burning brand from the fire and holding it aloft shouted at the Hottentot Corporal. 'Come on! We must save him!'

She ran forward to the lip of the bank before she realized she was alone, and unarmed.

She looked back. Not one of the men around the fire had followed her. They stood in a tight group, shoulder to shoulder, clutching muskets or axes or assegais, but rooted where they stood.

'He is finished.' The Corporal's voice shook with fright. 'Leave him. It's too late. Leave him.'

Robyn hurled the burning brand she held down into the river-bed below her feet, and before its flames faded and pinched out she thought she saw something big and dark and terrifying on the edge of the shadows.

Robyn ran back to the group and snatched a musket from one of the Hottentots. Thumbing back the hammer, she ran once more to the river bank and peered down into the dry bed. It was utterly dark, until suddenly there was somebody at her shoulder, holding high a burning branch from the fire.

'Juba! Go back!' Robyn snapped at the child. Juba was completely naked except for a single string of beads about her hips, and the firelight glinted on her sleek black body.

She could not answer Robyn, for tears were rolling down her plump cheeks and her throat was closed with terror, but she shook her head fiercely at the order to retreat.

Below them, outlined against the white sand of the dry river, was that grotesque dark shape. and the screams of the dying man blended with the grisly wet growls of the animal.

Robyn lifted the musket, but hesitated for fear of hitting the Hottentot. Disturbed by the light, the lion rose, becoming huge and black; swiftly it dragged the weakly wriggling body, dangling between its forelegs back into the darkness beyond the feeble circle of light from the flames.

Robyn drew a deep breath and the heavy musket shook in her hands, but she lifted her chin in a gesture of decision and holding up the skirts of her long nightdress in one hand, went down the path into the river-bed. Juba followed her like a faithful puppy, pressing so hard against her that they nearly lost their balance, but she kept the burning brand on high, though it shook, and the flames wavered smokily.

'Brave girl!' Robyn encouraged her. 'Good brave girl!'

They stumbled through the loose white sand that covered the ankles of their bare feet at each pace.

Ahead of them, at the extreme limit of their vision, moved the menacing black shadow, and the deep muttering growls seemed to fill the night around them.

'Leave it!' Robyn shouted, her voice quavering and breaking. 'Drop it – this instant!'

Unconsciously she was using the same commands as she had given her terrier as a child when it refused to deliver the rubber ball.

Ahead of her in the darkness Sakkie heard her, and bleated feebly. 'Help me – for God's love, help me.' But the lion pulled him away, leaving a long wet drag mark through the sand.

Robyn was tiring rapidly, her arms ached from the weight of the heavy weapon, each breath burned her throat as she panted, but she could not seem to get enough air, for an iron band of fear cramped her chest. She sensed that the lion would only retreat a certain distance before it lost patience with the shouting and harassment, and her instinct was right.

Suddenly she made out the full shape of the lion ahead of them. It had dropped the maimed body and stood over it now like a tomcat with its mouse, but it was as big as a Shetland pony, with the dark ruff of its mane fully erect, seeming to double its size.

In the light of the flames, its eyes glowed a bright ferocious gold, and it opened its jaws and roared. The very air dinned upon Robyn's eardrums, causing her actual physical pain as that great gust of sound struck her. It rose to an unbearable pitch, so that involuntarily she reeled backwards with Juba clinging to her. The child wailed with despair, losing control of her body so that in the light of the flames her urine shot in sharp little spurts down her legs, and as the lion launched into its charge she dropped the torch into the sand, plunging them all into complete darkness.

Robyn lifted the musket in front of her, as a defensive reflex rather than a planned act of aggression, and when the barrel was at waist-level she pulled the trigger with all her strength. The cap flashed, flaring brightly in the blackness and for an instant she saw the lion. It was so close that the long barrel of the musket seemed to touch its huge shaggy head. The mouth was wide open, still emitting those shattering gusts of sound, and the fangs that lined the deep, meat-red gape of jaws were long and white and cruel. The eyes burned yellow as living flames, and Robyn found that she was screaming, but the sound was lost completely in the roaring of the enraged animal.

Then an instant after the flash of the cap the musket fired, bucking so savagely in her hands that it almost tore itself from her grip, and the butt, not anchored against her shoulder, was driven back into her stomach with a force that expelled the air from her lungs, and sent her reeling in the loose white sand. Juba, clinging to her legs and wailing with despair, tripped her and she went over backwards, sprawling full length at the same moment that the full weight of the lion lunged into her.

If Robyn had not fallen, the charge would have stove in her ribs, and snapped her neck, for the lion was over four hundred pounds weight of driving bone and muscle. As it was, it knocked her out of her senses for she never knew how long, but she became conscious again, with the strong cat-reek of the lion in her nostrils, and an immense weight crushing her into the sand. She wriggled weakly, but the weight was suffocating her, and gouts of hot blood, so hot it seemed to scald her, were spurting over her head and neck.

'Nomusa!' Juba's voice, high with anguish and very close, but those shattering roars were silent. There was just the unbearable weight and the rank smell of lion.

Robyn's strength came back to her with a rush, and she struggled and kicked, and the weight above her rolled loosely aside, slithering off her, and she dragged herself free of it. Immediately Juba clung to her again, throwing her arms about Robyn's neck.

Robyn comforted her as though she were an infant, patting her and kissing her cheek that was wet and hot with tears.

'It's over! There, now. It's all over,' she mumbled, aware that her hair was sodden with the lion's blood, and that a dozen men, led cautiously by the Hottentot Corporal, had lined the high riverbank, each of them holding aloft a torch of burning grass.

In the dim yellow light the lion lay stretched out beside Robyn in the sand. The ball from the musket had struck him full in the nose, passed cleanly through the brain and lodged in the base of his neck, killing the great cat in mid-air, so the lifeless body had pinned Robyn to the sand.

'The lion is dead!' Robyn quavered as she called to the men, and they came down in a close bunch, timidly at first and then boldly when they saw the huge yellow carcass.

'It was the shot of a true huntress,' announced the Corporal grandly. 'An inch high and the ball would have bounced off the skull, an inch lower and it would have missed the brain.'

'Sakkie,' Robyn's voice still shook, 'where is Sakkie?'

He was still alive, and they carried him in his blanket up into the camp. His wounds were fearsome, and Robyn knew there was not the smallest chance of saving him. One arm from wrist to elbow had been chewed so that not a piece of bone bigger than the top joint of her finger remained. One foot was gone just above the ankle, bitten clean off and swallowed in one piece. He had been bitten through pelvis and spine, while through a tear in his diaphragm below the ribs the mottled pink of his lungs swelled out with each breath.

Robyn knew that to attempt to cut and sew that dreadfully torn flesh or to saw the splintered bone stumps would be inflicting futile agony on the little yellow man. She had him laid close to the fire, she plugged the worst holes gently, and then covered him with blankets and fur karosses. She administered a dose of laudanum so powerful as to be almost lethal in itself. Then she sat next to Sakkie and held his hand.

'A doctor must know when to let a man die with dignity,' her professor at St Matthew's had once told her. And a little before dawn Sakkie opened his eyes, the pupils dilated widely by the massive dose of the drug and smiled at her just once before he died.

His brother Hottentots buried him in a small cave in one of the granite kopjes and they blocked the opening with boulders that the hyena could not roll aside.

When the Corporal and his Hottentots came down from the hill, they indulged in a brief ritual of mourning which consisted mainly of emitting loud theatrical cries of anguish and firing their muskets in the air to speed Sakkie's soul on its journey, after which they ate a hearty breakfast of smoked elephant meat, and the Corporal came to Robyn, dry eyed and grinning broadly.

'We are now ready to march, Nomusa!' he told her, and with a stamp of his right foot, which began with the knee lifted under his chin, he gave her one of those widely extravagant salutes, a mark of deep respect that up to that date had been reserved exclusively for Major Zouga Ballantyne.

During that day's march, the porters sang again for the first time since leaving Zouga's camp at Mount Hampden.

'She is your mother and your father too,
She will dress your wounds
She will stand over you while you sleep
We, your children, greet you, Nomusa,
The girl child of mercy.'

It was not only the caravan's rate of advance under Zouga that had irritated and annoyed Robyn. It was also their complete failure to make contact with any of the indigenous tribes, with any of the inhabitants of the scattered and fortified villages.

To her it seemed completely logical that the only way that they would be able to trace Fuller Ballantyne through this wilderness was by asking questions of those who must have seen him pass, and almost certainly had spoken and traded with him.

Robyn could not believe that her father would have adopted the same high-handed actions to force a passage past anybody or anything that stood in the way of the caravan as Zouga had done.

When she closed her eyes she could still see clearly in her mind's eye the tiny falling body of the black man in the tall headdress, shot down ruthlessly by her brother. She had rehearsed in her mind how she or her father would have passed through the elephant road without gunfire and slaughter. The tactful withdrawal, the offering of small gifts, the cautious parley and eventual agreement.

'It was plain bloody murder!' she repeated to herself for the hundredth time. 'And what we have done since then has been blatant robbery.'

Zouga had helped himself to the standing crops of the villages they had passed, to tobacco, millet and yams, not even bothering to leave a handful of salt or a few sticks of dried elephant meat as token payment.

'We should try to communicate with these people, Zouga,' she had remonstrated.

'They are a sullen and dangerous people.'

'Because they expect you to rob and murder them – and, as God is my witness, you have not disappointed them, have you?'

The same argument had run its well-worn course many times, neither of them relenting, each holding stubbornly to their own view. Now at least she was free to attempt to establish contact with these people, Mashona, as Juba called them disparagingly, without her brother's impatience and arrogance to distract her and alarm the timid black people.

On the fourth day after leaving Zouga's camp, they came in sight of an extraordinary geological formation. It was as though a high dam wall had been constructed across the horizon, a great dyke of rock running almost exactly north and south to the very limit of the eye.

Almost directly in their line of march was the only breach in this rampart, and from the altered vegetation, the denser growth and deeper green, it was clear that a river flowed through the gap. Robyn ordered a small adjustment in their line of march and headed for the pass.

When they were still some miles distant Robyn was delighted to make out the first signs of human habitation that they had come across since leaving Mount Hampden.

There were fortified walls on the cliffs above the breach in the long low hill, high above the river bed, and as they drew closer, Robyn could see the gardens on the banks of the river, defended by high brush and thorn barriers with little thatched look-out huts standing high on stilts in the centre of the dark luscious green stands of young millet.

'We will fill our bellies tonight,' the Hottentot Corporal gloated. 'That corn is ripe enough to eat.'

'We will camp here, Corporal,' Robyn told him firmly.

'But we are still a mile . . .'

'Here!' Robyn repeated.

They were all puzzled and resentful when Robyn forbade entry to the tempting gardens, and confined them all to the perimeter of the camp, except for the water and wood parties. But resentment turned to genuine alarm when Robyn left the camp herself, accompanied only by Juba, and as far as they could see completely unarmed.

'These people are savages,' the Corporal tried to intercept her. 'They will kill you, and then Major Zouga will kill me.'

The two women entered the nearest garden, and carefully

approached the look-out hut. On the earth below the rickety ladder that rose to the elevated platform a fire had burned down to ash, but flared again when Robyn knelt and fanned it. Robyn threw a few dry branches upon it and then sent Juba for an armful of green leaves. The column of smoke drew the attention of the watchers on the cliff above the gorge.

Robyn could see their distant figures on the skyline, standing very still and intent. It was an eerie feeling to know that so many eyes were upon them, but Robyn was not relying entirely on the fact that they were women, nor was she relying on their patently peaceful intentions, nor even upon the prayers which she had offered up so diligently to protect them. On the principle that the Almighty helps those who show willing, she had Zouga's big Colt pistol stuffed into the waistband of her breeches and covered by the tail of her flannel shirt.

Next to the smoking beacon fire, Robyn left a half pound of salt in a small calabash gourd, and a bundle of sticks of black smoked elephant meat which was the last of her stock.

Early the next morning Robyn and Juba again visited the garden and found the meat and salt had been taken, and that there were the fresh footprints of bare feet overlaying their own in the dust.

'Corporal,' Robyn told the Hottentot with a confidence she did not feel, 'we are going out to shoot meat.'

Corporal grinned beatifically. They had eaten the last of the smoked meat, weevils and all, the previous evening, and he flung her one of his more flamboyant salutes, his right arm quivering at the peak of his cap, his fingers spread stiffly, the stamp of his right foot raising dust, before he hurried away shouting orders to his men to prepare for the hunt.

Zouga had long ago declared the Sharps rifle to be too light for elephant, and left it in camp, favouring the big four-to-the-pound smooth bores to the more expensive breech-loading rifle. Robyn took it now and inspected it with trepidation. Previously she had only fired it at a target, and now in the privacy of her grass hut she rehearsed loading and cocking the weapon. She was not sure that she would be capable of cold-bloodedly aiming it at a living animal, and had to reassure herself of the absolute necessity of procuring food for the many mouths and stomachs that now depended upon her. The Corporal did not share her doubts, he had seen her shoot a charging lion between the eyes, and trusted her now implicitly. Within an hour's walk they found a herd of buffalo in the thick reed beds along the river. Robyn had listened to Zouga talking of the hunt with enough attention to know the necessity of keeping below the wind – and in the reeds with visibility down to a few feet and with the commotion created by two hundred cows and bleating calves they crept up to a range at which nobody could miss.

Her Hottentots blazed away with their muskets, while Robyn herself fired grimly into the galloping bellowing bodies that charged wildly past her after the first shot had startled them.

After the dust had settled and the thick bank of powder smoke had drifted away on the faint breeze, they found six of the big black animals lying dead in the reedbeds. Her entourage were delighted, hacking the bodies into manageable chunks which they slung on long poles and carried singing up to the camp. Their delight turned to amazement when Robyn ordered that an entire haunch of fresh buffalo be taken out and left next to the hut in the millet garden.

'These people are eaters of roots and dirt,' Juba explained patiently. 'Meat is too good for them.'

'To kill this meat we have risked our lives,' the Corporal began his protest, then caught the look in Robyn's eye, broke off and coughed and shuffled his feet. 'Nomusa, could we not give them a little less than a haunch? The hooves make a good stew, and these people are savages, they will eat anything,' he pleaded. 'A whole haunch . . .'

She sent him away muttering and shaking his head sorrowfully.

During the night, Juba woke her, and the two of them sat and listened to the faint throb of drums and the singing that carried down from the hilltop village, clearly the sounds of feasting and jubilation.

'They have probably not seen so much meat at one time in all their lives,' Juba murmured sulkily.

In the morning Robyn found, in place of the buffalo meat, a bark basket containing fifteen hen's eggs the size of pigeons eggs, and two large earthen pots of millet beer. The look of the bubbling thin grey gruel almost turned Robyn's stomach. She gave the beer to the Corporal to distribute, and her followers drank it with such obvious relish, smacking their lips and nodding over it like connoisseurs over an ancient bottle of claret, that Robyn controlled her heaving stomach and tasted some; it was tart and refreshing and strong enough to set the Hottentots chattering and laughing raucously.

With Juba following her, each of them carrying a bundle of half-dried buffalo meat, Robyn returned to the gardens, certain that the exchange of gifts had proved it possible to establish friendly contact. They sat under the shelter and waited. The hours passed without a sign of the Mashona appearing. The hushed heat of noon gave way to long, cool shadows of evening – and then, for the first time, Robyn noticed a gentle stir amongst the millet plants that was neither wind nor bird.

'Do not move,' she cautioned Juba.

Slowly a human shape showed itself, a frail bent figure dressed in tatters of a skin kilt. Robyn could not tell whether it was man or woman, and she didn't dare stare openly at it, for fear of frightening it away.

The figure emerged from the stand of millet, crouched down on its haunches, and it hopped hesitantly towards them, with long pauses between each tentative hop. It was so thin and wrinkled and dried out that it looked like one of the unbandaged mummies that Robyn had seen in the Egyptian section of the British Museum.

It was definitely a man, she realized at last, sneaking a glance in his direction, for with each hop his shrivelled and stringy genitals flapped out from under the short kilt.

Closer still, Robyn saw that his cap of woolly hair was pure white with age, and in the seamed and pouched sockets his eyes wept slow tears of fright, as though these were the last drops of liquid that his desiccated old body contained.

Neither Juba nor Robyn moved or looked directly at him until he squatted a dozen paces from them, then slowly Robyn turned her head towards him. The old man whimpered with fear.

It was clear to Robyn that he had been selected as an emissary because he was the least valuable member of the tribe, and Robyn wondered what threats had been made to force him to come down from the hilltop.

Moving very slowly and calmly, as though she were dealing with a timid wild creature, Robyn held out a stick of half-cured buffalo meat. The old man stared at it, fascinated. As Juba had told her, these people probably existed almost entirely on their meagre crops and such roots and wild fruit as they could glean in the forest. Meat was a rare treat, and such an unproductive member of the tribe would be given only a very little of what there was.

The way he stared at the piece in Robyn's hand made her believe that the old man had not had so much as a taste of the buffalo haunch. He was more than half starved. He rolled his tongue loosely around in his toothless mouth, gathering his courage, and then shuffled close enough to hold out the claws of his bony fingers, palms cupped upwards in the polite gesture of acceptance.

'There you are, dearie.' Robyn placed the stick in his hands and the man snatched it to his mouth, sucking noisily upon it, worrying it with his smooth gums, drooling silver strings of saliva as his mouth flooded, his eyes streaming again, this time with pleasure rather than fear.

Robyn laughed with delight, and the old man rapidly blinked his eyes and then cackled around the stick of meat, the sound so comical that Juba laughed also, the laughter of the two younger women rippling and tinkling without restraint. Almost immediately, the dense leaves of the millet garden stirred and rustled, as other dark, half-naked figures came slowly forward, their anxiety relieved by the sound of laughing women.

The hilltop settlement consisted of not more than a hundred individuals, men, women and children, and every one of them came out to stare and laugh and clap as Robyn and Juba climbed the steep twisting path. The old silver-headed man, almost unbearably proud of his achievement, led Robyn by the hand possessively, screeching out explanations to those around, pausing every now and then to perform a little shuffling dance of triumph.

Mothers held up their infants to look at this marvellous being, and the children ran forward to touch Robyn's legs and then squeal with their own courage, skipping away ahead of her up the path.

The pathway followed the contours of the hillside, and it passed between defensive gateways and under terraced walls. Above the path at every steep place were piled boulders, ready to be hurled down upon an enemy, but now Robyn's ascent was a triumphant progress, and she came out into the village surrounded by a welcoming throng of singing, dancing women.

The village was laid out in a circular pattern of thatched and windowless huts. The walls were of plastered clay with low doorways and beside each hut was a granary of the same materials but raised on poles to protect it from vermin. Apart from a few diminutive chickens, there were no domestic animals.

The space between the huts, and the central courtyard was swept, and the whole village had an air of order and cleanliness. The people themselves were handsome, though none of them carried any excess flesh or fat. Robyn was reminded by their slim, lithe bodies that they were almost exclusively vegetarian.

They had alert and intelligent faces, and the laughter and singing with which they welcomed her was easy and unaffected.

'These are the people whom Zouga shot down like animals,' she thought, looking around her with pleasure.

They had set a low carved stool in the shade for her and Juba squatted beside her. As soon as Robyn was seated, the old man squealed importantly and a giggling young girl brought her a pot of the millet beer. Only when she had drunk a mouthful of the beer did the crowd fall silent, and draw aside to let a commanding figure come through.

On his head was a tall headdress of animal fur, similar to the one worn by the chieftain on the elephant road pass. He wore a cloak of leopard skin over his shoulders, the skins so worn that they must have been very old, probably the heredity symbol of his chieftainship. He sat down on another stool facing Robyn. He was a man of middle age, with a pleasant humorous face, and a lively imagination – for he followed Robyn's sign language with attention, and then acted out his own replies with facial expressions and gestures that Robyn understood readily.

This way he asked her from where she came and she showed him the north and made a circle of her hands towards the sun for each day's travel. He wanted to know who was her husband and how many children she had. That she was both unmarried and childless was a source of amazement to the whole village.

More beer was brought out in the clay pots and Robyn felt slightly light-headed, and her cheeks turned pink and her eyes shone. Juba was contemptuous of their hosts.

'They do not have even a goat!' she pointed out scornfully.

'Perhaps your brave young men have stolen them all,' Robyn answered tartly, and raised her beer pot in salute to the chief.

The chief clapped his hands, signalling his drummers to stoop to their instruments. The drums were hollowed tree trunks, beaten with a pair of short wooden clubs to a frantic rhythm that soon had the drummers running with rivulets of sweat and glassy-eyed with the mesmeric effects of the beat. The chieftain threw off his leopard-skin cloak and launched himself into the dance, swirling and leaping until his necklaces and bracelets jangled and rattled.

On his chest he wore a pendant of ivory, snowy-white polished ivory, and it caught the firelight, for by now the sun was long set. Robyn had not noticed the ornament before for it had been covered by the cloak, but now she felt her eye drawn repeatedly to the bouncing white disc.

The disc seemed too perfectly shaped, and as the chief came bounding up to her stool to perform a solo pass before her Robyn saw that it was decorated with a regular pattern around its border. The next moment her heart raced with excitement for the decoration was writing, she was not sure in what language, but it was Latin script, that was certain. Then the chief had gone, leaping away to prance in front of his drummers, exhorting them to greater efforts.

Robyn had to wait until the chief exhausted himself, and staggered panting back to his stool to quaff a pot of the thick grey beer, before she could lean forward and get her first close look at the ornament.

She had been mistaken. It was not ivory but porcelain, and its perfect shape and whiteness was immediately accounted for. It was an item of European manufacture, the lid of a small pot, the type in which tooth-powder or potted meats are sold. The writing was English, printed in neat capitals were the words:

'PATUM PEPERIUM – THE GENTLEMAN'S RELISH.'

She felt her skin go clammy with excitement. Clearly she remembered her father's rage when the pantry at King's Lynn had been bare of this delicacy. She remembered as a small girl running down the village street in the rain to the grocer to buy another pot.

'It is my one weakness, my only weakness,' she remembered her father's exact words while he spread the savoury paste on his toast, his anger mollified so that he came near to making a joke of it. 'Without my Gentleman's Relish, I doubt I would have had strength for the Transversa.'

When Robyn's mother left for Africa on that last ill-fated voyage, there had been a dozen cases of the relish in her luggage.

There was only one possible way that the porcelain lid could have reached here.

Robyn stretched out a hand and touched it, but the chief's expression changed instantly and he jumped back, out of reach. The singing and drumming came to an abrupt halt, and the consternation of the entire village made Robyn realize that the porcelain lid was a charm of great personal magic, and that it was a disaster that another hand had touched it.

She made an attempt to mollify the chief, but swiftly he covered himself with his leopard cloak and stalked away to his hut at the end of the village. The festivities were clearly ended. The rest of the villagers were subdued and crept away after the chief, leaving only the silver-haired toothless ancient, possessive as ever, to lead Robyn to the hut which had earlier been set aside for her.

She lay awake most of the night on the plaited reed sleeping-mat, excited at the evidence that her father had passed this way, and worried that she had ruined her relationship with the Mashona chief and would learn no more of the ornament and, through it, of her father.

She did not have an early opportunity to meet the chief again, and make amends for her breach of manners. The villagers kept away from her, obviously hoping she would go, but she stayed on stubbornly in the hilltop village, attended only by the faithful old man. For Robyn was the most important thing that had ever happened in his long life, and he was not going to relinquish her for the chief or for anybody else.

In the end, there was nothing for it but to send the chief an extravagant gift. She used the last *khete* of *sam-sam* beads and one of the double-bladed axes.

The chief could not resist such princely bribes, and though his attitude was cooler and more reserved than at first, he listened attentively while Robyn asked her questions, acting out little charades, which the chief discussed seriously with his elders, before giving his answers.

The answer was southwards again, south for five circles of the sun, and the chief would send somebody to guide Robyn. He was obviously pleased to be rid of her at last, for, though her gifts were welcome, the chief was still deeply troubled by the ill-fortune that her sacrilegious action must bring upon the tribe.

For a guide the chief chose the silver-headed old man, ridding himself of a useless mouth and an unwelcome visitor at one stroke.

Robyn had doubted that her guide's thin legs could carry him either very fast or very far. However, the old man surprised her. He armed himself with a long throwing spear which looked as old and frail as he did himself and on his head he balanced a rolled sleeping-mat and a clay cooking pot – these clearly constituted his total worldly possessions. He girded up his tattered kilts and set off southwards at a pace that had Robyn's porters grumbling again. Robyn had to restrain him.

It took a little time to get the old man to understand that he was now her language tutor. As they marched she pointed at herself, and everything around them, naming them clearly in English, and then looking at him enquiringly. He returned the look with equal enquiry in his rheumy old eyes. However, she persevered, repeating her own name 'Nomusa' as she touched her chest, and suddenly he understood.

He slapped his own chest. 'Karanga,' he squeaked. 'Karanga!' Once again his enthusiasm for this new activity was such that she had to restrain him. Within a few days Robyn had dozens of verbs and hundreds of nouns which she could begin stringing together, much to old Karanga's delight.

However, it was four days before Robyn realized that there had been an initial misunderstanding. Karanga was not the old man's name, but the name of his tribe. It was too late to rectify, because by that time everybody in the caravan was calling him 'Karanga', and the old man answered to it readily. It was difficult to get him to leave Robyn's side. He followed her wherever she went, much to Juba's disgust and undisguised jealousy.

'He smells,' she told Robyn virtuously. 'He smells very bad.' Which was true, Robyn had to admit.

'But after a while you do not notice it, so much.' There was one thing, however, which could not be so readily overlooked, it appeared from under the old man's kilts whenever he squatted, which he did whenever at rest. Robyn solved this by giving old

Karanga a pair of Zouga's woollen underwear and taking her chances with her brother's wrath later. The underwear filled old Karanga with almost unbearable pride. He preened and strutted like a peacock, as they flapped around his long thin legs.

Old Karanga led them cautiously wide of every occupied village along their route, although he assured Robyn they were also of the same tribe. There seemed to be no trade nor commerce between these settlements, each perched on its fortified hilltop in suspicious and hostile isolation.

By this time, Robyn could speak enough of the language to find out from Karanga more about the great wizard – from whom the chief had received the magical porcelain talisman, and the story filled her with excitement and anticipation.

Many rainy seasons ago, old Karanga was not sure how many, at his age every season blurred into the one before or the one after, anyway, at some not too far distant date an extraordinary man had come out of the forest, even as she had come, and like her he had been fair skinned. However, his hair and beard were the colour of flames (he showed her the camp fire), and he was without doubt a magician and prophet and rainmaker, for the day he arrived the long drought had broken with thunderous storms that filled the rivers for the first time in many years.

This pale wizard had performed other rare and wonderful feats, transforming himself first into a lion and then into an eagle, raising the dead from the grave, and directing the lightning with a wave of his hand. The tale had lost nothing in the retelling Robyn noted wryly.

'Did anybody speak to him?' Robyn asked.

'We were all too afraid,' Karanga admitted, shaking theatrically with terror, 'but I myself saw the wizard as an eagle fly over village and drop the talisman from the sky.' He flapped his skinny old arms in pantomime.

The strong anchovy smell would have attracted the bird to the discarded pot, Robyn reflected, but when it proved inedible the bird would have dropped it, by chance over Karanga's village.

'The wizard stayed a short time near our village and then went away to the south. We have heard that he travelled swiftly, obviously in his guise as a lion.

'We heard of his miracles, the word shouted from hilltop to hill-top or tapped out by the drums. How he cured others sick to death, how he challenged the ancestral spirits of the Karanga in their most sacred places shouting abuse at them so all who heard him trembled.

'We heard also how he slew the high priestess of the dead, an Umlimo of vast power in her own stronghold. This strange pale magician slew her and destroyed her sacred relics.'

In fact he had raged through the land like a man-eating lion, which of course he was, until finally he came to rest upon a dark hilltop far to the south, the mountain of iron, Thaba Simbi, where he stayed to perform diverse curses and miracles so that the people came to him from far and wide to buy his services with corn and other offerings.

'Is he still there?' Robyn demanded.

Old Karanga rolled his watery eyes and shrugged. 'It is always difficult and dangerous to predict the comings and goings of wizards and magicians,' that eloquent gesture seemed to say.

The journey was not so straightforward as Robyn had hoped, for the further he went from his own village the less certain old Karanga became of his direction, or of the exact location of the Iron Mountain, which he had told her of.

At the beginning of each day's march, he informed Robyn confidently that they would reach their destination that day, and as they went into camp each evening he told her apologetically that it would be the next day for certain.

Twice he pointed out rocky kopjes, 'That is indeed the Iron Mountain', but each time they were driven off with a hail of boulders and throwing spears from the heights.

'I was mistaken,' Karanga mumbled, 'there is a darkness in my eyes sometimes, even under the noonday sun.'

'Have you verily and truly seen this mountain?' Robyn demanded sternly, almost at the end of her patience, and Karanga hung his silver-wrinkled head and with great industry picked at his nostrils with a bony finger to hide his discomfiture.

'It is true that I have not personally seen this place, not with my own eyes, but I have been told by one who spoke with a man who himself . . .' he admitted, and Robyn was so angry that she shouted at him in English.

'You naughty old devil, why did you not say so before!'

Old Karanga understood the tone, if not the words, and his misery was so apparent that she could not sustain her anger for more than an hour, his gratitude when she once more allowed him to carry her water bottle and food bag was pathetic to see.

Robyn was now consumed with impatience. She had no way of knowing how far behind her was Zouga and his hunting-party. He might have returned to the camp at Mount Hampden and found her note the very day after her departure, or he might still be killing elephant a hundred miles away, completely unaware that she had marched without him.

Her disapproval of her brother, and her anger at his recent actions, had gradually evoked a sense of competition in her. She had come so far and accomplished so much on her own – from the contact with the Karanga village to following the traces of her father so far and so doggedly – that she fiercely resented the idea of his arrival when she was at the very point of making the prayed-for and long-delayed reunion with Fuller Ballantyne. She guessed how the tale would be told in Zouga's journal, and in the book that would follow it. She knew who would get all the credit for the arduous search, and its brilliantly successful conclusion.

Once she had thought that fame and praise meant little to her, she believed she would be content to leave that to her brother. She had believed that her own reward would be her father's embrace, and the deep personal knowledge that she had brought some comfort or some surcease to the suffering black peoples of her Africa.

'I still do not know myself all that well,' she admitted, as she called the third successive *tirikeza*, double-marching her porters relentlessly to keep ahead of Zouga wherever he might be.

'I want to find Pater, I want to find him alone, and I want the world to know I found him.'

'Pride is sinful, but then I have always been a sinner. Forgive me, Sweet Jesus, I will make it up in a thousand other ways. Only forgive this one small unimportant sin,' she prayed in her rude grass shelter, and as she did so she listened with one ear for the shouts of Zouga's bearers coming into camp, and her heart tripped at each sudden noise. She was tempted to break camp and call a night march towards the next distant hill they had seen on the horizon at sunset and which old Karanga had once again confidently declared to be the Iron Mountain. The moon was full and would rise in an hour, that one march might be all that was necessary to keep ahead of her brother.

However, her porters were exhausted, even Juba was complaining of thorns in her feet. It seemed that only she and old

Karanga were able to maintain this pace for day after day. She must let them rest.

The next morning she had them away when the grass was still bent under the weight of dew drops, and before she had gone a mile her breeches were soaked to the thighs. During the last few days' march the character of the land had altered. The elevated plateau of rolling grassland and open forest across which they had marched so long now seemed to be dipping southwards, and the single peak which she had seen the night before slowly evolved into a whole series of hills stretching across her horizon from west to east, and she felt her spirits sag.

What chance would she ever have of finding one man's camp, one single hilltop, amongst so many? But she slogged on doggedly, and she and Karanga reached the first foothills before noon well ahead of the column. She checked Zouga's barometer nestling in its velvet-lined wooden case, and found that the altitude was still well over 1,200 feet, though they had dropped two hundred feet in the last two days' march.

Then, followed closely by Karanga, and at a little distance by Juba, she climbed the rocky shoulder of one of the foothills and from its height had a clearer view ahead over the confused and broken ground. She could see that the hills descended sharply into the south. Perhaps they had crossed the highlands and before them lay the descent to one of the known rivers that Tom Harkness had marked upon his map. She tried to remember the names, Shashi and Tati and Macloutsi.

Suddenly she was starting to feel very lonely and uncertain again. The land was so vast, she felt like a tiny insect pinned to an endless plain beneath the high pitiless blue sky. She turned and looked back into the north, using the long, brass-bound telescope to search for any signs of Zouga's party. She was not certain if she was relieved or disappointed to find none.

'Karanga!' she called, and he scrambled to his feet readily and looked up at her on the pinnacle of rock on which she stood. His expression was trusting as that of a pet-dog.

'Which way now?' she demanded, and he dropped his eyes and stood on one bird-thin leg, scratching his calf with the other foot as he pondered the question. Then with an apologetic gesture he indicated the nearest half dozen promontories along the skyline ahead with a hesitant all-embracing gesture, and Robyn felt her heart sink further. She had to admit at last that she was lost.

She knew then that she would have to do one of two things. Either camp where she was until Zouga came up, or turn back along her own spoor until she met him. Neither alternative was attractive, and she put off the decision until the morrow.

There was water in the river-bed below her, the usual shallow warm green pools, foul with bird and animal droppings.

Suddenly she felt very tired. While the expectations of success had buoyed her up she had not noticed it, but now she felt deflated and the marrow of her bones ached with weariness.

'We will camp here,' she told the Corporal. 'Take two men and find meat.'

They had marched so hard and long since leaving Karanga's village that there had been no time to hunt. By this time the last of the dried buffalo meat smelt like badly cured hides and was full of bacon beetles. She could only eat it in a strong curry and the curry powder was almost finished. They needed fresh meat desperately, but she was too dispirited to lead the hunting party.

The porters had not finished thatching the low lean-to roof that would be her home for the night when she heard a fusillade of musket fire close by in the forest, and an hour later the Corporal came into camp. They had found a large herd of the lovely sable antelope, Harris buck, as Zouga insisted on calling them, and had succeeded in bringing down five fat chocolate-coloured cows. The porters, chattering happily, left en masse to help bring in the meat, and Robyn wandered listlessly down the river-bed, accompanied only by Juba, until she found a secluded pool.

'I must smell as good as old Karanga,' she thought, scrubbing herself with handfuls of white sand for she had weeks previously used the last of her soap. She washed out her clothing and spread it to dry on the smooth, water-worn rocks around the pool. Then, still naked, she sat in the sunlight and Juba knelt behind her and combed out her hair so that it could dry.

Juba was obviously pleased to have Robyn to herself again, without old Karanga hovering nearby. Even though Robyn was silent and dejected, Juba loved to play with her hair and delighted in the reddish lights that flared in the sunlight as the comb stroked through it.

She chatted merrily as she worked and gurgled with laughter at her own sallies, so that neither of them heard the footsteps in the sand, and it was only when the shadow fell at Robyn's feet that she realized that they were not alone. With a cry of alarm she rose, snatching up her still wet breeches and holding them to her breast to cover her nudity.

The woman who stood before her was unarmed, nervous as she was and shy. Not a young woman, though her skin was smooth and unlined and she had all her teeth still. She was almost certainly Mashona with the finer, more Egyptian features than the Nguni, and she wore the short kilt that left her upper body bare. Her naked breasts were large, out of proportion to the slim upright body, the nipples were raised and drawn-out as though she had recently been nursing an infant.

'I heard the guns,' she whispered shyly, and Robyn felt a lift of relief when she understood the language. It was Karanga. 'I came when I heard the guns. I came to lead you to Manali.'

Robyn felt the quick rush of tears scald her eyes at the name, and the leap of her heart made her gasp aloud.

Manali, the man who wears a red shirt – her father had always stoutly maintained that the colour red discouraged tsetse fly and other stinging insects, and that good thick flannel staved off the ague of fever.

Robyn jumped to her feet, completely oblivious now of her nudity and rushed to the woman, seizing her arm and shaking it.

'Manali!' she cried, and then in English. 'Where is he? Oh, take me to him this instant.'

It was more than mere chance, and old Karanga's faltering guidance, that had led her, Robyn decided exultantly as she followed her new guide along one of the narrow winding game paths. It was blood calling to blood. Instinctively, like a migrating swallow, she had flown straight to her father.

She felt like shouting aloud, singing her joy to the forest while the woman went swiftly ahead of Robyn, her narrow, smoothly muscled back and shoulders hardly moved above the gliding roll of her hips, that graceful walk of the African woman trained from childhood to carry a burden upon her head so smoothly that not a drop spills from a brimming pot.

She did not move swiftly enough for Robyn's expectations.

Already Robyn could imagine the powerful figure of her father striding towards her, the great flaming bush of his beard, the deep compelling voice as he called her name, and swung her high as he had when she was a child, then the crushing embrace of his arms.

She imagined his joy matching hers, and after the first heady moments of reunion, then the serious hours of discussion, the recital of the long years between, the growing trust and intimacy between them that they had lacked before, so that finally they could march together to a common goal. In the long years ahead, he could hand the torch to her confident that his faith and work would go forward in loving and loyal hands.

What would be his first words when he saw and recognized her? How immense his surprise? She laughed aloud breathlessly, of course, he would be deeply touched and grateful that she had come so far, so determinedly to be with him, and she, Robyn, knew that she would not be able to hold back her own tears of joy, she could imagine her father tenderly wiping them away. The tone of his voice would betray the pent-up love of all the intervening years that had parted them, and which would be so sweet that she could hardly bear it.

Ahead of her, in the fading light of a dying day the Mashona woman led them on to a steep pathway, climbing at a traverse across the western slope of the highest hill. Robyn laughed again when she realized that it was the same hill that old Karanga had pointed out from twenty miles away. He had been right in the end, she must praise him lavishly for that. In her own happiness she wanted to give joy to all the world.

The path came out on a level shelf just below the crest, with a shallow cliff at the back of it and the slope of the hill falling away steeply towards the sunset, and a breathtaking view across the forest and savannah. The entire land turned pink and gold in the low sun and the stupendous flat-topped thunderheads of cloud rose along the dark blue horizon. The setting was right for this magical moment, but Robyn glanced at it only once and then her full attention fastened on what lay ahead of her.

In the face of the cliff was the mouth of a low cave, the slanting rays of the sun struck fully into it showing that it was not very deep, but had been occupied for a long time. The roof and walls were blackened with the soot of the cooking fire, the floor had been swept bare except for the fire at the entrance, with its circle of blackened hearth stones and a small clay pot standing upon them.

The clearing in front of the cave was bare also, trodden by feet over many years, and there was the offal of human occupation scattered about it, the bare bones of small animals, scraps of fur, chips of wood and shards of broken pottery. There was the odour of rotting food fragments, unwashed leather garments, wood smoke and human excrement that confirmed the other evidence that men had lived here for a long time.

There was a single human figure crouched over the smoky little fire, an old crone, bowed by age, a mere bundle of filthy fur blankets, moth-eaten and ragged, looking more like an ancient ape than a human being. It did not stir, and Robyn barely glanced at it for something else held her attention.

In the back of the cave, lit by the last fleeting sunlight, stood a bed. It was made of rudely cut poles, and tied together with bark rope, yet it stood on four legs in European style, not the African sleeping-mat, and it was piled with a stained fur kaross that might have contained a human shape.

On a ledge directly above the bed stood a brass telescope, a teak box similar to the one that held Zouga's sextant and chronometer, but scarred and battered with age, and a small cheap tin chest. The chest was much battered also, most of the original paint chipped away so the bare metal showed.

Robyn remembered that box so vividly, open in Uncle William's study at Kings Lynn, the papers from it overflowing on to the desk top and her father bowed over them, steel-rimmed spectacles on the end of his beaked nose, tugging at his thick red beard as he worked.

Robyn gave a little choking cry, and ran forward passing the old crone sitting at the fire, crossing the cave, and flinging herself on her knees beside the crude bedstead.

'Pater!' Her voice husked over with emotion rasped her own throat. 'Pater! It's me – Robyn.'

There was no movement beneath the fur blanket and she put out a hand, then stopped before it touched.

'He is dead,' she thought miserably. 'I am too late!'

She forced her hand to move again, and touched the malodorous pile of old furs. They collapsed under her touch, and it took her seconds to realize that she had been mistaken. The bed was empty, the discarded blanket had fallen in the shape of a man, but the bed was empty.

Bewildered, Robyn rose to her feet and turned back towards the entrance of the cave. The Karanga woman stood by the fire, watching her expressionlessly, while little Juba hung back fearfully at the far side of the clearing.

'Where is he?' Robyn spread her hands to emphasize the question. 'Where is Manali?'

The Karanga woman dropped her eyes. For a moment Robyn did not understand, and then she too looked down at the grotesque figure that crouched by the fire at her feet.

She felt a cold steel band lock about her chest and squeeze her heart so that it took an effort of will to force her feet to move back across the swept floor of the cave.

The Mashona woman was watching Robyn expressionlessly. She had clearly not understood the English question, but she waited with the endless patience of Africa. Robyn was about to appeal to her again, when the skeletal figure across the smoky little fire started to rock from side to side agitatedly, and a querulous slurred old man's voice began to chant some strange litany, like a magical incantation.

It took Robyn some moments to realize that the accents were faintly Scots and the words, though blurred and jumbled, were a parody of the 23rd psalm.

'Yea! Though I walk through the valley of the shadow of death, I shall fear no evil.'

As suddenly as it had begun the chanting broke off, and the rocking ceased. The frail figure froze into stillness and silence again. Across the fire, the Mashona woman stooped and gently as a mother with a child, she drew back the kaross from the head and shoulder of the figure at her feet.

Fuller Ballantyne had shrivelled, his face lined and roughened like the bark of an old oak. It seemed as though the smoke of the fire had etched his skin, collecting in the creases, crusting it with soot.

His hair and beard had fallen out in clumps, as though from some disgusting disease, and what was left of it was pure white but stringed and darkened with dirt to a tobacco yellow at the corners of the mouth and at the nostrils.

Only his eyes still seemed to live, they rolled in their sockets, and it needed only one look at them for Robyn to realize that her father was mad. This was not Fuller Ballantyne, this was not the great explorer, the powerful evangelist and enemy of slavery. He had gone long ago, leaving a filthy shrivelled lunatic in his place.

'Pater,' she stared at him in disbelief, feeling the world spin and lurch beneath her. 'Pater,' she repeated, and across the fire the crouched figure gibbered with abrupt falsetto girlish laughter, and then began to rave incoherently, snatches of English giving way to a half-dozen dialects of Africa, the cries becoming more agitated, his thin pale arms thrown wildly in the air.

'I have sinned against thee, my God,' he screamed and clawed at his own beard, a tuft of the thin pale hair coming away in the hooked fingers. 'I am not worthy to be thy servant.' He tore at himself again, this time leaving a thin livid scratch down the pouched and wrinkled cheek, though it seemed that the wasted body had no blood left to shed.

The Mashona woman leaned over him and caught the bony wrist, restraining him. The action was so familiar that she must have performed it often. Then gently she stooped and lifted him. The body seemed to weigh no more than that of a child for she carried him without visible effort to the crude pole bed. One of his legs was bound up in a rudimentary splint and stuck straight out ahead of him.

Robyn stayed on beside the fire, hanging her head. She found that she was still shivering, until the woman came back to her, touching her arm.

'He is very sick.'

Only then could Robyn force back her revulsion and her horror. She stood, hesitated only a moment longer, and then went to her father. With Juba and the Mashona woman helping her, she began her examination, taking refuge behind her professional rituals and procedures while she regained control of her emotions. He was thinner than she had ever seen a living human body, thinner than the starved brats of gin-soaked slum sluts.

'There has been little food,' said the woman, 'and what there is, he will not eat. I have had to feed him like a small baby.' Robyn did not then understand what she meant, but she went on grimly with her examination.

The starved body was verminous, the bunches of little white nits hanging like grapes in the thin white pubic hair, and his whole body was crusted with filth and traces of his own incontinence.

Feeling under the staring rib cage her fingertips encountered the hard distended shape of liver and spleen, and Fuller Ballantyne screamed when she did so. The swelling and extreme tenderness were certain indications of massive malarial infection of long duration, and evidence of terrible neglect.

'Where is the medicine, the *umuthi*, of Manali?'

'It was long ago finished, together with the powder and shot for the gun. Everything was finished long ago,' the woman shook her head, 'long, long ago, and when it was finished, the people no longer came with gifts to feed us.' It was suicidal to remain in a malarial area without supplies of quinine. Fuller Ballantyne of all people knew that. The acknowledged world expert on malarial fever and its treatment – how could he have neglected his own often-repeated advice. She found the reasons almost immediately, as she opened his mouth, forcing open his lower jaw despite his feeble protests.

Most of his teeth had been rotted out by the disease, and his throat and palate were covered by the characteristic lesions. She released his jaw, allowing him to close the ruined mouth, and gently she touched the bridge of his nose, feeling the soggy collapsing bone and gristle. There could be no doubt at all, the disease was far advanced, had long ago begun its final assault upon the once magnificent brain. It was syphilis, in the terminal stages, the general paralysis of the insane. The disease of the lonely man that led inevitably to this lonely madman's death.

As Robyn worked, so her horror and revulsion gave way swiftly to the compassion of the healer, to the sympathy of one who had lived with human weakness and folly and had come far along the road of understanding. She knew now why her father had not turned back when his supplies of vital medicines ran perilously low, the half-destroyed brain had not recognized the dangers which he had previously described so clearly.

She found herself praying for him as she worked, praying silently but with the words coming more readily than they usually did.

'Judge him as he was, Oh Lord, judge him by his service in your name – not by his small sins, but by his great achievements. Look not upon this ruined pathetic thing, but on the strong and vital man who carried your work forward without flinching.'

As she prayed, she lifted the heavy kaross off his legs, and the smell of corruption made her blink and the frail figure began immediately to struggle with renewed strength, that needed both Juba and the Mashona woman to control.

Robyn stared at the legs, and realized the other reason why her father had never left this land. He had been physically unable to do so. The splints that held the leg had been whittled out of native timber. The leg had been fractured, probably at more than one place below the hip. Perhaps the hip joint itself had gone, that vulnerable neck of the femur. But what was certain was that the breaks had not mended cleanly. Perhaps the bindings of the splints had been too tight, for the deep suppurating ulcerations went down to the very bone, and the smell was a solid jarring thing.

Quickly she covered his lower body, there was nothing she could do until she had her medical chest and instruments, and now she was merely inflicting unnecessary pain and humiliation. Her father was still struggling and bleating like a petulant child, rolling his head from side to side, the toothless mouth darkly agape.

The Mashona woman leaned over him, and took one of her own dark tight breasts in her hand, squeezing out the nipple between her fingers, and then she paused and looked up shyly, imploringly at Robyn.

Only then did Robyn understand, and respecting the privacy of woman and the poor maimed thing that had been her father, she dropped her eyes and turned away towards the entrance of the cave.

'I must fetch my *umuthi*. I will return here later tonight.'

Behind her, the childlike bleats gave way abruptly to small snuffling sounds of comfort.

Robyn felt no shock or outrage as she went down the steep pathway in the moonlight. Instead she felt immense pity for Fuller Ballantyne who had made the full circle back to infancy. She felt also a deep gratitude to the woman, and a sense of wonder at her loyalty and dedication. How long had she stayed on with Fuller Ballantyne after all reason for staying was gone?

She remembered her own mother, and her devotion to the same man, she remembered Sarah and her child still waiting patiently beside a far-off river. And then there was Robyn herself, come so far and so determinedly. Fuller Ballantyne always had the power to attract as powerfully as he could repel.

Holding Juba's hand for her own comfort as well as that of the child, Robyn hurried along the moonlit path on the bank of the river, and with relief saw the glow of the camp fires in the forest ahead of her. On the return journey she would have bearers to carry her medical chest, and armed Hottentot musketeers as escort.

Her relief was short-lived, for as she answered the challenge of the Hottentot sentry and entered the circle of firelight, a familiar figure rose from beside the camp fire and came striding to meet her, tall and powerful, golden-bearded and handsome as a god from Greek mythology, and every bit as wrathful.

'Zouga!' she gasped. 'I didn't expect you.'

'No,' he agreed icily. 'I'm sure that you did not.'

'Why?' she thought desperately. 'Why must he come now? Why not a day later, when I have had time to clean and treat my father? Oh God, why now? Zouga will never understand – Never! Never! Never!'

Robyn and her escort could not hope to keep pace with Zouga. They fell swiftly behind him as he climbed the pathway in the night, months of hard hunting had toned him to the peak of physical condition and he ran at the hill.

She had not been able to warn him. What words were there to describe the creature in the cave on the hilltop. She had told him simply

'I have found Pater.'

It had deflected his anger instantly. The bitter accusations shrivelled on his tongue, and the realization dawned in his eyes.

They had found Fuller Ballantyne. They had accomplished one of the three major objectives of the expedition. She knew that Zouga was already seeing it in print, almost composing the paragraph that would describe the moment, imagining the newspaper urchins shouting the headlines in the streets of London.

For the first time in her life she came close to hating her

brother, and her voice was crisp as hoar-frost as she told him, 'And don't you forget it was me. I was the one who made the march and broke trail, and I was the one who found him.'

She saw the shift in his green eyes in the firelight.

'Of course, Sissy.' He smiled at her thinly, an obvious effort. 'Who could ever forget that? Where is he?'

'First I must assemble what I need.'

He had stayed with her until they reached the foot of the hill, and then had been unable to restrain himself. He had gone at the slope at a pace that none of them had been able to equal. Robyn came out in the little clearing in front of the cave. Her heart was racing and her breathing ragged from the climb so that she had to pause and fight for breath, holding one hand to her breast.

The fire in front of the cave had been built up to a fair blaze, but it left the depths of the cave in discreet shadow. Zouga stood in front of the fire. His back to the cave.

As Robyn regained her breath, she went forward. She saw that Zouga's face was deathly pale, in the firelight his sun-bronzing had faded to a muddy tone. He stood erect, as though on the parade ground, and he stared directly ahead of him.

'Have you seen Pater?' Robyn asked. His distress and utter confusion gave her a sneaking and spiteful pleasure.

'There is a native woman with him,' Zouga whispered, 'in his bed.'

'Yes,' Robyn nodded. 'He is very sick. She is caring for him.'

'Why did you not warn me?'

'That he is sick?' she asked.

'That he had gone native.'

'He's dying, Zouga.'

'What are we going to tell the world?'

'The truth,' she suggested quietly. 'That he is sick and dying.'

'You must never mention the woman.' Zouga's voice, for the first time that she could remember, was uncertain, he seemed to be groping for words. 'We must protect the family.'

'Then what must we tell about his disease, the disease that is killing him?'

Zouga's eyes flickered to her face. 'Malaria?'

'The pox, Zouga. The French sickness, the Italian plague – or, if you prefer it, syphilis, Zouga. He is dying of syphilis.'

Zouga flinched, and then he whispered, 'It's not possible.'

'Why not, Zouga?' she asked. 'He was a man, a great man – but a man nevertheless.'

She stepped past him. 'And now I have work to do.'

An hour later when she looked for him again, Zouga had gone back down the hill to the camp beside the river pools. She remained to work over her father for the rest of that night and most of the following day.

By the time she had bathed and cleaned him, shaved off the infested body hair and trimmed the stringy beard and locks of yellowed hair, treated the ulcerations of his leg, she was exhausted both physically and emotionally. She had seen approaching death too many times not to recognize it now. She knew that all she could hope for was to give comfort and to smooth the lonely road that her father must travel.

When she had done all that was possible, she covered him with a clean blanket and then tenderly caressed the short soft hair which she had so lovingly trimmed. Fuller opened his eyes. They were a pale empty shade of blue, like an African summer sky. The last sunlight of the day was washing the cave, and as Robyn leaned over him, it sparkled in her hair in chips of ruby light.

She saw something move in the empty eyes, a shadow of the man who had once been there, and Fuller's lips parted. Twice he tried to speak and then he said one word, so husky and light that she missed it. Robyn leaned closer to him.

'What is it?' she asked.

'Helen!' This time clearer.

Robyn felt the tears choke up her throat at the sound of her mother's name.

'Helen.' Fuller said it for the last time, and then the flicker of comprehension in his eyes was gone.

She stayed on beside him, but there was nothing more. That name had been the last link with reality and now the link was broken.

As the last light of the day faded, Robyn lifted her eyes from her father's face and for the first time realized that the tin chest was missing from the ledge at the back of the cave.

Using the lid of his own writing-case as a desk, screened from the camp by the thin wall of thatch, Zouga worked swiftly through the contents of the chest.

His horror at the discovery of his father had long ago been submerged by the fascination of the treasures which the chest contained. The disgust, the shame, would return again when he had time to think about it, he knew that. He knew also that there would be hard decisions to make then, and that he would have to use all his force of personality and of brotherly superiority to control Robyn, and make her agree to a common version of the discovery of Fuller Ballantyne and a tactful description of the circumstances to which he had been reduced.

The tin chest contained four leather and canvas-bound journals, each of five hundred pages, and the pages were covered on both sides either with writing or with hand drawn maps. There was also a bundle of loose sheets, two or three hundred of them tied together with plaited bark string. and a cheap wooden pen case with a partition for spare nibs, and cut-outs for two ink bottles. One bottle was dry, and the pen nibs had obviously been sharpened many times, for they were almost worn away. Zouga sniffed the ink in the remaining bottle. It seemed to be an evil-smelling mixture, of fat and soot and vegetable dyes that Fuller had concocted when his supplies of the manufactured item were exhausted.

The last journal and most of the loose pages were written with this mixture, and they had faded and smeared, making the handwriting that much more difficult to decipher, for by this stage Fuller Ballantyne's hand had deteriorated almost as much as his mind. Whereas the first two journals were written in the small, precise and familiar script, this slowly turned into a loose sloping scrawl as uncontrolled as some of the ideas expressed by it. The history of his father's madness was plotted therein with sickening fascination.

The pages of the leatherbound journals were not numbered, and there were many gaps between the dates of one entry and the next, which made Zouga's work easier. He read swiftly, an art he had developed when acting as regimental intelligence officer with huge amounts of reading, reports, orders and departmental manuals, to get through each day.

The first books of writing were ground that had been travelled before, meticulous observations of celestial position, of climate and altitude, backed up by shrewdly observed descriptions of terrain and population. Sandwiched between these were accusations and complaints about authority, whether it were the directors of the London Missionary Society, or 'The Imperial Factor' as Fuller Ballantyne referred to the Foreign Secretary and his department in Whitehall.

There were detailed explanations of his reasons for leaving Tete and travelling south with a minimally equipped expedition, and then, quite suddenly, two pages devoted to an account of a sexual liaison with an ex-slave girl, an Angoni girl whom Fuller had christened 'Sarah' and who he suspected was about to bear his child. His reasons for abandoning her at Tete were direct and without pretence. 'I know that a woman, even a hardy native, carrying a child would delay me. As I am on God's work, I can brook no such check.'

Although what Zouga had seen on the hilltop should have conditioned him for this sort of revelation, still he could not bring himself to terms with it. Using his hunting-knife, whetted to a razor edge, he slit the offending pages from the journal, and as he crumpled them and threw them in the camp fire he muttered, 'The old devil had no right to write this filth.'

Twice more he found sexual references which he removed from the journal, and by then the handwriting was showing the first deterioration, and passages of great lucidity were followed by wild ravings and the dreams and imaginings of a diseased mind.

More often Fuller referred to himself as the instrument of God's wrath, his blazing sword against the heathen and the ungodly. The weirdest and patently lunatic passages Zouga cut from the journal and burned. He knew he must work swiftly, before Robyn came down from the hilltop. He knew that what he was doing was right, for his father's memory and place in posterity and also for those who would have to live on after him, Robyn and Zouga himself, and their children and children's children.

It was a chilling experience to see his father's great love and compassion for the African people, and the very land itself changing and becoming a bitter unreasoning hatred. Against the Matabele people, whom he referred to as the Ndebele – or the Amandebele – he railed: 'These leonine peoples who acknowledge no God at all, whose diet consists of the devil's brew and half-cooked meat, both in vast quantities, and whose greatest delight is spearing to death defenceless women and children, are ruled over by the most merciless despot since Caligula, the most grossly blood-besotted monster since Attila himself.'

Of the other tribes he was at least as scornful. 'The Rozwis are a sly and secret people, the timid and treacherous descendants of the slave-trading and gold-mad kings they called the Mambos. Their dynasties destroyed by the marauding Ndebele and their monstrous Nguni brothers the Shangaans of Gungundha and the blood-smattered Angoni.'

The Karangas were 'cowards and devil-worshippers, lurking in their caves and hilltop fortresses, committing unspeakable sacrilege and offending in the face of the Almighty by their blasphemous ceremonies in the ruined cities where once their Monomatapa held sway'.

The reference to Monomatapa and ruined cities checked Zouga's eyes in the middle of the page. Then he read on eagerly, hoping for elaboration of the mention of ruined cities, but Fuller's mind had flown on to other ideas, the theme of suffering and sacrifice which has always been the spine of Christian belief.

'I thank God, my Almighty Father, that he has chosen me as his sword, and that as the mark of his love and condescension he has made his mark upon me. This dawn when I awoke there were the stigmata in my feet and hands, the wound in my side, and the bleeding scratches from the crown of thorns upon my forehead. I have felt the same sweet pain as Christ himself.'

The disease had reached that part of his brain that affected his eyes, and sense of feeling. His faith had become religious mania. Zouga cut out this and the following pages and consigned them to the flames of the camp fire.

Ranting madness was followed by cool sanity, as though the disease had tides which ebbed and flowed within his brain. The next entry in the journal was dated five days after that claiming the stigmata. It began with a celestial observation that placed him not far from where Zouga sat reading the words, always making allowances for the inaccuracy of a chronometer that had not been checked for almost two years. There was no further reference to the stigmata. They had healed as miraculously as they had bloomed. Instead there was a brisk and businesslike entry in the old neat script.

'The Karanga people practise a form of ancestor worship, which calls for sacrifice. It is extremely difficult to make any one of them discuss either this ceremony or even the basic precepts of this abominable religion. However, my command of the Karanga language is now sufficient to have earned the respect and trust of those members of the tribe with whom I have succeeded in making contact. The spiritual centre of their religion is in a place which they refer to as "the burial place of the kings", or in their language "Zimbabwe" or "Simbabwee" where the idols which represent their ancestors stand.

'It would seem that this place is situated to the south and east of my present position.

'The head of this foul belief is a priestess, referred to as the "Umlimo" who once dwelt in the "burial place of the kings" but fled from there at the coming of the Angoni marauders. She lives in another sacred place, and commands such sway that even the godless Ndebele, that sanguine tyrant Mzilikazi, send gifts for her oracle.

'So deeply ingrained is the power of this evil belief into the minds of all these people, that they are strongly resistant to the word of Christ which I bear.

'It has come to me in a revelation which can only be the voice of God Almighty himself that he has chosen me to march upon this citadel of evil, this "Simbabwee", and to throw down the images of the ungodly – even as Moses threw down and destroyed the golden calf on his descent from the mountain.

'God Almighty has further revealed to me that I have been chosen to seek out the High Priestess of evil in her secret place and to destroy her, and by so doing break the hold that she has over the minds of these people, that they might become receptive to the Holy Word of Christ which I bring them.'

Zouga raced on through the pages, it seemed as though they were being written by two different men, the rational being with the neat script and the raving religious maniac with the wild looping hand. In some passages the change came from one line to the next, in others the one character was maintained for page after page. Zouga could not afford to miss a word of it.

It was well after noon, and his eyes felt grainy and tender from continually scanning the cramped sheets, blurred and faded from the improvised ink which Fuller was now using.

'November 3rd. Position. 20° 05 S. 30° 50 E. Temperature 103° in the shade. Heat unbearable. Rain threatens each day and never comes. Have reached the lair of the Umlimo.'

The single laconic entry electrified Zouga. He almost missed it, for it was squeezed into the bottom of a page. He turned that page and on the next the madman had taken over again, writing in vaunting hyperbole and thunderous religious ecstasy.

'I praise God, my Maker. The one true and Almighty Saviour for whom all things are possible. Thy will be done!

'The Umlimo knew me as the instrument of God's wrath when I confronted her in that reeking charnel house, for she spoke in the voices of Belal and Beelzebub, the hideous voices of Azazel and Beliar, all Satan's myriad alter-egos.

'But I stood before her strong and proud in God's word, and when she saw she could not move me, she fell silent.

'So I slew her, and cut off her head and carried it out into the light. And God spoke to me in the night and said in his small still voice "Go on, my faithful and well-beloved servant. You cannot rest until the graven images of the godless are cast down."

'So I rose, and God's hand held me up and carried me onwards.'

How much of this was fact, and how much was the ranting of madness, fantasy of a diseased brain, Zouga could not know, but he read on furiously.

'And the Almighty guided me until I came at last alone to the foul city where the devil-worshippers commit their sacrilege. My bearers would not follow me, terrified of the devils. Even old Joseph who was always at my side could not force his legs to carry him through the gateway in the high stone wall. I left him cringing in the forest, and went in alone to walk between the high towers of stone.

'As God had revealed to me, I found the graven images of the heathen all decked with flowers and gold, the blood of the sacrifice not yet dried, and I broke them and cast them down and no man could oppose me for I was the sword of Zion, the finger of God's own hand.'

The entry broke off abruptly, as though the writer had been overwhelmed by the strength of his own religious fervour, and Zouga flipped through the next one hundred pages of the journal searching for further reference to the city and its gold-decked images, but there was none.

Like the miraculous blooming of the stigmata upon Fuller's hands and feet and body and brow, perhaps this was also the imaginings of a lunatic.

Zouga returned to the original entry, describing Fuller's meeting with the Umlimo, the sorceress whom he had slain. He wrote the latitude and longitude into his own journal, copied the rough sketch map and made cryptic notes of the text, pondering it for clues that might lead or guide him. Then, quite deliberately, he cut out the pages from Fuller's own journal and held them one at a time over the fire, letting them crinkle and brown, then catch and flare before he dropped them and watched them curl and blacken. He stirred the ashes to dust with a stick before he was satisfied.

The last of the four journals was only partially filled, and contained a detailed description of a caravan route running from 'the blood-soaked lands where Mzilikazi's evil impis hold sway' eastwards five hundred miles or more 'to where the reeking ships of the traders surely wait to welcome the poor souls who survive the hazards of this infamous road'.

'I have followed the road as far as the eastern rampart of mountains, and always the evidence of the passing of the caravans is there for all the world to see. That grisly evidence which I have come to know so well, the bleaching bones and the circling vultures. Is there not a corner of this savage continent which is free from the ravages of the traders?'

These revelations would interest Robyn more than they did him. Zouga glanced through them swiftly and then marked them for her attention. There was a great deal on slavery and the traders, a hundred pages or more – and then the penultimate entry.

'We have today come up with a caravan of slaves, winding through the hilly country towards the east. I have counted the miserable victims from afar, using the telescope and there are almost a hundred of them, mostly half-grown children and young women. They are yoked together in pairs with forked tree trunks about their necks in the usual manner.

'The slave-masters are black men, I have been unable to descry either Arabs or men of European extraction amongst them. Although they wear no tribal insignia, no plumes nor regalia, I have no doubt they are Amandebele, for their physique is distinctive, and they come from the direction of that tyrant Mzilikazi's kingdom. They are furthermore armed with the broad bladed stabbing spear and long ox-hide shields of that people, while two or three of them carry trade muskets.

'At this moment they are encamped not more than a league from where I lie, and in the dawn they will continue their fateful journey towards the east where the Arab and Portuguese slave-masters no doubt wait to purchase the miserable human cattle and load them like cargo for the cruel voyage half across the world.

'God has spoken to me, clearly I have heard his voice as he enjoined me to go down, and, like his sword, cut down the ungodly, free the slaves and minister to the meek and the innocent.

'Joseph is with me, that true and trusted companion of the years, and he will be well able to serve my second gun. His marksmanship is not of the best, but he has courage and God will be with us.'

The next entry was the last. Zouga had come to the end of the four journals.

'God's ways are wonderful and mysterious, passing all understanding. He lifteth up and he casteth down. With Joseph beside me I went down, as God had commanded, to the camp of the slave-masters. We fell upon them, even as the Israelites fell upon the Philistines. At first it seemed that we must prevail for the ungodly fled before us. Then God in all his knowing wisdom deserted us. One of the ungodly leapt upon Joseph while he was reloading, and though I put a ball through his chest he impaled poor Joseph from breast bone to spine with that terrible spear, before himself falling dead.

'Alone I carried on the fight, God's fight, and the slave-masters scattered into the forest before my wrath. Then one of them turned and at extreme range fired his musket in my direction. The ball struck me in the hip.

'I managed, I do not know how, to drag myself away before the slave-masters returned to slay me. They did not attempt to follow me, and I have regained the shelter which I left to make the attempt. However, I am sorely smitten and reduced to dire straits. I have managed to remove the musket ball from my own hip, but I fear the bone is cracked through and I am crippled.

'In addition I have lost both my firearms, Joseph's musket lies with him where he fell, and I was so badly hurt as to be unable to carry my weapon off the field. I sent the woman back to find them, but they have been carried away by the slave-traders.

'My remaining porters, seeing the state to which I have been reduced and knowing that I could not prevent it, have all deserted, but not before they had looted the camp and carried away almost everything of value, not excluding my medicine chest. Only the woman remains. I was angry at first when she attached herself to my party, but now I see God's hand in this – for although she is a heathen, yet she is loyal and true beyond all others, now that Joseph is dead.

'What is a man in this cruel land without a musket or quinine? Is there a lesson in this for me and posterity, a lesson that God has chosen me to teach? Can a white man live here? Will he not always be the alien, and will Africa tolerate him once he has lost his weapons and expended his medicines?'

Then a single poignant cry of agony.

'Oh God, has this all been in vain? I came to bring your Word and nobody has listened to my voice. I came to change the ways of the wicked and nothing is changed. I came to open a way for Christianity, and no Christian has followed me. Please, my God, give me a sign that I have not followed the wrong road to a false destination.'

Zouga leaned back and rubbed his eyes with the heels of both hands. He found himself deeply moved, his eyes stinging not only from fatigue.

Fuller Ballantyne was an easy man to hate, but a hard man to despise.

Robyn chose the place with care. The secluded pools on the river, away from the main camp, where nobody could overlook or overhear them. She chose the time, in the heat of midday – when most of the Hottentots and all the porters would be asleep in the shade. She had given Fuller five drops of the precious laudanum to quiet him, and left him with the Mashona girl and Juba to care for him while she went down the hill to Zouga.

They had barely exchanged a dozen words during the ten days since he had caught up with her. In all that time he had not returned to the cave on the hilltop, and she had seen him only once when she had gone down to the river camp for supplies.

When she had sent Juba down with a tersely worded note, demanding the return of Fuller's tin chest of papers, he had sent a porter with it immediately. In fact, with such alacrity that Robyn was immediately suspicious.

This distrust was a symptom of their rapidly deteriorating relationship. She knew that she and Zouga must talk, must discuss the future, before the opportunity to talk was past.

He was waiting for her beside the green river pools, as she had asked him to be, sitting in the mottled shade beneath a wild fig tree, quietly smoking a hand-rolled cheroot of native tobacco. He stood up courteously as soon as he saw her, but his expression was reserved and his eyes guarded.

'I do not have much time, Zouga dear.' Robyn tried to lessen the tension between them by using the small endearment, and Zouga nodded gravely. 'I must get back to Pater.' She hesitated. 'I did not want to ask you to come up the hill since you find it distasteful.' She saw the green sparks in his eyes kindle immediately, and went on quickly. 'We must decide what we should do now. Obviously we cannot stay on here indefinitely.'

'What do you suggest?'

'Pater is much stronger. I have subdued the malaria with quinine and the other disease,' she worded it tactfully, 'has responded to the mercury. It is only the leg that truly worries me now.'

'You told me he was dying.' Zouga reminded her levelly, and she could not help herself, despite her good intentions she flared at him.

'Well, I am sorry to disappoint you, then.'

Zouga's face stiffened into a handsome, bronzed mask. She could see the effort it took him to control his own temper, and his voice was thick with it as he answered.

'That's not worthy of you.'

'I'm sorry,' she agreed, and drew a deep breath. 'Zouga, he has rallied strongly. Food and medicine, care and his own natural strength have made an immense difference. I am even convinced that if we could get him to civilization to a skilled surgeon – we could cure the ulceration of his leg, and possibly even induce the bone to mend.'

Zouga was silent for a long time, and though his face was expressionless, she could see the play of emotion in his eyes.

He spoke at last. 'Father is mad.' She did not answer. 'Can you cure his mind?'

'No.' She shook her head. 'That will get worse, but with care and skilled attention in a good hospital, we can improve his body and he could live for many years still.'

'To what purpose?' Zouga insisted.

'He would be comfortable and perhaps happy.'

'And all the world would know that he was a syphilitic madman,' Zouga went on quietly for her. 'Would it not be kinder to let the legend stand untarnished? No, more than that, to add to it by our own account, rather than drag back this poor diseased and demented thing for all his enemies, his numerous enemies, to mock?'

'Is that why you tampered with his journals?' Robyn's voice was shrill, even in her own ears.

'That's a dangerous accusation.' He was losing his control also. 'Can you prove it?'

'I don't have to prove it; we both know it's so.'

'You cannot move him.' Zouga changed direction. 'He is crippled.'

'He could be carried on a litter. We have more than enough porters.'

'Which way would you take him?' Zouga demanded. 'He would never survive the route over which we have travelled – and the route southwards is uncharted.'

'Pater himself has charted the slave road in his journal. We will follow that. It will lead us directly to the coast.'

'With the major objectives of the expedition unfulfilled?' Zouga asked quickly.

'The major objectives were to find Fuller Ballantyne, and report on the slave trade, both of which we can accomplish if we march down the slave road to the sea.' Robyn broke off, and then made a show of dawning comprehension. 'Oh dear, how silly of me, you mean the gold and the ivory. Those were the major objectives all along, were they not, my dear brother?'

'We have a duty to our sponsors.'

'And none to that poor sick old man up there?' Robyn flung out one hand dramatically, and then spoiled the effect by stamping her foot. Angry with herself as well as with him, she yelled at him. 'I am taking Pater down to the coast, and quickly as I can.'

'I say you are not.'

'And I say the hell with you, Morris Zouga Ballantyne!' The

oath gave her a dark pleasure, and she turned and strode away from him, long-legged in her tight-fitting breeches.

Two days later Robyn was ready to march. All exchanges between Zouga and herself since their final meeting at the river had been in the form of written notes, and Robyn realized that her brother would be keeping copies of all this correspondence to justify his actions later.

She had briefly repudiated his written command not to attempt a march with the sick man. Zouga had listed half a dozen reasons, each neatly enumerated, why she should remain. Once he had her written defiance, his next note sent up the hill in Juba's sweating little hand was magnanimous, written for future readers other than herself, Robyn decided sourly.

'If you insist on this folly,' he began and he went on to offer her the protection of the entire force of Hottentot musketeers – with the exception of Sergeant Cheroot who had expressed a desire to remain with Zouga. Under the Corporal they would form an escort capable, as Zouga worded it 'of bringing you and your charge safely to the coast, and protecting you from any hazards upon the way'.

He insisted that she take most of the remaining porters. He would keep five porters to carry his essential stores, together with his four gunbearers, Matthew, Mark, Luke and John.

He also ordered her to take the Sharps rifle and all the remaining stores, 'leaving me only sufficient powder and shot, and the bare minimum of medicines to enable me to complete the further objectives of this expedition which I deem to be of prime importance'.

His final note reiterated all his reasons for keeping Fuller Ballantyne on the hilltop, and asked her once more to reconsider her decision. Robyn saved him the trouble of making fair copies by simply turning over the note and scribbling on it. 'My mind is made up. I will march at first light tomorrow for the coast.' Then she dated and signed it.

The next morning, before sun-up, Zouga sent a team of porters up the hill, carrying a litter of mopani poles. The poles had been peeled of their rough bark and bound together with raw-hide strips from the green hide of a freshly killed roan antelope, and the body of the litter was made from the same interwoven hide strips. Fuller Ballantyne had to be strapped into the litter to prevent him throwing himself out of it.

When Robyn brought them down again, walking beside the litter to try and calm the crazy old man on it, the Hottentot escort and the porters were ready to join her on the march. Zouga was waiting also, standing a little aside as though he had already dissociated himself, but Robyn went to him directly.

'At least we know each other now,' she said huskily. 'We may not be able to rub along together, Zouga. I doubt we ever could have, or ever will be able to, but that does not mean I do not respect you, and love you even more than I respect you.'

Zouga flushed and looked away. As she should have known, such a declaration could only embarrass him.

'I have made sure that you have a hundred pounds of gunpowder, that is more than you could ever need,' he said.

'Do you not wish to say farewell to Pater?'

Zouga nodded stiffly, and followed her to the litter, avoiding looking at the Mashona woman who stood beside it and spoke formally to Fuller Ballantyne.

'Good-bye, sir. I wish you a swift safe journey and a speedy return to good health.'

The wizened toothless face, revolved towards him upon its scrawny neck. The shaven head had a pale porcelain gloss in the grey dawn light, and the eyes were bird-bright, glittering with madness.

'God is my shepherd, I shall fear no evil,' Fuller cawed, mouthing the words so they were barely understandable.

'Quite right, sir,' Zouga nodded seriously. 'No doubt at all about that.' He touched his cap in a military salute and stepped back. He nodded to the porters and they lifted the litter and moved away towards the pale orange and yellow sunrise.

Brother and sister stood side by side for the last time watching the column of escort and porters file past, and when the last of them had gone and only little Juba remained beside her, Robyn reached up impulsively and threw her arms around Zouga's neck, embraced him almost fiercely.

'I try to understand you, won't you do the same for me?'

For a moment she thought he might unbend, she felt the hard erect body sway and soften, and then Zouga straightened again.

'This is not good-bye,' he said. 'Once I have done what is necessary, I shall follow you. We'll meet again.'

Robyn dropped her arms to her sides, and stood back.

'Until then,' she agreed wistfully, sad that he had not been able to make even a show of affection

'Until then,' she repeated, and turned away. Juba followed her away into the forest, after the departing column.

Zouga waited until the singing of the porters dwindled, and the only sound was the sweet wild bird chorus that greets each dawn in Africa, and the distant melancholy whooping of a hyena slinking away to its earth.

There were many emotions warring in him. Guilt that he had let a woman, however well supported, attempt the journey to the coast; worry that once she reached it, her accounts would be the first to reach London; doubt as to the authenticity of the clues which Fuller Ballantyne had left for him to follow, but overlying it all a sense of relief and excitement that he was at last answerable only to himself, free to range as fast and far as hard legs and harder determination would take him.

He shook himself, a physical purging of guilt and doubt, leaving only the excitement and soaring sense of anticipation. and he turned to where Sergeant Cheroot waited at the perimeter of the forlorn and deserted camp.

'When you smile, your face makes the children cry,' Zouga told him, 'but when you frown . . What troubles you now, oh mighty hunter of elephants?'

The little Hottentot lugubriously indicated the bulky tin box that contained Zouga's dress uniform and hat.

'Say not another word, Sergeant,' Zouga warned him.

'But the porters complain, they have carried it so far.'

'And they will carry it to the gates of hell itself, if I say so. Safari!' Zouga raised his voice, elated with the sense of excitement still strongly upon him. 'We march!'

Zouga was prepared for wide discrepancies in the positions that his father had fixed by celestial observation, and his own. A few seconds of error in the chronometers would put them many miles out.

So he treated with suspicion the terrain features which he saw ahead and which seemed to match with uncanny accuracy the sketch maps he had copied from Fuller's journals.

Yet as each day's march that he made opened up country that fitted his father's descriptions, he became more confident, more certain that the Umlimo and the ruined city were real and that they lay not many days' march ahead.

It was beautiful country they passed through, though the air was more sultry as they descended the sloping plateau towards the south and west. The long dry season, now drawing to its close, had seared the grasslands to the colour of fields of ripening wheat, and turned the foliage of the forests to a hundred shades of plum reds and soft apricots. Many of the trees were bare of all leaves, lifting arthritically contorted limbs to the sky as if beseeching it for the relief of rain.

Each day the thunderheads built up, tall silver ranges of cloud turning purple and sullen leaden blue, threatening rain, but never making good that threat, though the thunder muttered, and in the evenings the lightning flickered low on the horizon as though great armies were locked in battle far to the east.

The big game was concentrated on the remaining water, the deeper river pools and the strongest water-holes, so that each day's march was through a wonderland of wild animals.

In one herd Zouga counted thirty-two giraffe, from the old stink-bull almost black with age, his long neck taller than the trees on which he fed, to the pale beige splotched calves on their disproportionately long legs, galloping away in that slow rocking gait with their long tufted tails twisted up over their backs.

Every clearing had its family of rhinoceros, the cows with the distinctively long slender nose horn, running their calves ahead of them, guiding them with a touch of the horn on the flank. There were herds of Cape buffalo, a thousand strong, flowing in a black dense mass across the open glades, steaming with pale dust like the lava from an active volcano.

Then there were elephant. There was not one day they did not cut fresh spoor, veritable roads through the forest, tall trees pushed down or still standing but stripped of their bark so the trunks were naked and weeping with fresh sap, the earth beneath them strewn with chewed twigs and bunches of picked leaves only just beginning to wither, the huge piles of fibrous dung standing like monuments to the passing of the great grey beasts, and the baboon and the plump brown pheasant scratching and foraging enthusiastically in them for the half digested wild nuts and other tidbits.

Zouga could seldom resist him when Jan Cheroot looked up from his examination of the pad marks and said, 'A big bull, this one, walking heavy in the front quarters. Good teeth, I'd stake my sister's virtue on it.'

'A commodity which was staked and lost many years ago,' Zouga observed drily. 'But we will follow, none the less.'

Most evenings they could cut teeth and, having buried them, carry the bleeding heart to where they had left the porters, two men to carry the forty-pound hunk of raw flesh slung on a pole between them, a feast for the whole party. Because of the hunt, progress was slow and not always direct, but steadily Zouga identified and passed the landmarks that his father had described.

Then at last, knowing he was close, Zouga withstood the temptation to hunt, for the first time refusing to follow the fresh spoor of three fine bulls, and disappointing Jan Cheroot most grievously by doing so.

'You should never leave a good elephant, or a warm and willing lady,' he advised dolefully, 'because you never know where or when you are going to meet the next one.'

Jan Cheroot did not yet know the new object of their quest and Zouga's behaviour puzzled him. Zouga often caught him watching him with a quizzical sparkle in his bright little slitty eyes, but he avoided the direct question diplomatically and accepted Zouga's orders to abandon the spoor with only a little further grumbling, and they went on.

It was the porters who first baulked. Zouga never knew how they guessed, perhaps old Karanga had spoken of the Umlimo around the camp fire, or perhaps it was part of their tribal lore, although the gunbearers and most of the porters were from the Zambezi many hundreds of miles to the north. Yet Zouga had learned enough of Africa by now to recognize the strange, almost telepathic knowledge of far events and places. Whatever it was, and however they had acquired forewarning, there were thorns in the porters' feet for the first time in months.

At first Zouga was angry, and would have lived up to his nickname of 'Bakela', the Fist, but then he realized that their reluctance to continue towards the range of bald hills that showed above the horizon was confirmation that he was on a hot scent and close to his goal.

In camp that night, he drew Jan Cheroot aside and, speaking in English, explained what he was seeking and where. He was unprepared for the sickly expression that slowly spread over Jan Cheroot's wizened yellow features.

'Nie wat! Ik lol nie met daai goed nie!' The little Hottentot was driven in his superstitious terror to fall back on the bastard Cape Dutch. 'No what! I don't mess around with that sort of thing,' he repeated in English, and Zouga smiled tauntingly across the camp fire at him.

'Sergeant Cheroot, I have seen you run, with a bare backside, right up to a wounded bull elephant, and wave your hat to turn him when he charged.'

'Elephants,' said Jan Cheroot without returning the smile, 'is one thing. Witches is another thing.' Then he perked up and twinkled like a mischievous gnome.

'Somebody must stay with the porters or they'll steal our traps and run for home.'

Zouga left them camped near a muddy little water-hole, within an hour's march of the northernmost granite kopje. At the water-hole he filled the big enamelled water bottle, and wet its thick covering of felt to keep the contents cool, slung a freshly charged powder sack on one hip and a food bag on the other, and, with the heavy smooth-bore elephant gun over his shoulder set out alone while the shadows were still long on the earth, and the grass wet with the dew.

The hills ahead of him were rounded domes of pearly grey granite, smooth as a bald man's pate and completely free of vegetation. As he trudged towards them across the lightly forested plain, his spirit quailed at the task ahead of him.

With each step the hills seemed to rise higher and steeper, the valleys between them deeper and more sheer, the thorny bush that choked the gorges and ravines more dense. It could take months to search all of this broken wilderness, and he did not have a guide as his father had had. Yet, in the end, it was so easy that he was irritated with his own lack of foresight.

His father had written in the journals 'Even Mzilikazi, that sanguine tyrant, sends gifts for her oracle.'

He struck the well-defined road, leading out of the west, broad enough for two men to walk along it, and aimed directly into the maze of smooth, granite hills. It could only be the road used by the emissaries of the Matabele king.

It led Zouga up the first gentle slope of ground, and then turned abruptly into one of the gorges between peaks. The path narrowed, and jinked between huge round granite boulders, the bush so thick on each side that he had to duck below the thorny branches that interlinked to form a gloomy tunnel overhead.

The valley was so deep that the sunlight did not penetrate to the floor, but the heat was thrown out by the granite as though it had been baked in an open fire, and the sweat soaked Zouga's shirt and slid in cool, tickling drops down his flanks. The bush thinned and the valley narrowed, and then pinched out into a narrow neck between the converging rock walls. It was a natural gateway where a few good spearsmen could have held a regiment. On a ledge high above was a small thatched watch hut, and beside it an idle blue tendril of smoke rising from a watchfire into the still hot air. But if there had been a guard he had deserted his post at Zouga's approach.

Zouga grounded the butt of his elephant gun, and leaned upon it to rest from the climb and at the same time surreptitiously to search the cliffs above him for a hidden enemy, or for the spot from which one could send the familiar boulders bounding and clanging down upon him.

The gorge was silent, hot and deserted. There was not even the chittering of birds or the murmur of insects in the undergrowth. The silence was more oppressive than the heat, and Zouga threw back his head and hallooed up at the deserted watch-hut.

The echoes, boomed grotesquely back and forth across the gorge, and then descended through confused whispers to the same foreboding silence. The last white man to pass this way was the Sword of God, in person, intent on decapitating the oracle, Zouga thought bitterly. He could not expect a hero's welcome.

He shouldered the gun again and went into the natural granite gateway, his instinct telling him that the bold approach was the only one open to him. The narrow passageway was floored with crunching grey sand, full of mica chips that sparkled like diamonds even in the subdued light. The passage curved gently until he could see neither the entrance behind him nor the end of it. He wanted to hurry, for this was like a cage, or a trap, but he controlled his feet and showed neither fear nor indecision in his tread.

Around the curve the passageway fanned open, and from one wall a small freshet rippled down the granite cliff, spilled with a tiny liquid gurgle into a natural basin of rock and then overflowed to run down into the hidden valley beyond. Zouga came out of the natural gateway and paused again to stare about him. It was a pleasant valley, probably a mile long and half as wide. The rivulet watered it, and the grass was cool green.

In the centre of the valley was a huddle of neatly thatched huts, around which scratched a few scrawny fowls. He went down to them. The huts were all deserted, although there was everywhere evidence of very recent occupation, even the porridge in the cooking pot was still hot.

Three of the largest huts were crammed with treasures, leather bags of salt, tools and weapons of iron, ingots of smelted red copper, a pile of small ivory tusks, and Zouga guessed that these were the tributes and gifts sent by petitioners and supplicants to the oracle. Payments made for her intercession with the rain gods, fees for a spell cast upon an enemy, or to soften a coquette's heart.

The fact that these treasures were left unguarded was proof of the Umlimo's power, and her own belief in that power. However, if Fuller Ballantyne's journal was the truth 'the foul and midnight hag' as he referred to her was long ago dead, and her severed skull crunched by the hyenas or bleaching somewhere in the hot African sun.

Zouga stooped out through the low entrance of the last hut, into the sunlight once more. He called again, but again there was no answer. There were people here, many of them, but to make contact with them, and then to learn from them the location of the 'burial place of the kings' was going to be more difficult than he expected.

Leaning on the long gun he turned his attention to the steep side of the valley, and again it was the pathway that caught his eye and led it to the entrance of the cave. For the path continued beyond the village, running down the centre of the valley and climbed the far slope of the valley, then came to an abrupt end against the granite cliff. The mouth of the cave was low and wide, a narrow horizontal gash in the base of the cliff like a toad's mouth and the path led directly into it.

Zouga climbed the gentle slope to the cave entrance. He had left his food bag and water bottle at the village, and, lightly burdened, he strode upwards, tall and lithe, his beard sparkling like gold thread in the sunlight, so that any hidden watcher could not have doubted that this was a chieftain and warrior to treat with respect.

He reached the cave entrance and checked, not from fatigue, for the climb had not taxed him, but merely to take his bearings. The cave entrance was a hundred paces or so wide, and the roof so low that he could reach up and touch the rough rock.

There was a guard wall built to close off the opening, a wall of dressed granite blocks, fitted so closely that it would have been impossible to drive a knife blade between the joints, clearly the work of skilled masons, but done long ago for in places the wall had tumbled, the blocks piled upon each other in disarray. The path led into one of these gaps, and disappeared into the gloom beyond. It was a most unwelcoming entrance. Going in he would have the light at his back, and his eyes would be unaccustomed to the poor light, there would be many places where a man could wait with spear or axe. Zouga felt his first ardour cooling as he peered into that forbidding opening, and he called again in the Matabele language.

'I come in peace!'

He was answered almost immediately, in a childish piping voice speaking the same language, close behind his shoulder, so close that his heart tripped, and he whirled.

'White is the colour of mourning and death,' piped the voice, and Zouga looked about him in confusion. There was no child, no human, no animal even, the valley behind him was deserted, silent. The voice had emanated from the very air.

Zouga felt his mouth drying, and the skin on his forearms and at the base of his skull crawled with the loathsome little insects of fear, and while he stared another voice screeched from the cliff above him.

'White is the colour of war.'

It was the voice of an old woman, a very old woman, quavering and shrill. Zouga's heart jumped again, and then raced as he looked up. The cliff face was bare and smooth. His heart was fluttering against his ribs like a trapped bird, and his breath rasped and sawed in his throat.

'White is the colour of slavery,' sang a young girl's voice, filling the air about his head, having no direction and no substance, sweet and liquid as the burble of running water.

'She spoke in the voices of Belial and Beelzebub, the hideous voices of Azazel and Beliar, all Satan's myriad alter-egos,' his father had written, and Zouga felt the slow leaden spread of superstitious terror weighing down his legs.

Another voice, roaring like a bull, boomed from the mouth of the cave. 'The white eagle has cast down the stone falcons.'

He took a long slow breath, to bring his mutinous body under control, and he cast his mind back deliberately to a childhood memory. Brighton pier on August bank holiday, the small boy clutching his Uncle William's hand and staring up in wonder at the magician on the stage who made a doll come to life and speak in a quaint piping voice, answering the voice from the box too small to contain even a rabbit. The memory steadied him, and he laughed. It was a clear firm laugh, surprising himself even.

'Keep your tricks for the children, Umlimo. I come in peace to speak with you as a man.'

There was no reply, though he thought he caught the silken whisper of bare feet on stone, coming from the darkness beyond the turned stone wall.

'See me, Umlimo! I lay aside my weapons.'

He unslung the powder bag and dropped it at his feet, and then he laid the elephant gun across it and holding his empty hands before him advanced slowly into the cave.

As he reached the step in the wall, there was the crackling spitting snarl of an angry leopard from the shadows just ahead of him. It was a terrible sound, fierce and real, but Zouga had himself in hand now. He did not miss a pace but stooped under the sill through the gap, and straightened on the far side.

He waited for a minute while his eyes adjusted, and he could make out shapes and planes in the gloom. There were no other voices or animal sounds. There was a faint source of light somewhere ahead of him in the depths of the cave, and he could now make out a way amongst the scree and fallen rock that choked the cave, in some places as high as the low roof.

Zouga began to pick his way carefully forward. The light grew stronger, and Zouga realized that it was a single beam of sunlight, shining through a narrow crack in the roof.

Looking up, he stumbled and put out a hand to save himself. It was not rock that he touched but something sticklike that moved beneath his touch. There was a rattle, and a loose dry rush of debris. Zouga caught his balance and glanced down. A disembodied human skull gaped up at him from empty black eye sockets, the cheekbones still covered with a parchment of dried skin.

With a jolting little shock Zouga realized that what he had taken for loose scree and rock was instead piles of human remains, dried and desiccated corpses, lying in mounds and heaps, choking the passages and deepest recesses of the cave, here and there a single body, crouched or sprawled alone, bone shining dully from gaps in its covering of dark dried skin or through the rotting leather garments.

'That reeking charnel house,' Fuller Ballantyne had called it.

Instinctively Zouga wiped the hand that had touched the long-dead skeleton, and then went on towards the light. There was the smell of smoke now, and of human presence, and another sweet mousy odour that was hauntingly familiar but which Zouga could not place at that moment. The floor of the cave sloped downwards under his feet, and he turned a rocky shoulder and looked down into a small natural amphitheatre, with a floor of smooth granite.

In the centre of the floor burned a low fire of some aromatic wood, the smoke spiced the air and rose in a slow spiral towards the crack in the rocky roof, clouding the beam of sunlight with milky blue. There seemed to be other fingers of the cave leading further into the hillside, like the adits of a mine shaft, but Zouga's attention was focused on the figure that sat across the fire from him.

Zouga went slowly down on to the floor of the stone amphitheatre without taking his eyes from the figure.

'That foul and midnight hag,' his father had called the Umlimo, but this was no hag. She was young, in full physical prime, and as she knelt facing him Zouga realized that he had seldom seen such a fine-looking woman, certainly not in India or Africa, and very seldom, if ever, in the northern lands.

She had a long regal neck on which her head balanced like a

black lily on its stem. Her features were Egyptian, with a straight fine nose and huge dark eyes above high moulded cheekbones. Her teeth were small and perfect, her lips chiselled like the flutes of a pink seashell.

She was naked, her body slim, her limbs long and fine, her hands and feet narrow and delicately shaped with tapered fingers and pale pink palms. Her small breasts rode high and were perfectly round, her waist narrow but flaring into tight hard buttocks and hips like the curve of a Venetian vase. Her sex was a wide triangle, deeply cleft, the inner lips bursting out unashamedly, like the wings of a dark exotic butterfly emerging from its woolly chrysalis.

She was watching him with those huge dark eyes, and when he stopped across the fire from her, she made a slow gracious gesture with those delicately long fingers. Obediently Zouga squatted down opposite her and waited.

The woman took up one of the calabash gourds from the array beside her, holding it between the palms of her hands and poured from it into a shallow earthen bowl. It was milk. She set the calabash aside, and Zouga expected her to offer him the bowl, but she did not. She continued to watch him inscrutably.

'I come from the north,' Zouga said at last. 'Men call me Bakela.'

'Your sire slew the one before me,' said the woman. Her voice was compelling, for although the fluted lips barely moved, it was thrown with the power and timbre of the skilled ventriloquist. The sound of it seemed to quiver in the air long after she finished speaking and he knew now with certainty who had spoken in the voice of child and maid, of warrior and wild animal.

'He was a sick man,' Zouga replied, not questioning the source of her knowledge. Not querying how she had known that he was the son of the father.

Her words explained much to Zouga, and it was logical that the Umlimo was a hereditary duty, the office of high priestess being passed on down the years. This magnificent woman was the latest bearer of the title.

'My father was driven mad by the sickness in his blood. He did not know what he did,' Zouga explained.

'It was part of the prophecy.' The Umlimo's statement shimmered against the cave walls, but she did not stir while the silence spun out over many minutes.

'These,' Zouga spoke at last, indicating the dusty, crumbling piles of dead, 'who were they, and how did they die?'

'They are the people of the Rozwi,' said the woman, 'and they died by fire and smoke.'

'Who laid the fire?' Zouga persisted.

'The black bull from the south. The Angoni.'

Zouga was silent again imagining the tribe fleeing here, to their holy place, their refuge, the women carrying the children, running like driven game ahead of the beaters, looking back over their shoulders for a glimpse of the waving tufts on the crowns of the warshields and the plumed headdresses of the Angoni *amadoda*.

He imagined them lying here in the darkness listening to the ring of axes and shouts of the besieging warriors as they cut the timber and piled it in the mouth of the cave, and then the crackle of the flames as they put fire to it and the first choking acrid clouds of smoke boiled into the cave.

He could hear again in his imagination the screams and cries of the choking, dying victims, and the shouts and the laughter of the men beyond the flaming, smoking barricade of timber.

'That too was part of the prophecy,' said the Umlimo and was silent. In the silence there was a soft rustling sound like a leaf blown by the breeze across the tiles at midnight, and Zouga's eyes turned towards the sound.

A dark thing flowed out of the shadows at the back of the cave, like a trickle of spilt blood, black in the gloom but catching the firelight in pinpricks of reflected light. It rustled softly across the stone floor, and Zouga felt his skin crawl and his nostrils flare at the sweetish mousy odour which he had noticed before, but which he recognized now.

It was the smell of snake.

Zouga stared at it, frozen with fascinated horror, for the reptile was as thick as his wrist and the full length of it was lost in the recesses of the cave. The head slid into the circle of orange firelight. The scales glittered with a marble lustre, the lidless eyes fixed Zouga with an unblinking stare and from the slyly grinning lipless mouth the silken black tongue vibrated as it tasted his scent upon the air.

'Sweet Christ!' Zouga whispered hoarsely and dropped his

hand to the hilt of his hunting-knife on his belt, but the Umlimo did not move.

The snake lifted its head from the stone and dipped it over the bowl of milk. It began to drink.

It was a mamba, a black mamba, the most venomous of all the reptiles, the death it could inflict was swift but agonizing beyond all nightmares of pain. Zouga had not believed that a mamba could grow to such dimensions, for as he watched it drink half its length was still lost in the shadows.

After a minute the monstrous reptile lifted its head from the bowl and turned towards the Umlimo, it began to slide forward, the muscles under the glittering scales convulsing in little waves that came running down its length towards the broad spatulate head.

It touched the woman's bare knee with the flickering black tongue, seeming to use the tongue like a blind man uses his cane to grope its way along her thigh, licking briefly at the lips of her bulging sex, and then lifting itself up over her belly, over her breasts, still licking at her smoothly oiled skin, it rose up around her neck and then slid down over the other shoulder until it came to rest at last suspended around her neck, the head reaching out the length of a man's arm ahead of her at the level of her breasts; swaying slightly, it fixed Zouga once more with that cold ophidian stare.

Zouga licked his lips, and relaxed his grip on the hilt of the knife.

'I have come to seek wisdom,' he said hoarsely.

'I know what you seek,' replied the Umlimo. 'But you will find more than you seek.'

'Who will lead me?'

'Follow the little seeker of sweetness in the treetops.'

'I do not understand.' Zouga frowned, still watching the huge snake, and the Umlimo did not reply. Her silence was clearly an invitation to ponder the reply, and Zouga did so in silence, but found no explanation. He memorized the words, and would have asked another question but there was a silken rush out of the darkness near him, and he started half to his feet as a second snake slid swiftly past him.

It was another mamba, but a smaller snake, not much thicker than his thumb, and as long as twice the stretch of his arms. Half its length was raised arrow-straight in the air, and it sailed on its tail up to the kneeling woman with her grotesque living necklace.

The woman did not move, and the smaller snake stood before her, swaying gently from side to side, lowering itself gradually until it touched tongue to darting black tongue with the thick reptile around her neck.

Then it slid forward and began to roll itself around the body of the other snake, throwing turn after turn like a sailor lashing a sheet about a mast, and each time it rolled, it showed its soft white pulsating underbelly with the narrow scales reaching from flank to flank.

Neither the woman nor the bigger snake moved, nor removed their steadfast gaze from Zouga's fascinated pale face. The thinner lighter-coloured body of the second snake began a slow rhythmical and sensual movement, expanding and contracting about the thicker and darker body of the other and Zouga realized that they were a mating pair.

Two-thirds of the way down the underbelly of the male were the elongated scales that guarded the genital sac. As the male's excitement mounted so the scales gaped apart and the penis began to extrude. It was the colour and shape of the bloom of a night-flowering cactus, a pale lilac belled flower that gleamed like wet satin.

Insistently the male caressed the thick, dark body, and gradually his ardour was rewarded. The female rolled a portion of her own length, the white belly throbbing softly in acquiescence, exposing the scaled genital purse.

With a long shuddering movement the male slid his length down hers, white belly pressed to belly, and the swollen lilac flower prised open the female sexual purse, distorting the lips. The female mamba opened her mouth wide, and her throat was a lovely buttercup yellow. In her top jaw the small bony needles of her fangs were erect, each tipped with a pearly drop of venom, and she emitted a low sibilant hiss of ecstasy or pain as the male locked his penis deeply into her.

Zouga found he was sweating. A droplet slid down from his temple into his beard. The bizarre courtship and copulation had taken only minutes during which neither he nor the Umlimo had moved, but now she spoke.

'The white eagle has stooped on the stone falcons, and cast

them to earth.' She paused. 'Now the eagle shall lift them up again and they will fly afar.'

Zouga leaned forward, listening intently,

'There shall be no peace in the kingdoms of the Mambos or the Monomatapa until they return. For the white eagle will war with the black bull until the stone falcons return to roost.'

While she spoke, the slow convulsing copulation of those inter-locked bodies continued, giving to her words an obscene and evil weight.

'Generation will war with generation, the eaglet will strive against the bull calf – white against black, and black against black, until the falcons return. Until the falcons return.'

The Umlimo raised her narrow pink-palmed hands, and lifted the garland of intertwined serpents from off her own neck. She laid them gently on the stone floor of the cave and with a single flowing movement, she stood erect, and the firelight glinted upon her oiled satin body.

'When the falcons return,' she spread her arms, and the round breasts changed shape at the movement, 'when the falcons return, then once again the Mambos of Rozwi and the Monomatapa of Karanga will hold sway in the land.' She lowered her arms and her breasts sagged weightily. 'That is the prophecy. That is the whole prophecy,' she said, and turned away from the fire and, with a gliding walk, moved across the irregular stone floor, her back straight and her naked buttocks swaying in stately rhythm.

She disappeared into the dark shadows that shrouded one of the fingers of the cave beyond the amphitheatre.

'Wait!' Zouga called after her, scrambling to his feet and starting after her.

The huge female mamba hissed sharply, like the steam of a boiling kettle, and rose up as high as Zouga's head. The butter yellow mouth gaped again, and a crest of dark glittering scales came angrily erect down the length of her neck.

Zouga froze, and the snake hissed again and flared a little higher, the raised body arching gently into a taut 'S' shape. Zouga backed off, one pace and then another. The crest of scales subsided a little. He took another step backwards and the tense bow of the serpentine body relaxed, the head lowered a few inches. He moved steadily backwards towards the entrance of the cave, and before the amphitheatre was obscured by the shoulder of rock he saw the huge snake coiled in a knee-high pile of glinting scales still locked in sexual congress with her deadly consort.

The prophecy of the Umlimo, cryptic and unrevealed, stayed with Zouga during the long march back to where Jan Cheroot waited with his porters.

That night, by the firelight, Zouga copied it word for word into his journal, and afterwards the sweet smell of snakes haunted his nightmares – and lingered in his nostrils for long days after.

Now the wind turned fickle, sometimes completely still in the enervating hush and heat of noon, at other times dancing in the tall swaying vortex of the 'dust devils' across the plains, lifting leaves and dried blades of grass hundreds of feet in the yellow columns of dust, then again it gushed in turn from every point of the compass, one minute firm out of the north and the next as firmly from out of the south.

It was impossible to come up with elephant while the wind played so loosely. Often when the spoor was hot and true, and they had already laid aside their heavy traps and stripped down to light running order, Zouga would feel the cool touch of the breeze upon the back of his sweating neck and almost immediately afterwards hear the alarm squeal of an elephant ahead of them in the forest, and after that first alert, it was impossible to close with the herd, for they went into that long sloping gait that they could keep up for mile upon mile, hour upon hour, day upon night, that would kill a man who tried to match it for more than a few miles.

Thus they killed no elephant in the days following Zouga's meeting with the Umlimo, and once, when they had a good spoor which would have led them back into the north, away from the direction in which Zouga was convinced lay his quest, it was Zouga himself who called off the hunt. Jan Cheroot muttered bitterly for the rest of that day and the next while they made those seemingly aimless casts, eastward and then westward again, through the unmarked and uncharted wilderness.

Each day now the heat became fiercer, for the suicide month that ushers in the rains was upon them. Not even Zouga could march during the hours before and after noon. They would find the best shade and throw themselves down under it, sweating out the worst of the heat, trying to sleep when the buffalo flies would let them, but it was an effort to speak, an effort to wipe away the sweat that welled up on their bodies, and dried in white crystals on their skin and clothing. The salt rotted the fabric of Zouga's shirt and breeches so they tore like paper at the first touch of thorn or rock, and Zouga was gradually reduced to a beggar's rags, patched and stitched until little of the original material remained.

His boots had been resoled more than once with the raw-hide peeled from the inner surface of an elephant's ear, and his belt and webbing, the sling of his elephant gun renewed with uncured buffalo hide.

He made a strange gaunt figure, for hard hunting had burned all the fat and loose flesh from his body and limbs. His height was enhanced by his leanness and the breadth of his bony shoulders tapering sharply to his waist. The sun had burned his skin dark, yet bleached his hair and beard to white gold. His pale hair hung to his shoulders, and he tied it at the back of his neck with a leather thong. He kept his beard and whiskers trimmed neatly, using scissors to cut and the heated blade of his hunting knife to singe them.

The sense of well-being from his superb physical condition, together with the vaunting anticipation of a successful outcome to his search drove him onwards so that the days seemed too short for him and yet when the night fell he lay down on the hard earth and slept the deep dreamless refreshing sleep of a child, to awake again long before the dawn's first glimmering, impatient for what the new day would bring forth.

However, the time was passing. After each hunt, the powder bags were lighter, and though he dug the spent musket balls from the carcasses of his victims and recast them, there was always wastage.

The precious little store of quinine dwindled as swiftly, and the rains were coming. No white man could survive the rains without ammunition and quinine. Soon he would have to abandon the search for the ruined city with its idols decked in gold. He would have to march to beat the rains, south and west, five hundred miles or more, if his observations were still accurate, to cut his grandfather's road and follow it down to the mission station at Kuruman, which was the nearest outpost of European civilization.

The later he left it, the harder would he the march when he made it. Hard and fast, stopping for nothing, neither elephant nor gold, until he was out into the drier, safer land to the south.

The thought of leaving depressed him, for he knew with a certain deep gut feeling that there was something here, very close to where he now lay, and it irked him terribly that the oncoming rains would frustrate his search. But then he consoled himself that there would be another season, and he knew with the same deep gut certainty that he would return. There was something about this land – an insistent, irritating sound interrupted his thoughts. He pushed the cap up from his eyes and looked into the dense branches of the marula tree under which he lay. The harsh cries were repeated, and the drab little bird that uttered them hopped agitatedly from branch to branch, flirting its wings and tail with a sharp whirring. The bird was the size of a starling, its back dull brown and its chest and belly a muddy yellow.

Zouga rolled his head and saw that Jan Cheroot was awake also.

'Well?' he asked.

'I haven't tasted honey since we left Mount Hampden,' Jan Cheroot answered. 'But it's hot, and perhaps the bird is a liar, perhaps he will lead us to a snake or a lion.'

'He only leads you to a snake if you cheat him of his share of the comb,' Zouga told him.

'So they say,' Jan Cheroot nodded and then they were silent, considering the effort involved in following the honey guide, and weighing it against the possible rewards. The bird will very often lead a badger or a human being to a wild hive, and wait for its share of the wax and honey and bee grubs. The legend is that if his payment is not made, then next time he will lead the man who cheated him to a venomous snake or a man-eating lion.

Jan Cheroot's sweet tooth got the better of him. He sat up and the bird's cries were immediately shriller and more excited. It flashed away across the clearing to the next tree, flitting wings and tail noisily, calling them impatiently, and when they did not follow it darted back to the branches above them and continued its display.

'All right then, old fellow,' Zouga agreed resignedly, and stood up. Jan Cheroot took an axe from Matthew and the clay fire pot in its plaited bark carrying net.

'Make camp here,' Jan Cheroot told the bearers. 'We will bring you honey to eat tonight.'

Salt and honey and meat, the three greatest delicacies of the African bush. Zouga felt a twinge of guilt at wasting so much of the time that remained to him on this frivolous side-journey, but his men had worked hard and travelled fast and honey would revive their flagging spirits.

The little brown and yellow bird danced ahead of them, burring and rattling with a sound like a shaken box of Swan Vestas, darting from tree to bush, turning immediately it settled to make sure they were following.

For almost an hour it led them along a dry river course, and then it turned and crossed a rocky ridge of ground. At the saddle, they looked down into a heavily wooded valley bounded by the familiar rocky kopjes and hillocks.

'The bird is teasing us,' Jan Cheroot grumbled. 'How much further will he make us dance?'

Zouga shifted his elephant gun to the other shoulder. 'I think you are right,' he agreed, the valley ahead of him was forbidding, the floor choked with tall stands of the razor-edged elephant grass, higher than a man's head. It would be even hotter down there, and the dried seeds of the grass had arrowheads to them that could work themselves into the skin and cause festering little wounds.

'It comes to me that I am not so fond of honey as I thought I was,' Jan Cheroot cocked his head at Zouga.

'We will turn back,' he agreed. 'Let the bird find another dupe. We, will look for a fat kudu cow on the way back, meat instead of honey.'

They started back down the ridge and instantly the bird flashed back, and renewed its entreaties above their heads.

'Go and find your friend the *rattel* (honeybadger)!' Jan Cheroot shouted at it, and the bird's contortions became frantic. It dropped lower and lower, until it was in the branches barely an arm's length above their heads, and its cries were irritating and distracting.

'Voetsak!' Jan Cheroot yelled at it. The bird's cries would alert all wild game for miles about to the presence of man, and thwart

any chance of killing an animal for the night's meal. '*Voetsak*!' He stooped and picked up a stone to shy at the bird. 'Go away and leave us, little sugar mouth.'

The name stopped Zouga in his tracks. Jan Cheroot had used the bastard Dutch, '*klein Suiker bekkie*', and now he drew back his right arm to hurl the stone.

Zouga caught his wrist. 'Little sugar mouth,' he repeated, and the Umlimo's voice rang in his ears, that strange shimmering tone that he had memorized, 'the seeker of sweetness in the treetops.'

'Wait,' he told Jan Cheroot, 'Do not throw.'

It was ridiculous, of course it was. He would not make himself ludicrous by repeating the Umlimo's words to Jan Cheroot. He hesitated a moment. 'We have come so far, already,' he told the Hottentot reasonably, 'and the bird is so excited that the hive cannot be far.'

'It could be another two hours,' Jan Cheroot growled, but lowered his throwing arm. 'That makes six hours back to camp.'

'You don't want to grow fat and idle,' Zouga said. Jan Cheroot was lean as a whippet that had been coursing rabbit all season, and he had walked and run a hundred miles in the last two days. He looked pained at the accusation, but Zouga went on remorselessly, shaking his head in mock sympathy. 'But when a man grows older, he cannot march as far or as fast, and he is slower with the women too.'

Jan Cheroot dropped the stone, and went back up the ridge at a furious pace with the bird flitting and screeching ecstatically ahead of him.

Zouga followed him, smiling at the little man and at his own folly in placing any store on the words of that naked witch. Still the honey would be welcome, he consoled himself.

An hour later, Zouga was convinced that Jan Cheroot had been correct. The bird was a liar, and they were wasting what remained of the day, but there would be no turning Jan Cheroot now, he had been deeply insulted by Zouga's gibes.

They had crossed the valley, blundering through the stands of elephant grass, for the bird did not pick one of the game trails to follow. It moved on a direct line, and as they followed, the grass seeds showered upon them, working their way down the backs of their shirts and the sweat of their bodies activated them, as the first rains should have done, so that they began to worm like living things, trying to pierce the skin.

The view ahead was cut off by the tall grass, and they reached the far side of the valley with little prior warning. Suddenly there was a smooth rock cliff looming over them, almost obscured by the tall leafy trees of the forest, and by its own covering of lianas and dense climbing plants. It was not a very high prominence, perhaps forty feet, but it was sheer. They stopped below it and peered upwards.

The wild beehive was almost at the top of the cliff. The honey guide fluttered triumphantly above it, twisting its head to look down at them with a single bright beadlike eye.

The rock below the opening to the hive was stained with a dark dribble of old melted wax and the detritus of the hive, but it was almost entirely masked by a lovely creeping plant. The stem of the plant climbed the cliff, branching and twisting and doubling on itself, its pale leaves a cool green, but its flowers a lovely shade of cornflower blue.

The bees leaving and returning to the hive caught the sunlight like golden dust-motes, but their trajectory was swift and straight through the hot still air.

'Well, Sergeant, there is your hive,' Zouga said. 'The bird did not lie.' He felt a deep sense of disappointment. Although he had told himself to place no store on the Umlimo's words, yet there had been a sneaking anticipation, the forlorn hope persisting against common sense, and now that sense had prevailed, there was this regret.

Zouga leaned his gun against the bole of a tree, shed his traps, and threw himself down to rest and watch Jan Cheroot making his preparation to rob the hive. Jan Cheroot cut a square of bark from a mukusi tree, and rolled it into a smoking tube. He filled it with wood pulp scraped from a dead tree trunk.

Then he swung the clay fire pot on its carrying sling of bark rope, fanning it until the smouldering moss and wood chips that it contained burst into flame. He transferred fire to the smoking tube, and when it had fairly taken he hooked his axe over one shoulder and began climbing the interwoven branches of the flowering creeper up the sheer cliff.

The first of the defender bees buzzed fiercely about his head when he was a few feet from the opening to the hive, and pausing, Jan Cheroot lifted the bark tube to his mouth and blew a gentle stream of blue smoke towards his attacker. The smoke drove the insect away, and he resumed the climb.

Lying under the mukusi tree, idly swatting at the buffalo flies, picking at the grass under his shirt, and harbouring his disappointment, Zouga watched the Hottentot work.

Jan Cheroot reached the hive, and blew another stream of smoke over the hole in the cliff, stupefying the bees which had now formed a swirling defensive cloud about him. One of them darted in, despite the smoke, and stung him in the soft of the neck. Jan Cheroot swore bitterly, but he did not make the mistake of slapping at the attacker, or of trying to scratch away the barbed sting lodged in his flesh. He worked on calmly, unhurriedly, with the smoke tube.

Minutes later, the hive was sufficiently smoke-drugged to allow him to begin cutting away the screen of flowering branches that hid the entrance, and he balanced on a fork of the creeper, using both hands to swing the axe, perched like a little yellow monkey forty feet above where Zouga lay.

'What the thunder . . . 'He stopped after a dozen axe blows, and stared at the cliff face that he had exposed. 'Master, there is devil's work here.'

The tone of his voice alerted Zouga, and he scrambled to his feet.

'What is it?'

Jan Cheroot's body obscured the object of his amazement, and impatiently Zouga crossed to the foot of the cliff and climbed hand over hand up the serpentine stem of the creeper.

He reached Jan Cheroot's side and clung to a handhold.

'Look!' Jan Cheroot exhorted him. 'Look at that!' He pointed at the stone face that he had exposed with the axe.

It took Zouga a few seconds to realize that the entrance to the hive was through a geometrically perfect, sculptured aperture, one of a series which pierced the cliff face in a broad horizontal band, that seemed to extend unbroken in both directions along the cliff face. The decorated band was in chiselled stone blocks, arranged in a chevron pattern, a lattice work that was without question the work of a skilled stonemason.

The realization jolted Zouga so that he almost missed his hand-hold, and immediately afterwards he saw something else that up to that moment had been hidden by the dense covering of climbing plants and the thick coating of old outpouring wax from the beehive.

The entire cliff face was formed of perfect blocks of dressed stone, small blocks, so neatly fitted that they had appeared on casual inspection to be a solid sheet of rock. Zouga and Jan Cheroot were suspended near the top of the massive stone wall, forty feet high, so thick and long that it had seemed to be a granite hillock.

It was a monumental work of stonemasonry, to compare with the outer wall of Solomon's temple, a vast fortification which could only be the periphery of a city, a city forgotten and overgrown with trees and creepers, undisturbed over the ages.

'Nie wat!' whispered Jan Cheroot. 'This is a devil's place – this is the place of Satan himself. Let us go, master,' he pleaded. 'Let us go far away, and very fast.'

The circuit of the walls took Zouga almost an hour, for the growth was thicker along the northern curve of the stone rampart. The wall seemed to be laid out in an almost perfect circle, and without openings. At two or three likely points, Zouga hacked away the growth and searched the foot of the wall, looking for a postern or a gateway. He found none.

The decorative chevron pattern did not seem to extend around the entire circumference, but covered the eastern quadrant. Zouga wondered at the significance of that. The immediate explanation seemed to be that the decoration would face the rising sun. It seemed likely that the peoples who had built this massive edifice had been sun-worshippers.

Jan Cheroot trailed him reluctantly, prophesying the wrath of the devils and hobgoblins who guarded this evil place, while houga backed and chopped his way around the walls, completely oblivious of his advice.

'There must be a gateway,' he grumbled. 'How did they get in and out?'

'Devils got wings,' Jan Cheroot pointed out broodingly. 'They fly. Me, I wish I had wings also, to fly the hell away from here.'

They came again to the point in the wall where they had discovered the beehive, and by then it was almost dark, the sun had disappeared below the treetops.

'We'll search for the gate in the morning,' Zouga decided.

'We are not going to sleep here?' Jan Cheroot demanded, horrified.

Zouga ignored the protest. 'Honey for supper,' he suggested mildly, and for once he did not sleep that deep hunter's sleep, but lay under his single blanket, his imagination filled with golden idols and treasure houses built out of massive worked stone blocks.

Zouga resumed the search again when it was light enough to see the top of the wall silhouetted against the misty pearl sky of dawn. The previous day he had been blinded by his own eagerness and careless in his haste. He had missed the area, only a few yards from where they were camped, where the creepers covering the wall had once been hacked away and then had regrown, even more thickly than before. Now, however, a lopped branch beckoned him like a finger, the clean cut unmistakably made by an axe.

'Jan Cheroot,' Zouga called him from the cooking fire. 'Clean out this rubbish.' Zouga showed him the dense secondary growth, and Jan Cheroot sauntered away to fetch his axe.

While he waited for him to return, Zouga decided that only one person could possibly be responsible for these old overgrown and healed cut marks on the stems of the vine. Once again Fuller Ballantyne had been his guide, yet this time he did not resent it so fiercely; the experience of treading squarely in his father's footsteps was no longer new, and he had his excitement and anticipation to lessen the sting of it.

'Hurry,' he called to Jan Cheroot.

'It's been here a thousand years. It's not going to fall down now,' Jan Cheroot answered saucily, and spat on his palms before hefting the axe.

The little Hottentot was a great deal happier this morning. He had survived a night under the wall, without being assailed by even a single hobgoblin, and Zouga had passed the unsleeping hours in describing to him the treasures that might lie beyond that wall. Jan Cheroot's temporarily paralysed avarice had revived sufficiently to imagine himself with his pants filled with gold coin seated in his favourite tavern on the Cape Town dockside with a dozen butter yellow Hottentot beauties crowding close to him to hear the story, while the bartender prised the wax seal off another bottle of Cape Smoke. Now his enthusiasm almost matched that of Zouga himself.

He worked swiftly and when Zouga stooped and peered into the passage that he had cut through the dense secondary growth that had sprung up behind Fuller Ballantyne's axe, he saw the outline of the curved portals of the gateway, and the chiselled granite steps that led up to the narrow opening.

The steps had been worn into a smooth dish shape by the passage of thousands of feet over the centuries, but the gateway had been deliberately blocked with stone and rubble, not the neat stonework of the main wall, but a careless and hurried attempt to seal the entrance, probably in the face of an advancing enemy, Zouga thought.

Somebody, probably Fuller Ballantyne, had pulled down this barrier sufficiently to enter. Zouga followed his tracks, the loose stone rolling under foot, he squeezed his way through the gateway, and found that it turned abruptly to the left, into a narrow vegetation-choked passage, between high walls open to the sky.

His disappointment was intense. He had hoped that once he forced the gateway, all the city and its wonders and treasures would lie before him. Instead there were many hours of hard sweating labour facing him. It had been years, four years at least, since Fuller Ballantyne had entered through this gate and passageway, and it was as though he had never been.

Where the stonework had collapsed, Zouga clambered over it gingerly, the thought and dread of snakes was very much with him since the cave of the Umlimo. The long narrow passage, obviously constructed as a defensive measure against intruders, followed the curve of the main wall until abruptly it opened into a clear space, again choked with dense green thorny growth, and dominated by a tall cylindrical tower of lichen-covered granite blocks. The tower was immense, seeming in Zouga's excitement to reach to the very clouds.

Zouga started across the intervening courtyard, hacking impatiently at the bush and creepers, and halfway across he saw that there was a second tower, an identical twin to the first that had until that moment obscured it. Now his heart was pounding fiercely against his ribs, not from the exertion of swinging the axe – but with an intuitive belief that the towers were the centre of this strange ancient city, and that they held the key to the mystery.

He stumbled in his haste, and went down on his knees, tearing another long rent in his breeches and abrading a strip of skin from his shin, so he swore in his impatience and his pain. He had lost the axe but when he groped for it in the tangled roots and interwoven branches, he found it almost immediately, and at the same time, uncovered the stone that had tripped him.

It was not the granite of which the walls and tower had been constructed. That fact caught his attention, and still on his knees he used the axe to clear the bush around the stone. He felt his nerves thrill as he realized that it was a work of sculpture.

Jan Cheroot had come up behind him, and now he knelt also and tore at the plants with his bare hands – then the two of them rocked back on their heels, and still squatting examined the statue that they had uncovered. It was not large, probably weighed less than a hundredweight. It was carved in satiny, greenish soapstone, sitting on that familiar ornamental plinth, the simple pattern of triangles, like a row of shark's teeth.

The head was smashed off the statue, seemingly by a blow from a sledge hammer, but more likely from a rock used as a hammer. The body of the statue was still intact, the body of the raptor, with the folded pointed wings of a bird of prey, crouching on the point of flight.

Zouga slipped his hand into the opening of his shirt and drew out the little ivory charm on its leather thong, that he had taken from the body of the Mashona chieftain he had killed at the pass of the elephant road.

He let it nestle in the palm of his hand, comparing it with the statue. Beside him Jan Cheroot murmured, 'It is the same bird!'

'Yes,' Zouga agreed softly. 'But what does it mean?' He dropped the ivory charm back inside his shirt.

'It is from long ago.' Jan Cheroot shrugged. 'We will never know.' And dismissing it thus, he would have risen to his feet again, but something else caught his beady bright eye and he darted forward, his hand pecking at the loose earth beside the statue like a greedy hen, and held it up between thumb and forefinger to catch the slanted morning light.

It was a perfectly round bead of metal, pierced for the string of a necklace, a tiny bead only slightly bigger than the head of a wax Vesta, and it was irregular in shape, as though beaten out under the hammer of a primitive smithy, but the colour was red-yellow, and its surface was undulled by either tarnish or corrosion; there is only one metal that has that peculiar lustre and sheen.

Zouga held out his hand for it almost reverently, and it had the weight and the warmth of a living thing.

'Gold!' said Zouga, and beside him Jan Cheroot giggled ecstatically, like a young bride at her first kiss.

'Gold,' he agreed. 'Good yellow gold.'

Zouga was always aware of the very limited time left to him, and every hour or so as they worked he would lift his head to the sky with the sweat streaming down his face and neck, and greasing the flat hard muscles of his naked upper body, and always the clouds were taller and blacker, the heat more punishing, and the wind sullen as a captive tribe on the point of rebellion.

In the night he would start awake, breaking up through the drugged surface of exhausted sleep, to lie and listen to the thunder growling below the horizon like a man-killing monster.

Each dawn he shook his men from their blankets and drove them in a suppressed frenzy of impatience to their labour, and when Matthew, the gunbearer, refused to rise again after the short rest which Zouga allowed them in the hottest hour of the day, Zouga dragged him to his feet and hit him once, a short, perfectly timed chopping blow that sent him spinning backwards full length into his own excavation. Matthew crawled out again with blood dribbling from his chin, and picked up the crude sieve of plaited split bamboos with which he was sifting the earth from the digging, and began again working over the piles of loose earth and rubble.

Zouga drove himself harder than he drove his small band of temple plunderers. He worked shoulder to shoulder with them as they cut out all the undergrowth from the courtyard below the twin stone towers, exposing the broken cobbles, and piles of loose rubble amongst which lay the fallen statues.

He found six more of the bird carvings virtually undamaged, except for minor chips and the attrition of the ages, but there were the fragments of others that had been broken with a savagery which could only have been deliberate, so that he was uncertain of the original number of statues. Zouga spent little time puzzling over them. The loose earth and rubble on which they lay was rich ground for his band to pick over, though they were handicapped by the lack of tools. Zouga would have paid a hundred guineas for a set of good picks and spades and buckets. However, they had to make do with sharpened wooden stakes, the tips hardened in the fire, to dig out the loose stuff, and Jan Cheroot wove baskets of split bamboo, like the flat baskets used by the African women to winnow the stamped corn meal, and with these they sieved the fine earth after picking over it by hand.

It was tedious, back-breaking work, and the heat was murderous, but the harvest was rich. The gold was in small pieces, mostly in the pierced round beads, from which the string had long ago rotted away, but there were flakes and flecks of thinly beaten foil, which might once have been used to decorate a votive wooden carving, there were coils of fine gold wire, and more rarely small ingots of the metal the size and thickness of a child's finger.

Once the green stone birds must have stood in a circle, facing inwards like the granite columns of Stonehenge, and the gold had probably formed some part of the offerings and sacrifices made to them. Whoever had thrown down the statues had scattered and trampled the sacrifice, and time had corroded all except that lovely yellow incorruptible metal.

Within ten days of first hacking away the undergrowth that choked the inner courtyard, the temple yard, as Zouga called it, they had gleaned over fifty pounds weight of native gold, and the interior of the stone courtyard had been gutted, the earth rutted and harrowed as though a troop of wild bush pig had rooted it out.

Then Zouga turned his full attention to the twin towers. He measured them around the base, over a hundred paces, and inspected each joint in the masonry for a secret opening. There was none, so he built a rickety ladder of raw timber and bark rope and risking neck and limb reached the top of the tallest tower. From this vantage point he could look down into the roofless passageways and courtyards of the city. It was a maze, all of it choked with growth – but there was no other part as promising as the temple courtyard of the bird statues.

He turned his attention back to the tower on which he stood. There was again no sign of a secret opening, although he searched diligently for one. It puzzled him that the ancient architect would have built such a solid structure with no apparent use or motive, and the possibility occurred to him that it might be a sealed treasure house, built around an inner chamber.

The work of trying to penetrate the massive stonework, daunted even Zouga, and Jan Cheroot declared the attempt to be madness. But Zouga had exhausted the digging below the tower, and this seemed to be the only fruitful area left to him.

Complaining bitterly, a small team led by Matthew climbed the rickety ladder, and under Zouga's supervision began prising loose the small blocks from the summit of the tower. However, such was the skill and dedication of the original masons that progress in the demolition was painfully slow, and there was a long pause between each crash of one loose block into the courtyard below and the next. It needed three days' unremitting toil to break a jagged aperture through the first layer of dressed blocks and to discover that the interior of the tower consisted merely of a fill of the same grey granite.

Standing beside him on the summit of the tower, Jan Cheroot voiced Zouga's own disappointment.

'We are wasting our time. It's stone and more stone.' He spat over the side of the tower and watched the speck of phlegm float down into the ransacked courtyard. 'What we should look for is the place the gold came from.'

Zouga had been so obsessed by his search and plunder of the ruined and deserted city that he had paid no thought to the mines which must lie somewhere beyond the walls. Now he nodded his head thoughtfully.

'No wonder your mother loved you,' he said. 'Not only are you beautiful, but you are clever too.'

'Ja,' Jan Cheroot nodded smugly. 'Everybody tells me that.'

At that moment a fat weighty drop of rain struck Zouga's forehead, and ran down into his left eyeball so that his vision blurred. The drop was warm as blood, warm as the blood of a man racked by malarial fever.

Beyond the high walls there were other ruins, none of such

proportions or importance as the inner city, however, and all of them so scattered, so overgrown and thrown down as to make detailed exploration of them out of the question in the time still available to Zouga.

The kopjes around the city had been fortified, but were deserted, the caves empty as the eye-sockets of a long dead skull, smelling of the leopards and rock rabbits who were the latest tenants, but Zouga concentrated his search on the ancient mine workings which he had convinced himself had formed the backbone of this vanished civilization. He imagined deep shafts driven into a hillside, and dumps of loose rock like the ancient Cornish tin mines, and he scoured the densely wooded country for miles in each direction, eagerly checking each irregularity of ground, each eminence that could possibly be an abandoned mine dump.

He left Jan Cheroot to oversee the scratching and sweeping up of the last tiny scraps of gold in the temple yard, and all the men profited by the new relaxed supervision. They shared views with Jan Cheroot on the role of menial work in the life of a warrior and hunter.

The first spattering of rain had been only a warning of the fury to come, and it had barely wet Zouga's shirt through to the skin before passing, but it was a warning that Zouga realized he was ignoring at his own peril. Yet still the hope of the ancient mine workings with their fat golden seams of the precious metal tantalized him, and he spun out the days until even Jan Cheroot began to worry.

'If the rivers spate, we will be trapped here,' he brooded beside the camp fire. 'Besides we have taken all the gold. Let us now live to spend it.'

'One more day,' Zouga promised him as he settled into his single blanket, and composed himself to sleep. 'There is a valley just beyond the southern ridge, it will take me only another day to search it – the day after tomorrow—' he promised sleepily.

Zouga smelled the snake first, the sweet sickening stench of it filled his nostrils, so he drew each breath with difficulty, yet trying not to gasp or choke lest he called the snake's attention. He could not move, he was pinned under an immense dark weight which threatened to crush his ribs and the smell of snake suffocated him.

He could barely turn his head towards the place from which he knew the snake would come, and it came flowing sinuously, coil upon thick undulating coil. Its head was lifted, its eyes were unblinking and glassily fixed in the cold and deadly reptilian stare, the ribbon of its tongue flickered in a soft black blur through the icy smile of its thin curved lips. Its scales scratched softly across the earth, and they glittered with a soft metallic sheen, the colour of the polished gold foil that Zouga had gleaned from the temple courtyard.

Zouga could not move nor cry out, his tongue had swollen with terror to fill his mouth and choke him, but the snake slid past him, close enough to touch if he had had command of his arms to reach out. It slid on into the circle of soft wavering light, and the shadows drew back so the birds emerged from the darkness, each on its elevated perch.

Their eyes were golden and fierce, the cruel yellow curve of their beaks echoed by the proud pout of their russet-flecked breasts and the long pinions folded across their backs like crossed blades.

Though Zouga knew they were hunting falcons with belled tresses on their legs, yet they were the size of golden eagles. They were decked with garlands of flowers, crimson blossoms of King Chaka fire, and the snowy virginal white of arum lilies. They wore necklaces and chains of brightest gold about their arrogant necks, and as the serpent slid into the midst of the circle they stirred upon their perches.

Then as the serpent raised its glittering head with the crest of scales erect upon the back of its neck, the falcons burst into thunderous flight and the darkness was filled with the roar of their wings and the plaintive lament of their wild hunting cries.

Zouga lifted his hands to shield his face, and great wings beat all about him, as the flock of falcons took flight and the presence of the snake was no longer of significance – what was important was the departure of the birds. Zouga felt a tremendous sense of doom, of personal loss, and he opened his mouth, able to utter again. He shouted at the birds to call them back to roost.

He shouted into the darkness, after the soaring, buffeting thunder of the birds' wings and his own shouts and the cries of his servants woke him from the coils of the nightmare.

He woke to find the night was thunderous with the wind of the storm that swept down upon the camp. The trees tossed and thrashed their branches overhead, showering them with leaves and small twigs. and the rush of air was glacially cold. It stripped the thatch from their crudely built huts and it scattered ash and live coals from the fire. The coals, fanned into new life, were the only source of light, for overhead, the stars were obscured by the thick rolling banks of cloud that pressed close upon the earth.

Shouting to each other above the wind, they scrambled to collect their scattered equipment.

'Make sure the powder bags are kept dry,' Zouga bellowed, naked except for his tattered breeches, and barefooted as he groped for his boots. 'Sergeant Cheroot, where are you?'

The Hottentot's reply was lost in the cannon's roar of thunder that drove in their eardrums, and the flash of lightning that followed immediately seared their eyeballs, and imprinted on Zouga's vision the unforgettable picture of Jan Cheroot dancing stark naked on one foot, a red hot coal from the scattered fire stuck to the sole of the other, his wild curses lost in the drawn-out roll of the thunder and his face contorted like that of a gargoyle on the parapet of Notre Dame cathedral. Then the darkness fell on them again, like an avalanche, and out of it came the rain.

It came in cutting horizontal sheets like the blade of a harvester's scythe, so thick that it filled the air with water so they coughed and gasped like drowning men, it came with such hissing force that it stung their naked skins as though coarse salt had been fired at them from a shotgun barrel, and the cold chilled them to the bone, so that they crawled into a forlorn huddle, crowding together for comfort and warmth with the sodden fur blankets pulled over their heads, and stinking like a pack of wet dogs.

The cold gloomy dawn found them still huddled from the silver streams of falling rain, under the swollen bruised sky that pressed down upon them like the belly of a pregnant sow. Scattered and sodden equipment floated or was submerged in the ankle-deep flood of water that poured through the wind-shattered camp. The lean-to shelters had been wrecked, the camp fire was a muddy black puddle of ash, there was no prospect of rebuilding it, and with that went any chance of hot food or comfort for their stiff cold bodies.

Zouga had wrapped the powder bags in strips of oilskin, and he and Jan Cheroot had held them in their laps, like ailing infants, during the night. However, it was impossible to open the bags and check the contents for damp, for the rain still teemed down out of the low grey sky in long thin silver lances.

Slipping and sloshing in the muddy footing, Zouga drove his men to make up their loads for the outward march, while he made his own final preparations. In the middle of the morning they ate a miserable and hasty meal of cold millet cakes and the last scraps of smoked buffalo meat. Then Zouga stood, with a cloak of half-cured kudu skin draped over his head and shoulders, the rain dripping from his beard and plastering his patched clothing to his body.

'Safari!' he shouted. 'We march!'

'And not too damned soon either,' muttered Jan Cheroot, reversing his musket on its sling so the barrel pointed at the ground and the rain could not run into the muzzle.

It was then that the porters discovered the extra burden that Zouga had for them. It was lashed to carrying poles of mopani wood with bark rope, and protected by a plaited covering of elephant grass.

'They are not going to carry it,' Jan Cheroot told him, squeezing the rain from his woolly eyebrows with his thumb. 'I told you they would refuse.'

'They'll carry it.' Zouga's eyes were cold and green as cut emeralds, and his expression was fierce. 'They carry it – or they'll stay here with it, dead!'

He had carefully selected the best specimen of the carved stone birds, the only one that was completely undamaged and the one on which the carving was the most artistically executed, and he had packed and prepared it for porterage himself.

For Zouga the carving was physical proof of the existence of the ancient abandoned city, proof that could not be denied when even the most cynical critic read his account in far-away London. Zouga guessed that the intrinsic value of this relic probably surpassed the equivalent weight in pure gold. The value of the artefact was not the most important consideration in Zouga's determination to carry the carving out to civilization. The stone birds had come to have a special superstitious significance to him. They had come to symbolize for him the success of his endeavours, and by possessing one of them he had in some strange manner taken possession of this entire savage and beautiful land. He would return for the others, but he must have this single perfect specimen. It was his talisman.

'You and you.' He picked two of his strongest and his usually most willing porters, and when they still hesitated, he unslung the heavy elephant gun from his shoulder. They saw his expression and knew that his intention was serious, deadly serious. Sulkily they began breaking down their own loads and distributing them amongst their comrades.

'At least let us leave this other thundering piece of rubbish.' The rain and the cold had affected Jan Cheroot as much as the others, and he indicated the tin box that contained Zouga's dress uniform with a hatred and contempt usually reserved for animate objects. Zouga did not bother to reply, but gestured to Matthew to take it up.

It was noon before the bedraggled little column struggled through the long sodden grass that choked the valley floor and began to climb the far side, slipping and cursing in the mud.

It rained for five days and five nights, sometimes in thick drumming bursts that seemed to fall in solid sheets of water from the sky, at other times it was a cold drizzling mist, that swirled gently about them as they trudged on in the soft treacherous footing, a fine silver mist that blanketed and muted all sound except the eternal dripping of the forest and the soft sighing passage of the wind in the upper branches.

The fever vapours seemed to rise from the very ground, entering their lungs with each breath, and in the icy cold mornings they writhed and twisted like the wraiths of tormented souls down in the hollows of the valleys. The porters were the first to show the symptoms of the disease, for the fever was in their bones and the cold rain brought it out so they shivered in uncontrollable spasms and their teeth chattered in their jaws until it seemed they might crack like porcelain. However, they were seasoned to the rigours of the disease and they were still able to march.

The bulky statue in its ungainly packing of grass and bark

was borne painfully up the rocky ridges and down the other side by half-naked men staggering like drunks from the fever boiling in their veins, and when they reached the bank of another water course they dropped it gratefully and fell in the mud to rest without the will to cover themselves from the relentless rain.

Where there had been dried river-beds, with drifts of white sand shining like alpine snowfields in the sun, with quiet pools of still green water, and with steep high banks in which the brilliant kingfisher and little jewelled bee-eaters burrowed to nest, there were now maddened torrents of racing brown water, which brimmed over the high banks and carved out the roots of tall trees, toppling them into the flood and whisking them away as though they were mere twigs.

There was no possible means by which a man could cross these racing, foaming deluges; the corpse of a drowned buffalo with bloated pink belly and its limbs sticking stiffly into the air was borne downstream at the speed of a galloping horse, while Zouga stood morosely on the bank, and knew that he had left it too late. They were trapped by the spate.

'We will have to follow the river,' he grunted, and wiped his streaming face on the sleeve of his sodden hunting jacket.

'It goes towards the west,' Jan Cheroot pointed out with morbid relish, and it was not necessary for him to expand on the thought.

To the west lay the kingdom of Mzilikazi, King of the Matabele, and already they must be close to that vaguely defined area that old Tom Harkness had marked on his map.

'The Burnt Land – here Mzilikazi's impis kill all travellers.'

'What do you suggest, my ray of golden Hottentot sunshine?' Zouga demanded bitterly. 'Have you got wings to fly this?' He indicated the broad expanse of wild water, where the curled waves stood as stationary as carved sculptures as they marked the position of submerged rocks and hidden snags. 'Or what about gills and fins?' Zouga went on. 'Let me see you swim, or if you have neither wings nor fins, then surely you have good advice for me?'

'Yes,' Jan Cheroot answered as bitterly. 'My advice is that you listen to good advice when first it is given, and second that you drop those in the river.' He indicated the bundled statue and the sealed uniform box. Zouga did not wait for the rest of it, but turned his back and shouted.

'Safari! On your feet, all of you! We march!'

They worked slowly west and a little south, but too much westward for even Zouga's peace of mind, though his route was dictated by the network of rivers and flooded valleys.

On the sixth day the rain relented, and the clouds broke open, revealing a sky of deep aquamarine blue and a fierce swollen sun that made their clothing steam, and stilled the fever shakes of the porters.

Even with the accuracy of his chronometer in doubt, Zouga was able to observe the meridian passage that local noon and establish his latitude. He was not as far south as he had calculated by dead reckoning, so he was probably even further west than his suspect calculations of longitude suggested.

'The land of the Mzilikazi is drier,' Zouga consoled himself, as he wrapped his navigational instruments in their oilskin covers, 'and I am an Englishman, and the grandson of Tshedi. Not even a Matabele would dare deny me passage, despite what old Tom writes.' And he had his talisman, the stone bird, to add its protection.

Resolutely he faced west again, and drove his caravan onwards. There was one other misery to add to their sufferings. There was no meat, and there had been none since the day they left the abandoned city.

With the first onslaught of the rains, the great herds of game that had been concentrated upon the last few pools and waterholes had been freed to scatter widely across the vast land where every ditch and irregularity was now at last brimming with fresh sweet water and where the baked and sun-seared plains were already blooming green with the tender first shoots of new growth.

In five days' march in the rain, Zouga had seen only one small herd of waterbuck, the least palatable of all African game with its rank turpentine-scented musk which permeates the flesh. The heavily built bull, in his shaggy plum-brown coat led his small troop of hornless females at a frantic gallop across Zouga's front with his wide lyre-shaped horns cocked high and the perfect white circle over his buttocks flashing with each bound. He tore through the drizzling rain and dense wild ebony bush not twenty paces from Zouga. Zouga threw up the heavy gun and led on his driving shoulder.

Behind him his hungry, exhausted porters yipped like a pack

of hunting dogs with anticipation, and Zouga held his aim for an instant to make deadly certain and then squeezed off the trigger.

With a sharp crack, the cap exploded under the falling hammer, but there was not the long spurt of flame from the muzzle and the great clangour of the shot, followed by the heavy thumping impact of the lead ball into flesh. The gun had misfired and the handsome antelope led his harem away at full gallop, disappearing almost immediately into the bush and rain while the dwindling clatter of their hooves mocked Zouga. He swore with frustration as he laboriously drew the ball and charge with the corkscrew tool fitted to his ramrod, and found that the insidious rain had somehow entered the barrel, probably through the nipple and that the powder was as wet as though he had dipped it in the raging brown flood waters.

Those few hours of fierce sunlight on the sixth day gave Zouga and Jan Cheroot an opportunity to spread the coarse grey contents of their powder bags on a flat rock and dry it out so there would be less chance of another disastrous misfire, and while they did so the porters let drop their packs and limped off to find a dry spot to stretch their aching limbs.

Then too swiftly the sunlight was blotted out once more, and hurriedly they scooped the powder back into the pouches and as the fat raindrops began to hiss and splat about them they wrapped them in the worn oilskins, tucked them under their voluminous leather capes and resumed the westward trudge, heads bowed, silent and hungry and cold and miserable, Zouga's ears singing with the quinine-buzz, the first apparent side-effect of massive doses of the drug taken over long periods. The quinine-buzz that can lead to eventual, irreversible deafness.

Despite the heavy daily doses of the bitter powder, the morning arrived at last when Zouga woke with the deep ache in the marrow of his bones, the dull weight like a heavy stone lying behind his eyes and by midday he was shaking and shivering with the alternate flood of fierce heat and deathly sepulchre cold through his veins.

'The seasoning fever,' Jan Cheroot told him philosophically, 'it kills you, or hardens you.'

'Some individuals would appear to have a natural resistance to the ravages of this disease,' his father had written in his treatise, *The Malarial Fevers of Tropical Africa: Their Causes,*

Symptoms and Treatment, 'and there is evidence to suggest that this resistance is hereditary.'

'We'll see now if the old devil knew what he was talking about,' Zouga mumbled through chattering teeth, hugging the stinking wet leather coat around his shoulders. It never occurred to him even briefly to halt for his affliction; he had not accorded that courtesy to any of his men, and he did not expect it himself.

He trudged on grimly, with his knees giving a rubbery little bounce at each pace, his vision blurring and starring into little pinwheels of light, then emerging again though phantom worms and gnats still wriggled across his sight. Every now and then a touch upon his shoulder from the little Hottentot who marched behind him directed Zouga's stumbling feet back on to the path from which they had strayed.

The nights were hideous with the nightmares of his fever-inflamed brain, they were filled with the buffeting thunder of dark wings and the sickly stench of snakes so that he would wake panting and screaming, often to find Jan Cheroot holding him with a comforting arm around his shaking shoulders.

The lifting of that first bout of his seasoning fever coincided with the next brief break in the rains. It seemed that the bright sunlight, magnified by the lingering moisture in the air, burned away the mists from his mind and the poisonous miasma from his blood, leaving him clear-headed, with a fragile sense of well-being but a weakness in his legs and arms and a dull ache up under the right-hand side of his rib cage where his liver was still swollen and hard as a rock, the typical after-effect of the fever.

'You will be all right,' Jan Cheroot prophesied. 'You threw it off as quickly as I've seen any man with his first hit of the fever. Ja! You are a man of Africa – she will let you live here, my friend.'

It was while he still walked on wavering legs, light-headed, so that it felt as though his feet did not touch the muddy earth but danced inches above it, that they cut the spoor.

The weight of the great bull had driven the spoor a foot deep into the sticky red mud, so that it was a series of deep pot-holes, strung across the earth like beads on a necklace. The exact impression of the huge pads had been cast in the holes as though in plaster of Paris, each crack and fissure in the skin of the sole, each irregularity, even the outline of the blunt toe nails were there in precise detail, and at one place where the soft earth had been unable to bear his weight and the elephant had sunk almost belly deep, he had left the impression of his long thick ivories in the earth when he had used them to push himself free.

'It is him!' breathed Jan Cheroot, without looking up from the enormous spoor. 'I would know that spoor anywhere.' He did not need to say more to identify the great old bull that they had last seen so many months before on the high pass of the elephant road on the escarpment of the Zambezi river.

'Not an hour ahead of us,' Jan Cheroot went on in a reverential whisper, like a man at prayer.

'And the wind stands fair.' Zouga found he was whispering also. He remembered his premonition that he would encounter this animal again. Almost fearfully he looked up at the sky. In the east the storm clouds were rolling ponderously towards them once more, the brief respite was almost over. The next onslaught of the storm promised to be as fierce, and even those deep and perfect prints would soon dissolve into liquid mud and be washed into oblivion.

'They are feeding into the wind,' he went on, trying to put the threat of rain out of his mind and concentrating his still fever-dulled wits to the problem of the hunt.

The old bull and his remaining consort were feeding and moving forward with the wind into their faces. That way they would not walk into trouble. Yet these two old veterans, with their decades of accumulated experience, would not hold steadily into the wind for long, they would turn at intervals to get below the wind of a possible tracker.

Every minute now was of vital consideration, if the hunt was to succeed – for despite the weakness in his legs and the silliness in his head, Zouga had not for a single moment considered letting the spoor go. They might be a hundred miles within the borders of Mzilikazi's country with a Matabele impi of border guards closing swiftly, and the hours lost in following the two old bulls might make all the difference between escaping from these fever-haunted forests or leaving their bones here for the hyena to crunch, but neither Zouga nor Jan Cheroot hesitated. They began to shed their unneeded equipment, they would not need water bottles for the land was overflowing, the food bags were empty anyway, and the blankets sodden They would shelter tonight against the old bull's massive carcass.

'Follow at your best pace,' Zouga shouted to his heavily burdened porters, dropping his unwanted equipment into the mud for them to pick up. 'You can fill your bellies with meat and fat tonight, if you put your feet to it now.'

They had to gamble all Zouga's remaining strength on the opening play, using speed to beat the rain and to reach the bulls before they made a turn into the wind and took the scent. They ran at the spoor, going hard from the first, knowing that even a healthy man could not hold that pace beyond an hour or two at the most before his heart broke.

In the first mile Zouga's vision was starring and fragmenting again, sweat drenched his lean body and he reeled like a drunkard as his legs threatened to give under him.

'Run through it,' Jan Cheroot counselled him grimly.

He did it, by a sheer effort of will. He drove himself through to that place beyond the pain. Quite suddenly his vision cleared and though there was no feeling at all in his legs they drove on steadily under him so he seemed to float over the ground without effort.

Running at his side Jan Cheroot recognized the moment when Zouga broke the shackles and went clear of his own weakness. He said nothing but glanced sideways at him, eyes bright with admiration and he nodded once. Zouga did not see that nod, for his head was up and his dreaming gaze was fixed far ahead.

They ran the sun to its zenith, Jan Cheroot not daring to break the rhythm for he knew that Zouga would drop like a man shot through the heart if they stopped to rest. They ran on as the sun began to drop, pursued by the ponderous cohorts of the oncoming storm that threatened it with extinction, and their own shadows danced ahead of them along the deeply driven elephant-spoor. In a tight bunch behind Zouga, his four gunbearers matched him pace for pace, ready to hand him a weapon at the instant he required it.

The hunter's instinct warned Jan Cheroot. He twisted his head every few minutes to look back along the trail they had already run. That was how he picked them up.

They were two grey shadows, merging softly into the darker acacia shadows below the dripping trees, but they were moving with steadfast purpose, circling to strike their own spoor again, throwing a loop about their pursuers and taking the wind from them.

The bulls were half a mile away, moving with that swinging

deceptively leisurely gait that would bring them, within minutes, full on to the hot trail with which the small band of hunters had overlaid their own huge pug marks; the trail would be reeking with the rank odour of man, the air thick with it.

Jan Cheroot touched Zouga's arm, turning him back upon their own run without checking him nor breaking the driving rhythm of his numbed legs.

'We have to catch them before they cut our spoor,' he called softly. He saw Zouga's eyes come back into focus and the colour flare in his waxen pale cheeks as Zouga turned and saw for the first time the two huge shapes cruising serenely through the open forest, under the tall umbrella-shaped acacias, moving with a stately deliberation down towards the string of reeking man-prints in the red mud.

The big bull was leading, his gaunt frame too tall and bony for the wasted flesh over which the skin hung in deep folds and bags. The huge yellow tusks were too long and heavy for the ancient head, and his ears were ripped and torn into scarred tatters that dangled on to his creased cheeks. He had been wallowing in a mud hole and his body was slick and shining with wet red mud.

He stepped out on his long, heavily boned legs around which the thick loose skin bagged and drooped like a badly tailored pair of breeches, and close behind him strode his askari, a big heavily toothed elephant, but dwarfed by his leader.

Zouga and Jan Cheroot ran together, stride for stride, their breath hissing and gasping in their throats, as they spent their last reserves to get in gunshot range before the bulls took the scent.

They traded all stealth, any attempt at concealment for speed, trusting that the weak eyesight of the old bulls would betray them. This time, the vagaries of the weather favoured them, for as they ran, the storm burst about them again.

It had held off just long enough to allow them to come up, and now the thick streamers of pale grey rain were drawn across the forest like lace curtains and the bad light beneath the thick cloud banks gave them cover to cross the last few hundred yards unseen, and the tapping rain and the rush of the wind in the branches of the acacias muffled their racing footfalls.

A hundred and fifty yards ahead of Zouga the old bull hit the man spoor, and it stopped him as though he had run into the side of an invisible cliff of glass. He flared back on his hind quarters, his back humping and his wrinkled ivoried head flying up high, the ragged banners of his ears filling like the mainsail of a tall ship, and clapping thunderously as he flapped them against his shoulders.

He froze like that for a long moment, groping at the tainted earth with the tip of his trunk, then he lifted it to his mouth and sprayed the scent into the open pink buds of his olfactory organs. The dread and hated odour struck him like a physical force and he went back another pace, then his trunk lifted straight into the air above him, and he wheeled and like a well-trained pair of coach horses his tall askari wheeled with him, shoulder to shoulder, and flank to flank, they began to run – and Zouga was still a hundred yards behind them.

Jan Cheroot dropped on to one knee into the mud, and flung up his musket. At the same instant, the askari checked slightly and swung left, crossing his leader's rear. Perhaps it was unintentional, but neither Zouga nor Jan Cheroot believed that. They knew that the younger bull was drawing fire, protecting the other with his own body.

'You want it? Take it then, you thunder!' Jan Cheroot shouted angrily, he knew he had lost too much ground by pausing to fire.

Aiming for the younger bull, Jan Cheroot took the hip shot, and the bull staggered to it, flecks of red mud flying from his skin where the ball struck, and he broke his stride, favouring the damaged joint, swinging out of the line of his run, broadside to the hunters, while the great bull ran on alone.

Zouga could have killed the crippled bull with a heart shot, for the animal was down to a dragging, hump-backed trot and the range was less than thirty paces, but Zouga ran straight past him, never checking, hardly glancing at him, knowing he could leave Jan Cheroot to finish that business. He ran after the big bull, but despite his utmost endeavour, losing ground to him steadily.

Ahead of them, the ground dipped into a shallow open saucer, and beyond that it rose to another ridge on which the wild teak trees stood like sentinels in the grey rain. The bull went down into the saucer, still in his initial burst of speed, stretching out so that his padfalls sounded like the steady beat of a bass drum, opening the gap between himself and his hunter – until he reached the bottom of the dip, and then he was almost halted.

His weight broke the surface of the swampy ground, and he sank through almost to his shoulders, and had to lunge for each step, with the glutinous mud sucking and squelching obscenely at each of his frantic movements.

Swiftly Zouga closed the range, and his spirits took wing, his exultation driving back his weakness and fatigue. He felt intoxicated with battle lust. He reached the swampy ground, and leapt from tussock to tussock of coarse swamp grass, while the bull struggled on ahead of him.

Closer and closer still Zouga came up to him, almost point-blank range, less than twenty yards and at last he stopped and balanced on one of the little islands of grass roots.

Just ahead of him the bull had reached the far side of the swamp, and was heaving himself out on to the firm ground at the foot of the slope. The bull's front legs were higher than his still-bogged hindquarters, the whole slope of his back was exposed to Zouga, the knuckles of his massive spine stood out clearly through the mud-painted skin and the arched staves of his rib cage were like the frames of a Viking longboat. Zouga fancied he could actually see the pounding rhythm of the great heart beating against them.

There could be no mistake this time. In the months since their first encounter, Zouga had become a skilled huntsman, he knew the soft and vital places in the mountainous bulk of an elephant's body. At this range and from this angle, the heavy ball would shatter the spine between the shoulder blades without losing any of its velocity, and it would go on deep, to the heart, to those thick serpentine arteries that fed the lungs.

He touched the hair trigger, and with a pop like a child's toy the gun misfired. The great grey beast heaved himself clear of the mud, and went away up the slope, now at last settling into the swinging ground-eating gait which would carry him fifty miles before nightfall.

Behind him Zouga reached the firm ground and flung down the useless weapon, dancing with impatience as he screamed at his bearers to bring up the second gun.

Matthew was fifty paces behind him, slipping and staggering in the swampy ground. Mark, Luke and John were strung out behind him.

'Come on! Come on!' screamed Zouga, and snatched the second gun from Matthew, and dashed away up the slope. He had to catch the bull before he reached the crest of the slope, for down the other side he would go like an eagle on the wind.

Zouga ran now with all his heart, with all his will and the very last dregs of his strength, while behind him Matthew stopped, snatched up the misfired weapon from where Zouga had thrown it down, and, acting instinctively in the heat and excitement of the chase, he reloaded it.

He poured another handful of black powder on top of the charge and ball already in the barrel and tamped down a second quarter-pound ball of lead on top of it all. In so doing he changed the gun from a formidable weapon to a lethal bomb that could maim or even kill the man who attempted to fire it. Then Matthew slipped another percussion cap over the nipple and ran on up the slope after Zouga.

The bull was nearing the crest of the ridge, and Zouga was coming up on him, but slowly, the difference in their speed just barely discernible. At last Zouga's strength was failing, he could keep this pace for minutes more and he knew when he finally stopped he would be on the verge of total physical collapse.

His vision was swimming and wavering, and his feet stumbled and slipped on the wet lichen-covered rocks of the slope, and the rain beat into his face, almost blinding him. Sixty yards ahead of him the bull reached the crest, and there he did something that Zouga had never seen a hunted elephant do before – he turned broadside, flaring his ears, to look at his pursuers.

Perhaps he had been pushed too hard, perhaps he had been hunted too often and the hatred had accumulated like weed below the waterline of an old ship, perhaps this was his last defiance.

For a moment he stood tall, and glistening black with mud and rain, silhouetted against the low grey sky, and Zouga hit him in the shoulder, the gun ringing like a bronze cathedral bell, and the long lick of red flame blooming briefly in the gloom.

Both man and beast reeled to the shot, Zouga driven off-balance by the recoil and the bull taking the hardened lead ball through the ribs and going back on his haunches, the rheumy old eyes clenching tightly to the shock of it.

The bull kept his feet, though he was hard hit, and he opened his eyes and saw the man, that hated, evil-smelling and persistent animal that had persecuted him so relentlessly down the years.

He launched himself back down the slope, like an avalanche of dark grey granite, and his repeated blood squeals rang against the low sky, and Zouga turned and ran from the charging bull, while the earth trembled beneath his feet at the weight and nearness of the stricken beast.

Matthew stood his ground, even in the terrible press of the moment. Zouga loved him for that. He stood to do his duty, to deliver the second gun to his master.

Zouga reached him, just ahead of the charging bull, dropped his smoking weapon, snatched the second gun from Matthew, never suspecting that it had been double-shotted, and as he turned he thumbed the hammer back and swung up the long thick barrel.

The bull was on top of him, blotting out the rain-sodden sky, the long yellow ivories raised like roof-beams over his head, and the trunk already uncoiling to reach down and snatch Zouga up.

Zouga pressed the hair trigger, and this time the gun fired. With a shattering roar the barrel burst, the metal opening like the petals of a flower, and burning powder flew back into Zouga's face, singeing his beard and blistering the skin of his face. The hammer was blown clean off the barrel and it hit Zouga in the cheek, just under the right eye, cutting a jagged wound clean down to the bone. The shattered weapon flew out of his grasp, and slammed back into his shoulder with such force that he felt the ligaments and tendons tearing. Zouga was hurled into a backward somersault that carried him just beyond the grasp of the bull's questing trunk.

He fell heavily behind a pile of loose stone chips, and for a moment the elephant checked, going back on its hind legs to avoid the flashing flame and smoke of the explosion, blinded and unsighted for a moment – and then it saw the gunbearer still standing.

Matthew started to run, poor, loyal, brave Matthew, but the bull had him before he had gone a dozen paces. It took him about the waist with a single coil of its long trunk, and it threw him into the air as though he were light as a child's rubber ball. Matthew went up forty feet, with his arms and legs windmilling, his scream of terror unheard in the deafening squeals of the elephant. It sounded like the whistle of a steam engine blown by a crazed engineer, and Matthew seemed to rise very slowly into the air, hang for a long moment and then drop just as slowly downwards.

The bull caught him in mid-air and threw him again, this time even higher.

Zouga dragged himself into a sitting position. His right arm hung limply on its torn muscles and tendons, blood streamed from his ripped cheek into his beard and his eardrums were so tortured by the explosion that the elephant's squeals seemed muted and far off. He looked up groggily and saw Matthew high in the air, beginning to fall, saw him hit the ground, and the elephant begin to kill him.

Zouga dragged himself to his knees, and began to creep over the mound of loose stone towards the empty gun, the gun from which he had fired the first shot and which he had dropped when he snatched the double-shotted gun from Matthew, the gun which now lay five paces from him, five paces which seemed an infinite distance to drag his maimed body.

The elephant placed one foot on Matthew's chest and his ribs crackled like dry sticks in a fierce fire. It took his head in its trunk and plucked it from Matthew's shoulders, as easily as a farmer kills a chicken.

The elephant tossed Matthew's head aside and as it trundled down the slope close to where Zouga sat, he saw that Matthew's eyelids were blinking rapidly over his bulging eyeballs and that the nerves flickered under the skin of his cheeks.

Tearing his eyes from the gruesome object, Zouga lifted the empty gun into his lap and began to reload it. He had no use or feeling in his right arm, which still hung limply at his side.

Twenty paces away the elephant knelt over Matthew's decapitated body and drove one of the long yellow ivories through his belly.

Painfully Zouga poured a handful of powder into the gun muzzle, trying not to be distracted from his task.

Matthew hung impaled through the middle from the bloody tusk like a wet shirt on a laundry line, the elephant's trunk came up and coiled python-like about his battered body.

Zouga dropped a ball from his pouch into the barrel of the gun, and one-handed tamped it home with the ramrod.

The elephant tore an arm from the body, and Matthew slid from the point of the tusk and dropped once more to earth.

Moaning softly with the pain of each movement, Zouga primed the gun and hauled back the hammer against the powerful tension of the spring.

The elephant was kneeling with both front legs on what remained of Matthew, grinding him into a red mush against the rocky earth.

Dragging the gun with him, Zouga crawled back to the mound of rock chips behind which he had fallen. Using only his left hand, he balanced the stock of the big elephant gun over the top of the mound.

The elephant was still squealing in unabated fury as it crushed Matthew's corpse.

Grovelling flat on his belly, Zouga sighted over the thick barrel, but with only one hand it was almost impossible to hold the clumsy weapon true, and his vision swam and wavered with pain and exhaustion.

For an instant the shaking foresight aligned with the crude vee of the backsight, and he let the shot fly, in flame and a billowing cloud of burnt powder smoke.

The elephant's squeals stopped abruptly. As the powder smoke was blown aside on the cold breeze, Zouga saw that the bull had hoisted himself wearily upright and was swaying slowly from foot to foot. The massive head dropped under the weight of its blood-smeared tusks and its trunk hung as limply as Zouga's own damaged right arm.

The elephant was making a strange mournful humming sound deep in his chest, and from the second bullet wound just behind his bony shoulder joint, his heart blood spurted in short regular jets, to the beat of the huge heart, and poured down his body in a honey-thick stream.

The bull turned towards where Zouga lay, and shuffling like an old and very weary man came towards him, the tip of his trunk twitching with his last fading warlike instincts.

Zouga tried to drag himself away, but the bull came on faster than he could crawl, and the trunk reached out, touched Zouga's ankle, the vast bulk of the elephant filled the sky above Zouga, and he kicked out frantically but the trunk tightened its grip on his ankle with agonizing unbearable strength, and Zouga knew that it would tear his leg out of its socket at the hip.

Then the elephant groaned, a shuddering exhalation of air from the torn lungs, the grip on Zouga's ankle relaxed and the old bull died on his feet, his legs collapsed under him and he went down.

He fell with a weight and force that made the earth bounce and tremble under Zouga's prostrate body and with a thud that Jan Cheroot, who was crossing the swamp, heard clearly from a mile away.

Zouga dropped his head against the earth and closed his eyes, and the darkness overwhelmed him.

Jan Cheroot made no attempt to move Zouga from where he lay beside the old bull's carcass. He built a rough shelter of saplings and wet grass over him and then coaxed smoky flames from a fire at his head, and from another at his feet. This was all he could do to warm him until the porters came up with the blankets at sunset.

Then he helped Zouga into a sitting position and between them they strapped the damaged arm.

'God Almighty,' croaked Zouga, as he prepared the needle and thread from his sewing kit, 'I'd give both the tusks for a dram of good malt whisky.'

Jan Cheroot held the hand mirror, and using one hand only Zouga stitched the flap of his torn cheek back into place, and as he pulled the last knot tight and snipped the thread, he collapsed back into his damp and stinking fur kaross.

'I will die rather than march again,' he whispered.

'That is your choice exactly,' Jan Cheroot agreed, without looking up from the chunks of elephant liver and heart that he had begun wrapping in yellow fat before stringing them on a green twig. 'You can march or die here in the mud.'

Outside the hut the porters were wailing and chanting the mourning dirge for Matthew. They had gathered the fragments of his horribly mutilated body and made a package of them, wrapping them in Matthew's own blanket and binding it up with bark rope.

They would bury him the following morning, but until then they would keep up the haunting cries of mourning.

Jan Cheroot scraped coals from the fire and began to grill the kebab of liver and fat and heart over them, 'They will be useless until they have buried him, and we must still cut the tusks.'

'I owe Matthew a night of mourning at least,' Zouga whispered. 'He stood the bull down. If he had run with the second gun . . .' Zouga broke off, and groaned as a fresh stab of pain transfixed his shoulder. Using his good left hand, he scratched under the skin blanket on which he lay, moving the lumps of stone which had caused the discomfort.

'He was good – stupid, but good,' Jan Cheroot agreed. 'A wiser man would have run.' He turned the kebab slowly over the coals. 'It will take all day tomorrow to bury him and then cut the tusks from both elephants. But we must march the day after that.'

Jan Cheroot had killed his bull down on the plain, under the outspread branches of a giant acacia. Looking through the low opening of the hut Zouga could see the carcass of his own bull lying on its side not twenty feet away. Already it was swelling with trapped gas and the upper legs thrust out stiffly above the grey balloon of the belly. The tusks were unbelievable. Even as he stared at them Zouga thought they must be a fantasy of his exhaustion and agony. They were as thick as a girl's waist, and the spread of them must have been twelve feet from tip to tip.

'How much will they weigh?' he asked Jan Cheroot, and the Hottentot looked up and shrugged.

'I have never seen a bigger elephant,' he admitted. 'We will need three men to carry each of them.'

'Two hundred pounds?' Zouga asked, the conversation distracted him from the agony in his shoulder.

'More,' Jan Cheroot decided. 'You will never see another like him.'

'No,' Zouga agreed. 'That is true. There will never be another like him.' Deep regret blended with his pain, making it more intense. Regret for the magnificent beast and sorrow for the brave man who had died with him.

The pain and the sorrow would not let him sleep that night, and in the dawn when they gathered in the rain to bury Matthew, Zouga strapped his damaged arm into a bark sling and had two men help him to his feet, then he walked unaided but slowly and stiffly up the slope to the grave, using a staff to balance himself.

They had wrapped Matthew's body in his fur blanket and placed his possessions with him, his axe and spear, his food bowl and beer calabash, to serve him on the long journey ahead.

Singing the slow mournful song of the dead, they packed the rock over and around him so that the hyena would not dig him out. When they had finished, Zouga felt drained of strength and emotion. He staggered back to his hut and crawled under the dank blanket. He had only that day to gather his strength for the march that must be resumed in the dawn. He closed his eyes, but could not sleep for the thud of the axes into bone as Jan Cheroot supervised the chopping of the tusks from the casket of the old bull's skull.

Zouga rolled on to his back, and once again a loose rock chip dug into his aching body. He reached back and pulled it from under the blanket, was about to throw it aside when something caught his attention and he arrested the movement.

The rock was as white and as crystalline as the candied sugar that Zouga had loved so as a boy, a pretty little fragment, but that was not what had stopped his hand.

Even in the subdued light of the hut, the thin irregular seam of metal that wavered uncertainly between quartz crystals flicked a pin-prick of bright gold into his eyes. Zouga stared at it numbly, twisting the lump of quartz to catch the light and make it twinkle. There was a sense of unreality about the moment, as there always is when something sought for and longed for is at last held in the hand.

He found his voice at last, a hoarse croak through his swollen, blistered, powder-scorched lips, and Jan Cheroot came almost immediately.

'The grave,' he whispered urgently, 'Matthew's grave, it was dug so swiftly in such rocky soil.'

'No,' Jan Cheroot shook his head. 'It was there. There are other holes like it along the ridge.'

Zouga stared at him for a long moment, his face lopsided with the scabbed and stitched wound, his one eye a mere slit in the puffed and bruised flesh. He had let himself sink low from the wound. It had been under his nose and he had almost missed it. He started to drag himself out of his blanket.

'Help me!' he ordered. 'I must see them. Show me these holes.'

Leaning on Jan Cheroot's shoulder, stooped to favour his shoulder, he dragged himself along the ridge in the rain, and when at last he was satisfied, he limped back to the hut and used the last feeble light of that day to scrawl in his journal, holding it in his lap and bowing over it to protect the pages from the drip of rain through the rough thatching, using his left hand so the writing was barely decipherable.

'I have named it the Harkness Mine, for this must be very similar to the ancient workings that old Tom described. The reef is white sugar quartz and runs along the back of the ridge. It would appear to be very narrow but rich, for there is visible gold in many of the samples. My injury prevents me crushing and panning these, but I would estimate values well in excess of two ounces of fine gold to the ton of quartz.

'The ancient miners have driven four shafts into the hillside. There may be more that I overlooked, for they are heavily overgrown and an attempt has been made to refill the shafts, possibly to conceal them.

'The shafts are large enough to admit a small man crawling on hands and knees. Probably they used child-slaves in the diggings and the conditions of labour in these rabbit warrens must have been infernal. In any event they were only able to go down as far as the water table, and without sophisticated machinery to pump the flooded working, they would have been abandoned. This is probably what happened here at the Harkness Mine and there is almost certainly a great amount of gold-bearing ore to be recovered by modern methods.

'The rock dump on which stands my rude hut is composed almost entirely of the gold matrix, awaiting crushing and refining, and the miners were probably driven away by an enemy before they could complete their labours.

'I am couched upon a mattress of gold, and like King Midas all around me is the precious metal. Like that unfortunate King. there seems to be little profit in it for me that I can perceive at this moment—'

Zouga paused, and laid his pen aside, warming his icy hands at the smoky fire. He should have felt wildly elated. He picked up his pen once again. He sighed and then wrote tortuously,

'I have a huge store of ivory, but it is spread across this land, buried in small caches. I have fifty pounds and more of native gold in ingot and nugget, and I have discovered the mother lode of untold fortune, but it cannot buy me a pound flask of gunpowder nor an unguent for my grievous injuries.

'I will not know until tomorrow if I have the strength remaining to me to continue the march to the south, or if I am destined to remain here with Matthew and the great elephant as my only companions.'

Jan Cheroot shook him awake. It took a long time. Zouga seemed to be swimming up from great depths through cold and murky water, and when at last he surfaced, he knew immediately that his gloomy prophecy written in the journal the previous evening had become reality. There was no feeling or strength in his legs. His shoulder and arm were bound rock hard with spasmed muscle.

'Leave me here,' he said to Jan Cheroot, and the Hottentot heaved him to a sitting position, snarling at him when Zouga cried out at the agony of each movement, and forced him to drink the steaming hot soup made from elephant marrowbones.

'Leave one gun with me,' Zouga whispered.

'Here.' Jan Cheroot ignored the order and instead made him take the bitter white powder. Zouga gagged on the quinine.

It took two porters to get him on his feet.

'I am leaving that stone.' Jan Cheroot pointed to the packaged statue. 'We cannot carry both of you.'

'No!' Zouga whispered fiercely. 'If I go, the bird must go with me.'

'How?'

Zouga shrugged off their hands.

'I will walk,' he said. 'Carry the bird.'

They made less than five miles that day, but the following day the sun emerged again to cheer them on. Once it warmed Zouga's abused muscles, he could increase the pace.

That night he logged ten miles in his journal when they camped in open grassland. In the dawn Zouga was able to crawl from his blankets and gain his feet unaided. His injuries still stiff, he used the staff to leave the thorn *scherm* by its single gate and limp to the periphery of the camp. When he urinated his water was a dark amber colour from the fever and the quinine, but he knew now that he was going to be able to continue the march.

He looked up at the sky. It would rain again soon. They should start at once. He was about to turn back to the camp and rouse the porters when movement in the tall grass caught his attention.

For a moment he thought it might be a troop of wild ostrich passing the camp, then suddenly he realized that the whole plain was alive with swift but stealthy movement, the fluffy grass tops rustling and nodding with the passage of many bodies, only now and again there was a brief glimpse of ruffled plumes above the grass. The movement spread swiftly around both sides of the small camp, where Zouga's men still slept.

Zouga stared uncomprehendingly, leaning on his staff, still muzzy with sleep and fever and anchored by his injuries, he did not move until the swift encircling movement had been completed, and then the stillness and silence descended again so for a moment he believed he had been imagining phantoms.

Then there was a soft fluting whistle, like a blast on Pan's pipe, sweet and hauntingly melodious in the dawn, and immediately there was movement again, an encroaching movement, like a strangler's hand upon the throat. Zouga saw the ostrich plumes clearly now, snowy white and dead black they swayed and danced above the grass tops, and immediately afterwards he saw the war shields, long oval shields of dappled black and white cowhide. The long shields – the Matabele.

Dread was a cold, heavy lump under his ribs, yet instinct warned him that to show it would mean death, just when he had once again believed in life.

There were a hundred, he calculated swiftly as he glanced around the closing ring of warriors. No, there were more than that, at least two hundred Matabele *amadoda* in full war plumage, only the plumes and their eyes showing above the tops of the long dappled shields. The grey dawn light glinted on the broad-bladed stabbing spears, held underhand so the points protruded beyond the ring of shields. The ring was unbroken, shield overlapped shield, the encircling horns of the bull, the classic tactics of the Matabele, the finest and most ruthless warriors that the continent of Africa had ever spawned.

'Here Mzilikazi's border impis kill all travellers,' Tom Harkness had written.

Zouga drew himself up and stepped forward, holding up his one good arm with the palm extended towards the ring of shields.

'I am an Englishman. A commander of the great white Queen, Victoria. My name is Bakela, son of Manali, son of Tshedi – and I come in peace.'

From the ranks stepped a man. He was taller than Zouga and his tossing ostrich plumes turned him into a giant. He swept aside his shield, and he was lean and muscled like a gladiator. On his upper arms he wore the tassels of cow tails, each one awarded him by his King for an act of valour. The cow tails were thick bunches, layer upon layer. His short kilt was of spotted civet cat tails, and there were more cow tails bound around his calves just below the knees. He had the handsome smooth moonface of the true Nguni, with a broad nose and full sculptured lips. His bearing was noble, the carriage of his head proud.

He looked at Zouga slowly and with grave attention. He looked at his tattered rags, at the untidy bindings that held his damaged arm, the staff on which he leaned like an old man.

He studied Zouga's singed beard, and powder-burned cheeks, the blisters on his lips and the black scabs that clung obscenely on his swollen discoloured cheek.

Then the Matabele laughed. It was a deep musical laugh, and then he spoke.

'And I,' he said, 'am Matabele. An Induna of two thousand. My name is Gandang, son of Mzilikazi, son of the high heavens, son of Zulu, and I come with a bright spear and a red heart.'

Robyn Ballantyne realized within the first day's march that she had seriously miscalculated her father's strength and resilience when she made the decision to try for the coast. Perhaps Zouga had divined instinctively what she a trained physician should have known. That thought made her angry with herself. She found that since parting with Zouga her hostility and sense of rivalry towards him had, if anything, increased. It made her angry that he should have given the correct advice.

By noon of that first day Robyn had been forced to call a halt and to go into camp. Fuller Ballantyne was very weak, weaker than he had been when first she found him. His skin was burning hot and dry to the touch. The movement of the litter, the jolting and bumping over uneven ground had aggravated Fuller's leg. It was grotesquely swollen, and so tender that he screamed and fought at the lightest touch upon the discoloured skin.

Robyn had one of the bearers begin work on a cradle of green twigs and bark to place over the leg and keep the fur blanket off it, and then she sat by the litter applying a damp, cool cloth to her father's forehead and speaking to little Juba and the Mashona woman, not expecting nor receiving advice from them, but taking comfort from the human contact.

'Perhaps we should have stayed at the cave,' she fretted. 'At least he would have been more comfortable there, but then for how long could we have stayed?' She spoke her thoughts aloud. 'The rains will be on us soon. We could not have stayed, and even if we march as slowly as this, we will still be trapped here by them. We simply must increase the pace – and yet I do not know if he can survive it.'

However, on the following day Fuller seemed stronger again, the fever had cooled, and they made a full day's march, but in the evening when they went into camp he had once more sunk very low.

When Robyn removed the dressing from the leg, it seemed to be less sensitive, and she was relieved – until she saw the colour of the skin around the ulceration. When she lifted the soiled dressing to her nose and sniffed it, she caught the taint that her professor of medicine at St Matthew's had taught her to watch for. It was not the usual taint of benign pus, but a more pervasive odour, the smell of a decomposing corpse. Her alarm flared, and she threw the dressing on the fire and with dread returned to her examination of the leg.

From the inside of the groin, down the wasted thigh muscles, there were the unmistakable scarlet lines beneath the thin pale skin, and the extreme sensitivity of the area seemed to have passed. It was almost as though Fuller had no further feeling in the leg.

Robyn tried to console herself that the change and mortification in the leg was unconnected with having carried him two days in a litter over rough ground. But what other reasons were there? She could find no answer. Before the move, the ulceration had been stabilized, for it was almost eighteen months since the slaver's ball had shattered the bone.

The movement in the litter must have precipitated some serious change in the limb, and this was the result.

Robyn felt herself culpable. She should have listened to Zouga. She had brought this on her own father. Gas-gangrene. She could only hope that she was wrong, but she knew she was not. The symptoms were unmistakable. She could only continue the march and hope they would reach the coast and civilization before the disease swept to its inevitable climax – but she knew that hope was futile.

She wished that she had been able to develop the same philosophical acceptance that most of her fellow physicians cultivated in the face of disease or injury which were beyond their training and ability to alleviate. But she knew she never could, always she would be victim of this helpless sense of frustration, and this time the patient was her own father.

She bound up the leg in a hot compress and knew that it was a pathetic gesture, like trying to hold back the tide with a child's sand-castle. In the morning the leg felt cooler to the touch, and the flesh seemed to have lost resilience so that her fingers left depressions as though she had touched unleavened bread. The smell was stronger.

They made a full day's march, and Fuller was silent and comatose in the litter as Robyn walked beside it. He no longer chanted psalms and wild exhortations to the Almighty, and she thanked God that at least there was no pain.

In the late afternoon they met a broad pathway, well travelled and running east and west as far as Robyn could see it. It fitted exactly the description and the location that her father had written of in his journal. Little Juba burst into tears and was rendered almost helpless with terror when she saw the road.

They found an encampment of deserted and dilapidated huts, that might have been those used by the slave-traders, and Robyn ordered camp there. She left the Mashona woman and the still snivelling and shivering Juba to tend Fuller Ballantyne, and she took only old Karanga with her. He armed himself with his long spear, and strutted like an ancient peacock to be so honoured. Within two miles, the pathway climbed steeply to pass through a saddle in a line of low hills.

Robyn was seeking evidence that this was indeed the slave road, the Hyena Road, as Juba called it tearfully.

She found her evidence on the saddle, lying in the grass a few paces from the edge of the track. It was a double yoke, hewn from a forked tree trunk and roughly dressed with an axe.

Robyn had studied the sketches in her father's journal, and she recognized it immediately. When the slave-masters did not have chains and cuffs, they used these yokes to bind their captives around their necks; two slaves linked together and forced to do everything in concert, march, eat, sleep and defecate – everything except escape.

Now all that remained of the slaves who had once worn the yoke were a few fragments of bone that the vultures and hyena had overlooked. There was something terribly sad and chilling about that roughly carved fork of wood, and Robyn could not bring herself to touch it. She said a short prayer for the unfortunate slaves who had died on that spot and then, with her knowledge that she was on the slave road confirmed, she turned back towards the camp.

That night she held counsel with the Hottentot Corporal, old Karanga and Juba.

'This camp and road have not been used for this many days,' Karanga showed Robyn both hands twice with fingers spread, 'twenty days.'

'Which way did they go?' Robyn asked. She had come to have confidence in the old man's tracking ability.

'They were moving along the road towards the sunrise, and they have not yet returned,' quavered Karanga.

'It is even as he says,' Juba agreed, and it must have been an effort to agree with somebody for whom she had such disdain and jealousy. 'The slavers will make this the last caravan before the rains. There will be no trading after the rivers are full, and the Hyena Road will grow grass until the dry season comes again.'

'So there is a caravan of slavers ahead of us,' Robyn mused. 'If we follow the road we may overtake them.'

The Hottentot Corporal interrupted. 'That will not be possible, madam. They are weeks ahead of us.'

'Then we will meet them returning, after having sold their slaves.'

The Corporal nodded and Robyn asked him, 'Will you be able to defend us, if the slavers decide to attack our column?'

'Me and my men,' the Corporal drew himself to his full height, 'are a match for a hundred dirty slavers,' he paused and then went on, 'and you shoot like a man, madam!'

Robyn smiled. 'All right,' she nodded. 'We will follow the road down to the sea.'

And the Corporal grinned at her. 'I am sick of this country and its savages, I long to see the cloud on Table Mountain and wash the taste of dust from my throat with good Cape Smoke once again.'

The hyena was an old male. There were patches of fur missing from his thick shaggy coat, and his flat, almost snakelike head was covered with scars, his ears ripped away by thorns and a hundred snapping, snarling encounters over the decomposing carcasses of men and animals. His lip had been torn up into the soft of the nostril in one of these fights and had healed askew, so that the yellow teeth in one side of his upper jaw were exposed in a hideous grin.

His teeth were worn with age, so that he could no longer crush the heavy bones that made up the bulk of hyena diet, and unable to compete, he had been driven from the hunting-pack.

There had been no human corpses along the trail since the slave column had passed weeks before, and game was scarce in this dry country. Since then the hyena had subsisted on scrapings, the fresh dung of jackal and baboon, a nest of field mice, the long-abandoned and addled egg of an ostrich which had burst in a sulphurous geyser of gas and putrefied liquid when he pawed at it. However, even though the hyena was starving, he still stood almost three foot high at the shoulder and weighed 140 pounds.

His belly under the matted and scruffy coat was concave as that of a greyhound. From high ungainly shoulders, his spine slanted back in a bony ridge to his scraggy hindquarters.

He carried his head low, snuffling at the earth for offal and scourings, but when the scent came down on the wind to him, he lifted his head on high and flared his deformed nostrils.

There was the smell of wood smoke, of human presence, which he had grown to associate with a source of food, but sharper, clearer than all the others was a smell that made the saliva run from his twisted, scarred jaws in drooling silver ropes. He went lolloping into a swaying, uneven trot up into the wind following the tantalizing drift of that odour. The scent that had attracted the old dog hyena was the cloyingly sweet taint of a gangrenous leg.

The hyena lay on the outskirts of the camp. It lay like a dog, with its chin on its front paws and its hindlegs and its bushy tail drawn up under its belly, flat behind a clump of coarse elephant grass. It watched the activity about the smoking watch fires.

Only its eyes rolled in their sockets, and the ragged stumps of its ears twitched and cocked to the cadence of human voices, and the unexpected sounds of a bucket or an axe on a stump of firewood.

Once in a while a puff of wind would bring a whiff of the scent that had first attracted the hyena, and it would snuffle it, suppressing with difficulty the little anxious cries that rose in its throat.

As the evening shadows thickened, a human figure, a half-naked black woman, left the camp, and came towards its hiding-place. The hyena gathered itself to fly but before she reached the place where it lay, Juba paused and looked about her carefully without seeing the animal, then she lifted the flap of her beaded apron, lowered herself and squatted. The hyena cringed and watched her. When she stood and returned to the camp, the creature, emboldened by the oncoming night, crept forward and wolfed down that which Juba had left.

Its appetite was piqued and as the night fell, it inflated its chest, curled its bushy tail up over its back and uttered its drawn-out haunting cry, ascending sharply in key, 'Oooo-auw! Oooo-auw!' – a cry so familiar to every man and woman in the camp that hardly one of them bothered to look up.

Gradually the activity about the camp fires subsided, the sound of human voices became drowsy and intermittent, the fires faded, the flames sinking and the darkness crept in upon the camp, and the hyena crept in with it.

Twice a sudden loud voice put it to trembling flight and it galloped away into the bush, only to gather its courage at the renewed silence and creep back. It was long after midnight when the beast found a weak place in the protective *scherm* of thorn branches about the camp and quietly, furtively pushed its way through the opening.

The smell led it directly to an open-sided, thatched shelter in the centre of the enclosure, and with its belly low to the earth the huge dog-like animal slunk closer and fearfully closer.

Robyn had fallen asleep beside her father's litter, still fully dressed and in a sitting position; she merely let her head fall forward on to her crossed arms and then overwhelmed by fatigue and worry and guilt she at last succumbed.

She awoke to the old man's shrill shrieks. There was complete darkness blanketing the camp, and Robyn thought for a moment that she was blinded by a nightmare. She scrambled wildly to her feet, not certain where she was and she stumbled over the litter. Her outflung arms brushed against something big and hairy, something that stank of death and excrement, a smell that blended sickeningly with the stench of her father's leg.

She screamed also, and the animal growled, a muffled sound through clenched jaws like a wolfhound with a bone. Fuller's shrieks and her screams had roused the camp, and somebody plunged a torch of dried grass into the ashes of the watch fire. It burst into flames, and after the utter blackness the orange light seemed bright as noonday.

The huge hump-backed animal had dragged Fuller from his litter in a welter of blankets and clothing. It had a grip on his lower body, and Robyn heard the sharp crack of bone splintering in those terrible jaws. The sound maddened her and she snatched up an axe that lay beside the pile of firewood and struck out at the dark misshapen body, feeling the axe strike solidly, and the hyena let out a choking howl.

The darkness and its own starvation had emboldened it. It had the taste in its mouth now, seeping through the blankets into its locked jaws and it would not relinquish its prey.

It turned and snapped at Robyn, its huge round eyes glowing yellow in the light of the flames and those terrible yellowed fangs clashing like the snap of a steel man-trap, closing on the axe handle inches from her fingers, jerking it out of her hand. Then it turned back to its prey, and once more locked its jaws onto the frail body. Fuller was so wasted that he was light as a child and the hyena dragged him swiftly towards the opening in the thorn *scherm*.

Still screaming for help, Robyn stumbled after them and seized her father's shoulders, while the hyena had him by the belly. The woman and the animal fought over him, the blunted yellow teeth ripping and tearing through the lining of Fuller's belly as the hyena strained back on its hindquarters, the neck stretched out at the pull.

The Hottentot Corporal dressed only in unlaced breeches, but brandishing his musket, ran towards them in the firelight.

'Help me,' screamed Robyn. The hyena had reached the thorn fence, her feet were slipping in the loose dust, she was not able to hold Fuller.

'Don't shoot!' Robyn screamed. 'Don't shoot!' The danger from the musket was as great as from the animal.

The Corporal ran forward, reversing the musket and swung the butt at the hyena's head. It struck with a sharp crack of wood on bone, and the hyena released its grip. Finally, its natural cowardice overcame its greed. It turned and shambled through the opening in the thorn hedge and disappeared into the night.

'Oh, sweet merciful God,' Robyn whispered as they carried Fuller back to the litter, 'has he not suffered enough?'

Fuller Ballantyne lived out that night, but an hour after dawn that tenacious and tough old man at last relinquished his grip on life without having regained consciousness. It was as though a legend had passed, and an age had died with him. It left Robyn feeling numbed and disbelieving and she washed and dressed the frail and rotting husk for burial.

She buried him at the foot of a tall mukusi tree and carved into the bark with her own hand:

FULLER MORRIS BALLANTYNE
3rd Nov. 1788 17th Oct. 1860
'In those days there were giants upon the earth.'

She wished that she had been able to cut the words in marble. She wished that she had been able to embalm his body and carry it back to rest where it belonged in the great Abbey of Westminster. She wished that he had recognized and known who she was just once before he died, she wished she had been able to allay his suffering, and she was consumed with grief and guilt.

For three days she maintained the camp astride the Hyena Road, and she spent those days sitting listlessly beside the mound of newly turned earth under the mukusi tree. She drove old Karanga and even little Juba away, for she needed to be alone.

On the third day she knelt beside the grave and she spoke aloud. 'I make an oath to your memory, my dear father. I swear that I will devote my entire life to this land and its people, just as you did before me.'

Then she rose to her feet and her jaw-line hardened. The time for mourning was past. Now her duty lay plain before her – to follow this Hyena Road to the sea, and then to bear witness before all the world against the monsters who used it.

When the lions are hunting, the prey animals seem able to sense it. They are seized by a restlessness and will graze for only seconds at a time before throwing up their horned heads and freezing into that peculiar antelope stillness, only the wide trumpet-shaped ears moving incessantly; then, skittering like thrown dice, they rearrange themselves upon the grassy plains, snorting and nervous, aware of danger but uncertain of its exact source.

Old Karanga had the same instinct bred into him for he was Mashona, an eater of dirt, and as such he was natural prey. He was the first to become aware that there were Matabele somewhere close at hand. He became silent, nervous and watchful, and it infected the other bearers.

Robyn saw him pick a broken ostrich plume from the grass beside the path and study it gravely, puckering his lips and hissing quietly to himself. It had not fallen from the wing of a bird.

That night he voiced his fears to Robyn.

'They are here, the stabbers of women, the abductors of children—' He spat into the fire with a bravado that was hollow as a dead tree-trunk.

'You are under my protection,' Robyn told him. 'You and all the people in this caravan.'

But when they met the Matabele war party, it was without further warning, in the dawn when the Matabele always attack.

Suddenly they were there, surrounding the camp, a solid phalanx of dappled shields and nodding plumes, the blades of the broad stabbing assegai catching the early light. Old Karanga had gone in the night, and with him had gone all the other porters and bearers. Except for the Hottentots the camp was deserted.

Karanga's warning had not been in vain, however, and behind the thorn *scherm* all the Hottentot guards were standing to their muskets, with their bayonets fixed.

The encircling Matabele stood silent, and still as statues carved from black marble. There seemed to be thousands upon thousands of them – though common sense told Robyn that it was merely a trick of her heated imagination and the poor light. A hundred, at the most two hundred, she decided.

Beside her Juba whispered, 'We are safe, Nomusa. We are beyond the Burnt Land, beyond the border of my people. They will not kill us.'

Robyn wished she was as confident, and she shivered briefly, not merely from the dawn chill.

'See, Nomusa,' Juba insisted. 'The baggage boys are with them, and many of the *amadoda* carry their *isibamu* (firearms). If they intended to fight, they would not so burden themselves.'

Robyn saw that the girl was right, some of the warriors had rusty trade muskets slung upon their shoulders, and she remembered from her grandfather's writings that whenever the Matabele intended serious fighting they handed their muskets, which they neither trusted nor used with any accuracy, to the baggage boys and relied entirely upon the weapon that their ancestors had forged and perfected, the assegai of Chaka Zulu.

'The baggage boys carry trade goods, they are a trading party,' Juba whispered. The baggage boys were the young apprentice warriors, and beyond the ranks of fighting men they were still in column. As soon as Robyn recognized the boxes and bundles that the baggage boys carried balanced on their heads, her last qualms faded to be replaced by anger.

They were traders, that she was sure of now, and returning along the road from the east there was little doubt in Robyn's mind as to what they had traded for these paltry wares.

'Slavers!' she snapped. 'In God's name and mercy, these are

the slavers we seek, returning from their filthy business. Juba, go and hide immediately,' she ordered,

Then, with her Sharps rifle tucked under her arm, she stepped out through the opening in the wall of thorn bush, and the nearest warriors in the circle lowered their shields a little and stared at her curiously. This small change in attitude confirmed Juba's guess, their intentions were not warlike.

'Where is your Induna?' Robyn called, her voice sharp with her anger, and now their curiosity gave way to astonishment, Their ranks swayed and rustled, until a man came from amongst them, one of the most impressive men she had ever laid eyes upon.

There was no mistaking his nobility of bearing, the arrogance and pride of a warrior tried in battle and covered in honours. He stopped before her and when he spoke his voice was low and calm. He did not have to raise it to be heard.

'Where is your husband, white woman?' he asked. 'Or your father?'

'I speak for myself, and all my people.'

'But you are a woman,' the tall Induna contradicted her.

'And you are a slaver,' Robyn flared at him, 'a dealer in women and children.'

The warrior stared at her for a moment, then lifted his chin and laughed, it was a low clear musical sound.

'Not only a woman,' he laughed, 'but an insolent one also.'

He shifted his shield on to his shoulder and strode past her. He was so tall that Robyn had to lift her chin to look up at him. He moved with a sinuous balance and assurance of carriage. The muscles in his back shone as though they were covered in black velvet, the tall plumes of his headdress nodded and the war rattles on his ankles whispered with each pace.

Swiftly he moved through the gap in the thorn hedge and at Robyn's gesture the Hottentot Corporal lifted the point of his bayonet into the 'present' position and stepped back to let the Induna pass.

With a sweeping gaze the Induna took in the condition of the camp and laughed again.

'Your bearers have run,' he said. 'Those Mashona jackals can smell a real man a day's march away.'

Robyn had followed him into the camp and now she demanded with anger that was not feigned,

'By what right do you enter my kraal and terrify my people?'

The Induna turned back to her.

'I am the King's man,' he said. 'On the King's business.' As though that was all the explanation that was necessary.

Gandang, the Induna, was a son of Mzilikazi, the King and Paramount Chief of the Matabele and all the subservient tribes.

His mother was of pure Zanzi blood, the old pure blood of the south, but she was a junior wife and as such, Gandang would never aspire to his father's estate.

However, he was one of his father's favourites. Mzilikazi, who mistrusted nearly all of his sons, and most of his hundreds of wives, trusted this son, not only because he was beautiful and clever and a warrior without fear, but because he lived in strict accordance with the law and custom of his people, and because of his unquestioned and oft-proven loyalty to his father and his King.

For this and for his deeds, he was covered in honours to which the ox-tail tassels on his arms and his legs bore witness. At four and twenty summers, he was the youngest *indoda* ever to be granted the head-ring of the Induna and a place on the high council of the nation, where his voice was listened to with serious attention even by the old grey pates.

The ageing King, crippled with gout, turned more and more towards this tall and straight young man when there was a difficult task, or a bitter battle in the offing.

So when Mzilikazi learned of the treachery of one of his Indunas, a man who commanded the border guards of the south and eastern strip of the Burnt Land, he had not hesitated before summoning Gandang, the trusted son.

'Bopa, son of Bakweg, is a traitor.'

It was a mark of Gandang's favour that his father condescended to explain his orders as he issued them.

'At first, as he was ordered, he slew those who trespassed in the Burnt Land, then he grew greedy. Instead of killing, he took them as cattle and sold them in the east to the *Putukezi* (Portuguese) and the *Sulumani* (Arabs) and sent word to me that they were dead.' The old King shifted his swollen and painful joints and took snuff, before going on,

'Then because Bopa was a greedy man, and the men with whom he deals are greedy also, he began to seek other cattle to trade. On his own account, and secretly, he began to raid the tribes beyond the Burnt Land.'

Gandang, kneeling before his father, had hissed with astonishment. It was contrary to law and custom, for the tribes of the Mashona beyond the Burnt Land were the King's 'cattle', to be raided only at the King's direction. For another to usurp the powers and gather the booty that belonged to the King was the worst form of treason.

'Yes, my son,' the King agreed with Gandang's horror. 'But his greed was without frontiers. He hungered for the baubles and the trash which the *Sulumani* brought him, and when this supply of Mashona "cattle" was not enough, then he turned upon his own people.'

The King was silent and his expression one of deep regret, for though he was a despot with powers that were subject to neither check nor limitation, although his justice and his laws were savage, yet within those laws he was a just man.

'Bopa sent to me messengers accusing our own people, some of them nobles of Zanzi blood, one of treachery, another of witchcraft, another of stealing from the royal herds – and I sent the messengers back to Bopa ordering him to slay the offenders. But they were not slain. They, and all their people were taken along the road that Bopa had opened to the east. Now their bodies will not be buried in this land and their spirits will wander homelessly for all time.'

That was a terrible fate, and the King lowered his chin upon his chest, and brooded on it. Then he sighed and lifted his head. It was a small neat head and his voice was high-pitched, almost womanish, not that of a mighty conqueror and a warrior without fear.

'Take your spear to the traitor, my son, and when you have killed him, return to me.'

When Gandang would have crawled from his presence, the King halted him with one finger raised.

'When you have killed Bopa, you and those of your *amadoda* who are with you when the deed is done may go in to the women.'

It was the permission for which Gandang had waited for so many years, the highest privilege, the right to go in to the women and take wives.

Gandang shouted his father's praises as he crawled backwards from the royal presence.

Then Gandang, the loyal son, had done what his father commanded. He had carried his spear of retribution swiftly across all of Matabeleland, across the Burnt Land, and along the Hyena Road until he had met Bopa returning from the east laden with the spoils he so dearly coveted.

They had met at a pass through a line of granite hills, not a day's march from where Gandang now confronted Robyn Ballantyne.

Gandang's *Inyati* impi (buffalo) in their ostrich plumes and civet-tail skirts, carrying the dappled black and white oxhide shields had surrounded the slave-guards formed from selected warriors of Bopa's *Inhlambene* impi (the Swimmers). The slavers wore white egret plumes and kilts of monkey tails, while their war shields were of chocolate-red oxhide – but right was on the side of the Inyati, and after the swift *jikela* (encirclement) they raced in to crush the guilty and confused slave-guards in a few terrible unholy minutes of battle.

Gandang himself had engaged the grizzle-headed but powerfully built Bopa. He was a wily, scarred fighter and veteran of a thousand such conflicts. Their shields, the one dappled black and the other red, collided with a thud like charging bulls, and they wrestled for the advantage until Gandang, the younger and stronger, with a shift of weight and feet had hooked the point of his shield under the red shield of Bopa and prised it aside to open his enemy's flank.

'*Ngidla* – I have eaten!' Gandang sang out as he sent the broad blade cleaving between Bopa's ribs, and when it was withdrawn against the reluctant cling of flesh with a sucking noise like a man walking in thick ankle-deep mud, Bopa's heart blood burst out behind it and splattered against Gandang's shield, drenching the ox tail tassels on his arms and his legs.

Thus it was for good reason that Gandang had laughed when Robyn called him 'Slaver'.

'I am on the King's business,' he repeated. 'But what do you do here, white woman?' He knew very little of these strange people, for he had been a child when the impis of Mzilikazi had fought them in the land to the south, and had been driven by them northwards into what was now Matabeleland.

Gandang had met only one or two of them. They had been

visitors to his father's great kraal at Thabas Indunas, travellers and traders and missionaries who had been 'given the road' by the King and allowed to cross the strictly guarded frontiers.

Gandang was suspicious of them and their gaudy trade goods. He distrusted their habit of breaking pieces off the rocks along their path, he disliked their talk of a white man who lived in the sky and seemed to be in serious competition with the 'Nkulu-kulu', the great God of the Matabele.

Had he met this woman and her followers in the Burnt Land, he would have followed his orders without hesitation, and killed them all.

However, they were still ten days' march from the frontier and his interest in them was casual; he was impatient to return to his father and report to him the success of his expedition. He would not waste much further time.

'What is your business, woman?'

'I come to tell you that the Great Queen will no longer allow human beings to be sold like cattle for a few beads. I come to put an end to this evil business.'

'That is man's work,' Gandang smiled. 'And besides, it has already been seen to.'

The woman amused him, at another time he might have enjoyed bantering with her.

He would have turned and strode from the camp when suddenly a small movement seen through a gap in the thin thatch of one of the temporary shelters caught his attention. With uncanny speed for such a big man, he ducked into the hut and pulled the girl out by her wrist; holding her at arm's length he studied Juba gravely.

'You are of the people, you are Matabele,' he said flatly.

Juba hung her head and her face had a pale greyish sheen of terror. For a moment Robyn thought that Juba's legs would no longer bear her weight.

'Speak,' Gandang commanded in that low but imperious voice. 'You are Matabele!'

Juba looked up at him and her whisper was so soft that Robyn hardly caught it.

'Matabele,' she agreed, 'of Zanzi blood.'

The warrior and the maid considered each other carefully. Juba lifted her chin, and the greyness vanished from her face.

'Your father?' Gandang asked at last.

'I am Juba, daughter of Tembu Tebe.'

'He is dead, and all his children, at the King's orders.'

Juba shook her head. 'My father is dead – but his wives and his children are in the land of the *Sulumani* beyond the sea. I alone escaped.'

'Bopa!' Gandang said the name as though it were a curse. He considered a moment. 'It is possible that your father was wrongly sentenced, for Bopa sent false accusation to the King.'

Juba made no reply, but in the silence that followed, Robyn saw a subtle change coming over the girl, something altered in the carriage of her head, she shifted her weight, thrusting out one hip, a small but provocative movement.

Her eyes, when she looked up at the tall Induna, grew wider and softer, and her lips were held slightly apart so that the pink tip of her tongue just showed between them.

'What is this white woman to you?' Gandang asked, and there was just a trace of huskiness in his own voice. He held her wrist still, and she made no effort to pull away.

'She is as my mother was,' Juba replied, and as the Induna looked down from her face to her sweet young body the ostrich plumes fanned softly about his head, and Juba changed the angle of her shoulders slightly, offering up her breasts to his gaze.

'You are with her by your own will?' Gandang insisted, and Juba nodded.

'So be it.' It seemed to require an effort for the warrior to break his gaze, but he dropped Juba's wrist and turned back to Robyn. His smile was mocking once more.

'The slavers you seek are not far from here, white woman. You will find them at the next pass in the road.'

He went as swiftly and as silently as he had come, and his warriors followed him in a dense black column. Within minutes the last of them had disappeared along the winding narrow trail into the west.

Old Karanga was the first of the servants to return to the camp. He came in through the thorn *scherm* like a bashful stork on his thin legs.

'Where were you when I needed you?' Robyn demanded.

'Nomusa, I could not trust my temper with those Matabele dogs,' old Karanga quavered, but he could not meet her eyes.

Within the hour the other porters and bearers had crept down from the hills and out of the forest, all of them now endowed with amazing enthusiasm to continue the march in the opposite direction to that of the *Inyati* impi.

Robyn found the slavers where Gandang had promised her she would. They were scattered over the neck of the pass, they lay in knots and windrows, like leaves after the first storm of autumn. Nearly all of them had their death wounds in the chest or throat, proof that at the end they had fought like Matabele.

The victors had slit open the dead men's bellies to allow their spirits to escape, a last courtesy to men who had fought gallantly, but the vultures had used the openings to enter the belly pouches.

The birds hopped and flapped and squabbled raucously over the cadavers, tugging and dragging at them so that their dead limbs kicked and twitched as though they were still alive, and dust and loose feathers flew around them. The croaking and squawking of the birds was deafening.

In the trees and on the cliffs above the pass, the birds that had already gorged crouched somnolently, puffing out their feathers and hunching their naked scaly heads and necks upon their shoulders, digesting the contents of their bulging crops before returning to the feast.

The little caravan passed slowly, in fascinated horror at the carnage, speechless in the raucous chorus of the scavengers, stepping carefully over the ragged, dust-covered remains of brave men, reminded by them of their own mortality.

Once they had crossed the pass they hurried down the far slope with fearful backward glances. There was a stream at the bottom of the slope, a tiny trickle of clear water springing from the slope and threading its way from pool to small shaded pool. Robyn went into camp upon the bank, and immediately called Juba to follow her.

She had to bathe herself, she felt as though death had touched her with its putrid fingertips and she needed to wash away the taint of it. She sat under the trickle of clear water, waist deep in the pool below the waterfall and let the stream flow over her head, her eyes closed trying to blank out the horrors of the battlefield. Juba was not so affected, she was no stranger to death in its most malevolent forms, and she splashed and played in the green water, completely absorbed in the moment.

At last Robyn waded to the bank, and pulled her shirt and breeches over her still-wet body. In that heat, her clothes would dry upon her within minutes, and while she twisted her wet hair into a rope on top of her head she called to Juba to come out of the pool.

In a mischievous and rebellious mood the girl ignored her, and remained rapt in her own game, singing softly as she picked wild flowers from a creeper that hung over the pool and plaited them into a necklace over her shoulders. Robyn turned away and left her, climbing back along the bank towards the camp, and the first turn hid her from view.

Now Juba looked up and hesitated. She was not certain why she had refused to obey, and she felt a little chill of disquiet at being alone. She was not yet accustomed to this new mood of hers, this strange and formless excitement, this breathless expectancy for she knew not what. With a toss of her head she returned to her song and her play.

Standing above the bank, half screened by the trailing creeper and mottled like a leopard by the slanting dappled sunlight through the leaves of the forest, a tall figure leaned against the bole of a wild fig tree and watched the girl.

He had stood there, unseen and unmoving since he had been led to the pool by the sound of splashing and singing. He had watched the two women, comparing their nakedness – the bloodless white against the luscious dark skin, the skinny angular frame against sweet and abundant flesh, the small pointed breasts tipped in the obscene pink of raw meat against the full and perfect rounds with their raised bosses, dark and shiny as new-washed coal, the narrow hips of a boy against the proud wide basin which would cradle fine sons, the mean little buttocks against the fullness and glossiness that was unmistakably woman.

Gandang was aware that by returning along the trail he was for the first time in his life neglecting his duty. He should have been many hours' march away from this place, trotting at the head of his impi into the west, yet there was this madness in his blood, that he had not been able to deny. So he had halted his impi and returned alone along the Hyena Road.

'I am stealing the King's time, just as surely as Bopa stole his cattle,' he told himself. 'But it is only a small part of a single day, and after all the years I have given to my father, he would not grudge me that.' But Gandang knew that he would, favourite son or not, Mzilikazi had only one punishment for disobedience.

Gandang was risking his life to see the girl again, he was risking a traitor's death to speak a few words to a stranger, daughter of one who had himself died a traitor's death.

'How many men have dug their graves with their own *umthondo*,' he mused, as he waited for the white woman to leave the pool, and when she had covered her skinny boy's body with those stiff and ugly garments and called to the lovely child in the pool to follow her, Gandang tried to reach out with his own will to hold Juba there.

The white woman, clearly piqued, turned and disappeared amongst the trees and Gandang relaxed slightly, giving himself once more to the pleasure of watching the girl in the water. The wild flowers were a pale yellow against her skin, and the waterdrops clung to her breasts and shoulders like stars against the midnight sky. Juba was singing one of the children's songs that Gandang knew so well, and he found himself humming the chorus under his breath.

Below him the girl waded to the bank and standing in the sugar-white sand began to wipe the water from her body; still singing she bent forward to wipe her legs, encircling them with long slim pink-lined fingers and running her hands slowly down from thigh to ankle. Her back was to Gandang, and as she stooped he gasped aloud at what was revealed to him, and instantly the girl flew erect and spun to face him. She was trembling like a roused fawn, her eyes huge and dark with fright.

'I see you, Juba, daughter of Tembu Tebe,' he said, there was a husky catch to his voice as he came down the bank to her.

The expression in her eyes changed, they glowed with golden lights like sunshine in a bowl of honey.

'I am a messenger of the King, and I demand the right of the road,' he said, and touched her shoulder. She shivered under his fingers. He saw the little goose bumps rise upon her skin.

The 'right of the road' was a custom from the south, from the old country beside the sea. It was the same right which Senzangakhona had demanded of Nandi, 'the sweet one', but Senzangakhona had not respected the law, and he had penetrated the forbidden veil. From this transgression one had been born, the bastard 'Chaka', 'the worm in the belly', who had grown to become both the King and the scourge of Zululand, the same Chaka from whose tyranny Mzilikazi had flown with his tribe to the north.

'I am a loyal maiden of the King,' Juba answered him shyly, 'and I cannot refuse to comfort one who follows the road on the King's business.' Then she smiled up at him. It was neither bold nor provocative, but a smile so sweet, so trusting and filled with admiration, that Gandang felt his heart squeezed afresh.

He was gentle with her, very gentle and calm and patient, so that she found herself impatient to render the service he desired, found herself desiring it as strongly as he so evidently did. When he showed her how to make a nest for him between her crossed thighs, she responded instantly to his word and touch, and there was something wrong with her throat and her breathing, for she was unable to answer him aloud.

While she held him in this nest she felt herself gradually overwhelmed by a strange wildness of heart and body. She tried to alter the angle of her pelvis, she tried to unlock her tightly crossed thighs and spread them for him, she strove to engulf him for she could no longer bear that dry and tantalizing friction against the inside of her upper legs. She wanted to feel him breast the warm and welcoming flood that she sent down for him and she wanted to feel him gliding upon it deeply up inside her. But his resolve, his respect for custom and law, was as powerful as that muscular body that drove above her, and he held her captive until the moment when she felt his grip break and his seed spring strongly from him to waste itself in the white sand beneath them. At that moment she felt such a sense of loss that she could have wept aloud.

Gandang held her still, his chest heaving and the sweat forming little shiny runnels across that smooth dark back and down the corded neck. Juba clung to him with both arms wrapped tightly about him, her face pressed into the hollow between his shoulder and his neck, and for a long time neither of them spoke.

'You are as soft and as beautiful as the first night of the new moon,' Gandang whispered at last.

'And you are as black and as strong as the bull of the *Chawala* festival,' she instinctively chose the simile that would mean most to a Matabele, the bull as the symbol of wealth and virility and the *Chawala* bull the most perfect specimen of all the King's herds.

'You will be only one of many wives,' Robyn was horrified at the thought.

'Yes.' agreed Juba. 'First of all of them, and the others will honour me.'

'I would have taken you with me to teach you many things and show you great wonders.'

'I have already seen the greatest wonder.'

'You will do nothing but bear children.'

Juba nodded happily. 'If I am truly lucky, I will bear him a hundred sons.'

'I will miss you.'

'I would never leave you, Nomusa, my mother, not for any person nor reason in the world, except this one.'

'He wants to give me cattle.'

'Since the death of my family, you are my mother,' explained Juba, 'and it is the marriage price.'

'I cannot accept payment – as though you were a slave.'

'Then you demean me. I am of Zanzi blood and he tells me that I am the most beautiful woman in Matabeleland. You should set the *lobolu* as one hundred head of cattle.'

So Robyn called the Induna to her.

'The marriage price is one hundred head of cattle,' Robyn told him sternly.

'You make a poor bargain,' Gandang answered loftily. 'She is worth many times that amount.'

'You will keep the cattle at your kraal, against my coming. You will tend them carefully and see that they multiply.'

'It will be as you say, *amekazi*, my mother.' And this time Robyn had to return his smile, for it was no longer mocking and his teeth were so white and he was, as Juba had said, truly beautiful.

'Look after her well, Gandang.'

Robyn embraced the young woman and their tears mingled and smeared both their cheeks. Yet when she left Juba did not look back once, but trotted behind Gandang's tall erect figure carrying her rolled sleeping-mat balanced upon her head, and her buttocks jiggled merrily under the short beaded apron.

Man and woman reached the saddle of the pass and disappeared abruptly from view.

The Hyena Road led Robyn and her little party into the mountains, into the mist and the strangely desolate valleys of heather and fantastically shaped grey stone. It led her to the slave stockades which Juba had described to her, the meeting-place where the white man and black man made their trade for human life, where the slaves exchanged their carved yokes for cuff and chains. But now the stockades were deserted, the thatch already sagging and falling in untidy clumps, only the sour smell of captivity lingered, and the swarming vermin that infected the empty buildings. In a futile gesture, Robyn put fire to the buildings.

From the misty mountains the road led on, down through dark gorges and at last to the low littoral where once more the heat clamped down upon them from a sullen overcast sky and the grotesque baobab trees lifted their twisted arthritic branches to it like crippled worshippers at a healing shrine.

The rains caught them here upon the coastal plain. The flood swept three men away at a ford, four more, including one of the Hottentots, died of fever and Robyn herself was smitten with the first onslaught of the disease. Shivering, half demented by the phantoms of malaria, she toiled on along the rapidly overgrown trail, slipping and stumbling in the mud, and cursing the fever miasma that rose from the brimming swamps and hung like a silver wraith in the sickly green glades of fever trees through which they hurried.

Fever and the rigours of the last stage of the journey had tired and weakened them all. They knew that they were, at the most, only a few days' march from the coast, deep into Portuguese territory and therefore under the protection of a Christian king and a government of civilized men. It was for these reasons that the Hottentot sentries slept beside the smouldering watch fire of damp wood, and it was there that they died, their throats slit with a blade sharp enough to cut off the least cry.

So Robyn woke to rough hands upon her, twisting her arms

up between her shoulder blades and a bony knee in the small of her back, while steel cuffs clicked coldly about her wrists. Then the hands released her and she was wrenched cruelly to her feet, and dragged from the leaky hut beside the Hyena Road.

The previous evening she had been too tired and feverish to undress, so now she was still clad in a stained and rumpled flannel shirt and patched moleskin breeches. She had even kept the cloth cap on her head, covering her hair, thus in the darkness her captors did not realize that she was a woman.

She was bound with her own porters and Hottentots, forced to wear the light marching chains which were proof, if proof was needed, as to who her captors were. The dawn revealed them to be half-breeds and blacks, all of them dressed in the cast-off finery of European style, but carrying modern weapons.

These were the men she had crossed half a continent to meet, but now she cowered in the rags that were her only disguise. She shuddered to think on her fate if they should discover her sex, and she berated herself for having so blithely believed that she and her entourage would be safe from these predators merely because she was white and English. Their prey was human flesh, of whatever colour and condition and that was all she was now, human flesh on the hoof. A chained creature, of little real value, a few dollars on the auction block, and she knew that her captors would think nothing of taking their pleasure upon her, or of leaving her beside the road with a ball through the temple if she provoked them in any way. She kept silent and obeyed instantly the least word or gesture from her captors. Slipping and dragging in the mud they were marched on eastwards, forced to carry their remaining stores and equipment which had now become slavers' booty.

They were closer to the coast than Robyn had calculated, they smelt the iodine and salt of the sea from afar, and later as night began to fall, they caught the smell of woodsmoke and the unmistakable odour of captive humanity. Then at last they saw the firelight flickering in the darkness ahead, and the awful loom of the barracoons.

Their captors marched between the dark stockades of pole and daubed mud, from which the chilling dirge rose of men without hope singing of a land they would never see again.

At last they came into the central square around which the barracoons were built. It was an open area of trampled mud where a raised platform of rough-sawn planks had been built. Its purpose was immediately clear, for the first of Robyn's servants was dragged up the steps and stood upon the platform, while the fires around the clearing were heaped with dry wood to light the scene. The platform was the auction block, and it seemed that the sale was to take place immediately.

The auctioneer was clearly of pure Portuguese stock, a little man with the wrinkled, sun-browned face of a vicious gnome. He had the bland smile and the unblinking eyes of a serpent. He was dressed in elegantly cut jacket and breeches, and his boots and belt were of the finest Iberian leather, ornately tooled and with solid silver buckles. He carried a pair of expensive pistols in his belt, and wore the wide-brimmed flat-crowned hat of a Portuguese gentleman upon his small wrinkled head.

Before climbing up on the block, he sent one of his personal slaves with a casual kick and cuff to the carved wooden drum at the edge of the clearing. On it the slave began pounding out a summons to the buyers. The slave went to it lustily, his bare torso gleaming with sweat and raindrops in the firelight.

And in answer to the urgent staccato rhythm of the drum, men came from out of the shadows of the grove and from the living huts between the barracoons. Some of them had been drinking, they came arm in arm brandishing their rum bottles and bellowing in drunken chorus, others came singly and silently – but they came from every direction and gathered in a circle about the auction block.

The men who formed the circle seemed to be of every hue that the human skin is capable of assuming, from purple black through all the shades of brown and yellow to dead shark's belly white, and their features were African and Arabic, Asian and European. Even their dress differed widely, from the flowing robes of Arabia to the faded finery of embroidered jackets and high boots. They had only one thing in common, the hawk-fierce eyes and merciless mien of those who deal in human misery.

One at a time Robyn's servants were prodded up on to the block, and their ragged clothing was ripped away to expose their physique to the buyers. One of these might come forward to feel the muscle tone, or force open a slave's mouth to examine the teeth, like a gypsy horse-dealer at the fair.

Then, when the buyers had satisfied themselves as to the

quality of the wares on offer, the small Portuguese would step lightly to the front of the block and begin the bidding.

The men in the circle below him called him Alphonse and though they exchanged coarse banter with him, yet they all treated him with wary respect, there could be no clearer proof of the man's reputation than fear and respect from these men.

Under his control the sale went swiftly. The Hottentots, small wiry men, butter yellow and with flat pug-like features attracted little interest from the circle of buyers, knocked down for a few silver rupees apiece, while the porters, taller men and well muscled from many months of hard marching and porterage, fetched better prices – until they came to old Karanga, ancient and toothless, hobbling on to the block on storklike legs, seeming barely able to support the weight of his chains.

The laughter was derisive, and the little Portuguese pleaded in vain for a single bid before dismissing the old man with disgust. It was only when he was hauled down off the block and dragged away into the darkness beyond the fires that Robyn realized what was about to happen to him and, forgetting her resolve not to draw attention to herself, 'No – let him go!'

Hardly one of them glanced in her direction, and the man who held her chain hit her a careless open-handed blow across the side of her face that blinded her for a moment. She dropped to her knees in the mud, and through the buzzing in her ears heard the thud of a pistol shot from the darkness.

She began quietly to weep, and still weeping she was hoisted to her feet and in her turn dragged forward into the circle of firelight and hoisted by her chain on to the block.

'A young skinny one,' said the Portuguese. 'But white enough to make a choice bum-boy for the harems of Omani, once he has had his knackers clipped. Who will give me ten rupees?'

'Let's have a look at him,' a voice shouted from the circle, and the Portuguese turned to Robyn, hooked a finger into the top button of her flannel shirt and ripped it down to the level of her belt buckle.

She doubled over, trying to conceal her upper body, but the man behind her twisted the chain and forced her upright. Her breasts pushed out pertly through the torn shirt, and the ring of watchers growled and moved restlessly, the mood changing instantly.

Alphonse touched the butt of one of the pistols in his belt

significantly, and the growl of comment died, the ring of men drew back a little.

'Ten rupees?' Alphonse Pereira asked.

From across the circle a powerfully-built man swaggered into the firelight. Robyn recognized him instantly. He wore a tall beaver hat tilted back on his head, and from under the brim curled thick shiny black hair. His teeth, when he opened his mouth, sparkled in the light of the flames. His face was flushed with excitement, his voice was thick with it.

'Gold,' he shouted. 'I'll bid gold, a gold mohur of the East India Company, and a plague on any of you that goes above that.'

'A gold mohur,' called Alphonse, the slave-master. 'A gold mohur bid by my brother Camacho Pereira, and good luck to him,' he chuckled. 'Come now, who wants to deny my brother Camacho a fair tup at the wench?'

One of his men slapped Camacho's back.

'Sweet Christ, you always were a hot one, at that price you can have my turn on top of her.'

And Camacho laughed delightedly and came to the front of the block to stare up at Robyn, tipping the beaver hat forward he whispered,

'I've had to wait a long time—'

Robyn felt the little insects of loathing crawling over her skin, and she backed away to the limit of her chain.

'Come now,' Alphonse called. 'Who will go beyond a gold mohur for a fine piece—'

'She's mine,' Camacho told his brother. 'Strike the bargain.'

His brother lifted his hand to knock down the sale, when another voice stopped him.

'A double eagle, sir. Twenty golden dollars American bid.' The voice was not raised, yet it carried clearly to every man there, as it could carry from quarterdeck to maintop in a force eight gale.

Robyn started, and swung her chains disbelievingly in that direction; she would have known that lazy drawling inflection if she had not heard it for a lifetime. He stood at the very edge of the firelight, but as every head in the circle turned to him, he stepped forward.

The smile had frozen on Alphonse's face, and he hesitated.

'Call the bid!' The advancing figure in plain white shirt and dark breeches made the men about him seem small and grubby, and after a moment's hesitation, Alphonse obeyed him.

'A double eagle bid,' he said harshly. 'Captain Mungo St John of the clipper *Huron* bids a double golden eagle.'

Robyn felt her legs start to sag under her with relief, but the men behind her jerked her upright by her chain. Camacho Pereira had whirled to face the American, and to stare at him furiously. Mungo St John answered him with a smile, indulgent and patronizing. Robyn had never seen him look more handsome and dangerous, his dark wavy hair catching the firelight, and the gaze of his yellow-flecked eyes level and unflinching in the face of Camacho's fury.

'A thousand rupees, Camacho,' he said softly. 'Can you match it?'

Camacho hesitated, and then turned back quickly to his own brother, his voice low and urgent.

'Stake me?' he asked, and Alphonse laughed.

'I never lend money.'

'To a brother?' Camacho insisted.

'Especially not to a brother,' Alphonse answered. 'Let the wench go, you can buy a dozen better for fifty rupees each.'

'I must have her.' He whirled back to face Mungo St John. 'I must have her. It is a matter of honour. Do you understand?' He took the beaver from his head, and spun it away. One of his men caught it, and Camacho ran both hands through his thick black locks, and then stretched his arms down at his sides, flexing the fingers like a conjurer about to perform a sleight of hand.

'I will make one more bid,' he said ominously. 'I bid one mohur of gold – and ten inches of Toledo steel.' The knife seemed to appear in his hand from out of the air, he lifted the point to the level of Mungo St John's belt buckle.

'Walk away, Yankee, or I will take the woman *and* your gold double eagle.'

The watchers growled, a low blood-thirsty sound, and swiftly rearranged themselves into a ring about the two men, jostling for a better view.

'One hundred rupees says Machito slits the Yankee's guts.'

'Done!' And there was a rising hubbub as the wagers were called and accepted.

Mungo St John had not stopped smiling, but now he held out

his right hand without once taking his eyes off the Portuguese's face.

Out of the ranks of the watchers emerged a large, toadlike figure with a head as round and bald as a cannon ball. Tippoo moved with reptilian speed to Mungo St John's right side. He placed a knife in the outstretched hand, and then unknotted the embroidered sash from his waist and handed that to his Captain. Mungo wrapped the sash around his left forearm, still smiling softly to himself.

He had not once looked up at Robyn, though she had not been able to tear her own eyes from his face.

He seemed godlike to her at that moment, everything about him, the darkly classical features, the wide shoulders under the white cloth of his shirt, the narrow waist clinched with a broad belt of polished leather, the strong straight legs in tightly fitted breeches and soil leather boots, seemed to have come down directly from Olympus. She would have gladly thrown herself at his feet and worshipped him.

Just below Robyn, Camacho was stripping off his own jacket and wrapping his guard arm with it. Then with the long knife in his right hand he made a low swift cut, forehand and then backhand, so the steel whispered as it dissolved into a silver blur like the wing of a dragonfly in flight. At each stroke he ducked his head slightly and flexed his knees, loosening and warming his muscles like an athlete before the contest.

Then he moved forward, stepping lightly in the treacherous mud and weaving the point of the knife to distract and intimidate his adversary.

The smile went from Mungo St John's lips, to be replaced by a grave and attentive expression, like a mathematician considering a complex problem. He kept his own knife low, advancing his wrapped forearm, and balancing easily, stood his full height and turned gently to face the Portuguese as he circled. It reminded Robyn of the night she had watched him on the dance floor at Admiralty House, so tall and graceful, so balanced and controlled in each movement.

Now at last the watchers were silent, straining eagerly for the first glimpse of blood, but when Camacho charged they roared the way the crowd roars when the bull first bursts into the ring. Mungo St John barely seemed to move, swaying his body at the hips so the knife slid past him, and then he was facing Camacho again.

Twice more the Portuguese attacked, and both times Mungo St John moved effortlessly aside, but each time he gave a little ground, until he was backed up to the first rank of watchers, they began to fall back to give the American room to fight, but Camacho saw his opportunity as Mungo was crowded like a prize-fighter against the ropes and he swung back to attack. At the same moment, almost as though it had been rehearsed, a booted foot shot out from the crowd.

Nobody was sure whose foot it was, for the throng was closely packed and the light uncertain, but the kick to the back of Mungo St John's heel almost brought him down sprawling in the mud, he lunged to catch his balance, but before he could do so, Camacho hit him with the long bright blade. Robyn screamed and Mungo St John spun away from the sting of the steel with scarlet spreading wetly down his shirt-front like rich Burgundy wine spilled on a damask tablecloth, and his own knife flicked out of his hand and was lost in the red mud.

The crowd bellowed, and Camacho swarmed in eagerly, following the wounded man the way a good dog hunts a pheasant with a broken wing.

Mungo was forced to give him ground, falling back, clutching the wound, dodging and weaving, catching a forehand slash on his wrapped guard arm so the embroidered cloth split almost to the flesh beneath it.

Skilfully Camacho herded him towards the auction block, and when Mungo felt the poles catch in the small of his back, he froze for a moment as he realized that he was trapped. Camacho drove in at him, going for the belly, his lips drawn back baring his perfect white teeth.

Mungo St John caught the knife on his guard and then snatched a grip on the wrist with his right hand. The two men stood chest to chest, their arms entwined like vines on a trellis, swaying slightly as they strained together, and the effort brought a fresh flood of bright blood from Mungo's wound, but slowly he forced Camacho's knife hand upwards, bending it at the elbow, until the point was no longer aimed at Mungo's belly but at the night sky above them.

Mungo shifted his feet, gathering himself and then his face darkened, his jaw clenched and his breath sobbed with effort.

Slowly Camacho's wrist gave to the pressure, and his eyes widened as the point of his own knife reversed towards him.

Now he also was wedged against the side of the auction block and could not break away, and infinitely slowly but inexorably, the long blade moved towards his own chest. Both men stared down at it, their hands and arms interlocked, pitting their strength to hold each other, but the point touched Camacho's chest, a drop of blood welled up at the tiny prick.

On the block beside Robyn, Alphonse Pereira drew the pistol from his belt with a furtive movement – but before she could shout a warning there was a blur of movement and Tippoo the mate towered beside him, his own huge smooth-bore pistol pressed to the side of Alphonse's skull. The little Portuguese rolled his eyes sideways at Tippoo, and then hurriedly returned the weapon to his belt, and Robyn could watch again with fascinated horror the contest at her feet.

Mungo St John's face was congested with dark blood, every muscle in his shoulders and arms raised in knots under the thin shirt, his whole existence concentrated on the knife, and he slid his left foot back until it was anchored against the auction block, and then using it as a pivot hurled all his weight forward on to the knife, the final effort like the matador going over between the horns for the kill.

For a moment longer Camacho resisted him, and then the blade resumed its forward movement entering Camacho's chest as slowly as a python swallows a gazelle.

Camacho's mouth opened in a cawing burst of despair, and suddenly his fingers opened as all resistance and strength went out of them. His own blade with Mungo St John's full weight behind it shot its length into his chest with such force that the cross piece of the hilt struck against his ribs with a sharp thump.

Mungo St John released his grip and let him fall, face forward into the mud, while he himself caught at the edge of the auction block for support. Only then did he lift his chin to look up at Robyn.

'Your servant, ma'am,' he murmured, and Tippoo rushed forward to catch him before he fell.

Huron's seamen, all of them armed, formed a guard about them, and Tippoo led them holding aloft a bull's-eye lantern which he shone into the shadows as they hurried down the path.

Mungo St John was on his feet, but supported by Nathaniel, his bosun, and Robyn had bound up the wound roughly with a strip of linen torn from a seaman's shirt and had used the rest of the shirt to make a sling for Mungo's right arm.

Through a grove of mangroves they reached the bank of the creek on which the barracoons had been built and in the centre of the stream, her bare masts and yards silhouetted against the starry sky, lay the lovely clipper.

She had lanterns in her rigging and an alert anchor watch, for at Tippoo's first hail the whaler swung away from her side and was rowed swiftly to the bank where they stood.

Mungo climbed the ship's side unaided, but sank down with a grateful sigh on to his bunk in the stern cabin, the bunk that Robyn remembered so vividly.

She tried to force the memory from her mind, and keep her manner brisk and businesslike.

'They have taken my medical chest,' she said as she rinsed her hands in the porcelain basin at the head of the bunk.

'Tippoo.' Mungo looked up at his mate, and the bald, scarred head bobbed once and then Tippoo ducked out of the cabin. Mungo and Robyn were alone, and she tried to remain remote and professional as she made her first examination of the wound in good lantern light.

It was narrow, but very deep. She did not like the angle of the thrust, just below the collar bone but angled in towards the point of the shoulders.

'Can you move your fingers?' she asked. He lifted his hand towards her face and touched her cheek lightly.

'Yes,' he said, as he stroked her. 'Very easily.'

'Don't,' she said weakly.

'You are sick,' he said. 'So thin and pale.'

'It is nothing – lower your arm, please.'

She was terribly conscious of her matted hair and filthy mud-stained clothing, of the yellow tinges of fever on her skin and the dark smudges of fatigue and terror under her eyes.

'Fever?' he asked quietly, and she nodded as she went on working on the wound.

'Strange,' he murmured. 'It makes you seem so young, so fragile,' he paused, 'so lovely.'

'I forbid you to talk like that.' She felt flustered, uncertain of herself.

'I said I would not forget you,' he ignored the instruction, 'and I did not.'

'If you don't stop, I will leave immediately.'

'When I saw your face tonight in the light of the fires, I could not believe it was you, and at the same time it was as though all our lives we had a rendezvous to keep here tonight. As though it had been destined from the moment of our births.'

'Please,' she whispered, 'please stop.'

'That's better – please is better. Now I will stop.'

But he watched her face attentively as she worked. In the ship's medical chest which he kept in the locker below his bunk Robyn found most of what she needed.

He neither flinched nor grimaced as she laid the stitches in the wound, but went on watching her.

'You must rest now,' she said as she finished, and he lay back on the bunk. At last he looked tired and drained, and she felt a rush of gratitude, of pity, and of that other emotion which she had believed that she had long ago subdued.

'You saved me.' She dropped her eyes, no longer able to look at him and busied herself with repacking the ship's chest. 'I will always be grateful for that, just as I will always hate you for what you are doing here.'

'What am I doing here?' he challenged her lightly.

'Buying slaves,' she accused. 'Buying human lives, just as you bought me on the slaving block.'

'But for a much lower price,' he agreed as he closed his eyes. 'At twenty dollars gold a head there is not much profit in it, I assure you.'

She awoke in the small cabin, the same cabin in which she had sailed the length of the Atlantic Ocean and in the same narrow uncomfortable bunk.

It was like homecoming, and the first thing she saw after her eyes had adjusted to the harsh beam of sunlight through the skylight were the chests of her medical instruments, her remaining medicines and her few personal possessions.

She remembered the unspoken command that Mungo had

given to the mate the previous evening. Tippoo must have gone back ashore during the night, and she wondered what price he had paid or what threat he had made to get them back for her.

She rose swiftly from her bunk, ashamed of her sloth; whoever had left the chests, had also filled the enamel jug with fresh water. With relief she washed away the mud and filth and combed the tangles of her hair before finding worn but clean clothing in her chest. Then she hurried from her cabin down to the master's quarters. If Tippoo had been able to find her chests, then he might be able to find and free her people, the Hottentots and porters who had gone upon the auction block in the firelight.

Mungo's bunk was empty, the vest and bloodstained shirt bundled and thrown into a corner of the cabin, and the bedclothes in disarray. She turned swiftly for the deck, and as she came out into the sunlight she saw that it would be only a temporary respite from the monsoon, for already the thunderclouds were boiling up over the horizon.

She looked about her quickly. *Huron* lay in the centre of a broad estuary, with mangroves on each bank, and the bar and the open sea was not in sight, though the tide was ebbing, rustling down the ship's hull and leaving the mud flats half exposed.

There were other vessels in the roadstead, mostly big dhow-rigged buggaloos typical of the Arab coastal traders, but there was another fully rigged ship at anchor half a mile further downstream, flying the flag of Brazil at her peak. Even as Robyn paused to watch her, there came the clank of her capstan, and men ran up the ratlines and spread out along her yards. She was getting under way. Then Robyn realized that there was unusual activity all about her. Small boats were plying from the shore to the anchored dhows, and even on *Huron*'s deck there was a huddle of men on the quarter-deck.

Robyn turned towards them, and realized that the tallest of them was Mungo St John. His arm was in a sling and he looked drawn and pale, but his expression was forbidding, the dark curved brows drawn together in a frown, and the mouth a thin cruel line as he listened attentively to one of his seamen. So absorbed was he that he did not notice Robyn until she was only a few paces away. Then he swung towards her, and all the questions and demands stayed behind her lips for his voice was harsh.

'Your coming was an act of God, Doctor Ballantyne,' he said.

'Why do you say that?'

'There is a plague in the barracoons,' he said. 'Most of the other buyers are cutting their losses, and leaving.' He glanced downstream to where the Brazilian schooner had set reefed main and jib and was running down towards the bar and the open sea, and there was activity aboard most of the other vessels.

'But I have over a thousand prime blacks afattening ashore – and I'll be damned if I'll run now. At least, not until I know what it is.'

Robyn stared at him. Her mind was a whirl of doubts and fears. 'Plague' was a layman's word, it covered everything from the Black Death to syphilis, the grand pox, as it was called.

'I will go ashore immediately,' she said, and Mungo St John nodded.

'I thought you would say that,' he said, 'I will go with you.'

'No.' Her tone brooked no argument. 'You will aggravate that wound, and in your weakened condition you will be easy prey to this plague, whatever it is.' She glanced at Tippoo, and his face split laterally into that broad toadlike grin and he stepped up beside her.

'By God, ma'am, I've had them all,' said Nathaniel, the little pockmarked bosun. 'And none of them killed me yet.' And he stepped up to her other hand.

Robyn sat in the stern while Tippoo and Nathaniel handled the oars, and as they pulled across the ebb towards the shore the bosun explained what they would find ashore.

'Each of the traders has his own barracoon built and guarded by his own men,' he told Robyn. 'He buys from the Portos as the blackbirds are brought in.'

As Robyn listened to Nathaniel, she realized the answers to questions that had worried her and Zouga. This was the reason why Pereira had tried so desperately to persuade them not to bring the expedition south of the Zambezi river, and why, when all else had failed, he had attacked it with his armed brigands and tried to destroy it. He had been protecting his brother's trade routes and selling area. It was not mere avarice and lust, but a logical attempt to preserve this lucrative enterprise from discovery.

She went on listening to Nathaniel.

'Each trader fattens his wares ashore, like pigs for the market. That way they are stronger for the crossing, and he makes sure that they are healthy and not going to bring sickness aboard with them.

'There are twenty-three barracoons here, some small ones with twenty blacks or so, belonging to the small traders, right on up to the big ones like *Huron*'s, with a thousand and more prime blackbirds in the cage.

'We have the slave-decks set up in *Huron*'s hold, and we would have begun taking them aboard any day, but now—'

Nathaniel shrugged, and spat on the horny calloused palms of each hand in turn, and then plied himself to the oars once more.

'Are you a Christian, Nathaniel?' Robyn asked softly.

'That I am, ma'am,' he said proudly. 'As good a Christian as ever sailed out of Martha's Vineyard.'

'Do you think God approves of what you are doing here to these poor people?'

'Hewers of wood, ma'am, and drawers of water, like the Bible says,' the weather-beaten sailor told her, so glibly that she knew that the reply had been put in his mouth, and she guessed by whom.

Once they were ashore, Tippoo led the small party with Robyn in the centre and Nathaniel carrying her chest in the rear.

Captain Mungo St John had chosen the best site available for his barracoon, on a rise of ground at a distance from the river. The sheds were well built, with floors of sawn timber raised above the mud and good roofs thatched with palmetto leaves.

Huron's guards had not deserted, proof of the discipline which Mungo St John maintained and the slaves in the barracks had evidently been carefully chosen. They were all well set up men and women, and the copper cookers were filled with boiling farina so that their bellies bulged and their skins were glossy.

At Robyn's direction they were lined up and she passed swiftly down the ranks. There were some mild ailments, which she singled out for later treatment, but she found none of the symptoms which she so dreaded.

'There is no plague here,' she decided. 'Not yet.'

'Come!' said Tippoo.

He led her through the palm groves, and the next barracoon had been deserted by the traders who had built it and stocked it. Already the slaves were hungry and confused by their sudden liberation.

'You are free to go,' Robyn told them. 'Go back to your own land.'

She was not certain that they understood her. They squatted in the mud and stared at her blankly. It was as though they had lost all power of independent thought or action, and she knew that they would never be able to make their way back along the Hyena Road, even if they survived the coming epidemic.

With a flash of horror Robyn realized that without their slave-masters these poor creatures were doomed to a lingering death by starvation and disease. Their masters had cleared out the store rooms before they left, there was not a cupful of farina or corn meal left in any of the barracoons they visited that morning.

'We will have to feed them,' Robyn said.

'We have food for our own, that is all,' Tippoo told her impassively.

'He is right, ma'am,' Nathaniel confirmed. 'We feed them, then we'll starve our own blackbirds – besides, most of them are poor goods, not worth the price of a cup of farina.'

In the second barracoon Robyn thought that she had at last discovered the first plague victims, for the low thatched sheds were crammed with rows of prostrate naked figures, and their low moaning and whimpering was a heart-breaking sound, while the smell of corruption was thick and oily on the palate.

It was Tippoo who corrected her. 'China birds,' he grunted, and for a moment Robyn did not understand, and she stooped over the nearest body, then straightened immediately. Despite her training, cold blisters of sweat formed on her forehead.

By Imperial Decree from Peking, no black African slave could be landed on the shores of China unless he had been rendered incapable of reproducing his own kind. The Emperor was concerned that future generations would not be plagued by the growth of an alien population in their midst. The traders found it expedient to castrate their purchases in the barracoons, so that losses caused by the operation could be absorbed before the expense of the long voyage was incurred.

It was crudely done, a tourniquet applied to the root of the scrotum and then the entire scrotal sack removed at a single knife stroke and the wound cauterized immediately with a heated iron or a daub of hot pitch. About sixty per cent would survive the shock and subsequent mortification, but their price per capita was so enhanced that the trader could face forty per cent losses with equanimity.

There was nothing that Robyn could do for so many, she felt overwhelmed by the suffering and misery all around her, and she stumbled out on to the muddy pathway, blinded by her own tears. In the next barracoon, the one nearest to the central auction block, she found the first plague victims.

Once again the sheds had been deserted by the slave-masters, and the dimly lit thatched sheds were filled with naked figures, some squatting motionlessly, others lying on the damp earthen floor, knees drawn up, shaking with the cold of fever, and powerless to lift themselves out of their own bodily wastes. The sound of delirium and suffering was murmurous as of insects in an English orchard on a hot summer's day.

The first sufferer that Robyn touched was a young girl, just beyond puberty, and her skin was burning hot. She rolled her head from side to side, endlessly and senselessly, mouthing snatches of gibberish. Swiftly Robyn ran her fingertips down the girl's naked bulging stomach and immediately she felt the tiny lumps under the hot skin, like pellets of buckshot. There could be no doubt.

'Smallpox,' she said simply, and Tippoo drew back fearfully.

'Wait outside,' she told him, and he went swiftly and with obvious relief. She turned to Nathaniel. She had noticed the little pitted scars in his folded sun-toughened skin, and now there was no fear in his expression.

'When?' she asked.

'When I was a boy,' he said. 'It killed my old ma and my brothers.'

'We have work to do,' she told him.

In the gloomy stinking shed the dead were piled with the living, and on some of the wracked and furnace-heated black bodies the plague had already burst into full flower. They found it in all its stages. Papules beneath the skin had erupted into vesicles, bubbles of clear thin fluid that thickened into pustules, which in turn burst and released a custard-thick trickle of matter.

'These will live,' Robyn told Nathaniel. 'The plague is purging from their blood.' She found a man whose open pocks had already crusted over.

While Nathaniel held the man from moving, Robyn scraped away the crusty scabs with a spatula and gathered them in a wide-mouthed glass bottle that had once held quinine powder.

'This strain of the disease has been attenuated,' Robyn explained impatiently, and for the first time she saw fear in the flecked eyes of Mungo St John. 'The Turks first used this method two hundred years ago.'

'I would prefer to sail away from it,' Mungo St John said quietly, staring at the stoppered bottle which was half filled with damp yellow matter in which were small flecks of blood.

'It would be no use. The infection is already aboard.' Robyn shook her head firmly. 'In a week or less *Huron* would be turned into a stinking plague-ship filled with dying men.'

Mungo turned away from her and went to the ship's rail. He stood there with one hand clasped into a fist behind his back, the other still in its sling, staring at the shore where the thatched roofs of the barracoons just showed above the mangroves.

'You cannot leave those poor wretches,' Robyn said. 'They will starve. I alone could never find food to feed that multitude. You are responsible for them.'

He did not answer her for a moment, then he turned back to study her curiously.

'If *Huron* sailed, with her holds empty, would you stay here on this fever and smallpox-ridden coast to tend this multitude of doomed savages?' he asked.

'Of course.' She was still impatient, and he inclined his head. His eyes no longer mocked, but were sober, perhaps even filled with respect.

'If you will not stay for common humanity, then stay for self-interest.' She scorned him with her tone. 'A million dollars' worth of human cattle, and I will save them for you.'

'You would save them to be sold into captivity?' he insisted.

'Even slavery is better than death,' she replied.

Again, he turned away from her, taking a slow turn of the quarterdeck, frowning thoughtfully, puffing on the long black cheroot so that wreathes of tobacco smoke drifted behind him, and Robyn and half *Huron*'s crew watched him, some fearfully, others with resignation.

'You say that you have yourself undergone this – this thing.' His eyes were drawn back, with loathing fascination, to the little bottle that stood in the centre of his chart table.

For answer Robyn lifted the sleeve of her shirt and showed him the distinctive deeply pocked scar on her forearm.

A minute longer he hesitated, and she went on persuasively, 'I will give you a strain of the disease that is "passant" that has been weakened and attenuated by passage through another man's body, rather than the virulent form of the plague which you will breathe on the very air and which will kill most of you.'

'There is no risk?'

She hesitated and then replied firmly, 'There is always risk, but one hundred, nay a thousand times less risk, than if you take the disease from the air.'

With an abrupt gesture Mungo St John ripped open the sleeve on his left arm with his teeth and offered it to her.

'Do it,' he said. 'But in God's name do it quickly, before my courage fails.'

She drew the point of her scalpel across the smooth deeply tanned skin of his forearm and the tiny crimson droplets rose behind it. He did not flinch, but when she dipped the scalpel into the bottle and scraped up a speck of the noisome yellow stuff, he blanched and made as if to jerk his arm away, then with an obvious effort controlled himself. She smeared the pus over the tiny wound, and he stepped back and turned from her.

'All of you.' His voice was rough with his horror and disgust. 'Every last one of you,' he told the gaping terrified seamen.

With Nathaniel, the bosun, there were three others who had survived the disease, and were speckled by the small dimpled scars which were its stigma.

Four men were not enough to help Robyn care for a thousand slaves, and her losses were much higher than she had expected. Perhaps this strain of the disease was more virulent, or perhaps the black men from the interior did not have the same resistance as the Europeans whose forbears had for generations been exposed to smallpox.

She introduced the crusted pus into the scratches on their limbs, working in the noon sunlight on into the gloom of dusk and then by the lantern's gleam, and they submitted with dumb resignation of the slave which she found pitiful and repugnant, but which none the less made her work much easier.

The reaction began within hours, the swelling and fever and the vomiting, and she went out into the other deserted barracoons to gather more of the loathsome pus from the bodies of those who had survived the smallpox and were now dying of starvation and neglect – resigning herself to the fact that she had only the strength and time to care for those in *Huron*'s barracoons, resigning herself to the fact that there was farina to feed them only, and closing her mind to the cries and entreaty, to the silent dying stare from wizened faces that streamed pus from open pocks.

Even in her own barracoon the four of them working hour after hour, night and day, could give only perfunctory attention to each of the slaves, a handful of the cold pasty farina and a mugful of water once a day during the period of the most violent reaction to the inoculation. Those who survived this were left to care for themselves, to crawl to the water bucket when they could or to wolf a lump of farina from the spadeful that Nathaniel left on a wooden platter at intervals between the rows of supine figures.

Then when they were strong enough to stand they were put to work at piling the rotting bodies of their less fortunate peers upon a gun carriage and dragging them out of the barracoon. There was not the remotest chance of either burying or burning the bodies, and there were too many for the bloated vultures. They piled the corpses in heaps in the coconut grove, well downwind of the barracoon and went back for more.

Twice a day Robyn went down to the edge of the creek and hailed the anchor watch on *Huron*'s deck and had the whaler row her out to the ship, and she spent an hour in the stern cabin.

Mungo St John's reaction had been frighteningly severe, perhaps he had been weakened by the knife wound. His arm had swollen to almost twice normal size, and the scratch Robyn had inflicted turned into a hideous canker with a thick black crusty scab. His fever was intense, his skin almost painfully hot to the touch, and the flesh seemed to melt off his big-boned frame like candle wax under the flame.

Tippoo, himself suffering from a raging fever, his own arm swollen grotesquely, could not be made to leave the side of Mungo's bunk.

Robyn felt easier knowing that Tippoo was there, strangely gentle, almost like a mother with a child, to care for Mungo while she must go back ashore to the suffering multitude that choked the barracoons.

On the twelfth day when she went aboard *Huron*, Tippoo met her at the companionway with that wide toadlike grin which she had not seen for so long, and when she hurried into the cabin she saw why.

Mungo was propped up on the bolsters, thin and pale, his lips dry and dark purple bruises under his eyes, as though he had been beaten with a heavy club, but he was lucid and his skin cool.

'God's breath,' he croaked. 'You look awful!' And she felt like weeping with relief and chagrin.

When she had bathed and bandaged the shrinking canker on his forearm and was ready to leave, he took her wrist.

'You are killing yourself,' he whispered. 'When did you last sleep, and for how long?'

Only when he spoke did she realize the depth of her exhaustion – it had been two days previously and then only for a few hours that she had slept, and she felt *Huron*'s deck swing and lurch under her feet as though she rode a high sea and was not lying quietly at anchor in a placid creek.

Mungo drew her down gently beside him on to the bunk, and she did not have either the strength or will to resist. He made a cradle for her head on his shoulder, and almost immediately she was asleep, her last memory was the feel of his fingers smoothing back the dank ringlets from her temples.

She awoke with a guilty start, not sure how long she had slept, and still fuzzy with sleep struggled out of Mungo St John's arms brushing the hair out of her eyes with her fingers, trying ineffectually to straighten her rumpled and sweat-dampened clothing.

'I must go!' she blurted groggily, still exhausted and half asleep. How many had died while she slept, she wondered. Before he could prevent it, she was stumbling up the companionway to the deck calling for Nathaniel to row her ashore.

The few hours of rest had refreshed her so that she looked about the estuary with a new and lively interest again. It was the first time that she became aware that one other vessel, besides *Huron*, was still lying at anchor in the river. It was one of the small dhow-rigged buggaloos, the coastal slavers similar to the one from which she had rescued Juba. On impulse, she had Nathaniel row her alongside, and when nobody answered her hail, she went aboard. The vessel had clearly been overwhelmed by the plague before she could flee, perhaps she was the vessel from which the original infection had been carried ashore.

Robyn found the same conditions prevailing aboard as there were ashore, the dead, the dying, and those who would recover. Although they were slavers she was still a physician, and she had taken the Hippocratic oath. What she could do was very little, but she did it and the Arab captain, stricken and weakened, thanked her from his sleeping-mat on the open deck.

'May Allah walk beside you,' he whispered, 'and may he give me the opportunity to return this kindness one day.'

'And may Allah show you the error of your ways,' Robyn told him tartly. 'I will send some fresh water, before nightfall, but now there are others more deserving.'

In the days that followed, the plague ran its inexorable course, the weaklings died, some of them consumed by the terrible thirsts of fever crawled from the abandoned barracoons on to the mud flats of the estuary to fill their bellies with the salt water. Their bodies were twisted into grotesque contortions by the cramps of the salt in their blood, and their insane rantings were like the cries of seabirds across the water, extinguished at last by the incoming tide. The surface of the river was troubled by the swirl and splash of the crocodile and the big sharks that had come upstream to gather this grisly harvest.

Others had crawled away into the forest and groves; they lay under every bush and even before they died they were covered with a red mantle of the fierce safari ants that overnight picked the skeleton to gleaming whiteness.

Some of those that survived, encouraged by Robyn, crept weakly away towards the west. Perhaps a few would complete the long hazardous journey back to their razed villages and devastated countryside, she hoped.

However, most of the survivors of the plague were too weak and confused and demoralized to move. They stayed on in the squalid stinking barracoons, pathetically dependent upon Robyn and her tiny band of helpers for every mouthful of water and farina, watching her with the eyes of dumb and suffering animals.

All this time the piles of corpses in the palm groves grew taller, and the stench more penetrating. Robyn knew too well what would happen next.

'The battlefield plagues,' she explained to Mungo St John. 'They always follow when the dead are left unburied, when the rivers and wells are choked with bodies. If they strike now, then none will survive. All of us are weakened, we would be unable to resist the typhoid and enteric plagues. Now is the time to leave, for we have saved all those who are for saving. We must fly before the new onslaught, for unlike the smallpox, there is no defence against them.'

'Most of my crew are still sick and weak.'

'They will recover swiftly out on the open ocean.'

Mungo St John turned to Nathaniel to ask, 'How many slaves have survived?'

'More than eight hundred, thanks to the missus here.'

'We will begin to take them aboard at dawn tomorrow,' he decided.

That night Robyn came back to his cabin after dark. She could not stay away, and he was waiting for her, she could tell by his expression and the quickness of his smile.

'I was beginning to fear that you preferred the company of eight hundred plague-ridden slaves,' he greeted her.

'Captain St John, I wish to make one more appeal to you. As a Christian gentleman, will you not release these poor creatures and have them escorted and fed on the journey back to where they came—'

He interrupted her, his tone light and that smile hovering on his lips.

'And will you not call me Mungo, rather than Captain St John?'

She ignored the interruption, and went on. 'After all they have suffered, that terrible march down from the highlands, the error and humiliation of slavery and now this plague. If you would consent to release them, I would lead them back to their homes.'

He rose from the canvas chair and came to stand over her. His leanness and pallor made him seem even taller.

'Mungo!' he insisted.

'God would forgive you, I am sure of that, he would forgive you the sins that you have already committed against humanity—'

'Mungo!' he whispered, and placed his hands upon her shoulders. She felt herself begin to tremble uncontrollably.

He drew her to his chest. She could feel his ribs, he was so thin, and her voice choked up in her throat when she tried to continue her appeal. Slowly he stooped over her, and she closed her eyes tightly, her arms stiff at her sides, her fists clenched.

'Say Mungo,' he commanded quietly, and his lips were cool and soft on hers. Her trembling became uncontrolled shaking.

Her lips opened under his, and her arms went up around his neck.

'Mungo,' she sobbed. 'Oh, Mungo, Mungo.'

She had been taught that her naked body was shameful, but it was the one lesson that she had learned imperfectly, and much of her shame had been mitigated, firstly in the lecture rooms and dissection rooms of St Matthew's, and secondly in the company of Juba, the little Matabele dove, whose unaffected delight in her nudity she had transmitted to Robyn. Those childlike romps together in the cool green pools of an African river had served to blow away most of the cobwebs of shame.

Now Mungo St John's delight in and admiration for her body gave her joy and, far from shame, brought her pride that she had never known before. Their love-making was no longer accompanied by pain, there were no longer barriers between them – so locked together they could ride the dips and swings of emotion from Himalayan heights where the great winds blew, down to the sweet languorous depths where they seemed to be drowning in honey, each movement slowed, every breath drawn out as though it would last forever, their bodies damp and hot, pressed together and without form, like clay in the hands of a child.

The night was too short, while the wick of the lantern guttered and smoked, neglected and untrimmed. In the dawn, their loving seemed to have filled them with new strength, to have driven away the weakness of fever and the exhaustion of the past weeks.

It was only the sound of the first slaves coming aboard that roused Robyn and brought her back from that far frontier to the hot and cramped little cabin on a slave ship in a fever creek on a wild and brutal continent.

She heard the whisper of bare feet and the clank and drag of slave chains, the sound of men's voices raised, hectoring and impatient, on the deck above.

'Hurry them, or we load for a week.' Tippoo's voice.

Robyn raised herself on her elbow and looked down at Mungo. His eyes were closed but he was not asleep, she knew.

'Now,' she whispered. 'Now you cannot but release them. After last night, I know that something has changed in you.'

She felt a strange joy, the zeal of the prophet looking down upon a convert for whose soul she had wrestled with the devil and won.

'Call Tippoo,' she insisted, 'and give him the order to free the slaves.'

Mungo opened his eyes, even after the long night in which neither of them had slept, his eyes were clear. There was the shadow of new beard, dense and dark, carpeting his bony jawline. He was magnificent and she knew then that she loved him.

'Call Tippoo,' she repeated, and he shook his head – a little gesture of perplexity.

'You still do not understand,' he answered her. 'This is my life. I cannot alter that, not for you nor for anybody.'

'Eight hundred souls,' she pleaded, 'and you have their salvation in your hands.'

'No.' He shook his head again. 'You are wrong, not eight hundred souls but eight hundred thousand dollars – that is what I have in my hands.'

'Mungo.' His name still felt awkward on her lips. 'Jesus has said that it is easier for a camel to pass through the eye of a needle than that a rich man should enter the kingdom of Heaven. Let them go, you cannot judge human lives in gold.'

He laughed and sat up,

'With eight hundred thousand bucks, I can bribe my way into Heaven, if I want to, but between us, my dear, it sounds an awfully dull place. I think the devil and I might have more to talk about.'

The mocking gleam was back in his eye again, and he swung his legs out over the edge of the bunk, and naked crossed to where his breeches hung on a wooden peg from the bulkhead.

'We have lain too long abed,' he said briskly. 'I must see to the loading, and you had best begin your own preparations for the voyage.' He belted his breeches and stuffed his shirt into them. 'It will take us three days to load, I would be obliged if you would test the water barrels.' He came to sit on the edge of the bunk and began dragging on his boots, talking the while in crisp businesslike fashion, detailing the preparations that she should make for the welfare of the slaves during the voyage. 'We will have less than a full cargo, which will make it easier to exercise them on deck and keep the holds clean.' He stood up and looked down at her.

With a rush like a roused fawn she threw off the blanket that covered her and knelt on the edge of the bunk, seizing him about the waist with both arms.

'Mungo,' she whispered urgently, 'you cannot torture us so.' She pressed the side of her face to his chest, feeling the harsh springing curls of his body hair even through the linen of his shirt. 'I cannot offend further against my God and my conscience – unless you free these poor damned souls, then I can never marry you.'

His expression changed swiftly, becoming tender and concerned. He lifted his hand to stroke the dense russet locks of her hair, still damp and tangled from the loving of the night.

'My poor darling,' his lips formed the words, soundlessly, but her face was still pressed to his chest and she could not see his lips. He drew a deep breath, and though his eyes were still marked with regret and his expression sober, his tone was light and casual.

'Then it is just as well that I have no intention of freeing a single one of them – for what would my wife say otherwise?'

The words took many seconds to make sense to Robyn, and then her whole body spasmed, her grip around his waist tightened and then slowly relaxed. She released him. Slowly she sat back on her heels, naked in the midst of his disordered bunk, and she stared at him with an expression of desolation and disbelief.

'You are married?' Robyn's voice echoed strangely in her own ears, as though from the end of a long bare corridor, and Mungo nodded.

'These ten years past,' he answered quietly. 'A French lady of aristocratic birth, a cousin of Louis Napoleon. A lady of great beauty who with the three fine sons she has borne me awaits my return to Bannerfield.' He paused and then went on with infinite regret. 'I am sorry, my dear, I never dreamed that you did not know.' And he reached out to touch her cheek, but she cringed away as though he held a poisonous serpent in his hand.

'Will you go away, please,' she whispered.

'Robyn—' he began, but she shook her head violently.

'No,' she said. 'Please don't say any more. Just go. Go away! Please go away.'

Robyn locked the door of her cabin and sat down at the sea chest which she used for a desk. There were no tears. Her eyes felt dry and burning as though blasted by a wind off the desert. She had very little paper left and had to tear the end sheets from her journal. They were speckled with mildew and distorted from the heat and dryness of the highlands and the humidity of the monsoon-ridden littoral.

She smoothed out the first sheet carefully on the lid of her writing case, dipped her pen in the remaining half-inch of India ink and headed the sheet with a hand that was calm and unshaken.

16th November, 1860.
Aboard the Slaver *Huron*.

And then in the same clear unhurried script began to write:

My Dear Captain Codrington,
My trust in an all-merciful Providence and my belief in the

true and one God, and in his gentle son and our Saviour Jesus convinces me that this will come into your hands while there is still time for you to act.

Through a series of incredible adventures and misfortunes I now find myself devoid of friends or protectors, in the power of the notorious American Slave Master and trader Mungo St John. Against both my will and my conscience I am being forced to act as the physician for this infamous vessel which is at this moment preparing for the voyage around the Cape of Good Hope, across the Atlantic Ocean for a port in the Southern States of America.

As I write, I can hear the doleful sounds from the deck above me, and from the hold below where the poor creatures, eight hundred forsaken souls in all, wearing only their chains are being brought aboard and incarcerated for the voyage which many of them will not survive.

We are lying at anchor in a hidden creek, concealed from the open sea by a sweep of the channel and the mangrove swamps, a perfect hide-away for the nefarious business in hand.

However, I have been able to study the ship's chart and from the navigator's markings learn the name of the estuary and its exact position. The river is the Rio Save, and it lies 20° 58′ south latitude and 35° 03′ east longitude.

I will do all in my power to delay the sailing of this vessel, though at this moment I cannot think what that will be. If this letter reaches you in time, there will be no difficulty for an officer of your courage and experience to blockade the river mouth and seize this slave ship when she attempts to leave the river.

If we have sailed before your arrival, then I implore you to follow in the same course as the Captain of the *Huron* must set to round Good Hope, and I will pray for adverse winds and weather that will enable you to come up with us.

Robyn went on pouring out the tale of her capture, of the plague that had swept through the barracoons, of her fear and hatred of the slavers, the detailed accounts of their barbaric practices and cruelties, and suddenly she realized that she had filled many pages with her account, and she began her last paragraph.

You were gracious enough to express your belief that our destinies were linked in some mysterious way. I know that you share with me the same hatred of this abominable trade, and for these reasons I have made bold enough to appeal to you, confident that you will hearken to my anguished cry.

Robyn paused again, and then searched swiftly in her pen case and found the pair of the earring which she had given to Clinton Codrington so many months ago.

I enclose with this letter a token of my friendship and trust which I hope you will recognize, and I will search every day to see the topsails of your fine ship hurrying to give succour to myself and to the other unfortunates who are my shipmates on this cursed and iniquitous voyage.

She signed it with her bold, rounded signature and stitched the folded pages and the single item of cheap jewellery into a square of duck canvas.

There was only one address that she had for it. Clinton had told her that he was under orders to call at Zanzibar Island, and she knew that Her Majesty's Consul on the island was a man of substance and integrity, a staunch adversary of the slave trade, one of the few men that her father, Fuller Ballantyne, had ever written about with respect and affection.

When she had finished, she tucked the small canvas package up under her skirts, and went up on deck. Mungo St John was on his quarterdeck, gaunt and lean and pale, and he took a step towards her, but she turned from him immediately.

'Nathaniel,' she called to the bosun. 'I wish to visit the buggaloo.' She indicated the Arab dhow which was still anchored downstream from *Huron*.

'She's making ready to sail, ma'am.' Nathaniel knuckled his forehead. 'She'll be gone before we can get across—'

'She will if you continue talking,' Robyn told him briskly. 'I must see if there is aught they need, the poor devils, before they sail.'

Nathaniel glanced at his Captain, and after a moment's hesitation, Mungo nodded his assent and turned back to watch the stream of slaves coming aboard through the entry port.

The Arab Captain of the dhow, just strong enough to take his place at the tiller, greeted her respectfully and listened attentively while she spoke.

Nathaniel was waiting in the gig, out of sight below the level of the dhow's deck, and Robyn made sure that they were shielded from a casual watcher on *Huron*'s deck before she passed the canvas package to the Arab, and followed it with a gold English sovereign.

'There will be another sovereign for you, from the man you deliver it to,' she told him, and the Arab bit the coin, and smiled wanly as he tucked it into a fold of his turban.

'And I am Matabele. Induna of two thousand. My name is Gandang, son of Mzilikazi, son of Zulu, and I come with a bright spear and a red heart.'

Zouga understood the words with difficulty, for they were spoken rapidly, in accents that were strange to his ears, but there was no misunderstanding the Induna's intention. His tone was clear, the murderous determination in his voice evident, and around him the circle of long black shields was unbroken and steadfast.

Unconsciously Zouga had straightened, forcing his aching muscles erect, and he held the Induna's gaze without flinching. They stared at each other, and Zouga found himself exerting all his will, all the force of his personality, trying to stay the Induna's spear arm. He knew it needed only for the bright broad blade to drop and two hundred *amadoda* would sweep into the rudimentary camp. It would be over so swiftly, the resistance that Zouga and his tiny band could offer would be so puny that they would not even earn the compliment of disembowelment from the victors.

He knew that only his steady gaze and the completely fearless mien that he offered to the Matabele had so far stayed the spear arm, but the silence was drawing out. At any second the spell would snap. He must choose his next action and words as though his life depended upon them, as indeed they did.

Gandang watched the strange pale man before him with his features impassive, yet for possibly the first time in his life while on his father's service, he was uncertain.

The man who called himself Bakela had spoken familiar

names. Tshedi and Manali, they were names that his own father revered, yet that in itself would not have been enough to stay his hand, for the King's orders were clear: all who entered the Burnt Land must die. It was more than that. He knew who this man was. The maiden who he would soon take as wife had spoken of him. This was the brother of the white woman who had delivered Juba to his care, and who he had called *amekazi*, mother.

Juba had spoken of the man Bakela as she lay beside him on her sleeping-mat. She had spoken of him with admiration and awe, as a mighty hunter of elephant, as a warrior honoured by an all-powerful Queen who lived far beyond great waters. Juba had spoken of this man Bakela as a friend and a protector.

So Gandang paused before giving the order '*Bulala!* Kill them!'

A Matabele Induna is never influenced by the words or whims of a woman, if he has fifty wives their voices are still as the chattering of the waters over the rocks in the shallow rapids of the Nyati river, and a man does not heed them, or rather it must never be apparent that he heeds them.

Juba had travelled to strange places and spoken of wonders and witchery, and Gandang while seeming not to listen had indeed listened and been impressed. The girl was not only comely and high bred, but sensible far beyond that mere simpering giggling sexuality to which he was accustomed in other girls of her age.

Gandang was learning that a Matabele Induna is never influenced by the whims and words of a woman, unless those words are spoken and the whims expressed on the privacy of the sleeping-mat, by a senior wife whose good sense has been proven.

Then it is folly not to hearken, for a senior wife can make a man's life unbearable, even if that man is an Induna of two thousand, and the favoured son of the most powerful monarch in Africa.

Behind the dark impassive mask of his handsome face, Gandang was thinking furiously. Instinct and Juba's words had warned him that it would be folly to slay this man, yet the warriors at his back knew his orders, and if he failed to carry them out, that failure would immediately be construed as weakness, and his treason reported to the King.

Before him the tattered figure took a pace forward, his whole being ludicrously arrogant. Gandang could see no trace of fear in the steady gaze of his strangely coloured eyes.

'I come as an emissary to the great King Mzilikazi, ruler of the Matabele people – and I bring greeting from the White Queen from across the waters.'

At the words Gandang felt a small warm flame of relief. The fact that the white man spoke the language of the people, albeit with a strange accent, made it more plausible that he was indeed an emissary. It was plausible, also, that this Queen of his would want to seek the protection and favour of a king as powerful as his father, and that she should be so ignorant as to send her emissary through the Burnt Land instead of along the open road from the south. Zouga saw the shift of mood in the Induna's eyes, that tiny crack in his determination.

'Wait,' he said. 'There is something that I have for you.'

In Zouga's writing-case still reposed the impressive handwritten letters, with seals of wax and scarlet ribbon, that had been provided him by the Under-secretary at the Foreign Office, in the usual form.

> In the name of Her Britannic Majesty, Ruler of Great Britain and Ireland, Defender of the Faith – To the representatives of all foreign governments or to whosoever it may concern,
>
> We do, by these presents, request and require that our beloved Morris Zouga Ballantyne be allowed to pass freely without let or hindrance and that he be afforded that assistance of which he may stand in need.

Zouga turned his back on the silent menacing ranks of spearsmen, and walked back slowly through the gap in the *scherm* of cut thorn branches.

Jan Cheroot was waiting for him, his face the colour of the watch-fire ash. He and the gunbearers were crouched below the thorn barrier, staring through the chinks with expressions of such utter terror that Zouga felt emboldened in comparison

'Lay down those guns,' he snapped, for all the weapons were cocked and primed and a nervous finger on a hair-trigger could let fly the shot that brought a solid black wave of Matabele sweeping through the camp.

Gandang suddenly found himself in a position of uncertainty. From being the merciless bearer of the King's justice, he found himself waiting like a timid suitor outside the gate in the thorn barrier, and every second detracted from his dignity.

Behind him he heard the stir of one of his men, the soft tap of assegai spear on hide shield. His men were growing restless already, sensing the passing of advantage to the little group of ragged starvelings they had surrounded. Gandang turned slowly, and his stony gaze passed over the ranks. They froze once more into utter stillness.

'Gandang, son of Mzilikazi, Induna of two thousand. Come forward.'

The hail from beyond the thorn barrier was unexpected and startlingly loud, but it came the moment before Gandang reached the limit of his patience and loosed his eager warriors. Gandang moved forward to the gateway. His plumes nodding about his head, his tread dignified, his carriage proud, so that no men might guess at his uncertainty. At the gateway he paused, and though his expression did not alter nor his gaze waver, he experienced a profound relief that his own wisdom and the words of his little dove had stayed his blade.

Before him stood a figure of almost incredible beauty. It took him many seconds to recognize the ragged individual of a few minutes previously. The figure wore cloth of that same peculiarly rich shade of red of the bushshrike's chest, brighter than the colour of freshly spilled blood. Though this was enough to stop a man's breath, it was not all. Bright metal ornaments on breast and shoulders sparkled in the morning sunlight, the belt buckle was of the same metal. The belt and cross-straps were of the same blinding whiteness as an egret's wing. The tall shako swept down to an elegant point between the eyes, and the helmet badge blazed like a sunrise upon the man's forehead.

There was no doubt now in Gandang's mind that here was indeed an important man, and a soldier of repute, as Juba had warned him, and he made a silent resolution to listen to her words in future with even greater attention. He felt a little shiver of dismay at the thought that he might have followed his first instincts and had this man cut down as though he was a worthless Mashona, a mere eater of dirt.

The magnificent figure took one pace towards him and lifted a hand to the peak of that beautiful helmet in a formal gesture that Gandang answered instinctively with a sweeping salute of his stabbing spear.

'I, Bakela, request that my token be conveyed to your father, the honoured and victorious Mzilikazi, and that he be informed that I request from him the right of the road,' said the man in his atrocious Sindebele and Gandang accepted the token from his hand, the small package with strange signs and marks upon it, bound up with strips of coloured cloth so beautiful that they would have delighted the heart of even the most vain and spoiled woman.

'It shall be done,' he agreed.

In the moments of his confrontation with Gandang, Zouga had been thinking as furiously as the Matabele and making his own calculations of survival. Now that he had fallen in with a border impi he knew he must put aside any thought of escaping southwards. Apart from the fact that they were completely surrounded and heavily outnumbered, he knew that no unmounted man could run ahead of these warriors. They were like machines built for the pursuit and the annihilation of an enemy.

The meeting had not taken him completely unprepared. There had been many a night in the preceding weeks when he had woken in the darkest hours, and he had lain on the hard earth and dreaded a moment such as this.

He had mentally rehearsed his actions – from the concealment of any fear while he won time to don his dress uniform, to the demand to be taken to the King's kraal. When it had gone as he planned it, when the tall Induna had agreed, 'It shall be done,' it had taken another enormous extension of Zouga's will not to show relief. He had stood aloof, disinterested, while Gandang had picked and called out five of his swiftest runners and had recited a long message that they must memorize, and take to Mzilikazi.

It began with a long recitation of the King's praises which began,

'Great black elephant who shakes the earth with his tread –' went on to list the deeds that Gandang had performed since leaving the great kraal at Thabas Indunas, the march eastward, the battle at the pass and the slaying of Bopa, the slave master, right up to this day's encounter with the white man. After a flowery description of the man's magnificent finery (which

Gandang knew would intrigue his father), it ended with a repetition of Bakela's request to be 'given the road' to Thabas Indunas.

The chosen messengers, each in turn repeated the long message, and though he showed no change of expression Zouga was amazed that each of them had it word-perfect. It was an impressive demonstration of the developed memory of people who do not have the art of writing and reading.

Gandang handed them the sealed parchment envelope that contained Zouga's letter of credentials, and the messengers sprang to their feet from where they had squatted, saluted their Induna, formed file and trotted away towards the west.

Gandang turned back to Zouga. 'You will stay encamped here until the King sends word.'

'When will that be?' Zouga asked, and Gandang answered him sternly.

'Whenever the King is pleased to do so.'

Zouga's little party was left unmolested. Although there were a dozen Matabele *amadoda* positioned about the camp, guarding it day and night, not one of them attempted to enter the gateway in the thorn *scherm*. Until the moment when they might slaughter them, the persons and property of their prisoners were inviolate.

The main body of the impi camped a quarter of a mile downstream. Each evening the tall Induna visited Zouga and they sat for an hour or so across the fire from each other, speaking gravely and seriously.

As the days of waiting became weeks so the two men developed each for the other a deep respect, if not actual friendship. They were both warriors, and they had common ground when they spoke of old campaigns and of skirmishes and battles fought. They recognized in each other the strengths, the essential decencies of men who live by and respect the laws of their society, though those laws might diverge widely.

'I account him a gentleman,' Zouga wrote in his journal. 'One of nature's own.'

While Gandang, speaking to Juba on the sleeping-mat said merely, 'Bakela is a man.'

Gandang allowed Zouga's bearers to leave the enclosure, to cut and bring in thatch and timber to strengthen and improve the buildings, so that at last Zouga could sleep dry and warm.

This, together with the rest and respite from endless marching brought an immediate improvement in Zouga's health. The deep wound in his cheek healed cleanly, leaving a pink shiny scar. The shoulder mended, the bruising abated, and he no longer needed a staff or a sling for his arm. Within a week he knew he was well enough to shoot the heavy four-to-the-pound.

One evening he proposed to Gandang that they hunt together, and the Induna who by this time was finding the waiting as tedious as Zouga was, agreed with alacrity. Gandang's *amadoda* surrounded a herd of Cape buffalo, and drove them down in a bellowing, stampeding black wave to where they waited. Zouga saw the tall Induna rise from cover and race in, bare-footed, shieldless, and kill a mature bull buffalo with a single thrust of the broad-bladed assegai through the ribs behind the heaving shoulder. Zouga knew that he lacked both the skill and courage to emulate that feat.

Gandang watched when Zouga stood to meet the squealing, thunderous charge of an enraged bull elephant, and when the beast went down to the crash of the shot, dropping on to its knees in a storm of dust, Gandang stepped past Zouga and touched the little black hole that punctured the elephant's thick grey hide an inch above the first crease at the top of the trunk.

Gandang inspected the smear of blood on the tip of his forefinger, and said 'Hau!' quietly but with force, which is an expression of deep amazement. For Gandang, himself, owned a musket, a Tower Musket manufactured in London in 1837. When he first acquired the weapon, Gandang had fired it at buffalo, elephant and Mashona, all of whom had fled headlong, but unscathed.

Gandang understood that when firing it was necessary to close the eyes and the mouth firmly, to hold the breath and at the moment of discharge to shout a rebuke to the devil who lived in the gunpowder smoke, otherwise the devil could enter through the eyes or mouth and take possession of the marksman. In order to throw the musket ball to any distance, it was also necessary to pull the trigger with sudden and brutal force, as in hurling a spear. Furthermore, to minimize the recoil of the weapon, the butt should not touch the shoulder, but be held a hand's span from it. Despite all these precautions, Gandang had never succeeded in hitting the target at which he aimed, and had long abandoned the weapon to rust away, while he kept his assegai polished brightly.

Thus Gandang appreciated to the full the magnitude of the feat that Zouga performed with such apparent ease. So their mutual respect deepened with each day spent in each other's company, and became almost friendship. Almost, but not quite, there were chasms of culture and training between them that could never be bridged, and always the knowledge that on any day a swift runner might come from the west with a message for Gandang from his father.

'*Bulala umbuna*! Kill the white man!' And both of them knew that Gandang would hesitate not an instant longer.

Zouga had much time alone in camp, and he spent it planning his audience with the King. The longer he dwelt upon that the more ambitious became his plans. The memory of the ancient disused mine-shafts returned to plague these idle hours, and at first merely to amuse himself, and then with truly serious intent, Zouga began to draw up a document which he headed:

'Exclusive Concession to mine gold and hunt ivory in the Sovereign territory of Matabeleland.'

He worked on it each evening polishing and reshaping it in the gibberish that the layman takes for legal jargon and which he fondly believes will dignify his creation. 'Whereas I, Mzilikazi, ruler of Matabeleland, hereinafter referred to as the party of the first part—'

Zouga had completed this document to his entire satisfaction when a fatal flaw in his plans became evident. Mzilikazi could not sign his name. Zouga pondered this for a day and then the solution occurred to him. Mzilikazi should by this time have in hand the sealed package. The crimson wax seals must surely impress him, and in his writing-case Zouga had two full sticks of sealing wax.

Zouga began to design a great seal for King Mzilikazi. He sketched the design on the back cover of his journal, and the inspiration came from the first of the King's praise names.

'Great Black Elephant who shakes the earth.'

In Zouga's design the centre of the field depicted a bull elephant, with long tusks raised and ears spread wide. The upper border bore the legend, 'Mzilikazi Nkosi Nkulu'. And the lower border carried the translation, 'Mzilikazi, King of the Matabele'.

He started experimenting with various materials, clay and

wood, but the results did not please him – and the following day he asked Gandang for permission to send a party of his porters under Jan Cheroot back to the ancient workings at the Harkness mine to retrieve the ivory buried there.

It took two days of careful consideration for Gandang to agree, and when he did, he sent fifty of his men to accompany the caravan, with orders to kill them all at the first hint of flight or treachery. Jan Cheroot returned with the four huge tusks from the two bull elephants, and Zouga had not only the material from which to carve the King's great seal, but a gift fitting the King's importance.

Ivory was a treasure of which the Matabele had long ago realized the value in trade. It was, however, a scarce commodity, for even the bravest of men cannot kill a bull elephant with a stabbing spear. They had to rely on pick-ups from animals that had died of natural causes, or the very occasional victim of the pitfall.

Gandang's amazement when he saw the span and weight of the four tusks decided Zouga. The largest and most pleasingly shaped tusk would be Zouga's gift to Mzilikazi, if he were ever allowed to reach the great kraal at Thabas Indunas alive.

Not only was the threat of the King's wrath still hanging over him, but his supply of quinine powder was reduced to a few ounces. All around the camp steamed the swampy ground, fed each day by the interminable rains, and in the night he could even smell the evil fever-bearing vapours rising from the stagnant waters to waft over the camp. Yet he was forced to reduce his daily preventative dose of the bitter powder to perilously small quantities in an attempt to eke it out.

The inactivity and the dual threat of spear and disease wore on Zouga's nerves, until he found himself toying with suicidal plans to make an attempt to avoid the guarding impi and to escape on foot southwards. He thought of seizing Gandang and holding him as hostage, or using the remaining fifty pounds of black powder to manufacture a combustible with sufficient power to destroy the entire impi host at a blast. Reluctantly, one after another, he recognized these as plans of folly and abandoned them.

*

Gandang's impi came again in the dawn. Zouga was awakened by a stentorian voice calling him out of the thorn *scherm*. Zouga threw a fur kaross over his shoulders and went out into the grey and icy drizzle of rain, sloshing through the red mud to the gate, and he knew at a single glance that the King had at last sent his reply. The ranks of silent Matabele surrounded the camp, still as statues carved from the black wild ebony.

Zouga judged how swiftly he could reach the loaded gun beside his cot in the little thatched hut behind him, and guessed that he would probably be cut down before he could fire a single shot, yet he knew he would still make the attempt.

'I see you Bakela,' Gandang stepped from the dark and silent ranks.

'I see you Gandang.'

'The King's messenger has arrived—' Gandang paused a moment, solemn and stern, and then his perfectly square white teeth gleamed in the grey of dawn as he smiled. 'The King has given you the road, and bids you attend him at Thabas Indunas.'

The two men grinned at each other with relief, for both of them it meant life. The King had determined that Gandang had done his duty and correctly interpreted his commands, while Zouga had been accepted as an emissary and not as an enemy.

'We will march at once,' Gandang smiled still. 'Before the sun!' The King's summons brooked of no hesitations or delays.

'Safari!' Zouga roused his camp. 'We march at once!'

A natural delicacy and tact had made Gandang keep little Juba out of sight and hearing of Zouga's camp, nor had he mentioned the girl's name to Zouga while sentence of death still hung over the white man. However, that first night of the journey to Thabas Indunas after they had camped, he brought Juba to Zouga's hut, and she knelt and greeted him as 'Baba-father' and then with Gandang seated between them and listening attentively, he allowed them to talk for a short while.

Zouga was avid for news of his sister, and he listened in silence to the account of Fuller Ballantyne's death and his burial. It was better this way, and Zouga was already preparing his own fulsome tributes to the memory of his father.

While relieved also to hear that Robyn was safe, Zouga was

less happy with the swift progress she seemed to be making. It must have been nearly three months since Juba last saw her, almost within sight of the eastern mountain range, and by this time Robyn must have surely reached the coast, and could be on board a Portuguese trade ship, well on her way to Good Hope and the Atlantic.

He did not know how long he would be delayed by the Matabele King, and then how long the overland journey down half the length of Africa might take him. Robyn's manuscript could be in London a year or even more before his own.

Zouga had exchanged one worry for another, and on the following day's march he chivvied his porters, heavily laden though they were, to keep up with their captors. It was of little avail, and they struggled along behind the trotting impi until Zouga demanded of Gandang that his own bearers be ordered to help with the load of ivory and the even greater weightier package of bark and plaited grass which contained the granite bird which Zouga had plundered from the tomb of the Kings.

With each day's travel towards the west, so the land became drier, and the forests thinned out and gave way to level pasturage with sparsely dotted acacias, graceful, mushroom-shaped trees from whose branches hung the big protein-rich, bean-shaped pods so dearly loved by game and domestic animals alike.

The relief from the driving and endless rain-storms lifted their spirits, and the impi sang on the march, winding like a thick black serpent through the lovely parklike lands below the bald and rounded kopjes of granite.

Soon they came across the first of the King's herds. The small hump-backed cattle whose origins lay far back beyond the veils of history, perhaps it had taken them and their drovers four thousand years to travel down from the valley of the Nile or from the fertile plains enclosed by the twin rivers of the Euphrates and the Tigris.

The cattle were sleek, for the grass was dense and sweet, even here in the drier lands the rains had been good. The animals were of every colour and pattern, chocolate-red and black and white and yellow, piebald and skewbald, solid black or pure snowy white. They watched with a blank bovine stare as the column of men trotted past, and the small herd boys, naked except for the tiny apron of the *beshu*, came scampering to stare in silent wide-eyed awe at the fighting men in plume and tassel, for they were already pining for the day that they would be called into their own regiments and in turn follow the warriors' road.

They reached the first of the Matabele towns. It was situated on the banks of the Inyati river. Gandang explained that it was the headquarters of his own impi, the Inyati impi, and that it was not the largest of the regimental towns. The settlement was laid out around the central cattle-pen, a vast enclosure large enough to hold ten thousand head of the King's herds. The dwellings were of identical thatched beehive construction in the tradition that the wandering tribe had preserved since leaving their native Zululand. The outer stockade was of cut mopani poles, set deep in the earth and forming a stout defensive wall. The villagers streamed out to welcome the returning impi, lining both sides of the route, a singing, clapping and laughing throng, mostly of women and children.

'Most of the men and the marriageable maidens have left already for Thabas Indunas. In the full of this moon, the *Chawala* dance begins, and all the nation will assemble at the King's kraal. We will rest here only one night and then take the road again to reach Thabas Indunas before the moon.'

The road from the Inyati westwards was now a populous highway, as the nation went in towards the King's capital city to celebrate the festival of the first fruits. The men marched in their regiments, their distinctive dress and ornaments, the colour of their war shields identifying each from afar, from the scarred and silver-headed veterans who had fought the Basuto, the Griquas and the Boer in the south, to the young bloods eager for their first kill, eager to learn in which direction the King would hurl his war-spear at the conclusion of the *Chawala* – for that was the direction in which they would find their reputation, their manhood, their glory and possibly their deaths.

The regiments of young unmarried women, interspersed those of the warriors, and as they passed each other on the road, the girls preened and giggled, casting languorous sloe-eyes at the unmarried men, and the men pranced and leapt in the pantomine of battle, the *Giya*, showing bow they would wash their spears in blood and earn the privilege to 'go in to the women' and take wives.

With each day's march towards Thabas Indunas the roads became more congested, and their pace was reduced by the throng. They might wait half a morning to take their turn across a ford of the river, for the regiments drove the cattle which were their food supply ahead of them and dragged their baggage train behind. Each warrior's finery, his tassels and plumes and feathers, were carefully packed and carried by the young apprentice who was his personal bearer.

At last in the sweltering noon of high summer, Zouga's little party, still borne along on the river of humanity, came over a crest of ground and saw laid out ahead of them the great kraal and capital city of the Matabele.

It was spread out over many square miles of open plain below the bald-headed granite hills that gave it its name 'The Hills of the Chieftains'. The furthest hill was the 'Place of Killing', Bulawayo, and from its sheer cliffs those condemned to die were cast down.

The stockades formed concentric circles, dividing the city into its separate parts. Always the huge open cattle-pens were the centre of Matabele life, their cattle the source and store of their wealth, and now that the outlying herds had been brought in for the festival, every pen was filled with the multi-coloured herds of fat beasts.

Standing at Zouga's shoulder, Gandang used his stabbing-spear to point out with pride the city's features. There were sections for the unmarried girls, and the unblooded regiments, and another huge area for the married quarters; the huts were uniform in size and laid out in orderly patterns, the thatched roofs shining golden yellow in the sunlight. The earth between them was swept clean and beaten hard by the passage of bare feet.

'There is the King's hut.' Gandang pointed out a single huge conical structure in its own separate enclosure. 'And that is the compound of the King's wives,' a hundred other huts, within a high guarding stockade, 'and it is death to any man who enters that gate.'

Gandang led Zouga down to a small grove of acacia trees outside the main stockade. There was a stream within a few yards of it, and for the first time in days they were free of the close press of humanity. Although the plain without the city walls was thick with the temporary dwellings of the visiting impis, the area around the grove was empty, as if it had been placed out of bounds to the common people.

'When will I see the King?' Zouga asked.

'Not until after the festival,' Gandang answered. 'There is ritual and cleansing that the King must undergo but he has sent you gifts, you are much honoured.' And he pointed with his blade at the line of young maidens that left a gate in the stockade. Each girl carried a large earthenware pot balanced easily upon her head, and she did not use a hand to maintain that balance.

The girls moved with that peculiar straight-backed grace, hips swinging in lazy rhythm, the hard unripe fruits of their breasts bouncing and jostling at each pace. They came in to Zouga's little camp in the grove and knelt to offer the gifts they bore.

Some pots contained thick millet beer, tart and effervescent, others the clotted and soured cow's milk, *imaas*, that was so much a staple of the Nguni diet, and others again, big chunks of fatty beef, roasted on the open coals.

'You are much honoured by these gifts,' Gandang repeated, apparently himself surprised by the King's generosity. 'Yet Tshedi, your grandfather, was always his good and trusted friend.'

Once the camp was set up, Zouga found himself again the victim of idleness, with long days of waiting to fill. Here, however, he was free to roam about the city and its surrounds, save only the forbidden areas of the royal enclosure and women's quarters. He sketched the fascinating bustle of preparation for the festival. During the heat of the day the banks of the rivers were lined with men and women, their velvety black skins shimmering with water as they bathed and cleansed themselves for the dances. Every tree for miles about was hung with the kilts and furs, the feathers and plaited ornaments that were airing, the creases and rumples of travel and packing were being allowed to drop out of them as they billowed and flapped in the light breeze.

He passed groups of young girls plaiting each other's hair, smearing and rubbing each other's bodies with oil and coloured clays, and they giggled and waved at Zouga as he passed.

At first the problem of hygiene that this huge assembly presented puzzled Zouga, until he realized that there was an area of thick undergrowth beyond the city walls where both men and women went at dawn and in the short twilight. This area had its own population of crows and kites, of jackal and hyena that served as the city's cleansing service.

Interested further in the running of the city, he found that all bathing and washing of clothing was allowed only below a certain spot on the riverbanks marked by a distinctively large tree or other feature, and that the women filled the water pots for drinking and cooking above this point.

Even the huge cattle-pen in its very heart helped to keep the city clean. It acted as a vast fly-trap. The insects laid their eggs on the fresh cattle dung, but before they could hatch most of them were deeply trampled by the hooves of the milling herds. The brilliant sunlight and the untainted wind completed the process of keeping the area relatively clean and the smells interesting but not unbearable.

Zouga should have been content to have reached this haven, instead of leaving his assegai-riven corpse for a hyena's feast in the wilderness, but he was not.

He set himself tasks to fill the waiting days. He drew sketches and maps of the city, noting weaknesses in the fortifications, and where an attack would have the best chance of penetrating these and reaching the King's private quarters. He sketched the uniforms of the various impis. He noted the colours of their shields and other means of identifying them in the field. Asking innocent-seeming questions of Gandang, he was able to estimate the number of warriors each regiment contained, the ages and battle experience of the warriors, the names and personal idiosyncrasies of their Indunas, and the location of their regimental towns.

He found that much had changed in Matabeleland since old Tom Harkness had drawn his map, and Zouga noted these changes and drew his conclusions from them.

As a further exercise to pass the waiting days he began drawing up a battle plan for a campaign against the old King Mzilikazi, the requirements in men and weapons, the logistics of supply and resupply, the lines of march, and the most expedient methods of bringing the impis to battle – for Zouga was a soldier, a soldier with a dream which might one day become reality only through military action.

Unsuspecting, Gandang was flattered by Zouga's interest and

he answered every question with pride in his nation's might and its achievements. Despite this work Zouga had given himself, the days dragged past.

'The King will not give you audience until after the festival,' Gandang repeated, but he was wrong.

The evening before the festival began, two elderly Indunas, blue heron feathers nodding above the silvery woollen caps of close-cropped hair, entered the camp in the acacia grove and Gandang greeted them with deep respect, listened to them attentively, and then came to Zouga.

'They have come to take you to the King,' he said simply.

There were three small fires burning before the King's hut, and over the middle one crouched a wizened ape-like figure, who crooned a low incantation through toothless gums, rocking on his haunches and occasionally adding a pinch of powder, or a sprig of herb into one of the large earthenware pots that bubbled over the flames.

The witchdoctor was festooned with the grisly accoutrements of his profession, the dried skins of reptiles, the claws of eagle and leopard, the inflated bladder of a lion, the skull of ape and the teeth of crocodile, small stoppered gourds of potions and powders, the horn of duiker to be used as a blooding cup, and other unidentifiable charms and elixirs.

He was the orchestrator of the entire festival, the most important event in the Matabele calendar, the gathering of the first fruits of the harvest, the blessing of the nation's herds, and the setting of the warlike campaigns which would occupy the amadoda during the coming dry season. Thus the assembled Indunas watched his preparations with attention and awe.

There were thirty or so men in the squatting circle of elders, the senior Indunas of the nation, the King's privy council. The small courtyard was crowded. The tall thatched sloping side of the King's hut towered thirty feet or so above them all, the top of it lost in darkness.

The thatching was skilfully done, with intricate patterns worked into the grass, and before the low doorway stood an armchair of European design and construction. With a small prick of recognition Zouga realized that this must be the same chair given to the King by his own grandfather Moffat, Tshedi, nearly twenty years before.

'Bayete! Mzilikazi, the bull elephant of the Matabele.'

Gandang had coached Zouga in the correct etiquette, the formal greetings and the behaviour which the King would expect.

As Zouga crossed the narrow yard of bare earth, he intoned the King's praise names, not shouting them aloud, not crawling on his knees as a subject would have done, for he was an Englishman and an officer of the Queen.

Nevertheless, at a distance of ten feet from the King's chair Zouga squatted down, his own head below the level of the King's, and waited.

The figure in the chair was much smaller than he had expected for a warrior of such fearsome reputation, and as his eyes adjusted to the gloom, Zouga saw that the King's feet and hands were small and delicately shaped, almost feminine, but that his knees were grotesquely swollen and distorted by the gout and arthritis that was attacking them.

The King was an old man now, nobody knew how old, but he had been a fighting warrior at the turn of the century. His once fine muscles had sagged so that his belly bulged out on to his lap, the skin stretched and riven with stria like that of a pregnant woman.

His head seemed too big for the narrow shoulders, and the neck hardly strong enough to support it, but the eyes which watched Zouga intently from the seams of wrinkles and loose, bagged skin, were black and bright and lively.

'How is my old friend Tshedi?' the King asked in a piping high-pitched voice.

Zouga had last seen his maternal grandfather twenty years previously; the only memory that persisted was of a long flowing white beard.

'He is well and happy,' Zouga replied. 'He sends you his greeting and respect.'

The old man in the armchair nodded the big ungainly head contentedly.

'You may present your gifts,' he said, and there was a buzz of comment from the Indunas, and even the witchdoctor at the fire looked up as the ivory tusk was carried in by three of Gandang's warriors, staggering under its weight, and laid before the King's chair.

The witchdoctor clearly resented this interruption of the ritual cleansing and the diversion of interest and attention from himself, and now with two of his assistants to help him he made an officious show of carrying one of the steaming pots from the fire and placing it between the King's feet.

Then he and his assistants raised a large kaross of stitched leopard skins and spread it like a tent over the King and his chair so the steam from the pot was trapped beneath it. Within a minute, there was a paroxysm of gasps and coughing from under the fur blanket, and when at last the witchdoctor removed it, the King was streaming sweat and choking for breath, his eyes inflamed and pouring tears, but any demons had been expelled by the coughing, and impurities washed away by the sweat and tears.

The gathering waited in respectful silence, while the King recovered his breath, and the witchdoctor withdrew to prepare the next potion. With his breath still wheezing and whistling in his throat, Mzilikazi reached into the small chest beside his chair and brought out the sealed package which Zouga had sent him.

'Speak the words.' The King handed it to Zouga, demanding that he read the letter.

Although he was illiterate, the King understood clearly the uses of the written word. For twenty years he had corresponded with Zouga's grandfather, who always sent one of his mission students to deliver his letters, to read them to the King, and to record the King's reply.

Zouga stood erect and opened the package. He read aloud, translating from the English as he went along, and adding a few small embellishments to the original text.

When he had finished, there was a respectful silence from the tribal elders, and even the King studied the tall and magnificently attired figure before him with new attention. The firelight danced on the burnished brass buttons and badges of Zouga's dress uniform, the scarlet cloth of his coat seemed to glow like the very flames of the fire.

The witchdoctor would have intervened again, coming forward with a brew of steaming medicine for the King to swallow, but Mzilikazi waved him away irritably.

Knowing that this was the moment when the King's interest was at its zenith, Zouga asked smoothly, 'Does the King see these signs of my Queen? They are her special marks, and every ruler should have such a mark to prove his power and the rocklike nature of his words.'

Zouga turned and beckoned the bearer who knelt in the gateway behind him and the terrified man crawled to Zouga's feet, not daring to look up at the King, and handed to Zouga the small tea caddy that contained the carved ivory seal and the sticks of wax.

'I have prepared one of these for the King, that his dignity and power may be known to all men.'

Mzilikazi was unable to contain his interest; he craned forward in his chair and called Zouga closer. Kneeling before him, Zouga prepared the wax, melting it on to the lid of the tea caddy with a taper lit from the fire. Then he made the impression of the seal upon it, and when it had hardened, handed it up to the King.

'It is an elephant.' The King recognized the beast with unconcealed amazement.

'The great black bull elephant of the Matabele,' Zouga agreed.

'Speak the words.' The King touched the lettering on the border, and commanded Zouga to translate it.

'Mzilikazi, Nkosi Nkulu!'

The King clapped his hands with delight, and passed the seal to his senior Induna. Soon they were all clucking and exclaiming over the imprint, the wax impression passing from hand to hand.

'Bakela,' the King told Zouga, 'you must come to me again on the day following the *Chawala* ceremony. You and I have much to discuss.'

Then with a wave of his hand he dismissed the splendid young man from his presence, and patiently, resignedly, gave himself up to the ministrations of the hovering doctor.

The full moon rose well past midnight, and the fires were stacked with new logs to welcome it, and the singing and drumming began. No man nor woman had dared to pick a single grain of corn from the harvest before this moment, for the rise of the moon heralded the *Chawala*, the dance of the first fruits, and the entire nation gave itself up to rejoicing.

The ceremony began in the middle of the first morning. The massed regiments assembled before their King, filing in column into the vast arena of the cattle stockade, and the earth shook to the crash of bare feet lifted in unison, twenty-five thousand at a time, lifted to the level of the shoulder and then brought down with the full force of the muscular, hardened bodies of highly trained warriors.

'Bayete!' they greeted the King with the royal salute.

'Bayete!' the crash of feet once more.

'Bayete!' a third time, and then the dancing began.

One regiment at a time coming forward in swaying, singing ranks, to perform before Mzilikazi's armchair throne. The perfect timing and execution of the intricate steps made it seem as though they were a single living organism, the shields interlocking and revolving and twisting together like the scales of some gigantic reptile, the dust rising and swirling through their ranks like smoke so that they appeared as wraiths, and their cloaks of furs and their kilts of civets' tails and monkeyskins, of the pelts of foxes and cats, swirled about their legs so they appeared to be divorced from earth, suspended above it on the moving cloud of dust and the soft waves of fur.

From the ranks sprang the great champions and the heroes of each regiment, to *giya* in their pride. Leaping as high as their own heads, and stabbing furiously at the air, screaming challenge and triumph, the sweat greased their muscles and flew in explosive droplets in the sunlight.

Mzilikazi was caught up in the building sea of excitement, and he quaffed from the beer pots that the maidens brought him until his eyes rolled in his head and he could not contain himself further. He struggled from his chair, and hobbled out on his swollen and deformed legs, and the champions fell back to give him place.

'My father is the finest dancer in all of Matabeleland,' said Gandang, squatting beside Zouga.

The old King tried to leap, but his feet did not leave the ground. He shuffled back and forth, making little pawing gestures, hacking at the air with his toy war spear.

'Thus I struck down Barend the Griqua, and thus his sons died.'

The nation roared.

'The bull elephant dances, and the earth shakes.' And the slamming of ten thousand feet goaded the King to circle in a painful and pathetic parody of the young champions' wild gyrations.

'Thus I spurned the tyrant Chaka, and thus I cut the plumes from the headdress of his messengers and sent them back to him,' squealed Mzilikazi.

'Bayete!' thundered the nation. 'He the father of the world.'

Exhausted within minutes, the ancient King sank into the dust, and Gandang and two other of the King's sons leapt to their feet from the half circle of Indunas and raced to his side.

Gently they bore him up and carried him back to his chair, and Lobengula, the King's senior son, held a beer pot for him to drink from. The beer dribbled from his chin and ran down the King's heaving chest.

'Let the nation dance,' gasped the King, and Gandang returned to Zouga's side and squatted beside him.

'After war, my father loves best the dance,' he explained.

The maidens came, rank upon lovely rank, their naked skin shimmering in the glaring sunlight of noon. The tiny beaded apron that barely covered their little triangular sex was all they wore, and their singing was sweet and clear.

Mzilikazi hoisted himself from his chair once more, and hobbled out to dance with them, passing along the foremost rank, directing the singing with his ritual war-spear pointed to the skies. The King danced until he dropped once more, and was again carried back to his chair by his sons.

By nightfall, Zouga was exhausted. His sweaty neck was chafed by the high stock of his dress coat, and sweat had soaked through the thick scarlet serge in dark patches. His eyes were bloodshot and inflamed from the dust and the glare, his head ached from the cacophony of drums and the roar of Matabele voices, his tongue felt thick and furry from the draughts of sorghum beer that had been pressed upon him and his back and legs ached from the unfamiliar squatting attitude he had been forced into all that day – but the King was still dancing, hobbling and prancing and squeaking on those twisted and deformed legs of his.

The following morning Mzilikazi was on his throne again, so undaunted by the previous day's exertions, that when the

Chawala bull was loosed into the arena his sons had bodily to restrain him from rushing out to slay it with his bare hands.

A champion from each regiment had been chosen, and stripped down to a loin-cloth. They waited in squatting ranks on each side of Mzilikazi's chair.

The bull came into the ring at the charge, horned head held high, red dust spurting from under his hooves, and his wild eyes glaring. He was pure, untainted black, with a huge humped back and glossy burnished hide.

Carefully picked from all the King's herds, he was the finest animal in the whole of Matabeleland and he made an arrogant circuit of the arena, stepping high, snorting and dropping his head to hook with curved horns at anything in his path.

The King, held by his sons, but struggling against their grip, was almost incoherent with excitement, and now he lifted his spear and his arms shook violently as he screamed,

'*Bulala inkunzi!* Kill the bull!'

The waiting men leapt to their feet, saluted the King, and then raced out, spreading into a half-moon-shape line, instinctively adopting the *jikela*, the movement of encirclement.

The black bull swung to meet them, came up short on locked front legs, his head swinging as he measured his charge; then the great rounded quarters bunched under him and he surged forward, picking a man in the centre of the line and thundering down on him.

The man he had chosen stood his ground, spreading his arms in a welcoming gesture and the bull dropped his head and hit him. Clearly Zouga heard the brittle snap of bone as the warrior absorbed the shock of impact against his chest, and then locked his arms around the animal's neck and held on.

The bull tried to toss him, hooking and throwing his head high, but the man held on, and was cruelly thrown about, but his body blocked the bull's sight and brought him to a halt. The racing line closed about him instantly, and abruptly the bull's great humped body was smothered by the rush of naked black men.

For long seconds the bull struggled to remain upright, but they bore him down and tore his legs out from under him so he hit the dusty earth with a heavy thump and a groaning bellow. A dozen men seized the long horns, and, using their leverage, began to twist them against the massive inert weight of his pinned body. Slowly, sweating and straining, they forced his head around, and the bull kicked his hooves in the air, his bellows becoming more desperate and strangled.

The King leapt up and down in his chair, screaming with excitement, and the roar of voices was like the sound of surf on a gale-driven coast of rock.

Inch by inch, the huge horned head revolved, and then suddenly there was no longer resistance. Zouga heard the crack of the vertebrae, sharp as a musket shot even above the thunder of the assembled nation. The horned head flicked through another half turn, the legs stiffened skywards for a moment, and the bull's bowels voided in a liquid green stream.

The sweat-drenched warriors lifted the carcass shoulder high and bore it bodily across the arena to lay it at Mzilikazi 's feet.

On the third and last day of the ceremony, Mzilikazi stalked out into the centre of the cattle-pen. He made a frail and bent figure in the vast open space, and the noon sun burned down from above so that there was almost no shadow under him. The nation was quiet, forty thousand human beings watching one old man and there was not a whisper, nor a sound of breathing.

In the centre of the arena Mzilikazi paused and raised his war-spear above his head. The watching ranks stiffened as he revolved slowly, and then stopped facing towards the south. He drew back his spear arm, poised for a moment while the tension in the watchers was a palpable emanation from forty thousand charged bodies.

Then the King gave a little hop, and began slowly to revolve, the crowd sighed and swayed and then grew silent as again the King poised with his blade pointed towards the east. Then another little hop as he teased them deliberately, drawing out the moment with the timing of a natural showman.

Then suddenly his spear arm shot forward and the tiny toylike weapon flew from his hand in a high sparkling parabola, and dropped to bury its point in the baked earth.

'To the north!' thundered the nation. 'Bayete! The great bull has chosen the north!'

'We go northwards to raid the Makololo,' Gandang told Zouga. 'I will leave with my impi in the dawn.' He paused, and then smiled briefly. 'We will meet again, Bakela.'

'If the gods are kind,' Zouga agreed, and Gandang laid one hand on his shoulder, squeezed briefly, and then turned away.

Slowly, without looking back, Gandang walked away into the darkness which was clamorous with the singing and the sound of the drums.

'Your guns would be terrible weapons if they did not have to be reloaded,' Mzilikazi piped in his querulous old man's voice. 'But to fight with them a man must have a fast horse, so that he may fire and then gallop away to reload.'

Zouga squatted by the King's chair in the royal enclosure as he had for almost thirty successive days. The King sent for him each day, and he must listen to Mzilikazi's wisdom and eat huge quantities of half-raw beef washed down by pot after pot of beer.

'Without a horse my warriors will overrun them before they can reload, even as we did to the Griquas, and afterwards we picked up over three hundred of their precious guns from the battlefield.'

Zouga nodded his agreement, smiling inwardly as he imagined the *amadoda* trying those tactics on a square of British infantry.

Mzilikazi broke off to lift the beer pot. and then as he lowered it the sparkle of one of Zouga's tunic buttons caught his eye, and he leaned across to pluck at it. Resignedly Zouga took the clasp knife from his pocket and carefully cut the threads that held the button. He handed it to the King, and Mzilikazi grinned with pleasure and held it to the sunlight.

'Only five to go,' Zouga thought ironically. He felt like the Christmas turkey being plucked a feather at a time. His lapel badges and field officer's pips had long since been taken by the King, as had his belt buckles and helmet badge.

'The paper,' Zouga started and the King waved airily, dismissing the reference to the concession.

He might be on the verge of senility and certainly he was an alcoholic, drinking seven gallons of beer each day, by Zouga's count, but still Mzilikazi possessed a cunning and devious intellect with a natural grasp of his own bargaining weaknesses and strengths. He had teased Zouga for thirty days, just as he had teased the watching nation on the third day of the *Chawala*, while they had waited for him to hurl the war-spear.

Now the King turned away from Zouga at the mention of the concession, and transferred his attention to the young couple who knelt before him. They had been accused, and come before the King for judgement.

That day, in between chatting with Zouga, Mzilikazi had received emissaries bearing tribute from two of his vassal chieftains, he had rewarded a young herdboy for saving his herd from a marauding lion, he had sentenced to death another who had been seen drinking milk directly from the udder of one of his charges, he had listened to the reports of a messenger from the impis campaigning in the north against the Makololo, and now his attention was on the accused couple before him.

The girl was a lovely creature, with long delicately formed limbs and a sweetly rounded face with full flaring lips over small very white teeth. She kept her eyes tightly closed, so as not to look upon the King's wrath, and her body was shaken with tremors of terror as she knelt before him. The man was a finely muscled young warrior, from one of the unmarried regiments, who had still to win the honour of being allowed to 'go in to the women'.

'Rise up, woman, that the King may see your shame,' the voice of the accuser rang out, and hesitantly, timidly, still with her eyes tightly closed, the girl lifted her forehead from the dusty earth, and sat back on her heels.

Her naked stomach, drum tight and round as a ripening fruit, bulged out above the tiny beaded apron.

The King sat hunched in his chair, brooding silently for many minutes, then he asked the warrior,

'Do you deny this thing?'

'I do not deny it, Nkosi Nkulu.'

'Do you love this wench?'

'As I love life itself, my King.' The man's voice was low and husky, but firm and without a quaver to it.

The King brooded again.

Zouga had sat by and watched the King give judgement on a hundred such occasions. Sometimes the decision had been worthy of a black Solomon, at others Zouga had been appalled by the barbaric savagery of the sentence.

Now the King stared at the man before him, and he fiddled with the toy spear in his right hand, frowning and shaking his head softly, then he reached a decision, and leaning forward he proffered the weapon to the man who knelt before him.

'With this blade, open the womb of the woman you love, take out from it that which offends against law and against custom – and place it in my hands.'

Zouga did not sleep that night, and once he threw off his blankets and hurried to the fringe of the acacia grove to retch and heave, vomiting up his horror at what he had witnessed.

In the morning the memory of the girl's screams had not faded but the King was jocular and garrulous, pressing pot after pot of sour beer on Zouga's rebellious stomach, recounting episodes from his long and eventful life, describing vividly the scenes from his childhood and youth in far-off Zululand with a certain old man's wistful nostalgia.

Then suddenly, without any prior hint that he would do so, he commanded Zouga, 'Speak the words of your paper.'

He listened silently as Zouga translated the terms of the concession he was seeking, and at the end he mused a moment.

'To hunt elephant and to dig a hole,' he mumbled at last. 'It is not so very much you wish for. Write that you will do these things only in the land below the Zambezi, east of the Inyati River and above the Limpopo.'

Not quite convinced that the King was this time serious, Zouga quickly added the proviso to the foot of his home-grown legal document.

Then he directed the King's trembling hand to form the big uncertain cross below it.

'Mzilikazi: his mark.'

The King's pleasure in affixing the wax seal beside his mark was childlike and unaffected. After it was done he passed it to his Indunas to admire, and leaned forward towards Zouga.

'Now that you have what you want from me, you will wish to leave.' There was regret in the rheumy eyes, and Zouga felt a pang of guilt, but he replied directly.

'I cannot hunt in the rains, and there is much work for me to accomplish in my own land across the sea. I must go, but I shall return, Nkosi Nkulu.'

'I give you the road to the south, Bakela the Fist. Go in peace and return to me soon, for your presence pleases me, and your words are wise for one still so young.'

'Stay in peace, Great Elephant.' Zouga rose and left the King's courtyard, and his step was as light as his spirits were gay. He had the concession buttoned into the breastpocket of his tunic, fifty-six pounds of native gold in his chest, the stone bird of Zimbabwe, and three fine tusks of ivory to buy his way. The road to the south, to Good Hope and to England lay open before him.

The wind was offshore, a faint backlash of the monsoon, but the sky was low and grey and the twisting squalls of rain fell from it like pearl dust.

Ensign Ferris, *Black Joke*'s most junior officer, was taking his sights off the traverse board as the gunboat closed the land, calling them quietly to the signals yeoman who swiftly worked out the distance offshore, and wrote this down on the navigation slate, so that any moment the Captain could glance down at it to confirm his own observations.

There was a man in the bows with a leadline, chanting the depth as he read it from the markings on the line, then twirling the weight and hurling it out ahead of *Black Joke*'s creeping bows, letting it sink and then reading the mark again as the ship passed over it.

'By the deep six.'

Clinton Codrington was conning his ship in by the leadsman's chant, by the angles that Ferris was shooting off the land features which they had identified, by the colour shadings of the water, by the break and swirl of the tide on shoal and bank, and by a seaman's instinct. The chart surveyed thirty years previously by Captain Owen, R.N., he trusted not at all.

'Bring her around a point,' he told the helmsman quietly, and as the ship swung towards the land, they smelt it on the wind.

'Slave stink!' exclaimed Denham fiercely, and as he said it the masthead lookout sang out sharply,

'Smoke! Smoke from the right bank of the river.'

'How far up stream?'

'Two miles or more, sir!'

For the first time since sailing from Zanzibar harbour, Clinton allowed himself to believe that he was in time, that he had reached the Rio Save in time to answer the heartrending appeal of the woman he loved.

'We will clear for action, if you please, Mr Denham, but don't run out the guns.' He kept his voice level and formal, but his Lieutenant grinned at him.

'A fair cop, by Jove. Congratulations, sir,' and the crew laughed and skylarked as they lined up at the arms chest to receive their pistol and cutlass.

As *Black Joke* breasted the breaking white water of the bar, touched sand bottom for a moment and then broke the grip of it, and surged forward into the dark green and still waters of the estuary, Clinton nodded at Denham.

'You may run out the guns now.'

He had delayed until this moment to avoid altering the ship's trim during the critical passage of the bar. With the carriages rumbling ominously, *Black Joke* bared her fangs and under fighting sail, her bronze propeller thrashing exultingly, her crew armed and eager, she went into the labyrinth of the Rio Save like a ferret into the warren.

Clinton took her around the first bend, following the deep green sweep of the channel between the paler sandbanks. It was two hours past low tide and the flood was pushing strongly, the leadsman calling good bottom and Clinton was trying to conceal his impatience and eagerness by the calm controlled tone in which he called his orders to the helm.

'Would you just look at that!' exclaimed Ferris, and pointed over the side. Beside them floated what looked like an ebony log. It was only as they passed and it bobbed and rolled in their wake that Clinton realized that it was a human corpse, stomach distended, round and shiny with gas and limbs twisted like the branches of a tree blasted by lightning. Clinton transferred his attention back to the ship, with a small grimace of distaste.

'Meet her,' he told the helmsman and then as they tore around the broad curve of water between the mangrove forests and the full stretch of the estuary opened ahead of them, he said, 'Midships!'

His voice was flat, unemotional, neither triumphant nor

dejected. Smoke rose from the bank of the river, and through his glass he could see the smouldering remains of a series of long low buildings, roofs burned through and collapsed inwards. They seemed to have been deliberately fired.

In the smoke soaring and circling on spread wings rose a host of birds, buzzards and kites and vultures and the carrion-eating marabou storks. They seemed to reach up with the smoke to the belly of the lowering monsoon clouds, dimming the light of day with their wings. The oppressive towering silence was broken only by the faint high cries of the birds, and the river was empty.

Clinton and his officers stared silently at the wide deserted sweep of the Rio Save, green and smooth from bank to mangrove-clad bank. No one spoke as *Black Joke* bore on, close in to the ruined and blackened barracoons. They stared at the piles of corpses, their faces stiff and expressionless, concealing their horror at the foul plague that lurked there in the palm groves, concealing also their disappointment and chagrin at finding the anchorage deserted and *Huron* gone.

'Stop engine,' Clinton broke the silence. 'Let go port anchor.'

Denham and Ferris turned to look at their Captain, their carefully controlled expressions cracking with disbelieving dread; he was going to send a party ashore. They would come back aboard carrying the plague with them, they would all be doomed.

The bow anchor hit the mud of the estuary bottom, and *Black Joke* turned sharply, the flow of the tide swinging her across the narrow channel in her own length, the anchor holding her head until she was pointed directly back down the river towards the sea. Immediately Clinton gave the order, 'Slow ahead,' and, as the ship breasted the tide, 'Up anchor,' and the steam winch clattered merrily. The officers relaxed visibly, and Denham allowed himself to smile with relief. The Captain had used the anchor merely to turn the ship as swiftly as possible without going through the dangerous business of backing and filling in the narrow channel against the push of the tide.

As the anchor came back aboard with the gluey black mud clinging to its flukes, Clinton gave another series of orders.

'Half ahead.' That was as fast as he dared push for the open sea.

'Secure from action stations.'

There was no enemy to fight and as the heavy long-barrelled

thirty-two pounder guns were run in, *Black Joke* handled more easily.

'Mr Ferris, we will fumigate the ship.'

The smoke from the pails of burning sulphur would redden all their eyes and for days would taint the food and water, but Clinton's dread of smallpox outweighed such small considerations as comfort, and, besides, he smiled wryly to himself, any change to the taste of *Black Joke*'s bullied beef and hard bread could only be an improvement.

The smile was fleeting. He was sickened by his brief glimpses of the barracoons, and his anger was a cold sharp thing like the blade of the cutlass on his belt.

'Mr Denham,' he said quietly, 'please plot a course for Good Hope. We'll come on to it the moment we clear the land.'

He moved to the rail, half his mind on the job of conning *Black Joke* out of this stinking green river into the open sea, the other half of his mind running swiftly over the problem of bringing his ship into action against *Huron*.

How long was the start that the tall clipper had over his gunboat? Robyn Ballantyne's letter had been dated 16th November, today was the 27th November. Eleven days. That was too much. He could only hope that Robyn had been able to delay the sailing, as she had promised.

Clinton glanced back over his shoulder at the blue smoke column that blurred the horizon. How long had those fires in the barracoons been burning? Not more than three or four days, he guessed, with more hope than conviction. Yet even that was still too long a start. He had seen *Huron* on a wind and she was swift as a swallow, and light as a witch. Even with eight hundred slaves in her holds, and her water casks filled, she would toy with *Black Joke* in any wind better than a light breeze. His only advantage would be in the offing that Huron must make to get on the trades and weather the bulge of the continent, while *Black Joke* could cut across the other arm of the triangle, hugging the land. It was small advantage, a few hundred leagues, and in the end it would all depend on the wind.

Clinton found he was pounding his clenched fist on the ship's rail, that he was glaring ahead with such ferocity that the idle hands of the lee rail were watching him curiously.

With an effort he forced his features to relax, and linked his hands at the small of his back, beneath the tails of his uniform coat, but his eyes still glittered pale sapphire blue and his lips were chalky with stress. It seemed too long for his patience before he could at last bring *Black Joke* on to her true course, and bend to the engine room voice-tube.

'I want all the speed you can squeeze out of her,' he told his engineer. 'There is twenty thousand pounds of prize money just below the horizon, but it's running like a fox and I'll need every pound of steam you can give me.'

He straightened up and the wind whipped his pale golden hair against his sun-gilded cheeks and forehead. He glanced up at the sky and saw the ponderous roll of the monsoon clouds on the wind.

Huron would have it full and boisterous on her port beam, with that hull and rigging it was probably her best point of sailing.

He knew that there was not the remotest chance of finding the clipper on the open sea, there were millions of square miles of ocean to cover – not even a battle fleet with a full squadron of frigates ideally placed ahead of the fugitive would have much chance of finding a single ship in that infinity of water.

Clinton knew that his only chance was to reach the southern tip of the continent ahead of *Huron* and to take up station athwart the narrow shipping-lane that was threaded around Cape Point. However, once *Huron* rounded the southern cape, the whole of the wide Atlantic would lie ahead of her and she would be gone again. Clinton's jawline clenched spasmodically at the thought of the American escaping into that limitless expanse of sea. If she had indeed eleven days' lead on him with this wind holding fair, she could even at this moment be raising the rocky cliffs of Cape Point. He put the thought from his mind and concentrated on coaxing every inch of speed from his ship over the long days and nights ahead.

Robyn had searched in vain for a subterfuge to delay *Huron*'s departure from the Rio Save, even though she knew that if she succeeded she would be endangering the lives of all aboard her. However, Mungo St John had swiftly regained his energy and determination as his wound healed and the effects of the inoculation passed. Affected by Robyn's warning about the danger of battlefield plagues, he forced the pace of his crew in loading the slaves. They worked through the night by the light of tar-dipped rope torches, as well as by day, the crew every bit as eager as their Captain to be away from this cursed river. Four days after the loading began, *Huron*'s slave-decks were in place and her cargo of slaves aboard, and that evening at the full of the tide, using the last of the light and the first gusts of the offshore night breeze, *Huron* slipped over the bar, shook out her reefs and settled down to make her offing during the night.

At dawn they caught the steady push of the trades and Mungo brought her round on to a more southerly heading, close-hauled to make good their eastings before running for the bulge of Agulhas with the wind on the beam.

The sweet clean air of the open sea that had travelled thousands upon thousands of miles since last having touched land, swept through the ship, cleansing it of the dreadful stench of the plague barracoons, and Mungo's strict hygienic discipline helped to keep the holds free of the slave stink and impressed even Robyn, though reluctantly, with his forethought and his precautions.

By sacrificing a single slave deck, raising the space between each from the traditional 20 inches to 32 inches, he allowed not only greater comfort but easier access. In these mild conditions of wind and sea, the slaves were exercised during all of the daylight hours, the higher headroom and wider ladderways enabled even those in the lowest decks to be brought up on deck in batches of fifty at a time. On the maindeck they were forced to dance to the rhythm of a tribal drum beaten by a tattooed naked tribesman, the rattle and clink of their chains made a mournful background music to the drum and the sweet sound of the singing slaves.

'Funny business, that tattooing.' Nathaniel stopped to chat with Robyn as she stood watching the dismal show. 'They started tattooing their children to make them repulsive to us slavers, some of them file or knock out their teeth like that one there.' He pointed at a muscular black man in the circle of dancing slaves whose teeth had been filed to sharp points like those of a shark. 'Some of them put bones through the noses of their daughters, and others stretch their tits – begging your pardon at the plain speaking, ma'am – or they put rings of copper around their necks until they look like giraffes, all so the slavers will leave them alone. They do say now that these have become marks of beauty amongst the heathen. No accounting for taste, is there, ma'am?'

Robyn saw how the extra space and regular exercise would affect the well-being of the slaves, and while they were up on the maindeck, in the open air, their empty slave decks were flushed out with sea water from the ship's pumps and then scrubbed down with a strong lye mixture. Though even this was not enough to prevent the slave stink slowly impregnating the ship.

Each slave spent two hours on deck each second day, and while they were there, Robyn held clinic and examined each of them for any signs of disease or injury. Before going below once more, they were each forced to drink a decoction of molasses and lime juice to supplement the plain diet of boiled farina and water, and to ward off the dreaded scourge of the scurvy.

The slaves responded well to this treatment, and, incredibly, began to put on the weight that they had burned off during the fevers that were the result of the inoculation against the smallpox. The mood of the slaves was resigned and compliant, although there were isolated incidents. One morning, while a batch of slaves were being brought up, one of them, a fine-looking naked woman, managed to work free the shackle of her chain and the moment she reached the deck she rushed to *Huron*'s side and leapt over it, into the creaming blue wake of the racing clipper.

Despite the fact that she still wore the iron cuffs on her wrists, she managed to keep afloat for many long minutes; her struggles were pitiful to watch as she was slowly drawn down lower and lower in the water.

Robyn had run to the rail to watch the woman's efforts, expecting Mungo to heave-to and lower a boat to rescue her, but he remained detached and silent on his quarterdeck, barely glancing over the stern before occupying himself once more with the management of his ship, while *Huron* tore away and the woman's head dwindled to a speck on the blue water, then was drawn inevitably below the surface by the weight of her iron cuffs.

Although Robyn realized that it would have been impossible to stop the clipper and reach the woman before she drowned, yet she glared at Mungo across the length of the deck, wishing that there were words to express her fury and indignation.

That night she lay awake in her tiny cabin, hour after hour, racking her imagination for some ruse that could be used to delay the tall clipper's full flight towards the Southern Cape.

She thought of stealing one of the ship's boats and casting herself adrift during the night, forcing Mungo to turn back and to search for her. It took only a few minutes' reflection to realize that it would take a dozen strong men to free the whaler from its lashings and lower it on its davits over the ship's side – and even if she managed to accomplish that, it was far from certain that Mungo would delay even a minute. He was more likely to sail away and leave her, as he had left the slave woman.

She thought of setting fire to the ship, overturning a lantern in the mainsail locker, and creating so much damage that *Huron* would be obliged to call at the nearest port, Lourenç Marques or Port Natal, to effect repairs, and to give *Black Joke* an opportunity to come up with her. Then she imagined eight hundred chained slaves burning to death in the hold when the fire got out of control, and she shuddered, thrust that idea from her and hopelessly composed herself to a sleep which would not come.

In the end her opportunity came from a most unexpected source, Tippoo. The huge mate had a weakness, a single weakness that Robyn could observe. He was a trencherman and, in his own taste, a gourmet. Half the lazaretto was filled with delicacies that Tippoo had hoarded and which he shared with no others. There were dried and smoked meats and sausages, cheeses the smell of which brought tears to the eyes, and wooden crates of cans and bottles of preserved foods, though as a strict Moslem, he took no alcohol. He made up what he lacked in the glass with his spoon.

His appetite was one of the ship's jokes, and Robyn had heard Mungo chaffing him across the wardroom table.

'Were it not for the tucker you brought aboard, Mr Mate, we'd have room for another hundred blackbirds in our hold.'

'I'll wager that belly of yours costs you more to sustain than a harem of extravagant wives.'

'Sweet merciful heavens, Mr Tippoo, but whatever you are eating should have been given a Christian burial a month ago.'

One of Tippoo's favourite appetizers was a particularly virulent bloater paste, packed in half-pound tins. The instruction printed on the tin read 'Spread thinly on biscuit or toast', and Tippoo would spoon it directly from the tin, consuming the entire half pound without once breaking the rhythmic dip and lift of his soup spoon, his eyes half closed and a cherubic smile buckling the wide line of his toad's mouth.

The fourth night out of the Rio Save he began his dinner with a can of bloater paste, but as he pierced the lid with his clasp knife, there was a sharp hiss of escaping gas, and Mungo St John glanced up from his own plate of pea soup.

'It is blown, Mr Tippoo. I would not eat it if I were you.'

'No,' Tippoo agreed. 'But you not me.'

They called Robyn a little before midnight. Tippoo was in convulsions, doubled up with agony, his belly swollen and hard as a yellow agate boulder. He had vomited until now he was retching only a little blood-flecked bile.

'It's ptomaine poisoning,' Robyn told Mungo St John. It was the first time she had spoken directly to him since that morning in the Rio Save, and her voice was cool and formal. 'I do not have the medicines to treat it. You will have to put into a port where he can receive treatment. There is a military hospital at Port Natal.'

'Doctor Ballantyne,' Mungo answered her as formally, but his infuriating smile lurked behind the gold-flecked eyes. 'Mr Tippoo's mother was an ostrich, he can digest stones, nails and lumps of broken glass. Your concern, touching as it may be, is entirely misplaced. He will be ready to fight, flog, or devour an ox by noon tomorrow.'

'And I tell you that without proper treatment he will be dead in a week.'

However, Mungo's prognosis proved to be correct, for by morning the vomiting and retching had abated and Tippoo seemed to have purged his bowels of the poisoned fish. Robyn was forced to a decision which she made on her knees in her cabin.

'Forgive me, oh Lord, but there are eight hundred of your children chained below decks in this foul prison, and I will not kill him – at least, with your help, I will not kill him.'

Then, off her knees she went briskly to work. She used a solution of peppermint tincture to disguise the taste, and let fall fifteen drops of essence of ipecacuanha into the medicine glass, which was three times the recommended dosage for the most powerful emetic known to the medical science.

'Drink it down,' she told Tippoo. 'It will soothe your stomach, and cure the diarrhoea.'

Late that afternoon she repeated the dose, but the wardroom steward had to help her lift Tippoo's head from the bolster and pour the draught down his throat. The effect was enough to alarm even Robyn.

An hour later she sent for Mungo, and the steward came back with the message, 'Captain says as how the ship's safety demands all his attention at the moment, begging your pardon, Doctor.'

When Robyn herself went on deck, Mungo was at the weather rail, sextant in hand, waiting for the sun to appear in a gap in the clouds.

'Tippoo is dying,' she told him.

'And this will be my first sight of the day,' Mungo replied without taking his eye from the eyepiece of the instrument.

'I at last believe that you are a monster with no human feelings,' she whispered fiercely, and at that moment blazing sunlight struck the deck, as the sun showed briefly through the ragged hole in the cloud.

'Stand by the chronometer,' Mungo called to the signals yeoman, and then 'Mark!' as he brought the sun's image down to bounce lightly as a green rubber ball on the dark line of the horizon.

'Excellent,' he murmured with satisfaction, as he lowered the sextant and read off the height of the sun, and called it to the yeoman to mark on his slate. Only then did he turn back to Robyn.

'I am sure you have misjudged the severity of Tippoo's ailment.'

'See for yourself,' she invited.

'That is my intention, Doctor.'

Mungo stooped into Tippoo's cabin, and paused. His expression changed, suddenly the light mocking smile was gone. It was evident that Tippoo was indeed dangerously ill.

'How are you, old friend?' Mungo asked quietly. It was the first time Robyn had ever heard him use that form of address. He lifted his hand and laid it on the mate's sweat-beaded forehead.

Tippoo rolled the bald yellow cannon ball of his head towards Mungo, and he tried to smile. It was a brave effort. Robyn felt a terrible guilty pang, at the suffering she was inflicting and at being the witness to this private, and strangely intimate, moment between these two hard and dangerous men.

Tippoo tried to lift himself, but the effort brought a long dragging groan rattling up his throat, and he clutched at his stomach with both hands, drawing his knees up with agony, and then desperately twisting his head as a fresh bout of heaving and retching racked his body.

Mungo snatched the bucket off the deck and with one arm around Tippoo's shoulders held it for him – but all that Tippoo could bring up was a little splash of blood and brown bile, and when he fell back on the bunk he was gasping unevenly, bathed in fresh sweat and his eyes rolled back in his skull until only a little half moon of the iris still showed.

Mungo stood beside his bunk for a full five minutes, bowed and attentive, swaying slightly to the ship's movement, but otherwise still and silent. His brow was creased with thought and his gaze remote, and watching him, Robyn knew he was making the dire decision – the throw of the dice of life, friendship against the loss of his ship and perhaps even his own liberty, for to go into a British port with slaves in his holds was an awful risk.

Strange, now that he was showing this gentler side of his nature, that her affection came flooding back at full strength, she felt mean and cheap for playing on his deepest emotions, and for torturing the huge yellow Moslem on the narrow bunk.

Mungo swore quietly but decisively, and, still stooped under the low deck, strode from the cabin.

Robyn's affection turned to disgust and disappointment. Disgust that even the life of an old and loyal friend meant nothing to this cruel and merciless man whom she was doomed to love, and intense disappointment that her ruse had failed, that she had inflicted this dangerous suffering on Tippoo to no avail.

She sank down wearily and bitterly beside his bunk, took a cloth soaked in sea water and bathed the sweat-basted yellow head.

During their long voyage down the Atlantic, Robyn had grown sensitive to all *Huron*'s moods, to the feel of the deck underfoot at every point of sailing, and to the sounds that her hull made in different sea and wind conditions, and now abruptly she felt the deck cant sharply beneath her. She heard the stamp of bare feet on the deck above as her yards were trained around and

Huron's action became easier, the sounds of her hull and rigging muted as she took the wind in over her stern quarter and rode more easily.

'He's altered course towards the west,' she breathed as she lifted her head to listen. 'It worked. He is going in to Port Natal. Oh thank you Lord, it worked.'

Huron anchored well offshore, out on the thirty-fathom line of the shelving coast, so that she could not benefit from the shelter of the huge whale-backed bluff that protected Port Natal's natural harbour. Even with a powerful telescope, a watcher on the shore would be unable to make out any significant details of *Huron*'s cargo, nor of her true occupation. However, the ship paid for her offshore berth by taking the unfettered scend of the sea and the wind. She pitched and she rolled and she jerked at her anchor chain.

At her peak she flew the stars and stripes of her country – and below that the yellow 'Quebec', the plague flag which warned, 'Stay away from me! I have plague on board!'

Mungo St John placed an armed watch on both sides of the ship and others at her bow and stern, and, despite Robyn's strident protest, she was confined to her cabin for the duration of the ship's call, with another armed guard outside her door.

'You are very well aware of the reason, Doctor Ballantyne.' Mungo answered her protests calmly. 'I do not wish you to have any communication whatsoever with your countrymen ashore.'

The whaler, when it took Tippoo ashore, was rowed by men that Mungo selected personally, and they were instructed to inform the Harbour Master that there was smallpox aboard, and to request that no other vessel be allowed near *Huron*.

'I can only wait three days for you.' Mungo stooped over the litter on which Tippoo was carried on deck. 'That is all I can risk. If you are not sufficiently recovered by then, you will have to stay here until my return. That cannot be more than five months.' He tucked a leather draw-string purse under Tippoo's blanket. 'And that will pay your expenses in the meanwhile. Get well, Mr Tippoo, I need you.'

Robyn had administered another dose of the peppermint and

ipecacuanha a few minutes previously, and Tippoo could reply only in an agonized whisper.

'I will wait for you, Captain Mungo, as long as she takes.'

Mungo's voice was husky as he straightened and spoke to the seamen carrying the litter.

'Handle him easy, you hear me.'

For three days Robyn sweated and fretted in the stuffy little cabin, trying to occupy her time with writing up her journals but distracted by any loud noise from the deck above, her heart pounding as she both hoped for and dreaded the hail from a British gun-boat, or the rush of a boarding-party coming in over *Huron*'s side.

On the third morning Tippoo was rowed back to the ship, and he climbed up the side and in through the entry port unaided. Without further doses of ipecacuanha, his recovery had amazed the military surgeons ashore, but he was so thin that the skin hung in folds from his jowls like a bulldog, his belly had shrunk so that he had tied his breeches with a length of rope to keep them from sinking down past his flattened belly, but still they flapped around his shrunken buttocks.

His skin was the pale yellow of ancient ivory, and he was so weak he had to pause to rest when he reached the deck.

'Welcome aboard, Mr Tippoo,' Mungo called from the quarter-deck. 'And if you have finished your holiday ashore, I'll thank you to get this ship under way immediately.'

Twelve days later, having struggled with flukey and variable winds, Mungo St John played the field of his glass down the open gaping maw of False Bay. On his right hand rose the distinctive curved black peak of Hangklip, shaped from this angle like a shark's dorsal fin, and directly opposite it across the mouth of the bay the southernmost tip of the African continent, Cape Point, with its lighthouse perched high above the steep wet cliffs.

It was a magnificent Cape summer's day, a light and fickle breeze scratching dark patches on the surface of the rolling dark blue sea, leaving the rest of it with a satiny gloss. There were seabirds working, their wings twinkling like flurrying snow flakes in the sunlight, huge flocks of them that stretched low across the horizon.

Creeping along on the breeze, lying for minutes at a time completely becalmed, *Huron* took half a day to round the point and came on to west-north-west and a point north, the course that would carry her up the Atlantic, across the equator and finally into Charleston Roads.

Once they were on their new course, Mungo St John had leisure to inspect the other sails that were in sight. There were nine, no, ten other vessels in view now, for there was another far out to sea, just her topsails showing. They were small fishing craft out from Hout Bay and Table Bay, and the seabirds clouded the air about them, most of them were between *Huron* and the land, and all of them were bare-masted or under working sail as they plied their lines or their nets. Only the vessel furthest out was carrying topsails, and though she was hull down she gave to Mungo's seaman's eye the impression of being a bigger ship than the rest of the fishing fleet.

'There's a ship for you!' Tippoo exclaimed, touching Mungo's arm to draw his attention and when he swung his glass back towards the land Mungo murmured with pleasure as a square-rigged East Indiaman came into view around the headland that guarded the entrance to Table Bay itself.

She was as splendid a sight as *Huron* was herself, canvas piled to the sky and her paintwork gleaming in snowy white and Burgundy red, the two lovely ships on reciprocal courses passed each other by two cables' length, the officers eyeing each other through their telescopes with professional interest and appraisal as they paid passing honours.

Robyn was also at *Huron*'s rail, pining towards the land. The proximity of the beautiful ship interested her hardly at all, it was that flat-topped mountain from which she could barely tear her gaze. It was so very close, marking as it did her one hope of succour, her friends there, the British Governor and the Cape Squadron, if they only knew that she was a prisoner aboard this slave ship.

The thought was interrupted by an abrupt movement that she caught from the corner of her eye – strange how receptive she was to Mungo St John's smallest movement, to his slightest change of expression – and now she saw that he had turned his back on the East Indiaman as she dwindled away astern, and instead he was peering intently over *Huron*'s port side, his expression rapt, his whole body seemed charged with latent energy, and the hands that gripped the barrel of the telescope were ivory knuckled with tension.

Quickly she followed his gaze, and for the first time noticed a tiny shred of white on the horizon that did not fade like the white caps of the waves, but stood constant and bright in the sunlight, though even as she watched it seemed to alter its shape slightly and – was it her imagination, or was it a thin dark wavering line that seemed to appear behind it and spread slowly away in the direction of the wind?

'Mr Tippoo, what do you make of that sail?' She heard the timbre of concern and alarm in Mungo St John's tone, and her heart leapt wildly, with hope and a Judas dread.

For Clinton Codrington it had been a desperate run down the eastern coastline of southern Africa, long days and sleepless nights of unceasing strain, when hope and despair pendulumed against each other. Each shift or change in the wind either alarmed or encouraged him, for it would either aid or hinder the tall clipper ship he was racing to head. The calms elated him, and the revival of the south-easterly prevailing winds sent his spirits plunging.

On the last days there was another worry to plague him. He had burned his coal like a spendthrift on the long thousand-mile run southwards, and his engineer came up on deck, a small red-headed Scot with the grease and coal-dust etched into his skin so that he seemed to be suffering from some debilitating and incurable disease.

'The stokers' shovels be hitting the bottom of the bunkers already,' he told Clinton with mournful relish. 'I warned ye, sir, that we'd not make it if you—'

'Burn the ship's furniture if you must,' Clinton snapped at him. 'You can start with my bunk, I'll not be needing it.'

And when the engineer would have argued further Clinton added, 'I don't care how you do it, Mr MacDonald, but I want a full head of steam on your boiler until I reach Cape Point, and another full head of steam when I bring this ship into action.'

They raised the Cape Point lighthouse a few minutes after midnight the following night, and Clinton's voice was hoarse with fatigue and relief as he stooped over the voice pipe.

'Mr MacDonald, you can let your fires damp down, but keep

your furnaces warmed and ready to stoke. When I ask for steam again, I'll need it in a hurry.'

'You'll be calling at Table Bay to take on fresh bunkers, of course, sir?'

'I'll let you know when,' Clinton promised him, and snapped the lid of the speaking tube closed and straightened up.

The Cape naval base, with all its amenities lay only a few hours steaming away. By dawn he could be filling *Black Joke* with coal and water and fresh vegetables.

However, Clinton knew that within minutes of dropping anchor in Table Bay, Admiral Kemp or one of his representatives would be on his way out to the ship, and Clinton's term of independent command would be over. He would revert to being a very junior commander, whose recent actions needed a great deal of explanation.

The closer that Clinton drew to Admiralty House, the louder the warnings of Sir John Bannerman rang in his ears, and the more soberly he was forced to review his own position. The excitement of storming Arab barracoons and of seizing slave-laden dhows on the high seas had long ago cooled, and Clinton realized that once he entered it he would not be able to escape again from Table Bay for weeks, or possibly months. It would not even suit his immediate plans to be seen and recognized from the land, for a boat would immediately be sent out by Admiral Kemp to order him in to face judgement and retribution.

Clinton felt not the least trepidation about the Navy's ultimate judgement, he was so indifferent to the threat hanging over his career that he surprised even himself. There was only one desire, one object in his mind, that overshadowed all else. He must have his ship in position to intercept *Huron* as she rounded the Cape, if she had not already done so. Nobody and nothing must prevent him from doing so. After that he would face his accusers with complete equanimity. *Huron* and Robyn Ballantyne first, beside them all else was pale and insignificant.

'Mr Denham,' he called his Lieutenant across the dark deck. 'We will take up night patrol station ten miles off Cape Point, and I am to be called immediately the lights of any ship are sighted.'

As Clinton threw himself down, fully dressed and booted, upon his bunk, he experienced the first peace of mind since leaving Zanzibar harbour. He had done all that was in his power to reach Cape Point ahead of *Huron*, and now the rest was in the hands of God – and his trust in God was implicit.

He fell asleep almost instantly, and his steward woke him again an hour before dawn. He left the mug of coffee to grow cold beside his bunk and hurried on deck, reaching it a few seconds ahead of Lieutenant Denham.

'No ships during the night, sir,' Ferris, who had the watch, saluted him.

'Very well, Mr Ferris,' Clinton acknowledged. 'We will take up our daylight patrol station immediately.'

By the time the light was strong enough for a watcher on the shore to make out any details, *Black Joke* had retreated tactfully below the horizon and it would have taken a sharp eye to pick out the occasional flash of her topsails, let alone to identify the gunboat and to speed a report to Admiral Kemp that his prodigal had returned.

From *Black Joke*'s masthead the land was a low irregular distortion of the horizon, but a ship rounding the Cape would be many miles closer than the land. *Huron*'s mainmast was almost one hundred and fifty feet tall, her sails would shine like a flaming beacon and as long as the fog did not come down, which was unlikely at this season of the year, Clinton was confident that she could not slip by him.

The only disquiet that scratched him like a burr as he paced his deck, and the gunboat settled down into the regular four-sided box-patterned legs of her patrol, was that *Huron* had long ago flown northwards on this fine wind that at last bore steadily out of the south-east at almost gale force, and that she was already lost in the endless watery green wastes of the southern Atlantic Ocean, leaving *Black Joke* to guard the gate of an empty cage.

He was not left long to brood, the first sighting was called down to the deck from the look-outs in the crow's nest at the main peak, and Clinton's nerves jumped tight and his expectations flared.

'What do you make of her?' he called up through the voice trumpet.

'Small lugger—' and his expectations plunged. A fishing-boat out of Table Bay, there would be many of them, but each time he could not control the wild surge of excitement when another sail was sighted, so that by nightfall his nerves were ragged, and his body ached with exhaustion as he gave the order for *Black Joke* to take up her inshore patrol station for the night.

Even then he could not rest, for three times during the night he was called from his bunk, and he stumbled owl-eyed on deck as *Black Joke* went down to investigate running lights that winked ruby red and emerald green out of the darkness.

Each time the same leap of expectation, the steeling of nerves for instant orders and swift action, and then the same let down as the lights proved to belong to small trading vessels, and the gunboat sheered away quickly, lest she be recognized and her presence off the Cape be reported in Table Bay.

In the dawn, Clinton was on deck again, as the gunboat moved further offshore to take up her daylight patrol station. He was distracted by the sighting reports as his masthead look-out picked up the first sails of the fishing fleet coming out for the day's business, and by the lugubrious report of his coal-stained Scottish engineer.

'Ye'll not last out the day, sir,' MacDonald told him. 'Even though I am burning just enough coal to keep the furnace warm – we've not more than a bucket or two left.'

'Mr MacDonald,' Clinton interrupted him, trying to keep his temper under control and to disguise his exhaustion. 'This ship will stay on station until I give the order, I don't care what you burn, but you are to give me steam when I ask for it – or kiss good-bye to the fattest bundle of prize money that will ever come your way.'

Despite this brave promise and threat, Clinton's hopes were sinking swiftly. They had been on station for more than a day and a night already – he could not bring himself to believe that he had beaten the swift clipper to the Cape by that margin, not unless she had been somehow miraculously delayed, and every hour increased the certainty that she had run clear away from him, taking her cargo and the woman he loved out of his life for ever.

He knew he should go below to rest, but his cabin was stifling in the rising summer heat, and in it he felt like a trapped animal. He stayed on deck, unable to keep still for more than a few moments at a time, poring over the chart table and fiddling with the navigational instruments before throwing them down and resuming his nervous pacing, shooting quick glances up at the masthead, and then roaming the ship so obviously intent on finding fault or criticizing the ship's running that his officers followed his lanky figure with troubled expressions, while the watch on deck was silent and subdued, not one of them daring to glance in his direction until Clinton's voice rose in a coldly furious cry that froze them all.

'Mr Denham,' the Lieutenant almost ran to the summons, 'this deck is a pig-sty. What animal is responsible for this filth?'

On the white holystoned deck planking was a brown splash of tobacco juice, and Denham stared at it for an instant before wheeling away to bellow a series of orders that had a dozen men scampering. The activity was so intense, the atmosphere electric, as Captain and Lieutenant stood over four men on their knees scrubbing furiously at the offending stain while others carried buckets of sea water and still others rigged the deck pump, that the hail from the masthead was almost ignored,

It was left to Ferris to acknowledge it, and to enquire through the voice trumpet,

'What do you make of her?'

'She's hull down, but she's a four-masted ship, square rigged—'

The activity on the deck ceased instantly, every head lifting as the look-out went on elaborating on his sighting.

'She's on a course to weather the Cape, now she's coming round on to a heading of north-north-west or thereabouts.'

Clinton Codrington was the first to move. He snatched the telescope out of Lieutenant Denham's hand and ran to the ratlines. With the telescope tucked in his belt he began to climb, hand over hand.

He went up steadily, never pausing nor faltering, not even when he reached the futtock shrouds and for a few moments hung over backwards one hundred feet above the swaying deck. However, when he reached the crow's nest at the main peak and tumbled into it thankfully, his breath was sawing dryly in his throat and the blood sang in his ears. He had not climbed like that since he had been a midshipman.

The look-out tried to make himself as small as possible, for they were crowded together in the canvas bucket, and he pointed out the ship to his Captain.

'There she be, sir.'

Black Joke's roll was emphasized up here on the tall pendulum of the mast, and the horizon swung giddily through the field of

Clinton's telescope as he tried to keep it focused. It was an art that he had never completely mastered, but that was of little consequence for the first time the little regular white pyramids popped up in the field of his glass the last doubts were dispelled, and Clinton felt his heart leap fiercely against his ribs.

His voice was strangled with triumphant emotion as he shouted down at the tiny foreshortened figures on the gleaming white quarterdeck far below.

'Bring her round to due east, Mr Denham. Order a full head of steam on the boiler–'

Though he had not yet fully recovered his breath, he threw himself out of the crow's nest and scrambled down faster than he had climbed. In his haste he slid the last fifty feet down the backstay and barely noticed the rough hempen rope scorching the palms of his hands.

By the time his feet hit the deck, *Black Joke* was coming around on to her new heading, and in anticipation of Clinton's next order, Denham had already called the watch below, and they came boiling out on to the deck.

'And we will clear for action, Mr Denham, if you please,' gasped Clinton, his face dark with blood under his deepwater tan and the sapphire eyes alight with battle lust.

All *Black Joke*'s officers carried swords on their belts, only Clinton had selected a cutlass, for he preferred the stouter and heavier weapon, and he fiddled with the hilt even now as he spoke to them quietly and seriously.

'Gentlemen, I have documented proof that the ship ahead of us has a cargo of slaves aboard her.'

Denham coughed nervously and Clinton forestalled him. 'I am also aware that she is an American vessel, and in ordinary circumstances we would be helpless to oppose her passage.' Denham nodded with relief, but Clinton went on remorselessly, 'However, I have received an appeal from one of Her Majesty's subjects, Dr Robyn Ballantyne whom you all know well, who is being abducted aboard the *Huron* against her will. I am certain what my duty is in these circumstances. I intend to board her, and if she resists me, I intend to fight her.' He paused and their faces were shocked, strained. 'Those of you who have objections to this course of action should immediately note them in the ship's log, and I will sign them.'

Their relief and gratitude was immediate, few other captains would be so lenient.

He signed his name neatly beneath the entry in the ship's log, and then returned the pen to its holder.

'Now that the formalities have been seen to, gentlemen, shall we get on with earning our hire?' And Clinton was smiling for the first time since they sailed from Zanzibar harbour as he indicated the pile of snowy white sails that was now clearly visible from the deck ahead of *Black Joke*'s bows, and as he spoke there was an eruption of dark tarry-smelling smoke from the tall single stack above them, and the engine telegraph clanged sharply as the pointer moved to 'Engine Standing By' position on the repeater. *Black Joke* had steam in her boiler.

Clinton stepped to the telegraph, thrust the handle fully around the dial to the 'Full ahead' position, and the deck vibrated under his feet as the propeller shaft began to spin and *Black Joke* lunged forward eagerly, breaking the swells off her shoulders in explosions of white spray.

'By God, he's got us pinned against the land –' Mungo drawled the words out nonchalantly, even smiling slightly at Tippoo as he lowered the glass from his eye for a moment and polished the lens on his shirt-sleeve. 'We'll have to run like the very devil to get round him, and make the open sea. Mr Tippoo, will you be good enough to shake out every last reef and crack on all the sail we can carry right up to the sky sails?' He lifted the glass to his eye again as Tippoo began bellowing the orders. 'It's a little bit too much luck for any one man,' Mungo murmured aloud. 'It's too much coincidence that the one man I would not wish to meet be lying in the one place on all the oceans where I would not wish to meet him.' Again he lowered the glass and strode to the poop rail to look down on to the maindeck.

Robyn Ballantyne was at the ship's side, staring out across the indigo blue waters at the sail and the smear of dark smoke, still far out to sea, but every moment converging on them, headed to a point far ahead of *Huron*'s elegant bows where the courses of the two ships would meet. She sensed Mungo's eyes upon her, and she lifted the shawl off her head so that her dark russet hair tumbled out and snapped and danced around her cheeks. Her skirts were flattened against her legs by the wind, so that she had to lean slightly forward to balance herself.

She lifted her chin and stared up at Mungo, her expression defiant and she watched him as he carefully bit the end off one of his long thin black cheroots and cupped his hands around the sulphurous flare of the Vesta match and lit the cheroot without once breaking the steady gaze that held her own.

Then he sauntered easily down the poop-ladder to her side.

'A friend of yours, Doctor Ballantyne?' The smile was on his lips alone. His eyes were frosty.

'I have prayed every night for him to come. Ever since I sent the letter that summoned him.'

'You do not deny the betrayal?'

'I am proud I was able to perform my Christian duty.'

'Who carried your letter?'

'No member of your crew, sir. I sent it by the master of the Omani buggaloo.'

'I see.' His voice was low, but stinging as dry ice. 'And what of Tippoo's illness, would a physician, per chance, stoop to poisoning a patient?'

She dropped her eyes, unable to meet that accusation.

'Will you be so kind, Doctor Ballantyne, as to return to your cabin immediately and stay there until I give you permission to leave it. There will be an armed guard at the door.'

'I am to be punished?'

'No man would blame me for dropping you over the side, and leaving you to be picked up by your countrymen. However, it is your safety I am thinking of. This deck could become an unhealthy spot in the very near future, and we will all be too much occupied to care for you.'

His attention left her, and he was staring ahead, and then glancing back at *Black Joke*'s smoke, judging speeds and angles with a seaman's eye. Then he smiled.

'Before you go, I would like you to know that all your efforts have really been a fine waste of time – look there!' He pointed ahead along the sheer and mountainous coastline, and following his arm she saw for the first time that ahead of them the sea was as black and broken as new coal cut from the face, glittering with wild jumping wavelets, each flecked with pretty white crests.

'There is the wind,' Mungo said. 'That's where it comes through the mountains, and we will be into it before you are safely tucked up in your cabin.' He chuckled now comfortably, confidently. 'Once we get on that wind, there are few ships on all the oceans, either steam or sail, that would match *Huron* for a moment, and God knows, there are none who could run her down.' He gave her a small mocking bow, parody of gracious southern manners. 'Take a good look at that ugly little steam packet, before you go, ma'am, you'll not be seeing her again. And now, if you'll be good enough to excuse me—'

He turned from her and ran lightly back up the poop-ladder.

Tears of anger dimming her eyes, Robyn clutched the rail and stared across the narrowing strip of sea at the bustling, puffing little gunboat, already she could catch glimpses of the hull, and its painted chequer-board gun-ports. She began to hope that Mungo St John's boast had been mere bravado, for *Black Joke* seemed to be keeping pace with the tall clipper, the wind was still a long, long way ahead.

There was a respectful touch on Robyn's shoulder, and old Nathaniel stood beside her.

'Captain's orders, ma 'am, and I am to see you safe in your cabin.'

Clinton leaned forward, all his weight on the balls of his feet, almost as though he were trying to urge his ship on by the balance of his body, the way a rider leans forward into the jump. He also had seen the wind pattern on the surface of the sea, and knew what it heralded.

The tall clipper ship looked lazy now, indolent in her flounces and ruffles as a lady of high fashion, and *Black Joke* was snorting and snuffling busily down the short leg of the triangle. If they both maintained this speed and course they would meet about eleven nautical miles ahead. Clinton could visualize the exact spot clearly just beyond the spit of land marked on his chart as 'Bakoven Point'.

Huron was committed to her present course. She could not bear up for the land lay close under her weather rail, and the chart showed breaking shoals well offshore – there was one of them now, close on her starboard beam, showing its round black granite back and blowing like a whale. *Huron* was in a trap, and her only escape would be to find the extra turn of speed which would carry her away out of gunshot range – and there it was, the wind, less than three miles ahead of her.

There was a loud banging from the deck below Clinton's feet, and he glanced irritably at Ferris.

'See what that is,' he snapped, and turned his full attention back to the clipper. Three short miles she had to go, but even as Clinton stared at her through his glass he saw her huge square mainsail quiver and then shake gently as she luffed in the flukey airs below the mountains.

'Please God!' Clinton whispered, and *Huron*'s speed bled off perceptively, all her sails were losing their taut clean shape and she checked away, baulking like a weary animal.

'She's found a hole in the wind,' Lieutenant Denham called exultantly. 'We've got her now, by God!'

'I'll thank you not to blaspheme on this quarterdeck, Mr Denham,' Clinton told him sharply, and Denham's expression was instantly crestfallen.

'I beg your pardon, sir.' At that moment Ferris arrived breathlessly back on deck.

'The stokers, sir,' he panted. 'They are knocking out all the furniture from the officers' quarters. Your bunk's gone, sir, and your desk also.'

Clinton barely glanced at him, he was studying the clipper, evaluating each yard of difference in their speeds, judging as finely as he dared the angle of his interception.

Yes, he decided, with *Huron*'s loss of speed, he could edge in a touch more.

'Bring her up a point to starboard,' he told the helmsman, and then he glanced up at his own sails that were helping the big bronze screws under the stern to hurl *Black Joke* forward. The alteration of course had affected them.

'Mr Ferris, see to the trim of your jib, if you please.'

Ferris bellowed an order to the foredeck watch, and watched critically as they hardened up the long triangular sail.

All *Huron*'s sails shivered, and then refilled, once more taking on their true shape, and she spurted away, a curl of white sparkling under her bows. The dark windswept water was much closer ahead of her.

It had been Denham's unnecessary blasphemy, Clinton was sure of it, and he glanced darkly at his Lieutenant, and then reluctantly gave the order.

'Let her fall off a point.' *Huron* was head-reaching again. If *Black Joke* held on she would be aiming to cut behind the clipper's stern. The alteration was an acknowledgement of the advantage changing hands once again.

The engine voice pipe squealed, and it was a relief to have even the small distraction.

'Engine room, Captain,' he snapped into the mouthpiece. 'Coal long ago gone, sir. Pressure down to 100 pounds, sir – and falling.'

'Burn everything you can find.'

'Wood goes up like paper, sir. No body to it – and it chokes the flue.' MacDonald seemed to relish the gloomy news, and Clinton felt his irritation turn to anger.

'Do your best, man, nobody can ask more than that,' and he snapped the voice pipe closed.

Was he close enough yet to try a shot with his bow-chaser, he wondered? The long sixteen-pounder had almost twice the range of the big thirty-two pounders that made up *Black Joke*'s main armament. A lucky shot might carry away one of the clipper's spars, might even bring down a yard – and at that moment he distinctly felt the change in the engine vibrations coming up through the deck, *Black Joke* was faltering, the steam in her boilers losing pressure.

'Mr Ferris, break out the colours, if you please.'

As the Ensign unfurled at the peak, spread gloriously against the pale blue sky, crimson and silky white, shouting a challenge on the wind, Clinton felt that tightness in his chest, that swell of pride which never failed him.

'*Huron*'s replying,' Denham muttered, and Clinton lifted his glass, and watched the American's colours bloom like a flower high above her shimmering piles of white canvas.

'And be damned,' Denham interpreted the show of colours. *Huron* was scorning their challenge.

'Mr Ferris, we'll give her a gun now,' Clinton decided grimly. 'Put one over her bows.' And Ferris scrambled away to the bows to supervise the loading and laying of the bow-chaser.

The shot when it came was a puny little pop of sound, muted by the wind and the long spurt of grey powder smoke was whipped away almost before it could form. Though they were all watching avidly through the telescopes, not one of them could spot the fall of shot, and Denham spoke aloud for all of them.

'She's not altering. She's ignoring us.'

'Very well.' Clinton kept his voice low. 'We'll try one into her rigging.'

The sixteen-pounder banged again, like an unlatched door in a high wind, and this time they both exclaimed in unison. A pinprick of light appeared in one of the *Huron*'s studding sails, pierced by shot; it held its shape for an instant and then burst like a paper packet and was blown to tatters.

Clinton saw the bustle of *Huron*'s seamen on the decks and yards, and before the bow-chaser could be reloaded, the ruined sail was hauled down and another clean new sail spread open in its place. The speed with which the sail change was made impressed even Clinton.

'The devil is a good sailor, I'll grant him that—' And then he broke off, for *Huron* was turning boldly, seeming to aim to cut the gunboat's bows, and Clinton realized what her Captain was doing. He was anticipating the rush of the wind, and as Clinton watched it struck her.

It came roaring aboard the clipper, howling through her rigging, like a pack of hunting wolves, and the tall ship heeled and seemed almost to crouch, gathering herself like a blood stallion feeling the cut of the lash, and then she hurled herself forward and was away.

The dark wind-scoured sea burst open before the long lithe knifing hull, and joyously *Huron* tossed the dashing white spray over her bows.

'She's making twenty knots,' Denham cried with disbelief, as *Black Joke* seemed to come up dead in the water, a wallowing log when compared to the swift and lovely ship that cut daringly across her bows, just out of cannon shot, and dashed away into the open Atlantic Ocean.

Through his glass Clinton saw that the seamen who lined *Huron*'s yards were gambolling and waving their caps, mouths wide open and they cheered and jeered, and then he focused the glass on *Huron*'s deck.

There was a tall figure at *Huron*'s near rail, clad in a plain dark blue jacket. Clinton could not make out the man's features at this distance, but he recognized the set of wide shoulders, the arrogant carriage of head, that he had last seen over the sights of a duelling pistol.

The acid bile of hatred rose to scald his throat as the figure lifted a hand in a laconic salute, a taunting gesture of farewell, and then turned away from the rail unhurriedly.

Clinton snapped his telescope closed.

'Stern chase!' he ordered. 'We'll keep after her!'

He did not dare look at his officers' faces, lest one of them wore an expression of pity.

Lying on her bunk, her arms held stiffly at her sides and hands clenched painfully, Robyn heard the creak and squeal from the deck below her that meant *Huron* was altering course, and that the eight-inch thick rudder-lines were running through their blocks as the helmsman spun the wheel. It was a sound she had long become accustomed to, and she braced herself instinctively as the rudder lines attached to the pintles trained around the enormous wooden rudder under *Huron*'s stern and the ship altered her action through the water.

Seconds later there was a thunderous commotion from the deck above her, the blustering roar of the gale socking into the rigging, the crash of tackle coming up taut, the slam of the great sails as their awesome power was transferred into the hull, and Robyn was almost hurled from her bunk as *Huron* heeled wildly.

Then the cabin was filled with the exultant thrumming of the hull through water, as though she were the body of a violin as the bow was drawn across the bass strings, and *Huron* trembled with life, lifting and dropping to the new urgency of her run.

Very faintly Robyn could hear above it all the sound of men cheering. She jumped from the bunk and clutching for handholds crossed the cabin and pounded her fist upon the door.

'Nathaniel,' she called. 'Answer me this instant.'

'Captain says as how I'm not to talk to you.' His voice was muffled.

'You cannot torment me so,' Robyn yelled back. 'What is happening?'

A long pause while Nathaniel considered his duty and then weighed it against his affection for this spirited young woman.

'We are on the wind, ma'am,' he told her at last. 'And going like all the devils of hell with a crackerjack tied to their tails.'

'What of *Black Joke*?' she pleaded. 'What of the British gunboat?'

'Ain't nothing will catch us now. Reckon the puffing Billy will be out of sight before nightfall. From here she looks like she's dropped her anchor.'

Slowly Robyn leaned forward until her forehead pressed against the planking of the door. She closed her eyes very tightly, and tried to fight down the black waves of despair that threatened to overwhelm her.

She stayed like that for a long time until Nathaniel's voice roused her. It was rough with concern.

'Are you all right then, missus?'

'Yes, thank you, Nathaniel. I'm just fine,' she replied tightly, without opening her eyes. 'I'm going to take a little nap now. Don't let anybody disturb me.'

'I'll be right here, missus. Ain't nobody going to get past me,' he assured her.

She opened her eyes and went back to the bunk, and knelt before it and began to pray – but for once she could not concentrate. Jumbled images kept intervening, and, when she closed her eyes, the face of Clinton Codrington was there, with those pale beautiful eyes in the darkly tanned mahogany of his face that accentuated the sun-bleached platinum of his hair. She longed for him as she had never done before – he had become a symbol for her that was good and clean and right.

Then her mind darted away and it was that distant mocking smile, the taunting gold-flecked eyes of Mungo St John. She trembled with humiliation, the man who had violated her and turned her own emotions traitor, who had dallied with her and allowed her to hope, nay, to pray that she could bear his children and become his wife. Her despair turned to hatred once again, and hatred armed her.

'Forgive me, Lord – I'll pray later – but now I *have* to do something!'

She started to her feet, and the cramped little cabin was a cage, suffocating and unbearable. She hammered her fists on the door and Nathaniel replied immediately.

'Nathaniel, I cannot bear it in here a moment longer.' she cried. 'You must let me out.'

His voice was regretful but firm. 'Can't do that, missus. Tippoo would have a look at my back bone!'

She flung away from the door, angry, confused, her mind in a turmoil.

'I cannot let him carry me away to–' She did not go on, for she could not imagine what awaited her at the end of this voyage unless – and she had a vivid mental image of *Huron* coming into dock, while standing on the quay was a beautiful tall and aristocratic French woman in crinolines and velvets and pearls with three small sons standing at her side waving up at the tall arrogant figure on *Huron*'s quarterdeck.

She tried to close her mind to it, and she concentrated instead on the sound that *Huron* made as she bore away joyously on the wind, the drumming of her hull, and the pop and creak of her planking, the clatter of tackle and the stamp of bare feet on her deck as a party of seamen walked away with a fall, training one of the yards more finely to the wind. From beneath her feet came another muted squeal, like a rat in the cat's jaws, as the helmsman made a small adjustment to *Huron*'s heading, and the rudder tackle ran protestingly through the blocks.

The sound triggered a memory, and Robyn froze, trembling again, but this time with anticipation. She remembered Clinton Codrington describing to her how as a young Lieutenant he had been in command of a cutting-out party sent into a river estuary that was crammed with small slaving craft, buggaloos and dhows.

'I didn't have enough men to take them all as prize at once, so we jumped from one to the other, cut their rudder lines and left them drifting helplessly, until we could pick 'em up later – those that hadn't gone aground, that is.'

Robyn roused herself from the memory and rushed to the corner of her cabin. She had to wedge her back against the bulkhead and push with both her feet to move her wooden chest into the centre of the cabin. Then she dropped to her hands and knees.

There was a small trap-door in the deck, so neatly fitted that its joints were knife edges, but there was a small iron ring let flush into the woodwork. Once on the long voyage down the Atlantic, she had been disturbed by a very apologetic carpenter's mate and she had watched with interest while he had dragged her chest aside and opened the hatch, to descend through it with a grease pot.

She tried now to open it, but the hatch was so tight-fitting, that it resisted her efforts. She snatched a woollen shawl from her chest, and threaded it through the iron ring. Now she could get a fairer purchase. Once more she strained back, and the hatch moved inchingly and then abruptly flew open with a crash that she was sure must have alerted Nathaniel. She froze again, listening for a half minute, but there was no sound from beyond the cabin door.

On her hands and knees again she peered into the open hatchway. There was a faint breeze of air coming up out of the dark square hole, and she could smell the thick grease, the reek of the bilges and the awful slave stink that not all the lye and scrubbing had been able to cleanse – her gorge rose at the taint. As her eyes adjusted, she made out the low and narrow tunnel that housed *Huron*'s steering gear. It was just high enough for a man to crawl along, running fore and aft along the hull.

The rudder lines came down from the deck above, ran through heavy iron blocks bolted into one of *Huron*'s main frames, and then changed direction and ran directly astern down the narrow wooden tunnel. The pulley wheels of the blocks were caked with black grease, and the rudder lines were of new yellow hemp. They seemed as thick as a man's leg, and she could sense the enormous strain on them, for they were as rigid as steel bars.

She looked around for a means of damaging them, a knife, one of her scalpels, perhaps, and almost immediately realized the futility of anything so puny. Even a strong man with a double-headed axe would be hard pressed to hack his way through those cables, and there was no room in which to swing an axe in that narrow tunnel. Even if a man had succeeded in severing one of them, he would have been cut to bloody tatters as the cable whiplashed.

There was only one means, one sure means, and she quailed at the thought of what would happen if it got out of control, and if *Black Joke* was not very swiftly alongside to render assistance with her steam-driven pumps and hoses. She had once already rejected the idea of using fire, but now with help so close astern, with the last chance rapidly fading, she was ready to accept any risk.

She reached across and pulled off the wooden bunk one of her grey woollen blankets and wadded it into a bundle, then she stood up and lifted the oil lamp from its gimbals in the deck above her. Her fingers were clumsy with haste as she unscrewed the cap of the oil reservoir in the base of the lamp.

She soaked the blanket, and then looked round for anything else that was inflammable – her journals? No, not them, but she pulled her medical manuals out of the chest and ripped the pages out of them, crumpling them so they would burn more readily, and she made a sack of the oil-soaked blanket and wadded the paper into it.

She stuffed it down the hatch and it fell across the straining rudder lines, and entangled itself in the iron pulleys.

The mattress on the bunk was filled with coir, the dry coconut fibre would burn fiercely; she dragged it off the bunk and pushed it into the hatch. Then the wooden slats off the bunk followed it, then the navigational books from the narrow bookshelf behind the door. She looked about her swiftly, but there was nothing else in the cabin that would burn.

The first Swan Vesta that she dropped burning down the hatchway flickered once and then went out. She tore the end sheet out of her journal and twisted it into a spill, when it was blazing strongly she let it fall into the dark square opening, and as it floated down it illuminated the gloomy recesses of *Huron*'s bilges, and the rough planking of her underbelly.

The burning spill landed on the oil-soaked blanket, and pale blue flames fluttered over it as the evaporating gases flashed off, then a crumpled ball of paper caught and little orange flames peaked up and danced merrily over the blanket and the linen covering of the mattress. A rush of heat came up through the hatchway, scorching Robyn's cheeks, and the sound of the flames was higher than that of the rushing seas along the outside of the hull.

Using all her strength, Robyn swung the hatch cover over and let it drop back on to its seating with a thump that alarmed her anew, but immediately the sound of the flames was cut off.

Panting with the effort and a savage excitement, Robyn backed away and leaned against the bulkhead to rest. Her heart was pounding so fiercely that the blood in her ears nearly deafened her, and suddenly she was afraid.

What if *Black Joke* had abandoned the unequal contest, and there was nobody to rescue the eight hundred miserable souls chained below *Huron*'s decks before the flames reached them?

That first wild assault of the wind, as it came boiling down off the mountains, had settled to a steady blast, not so furious, but constant and reliable.

'There will be no flukes or holes in this gale of wind,' Mungo thought with satisfaction, pausing in his pacing to look up at the small scudding wind-torn shreds of cloud that seemed to scrape the tops of his masts, and then turning to survey an indigo Atlantic that stretched to every corner of the horizon, dark with the wind rush and dappled with the prancing white horses that curled from every wave crest.

His leisurely survey ended over *Huron*'s stern rail. The land was already out of sight, so swiftly had *Huron* run the great flat-topped mountain below the horizon, and *Black Joke* was hull down. Only her topsails showed, not a trace of furnace smoke.

The absence of smoke puzzled Mungo a little and he frowned, considering it, and finding no plausible answer, he shrugged and resumed his pacing. *Black Joke* would be out of sight, even from *Huron*'s towering masthead, before sunset, and Mungo was planning the evolutions he would make during the night to confuse thoroughly any pursuit, before settling on to his final course to run through the doldrums and cross the equator.

'Deck, masthead.' A faint hail reached him, breaking his line of thought, and he stopped again, threw back his head and with both hands on his hips stared up at the masthead as it dipped and swung across the sky.

Tippoo answered the hail with a bull bellow, and the look-out's voice was strained, his anxiety evident even against the wind and at that remove.

'Smoke!'

'Where away?' Tippoo's voice was angry, the reply should have given both distance and bearing from *Huron* – already every man on *Huron*'s deck was twisting his head to sweep the horizon.

'Dead astern.'

'That will be the gunboat,' Mungo thought comfortably. 'She's got her boiler going again – and much good may it do her.' He dropped his fists from his hips and took one more pace before the look-out's voice rang out again.

'Smoke dead astern, we are trailing smoke!'

Mungo stopped dead in his tracks, his foot still an inch from the deck. He felt the icy spray of fear chill his guts.

'Fire!' bellowed Tippoo.

It was the one most dreaded word to men who lived their lives in the tinder hulls of wooden ships, whose seams were caulked with tar and pitch, and whose sails and rigging would burn like straw. Mungo completed that suspended pace, spinning on the ball of his foot as it struck the deck, and the next pace carried him to *Huron*'s rail. He leaned far out, peering back over the stern, and the smoke was a pale wisp, thin as sea fret, lying low against the dark blue sea, drifting away behind them, and dissipating even as he watched it.

Dry oak planks burn with a fine clean flame and little smoke, Mungo knew that, he knew also that the first thing he must do was starve the flames of air, heave the ship to, to reduce the wind of her passage while the extent of the flames could be explored and the ship's pumps—

He turned again, his mouth opening to begin shouting his commands. The quartermaster and his mate stood directly ahead of him, both of them balancing easily before the massive mahogany and brass wheel. Larger than the driving-wheel on a steam locomotive, it required the strength of two men to hold *Huron*'s head in this wind and on this point of sailing, for the huge spread of her canvas was opposed by the massive oak and copper rudder under her stern.

Down in the steering tunnel, the flames were being fed by the strong breeze that the canvas scoops on *Huron*'s foredeck were directing down into her own slave-decks in an attempt to keep them sweet.

The draught forced its way through the companionways and ladderways, through the ports and cracks in *Huron*'s bulkheads, and this steady breeze at last found its way into the long narrow tunnel that housed her steering-gear.

The bright rustling flames were almost smokeless, but intensely hot. They frizzled the loose fibres of hemp off the thick hairy rudder lines, and then swiftly blackened the golden brown cords, began to eat through them so that here a strand parted with a snap that was lost in the rising crackle of burning timbers and the strand unravelled, spinning upon itself and bursting in another tiny new explosion of light.

The two quartermasters were ten feet from where Mungo stood, poised to give his commands, composing the orders in his head, when suddenly the massive wheel no longer resisted the thrust of the brawny men who held it over.

Deep down in *Huron*'s hull, in the long wooden tunnel that had been turned into a raging blast furnace, the rudder lines had burned through, and as they snapped, they snaked and whipped viciously, smashing through the burning deck timbers, scattering flaming brands into the hold below, and letting in a fresh whistling gush of air that forced the flames higher.

Under the helmsman's hands the wheel dissolved in a spinning blur of glittering brass and the quartermaster was hurled the length of the deck, striking the bulwark with jarring force that dropped him to the planking wriggling feebly as a crushed insect. His mate was less fortunate, his right arm was caught in the polished mahogany spokes of the wheel and it twisted like a strip of rubber, the bone of his forearm breaking up into long sharp splinters whose points thrust out whitely through the tanned skin, and the head of the long humerus bone was plucked from its socket in the scapula and the whole upper arm screwed up in a twist of rubbery flesh.

With the press of the rudder under the stern no longer controlling the rush of *Huron*'s hull through the water, the tremendous pressure of the wind in her sails took over unopposed, and *Huron* became a giant's weathercock. She spun in almost her own length, her bows flying up into the wind and every man on her deck was hurled to the planking with stunning force.

The yards came crashing about, tackle snapping like cotton, one of the upper yards tearing itself loose, falling in a twisted web of its own canvas and rigging, and *Huron* was taken full aback, the neat geometrical pyramids of her sails disintegrating into flapping, fluttering chaos, wrapping around the stays and halyards, flogging against their own yards and masts.

With the gale of wind flying fully into the front of the sails, from the diametrically opposite direction to that for which they had been designed, the tall masts flexed and arched dangerously backwards, the backstays drooping slackly, adding to the confusion of sail and rigging, while all the forestays were humming with unbearable tension – and one of them parted with an ear-jarring crack and the foremast shifted a few degrees and then hung askew.

Mungo St John dragged himself to his feet and clung to the rail. The screams of the maimed helmsman dinning in his ears, he looked, about him, and disbelief turned to bitter despair, as he found his beautiful ship transformed to an ungainly shambles. Wallowing drunkenly, *Huron* was beginning to make sternway, as the wind pushed her backwards and the waves came tumbling aboard her.

For long seconds Mungo stared about him numbly. There was so much damage, so much confusion, and so much mortal danger, that he did not know where to begin, what his first order must be. Then over *Huron*'s heaving bows, in the opposite direction to which he had last seen it, the distant but suddenly dreadfully threatening speck that was *Black Joke*'s topsails showed in a pale flash above the horizon, and it galvanized Mungo.

'Mr Tippoo,' Mungo called. We'll reef the mains and send down all her top hamper.'

The logical sequence of orders began to arrange themselves in his mind, and his voice was calm and clear, without the strained and panicky timbre they had expected.

'Mr O'Brien, go below and give me a fire report, quick as you like.'

'Bosun, rig port and starboard pumps, and stand by to hose down the fire.'

'Mr Tippoo, send a party to batten all her hatches and strike the air scoops.' They must try to prevent air reaching the flames, he was sealing the hull.

'Coxswain, have the whaler off her davits and launch her.' He would attempt to tow the heavy boat astern, to act as a drogue, a sea-anchor. He was not sure that it would provide a solution, but he intended to work *Huron*'s bows around with the delicate use of her forward sails – and with the drogue holding her tail in place of the rudder, he might be able to run directly before the wind. It was not his optimum course, and it would be fine and dangerous work with the deadly risk of gibing and broaching, but at the least it would give him respite while he rigged the emergency steering tackle to her useless rudder, and get *Huron* under control once more.

He paused for breath, but once more glanced forward. *Huron* was moving rapidly astern, dipping and staggering into the swells so they came flurrying aboard her in spray and solid green gouts of water, while over her bows the British gunboat was closer – so close that Mungo glimpsed a little sliver of her painted hull, and it seemed that her action through the water was more boisterous and cocky, like a game rooster erecting its coxcomb and ruffling its feathers as it bounces across the sandy floor of the cockpit.

Unable to endure the company of his junior officers a moment longer, stifled and filled with a sense of helplessness by his inability to prevent the tall American clipper from romping away from him, desperate for some activity to help his nerves from fraying further, Clinton Codrington had taken his telescope and gone forward into *Black Joke*'s bows.

Oblivious to the spray that splattered over him, soaking the thin linen shirt and chilling him so that his teeth chattered even in the brilliant sunlight, Clinton clutched for a hand hold in the ratlines, balancing on the narrow bulwark and staring ahead through eyes that swam not only with the stinging spray and wind, but as much with humiliation and frustration.

Just perceptibly, *Huron*'s tower of canvas was sinking below the irregular watery horizon, by sunset she would be gone. She and Robyn Ballantyne. His chance had come and he had missed it. His spirits could sink no lower.

To add to his suffering, his streaming eyes were playing him false, and what he could still make out of the clipper became distorted, changing shape as he still stared after her. Then the hail from the look-out high above him broke the grip of his despair,

'Chase is altering!' Clinton could not yet believe the high-pitched shriek from the masthead. 'She's coming about!' The hail was almost incoherent with excitement and surprise.

Clinton whipped the telescope to his eye, and once again doubted his eyesight. *Huron*'s masts had been almost dead in line, but now they showed individually. She was coming about, already *Huron* was almost broadside, and Clinton stared. For a few moments more the orderly mass of sails retained their perfect snowy shape, and then the pattern began to break up. The ponderous belly of the mainsail wobbled and trembled, then began to flutter and shake like a pennant in the gale, it spilled its wind and collapsed like a bursting paper bag and lashed itself in a petulant fury around its own mainmast.

Huron was a shambles. Through the glass Clinton could see her beginning to tear herself to pieces, sails ripping, yards tumbling – her foremast sagging out of true, and he still could not believe it was happening.

'She's taken full aback.' He heard Denham's triumphant yell, and other voices took up the cry.

'She fast in irons!'

'We've got her, by God, we've got her now!'

Though his vision blurred and the wetness running down his cheeks was not all splattered spray, Clinton went on staring incredulously through the telescope.

'There is smoke, she's on fire!' Denham again, and Clinton picked up the fine pale mist of smoke spreading away from her; and at that moment a fresh burst of spray over the bows drenched the lens of his telescope, and he lowered it.

He took a silk bandanna from his hip pocket, and wiped his face and eyes of spray and the other wetness, then he blew his nose noisily, stuffed the handkerchief back into his pocket, jumped on to his deck and strode back to his quarterdeck.

'Mr Ferris,' he said crisply, 'please send up a flag hoist under *Huron*'s name and make the following "I am sending a boarding party to you." ' The pale sapphire eyes shone with a zealot's intensity. '"If you resist I shall fight you." '

It was a long message, and while Ferris called for the pennants from the flag locker, Clinton turned to Denham. His voice shook with passion.

'Please clear the ship for action, Mr Denham – and we'll run out our guns now.'

Above the gale Clinton heard the clatter of the opening gunports, the rumble of the gun carriages, but all his attention was concentrated ahead upon the crippled slave ship.

He saw and understood the desperate attempts that her Captain was making to get her before the wind. He knew what a feat it had been to take down that tangled mast of canvas and rope in such a short time, yet he felt no admiration, only cold fighting fury.

Huron was showing only a storm jib.

St John was clearly trying to break the grip of the gale upon her for she was fast 'in irons' – her bows to the wind, and he was attempting to bring her round, but the tall ship that was usually so compliant and obedient was baulking, resisting him, and every minute *Black Joke* was swarming down upon her, closer and still closer.

'She's got serious structural damage,' Denham gloated aloud. 'I'd hazard a guess that she's lost her rudder.'

Clinton did not answer him, he strained ahead, half exultant, half fearful that St John's efforts would succeed and he would watch helplessly as *Huron* turned her stern to him once more, and went plunging away at the speed which *Black Joke* could never hope to match.

Then, as he watched, it happened. *Huron* swung her long, low length nearly broadside to him, beam on to the wind once again, and hung there for infinite seconds, then she shuddered and shook herself free of the gale's grip and went through the eye of the wind. Instantly the scraps of sail on her foremast snapped open, she came around presenting her stern to *Black Joke* and was sailing again.

Even in his bitter chagrin, Clinton could at last feel admiration for that barely credible feat of seamanship, but beside him his officers were struck dumb, paralysed with disappointment to see their prey slipping away from them once more.

More sails bloomed upon her tall bare masts, and the gap between the two ships was no longer narrowing; instead, it began to widen once more; slowly, infinitely slowly, *Huron* was forging away, and the night was coming.

'She's streaming a warp behind her,' Denham lamented quietly.

'It's a small ship's boat,' Ferris corrected him. They were already close enough to make out such details, *Huron* was only three or four nautical miles ahead of them, all her hull was in plain sight and they could even make out the tiny human figures on her decks with the naked eye. 'Damned clever, what!' Ferris went on with professional interest. 'Who would have believed it would work. Like as not the damned Yankee has the legs of us still.'

Clinton's chagrin turned to anger at his junior's unnecessary commentary.

'Mr Ferris, instead of chattering like a washerwoman, will you not read the signal *Huron* is flying?'

Huron's signal flags were blowing almost directly away from the watchers on *Black Joke*'s deck, making them difficult to spot and interpret, and Ferris, who had been fixing all his attention on the towing whaler, started guiltily, and then dived for his signal book and began busily scribbling on his slate.

'*Huron* sends under our name, "Stay clear of me, or I will fire upon you." '

'Good.' Clinton nodded and drew an inch of bare steel from the scabbard of his cutlass to make sure the weapon was free before thrusting it back to the hilt. 'Now we all know where we stand!'

But, slowly, inexorably, *Huron* even partially crippled, and steering only by the sails on her foremast, was drawing away from them, and she was still far out of random cannon shot.

'The fire has taken hold in the steering-gear under the doctor's cabin.' The third mate came hurrying back on deck to make his damage report. 'I got her out of there.' He jerked a thumb as Robyn came up on deck clutching her black leather valise into which she had hastily crammed her journals and other small valuables.

'It's got through into the cable tier and the lazaretto, it will be into the sternquarters in a minute.' The mate's arms and face streamed with oily sweat, and the soot had blackened them like a chimney sweep.

'Put the hoses in through the poop companionway,' Mungo told him calmly. 'And flood the stern section abaft the main hold.'

The mate hurried away and within seconds there was the tolling clangour of the pumps as a dozen men threw their combined weight on the handles and the canvas hoses filled and stiffened, ejaculating solid jets of seawater down the stifling ladderways where already the air was trembling with heat like a desert mirage. Almost immediately hissing clouds of white steam began to boil from the ports and stern lights.

Satisfied, Mungo turned away, shot one glance over the stern to make sure that the gunboat was still falling away behind the limping clipper, then let his gaze linger a moment longer on the thick hawser that was secured to the port stern stanchions and ran through the fairlead to the bobbing whaler that *Huron* was dragging half a cable's length astern. The whole complex arrangement of the wind and sails and drogue was critical and unstable, the slightest change might upset it. He decided he could not risk hoisting another square inch of canvas, nor could he send a party below to rig a jury tackle on the useless rudder until the fire was brought under control.

He lit a cheroot, frowning with concentration over the simple and familiar task, and then he raised his eyes to look directly at Robyn for the first time since she had come up on deck.

For a second they stared at each other, and then Robyn looked astern at the ugly little gunboat that was still plugging along after them.

'I keep making the mistake of trusting you,' Mungo said beside her.

'I only made that mistake once – with you,' she replied, and he inclined his head slightly, accepting the riposte.

'How did you get into the steering gear,' he began to enquire, then snapped his fingers irritably at his own oversight. 'Of course, the inspection hatch. Yet, your ingenuity, Doctor, has been of no avail. Your friends still cannot hold us and as soon as it is dark, I will have the rudder cables repaired.'

For the last minute Mungo had been studying her face, oblivious to the sea and the ship and the gale. He did not see the fresh squall racing down upon *Huron*. When it struck, there was no helmsman to hold her. She saw the flash of alarm in his eyes, the realization of danger. His voice, as he yelled an order down the length of the deck, had for the first time the crack of fear in it.

'Get the sails off her, Mr Tippoo. Quick as you can!'

For the squall had upset the nice balance of *Huron*'s drogue and sail. The ship lunged forward sharply, the long bellied length of cable trailing astern lifted itself above the broken surface of the sea, straightening and coming under such strain that the seawater spurted from the hemp cords in tiny feathery jets.

The empty whaler, with her tarpaulin cover still lashed down over her in an attempt to keep her dry, was at that instant canted steeply over the crest of a breaking swell. The shattering impact transmitted by the taut cable to her bows pitched her forward and heaved her clear of the crest, so that for a moment she was airborne, like a leaping porpoise and then she struck bows first and was snatched below the surface.

For an instant *Huron* staggered to the enormous increase in drag upon the trailing cable, and then the whaler disintegrated in a boiling flurry of white disturbed water. Her broken planking popped to the surface and the cable freed of its wearying weight flicked high in the air like the tail of an angry lioness. Without restraint, *Huron* gibed fiercely, spinning once more across the wind, and this time being blown flat, her tall bare masts swinging over almost parallel to the sea's surface.

The lee rail dug deeply into the sea, and the water came aboard her in a sweeping torrent, like a bursting dam wall.

It caught Robyn and hurled her against Mungo St John's chest; if it had not done so, she would have been carried overboard, but he caught her to him and held her as they were tumbled down the steeply canted deck – and then *Huron* was righting herself again, the water cascading off her in silver spouts.

She wallowed helplessly, taking the gale-driven seas on her beam, her desperate rolling accentuated by the pendulum of her high bare masts, but at least that drenching wall of sea water had poured into her hull through every opening and had extinguished her fires on the instant.

Mungo St John dragged Robyn by the wrist across the flooded deck, sloshing and slipping knee deep with loose tackle slithering and floating around them.

At the break of the poop he stopped, both of them panting for breath, their clothing and hair streaming sea water, the deck heaving and dropping crazily under them so he had to cling to the weather rail for support. He stared across at *Black Joke*.

The race was run. The gunboat was crowding down upon them exultantly, so close that he could see the cannon protruding from her open ports and the heads of the gunners above the bulwarks. Her challenging flag hoist still flew in her rigging, gaudy and gay as Christmas decorations. She would be up to the wallowing clipper in minutes, long before Mungo could ever hope to get his ship sailing again.

Mungo shook the water from his sodden dark locks like a spaniel coming ashore, and he filled his lungs.

'Mr O'Brien, a pair of slave cuffs here,' he bellowed, and Robyn, who had never heard him raise his voice, was stunned by the volume of sound that came up out of that muscular chest. She was still dazed and confused as she felt the cold kiss of iron on her wrists.

Mungo snapped the cuff on her left wrist, took two swift turns of chain around *Huron*'s rail and then snapped the second cuff on her right wrist.

'I have no doubt your friends will be delighted to see you – in the cannon's mouth,' he told her, his face still set with anger, the rims of his nostrils white as bone china. He turned from her, running his fingers through his dark curls, throwing the hair back from his forehead and eyes.

'Mr O'Brien, muskets and pistols to every hand. Run out the guns and load with ball, we'll change to grape as the range closes.' The mate shouted his orders as he ran, and the crew scattered from the futile task of attempting to bring the clipper under control. They stumbled across the wave-swept deck, dodging fallen and broken tackle, hurrying to arm themselves and to man *Huron*'s guns.

'Mr Tippoo!' Mungo's voice cut through the cacophony of gale and shouted orders.

'Captain Mungo!'

'Bring up the first deck of slaves.'

'We deep-sixing them?' Tippoo asked, for he had served before under slave captains, who, when capture by a naval vessel was imminent, would deep-six their cargo of blackbirds, drop them overboard, chains and all, and rid themselves of the most damning evidence against them.

'We'll chain 'em to the weather rail, Mr Tippoo, with the woman.' Mungo used neither Robyn's title nor her name. 'Make the limejuicer think a spell before he opens fire.' And Tippoo let an explosive chuckle of laughter come bouncing up his throat as he bounded away on those thick bowed legs, to get the gratings off the main hatch.

'Sir!' Denham's voice was incredulous, shocked. 'Sir!'

'Yes, Mr Denham,' Clinton answered him quietly, without lowering his telescope. 'I have seen it–'

'But, sir, that's Doctor Ballantyne—'

'And black slaves.' Ferris could hold his tongue no longer. 'They're chaining them to the rail.'

'What manner of man is that Yankee!' Denham burst out again.

'A damned clever one,' Clinton answered him quietly. He was watching the woman he had come to rescue through the glass. He could already recognize her features. Her eyes seemed too large for her deathly white face, her sodden and rumpled clothing stuck to her body. Through a rent in her blouse he could see the pale skin of her shoulder and upper arm gleaming with a pearl-like lustre in the sunlight.

'Mr Denham,' Clinton went on speaking. 'Warn the crew that we will be receiving fire in about five minutes, and we will be unable to return it.'

He watched the ranks of naked black slaves still coming up on to the clipper's maindeck and taking their place along the rail, their gaolers fussing about them, chivvying them into place and securing their chains.

'We are fortunate in having a gale of wind, so we will be exposed to fire for a short period, but warn the men to lie flat upon the deck below the bulwark.'

Black Joke's fragile eggshell plating would give some protection at extreme range, but as they closed with the slave ship, he could expect even grape shot to penetrate their sides. One blessing, they would be spared the lethal flying splinters that were so much dreaded in wooden ships.

'I am going to lay her alongside the Yankee's stern,' Clinton went on. That way she would be exposed to the clipper's broadsides while the two ships were bound to each other. 'But she stands taller than we do. I want your best men with the grappling irons, Mr Denham.' *Huron*'s maindeck was ten feet higher than the gunboat's. There would be nice work ahead when they leapt the gap, and scrambled up *Huron*'s stern with its pronounced tumble home.

'By God! She's running out her guns. She means to fight us after all,' Denham cut in, and then, penitently, 'I beg your pardon, sir.' He excused himself for the interruption and the blasphemy.

Clinton lowered the telescope. They were so close now that he no longer needed it.

The clipper had six light cannons on each side of her, mounted on the maindeck. The barrels were almost twice as long as *Black Joke*'s own heavy carronades. However, the bore of the muzzles was much smaller in diameter, and as Clinton watched, they began to train around towards him, one at a time beginning at the stern.

Even without the glass, Clinton could make out the tall lean figure in the plain blue jacket moving at a deceptively leisurely pace from one gun to the next, laying each of them personally, gesturing at the gun crews to strain on the tackles and traverse the long cannon on to their target.

Clinton saw St John reach the bow gun and make a careful adjustment, working over it a few seconds longer than he had the others, and then he leapt to the clipper's bulwark and balanced there with the assurance of an acrobat against the rudderless hull's unpredictable movements.

The scene engraved itself upon Clinton's mind, it seemed so theatrical, like the cast of a stage production lined up at the end of the performance to receive the applause of the spectators. The file of naked black bodies, standing almost shoulder to shoulder with their arms extended in unison, like the trained chorus, their wrists locked to the teak rail by the slave cuffs. Then the principal, the figure of the woman, slim and somehow delicate and tiny in their midst. The bodice of her dress, a buttercup yellow, was a gay spot of colour that drew Clinton's eye irresistibly. It was a distraction that he could not afford at this moment.

The American seemed to be watching Clinton, seemed to have singled him out from the group of officers, and even across the wide stretch of water that still separated them, Clinton was aware of the mesmeric pull of those golden-flecked eyes, the eyes of a predator, a leopard perhaps, poised with a lithe and patient grace upon the bough above the waterhole, awaiting the moment when the prey moved beneath him.

At the level of Mungo St John's knees were the heads of his gun crews, little knots of pale tense faces, contrasting starkly with the quiescent rank of black slaves. They crouched over their weapons, and the long slim barrels were reduced to small dark circles as Clinton stared directly down the bores.

There were men also in *Huron*'s rigging, roosting in the crosstrees of the yards and masts, and the long barrels of their muskets were clear to see against the backdrop of the wind-driven sky. They would be picked marksmen, *Huron*'s best, and their preferred and special target would be the small group of officers on the gunboat's quarterdeck. Clinton hoped that the clipper's wild action in the gale would throw out their aim.

'Gentlemen, I advise you to take cover until we can bring the ship into action,' he told Denham and Ferris quietly, and felt a little prick of pride when neither of them moved. It was the tradition of Drake and Nelson not to flinch from the coming storm of fire, and Clinton himself went on standing at his ease, hands clasped at the small of his back, calling a small adjustment to the helm as *Black Joke* drove in eagerly, the terrier going for the hold on the bull's nose.

He saw the American move his head, a final judgement of range, considered against the clipper's rolling and beside him Ferris murmured the age-old blasphemy which Clinton this time could not find it in him to resent, for it was also a part of the great tradition.

'For what we are about to receive—' said Ferris, and as if he had heard the words, the American drew the sword from the scabbard on his belt, and raised it above his head. Involuntarily all three naval officers drew breath together and held it. *Huron* was at the bottom of her roll, her cannon pointing down into the sea close alongside, then she was coming up, the barrels rising – levelled, and the sword arm fell.

The six cannon leaped together, in perfect concert, and the startling white gusts of smoke shot fifty feet from her sides, completely silent, for the sound had not reached them, and for a fleeting part of a second they could believe that *Huron* had not loosed her broadside.

Then the very air beat in upon them, shocking the eardrums, seeming for a moment to suck their eyeballs from the sockets with the vast disruption of air caused by passing shot, and close above Clinton's head a stay parted with a whiplash crack.

That was one ball high, but under Clinton's feet, the deck jumped with the multiple impact of ball into her, and the hull rang like the strokes of a gigantic brass gong.

A single ball came through at deck level. It struck a burst of sparks from the steel hull, like Brocks fireworks at Crystal Palace, brilliant orange even in the strong sunlight, and the hole it tore through *Black Joke*'s plating was fringed with bare jagged tongues of metal like the petals of a silver sunflower.

A seaman in striped vest and baggy canvas breeches, who was kneeling behind the bulwark, took the ball full in his chest.

His severed limbs were strewn untidily across the gunboat's spotless deck and the ball went on to strike the foot of *Black Joke*'s mast, shivering it like a tall tree struck by lightning, and tearing a long white splinter from the seasoned Norwegian pine. Then, with its force mainly spent the ball rolled the length of the deck, smoking and stinking of scorched metal until it thumped into the scuppers and rolled idly back and forth. Only then, seconds after the broadside struck, did the crash of the discharge reach their ears across the turbulent waters that separated the two vessels.

'Not bad shooting for a Yankee,' Ferris grudged them, raising his voice above the gun thunder, and Denham had his watch out and was timing how long it took for the clipper's gun crews to reload.

'Forty-five seconds,' Denham intoned, 'and not a single gun run out again. A bunch of fairground tinkers could do better.'

Clinton found himself wondering if it was merely bravado, or complete indifference to danger and violent death which allowed the two younger officers to chat so casually, while the seaman's severed arms still twitched on the deck, not twenty feet away.

Clinton was afraid, afraid of death and afraid of failing in his duty and afraid of being seen to be afraid, but then he was older than they, for despite their manly airs Ferris was a boy and Denham barely twenty – so perhaps it was not courage but ignorance and lack of imagination.

'Fifty-five seconds!' Denham grunted scornfully, as the next ragged broadside crashed into *Black Joke*'s iron hull, and somebody started to scream below decks, a high mindless keening like steam from a kettle.

'Send somebody to stop that fellow,' Ferris murmured to the seaman who crouched nearby, and doubled over still the man hurried away. Seconds later the screaming stopped abruptly.

'Good work,' Ferris told the seaman as he took his place at the bulwark again.

'Dead, sir, he is, poor devil.'

Ferris nodded without change of expression, and moved closer to listen to his Captain.

'Mr Denham, I am going to lead the boarding-party. You are to be ready to sheer off and leave us to it, should there be any danger to the ship—' There was a sharp fluting sound, like the flight of a giant insect past their heads, and Clinton glanced up irritably. The marksmen in *Huron*'s rigging had opened fire, the pop of their muskets seemed muted and without menace. Studiedly Clinton ignored them and went on issuing his final orders, raising his voice to compete with the crash and roar of shot and the strike of it into the gunboat's hull.

As Clinton finished speaking, Denham blurted abruptly, 'It's hell not being able to reply.' He was staring across at the clipper whose silhouette was blurred with a bank of pale gunsmoke that even the gale could not disperse rapidly enough. 'It's bad for the men,' he corrected himself swiftly, and Clinton had his answer. Denham was afraid as he was, and the knowledge gave him no comfort at all. If only they could do something, anything, instead of having to stand here in the open and make studied conversation, while *Black Joke* tore across the last few hundred yards of white crested sea that still separated them.

The crash of cannon shot tearing into *Black Joke*'s vitals was almost continuous now as the fastest gunners aboard *Huron* outstripped the others. The bow cannon that the American Captain was supervising and laying was firing three times to the other's twice, Clinton had been counting the plumes of muzzle smoke, this would be the sixth ball they sent into the little gunboat since the American had given the order to fire as many minutes ago.

He watched the gunsmoke bloom again from the cannon's maw, and this time the gunboat's deck was swept as if by hail stones, but leaden hail stones as big as ripe grapes that pierced the thin steel bulwarks with pricks of sunlight and clawed chunks of wood from the maindeck, a deck that was now threaded with meandering scarlet snakes of blood and slick little puddles of it that spread from beneath the inert and crumpled figures that seemed to be scattered in purposeless profusion wherever Clinton looked.

Black Joke was taking merciless punishment, perhaps already more than she could afford, but they were close now, very close, seconds only left to go.

He could hear the cheering of the clipper's gun crews, the terrified wailing of the slaves who were huddled down in pathetic little heaps upon *Huron*'s decks, he could clearly hear the rumble of the sixteen-pounders run out against the straining tackles, and hear the shouted commands of the gun captains.

The girl at the rail still stood rigidly erect, staring white-faced across at him, and she had seen and recognized him now. She tried to raise a hand to wave a greeting, but the iron slave cuff on her wrist hampered the movement. As Clinton stepped forward the better to see her, something tugged sharply at the sleeve of his jacket and behind him Ferris gasped.

Clinton looked down at his arm, the sleeve was torn and the white lining showed in the tear – it was only then he realized that it was a musket ball fired from *Huron*'s crosstrees which might have struck him squarely had he not moved, and he turned quickly to Ferris.

The boy was pressing a wadded handkerchief to his chest, standing very upright.

'You are wounded, Mr Ferris,' said Clinton. 'You may go below.'

'Thank you, sir,' wheezed Ferris. 'But I'd just as soon not miss the kill.' As he spoke, a droplet of blood formed in the corner of his mouth, and with a chilling little jolt, Clinton realized that the boy was probably mortally struck – blood in the mouth would almost certainly mean a lung hit.

'Carry on then, Mr Ferris,' he said formally, and turned away. He must not let the doubts assail him now, he must not question whether his decision to board *Huron* had been correct, or if his execution of the attack had been properly carried out – or if he was responsible for those dismembered corpses that littered *Black Joke*'s deck, or for the dying lad who still determinedly kept erect. He must not let his resolve weaken.

Instead he slitted his eyes against the lowering sun that outlined *Huron*'s bare masts with golden haloes, and stared across at her with true hatred. It was then he realized suddenly that at last her bow cannons could no longer bear, the terrible battering of close-range grape shot was abating as they sailed into *Huron*'s stern quadrant.

'Bring her up two points,' he snapped, and the *Black Joke* cut in sharply under *Huron*'s stern. She loomed suddenly high above them and there was no more cannon fire from her while the clipper's tall hull shielded them from the gale. The sudden silence was ghostly, unnerving, as though the cannon fire had damaged his ears and he was rendered deaf.

Clinton shook off the sense of dreamlike unreality, and strode down the length of his deck.

'Up the Jokers!' he shouted, and his crew rose from where they had been crouching under the fragile bulwark.

'You've shown you can take it, boys, now let's show those damned Yankees we can hand it out.'

'A tiger for Tongs!' yelled a voice, and suddenly they were all cheering, crowding the gunboat's side, so he had to cup his hands to his mouth to give the order.

'Helm a lee, let fly all!' and *Black Joke* spun up sharply under *Huron*'s counter, spilling her wind, while the seamen in her rigging stripped the canvas off her.

The two ships came together with a rending crackling crash, the gnashing of steel plate against timber and the shattering of glass in *Huron*'s sternlights.

A dozen of *Black Joke*'s sailors hurled the three-pronged grappling hooks high over the clipper's gunwale with the lines snaking up after them, and then heaved them up tight and made them fast to the portside cleats, and a swarm of seamen cheering wildly went up *Huron*'s stern, like a troop of vervet monkeys pursued into the trees by a hunting leopard.

'Take command, Mr Denham,' Clinton shouted above the hubbub.

'Aye, aye, sir,' Denham's lips moved and he saluted as Clinton thrust his cutlass back into his scabbard and headed the next rush of his men, those who had been freed by the heaving-to of her sails.

The two hulls were working against each other as viciously as millstones, grinding and bumping, the gap opening and closing as the wind and the seas tore at them.

At *Huron*'s rail a dozen of her crew were hacking at the grappling lines with axes, the clunking of the blades into her timber blended with the popping of pistols and muskets as their mates blazed down on the swarm of seamen climbing up from the gunboat's deck.

One of *Black Joke*'s sailors climbed swiftly hand over hand, pushing off with his feet from the clipper's raked stern like a mountaineer, and he had almost reached the rail when an American sailor appeared above him, an axe held high and then sent thudding down into the woodwork, severing the line at a single blow.

The sailor dropped like a windblown fruit from the bough into the gap between the hulls. He floundered for an instant in the surging water and then the two ships came together again, with the shriek of rending timbers, chewing the man like a pair of monstrous jaws.

'More lines,' Clinton howled, and another grappling hook flew over his head, thrown by a stout British arm, and the line whipped around Clinton's shoulders.

He seized it, heaved once upon it to set the hook and then swung across the gap and his boots thudded on *Huron*'s stern. He had seen his seaman drop on the severed line, so he climbed with the strength and agility of terror and desperation, and only as he swung one leg over *Huron*'s rail did the battle rage seize him, the world changed colour before him, seen through a reddish haze of hatred and fury, hatred for the slave stink that rose to offend his soul and fury for the death and punishment that his ship and his seamen had suffered.

His cutlass sprang from its scabbard with metallic rasp, and there was a man rushing down upon him, and the man naked to the waist with a bulging hairy belly and thick heavily muscled arms. He was brandishing a double bladed axe above his head, and Clinton uncoiled his lanky frame as though it were the 'S' in an adder's body, straightening as it strikes. He drove the point of the cutlass through the axe man's furry silvered beard and the axe flew from his raised hands and went sliding away across the deck.

Clinton stood over the man he had killed, placed his foot on his chest and yanked the cutlass blade out of his throat. A bright scarlet carotid fountain followed the blade out, splattering Clinton's boot.

Half a dozen of his seamen had reached *Huron*'s deck ahead of Clinton, and without a word of command spoken, they bunched to guard the grappling lines over the stern, holding off *Huron*'s axe men with cutlass and point-blank pistol fire. Behind them, *Black Joke*'s men came swarming aboard, unopposed, surging forward, their cheers rising into a triumphant chorus.

'At 'em the Jokers!'

'All together, boys,' howled Clinton, the madness had taken complete hold of him now. There was no fear, no doubts, not even conscious thought. The madness was infectious, and his men howled with him, hunting as a pack like the wolf or the wild dog they swept across *Huron*'s deck to meet the wave of her own seamen rushing back from *Huron*'s bows.

The two waves of running, screaming men met.just below the break of the poop, were transformed into a struggling mass of closely locked humanity, and their cries and curses mingled with the animal howl of terrified slaves. The pistols and muskets had all been discharged and there was no chance to reload. It was steel against steel now.

Black Joke's crew were battle-hardened, they had fought together fifty times in the past year, they had stormed glacis and barracoon and withstood fire and steel. They were blooded fighting men and proud of it.

Huron's men were commercial seamen, not warriors, most of them had never swung a cutlass nor fired a pistol at another man before, and the difference was evident almost immediately.

For a minute or less the closely engaged mass of men swayed and churned like the meeting of two strong currents at the tidal line of the ocean, and then *Black Joke*'s sailors began to forge forward.

'Up the Jokers!' They sensed their advantage.

'Hammer and tongs, boys. Give 'em hell!'

At only one point was the tide of British sailors checked, at the foot of *Huron*'s mainmast two men stood almost shoulder to shoulder.

Tippoo seemed immovable on the solid foundation of those massive bared legs. Like a Buddha carved from solid rock, he spurned the press of men around him, and their ranks parted and drew back.

His loin-cloth was drawn up between his legs, and his smooth belly bulged over it, again as hard as mountain rock, with the deep cyclops eye of his navel in its centre.

The golden thread of his embroidered gilet sparkled in the sunlight, and he held his great round head low on his shoulders as he swung a double-bladed axe as easily as though it were a lady's parasol, and the axe hissed fiercely at every stroke and *Black Joke*'s seamen gave him ground.

A pistol ball had nicked the scarred flesh of his bald head, and blood poured copiously from the shallow wound, turning his face to a glaring gory mask.

His wide toad's slit of a mouth opened as he laughed and

shouted his contempt of the men who swarmed about him like pygmies about an ogre.

Beside him fought Mungo St John. He had stripped off his blue jacket to free his sword arm, and his white linen shirt was open to the belt, the buttons torn from their threads by a clutching enemy hand. He had knotted a silk bandanna around his forehead to keep the sweat from running into his eyes, but sweat poured down his naked chest, and had soaked through his shirt in patches. He had a sword in his right hand, a weapon with a plain silver steel guard and pommel, and he cut and parried and thrust without a break in the rhythm of his movements.

He was unmarked, the droplets of thrown blood that stained the full sleeve of his white shirt and which had been diluted by his sweat to a dirty brown, were not his blood.

'St John!' Clinton called to him. They were both tall enough to look over the heads of the men between them, and they stared at each other for a moment.

Clinton's eyes were pale fanatical blue, and his lips white with fury. Mungo's expression was grave, thoughtful almost, and his gaze troubled, almost grieving, as though he knew he had lost his ship and that his life and the lives of most of his crew were forfeit.

'Fight me!' Clinton challenged him, his voice strident, ringing with triumph.

'Again?' Mungo asked, and the smile touched his lips fleetingly, then was gone.

Clinton shouldered his way roughly through the press of his own men. The last time it had been pistols, Mungo St John's choice of weapon, but now Clinton had the familiar weight and balance of a naval cutlass in his right hand – his weapon, that he had first swung as a midshipman of fourteen years old, and the whip cord muscles in his long right arm were seasoned to the use of the blade, and every evolution in its use, every trick and subterfuge had been drilled until they were instinctive.

As they came together, Clinton feinted and cut backhanded and low, going for the hip to cripple and bring the man down. As the stroke was parried he felt the strength of Mungo's sword arm for an instant before he disengaged, and switched his attack fluidly, going on the thrust leading with his right foot, a full stroke, and again the parry was strong and neat, but only just strong enough to hold the heavier, broader steel of the cutlass.

Those two brief contacts were enough for Clinton to judge his adversary and find his weakness, the wrist. He had felt it through the steel the way a skilled angler feels the weakness of the fish through line and rod – it was the wrist. St John did not have the steely resilience that comes only from long and dedicated exercise and practice.

He saw the flare of alarm in St John's strangely flecked eyes. The American, too, had felt his own inadequacy, and he knew he did not dare to draw out the encounter. He must try to end it swiftly, before the Englishman's superiority could wear him down.

With the swordsman's instinct, Clinton translated the little flicker of the golden yellow eyes. He knew that Mungo St John was going on the attack, so that as the stroke came an instant later, he caught it on the broad curved blade of the cutlass; then he shifted his weight forward and, with a twist of his own iron wrist, prevented the disengagement, forcing St John to roll his own wrist, the two blades milling across each other, the steel screeching sharply on a harsh abrasive note that set their teeth on edge. Clinton forced two and then three turns, the classic prolonged engagement from which Mungo St John could not break without risking the thunderbolt of the riposte, and Clinton felt the other's wrist give under the strain. He lunged his weight against it, slid the guard of the cutlass high up the blade and used the rolling momentum of two blades and the leverage of his wrist and the curved guard of the cutlass to tear the hilt out of Mungo St John's fingers.

The American's sword clattered to the deck between them, and Mungo St John threw up both hands, sucked in his belly and flung himself back against the mainmast in an attempt to avoid the thrust of the heavy cutlass blade which he knew would follow. In the fury of hatred that possessed Clinton, there was no thought of giving quarter to the man whom he had disarmed.

The thrust was full-blooded, driven by all the strength of wrist and arm, of shoulder and of Clinton's entire body weight, the killing stroke.

Clinton's whole being had been concentrated on the man before him, but now there was movement in the periphery of his vision. Tippoo had seen his Captain disarmed in the same instant that he had just completed a swing with the axe. He was off balance, it would take only a shaded instant to recover that balance, to raise the axe again, but that instant of time would be too long, for he saw the cutlass stroke already launched, and Mungo St John trapped helplessly against the mainmast, his belly unprotected and his empty hands held high.

Tippoo opened his huge paws and let the axe go spinning away, like a cartwheel, and then he reached out and seized the gleaming cutlass blade in one bare hand.

He felt the blade run between his fingers and the terrible sting of the razor-sharp edge cutting down to the bone, still he heaved with all his weight, pulling the point away from the helpless man against the mainmast, deflecting it but unable to hold it for the tensed tendons in his lacerated fingers parted, and the blade ran on driven by the full weight of the tall platinum-headed naval officer.

Tippoo heard the point of the cutlass scrape over one of his ribs, and then a numbness filled his chest, and he felt the steel guard of the hilt strike his rib cage, a thud like that of a butcher's cleaver striking the chopping board, as the cutlass blade reached the limit of its travel.

Even the savage force of that blow was not enough to knock Tippoo off his feet, though it drove him back a pace. He stood solidly. His eyes screwed up into slits of skin, staring down at the blade that transfixed his chest, his bleeding hands still clutching the guard of the cutlass.

Only when Clinton leaned back and pulled the blade from his flesh, did Tippoo begin to sag slowly forward, his knees buckling, and he fell, his body slack and unresisting.

Clinton freed his cutlass blade, and it was thinly smeared along its full length, so that it blurred redly as he went on to the forehand cut, going once more for the man who was still pinned against the mainmast.

Clinton did not complete the stroke. He arrested it in mid-air, for Mungo St John had been borne to the deck beneath a wave of struggling British seamen.

Clinton stepped back and rested on his cutlass. The fight was over, all around him the crew of *Huron* were throwing down their weapons.

'Quarter, for the love of God, quarter!'

They were dragging Mungo St John to his feet, two seamen on each of his arms. He was unwounded, and Clinton's hatred was unabated. It took an enormous effort to prevent himself driving the point of the cutlass into Mungo's belly. Mungo was struggling to throw off the hands of the men who held him, straining to reach the massive body of the half-naked Moslem mate that lay at his feet.

'Let me free,' Mungo cried. 'I must see to my mate.' But they held him remorselessly, and Mungo looked up at Clinton.

'In the name of mercy,' he was pleading, and Clinton had never expected that. He took a deep ragged breath, the madness began to fade.

'I give you my word, sir,' Mungo was stricken, there was no mistaking his consuming grief, and Clinton hesitated. 'I am your prisoner,' Mungo told him. 'But this man is a friend—'

Clinton let out his breath slowly, and then he nodded to the seamen who held Mungo St John.

'He has given his word.' And then to Mungo, 'You may have five minutes.' And the seamen released him. Mungo sank swiftly to his knees beside the inert figure.

'Old friend,' he whispered, as he tore the bandanna from off his own head and pressed it to the obscene little slit between Tippoo's ribs, 'old friend.'

Clinton turned away, slipping the cutlass back into its scabbard and he ran across the deck to the weather rail.

Robyn Ballantyne saw him coming and she strained towards him, unable to lift her arms for the slave cuffs that still bound her, but as he embraced her she put her face against his chest and her whole body trembled and shook as she sobbed.

'Oh, I give thanks to God—'

'Find the keys,' Clinton ordered brusquely, and as the cuffs fell from Robyn's wrists he snatched them up and handed them to one of his men. 'Use these on the slaver's Captain,' he ordered.

With that gesture, the last of his madness was gone.

'Forgive me, Doctor Ballantyne. We will speak later, but now there remains much to be done.' He bowed slightly and hurried away calling his orders.

'Carpenter's mate, go below immediately, I want the damage to this ship repaired at once. Bosun, disarm her crew, and have them sent below under lock and key with a guard on the companionway. Two men on her wheel, and a prize crew to work her. We'll sail her into Table Bay with the dawn, my boys, and there'll be prize money for your fancy.' His men were still drunk on excitement and battle lust, and they cheered him hoarsely as they rushed to obey the string of orders.

Rubbing her chafed wrists, Robyn picked her way across the littered deck and through the throngs of bustling British seamen as they hustled their captives and the still-chained files of slaves below.

Almost timorously she approached the ill-assorted pair at the foot of the ship's mainmast. Tippoo lay on his back, the mound of his naked belly pressing upwards like a woman in labour, the soiled bandanna hiding the wound. His eyes were wide, staring up at the mast that towered above him, and his lower jaw sagged.

Mungo St John held the huge bald cannon-ball head on his lap. He sat with his legs thrust out straight ahead of him, his back against the mast and as Robyn approached, he closed the lids over Tippoo's staring eyes, one at a time, with his thumb. His head was bowed, his hands gentle as those of a mother with her infant as he lifted the bandanna and used it to bind up the sagging jaw.

Robyn went down on one knee and reached out to Tippoo's chest, to feel for the heart beat, but Mungo St John raised his head and looked at her.

'Don't touch him,' he said softly.

'I am a doctor—'

'He no longer needs a doctor,' Mungo's voice was low and clear, 'especially if that doctor is you.'

'I am sorry.'

'Doctor Ballantyne,' he told her, 'you and I have no reason to apologize to each other, nor for that matter to speak to each other, ever again.'

She stared at him, and his face was cold and set, the eyes that stared back at her were devoid of all emotion, and it was in that moment she knew she had lost him, irrevocably and forever. She had thought that was what she wanted, but now the total knowledge left her devastated, without the strength to break her gaze, without the power of speech, and he stared back at her remotely, hard and unforgiving.

'Mungo,' she whispered, finding at last the strength and will to speak. 'I did not mean this to happen, as the Almighty is my witness, I did not mean it.'

Rough hands dragged Mungo St John to his feet, so that

Tippoo's dead head slipped from his lap and the skull thumped against the wooden deck.

'Captain's orders, me old cock, and you are to 'ave a taste of your own chains.'

Mungo St John did not resist as the slave cuffs were fastened on his wrists and ankles. He stood quietly, balancing to *Huron*'s wild gale-driven lunges, looking about the fire-blackened ship with its decks covered with fallen and tangled rigging, stained with the blood of his crew, and though his expression did not change, there was a limitless grieving in his eyes.

'I am sorry,' whispered Robyn, still kneeling beside him. 'I am truly sorry.'

Mungo St John glanced down at her, his wrists fastened at the small of his back by the cold black links of chain.

'Yes,' he nodded. 'So am I.' And a seaman thrust the palm of a horny hand between his shoulder blades, shoving him away towards the *Huron*'s forecastle, and the slave chains clanked about his ankles, as he staggered.

Within a dozen paces he had recovered his balance, and shrugged off the hands of his gaolers. He walked away with his back straight and his shoulders thrown back, and he did not look back at Robyn kneeling on the blood-stained deck.

Mungo St John blinked at the brilliant sunlight as he followed the scarlet uniform coat and white cross-straps of his escort out into the courtyard of the Cape Town castle.

He had not seen the sun for five days; the cell in which he had been confined since he had been escorted ashore, had no external windows. Even in midsummer, the dark and chill of the past winter still lingered in the thick stone walls, and the air that entered through the single barred opening in the oaken door was stale and sullied by the gaol odours, the emanations from the dozen or so prisoners in the other cells.

Mungo filled his lungs now, and paused to look up at the ramparts of the castle. The British flag spread jauntily above the Katzenellenbogen redoubt, and beyond it the seagulls planed and volleyed on the fresh south-easterly wind. Force five and standing fair for a ship to clear the bay and make the open Atlantic, Mungo noted instinctively.

'This way please.' The young Subaltern who commanded the prison escort urged him on, but Mungo hesitated a moment longer. He could hear the murmurous song of the surf-break upon the beaches just beyond the castle walls, and from the ramparts he would have a clear view across Table Bay to Bloubergstrand on the far curve of the land.

Huron would be lying at anchor close inshore, still under her prize crew, and he longed for just a single glimpse of her, longed to know if the stern quarters were still smoke-blackened and gutted, or if O'Brien had been allowed to make the repairs to her hull and her steering-gear.

'If only Tippoo,' he began the thought, and then stopped himself, shivered briefly in the sunlight not only from the prison chill in his bones. He squared his shoulders and nodded to the Subaltern.

'Please lead the way,' he agreed, and the hobnailed boots of the escort gnashed the cobbles as they crossed the courtyard and then climbed the broad flight of steps to the Governor's suite of offices.

'Prisoner and escort, halt.'

Upon the portico a naval Lieutenant waited to receive them in his navy-blue and gold jacket, white breeches and cocked hat.

'Mr St John?' asked the Lieutenant. He was old for his rank, grey and worn-looking, with a weary disinterested eye, and Mungo nodded disdainfully.

The Lieutenant turned to the officer of the escort.

'Thank you, sir, I will take over from here,' and then to Mungo. 'Kindly follow me, Mr St John.'

He went in through the magnificent teak doors, carved by the master craftsman Anreith, into the Governor's antechamber with its polished floors of butter-coloured Cape deal, the high hewn rafters of the same timber, and with the thick walls hung with the treasures of the Orient gathered so assiduously by that great plunderer, the Dutch East India Company, which had in turn succumbed to an even more powerful predator.

The Lieutenant turned right, avoiding the brass and mahogany double doors of the Governor's private office to which Mungo had expected to be led; instead they went to a less pretentious single door set in a corner of the antechamber. At the Lieutenant's knock, a voice bade them enter, and they went in to a small office, clearly belonging to the Governor's Aide-de-camp whom Mungo had met before.

The Aide-de-camp sat at the plain oak desk facing the door, and he did not rise nor did he smile as Mungo entered. There were two other men in the room, both seated in armchairs.

'You know Admiral Kemp,' said the Aide-de-camp.

'Good morning, Admiral.'

Slogger Kemp inclined his head, but made no other gesture of recognition.

'And this is Sir Alfred Murray, Chief Justice of the Supreme Court of the Cape Colony.'

'Your servant, sir.' Mungo neither bowed nor smiled, and the judge leaned forward slightly in his armchair, both hands on the gold and amber handle of his walking-stick, and stared at Mungo from under beetling white brows.

Mungo was pleased that an hour previously his gaoler had provided him with hot water and razor and that he had been allowed to contract with the ex-slave Malay washerwoman who laundered for the castle's officers. His breeches were clean, his boots polished and his shirt crisply ironed and snowy white.

The Aide-de-camp picked up an official document from the desk before him.

'You are the Captain and owner of the clipper *Huron*?'

'I am.'

'The ship has been seized as prize by the Royal Navy under Articles Five to Eleven of the Treaty of Brussels, and presently lies under prize crew in British territorial waters.'

That did not need reply, and Mungo stood silently.

'The case has been considered by the Courts of Mixed Commission for the colony, under the presidency of the Chief Justice, and after hearing evidence from the Officer Commanding the Cape Squadron and others, the Court has determined that as the *Huron* was taken on the high seas, the Cape Colony has no jurisdiction in this matter. The Chief Justice has recommended to His Excellency, the Governor of Cape Colony, that the – ahem –' the Aide-de-camp paused significantly, 'the cargo of the clipper ship *Huron* be impounded by Her Majesty's Government, but that the clipper be released under the command and connaissance of its owner and that the owner be ordered to proceed with all despatch to place himself and his vessel under the jurisdiction of a properly constituted American Court and there to answer such charges as the President of the United States deems fit to bring against him.'

Mungo let out a long slow breath of relief. By God's breath, the Limeys were going to duck the issue! They were not about to chance the wrath of the new American President-elect. They had taken his slaves, eight hundred thousand dollars worth, but they were giving him back his ship and they were letting him go.

The Aide-de-camp went on reading without looking up.

'The Governor of Cape Colony has accepted the Court's recommendation and has so decreed. You are required to make your ship ready and safe for the voyage with all speed. In this respect, the officer commanding the Cape Squadron has agreed to place at your disposal the repair facilities of the Naval Station.'

'Thank you, Admiral.' Mungo turned to him, and Slogger Kemp's brows came together, his face mottled with passion, but his voice was very quiet and clear.

'Sixteen of my men dead, and as many maimed by your actions – sir – each day the smell of your filthy ship blows in to the windows of my office.' Admiral Kemp lifted himself with an effort from his armchair, and glared at Mungo St John. 'I say rot you, and your thanks, Mr St John, and if I had my way we wouldn't be playing coy and cute with Mr Lincoln, and I would have you swinging at the mainyard of a British man-of-war rather than sailing out of Table Bay in your stinking slaver.'

Slogger Kemp turned away and went to stare out of the single window, into the courtyard of the castle where his carriage waited.

The Aide-de-camp seemed not to have noticed the outburst. He went on smoothly,

'A representative of the Royal Navy will accompany you aboard your ship and remain there until he determines that your vessel is seaworthy.'

The Aide-de-camp reached back and tugged the bell-pull behind his shoulder, and almost immediately the door opened and the naval Lieutenant reappeared.

'Just one other thing, Mr St John, the Governor has declared you to be an undesirable alien and you will immediately be arrested if you are ever again so rash as to set foot in Cape Colony.'

The tall figure came striding up the yellow gravel pathway, under the avenue of tall date palms, and Aletta Cartwright called gaily across the rose garden,

'Here comes your beau, Robyn. He is early today.'

Robyn straightened, the basket full of rose blossoms hanging on her arm, the wide straw hat shading her face from the flat glare of the Cape noonday. She watched Clinton coming towards her with the warmth of affection. He looked so gangling and boyish and impetuous, much too young ever to have led that rush of fighting seamen over *Huron*'s stern.

She had grown accustomed to him over the past weeks while she had been a guest once more of the Cartwright family, and each afternoon Clinton had walked up the hill from his modest lodgings in Waterkant Street. She looked forward to his visits, to their serious conversations after the frivolity and inconsequences of the Cartwright daughters. She found his admiration and his adoration flattering and deeply comforting. She felt it was something that would never change, something constant, a pole-star in the confusion and uncertainty that had been her life to this time.

She had learned to value his good sense, and his judgement. She had even allowed him to read the manuscript which was occupying most of her days now, and his comments and criticisms were always well based.

Then she had found that he filled a part of her life that had been empty for much too long. She needed something or someone to cherish and protect and comfort, somebody who needed her, someone on whom to lavish the bounty of her compassion.

'I do not believe I could ever live without you, my dear Doctor Ballantyne,' he had told her. 'I do not believe I could have endured this terrible period of my life without your help.'

She knew it was probably true, not just the hyperbole of the love-sick swain, and Robyn was entirely unable to resist the appeal of anybody in pain or in suffering.

It was many weeks since that heady day when *Black Joke* had sailed into Table Bay with her bulwarks and upperworks riddled with shot, her rigging in heroic and picturesque ruins, and her huge captive, blackened with smoke and limping under jury rigging and makeshift steering-gear, herded submissively under the menace of her carronades to an anchorage close inshore at Rogger Bay.

How the townsfolk had swarmed to the beachfront to gawk and exclaim, and how the other naval vessels in the bay had lined their rails and yards with seamen to cheer them in.

She had been standing at Clinton Codrington's side when the two contingents of naval officers from the Cape Squadron's headquarters had been rowed out to *Black Joke*'s anchorage. The first had been headed by a naval Commander, some years junior to Clinton.

'Captain Codrington,' he saluted. 'I am under orders to take over command of this ship from you forthwith, sir.'

Clinton accepted this without change of expression.

'Very well, sir, I will have my gear removed, and in the meantime we should complete the formalities, and I will introduce you to the remaining officers.'

When Clinton had shaken hands with his officers and his sea chest was at the entry port, the second longboat which had been lying on its oars a few yards off, now came alongside and a senior Captain came aboard. Everyone on *Black Joke*'s deck knew what was about to happen, and Denham stepped close to Clinton and said softly, 'Good luck, sir, you know you can count on me when the time comes.'

They both knew what he was referring to – the day they would meet again in the court-martial chamber.

'Thank you, Mr Denham,' Clinton replied, then he went forward to where the senior Captain waited.

'Captain Codrington, it is my duty to inform you that you have been called upon by the Officer Commanding the Squadron to answer certain charges concerning the conduct of your duties. Therefore, you are to consider yourself under open arrest and to hold yourself in readiness to answer those charges as soon as a court martial can be convened.'

'I understand, sir.'

Clinton saluted him, and then preceded him through the entry port and down the ladder into the waiting boat.

A single voice called out, 'Give 'em hell, Tongs.'

And suddenly they were all cheering. *Black Joke*'s crew lined her side and hung in her rigging and they cheered as though their throats would crack.

'Hammer and Tongs!' They tossed their caps on high.

'At 'em the Jokers!'

As the boat pulled away and rowed for the beach, Clinton

Codrington stood in the stern and stared back at them without expression, and his bare head shone like a beacon fire in the sunlight.

That had been so many weeks ago. Still the opportunity of assembling enough senior officers in a small station like the Cape Colony to act as his judges might not occur for weeks still or even months.

Clinton had spent his nights in the cheap lodgings on Waterkant Street. Ostracized by his brother officers, he had spent most of his days alone upon the waterfront staring out at the little gunboat that was making her repairs at the anchorage, and at the bare-masted clipper.

He had watched while the slaves were brought ashore from *Huron*'s holds, and their chains were struck off by a blacksmith from the castle. He had seen the bewildered blacks put their marks upon the indenture contracts, and then be led away by the Dutch and Huguenot farmers to learn their new duties, and he had wondered at this other fate to which he had delivered them.

Then in the afternoons he had climbed the hill to the Cartwright mansion set in its green and pleasant garden to pay his court to Robyn Ballantyne.

This day he was early, the noonday gun banged from the top of Signal Hill as Clinton came striding up the pathway, almost breaking into a run when he saw Robyn in the rose garden. He left the pathway and cut across the velvety green carpet of the lawn.

'Robyn! Doctor Ballantyne!' His voice was strange, and his pale eyes wild.

'What is it?' Robyn handed the basket to Aletta and hurried across the lawn to meet him.

'What is it?' she repeated with concern, and he seized both her hands in his.

'The slaver!' he was stuttering with the force of his emotion, 'The American – *Huron!*'

'Yes?' she demanded. 'Yes?'

'She is sailing – they are letting her go!'

It was a cry of outrage and despair, and Robyn froze, her face suddenly pale.

'I do not believe it.'

'Come!' said Clinton. 'I have a carriage at the gate.'

The coachman whipped the horses at the slope, with Clinton shouting to him to hurry still, and they came out on the crest of Signal Hill in a lather, with froth splattered on their chests and forelegs.

The moment the coach braked, Clinton jumped down and led Robyn to the side of the roadway facing down the steep hillside out over the bay. The tall American clipper slid silently and gracefully over a green sea that was speckled by the dancing white caps of the south-easterly wind.

As she cleared the low dark shape of Robben Island, she altered her heading a fraction and more sail bloomed upon her yards, white as the first flowers of spring. Silently, the man and the woman stared after the beautiful ship, and neither of them spoke as she merged with the milky sea fret, became a ghostly silhouette, and then quite suddenly was gone.

Still in silence the couple turned back and climbed into the waiting carriage, and neither of them spoke until it drew up before the gates of the Cartwright estate. Clinton looked at her face. It was completely bloodless, even her lips were ivory white and quivering with suppressed emotion.

'I know how you feel. After all we endured, to see that monster sail away. I share your distress,' he said quietly, but she shook her head once vehemently and then was still again.

'I have other news,' he told her when at last he judged she had recovered, and a little colour had returned to her cheeks.

'There is a Rear-Admiral on the passenger list of the East Indiaman that anchored in the bay yesterday. Slogger Kemp has asked him to make up the numbers at the court-martial. It begins tomorrow.'

Immediately she turned to face him, her expression softening with concern and alarm.

'Oh, I will pray for you every moment.' She reached out her hand impulsively, and he seized it with both of his, and clung to it.

It was as though the contact had loosened something in her that she had locked away tightly and at last the tears welled up in her hot dry eyes.

'Oh my dear Doctor Ballantyne,' Clinton whispered. 'Please do not fret for me.' But through the tears Robyn was still seeing the ghostly image of a tall and beautiful ship fading away into the pearly curtain of sea fret, and the first sob shook her body.

The floor of the ballroom of Admiralty House was laid out in chessboard squares of black and white marble, and the human characters like chess pieces were ranged upon it haphazard, as though by the vagaries of a hard-fought end-game.

Robyn Ballantyne in skirt and blouse of sober green stood by the head of the board, a solitary queen, while arranged opposite her were the rooks of the legal council: two naval officers in full uniform and sword who were playing the roles of prosecutor and defender. They had been chosen arbitrarily, and neither of them relished the unfamiliar task.

They had isolated themselves from the rest of the company, and each of them busied himself with the sheaf of documents he carried, not looking at the man who they were destined to save or condemn, depending on the deliberations of the senior officers who were even now closeted behind the tall double doors at the far end of the ballroom.

The other witnesses, Denham of *Black Joke* bearing the ship's log under his arm, MacDonald the engineer hiding his grey coal-stained hands behind his back, the colony's agent and Honorary Consul for the Sheikh of Omani, a prosperous Asian trader, were like the scattered pawns of the game around the edge of the board.

Only the officer accused and on trial for his life was not at rest. Captain Clinton Codrington paced at random about the ballroom floor, his heels clicking on the marble slabs, his cocked hat clasped under one arm, his pale blue eyes staring dead ahead. He paced without pattern, like the roving knight of the chess board.

The tension seemed to charge even this huge room, increasing rather than lessening with every minute. Only the two red-coated marines on each side of the double doors seemed totally unaffected.

They stood stolidly, their musket butts grounded beside the polished toe caps of their right boots, their expressions blank and their eyes fixed directly ahead.

Once Clinton stopped in front of Robyn and drew his watch.

'Fifty minutes,' he said.

'It could be hours yet,' she answered quietly.

'I can never thank you for the evidence you gave.'

'It was nothing but the truth.'

'Yes,' he agreed. 'But without it—' He broke off, and resumed his restless pacing.

The prosecuting officer who had attempted for the two previous days to damn him and send him to the gallows, glanced up at Clinton, and then hurriedly, almost guiltily, returned his eyes to the documents he held in his right hand. Robyn was the only one who watched him openly, and her eyes were dark with worry and concern, yet when he caught her eye again a few minutes later, she smiled at him bravely, trying to hide her doubts.

The four senior officers, before whom she had given her evidence, had listened attentively, but she had seen no warmth nor compassion in their faces.

'Madam,' Admiral Kemp had asked her at the end, 'is it true that you obtained a medical degree by impersonating a man, and if your answer is 'Yes', would you not then believe us justified in doubting your allegiance to the truth?'

Robyn had seen the faces of the senior officers flanking Kemp harden, their eyes become remote. The Sultan's agent had been blatantly hostile, as the prosecuting officer had led him dutifully through a long list of aggressions and warlike acts against his master's sovereign territory and against his subjects.

Denham and MacDonald could only recite the facts, and their own repudiation of their Captain's orders was recorded in the ship's logbook.

The only thing that surprised Robyn was that the court had deliberated so long, and then she started involuntarily as, with a crash that echoed around the walls of the empty ballroom, the double doors were thrown open, and the two marine guards stamped to attention.

Through the doors she could see the naval officers seated down the length of the long dining-room table facing the ballroom. Their frogging and epaulettes gleamed with gold lace and Robyn was too far to be certain of their expressions. Though she took a step forward and craned to see the polished top of the table in front of the grim line of judges, she could not be certain of the hilt and point of the single weapon that lay upon it, and then her view was blocked by the backs of the three men who lined up facing the doors.

Clinton was in the centre with the prosecution and the defending officers flanking him. At a muttered command, they marched briskly through the open doors. The doors closed behind the trio, and still Robyn could not know which way the naval dirk on the table was pointing, whether it was in its sheath or if the blade was naked.

Clinton had explained to her the significance of that weapon. It was only placed upon the table when the judges had reached their decision. If the blade was sheathed, and if the hilt was pointed towards the prisoner when he entered, then the judgement was 'not guilty'. When the bare blade was pointed towards him, then he knew that the wrath of the service was about to descend upon him – and he might be called to pay his penalty upon the flogging grating, or upon the gallows itself.

Clinton kept his gaze fixed upon a point above Admiral Kemp's head, while the doors were banged closed behind him, and he and the officers flanking him came to attention five paces from the long polished table behind which sat his judges.

Only then did he allow himself to glance down at the dagger upon the table top. The bare blade glinted a bluish-silver in the late sunlight that slanted in from the tall french windows, and the bright point was aimed at Clinton's stomach.

He felt the cold drive of despair in his guts, as though the dagger had been plunged through them. The shock of the injustice of the verdict, the disbelief that his whole life had been brought down at a single stroke, the shame and disgrace of a career shattered and a reputation indelibly besmirched, left him numbed and blind to all but the wicked blade before him, and deaf to all but the voice of Admiral Kemp.

'Guilty of flagrant disregard of the orders of his superior officer.'

'Guilty of acts of piracy upon the high seas.'

'Guilty of destroying the property of the subjects of a friendly power.'

'Guilty of flouting the terms of a treaty between her Britannic Majesty's Government and the Sultan of the Omani Arabs.'

It must be death, Clinton realized, the verdict was too detailed, the list of his transgressions too long and his guilt too serious. It must be death by the noose.

He lifted his eyes from the accusing weapon, and he stared

out of the french windows beyond his judges. The high stock of his uniform collar felt as tight as the hangman's noose as he tried to swallow.

'I have never feared death, Lord,' he prayed silently. 'There is only one thing I will regret – that I must leave the woman that I love.'

To be deprived of honour, and of life was sufficient punishment, but to lose his love as well was the final injustice.

'The Court has deliberated at length on the sentence,' Admiral Kemp paused and shot a sideways glance at a lean, tanned and silver-haired Rear-Admiral beside him, the passenger from the visiting East Indiaman, 'and has heard and been swayed by the eloquent arguments of Admiral Reginald Curry.'

He paused again and puffed out his lips, indicating clearly that he did not agree with those eloquent arguments, before going on.

'The sentence of this Court is that the prisoner be stripped of all rank, privileges and pay and that the Queen's Commission which he holds shall be withdrawn, and that he be *dishonourably* discharged from the naval service.'

Clinton steeled himself, the stripping of rank and discharge would precede the main body of the sentence.

'Furthermore,' Kemp paused and cleared his throat. 'Furthermore it is the sentence of the Court that the prisoner be taken from here to the castle and that he be there –'

The castle was the place of execution, the gallows would be erected on the parade ground before the main gates.

'That he be there imprisoned for a period of one year.'

The judges were standing up, were filing out of the room. As the lean silver-haired Admiral came level with Clinton, a small conspiratorial smile touched his lips, and for the first time Clinton realized that it was not death.

'A year,' said the Lieutenant who had prosecuted, as the door closed, 'not a flogging, nor a hanging – damned generous, I'd say.'

'Congratulations.' Clinton's defending officer was grinning incredulously. 'It was Curry, of course, he commanded the west coast anti-slavery squadron himself. What a stroke of luck to have him on the Board.'

Pale, voiceless, swaying slightly on his feet, Clinton was still staring blindly through the open windows.

'Come on, my dear fellow, a year will soon be past,' the defending officer touched his arm, 'and after that, no more bully beef and hard bread – do pull yourself together.'

Twenty miles a day since leaving grandfather Moffat's mission-station at Kuruman, Zouga had pushed the mules and his servants hard all the way, and now at the crest of the pass he reined in the tall sway-backed mule and stared out across the sweeping panorama of the Cape peninsula.

Directly below him was that strange pale hill of smooth rock, Die Paarl as the Dutch burghers had named it, 'the Pearl', and it shone with an almost translucent lustre in the Cape sunlight of high summer.

Beyond that the wheatlands and vineyards dotted the flat land that stretched away to the Paarde Berg, the Horse Mountains, where once the wild mountain zebra had roamed, and the Tyger Berg. The leopard to the Dutch burghers was a tiger and the zebra was a horse.

'Nearly home now, Sergeant,' Zouga called to Jan Cheroot.

'Just look at that—' The little Hottentot pointed to the smoky blue flat-topped mountain that stood up tall and massive against the southern horizon.

'We will be there before dark tomorrow night.'

Jan Cheroot puckered his lips and blew a kiss towards it. 'Pull the cork and tell the Cape Town ladies that my mama didn't call me big cheroot for nothing.'

His mule flicked its long hairy ears to the sound of his voice and gave a little half-hearted buck. 'You feeling it too, you old thunder!' Jan Cheroot chuckled. 'Let's go then!' and he whipped the animal up and went clattering away down the steep and rocky roadway.

Zouga stayed to watch the battered little two-wheeled Cape cart follow him at a more sedate pace, carrying its precious burden of ivory and sculptured green soapstone, as it had for a thousand miles and more.

It was a month before Robyn was allowed to pay her first visit to the castle. After the guard at the gates inspected her pass, she was led to a small whitewashed guard room, devoid of all furniture except three high-backed uncushioned chairs.

She remained standing for ten minutes before the low door opposite her was opened and Clinton stooped through it. He stopped, facing her, and she was struck instantly by the prison pallor of his skin. His deepwater tan had faded to a tobacco stain of yellow, and the roots of his hair, no longer bleached by salt and strong sunlight, had darkened.

He looked older, tired and dejected.

'You at least have not deserted me in my disgrace,' he said simply.

The Subaltern of the guard took the third chair and tried to look as though he was not listening to their conversation. Robyn and Clinton sat facing each other stiffly, on the uncomfortable chairs, and their conversation was at first as stilted, a polite series of enquiries after each other's health.

Then Robyn asked, 'Have you received the newspapers?'

'Yes. The warder has been good to me.'

'Then you have read what the new American President has promised at his inauguration.'

'Lincoln was always a staunch enemy of the trade,' Clinton nodded.

'He has granted the ships of the Royal Navy the right of search at last.'

'And six of the Southern States have seceded already,' Clinton told her grimly. 'There will be fighting, if he tries to force it.'

'It's so unfair,' Robyn cried. 'Just a few short weeks and you would have been a hero instead of a—' she broke off with her hand to her mouth, 'I am sorry, Captain Codrington.'

'Captain no longer,' he said.

'I feel so much to blame – had I not sent that letter—'

'You are so kind, so good,' then he blurted abruptly, 'and so beautiful that I can scarcely bear to look at you.'

Robyn found herself blushing hotly, and she glanced at the listening guard officer. He was studying the rough plaster ceiling of the cell.

'Do you know what I thought when I entered the chamber and saw the dirk pointed at me?' Clinton went on, and she shook her head. 'I thought I was going to lose you. That they would hang me and I would never see you again.' His voice was shaking with such emotion, that the listening officer rose to his feet.

'Doctor Ballantyne, I will leave the room for five minutes,' he said. 'Do I have your word that you will not attempt to pass a weapon or a tool to the prisoner in my absence?'

Robyn nodded jerkily and whispered, 'Thank you.'

The moment the door closed, Clinton launched himself across the gap between them and dropped to his knees before Robyn. He encircled her waist with both arms and pressed his cheek to her bosom.

'But now I have nothing to offer you, I have nothing to share with you but my disgrace.'

Robyn found herself stroking his hair as though he were a child.

'Soon I will go back to that beautiful land below the Zambezi river. I know now that is where my destiny lies,' she said quietly. 'To minister to the souls and the bodies of those who live there.'

She paused a moment and looked down fondly on the dense pale locks of his hair.

'You say you have nothing to offer, nothing to share, but I have something to offer you, and to share with you.'

He raised his head and looked up at her questioningly, hope starting to dawn in his pale sapphire eyes.

'Will you not offer yourself to be ordained in God's service as a missionary, and come with me into the wilderness, to the land of Zambezia?'

'To share my life with you, and with God.' His voice was hush and choked. 'I never dreamed I was worthy of such an honour.'

'The fellow is a prig,' said Zouga firmly. 'And, damn me, but now he is a gaol-bird to boot. Neither of you will be able to hold up your heads in society.'

'He has a true and noble spirit, and now he has found his true calling in God's service,' Robyn replied hotly. 'Neither of us intend spending much of our time in society, you may be certain of that.'

Zouga shrugged and smiled. 'Of course, that is your affair. At least he has made a pretty packet of prize money which they can't take away from him.'

'I assure you that money had nothing to do with my decision.'

'I will believe that.' Zouga's smile infuriated her, but before she could find a scathing enough retort, he turned away and sauntered the length of the long veranda under the trellised vines and stood with his hands thrust into his pockets, staring out across the Cartwrights' gardens to the far glimpses of blue bay seen through the oaks and the rustling palms.

Robyn's anger subsided and gave way to regret. It seemed now that the two of them must always be squabbling, their desires and their motives always directly opposed.

At first her relief at his safety had been almost as strong as her sisterly delight at seeing him again. She had barely recognized him as he rode the bony sway-backed mule up the path to the Cartwright mansion. It was only when he dismounted and lifted the stained old hat from his head that she screamed with joy, leapt up from the luncheon table and ran down off the terrace to hug him.

He was so lean and hard and bronzed, and somehow endowed with new authority, charged with purpose and presence, that she glowed with pride as he recounted his experiences and all the company hung avidly on each word.

'He is like a Greek god!' Aletta Cartwright had whispered to Robyn, which was not an original description – but then Aletta did not run much to original thought, and Robyn had to agree that in this case it was accurate.

She had followed his description of the land of the Matabele, and of the long trek southward with all her attention, asking such acute questions that Zouga had asked sharply,

'I hope that you will not be using any of this in your own account, Sissy?'

'Of course not,' she assured him, but still that had been the first sour note, and he had not spoken further of his adventures, except to give her the greetings and news of their grandfather, Robert Moffat at Kuruman.

'You would never believe that he was seventy-five years old this past December. He is so bright and alive that he has just finished translating the Bible into the Sechuan language. He gave me every courtesy and help, and it was he who arranged for mules and for the cart which made the last portion of the journey so much easier. He remembered you as a little girl of three years old, and he has received your letters and gave me this in reply.' It was a thick packet. 'He tells me that you have asked him about leading a missionary expedition to Zambezia or Matabeleland.'

'That is correct.'

'Sissy, I do not think that a woman on her own,' he had begun, but she had forestalled him.

'I shall not be alone. Captain Clinton Codrington has decided to seek ordination as a missionary, and I have consented to become his wife.'

That had led to the explosion which had once more marred their relationship. As her anger faded, she made another determined effort to avert the new clash of temperament.

'Zouga,' she went down the length of the terrace and took his arm. 'I would be grateful if you would consent to give me away at the wedding.'

Some of the hardness went out of his arm as his muscles relaxed.

'When will that be, Sissy?'

'Not for seven months. Clinton has that much longer of his sentence.'

Zouga shook his head. 'I will not be here. I have booked passage on the P. & O. steamer that sails for home at the beginning of next month.' They were both silent, and then Zouga went on, 'But I wish you joy and happiness – and I apologize for the remark I made about your future husband.'

'I understand.' She squeezed his arm. 'He is a different kind of man from you.'

Zouga almost exclaimed, 'Thank God for that,' but caught the blasphemy before it reached his lips, and again they were silent.

Zouga was considering the problem that had concerned him so intimately since his return to Cape Town – how to find out from Robyn what she had written in her manuscript, and if possible to influence her into amending those portions of it which might offend the family reputation.

Now that he had learned that she would not be returning to England, the natural opportunity had presented itself.

'Sissy, if your manuscript is prepared, I will be happy to take it with me and to make certain that it is delivered safely to Oliver Wicks.'

The voyage to England would give Zouga ample opportunity to study Robyn's work, and if the delivery was delayed for a month or so after his arrival, then Zouga's own published account of the expedition would skim the cream off the pool of interest and critical literary attention.

'Oh, did I not mention it to you?' Robyn lifted her chin, and her smile was spiced with a little spiteful relish. 'I sent my manuscript on the mail steamer a month before your arrival here. It will be in London already, and I should not be surprised if Mr Wicks has not published it already. I expect he will have sent the reviews, and we will have them on the next mailship.'

Zouga jerked his arm out of her grip, and his eyes were steely as he glared down at her.

'I really should have mentioned it,' she added sweetly. His reaction confirmed her suspicions. and she knew that what last small chance they had was finished. From now on they would be enemies, and somehow she knew that the centre of their enmity would always be the land and peoples of that faraway country between two great rivers which Zouga had named Zambezia.

At the end of the Woodstock road, on the bank of the Liesbeeck river, not far from the domed roof of the Royal Astronomical Observatory, stands the Cartwright warehouse. It is a rambling whitewashed building of a burnt Kimberley brick with a corrugated iron roof.

Against the rear wall of the main storeroom stood three articles left there in storage and for later collection by Major Morris Zouga Ballantyne, presently on passage aboard the Peninsular and Orient Steamship S.S. *Bombay* from India to the Pool of London. The three bulky articles were almost completely screened by the bays and hillocks of bales and crates, and of barrels and bags, which reached almost to the high ceiling.

The two huge elephant tusks formed a perfect frame with their curved yellow ivories for the third package. The carved soapstone figure was still contained in its protective covering of plaited elephant grass and twisted bark rope. It stood upright on its wide heavy base, and it was merely chance that it faced towards the north.

The grass covering had been torn away from the head by careless handling and long months of travel on the shoulders of porters and on the buckboards of an unsprung Cape cart.

The cruel proud head of the bird of prey protruded from its wrappings. The stony sightless eyes stared across forest and mountain and desert, one thousand five hundred miles, to a walled and ruined city and the words of the Umlimo's prophecy seemed to hover in the air above the graven head of the bird like living things.

'The white eagle has stooped on the stone falcons and cast them to earth. Now the eagle shall lift them up again and they will fly afar. There shall be no peace in the kingdoms of the Mambos or the Monomatapas until they return. For the white eagle will war with the black bull until the stone falcons return to roost.'

Men of Men

This book is for my wife, Danielle,
with all my love for ever

It had never been exposed to the light of day, not once in the 200 million years since it assumed its present form, and yet it seemed in itself to be a drop of distilled sunlight.

It had been conceived in heat as vast as that of the sun's surface, in those unholy depths below the earth's crust, in the molten magma that welled up from the earth's very core.

In those terrible temperatures all impurity had been burned from it, leaving only the unadulterated carbon atoms, and under pressures that would have crushed mountains these had been reduced in volume and packed to a density beyond that of any other substance in nature.

This tiny bubble of liquid carbon had been carried up in the slow subterranean river of molten lava through one of the weak spots in the earth's crust, and it had almost, but not quite, reached the surface before the laval flow faltered and finally stopped.

The lava cooled over the ensuing millennium, and it altered its form and became a mottled bluish rock, composed of gravelly fragments loosely cemented in a solid matrix. This formation was naturally unassociated with the country rock which surrounded it, and filled only a deep circular well whose mouth was shaped like a funnel almost a mile in diameter and whose tail descended sheer into the uncounted depths of the earth.

While the lava was cooling, the purged bubble of carbon was undergoing an even more marvellous transformation. It solidified into an eight-faced crystal of geometrical symmetry the size of a green fig, and so thoroughly had it been purged of impurity in the hellish furnace of the earth's core that it was transparent and clear as the sun's own rays. So fierce and constant had been the pressures to which the single crystal had been subjected and so evenly had it cooled that there was no cracking or shearing within its body.

It was perfect, a thing of cold fire so white that it would appear electric blue in good light – but that fire had never been awakened, for it had been trapped in total darkness across the ages, and no single glimmer of light had ever probed its lucid depths. Yet for all those millions of years the sunlight had been no great distance away, a matter only of two hundred feet or less, a thin skin of earth when compared to the immense depths from whence its journey to the surface had begun.

Now, in the last wink of time, a mere few years out of all those millions, the intervening ground had steadily been chipped and whittled and hacked away by the puny, inefficient but persistent efforts of an antlike colony of living creatures.

The forebears of these creatures had not even existed upon this earth when that single pure crystal achieved its present form, but now with each day the disturbance caused by their metal tools set up faint vibrations within the rock that had been dormant so long; and each day those vibrations were stronger, as the layer between it and the surface shrank from two hundred feet to a hundred and then to fifty, from ten feet to two, until now only inches separated the crystal from the brilliant sunlight which would at last bring to life its slumbering fires.

Major Morris Zouga Ballantyne stood on the lip of the aerial rope-way high above the deep circular chasm where once a small hillock had risen above the flat and dreary landscape of the African continental shield.

Even in the fierce heat he wore a silk scarf at his throat, the tail of which was tucked into the buttoned front of his flannel shirt. Though recently washed and pressed with a heated stroking-iron, his shirt was indelibly stained to a dull reddish ochre colour.

It was the pigment of the African earth, red earth, almost like raw meat, where the iron-shod wheels of the wagons had cut it or the shovels of the diggers had turned the surface. Earth that rose in dense red dust clouds when the hot dry winds scoured it, or turned to bleeding glutinous red mud when the thunderstorms thrashed its surface.

Red was the colour of the diggings. It stained the hair of dogs and beasts of burden, it stained the clothing of the men and their beards and the skin of their arms, it stained their canvas tents and coated the corrugated iron shanties of the settlement.

Only in the gaping hole below where Zouga stood was the colour altered to the soft yellow of a thrush's breast.

The hole was almost a mile across, the rim of it nearly a perfect circle, and its bottom already two hundred feet deep in places. The men working down there were tiny insect-like figures, spiders perhaps, for only spiders could have spun the vast web that glittered in a silvery cloud over the entire excavation.

Zouga paused a moment to lift the wide-brimmed hat, its pointed peak stained by his own sweat and the blown red dust. Carefully he mopped the beads of sweat from the smooth paler skin along his hairline, and then inspected the damp red stain on the silk bandanna and grimaced with distaste.

His dense curling hair had been protected by the hat from the fierce African sunlight and was still the colour of smoked wild honey, but his beard had been bleached to pale gold and the years had laced it with silver strands. His skin was dark also, baked like a crust of new bread, only the scar on his cheek was porcelain white where the elephant gun had burst so many years before.

There were little creases below his eyes from squinting in the sunlight at far horizons, and harsh lines cut his cheeks from the corner of his nose and ran down into the beard – lines of hardship and heartbreak. He looked down into the gaping pit below him and the green of his eyes clouded as he remembered the high hopes and bounding expectation that had brought him here – was it ten years before? It seemed like a day and an eternity.

He had first heard the name, Colesberg kopje, when he had stepped out of the bum-boat onto the beach at Rogger Bay below the vast square monolithic bulk of Table Mountain, and the sound of it had made his skin tingle and raised the hair at the nape of his neck.

'They have struck diamonds at Colesberg kopje, diamonds big as grapeshot and so thick they'll wear out the soles of your boots just walking across them!'

In a clairvoyant flash he had known that this was where his destiny would lead him. He knew that the two years he had just spent in old England, trying desperately to raise backing for his grand venture in the north, had been marking time for this moment.

The road to the north began in the diamond gravels of Colesberg kopje. He knew it with certainty as he heard the name.

He had one single wagon left, and a depleted span of draught oxen. Within forty-eight hours they were plodding through the deep sands that clogged the track across the Cape Flats, northwards six hundred miles to that kopje below the Vaal river.

The wagon carried all his possessions, and there were precious few of these. Twelve years following a grandiose dream had wasted his substance all away. The considerable royalties from the book that he had written after his travels to the unexplored lands below the Zambezi river, the gold and ivory that he had brought back from that remote interior, the ivory from four more hunting expeditions to that same haunting and yet sadly flawed paradise – all of it was gone. Thousands of pounds and twelve years of heartbreak and frustration, until the splendid dream had become clouded and soured and all he had to show for it was a tattered scrap of parchment on which the ink was beginning to yellow and the folds were almost worn through so that it had to be glued to a backing sheet to hold it together.

That parchment was 'The Ballantyne Concession' title for one thousand years to all the mineral wealth of a huge tract of the wild African interior, a tract the size of France which he had cajoled from a savage black king. In that vast territory Zouga had panned red native gold from the outcropping quartz reef.

It was a rich land and all of it was his, but it needed capital, huge amounts of capital, to take possession of it and to win the treasures that lay below it. Half his adult life had been spent in struggle to raise that capital – a fruitless struggle, for he had not yet found a single man of substance to share his vision and his dream with him. Finally, he had in desperation appealed to the British public. He had journeyed to London once more to promote the formation of the 'Central African Lands and Mining Co.' to exploit his concession.

He had designed and had printed a handsome brochure, extolling the riches of the land he had named Zambezia. He had illustrated the pages with his own drawings of fine forests and grassy plains abounding with elephant and other game. He had included a facsimile of the original concession, with the great elephant seal of Mzilikazi, King of the Matabele, at its foot. And he had distributed the brochure throughout the British Isles.

He had travelled from Edinburgh to Bristol lecturing and holding public meetings, and he had backed up this campaign with full-page advertisements in *The Times* and other reputable newspapers.

However, the same newspapers that had accepted his advertising fees had ridiculed his claims, while the attention of the investing public was seduced by the flotations of the South American railway companies which unhappily coincided with Zouga's promotion. He had been left with the bill for printing and distribution of the brochure, the fees for advertising and for the lawyers and the expenses of his own travelling, and when he had paid them and his passage back to Africa there remained only a few hundred sovereigns from what had once been considerable wealth.

The wealth was gone, but the responsibilities remained. Zouga looked back from the head of the span of dappled black oxen.

Aletta sat on the wagon box. Her hair was still pale gold and silky in the sunlight, but her eyes were grave and the line of her lips no longer sweet and soft, as though she had set herself against the hardships that she knew lay ahead.

Looking at her now it seemed impossible that she had once been a pretty carefree butterfly of a girl, the pampered darling of a rich father, with no thought in her head beyond London fashion newly arrived on the mailship and the preparations for the next ball in the glittering social whirl of Cape society.

She had been attracted by the romance surrounding young Major Zouga Ballantyne. He was the traveller and adventurer in far places of the African continent. There was the legend of the great elephant hunter that surrounded him, the glamour of the book that he had recently published in London. All Cape Town society was agog with this young man and envied her his suit.

That had been many years ago, and the legend had tarnished.

Aletta's delicate breeding had not been equal to the rigours of the savage interior beyond the gentle and temperate airs of the Cape littoral – and the rough country and rougher peoples had appalled her. She had succumbed swiftly to the fevers and pestilences which had weakened her so that she suffered repeated miscarriages.

All her married life she seemed to be in childbed, or lost in the mists of malarial fever, or waiting interminably for the golden-bearded, godlike figure whom she worshipped to return from across an ocean or from the hot and unhealthy hinterland to which she could no longer follow him.

On this journey to the diamond fields, Zouga had taken it for granted that she would once again remain at her father's home at the Cape, to guard her failing health and to care for their two boys, fruit of the only pregnancies which she had succeeded in bringing to full term. However, she had suddenly shown an uncharacteristic determination, and none of his arguments to make her remain behind had prevailed. Perhaps she had some premonition of what was to follow – 'I have been alone too long,' she answered him, softly but stubbornly.

Ralph, the eldest boy, was old enough by then to ride ahead of the wagon with his father and take his shot at the springbuck herds which drifted like thin pale brown smoke across the scrubby plains of the wide Karroo. Already he sat his rugged little Basuto pony with the panache of a hussar and he shot like a man.

Jordan, the younger boy, would sometimes take his turn at leading the fore oxen of the span, or wander away from the wagons to chase a butterfly or pick a wild flower; but mostly he was content to sit beside his mother on the wagon box while she read aloud from a small leather-bound book of romantic poetry, his green eyes sparkling with the thrilling sound of the words that he was still too young properly to understand and the brilliant Karroo sunlight turning his golden curls into an angel's halo.

It was six hundred miles from Good Hope to the fields, a journey that took the family eight weeks. They camped each night on the open veld and the night sky was clear and cold and brilliant with white stars that shone like the diamonds that they were certain awaited them at the end of the journey.

Sitting beside the watch-fire with his two sons flanking him, Zouga would talk in that magnetic compelling tone that had the two small boys rigid with attention. He spun descriptions of great elephant hunts and ancient ruined cities, of graven idols and red native gold in the land to the north, the land to which he would one day take them.

Listening quietly from across the fire, wrapped in a shawl

against the night chill, Aletta would find herself enchanted with the romantic dream, as she had been as a girl, and she wondered again at herself and the strange attraction of this intense golden-bearded man who was her husband of so many years and still so often seemed a stranger to her.

She listened as he told the boys how he would fill their caps with diamonds, fat glistening diamonds, and then at last they would set out on the final journey northwards.

She found herself believing it all again, though she had long ago experienced the first disillusion. He was so persuasive, so vital and strong and convincing, that the failures and the frustrations seemed of no account, only a temporary check on the destiny he had set for all of them.

The days rolled by at the leisurely pace of the wagon wheels and became weeks, weeks in which they travelled across a great sun-washed plain that was furrowed by steep dry watercourses and studded with the dense dark-green camel-thorn trees in whose branches hung the enormous communal nests of thousands of dry-land weaver birds, each nest the size of a haystack, growing until it snapped off the sturdy branch that supported it. The monotonous line of the horizon was relieved by the occasional low hillock, the kopje of the African continent, and the track led them directly towards one of these.

Colesberg kopje. It was only weeks after they had arrived at it that Zouga heard the story of how the diamond hillock had been discovered.

A few miles north of Colesberg kopje the plain was broken by the bed of a wide shallow river, along whose banks the trees were taller and greener. The trek Boers had called it the Vaal river, which in the African Dutch taal means 'the grey river', the colour of its sluggish waters. From its bed and from the alluvial gravels of the flood plains along its course, a small colony of diamond diggers had for years been gleaning the odd sparkling stone.

It was dreary, back-breaking work and after the first rush of hopeful diggers only the hardiest had remained. These doughty souls had known for years that it was possible to pick up an occasional small diamond of inferior quality on the dry ground thirty miles south of the river, in fact the surly old Boer named De Beer who owned the ground in that area was selling licences to diamond claims on his property – although he favoured diggers of his own people and was notoriously prejudiced against granting 'briefies' to Englishmen.

For these reasons, and also for the more pleasant living conditions along the river, the diggers had not taken too much interest in the 'dry diggings' to the south.

Then one day a Hottentot servant of one of the river diggers rendered himself blind falling-down drunk with Cape Smoke, the fierce Cape brandy, and while in that state accidentally set fire to his master's tent and burned it to the ground.

When he was once again sober, his master beat him with a sjambok whip of cured rhinoceros-hide until he was once more unable to stand. When he recovered from his treatment, his master ordered him, still in disgrace, to go into the dry country 'and dig until you find a diamond'.

Chastened and still wobbly on his feet, the Hottentot had shouldered his shovel and pack and limped away. His master promptly forgot him, until he returned unannounced two weeks later and placed in his master's hand half a dozen fine white stones – the largest the size of the first joint of a lady's little finger.

'Where?' demanded Fleetwood Rawstorne, the single word all that he could choke through a throat suddenly parched and closed with excitement.

Minutes later, Fleetwood galloped furiously out of camp, a cartload of scrapings from the river bed left untreated and his diamond 'cradle' abandoned halfway through the process of concentrating the heavier diamondiferous gravel. Daniel, the Hottentot servant, hung from his stirrup leather, his bare feet kicking up little puffs of dust as they skimmed the dry earth, and the red woollen cap that was the insignia of Fleetwood's party blowing back from his bald head to flap like a flag beckoning others to follow.

Such behaviour instantly precipitated a wild panic amongst the fiercely competitive little community of diggers along the river. Within an hour a tall column of red dust rose above the flat dry land; a headlong column of horsemen flogged their mounts while behind them the Scotch carts rumbled and the less fortunate stumbled and slipped in the sandy footing as they ran the miles back southwards to old man De Beer's barren hardscrabble little farm on which rose another bald stony little kopje, just like ten thousand others, that studded the plains.

The kopje was that same day in the bleak, dry winter of 1871 named 'Colesberg' kopje, for Colesberg was Fleetwood Rawstorne's birthplace, and De Beer's New Rush came swarming out of the dusty sun-bleached distances towards it.

It was almost dark when Fleetwood reached the kopje, only just ahead of his followers. His horse was blown, lathered with sweat and white froth, but the Hottentot servant clung to the stirrup leather still.

Master and servant flung themselves from the heaving staggering animal and ran at the slope. Their scarlet caps bobbing above the scrub thorn could be seen from a half mile distance, and a hoarse excited cheer went up from the ragged column that pursued them.

On the crest of the hill, the Hottentot servant had burrowed a shaft ten feet into the hard earth, a tiny scratch when compared to what was to follow. Frantic with haste, casting fearful glances down the hillside at the horde that raced up towards him, Fleetwood drove the centre line of his claim pegs across the narrow mouth of the shallow prospect shaft.

Night fell over a battlefield on which brawny diggers cursed each other and swung punches and pick-handles to clear the ground and drive their own claim pegs. By noon the next day, when farmer De Beer rode across from his primitive two-roomed dwelling to begin writing out the 'briefies', which was taal for 'letters', the entire kopje was covered with claim pegs; even the flat plain for a quarter of a mile below the slopes was bristling with pegs.

Each claim was thirty feet square, its centre and corners marked with a sharpened wood stake cut from a camel-thorn branch. On payment of an annual fee of ten shillings to farmer De Beer, the digger received his written 'briefie' which entitled him to hold and work the claim in perpetuity.

Before nightfall that first day the lucky diggers who had pegged the centre of the new rush had merely scratched the stony earth, but had turned up over forty stones of the first water; and already horsemen were away southwards carrying the word to the world that Colesberg kopje was a mountain of diamonds.

When Zouga Ballantyne's single wagon creaked the last few miles down the rutted red earth track towards Colesberg kopje, it was already half demolished, eaten away as though by the maggots in a rotten cheese, and men still swarmed over what remained. On the dusty plain below it were encamped almost ten thousand souls, black and brown and white. The smoke from their cooking fires blurred the high china-blue sky with dirty grey, and for miles in each direction the diggers had almost denuded the plain of the beautiful camel-thorn trees to feed those fires.

The settlement was strewn about under dirty weather-worn canvas, although already some sheets of the ubiquitous corrugated iron had been laboriously transported from the coast and knocked up into boxlike shanties. Some of these, with a fine sense of order, had been arranged in an approximation of a straight line, forming the first rudimentary streets.

These belonged to the 'kopje-wallopers', the previously nomadic diamond buyers who had until recently roamed the diggings, but who had now found it worth their while to set up permanent shop below the crumbling remains of Colesberg kopje. According to the infant diamond laws of the Boer Free State, each licensed buyer was obliged to display his name prominently. This they did in crudely lettered signs upon the little iron sweat-box offices, but most of them went further and flew a disproportionately large gaudy and fancifully designed flag from a mast on the roof to announce to the diggers that the incumbent was in office and ready to do business. The flags lent a carnival air to the settlement.

Zouga Ballantyne walked beside the offside lead ox of his team, following one of the narrow meandering rutted tracks that ran through the settlement. Occasionally the team had to be swung to avoid the tailings that had spilled into the track from one of the recovery stations, or to avoid a deep morass formed by spilled sewerage and washings from the sorting-tables.

The settlement was densely crowded upon itself – that was the first impression that struck Zouga. He was a man of the plains and savannah forests, accustomed to long uninterrupted horizons, and the crowding jarred upon his senses. The diggers lived within touching distance of each other, every man attempting to get as close to his claim as he could so that the gravel that he won from it would not have to be carried too far to the place where he would process it.

Zouga had hoped to find an open space upon which to outspan his wagon and erect the big bell tent, but there was no open space within a quarter of a mile of the kopje.

He glanced back at Aletta on the box. She was sitting very still, moving only as the wagon jolted, looking straight ahead as though oblivious of the almost naked men, many wearing merely a scrap of trade cloth about the loins, who milled the crunchy lumps of yellow gravel and then shovelled it into the waiting cradles. Swearing or singing as they worked, all of them oiled with their own sweat in the cruel white sunlight.

The filth appalled even Zouga, who had known the kraals of the Mashona in the north and had lived in a bushman settlement with the little creatures who never bathed in their entire lifetimes.

Civilized man generates particularly loathsome wastes, and it seemed that every square inch of the dusty red earth between the tents and the shanties of the settlement was covered with a litter of rusty bully beef tins, broken fragments of bottles and porcelain that glittered in the sunlight, a snowstorm of paper scraps, the decomposing corpses of stray kittens and unwanted dogs, the scrapings from the cooking pots, the excrement of those too lazy to dig a latrine in the hard earth and screen it with a thatch of the silvery Karroo grass, and all the other unidentifiable offal and castings with which ten thousand human beings without control or sanitary regulations had surrounded themselves.

Zouga caught Aletta's eyes and smiled at her reassuringly, but she did not return the smile. Her lips were set bravely, but her eyes were huge and brimming with tears that lapped at her lower lids.

They squeezed past a transport rider who had brought up a wagonload of goods from the coast, six hundred miles, and had set up shop from the tailboard of his wagon, displaying a sign on which he had chalked up a price list:

Candles – £1 a pkt
Whisky – £12 a case
Soap – 5/- a piece

Zouga did not look back again at Aletta, the prices were twenty times higher than those prevailing at the coast. De Beer's New Rush was probably at that moment the most expensive spot on the surface of the globe. The remaining sovereigns in the wide leather money-belt around Zouga's waist seemed suddenly feather light.

By noon that day they had found space to outspan the wagon on the periphery of the huge circular encampment. While Jan Cheroot, Zouga's Hottentot retainer, drove the cattle away to find grazing and water, Zouga hurriedly erected the heavy canvas tent, Aletta and the boys holding the guy ropes while he drove the pegs.

'You must eat,' Aletta mumbled, still not looking at him as she squatted over the smouldering cooking fire and stirred the cast iron stew pot that contained the remains of a springbuck that Ralph had shot three days before.

Zouga went to her, stooped and with his hands on her shoulders lifted her to her feet. She moved stiffly as an old woman, the long hard journey had taken a heavy toll of her frail body.

'It will be all right,' he told her, and still she would not look at him, perhaps she had heard that assurance too often. He cupped her chin and lifted her face, and the tears broke at last and slid down her cheeks, leaving little runnels through the red dust that powdered her skin. The tears angered Zouga unreasonably, as though they were an accusation. He dropped his hands and stepped back from her.

'I will be back before dark,' he told her harshly and, turning from her, he strode away towards the ruined silhouette of the Colesberg kopje which stood out starkly, even through the stinking miasma of smoke and dust that hovered over the camp.

Zouga might have been a wraith, a thing of air, invisible to human eyes. They hurried by him on the narrow track, or remained stooped over mill and cradle while he passed, without an inclination of head or even a casual glance, an entire community living for one thing only, completely absorbed and obsessed.

From experience Zouga knew there was one place where he might be able to establish human contact, and through it glean the information he so desperately needed. He was looking for a canteen that sold hard liquor.

Below the kopje there was an open space, the only one in the camp. It was roughly square in shape, bordered by shacks of canvas and iron, cluttered with the wagons of the transport riders.

Zouga selected one of the shacks that grandly announced itself as 'The London Hotel' and on the same board advertised:

Whisky 7/6. Best English Beer 5/- a schooner.

He was picking his way across the littered, rutted market square towards it when ragged cheers and a bellowed chorus of 'For he's a jolly good fellow' from the direction of the kopje checked him. A motley band of diggers came stamping through the dust carrying one of their number upon their shoulders, singing and yelling, their faces brick red with dust and excitement. They shouldered their way into the rickety bar ahead of Zouga, while from the other canteens and from the parked wagons men came running to find the cause of the excitement.

'What happened?' the question was yelled.

'Black Thomas pulled a monkey,' the reply was hurled back.

It was only later that Zouga learned the diggers' parlance. A 'monkey' was a diamond of fifty carats or more, while a 'pony' was that impossible diggers' dream, a stone of one hundred carats.

'Black Thomas pulled a *monkey*.' The reply was picked up and called across the square and through the encampment, and soon the crowd overflowed the rickety canteen so that the frothing schooners of beer had to be passed overhead to the men on the fringes.

The fortunate Black Thomas was hidden from Zouga's view in the crowd that pressed about him, everybody trying to draw close as though some of the man's luck might rub off onto them.

The kopje-wallopers heard the excitement, hastily lowered their flags and hurried across the square, gathering like carrion birds to the lion's kill. The first of them arrived breathless on the fringe of the revellers, hopping up and down for a glimpse of the man.

'Tell Black Thomas that Lion-heart Werner will make an open offer – pass it on to him.'

'Hey, Blackie, Lion-arse will go open.' The offer changed shape as it was yelled through the packed doorway. An 'open offer' was firm and the digger was free to tout the other buyers. If he received no higher bid for his diamond, he was entitled to return and close with the open offer.

Once again Black Thomas was raised by his fellows until he could see over their heads. He was a little gypsy-dark Welshman and his moustache was rimed with beer froth. His voice had the sweet Welsh lilt as he sang his defiance:

'Hear me, then, Lion-arse the robber, I would sooner—' what he proposed to do with his diamond made even the rough men about him blink and then guffaw with surprise '—rather than let you get your thieving paws on it.'

His voice rang with the memory of a hundred humiliations and unfair bargains that had been forced upon him. Today Black Thomas with his 'monkey' was king of the diggings, and though his reign might be short, he was determined to reap all the sweets that it promised.

Zouga never laid eyes on that stone; he never saw Black Thomas again; for by noon the following day the little Welshman had sold his diamond, and sold too his 'briefies', and taken the long road south on the beginning of his journey home to a fairer, greener land.

Zouga waited in the press of hot sweat-stinking bodies that filled the canteen, choosing a man with care while he listened to the voices grow louder and the chaff coarser as the schooners went down.

He selected one who by his comportment and speech was a gentleman, and home-bred rather than colonial born. The man was drinking whisky, and when his glass was empty Zouga moved closer and ordered it refilled.

'Very decent of you, old man,' the man thanked him. He was in his twenties still and remarkably good-looking, with fair English skin and silky sideburns. 'The name is Pickering, Neville Pickering,' he said.

'Ballantyne – Zouga Ballantyne.' Zouga took the proffered hand and the man's expression altered.

'Good Lord, you are the elephant hunter.' Pickering raised his voice. 'I say, fellows, this is Zouga Ballantyne. You know, the one who wrote *Hunter's Odyssey.*'

Zouga doubted half of them could read, but the fact that he had written a book made him an object of wonder. He found the centre of interest had shifted from Black Thomas to himself.

It was after dark when he started back to the wagon. He had always had a strong head for liquor and there was a good moon, so he could pick his way through the ordure that littered the track.

He had spent a few sovereigns on liquor, but in return he had learned a great deal about the diggings. He had learned of the diggers' expectations and fears. He knew now the going price for 'briefies', the politics and economics of diamond pricing, the geological composition of the strike and a hundred other related facts. He had also made a friendship that would alter his whole life.

Although Aletta and the boys were already asleep in the wagon tent, Jan Cheroot, the little Hottentot, was waiting for him, squatting beside the watch-fire, a small gnome-like figure in the silver moonlight.

'There is no free water,' he told Zouga morosely. 'The river is a full day's trek away, and the thieving Boer who owns the wells sells water at the same price as they sell brandy in this hell-hole.' Jan Cheroot could be relied upon to know the going price of liquor ten minutes after arriving in a new town.

Zouga climbed into the wagon body, careful not to jolt the boys awake; but Aletta was lying rigidly in the narrow riempie bed. He lay down beside her and neither of them spoke for many minutes.

Then she whispered. 'You are determined to stay in this,' her voice checked, then went on with quiet vehemence, 'in this awful place.'

He did not reply, and in the cot behind the canvas screen across the body of the wagon Jordan whimpered and then was silent. Zouga waited until he had settled before he replied.

'Today a Welshman named Black Thomas found a diamond. They say he has been offered twelve thousand pounds by one of the buyers.'

'A woman came to sell me a little goat's milk while you were away.' Aletta might not have heard him. 'She says there is camp fever here. A woman and two children have died already and others are sick.'

'A man can buy a good claim on the kopje for one thousand pounds.'

'I fear for the boys, Zouga,' Aletta whispered. 'Let us go back. We could give up this wandering gypsy life for ever. Daddy has always wanted you to come into the business–'

Aletta's father was a rich Cape merchant, but Zouga shuddered in the darkness at the thought of a high desk in the dingy counting-room of Cartwright and Company.

'It is time the boys went to a good school, else they will grow up as savages. Please let us go back now, Zouga.'

'A week,' he said. 'Give me a week – we have come so far.'

'I do not think I can bear the flies and filth for another week.' She sighed and turned her back to him, careful not to touch him in the narrow cot.

The family doctor in Cape Town, who had attended Aletta's own birth, the birth of both boys and her numerous miscarriages, had warned them ominously.

'Another pregnancy could be your last, Aletta. I cannot be responsible for what may happen.' For the three years since then she had lain with her back to him, on those occasions when they had been able to share a bed.

Before dawn Zouga slipped out of the wagon while Aletta and the boys still slept. In the darkness before first light he stirred the ashes and drank a cup of coffee crouching over them. Then in the first rosy glow of dawn he joined the stream of carts and hurrying men that moved up for the day's assault on the hill.

In the strengthening light and rising heat and whirls of dust he moved from claim to claim, looking and assessing. He had long ago trained himself as an amateur geologist. He had read every book that he could find on the subject, often by candlelight on the lonely hunting veld; and on his infrequent returns home he had passed days and weeks in the Natural History Museum in London, much of the time in the Geological Section. He had trained his eye and sharpened his instinct for the lie of the rock formations and for the grain and weight and colour of a sample of reef.

At most of the claims his overtures were met with a shrug and a turned back, but one or two of the diggers remembered him as the 'elephant hunter' or the 'writer fellow' and used his visit as an excuse to lean on their shovels and talk for a few minutes.

'I've got two briefies,' a digger who introduced himself as Jock Danby told Zouga, 'but I call them The Devil's Own. With these two hands,' he held up his huge paws, the palms studded with raised calluses, the nails chipped away and black with dirt, 'with my own hands I've shifted fifteen thousand tons of stuff, and the biggest stone I've pulled is a two. That there,' he pointed to the adjoining claim, 'was Black Thomas's claim. Yesterday he pulled a monkey, a bloody fat stinking monkey, only two feet from my side peg. Christ! It's enough to break your heart.'

'Buy you a beer.' Zouga jerked his head towards the nearest

canteen, and the man licked his lips then shook his head regretfully.

'My kid is hungry – you can see the ribs sticking out of the little bugger and I have to pay wages by noon tomorrow.' He indicated the dozen half-naked black tribesmen labouring with pick and bucket in the bottom of the neatly squared off excavation with him. 'These bastards cost me a fortune every day.'

Jock Danby spat on his callused palms and hefted the shovel, but Zouga cut in smoothly.

'They do say the strike will pinch out at the level of the plain.' At this point the kopje had been reduced to a mere twenty feet above the surrounding plain. 'What do you think?'

'Mister, it's bad luck to even talk like that.' Jock checked the swing of his shovel and scowled heavily up at Zouga on the roadway above him, but there was fear in his eyes.

'You ever thought of selling out?' Zouga asked him, and immediately Jock's fear faded to be replaced by a sly expression.

'Why, mister? You thinking of buying?' Jock straightened. 'Let me give you a little tip for free. Don't even think about it, not unless you got six thousand pounds to do the talking for you.'

He peered up at Zouga hopefully, and Zouga stared back at him without expression.

'Thank you for your time, sir, and for your sake I hope the gravel lasts.'

Zouga touched the wide brim of his hat and sauntered away. Jock Danby watched him go, then spat viciously on the yellow ground at his feet and swung the shovel at it as though it were a mortal enemy.

As he walked away Zouga felt a strange sense of elation. There was a time when he had lived by the turn of a card and the fall of a die, and he felt the gambler's instinct now. He knew the gravel would not pinch out. He knew it sank down, pure and rich into the depths. He knew it with a deep unshakable certainty, and he knew something else with equal certainty.

'The road to the north begins here.' He spoke aloud, and felt his blood thrill in his veins. 'This is where it begins.'

He felt the need to make an act of faith, of total affirmation, and he knew what it must be. The price of livestock on the diggings was vastly inflated, and his oxen were costing him a guinea a day to water. He knew how to close the road back.

By mid-afternoon he had sold the oxen: a hundred pounds a

head, and five hundred for his wagon. Now he was committed, and he felt the currents of excitement coursing through his body as he paid the gold coin over the raw wooden counter of the tin shack that housed the branch of the Standard Bank.

The road back was cut. He was chancing it all on the yellow gravel and the road northwards.

'Zouga, you promised,' Aletta whispered when the buyer came to Zouga's camp to collect the oxen. 'You promised that in one week –' Then she fell silent when she saw his face. She knew that expression. She drew the two boys to her and held them close.

Jan Cheroot went to each of the animals in turn and whispered to them as tenderly as a lover, and his stare was reproachful as he turned to Zouga while the span was led away.

Neither man spoke, and at last Jan Cheroot dropped his gaze and walked away, a slight, bare-footed, bow-legged little gnome.

Zouga thought he had lost him, and he felt a rush of distress, for the little man was a friend, a teacher and a companion of twelve years. It was Jan Cheroot who had tracked his first elephant, and stood shoulder to shoulder with him as he shot it down. Together they had marched and ridden the breadth of a savage continent. They had drunk from the same bottle and eaten from the same pot at a thousand camp fires. Yet he could not bring himself to call him back. He knew that Jan Cheroot must make his own decision.

He need not have worried. When 'dop' time came that evening, Jan Cheroot was there to hold out his chipped enamel mug. Zouga smiled and, ignoring the line that measured his daily ration of brandy, he filled the mug to the brim.

'It was necessary, old friend,' he said, and Jan Cheroot nodded gravely. 'They were good beasts,' he said. 'But then I have had many fine beasts go from my life, four-legged and two-legged ones.' He tasted the raw spirit. 'After a little time and a dram or two, it does not matter so much.'

Aletta did not speak again until the boys were asleep in the tent.

'Selling the oxen and the wagon was your answer,' she said.

'It cost a guinea a day to water them, and the grazing has been eaten flat for miles about.'

'There have been three more deaths in the camp. I counted thirty wagons leaving today. It's a plague camp.'

'Yes.' Zouga nodded. 'Some of the claim holders are getting nervous. A claim that I was offered for eleven hundred pounds yesterday was sold for nine hundred today.'

'Zouga, it's not fair to me or the children,' she began, but he interrupted her.

'I can arrange a passage for you and the boys with a transport rider. He has sold his stock and he leaves in the next few days. He will take you back to Cape Town.'

They undressed in darkness and silence, and when Aletta followed him into the hard narrow cot the silence continued until he thought she had fallen asleep. Then he felt her hand, smooth and soft, touch his cheek lightly.

'I am sorry, my darling.' Her voice was as light as her touch, and her breath stirred his beard. 'I was so tired and depressed.'

He took her hand and held the tips of her fingers to his lips.

'I have been such a poor wife to you, always too sick and weak when you needed someone strong.' Timidly she let her body touch his. 'And now when I should be a comfort to you, I do nothing but snivel.'

'No,' he said. 'That's not true.' And yet over the years he had resented her often enough for just those reasons. He had felt like a man trying to run with shackles on his ankles.

'And yet I love you, Zouga. I loved you the first day I laid eyes on you, and I have never ceased to love you.'

'I love you too, Aletta,' he assured her, yet the words came automatically; and to make up for the lack of spontaneity, be placed his arm around her shoulders and she drew closer still and laid her cheek against his chest.

'I hate myself for being so weak and sickly,' she hesitated, 'for not being able to be a real wife any more.'

'Shh! Aletta, do not upset yourself.'

'I will be strong now – you will see.'

'You have always been strong, deep inside.'

'No, but I will be now. We shall find that capful of diamonds together, and afterwards we shall go north.' He did not reply, and it was she who spoke again. 'Zouga, I want you to make love to me – now.'

'Aletta, you know that is dangerous.'

'Now,' she repeated. 'Now, please.' And she took his hand down and placed it under the hem of her nightdress against the smooth warm skin of her inner thigh. She had never done that before, and Zouga found himself shocked but strangely aroused, and afterwards he was filled with a deep tenderness and compassion for her that he had not felt for many years.

When her breathing had become regular once more, she pulled his hands away gently and slipped out of the cot.

Leaning on one elbow he watched her light the candle and then kneel by the trunk that was lashed to the foot of the cot. She had plaited her hair with a ribbon in it, and her body was slim as a young girl's. The candlelight flattered her, smoothing out the lines of sickness and worry. He remembered how lovely she had been.

She lifted the lid of the trunk, took something from the interior and brought it to him. It was a small cask with an ornate brass lock. The key was in the lock.

'Open it,' she said.

In the candlelight he saw that the cask contained two thick rolls of five-pound notes, each bound up with a scrap of ribbon, and a draw-string pouch of dark green velvet. He lifted out the pouch and it was heavy with gold coin.

'I was keeping it,' she whispered, 'for the day it was really needed. There is almost a thousand pounds there.'

'Where did you get this?'

'My father, on our wedding day. Take it, Zouga. Buy that claim with it. This time we will make it all right. This time is going to be all right.'

In the morning the purchaser came to claim the wagon. He waited impatiently while the family moved their meagre possessions into the bell tent.

Once Zouga had removed the cots from the tented half of the wagon body he was able to lift the planking from the narrow compartment over the rear wheel truck. Here the heavier goods were stored to keep the vehicle's centre of gravity low. The spare trek chain, the lead for moulding into bullet, axe heads, a small anvil – and then Zouga's household god which he and Jan Cheroot strained to lift from its padded bed and lower to the ground beside the wagon.

Between them they carried it to the tent and set it upright against the far screen of the bell tent.

'I've lugged this rubbish from Matabeleland to Cape Town and back,' complained Jan Cheroot disgustedly as he stood back from the graven birdlike figure on its stone plinth.

Zouga smiled indulgently. The Hottentot had hated that ancient idol from the very first day they uncovered it together in the overgrown ruins of an ancient walled city, a city they had stumbled on while hunting elephant in that wild untamed land so far to the north.

'It's my good-luck charm,' Zouga smiled.

'What luck?' Jan Cheroot demanded bitterly. 'Is it luck to have to sell the oxen? Is it luck to live in a tent full of flies amongst a tribe of white savages?' Muttering and mumbling bitterly, Jan Cheroot stamped out of the tent and snatched up the halters of the two remaining horses to take them down to water.

Zouga paused for a moment in front of the statue. It stood almost as high as his head on its slim column of polished green soapstone. Atop the column crouched a stylized bird figure on the edge of flight. The cruel curve of the falcon beak fascinated Zouga, and in a habitual gesture he stroked the smooth stone and the blank eyes stared back at him inscrutably.

Zouga opened his lips to whisper to the bird, and at that moment Aletta stooped into the triangular opening of the tent and saw what he was doing.

Quickly, almost guiltily, Zouga dropped his hand and turned to face her. Aletta hated that stone image even more bitterly than did Jan Cheroot. Now she stood very still. Her arms were filled with a pile of neatly folded linen and clothing – but her eyes were troubled.

'Zouga, must we have that thing in here?'

'It takes up no room,' he told her lightly, and came to take her burden from her, place it on the truckle bed, and then turn back to take her in his arms.

'I will never forget what you did last night,' he told her, and felt the rigidity go out of her body. She swayed against him and lifted her face to his. Once again he felt his chest squeezed with compassion as he saw the lines of sickness and worry at the corners of her eyes and mouth, saw the grey patina of fatigue on her skin.

He bowed his head to kiss her lips, feeling awkward at such unaccustomed demonstration of affection; but at that moment the two boys burst into the tent, raucous with laughter and excitement and dragging between them a stray puppy on a string, and Aletta broke hurriedly from Zouga's embrace and, flushing with embarrassment, adjusted her apron, beginning to scold her offspring fondly.

'Out with it! It's covered in fleas.'

'Oh please, Mama!'

'Out, I say!'

She watched Zouga set off into the sprawling settlement, striding down the dusty track with his shoulders squared and the old jaunty spring in his step, then she turned back to the cone of soiled canvas set on a bleak dry plain under the cruel blue African sky, and she sighed. The weariness came upon her again in waves.

In her girlhood there had been servants to perform the menial tasks of cooking and cleaning. She still had not mastered the smoky fluttering open flames of the camp fire, and already a fine red coating of dust had settled upon everything, even the surface of the goat's milk in its earthenware jug. With an enormous effort of will, she gathered her resolve and stooped determinedly into the tent.

Ralph had followed Jan Cheroot down to the wells to help with the horses. She knew that the two of them would not return until the next mealtime. They made an incongruous pair, the wizened little old man and the handsome reckless child already taller and more sturdy than his inseparable protector and tutor.

Jordan stayed with her. He was not yet ten years of age, but without his companionship she doubted that she could have borne the terrible journey across those bone-breaking miles, the burning dusty days and the frosty nights of aching cold.

Already the child could cook the simple camp dishes, and his unleavened bread and griddle scones were family favourites at every meal. She had taught him to read and write, and given to him her love of poetry and fine and beautiful things. He could already darn a torn shirt and wield the heavy coal-filled stroking iron to smooth a shirt. His sweet piping tones and angelic beauty were constant sources of intense joy to her. She had grown his golden curls long for once, resisting her husband when he wanted to scissor them short as he had done Ralph's.

Jordan stood below her now, helping her to string a canvas screen across the tent that would divide the sleeping and living areas. She was suddenly compelled to lean down and touch those soft fine curls.

At the touch he smiled sweetly up at her, and abruptly her senses spun dizzily. She swayed wildly on the rickety cot, trying to keep her balance and, as she fell, Jordan struggled to hold and steady her. He did not have the strength and her weight bore them both to the ground.

Jordan's eyes were huge and swimming with horror. He helped her half crawl, half stagger back to the cot and collapse upon it.

Waves of heat and nausea and giddiness broke over her.

Zouga was the first customer at the office of the Standard Bank when the clerk opened the door onto Market Square. Once he had deposited the contents of Aletta's casket and the clerk had locked it in the big green iron safe against the far wall, Zouga had a balance of almost £2,500 to his credit.

That knowledge armed his resolve. He felt tall and powerful as he strode up the ramp of the central causeway.

The roadways were seven feet wide. The mining commissioner, after the lesson of the diggings at Bultfontein and Dutoitspan, had insisted that these access roads be left open to service the claims in the centre of the growing pit. The workings were a mosaic of square platforms, each precisely thirty feet square. Some of the diggers, with more capital and better organization, were sinking their claims faster than others, so that the slower workers were isolated on towers of golden yellow earth, high above their neighbouring claims, while the fastest miners had sunk deep square shafts at the bottom of which toiled the naked black labourers.

For a man to move from one claim to another was already a laborious and often downright dangerous journey: crossing rickety board walks above the dizzying shaft of a deep claim, scrambling up high swaying rope ladders or down the steps of a pole ladder, lengths of native timber lashed together with cross-steps that creaked and gave with a man's weight.

Standing on the crumbling roadway with the workings gaping below him, Zouga wondered what would be the outcome if the strike continued to great depth. It already required a level head and strong stomach to chance the uneven pit, and he wondered again at man's determination to accumulate wealth against any odds, in the face of any danger.

He watched while from the bottom of the workings a leather bucket, brimming with broken lumps of the compacted yellow gravel, was hauled up, swinging at the end of a long rope, two sweating black men dipping and swinging over the windlass, their muscles swelling and subsiding in the bright sunlight.

The bucket reached the lip of the roadway, and they seized it, lugged it to the waiting cart with its patient pair of mules, and dumped the contents into the half-full body. Then one of them dropped the empty bucket over the side of the roadway to the waiting men fifty feet below. At hundreds of points along the fourteen causeways the same operation was being repeated, endlessly the loaded buckets came swinging up and were dropped back empty.

Occasionally, breaking the monotonous rhythm, the seam of a leather bucket would burst, showering the men below with jagged chunks of rock, or a worn rope would snap and, with warning shouts, the toilers at the bottom of the pit would hurl themselves aside to avoid the plunging missile.

There was an impatient humming excitement that seemed to embrace the entire workings. The urgent shouted commands between pit and roadway, the squeal of rope sheaves, the thudding jar of pick and swinging shovel, the rich lilting chorus of a gang of Basuto tribesmen singing as they worked, small wiry little mountaineers from the Dragon Range.

The white diggers, bullying and bustling, scrambled down the swaying ladderworks or stood over their gangs on the pit floor, hawk-eyed to forestall a 'pick-up': the possibility of a valuable diamond being exposed by a spade and swiftly palmed by one of the black workers, to be slipped into the mouth or other body opening at the first opportunity.

Illegal diamond selling and buying was already the plague of the diggers. In their eyes, every black man was a suspect. Only men with less than one quarter black blood were allowed to hold and work claims. This law made it easier to apportion blame, for a black face with a diamond in his possession was guilty without appeal. However, this law could not control the shady white men that hung around the diggings, ostensibly travelling salesmen, actors or proprietors of infamous drinking canteens but in reality all I.D.B., Illegal Diamond Buyers. The diggers hated them with a ferocity that sometimes boiled over in a night of rioting and beating and burning in which innocent merchants, as well as the guilty, lost all their possessions in the flames, while the mob of diggers danced about the burning shacks chanting: 'I.D.B.! I.D.B.!'

Zouga moved cautiously out along the crest of the roadway, at times pushed perilously close to the edge by a passing cart laden with diamondiferous earth.

He reached the point above Jock Danby's claims from which he had spoken to the friendly digger the previous day.

The two claims were deserted, the leather bucket and rope coils abandoned, a pick handle standing upright with its point driven into the earth far below the level of the roadway.

There was a big bearded digger working the adjoining claim, and he scowled up in response to Zouga's hail.

'What you want?'

'I'm looking for Jock Danby.'

'Well, you are looking in the wrong place.'

The man turned and aimed a kick at the nearest labourer. 'Sebenza, you black monkey!'

'Where will I find him?'

'Other side of Market Square, behind the Lord Nelson.' The man answered off-handedly without turning his head.

The dusty pitted open square was as littered with filth as the rest of the settlement, and crowded with the wagons of the transport riders and the carts of farmers who had come in to sell milk or produce and of the water sellers, peddling the precious stuff by the bucket.

The Lord Nelson was stained red dusty canvas over a wooden frame. Three of the previous night's drinkers were laid out like embalmed corpses in the narrow alley beside the canteen, while the single bar-room was already filling with the early morning customers.

A pariah-dog sniffed the breath of one of the unconscious drunks, and recoiled with shock before slinking away to raid the open drum that served as a rubbish bin behindthe shack.

Zouga stepped over the sprawling bodies and gingerly made his way into the noisome slum beyond. He had to make half a dozen further enquiries until he found Jock Danby's hut. So obsessed were the diggers with their own race for the hidden glitter of wealth, and so transient the population of the diggings, that a man seemed to know only the names of his immediate neighbours. It was a community of strangers, every man caring only for himself, completely uninterested in the other human beings about him, except in as much as they could either hinder or help him in his quest for the bright stones.

Jock Danby's hut was hardly distinguishable from a thousand others. Two rooms built of adobe bricks and covered with thatch and tattered canvas. There was a lean-to at one end, with a smoking cooking fire on which stood a sooty black three-legged pot.

In the cluttered dusty yard stood the inevitable diamond sorting-table, a low structure with sturdy wooden legs, the top covered with a sheet of flat iron which was scoured shiny bright by the diamondiferous pebbles that had brushed over the surface. The wooden scrapers lay abandoned on the table top, and a heap of sieved and washed gravel formed a glittering pyramid in the centre of the table.

A two-wheeled cart stood in front of the main door of the hut, two somnolent donkeys still in the traces, flicking their ears at the swarming black cloud of flies. The cart was piled with lumps of yellow earth, but the yard was deserted.

Incongruously there were a few straggling scarlet geraniums growing in galvanized one-gallon syrup cans on each side of the doorway. There were also dainty lace curtains in the single window, so freshly washed that they had not yet turned ochre red with dust, nor become speckled with the excrement of the swarming flies.

The touch of a woman was unmistakable, and to confirm Zouga's guess there was the faint but harrowing sound of a woman weeping from the open doorway.

As Zouga hesitated in the yard, disconcerted by the sounds of grief, a brawny figure filled the doorway and stood blinking in the sunlight, shading his eyes with a gnarled and dirt-ingrained hand.

'Who are you?' Jock Danby demanded, with unnecessary roughness.

'I spoke to you yesterday,' Zouga explained, 'up at the pit.'

'What do you want?' the digger demanded, showing no sign of recognition, his features screwed up in an expression of truculence and something else, some other emotion which Zouga did not immediately recognize.

'You spoke of selling your briefies,' Zouga reminded him.

Jock Danby's face seemed to swell and turn dark ugly red; the veins and cords stood out in his throat as he ducked his head down on the thickly muscled shoulders.

'You filthy bloody vulture,' he choked, and he came out into the sunlight with the heavy irresistible crabbing rush of a gut-shot buffalo bull.

He was taller than Zouga by a head, ten years younger and fifty pounds heavier. Taken completely by surprise, Zouga was a hundredth part of a second late in ducking and spinning away from the man's charge. A fist like a cannon ball smashed into his shoulder, a glancing blow but with the force to send Zouga reeling to sprawl on his back across the sorting-table, scattering diamondiferous gravel across the dusty yard.

Jock Danby charged again, his swollen face working, his eyes mad, his thick stained fingers hooked as they reached for Zouga's throat. Zouga jack-knifed his legs, drawing himself into a ball, tense as the arch in an adder's neck at the moment before it strikes, and he drove the heels of his boots into the man's chest.

The breath whistled out of Jock Danby's throat, and he stopped in mid-charge as though hit in the chest with a double charge of buck-shot. His head and arms snapped forward, nerveless as a straw-man, and he flew backwards, crashing into the unbaked brick wall of the hut and beginning to slide down onto his knees.

Zouga bounded off the tabletop. His left arm was numb to the fingertips from the unexpected blow, but he was light on his feet as a dancer, and the quick rush of cold anger armed and strengthened him. He closed the gap between them with two swift strides and hooked Jock Danby, high in the side of his head just above and in front of his ear; the shock of the punch jarred his own teeth but sent the man spinning along the wall to slump on his knees in the red dust.

Jock Danby was stunned and his eyes were glazing over, but Zouga jerked him to his feet and propped him against the side of the cart, setting him up carefully for the next punch. His anger and outrage driving him on to revenge that unprovoked and senseless attack, Zouga shifted his weight, holding Jock Danby steady with his left hand and pulling back the right fist for a full-blooded swing.

Then he froze. He never threw the punch. Instead he stared incredulously. Jock Danby was blubbering like a child, his heavy shoulders shaking uncontrollably, tears greasing down the sun-raddled cheeks into the dusty beard.

It was somehow shocking and embarrassing to see a man like this weep, and Zouga felt his anger swiftly extinguished. He dropped his fist and unclenched it at his side.

'Christ –' Jock Danby choked hoarsely. 'What kind of man are you to try and make a profit of another man's grief?'

Zouga stared at him, unable to answer the accusation.

'You must have smelt it, like a hyena or a fat bloody vulture.'

'I came to make you a fair offer – that's all,' Zouga replied stiffly. He took the handkerchief from his jacket pocket and handed it to Jock Danby. 'Wipe your face, man,' he ordered gruffly.

Jock smeared his tears and then studied the stained linen. 'You didn't know then?' he whispered. 'You didn't know about the boy?' He looked up and studied Zouga's face sharply and, seeing his answer, he handed back the handkerchief and shook his head like a spaniel shaking off the water from its ears, trying to steady his reeling senses. 'I'm sorry,' he grunted. 'I thought somehow you had learned about the boy – and come to buy me out.'

'I don't understand,' Zouga told him, and Jock Danby started for the door of the shack.

'Come,' he said, and led Zouga through the hot stuffy little front room. The chairs covered with dark green velvet were too bulky for the size of the room, and the family treasures – Bible and faded ancestral photographs, cheap cutlery and a porcelain dish commemorating the Queen's wedding to Prince Albert – were on display upon the central table.

In the door of the back room Zouga paused, and felt a sickening little lurch in the pit of his stomach. A woman knelt beside the bed. She had a shawl spread over head and shoulders. Her hands clasped before her face were roughened and reddened by the drudgery of labour over the diamond sorting-table.

She lifted her head and looked at Zouga in the doorway. She might once have been a pretty girl, but the sun had coarsened her skin and her eyes were swollen and reddened with grief. The wisps of hair that hung lankly from under the shawl were greasy and prematurely greyed.

After that one glance she lowered her head again and her lips moved silently as she prayed.

A child lay upon the bed, a boy no older than Jordan. His eyes were closed, his features very pale, bloodless as candlewax, but infinitely peaceful. He was dressed in a clean nightshirt, his limbs neatly arranged, the hands folded on his chest.

It took Zouga a full minute to realize that he was dead. 'The fever,' whispered Jock at Zouga's side. He broke off and stood dumb and massive as an ox awaiting the butcher's stroke.

Zouga took Jock Danby's cart down to Market Square and purchased a dozen rough-sawn planks of lumber, paying the transport rider's price without haggling.

In the dusty yard in front of Danby's shack he stripped to his shirtsleeves and planed the raw planks, while Jock sawed and shaped them. They worked in silence except for the whicker of plane and saw.

The rough coffin was ready before noon, but as Jock lifted his son's body into it Zouga caught the first whiff of corruption; it happens very swiftly in the African heat.

Jock's wife rode on the battered cart with the coffin and Zouga walked beside Jock Danby.

The fever was ravaging the camp. There were two other carts already at the burial ground, a mile beyond the last tents on the Transvaal road, each surrounded with a silent knot of mourners; and there were graves ready dug, and a grave-digger to demand his guinea.

On the way back from the burial ground Zouga stopped the cart in front of one of the canteens that fronted the market square, and with the remaining coins in his pocket he bought three bottles of Cape brandy.

He and Jock sat facing each other on the over-stuffed green velvet chairs, with an open bottle and two tumblers on the table between them. The tumblers were embossed with cheery gold letters:

'The Queen, God Bless Her.'

Zouga half-filled the tumblers and pushed one across to Jock.

The big man studied the contents of the tumbler, holding it in his huge fists between his knees, hunching his shoulders and drooping his head.

'It was so quick,' he muttered. 'Yesterday evening he ran to meet the cart, and rode home on my shoulder.' He took a swallow of the dark liquor and shuddered. His voice was husky as he went on. 'He was so light. No meat on his little bones.'

They drank in unison.

'There was a jinx on me from the moment I drove my first peg on these bloody claims.' Jock shook his great shaggy head. 'I should have stayed on the river-diggings, like Alice told me.'

Outside the single lace-covered window the sun was already setting, a lurid red show through the dust clouds; and as the gloom gathered in the room, Alice Danby came through and placed a smoky hurricane lantern on the table between them and followed it with two bowls of Boer-meal porridge swimming in a thin and oily mutton stew. Then she disappeared silently into the back room and, from time to time during the long night, Zouga heard her gentle sobs through the thin dividing wall.

In the dawn Jock Danby lolled in the green velvet armchair, his shirt open to the navel and his hairy stomach bulging out of it. The third bottle was half empty.

'You are a gentleman,' Jock slurred unevenly. 'I don't mean a swell or a toff but a bloody gentleman, that's what you are.'

Zouga sat upright, grave and attentive; except for a slight reddening of his eyes he seemed totally unaffected by the night's drinking.

'I wouldn't want to wish the Devil's Own on a gentleman like you.'

Zouga said quietly, 'If you're going, you have to sell to someone.'

'They're jinxed, those two claims,'mumbled Jock. 'They've killed five men already, they've broken me, they've given me the worst year of my life. I've seen men on each side of me pull big stones; I've seen them become rich – while me –' he made a drunken gesture that encompassed the sordid little shack, 'look at me.'

The canvas that screened the connecting doorway was jerked aside and Alice Danby stood bareheaded beside her husband. It was evident by her drawn grey features that she had not slept either.

'Sell them,' she said. 'I cannot stay here another day. Sell them, sell everything – let's go, Jock, let's get away from this dreadful place. I cannot bear to spend another night here.'

The mining commissioner was a dour little magistrate appointed by President Brand of the fledgling Boer Free State, who laid claim to the diggings.

Brand was not the only one to have done so. Old Waterboer, the chief of the Griqua Bastaards, made cross claim to the arid plains where his people had lived for fifty years and more. In London, Lord Kimberley, Secretary of State for the Colonies, had only just awakened to the potential wealth of the diamond diggings, and for the first time was listening attentively to the pleas of the Imperialists to support old Nicholaas Waterboer's claim and take Griqualand into the sphere of British influence.

In the meantime the Free State mining commissioner was trying, with only qualified success, to maintain some order over the unruly diggers. Just as his roadways were crumbling into the surrounding pits on Colesberg kopje, so his authority was eroding before the onrush of events with the gathering of national interests and the emergence from obscurity of the first powerful figures as the financial aristocracy of the fields.

Zouga and Jock Danby found the commissioner bewailing his task over a liquid breakfast in the bar of the London Hotel and, supporting him by each elbow, they escorted him back across Market Square to his office.

By mid-morning that day, the commissioner had copied the details of the Devil's Own, claims Nos 141 and 142 held under perpetual quit-rent letter, from J. A. Danby, Esq. to Major M. Z. Ballantyne, and noted payment in full in the sum of £2,000 by cheque drawn on the Standard Bank.

An hour after noon, Zouga stood at the corner of Market Square, and watched the cart piled high with the green velvet armchairs and the brass bedstead pull away towards the northern corner of the square. Jock Danby led the team, and his wife sat thin and erect upon the load. Neither of them looked back at Zouga, and the moment they disappeared into the maze of narrow alleys and shanties Zouga turned towards the kopje.

Despite the night of sleep that he had missed, he felt no fatigue, and his step was so light that he almost ran out along the narrow causeway that intersected the jumble of claims and workings.

The Devil's Own were deserted, two forlorn patches of raw yellow earth, neatly squared off and littered with abandoned equipment. Jock Danby's black workers had gone, for there was always a desperate shortage of labourers on the diggings. When Jock had not mustered them the previous dawn they had simply wandered away to take daily hire with one of the other diggers.

Most of the mining gear left on the claims seemed worn out, the buckets on the point of bursting and the ropes furry as fat yellow caterpillars. Zouga would not trust them with his own weight.

Gingerly he climbed down the swaying ladder, his cautious movements alerting the diggers on the neighbouring claims that he was an outsider.

'Those are Jock Danby's briefies, man,' one of them shouted a challenge. 'You breaking the diggers' law. That's private ground. You better clear out – and bloody quick, at that.'

'I bought Jock out,' Zouga shouted back. 'He left town an hour ago.'

'How do I know that?'

'Why don't you go up to the commissioner's office?' Zouga asked. The challenger scowled up at him uncertainly, the level of his claim twenty feet below the Devil's Own.

Men had stopped work along the length of the irregular pit, others had lined the causeway high above, and there was an ugly mood on all of them – that was broken by a clear young voice speaking in the cadence and intonation of a refined English gentleman.

'Major Ballantyne – that is you, is it not?' And, peering up at the causeway, Zouga recognized Neville Pickering, his drinking companion from the first day in the London Hotel.

'It is indeed, Mr Pickering.'

'That's all right, fellows. I'll vouch for Major Ballantyne. He is the famous elephant hunter, don't you know?'

Almost immediately they lost interest and turned away to become absorbed once more in their own race to get the buckets of gravelly yellow stuff to the surface.

'Thank you,' Zouga called up to the man on the causeway above him.

'My pleasure, sir.' Pickering flashed a brilliant smile, touched the brim of his hat and sauntered away, a slim and elegant figure in the press of bearded dust-caked diggers.

Zouga was left alone, as alone in spirit as he had ever been in any of his wanderings across the vast African continent. He had spent almost the last penny he owned on these few square feet of yellow earth at the bottom of this hot and dusty pit. He had no men to help him work it, no experience, no capital – and he doubted that he would recognize an uncut diamond if he held one in the palm of his hand.

As suddenly as it had descended upon him, the gambler's elation, the premonition of good fortune that awaited him here evaporated. He was instantly overwhelmed by his own presumption and by the enormity of the gamble he was taking.

He had risked it all on claims that so far had not yielded a single good stone, the price of diamonds was plummeting, the 'pool goods', small splints of half a carat or less which formed the vast bulk of stones recovered, were fetching only five shillings each.

It was a wild chance, and his stomach slid sickeningly as he faced the consequences of failure.

The sun was almost directly overhead, burning down into the bottom of the workings; the air around him wavered with the heat and it came up through the leather of his boots to scorch the soles of his feet. He felt as though he were suffocating, as though he could not bear it another moment, as though he must scramble up out of this loathsome pit to where the air was cooler and sweeter.

He knew then he was afraid. It was an emotion to which he was not accustomed. He had stood down the charge of a wounded bull elephant, and taken his chance – man to man, steel to steel – on the frontiers of India and in the wild border wars of the Cape.

He was not accustomed to feeling fear, but the waves of panic rose up out of some dark place in his soul and he fought to control them. The sense of impending disaster crushed down upon him. Under his feet he could almost feel the sterility of the baking earth, the barren earth which would cripple him at last, and destroy the dream which had been the fuel on which his life had run for all these years.

Was it all to end here in this hot and hellish pit?

He took a deep breath, and held it for a moment, fighting off the waves of blind panic, and slowly they receded, leaving him feeling weak and shaken as though from a heavy dose of malarial fever.

He went down on one knee and took a handful of the yellow stuff, sifting it through his fingers, and then examined the residue of dull and worthless pebbles. He let them drop and dusted his hand against his thigh.

He had beaten back the engulfing panic, but he was left with a terrible sense of despondency, and a weariness that ached in his bones so that he hardly had strength enough to climb the swaying rope ladder and his feet dragged and scuffed the ochre-red earth of the track, while around him the encampment swam and wavered in the heat and dust as he started back towards the outspan.

Above the hubbub of the camp a clear childish voice rang, and Zouga lifted the golden beard from his chest, his mood lightening as he recognized his son's sweet piping tones.

'Papa! Oh Papa!'

Jordan was racing towards him, wild abandon in every frantic pace, his arms pumping and his feet flying over the rutted track, while the mass of silken curls flew about his lovely face.

'Oh Papa, we have searched for you – all night, all day.'

'What is it, Jordan?' The child's distress alarmed Zouga afresh, and he started forward.

Jordan reached him and threw both arms about Zouga's waist, he pressed his face to Zouga's coat front so that his voice was muffled and he trembled like a frightened little wild animal.

'It's Mama! Something has happened to Mama! Something terrible has happened.'

The delirium of typhoid fever came upon Aletta in hot grey fog banks that blotted out reality and filled her head with phantoms and fantasies which cleared abruptly, leaving her too weak to sit upright, but with her senses enhanced so that her hot skin was hypersensitive to the touch of the clammy flannel against her face and the oppressive weight of her clothing threatened to smother her.

Her vision was sharp and the images enlarged as though seen through a fine reading glass. She could study each long curved eyelash that made up the dense fringe about Jordan's beautiful green eyes. She could see each individual pore in the satiny skin of his cheeks, could delight in the texture of his perfectly bowed lips that trembled now with his agitation and fear as he stooped over her.

She was lost in wonder at her son's beauty, and then the roaring started in her ears again and the beloved child's face receded, until she was looking at it down a long narrow tunnel through the roaring darkness.

She clung desperately to the image, but it began to turn, slowly at first like the wheel of a carriage, then faster still until Jordan's face blurred dizzily and she felt herself tumbling down into the humid darkness again like a leaf upon the roaring wind.

Again the darkness opened, a veil drawn aside in some deep place in her head, and with joy she sought the boy's face again – but instead she saw the falcon high above her.

It was the bird figure of the graven idol that had always been a part of her life since Zouga had come into it. At every cottage, at every outspan or room that they had called home for a day or a week or a month, that stone idol seemed to have been there with them, silent, implacable, heavy with a brooding and ancient malevolence. She had always hated that idol, had always sensed the aura of evil that surrounded it – but now her hatred and her fear could focus fully upon the stone bird that stood tall above the cot on which she lay.

She cursed it weakly, silently, lying on her back on the narrow cot, the robe she wore clinging damply to her skin with the fever-sweat; and she mouthed her hatred at the stone image that towered above her on its polished green soapstone column. Again her vision narrowed, became concentrated so that the falcon head was her whole existence.

Then miraculously the blank stone eyes began to glow with a strange golden light; they revolved slowly in the sockets of the polished stone skull, and suddenly they were looking down at her. The pupils were black and glossy, alive and seeing – but cruel and so truly evil that she quailed in terror, staring up at the bird.

The curved stone beak opened, the tongue was sharp as an arrow-head, and from its tip was suspended a single perfect ruby drop of blood in which a star of light glowed – and Aletta knew it was the blood of the sacrifice. The darkness about the bird was filled with moving shadows, the wraiths of the sacrificial victims, the shades of the falcon-priests dead these thousand years, gathering again to reinforce the powers, gathering again to welcome her –

She screamed, again and again, her terror ringing insanely in her own ears – and then firm hands were shaking her gently, tenderly. Her vision cleared again, but not completely. Everything was dim and blurred, so she screwed up her eyes, still panting wildly from her screams.

'Ralph, is that you?' The strong dark features, already taking on the set of manhood, so different from the sweet angel face of his brother, were close above her.

'Don't take on so, Mama.'

'Ralphie, why is it so dark?' she mumbled.

'It's night time.'

'Where is Jordie?'

'He is asleep, Mama; he could not keep awake. I sent him to sleep.'

'Call Papa,' she whispered.

'Jan Cheroot is searching for him – he will come soon.'

'I'm cold.' She was trembling violently, and felt him draw the rough blanket up beneath her chin before she sank back into the darkness.

In the darkness she saw the shapes of men hurrying forward, pressing about her; she caught their urgency, the passion of their terrible purpose, and she saw their arms glint in the shadows, the flash of white steel, bared and honed for war. She heard the snick of breech-block, the rattle of bayonet in the scabbard, and here and there in the press she recognized a face, faces she had never seen before but which she recognized instantly with a clairvoyant flash of intuition. One was a man full grown, bearded, strong, who was her son – riding into war – and others, so many others, her blood, her flesh, her bones going forward in that awful expectant throng. She was consumed with terrible grief for them, but she could not weep. Instead, she lifted her eyes and saw the falcon on high, clear in the single brilliant shaft of sunshine that pierced the sombre and ominous clouds that rolled from horizon to horizon, the dun and terrible clouds of war.

The falcon hovered on outstretched pinions against the belly of the clouds, twisting the cruelly beautiful head to peer down, then the long pointed wings folded and the bird dropped in a stoop like the lightning bolt, the great talons reaching forward in the strike. She saw them hook into living flesh, saw the grimace on the face that she had never seen before but knew as deeply as she did her own.

And she screamed again. Then strong arms held her, the familiar beloved arms for which she had waited so long. She looked up at him. The clear emerald eyes so close to hers, the powerful jut of his jaw-line half-masked by the full golden-streaked beard.

'Zouga,' she breathed.

'I am here, my love.'

The phantoms receded, the terrible nightmare world of her delirium was gone, and she found herself in a tent upon a dusty plain beneath a half-ruined hillock, and the bright African sunlight through the tent opening cut a stark slash of white light across the powdered red dust floor. She was mildly amazed by the swift transition from night to noonday, from fantasy to reality, and her mouth and throat were filled with the dry chalk of terrible thirst.

'I am thirsty,' she whispered huskily.

He held the pitcher to her cracked lips, and the coolness and the sweetness of the liquid in her throat made her vision swim with delight.

But immediately afterwards, the memory of the nightmares assailed her and she darted a fearful glance across the tent at the silent statue. It seemed suddenly harmless, insignificant, the image blind and dumb, but a flicker of the night's terror remained.

'Beware the falcon,' she whispered, and she saw in his green eyes that he thought her words were still fever ravings. She wanted to convince him but she was terribly, deadly tired, and she closed her eyes and slept in his arms.

When she awoke, the sun's rays had mellowed to a glorious orange light that filled the whole tent and lit little stars in Zouga's beard and curls. She was filled with a deep sense of peace. His arms were so strong, so all-encompassing.

'Look after my babies,' she said softly, but very clearly, and then she died.

Aletta's grave was just another mound of red dirt in the long, neat row of freshly turned mounds.

After he had buried her, Zouga sent the boys back to the outspan with Jan Cheroot. Jordan was weeping inconsolably, his lovely face smudged with grief. Ralph sat behind his brother on the back of the gaunt bay gelding, holding the smaller child with both arms clasped about his waist. Ralph was silent, stoic, but his body was rigid with controlled emotion, and his eyes, the same clear deep green of his father's, smouldered with unexpressed grief.

Jan Cheroot led the bay, and the two boys seemed as frail and forlorn as swallows left on a fence rail long after the others had flown the oncoming winter.

Zouga stood beside the grave with military bearing, as expressionless as his elder son had been, but behind the handsome mask he was stunned by his own sorrow and pervading sense of guilt.

He wanted to speak aloud, to tell Aletta that he was sorry, that he knew that he was responsible for this lonely grave so far from her loving family and the beautiful forested mountains of Good Hope which he had loved so dearly. He wanted to ask for forgiveness for sacrificing her to a dream, an impossible grandiose dream. Yet he knew that words were futile and the red earth stopped Aletta's ears.

He stooped and with his bare hand dressed the mound where the earth had collapsed at one corner.

With the first diamond I will buy the headstone, he promised himself silently. The red earth had stained under his fingernails, little half-moons the colour of blood.

With a supreme effort he overcame his sense of futility, overcame the self-consciousness sufficiently to speak aloud to someone who could not hear.

'I will look after them, my dear,' he said. 'That is my last promise to you.'

'Jordie will not eat, Papa.' Ralph greeted him as he stooped into the tent, and Zouga felt the leap of alarm swamp his sorrow and his guilt. He strode to the cot on which the child lay, facing the canvas wall of the tent with his knees drawn up to his chest.

Jordan's skin was burning hot as the sun-scorched rocks that littered the plain outside the tent, and his silken cheeks smeared with tears were flushed a furious fever red.

By morning Ralph was feverish also, both boys tossing and muttering in delirium, their bodies hot as two little furnaces, the blankets sodden with their sweat and the tent reeking with the carrion stench of fever.

Ralph fought the fever.

'Ja, just look at him.' Jan Cheroot paused fondly in the act of sponging down the robust strong-boned body. 'He takes the sickness like an enemy, and struggles with it.'

Helping him, kneeling on the opposite side of the cot, Zouga felt the familiar glow of pride surface through his concern as he looked down at him. Already there were little smoky wisps of hair under Ralph's arms, and a darker explosion of curls at the base of his belly; and his penis was no longer the little wormlike appendage with a childish cap of wrinkled loose skin. His shoulders were squaring and filling with muscle, and his legs were straight and sturdy.

'He will be all right,' Jan Cheroot repeated, and Ralph thrashed out angrily in his delirium, his features scowling and dark with determination.

The two men drew the blanket up over him and turned to the other cot.

Jordan's long thick lashes fluttered like the wings of a beautiful butterfly, and he whimpered pitifully, unresisting as they stripped and sponged him. His little body was as sweetly formed as his features, but clad still in its puppy-fat so that his buttocks were round as apples and plump as a girl's; but his limbs were delicately boned and shapely, his feet and hands long and narrow and graceful.

'Mama,' he whimpered. 'I want my Mama.'

The two men nursed the boys, taking turns day and night, everything else neglected or forgotten, an hour snatched here to water and tend the horses, another hour for a hurried journey into the camp to purchase patent medicine from a transport rider or scramble for the few vegetables offered for sale on the farmers' carts. But diamonds were forgotten, never mentioned in the hot little tent where the struggle for life went on, and the Devil's Own claims were abandoned and deserted.

In forty-eight hours Ralph had regained consciousness, in three days he was sitting up unaided and wolfing his food, in six days they could no longer keep him in his cot.

Jordan rallied briefly on the second day, becoming lucid and demanding his mother fretfully, and then remembered that she was gone, began weeping again and immediately began to sink.

His life teetered, the pendulum swinging erratically back and forth, but each time he fell back the presence of death grew stronger in the baking canvas tent, until its stench overpowered the odour of fever.

The flesh melted from his body, burned away by the fever, and his skin took on a pearly translucent sheen, so that it seemed in that uncertain light of dusk and early dawn that the very outline of the delicate bone-structure showed through.

Jan Cheroot and Zouga nursed him in turns, one sleeping while the other watched – or, when neither could sleep, sitting together, seeking comfort and companionship from each other, trying to discount their helplessness in the face of onrushing death.

'He's young and strong,' they told each other. 'He will be all right also.'

And day after day Jordan sank lower, his cheekbones rising up out of his flesh, and his eyes receding into deep cavities the colour of old bruises.

Exhausted with guilt and sorrow, with helpless worry, Zouga left the tent each dawn before sunrise to be the first at Market Square – perhaps there was a transport rider freshly arrived with medicines in his chests, and certainly there would be Boer farmers with cabbages and onions and, if he was lucky, a few wizened and half-green tomatoes, all of which would be sold half an hour after dawn.

On the tenth morning, as Zouga hurried back to the tent, he paused for a moment at the entrance, frowning angrily. The falcon statue had been dragged from the tent, and there was a long furrow scraped by its base in the loose dust. It stood now at a careless angle, leaning against the trunk of the scraggy camel-thorn tree that gave meagre shade to the camp.

The branches of the tree were festooned with black ribbons of dried springbuck meat, with saddlery and trek gear – so that the statue seemed to be part of this litter. There was one of the camp's brown hens perched on the falcon's head, and it had dropped a long chalky smear of liquid excrement down the stone figure.

Still frowning, Zouga ducked into the tent. Jan Cheroot squatted beside Ralph's cot, and the two of them were deeply involved in a game of five stones, using polished pebbles of agate and quartz for the counters.

Jordan lay very still and pale, so that Zouga felt a lurch of dismay under his ribs. It was only when he stooped over the cot that he saw the rise and fall of Jordan's chest and caught the faint whisper of his breathing.

'Did you move the stone falcon?'

Jan Cheroot grunted without looking up from the shiny stones. 'It seemed to trouble Jordie. He woke up crying again – and kept calling to it.'

Zouga would have taken it further, but suddenly it did not seem worth the effort. He was so tired and dispirited. He would bring the statue back into the tent later, he decided.

'There are a few sweet potatoes – nothing else,' he grunted as he took up the vigil beside Jordan's cot.

Jan Cheroot made a stew of dried beans and mutton, and mashed this with the boiled potatoes. It was an unappetizing mess, but that evening, for the first time, Jordan did not roll his head away from the proffered spoon, and after that his recovery was startlingly swift.

He asked only once more after Aletta, when he and Zouga were alone in the tent.

'Has she gone to heaven, Papa?'

'Yes.' The certainty in Zouga's tone seemed to reassure him.

'Will she be one of God's angels?'

'Yes, Jordie, and from now on she will always be there – watching over you.'

The child thought about that seriously and then nodded contentedly, and the next day he seemed strong enough for Zouga to leave him in Ralph's charge while he and Jan Cheroot went up to the kopje and walked out along No. 6 Roadway to look down on the Devil's Own claims.

All the mining equipment, shovels and picks, buckets and ropes, sheave wheels and ladders had been stolen. At the prices the transport riders were charging it would cost a hundred guineas to replace them.

'We will need men,' Zouga said.

'What will you do when you have them?' Jan Cheroot asked.

'Dig the stuff out.'

'And then?' the little Hottentot demanded with a malicious gleam in his dark eyes, his features wrinkled as a sour windfallen apple. 'What do you then?' he insisted.

'I intend to find out,' Zouga replied grimly. 'We have wasted enough time here already.'

'My dear fellow,' Neville Pickering gave him that charming smile. 'I'm delighted that you asked. Had you not, then I should have offered. It's always a little problematic for a new chum to find his feet,' he coughed deferentially, and went on quickly, 'not that you are a new chum, by any means –'

That was a term usually reserved for the fresh-faced hopefuls newly arrived on the boat from 'home'. 'Home' was England, even those who were colonial-born referred to it as 'home'.

'I'd bet a fiver to a pinch of giraffe dung that you know more about this country than any of us here.'

'African born,' Zouga admitted, 'on the Zouga river up north in Khama's land; accounts for the odd name – Zouga.'

'By jove, didn't realize that, I must say!'

'Don't hold it against me.' Zouga smiled lightly, but he knew that there were many who would. Home born was vastly superior to colonial born. It was for that reason that he had insisted that Aletta should make the long sea voyage with him when it seemed that her pregnancies would reach full term. Both Ralph and Jordan had been born in the same house in south London, and both had arrived back at Good Hope before they were weaned. They were homeborn: that was his first gift to them.

Pickering glossed over the remark tactfully. He did not have to declare his own birth. He was an English gentleman, and nobody would ever mistake that.

'There are many parts of your book that fascinated me. I'll teach you what I know about sparklers if you'll answer my questions. Bargain?'

Over the days that followed they bombarded each other with questions, Zouga demanding every detail of the process of raising and sorting the yellow gravel from the deepening pit, while Pickering kept turning the conversation back to the land to the north, asking about the tribes and the gold reefs, about the rivers and mountains and the wild animals that swarmed upon the plains and in the lonely forests that Zouga had conjured up so vividly in *Hunter's Odyssey.*

Each morning an hour before the first light, Zouga would meet Pickering at the edge of the roadway above the workings. There would be an enamelled kettle bubbling on the brazier and they drank black coffee that was strong enough to stain the teeth, while around them in the gloom the black mine-workers gathered sleepily, still hugging their fur karosses over their shoulders, their voices muted but musical, their movements stiff and slow with sleepiness and the dawn chill.

At a hundred other points around the growing pit the gangs assembled, waiting for the light; and when it glimmered on the eastern horizon the men went swarming down into the workings, like columns of ants along the board walks and down the swaying ladders, spreading out on the chequer board of claims, the hubbub rising, the chant of tribesmen, the squeal of ropes, the hectoring shouts of the white overseers, and then the rattle of bucket loads of yellow gravel into the waiting carts upon the roadway.

Pickering was working four claims, which be owned in partnership.

'My partner is down in Cape Town. Heaven knows when he will be back.'

Neville Pickering shrugged with that deceptively indolent air which he cultivated. 'You'll meet him one of these fine days, and it will be an experience—memorable but not necessarily enjoyable.'

It amused Zouga to see how Neville contrived to maintain his foppish elegance of dress, how he could walk the length of the No. 6 Roadway without the dust hazing the shine of his boots; how he could scramble across the ladderworks without dampening his shirt with sweat, or exchange a flurry of blows with a brawny digger who was encroaching on his claims without it seeming to affect the drape of his Norfolk jacket. His casual sauntering gait carried him from one end of the diggings to the other, at a pace which had Zouga stretching his own legs.

The four claims were not in a single block, but each separated from the others by a dozen or so intervening claims, and Pickering moved from one to the other co-ordinating the work, pulling a gang of half-naked black men from one claim and leading them across to another where the work had fallen behind.

Abruptly he was on the roadway, checking the loading of the carts, and then again, just as abruptly, at the fenced-off plot beyond Market Square where his black workers were rocking the cradles of gravel.

The diamond cradles were like giant versions of the old-fashioned baby cradles from which they took their name. Standing on their half-moon-shaped feet, a man on each side kept them swinging easily from side to side while a third worker shovelled the yellow gravel into the top deck of the cradle from the mound that the cart had dumped. The top deck was a coarse steel sieve, with inch and a half openings in the mesh.

As the cradle rocked rhythmically, the gravel tumbled and bounced across the sloping sieve, the finer stuff under one and a half inches in diameter dropping through onto the second deck of the cradle while the coarse pebbles and waste rolled over under the surveillance of the two cradle men, who watched for the highly unlikely flash of a diamond too big to fall through onto the second deck.

A diamond more than one and a half inches across would be the fortune-maker, the finder's passport to great wealth, the almost impossible 'pony' of the diggers' dreams, a stone heavier than one hundred carats.

On the second deck the mesh was much finer, half-inch square, and a yellow dust blew away like smoke as the cradle agitated it, while on the third deck the mesh was finer still, allowing only the worthless tailings to drop to waste, stuff smaller than the crystals of refined sugar.

From the third deck the gravel was gathered with reverential care, and this was washed in a tub of precious water, every drop of which had been transported thirty miles from the Vaal river.

The gravel was washed in a circular sieve of the No. 3 mesh, the finest of all. The worker agitating and dipping over the tub, muddy to the elbows. Finally the contents of the sieve, cleansed of mud, were dumped onto the flat metal surface of the sorting-table, and the sorters began picking over it with the flat wooden blades of their scrapers.

Women were far away the best sorters, they had the patience, the manual dexterity and the fine eye for colour and texture that was needed. The married diggers kept their wives and daughters at the sorting-table from the minute the mellow morning light was strong enough until the dusk faded each evening.

Pickering was not lucky enough to have women working his

tables, but the Africans he had were carefully trained, although never trusted.

'You would never credit what they do with a good stone to try and get away with it. I smile sometimes at what the Duchess would think if she knew that the shiner hanging around her neck had been up the tail end of a big black Basuto,' Pickering chuckled. 'Come, I'll show you what to look for.'

The wiry little black sorter at the head of the table advertised his superior status by his European finery, embroidered waistcoat and Derby hat, but his feet were bare and he carried his snuff-horn in the pierced lobe of his ear. He vacated his seat at the table cheerfully, and Neville Pickering took up the scraper and began to sift through the gravel, a few pebbles at a time.

'There!' he grunted suddenly. 'Your first wild diamond, old man! Take a good look at it, and let's hope it isn't your last.'

Zouga was surprised. It was not what he had expected, and then his surprise was replaced immediately by disappointment. It was a drab little chip of stone, barely the size of one of the sand fleas which swarmed in the red dust of the camp.

It lacked the fire and flash that Zouga had expected, and its colour was a dingy yellow: the colour of champagne perhaps, but without that wine's sparkle.

'Are you sure?' Zouga asked. 'It doesn't look like a diamond to me. How can you tell?'

'It's a splint-chip, probably a piece of a larger stone. It will go ten points, that's a tenth part of a carat, and we will be lucky to get five shillings for it, but it will pay the wages of one of my men for a week.'

'How do you tell the difference between that – and those?' Zouga indicated the mound of gravel in the centre of the table, still wet from the washing-tub, glistening in a thousand different shades of red and gold, anthracite black and flesh pinks, the gaudy show of diamondiferous gravel.

'It's the soapiness,' Pickering explained, 'the soap texture. You will train your eye to it soon, don't bother about the colour – look for the soap.' He took the stone in the teeth of a pair of wooden tweezers and turned it in the sunlight. 'A diamond is unwettable, it repels water; so in the wet gravel it stands out, and the difference is that soapy look.'

Neville proffered the stone. 'There, I tell you what, you keep it as a gift, your first diamond.'

They had been hunting for nearly ten days now, and had gradually moved farther and farther north.

Twice they had sighted quarry, small groups, but each time the quarry had scattered at the first approach.

Zouga was getting desperate. His claims were lying abandoned in the New Rush workings, the level of the surrounding claims would be sinking swiftly, making his more difficult to work and every day increasing the danger of rock slide. Those claims had already killed five men. Jock Danby had warned him.

He was lying now, belly down, on a tiny rocky kopje fifty miles north of the Vaal river, eighty miles from New Rush, and he was still not certain when he could finish this business and turn southwards again.

Jan Cheroot and the two boys were farther down the slope with the horses, holding them in a shallow ravine that was choked with scrub thorn. Jordan's girlish tones carried to where Zouga sat, blending with the cries of circling birds, and Zouga lowered the binoculars to rest his eyes and to listen to his son's voice.

He had worried about taking the boy on this rough journey, especially so soon after that bout of camp fever, but there had been no alterative, no safe place to leave him. Once again Jordan's stamina had belied his delicate looks. He had ridden hard and kept up well with his brother, at the same time recovering the flesh that the fever had burned from his body; and in the last days the deathly pallor of his skin had been gilded to velvety peach.

Thinking about Jordan led directly to memories of Aletta, memories still so filled with sorrow and raw guilt that he could not bear them and he lifted the binoculars again and raked the plain, seeking distraction. He found it with relief.

There was unusual movement far out on the wide plain. Through the lens Zouga picked up a herd of a hundred wildebeest, the 'wild cattle' of the Boers. These ungainly animals, with their mournful Roman noses and scraggly beards, were the clowns of the veld. They chased each other in aimless circles, nose to earth and heels kicking at the sky, then abruptly they ceased this lunatic cavorting and stood snorting at one another with wild-eyed expressions of amazement.

Beyond them Zouga caught a flicker of other movement: until that moment it had been hidden by the dust kicked up by the splayed wildebeest hooves. Carefully he adjusted the bevelled focus ring of his binoculars, and the heat mirage trembled and melted before his gaze, turning the movement into a serpentine wriggle that seemed to float above the plain on a lake of silver shimmering water.

'Ostriches!' he thought disgustedly. The distant shapes seemed to wriggle like long black tadpoles in the watery wavering mirage of distance. The long-legged birds seemed to float free of the earth, blooming miraculously in the tortured air above the plain. Zouga tried to count them, but they changed shape and coagulated into a dark wavering mass, their plumed backs bobbing.

Suddenly Zouga sat up. He dropped the binoculars and polished the lens with the tail of the silk bandanna around his throat, then quickly lifted them to his eyes again. The grotesque dark shapes had separated, the lumpy wriggling bodies fined down, the elongated legs had assumed normal proportions.

'Men!' whispered Zouga, and counted them eagerly, as eagerly as he had ever made a first sighting of the huge ivory-carrying grey bull elephants in the hunting veld. He reached eleven before another layer of heated air intervened and altered the distant man-shapes to grotesque unsteady monsters once again.

Zouga slung the binoculars over his shoulder and went down the slope with the loose scree rolling under his boots. Jan Cheroot and the boys lay in the bottom of the ravine on their saddle blankets, their saddles propped behind them as bolsters.

Zouga slid down the bank and landed between them before they had returned from the fairyland that Jan Cheroot had been spinning for them.

'A good bunch,' he told Jan Cheroot.

Zouga reached down and withdrew the short Martini-Henry carbine from the leather bucket of Ralph's saddle. He levered the breech-block down and checked the weapon was empty.

'We aren't after springbuck. Don't you load until either Jan Cheroot or I tell you,' he ordered sternly.

Jordan was still too little to handle the heavy rifle, but he rode well enough to make the encircling sweep with which they would try to close the net.

'Remember, Jordie, that you stay close enough to Jan Cheroot to hear what he tells you,' Zouga told him, glancing up at the sun as he did so.

It was well past noon; he would have to move fairly soon – for if they could not surround the little band of black men at the first attempt, if they did not achieve surprise, then it would be the old time-consuming business of spooring them down individually. So far attempts at doing so had always been interrupted by the sudden African nightfall.

'Saddle up,' Zouga ordered, and they scrambled to their horses.

Zouga swung up onto the bay gelding and glared sternly at Ralph.

'Now you do what you are told – or I'll warm your tail feathers for you, young man.'

He swung the horse's head and pointed it down the ravine, while behind his back Ralph grinned at Jan Cheroot conspiratorially, his face flushed with excitement, and the little Hottentot closed one eyelid briefly but kept his flat wrinkled oriental features expressionless.

Zouga had chosen the kopje with care; from it a ravine meandered out across the plain in an approximate east to west direction – and he followed it now, slouching in the saddle to keep his head below the level of the banks and keeping the gelding down to a walk so as not to raise dust.

After half a mile he removed the wide-brimmed hat from his head and raised himself cautiously in the stirrups until his eyes were just above the bank, and he darted a quick glance into the north and then immediately ducked down again.

'Station here,' he told Ralph. 'And don't move until I do.'

They moved on down the ravine, while Zouga placed Jan Cheroot and Jordan side by side in a bend of the ravine where the bank had collapsed and formed an easy ramp up which they could launch their charge.

'Keep Jordie close,' Zouga cautioned Jan Cheroot, and swung the gelding around with the saddlery creaking as the animal turned in the narrow gut of the ravine; then Zouga trotted back until he was in the centre of the waiting line, and there he halted and contained his impatience, glancing up repeatedly at the lowering sun.

There would probably not be another chance for many days, and each day was vital for those untended claims. Zouga jerked the rifle from the leather bucket at his knee, selected a cartridge from the bandolier around his waist and slipped it into the breech. Then he returned the weapon uncocked to the bucket.

It was merely a precaution, but he had no means of knowing what manner of men those approaching figures were.

Even if their intentions were peaceable, and their ultimate object identical to Zouga's own, yet they would be armed and nervous, so nervous that they had avoided the road from the north and were travelling over the open veld. They were in company for defence, and Zouga knew they would have been harassed often along the way, by black men and white: the black men trying to rob and cheat them of their meagre possessions, the white men of something infinitely more valuable, their right to contract their labour to the highest bidder.

On the day that Zouga thanked Neville Pickering for his tuition and began preparing to work the Devil's Own claims for his personal account, he had faced the problem that was already wracking the entire sub-continent.

Only black men could stand the conditions of physical labour in the diggings. Only black men would work for a wage that made the diggings profitable, and even that beggarly wage was many times more than the Boer farmers of the surrounding backveld republics could afford to pay.

The diamond diggings had denuded the countryside of labourers for five hundred miles around; and the Boers resented that as fiercely as they resented the nest of adventurers and fortune seekers that the diggings supported.

The diamonds had caused an upheaval in the Boers' traditional way of life; not only were the miners threatening the supply of cheap labour, which only just allowed a diligent and frugal farmer to eke out a living for himself and his family from the savage land, but the diggers were doing something else that from the Boer point of view was unforgivable, that went against all their deeply held beliefs and threatened not just their livelihood but their very physical existence.

The diamond diggers were paying the black tribesmen with *guns.* The Boers had fought the tribes at Blood River and Mosega, they had stood to the laager in ten thousand threatening dawns, the favourite hour of attack. They had seen the smoke rising from their burning homesteads and crops, they had ridden out on commando on the spoor of their stolen herds, and they had buried the pale corpses of their children, the blood drained from the frail bodies through the gaping and terrible wounds of the assegai. They had buried them at Weenen – the Place of Weeping

– and at other accursed and abandoned grave sites across the land.

The payment of black men with guns went against every one of their instincts; it flew full in the face of their laws and offended the memories of their dead heroes.

For these reasons Boer commandos from the little backveld republics were sweeping the land and patrolling the lonely roads from the north to try and prevent the tribesmen reaching the diggings and instead press them to work upon the land.

However, five shillings a week and a musket at the end of a three years' contract were a lure that brought the tribesmen, on foot, against a hundred hazards, on a journey of hundreds of miles, daring the commandos and all else, to reach the diggings.

They came in their hundreds, but still not enough of them arrived to fill those hungry diamond pits. In vain Zouga and Jan Cheroot had ridden the workings. Every black man was signed on contract, and jealously guarded by his employer.

Zouga had told Jan Cheroot, 'We'll offer seven shillings and sixpence a week.'

They signed five men that same day at the higher wage, and the next day there were a dozen deserters waiting outside Zouga's camp, eager for the new coin.

Before Zouga could sign them, Neville Pickering sauntered up. 'Official visit, old man,' he murmured apologetically. 'As a member of the jolly old Diggers' Committee, I have to tell you the rate is five shillings not seven and six.'

When Zouga opened his mouth to protest, Pickering smiled easily and held up his hand.

'No, Major. I'm sorry. It's five shillings, and not a penny more.'

Zouga was already in no doubt about the sweeping powers of the Diggers' Committee. An edict from the elected body was enforced firstly by a warning, then a beating, and finally by the full aggression of the entire community of diggers which could end in a burning or even a lynching.

'What do I do for a gang, then?' Zouga demanded.

'You do what we all do; you go out and find a gang, before another digger or a Boer commando grabs them.'

'I might have to go as far north as the Shashi river,' Zouga snapped sarcastically, and Pickering nodded in agreement.

'Yes, you might.'

Zouga smiled thinly at the memory of his first lesson in digger labour relations, and now he settled his hat firmly and gathered up his reins.

'All right,' he muttered, 'let's go recruiting!' And he put his heels into the gelding's flanks and went lunging up the bank of the ravine onto the open plain.

The tribesmen were five hundred yards dead ahead, and he counted swiftly: sixteen of them. If he could take them all he could start back for New Rush in tomorrow's dawn. Sixteen men were sufficient to work the Devil's Own, and at that moment they had, for Zouga, the same value as a fifty-carat diamond. They were in single file, moving swiftly, the trotting gait of the fighting impis of Zulu, no women or children with them.

'Good,' grunted Zouga as the gelding stretched out under him, and he held him back in an easy canter as he glanced right.

Jan Cheroot was tearing across the plain, Jordan plugging along in his dust fifty strides behind. At this distance Jordan did not look like a child; they might have been a pair of armed riders, and Jan Cheroot was swinging wide, trying to get behind the little group of men, pinning them before they scattered, pinning them long enough for Zouga to get within hail.

Zouga glanced left and scowled as he saw that Ralph was at full gallop, leaning low over his horse's neck, brandishing the Martini-Henry rifle – and Zouga hoped it was still unloaded, wished that he had specially ordered Ralph not to show the rifle, and yet even in that moment of anger he experienced a little prickle of pride as he watched his son ride; the boy was born to the saddle.

Zouga checked the gelding again, bringing him down to a trot, giving his flank men time to complete the circle, and at the same time trying to reduce the dramatic effect of his approach. He knew that they would appear to the tribesmen to be an armed commando, their intentions warlike, and he tried to soften this by lifting his hat and waving it over his head.

Then suddenly Jan Cheroot was reining in, gesturing to Jordan to do the same. They had got behind the band, and opposite them, facing them across the wide circle, Ralph was wheeling his filly and bringing her up sharply on her hind legs, rearing and shaking out her mane theatrically.

In the centre the tribesmen had moved swiftly, and with the concerted action of trained fighting men.

They had dropped the rolled bundles of sleeping-mat, cooking-pot and leather grain bag that they had been carrying on their heads, and they had bunched into a defensive circle shoulder to shoulder, war shield overlapping war shield, while above them the steel of their assegais flicked little pinpricks of sunlight.

They did not wear the full regalia of their fighting regiments, the kilts of monkey tails, the cloaks of desert fox furs, the tall headdress of ostrich and widow-bird feathers, they were travelling with weapons only; but the shields they presented to the approaching horseman and the glint of steel told Zouga all he wanted to know. The shields gave the tribe its name, the Matabele – the people of the long shields.

The little group of men who stood impassively in the sunlight and watched Zouga ride up were the finest warriors that Africa had ever spawned. Yet they were almost five hundred miles south of the borders of Matabeleland.

'I set for a covey of partridge,' Zouga smiled to himself, 'and I have trapped a brood of eagles.'

A hundred yards from the ring of shields, Zouga reined in; but the gelding, infected by the tension, fidgeted under him.

The long shields were made of dappled black and white oxhide, every regiment of the Matabele carried a distinctive shield.

Zouga knew that black dappled with white was the regimental colour of the Inyati, the Buffaloes Regiment, and again he felt a twist of nostalgia.

Once the induna who commanded the Inyati had been a friend; they had travelled together across the mimosa-clad plains of Matabeleland; they had hunted together and shared the comfort of the same camp fires. It was all so long ago, on his first visit to the land below the Zambezi river, but Zouga was carried back so vividly that it required an effort of will to shake off the memory.

He lifted his right hand, fingers spread in the universal gesture of goodwill.

'Warriors of Matabele, I see you,' he called to them, speaking their language as fluently as one of them, the words returning to his tongue readily.

He saw the small stir behind the war-shields, the shift of heads with which they greeted his words.

'Jordan!' Zouga called, and the child circled out and reined in his pony at Zouga's side. Now the difference in size between man and boy was apparent.

'See, warriors of King Lobengula, my son rides with me.' No man took his children to war. The ring of shields sank a few inches so Zouga could see the dark and watchful eyes of the men behind them; but as Zouga pushed the gelding a few paces forward, the shields were immediately lifted again defensively.

'What news of Gandang, induna of the Inyati Regiment, Gandang who is as my brother?' Zouga called again persuasively.

At the mention of the name one of the warriors could no longer contain himself, swept aside his shield and stepped from the ring of spears.

'Who calls Gandang brother?' he demanded in a clear firm voice, a young voice, yet with the timbre and inflection of one used to authority.

'I am Bakela, the Fist,' Zouga gave his Matabele name, and he realized that the warrior facing him was still a youth, barely older than Ralph. But he was lean and straight, narrow in the hips and with muscle in the shoulder and arms built up in the games of war. Zouga guessed he had probably already killed his man, washed his spear in blood.

Now he crossed the open ground towards Zouga, his stride lithe, his legs long and shapely beneath the short leather kilt.

'Bakela,' he said, as he stopped a dozen paces from the gelding's head. 'Bakela.' He smiled, a brilliant show of white even teeth in the broad and handsome Nguni face. 'That is a name I took with the first draught of my mother's milk, for I am Bazo, the Axe, son of the same Gandang whom you call brother, and who remembers you as an old and trusted friend. I know you by the scar on your cheek and the gold in your beard. I greet you, Bakela.'

Zouga swung down off the gelding, leaving the rifle in the saddle scabbard, and, grinning broadly, went to clasp the youth's upper arms in an affectionate salute.

Then, turning with his fists on his hips, still smiling, Zouga shouted to Ralph. 'Go and see if you can shoot a springbuck, or better even, a wildebeest; we'll need plenty of meat for tonight.'

Ralph let out a whoop at the command, and provoked the filly with his heels, forcing her to rear again and then come down in full run, mane flying, hooves pounding as she bore away. Without being ordered, Jan Cheroot shook his bony mare into a canter and followed the flying filly.

The two riders returned in the dusk, and the hunt had gone well. They had found rare quarry, a bull eland so old that his neck and shoulders had turned blue with age and the swinging dewlap almost swept the dusty earth between his stubby fore-legs.

He was as big as a prize stud bull, with a chest round as a brandy cask of Limousine oak, and Zouga guessed he would weigh not much under a ton, for he was fat and sleek; there would be a tubful of rich white lard in the chest cavity, and thick layers of yellow fat beneath the glossy hide. He was a prize indeed, and the little band of Matabele drummed their assegai against the hide shields and shouted with delight when they saw him.

The bull snorted at the hubbub and broke into a lumbering gallop, trying to break away, but Ralph swung the filly to head him off and within a hundred yards the bull changed the gallop for a short winded trot and allowed himself to be turned back towards the group of waiting men.

Ralph reined in the filly, kicked his feet from the stirrups and jumped easily to the earth, throwing up the carbine as he landed cat-like on his toes and seeming to fire in the same instant.

The bull's head flinched at the shot, blinking the huge shining eyes convulsively as the bullet slammed into his skull between them, and he collapsed with a meaty thud that seemed to tremble in the earth.

The Matabele streamed out like a pack of wild dogs, swarming over the mountainous carcass, using the razor edge of their war-assegai as butchers' knives, going for the tidbits, the tripes and the liver, the heart and the sweet white fat.

The Matabele gorged on fat eland meat, grilling the tripes over the coals, threading garlands of liver and fat and succulent heart onto wet white mimosa twigs from which they had peeled the bark, so that the melting fat sizzled and bubbled over the layers of meat.

'We have killed no game since we left the forests,' Bazo explained their ravenous appetites. Though the desert teemed with springbuck herds, they were not the type of game that a man on foot, armed only with a stabbing spear, could run down easily.

'Without meat a man's belly is like a war drum, full of nothing except noise and wind.'

'You are far from the land of the Matabele,' Zouga agreed. 'No Matabele has been this far south since the old king took the tribe north across the Limpopo, and in that time even Gandang, your father, was a child.'

'We are the first to make this journey,' Bazo agreed proudly. 'We are the point of the spear.'

In the firelight the warriors about him looked up and their expressions echoed his pride in their achievement. They were all youths, the eldest only a few years older than Bazo, not one of them over nineteen years of age.

'Where does this long journey take you?' Zouga asked.

'To a wonderful place in the south from which a man returns with great treasures.'

'What manner of treasures?' Zouga asked again.

'These.' Bazo reached across the circle to where Ralph leaned against his saddle, using it as a pillow, and Bazo touched the polished wooden butt of the Martini-Henry that protruded from the gun bucket.

'*Isibamu* – guns!' said Bazo.

'Guns?' Zouga asked. 'A Matabele *indoda* with a gun?' His voice mildly derisive. 'Is not the assegai the weapon of the true warrior?'

Bazo looked uncomfortable for a moment and then recovered his aplomb.

'The old ways are not always the best,' he said. 'The old men tell us that they are, so that young men will consider them wise.' And the Matabele in the circle about the fire nodded and made little sounds of agreement.

Although he was certainly the youngest of the group, Bazo was clearly their leader. Son of Gandang, he was therefore the nephew of King Lobengula, grandson of old King Mzilikazi himself. His noble birth assured him preference, but it was clear that he was quick and clever also.

'To earn the guns you covet a man must work hard, in a deep pit in the earth,' Zouga said. 'He must milk himself of his sweat by the calabash full every day for three years, before he is paid with a gun.'

'We have heard these things,' Bazo nodded.

'Then you shall have your guns, each of you a fine gun, at the end of three years. I, Bakela, the Fist, give you my word on it.'

It was a custom of the diggings, a ceremony of initiation, that when a gang of raw tribesmen arrived at New Rush the established black labourers would rush to line each side of the track, most of them dressed in cast-off European finery as a badge of their sophistication.

They would jeer their newly arrived brethren:

'Behold, the baboons have come down from the hills.'

'Nay! Baboons are cunning; these cannot be baboons.' And they pelted the newcomers with pieces of filth as well as insults.

Bazo's group were the first Matabele to reach the diggings. The Matabele language is almost identical to that of Zululand, and very closely associated to the Southern Xhosa. Bazo understood every word of the banter, and he gave a quiet but grim order to his little group.

His men dropped their sleeping-mats and the long shields rattled one against the other, the broad bright assegais whispered in the sunlight as they were bared, and the taunts and derisive laughter dried on the instant, to be replaced with expressions of astonishment and real dismay.

'*Manje*! Now!' hissed Bazo. The ring of shields exploded outwards, and the crowd fled before it in disordered panic.

From the back of the gelding, Zouga had a grandstand view of the charge, and he had no illusions as to the danger of the moment. Even such a tiny war party of Matabele *amadoda* on the rampage through the camp could cause chaos and frightful slaughter amongst the unarmed black labourers.

'Bazo! Kawulisa! Stop them!' he roared, spurring across the front of the murderous rank of rawhide shields and steel.

The erstwhile tormentors ran with their heads twisted backwards, yelling with terror and eyes popping. They knocked each other down and the fallen grovelled in the dust. A portly black man, dressed in grubby duck breeches many sizes too small and a frock coat many sizes too large, ran into the side of one of the shacks lining the track, the home of one of the less affluent diggers, and the canvas wall burst open before the power of his run, the thatch roof collapsed on top of the fugitive, covering him completely with a haystack of dried grass and probably saving his life – for the point of a Matabele assegai had been inches from the straining seam of his bulging breeches at the moment the shack collapsed.

Bazo gave a single blast on the buckhorn whistle that hung on a thong at his throat, and the spearsmen froze. The charge stopped dead on the instant, and the Matabele trotted back to where they had dropped their baggage, all of them grinning with delight; as they formed up again, Bazo sang the first line of the Inyati regimental war chant in a high ringing voice:

'See the war shields black as midnight,
white as the high storm clouds at noon –'

And the men behind him came crashing in with the chorus:

'Black as the Inyati bull, white as the egrets
that he carries upon his back –'

The entry of the little band of warriors to the New Rush diggings became a triumphal procession. Riding at their head Zouga felt like a Roman emperor.

Yet not one of the young warriors had ever swung a pick or hefted a shovel. Jan Cheroot had to place the tools in their hands, positioning their fingers correctly on the handles, all the while muttering his disdain of such ignorance. However, they had the knack of it within minutes, and the velvety black muscles, forged in war and the training for war, changed the mundane tools into lethal weapons; they attacked the yellow earth as though it were a mortal adversary.

Confronted with a wheelbarrow for the first time, two of them lifted it bodily and walked away with it and its contents. When Ralph demonstrated the correct use of the vehicle, their wonder and delight was childlike, and Bazo told them smugly: 'I promised you many wonders, did I not?'

They were a highly disciplined group of young men, accustomed since childhood firstly to the strict structure of family life in the kraals and then from puberty to the communal training and teamwork of the fighting regiments.

They were also fiercely competitive, delighting in any challenge to pit their strength or skill against one another.

Zouga, knowing all these things, organized them in four teams of four men, each named after a bird – the Cranes, the Hawks, the Shrikes and the Khorhaans – and each week the team with the best performance in lashing the gravel was entitled to wear the feathers of their adopted bird in their hair and to a double ration of meat and mealie-meal and *twala*, the African beer fermented from millet grain. They turned the work into a game.

There were some small adjustments to be made. The Matabele were cattle-men, their whole lives devoted to raising, protecting and enlarging their herds, even if these expansions were often at the expense of their less warlike neighbours. Their staple diet was beef and *maas*, the calabash-soured milk of the Nguni.

Beef was an expensive item on the diggings, and it was with patent distaste that they sampled the greasy stringy mutton that Zouga provided. However, hard physical labour builds appetites, and within days they were eating this new diet if not with relish at least without complaint.

Within those same few days the labour was apportioned and each man learned his task.

Jan Cheroot could not be inveigled down into the workings.

'Ek is nie 'n meerkat nie,' he told Zouga loftily, reverting to the bastard Dutch of Cape Colony. 'I am not a mongoose; I do not live in a hole in the ground.'

Zouga needed a trusted man on the sorting-tables, and that was where Jan Cheroot presided. Squatting like a yellow idol over the glittering piles of washed gravel, the triangular shape of his face was emphasized by the scraggy little beard on the point of his chin – by the high oriental cheekbones and slanted eyes, each in their spider-web of wrinkles.

He was quick to pick out the soapy sheen of the noble stones in the piles of dross, but there was another pair of eyes sharper and quicker. Traditionally the women made the best sorters, but little Jordan proved immediately to have an uncanny talent at picking out diamonds, no matter what their size or colour.

The child picked the very first stone from the very first sieveful. It was a minute stone, twenty points, a fifth part of a carat, and the colour was a dark cognac brown, so that Zouga doubted its integrity. But when be showed it to one of the kopje-wallopers, it was a veritable diamond and the buyer offered him three shillings for it.

After that nobody questioned Jordan, instead a doubtful stone was passed to him for judgement. Within a week he was the Devil's Own chief sorter.

He sat opposite Jan Cheroot at the low metal table, almost the same size as the Hottentot. He wore a huge sombrero of platted maize stalks to protect his delicate peachlike skin from the sun, and he sorted the gravel as though it were a game of which he never tired. Competing with Jan Cheroot avidly, a high-pitched shriek of excitement signalled each discovery, and his neat little hands flew over the gravel like those of a pianist over the ivory keyboard.

Zouga had found a woman to give both Ralph and Jordan their lessons. The wife of a Lutheran preacher, she was a plump-breasted, sweet-faced woman with iron-grey hair swept up into an enormous bun at the back of her head. Mrs Gander was the only schoolmistress within five hundred miles, and for a few hours each morning she gave a small group of diggers' children their reading, writing and arithmetic in the little galvanized-iron church at the back of Market Square.

It was a daily ritual to which Ralph had to be driven by his father's threats, and to which Jordan hurried with the same enthusiasm as he did to the sorting-table after school was out. With his angelic looks, and the intense interest in the written word that Aletta had germinated in him, Jordan was instantly Mrs Gander's darling.

She made no effort to conceal her preference. She called him 'Jordie-dear' and gave to him the task of wiping clean the black-board, which immediately made it an honour for which the dozen other children in the class would have scratched out his lovely densely-lashed angel eyes.

There was a pair of twins in Mrs Gander's class. The tough sons of a tough out-of-luck digger from the Australian opal fields, they were a matched pair, with shaven heads to inhibit the breeding of lice, bare-footed, for their father was working a poor claim on the eastern edge of the diggings, their braces supporting patched canvas breeches over faded and frayed shirts. Henry and

Douglas Stewart made a formidable pair, acting in complete concert, quick with a cruel jibe too soft for Mrs Gander to hear or a crafty jab with the elbow or a tug of the hair too quick for her to see.

Jordan was natural prey. 'Jordie-girl' they christened him, and his soft curls felt good between their fingers, and his tears were enormously satisfying – especially when they realized that Jordan for some strange reason of pride would not appeal to his big brother for protection.

'You tell Goosie-Gander that I've a belly ache,' Ralph instructed Jordan. 'And that Papa says I am too sick to come to class.'

'Where are you going?' Jordan demanded. 'What are you going to do?'

'I'm going to the nest – I think the chicks may be ready.' Ralph had discovered a lanner falcon's nest on the top ledge of a rocky kopje five miles out on the Cape road. He was planning to take the chicks and train them as hunting falcons. Ralph always had exciting plans; it was one of the many reasons why Jordan adored him.

'Oh, let me come with you. Please, Ralph.'

'You're still just a baby, Jordie.'

'I'm nearly eleven.'

'You're only just ten,' Ralph corrected him loftily, and from experience Jordan knew there was no profit in arguing.

Jordan delivered Ralph's lie for him in such sweet piping tones and with such a guileless flutter of the long lashes, that it never occurred to Mrs Gander to doubt it, and the Stewart twins exchanged a quick glance of complete accord.

There was a latrine at the back of the church, a sentry box of corrugated iron, a boxwood seat with an oval cut from it suspended over a galvanized steel bucket. The heat in the tiny room was ovenlike and the contents of the bucket ripened swiftly. The twins trapped Jordan there in the mid-morning break.

They had hold of an ankle each and were standing on the wooden seat, the hole between them, and Jordan was dangling upside down, clinging desperately to the boxwood seat as they tried to force his head and shoulders through the opening and into the brimming bucket.

'Stamp on his fingers,' Douglas panted. Jordan had offered unexpected opposition. Douglas had a red scratch down his neck, and they had had to pry Jordan's jaws open to release their grip on Henry's thumb. The injuries had changed the mood of the twins. They had started out with laughter, spiteful laughter, but laughter all the same; now they were angry and vicious, their self-esteem smarting as much as their injuries.

'Shut up, you little sissy,' blurted Henry, as he obeyed his brother and brought down his horny heel on Jordan's white knuckles. Jordan's shrieks of agony and horror and terror reverberated in the tiny iron shed as he kicked and fought.

Against their combined strength, Jordan's wildest efforts were ineffectual. His fingernails scratched white splinters from the wooden seat, and his shrieks mounted hysterically, but his head was forced down. The stench was suffocating, the disgust choked his throat and strangled his cries.

At the moment that he felt the cold wet filth soaking into his golden curls the door of the shed was wrenched open and Mrs Gander's motherly bulk filled the opening.

For a moment she stared incredulously, and then she began to swell with outrage. Her right arm, muscled from kneading bread and pounding wet washing, flew out in a round open-handed blow that knocked both twins flying into a corner of the latrine and she gathered Jordan up, holding him at arms' length. With her flushed face wrinkling at the smell of his soaked curls, she rushed out with him, shouting to her husband to bring a bucket of precious water and a bar of the yellow and blue mottled soap.

Half an hour later Jordan reeked of carbolic soap and his curls were fluffing out again as the sun dried them into a shining halo, and from behind the closed doors of the vestry the yells of pain emitted by the twins were punctuated by the clap of the Reverend Gander's Malacca cane walkingstick as his wife urged him on to greater endeavour.

Around the whittled remains of Colesberg kopje had grown up a miniature range of man-made hillocks. These were the tailings from the diamond cradles, dumped haphazardly on the open ground beyond the settlement. Some of these artificial hills were already twenty feet high, and they formed a wasteland where no tree nor blade of grass grew. A maze of narrow footpaths laced the area, made by the daily pilgrimage of hundreds of black workers to the pit.

The shortcut between the Lutheran church and Zouga's camp followed one of these footpaths, and in the heat-hushed hour of noon, the labourers were still in the workings and the hills were deserted. The sun directly overhead threw only narrow black strips of shade below the mounds of loose gravel as Jordan hurried along the dusty path, his eyes still red-rimmed with weeping the tears of humiliation and stinging from the foam of carbolic soap.

'Hello Jordie-girl.' Jordan recognized the voice instantly, and it stopped him dead, blinking his swimming eyes in the sunlight, peering up at the summit of one of the gravel mounds beside the path.

One of the twins stood silhouetted against the pale blue noon sky. His thumbs hooked into his braces, his shaven head thrust forward, his eyes with their thin colourless lashes as vicious as those of a ferret.

'You told, Jordie-girlie,' the twin accused flatly.

'I never told,' Jordan denied, his voice squeaking uncertainly.

'You screamed. That's the same as telling – and now you are going to scream again, but this time there isn't going to be anyone to hear you, Jordie-girl.'

Jordan spun around, and in the same movement he was running with all the desperation and speed of a gazelle pursued by a hunting cheetah; but he had not gone a dozen frantic paces when the second twin slid down the sloping bank, the gravel hissing around his bare feet, full into the narrow pathway ahead of Jordan, his arms spread in welcome, his mouth twisted into a grin of anticipation.

They had laid the trap with care. They had caught him in a narrow place, where the gravel banks were highest, and behind him the first twin slid adroitly down to block the path, keeping his balance on the little avalanche of rolling gravel under his bare feet until he hit the level pathway.

'Jordie-dear,' called one twin.

'Jordie-girl,' echoed the other, and they closed from each side, slowly, tantalizing themselves, so that Henry giggled almost breathlessly.

'Little girls shouldn't tell tales.'

'I'm not a girl,' whispered Jordan, backing away from him.

'Then you shouldn't have curls; only girls have curls.' Douglas groped in his pocket and brought out a bone-handled clasp knife. He opened the blade with his teeth.

'We are going to turn you into a boy, Jordie-girl.'

'Then we are going to teach you not to tell tales.' Henry brought out his hand from behind his back. He had cut a camel-thorn branch, and stripped the bunches of lacy leaves, but not the thorns. 'We are going to do the same to you as old Goosey-Gander did to us. Fifteen cuts each. That's thirty for you, Jordie-girl.'

Jordan's gaze fastened on the branch with sickened fascination. It was twice as thick as a man's thumb, more a club than a cane, and the thorns were half an inch long, each on a little raised knob of rough black bark. Henry swung it in an experimental cut and it hissed like an adder.

The sound galvanized Jordan, he whirled and flew at the high bank of gravel beside him; it slid treacherously under his feet so that he had to use his hands to claw his way towards the summit.

Behind him the twins yipped with excitement, like the hunting call of a pack of wild dogs, and they raced after him, scrambling up the soft collapsing bank.

Their weight buried them at each pace above the ankles, so that Jordan, lighter and buoyant with terror, reached the top of the bank ahead of them, and he raced silent and white-faced across the flattened table of the summit, opening the gap further.

Henry snatched up a stone as he ran, a lump of quartz as big as his own fist, and he used his own momentum to hurl it. It flew an inch past Jordan's ear, and he flinched and whimpered, losing his balance, stumbled at the far edge of the dump, and went tumbling down the steep slope.

'Stop him,' yipped Douglas, and launched himself over the edge.

At the bottom Jordan rolled to his feet, dusty and wildly dishevelled, his curls bushed out and dangling in his eyes. He wasted a second, glancing about desperately, and then darted away along the narrow footpath through the gut of the pass between the gravel dumps.

'Catch him. Don't let him get away.' The twins yelled at each other, panting with laughter, like two cats with a mouse, and here on the flat their longer legs quickly narrowed Jordan's lead.

He heard their bare feet slapping on hard earth in a broken rhythm close behind him, and he twisted his head back over his shoulder, almost blinded with his own sweat and dancing curls, his breath sobbing, his skin white as bone-china and his huge brimming eyes seeming to fill his whole face.

Henry steadied himself, poised with his right arm held back at full stretch and then he threw the thorn stick, cartwheeling it low over the ground so that it slammed into the back of Jordan's knees, the thorns ripping the soft bare skin, raising deep parallel scratches as though from the slash of a cat's claws.

Jordan's legs folded under him and be went down, sliding on his belly, the wind driven from his lungs as he hit the baked earth of the pathway. Before he could raise himself, Douglas landed with all his weight between Jordan's shoulder blades and shoved his face, cheek down, against the ground, while Henry snatched up the thorn branch and danced about them, looking for an opening, the branch held in both hands above his head.

'His hair first,' gasped Douglas, choking with laughter and his own excitement. 'Hold his head.'

Henry dropped the cane and stooped over Jordan, grabbing a double handful of the fine curls and leaning back against it with all his weight so that Jordan's neck was stretched out. Douglas was still perched between Jordan's shoulder blades. Pinning him against the earth and brandishing the open clasp knife, he told his twin, 'Hold him still.' The fine golden hair was stretched like the strings of a violin and Douglas hacked at it.

It came away in tufts in Henry's fists, some of it cut through, some of it torn out at the roots, like feathers from the carcass of a slaughtered chicken, and he threw it high in the air, shouting with laughter as it sparkled in the sunlight.

'Now you will be a boy!'

All the resistance went out of Jordan. He lay crushed against the earth, shaken only by his own sobs, and Henry grabbed another handful of his curls.

'Cut closer,' he ordered his twin, and then shrieked with shock and pain.

The thin tapered end of a rhinoceros-hide riding whip curled with a snap around the seat of Henry's breeches, over the fresh bruises raised by the Reverend Gander's Malacca cane, and

Henry shot erect clutching at his own buttocks with both hands and hopping up and down on the same spot.

A hand closed on the collar of his shirt and he was yanked into the air and held suspended, kicking, a foot above the ground, still clutching the seat of his breeches that felt as though they were filled with live coals.

His brother looked up from his seat on Jordan's back. In the excitement of tormenting the smaller boy, neither of the twins had heard or seen the horseman. He had walked his horse around the bend in the footpath between the gravel heaps and come across the squirming yelling knot of small bodies in the middle of the path. He recognized the twins immediately; they had earned quick notoriety on the diggings, and it had taken only another second to guess the cause of the commotion, to understand who were the attackers and who the victim.

Douglas was quick to realize the changed circumstances as he looked up at his twin, dangling like a man on the gallows from the horseman's fist. He scrambled to his feet and darted away, but the horseman turned his mount with his heels and, like a polo player, cut back-handed with the long rhino-hide sjambok, and the agony of it paralysed Douglas. But for the thick canvas breeches it would have opened his skin.

Before he could begin to run again the horseman stooped in the saddle, seized his upper arm and lifted him easily. On each side of the horse, the twins wriggled and whimpered with the sting of the lash and the rider looked down at them thoughtfully.

'I know you two,' he told them quietly. 'You are the Stewart brats, the ones who drove old Jacob's mule into the barbed wire.'

'Please, sir, please,' blubbered Douglas.

'Keep quiet, boy,' said the rider evenly. 'You are the ones that cut the reins on De Kock's wagon. That cost your daddy a penny, and the Diggers' Committee would like to know who set fire to Carlo's tent then–'

'It weren't us, Mister,' Henry pleaded. It was clear they both knew who their captor was, and that they were truly afraid of him.

Jordan crawled to his knees and peered up at his rescuer. He must be somebody very important – perhaps even a member of the committee he had mentioned. Even in his distress Jordan was awed by that possibility. Ralph had explained to him that a committee member was something between a policeman, a prince and the ogre of the fairy tales which their mother used to read to them.

Now this fabulous being looked down at Jordan as he knelt in the pathway, with his cheek smeared with dust and tears, his shirt torn and the buttons dangling on their threads, while the backs of his knees were criss-crossed with bloody welts.

'This little one is half your size,' the horseman said. His eyes were blue, a strange electric blue – the eyes of a poet – or of a fanatic.

'It was just a game, sir,' mumbled Henry; the collar of his shirt was twisted up under his ear.

'We didn't mean nothing, Mister.'

The horseman transferred that glowing blue gaze from Jordan to the two wriggling bodies in his hands.

'A game, was it?' he asked. 'Well, next time I catch you playing your games, you and your father had better have a story for the committee, do you hear me?'

He shook them roughly. 'Do you understand me clearly?'

'Yes, sir –'

'So you enjoy games, do you? Well then, here is a new one, and we shall play it every time you so much as lay a finger on a child smaller than you are.'

He dropped them unexpectedly to earth, and before the twins could recover their balance had cut left and right with the sjambok, starting them away at a run, and then he cantered easily along behind them for a hundred yards or so, leaning from the saddle to flick the whip at the back of their legs to keep them at their best speed. Then abruptly he let them go and wheeled the horse, cantering back to where Jordan stood trembling and pale in the pathway.

'If you are going to fight, then one at a time is the best policy, young man,' said the rider and stepped down easily from the stirrup and threw the reins over his shoulder as he squatted on his haunches facing Jordan.

'Now where does it hurt most?' he asked.

It was suddenly terribly important to Jordan that he did not appear a baby. He gulped noisily as he fought his tears, and the man seemed to understand.

'Good fellow,' he nodded. 'That's the spirit.' And he drew a cotton handkerchief from his pocket and wiped away the muddy tears.

'What's your name?'

'Jordie – Jordan,' he corrected himself and sniffed noisily.

How old are you, Jordan?'

'Almost eleven, sir.'

The sting of his injuries and of his humiliation began to recede, to be replaced by a warm flood of gratitude towards his rescuer.

'Spit!' ordered the horseman, proffering the handkerchief, and Jordan obeyed, dampening a corner of the cloth with his saliva.

The man turned him with a hand on his shoulder, and with the handkerchief cleaned the bloody lines on his legs. It was perfunctory treatment, and the man's touch was masculine and ungentle, but Jordan was powerfully reminded of his mother by the attention, and that empty place inside him ached so that he almost began weeping again. He held back the tears, and twisted his neck to watch the man work on his injured legs.

The fingers were square and powerful, but a little uncoordinated. The nails were big and strong and even, cut short, with a pearly translucent lustre. The back of his hands were covered with fine golden hairs that caught the sun.

The man glanced up from his task at Jordan. His face was fair, the skin was smooth-shaven and unblemished except for the small fine moustache. His lips were full, high-coloured, sensual. His nose was large, but not too large for the big round head and the thick waves of light-brown hair.

He was young, probably ten years older than Jordan, though he had such a powerful presence, such a sense of maturity and of power seemed to invest him, that he appeared much older.

Yet there was something else about him that seemed to contradict the first appearance. The high colour in his lips and cheeks was not the flush of health and the open air life. It was a shade hectic, and though the skin was unlined, there were the subtle marks of suffering and pain at the corners of his eyes and mouth, while behind that penetrating gaze, that compelling intensity, there was a tragic shadow, a sense of sadness that was perhaps only readily apparent to the uncomplicated view of a child.

For a moment the man and the boy looked into each other's eyes, and something twisted almost painfully deep in Jordan's soul, a sweet pang – gratitude, puppy love, compassion, hero-worship – it was all of those and something else for which he would never have words.

Then the man stood; he was tall and big built, over six foot in his riding boots, and Jordan only reached as high as his ribs.

'Who is your father, Jordan?' And Jordan was grateful that he did not use the diminutive . The rider nodded at his reply.

'Yes,' he said. 'I have heard of him. The elephant hunter. Well, then, we had best get you home.'

He stepped up into the stirrup and from the saddle reached down, took Jordan by the arm and swung him up onto the horse's rump. Jordan sat sideways, and as the horse started forward, he put both arms round the rider's waist to balance himself.

Jan Cheroot came hurrying from the sorting-table as they trotted into Zouga's camp, and when the rider reined in, he reached up and lifted Jordan down.

'He has been in a fight,' the rider told Jan Cheroot. 'Put a little iodine on his cuts, and he'll be all right. The boy has spirit.'

Jan Cheroot was obsequious, almost cringing, far from his usual acerbic and cynical self. He seemed to be rendered speechless by the direct and startling gaze of the big man on the rangy horse. He held Jordan with one hand and with the other lifted the old regimental cap from his head and held it against his chest, nodding in servile agreement with the orders the man gave him.

The rider transferred his steady gaze back to Jordan, and for the first time he smiled.

'Next time pick on somebody your own size, Jordan,' he advised, took up the reins and trotted out of the camp without looking back.

'You know who that was, Jordie?' Jan Cheroot asked portentously, staring after the rider and not waiting for Jordan's reply. 'That's the big boss of the Diggers' Committee, that's the most important man on New Rush, Jordie –' he paused theatrically, and then announced, 'That's Mr Rhodes.'

'Mr Rhodes.' Jordan repeated the name to himself, 'Mr Rhodes.' It had a heroic sound to it, like some of the poetry that his mother had read to him. He knew that something important had just happened in his life.

Every member of Zouga's family and following quickly found his place in the work, almost as though a special niche had been reserved for each of them: Jan Cheroot and Jordan at the sorting-table, the Matabele *amadoda* in the open diggings, and, naturally there was only one place for Ralph – in the diggings with them.

So they found the stones; they won them from the tiny squares of ground in the depths of the growing pit, and carried them to the surface in the swinging buckets, and carted them out along the rotten crumbling roadways which each day became more dangerous and they washed and sieved them, until at last Jan Cheroot or Jordie could pounce upon them on the sorting-table.

Then in the evening there might be three or four of Zouga's Matabele workmen waiting under the camel-thorn tree beside Zouga's tent.

'Let me see,' Zouga would grunt, and with a deal of showmanship the man would unknot a scrap of grubby cloth to display a chip of stone or a small transparent crystal.

These were the 'pick-ups' from the claims. As the Matabele handled the stuff, shovelling it and emptying the leather buckets, a glitter or shine of a pebble may catch their eye – and there was a reward for a diamond 'picked-up' and handed in.

Most of these 'pick-ups' were not veritable diamonds, for they took anything that sparkled, or anything pretty and unusually coloured. They brought in agate and quartz, feldspar and rock crystal, jasper and zircons – and once in a while a diamond; and then for each diamond, large or small, clear or discoloured, Zouga would hand over a golden sovereign from his dwindling hoard and add the diamond to the contents of the little chamois leather drawstring bag that he carried buttoned into his breast pocket, and which was under his pillow when he slept at night.

Then each Saturday morning, while Jan Cheroot and the two boys gathered around the camp table under the camel-thorn tree beside the tent, Zouga would carefully tip the contents of the leather bag onto a sheet of clean white paper, and they examined and discussed the week's recovery; and always Zouga tried to cover his disappointment, tried to ignore the nauseating bite of worry in his guts as he looked at the tiny, discoloured and flawed diamonds which the Devil's Own so reluctantly yielded up.

Then with the chamois bag buttoned into his pocket once again, his riding boots freshly waxed and polished by Ralph, his frayed shirt collar neatly darned and the buttons replaced by Jordan, and the gelding curried to a gloss by Jan Cheroot, Zouga would ride into the settlement, putting on the best face he could muster, smoking a cigar to show how little he really needed the money, and he would hitch the gelding at the door of the first diamond-buyer's galvanized iron shack.

'The Devil's Own.' The first kopje-walloper was a Hollander, and his accent was difficult to understand, but Zouga's brave show did not deceive him, and he sucked his teeth and shook his head dismally over Zouga's offering. 'The Devil's Own,' he repeated. 'It killed five men, and broke three others. Jocky Danby was lucky to get out at the price you paid him.'

'What's your offer?' Zouga asked quietly, and the buyer prodded the scattering of tiny stones.

'You want to see a real diamond?' he asked, and without waiting for Zouga's reply, swivelled his chair and opened the iron safe on the wall behind his desk.

Reverently he unfolded a square of white paper and displayed the beautiful flashing crystal, almost the size of a ripe acorn.

'Fifty-eight carats,' he whispered, and Zouga stared at it with the sour acid of envy in the back of his throat. 'I bought it yesterday.'

'How much?' he asked, hating himself for the weakness.

'Six thousand pounds!' said the buyer and carefully refolded the paper, placed the diamond back in the safe, locked the thick iron door, hung the key on his watch chain and glanced at Zouga's stones.

'Forty pounds,' he said off-handedly.

'The lot?' Zouga asked quietly. He had sixteen men to pay and feed and he needed new rope, and he would have to pay the piratical prices of the transport riders for it.

'The price of pool goods is right down.' The buyer shrugged. 'Every digger south of the Vaal is bringing in rubbish like this.'

Zouga refilled the bag and stood up.

'I made you that price as a favour,' warned the buyer. 'If you come back later, it will be thirty pounds.'

'I'll take that chance.' Zouga touched the brim of his hat and strode out into the sunlight.

The second buyer he visited poured the diamonds into the bowl of the diamond balance and then carefully added weights to the other arm until the scale was in balance.

'You should have stuck to elephant hunting,' he said, as he wrote down the weights and made his calculations in a leather notebook. 'The diamond market is flooded. There is a limit to the number of rich ladies who want to hang baubles round their necks, and here on the Vaal diggings we have mined more stones in a few years than were found in the six thousand years before that.'

'They are using them in watch movements, and tools for cutting glass and steel,' Zouga said quietly.

'A fad,' the buyer waved his hands in dismissal. 'Diamonds are finished. I'll give you fifty-five pounds for this lot and that's generous.'

One morning Zouga found Ralph working side by side with Bazo in the bottom of the pit, swinging the pick in rhythm with the Matabele chant. He stood there watching for a few minutes, saw the shape of mature muscle emerging from the soft flesh of childhood, saw the breadth of shoulder. Ralph's belly was greyhound slim and the cloth of his breeches, that were suddenly many sizes too small, strained over neat round buttocks as he stooped to break the point of the pick from the compacted yellow earth.

'Ralph,' he called him at last.

'Yes, Papa.' His throat was greasy with sweat, and it had cut little runnels down through the dust that coated his upper body, fat glistening drops clung in the little nest of fine dark curls that had abruptly appeared in the centre of his chest.

'Put your shirt on,' Zouga ordered.

'Why?' Ralph looked surprised.

'Because you are an Englishman. By God's grace and, if necessary, the strength of my right arm you are going to be a gentleman as well.'

So Ralph worked booted and buttoned to the throat beside the naked Matabele, and he earned firstly their respect and then their affection and friendship.

From the first day when they had met in the open veld, the Matabele had been impressed with his horsemanship, and with the marksmanship which had brought down the old eland bull. Now they began to accept him amongst them, first in the patronizing manner of elder brothers, then gradually on more and more equal terms, until Ralph was competing with them in all they did, their work and their sport. He was not yet as tall or strong as the Matabele, so he won very seldom; and when he failed or was beaten, he scowled until his face darkened and the heavy brows met above the big nose.

'A good sportsman knows how to lose graciously,' Zouga told him.

'I don't want to be a sportsman, I don't want to learn how to lose,' Ralph replied. 'I want to learn how to win.' And he threw himself back at the task with fiercely renewed determination.

It seemed that his strength grew with each day in the diggings, the puppy fat was burned away, and he made that final spurt to his full height without outstripping his strength. And he learned how to win.

He began to win the contests with Bazo at lashing gravel, frenziedly filling bucket after huge leather bucket so that the yellow dust flew in choking clouds. He won one of the dangerous races down the ladderworks from the roadway to the bottom of the pit, scorching his palms on the ropes and swinging out over the drop to pass another man on the reverse side of the ladder, using the pole of a gantry to cross a deep void between two claims, running across it upright, like a tight-rope walker, without looking at his feet or the hundred-foot drop beneath him. Even Bazo shook his head and said 'Hau!' which is an exclamation of deep amazement, and Ralph stood panting in the bottom of the pit, looking up at Bazo, and shouted with triumphant laughter.

Then Ralph learned to use the fighting sticks the hard way – for this was the game the Matabele had played since their first day as herd boys in the veld. Before he mastered the art of the sticks he had, perforce, to learn how to staunch a bleeding cut in his own scalp inflicted by Bazo's stick by plugging it with a handful of dust snatched in the midst of the contest.

A week short of his sixteenth birthday, Ralph beat Bazo for the first time. They fought behind the thatched beehive huts that the Matabele had built on the open veld beyond Zouga's camp.

It started light-heartedly, Bazo the instructor, hectoring his pupil, executing the weaving steps of the traditional combat with indolent grace like a sleepy black panther, a fighting stick held in each hand and flourished with studied artistry of movement to form a fluid screen from which a vicious cutting attack could be launched with either hand.

Ralph turned to face him so that they revolved smoothly as a balanced wheel, like a pair of trained dancers, and when they taunted each other Ralph's repartee was in fluent and colloquial Matabele. He was stripped to the waistband of his riding breeches, and his torso, which had at Zouga's orders been so long protected from the sun, was creamy pale; only his arms and the deep V at his throat were sun dark.

'I once had a pet baboon,' Bazo told him. 'It was an albino baboon, white as the moon, and so stupid it never learned even a simple trick. That baboon reminds me of somebody, though I cannot think who.'

Ralph smiled with his lips only, exposing square white teeth, but the black brows were joined above his nose. 'I am only surprised that a Matabele thought he could teach a baboon – surely it should be the other way around.'

Bazo jumped back and hooted, beginning the *giya* – the challenge dance of the warrior – leaping high and making the kerries sing in the air until they blurred like the wings of a sunbird in flight.

'Let us see if your sticks are as quick as your tongue,' he shouted; and then suddenly he was attacking, the song of the fighting sticks rising to a shriek as he cut for Ralph's knee, the shriek ending with a crack like a rifle shot as Ralph caught it on his guard; and instantly Bazo cut with the other hand, for the elbow and – crack – again as Ralph warded off the blow with his own kerrie.

The sticks clattered against each other in a rising tempo, and the circle of Matabele watchers encouraged them with the deep drawn-out 'Jee!' as a stroke was skilfully countered and turned into a hissing riposte to be countered in its turn.

Bazo broke first, jumping back with a light sheen of sweat turning his muscles to black velvet, his chest swelling and subsiding, his chuckle only slightly hoarse.

There should be a pause now, as the combatants circled each other again, in that stylized shuffling dance, trading light insults, catching breath, stooping to dry their hands in the dust to improve their grip on the sticks – but, not this time, for as Bazo broke and jumped back and for an instant dropped his right hand, so Ralph went in.

Even the pretence of a smile was gone from Ralph's mouth. His jaw was clenched, lumps of muscles knotted with determination beneath his ears. Bazo's right guard had dropped, and his attention had switched to the audience of Matabele faces, for whose benefit he was already composing the next jibe.

'Jee!' They shouted encouragement and warning, and Bazo tried desperately to raise his guard and swivel to face the unexpected attack. He managed a touch of stick against stick, just enough to cushion the blow, otherwise it would have broken bone. Ralph's kerrie smashed into the point of his shoulder, and abruptly it was no longer a game.

The blow to Bazo's shoulder raised a welt as thick as a finger across the muscle, and almost paralysed the arm to the fingertips. So as he caught Ralph's next cut he felt the kerrie jerk and turn in his numb fingers, almost breaking his grip, and the shock of it was transferred into the abused muscle so that he grunted involuntarily, a little grunt of agony that seemed only to goad Ralph.

His sun-dark features were a mask of fighting fury, his eyes cold and green, and little droplets of sweat flew from his long black hair with the force of every blow that he swung.

The Matabele had never seen him like this, but they recognized the killing madness, for they had themselves all been in battle and killed, and it infected them so that they danced and stamped with excitement and spurred Ralph with their voices.

'Jee!' they sang, and Bazo fell back, giving ground to Ralph's attack as the sticks cracked and rattled. His mouth was wide open now as he gasped for air and his throat was a deep pink cavern. Blood ran in a thin shining slick down behind his ear, spreading over his straining throat and then onto his right shoulder like a mantle. A glancing blow above his eye had not opened the flesh, but had formed a blister of black blood as large as a walnut under the skin. It hung from Bazo's forehead like some bizarre bloodsucking leech, and still the blows hissed and cracked about him, thick as tropical rain, falling on his guard so that the shock was carried through arm and shoulder and jarred his head upon the thick black column of his neck.

Then another blow went through and the ivory flash of Bazo's teeth was dulled with a film of blood that snaked down from one nostril into his mouth, and another blow went through, on the line of his thigh, the swelling rising instantaneously, the skin stretched glossy and black, and almost crippled Bazo who was pinned by the injured leg – and Ralph was still attacking, instinctively swinging him against the bad leg so that Bazo was slow and clumsy in the turn, and again one of Ralph's sticks fluted and thumped into rubbery muscle and Bazo reeled and almost went down, recovering with an immense effort, his counter-stroke loose and lacking power, so that Ralph spurned it aside and used his point.

He drove the end of his right-hand kerrie through Bazo's guard, using it as though it were a sword rather than a club, and Bazo was not ready for it. With all Ralph's weight behind it, the kerrie tore into Bazo's belly muscles, up under the heavy ribcage, and the Matabele doubled over the blow, one kerrie flying from his hand the other dropping to dangle uselessly at his side.

He dropped on his knees, head bowed to expose the back of his neck, the knuckles of his spine standing out between the ridges of hard black muscle.

Ralph's eyes were fastened on the unprotected neck, and they were glazed over with the same soapy sheen as an uncut diamond, his movements too swift to be anything but instinctive. He threw the kerrie on high and shifted his weight from the back foot to the leading foot, and all his strength flowed into his back and shoulders as he went into the killing stroke.

'Jee!' roared the watchers, themselves carried beyond the frontiers of sanity on the hot wave of fighting madness, crowding forward for the death.

Ralph froze like that, right arm high, his entire body arched like a drawn bow, the fallen Matabele at his feet – and then slowly the tension went out of his limbs and he shook his head with the fumbling uncertainty of a man awaking from a nightmare. He looked about him with stunned disbelief, blinking his eyes as though to clear them of that opaque glittering madness, and suddenly his legs were trembling, unable to hold his weight. He sank down in front of Bazo, knelt facing him and put out one arm and wrapped it around the Matabele's neck, and laid his cheek against Bazo's.

'God,' he whispered. 'Oh God – I nearly killed you.'

Their blood and their sweat mingled, and both of them were pumping for air, their chests heaving, their bodies racked for the precious stuff.

'Never teach an albino baboon a trick,' Bazo spoke at last, his voice was husky and unsteady. 'He might learn it a little too well.'

Then they were dragged to their feet by the laughing, hooting Matabele and carried to the nearest hut.

Ralph drank first from the calabash of gruel – thick bubbling millet beer – and then handed it across to Bazo.

Bazo washed the blood from his mouth and spat it on the ground, then he drank with his head tilted back, a dozen deep swallows before he lowered the gourd and looked at Ralph.

For a moment they were grave, green eyes holding the gaze of smouldering black, and then suddenly they were both laughing, great gusts of shaking uncontrolled laughter, so that the men that squatted in the circle about them began to chuckle also, and then to laugh with them.

Still laughing, Bazo leaned across and gripped Ralph's right forearm briefly. 'I am your man,' he said, through his laughter, and through the blood in his mouth.

When Zouga stepped off the ladder in the bottom level of the Devil's Own, the heat was already enough to bring out a dark patch of sweat between the shoulder blades of his blue flannel shirt. He lifted his hat to mop the dewdrops along his hairline and then paused and frowned quickly.

'Ralph!' he snapped, and his son sank the pickhead into the yellow gravel, let it stand like that and then straightened with his hands on his hips.

'Just what do you think you are doing?' Zouga demanded.

'I've worked out a new way of doing it,' Ralph told him. 'First Bazo's gang breaks rock, then Wengi comes along behind and–'

'You know what I'm talking about.' Zouga cut in impatiently. 'It's Monday; you are supposed to be at school.'

'I'm sixteen now,' Ralph told him. 'And besides, I know how to read and to write.'

'Don't you think you might have mentioned your decision,' Zouga asked with deceptive mildness, 'if only in passing?'

'You were busy, Papa, I didn't want to worry you with something so unimportant. You've got enough to worry about without that.'

Zouga hesitated. Was that just his usual clever twisting, or did Ralph truly realize how finely stretched they were, just how much Zouga truly did have to worry about?

Ralph sensed his advantage. 'We need every pair of hands we can get, and these are free.' He held them up, and Zouga noticed for the first time that they were powerful and broad with yellow callouses on the palms.

'Just what is this new idea of yours?' Zouga's scowl smoothed away, and Ralph grinned as he realized that he was no longer a schoolboy; and he began to explain, gesturing with spread hands while Zouga nodded.

'All right,' he said at last. 'It makes sense. We'll try it.'

Zouga turned and walked away, and Ralph spat on his hands and shouted in Matabele.

'Come on, you are not a bunch of women hoeing for yams; let's break ground.'

On Claim No. 183 an American digger named Calvin Hine hit an enrichment, a tiny pocket, and in a single bucket he took out two hundred and sixteen diamonds, the biggest over twenty carats. In a stroke he was transformed from a ragged, bearded sun-blackened beggar grovelling in the yellow dust into a rich man.

Calvin was there that night when Diamond Lil climbed up onto the wooden counter of her grog-shop, with her ostrich feathers swirling and her sequins aglitter in the lamplight. She asked in Cockney that chimed like Bow Bells:

'Will some sporting gent name me a price for these fancy goods?' and squeezed out her own big round breasts between painted red fingertips, so that they bulged over the top of her crimson velvet bodice, the skin smoother than the velvet and the big pink coin of a nipple coming up like the dawn over the horizon of her neckline.

'Come on, dearies, one night of paradise, one little glimpse of heaven, me loves.'

'Tenner, Lil darling. Ten iron men,' shouted a digger at the back of the bar, and Lil turned and flipped up the back of her skirts at him.

'Shame on you, for a mean little man,' she chided him over her white shoulder; and the laced and beribboned pantaloons beneath her rustling skirts had no crotch to them, so for a fleeting part of a second they saw what she was selling, and bellowed like trek-oxen five days in the desert when they smell the waterhole.

'Lil, my beauty.' Calvin climbed unsteadily onto the packing case that acted as a table. He had been drinking since noon when he left the kopje-walloper's office. 'Lily, the moon of my soul,' he crooned, 'every night for a year and more I dreamed of this moment.'

He dug into the back pocket of his coat and held up a fistful of crumpled five-pound notes.

'I don't know how much that is,' he blurted, 'but it's yours.'

For a moment Lily's plucked and pencilled eyebrows contracted as she made a rapid calculation of the proffered wad of banknotes; and then she smiled so that the tiny diamond set in her front tooth sparkled like the evening star.

'You beautiful boy,' she sang. 'Tonight I am your bride. Take me in your arms, my lover.'

The next day someone took a thirty carat stone on the eastern section, a lovely white stone of the first water, and the day after that a huge champagne-coloured diamond came from Neville Pickering's block.

'You'll be leaving now?' Zouga asked him when they met on the roadway above the Devil's Own, and he hoped that the envy did not show in his smile.

'No.' Pickering shook his head, and answered with his own charming sunny smile. 'I always bet on a winning streak. My partner and I are staying in the game.'

It seemed that the diamond god was intent on showering sudden largesse on the New Rush, and a fever of expectation and excitement gripped them all so that the great pit at noon sounded like a hive of wild bees when the acacia forests are in yellow bloom. Three great finds in three days; nobody had seen it happen before.

At night around the camp fires, and in the lantern-lit grog-shops and canteens, the wild theories were aired by dusty diggers drunk on bad liquor and reborn hope.

'It's a stratal enrichment,' pontificated one. 'It's a layer of fat babies right across the kopje. You mark my words, somebody will take a pony before the week is out.'

'Hell no,' argued another. 'The stones are lying in pot-holes. Some lucky bastard is going to scoop the pot again, like Calvin's two one six or Pickering's monkey.'

Thursday night of the crazy week it rained. Here on the fringes of the Kalahari desert the rainfall was less than twenty inches a year. They had almost half of that on that single night.

The rain was a slanting curtain of silver arrow shafts in the brilliant crackling blue flare of the lighting. The clouds piled to the heavens banged against one another like fighting bulls, mountainous in the lightning bursts, and the thunder jarred the earth while the rain hissed down.

In the dawn it was still raining, and at another time the diggers might have stayed out of the pit and waited for it to dry out. But not on this day, not with the fierce excitement that gripped the entire settlement. That day nothing would keep them out of the pit.

The diggings were greasy with yellow mud. The lowest claims were knee deep with the insidious clinging stuff. It coated the bare legs of the black workmen to the thigh; it built up in mud bricks on the boots of the white overseers, weighing them down like convicts shackled to a ball and chain.

The thick red mud on the roadways clogged the wheels of the gravel carts and had to be prised clear with the point of a crowbar. They shovelled the slush into the buckets and as they were hoisted the thin watery mud cascaded down on the men below, so that it was no longer possible to tell black man from white behind their slick and glistening yellow masks.

What none of the men in the workings realized was that, apart from the discomfort and filth that the downpour of the night's thunderstorms had brought to the pit, they had created a less obvious but infinitely graver change in the riddled remains of Colesberg kopje.

The rushing rivulets had found a fissure at the neck of No. 6 Roadway and had poured into it, carving and cutting and weakening; and the slimy yellow mud had hidden the deep vertical cracks in the hundred-foot high earthen embankment.

There were sixteen mule carts crowded onto the causeway, most of them fully laden with the first load of the morning, the drivers swearing at each other, the long trek whips firing explosively as they tried to clear a path to get their load out to the waiting cradles.

Down on the Devil's Own the Matabele teams were working side by side, but the icy sting of the rain on bare shoulders and backs slowed the swing of the picks, and at each forward pace they slithered and slipped in the treacherous footing. The work chant sounded like a dirge; Zouga snarled at them to keep them moving, and the mood was ugly.

Up on the roadway an overladen gravel cart began to slide sideways in the mud, and the wheeler mule was pulled down on his knees, unable to hold it. The off wheel dropped over the edge, and the cart sagged drunkenly and then hung out over the pit. The team slewed across the narrow causeway in tangled traces while the unequal weight of gravel snapped the outer axle of the cart. Zouga's cart was directly behind the stranded team, facing in the same direction, and Ralph jumped down off the driver's seat and shouted furiously.

'You damned fool – you've jammed us in.'

'You cheeky puppy,' the driver of the bogged-down vehicle yelled back. 'You need a lick of the whip across your backside.'

Immediately half a dozen diggers were joining in, taking sides, shouting advice or abuse.

'Cut the traces, get those bloody animals off the roadway.'

'Dump the gravel out, you're overloaded.'

'You don't touch my rig,' yelled the driver of the stricken cart. Ralph had drawn the sheath knife from his belt and run forward.

'That's the ticket, Ralph.'

'That little blighter needs a lesson.'

Men and vehicles and mud-smeared beasts formed an angry, unstable knot at the top of the high earthen wall. In the bottom of the diggings, Zouga threw his head back and cupped his hands to his mouth.

'Ralph!' he bellowed. He could see how dangerous the tangle had become. Tempers were flaring; he could sense how close they were to mortal danger as fighting men lost control of panicking animals.

In the uproar Zouga's voice was almost drowned, and if Ralph heard him, he gave no sign of doing so. He was kneeling beside the downed wheel mule, hacking at the thongs of the traces with his sheath knife.

'Get away from there,' howled the driver, and reared back, the long trek whip flying out high above his shoulders and then snaking forward, twenty feet long, whispering like the wing of a wild duck in flight.

Ralph saw it, and ducked behind the mule's heavy barrel-like body; the lash exploded in the air like a bursting grenade, and the mule lunged wildly, swinging the disselboom of the cart across the causeway so that the broken axle collapsed before the snapping of the half-severed leather thongs allowed the mule to regain its feet and then gallop away down the muddy track to firmer ground.

Ralph leaned out and ran to his own team. He called to his wheeler mule, 'Pull, Bishop!' The wheels sucked and farted in the mud as Ralph drove them at the narrow gap, the stranded cart on one side, sprawled half across the track, on the other the sheer unguarded drop into the open workings.

'Ha, Rosie!' Ralph grabbed the bridle of the lead mule and, running at her head, guided her into the gap.

'Ralph, damn you!' Zouga roared. 'Stop! Do you hear me, stop!'

But he was a helpless spectator. It would take five minutes or longer to reach the causeway across the complicated system of ladderworks and board walks. There was nothing he could do to prevent the developing tragedy.

The infuriated owner of the stranded cart was still on the body of the vehicle, brandishing his long whip and howling with anger and frustration. He was not a big man, an inch or so shorter than Ralph – but heavy in the shoulder and the belly, not flabby fat but work-braided muscle, and his hands on the stock of the whip were rough as oak bark, baked by the sun and scoured by gravel and the haft of pick and shovel.

'I'll settle your account, you little bugger,' he shouted, and again threw back the whip; again Ralph ducked under the flailing lash, but it caught the sleeve of his faded and patched shirt, splitting the rotted material and opening the skin of Ralph's upper arm in a thin red razor cut from which the bright blood bloomed instantly.

Rising from his crouch in the mud, Ralph placed one hand on the wheel mule's withers and used his own impetus and the leverage of his arm to leap high in the air. It was a trick that Jan Cheroot had taught him, the way a good teamsman crosses from one side of the span to another. In mid-air Ralph tucked his legs and swung his body, vaulting cleanly over the mules' backs and landing on the far side of the team alongside the leading wheel. His next jump carried him onto the truck of the cart, and with the same movement he had snatched his own long trek whip from its slot beside the brake handle.

The handle was ten feet long, and the tapered lash another

twenty. A skilled teamsman could cut a fly off the tip of the lead mule's ear with the lash, and Jan Cheroot had trained Ralph: he was good with the whip, very good.

Ralph's lips were a thin chalky white line, his eyes green and furious. The sting of the whip had driven him into murderous, unthinking rage.

'Ralph!' Zouga shouted vainly. He had seen his son like this before. It frightened him. 'Ralph! Stop!'

Standing high on the cart bed Ralph shot the lash out to full stretch behind him. It was an easy graceful movement like a salmon fisherman putting up the fly, and in the same action he brought the tip of the whip stock forward, all wrist and shoulders, and the lash whined and reached out to the other driver.

It cut him like a sword stroke, from breast to belt buckle, and only the heavy wet oilskin he wore protected him from serious injury. The torn fabric flapped about his body, and the rain diluted the dribble of blood from the shallow wound.

Ralph's mules swung from the crack of the whip, and the off wheel hooked that of the stranded cart, locking both vehicles hopelessly in the soft mud.

Ralph was too close now to the other driver to stretch the lash, and he reversed the whip stock, using it like a club, and swung it at the man's head.

Below them in the diggings, the Matabele were encouraging their favourite with the fighting 'Jee!' and it goaded Ralph. He was quicker than the other driver, nimble to avoid his swinging stock, using his own like the fighting sticks with which he had trained so assiduously.

The mules were panicked by the uproar, the crack of whips, the Matabele war chant, the shrieked insults and the bellow of the watchers.

Rosie reared and cut with her fore-hooves, whinnying hysterically, and her team mate lunged and struggled against the jammed off wheel.

Bishop shirked the yoke, turned from it; his hind legs scrabbled on the crumbling edge of the causeway and he went over, hanging in the tangle of reins and chains, kicking and pawing at the air and shrieking wildly.

Then quite gently, like a sleeper awaking from deep slumber, the yellow earthen causeway shook itself.

The movement started below the wheels of the locked carts and the trampling hooves of the terrified mules – and then it rippled along the embankment to the neck where it joined the rim of the pit – and at that point a deep vertical crack opened miraculously in the muddy yellow wall. It opened with only a soft wet sound like an infant suckling at the breast, but it silenced the shouting, chanting men who watched.

Suddenly the only sound in the open diggings was the rustle of the falling rain and the shrieks of the dangling mule. On the cart Ralph stood poised like a Greek statue of an athlete, the whip stock thrown back, the cords in his throat relaxing, the insane rage in his green eyes clearing to leave a bemused expression of disbelief; for beneath his feet the earth was moving.

'Ralph!' This time Zouga's voice reached him clearly, and he looked down into the pit, saw their faces, the shock, the terror upon them.

'Run!' shouted Zouga, and the urgency galvanized Ralph. 'Get off the roadway.'

Ralph threw the whip aside and jumped down off the cart. The sheath knife in his hand again.

The rein that held Bishop, the big grey mule, was stretched tight as an iron bar. It parted cleanly to the touch of the blade and the mule dropped free, twisting in the air so that the men below scattered away, and the heavy body smacked into the mud. Then the beast scrambled to its feet and stood trembling miserably, belly deep in the yellow mud that had saved it.

The earth trembled like jelly under Ralph's feet as he hacked at the traces that held the other three mules and the moment they were free of the trapped cart he drove them ahead of him along the causeway, yelling them into a gallop. The yellow mud shook and tilted as the cracks yawned open, and the entire causeway began to sag.

'Run, you bloody fool,' Ralph panted at the man he had been fighting, as he stood in the rain and looked about him, the tattered oilskins dangling about his legs, his expression bewildered.

'Come on, run,' and Ralph grabbed his arm and dragged him after the galloping mule team.

One after another the gantries that lined the roadway, some of them with the huge buckets still hanging from the sheaves, began to topple over into the pit, the timber crackling and twisting, the ropes tangling and snapping like strands of cotton.

Ahead of Ralph the three yoked mules reached firm ground and galloped away, whisking their tails and kicking out skittishly at relief from their burden.

The causeway tilted and sagged, so that suddenly Ralph seemed to be running up a steep hill. The driver beside him missed his footing and went down on his knees, and then as he started to slide backwards he threw himself face down and spread his arm as though to hug the earth.

'Get up.' Ralph checked his own run, and stood over him.

Behind them the earth growled like a voracious animal, moving gravel grinding upon itself; and there were still fourteen carts out on the collapsing causeway. Half a dozen of the drivers had abandoned their teams and were running back along the trembling, sagging roadway, but they had left it too late. They stopped in a little group. Some of them fell flat and clung to the earth. One turned and leapt boldly from the edge into the gaping pit.

He plugged into the mud, and three black workers seized him and dragged him to safety, a broken leg twisting and slithering over the mud behind him.

One of the laden carts, with four mules in the traces, toppled over and, as it hit the bottom of the diggings, the weight of gravel shattered it to ragged splinters of raw white wood, and a shaggy black mule impaled on the disselboom screamed with shockingly human agony and kicked wildly. tearing out its own entrails from the gaping wound in its flank.

Ralph stooped and dragged the driver to his feet, pulling him up the steepening incline, but the man was semi-paralysed by terror and hampered by the flapping tails of his heavy oilskins.

The centre of the roadway cracked through abruptly and a hundred feet of it collapsed sideways with a swift rumbling rush, hurling carts and animals into the pit as though from some gigantic catapult.

Ralph glanced once over his shoulder at the terrifying carnage and saw that the whole roadway was going, starting from that centre point and running swiftly towards him, a breaking wave of soft yellow earth seeming to be of some thick and viscid fluid, breaking with that grinding whisper.

'Come on,' Ralph grunted at the man on his arm, and suddenly the earth beneath their feet lunged the other way, throwing them forward towards the rim of the pit – and safety.

They went forward with a rush, the driver clutching at Ralph's shoulder for support. A dozen paces to go to firm ground, and Ralph did not look back again. The hideous sounds from the pit were unnerving, and he sensed that another glimpse of that onrushing wave of collapsing earth might paralyse his own legs.

'Come on,' he gasped. 'We'll make it – almost there. Come on!' And as he said it the earth opened in front of their feet as though from a giant's axe stroke. It opened with a smacking sound, as of kissing lips, and the mouth of it was sheer, eighty feet deep and three feet across, but in the brief seconds that they tottered on the edge it gaped wider, six feet, eight feet, and the causeway tilted sideways – the final convulsion.

'Jump!' said Ralph. 'Jump for it, man.' And he shoved the driver at it, forcing him at that frightful crack that seemed to split the earth to its very core.

The man stumbled off balance, his arms waving wildly for control, and then he made a clumsy scrambling leap out over the drop. The torn oilskins tangled with his limbs and fluttered about his head. He hit the far lip of the crack with his chest, his legs hanging into the drop and kicking hopelessly, and clawed at the muddy lip. But there was no purchase and inexorably he began to slide backwards.

Ralph knew there was no chance of making a run-up to the jump. He had to take it from a standstill, and it was gaping wider with every second, ten feet or more now – and the quivering bank of collapsing earth was an unstable platform.

He sank on one knee, steadied himself with a clenched fist against the earth, and then straightened his legs and body in a sudden burst of energy like a released coil-spring, jumping high because the causeway had already sagged below the level of the rim.

The power of that leap surprised even Ralph; he cleared the driver's wriggling body and landed deep, on firm and rock-steady ground, stumbled with his own forward impetus and then ran on half a dozen paces.

Behind him the driver wailed and slid back a few inches, and around his spread fingers opened a mesh of smaller cracks, running parallel to the gaping sheer line. Ralph spun and ran back. He threw himself flat and reached for the driver's wrist.

It was greasy with mud, slippery as a freshly netted trout, and he knew he could not hold him for long.

Over the driver's head Ralph stared down into the diggings. He watched the final collapse of the causeway, a massive rush of earth, some of it liquid mud, mixed with huge chunks of compacted gravel that ground together like the jaws of some mindless monster, crushing and smothering men and animals between them.

The entire No. 6 Roadway was gone, and across the floor of the pit, deep dark cracks spread out like a grotesque spider's web.

In the bottom of the diggings the figures of men seemed frail and insectlike, their cries feeble and without consequence, their pathetic scurrying without purpose.

Ralph suddenly recognized his father. He alone was standing firm, his head thrown back, and even across that dizzy space Ralph could feel the strength of his gaze.

'Hold on, boy!' Zouga's voice carried faintly above the pandemonium. 'They're coming. Hold on!'

But under Ralph's belly the earth whispered and shrugged impatiently and the driver's weight pulled him another inch towards the drop.

'Hold on, Ralph!'

Across that aching breathless space Zouga was reaching out with both hands, a gesture that was more eloquent than *any words* – a gesture of suffering and helpless love.

Then suddenly Ralph felt rough hands seize the ankles of his muddy boots, the shouts of many men behind him, the rasp of a hairy manila rope against his cheek, the noose dangling in front of his face – and with a huge surge of relief he saw the dangling driver thrust his free arm through the noose and saw it drawn tight.

Ralph could let the muddy wrist slip from his grip, and he crawled back from the edge.

He looked down at his father. It was too far for either of them to see the expression on each other's face.

For a moment longer Zouga stared up at him. Then he turned away abruptly, his stride businesslike, his gestures imperative as he ordered his Matabele forward to the rescue work.

The rescue went on all that day. For once every digger on New Rush was united by a common purpose.

The Diggers' Committee closed the workings and ordered every man out of the unaffected areas. The five other roadways that had not collapsed were declared out of bounds to all traffic and they stood high and menacing in the silver clouds of drifting rain.

On the churned and collapsed remnants of No. 6 Roadway the rescuers swarmed. These were the men who had been trapped on the floor by the severed ladderworks and the fallen system of gantries.

There were no members of the Committee in the No. 6 area, and Zouga Ballantyne with his natural air of authority was quickly accepted as the leader. He had marked the position of the gravel carts and drivers on the roadway at the moment of the cave-in, and be split the available men into gangs and set them to digging where he guessed men and vehicles were buried. They attacked the treacherous shapeless mass of earth with a passion which was a mixture of hatred and stale fear, an expression of their own relief at having escaped that smothering, entombing yellow cascade.

For the first hour they dug men out alive, some miraculously protected by an overturned cart or the body of a dead mule. One of these survivors rose shakily to his feet unaided when the earth was shovelled away, and the rescuers cheered him with a kind of wild hysteria.

Three mules had survived the drop (one of these was Zouga's old grey Bishop) but others were fearfully mutilated by the wrecked carts. Someone lowered a pistol and a packet of cartridges from the ground level and Zouga slipped and slid from one team to the other and shot the unfortunate beasts as they lay screaming and kicking in the mud.

While this was going on there were teams of men busy above them at ground level. Under the direction of the Diggers' Committee they were rigging rope ladders and a makeshift gantry to bring up the dead and the injured. By noon that day they could begin taking the injured out, strapped to six-by-three timber boards and hoisted on the new gantry, swaying up the high wall of the pit.

Then they began to find the dead men.

The last of the missing men was locked like a foetus into the cold muddy womb of the earth. Zouga and Bazo stooped shoulder to shoulder into the mouth of the excavation, seized the limp wrist that protruded from the bank and, straining together, freed the corpse. It came out in a rush of slippery mud, like the moment of birth, but the man's limbs were convulsed in *rigor mortis* and his eye sockets packed with mud. Other hands lifted the corpse and carried it away, and Zouga flexed his back and groaned. Cold and weariness had tied knots in his muscles.

'We are not finished yet,' he said, and the young Matabele nodded.

'What is there still to do?' he asked simply, and Zouga felt a rush of gratitude and affection towards him. He placed his hand on Bazo's shoulder and for a moment they considered each other gravely, then Bazo asked again, 'What must be done?'

'The roadway is gone. There will be no work on these claims – not for a long time,' Zouga explained, his voice dulled and his hand dropping wearily from Bazo's shoulder. 'If we leave any tools or equipment down here, they will be stolen.'

They had lost the gravel cart, the hoist with its iron sheave wheels and valuable rope, and the gravel buckets.

Zouga sighed, and the fatigue swept over him like a cold dark wave. There was no money to replace those essentials. 'We must save what we can from the vultures.'

Bazo called to his men in their own language and led them along the shapeless bank of broken earth from which protruded shattered pieces of equipment and tangles of sodden rope, to the deserted Devil's Own claims.

The fallen roadway had buried the eastern corner of No. 142, but the rest of the claims were clear. However, a pressure crack had opened in a deep zigzag across the floor and some of Zouga's equipment had fallen into it and lay half submerged in muddy water.

Bazo clambered down into the fissure and groped for the mess of rope and tools, passing it up to the Matabele on the bank above his head. Here Zouga supervised them as they tied the tools into bundles and then staggered away with them to the high eastern bank, there to wait their turn for the single functioning gantry to hoist the bundles out to ground level.

As they worked the last pale rays of the sun pierced the mass of low cloud and struck down into the huge man-made pit.

In the bottom of the fissure Bazo found the last missing pick, passed it up, and then leaned against the bank to rest for a few moments. He felt that he no longer had the strength to climb out of the deep crack. The cold had numbed his legs and softened his skin until it was wrinkled and water-logged like that of a drowned man. He shivered and laid his forehead on his arm, bracing himself against the bank of yellow earth. He felt that if he closed his eyes he would fall asleep on his feet.

He kept them open with an effort, and stared at the earth in front of his face. A trickle of rainwater was still running down from the level above his head; it had cut a narrow runnel a few inches wide and deep. Most of the mud had settled out of this little streamlet, and it was almost clear, only slightly milked with colour.

At one point in its trickle down the mud wall it had encountered an obstacle, and was pouring over it, forming a little plume of running water.

Suddenly Bazo was thirsty. His throat was rough and dry. He leaned forward, and let the trickle flow over his lips and tongue, and then slurped a mouthful.

The watery sun touched the bank, and a strange brilliant light flared inches from Bazo's face. It came pouring up, powerful and pure and dancing white, from the tiny freshet from which he was drinking.

He stared at it dully, and slowly it dawned upon him that the obstruction over which the water was pouring was something embedded in the gravel bank, something that glowed and flickered as the random beam of sunlight played upon it, something that seemed to change shape and substance through the trickling yellow-tinged waters.

He touched it with his forefinger, and the cold water ran down his forearm and dripped from his elbow. He tried to work it loose, but it was firmly implanted, and soapy feeling in his raw numb fingers so that he could not get a fair grip upon it.

He took the buckhorn whistle from around his neck and used the point to prise the pretty fiery object loose, and it dropped heavily into the raw pink palm of his hand, almost filling it.

It was a stone, but a stone such as he had never seen before. He held it under the trickle of rainwater, and with his thumb rubbed off the clinging mud until it was clean. Then he looked at it again, turning it curiously in the weak sunlight.

Until Bazo had arrived at New Rush he had never thought

about rocks and stones as being different from one another, any more than one drop of water differed from another or one cloud in the sky was more valuable or useful than the others. The Matabele language did not differentiate between a granite pebble and a diamond, they were both simply '*imitshe*'. Only the white men's maniacal obsession with stones had made him look at them afresh.

In all these months he had spent toiling in the diggings, he had seen many strange things and learned much of the white men and their ways. At first he had not been able to believe the extraordinary value they placed on the most trivial items. That a single pebble could be exchanged for six hundred head of prime cattle seemed some grotesque madman's dream, but at last he had seen that it was true and he and his little band of *amadoda* had become fanatical gatherers of pebbles. Every sparkling or coloured stone they had pounced upon like magpies and carried proudly to Bakela for their reward.

This initial enthusiasm had swiftly waned, for there was neither logic nor system in the white man's mind. The showiest stones were discarded contemptuously. Lovely shiny red and blue pebbles, some of them shot through with different colours like ceramic beads, Bakela handed back to them with a grunt and a shake of the head. While occasionally, very occasionally, he would select some dull and uninteresting little chip and hand the delighted finder a gold coin.

At first, payment in coin had confused the Matabele, but they learned fast. Those little metal discs could be exchanged in their turn for anything a man desired, as long as he had enough of them he could have a gun, or a horse, a woman or a fine ox.

Bakela had tried to explain to Bazo and his Matabele how to recognize the stones for which he would pay a red gold coin. Firstly, they were small, never much bigger than the seed of the camel-thorn tree.

Bazo considered the stone in his palm. It was huge; he could barely close his fingers over it. The stones that Bakela wanted were usually of a certain shape, a regular shape with eight sides, one for every finger less the thumbs. This huge stone was not so shaped. It had one clean side, as though cut through with a knife blade, and the rest of it was rounded and polished to a strange soapy sheen.

Bazo held it under the trickle of rainwater again, and when

he brought it out the film of water that covered the surface instantly coagulated into little droplets and shrank away, leaving the stone dry and glittering.

That was strange, Bazo decided, but the stone was the wrong colour. Bakela had explained that they must look for pale lemon, or glossy grey, even brown colour. This stone was like looking into a clear pool in the mountains. He could see the shape of his own hand through it, and it was full of stars of moving light that hurled little darts of sunlight into his eyes as he turned it curiously. No, it was too big and much too pretty to be of value, Bazo decided.

'Bazo! *Checha*!' Bakela was calling him. 'Come on, let's go where we can eat and sleep.'

Bazo dropped the stone into the leather pouch at his waist and scrambled up out of the open fissure. Already the file of Matabele workers led by Zouga were plodding away through the mud, each of them bowed under a bundle of spades or picks, one of the big leather buckets or a coil of sodden muddy rope.

'He has the lives of six men on his hands. I was there, I saw it all happen. He drove his team into Mark Sanderson's gravel bucky.' The accuser was a tall digger with a huge shaggy head of greying hair, heavy shoulders and heavier paunch. He was working himself up into a boil of righteous indignation, and Zouga saw that it was infectious, the crowd was beginning to growl and surge restlessly around the wagon body.

The New Rush Diggers' Committee was in public session. Ten minutes previously they had formed themselves into a Board of Enquiry into the cave-in of No. 6 Roadway.

A wagon had been dragged into the centre of Market Square to provide a platform for their deliberations, and around it was a solid packed crowd of diggers from the No. 6 Section. Since the cave-in, they had not been able to get back into the diggings to work their claims and they had just come from the mass funeral of the six men that had been crushed to death by the treacherous yellow gravel. Most of them had begun the wake for their mates and were carrying uncorked green bottles.

Mixed with the diggers were all the loafers of New Rush, the transport riders and merchants; even the kopje-wallopers had closed their offices for the meeting. This was something that affected all their futures directly.

'Let's have a look at the little blighter,' somebody yelled out at the back of the crowd, and there was a menacing growl of agreement.

'Right, let's see him.'

Zouga stood beside the tall back wheel of the wagon, hemmed in by the press of bodies, and he glanced at Ralph who stood at his shoulder. He no longer had to look down at his son, their eyes were on a level.

'I'll go up and face them,' Ralph whispered huskily. Under the dark tan, his skin was grey and his eyes dark green and worried. He knew as well as Zouga did how grave was his position: he was to be tried by a mob that was angry and vindictive and mostly filled with cheap liquor.

The collapse of the roadway had destroyed the value of their claims. They could no longer get the gravel out; their claims were isolated, cut off from ground level, and they were spoiling to place the blame and extract vengeance. That vengeance would be brutal.

Ralph put one hand on the spokes of the wagon wheel, ready to climb up onto the wagon body where the dozen members of the Committee were already waiting.

'Ralph.' Zouga stopped him with a hand on his arm. 'Wait here.'

'Papa–' Ralph began to protest quietly, the fear still dark in his eyes.

'Stay,' Zouga repeated softly, and vaulted up onto the wagon body lightly.

He nodded briefly to the members of the Committee and then turned to face the mob. He was bare-headed, his beard catching the sunlight and jutting aggressively as he placed his clenched fists on his hips and set his feet easily apart.

'Gentlemen,' he said, and his voice carried clearly to the last row of the crowd, 'my son is only sixteen years old. I am here to answer for him.'

'If he's old enough to kill six men, then he's old enough to face the music himself.'

'He killed nobody,' Zouga answered coldly. 'If you look to place the blame, then put it on the rain. Go down to the pit, and you will see where it undercut the bank.'

'He started fighting,' the shaggy-headed accuser bellowed. 'I saw him use his whip on Mark Sanderson.'

'There is a fight on one of the causeways every hour of every day,' Zouga shot at him. 'I've seen you throwing punches out there, and getting your arse whipped at that.'

There was a ripple of laughter, a lightening of the mood, and Zouga took his advantage.

'In the name of all that's holy, gentlemen, there is not one of us here who does not protect his rights. My son was doing that, against a man older and stronger than himself, and if he's guilty for that, then so are all of you.'

They liked that, liked being told they were tough and independent, proud of being hard fighters and hard livers.

'Are you telling me that one boy with a trek whip brought down the No. 6 causeway all on his own? If so, then I'm proud that boy is my son.'

They laughed again, and on the wagon behind Zouga the tall blond untidily dressed man with the cleft chin and pale blue eyes smiled thoughtfully and murmured to the Committee member beside him.

'He's good, Pickling,' using Neville Pickering's familiar nickname. 'He talks as well as he writes, and that's well enough.'

'No, gentlemen,' Zouga changed pace. 'That causeway was a death-trap, ready to go off before the first gravel bucky went out on it Friday morning. The collapse was nobody's fault; we had just dug too deep, and there was too much rain.'

Heads were nodding now, their expressions concerned and grave as Zouga went on.

'We are too deep on the New Rush, and unless we work out a new system of getting the stuff out of our claims, then there are going to be a lot more dead men for us to bury.'

Zouga glanced down as one of the diggers shouldered his way through the crowd and climbed up onto the disselboom of the wagon.

'Now you pay attention, you bunch of dirt-hounds,' he yelled.

'The chair acknowledges Mister Sanderson,' Neville Pickering murmured sarcastically.

'Thanking you, Guv.' The digger lifted his battered Derby hat, finery that he had donned especially for this meeting, then turned and scowled at the crowd. 'This nipper of Zouga Ballantyne's is going to be a bad one to mess with, and a good one to have at your side when things get hard.' Still scowling, he turned and called to Ralph. 'You come up here, young Ballantyne.'

Still pale and worried, Ralph hung back, but rough hands pushed him forward and hoisted him onto the wagon.

The digger had to reach up to put his arm around Ralph's shoulder.

'This boy could have let me drop into the pit like a rotten tomato, and squash the same way when I hit the bottom.' He made a vaguely obscene squelching sound with his lips to illustrate his own demise. 'He could have run and left me, but he didn't.'

'That's 'cause he's young and stupid,' someone called. 'If he had any sense he'd have given you a shove, you miserable bastard.'

There was a hubbub of cheers and hooted derision.

'I'm going to buy this boy a drink,' announced Sanderson belligerently.

'That will be some sort of record. You ain't never bought nobody a drink yet.'

Sanderson ignored them haughtily. 'Just as soon as he turns eighteen, I'm going to buy him a drink.'

The meeting started to break up in a storm of friendly catcalls and laughter, the diggers streaming away across the square to the canteens.

It was obvious to even the most bloody-minded of them that there wasn't going to be a lynching, and hardly any of them bothered to wait for the Committee's verdict. It was more important to get a good place at the bar.

'Which doesn't mean we approve of your behaviour, young man,' Pickering told Ralph severely. 'This isn't Bultfontein or Dutoitspan. Here on New Rush we try to set an example to the other diggings. In future, do try and behave like a gentleman. I mean fists are one thing, but whips–' He raised one eyebrow disdainfully and turned to Zouga. 'If you have any ideas about how we are going to work the No. 6 area now that the causeway has gone, we'd like to hear them, Major Ballantyne.'

Hendrick Naaiman would have called himself a 'Bastaard', and would have used the term with a deep sense of pride. However, the British Foreign Office had found the word awkward, possibly the double 'A' in the spelling offended the proper order of official correspondence and treaties, especially if one of those treaties should ever be laid for signature before Queen Victoria. So the nation was now referred to as Griqua, and the land on which New Rush stood was renamed Griqualand West, a definition which made it easier for Whitehall to champion old Nicholaas Waterboer, the Bastaard captain's claim to the area, over that of the Boer presidents of the backveld republics which also claimed the area as part of their dominions.

It was remarkable how before the discovery of the bright stones nobody, and especially not Great Britain, had shown the slightest interest in this desolate and arid plain, no matter what it was called.

In Hendrick Naaiman's veins flowed the rich intermingled blood of numerous peoples.

Its basis was that of the Hottentot, the sturdy golden-skinned, dark-eyed people who had met the first Portuguese circumnavigators of the globe when they stepped onto the gleaming white beach sands of Good Hope.

Added to the Hottentot was the blood of the captured yellow bushman girls. Tiny doll-like creatures whose buttery yellow skins and dainty triangular faces with orientally slanted eyes and flattened pug features were only part of their attraction. To a people who regarded a large female posterior as a mark of beauty, the buttocks of the bushmen girls were irresistible, a bountiful double bulge that stood out behind them like the hump of a camel – and in the arid deserts of the Kalahari served the same purpose.

To this blood mixture was added the contribution of outcast Fingo and Pondo tribesmen, fugitives from the wiles of their own cruel chiefs and merciless witchdoctors, and Malayan slaves, escaped from their Dutch burgher masters, who had found their way through the secret passes of the mountains that defended the Cape of Good Hope like the turreted walls of a great castle. They also joined the bands of wandering Griquas on the vast plains of the interior.

This blood mixture was compounded with that of little English girls, orphaned survivors of shipwrecked East India men that had perished on the treacherous rocks scoured by the Agulhas current, and taken to wife at puberty by their darker-skinned rescuers. And there was other northern blood, that of British seamen, pressed into the Royal Navy's service in the time of Napoleon's wars and desperate to exchange that harsh duty even for the life of deserter in such a wild and desert land as Southern Africa. Others had fled into the same wilderness, escaped convicts from the transport ships that had called at Good Hope to reprovision for the long eastern leg of the voyage to Australia and penal settlement of Botany Bay.

Then came travelling Jewish pedlars, Scottish missionaries taking God's injunction 'Be fruitful' as their text for the day – riders on commando, collecting slaves and taking others of the traditional spoils of war in a dusty donga or behind a thorn bush under the inscrutable African sky. The old hunters had passed this way at the century's turn, and had paused in their pursuit of the great elephant herds to take on more tender game at closer range.

These were Hendrick Naaiman's ancestors. He was a Bastaard and proud of it. He had dark gypsy ringlets that dangled to the collar of his tanned buckskin jacket. His teeth were square and strong and starred with tiny white specks from drinking the lime-rich waters of the Karroo wells since childhood.

His eyes were black as tarpits, and his toffee-coloured skin thickly sown with the darker coin-like scars of smallpox, for his white ancestors had bestowed upon the tribe many of the other virtues of civilization: gunpowder, alcohol and more than one variety of the pox.

Despite the scarring, Hendrick was a handsome man, tall, broadshouldered, with long powerful legs, flashing black eyes and a sunny smile. He squatted across the fire from Bazo now, with his wide-brimmed hat still on his head; the ostrich feathers nodded and swirled above the flat crown as he gestured widely, laughing and talking persuasively.

'Only the ant-bear and the meercat dig in the earth for no reward more than a mouthful of insects.' Naaiman spoke in fluent Zulu, which was close enough to their own tongue for the Matabele to follow him readily. 'Do these hairy white-faced creatures own all the earth and everything upon and beneath it? Are they then some kind of magical creature, some god from the heavens that they can say to you "I own every stone in the earth, every drop of water in the–" ' Hendrick paused, for he was about to say oceans, but he knew that his audience had never seen the sea, " '– every drop of water in the rivers and lakes." '

Hendrick shook his head so that the ringlets danced on his cheeks. 'I tell you then to see how, when the sun burns away their skin, the red meat that shows through is the same coloured meat as yours or mine. If you think them gods, then smell their breath in the morning or watch them squatting over the latrine pit. They do it the same way as you or me, my friends.'

The circle of black men listened fascinated, for they had never heard ideas like these expressed aloud.

'They have guns,' Bazo pointed out, and Hendrick laughed derisively.

'Guns,' he repeated, and patted the Enfield in his own lap. 'I have a gun, and when you finish your contract you also will have a gun. Then we are gods also, you and me. Then we own the stones and the rivers also.'

Cunningly Hendrick used 'we' and 'ours', not 'me' and 'mine', although he despised these naked black savages as heartily as did any of the other bigots on New Rush.

Bazo took the stopper from his snuff-horn and poured a little of the fine red powder onto the pink palm of his hand, a palm still riven and scabbed from the rescue in No. 6 Section, and he closed one nostril with his thumb and with the other sniffed the powder deep, left and right, and then sat back blinking deliciously at the ecstatic tears before passing the snuff-horn on to Kamuza, his cousin, who sat beside him.

Hendrick Naaiman waited with the patience of a man of old Africa, waited for the snuff-horn to complete the circle and come into his own hands. He took a pinch in each nostril and threw back his head to sneeze into the fire, then settled into silence again, waiting for Bazo to speak.

The Matabele frowned into the living coals, watching the devils form and fade, the figures and faces of strange men and beasts, the spirits of the flames – and he wished they had counsel for him.

At last he lifted his gaze to the man across the fire, once again studying the laced velskoen on his feet, the breeches of fine corduroy, the Sheffield-steel knife on this brass-studded belt, the embroidered waistcoat of beautiful thread and velvet and the flaming silk at his throat.

He was without doubt an important man, and a rogue. Bazo

did not trust him. He could almost smell the deceit and cunning upon him.

'Why does a great chief, a man of worth, like yourself, come to tell us these things?'

'Bazo, son of Gandang,' Hendrick intoned, his voice becoming deep and laden with portent, 'I dreamed a dream last night. I dreamed that under the floor of your hut lie buried certain stones.'

For a moment the eyes of every Matabele warrior swivelled from Hendrick's face to the mud-plastered floor at the back of the low, smoky thatched hut, the darkest area of the circular room, and Hendrick suppressed the smile that crowded his lips.

Treasure was always buried under the floor of the hut, where a man could spread his sleeping-mat over it at night and guard it even in his sleep. It had not been difficult to guess where, the only question had been whether or not the gang of Matabele had yet learned the value of diamonds and begun gathering their own, as every other gang on the diggings was doing. Those furtive, guilty glances were his answer, but he let no trace of satisfaction show as he went on quietly.

'In my dream I saw that you were cheated, that when you took the stones to the white man, Bakela, he gave you a single gold coin with the head of the white queen upon it.' Hendrick's broad handsome face darkened with melancholy. 'My friend, I come to warn you. To save you from being cheated. To tell you that there is a man who will pay you the true value of your stones, and that you will have a fine new gun, a horse with a saddle, a bag of gold coins; whatever you desire will be yours.'

'Who is this man?' Bazo asked cautiously, and Hendrick spread his arms and for the first time smiled.

'It is me, Hendrick Naaiman, your friend.'

'How much will you give? How many white queens for these stones?'

Hendrick shrugged. 'I must see these stones. But one thing I promise, it will be many, many times more than the single coin that Bakela will give you.'

Again Bazo was silent.

'I have a stone,' he admitted at last. 'But I do not know if it has the spirit you seek, for it is a strange stone, like none other we have ever seen.'

'Let me see it, my old friend,' Hendrick whispered encouragingly. 'I will give you the advice of a father to his favourite son.'

Bazo took the snuff-horn and turned it over and over between his fingers, the muscles in his shoulders and arms bulged and subsided and his smooth regular features, knitted now in thought, seemed to be carved from the wood of the wild ebony.

'Go,' he said at last. 'Return when the moon sets. Come alone, without a gun, without a knife. And know you that one of my brothers will stand always at your back ready to drive the blade of his assegai out of your breastbone if you so much as think a treacherous thought.'

When Hendrick Naaiman crawled through the low doorway again it was past midnight; the fire had sunk to a puddle of ruddy ash, the smoke swirled like grey phantoms in the light of the bull's-eye lantern he carried, and the naked blades of the short broad stabbing spears flickered blue and deadly in the shadows.

He could smell the nervous sweat of the men that wielded those dreadful weapons, and the vulture wings of death seemed to rustle in the dark recesses of the hut. Hendrick knew how close that dark presence could crowd about him, for frightened men are dangerous men. It was part of his trade, this ever-present threat of death, but he could never accustom himself to it, and he heard the quaver in his own voice as he greeted Bazo.

The young Matabele sat as he had last seen him, facing the single door of the hut, his back protected by the thick mud wall and his assegai at his side, the shaft ready to his hand.

'Sit,' he instructed the Griqua, and Hendrick squatted opposite him.

Bazo nodded to two of his men and they slipped away as silently as hunting leopards to stand guard in the starlight, while two others knelt at Hendrick's back, their assegais in their right hand, the points merely inches from his cringing spine.

There was the weird 'woo woo' call of a nightjar out in the starlight, clearly the signal for which Bazo waited; one of his Matabele assuring him that they were unobserved. Hendrick Naaiman nodded in approval, the young Matabele was clever and careful.

Now Bazo lifted into his lap a small cloth-wrapped package on which fresh earth still clung in little yellow balls. He unwrapped it swiftly and, leaning forward across the smouldering fire, placed the contents in Hendrick's cupped hands.

The big Griqua sat paralysed like that, his cupped hands before his face, his dark pock-marked features frozen in an expression of disbelief, of utter astonishment. Then his hands began to tremble slightly, and quickly he placed the huge glittering stone on the hard-packed mud floor as though it had burned his fingers, but his tar-dark eyes seemed to bulge from their deep sockets as he stared at it still.

Nobody spoke or moved for almost a minute, and then Hendrick shook himself as though he were waking from deep sleep, but his eyes never left that stone.

'It is too big,' he whispered in English. 'It cannot be.'

Then suddenly he was hasty; he snatched up the stone and dipped it and his hand wrist-deep into the calabash of drinking water which stood beside the fire; then, holding it up in the lantern light, he watched the great stone shed water as though it had been greased, as though it were the feather of a wild goose.

'By my daughter's virgin blood,' he whispered again, and the men watching him stirred darkly into the shadows. His emotions had infected them with restless excitement.

Hendrick reached for the side pocket of his buckskin coat, and immediately the point of the assegai pricked the soft skin behind his ear.

'Tell him!' Hendrick blurted, and Bazo shook his head. The prick of steel ceased and Hendrick took from his pocket a shard of curved dark green glass, part of a shattered champagne bottle discarded in the veld behind one of the grog-shops.

Hendrick set it firmly on the floor of the hut, pressing the sharp points of glass into the clay. Then he closely examined the stone for a moment. One plane of the crystal had sheared through cleanly, leaving a sharp ridge around the rim, and the curved upper surface fitted neatly into Hendrick's cupped hand.

He placed the sharp ridge of the stone against the polished dark green curve of the broken bottle, then pressed down with the full strength of his right forearm and began to draw the edge across the glass. There was a thin abrasive screech that set his big white-starred teeth on edge, and behind the moving edge of the glittering stone a deep white groove appeared in the green glass, the stone had cut it as a hot knife cuts cheese.

Reverently the Griqua placed the stone in front of him, on the bare floor, and it seemed to be moving as the light played within its limpid depths, turned to magical stars of mauve and green and flaming crimson.

His voice had dried, his throat cleaved closed, he could barely breathe for iron bands of avarice had bound his chest, but his eyes glittered like a wolf in the firelight.

Hendrick Naaiman knew diamonds as a jockey knows fine horse flesh or a tailor the feel of good tweed cloth between his fingers. Diamonds were his salt, his bread, his very breath, and he knew that before him on the swept mud floor of this smoky little thatched hut lay something that would one day repose in the treasure house of the palace of some great king.

It was a living legend already: something that only a king could buy, something whose value, when converted to gold pounds or dollars, would stun even a rich man.

'Has this stone the spirit you seek?' Bazo asked quietly, and Hendrick swallowed before he could talk.

'I will give you five hundred gold queens for this stone,' he answered, and his voice was hoarse, ragged as though he were in pain.

His words struck the dark group of Matabele the way the east wind off the sea strikes the forests of Tzikhama, so that they swayed and rustled with the shock.

'Five hundred,' repeated Hendrick Naaiman. 'Which will buy you fifty guns or many fine cattle.'

'Give the stone to me,' Bazo ordered, and when Hendrick hesitated, the assegai pricked him again so that he started violently.

Bazo took the stone and stared at it broodingly, then he sighed.

'This is a heavy matter,' he said. 'I must think on it. Go now and return tomorrow at the same time. I will have an answer for you then.'

Long after the Griqua left, the silence persisted in the darkened hut, broken at last by Kamuza.

'Five hundred gold pieces,' he said. 'I long to see the hills of Matopos again; I long for the sweet milk of my father's herds again. With five hundred gold queens we could leave this place.'

'Do you know what the white men do to people who steal these stones?' Bazo asked softly.

'Not their stones. The Bastaard told us –'

'No matter what the yellow Bastaard told you, you will be a very dead Matabele if the white men catch you.'

'One man they burned alive in his hut. They say he smelled like a roasting joint of warthog meat,' one of the others murmured.

'Another they tied by his heels and dragged behind a galloping horse as far as the river. When they were finished, he no longer looked like a man at all.'

They thought about these atrocities a while, not shocked by them for they had seen men burned alive before. On one of the cattle raids to the east of Matabeleland their own regiment had chased two hundred Mashona men and women and children into the maze of caves that honeycombed the kopjes above their village.

It would have been a tedious task to hunt them out of the dark belly of the hills, so they had packed every entrance to the underground passages with branches of mopani trees and then put in fire. At the end some of the Mashona had run out through the flames, living torches of shrieking flame.

'Fire is a bad way to die,' said Kamuza, and uncorked his own snuff-horn.

'And five hundred pieces is a great deal of gold,' one of his friends answered him across the fire.

'Does a son steal the calves from his father's herd?' Bazo asked them, and now they were shocked indeed. To the Matabele the great herds of cattle were the nation's wealth, and the harsh laws and penalties that governed the management of the herds they had learned as part of their existence as '*mujiba*', the apprenticeship as herd boys which every Matabele boy must serve.

'It is death even to squirt the milk of another man's cow into your mouth,' Bazo reminded them; and they all remembered how they had taken that chance at least once in the solitude of the bush, spurting it directly from the teat so that it dribbled down their chins onto their naked chests – risking their lives for a mouthful of warm sweet milk and the respect of their peers.

'It is not a calf,' Kamuza reminded, 'but a single little stone.'

'Gandang, who is my father, looks upon the white man Bakela

as a brother. If I take anything from Bakela, then it is as taking from my own father.'

'If you take this stone to Bakela he will give you a single coin. If you take it to the Bastaard he will give you five hundred.'

'It is a heavy matter,' Bazo agreed. 'I will think on it.' And long after all the others had curled on their reed sleeping-mats under the karosses of fur, he sat alone over the dying fire with the great diamond burning coldly in his right hand.

Three men rode into Zouga's camp that Monday morning, and Zouga stooped out of his tent to meet them, standing bareheaded in the sunlight.

Neville Pickering led the party, and as he stepped down from the stirrup, he said, 'I hope we do not disturb you, Major, but I'd like you to meet some friends of mine.'

'I know Mr Hayes.' Zouga shook the hand of the lanky Texan engineer and then turned to the third man.

'And of course I know Mr Rhodes by sight and reputation.'

Rhodes' hand was cool, the skin dry and the knuckles large and bony. It had the feel of strength, although his grip was quick and light. Zouga found the pale blue eyes on a level with his. The man was tall, and startlingly young, he could be very little older than twenty, young to have earned such a formidable reputation.

'Mr Rhodes.' Nobody, not even Pickering, used his Christian name. It was said he even signed his letters to his own mother 'Your affectionate son, C. J. Rhodes'.

'Major Ballantyne.' Zouga was startled again, for Rhodes had a slight voice, pitched high and with a breathless quality. 'I am delighted to meet you at last. Of course, I have read your book, and there are many questions I should like to ask you.'

'Jordan, take the horses,' Zouga called, and began to lead his guests towards the scant shade of the camel-thorn tree. But Rhodes paused as Jordan scurried from the tent, obedient to his father's order.

'Good morning, young Jordan,' he said, and the child stopped abruptly and stared up at him speechlessly, beginning to blush a deep pink with transparent hero-worship, overcome at being recognized and addressed by name.

'I see you have taken to reading rather than fisticuffs now.'

In his haste Jordan still carried a book in his hand. Rhodes stooped and took it from him.

'Good Lord –' he said. 'Plutarch! You have cultivated taste for one so young.'

'It's a fascinating book, sir.'

'Indeed it is, one of my favourites. Have you yet read Gibbon?'

'No, sir,' Jordan whispered shyly, the blush subsiding to leave him only faintly pink. 'I do not know where I could find a copy.'

'I will lend you one, when you have finished this.' He handed the battered dog-eared copy of Plutarch's *Lives* back to Jordan. 'Do you know where my camp is?'

'Oh, yes, Mr Rhodes.'

Every day of his life Jordan made a detour on his way back from his lessons in the church, a detour that passed the tented and thatched camp where Pickering and Rhodes kept a bachelor mess, and Jordan passed with dragging footsteps. Twice he had glimpsed his idol at a distance and each time overcome with shyness had scampered away.

'Good. Call in when you are ready for it.' For a moment longer he studied the angelic child, and then turned and followed the other men to the shade of the tree.

There were empty packing cases and logs to sit on, and the four men arranged themselves in a casual circle. Zouga was relieved that it was too early to offer his guests liquor. He had barely sufficient money to buy food for his family, let alone to afford whisky, and he guessed that a bottle would not last long in this company; all three guests were drinking men.

They sipped coffee and swapped the news of the settlement for a few minutes before Pickering brought up the real business of their visit.

'There are only two schemes we have come up with to get the No. 6 area back to work,' he said. 'The first is the ramp –'

'I'm against that,' Rhodes said brusquely, impatiently. 'Within months we'll be back at the same problem – just too damned deep!'

'I would agree with Mr Rhodes,' said Hayes, the engineer. 'At best it would be only a temporary measure. Then the ramp itself would start collapsing.'

'Major Ballantyne's idea is the only one worth considering,' Rhodes cut in, and Zouga was struck forcibly by the man's manner of cutting through unnecessary discussion and getting to the core of a problem. 'The idea of building stagings on the rim of the workings, and running wires to the floor of the diggings is the only one that will beat the problem of depth. Hayes, here, has done some drawings.'

The engineer unrolled the plans he carried, spread them on the dusty earth at his feet and anchored the corners with diamondiferous pebbles from Zouga's tailing dump which had spilled into and was threatening to engulf the entire camp.

'I have considered a cantilever design.' Hayes began to explain the drawings in crisp technical terms, and the others moved their seats closer and bowed over the plans. 'We will have to use hand winches, and perhaps horse whims, until we can get a steam engine to do the haulage.'

They discussed it quietly, asking penetrating questions and, when the answers were obscure, cutting down for them with sharp minds and quick words. There was no waste of words, no repetitions, no drawn-out discussion and the work went swiftly.

The stagings would be tall scaffoldings built on the edge of the pit, and they would house the haulage winches.

'We will have to use steel hawsers. Manila will never do the job,' Hayes told them. 'There will have to be a single wire to each individual claim. A lot of wire.'

'How long to get it out?'

'Two months to Cape Town.'

'How much is this going to cost?' Zouga asked the question which had been burning his lips all morning.

'More than any of us can afford,' smiled Pickering. A man with a thousand guineas in his pocket was a rich man on New Rush in these days.

'What we cannot afford is not to do it,' Rhodes answered him without a smile.

'What about those diggers who cannot afford their share of the stagings?' Zouga persisted, and Rhodes shrugged.

'Either they find the money, or they will not have a wire down to their claims. From now on it's going to take capital to work a claim on New Rush.'

'Those who haven't got it, will have to sell out – it's as easy as that.'

'Since the cave-in the price of claims in the No. 6 has dropped to £100,' Zouga said. 'Anybody who sells now is going to take a hell of a knock.'

'And anybody who buys at £100 is going to make a killing,' Rhodes answered him, and lifted his pale blue eyes from Hayes' plans, and for a moment held Zouga's gaze significantly. He was giving advice, Zouga realized, but what impressed Zouga was the strength and determination behind that level gaze. He no longer wondered why somebody so young commanded such widespread respect on the diggings.

'Are we all agreed, then?' he asked.

With less than twenty pounds cash in the world and his claims cut off eighty feet below ground level and partially covered by the earth fall of the roadway, Zouga hesitated.

'Major Ballantyne.' They were all looking at him. 'Are you in?'

'Yes,' he nodded firmly. 'Count me in.' He would find the money, somewhere, somehow.

They all relaxed, and Pickering chuckled. 'It's never easy to play it all on one card.' He understood.

'Pickling, didn't I hear your saddle-bag clink when you dismounted?' Rhodes asked, and Pickering laughed again and went to fetch the bottle.

'Cordon Argent,' he said as he pulled the cork. 'The right juice for such an occasion, gentlemen.'

They swished the coffee grounds from their mugs and held them out for a dram of the cognac.

'The No. 6 stagings – fast may they rise and long may they stand!' Pickering gave them the toast, and they drank together.

Hayes wiped his whiskers with the back of his hand and stood up. 'I'll have the quantities ready to send off on the noon coach tomorrow,' he said, and hurried to his mount. Men who worked for Rhodes were always in a hurry. But neither Pickering or Rhodes moved to follow him.

Instead, Rhodes stretched out his long legs in the stained white cricket flannels and crossed his dusty riding boots at the ankles, at the same time offering his coffee mug to Pickering.

'I'll be damned if we don't have something else to celebrate this day,' he said as Pickering glugged cognac into their mugs.

'The Imperial Factor,' Pickering suggested.

'The Imperial Factor,' Rhodes agreed, and when he smiled the cleft in his smooth chin deepened and the melancholy line of his full lips under the fair moustache relaxed. 'Even this awful creature Gladstone has not been able to halt the march of Empire northwards through Africa. The Foreign Office has moved at last. The Griquas are to be recognized as British subjects, and Waterboer's request has been granted. Griqualand West is to become part of Cape Colony, and of the Empire. We have lord Kimberley's assurance on it.'

'That's wonderful news,' Zouga interrupted.

'You think so?' The pale blue eyes sought and held Zouga's.

'I know it to be so,' Zouga told him. 'There is only one way to bring peace and civilization to Africa and that is under the Union Jack.'

Immediately there was a relaxation of the relationship between the three men, an unspoken accord, so that even without moving they seemed to have drawn closer, and their talk was easier, more intimate.

'We are the first nation in the world and anything less than our total duty is unworthy of us,' Zouga went on, and Rhodes nodded. 'We destroyed the slave trade on this continent; that was only a beginning. When you have seen the conditions that still exist, the savagery and barbarism, to the north of us, only then can you appreciate how deep that duty still is.'

'Tell me about the hinterland,' Rhodes demanded in that thin, almost querulous voice that so ill-suited his big loose knit frame.

'The hinterland.' It was an unusual term, but it stuck like a burr, and Zouga heard himself use it as he described that wilderness through which he had travelled and hunted and prospected.

Rhodes sat on a log of firewood, the shaggy leonine head sunk forward, brooding and silent, only his eyes quick and attentive, listening with an almost religious fervour, rousing himself every few minutes, lifting his head to ask a question and then letting it sink again to the answer.

Zouga spoke of the wide slow rivers that ran in their deep valleys where the cream of tartar trees grew upon the banks and in the green shallows herds of hippopotamus challenged the traveller with gaping pink mouths and curved white tusks.

He described the deadly malarial swamps, vast stands of papyrus reeds swaying like dancers from horizon to horizon, where the sky pressed down, smothering the world under a heavy blue blanket sodden with steamy vapours, and he told of the relief of climbing the steep rocky escarpments to the cool high plateau of golden grasslands.

With words he showed them the vast and empty spaces, the plains dotted with moving herds of wild game, the cool green forests of standing timber, the streams of sweet water, crystal cold, from which a man could water his herds or his homestead.

He talked of vanished kingdoms of long dead kings, the Mambo and the Monomatapa, who had built cities of massive grey stone and left them to the smothering vines – their idols thrown down and shattered, the foundations of the walls menaced by the twisted grey python roots of the wild fig trees which found the joints in the stonework and forced them inexorably apart.

He told them of the square mine shafts that these vanished people had driven into the matrix and then abandoned, leaving the gold-bearing quartz where they had piled it before they fled.

'Visible gold,' he told them, 'thick as butter in the reef. Lying out there in the bush.'

He spoke of the people, the remnants of the subjects of the Monomatapa, their glories long past, decimated by war. He told them of the conquerors, the Matabele, the cruel legions from the south, calling the subservient tribes 'cattle' and, contemptuously, 'Mashona – eaters of dirt', taking them as slaves, killing them as sport, to prove their manhood, or merely on the king's whim.

He described the wealth of the Matabele, their uncountable herds of cattle, thousands upon tens of thousands of fine beasts, glossy hump-backed bulls whose blood lines ran back to Egypt and the land between the Tigris and Euphrates, big rangy animals with widespread horns and hides of every colour from unrelieved black to purest white.

He told them of deep and secret caverns in the hills where the priests of the vanished kings still conducted their mysteries and sustained the oracle, weaving a gossamer net of witchcraft and magic which enfolded even their proud and arrogant Matabele overlords.

Then, as the day wasted away and the sun began to set behind a flaming curtain of red dust, Zouga told them of the kraals of the Matabele, the impis trained into the most merciless killing machine Africa had ever brought forth, racing barefoot into battle behind their tall rawhide shields, the plumes nodding and streaming from their dark heads and the dazzle of their assegais lighting the plains as the stars light the night sky.

'How would you fight them, Ballantyne?' Rhodes fired the question harshly, and it checked Zouga in full lyrical flow. They stared at each other for a moment, but a moment that was fraught with portent, a moment in which the lives of many thousands – black men and white teetered in the balance. Then slowly the arm of the balance came down on one side, and the destiny of a continent moved, like a fiery planet shifting its orbit through the universe.

'I would thrust for the heart,' Zouga said, suddenly his eyes cold and green, 'a small mobile force of mounted men –'

'How many men?'

And suddenly they were talking war as the sun fell below the dusty mauve and purple plain, leaving the sinister shadows to draw in around the little group under the camel-thorn tree.

Jan Cheroot threw logs on the fire and they sat on in the ruddy wavering light and the talk was of gold and of war, diamonds and gold and war, Empire and war, and their words conjured columns of armed and mounted men from the night, dark phantoms riding into the future.

Suddenly Zouga checked in the middle of a sentence, his expression changed as though he had seen a ghost or recognized an old implacable enemy in the shadows under the camel-thorn tree.

'What is it, Ballantyne?' Rhodes asked sharply, swivelling the big untidy head to follow the direction of Zouga's gaze.

Against the bole of the thorn tree stood the tall green soapstone bird-statue. Unnoticed until now, hidden by the welter of harness and loose equipment that festooned the branches around it, some trick of the flames, the fall and flare of one of the burning logs, had illuminated it with sudden and dramatic firelight.

It stood taller than the seated men, seeming to preside over their counsels, listening to and directing the talk of gold and of blood. The falcon head, timeless as evil itself, as ancient as the hills of the far land from which it had been hewn, stared back at Zouga with sightless, yet somehow all-seeing, blank eyes, the cruel curve of the beak seemed on the point of opening to emit the falcon's hunting cry – or to bury itself in living flesh. To Zouga it seemed that in the darkness above the statue the words of the prophecy, spoken so long ago in that deep cavern of the Matopos hills by the beautiful naked witch who was the *Umlimo* of Monomatapa, still persisted, hovering in the shadows like living things:

> The stone falcons will fly afar. . . . There shall be no peace in the kingdoms of the Mambos or the Monomatapas until they return. For the white eagle will war with the black bull until the stone falcons return to roost.

In his memory Zouga heard the words again, spoken by that silken voice, and they seemed to echo against the dome of his skull and fill the drums of his ears.

'What is it, my dear fellow?' Pickering repeated the question and something slithered along Zouga's spine and crawled upon the skin of his forearms so that the hair came erect and he had to shudder to free himself of it.

'Nothing,' he answered, huskily. 'It's nothing; a grey goose walked over my grave.' But he stared still at the statue and Rhodes followed his gaze.

'By Jove. Isn't that the bird you wrote about in the book?' Rhodes sprang to his feet.

Eagerly he strode to where it stood and paused before it for a long silent moment before he reached out and touched the head.

'What an extraordinary piece of work,' he said softly, and went down on one knee to examine the shark-tooth pattern that was carved into the plinth. In that attitude he seemed like a worshipper, a priest conducting some weird rite before the idol.

Again Zouga felt that superstitious flutter of nerves crawl like insects upon his skin, and to break the mood he called loudly for Jan Cheroot to bring a lantern.

In the lantern's beam they scrutinized the polished greenish stone, and as Rhodes ran his big large-knuckled hand over it his expression was rapt, the gaze of those strange pale eyes remote, like a poet hearing words in his head.

Long after Pickering and Zouga had returned to their seats by the log fire, Rhodes stood alone under the camel-thorn tree with the falcon – and when at last he left it to join them once more, his tone was brittle with accusation.

'That thing is a treasure, Ballantyne. It is unforgivable to leave it lying out under a tree.'

'It's lain in worse conditions for hundreds, perhaps thousands of years,' Zouga replied drily.

'You are right.' Rhodes sighed, his attention straying back to the bird. 'It's yours to do with as you wish.' And then, impulsively, 'I wish to purchase it from you. Name a price.'

'It's not for sale,' Zouga told him.

'Five hundred pounds,' said Rhodes.

The sum startled Zouga, but his reply was immediate.

'No.'

'A thousand.'

'I say,' Pickering intervened. 'You can pick up ten claims in No. 6 Section for that.'

Rhodes did not glance at him, but he nodded. 'Yes, you could, or Major Ballantyne could pay for his share of the new stagings with a thousand pounds.'

A thousand pounds. Zouga felt himself tempted. A thousand pounds would see him clear.

'No.' He shook his head. 'I'm sorry.' He felt he had to explain. 'It has become the household god, my personal good-luck symbol.'

'Good luck!' snorted Jan Cheroot from across the fire, and all three of them turned their heads in his direction. None of them noticed him sitting on the edge of the shadows like a wizened little yellow gnome.

'Good luck!' the Hottentot repeated scornfully. 'Since we picked up that verdamned bird we haven't seen a day's good luck.' He spat into the fire, and his phlegm sizzled and exploded in a little puff of steam. 'That bird has put blisters on our feet and rubbed the skin from our backs, it has broken the axles of our wagons and lamed our horses. It has brought us fever, and sickness and death. Miss Aletta died looking at that bird, and Jordie would have followed her if I hadn't thrown the verdamned thing out.'

'That's nonsense,' Zouga snapped sharply. 'That's an old Hottentot maid's superstition.'

'Ja,' Jan Cheroot challenged him hotly. 'Is it an old Hottentot superstition that we are sitting in the dust of this hell-hole, swatting flies and rubbing empty bellies? Is it superstition that all around us they are pulling fat diamonds and we find only the droppings and manure? Is it superstition that the earth has fallen on our claims, and that it nearly swallowed Ralph? Is that your good luck that you boast the bird brings you, Master Zouga? If it is, then hear the words of old Jan Cheroot and take the thousand pounds that Mr Rhodes offers you; take it with both hands, and thank him for getting rid of that – that –' Jan Cheroot ran out of words and glared across the fire at the birdshape under thc thorn tree.

'Damn me,' Pickering smiled. 'But you nag like a wife.'

None of them were surprised at the familiar address between servant and master. In Africa relationships like this were common; the servant considering himself to be part of the family with a voice in the affairs of the family, and his claim was accepted by all.

'Jan Cheroot has hated the idol since the day we discovered it.'

'Tell me about that day, Jan Cheroot,' ordered Rhodes brusquely; and Jan Cheroot puffed up visibly with self-importance. There were few things he enjoyed more than an important and attentive audience and a good story to tell them. While he made a show of packing his clay pipe with black Magaliesberg shag tobacco and lighting it with an ember from the fire, the two boys crept out of the tent drawn by the prospect of a story. They glanced cautiously at Zouga and, when he made no move to send them back, they were emboldened.

Jordie sat next to Jan Cheroot and leaned his curly golden head against the Hottentot's shoulder, while Ralph came diffidently to sit with the men beside the fire.

'We had been one year in the bush,' Jan Cheroot began, 'one year without seeing a civilized man, one year trekking and hunting–' And the boys settled down with delicious anticipation. They had heard the story a hundred times before and enjoyed each telling more than the last.

'We had killed two hundred great elephant since leaving the Zambezi river, and we had fought bad men and savages. Our porters had mostly deserted or died of disease and wild animals, our provisions were long finished, no salt, no tea, no medicine and little gunpowder. Our clothes were rags, our boots worn through and repaired with the wet hide of buffalo.

'It had been a killing journey, over mountains with no passes and rivers with no names, and ordinary men would long ago have fallen and the birds would have picked their bones white. Even we were tired and sick and we were lost. Around us, as far as our eyes could see, there was nothing but wild hills and bad bush through which only the buffalo could pass.'

'And you needed honey for your strength,' Jordie burst out, unable to contain himself, and knowing the story word perfect. 'Otherwise you would have died in the bush.'

'And we needed honey for our strength or we would have died in the bush,' Jan Cheroot agreed solemnly.

'Out of the bush came a little brown honey guide, and he sang thus –' Jan Cheroot imitated the high-pitched burring call and fluttered his fingers in an uncanny imitation of the bird. ' "Come!" he called to us. "Come, follow me, and I will lead you to the hive." '

'But he wasn't a real honey-bird, was he, Jan Cheroot?' Jordie cried excitedly.

'No, Jordie, he wasn't a real honey-bird.'

'And you followed him!'

'And we followed him for many days through bad country. Even when Master Zouga, your father, would have turned back, old Jan Cheroot was firm. We must go on, I told him, for by this time I, who have a deep knowledge and understanding of ghosts and spirits, realized that this was not a real honey-bird but a hobgoblin in the guise of a bird.'

Zouga smiled softly. He remembered the incident differently. They had followed the bird for some hours, and it was Jan Cheroot who had lost interest in the hunt and had to be prodded and cajoled to continue.

'Then suddenly –' Jan Cheroot paused and flung out both hands theatrically, '– before our eyes, a wall of grey stone rose out of the bush. A wall so high it was like a mountain. With my axe I chopped away the vines and found a great gateway, guarded by fierce spirits –'

'Spirits?' Zouga smiled.

'They were invisible to ordinary eyes,' Jan Cheroot explained loftily. 'And I put them to flight with a magical sign.'

Zouga winked at Pickering, but Jan Cheroot ignored their smiles.

'Beyond the gateway was a temple yard, in which lay the falcon statues, cast down, some of them shattered, but all of them covered with heaps of gold, mountains of gold.'

Zouga sighed. 'Fifty pounds weight to be exact. Fragments and tiny pieces which we had to sift from the soil. How I wish it had been a mountain.'

'We gathered the gold from where it lay, and we took up that statue on our shoulders and carried it one thousand miles–'

'Complaining every step of the way,' Zouga pointed out.

' – until we reached Cape Town again.'

It was after midnight when Jan Cheroot brought the saddled horses to the camp fire, and as Rhodes took the reins he paused in the act of mounting.

'Tell me, Major, this land to the north, this Zambezia as you call it in your book – what is it that keeps you from it? What are you doing here?'

'I need money,' Zouga told him simply. 'And somehow I know that the road to the north begins here. The money to take and hold Zambezia will come from the workings of New Rush.'

'I like a man who thinks big, a man who counts not in ones and twos but in tens of thousands,' Rhodes nodded approval.

'At this moment I count my fortune in ones and twos.'

'We could change that.' Rhodes shot a pale piercing glance towards the bird carving, but Zouga chuckled and shook his head.

'I would like first refusal,' Rhodes persisted.

'If I sell, it will be to you,' Zouga agreed, and Rhodes stepped up in the stirrup, swung a leg over the horse's rump, settled in the saddle and rode out of the camp.

Pickering edged his mount closer to Zouga and leaned down from the saddle to tell him seriously:

'He will have it from you – in the end he will have it.'

'I think not.' Zouga shook his head.

But Pickering smiled. 'He always gets what he sets his heart on. Always.'

He saluted Zouga with the hand that held the reins and then started his horse into a canter and followed Rhodes out onto the dusty starlit track.

'Give the stone to the yellow man,' Kamuza urged quietly. 'Five hundred gold queens, and we will return to our own people with treasures. Your father, the induna of Inyati, will be pleased, even the king will call us to the great kraal at Thabas Indunas for audience. We will become important men.'

'I do not trust the Bastaard.'

'Do not trust him. Trust only the yellow coins he brings.'

'I do not like his eyes. They are cold and he hisses like a yellow cobra when he speaks.'

They were silent then, a circle of dark figures in the smoky hut, squatting around the diamond as it lay on the clay floor and flickered with weird lights in the reflection of the fire.

They had argued since the sunset had released them from their labours. They had argued over the meal of stringy mutton with its rind of greasy fat and maize porridge baked until it was stiff as cake.

They had argued over the snuff-horn and beer pot, and now it was late. Soon, very soon, there would be a scratching at the door of the hut as the Bastaard came for his answer.

'The stone is not ours to sell. It belongs to Bakela. Does a son sell the calves from his father's herds?'

Kamuza made a clucking sound of exasperation. 'Surely it is against law and custom to steal from the tribe, from the elders of the tribe, but Bakela is not Matabele. He is *buni,* white man, it is not wrong doing to take from him any more than it is against law and custom to send the assegai through the heart of a Mashona dog, or to mount his wife in sport, or to take the cattle of a Tswana and put fire into his kraal to hear his children squeal. Those are natural and right things for a man to do.'

'Bakela is my father, the stone is his calf, given into my care.'

'He will give you a single coin,' Kamuza lamented, and Bazo seemed not to hear him.

He picked up the diamond again and turned it in his hand.

'It is a large stone,' he mused aloud, 'a very large stone.' He held it to his eye and looked into the stone as though it were a mountain pool, and he watched with awe the fires and shapes move within it.

Still holding it to his eye, he said, 'If I bring my father a newborn calf, he will be happy and give me a reward. But if I bring him one hundred calves how much greater will be his joy, and one hundred times greater the reward that he will give me.'

He lowered the stone and gave a series of orders that sent his men hurrying out into the night, to return immediately with the tools Bazo had sent them to fetch.

Then in silence they watched him make his preparations.

Firstly he spread a kaross of silver jackal pelts on the earth floor and then in the centre of the fur he placed a small steel anvil at which he had watched Zouga shaping horse-shoes and working the iron hoops to repair the wagon wheels.

On the anvil Bazo placed the diamond, and then he threw aside his cloak so that he stood stark naked in the firelight, tall and lean and hard, his belly muscles standing up in concentric ridges under the dark satiny skin and the wide rangy shoulders overdeveloped by practice with shield and spear.

With his legs braced wide, he stood over the anvil, and hefted the sweat-polished handle of the pick, feeling the balance and weight of the steel head that had become so familiar.

Bazo narrowed his eyes, measuring his stroke, and then he reared back with the pick almost touching the thatched roof. He drove his body weight into the stroke, and the steel pick head came hissing down from on high.

The point caught the diamond exactly on the high centre of its curved upper surface, and the great stone exploded as though a bucketful of mountain water had been dashed to the earth. The sparkling drops, the shattered fragments, the glowing chips of priceless crystal, seemed to fill the whole hut with a burst of sunlight.

They pattered against the thatched walls, stung the naked skins of the watching Matabele, kicked little puffs of grey ash as they fell into the fire, and scattered on the lustrous fur of the silver jackal kaross, shining there like live fish in the net.

'Son of the Great Snake,' hooted Kamuza joyously. 'We are rich men.' And the laughing Matabele flung themselves into the task of gathering up the fragments.

They picked them from the ashes, swept them up from the earthen floor, shook them out of the jackal skin kaross – and piled them into Bazo's cupped hand until it was filled to overflowing. Even then they missed some of the tiny chips that had fallen into the dust or the fire and were lost for ever.

'You are a wise man,' Kamuza told Bazo with unaffected admiration. 'Bakela has his stones – a hundred calves – and we will have more coins than the yellow Bastaard would give us.'

*There was no work in the collapsed No. 6 Section, no need to rise before dawn, so the sun was clear of the horizon when Zouga strode out of the tent, clinching his belt as he joined Jan Cheroot and the two boys under the camel-thorn tree.

The table was a packing-case, the lid stained with candle grease and spilled coffee, and breakfast was maize-meal porridge in chipped enamel bowls, unsweetened, for the price of sugar had recently risen to a pound a pound on the diamond fields.

Zouga's eyes were red-rimmed, for he had slept little the previous night, but had lain awake worrying and scheming, going over and over in his mind every detail of the plans for the new staging – and coming back each time to the most important detail, the one for which there seemed to be no solution: the cost, the enormous cost of it all.

The two boys saw his face, recognized his mood, and were immediately silent, applying themselves with complete absorption to the unappetizing grey gruel in their bowls.

A shadow fell across the group, and Zouga looked up irritably, squinting into the early sunlight with the spoon half raised to his lips. 'What is it, Bazo?'

'Pick-ups, Bakela.' The tall young Matabele used the English words. 'Pick-ups.' Zouga grunted.

'Let me see it.' Zouga was immediately uninterested. Almost certainly it would be a worthless chip of quartz or rock crystal. But Bazo placed a small bundle wrapped in a dirty scrap of cloth beside Zouga's bowl.

'Well, open it,' Zouga ordered; and Bazo picked the knot, and spread the cloth.

'Glass!' thought Zouga disgustedly. There was almost a handful of it, chips and pieces, the biggest not much bigger than the head of a wax Vesta.

'Glass!' and he made the gesture of sweeping it away, and then stayed his hand as the sunlight fell on the pile and a shaft of it pricked his eyes in a rainbow burst of colours.

Slowly, disbelievingly, he changed the gesture of dismissal and reached hesitantly, almost reverently for the glittering heap, but Jordan forestalled him.

With a shriek of joy the child's small graceful fingers danced over the pile.

'Diamonds, Papa,' he screamed. 'They are diamonds, real diamonds.'

'Are you sure, Jordie?' Zouga asked the question unnecessarily, his voice hoarse, realizing it was too good to be true. There must be many hundreds of precious stones in the pile, small, very small, but of what superb colour, white, ice-white, seeming to crackle like lightning they were so bright.

Still hesitantly Zouga took onc of the largest stones from Jordan's fingers.

'Are you sure, Jordie?' he repeated.

'They are diamonds, Papa. All of them.'

Zouga's last doubts faded, to be replaced immediately by a deeper uncertainty.

'Bazo,' he said. 'There are so many–' And then something else puzzled him. Quickly he picked out twenty of the largest stones and stood them in a row across the top of the packing case.

'The same colour, they are all the same colour, exactly!'

Zouga shook his head, frowning, confused; and then suddenly the shadows in his eyes cleared.

'Oh my God,' he whispered, and slowly all blood drained from his face, leaving the skin dirty yellow like a man ten days gone in malaria fever.

'The same; they are all the same. The breaks are clean and fresh.'

Slowly he lifted his eyes to Bazo's face.

'Bazo, how big –' his voice roughened and dried, so that he had to clear his throat, 'how big was the stone before – before you cracked it?'

'This big.' Bazo clenched and showed his fist. 'With my pick I made it into many stones, for you, Bakela, knowing how you value many stones.'

Zouga's voice was still a husky whisper. 'I will kill you,' he said in English. 'For this, I will kill you.'

The scar across his cheek turned slowly into an ugly inflamed weal, the stigmata of his rage, and now he was shaking, his lips trembling as he rose slowly to his feet.

'I will kill you.' His voice rose to a bellow, and Jordan shrieked again, this time with terror. He had never seen his father like this before; there was a terrifying maniacal quality about him.

'That was the stone I was waiting for, you bastard, you black bastard, that was it. That was the key to the north.'

Zouga snatched the Martini-Henry rifle from where it leaned against the bole of the camel-thorn tree beside the falcon carving.

The steel clashed and snickered as he pumped a cartridge into the chamber and in the same moment swung up the barrel.

'I'm going to kill you,' be roared, and then checked.

Ralph had jumped to his feet, and now he faced his father, stepping forward until the muzzle of the loaded and fully cocked rifle almost touched the entwined brass snakes of his belt buckle.

'You will have to kill me first, Papa,' he said. He was as pale as Zouga, his eyes the same deep haunted green.

'Get out of the way.' Zouga's voice sank into that croaking, husky whisper and Ralph could not answer him, but he shook his head, his heavy jaw clenched so determinedly that his teeth grated audibly.

'I warn you, stand aside,' Zouga choked, and they stood confronting each other, both trembling with tension and outrage.

Then the muzzle of the heavy rifle wavered in Zouga's hands, lowered slowly until it pointed to the dusty red earth between the toes of Ralph's boots.

The silence went on for many seconds; then Zouga took a full breath and the barrel of his chest swelled under the faded blue flannel shirt.

With a gesture of utter frustration he hurled the rifle against the treetrunk and the butt snapped through. Then he sank back into his seat at the packing-case table and his golden head sank slowly into his hands.

'Get out.' All the fire and fury had gone from his voice; it was quiet and hopeless. 'Get out, all of you.'

Zouga sat on alone under the thorn tree. He felt burned out with emotion and anger, empty and blackened and devastated within, like the veld after fire has swept through it.

When at last he lifted his head the first thing he saw was the falcon squatting opposite him on its greenstone plinth. It seemed to be smiling, a cruel and sardonic twist to the predator's beak, but when he stared at it Zouga saw that it was merely a trick of shadow and sunlight through the thorn branches.

The kopje-walloper was a small man, with legs so short that his polished high-heeled boots did not touch the floor when he sat on the swivel piano stool behind his desk.

The desk filled most of the tiny galvanized-iron hut, and it was furnace-hot in the room; the heat quivered and danced down from the roof. On the raw deal planks of the desk stood the accoutrements of the kopje-walloper's trade. The whisky bottle and shot-glasses to mellow the man with stones to sell; the sheet of white paper on which to examine the goods for colour; the wooden tweezers, the jeweller's eye-glass, the balance and scales, and the cheque book.

The cheque book was the size of a family Bible, each cheque form embossed in gold leaf and printed in multi-colours, the border depicting choirs of heavenly angels, sea nymphs riding in half clam shells drawn by teams of leaping dolphins, the Queen as Britannia with helmet, shield and trident, twisting cornucopia from which poured the treasures of Empire and a dozen other patriotic symbols of Victorian might.

The cheque book was by far the most impressive item in the hut, not excepting the buyer's flowing silk Ascot tie and the yellow spats that covered his boots. It was unlikely that a digger would be able to refuse payment offered in such flamboyant style.

'How much, Mr Werner?' Zouga asked.

Werner had swiftly sorted the glittering heap of diamond chips into separate piles, grading them by size alone for each stone was of the same fine white colour.

The smallest stones were three points, three hundredth parts of a carat, barely bigger than a grain of beach sand, the largest was almost a carat.

Now Werner laid aside his tweezers and ran his hand through his dark locks.

'Have another whisky,' he murmured, and when Zouga refused, 'Well, me, I'm having one now.'

He poured both glasses full to the brim, and despite Zouga's frown pushed one across to him.

'How much?' Zouga persisted.

'The weight?' Werner sipped the whisky and smacked his thick liver-coloured lips. 'Ninety-six carats, all told. What a diamond it must have been. We will never see the likes again–'

'How much in cash?'

'Major, I would have offered you fifty thousand pounds, if that had been a single stone.'

Zouga winced and blinked his eyes closed for an instant, as though he had been slapped across the face with an open hand.

With fifty thousand pounds he could have taken Zambezia – money for men, horses and guns, money for wagons and bullock teams, machinery to mine the reef and mill the gold, money for the farms, the seed and implements. He opened his eyes again.

'Damn you, I'm not interested in what might have been,' he whispered. 'Just tell me how much you will pay for that.'

'Two thousand pounds; that's my top price, and it's not an "open" offer.'

The stone had splintered into almost two hundred chips. That meant a 'pick-up' payment to Bazo of that many sovereigns. Zouga would intensely resent having to make that payment, but he owed it and he would make it. Of what remained after paying Bazo, at least a thousand would go for his share of the new stagings on the No. 6 Section.

Eight hundred left, and it cost him a hundred a week to work his claims, so he had won himself two months. Sixty days, instead of a land. Sixty days instead of a hundred thousand square miles of rich land.

'I'll take it,' he said quietly, picked up the whisky glass and drained it. It burned away the bitter taste at the back of his throat.

Ralph's bird was a lanner, one of the true members of the family *Falco*, long-winged and perfect for hunting the open plains of Griqualand. At last, after many attempts, he had found her and taken her for his own, a falcon and therefore bigger than the male bird, which was not a falcon but a tercel or, in the case of a lanner, a 'lanneret'.

She was 'eyas', the falconers' term for a wild bird taken at the nest when almost full-fledged. Ralph had climbed to the nest high on the top branches of a giant acacia and brought the bird down in his shirt, bleeding where she had raked him with her talons across his belly.

Bazo had helped him fashion the hood and jesses of soft glove leather for the proud head, but it was Ralph who walked her on his hand, hour after hour, day after day, stroking and gentling her, calling her 'darling' and 'beauty' and 'lovely' until she would eat from his fist and greet him with a soft 'Kweet! Kweet!' of recognition when she saw him. Then he introduced her to the lure of stuffed pigeon feathers, teaching her to hit it as he swung it on its long cord.

Finally, in the traditional ritual of the falconer, he sat up all night with the bird on his fist and a candle burning beside him. He sat with her in the trial of wills which would prove his domination over her, staring into her fierce yellow eyes, in the candlelight, hour after hour, outlasting her until the lids closed over her eyes and she slept perched upon his fist and Ralph had won. Then at last he could hunt her.

Jordan loved the bird for her beauty, and once she was trained Ralph occasionally let him carry her and stroke the hot sleek plumage under his gentle fingers. It was Jordan who found her name. He took it from Plutarch's *Lives*, which he was re-reading, and so the falcon was named Scipio, but Jordan accompanied the hunt only once, disgracing himself irretrievably by bursting into tears at the moment of the kill. Ralph never invited him again.

The same rains that had undermined the No. 6 causeway had flooded every depression and vlei for a hundred miles around the New Rush diggings. Slowly, in the hot dry months since that deluge, the shallower pools and swamps had dried out; but five miles south on the Cape Road, halfway to the low line of blue Magersfontein hills, there was still a wide body of open water, and already reed-beds had grown up around its perimeter and colonies of scarlet and ebony bishop birds had woven their hanging basket nests on the nodding reed staffs. Amongst the reeds Ralph and Bazo built their blind.

They drew the long, leafy fronds down over their own heads, careful not to slice their hands on the razor-edged leaves; the fluffy white silks snowed down on them from the laden seed heads of the reeds, and they plaited the roof of stems in place, concealing themselves from the open sky.

Ralph scooped a handful of black mud and smeared it over his face. He knew that his white face turned upwards would shine like a mirror, catching the eye of even a high-flighted bird.

'You should have been born Matabele, then you would not need mud.' Bazo chuckled as he watched him, and Ralph made an obscene sign at him with his fingers before they settled down to wait.

It was fascinating to see how Scipio, blind under the leather hood, could still pick up the beat of approaching wings long before the men could see or hear them, and they were alerted by the set of her head and the anticipatory stretch of her talons.

'Not yet, darling,' Ralph whispered. 'Soon now, darling.'

Then Bazo whistled sharply and pointed with his chin.

Across the swamp, still two miles out, very high against the empty sky, Ralph saw them. There were three of them, big black wings curving on the downbeat in that characteristic unhurried, weighty action.

'Here they come, my love,' Ralph murmured to Scipio, and touched the russet-dappled breast with his lips and felt the beat of the fierce heart against his face.

'God, but they are big,' Ralph murmured, and the tiny shapely body on his arm was feather light. He had never flown her against geese before, and he was torn with doubts.

The V-shaped flight of geese went far out across the swamp in a leisurely descending circle and then they were coming back, low, flying into the sun. It was perfect. Scipio would have the sun behind her when she towered, and Ralph thrust his doubts aside.

He slipped the soft leather hood off Scipio's beautiful dove-grey head, and the yellow eyes opened like full moons, focusing swiftly. She shook out her feathers, swelling in size for a moment, puffing out her breast – until she saw the thick black skein of geese against the sky, and her plumage flattened, going sleek and polished, steely in the early sunlight, and she crouched forward on Ralph's wrist.

Turning with her to follow the flight of the geese, Ralph could feel the rapier points of her talons through the cuff of his leather gauntlet and sense the tension of the small neat body. She seemed to vibrate like a violin's strings as the bow is drawn lightly across them.

With his free hand he broke the quick-release knot that secured the jesses to Scipio's leg.

'Hunt!' he cried, and launched her, throwing her clear of the reed; and she went on high like a javelin, towering swiftly for the sun on wings shaped like the wicked blades of a pair of fighting knives.

The geese saw her instantly, and stalled back on great wings that were suddenly ungainly with shock. Their tight V-formation broke up as each bird turned away – two of them rising, driving hard for height while the third bird swung north again towards the river, dropped height steeply to pick up the speed he had lost in the initial stall of shock, and then levelled out low and winged hard, neck outstretched, webbed feet tucked up under his tail.

Scipio was still towering, going up on wings that blurred with speed and turned to golden discs in the early slanting sunlight.

Her tactics were those of the instinctive killer. She needed every inch of height that she could achieve. She needed it to exchange for speed when she began her stoop, her body weight was many times lighter than the huge birds she was hunting, and she had to kill with shock and speed.

Even as she went up her head was twisted to the side, watching, judging, as the game scattered away below her.

'Don't duck, my sweeting,' Ralph called to her.

There was very real danger of it, for though Scipio was hungry to hunt, she had never been flown against birds such as these. Geese were not her natural prey; nature had not equipped her for the shock of binding to something so massive.

As she climbed so the difference in size of hunter and hunted was emphasized; and then abruptly Scipio was at the height she judged sufficient and she hovered, ten beats of Ralph's own heart as he watched her standing in the air.

She was daunted, the game was too big, she was going to duck.

'Hunt, darling, hunt!' he called to her and she seemed to have heard him. She screamed that terrible death cry of the falcon, high and shrill and fierce, and then she folded her wings and dropped into her stoop.

'She's taking the low bird,' Ralph shouted his triumph; she was not going to duck, she had selected the goose that had dropped close to earth and was now crossing her front at an acute angle.

'There is the liver of a lion in that small body.' Bazo's voice was full of wonder as he stared upwards at the tiny deadly dart that fell against the blue.

They could hear the wind hissing through her half-cocked wings, see the infinitesimal movements of her tip feathers with which she controlled that terrible headlong plunge.

The goose flogged at the air, heavy, massive, black flashed

with frosty white, its panic evident in every beat of its frantic wings.

The speed with which Scipio closed was chilling. Ralph felt the hair on the nape of his neck come erect as though an icy wind had touched him as Scipio reached forward with her steely talons.

This was the moment for which he and the bird had worked and trained so long. The supreme moment of the kill – an involuntary cry burst from his throat, a primeval and animal sound, as Scipio bound to the great goose and the sound of the hit was like a single beat of a bass drum that seemed to shake the very air about Ralph's head.

The goose's spread wings spun like the spokes of a wheel, and a burst of black feathers filled the air as though a shrapnel shell had been fired from a heavy cannon; and then the goose's body collapsed under the shock, one wing snapped and trailed down the sky as it fell, the long serpentine goose neck was arched back in the convulsion of death, and Scipio was bound to the gigantic black body, her talons locked deep into the still frantically beating heart. The impetus of Scipio's stoop had shattered bone in the big body and burst the pulsing blood vessels around the goose's heart.

Ralph started to run, whooping with excitement, and Bazo was at his shoulder, laughing, head thrown back, watching the birds fall, leaving a tracery of feathers like the plume of a comet in the sky behind them.

A hawk binds to its prey, from the moment of strike unto the earth. A falcon does not. Scipio should break, and let the goose fall, but she had not; she was still locked in, and Ralph felt the first frost of worry cool his excitement. Had his bird broken bone, or otherwise injured herself in that frightful impact?

'Beauty!' he called to her. 'Unbind! Unbind!' She could be caught under the heavy goose and crushed against the earth. It was not her way to hold on all the way in.

'Unbind!' he screamed again, and saw her flutter, stabbing at the air with those sharp-bladed wings. She was stunned, and the earth rushed up at her.

Then suddenly she lunged, unbinding, breaking loose from her kill, hovering, letting the goose go on to thud into the rocky earth beyond the swamp, only then sinking, dainty and poised, and settling again upon the humped black carcass. Ralph felt his chest choked with pride and love for her courage and her beauty.

'Kweet,' Scipio called, when she saw Ralph. 'Kweet,' the recognition call, and she left the prize that she had risked her life to take and came readily to Ralph's hand.

He stooped over her, his eyes burning with pride, and kissed her lovely head.

'I won't make you do it again,' he whispered. 'I just had to see if you could do it – but I won't ever make you do it again.'

Ralph fed the goose's head to Scipio, and she tore it to pieces with her curved beak, between each morsel pausing to stare at Ralph.

'The bird loves you,' Bazo looked up from the fire over which he was roasting chunks of fat goose, the grease dripping onto the coals and frizzling sharply. Ralph smiled, lifted the bird and kissed its bloody beak.

'And I love her.'

'You and the bird have the same spirit. Kamuza and I have spoken of it often.'

'Nothing is as brave as my Scipio.'

Bazo shook his head. 'Do you remember the day that Bakela would have killed me? In the moment that he took the gun to me he was mad, mad to the point of killing.'

Ralph's expression changed. It was many months since he had intervened to save the young Matabele from the wrath of his father.

'I have not spoken of it before.' Bazo held Ralph's eyes steadily. 'It is not the kind of matter about which a man chatters like a woman at the water hole. We will probably never speak of it again, you and I, but know you that it will never be forgotten –' Bazo paused, and then he said it solemnly. 'I shall remember, Henshaw.'

Ralph understood immediately. 'Henshaw, the hawk.' The Matabele had given him a praise name, a thing not lightly done, a mark of enormous respect. His father was Bakela, the Fist, and now he was Henshaw, the Hawk, named for the brave and beautiful bird upon his wrist.

'I shall remember, Henshaw, my brother,' repeated Bazo, the Axe. 'I shall remember.'

Zouga was never entirely sure why he kept the rendezvous; certainly it was not merely because Jan Cheroot urged him to do so, nor the fact that the payment of £2,000 for the shattered chips of the great Ballantyne diamond had not lasted him as long as he had hoped, nor that the cost of the new stagings was rising all the time. His share looked to be more like two thousand than a thousand pounds. Sometimes in his least charitable moods Zouga suspected that Pickering and Rhodes and some other members of the committee were content to see the costs of the stagings rise and the pressure begin to squeeze out the smaller diggers. The going price of claims in the collapsed No. 6 Section continued to drop as the cost of the stagings rose; and somebody was buying, if not Rhodes and his partners, then it must be Beit or Werner, or even the newcomer, Barnato.

Perhaps Zouga kept the rendezvous to distract himself from these grave problems, perhaps he was merely intrigued by the mystery that surrounded it all, but when he looked at himself honestly it was more likely the prospect of profit. The whole affair reeked of profit, and Zouga was a desperate man. He had very little left to sell apart from the claims themselves. To sell the claims was to abandon his dream. He was ready to explore any other path, to take any risks, rather than that.

'There is a man who wishes to speak with you.' Jan Cheroot's words had started it, and something in his tone made Zouga look up sharply. They had been together many years and there was little they did not know of each other's moods and meanings.

'That is simple enough,' Zouga had told him. 'Send him to the camp.'

'He wishes to speak secretly, at a place where no other eyes will be watching.'

'That sounds like the way of a rogue,' Zouga frowned. 'What is the man's name?'

'I do not know his name,' Jan Cheroot admitted, and then when he saw Zouga's expression, he explained. 'He sent a child with a message.'

'Then send the child back to him, whoever he is. Tell him he will find me here every evening, and anything he has to discuss I will be pleased to listen to in the privacy of my tent.'

'As you wish,' Jan Cheroot grunted, and the wrinkles on his face deepened so that he looked like a pickled walnut. 'Then we will continue to eat maize porridge.' And they did not discuss it again, not for many weeks, but the worm was planted and it gnawed away at Zouga until he was the one who asked.

'Jan Cheroot, what of your nameless friend. What was his reply?'

'He sent word that it was not possible to help a man who refused to help himself,' Jan Cheroot told him airily. 'And it is clear to all the world that we have no need of help. Look at your fine clothes, it is the fashion now to have the buttocks hanging out of the pants.'

Zouga smiled at the hyperbole, for his breeches were neatly patched. Jordan had seen to that.

'And look at me,' Jan Cheroot went on. 'What reason do I have for complaint? I was paid a year ago, wasn't I?'

'Six months ago,' Zouga corrected him.

'I cannot remember,' Jan Cheroot sulked. 'The same way I have forgotten what beef tastes like.'

'When the stagings are completed –' Zouga began, and Jan Cheroot snorted.

'They are more likely to fall on our heads. At least then we won't have to worry about being hungry.'

Serious defects had shown up in the design of the stagings. They had been unable to support the weight of cable. The cables between them weighed over three hundred tons and they had to be stretched to sufficient tension to carry the gravel buckies without sagging excessively.

The very first day of operation the stagings at the north end of the section gave under the strain. Two winches tore loose and the wires fell twanging and snaking into the diggings. There had been a gravel bucky on the rope, carrying five black workmen down to the floor of the workings to begin re-opening the long deserted claims. They screamed the whole way down as the bucky spun and twisted, throwing them clear, and the tangle of snapping silver cables caught them up like the tentacles of some voracious sea-monster.

It took the rest of the day to bring out the fearfully mutilated bodies, and the Diggers' Committee closed the No. 6 Section again while modifications were made to reinforce the stagings.

The No. 6 Section was still closed.

Zouga had one bottle of Cape brandy left which he had been saving, but now he fetched it from his locker, pulled the cork with his teeth and poured into their two mugs.

He and Jan Cheroot drank in moody silence for a while, and then Zouga sighed.

'Tell your friend I will meet him,' he said.

Pale dust chalked the sky above the plain, so that the distances drifted away, dreamlike and insubstantial, to an indefinite horizon.

There was no living thing, no bird nor vulture in the milky blue sky, no ripple of flocks nor smoky drift of springbuck herds through the low scrub.

In this loneliness the little cluster of buildings stood forlorn, long deserted, roofs sagging and the adobe plaster falling from the walls in chunks exposing the unsawn timber frames beneath.

Zouga touched the reins and brought the gelding down to a walk, while he slouched in the saddle, riding with long stirrups and the disinterested mien of a man on a long and boring journey – but his eyes under the brim of the wide hat were quick and restless.

He was uncomfortably aware of the empty rifle scabbard under his right knee.

'Unarmed.' The invitation had been unequivocal. 'You will be watched.'

The man had chosen an ideal rendezvous. There was no approach to this deserted farmhouse except across miles of bare veld, no cover higher than a man's knee – and it was good shooting light, with the sun in the west. Zouga shifted his weight restlessly in the saddle, and the big ungainly Colt revolver under his coat dug into his side, a pain he did not resent – although the comfort it gave him was illusory. A man with a rifle could pick his shot and take his time as Zouga rode in.

The sheep kraal was part of the homestead, unplastered stone walls, and there was a well in front of the house, again with a stone coping. Beside the well lay the remains of a wagon, three wheels and the disselboom missing, the paint dried and cracked away, the weed growing up through the wagon bed.

Zouga touched the gelding's neck and he stopped beside the wagon. He dismounted swiftly, dropping off on the side farthest from the building, using the horse as cover, and while he made a show of adjusting the girth, he studied the empty building again.

The windows were dark empty holes, like missing teeth, and there could be an unseen marksman standing well back in the gloomy interior. The front door was blanched by the sun; Zouga could see the light through the cracks. It banged aimlessly and unrhythmically in the wind, and the wind hooted and moaned in the eaves and through the empty windows.

Behind the gelding's body Zouga loosened the revolver in his belt, making certain that it was ready to hand. He tied the gelding's reins to the wagon body with a slippery knot that would come undone at a tug, and then he consciously steeled himself, drew breath and squared his shoulders and stepped out from behind the horse.

He began to walk towards the front door, but his right hand was on his hip, under the tail of his jacket, almost touching the checkered grip of the revolver.

He reached the doorway, keeping clear of the entrance, and then flattened his back against the wall.

With faint surprise he realized that his breathing was rough, as though he had been running. Then another surprise – he was enjoying his own fear, the feeling of heightened sensitivity of his skin, the enhanced clarity of vision, the singing of the adrenalin in his blood, the nervous tension of his sinew and muscle, the awareness of being alive in the threat of death. He had been too long without this stimulant.

He placed one hand on the sill of the window and vaulted through it lightly, dropping to the earthen floor as he landed and rolling swiftly to his feet again in the corner, facing the room. It was small and empty, bunches of dusty cobwebs hung from the rafters, and the floor was scattered with the white-flecked droppings of gecko lizards.

Zouga moved down the wall, keeping his back covered, and stepped through into the second room. The kagel fireplace was blackened with soot, and the smell of dead ash caught in his throat. He looked through the open doorway into the sunlit sheep kraal beyond. There was a riderless horse tethered in the angle of the wall. A grey, dappled quarters, uncropped dark mane and full tail almost sweeping the ground. The rifle scabbard on the saddle was empty, and Zouga's nerves fizzed. The unknown rider must have the gun with him.

Zouga loosed the long barrel of the Colt revolver in his belt, peering out into the sunlight.

'Keep your hand away from that gun.' The voice came from behind him, from the empty front room through which Zouga had just passed. 'Don't draw it, and don't turn around.'

The voice was quiet, controlled and very close. Zouga obeyed it, standing awkwardly with his right hand under his coat, and he felt the touch of steel between his shoulder blades. It had been well done; the man had been lying outside, had let him walk through the house and then had come in behind him.

'Now very slowly bring out the gun and put it on the floor between your feet. Very slowly, please, Major Ballantyne. I don't want to have to kill you, but if I hear the hammer cocked I will – believe me, I will.'

Slowly Zouga freed the heavy pistol and stooped to place it on the littered kitchen floor. He glanced back between his own legs and saw the man's feet. He was wearing velskoen of tanned kudu hide and leather leggings, big feet, big man, strong legs.

Zouga straightened up, holding his hands well away from his body.

'You should not have brought a gun, Major. That is very distrustful of you, and dangerous for both of us.' He could hear the relief in the man's tone, and the voice was familiar, he searched his memory. That strange accent, where had he heard it? The footsteps retreated across the kitchen.

'Slowly now, Major, very slowly, you may turn around.'

The man stood in the gloom of the soot-darkened walls, but the shaft of sunlight from the high window fell on his hands and the weapon they held.

It was a shotgun. Both big fancy hammers were at full cock, and the man's fingers were hooked around the triggers.

'You!' said Zouga.

'Yes, Major, me!' The pockmarked Griqua Bastaard smiled at him, white teeth in the darkly handsome face and the gypsy ringlets dangling to his collar. 'Hendrick Naaiman, at your service, once again.'

'If you are buying cattle, it's a hell of a way to do business.' The Griqua was the one who had bought Zouga's bullock team, the money he had used to buy the Devil's Own.

'No, Major, this time I am selling.' And then sharply, 'No, Major, do not move, and keep your hands there, where I can see them. I have loaded with Big Loopers – lion-shot, Major. At this range it will cut you in half.'

Zouga lifted his hands away from his sides.

'What are you selling?'

'Wealth, Major, a new way of life for you, and for me.'

Zouga smiled bleakly, sarcastically.

'I am truly grateful for your kindness, Naaiman.'

'Please call me Hendrick, Major – if we are to be partners.'

'We are?' Zouga inclined his head gravely. 'I am honoured.'

'You see, you have something I need and I have something you need.'

'Go on.'

'You have two excellent claims, they are truly excellent claims in all except they yield very few diamonds.'

Zouga felt the scar on his cheek heating up, but he kept his expression neutral.

'And as you know, Major, my ancestry, the touch of the tar-brush, I think is the polite term, or more succinctly my kaffir blood, precludes me from owning claims.'

They were silent then, regarding each other warily across the darkened kitchen. Zouga had abandoned any idea of going for the shotgun. He was starting to become intrigued by the articulate and persuasive voice of the tall Griqua.

'For that reason I cannot sell you my claims, not even at gunpoint,' Zouga said quietly.

'No, no, you do not understand. You have the claims but no diamonds, while I have no claims but –'

Hendrick drew a drawstring tobacco bag from his inner pocket and dangled it by its string from his forefinger.

'—But I have diamonds.' He finished the sentence and tossed the bag across the room.

Instinctively Zouga reached out one hand and caught it. The bag crunched in his hands like a bag of humbugs, bringing back childhood memories. He held it, staring still at Hendrick Naaiman.

'Open it, please, Major.'

Slowly Zouga obeyed, pulling open the mouth of the cloth bag, and then peered into it.

The light was bad, but in the bag something gleamed like the coils of a sleeping serpent.

Zouga felt the diamond thrill close its fist upon his chest. It never failed, he thought, always that choking feeling when the stones shine.

He tipped the bag and spilled a small rush of uncut diamonds into his hand. He counted them quickly; there were eight of them altogether.

One was a canary bright stone, twenty carats if it was a point. Two thousand pounds' worth, Zouga estimated.

'These are just samples of my wares, Major, a week's takings.'

There was another perfect eight-sided crystal, slick and soapy silver-grey, bigger than the yellow diamond, at least three thousand pounds' worth.

Another of the stones was a symmetrical triangular shape, like those throat lozenges that tasted of liquorice, more childhood memories. A clear silver stone, limpid and lovely. Zouga picked it up between thumb and forefinger and held it to the light of the high window.

'These are I.D.B?' he asked.

'Dirty words, Major; they offend my delicate breeding. Do not concern yourself further with where they come from, or how I get them. Just be certain that there will be more, many more, every week there will be a parcel of first water stones.'

'Every week?' Zouga asked, and heard the greed in his own voice.

'Every week,' Hendrick agreed, watching Zouga's expression, and he knew the fly had touched the sticky strands of his web. He let the barrel of the shotgun sag towards the mud floor, and he smiled that flashing flamboyant smile. 'Every week you will have a parcel like this to seed into your own cradle, to throw out on your own sorting-table.'

There was another stone in his palm. At first Zouga had thought it to be black boart, the almost worthless industrial diamond; but his heart bounced suddenly as the poor light caught it and he saw the deep emerald colour flash from its heart. His fingers trembled slightly as he lifted it.

'Yes, Major.' Hendrick Naaiman nodded approval. 'You have a good eye; that's a green dragon.'

A freak stone, a green diamond, a 'fancy' in the parlance of the kopje-wallopers. There were fancy diamonds the colour of rubies, or sapphires or topaz, and fancies commanded whatever the trade would bear. It was not impossible that this green dragon would fetch ten thousand pounds, and end up in the crown jewels of an emperor.

'You said partners?' Zouga asked softly.

'Yes, partners,' Hendrick nodded. 'I will find the stones. Let me give you an example. I paid three hundred to one of my men for that green dragon. You put it across your table and register it from the Devil's Own –'

Zouga was staring at him fixedly, hungrily, his hands still trembling, and Hendrick stepped towards him confidently.

'– You should get four thousand pounds for a stone like that, a profit of three thousand seven hundred; and we share that fiftyfifty, because I am not a greedy man. Equal partners, Major, eighteen fifty for you and eighteen fifty for me.'

Zouga poured the glittering stones into his left hand. His eyes had not left Hendrick Naaiman's lips.

'What do you say, Major? Equal partners.' Hendrick transferred the shotgun to his left hand and reached out with his right.

'Equal partners,' he repeated. 'Let's shake hands on it.'

Slowly Zouga stretched out his own right hand, fingers open, palm upwards. And then, as their fingers touched, he hurled the handful of diamonds into Hendrick Naaiman's face. All Zouga's strength was behind the throw, all his anger at being so sorely tempted, all his outrage at this devilish assault upon his own self-esteem.

The diamonds tore into Hendrick Naaiman's flesh, one sharp-sided crystal ripped open his smooth olive-skinned forehead above the right eye, another sliced his lip.

Involuntarily Hendrick threw up his hands, lifting the shotgun muzzle high before his face as he staggered back from this unexpected assault, but at the same instant his right hand closed over the pistol grip and his forefinger hooked for the triggers. The gun was still at full cock, each barrel loaded with lion-shot. Hendrick started to drop the muzzles, pointing for Zouga's belly.

Zouga grabbed the barrel six inches below the gaping muzzles and forced the gun upwards, grasping with his left hand for Hendrick's right wrist. The big Griqua jerked backwards with both arms, and Zouga made no effort to resist him; instead he lunged forward, thrusting the gun into Hendrick's own face. The blue steel barrels cracked against his cheekbone, and Hendrick gasped at the blow and reeled backwards. Zouga drove at him again, forcing him into the soot-blackened wall so that he grunted with pain, pinned there for a moment with the shotgun pointing at the roof. In these seconds Zouga reached with his left hand, hooked his thumb through the trigger guard and jerked back against the triggers.

Both barrels fired simultaneously.

The burst of gunfire in the tiny confined kitchen was deafening. The bright orange muzzle flashes lit the gloom like a lightning strike, and the charges of shot crashed through the rotten roof, blowing gaping holes through which the sun shot long bright shafts of light.

The massive recoil of the double-shotted gun drove the butt back into Hendrick's own belly, and he doubled over with a gasp of shock and agony.

The gun was empty, harmless. Zouga let it go and dived full length across the dusty floor. At full stretch his fingers touched the cool checkered grip of the ugly black Colt revolver. As he fumbled for it desperately, he heard the light crunch of footsteps across the earthen floor behind him, and rolled right, flicking over on his back without raising his head.

Hendrick was over him, the empty shotgun raised above his head with both hands like an executioner's axe, and he had already launched the stroke. The gun swung down in a wide arc, the blue steel glittering sullenly in the gloom and the hiss of it like the sound of a goose's wing. Zouga rolled again flipping his body aside. But the butt of the shotgun caught him.

It was only a touch, high in the shoulder, but it jerked his head so that his teeth clashed in his skull, and his right arm was instantly nerveless, numb from his shoulder to fingertips. The Colt revolver went flying from his grip, spinning away across the kitchen floor until it hit the far wall.

Instantly Hendrick turned to chase the pistol, and Zouga kicked out at the back of his knee, landing solidly with the heel of his boot. Hendrick's leg folded under the blow, and he would have gone down but the wall was there to hold him. He fell against it, pinned for a moment by his crippled leg, and Zouga rolled to his feet.

He stabbed with his good left hand, feeling the solid shock of the Griqua's jawbone under his fist. Then again Zouga caught him with the left and heard the gristle in the beaky nose give with a crunch like chewing on a ripe apple, and the fresh blood from Hendrick's nostrils gave him a fierce joy.

He was going to beat this man to a bleeding pulp.

'Wait!' Hendrick shouted. 'Please! Don't hit me again.'

The appeal was so frantic, the terror on the Griqua's bloody face so pitiful, that even in his own cold killing anger, Zouga checked.

He stepped back and lowered his hands, and the Griqua hurled the empty shotgun at Zouga's face. It was completely unexpected, Zouga was off-guard, and even as he started to duck, Zouga knew it was too late, and he hated himself for a fool.

It felt as though somebody had slammed a door behind Zouga's eyes, and his vision was suddenly narrowed and dimmed with blood. He hurled himself forward, and dived again for the revolver. He got a hand on the barrel, and as he touched it the full weight of Hendrick's charging body crashed into his back, driving him into a heap against the doorjamb. But he still had a grip on the pistol barrel, and he struck out blindly using it like a club.

He felt the steel butt sock into flesh, and he hit again and again, some of the blows dying in the air, others thudding into the floor, but others cracking against bone.

He was sobbing and panting, blinded by his own blood, and for seconds he did not realize that Hendrick no longer clutched and tore at him.

Zouga shrank back against the wall and wiped the blood from his eyes. Then he peered like an old man through the red film. Hendrick was beside him. He was on his back, his arms flung wide as a crucifix and the blood snored and bubbled from his nostrils. He lay very still, his breathing the only sign of life.

Zouga lowered the pistol, and used the wall to hoist himself to his feet. He stood there swaying, his head hanging, the pistol dangling from his hand that was suddenly so weak that he could barely support its weight.

'Master Zouga!' Jan Cheroot dashed into the yard, panting from his run, carrying the Lee-Enfield rifle at high port across his chest, sweat streaking down from under his brimless pillbox infantry cap and his face crumpling with dismay as he saw Zouga's bloody torn face.

'You took your time,' Zouga accused him huskily, still clinging to the door for support. He had left Jan Cheroot with the rifle hidden in a ravine half a mile out across the dusty plain.

'I started running as soon as I heard the shots.'

Zouga realized that the fight had lasted only a few minutes, as long as it takes a man to run half a mile. Jan Cheroot unslung the water bottle from his shoulder and tried to wash a little of the blood from Zouga's face.

'Leave that.' Zouga pulled away brusquely. 'See if there is a rope in the Bastaard's saddle bags, something to tie him, a knee halter, anything.'

There was a coil of braided rawhide rope on the pommel of the grey mare's saddle. Jan Cheroot hurried back with it and then paused in the door of the derelict shanty.

'I know him.' He stared at Hendrick Naaiman's bloody snoring face. 'I think I know him, but you made such a mess of him.'

'Tie him,' Zouga whispered, and drank from the water bottle. Then he unwound the silk scarf from around his throat and wetted it from the bottle before tenderly wiping away the blood and dust from his cuts and scratches.

The worst injury was in his hairline, where the breech of the broken shotgun had caught him; by the feel of it, it needed to be stitched.

Jan Cheroot was muttering insults and abuse at Hendrick Naaiman as he worked.

'You yellow snake.' He rolled the Griqua onto his back. 'You got shoes on your feet and pants covering your black arse, and you think you are a gentleman.'

He pulled Hendrick's arms up behind him and trussed them, quickly and expertly, at wrist and elbow.

'You'd give a vulture a bad name.' Jan Cheroot looped the rawhide around his ankles and pulled it up tight. 'Even the hyenas wouldn't eat dung alongside of you, my beauty.'

Zouga capped the water bottle and picked up the empty tobacco bag. Then he hunted for the diamonds. They had been kicked and scattered about the kitchen. The eighth and last was the green dragon, dark and inconspicuous in one gloomy corner.

Zouga tossed the bag to Jan Cheroot, and he whistled as he peered into it.

'I.D.B.,' he muttered, his wrinkled brown face puckering into a sculpture of pure avarice. 'The yellow snake was I.D.B.'

'He wanted us to run those stones across our sorting-tables.'

'What shares?' Jan Cheroot demanded, playing with the stones.

'Half shares.'

'That's a good deal. We could be rich in six months and get out of this god-damned and blasted desert for ever.'

Abruptly Zouga snatched the bag back again. He had been through the temptation once already.

'Get his horse,' he ordered angrily.

They hoisted the Griqua's inert body and threw it over the grey's saddle. As Jan Cheroot was tying the Griqua to the horse, Hendrick kicked his legs weakly and tried to raise his head, twisting his neck to peer blearily at Zouga.

'Major,' he croaked, only half conscious. 'Major, let me explain. You don't understand.'

'Shut your mouth,' Zouga growled at him.

'Major. I am not a thief, let me explain about those diamonds.'

'I told you to hold your mouth,' Zouga warned, and wrenched the Griqua's jaw open, roughly digging his thumbs into the sallow bloody cheeks; then he thrust the bag of diamonds into his slack mouth.

'Choke on your bloody diamonds, you thieving, treacherous bastard,' he told him grimly as he bound the man's mouth closed with his scarf, jamming the bag in place, while Hendrick squawked and rolled his eyes, jerking his head from side to side, his cries muffled and his spittle soaking the gay band of silk.

'That will keep you quiet until we get you in front of the Committee.'

Jan Cheroot sat up behind the trussed Griqua on the grey's back and followed Zouga on the gelding.

He sucked his teeth mournfully, sighed and shook his head.

'What a waste!' he grumbled just loud enough for Zouga to hear. 'That bag would take us back to the north.'

He rolled his eyes sideways at Zouga, but there was no reaction.

'The Committee is going to see this yellow bastard lynched anyway. He is as good as vulture breakfast already –'

Hendrick wriggled helplessly and snuffled through his swollen nose.

'– If we just did the job for them, nice and quietly, a bullet in the head, and leave him for his brothers and sisters, the jackals and the hyena, man, nobody will ever know.'

He glanced hopefully at Zouga again. 'What's in that bag will take us north again, as far as we want to go.'

Zouga kicked the gelding into a canter, and ahead of them the iron roofs and dusty tent cones of New Rush glowed ruddily in the slanting rays of the sunset. Jan Cheroot sighed, swatted the double-laden grey across the quarters and followed Zouga into the camp.

Pickering and Rhodes messed with a few other bachelor diggers directly beyond Market Square, at the edge of the main tailing dumps. There were two good spreading acacias to give them shade, and they had planted a hedge of milkbush around the cluster of iron huts and walled shanties.

Every member of the mess owned good claims and was recovering stones; he had to do so to afford the mess bills for champagne and old cognac that seemed to form the group's staple diet. One of them was the younger son of a belted earl, another was a baronet in his own right, although merely of the Irish aristocracy. Most of them were members of the Diggers' Committee, and their style had earned the group the title of 'The Swells'.

When Zouga rode into their camp, half a dozen of the Swells were lounging under the acacia trees, dining on Veuve Cliquot champagne, although the sun was still above the horizon, and wrangling amiably over the heavy wagers that they were placing against how many flies would settle on the sugar lumps that each had on the camp table in front of him.

Pickering looked up, his fair open features for once puckered in astonishment, as Zouga rode into the camp.

'Gentlemen,' Zouga announced grimly. 'I have something for you.'

He leaned out of his saddle and cut the thongs that secured Hendrick Naaiman's heels to the saddle girth of the grey mare, and then tipped him off the horse, letting him fall head-first into the dust in front of the seated group of Diggers' Committee members.

'I.D.B.,' Zouga told them, as they stared at him.

Pickering moved first. He jumped to his feet.

'Where are the diamonds, Major?' he asked.

'In his mouth.'

Pickering went down on one knee next to the Griqua, and he undid the scarf.

He worked the saliva-drenched bag out of Hendrick's broken mouth, and poured the contents onto the camp table amongst the flies and sugar lumps and champagne bottles.

'Eight,' Rhodes counted them swiftly, and looked immensely relieved. 'They are all there.'

'I told you not to worry. I bet fifty guineas on them all being there. Don't forget it.'

Pickering smiled at Rhodes and turned back to the Griqua, who was flapping around in the dust like a trussed chicken.

Pickering helped him solicitously to his feet.

'My dear fellow,' he asked. 'Are you all right?'

'He nearly killed me,' Hendrick bleated bitterly. 'He's a madman!'

'I told you to be careful,' Pickering agreed. 'He's not a man to trifle with.'He patted the Griqua's back. 'Well done, Hendrick; you did a good job.'

Then Pickering turned to Zouga. 'We owe you a little apology, Major.' He spread his hands and smiled winningly.

Zouga had been staring at him, unable to speak, his face so pale that his scratches and gouges stood out lividly. But now the scar under his eyes began to glow and he found his voice.

'A trap!' he whispered. 'You set a trap for me.'

'We had to be sure of you,' Rhodes explained reasonably. 'We had to know what kind of man you really were before we got you onto the Diggers' Committee.'

'You swine,' Zouga husked. 'You arrogant swine.'

'You came out of it with flying colours, sir,' Rhodes told him stiffly. He was not accustomed to being addressed in those terms.

'If I had fallen for your trap, what would you have done?'

Rhodes shrugged his heavy shoulders. 'The question doesn't arise. You acted like a true English gentleman.'

'You will never know how close it was,' Zouga told him.

'Oh yes, I do. Most of us here have been tested.'

Zouga turned to Pickering. 'What would have happened, a lynching party?'

'Oh, my dear fellow, probably nothing so theatrical. You just might have slipped on the roadway and taken a tumble into the diggings, or had the misfortune to be standing under a gravel bucky when the rope parted.' He laughed merrily, and the men at the table laughed with him.

'You need a glass of Charlie Champers, Major, or something stronger perhaps.'

'Do join us, sir,' cried another, making room for him at the table. 'An honour to drink with a gentleman.'

'Come along, Major.' Pickering smiled. 'I'll send for the quack to see to that cut on your head.'

Then Pickering stopped and his expression changed.

Zouga had kicked his feet loose from the stirrups and jumped down to face him. They were of an even height, both big men, and the group at the camp table was instantly enchanted. This would be more diverting than watching bluebottles settling on sugar lumps.

'By gad, he's going to bang Pickling's head.'

'Or Pickling his.'

'Ten guineas the elephant hunter to win.'

'I don't approve of brawling,' murmured Rhodes, 'but I'll take Pickling for ten.'

'I say, the other horse has run a fair chase already. I do think you might offer some odds.'

Pickering's smile had turned frosty, and he was on his toes, his fists clenched, and his guard half raised.

Zouga dropped his own guard and turned disgustedly to the group under the acacia.

'I've provided you with enough amusement for one day,' he told them coldly. 'You can take your bloody diamonds, and your damned Committee and you can –'

There was a burst of clapping and laughing cheers to cover Zouga's outburst. Zouga swung back onto the gelding's back and kicked him into a gallop, and the ironical applause followed him out of the camp.

'I hope we haven't lost him.' Pickering lowered his fists and stared after Zouga. 'God knows, we need honest men.'

'Oh, don't worry,' Rhodes told him. 'Give him time to simmer down and then we'll square him.'

'Henshaw.' Bazo held the woven reed basket on his lap and peered into it mournfully.

'Henshaw, she is not ready to fight again so soon.'

They sat in a circle about the cooking fire in the centre of the thatched beehive. Ralph felt more at home here than in the tent under the camel-thorn tree. Here he was with friends, the closest friends he had ever known in his nomadic life, and here also he was beyond the severe and unrelenting surveillance of his father.

Ralph dipped into the communal three-legged black pot with his left hand and scooped up a little of the stiff fluffy white maize porridge. While he rolled it into a ball between his fingers he argued with the Matabele princeling opposite him.

'If it were you to decide, she would never fight again,' Ralph told him, and dipped the maize ball into the flavouring of mutton gravy and wild herbs.

'Her new leg is not strong enough yet,' Bazo shook his head.

Ralph popped the morsel and chewed as he talked. 'The leg is hard and bright as a knife.'

Bazo puffed out his cheeks and looked even more lugubrious, and on her perch in the shadows behind him Scipio, the falcon, shook out her feathers and 'kweeted' softly as though in sympathy with him.

Bazo's decision, although heavily influenced by Ralph's arguments and by the urgings of the other young Matabele, would be final. For it was Bazo who had made the original capture of the animal under discussion.

'Every night that she does not fight, we, your brothers, are the poorer,' Kamuza came in to support Ralph. 'Henshaw is right. She is fierce as a lioness and ready to earn us all many gold queens.'

'Already you speak and think like a white man,' Bazo replied loftily. 'The yellow coins fill your head day and night.'

'What other reason for that,' Kamuza shuddered slightly as he pointed at the basket, 'that thing. If it stings you, the spear of your manhood will shrivel like a rotten fruit until it is no bigger than the finger of a new born baby.'

'What a shrivelling that would be,' Ralph chuckled. 'Like a bull hippopotamus shrivelling into a striped field mouse.'

Bazo grinned and made the gesture of placing the tiny basket on Kamuza's lap. 'Come, let her suckle a little to give her strength for the conflict,' he suggested, and the circle exploded with a roar of delighted laughter at Kamuza's patent horror as he yelled and leapt violently away.

The noisy jeers covered their own uneasiness at the close proximity of the basket, and they were immediately silent as Bazo cautiously lifted the lid.

They craned forward with sickly fascination, and in the bottom of the basket something dark and furry and big as a rat stirred.

'Hau! Inkosikazi!' Bazo greeted it, and the creature reared up on its multiple legs, raising the front pair defensively, and the rows of eyes glittered in the softly wavering firelight. Bazo lifted his own right hand to return the salute of long hairy legs.

'I see you also, Inkosikazi.'

Bazo had named her Inkosikazi, the queen, for, as he explained to Ralph, 'She is right royal in her rage, and as thirsty for blood as a Matabele queen.'

He and Ralph had been unloading timber baulks at the eastern end of the new stagings, and as one load had swung upwards in the slings the great spider had come out from its nest between the sawn planks, and, raising its swollen velvety abdomen, had scampered over Ralph's arm and leapt ten feet to the ground.

The spider was the size of a dinner plate when its legs were extended. Its hirsute appearance and its extraordinary jumping prowess had given the species the common name of baboon spider.

'Get him, Bazo!' Ralph yelled from the top of the loaded wagon.

For now that Griqualand West and the New Rush diggings were part of Cape Colony and the British Empire there had been changes.

New Rush had been re-named Kimberley, after Lord Kimberley, the Colonial Secretary in London, and the town of Kimberley was starting to enjoy the benefits of British civilization and Victorian morality, amongst which was the total ban on cock fighting which was strictly enforced by the new administrator. The diggers, always eager for distraction, had not taken long to find an alternative sport. Spider fighting was the rage of the diggings.

'Don't let him get away!' Ralph vaulted down from the wagon, ripping off his shirt, but Bazo was quicker. He whipped the loincloth from his waist and flared it at the spider like a matador caping the bull, bringing the huge arachnid to bay on its hind legs, threatening him with its waving arms, then, naked and triumphant, Bazo had flipped the cloth over it and swiftly bundled it into a bag.

Now he slowly but deliberately extended his own hand into the basket, and the spider raised itself higher, the wolflike mandibles chewing menacingly, and between them the single curved red fang rising from its shallow sheath, a pale droplet of venom shining upon the needlesharp tip.

There was not even the sound of breathing in the dark hut, and the soft tick and rustle of the ashes sounded deafening in the silence as they watched Bazo's open hand draw closer and closer to the creature.

Then he touched it with his fingertips and began to stroke the soft furry carapace. Slowly the spider subsided from her threatening posture, and the watchers sighed and began to breathe again.

Inkosikazi had fought five times, and five times she had killed, although in the last conflict against another huge and ferocious female she had lost one of her legs, chewed through at the elbow joint. That had been almost three months previously; but the severed limb had now regenerated itself, and the new leg was lighter coloured than the others like the fresh shoots on a rose bush.

Slowly Bazo turned his hand palm upwards and the spider scuttled up into it and crouched there, filling it completely without extending her many jointed legs.

'A queen,' he said, 'a veritable queen.' And then, frowning, he told her, 'Henshaw would like to see you fight again.' He glanced up at Ralph, and there was a mischievous twist to his full lips. 'Go to Henshaw and tell him if you will fight or no.' And he offered the spider to Ralph.

Ralph felt the crawling of the tiny feet of horror across his skin as he stared at the spider crouching like a hairy toad before his face.

'Come, Henshaw,' Bazo smiled. 'Talk to her.'

It was a challenge, and the watchers stirred with anticipation. If the challenge was not taken up, then their mockery would be merciless. Ralph tried to force himself to move, but his loathing was a cold nauseating lump under his ribs, and the sheen of sweat on his forehead was suddenly glacially cold.

Bazo was still smiling, but the challenge in his direct gaze was slowly changing to taunting disdain. With an enormous effort Ralph raised his hand, and at the movement the spider lifted itself and the soft bloated abdomen seemed to pulse softly, obscenely.

Only one person had ever handled Inkosikazi, and her reaction to a strange touch was totally unpredictable; but Ralph forced himself to reach out towards her.

Slowly his fingertips drew closer, six inches, two inches from the hairy body, and then the spider sprang. It launched itself in a high parabola, and landed on Ralph's shoulder.

The circle of watchers broke up in comic panic, yelling with terror and falling over one another to reach the single low doorway. Only Bazo and Ralph had not moved. Ralph sat with his hand still extended and the spider squatted massively on his shoulder. Infinitely slowly Ralph cocked his head and peered down at it, and it began to move; lifting the long bristled legs with a chilling daintiness, it crept sideways into the hollow of Ralph's neck – so that he could no longer see it but suddenly he felt the sharp points of its feet scratching the soft of his throat.

There was a horrified yell locked in the back of Ralph's throat, but he kept it there with a total effort of will. The spider climbed his chin and hung upside down for a moment like a huge hairy bat, and Ralph did not move.

Instead he lifted his gaze and held that of the Matabele opposite him. The mockery was gone from Bazo's eyes, and behind him the other watchers drew closer, fascinated and fearful. Perhaps for a minute they sat like that, and then Ralph lifted his hand. The gesture was so calm, so controlled, that the spider showed only perfunctory symptoms of alarm, and then quite willingly scuttled onto the inviting fingers and Ralph transferred her gently back into her basket.

Ralph wanted to leap up and run out into the darkness, to be alone while he vomited up his horror, but he forced himself to sit and stare impassively at Bazo until the Matabele lowered his eyes.

'She will fight,' he said softly. 'As you wish, Henshaw, she will fight again tomorrow.' And he closed the lid of the basket.

Inkosikazi had not fought for almost three months, and the

punters, always fickle, had forgotten her. Other champions had emerged in her absence and commanded the fanatic loyalty of their followers. They gathered four deep around the handlers, trying to peer into the baskets and assess the fighting metal of the caged creatures, as they waited for the first bout of the afternoon.

Although lantern-lit contests were held each evening behind Diamond Lil's canteen, Sunday afternoon was the main event of the week when every digger in Kimberley was free to crowd the western corner of Market Square and pick his fancy.

The arena was a square wooden structure, six feet by six and three deep, covered by a sheet of clear glass. This sheet of glass was the largest in Griqualand; originally intended as a display window for a ladies' dress shop on Main Street, it had miraculously survived the long wagon journey from the coast – and was now probably one of the most cherished items in Kimberley. Without it the sport would die, and Sunday afternoons would be tedium indeed.

The sheet of glass and the wooden arena were owned by a onetime kopje-walloper who had found there was more money in spiders than in diamonds. Ownership of the glass gave him a monopoly of the game and allowed him to charge a cruel entrance fee, and take a lion's share of the winnings.

Half a dozen wagons had been drawn up in a square around the arena to make grandstand accommodation for the crowds. The canteens around the square provided *al fresco* service, their waiters staggering under trays laden with foaming schooners of beer to quench the raging thirsts that men had built up during a week in the pit.

The female population had doubled and re-doubled since Kimberley had become part of the Empire, and the ladies used the occasion to show off a pretty hat and a nicely sculptured ankle. Their delighted squeals of horror when the fighting spiders were released into the arena added to the feverish air of excitement.

In one of the alleys that led into the square, Ralph and his Matabele were huddled in solemn discussion.

'I do not know what that name means,' Bazo was protesting to Ralph.

'It is the name of a dangerous woman, who danced so beautifully that when she asked for it the king cut off a man's head and gave it to her.'

They all looked impressed. It was the kind of story which appealed to a Matabele.

'What is the name again?'Bazo asked thoughtfully.

'Salome –'

'But why cannot she fight under her real name?' Bazo glanced down at the basket under his arm. 'Why must we change Inkosikazi's name for this fight? It is not a good omen.'

Ralph looked exasperated. 'If we use that name they will know it is the same Inkosikazi who has already killed five times. If we call her Salome, why, one spider looks like another. They will not recognize her. They will believe her to be unblooded, and we shall win more money.'

'That is a good reason,' Kamuza cut in, and Bazo ignored him.

'Who found this name?' Bazo insisted.

'Jordie. He found it in the big book.' That decided it. Bazo had vast respect for the lovely gentle boy and his knowledge of books.

'Salome.' He nodded. 'It is agreed, but only for today.'

'Good.' Ralph rubbed his palms together briskly. 'Now where is the money?' And they all looked to Kamuza. He was the treasurer of the group. In their years of unbroken labour the gang of young Matabele had accumulated a hoard of gold and silver coin, for to their wages they had added the bounty on 'pickups'. Then of course there were the considerable winnings from Inkosikazi's previous bouts.

Kamuza kept this treasure buried under the floor of the communal hut, but he had reluctantly exhumed part of it the evening before, and now he produced a soft furry white bag, made from tanned scrotal skin of a springbuck ram, and reluctantly counted out coins into Ralph's hand. No white bookmaker would accept a wager from a black man, so Ralph was frontman for the Matabele syndicate.

'Make a book,' Kamuza said, and Ralph scribbled a receipt for sixteen sovereigns on a page of his notebook, tore it out and handed it to Kamuza, who examined it minutely. He trusted Ralph without question. He could not read, but the rituals of European commerce fascinated Kamuza and he had seen white men passing slips of paper whenever they exchanged coin.

'Good.' He tucked the receipt into the springbuck-skin wallet.

'I have four gold queens of my own.' Ralph displayed his life savings. 'I will pay my share of the entrance fee and bet the rest of it.'

'May the gods go with us all, Henshaw,' said Bazo, and handed Ralph the precious little basket.

Ralph adjusted his cap to an angle that would hide as much of his face as possible. It was unlikely that his father would be amongst the crowd, and if he was, the cap would hardly disguise his firstborn sufficiently for him not to be recognized – so the gesture was instinctive, as was his fear of his father's wrath.

'I will wait here for the money,' Kamuza told him.

'If she wins,' Ralph agreed.

'She will win,' said Bazo darkly. 'Would that I could serve her with my own hands.'

There was no law to prevent a black man entering a fancy in the lists, but none of them had ever done so. The niceties of this complex society were unwritten but understood by all.

Ralph slipped out of the alley and mingled with the crowd, working his way through the press until he was on the outskirts of the group of handlers, each of them with his woven basket, as they waited to enter their fancy.

'Ah, young Ballantyne.' Chaim Cohen looked up from his register, the wire-rimmed spectacles on the end of his nose, sweating jovially in the dust and blazing sun. 'Haven't seen you in some time.'

'Didn't have a fancy, Mr Cohen. Caught a new one now,' Ralph lied glibly.

'What happened to – what did you call her, some kaffir name?'

'She died. Lost a leg and died after her last fight.'

'What is your new lady's name?'

'Salome, sir.'

'Salome it is, then. That will be two pounds, young Ballantyne.' The coins disappeared with uncanny speed into the enlarged pocket that Cohen had sewn into the inside of his long frock coat, and with relief Ralph sidled into the crowd, trying to lose himself until the draw was announced.

He found a place near the tailboard of one of the wagons, where he was partly concealed and from where he could watch the ladies in the crowd. Some of them were young and pretty, and they knew it. Every few minutes one would pass close enough to Ralph for him to hear the frou-frou of her petticoats and to smell her, for the heat brought out the subtle musk of womankind that was emphasized and not concealed by the sweet reek of French perfume. It seemed to catch in Ralph's throat, too poignant to breathe, and there was a hollow aching place at the base of his belly and weird thoughts in his head.

The fruity smell of cognac suddenly blotted out that French perfume and a hoarse voice close to his ear put the imaginings to flight.

'You are fighting a new fancy, I see, young Ballantyne.'

'Yes, sir. That's right, sir, Mr Lennox.'

Mr Barry Lennox was a big man, a brawler with a reputation for quick fists that was respected as far as the river workings. He was a plunger, who had bet a thousand guineas on a single cock fight, and won. That was in the days before civilization had reached the diggings, but now he chanced as much on the spider fights. He was a rich man by the standards of New Rush, for he owned eighteen claims in the No. 4 Roadway block. He had the red-veined cheeks and husky voice of the heavy drinker, but what intrigued Ralph most about this man was that he employed three young women, not one but three women to keep house for him. One was a pretty pug-faced daffodil-yellow Griqua girl, another a bold-eyed Portuguese mulatto from Mozambique, and the third a mulberry black Basuto with haunches on her like a brood mare. Whenever Ralph thought about this dusky trio, which was often, his imagination conjured up a garden of forbidden delights.

Of course, neither Ralph's father nor any other member of the Committee would acknowledge Lennox's existence and cut him elaborately on the street. Lennox's application to join the Kimberley Club had been met with a record-breaking fifty-six black balls. But Ralph removed his cap respectfully now, as Lennox asked throatily:

'What happened to Inkosikazi? I made a bundle on her.'

'She died, Mr Lennox. Old age, I suppose.'

'Baboon spiders live nearly twenty years and more,' Lennox grunted. 'Let's have a look at your new lady.'

'I don't like to unsettle her – not just before a bout, sir.'

'Does your daddy know where you spend your Sunday afternoons, young Ballantyne?'

'All right, sir.' Ralph capitulated swiftly and lifted the lid of the basket a crack. Lennox cocked a bloodshot but knowledgeable eye at it.

'That looks like a strong left front – new grown.'

'No, sir. Well, it might be. Caught her just the other day. Don't know her history, Mr Lennox.'

'Boy, you wouldn't be running a ringer, would you! 'Fess up now.' Lennox looked sternly into Ralph's eyes, and Ralph dropped them.

'You don't want to go up before the Diggers' Committee, do you? The shame you would bring on your daddy. It might break his heart.'

It might not break Zouga Ballantyne's heart, but it would certainly break Ralph's head.

Miserably Ralph shook his head. 'Very well then, Mr Lennox. It's Inkosikazi, she grew a new leg. I thought I'd get better odds – but, I'll withdraw her now. I'll go tell Mr Cohen I lied.'

Barry Lennox leaned so close that his lips touched Ralph's ear and the smell of fine old cognac on his breath almost overpowered him.

'You don't do anything so stupid, Ralph, my lad. You fight your fancy, and if she wins there will be a special treat for you. That's a promise. Barry Lennox will see you right – and then some. Now, if you will excuse me, I've got some business to attend to.' Lennox twirled his cane and drove a wedge into the crowd with his bow-fronted belly.

Chaim Cohen climbed up onto the disselboom of the nearest wagon to the arena and began chalking up the draw on a green-ruled board, and the bookmakers craned for the matchings and then began calling their odds for each bout.

'Threes on Mr Gladstone in the first.'

'Dreadnought even money. Buttercup fives in the second.'

Ralph waited as bout after bout was drawn, and each time that Inkosikazi's name was omitted his nerves stretched tighter. There were only ten bouts, and Mr Cohen had finished chalking the ninth already.

'Bout No. 10,' he called as he wrote. 'This is a biblical match, gentlemen and ladies, a diamondiferous bout straight out of the Old Testament.' Chaim Cohen used the adjective 'diamondiferous' to describe anything from a thoroughbred horse to a fifteen-year-old whisky. 'A pure diamondiferous match, the one and only, the great and deadly, Goliath!' There was a burst of applause and whistles of approval. Goliath was the champion spider of the diamond fields, with twelve straight kills to her credit. 'Matched against your favourite is a pretty little newcomer, Salome!'

The name was greeted with indifference as the punters scrambled to get money onto the champion.

'I'm giving tens on Salome,' called one desperate bookie as he tried to stem the flow of wagers. They were taking Goliath at odds on, and Ralph shared his distress.

Leaden-footed he traipsed back to the alleyway. Kamuza had heard the draw announced.

'Give us back the sixteen queens,' he greeted Ralph; but the demand stung Bazo:

'Inkosikazi will drink her blood –'

'The other is a giant –'

'Inkosikazi is quick, fast as a mamba, brave as a honey badger.' Bazo chose the most fearless and indomitable fighters of the veld as comparisons for his fancy.

They argued while the sudden roar of voices from the Square signalled the beginning of the first bout, and the squeals of the ladies told that the kill had been swiftly made.

They argued fiercely, Bazo becoming so agitated that he could no longer sit still. He leapt up and began to *giya*, the challenge dance of the Matabele warrior preparing for battle.

'Thus Inkosikazi sprang, and thus she drove her assegai into the chest of Nclo,' Bazo shouted, as he imitated the death stroke of his fancy; but the Matabele always found difficulty in pronouncing the letter 'R', and the Roman Emperor's was mutilated in the recounting of the battle.

'You must decide,' Ralph broke in on his heroics, and Bazo abruptly ended his *giya* and looked at Kamuza.

In matters of money Kamuza was without question the leader of the group, just as Bazo was in all else.

'Henshaw,' Kamuza asked gravely. 'Are you risking your four queens against this monster?'

'Inkosikazi is risking her life,' Ralph replied, without hesitation. 'And I am risking my money for her.'

'So be it, then. We will follow you.'

There were only minutes left before the tenth bout of the afternoon. Already Chaim Cohen was upending his schooner of beer and, considerably refreshed, wiping the froth from his whiskers. At any moment he would climb back onto the wagon and call for the handlers to bring their fighters to the arena for the final bout.

Ralph still had five sovereigns to place.

'You said twelves,' he argued desperately with the ferret-eyed bookmaker in the flowing Ascot tie.

'If you are betting your own fancy, then it's tens.'

'That's welshing.'

'Life is all a welsh,' the bookie shrugged. 'Take it or leave it.'

'All right, I'll take it.' Ralph snatched the slip and pushed towards the circle of wagons, and once again found his way blocked by the grand belly of Barry Lennox.

'Are you betting her yourself?'

'With everything I've got, sir.'

'That's all I wanted to know, Ralph me boy.' And he strode to the nearest bookmaker, pulling his purse from his hip pocket just as Chaim Cohen crowed from his perch on the wagon.

'Lovely ladies and sporting gentlemen! The tenth and final bout of the day! The mighty Goliath meets the dancing lady Salome!'

Goliath crabbed into the glass-topped arena. Her four pairs of legs undulated sinuously so that her progress was stately and deliberate.

She was a huge beast, newly moulted, for her chintyl armoured covering was a lustrous coppery colour and the long hairs that covered her abdomen and legs were burnished like newly spun gold wire. She left a double necklace of tiny stippled footprints in the swept sand of the arena floor, and the crowd cheered her. Their inhibitions had long been lost in the primeval conflicts in the little arena, and most of them had been drinking since noon: there was a peculiar ring of ferocity and cruelty in their voices.

'Kill her!' screamed a pretty blond girl with gold ringlets and flowers in her hat. 'Rip her to pieces!' Her face flushed feverishly and her eyes were glittering.

'All right, Mr Ballantyne. Put your fancy in,' Chaim Cohen commanded, raising his voice to be heard above the uproar. But Ralph delayed a few seconds longer, letting the other spider complete its circuit and face away from his side of the cage. Then he lifted the sliding door and tapped the basket to rouse Inkosikazi.

She crawled forward cautiously, lifting her abdomen clear of the sand, stepping on the spiked toes of her ranked legs, and then freezing as she saw her adversary across the cage. Her multiple jewelled eyes were sparkling like chips of black diamond.

Goliath sensed her presence and leaped high, turned in the air and landed facing her. The two spiders confronted each other across the smoothly swept floor of white river sand – and only now was the difference in their sizes apparent. Goliath was enormous, swelling in rage, the long silken mane of burnished hair rising like the quills of a porcupine to enhance her size as she began to dance her challenge to her smaller adversary.

Immediately Inkosikazi replied to the challenge, raising and lowering her abdomen in time to the rhythmic swaying of her carapace, lifting her legs in pairs and weaving them with an awful grace, like the many-armed Hindu god, Shiva.

An utter silence had fallen on the watchers as they strained to catch every nuance of this stylized dance of death – and then a lust-choked roar burst from them as Goliath sprang.

She exploded into flight, soaring with her talons fully extended, clearing the length of the arena without effort and landing precisely where Inkosikazi had stood a thousandth part of a second before. Inkosikazi had evaded that flashing leap with a bouncing side jump of her own, and now she faced the huge enraged creature and danced her defiance.

The dazzling agility of these great spiders was the essential attraction that drew such a following of eager spectators. There was no preliminary bracing or crouching to herald one of those swallowlight bounds. The spiders fired themselves like bullets, suddenly and unerringly at their rival, and reacted as swiftly to the counter-attack. Then between each onslaught that mesmeric and chilling dance resumed.

'Jee! Jee!' The tightly drawn silence was interrupted by the chilling, killing cry of a Matabele warrior.

'Jee! Jee!' The deep hissing chorus that had carried a black wave of naked bodies across a continent, a wave crested by the plumes of the war bonnets and lit by the glitter of the bright silver assegais.

Bazo had not been able to skulk in the alley beyond the square. He had edged forward into the crowd until he reached the wagons, but as the conflict mounted, so had his warrior passions. He thrust forward through the packed ranks and now he was in the forefront, and he could not contain himself further.

'Jee! Jee!' He hissed his battle cry, and Ralph found himself echoing it.

Inkosikazi was fighting instinctively, reacting mindlessly to the presence of another female in deadly sexual rivalry. It was the waving arms of the gigantic female across the cage which infuriated her, and it was mere coincidence that her first attacking leap was synchronized with the war chant.

Twice she launched herself, and twice Goliath gave her ground. and then on her third leap Inkosikazi vaulted too high and touched the glass roof of the arena. The impact broke the perfect parabola of her flight, and she fell short and out of balance, scrabbling frantically in the fine white sand as Goliath saw her chance and flew in for the kill.

The men howled with cruel glee, the women trilled with delicious horror as the two huge furry bodies came together chest to chest and entangled each other's limbs in a hideous octopus embrace.

The impetus of Goliath's leap sent them rolling across the arena like an india-rubber ball, until they struck the far wall and wrestled in a flurry of serpentine limbs. Both their long hooked fangs were fully erect, and they slashed at each other with their hairy wolf mouths, the needle points of the fangs striking the impenetrable shiny armour of carapace and jointed legs, glancing off the polished surface and leaving minute dribbles of colourless honey-thick venom on each other's chests.

Instinctively they were holding their vulnerable abdomens clear, while straining to tear from the embrace for a chance to strike into the soft skin of the other. They came up on their hind legs and wrestled together, and immediately Goliath's weight began to take effect.

With a sharp crackling sound, like a walnut in the jaw of a silver nutcracker, one of Inkosikazi's legs was torn bodily from the joint of her carapace, and she jerked convulsively, contracting her soft belly in a dreadful spasm.

'Kill her! Rip her to pieces!' screamed the pretty blond girl, and tore at her perfumed silk handkerchief, shredding it between her fingers. Her face was swollen and inflamed and her eyes wild.

Goliath shifted the grip of her many legs, groping for a soft spot into which to plunge the jerking red fang.

'Jee! Jee!' sang Bazo, his eyes bloodshot with passion, and Inkosikazi strained with all her remaining legs to break the grip that was slowly smothering her under the huge hairy body. Again there was that grisly crackling, one of her front legs broke off in a little spurt of body juices, and instinctively Goliath lifted the severed limb to her mouth.

The distraction was sufficient, and Inkosikazi tore herself free and bounded halfway across the arena, landing in an unbalanced sprawl, her body fluids oozing from the leg stumps, but gathering herself swiftly. Goliath was still worrying the severed legs, the smell of her opponent's blood enrapturing her so that she mouthed the twitching limbs, striking at them with her fang, her full attention upon them – and Inkosikazi rebounded like a rubber ball thrown against a brick wall.

She dropped lightly onto Goliath's broad furry back, locked in with her remaining legs, and then plunged the long blood-red fang into Goliath's abdomen, her head pumping as she forced a steady gush of poison into the bloated body.

Goliath's body arched, her long jointed legs straightened into an agonized rictus, and the balloon of her belly spasmed and convulsed as the venom pulsed into her. Crouched upon her back like some grotesque incubus, Inkosikazi squirted in the fatal fluid until the bigger creature's limbs wilted and crumpled under her and her belly sagged gradually to the white sand of the arena.

In the roaring consternation of disappointed punters and squeaks of women, both loathing and gloating at the same time, Ralph and Bazo rushed together and embraced with whoops of triumph. In the glassed arena Inkosikazi slowly withdrew the long curved hypodermic fang. Her venom not only paralysed and killed but also liquefied the body tissue of her prey. Her jaws opened and then locked into the jelly-soft passive body beneath her, and her own abdomen began to swell and subside as she sucked her vanquished adversary's fluids from her – while she still lived.

Ralph broke from the embrace of Bazo's thickly muscled arms.

'Get her out of the cage,' he told him. 'I'll go and get the money.'

Bazo bore the basket high on the return from the conflict. His bare-chested Matabele ran behind him, in that floating stylized gait, half dance, half trot, and they brandished their fighting sticks and sang the praise song which Kamuza had composed in Inkosikazi's honour:

'See with your thousand eyes,
Hold hard with many arms of steel,
Kiss with your long red assegai,
Taste the blood, is it not richer
than the milk of Mzilikazi's herds?
Taste the blood, is it not sweeter
than the wild honey in the comb?
Bayete! Bayete!
Royal greetings, Black Queen,
Loyal greetings, Great Queen.'

Ralph dearly wanted to run with them in that triumphant procession, but he knew what his father would say if he heard that his son had joined such a barbaric display through the dusty streets, past the very portals of the Kimberley Club where Zouga Ballantyne was almost certainly passing his Sunday afternoon.

Ralph followed them in a fashion that better suited Zouga's idea of how a young English gentleman should comport himself, but his cap was on the back of his head, his hands were thrust deeply into pockets jingling the gold coin, and there was a beatific grin on his face. The smile broadened further as a familiar big-gutted figure rolled out through the doors of Diamond Lil's canteen.

'Mr Ballantyne,' bellowed Barry Lennox across the street. 'Mr Ballantyne, will you do me the very great honour of taking a glass with me?'

'Enchanted indeed, sir.' Ralph felt cocky enough to reply facetiously, and Lennox guffawed and flung an arm around Ralph's shoulders and led him into the canteen.

Ralph looked about him quickly; it was the first time he had ever entered a place such as this. He hoped to see naked women dancing on the tables and gamblers in flowered waistcoats fanning open hands full of aces and kings and sweeping up pots of gold sovereigns.

The only partially nude figure was that of Charlie, the undertaker, snoring on the sawdust floor with his shirt open to his hairy belly button; and the gamblers were all familiar faces, men beside whom Ralph worked every day on the stagings or in the pit. They were dressed in their work clothes and the cards were dog-eared and greasy and the pot was a small pile of copper and worn silver.

'Ralph,' said one of them, looking up. 'Your daddy know where you are?'

'Does yours?' Ralph shot back, the cockiness unabated. 'And do you know *who* he is?'

There was a hoot of laughter from the others, and the man grinned good-naturedly. 'Damn me, but the boy has a sharp enough tongue.'

'Give my sporting friend a beer,' Lennox told the barman, and he looked dubious.

'How old is your sporting friend?'

'He will be forty years old on one of his future birthdays. However, sir, I consider that question to be a direct slur on my sporting friend's honour. I have broken jaws that asked less impertinent questions.'

'Two beers coming up, Mr Lennox.'

Barry Lennox and Ralph saluted each other with the schooners, and Lennox gave them a toast.

'To a lady of our mutual acquaintance, bless her bright eyes and all her lovely legs.'

The beer was faintly warm and tasted like soap and quinine, but Ralph forced down a mouthful and smacked his lips appreciatively. He would have much preferred a cool green bottle of ginger beer with a pop up marble in the neck.

'Cigar?' Lennox opened his silver case, and Ralph hesitated only a moment, then selected one of the thick Havanas and bit off the end in a faithful imitation of Zouga Ballantyne.

He sucked from the Vesta that Lennox held for him, and cautiously held the smoke in his mouth. That was the last draw he took, and after that he used the cigar like a conductor's baton, waving it airily and creating about himself a cloud of perfumed blue without actually touching it to his lips again. Somehow he was able to impart the impression of swagger while standing at the rough-sawn bar counter.

'– I mean, anybody knows the classic Zulu battle tactics. They wait for bad ground and thick bush, there are few soldiers who use cover and defilade the way they do.' Ralph sipped his beer and waved his cigar as he discussed Lord Chelmsford's current campaign against the Zulu King Cetewayo. The views he was expressing were those of Zouga Ballantyne, learned by heart and unadulterated; so though his listeners winked and nudged at his pretensions, they could not fault his logic. 'The device of decoying Chelmsford's flying column out of the camp and then doubling back to destroy the base with its depleted defences is as old as Chaka Zulu himself. Chelmsford was at fault, there, no doubt on it.'

There was a gloomy shaking of heads, as there always was when anyone mentioned the catastrophic reversal of British arms that Chelmsford had been manoeuvred into at the Hill of the Little Hand, Isandhlwana, across the Buffalo River in Zululand.

The corpses of seven hundred British dead, militia and regular regiments, had already lain for six months on the bleak grassland below the little hill. Lord Chelmsford had abandoned the field, and his dead lay where they had fallen, their bellies ripped open by Zulu assegais to allow their souls to escape, the litter of wagons and broken equipment scattered about them, their flesh taken off the bone by vulture and jackal and hyena.

The thought of leaving British soldiers unburied on the battlefield seemed to threaten the very foundation of the greatest empire the world had ever known.

'Chelmsford must retake the field,' said one of the men at the bar.

'No, sir,' Ralph shook his head firmly. 'That will be inviting another disaster for a sentimental gesture.'

'What do you propose, Mr Ballantyne?' the man asked sarcastically.

'A page from the Boer book.' Ralph had an audience of grown men listening to him – perhaps not with respect, but at least with attention. This was heady stuff, even though the ideas were his father's, and Ralph threw in an oath. 'By God, those fellows know how to fight the tribes. Mounted men as a screen around a column of wagons that can be thrown into laager within minutes. Go for the heart of the Zulu nation – their cattle herds – pull the impis into the open, make them come in across good shooting ground against the laagered wagons –' Ralph did not finish his plan of battle; abruptly he lost his sequence of ideas and began to stutter like an idiot, a blush darkening his tanned, handsome young face.

Barry Lennox followed the direction of Ralph's gaze, and then he grinned delightedly.

Diamond Lil had entered the canteen through the rear door. It was six o'clock in the evening and an hour before she had risen, stretching and yawning like a sleepy leopard, from the brass bed in the darkened room behind the canteen.

A servant had filled the enamelled hip bath with buckets of steaming water, and Lil had poured in a vial of perfume before stepping into the bath and settling luxuriously into the fragrant water, shouting for her canteen manager.

She listened attentively, a small frown cracking the perfect pale skin of her forehead, as he recited the figures of the previous night's take, his eyes averted from the white skin of her shoulders and the tight pink-tipped bosom that peeked through the hot suds. Then she had dismissed him with a wave of her hand and stepped naked from the bath, glowing pinkly from the hot water, her steam-damp hair dangling down the sleek white body. She poured a little gin into a coloured Venetian glass and sipped it neat as she started the powdering and the painting, rolling her eyes at herself in the mirror, practising her professional smile with the tiny diamond twinkling in the centre of the wide display of white teeth, then, at last, considering herself levelly and appraisingly.

She was twenty-three years old, and she had come a long hard way from the house in Mayfair where Madame Hortense had sold her maidenhood to an elderly Whig minister of state for one hundred guineas. She had been thirteen years old then, only ten years ago, but it seemed like a dozen lifetimes.

The house in Mayfair was truly the only home she had ever known, and she often thought back with nostalgia to those days. Madame Hortense had treated her more like a daughter than a house girl. There was always a pretty bonnet or a new dress on her birthday and at Christmas, and she had had special privileges. Lil would ever be grateful for what she learned about men and money and power from Hortense.

Then one Saturday evening a half dozen young officers from a famous cavalry regiment, celebrating their orders for foreign service, had visited the house in Mayfair. Amongst them was a young captain, dashing, rich and beautiful; he saw Lil across the salon the moment he entered. Ten days later Lil had sailed with him for India on the Peninsular and Orient mailship, while Madame Hortense wept on the quay and waved until the ship cleared the pool of London and disappeared beyond the first bend of the river. Forty days later Lil found herself abandoned by her protector.

From an upper window of the Mount Nelson Hotel in Cape Town she watched her cavalry captain's ship clear Table Bay for Calcutta, her sorrow at parting alleviated by the luxurious surroundings in which her protector had left her. Lil shrugged off her grief, drank a glass of gin, bathed and re-painted her face, then sent for the manager.

'I cannot pay my bill,' she told him and, taking his hand, led him unprotestingly into the bedroom of her suite.

'Madame, may I give you some advice?' he asked a little later as he retied his Ascot and shrugged into his waistcoat.

'Good advice is always welcome, sir.'

'There is a place called New Rush five hundred miles north of here and there are five thousand diggers there, each with a pocket full of diamonds.'

Now Lil entered her canteen. It was still early for a Sunday. It was one of the things she had learned from Madame Hortense, always be there long before you are expected. It keeps clients satisfied and employees honest.

Quickly she checked her clientele. It was the usual Sunday afternoon crowd. It would be better soon. She stooped and counted the bottles under the bar counter, examining the wax seals to make certain they had not been tampered with.

'Never be greedy, darling,' Hortense had taught her. 'Water the beer, they expect that, but keep good whisky.'

She straightened and opened the huge ornate cash register with a chime of bells, making certain that it flagged the correct price, and then touched the line of gold sovereigns in their special slotted drawer. The metal had a marvellous feel under her fingertips, and she picked up a coin as though merely to feel the weight and take pleasure from it. Gold was the only thing in all the world she trusted. Her barman was watching her in the mirror as he swabbed the counter top; she pretended to replace the sovereign in its slot, letting it clink and then palmed it smoothly and closed the drawer of the register. The barman was new. It would be interesting to see if he covered the shortage or reported it, little things like that had made her rich at the age of twenty-three.

She glanced up into the mirror, once again appraising her own face and shoulders in the less flattering sunlight that streamed into the canteen. Her eyes were sharp as a stropped razor, but the skin around them was clear and fresh as rose petals without the first sign of wrinkling.

'You will wear well, my dear,' Hortense had told her, 'if you use the gin and don't let it use you.' She had been right, Lil decided. She looked as she had when she was sixteen years old.

She shifted her gaze from her own face, and swept the canteen. The mirror was imperfect, and the silvering was beginning to go in dark spots, slightly distorting the young face that was watching her intently. Her gaze flicked over it, and then came back.

The boy was blushing as he studied her avidly, that was the only thing that had caught her attention. Now when she looked at him again she realized he was probably under-age, and she already had trouble with the Committee. He wore a boy's cloth cap on the back of his head and he was very obviously still growing, his Norfolk jacket straining around the sturdy arms and across the shoulders.

Too young and certainly penniless. She had to get him out fast, and she turned quickly, her fists on her hips, her blond head cocked aggressively.

'Good afternoon, Miss Lil.' Ralph was stunned by his own audacity at addressing this heavenly presence directly. 'I was about to buy my friends a round of drinks. We should be honoured if you would take a glass with us, ma'am.' Ralph slapped the counter with a sovereign, and Lil uncocked her head and raised one hand from her hip to touch her hair.

'I like a big spending gent.' She flashed the little diamond in her front tooth at him and nodded to the barman. He would pour from her special bottle labelled Booth's Gin but filled with rain water from the galvanized tank beside the backdoor.

Suddenly she realized that the boy was bonny, with a strong jaw and good white teeth. Now that his blush had subsided, his skin was clear and smooth as her own, and his eyes a penetrating emerald green. And the eagerness and freshness that he exuded was so different from that of the hairy diggers, caked with red dirt and smelling like goats, that formed her usual clientele.

Let the boy pay for his round of drinks, and there would be time to get rid of him after that. In the meantime his transparent adoration was amusing and flattering.

'Lil, me darling.' Barry Lennox leaned across the counter and she did not flinch from his breath. 'Give me your pearl-like little ear.'

Smiling her bright smile she held her ear to his lips, and cupped her hand in an exaggerated pantomime of secrecy.

'Are you working tonight, Lil?'

'I'm always ready for a quick rattle of the dice with you, my sweet. You want to go right now or finish your drink?'

'No, darling, not me. How would you like to be first to put the saddle on an unbroken colt?'

Her eyes flicked to Ralph's face again, and her hard bright smile softened thoughtfully. He was a lovely boy, and for the first time since her cavalryman had left her in Cape Town she felt the prickle of her loins and bitter sweet catch in her throat, so that she did not trust her voice entirely.

'It's still early, Lil, and business isn't good this time on Sunday, Lil dearie.' Barry Lennox wheedled and chuckled beerily at the same time. 'He is a pretty boy, and I should charge you for the pleasure, but I'll just let you make me a special price instead.'

Lil's throat cleared instantly and the languid expression disappeared. Her reply was crisp.

'I'll not charge you school fees, Barry Lennox, just the usual ten guineas.'

Lennox shook his head. 'You are a hard one, Lil. I'll send him to you, love. But just one thing, make it good, make it something that he will remember if he lives a hundred years.'

'I don't teach you to dig diamonds, Barry Lennox,' she said, and without looking back swept from the canteen. They heard the door of her bedroom bang, and Ralph stared after her in dismay – but Barry Lennox put an arm around his shoulders and as he talked quietly, punctuating each sentence with a throaty lewd chuckle, all the colour fled from Ralph's face.

*

'Come in.' Her voice reminded Ralph of the gentle contented cooing that the plump wild pigeons made at sunset in the top branch of the camel-thorn tree above Zouga's camp.

With his hand on the brass doorknob, he lifted his feet one at a time and polished the toe-cap of his boots against the back of his trouser leg. He had doused his head under the tap of the rainwater tank and combed his hair while it was still wet, sleeking it away from his forehead, and the droplets had run down his neck, turning the dust on his darned shirt collar into damp red mud.

He glanced down at his hand on the doorknob, saw the black rinds under his finger nails and lifted it quickly to his mouth, trying desperately to pick out the dirt with his eye tooth.

'Come in!' The command was repeated; but this time there was no cooing of pigeons, but a sharp imperious command, and Ralph lunged for the door handle. There was no resistance, the door flew open, and Ralph went with it. He entered Diamond Lil's boudoir like a cavalry charge, tripped on the frayed edge of a cheap oriental carpet and sprawled headlong across the brass bed.

There was a Chinese lacquer screen across one corner of the small violently furnished room, and over the top of it rose Diamond Lil's magnificently sculptured blond coiffure.

'Oh,' she said sweetly, the sharp slanted eyes widening with amusement. 'Are you going to start without me then, darling?'

Ralph scrambled untidily to his feet like a puppy with oversized paws and stood to attention in the middle of the floor, holding his cloth cap to his stomach with both hands.

From behind the screen came the most evocative sounds he had ever heard. The rustle of lace and cloth, the clink of china and the gurgle of water poured from a jug. The lacquer screen was ornamented with oriental figures, women bathing in a willow-screened pool with a waterfall in the background. The women were all naked, and the artist had lingered on their physical charms. Ralph felt his ears and neck heating again – and hated himself for it.

He wished he had kept the cigar, as a proof of his manhood. He wished that he had worn a fresh shirt, he wished – but then there was no further time for wishing.

Lil stepped out from behind the screen. She was barefooted,

and her toes were chubby and rosy pink like those of a little girl.

'I have seen you on the street, Mr Ballantyne,' Lil told him quietly. 'And I have admired your manly disposition. I am so glad we have had an opportunity to meet.'

The words worked a miracle. Ralph felt himself growing in stature, the trembling in his legs stilled and they felt strong and sure under him.

'Do you like my robe?' Lil asked, and took the long skirts in her hands, turning to make them flare.

Ralph nodded dumbly, his new-found strength had not yet reached his tongue, but his eyes were wide and feverish.

She came to him and without her heels she stood only as high as his shoulder. 'Let me help you with your coat.' And when he was in his shirtsleeves, she said, 'Come and sit on the sofa.' She took his hand and led him across the room.

'Do you like me, Mr Ballantyne?'

At last he could speak, 'Oh yes. Oh yes!'

'May I call you Ralph? I feel I know you so well.'

Very early one January morning long ago she had left the Mayfair house, and reached the deserted park where it had snowed during the night. The snow lay white and smooth and unmarked. She left the gravelled path, and the snow crumbled like sugar under her feet. When she looked back her tiny footprints were strung out across the unblemished snow, as though she were the first and only woman in the world. It gave her an extraordinary feeling of her own importance. Now as she lay on the wide bedstead beside the lad, she experienced that same feeling.

He was not a lad, but she thought of him as that. His body was fully matured, but his innocence made him as vulnerable as an unweaned infant, and his body was like the snow which no other feet had trodden.

The sun had stained his throat in a deep V down onto his chest, but the skin of his chest and flat belly were the lustrous white of watered marble or of freshly fallen snow. She touched it with her lips and when his little dusty rose nipples puckered and started her own skin crawling deliciously, she took his hands. His palms were rough and callused from work on the stagings and in the pit. The fingernails were torn and cracked, with ingrained dirt beneath them. But it was honest dirt, and the hands were shapely, long and graceful. She had learned to judge men by the shape of their hands, and now she lifted Ralph's to her lips and kissed them lightly, watching his eyes as she did so.

Then slowly she took his hands down and cupped them over her own soft breasts. She felt the rough skin rasp her own nipples, and they popped out like full moons, pale pink and tense.

'You like that, Ralph?'

She asked that same question five times, and the last time was when the room was almost dark and he was convulsed and shaking within the circle of her arms and her pliant thighs, drenched with his own sweet young sweat, and breathing in little choking sobs.

'You like that, Ralph?' And his reply was broken and ragged:

'Oh yes. Oh yes, Miss Lil.'

Suddenly she was sad. The snow was trodden, the magic was passing, just as the power she had wielded was transitory.

She had not cried in ten long hard years, not since that first evening in the Mayfair house, but now she was shocked to find the constriction in her throat and the burning behind her eyes.

'What is there to cry for?' she wondered desolately. 'It's far too late for tears.'

She rolled Ralph expertly onto his back, his body limp and unresisting – and for a moment she stared at him hatefully. He had touched something in her which had hurt unbearably. Then the hating passed and there was only the sadness.

She kissed him once more, softly and regretfully.

'You must go now, Ralph,' she said.

He lingered at the door, with his jacket over his arm and his cap in his hand.

'I will come and see you again, Lilly.'

She formed a bow with her lips and painted them with quick deft strokes before she replied, but while she worked she was watching him in the mirror.

He was altered already, she saw. He stood four-square, his shoulders wide and his neat young head proud on the column of his sun-tanned neck. The sweet diffidence was gone, the appealing shyness evaporated. An hour before he would have said:

'Please can I come and see you again, Miss Lil.'

She smiled at him in the mirror, that bright burnished smile, and the diamond in her tooth winked sardonically.

'You come any time, dearie – any time you have saved ten guineas.'

It was only surprising that the full report of Ralph's foray into the lilac fields of Venus took so long to reach Zouga, for Barry Lennox had repeated the story with zest and embroidery to anyone who would listen, and the chaff and banter had flown like a Kalahari dust-storm every evening in Diamond Lil's canteen.

'Gentlemen, you are speaking about the eldest son of one of the pillars of Kimberley Society,' Lil admonished them saucily. 'Remember that Major Ballantyne is not only a member of the Kimberley Club, but a respected ornament of the Diggers' Committee.' She knew that one of them would soon succumb to the temptation to take the story to Zouga Ballantyne. 'I would love to hear what that cold-bellied, stuck-up prig will say when he hears,' she told herself secretly. 'Even the iced water in his veins will boil.'

'Whores and whore masters,' said Zouga. He stood on the wide verandah, in the shade of the thatched roof which had replaced the original tent of the first camp.

Ralph stood below him in the sunlight, blinking up at his father.

'Perhaps you have no respect for your family, for the name of Ballantyne – but do you have none for yourself and for your own body?'

Zouga was barring the front door to the cottage of raw unbaked brick. He was bare-headed, so that his thick dark gold hair shone like a war helmet and his neatly-cropped beard emphasized the jut of his heavy jaw, and the long black tapered hippohide kurbash whip hung from his right hand, touching the floor at the toe of his riding boot.

'Do you have an answer?' Zouga's tone was quiet, and deadly cold.

Ralph was still dusty as a miller from the pit. The dust was thick and red in his hair, and outlined the curl of his nostrils and ran like tears from the corners of his eyes. He wiped his forehead on his shirtsleeve, an excuse to break the gaze of his father's eyes, and then examined the muddy smear with attention.

'Answer me,' Zouga's voice did not alter. 'Give me a reason – just one reason why I should not throw you out of this home – for ever.'

Jordan could bear it no longer, the thought of losing Ralph overcame his terror of his father's wrath.

He ran down the length of the verandah, and seized the arm that held the whip.

'Papa! Please, Papa – don't send him away.'

Without glancing at Jordan, Zouga lashed out and the blow caught Jordan across the chest and hurled him back against the verandah wall.

'Jordie did nothing,' said Ralph, as quietly as his father had spoken.

'Oh, you do have a tongue?' Zouga asked.

'Get out of it, Jordie,' Ralph ordered. 'This is not your business.'

'Stay where you are, Jordan.' Zouga still did not look at him, his gaze was riveted on Ralph's face. 'Stay here and learn about whores and the kind of men who lust after them.'

Jordan was stricken, his face like last night's camp-fire ashes, his lips dry and white as bone. He knew what they were talking about – for he had listened while Bazo and Ralph wove their fantasies aloud, and with his interest piqued, he had questioned Jan Cheroot furtively – and the replies had disgusted and terrified him.

'Not like animals, Jan Cheroot, surely not like dogs or goats.'

Jordan's questions to Jan Cheroot had been generalized – men and women, not any person he knew or loved or respected. It had taken him days fully to appreciate Jan Cheroot's reply, and then the terrible realization had struck – all men and women, his father who epitomized for him all that was noble and strong and right, his mother, that sweet and gentle being who was already a fading wraithlike memory – not them, surely not them.

He had been physically sickened, vomiting and wracked by excruciating bowel cramps so that Zouga had dosed him with sulphur and treacle molasses.

Now they were talking about that thing, that thing so dreadful that he had tried to purge his memory of it. Now the two most important people in his world were talking about it openly, using words he had only seen in print and which had even then shamed him. They were mouthing those words and the air was full of shame and hatred and revulsion.

'You have wallowed like a pig where a thousand other pigs have wallowed before you, in the foetid cesspool between that scarlet whore's thighs.'

Jordan crept away along the wall, and reached the corner of the stoep. He could go no further.

'If you were not ashamed to muck in that trough, did you not give a thought to what those other rutting boars had left there for you?'

His father's words conjured up vivid images in Jordan's mind. His stomach heaved, and he covered his mouth with his hand.

'The sickness a harlot carries there is the curse of God upon venery and lust. If you could only see them in the pox hospital at Greenwich, raving idiots with their brains eaten half away by the disease, drooling from empty mouths, their teeth rotted out, their noses fallen into black festering holes, blind eyes rolling in their crazed skulls –'

Jordan doubled over, and sicked up on his own rawhide boots.

'Stop it,' said Ralph. 'You have made Jordie sick.'

'I have made him sick?' Zouga asked quietly. 'It is you who would make any decent person sick.'

Zouga came down the steps into the dusty yard, and he swung the whip, cutting the air with it, across and back and the lash fluted sharply.

Ralph stood his ground, and now his chin was up defiantly.

'If you take that whip to me, Papa – I shall defend myself.'

'You challenge me,' Zouga stopped.

'You only use a whip on an animal.'

'Yes,' Zouga nodded. 'An animal – that's why I take it to you.'

'Papa, I warn you.'

Gravely Zouga inclined his head and considered the young man before him. 'Very well. You claim to be a man, make good that claim.' Zouga tossed the hippohide whip casually onto the verandah, and then turned back to his son.

Ralph was prepared, his weight balanced on the balls of his feet, although his hands were held low before him, they were balled into fists.

He never saw it. For a moment he thought that someone else

had used a club on him from behind. The crack of it seemed to explode under the dome of his skull. He reeled backwards, his nose felt numb and at the same time swollen horribly. There was a tickling warmth on his upper lip and dumbly he licked it. It tasted of coppery salt, and he wiped at it with the back of his hand and then stared at the smear of blood on the back of his wrist.

His rage came on him with startling ferocity, as though a beast had pounced upon his back, a black beast that goaded him with its claws. He heard the beast growl in his ears, not recognizing his own voice, and then he rushed forward.

His father's face was in front of him, handsome, grave and cold, and he swung his fist at it with all his strength, wanting to feel the flesh crush under his knuckles, the gristle of that arrogant beaked nose break and crackle, the teeth snap out of that unforgiving mouth.

His fist spun through air, meeting no check, swinging high about the level of his own head, and the blow died there, the sinews of his shoulder wrenched by the unexpected travel of his arm.

Again that burst of sound in his skull, his teeth jarring, his head snapping back, his vision starring momentarily into pin-points of light and areas of deep echoing black, and then clearing again so that his father's face floated back towards him.

Until that instant the only feelings he had ever had for Zouga were respect and fear and a weighty monumental love, but suddenly from some deep place in his soul rose a raging unholy hatred.

He hated him for a hundred humiliations and punishments, he hated him for the checks and frustrations with which be filled each precious day of Ralph's life, he hated him for the reverence and deep respect in which other men held him, for the example that he knew he would be expected to follow faithfully all his life and doubted that he could. He hated him for the enormous load of duty and devotion he owed him and which he knew he could never discharge. He hated him for the love he had stolen from him, the love his mother had given unstintingly to his father and which he wanted all for himself. He hated him because his mother was dead, and his father had not prevented her going.

But most of all he hated him because he had taken something

which had been wonderful and made it filthy, had taken a magical moment and made him ashamed of it, sick and dirty ashamed.

He rushed back at Zouga, swinging wildly with both fists meeting only air, and the blows that landed on his own head and face sounded as though somebody far away was chopping down a tree with a steel axe.

Zouga fell away neatly before each charge, swaying his head back or to the side, deflecting a blow with his arms, ducking carefully under a flying fist, and counter-punching only with his left hand, flicking it in with deceptive lightness, for at each shot Ralph's head snapped backwards sharply and the blood from his nose and his swollen lips slowly turned his face into a running red mess.

'Stop it, oh please stop it!' Jordan crouched against the verandah wall with the yellow vomit staining his shirt front. 'Please stop it!'

He wanted to cover his face with his hands, to blot out the violence and the blood and the terrible black hatred – but he could not. He was locked in an awful fascination, watching every stinging cruel blow, every droplet of flung blood from his brother's face.

Like a corrida bull Ralph came up short at last, and stood with his feet wide apart, his knees giving like reeds overweighted with dew, trying feebly to shake the blackness from his head and the blood from his eyes, his fists bunched up still but too heavy and weak to lift above his waist, his chest heaving for air, swaying and catching his balance every few seconds with an uncontrolled stagger, peering blindly about him for his tormentor.

'Here,' said Zouga quietly, and Ralph lurched towards the voice and Zouga used his right hand for the first time. He chopped him cleanly under the ear, a short measured blow, and Ralph flopped face forward into the dust and snored into it, blowing little red puffs with each breath.

Jordan flew down the steps and dropped to his knees beside his brother, turning his head to one side so he could breathe freely and dabbing ineffectually at the blood with his fingers.

'Jan Cheroot,' Zouga called. He was breathing deeply but slowly; there was colour in his cheeks above his beard, and he touched a few beads of perspiration on his forehead with the kerchief from around his throat.

'Jan Cheroot!' he called again irritably, and this time the little Hottentot roused himself and hurried down the steps.

'Get a bucket of water,' Zouga told him.

Jan Cheroot dashed the contents of a gallon bucket into Ralph's face, washing away the bloody mask, and Ralph gasped and snorted and tried to crawl to his knees.

Jan Cheroot dropped the bucket and grabbed his arm; Jordan stooped and got his head under Ralph's other armpit and between them they lifted him to his feet.

They were both much smaller than Ralph and he hung between them like a dirty blanket on a washline, with the mixture of water and blood dripping to form pale pink rosettes on his shirt front.

Zouga lit a cheroot, studied the ash to be sure it was drawing evenly, then replaced it between his teeth.

He stepped up to his eldest son. With his thumb he pulled down each lower eyelid in turn and peered into his pupils, then grunted with satisfaction. He studied the cut in Ralph's eyebrow, then took his nose between his fingers and moved it gently from side to side to check it for damage, then finally he pulled back Ralph's lip and inspected his teeth for chips or breakage and stepped back

'Jan Cheroot, take him down to Jameson's surgery. Ask Doc to stitch that eye and give him a handful of mercury pills for the pox.'

Jan Cheroot started to lead Ralph away but Zouga went on, 'Then on your way back stop at Barnato's Gymnasium and sign him up for a course of boxing lessons. He'll have to learn to fight a bit better than that or he's going to get his head beaten in even before he dies of the clap.'

On the way back from Market Square Jan Cheroot and Ralph walked with their heads together, talking seriously.

'Why do you think they call him Bakela, the Fist?' Jan Cheroot asked, and Ralph grimaced painfully.

His face was lumpy and the colour was coming up in his bruises, deep plum and cloudy blue like summer thunderclouds.

The horsehair stitches stuck up stiffly out of his eyebrow and lip, and the cuts were soft-scabbed like cranberry jam.

Jan Cheroot grinned and clucked with sympathy, and then asked the question that had burned his tongue since first he had learned the cause of Zouga's wrath.

'So how did you like your first taste of pink sugar?'

The question stopped Ralph in his tracks while he considered it seriously, then he answered without moving his damaged lip.

'It was bloody marvellous,' he said.

Jan Cheroot giggled and hugged himself with delight. 'Now you listen to me, boy, and you listen good. I love your daddy, we been together so many years I can't count, and when he tells you something you can believe it – nearly every time. But me, I have never in my life passed up a chance for a slice of that warm stuff – never once, old or young or in between, ugly as a monkey or so pretty it would break your heart, whenever it was offered and lots of times when it wasn't, old Jan Cheroot grabbed it, boy.'

'And it never killed you.' Ralph supplied the summation.

'I guess I would have died without it.'

Ralph started walking again. 'I hope Bazo will fight his fancy again next Sunday. I'm going to need ten guineas pretty badly by then.'

The moon was lipping the horizon, putting the stars to pale shame. It was still a few days short of full, but on the stoep of Zouga's cottage it was light enough to read the headlines of a crumpled copy of the *Diamond Fields Advertiser* that lay beside Zouga's empty riempie chair.

The only sounds were the distant baying of a moon-crazy hound, and the flirt of bats' wings as they spun high parabolas in the moonlight or came fluttering in under the overhang of the verandah roof to pick a moth from the air. The front door was stopped wide open to allow the night's cool to penetrate the inner rooms of the cottage. Jordan crept through it timidly.

He was bare-footed, and the old flannel shirt he wore as a nightdress was one of Zouga's cast-offs. The tails flapped around his bare knees as he moved down the verandah and stopped before the tall falcon-headed carving that stood on its pedestal at the end of the covered stoep.

The slanting moonlight lit the graven bird image from the side, leaving half of it in black mysterious shadow.

Jordan stopped before the image. The clay floor was cold on his bare soles, and he shivered not entirely from the cold, and looked about him surreptitiously.

Zouga's camp slept, that deep pre-dawn sleep.

Jordan's curls, bushed wildly from the pillow, sparkled like a halo in the moonlight, and his eyes were in shadow, dark holes like those of a skull. All night he had lain rigid in his narrow bed and listened to his brother's heavy breathing through his swollen nose.

Lack of sleep made Jordan feel light-headed and fey. He opened the little twist of newspaper which he had hidden under his pillow when he went to bed.

It contained half a handful of rice and a thin slice of cold roasted lamb. He laid it at the foot of the soapstone column, and stepped back.

Once more he looked about him to make sure that he was alone and unobserved. Then he sank down to his bare knees with the book held against his chest, and bowed his head.

The book was bound in blue leather with gold leaf titling on its spine: *Religions of the American Indians.*

'I greet you, Panes,' Jordan whispered, his swollen eyelids tightly closed.

'The Indians of California, the Acagchemem tribe adore the great buzzard Panes.' The book Jordan held to his breast had become far and away the most precious of all his possessions. He did not like to remember how he had obtained it. It was the only thing he had ever stolen in his life, but he had been forgiven for that sin. He had prayed to the goddess and been forgiven.

'The Panes was a woman, a young and beautiful woman, who had run off into the mountains and been changed into a bird by the god Chinigchinich.'

Jordan knew with all his being whom this description depicted. His mother had been young and beautiful, and she had run away to the black mountain of Death without him.

Now he opened the book and bowed his head over it. It was not light enough to read the fine print of the text, but Jordan knew the invocation to the goddess by heart.

'Why did you run away?' he whispered. 'You would have been better with us. Are we not the ones who love you? It was better that you stayed, for now you are Panes. If we make you a sacrifice of rice and meat, will you not come back to us? See the sacrifice we set for you, great Panes.'

The morning wind stirred, and Jordan heard the branch of the camel-thorn scrape upon the roof before the wind touched him. It was a warm, soft wind, and it ruffled his hair.

Jordan clenched his eyes even tighter, and the little insects of awe crawled upon his skin. The goddess had many ways of showing her presence. This was the first time she had come as a soft warm wind.

'Oh great Panes, I don't want to wallow in filth like Ralph. I don't ever want to smell the trough where a thousand pigs have wallowed. I don't want to go mad, and have my teeth rot out of my mouth.' He whispered softly but ardently, and then the tears began to squeeze out from between his lids.

'Please save me, great Panes.' He poured out all his horror and disgust to the sacred bird-woman. 'They were hitting each other. They were hating each other, and the blood, oh the blood –'

At last he was silent, head bowed, shivering, and then he rose to his bare feet, and for the first time looked at the image.

The bird stared back at him stonily, but Jordan cocked his lovely golden head as though he were listening, and the moonlight silvered his skin.

He turned, still clutching the book, and crept back along the verandah. As he turned the far corner there was a furry rush of dark bodies out of the shadows, and the soft squeals of the bush rats as they squabbled over the sacrifice.

Jordan pushed open the door of the kitchen and it smelled of woodsmoke and curry powder and carbolic soap.

He stooped to the ashbox of the black iron stove, and when he blew lightly through the grating the ashes glowed.

He pushed a long wax taper through the bars and blew again and a little blue flame popped into life. He carried it carefully across the kitchen, sheltering it with his cupped hand, and transferred the flame to the stump of candle in the neck of the dark green champagne bottle. Then he blew out the taper and placed the bottle on the scrubbed yellow deal table and stepped back.

For a few seconds longer he hesitated, then he took the skirts of the faded and patched nightshirt, lifted them as high as his shoulders and looked down at his body.

The puppy fat had disappeared from his belly and hips. His navel was a dark eye in the flat clean plain of his trunk, and his legs were gracefully shaped. His buttocks lean and tight, like immature fruit.

His body was smooth and hairless except for the golden wisps at the juncture of his legs. It was not yet thick enough to curl, and was sparse and fine as silk thread freshly spun upon the cocoon.

From the centre of this cloudy web his penis hung down limply. It had grown alarmingly in the last few months, and in Jordan's horrified imagination, he foresaw the day when it would be thick and heavy as his arm, a huge shameful burden to carry through life.

At this moment it looked so soft and white and innocent, but when he woke in the mornings it was hard as bone, hot and throbbing with a sinfully pleasurable ache.

That was bad, but in these last weeks that terrible swelling and stiffening had come upon him at the most unexpected times: at the dinner table with his father seated opposite him, in the schoolroom when the new schoolmistress had leaned over him to correct his spelling, seated at the sorting-table beside Jan Cheroot, on the gelding's back when the friction of the saddle had triggered it, and that awful stiff thing had thrust out the front of his breeches.

He took it in his hand now and it seemed helpless and soft as a newborn kitten, but he was not deceived. He stroked it softly back and forth and instantly he felt it change shape between his fingers. He released it quickly.

The joint of mutton that the family had dined off the previous evening stood on the deal table, under a steel mesh fly-cover. Jordan lifted the cover, and the leg was hacked down to the bone.

His father's hunting knife lay beside the cold joint. The handle was stag-horn and the blade was nine inches long, sweeping up to a dagger point, and the white mutton fat had congealed upon the blade.

Jordan picked up the knife in his right hand.

The previous evening he had watched his father flicking the edge of the blade across the long steel. It always fascinated him, because Zouga held the razor edge towards his own fingers as he worked.

The proof of his father's expertise with the steel was the way in which the heavy knife seemed to glide effortlessly through the meat of the joint. It was wickedly sharp.

Jordan looked down again at that long white thing that stuck out of his body. The loose skin at the tip was half retracted so that the pink acorn pushed out from beneath it.

He tucked the tail of his shirt under his chin to free both hands and seized himself at the root, enclosing within the circle of his fingers the wrinkled bag with its tender marbles of flesh, and he pulled it out, stretching it out like the neck of the condemned man upon the headsman's block, while with the other hand he brought the knife down and laid the blade against his own belly, just above the fine golden fluff of pubic hair.

The blade was so cold that he gasped, and the mutton fat left a little greasy smear on his belly. He took a long breath to steel himself, and then slowly began to draw the blade downwards, to free himself for ever of that shameful wormlike growth.

'Jordie, what are you doing?' The voice from the doorway behind him startled him so that he cried out aloud. He threw the knife onto the table and at the same time dropped the shirt to cover himself.

'Jordie!'

He turned swiftly, breathing in sharp little gasps, and Ralph came towards him from the kitchen door. He wore only a pair of baggy shorts, and there were goose-bumps on the smooth bare skin of his chest from the pre-dawn chill.

'What were you doing?' he repeated.

'Nothing. I wasn't doing anything.' Jordan shook his head wildly.

'You were whacking your old winker, weren't you?' Ralph accused and grinned. 'You dirty little bugger.'

Jordan let out a choking sob and fled past him to the door, and Ralph chuckled and shook his head.

Then he picked up the stag-handled knife and cut a thick slab of mutton off the joint, dipped the blade into the stone pot and smeared a gob of yellow mustard over the meat, and munched it as he went about building up the fire in the stove and setting the coffee water to boil.

The following Sunday afternoon on the white sand of the fighting arena, Inkosikazi, the spider, died an agonizing death in the ghastly embrace of a smaller more agile adversary.

Bazo mourned her as he would a lover, and Kamuza sang the dirge with him just as sadly, for the Matabele syndicate had lost twenty sovereigns with her passing.

The return from Market Square to Zouga's camp resembled Napoleon's retreat from Moscow, headed by Ralph and Bazo bearing between them the basket and its sorry contents.

Opposite Diamond Lil's canteen, Ralph halted the cortege for a moment and wistfully contemplated the painted windows across the street, and listened for a moment to the sounds of laughter from beyond the green door – imagining that he could distinguish Lil's tinkling chimes.

When they reached the thatched beehive communal hut, Kamuza passed Ralph the clay pot of bubbling millet beer.

'How much did you lose, Henshaw?'

'Everything,' Ralph replied tragically. 'The very reason for living.' He took a long swallow of the thick gruel-like beer.

'That is bad; only a foolish man keeps all his cows in the same kraal.'

'Kamuza, your words are always a great solace,' Ralph told him bitterly. 'But I am unworthy of such wisdom. Keep those treasures for yourself alone.'

Kamuza looked smug and turned to Bazo. 'Now you know why I would not lay fifty gold queens, as you bid me.'

Bazo shot a glance at Ralph, and they acted together.

Ralph draped a seemingly brotherly arm over Kamuza's shoulders, but it was a steely yoke that held him helpless, and with the other hand he pulled open the front of Kamuza's loincloth – and Bazo scooped the soft furry carcass of the great spider out of the basket and dropped it into the opening.

As Ralph released him, Kamuza went up into the air, rearing like an unbroken stallion feeling the saddle and spur for the first time, whinnying wildly with horror, beating at his own loins with both hands.

If Ralph had not caught him, Bazo, in a shaking paralysis of mirth, might have fallen into the fire in the centre of the hut.

*

Kamuza had been gone almost three years.

When Bazo and the other Matabele had signed their contracts for a third period, Kamuza alone had asked Bakela to *'Bala Isitupa'*, to write off the contract as complete, and he had taken the road north back to Matabeleland.

Bazo had missed him deeply. He had missed the spiked tongue and shrewd acerbic counsel. He had missed Kamuza's intuitive understanding of the white man's ways of thinking, ways which Bazo still found unfathomable.

Even though Henshaw was his friend, had worked at Bazo's shoulder for all those long years, though they had hawked and hunted together, dipped into the same baking of maize porridge and drunk from the lip of the same beer-pot – though Henshaw spoke his language so easily that sitting in the darkness when the fire had burned down to embers it might have been a young Matabele buck talking, so faithfully did Henshaw echo the deep cadence of the north, so complete was his command of the colloquial, so poetic the imagery he used – yet Henshaw would never be Matabele as Kamuza was Matabele, could never be brother as Kamuza was, had never shared the initiation rites with Bazo as Kamuza had, had never formed the 'horns of the bull' with him as the impi closed for the kill, and had never driven the assegai deep and seen the bright blood fly as Kamuza had.

Thus Bazo was filled with joy when he heard the word.

'Kamuza is amongst us again.'

Bazo heard it first whispered by another Matabele as they formed a line at the gate of the security compound.

'Kamuza comes as the king's man,' they whispered around the watch-fires, and there was respect, even fear, in their voices. 'Kamuza wears the headring now.'

Many young Matabele had come to work at *Umgodi Kakulu*, 'The Big Hole', these last few years, and each month more came down the long and weary road from the north, small bands of ten or twenty, sometimes only in pairs, or threes and occasionally even a man travelling alone.

How many had reached Kimberley? There was nobody to keep a tally, a thousand certainly, two thousand perhaps, and each of them had been given the road southwards by the great black elephant, each of them had the king's permission to journey beyond the borders of Matabeleland, for without it they would have been speared to death by the bright assegais of the impis that guarded every road to and from the king's great kraal at Thabas Indunas – the Hills of the Chiefs.

Even in exile these young Matabele formed a closeknit tribal association. Each newcomer from the north carried tidings, long messages from fathers and indunas, repeated verbatim with every nuance of the original. Just as every Matabele who left the diamond fields, whether he had worked out his three-year contract or was bored and homesick or had fallen foul of the white man's complicated and senseless laws and was deserting, carried back with him messages and instructions that he had committed to the phenomenal memory of a people who did not have the written word.

Now the word passed swiftly from Matabele to Matabele.

'Kamuza is here.'

Kamuza had never warranted such attention before. He had been one amongst a thousand; but now he had returned as the king's man, and they lowered their voices when they spoke his name.

Bazo looked for him each day, searching the faces on the high stagings and on the running skips. He lay sleepless on his mat beside the cooling watch-fire, listening for Kamuza's whisper in the darkness.

He waited for many days and many nights, and then suddenly Kamuza was there, stooping through the low entrance and greeting Bazo.

'I see you, Bazo, son of Gandang.'

Bazo stifled his joy and replied calmly.

'I see you also, Kamuza.'

And they made a place for Kamuza in the circle, not pressing him too closely, giving him space, for now Kamuza wore the simple black tiara upon his close-cropped pate, the badge of the Councillor, the induna of the king of Matabeleland.

They called him 'Baba', a term of great respect, and even Bazo clapped his hands softly in greeting and passed him the beer pot.

Only after Kamuza had refreshed himself could Bazo begin to ask the questions of home, disguising his eagerness behind measured tones and an expression of calm dignity.

Kamuza was no longer a youth, neither of them were; the years had sped away and they were both in the full flowering of their manhood. Kamuza's features were sharper than the true

Matabele of Zanzi blood, the old blood from Zululand, for his was mixed with Tswana, the less warlike but shrewd and cunning peoples of King Khama. Kamuza's grandmother had been captured as a maiden, still short of puberty, by one of King Mzilikazi's raiding impis, and taken to wife by the induna who commanded her captors. From her Kamuza had inherited his mulberry black skin and the Egyptian slant of his eyes, the narrow nostrils and the thin and knowing twist of his lips.

There were very few Matabele who could still trace their bloodline back to the pure Zanzi, to the line of Chaka and Dingaan, the Zulus, the Sons of Heaven, and Bazo was one of those. Yet it was Kamuza who wore the ring of the induna on his head now.

In the time of Mzilikazi, a man would have the hoar frost of wisdom and age powdering his hair, and the cowtails bound about his elbows and knees would proclaim his deeds in battle to the world before the king ordered him to take the *isicoco.* Then his wives would plait and twist the headring into his own hair and cement it permanently into place with gum and clay and ox blood, a permanent halo of honour that entitled the wearer to his seat on the Council of the Matabele nation.

However, the old times were changing. More cunning than fierce, Lobengula, son of Mzilikazi, looked for cunning in those about him. Mzilikazi had been a warrior and lived by the white flash of the assegai. Lobengula, though he had blooded his spear, had never been a warrior, and he scorned the warriors' simpleness of thought and directness of action. As his father's greybeards faltered, he replaced them with men who thought as swiftly as the old ones had stabbed.

He had no patience with the old men's preoccupation with a world that was passing, and he sought out the young ones with clear fresh eyes, men who could see with him the dark clouds gathering on the southern borders like the soaring thunderheads of high summer.

Men who could sense the change and terrible events which his wizards and his own divinations warned him would soon rush down upon him like the fires that sweep the papyrus beds of the Zambezi swamps at the end of the dry season.

Lobengula, the great Black Elephant, whose very tread shakes the earth's foundations, and whose voice splits the skies, was choosing young men with eyes to see and ears to hear.

Thus Kamuza now wore the *isicoco* of the induna and, as he spoke over the fire in his dry whisper, his slanted eyes black and bright as those of a mamba in the firelight, men listened – and listened with great attention.

It was a measure of the gravity of the news he carried from the north that Kamuza began the council – the *indaba* – with a recital of the history of the Matabele nation. Each of them had heard it first with their mother's breast in their mouths, had drunk it in with her milk, but they listened now as avidly as then, reinforcing their memories so that when the time came they would be able to repeat it perfectly in each detail to their own children, that the story might never be lost.

The history began with Mzilikazi, war chief of the impis of Zulu, warrior without peer, beloved comrade and trusted intimate of King Chaka himself. It told of the black sickness of King Chaka, driven mad with grief at the death of his mother Nandi, the Sweet One. Chaka ordering the year of mourning in which no man might sow seed, on pain of death; in which the milk from the cows must be thrown upon the earth, on pain of death; in which no man might lie with his woman, on pain of death.

Mad Chaka brooded in his great hut and looked for cause to strike down all around him, even the most trusted, even the most beloved.

So it was that Chaka's messengers came to Mzilikazi, the young war chieftain. They found him in the field with his impis about him, five thousand of Zululand's bravest and finest, all of them still hot from battle, driving before them the spoils they had taken – the captured herds, the young and comely girls roped neck to neck.

The king's messengers wore the long tail feathers of the stately blue cranes in their headdress, token of their solemn mission.

'The king accuses the induna Mzilikazi,' began the first messenger, and looking into his arrogant face Mzilikazi knew that he looked upon the face of death. 'The king accuses Mzilikazi of stealing the king's share of the spoils of war.'

Then the second messenger spoke, and his words were an echo of the king's black madness, so that the words of King Chaka stood in the air above Mzilikazi's impis the way that the vultures circle above the battlefields on wide and motionless pinions.

If the sentence of death had been upon him alone, Mzilikazi

might have gone to his king and met it with courage and dignity. But his five thousand fighting men were doomed also, and Mzilikazi called them his children.

So Mzilikazi reached out and seized the king's messengers, and for a moment the earth seemed to lurch in its courses, for to touch these who wore the blue crane feathers was to touch the person of the king himself. With the razor edge of his assegai, Mzilikazi slashed the blue feathers from their heads, and threw them into the faces of the grovelling messengers.

'That is my reply to Chaka – who is no longer my king.'

Thus began the great exodus towards the north and, seated over the watch-fire, Kamuza, the king's man, related it all again.

He told the battle honours of Mzilikazi, the renegade. He told how Chaka sent his most famous impis after the fleeing five thousand, and how Mzilikazi met them in the classic battle tactics of the Nguni, how he waited for them in the bad ground.

Kamuza told how Mzilikazi threw the 'horns of the bull' around the impis of Chaka, and how his young men shouted '*Ngi dhla!* I have eaten!' as they drove in the steel; and the listeners in the dark hut murmured and moved restlessly, and their eyes shone and their spear hands twitched.

When it was over, the survivors of Chaka's shattered impi came to Mzilikazi and, on their knees, swore allegiance to him, to Mzilikazi who was no longer a renegade, but a little king.

Kamuza told how the little king marched north with his swollen impi, and how he defeated other little kings and became a great king.

Kamuza told how after Chaka was murdered by his brothers, Dingaan, the new leader of the Zulu nation, did not dare to send out more impis to pursue Mzilikazi. So Mzilikazi flourished, and like a ravaging lion he ate up the tribes. Their warriors swelled his fighting impis, and his Zanzi, the pure-blooded Zulu, bred upon the bellies of the captured maidens and the Matabele became a nation and Mzilikazi became a black emperor whose domain overshadowed even that of Chaka.

The men about the fire listened and felt their hearts swell with pride.

Then Kamuza told how the *buni*, the strange white men, crossed the river in their little wagons and outspanned upon the land that Mzilikazi had won with the assegai. Then Mzilikazi paraded his impis, and they danced with their war plumes aflutter, and their long shields clashing as they passed before him.

After he had reviewed the might of his nation, Mzilikazi took the little ceremonial spear of his kingship, and he poised before his impis and then hurled the toy-like weapon towards the banks of the Gariep river on which the white men had outspanned their wagons.

They took them in the hour before dawn, at the time of the horns, when the horns of the cattle can first be seen against the lightening sky. The front ranks of racing black warriors received the first volley of the long muzzle-loading guns, absorbing it as though it were a handful of pebbles thrown into a stormy black sea.

Then they stabbed the bearded men as they worked frantically with powderhorn and ramrod. They stabbed the white women as they ran from the wagons in their nightdresses, trying to carry the second gun to their men. They snatched the infants from their cradles on the wagonbed, and dashed out their brains against the tall steel-shod wheels of the wagons.

Oh, it was a rare feast that they set for Mzilikazi's chickens, the grotesque naked-headed vultures. They believed it was an ending – but it was only a beginning, for the Matabele were about to learn of the persistence and the dour courage of these strange pale people.

The next wave of white men came out of the south, and when they found the abandoned wagons and the jackal-chewed bones on the banks of the Gariep, theirs was a fury such as the Matabele had never encountered in all their wars.

So the *buni* met the impis on the open ground, refusing to be drawn into the ravines and thorn scrub. They came in pitifully small squadrons on shaggy ponies to dismount and discharge their volleys in a thunder of blue powder smoke. Then they went up into the saddle to wheel away from under the wall of charging rawhide shields, and reload and circle back to let loose the thunder again into the mass of half-naked bodies glistening with oil and sweat.

The *buni* built fortresses on the open plain, fortresses with their wagons' bodies which they lashed wheel to wheel; and they let the impis come to die upon the wooden walls of the fortress, while their womenfolk stood close behind them to take the gun while the barrel was still hot and pass up the second gun, charged and primed.

Then when the impis drew back, mauled and shaken, the wagons uncoiled from their circle, like a slow but deadly puff-adder, and crawled forward towards the kraal of Mzilikazi. And the dreadful horsemen galloped ahead of them, firing and circling, firing and circling.

Sadly Mzilikazi counted his dead and the price was too high, the red mud through which the iron-shod wheels churned was puddled with the blood of Zanzi, the blood of Heaven.

So he called his nation, and the herd boys brought in the herds, and the women rolled the sleeping-mats, and the little girls balanced the clay cooking-pots upon their heads, and Mzilikazi put fire into his kraals and led the Matabele nation away. A vast throng of people and animals were guarded by the depleted impis, while the white men on their sturdy ponies drove them and pointed them the way the sheepdog works the flock. Mzilikazi led them northwards until they crossed the great river into a new land.

'Now the white birds are gathering again,' Kamuza told the young men about the watch fire. 'Each day they come up the road to Thabas Indunas, and they bring their tawdry gifts and the little green bottles of madness. Their words are sweet as honey on the tongue, but they catch in the throat of those who try to swallow them as though they were the green bile of the crocodile.'

'What is it they seek from the king?' Bazo asked the question for all those who listened, and Kamuza shrugged.

'This one asks for the right to hunt elephant and take the teeth, this one asks for the young girls to be sent to his wagon, another wants to tell the nation of a strange white god that has three heads, another wishes to dig a hole and look for the yellow iron, yet another wishes to buy cattle. One says he wants only this, and another only that, but they want it all. These people are consumed by a hunger that can never be appeased, they burn with a thirst that can never be assuaged. They want everything they see, and even that is never enough for them. They take the very earth, but that is not enough, so they tear it open like a man tearing a child from the mother's womb. They take the rivers, and that is not enough, so they build walls across them and turn them into lakes. They ride after the elephant herds and shoot them down, not just one or two, not just the big bulls, but all of them – the breeding cows and the calves with ivory no longer than your finger. Everything they see they take; and they see everything, for they are always moving and searching and looking.'

'Lobengula must eat them up,' Bazo said. 'He must eat them up as Mzilikazi his father would have eaten them.'

'Hau!'Kamuza smiled his thin twisted smile. 'Such wisdom from my brother. He recalls how Mzilikazi ate the white men on the banks of the Gariep, and lost a land. Listen to Bazo, my children. He counsels the King Lobengula to throw the war spear and loose his impis as Cetewayo the King of Zulu did at the Hill of the Little Hand. How many Englishmen did Cetewayo slay? There was no counting, for their red jackets lay one upon the other like the snows of the Dragon Mountains when the sunset turns them to fire, and their blood fed the land so that the grass still grows greener and thicker and sweeter upon the slopes of the Little Hand to this day. Oh a fine killing, my children, a great and beautiful stabbing – and afterwards Cetewayo paid for it with the spear of his kingship. He paid for it with his royal herds, he paid for it with the liver and heart of his young men, with the grassy hills of Zululand. For after the avengers had made the great slaughter at Ulundi they took it all, and they placed chains of iron upon Cetewayo's wrists and ankles and they chained his indunas and his war captains and led them away. Now Bazo, the wise, would have you know what a good bargain King Cetewayo made, and he urges Lobengula to make the same bargain with these white men.'

Bazo's expression remained grave and dignified while Kamuza chided and mocked him but he twisted the snuff-horn between his fingers and once he glanced to the dark corner of the thatched hut where the long war shields and the broad assegai were stacked.

But when Kamuza finished, Bazo shook his head. 'No one here dares counsel the king; we are his dogs only. No one here doubts the might and resolve of the white men, we who live each day with their strange and wonderful ways. All we ask is this: what is the king's word? Tell us what Lobengula wishes – for to hear is to obey.'

Kamuza nodded. 'Hear then the king's voice, for the king has travelled with all his senior indunas – Babiaan and Somabula and Gandang – all the indunas of the house of Kumalo – they have gone into the hills of Matopos to the place of the Umlimo –'

A superstitious tremor shook the group, a little shiver as though the name of the wizard of the Matopos had crawled upon their skins like the sickle-winged tsetse fly.

'The Umlimo has given the oracle,' Kamuza told them, and then was silent, the pause theatrical, to pique their attention, to dramatize the effect of his next words.

'On the first day the Umlimo repeated the ancient prophecy, the words that have come down from the time of Monomatapa. On the first day the Umlimo spoke thus:

> "The stone falcons will fly afar. There shall be no peace in the kingdoms of the Mambos or the Monomatapas until they return. For the white eagle will war with the black bull until the stone falcons return to roost."

They had all of them heard the prophecy before, but now it had a new and sinister impact.

'The king has pondered the ancient prophecy, and he says thus: "The white birds are gathering. Eagle and vulture – all of them white, they roost already upon the roof of my kraal." '

'What is the meaning of the stone falcons?' one of his listeners asked.

'The stone falcons are the bird gods that the ancient ones left at the burial place of the old kings, Zimbabwe.'

'How will stone birds fly?'

'One has flown already,' Bazo answered this time. 'One of the stone falcons stands close by us now. It stands under the roof of Bakela, the Fist. It was he who took the falcon, and carried it away.'

'When the other birds fly, then war will sweep over Matabeleland,' Kamuza affirmed. 'But listen now to the oracle of the Umlimo.' And their questions were stilled.

'On the second day the Umlimo prophesied thus:

> "When the midnight sky turns to noon, and the stars shine on the hills – then the fist will hold the blade to the throat of the black bull."

'This was the prophecy of the second day.'

Again they were silent as they pondered the words then, mystified, they looked to Kamuza for the meaning of the prophecy.

'Lobengula, the Black Elephant, alone understands the meaning of the prophecy of the second day. Is he not versed in the mysteries of the wizards? Did he not pass his childhood in the caves and secret places of the wizards? Thus says Lobengula. "This is not yet the time to explain the words of the Umlimo to my children, for they are momentous words indeed, and there will be a time for the nation to understand." '

Bazo nodded and passed his snuff-horn. Kamuza took it and drew the red powder up into his nostrils with two sharp inhalations of breath and, watching him, Bazo did not dare to voice his own suspicion that perhaps Lobengula, the mighty thunder of the skies, was as mystified by the prophecy of the second day as was the little group around the fire.

'Was this all the oracle?' Bazo asked instead, and Kamuza shook his head.

'On the third day the Umlimo prophesied for the last time:

> "Sting the mamba with his own venom, pull down the lion with his own claws, deceive the clever chacma baboon with his own trickery."

'This was the prophecy of the third and final day.'

'Does the king intend that we, his humble cattle, should know the meaning of the prophecy of the third day?'

'Thus spoke Lobengula: "We the Matabele cannot prevail until we arm ourselves as our adversary is armed, until we gather to ourselves the strength that is found only in the yellow coins and shining stones. For it is these things which have made the white man strong." '

Nobody interrupted the silence that followed, for they all sensed that there was more to come.

'Thus the king summoned me to the royal kraal and bid me carry his word to all the Matabele who live beyond the borders of the king's domains. For thus spoke the king: "Bring me guns to answer the smoke of the white man's guns. Bring me diamonds and bring me the yellow coins that I may grow as strong as the white Queen who lives beyond the sea. For then her soldiers will not dare to come against me." '

Bazo replied for them all. 'Let Lobengula know that what he requires of us he shall have. Guns he shall have, for it is part of our contract with the white man. Each of us will carry a gun when we return to Matabeleland, some of us who have worked out two *Isitupa* will carry two guns when we return. Some of us will bring three guns.'

'That is known,' Kamuza nodded.

'Lobengula will have gold coins, for we are paid in coin, and what we bring home to Thabas Indunas belongs to the king.'

'That is right and proper.'

'But diamonds?' Bazo asked. 'The diamonds belong to the white man. They are fierce for them as a lioness is fierce for her cubs. How are we to bring diamonds to the king?'

'Listen to me,' whispered Kamuza. 'There will be no more "pick-ups". When one of you turns up the shine of a diamond in the yellow gravel, then that diamond belongs to Lobengula.'

'It is against the law.'

'Against the white man's law only, not against the law of Lobengula, who is your king.'

'To hear is to obey,' Bazo grunted, but he thought of Bakela, the Fist, who was his father, and Henshaw, the Hawk, who was his brother, and he did not relish stealing the stones for which they laboured as hard as Bazo did himself.

'Not only in the pit,' Kamuza went on. 'Each of you will watch for the chance on the sorting-tables, you, Donsela –' He picked out a Matabele across the fire from him, a young man with a deep intelligent brow and strong jaw. 'You have been chosen to work in the new grease house.'

'The tables are guarded,' Donsela replied. 'They are covered with a steel screen.'

They had all of them heard Donsela speak of the marvel of the new grease house.

Once again the ingenuity of the white men had put the diamond's unique qualities to his own advantage. The diamond was unwetable, shedding moisture like the body feathers of a goose. So while wet gravel would roll across a steel table smeared with thick yellow grease, the dry diamond would stick fast.

The pipeline from the Vaal river had at last reached Kimberley, and this water supply was augmented by the subterranean water pumped up from the depths of the vast excavation. There was water enough now to wash the gravel, instead of laboriously dry-sorting it, water enough to wash the sieved gravel over the slanting grease tables. The diamonds stuck like fat little blisters, half embedded in the grease, ready to be scraped off with a steel spatula at the end of each shift.

'There is a steel screen over the tables,' Donsela repeated, and Kamuza smiled and passed him a thin reed, cut from the riverbank. On the tip of the reed was a little lump of beeswax.

'The reed will pass through the mesh of the screen,' Kamuza told him. 'The diamond will stick more firmly to the wax than to the grease.'

Donsela examined the reed cautiously. 'Last week a Basuto was found with a stone. That same day he fell from the skip as they were bringing him out of the pit. Men who steal stones have accidents. Those accidents always kill them.'

'A warrior's duty is to die for his king,' Kamuza told him drily. 'Do not let the overseer catch you, and pick out only the biggest and brightest stones.'

In the three years between Kamuza's departure from Kimberley and his abrupt return, Ralph had reached his full growth. Only months short of his twenty-first birthday, he stood as tall as Zouga; but unlike his father, he was cleanshaven except for the thick dark moustache which he allowed to curl down at the corners of his mouth.

At rare intervals he was still able to gather together the ten gold sovereigns necessary to keep his surreptitious friendship with Diamond Lil alive. Then suddenly that was no longer relevant, for Ralph fell in love.

It happened in the street outside that exclusive institution, already the most famous in Africa south of the equator, membership of which conferred enormous prestige and a semi-mystical entrée to the elite band of men who wielded the growing wealth and burgeoning power of the diamond fields.

Yet the Kimberley Club was merely a single-storeyed wood-and-iron building as drab as any on the diggings. True it boasted a billiard room with a full-sized table, a picket fence of ornate cast iron and a stained-glass front door – but it was situated in the noisiest street just off Market Square, and it enjoyed its fair share of the flies and the all-pervading red dust.

It was mid-morning and Ralph was bringing one of the gravel carts back from the blacksmith who had replaced the iron tyres on the wooden-spoked wheels.

There was a stir in the street ahead of him. He saw men run

from the canteens and kopje-wallopers' offices, most of them bareheaded and in shirtsleeves.

A vehicle came bowling out of the Square – an extraordinary vehicle, light and fast, with high narrow wheels, so cunningly sprung that it seemed to float behind the pair that drew it. They were matched, a strange pale brazen colour, softer than the colour of honey, and their manes were white blond.

Both horses were martingaled to force them to arch their necks, and the long-combed platinum manes flew like the battle colours of a famous regiment.

The driver, either by chance, but more probably by skill, had them leading with their off fores in perfect unison, and their gait was an exaggerated trot in which they threw their forehooves so high that they seemed almost to touch the shining heads as they nodded to the rhythm of their run.

Ralph was stabbed by such a pang of envy that it was a physical pain. He had never seen anything so beautiful as those pale glistening animals and the vehicle that they drew – until he raised his eyes to the driver.

She wore a tricorn hat of midnight blue, set at a jaunty angle over one eyebrow. Her eyebrows were jet black, narrow and exquisitely arched over huge drop-shaped eyes.

As she came up to the plodding gravel cart she barely lifted the gloved hand that held the reins, and the plunging pair of pale horses swerved neatly and the elegant vehicle flashed past so close that, had he dared, Ralph might have reached up and touched one of those slim ankles in its high-buttoned patent leather boot which just showed under the tailored skirt of moire taffeta.

Then she dropped her hand again, and the matched pair swung the carriage in neatly before the wrought-iron gate of the Kimberley Club and stopped, shaking out their manes fretfully and stamping their forefeet.

'Bazo, take them,' Ralph called urgently. 'Go on to the stagings. I'll follow you.'

Then he darted across the street and reached up to seize the head of the nearest thoroughbred.

He was only just in time, for half a dozen other loiterers had raced him to it. Ralph removed his cap and looked up at the woman on the buttoned leather seat of the carriage. She glanced down at him and fleetingly smiled her thanks, and Ralph saw that her eyes were the same midnight blue as the hat on her head. Those eyes touched him for only an instant and then went back to the stained-glass front door of the club, but Ralph felt a physical shock from her gaze like a blow in the chest, so that he could not catch his breath.

Ralph was aware of voices, men's voices, from the direction of the club, but he could not tear his eyes from that lovely face. He was absorbing each fine detail, the braid of her hair, the colour of freshly-washed coal, thick as the tail of a lioness, which dropped from under the hat over her shoulder and hung to her waist. The fine peppering of dark freckles high on her cheekbones seemed to emphasize the purity of the rest of her skin. Her small pointed ears were set at an alert listening angle which gave a peculiar vivacity to her face. The dark V of the widow's peak below the brim of her hat pointed up the depth of forehead. Her nose was narrow and straight with elegantly flared nostrils that gave her expression an hauteur that was instantly belied when she smiled, as she was smiling now, but not at Ralph.

She was smiling at the group of men who came out onto the porch of the club, chatting animatedly as they adjusted their hats.

'A splendid lunch, sir.' The only stranger to Ralph in the group thanked his host and then led them down the short walk to the street.

He was a tall, well-proportioned man. His dress was sober. The cut was not English but he wore it with a dash that made the dark colours appear flamboyant.

He wore a dark patch over one eye, and it gave him a piratical air. His beard was trimmed to a point, and touched with silver.

'He is at least forty years old,' Ralph thought, bitterly, as he realized that the woman was smiling directly at this man.

At his right hand was a small neat figure, a man with an unremarkable face and thin receding hair, a small moustache of indeterminate colour – but eyes so intelligent and humorous that they altered the man's appearance – made it striking and interesting.

'Ah, Ralph,' this man murmured, as he noticed the young man standing at the horse's head; but Ralph could not meet his eyes.

Doctor Leander Starr Jameson was an intimate friend of his father's, and privy to Ralph's shame and disgrace. It was he who had administered the mercury tablets, and washed them down with a stern admonition to avoid in future the snares of harlotry. For a moment Ralph wondered if the doctor would impart his vile secret to the lovely lady on the seat of the carriage – and the thought burned his soul like hoar frost.

On the bearded man's other hand was Mr Rhodes, big and serious, his dress untidy, the knot of his tie slipping and his breeches baggy, but with that sense of determination and certainty about him that always awed Ralph.

Behind them all followed the stooped scholarly figure of Alfred Beit, like Mr Rhodes' shadow.

The four men paused in a group beside the carriage, and the tall stranger reached up and took the woman's hand.

He touched her fingers to his lips.

'Gentlemen, may I present my wife, Mrs St John.' The big man's accent was unmistakable, even Ralph recognized the soft drawl that emanated from the Southern States of America.

However, it was the title the man used and not the accent which struck like a fiery dart into Ralph's breast.

'– Mrs St John, my wife – Mrs St John.'

While Ralph stood rigid at the horse's head, destroyed by his adoration which he now knew was hopeless, the group ignored him and the men made their bows.

'Louise, my dear, this is Mr Rhodes of whom you have heard so much –'

The formal phrases might have been spoken in a foreign language as far as Ralph was affected by them. Her name was Louise, and she was married. That is all that he understood.

General St John climbed up beside his wife. He moved lithely for such a big man, and one so old, Ralph conceded reluctantly, and hated him anew for that. St John took the reins from Louise's gloved hand, lifted his hat to the three men and started the horses. Ralph had to jump back to avoid being knocked down, and Louise was talking animatedly to the General. Neither of them glanced at Ralph again, and the carriage whirled away, down the street.

Ralph stared after it wistfully.

Jordan decorated the borders of the menus with romanticized

scenes of the diggings: the stagings soaring above the gaping pit, heroic figures working on the walls of yellow earth, a sorter at his table – and at the head of the sheet a man's cupped hands overflowing with uncut diamonds – and he coloured the illustrations with water paints.

'What's Velouté de la Nouvelle Ruée?' Ralph asked.

'Soup New Rush,' Jordie told him without looking up from his artistic labours.

'What's going to be in it?'

'Marrow bones and pearl barley.'

'– And what's Quartier de Chevreuil Diamant Bleu?'

'Haunch of springbuck in the style of a blue diamond.'

'I don't know why we can't just speak English,' Ralph complained. 'What's the style of a blue diamond, anyway?'

'Lard the haunch with bacon fat, marinade it in olive oil and cognac with wild garlic, and then bake it in a pie crust.'

Ralph swallowed his saliva. Jordan's culinary skills were always a source of delight to him.

'All right – I'll eat it.'

Jordan licked his brush, leaving a streak of Prussian blue on his tongue, and then looked up at his brother.

'You are going to serve it, not eat it –' Jordan paused portentously, 'Mr Rhodes is coming to lunch,' as though that explained it all.

'Well, if I'm not good enough to sit at the same table as your famous Mr Rhodes – I'll be damned if I'll play waiter. You can get Donsela. For a shilling Donsela will spill soup on Mr Rhodes, for a shilling Donsela would throw soup on King Lobengula himself. I'm going to bribe him.'

However, in the end curiosity and Jordan's promise of the leftovers prevailed and Ralph dressed himself in the ridiculous monkey-jacket that Jordan had designed and tailored for him and carried the tray of Velouté out on the wide verandah of Zouga's camp – and there nearly dropped it.

'Madame, you remind me of the heroine from Mr Longfellow's poem,' Neville Pickering complimented Louise St John, and she smiled back at him from her seat at the centre of the luncheon table.

'Thank you, sir.'

Her jacket was in pale creamy buckskin with tasselled sleeves, and the bodice was crusted with bright-coloured beads in bold geometrical patterns. Louise had parted her thick black hair in the centre, braided a blue ribbon into each of the thick tresses, bound them with a band about her forehead, and then let them hang onto her bosom. The soft tanned buckskin was divided into ankle-length culottes, and her boots were also of soft beaded leather.

Louise was the only woman at the long trestle table on the open verandah of Zouga's camp. The men seated on each side of her were already emerging as the most influential subjects on this continent of an omnipotent queen. Like the men that another English queen had sent out to the corners of the earth, these were the new Elizabethans, most of them already rich – all of them restless and consumed with their lust for power, for wealth, for land. Each with a separate dream that he would follow relentlessly all his life, every one of them driving, ruthless men.

Ballantyne. Beit. Jameson. Rhodes. Robinson. The list of names read like a roll-call for a regiment of filibusters, and yet here they were listening to a discourse on women's fashion as though it were a company report on tonnage treated and cartage recovered.

Only Zouga Ballantyne was not smiling. The woman offended Zouga. Her beauty was too flamboyant, her colouring too vivid. Zouga preferred the pale gold blond hair and the complexion of sugared cream and strawberries. An Englishman's idea of beauty.

This woman's dress was outrageous, the styling of her hair pretentious. Her gaze was too direct, her eyes too blue, her conversation too easy and her style of address too familiar. Of course American women had the reputation of affecting masculine manners, but Zouga found himself wishing that Louise St John had kept those manners on the other side of the Atlantic Ocean where they belonged.

It was enough that she had galloped into his camp ahead of her husband, riding astride, and dismounted by freeing both of her narrow booted feet from the stirrups and vaulting lightly to the ground; but then she had come up onto the stoep with an assured stride and smile, her right hand out like a man, and without waiting for her husband to introduce them had said: 'You must be Zouga Ballantyne. I'd recognize you anywhere by Mungo's description of you.'

Her hand was narrow, the skin warm but dry, but the grip of

her fingers was unfemininely firm, the grip of a skilled horsewoman.

These leisurely Sunday luncheons at Zouga's camp were his one extravagance, and they had become one of the traditions of Kimberley, when excellent fare and good liquor and the company of intelligent men made for memorable afternoons.

Women were very seldom invited to these gatherings, and Louise St John would not have been there if Zouga had been able to have her husband come alone, but Mungo St John had replied pointedly to the invitation, 'General *and Mrs St John* have pleasure in accepting.'

The friendship between St John and Zouga had begun many years previously, and he was the kind of man whom Zouga could admire: a man like himself, hard and determined, one who lived by his own code without compromise. One who expected no preference nor favour, but whose triumphs were of his own engineering and whose disasters were met with fortitude, without plea or excuse, even when occasioned by cruel circumstances beyond his control.

In the late 'fifties St John had built up a commercial empire, a fleet of trading vessels which had carried the black ivory of slaves from the African continent to that of North America. Legend was that in three voyages, in the course of a single period of twelve months, across the notorious middle passage of the Atlantic, he had transported almost two million dollars' worth of slaves, and with those profits he had acquired vast estates in Louisiana.

It was at this time that Zouga had first met him. Zouga had travelled as a passenger on St John's magnificent clipper *Huron* out of the Port of Bristol in southern England to the Cape of Good Hope. The irony of that voyage had been that Zouga at the time had not been aware that St John was engaged in the trade, and Zouga had been accompanied on the voyage by his only sister, Robyn Ballantyne, a medical missionary whose declared goal in life was the extinction of the trade on the African continent.

When Robyn Ballantyne had discovered that St John was not sailing to Africa to barter beads and copper wire for ivory and ostrich feathers, for gumcopal and alluvial gold dust from the kingdom of Monomatapa, but was seeking richer, living black cargo, her hatred was rendered more implacable by her shame at having travelled in company with such a man.

It was Robyn Ballantyne who had called up the avenging spectre of the Royal Navy. She had been the chief instrument in delivering St John and his beautiful clipper *Huron*, with her cargo of five hundred prime slaves, to the gunboats of the British anti-slavery squadron.

St John, as was his right as an American captain, had resisted the British boarders, and in the savage action that followed, half his crew had been killed or maimed and his lovely ship so badly mauled that she had to be towed into Table Bay by her captors.

Though after imprisonment in Cape Town castle, the British governor had finally released St John and allowed him to sail away, still his cargo of slaves were seized and released from their chains, and the African coast was closed for ever to his ships.

It was then that Zouga had lost contact with him; but after Zouga's book *A Hunter's Odyssey* had been published, St John had written to him care of his London publishers, Messrs Rowland Ward, and since then they had corresponded at irregular intervals. Indeed it was Zouga's description of the diamond fields in one of these letters that was responsible for St John's presence here now.

Through the exchange of letters Zouga had been able to follow St John's career, and he learned how after his release from the Cape Town castle, St John had returned to Fairfields, his cotton and sugar estates near Baton Rouge, only weeks before the first cannon shots were fired at Fort Sumter.

Louisiana had voted for secession from the Union, and when the war began, Mungo raised his own force of irregular cavalry and led them in a brilliant series of hit-and-run raids against the supply lines and rear bases of the Federal army. So successful were these depredations that the northeners christened him 'Murdering Mungo', declared him an outlaw and placed a reward of fifty thousand dollars on his head. Promoted to major-general, he was later struck in the left eye by a red-hot splinter of shrapnel and dragged over a mile when his horse bolted. By the time he was discharged from the hospital, Vicksburg had fallen. Recognizing this as a fatal stab in the heart of the Confederacy, he had limped back along the empty road to Fairfields.

The reek of fermenting sugar juices mingled with that of charred flesh was more revolting than any battlefield Mungo had ever smelled. Four colonnades stood above the ashes of his homestead, like monuments to all his dreams.

Now, all these years later, St John had come up the road from Good Hope, driving a pair of magnificent pale gold horses with flowing white manes that he called 'Palaminos', a long black cigar between his white teeth, an eagle gleam in his single eye and this strangely disturbing woman on the seat of the phaeton beside him.

St John's first act in Kimberley had been to walk into the office of the Standard Bank on Market Square and present a letter of credit to the flabbergasted clerk. The letter of credit was on heavy, expensive paper, the printing embossed in rose and gold, the wax seal that of Messrs Coutts and Co. in the Strand, and the sum for which it was drawn was half a million of sterling.

St John had drawn a modest hundred pounds against that formidable total, and taken rooms for himself and his wife at the Craven Hotel, Kimberley's most fashionable and comfortable. When he recovered from his shock, the bank-clerk had excitedly begun to spread the news. There was an American general on the fields who disposed of a half million pounds in cash.

The following noon St John had casually accepted an invitation to lunch at the Kimberley Club and smiled indulgently as his name was proposed for membership by Mr C. J. Rhodes and seconded by Dr Leander Starr Jameson. There were men, rich and influential men, who had tried in vain since the foundation of the Club to obtain membership.

St John was smiling that same indulgent smile now as he leaned back in his chair, twisting the stem of his champagne glass between his fingers and watching the other guests at the table fawning over his wife.

Even Mr Rhodes, who was famous for his immunity to female wiles, and who usually bluntly terminated any frivolous conversation, was responding to her artless questions and chuckling at her sallies.

With an effort, Zouga tore his own attention from Louise and turned to Mungo St John. Quite pointedly he changed the discussion from the split skirts which allowed his wife to ride astride to Mungo's own doings since their last meeting.

The reason for the change of subject was not missed by Louise. She shot a sharp speculative glance at Zouga, but then smiled graciously and relapsed into dutiful silence while the conversation became at last serious and important.

St John had been in Canada and Australia, and without being specific they all understood that both journeys had been rewarding, for St John spoke of wheat and opals and wool and gold, and they listened avidly, shooting their questions like arrows and nodding to the deft replies, until at last St John ended: 'Well, then I heard from my dear friend Zouga what you gentlemen have been doing here, and thought it was time to come and have a look.'

Almost on cue Ralph came down the verandah carrying the scrubbed carving board with its cargo of roasted venison enclosed in a crisp brown envelope of pastry. The company applauded with exclamations of delight and approbation.

Zouga stood up to carve the roast and while he stropped the hunting knife against steel, he glanced at Ralph who still lingered on the verandah.

'Are you feeling well?' he asked out of the side of his mouth, and Ralph roused himself, tearing his adoring gaze from Louise St John.

'Oh yes, Papa, I'm fine.'

'You don't look fine. You look as if you have a belly ache. Better get Jan Cheroot to give you a dose of sulphur and treacle.'

Jan Cheroot, dressed in his old regimental jacket with burnished buttons and his scarlet cap set at a rakish angle, brought in fresh bottles of champagne, the buckets packed with crushed white ice.

'Ice!' Louise clapped her hands with delight. 'I never expected such sophistication here.'

'Oh, we lack very little, ma'am,' Rhodes assured her. 'My ice-making factory has been in operation for a year or more. In a year or so the railway line will reach Kimberley and then we shall become a city, a real city.'

'And all this on woman's vanity.' Louise shook her long black tresses in mock dismay. 'A lady's baubles, a city built on engagement rings!'

Despite Zouga's best efforts, the focus of attention had shifted again. They were all hanging on her words with that slightly bemused expression which overcomes even the most sensible of men when he looks at a beautiful woman.

'Beautiful woman.' It was the first time Zouga had acknowledged that fact, even to himself, and for some reason it increased his resentment of her.

'Do you know, Mr Rhodes,' she leaned across the table confidentially, 'I have been here for five days now – and although I have searched the sidewalks diligently, I have not seen a single diamond – and I was assured the streets of Kimberley were paved with diamonds.'

They all laughed, more heartily than the witticism warranted, and Rhodes murmured a few words to Pickering before turning back to Louise.

'We shall do what we can to remedy that, Mrs St John,' and while he spoke Pickering scrawled a note and then summoned one of the coloured grooms who was lolling and smoking in the shade of the camel-thorn tree.

'Major, may I borrow one of your champagne buckets?' Pickering asked, and when Zouga agreed, he handed the empty bucket and the note to the groom.

Zouga was carving seconds off the roast when the groom returned. He was followed by a nondescript white man with an uncertain seat on his placid steed. He came up onto the verandah carrying the bucket as though it were filled with Mr Alfred Nobel's new-fangled blasting gelatine.

He placed the bucket on the table in front of Rhodes with a timid flourish, and then seemed to disappear from sight. With his thin colourless hair and myopic eyes behind pebble-lens wire-rimmed spectacles, his dark jacket shiny with wear at elbows and cuffs, he blended like a chameleon with his background.

'Where is young Jordan?' Rhodes asked. 'That boy loves diamonds as much as any of us do.'

Jordan came from the kitchen in his apron and with his colour high from the heat of his stove. He greeted Rhodes shyly.

'Ladies and Gentlemen, Mr Jordan Ballantyne is not only the finest chef on the diggings – but he is also one of the best diamond sorters that we have.' Rhodes was expansive as few of them had ever seen him. 'Come and stand by me, Jordan, where you can have a good view.'

When Jordan was beside his chair, Rhodes tipped the bucket carefully and even Zouga heard himself gasp with shock, while Louise St John cried out aloud.

The bucket was filled to the brim with uncut diamonds, and

now they cascaded onto the white tablecloth in a sullenly glowing pyramid from which random darts of light sped to astound the eye.

'All right, Jordan. Tell us something about them,' Rhodes invited. And the boy stooped over the fabulous pile of treasure, his long tapered fingers flying lightly over the stones, spreading and sorting them into piles. While he worked he talked, and his voice was as lovely as his face, low and melodious. Fluently he explained the shapes of the crystals, pointed out the flaws in one, placed two side by side to compare the colours, twisting one to the light to bring up its smouldering fires.

Zouga was puzzled. This little act was too theatrical to be Rhodes' usual style, and he would never go to such lengths to impress a woman, even a beautiful one; for by jumbling up a bucket of stones he had given his own sorters many days of extra work. Every one of those stones would have to be re-graded and appraised and returned to its own little white envelope.

'Here is a perfect stone,' Jordan picked a diamond the size of a green pea. 'Look at that colour, blue as a bolt of lightning and as full of fire.'

Rhodes took it from him, considered it a moment, holding it between thumb and forefinger, then he leaned across the table and placed it before Louise St John.

'Madam, your first diamond. I sincerely hope not your last,' said Rhodes.

'Mr Rhodes, I cannot accept such a generous gift,' said Louise, her eyes wide with delight, and she turned to Mungo St John. 'Can I?'

'If I agreed with you, you would never forgive me,' Mungo St John murmured, and Louise turned back to Rhodes.

'Mr Rhodes, my husband insists, and I can find no words to express my gratitude.'

Zouga watched the scene attentively; there was so much happening here, so many nuances, so many undercurrents.

It was on the surface merely a demonstration of the remarkable effect that these bright hard pebbles had upon a woman. That was their true value, perhaps their only value. When he looked at Louise St John's face he could see that it was not avarice that lit it so, but a mystical emotion not far removed from love – the love of a living thing, a child, a horse, a man, a warming thing to watch.

Quite suddenly Zouga found himself wishing that he had been the author of such joy. That it had been he and not Rhodes who had made the gift which had transformed her, and it took a moment for him to free himself of that desire, so that he almost missed the glance that Rhodes shot beyond the woman's face.

Suddenly it was clear to Zouga. Rhodes was not baiting for the woman; he was fishing for the man. That display of treasure was for Mungo St John, the man with half a million sterling to dispose of.

Rhodes needed capital. When a man sets out to buy up every single claim on the Kimberley field, and when he is in a desperate hurry to do it, he must always be starved of capital. Rhodes' ambition was no secret. Zouga himself had been present at the long bar of the Kimberley Club when Rhodes had made the declaration of his intent.

'There is only one way to stabilize the price of the goods –' Rhodes' euphemism for diamonds – 'and that is an orderly, centralized marketing policy. There is only one way to stop the stealing of goods by the I.D.B., and that is through the institution of a rigorous security screen; and there is only one way to achieve both these objects, and that is to have every claim on the fields owned by one company.' Everyone listening to him had known who Rhodes intended that the head of that company should be.

That had been a year previously, and now the bucket of diamonds on Zouga's luncheon table was proof of how far Rhodes had made good his threat and had eaten up the field. Already he was more than halfway towards his goal, but he had been forced to take in partners and still he was short of capital, desperately short.

For the serious obstacle that stood between him and complete ownership of the field was Barney Barnato's company. He would need millions – literally millions of sterling – for that final step.

So the reason for the little charade was clear to Zouga now, and he was about to turn his head to study General Mungo St John's reaction to it when the tableau at the far end of the table struck him forcibly.

The untidily dressed young man, heavy in the shoulders, hunched forward in his chair, unruly curling hair spilling over onto the broad forehead above the florid meaty face, thick arms and square powerful hands enclosing a glittering mound of treasure. At his shoulder the slim and graceful figure of the boy with the bright and lovely face, and behind them both, towering above them, holding them both in its thrall, the graven statue of the falcon god.

Zouga shivered, touched for the first time in the presence of the falcon by a superstitious chill. For the first time he was aware of the sense of evil that the old Hottentot had immediately detected in the statue's stony eyes. For one horrifying instant Zouga was convinced that the bird was about to spread its sharp blade-shaped wings and hold them like a possessive canopy over the two human figures beneath it – and then the moment was past. The tableau broke up.

Rhodes was sweeping the gems back into the bucket, talking quietly to Jordan.

'Are you still studying the book of Mr Pitman's shorthand that I sent you, Jordan?'

'Yes, Mr Rhodes.'

'Good – you'll find it of great value one day.'

The boy understood the dismissal and slipped away down the verandah to his kitchen, while Rhodes casually handed the bucket of diamonds to his clerk and addressed General St John directly.

'In the section of the workings that we own we are recovering an average of ten carats to each ton of gravel that we process, to that we must add at least another two carats a ton which is being stolen by the labourers between the pit floor and the grading room. As our security system becomes more efficient and as we have better laws to control the I.D.B. we can expect to eliminate that wastage –' Rhodes was talking in that high-pitched voice so incongruous in such a big man, gesturing with strong square hands, persuasive and articulate. Reeling off figures for production costs and anticipated recovery, the expectations of profits on tonnage worked, returns on capital outlaid, he was addressing himself to one man only, the erect bearded figure with the black eye-patch, yet his manner was so persuasive that every one of them was listening with full attention, even Louise St John.

Zouga glanced at her and saw that she was concentrating on the confusing jumble of figures, and that she seemed to be able to absorb them. She proved that immediately.

'Mr Rhodes, you said earlier that working costs on the No. 9

Section were ten shillings and sixpence; now you use a new figure – twelve shillings?' She challenged unexpectedly, and Rhodes paused, gave a little nod of recognition for her perception before he replied.

'At the deeper levels the costs rise. Ten and six is our present cost, twelve shillings our projected cost for twelve months hence.' His voice had a new note of respect. 'I am flattered that you have followed my discourse so closely, madam.' Then he turned back to St John. 'From this you will see, General, that the returns on capital invested are about the best you will find anywhere: ten per cent is certain, fifteen per cent is possible.'

St John had been holding an unlit cigar between his teeth; now he removed it and stared hard at Rhodes with his single eye.

'So far, Mr Rhodes, you have not mentioned the blue.'

'The blue.' Every single one of them at the long table froze.

'The blue.' It was as if St John had spoken a gross obscenity, shocking them all into silence.

'The blue' was the main reason why Rhodes was hungry for capital.

'The blue' was the reason why the banks were calling on all diggers who had borrowed against the collateral of their claims to reduce their overdrafts by fifty per cent; and Rhodes had borrowed a million pounds to finance his attempt to acquire every single claim on the New Rush field. As he had acquired each block, Rhodes had immediately used it as security to borrow money to buy the next block, pyramiding loan upon loan, debt upon debt.

Zouga was one of the few who so far had resisted Rhodes' advances, resisted with pain and heart-searching an offer of £5,000 for his claims on the Devil's Own. The offer had been made six months before, before those dreaded words 'the blue' were whispered in the inner sanctum of the long bar of the Kimberley Club.

Nobody would offer Zouga £5,000 for his claims now. On the contrary, a week after he first heard those two dreaded words, the manager of the Standard Bank had sent a note asking him to call.

'Major Ballantyne, in view of recent developments, the bank has been forced to review the value of collateral securing our clients' overdrafts. We have calculated the present market value of your claims as five hundred pounds each.'

'That's ridiculous, sir.'

'Major, the blue has shown on the claims of the Orphen Company.' The bank manager did not have to elaborate. The Orphen block was only separated from the Devil's Own by a dozen intervening claims. 'I don't enjoy doing this, Major, but I must ask you to reduce your overdraft to one thousand pounds.'

'The blue' was the reason why many of the town's merchants were running down their stocks, preparing themselves to pull out.

'The blue' was the reason why many of the transport riders were re-routing their wagons to the new goldfields at Pilgrims' Rest.

'What is the blue?' asked Louise St John, and when none of the others spoke, Zouga's duty as host placed the burden of reply upon him.

'The blue is the diggers' name for a type of rock formation, Mrs St John. A volcanic conglomerate, dark blue in colour and very hard – too hard to work easily.' Zouga picked up his champagne glass, sipped the yellow wine and then studied the rising pinpricks of bubbles.

'Is that all?' Louise asked quietly.

'It has zircons in it, small zircons the size of sugar grains, but there is no market for zircons,' Zouga went on grudgingly.

'What is the significance of this – blue?' Louise persisted.

Zouga paused to pick his words with care.

'The diamondiferous earth is a friable yellow gravel – friable means crumbling.'

'Thank you,' Louise smiled without rancour. 'I do know the word.'

'Well, then, on some of the deeper claims in the northern section the yellow gravel has pinched out, and we have come up short against this hard blue floor, hard as marble and just as sterile.'

'That hasn't been proved,' Rhodes cut in sharply, and Zouga inclined his head in acceptance.

'No, it hasn't been proved, but that is what we all fear. That we have come to the end. That the fields are worked out.'

They were all silent then, contemplating that terrifying eventuality.

'When will you know for certain?' Mungo St John asked. 'When will you know that this blue ground underlies the entire field, and that there are no diamonds in it?'

'It will be many months still before the shallower claims can be worked down to the level of those that have run into the blue,' Rhodes answered. 'Then if we do find it covers the whole field, we will have to drive pot-holes through it to make sure that it is not a thin layer, and that the yellow gravel does not recur below it.'

'I see,' St John nodded. 'It seems that I was fortunate to delay my visit to Kimberley until after this blue ground was encountered, or I might have found myself the owner of a mountain of blue marble and no diamonds.'

'You have always been a fortunate man, Mungo.' Louise flashed a smile at him, and he replied to it gravely.

'You, my dear, are the greatest of all my good fortunes.'

With obvious relief the company abandoned the subject of the dreaded blue ground and turned to lighter topics. Only Rhodes did not join them, but sat silent and brooding at the head of the long table.

Though Zouga smiled and nodded at the repartee, he also was distracted by the talk of lurking disaster, and his thoughts were a barrier between him and the company, so that Louise St John had to repeat his name to gain his attention.

'Is that possible, Major Ballantyne?'

Zouga roused himself and turned to her. 'Forgive me, Mrs St John. Will you repeat the question?'

Louise was not accustomed to having a man's thoughts wander when she was talking to him. This cold and correct Englishman was truly beginning to irritate her, and she found herself wanting to shock some natural reaction out of him. She had thought of including a man's word, one of Mungo's soldier's words, in her conversation, but good sense warned her that he would merely raise an eyebrow at such gaucherie. She had thought of ignoring him, but intuition warned her that he would probably welcome that treatment. The best course open to her was to direct her queries at him and force him to recognize her existence, and let it nettle him.

'I was led to understand that you were the Chairman of the Kimberley Sporting Club?'

'I have that honour,' Zouga agreed.

'I have heard also that your steeplechases or point-to-point races – I am never quite sure of your British terminology – are the most popular diversions on the diamond fields.'

Zouga shook his head and smiled. 'I'm not sure of the terminology myself. They certainly are not steeplechases, we are critically short of steeples out here, and they are not point-to-point exactly, for we throw in a little rifle drill. So, we prefer to call them rough rides. A fairly accurate description, I think.'

'I thought to enter one of my horses – in a rough ride,' Louise said.

'We would welcome your participation,' Zouga agreed. 'I could prepare a list of our better riders from which you could choose.'

'I prefer to ride myself,' Louise shook her head.

'I am afraid that would not be possible, Mrs St John.'

'Why not?'

'Because you are a woman.'

Her expression gave Zouga his first truly satisfying moments in her company. She had turned waxen pale so that the freckles stood out boldly on her cheeks and her eyes glowed a lighter, brighter, angry blue.

Zouga waited for her retort, but she sensed his anticipation and, with a huge effort, denied him the satisfaction. Instead she turned to her husband.

'It's after three o'clock. It has been a very pleasant luncheon, but I should like to return to the hotel now.' She stood up quickly, and Mungo St John shrugged resignedly and stood up beside her.

'Please do not let us break up this delightful gathering.' His smile and his tone asked their indulgence for a womanly whim.

The groom brought her horse to her and she caressed its pale silken muzzle. Then she gathered the reins, looked up at the group of men on the stoep, held Zouga's eye for a moment, before deliberately turning away.

She placed one neat gloved hand on the stallion's withers where the long white mane rose into the crest of the shoulders, and then in the next instant she was seated on the broad and powerful back, her small feet thrust deeply into the silver-starred Mexican-type stirrups.

Zouga was astounded. He had never seen a woman vault to the saddle. Usually it took a groom to hold the head and another to form a bridge of linked fingers to boost her to the height of the horse's back.

Louise St John had gone up so lightly and easily that she might have flown, and the movement of her left hand that made the stallion rear was only apparent to someone looking for it.

The huge horse went up on its hind legs, walking backwards in a circle, cutting at the air with its forehooves, until it faced the five-foot barbed-wire fence that marked the division between Zouga's camp and the public road.

Then Louise moved her hand again and the stallion dropped into a dead run, straight at the fence.

The watching men exclaimed in alarm for the stallion had a bare twenty strides to build up momentum for the jump, yet he flew at it with his pink nostrils flaring and the serpentine veins beneath the burnished skin of his cheeks swelling with the pumping of the great heart.

Louise's thick black braids were flung out tautly behind her head by the power of the stallion's acceleration, and then she lifted him into the jump with her knees and her hands.

For an instant of time the horse and the tiny figure upon its back seemed to hang suspended against the pale blue of the sky, the horse with its forefeet drawn up beneath its noble head and the woman rising in the saddle to cushion the shock of take-off and landing – and then they were over.

The stallion landed neatly, with his rider in perfect balance, and the golden body flowed smoothly into the continuation of his run.

There was a soft involuntary sigh from the group on the verandah, and Zouga felt a surge of relief as powerful as the driving leap of the stallion. He had had a mental image of the woman caught up in the bloody strands of barbed wire, like a wild bird in the trapper's net, with torn body and broken wings.

Zouga stood on top of the central stagings. He was as high above the level of the plain as a three-storey building, and from his vantage point he could see as far north as the Vaal river. The dark-green stain of the lusher scrub and grass along its course looked like cloud shadow upon the dust-pale earth, but there were no clouds in the high vault of the sky, and the brutal sun threw stark shadows below the high stagings, geometrical patterns that parodied in two-dimensional plan the intricate structure of timber and iron and steel wire. The stagings clung perilously to the sheer precipice that fell into the depths.

It was as though a gigantic meteor had ploughed into the yellow earth, gouging this bowl-shaped dish through the earth's crust. In the deepest sections it was almost two hundred feet deep already, and each spadeful of gravel had been dug out by hand, lifted to the surface and laboriously picked over before being discarded in the mountainous waste dumps. It was a monument to the persistence of those antlike creatures that swarmed down there on the pit floor.

Zouga wiped the black grease off his hands with a wad of cotton waste, and nodded to the Matabele winchman who threw in the gear lever of the steam winch.

Once again the numbing clatter hammered against Zouga's skull and the slender thread of shining steel cable slithered in over the drums. The winch and steam boiler had cost Zouga over a thousand pounds, the entire winnings of an unusually productive week's labour when Jordan had picked eleven good diamonds off the sorting-table. That week's recovery had been one of the false promises that the Devil's Own had whispered to him, like an unfaithful wife.

Zouga moved to the front of the stagings to escape the painful sound of the winch. He was on an unguarded wooden balcony with the drop sucking seductively at him, but he ignored it.

He had ten minutes to rest now, the time that it took the gravel skip to travel up from the claims to the surface. He could see it lifting off the floor below like a fat spider creeping up its individual silken thread towards him, still too deep for him to recognize for certain the human figure riding on the enormous steel bucket.

Zouga lit a cheroot, and it tasted of engine grease from his fingers. He looked down again, and decided that instead of an ant's nest the pit reminded him more of a beehive. Even at these deep levels the precise shape of each claim had been maintained, and the geometrical shapes were like the individual cells in a honeycomb.

'If only mine would yield a little more honey,' he thought.

The skip was close enough now for there to be no doubt of the tall young figure standing casually on the lip of the steel bucket, balancing easily with both hands on his hips as the drop grew steadily deeper under him.

It was a matter of pride amongst the younger diggers to ride the skip in the most casual or spectacular manner possible. Zouga had forbidden Ralph to dance on the skip, a fad that had been started by a young Scot who had once danced between the floor and the stagings, accompanying himself on the bagpipes.

Ralph drew steadily closer, rising up through the glistening web of steel cables that hung over the pit like a silver cloud. Hundreds of cables, one for each individual claim, every strand polished by the pulley wheels, by the friction over the winding drums, until they caught the sunlight and shimmered into a silver mist that hung like an aura over the pit – ethereal and lovely, hiding the harsh reality of that gouged raw earth, with its dangers and disappointments.

While he waited for the skip to reach him, Zouga cast his mind back to that first day when he had led the single oxen into the sprawling encampment with Aletta on the wagon box beside him, and they had looked up at the riddled and torn kopje.

So much earth had been moved since then, so many men had died in this terrible pit where that kopje had once stood and so many dreams had perished with them.

Zouga lifted the wide-brimmed hat. Carefully he mopped the beads of sweat from the smoother paler skin along his hairline, and then he inspected the damp red stain on the silk bandanna and grimaced with distaste. It looked like blood.

He re-knotted the silk about his throat, still peering down into the depths, and his eyes clouded with disenchantment as he remembered the high hopes and bounding expectation that he had brought with him on that day – was it really ten years ago? It seemed like a day and an eternity.

He had found himself dreaming, the random events from those lost years replaying through his mind, the sorrows and the joys magnified by his imaginings and by the passage of time.

Then, after a few minutes, Zouga roused himself. Dreaming was an old man's vice. The past was beyond regret; today was all that counted. He straightened his shoulders and looked down at Ralph in the swinging skip. Something jarred him, scattering the last of his dreams.

The skip was riding differently, it did not have the accustomed weight to it, he could not yet make out the heaped yellow gravel, which, despite his orders, Ralph usually over-loaded high above the steel sides of the skip.

It was empty, and Ralph was alone. He was coming up without the Matabele gang to help run the skip over the bars and up-end its burden of gravel into the chute, down which it would be carried to the waiting cart.

Zouga cupped his hands to his mouth to shout an enquiry – but the words stayed in his throat.

Ralph was close enough now for Zouga to see the expression on his face. It was tragic, stricken with some terrible emotion.

Zouga lowered his hands and stared at his son in dread anticipation. The skip hit the end bars with an iron clash and the winchman threw out the gear lever, expertly braking the steel skip against the bars.

Ralph jumped lightly across the narrow gap onto the platform, and stood there, still staring at Zouga.

'What is it, my boy?' Zouga asked quietly, fearfully – and for answer Ralph turned away and glanced down into the empty body of the skip.

Zouga stepped up beside him, and followed his glance. He saw that he had been mistaken – the skip was not empty.

'It has taken us all morning to hack that out of the east face,' Ralph told him.

It looked like a roughly cut gravestone, before the inscription was chiselled in, as wide as the stretch of a man's arms and imperfectly squared up, the marks of the steel wedges and pick-axe still fresh upon it.

'We broke three pick handles on it,' Ralph went on grimly, 'and we only got it out because there was a natural fracture line that we could crack open with wedges.'

Zouga stared at the ugly cube of stone, not wanting to believe what it was, trying to close his ears against his son's voice.

'Underneath it's the same, solid, hard as a whore's heart, no faults, no cracks.'

The lump of stone was a dull ugly mottled thing, across which the steel tools had left paler weals and furrows.

'Sixteen of us,' Ralph went on. 'We worked on it all morning.' He opened his hands, and showed them palms upwards. The horny yellow calluses had been torn open, the raw flesh beneath was mushy and caked with dust and earth. 'All morning we broke our hearts and our picks on it – and that bloody little chip weighs less than half a ton.'

Slowly Zouga stooped over the edge of the skip and touched the stone. It was as cold as his heart felt – and its colour was dark mottled blue.

'The blue,' Ralph confirmed quietly. 'We have hit the blue.'

'Dynamite or blasting gelatine,' Ralph said. 'That's the only way we'll ever move it.'

He was stripped to the waist, a polish of sweat on his arms, and little drops of it hanging like dew in the thick hair of his chest.

The tombstone of blue marble lay at his feet, and Ralph rested on the shaft of the sledgehammer. The blows he had swung at the rock had raised bursts of sparks and tiny puffs of white dust that stung their nostrils like pepper – but had not cracked the rock through.

'We cannot blast in the pit,' Zouga said tiredly. 'Can you imagine two hundred diggers firing away dynamite, every one doing it when and how he wanted?' He shook his head.

'There is no other way,' Ralph said. 'No other way to get it out.'

'And if you do get it out?' Jordan asked from the verandah where he had stood without speaking for the past hour.

'What do you mean?' Zouga demanded. He could hear the strain in his own voice, and knew how close his anger and frustration were to the surface.

'What will you do with it when you do get it out?' Jordan persisted, and they all stared at the awful blue lump.

'There are no diamonds in that stuff.' Jordan said it for them.

'How do we know that?' Ralph snapped at him, his voice rough and ugly with the same tension that gripped Zouga.

'I know it,' Jordan said flatly. 'I can sense it – just look at it. It's hard and bleak and bare.'

Nobody replied to that, and Jordan shook his curls regretfully. 'Even if there were diamonds in it, how would you free them from the blue? You can't smash them out with sledgehammers. You'd end up with diamond dust.'

'Ralph,' Zouga turned away from Jordan, 'this stuff, this blue – it's only on the east face, isn't it?'

'So far.' Ralph nodded. 'But –'

'I want you to cover up the east face,' Zouga told him bluntly. 'Shovel gravel over the exposed rock. Nobody else must see it. Nobody else must know.'

Ralph nodded, and Zouga went on, 'We will keep on raising the yellow gravel from the other sections as though nothing has happened; and nobody, not one of you, is to say a word about – about us having struck the blue.' He looked directly at Jordan. 'Do you understand, not a word to anybody.'

Zouga sat easily in the saddle, riding with the long stirrups of a Boer hunter or of a born colonial.

He knew that Rhodes was leaving in the next few weeks, to keep his term at Oxford University. Perhaps his imminent departure would make his judgement hasty.

'Let's hope so, anyway.' And his mount flicked his ears back to listen to his voice.

'Steady, old man.' Zouga touched his withers, feeling a quick twist of guilt at his intentions. He knew he was going to try and sell faulty goods, and he steeled himself against his own conscience.

He touched his mount's flank with his knee and turned him off the rutted dusty track through the break in the milkwood fence and into Rhodes' camp.

Rhodes sat with his back to the mud wall of the shack, a mug in his hand, the big shaggy leonine head cocked to something that Pickering was saying.

The talk of the diggings was that he was already a multi-millionaire, at least on paper, and Zouga had seen the champagne bucket of uncut diamonds poured out onto his lunch table. Yet here Rhodes was sitting on a soap box in the dusty yard, dressed in shabby ill-fitting clothes, drinking from a chipped enamel mug.

Zouga dropped his reins and his horse stopped obediently, and when he slipped off its back there was no need for him to tether it. It would stand as long as Zouga wanted it to.

He crossed the yard towards the small group of men, and

Zouga smiled to himself. Rhodes' mug might be chipped – but it contained a twenty-year-old cognac. Rhodes' seat might be a soapbox, but he sat it as though it were a throne, and the men that sat around him like courtiers or supplicants were all rich and powerful men, the new aristocracy of the diggings.

One of these rose now and came to meet Zouga, laughing lightly and brandishing a rolled newspaper.

'By gad, Major, they say you need only speak of the devil.' He clapped Zouga's shoulder. 'I hope you are taking this assault on our masculine pride as seriously as we are – and have come to offer to champion our cause.'

'I don't understand.' Zouga's protest was lost in the laughter and friendly pummelling as they came to crowd around him. Only Rhodes had not left his seat against the wall, but even he was smiling.

'Let him read it for himself, Pickling,' Rhodes suggested mildly, and Pickering handed Zouga the news sheet with a flourish.

It was a copy of the *Diamond Fields Advertiser* – so newly printed that the ink smudged beneath Zouga's fingers.

'Front page,' said Pickering gleefully. 'The headline.'

GAUNTLET THROWN DOWN
LADY INSULTED
SEEKS SATISFACTION

This morning your editor was privileged to receive a visit from a beautiful and distinguished visitor to Kimberley. Mrs Louise St John is the wife of a hero of the American Civil War, and in her own right a noted equestrienne.

Her stallion 'Shooting Star' is a remarkable example of the recently developed American breed known as Palamino. He is a former Louisiana champion of breed, and quite one of the most magnificent animals ever to be seen on the Diamond Fields.

Mrs St John attempted to enter her mount in the regular point-to-point meetings organized by the Kimberley Sporting Club – but was informed by Major Ballantyne, the Club President, that she was barred from riding –

Zouga skipped quickly over the next few paragraphs:

'Simply because I happen to be a woman. . . . Insufferable masculine arrogance.'

He smiled and shook his head.

'Challenge the good major to ride against me over any course of his choice for any purse he stipulates.'

Now Zouga laughed delightedly, and tossed the paper back to Pickering.

'The lady has good bottom', he admitted, 'in both senses of the word.'

'I will lend you King Chaka,' Beit promised. He was a strong hunter, English and Arab blood, from one of the famous Cape studs. Beit had paid three hundred guineas for him.

Zouga shook his head and shot an affectionate glance at his own hunting horse standing across the yard. 'That won't be necessary, I shan't be riding.'

There was a howl of jovial protest from them all.

'By God, Ballantyne, you can't let us down.'

'This damned vixen will say you funked it, old man.'

'My wife will crow for a week – you'll ruin my marriage.'

Zouga held up his hands. 'I'm sorry, gentlemen. This is merely a bit of female nonsense – and you can quote me.'

'You won't ride, then?'

'Certainly not.' Zouga was smiling, but his voice had a brittle edge. 'I have more serious matters to concern me.'

'You are right, of course.' Rhodes' piping voice stilled them all into respectful silence. 'That pale brute is a flying devil and the lady rides like a witch – we have all seen that.'

The scar on Zouga's cheek turned pale pink, and there was a sudden green glint in his eye; but the smile stayed on his lips.

'That fancy high-stepper moves well on the flat, I grant you, but over the course I would choose he would be lucky to finish, let alone win.'

'You'll ride then?' They were clamouring again immediately.

'No, gentlemen. That's my final word.'

Long after the others had left, the three of them sat on: Pickering, Rhodes and Zouga. The sun had set, and just the orange glow of the fire lit their faces. The first bottle of cognac was empty and Pickering had opened another. Now Rhodes was staring into his mug, and he spoke without lifting his eyes.

'So, Major, at last you are ready to sell, and I ask myself a question, a simple little question – why?'

Zouga did not reply, and after a moment Rhodes lifted his head.

'Why, Major?' he repeated. 'Why now suddenly?'

Zouga found that the lie he had prepared would not come to his lips. He was dumb, but he held the gaze of those pale blue eyes – and it was Rhodes who broke the silence.

'I have trusted very few men in my life,' and involuntarily his eyes flickered to Pickering and then back to Zouga, 'but now, Major, you are one of them.'

He picked up the cognac bottle and spilled a little of the honey-dark liquor into Zouga's mug.

'Once you were offered a hundred thousand pounds in illicit diamonds – and you couldn't bring yourself to take them.' Rhodes was speaking so softly that Zouga had to lean forward to catch the words. 'Yesterday your son brought up the first hunk of blue ground from the Devil's Own – and still you could not bring yourself to lie.'

'You knew!' Zouga whispered, and Rhodes nodded and then sighed.

'By God, I wish I knew more like you.' He shook the big curling head and his voice was become brusque and businesslike. 'Once I offered you five thousand pounds for your claims. All right, I will make the same price –'and he lifted one meaty hand to still Zouga. 'Wait! Listen to the rest of it, before you thank me. The bird goes with the claims.'

'What?' For a moment Zouga did not understand.

'The stone bird, the statue. It becomes part of the deal.'

'Damn it!' Zouga half rose from the log on which he was sitting.

'Wait!' Rhodes stopped him again. 'Listen – before you refuse,' and Zouga sank back. 'You'll ride for it.'

Zouga shook his head, not understanding.

'You'll ride against this woman, St John, on her terms, and if you win you keep the claims and the bird and my five thousand.'

The silence stretched out for a full minute – and then Zouga asked with a harsh gravelly sound in the back of his throat:

'And if I lose?'

'You yourself have said there is little chance of that,' Rhodes reminded him.

'And if I lose?' Zouga persisted.

'Then you leave these fields as you came – with nothing.'

Zouga looked away to the horse standing at the edge of the shadows. He had named him Tom, after a friend, the old hunter who had first told Zouga about the land to the north and how to reach it, Tom Harkness, now dead these many years.

The horse was part of Zouga's dream of the north, the mount that would carry him back to Zambezia. Zouga had selected him with more care than a man usually gives to choosing his wife – and beauty was the last thing he looked for.

Tom was a mixture of many bloodlines, the wide nostrils and big chest of the Arab for staying power, the sturdy legs and sure feet of the Basuto, the canny eye and hammer head of a wild Mustang, the heart and strength of an English hunter. However, Tom was a drab unrelieved dun-colour. His coat was long and thick, brushed but not curried, protection from the night frost and the noon sun, from flying pebbles thrown by frantic hooves of the quarry in a stern chase or from the rip of red-tipped 'wait-a-bit' thorns.

Tom had proved that the intelligent gleam in his eye was no illusion. He learned swiftly and well. He learned to stand when the reins were dropped on his neck, giving his rider both hands for the rifle, and he remained stone-still while gunfire crashed about his head, only the twitching of his ears signalling his consternation.

When Zouga took him out into the open veld to continue his training, Tom displayed nimble feet on the rocky slopes of the kopje and a buffalo skin through the thorn bush; he learned to hunt, and seemed to enjoy it the way a good polo pony revels in the crack of the bamboo root and the riotous chase.

He seemed instinctively to understand stalking, keeping his own body between Zouga and the game, angling off his approach, never heading directly at the quarry, and the herds of springbuck let the seemingly riderless horse walk up into easy rifle shot. Then Tom would carry the freshly killed carcass on his back, without shying and fussing about the blood.

Tom was ugly, with a Roman nose, ears a little too long, legs a little too short, and he ran with an awkward hump-backed gait – which he could keep up all day, over any ground.

He was an incorrigible thief. Jordan's vegetable garden had to be fenced, but still Tom left tufts of his drab hair on the spikes of the barbed wire. He had a trick of plucking the carrots out of the ground with a delicate grip between his square white teeth, and then knocking the earth off them against his forehooves.

He learned to push open the kitchen window and reach the fresh loaves of bread that were cooling on the marble sink, and once when Jan Cheroot left the door to the storeroom off the latch, Tom got in and ate half a bag of sugar – at twenty shillings a pound.

However, he would follow like a dog, and when ordered he would stand for hours – and Zouga, who was not sentimental about animals, had come to love him.

Zouga looked back from the horse to the young man across the log fire.

'Agreed,' he said without emphasis. 'Do we need to have further witnesses?'

'I don't think so, Major,' said Rhodes. 'Do you?'

'At the gun the competitor will ride out to the first flag –' Neville Pickering was the steward-in-chief, and his voice through the speaking trumpet carried to every member of the huge Sunday crowd that spilled out across the dry veld below the Magersfontein hills.

'At the first red flag they will fire upon the standing targets. When they have demolished all four targets to the satisfaction of the stewards, they will be free to round the second yellow flag, and thereafter to return to the finish line.' He pointed to the twin poles each with its crown of coloured bunting. 'The first rider to pass between them will be declared the winner.'

Pickering paused and drew fresh breath before going on.

'Are there any questions?'

'Would you recite the rules, please, Mr Pickering,' Louise St John called. She looked like a child on the great glistening pale stallion's back. She was walking him in circles, leaning forward to pat his neck for the crowds had made him nervous. He was chewing the light snaffle and sweating in dark patches on the rippling muscled shoulders.

'There are no other rules, ma'am.' Pickering answered her loudly enough for those at the back of the crowd to hear.

'No rules – barging and fouling?'

'There are no fouls, ma'am,' Pickering replied. 'Though if one of you deliberately shoots an opponent, he or she might have to face criminal charges, but not disqualification.'

Louise turned her head towards the figure on the front seat of the high-wheeled phaeton which was parked beyond the course markers. Her face was pale, the freckles standing out on her cheeks; and her head was bared so that the thick dark braid of hair thumped against her shoulder.

Mungo St John smiled back at her over the heads of the crowd, and shrugged slightly, so that Louise was forced to turn back to Pickering.

'Very well, then,' she agreed. 'But the stake. We have not agreed the stake.'

'Major Ballantyne,' Pickering called to where Zouga stood at Tom's head. 'You have laid out the course. Now will you be good enough to name the stake.'

Then a strange thing happened. For the first time since Zouga had met her, Louise St John was uncertain of herself. Nobody else seemed to notice it, perhaps it was merely that Zouga had become highly receptive to every shade of her voice and expression. But he was certain that he saw something dark move in the blue depths of her eyes, like the shadow of a shark beneath the surface of the sea, and she took a pinch of her soft lower lip between her white teeth and again she glanced almost furtively at Mungo St John.

It was not Zouga's imagination. Mungo St John did not return Louise's glance with his usual amused indulgence. He was looking at Zouga and under his calm was a small undercurrent of unease, like an eddy at highwater when the tide turns.

Zouga raised his voice so that it would carry to St John.

'Firstly, the loser will publish at his or her own expense upon the front page of the *Advertiser* in terms dictated by the winner, an acknowledgement of defeat.'

'A composition I shall enjoy.' Louise had swiftly recovered her poise. 'And what else, Major?'

'A payment by the loser to a charity of the winner's choice of,' Zouga paused, and both man and woman watched his face with outward calm, 'of the sum of one shilling!'

'Done!'

There was a slightly jarring note in Louise's laugh, relief perhaps, and though Mungo St John's expression did not alter, the tension went out of his shoulders.

'Mrs St John. You are under starter's orders,' Pickering called through his speaking trumpet. 'Be so good as to bring your mount under control.'

'He is under perfect control, sir,' she called back, and Shooting Star put his head down and lashed out with both back hooves towards the crowd.

'If he is under control, Missus, then so is my mother-in-law,' called a wag, and there was a hoot of laughter.

'On the count of three then,' Pickering intoned, his voice hollow and solemn through the trumpet. 'One.'

Shooting Star backed up against the crowd, and they scattered as he bucked.

'Two.'

He went into a tortured high-stepping circle, so tight that his nose almost touched the toe of Louise's boot in the fancy silver stirrup.

'And three.' Louise lifted her left hand. Shooting Star came smoothly out of the circle, for the first time facing the start line, beginning to pace towards it majestically, and the pistol shot was a brief blurt of sound which sent the stallion sweeping away with an irresistible rush that made the slight figure on his wide back seem vulnerable and childlike.

There was no horse on the diamond fields that could match that first blazing burst of speed, the gap between the two horses opened, but not so dramatically as the watchers had expected. Tom's awkward gallop took him over the ground at surprising speed, and he was not following directly in Shooting Star's tracks.

'She's going wide, Thomas,' Zouga told him with satisfaction, and Tom cocked his ears back to listen. 'They aren't going to chance the river. Well, we didn't really think they would, did we?'

Directly ahead of Zouga the river started a lazy series of loops, symmetrical hairpin turns, winding back upon itself like a dying python.

Zouga had placed the red flag so that the direct line would cross the river-bed twice, and like most southern African rivers the banks were sheer, dropping ten feet to the dry sand and isolated rocky pools strung along the course. Each crossing was a trap in which a horse could break a leg and a rider his neck.

The alternative to the crossings was to ride wide, taking a circuit out beyond the meandering river course; but that almost doubled the distance to run to the first flag.

Already Shooting Star was a distant flying shape far out on the right, showing at intervals through gaps in the thorn scrub, marked by a little pale feather of dust flung up by his hooves.

'Here we are,' said Zouga, and under Tom's ugly Roman nose the ground opened abruptly.

Zouga gave him a slack rein, and Tom hardly checked on the brink of the steep clay bank. He sat down, and skidded over the edge on his fat round haunches, his forelegs sticking out stiffly ahead of him, and they toboganed down into the river bed and hit the sand in a scrambling tangle; and then Tom was up and lunging for the far bank, going half up before the dried clay crumbled under his hooves and they slid back again, Tom stiff-legged and trembling with exertion.

Zouga circled him once in the clinging white sand, and then put him to the bank again, and he went up in a determined series of buck-jumps, shifting his weight before the clay could break under his hooves, and they flew out over the top and were running again, the next bend of the river a quarter of a mile ahead.

At the next crossings Tom had the knack of it and they went down the bank and out the other side without a check. Under Tom's hooves the grass exploded into a whirl of noisy wings, and, with a wild harsh cry that would have panicked another horse, a big black-bellied bustard shot up into the air. Tom rolled a disdainful eye at the bird, steadied and gathered himself on the river bank of the last crossing and went down into it in a slide of dust and rolling pebbles.

As they came up the far bank the red flag was two hundred paces dead ahead.

Zouga swivelled in the saddle and looked out on his right hand.

'Good for you, Tom,' he called. 'You've made a mile on them.'

Far out across the plain, the golden horse was just swinging wide of the last bend of the river, and Louise was bent low on his neck, pushing him at reckless speed over the rough going.

'If she rides like that for a shilling – 'Zouga broke off, and himself leaned into the rhythm of Tom's gallop. A mile was such a slim margin, and the stakes he was riding for were enormous. His fortune, his dream – nay his very existence – was at stake.

'Go, Thomas, go!' Zouga whispered grimly into the long furry ears, and Tom stabbed at the earth with his awkward hump-backed gait.

Zouga did not look back again; he knew the stallion was bearing down on them, fast, too fast, but Zouga dismissed them from his attention and slid the carbine from the leather boot at his knee and opened the breech, checking the load.

The targets were white china soup plates, the range two hundred yards, extreme range after a gallop like this. The stewards were waving their hats to guide him up to the firing line.

'This way, Major.'

Zouga dropped the reins as he reached the low barrier of thorn branches that marked the firing line, and Tom came up short. He swung up the carbine, and fired as the butt slapped into his shoulder. One of the far-off specks of white burst and vanished. He cranked another round into the chamber, and glanced over his shoulder. The stallion was still half a mile away, but coming on with a war drum of hooves.

Zouga fired again, but Tom was blowing between his knees, heaving with the effort of the wild gallop.

'Damn it to hell.'

Haste would be fatal now, but his fingers fumbled the reload and a shiny brass cartridge slipped and struck his boot before it fell into the sand. He thrust another into the breech, took a long slow breath, and judged Tom's movements beneath him.

The rifle jumped against his shoulder, and the acrid plume of gunsmoke blew into his face. The second target exploded.

'Two down, Major,' one of the stewards shouted, and then as he fired again,

'Three down – one to go!'

Then beside Zouga the golden stallion came plunging to a halt, coming back low on glossy bunched quarters.

Louise vaulted from his back in a swirl of beaded buckskin skirts. There was a flash of the silky skin of her upper calf above the boot, and the back of a dimpled knee. Even in the press of the moment, he found the pale beautiful flesh disturbing enough to spoil his aim – and he swore as his next shot flew wide.

Louise was shooting the latest model of the legendary '73 Winchester repeater, the original polished brass frame replaced by blued steel, and Zouga knew that the modern centre-fire ammunition drove the heavy lead bullet with amazing power and accuracy.

She threw the stallion's rein over her left shoulder, and braced herself to fire from a standing position, leaning forward to absorb the recoil of the Winchester, and let her first shot fly.

She shot in the American style, throwing the rifle to her shoulder and firing in the same movement, not holding her aim nor giving the barrel time to wander. It was fine shooting.

'One hit to Mrs St John,' yelled the steward. But the crash of the shot had startled Shooting Star and he reared wildly and backed off on his hind legs, heaving at the reins that were looped over Louise's shoulder, jerking her over backwards so that her second shot flew in a long spurt of powder smoke towards the sky; and then she was down on her back, being dragged away, her skirts tangled about her legs, and the Winchester rifle was flung from her hand.

The stallion came down on his forelegs again. One hoof, sharp as a woodman's axe, grazed the tender spot at the nape of Louise's neck, just below the thick plait of dark hair, leaving an angry pink blaze on the pale skin but not breaking it.

Zouga felt the sweat on his throat turn so cold that he could not swallow. He swung Tom around to head off the stallion.

For unholy seconds Louise's body was hidden by flying dust and trampling hooves; Zouga tried to shout to her to let the horse go, but his voice had choked, and then abruptly Louise was on her knees.

She was facing Shooting Star, clinging stubbornly to his reins with both hands, and when he reared again she used his strength to let him boost her to her feet.

'Steady!' she called to him. 'Steady, I tell you.'

She was dusty and a tendril of dark hair had escaped the plait and hung into her eyes, but she was safe and very angry. Her voice crackled like breaking ice. Zouga's relief was immediate, but he mocked her as he swung Tom back to the firing line for his last target.

'I advise you to have that animal properly trained, madam.'

'To hell with you, Major Ballantyne!' she told him in the same tone as she had quelled her mount. Somehow the oath on her lips was not shocking at all, but strangely titillating.

Zouga gave Tom a few seconds to settle and regulate his breathing, and then swung up the rifle, held a full bead on the distant white speck and touched off the shot.

'Four hits – you are free to ride on, Major,' shouted the steward.

Louise was dragging Shooting Star by the reins to a wild plum tree, a tree with low and sturdy branches. Swiftly she lashed the stallion's reins to a branch, and now she was running back holding her skirts up to just below the knee, and the stewards gawked at her ankles in the tight-fitting buttoned boots.

She snatched the Winchester from a clump of sansevieria and ran up towards the firing line, reloading as she came. Zouga could see that there were little blisters of perspiration across her forehead, and knew that she was badly shaken, for when she threw up the rifle she held the shot and the heavy weapon wavered unsteadily.

She lowered it, and her shoulders were trembling. She took two long deep breaths and then lifted the Winchester again, firing on the toss up.

'Hit!' yelled the steward.

Louise's lower lip was quivering and she bit down on it fiercely, and shot again.

Zouga slid the carbine back into its leather scabbard, touched the brim of his helmet to Louise in a cavalier salute. 'Good shooting, ma'am.'

He turned Tom's head away from the firing line.

As they reached the wild plum, Zouga leaned out from the saddle. Louise had tied Shooting Star's reins to the branch with a slippery fisherman, it was a sailor's knot, a quick-release knot for a fast getaway.

Zouga twitched the loose end and the knot fell apart, then he slapped Shooting Star across the cheek with his open hand. 'Go on,' he said. 'Get out of it!'

The stallion jerked his head, found that he was free and kicked his heels high.

Zouga looked back as he reached the next low fold in the plain.

The stallion was grazing head down, but even at that distance it was apparent that he was keeping a wary eye on the lonely figure that ran after him in hampering skirts. As soon as Louise came within arm's length of his bridle, he tossed up his head and trotted away to the next clump of grass, leaving her blundering behind.

'Come, Tom.' He turned away, trying not to let his conscience trouble him. There were no rules, any ruse was acceptable, but it still felt bad – until he reminded himself of the stakes. A shilling against all he owned – and he set Tom to run in earnest.

Another mile and he glanced back, just in time to see Shooting Star and his rider come over the rise. They seemed to fly clear of the earth, borne along by the floating carpet of their own dust.

'Run! Tom! Run!' Zouga swept the hat off his head and slapped it against Tom's neck, goading him to his best speed.

Within another half mile Tom's shoulders were hot and slick with salt sweat. Ropes of saliva spilled from the corners of his lips and splattered onto Zouga's boots – but the yellow flag was in sight.

'Not far,' Zouga called to him anxiously. 'We must beat them to the flag.'

He looked back. He could not believe they were so close.

The stallion's head was driving like a hammer to each stride, and his neck and shoulders were black with sweat. She had pushed him fearfully. Louise was driving him with her arms and the rhythmic force of her body. Her hair was a wild tangle about her face, and her eyes were a blaze of blue.

Yet as she came up to them she straightened in the saddle, her chin lifted high, and she looked at Zouga coldly, expressionlessly, the way a queen might glance at an urchin running at the wheel of her coach.

Zouga lifted his right hand to salute her achievement. It had been a tremendous run, to make up so much ground. He was turned slightly towards her – and her expression of cold disinterest lulled him for the vital instant that it took her to bring Shooting Star level with Tom's shoulder.

Zouga never saw the command, probably the toe of her boot on the far side of Shooting Star's heaving chest; he had certainly not expected a show horse to have learned the low tricks of a polo pony. Shooting Star's huge sweat-streaked shoulder crashed into Tom, taking him in the short ribs with a force that drove the air out of him in a belching grunt, and as he was spun aside Tom chopped desperately to keep from falling, twisting and dropping to his knees, his nose on the ground, too tired and taken too unawares to meet the power of that ferocious barge.

Zouga lost a stirrup and was thrown onto Tom's neck. He clung desperately, feeling the saddle shift under the unequal transfer of weight; then Tom heaved again and Zouga went over, landing on his shoulders and the back of his neck.

He seemed to strike solid rock and blackness crushed down from the dome of his skull. When it cleared, he was standing again, swaying like a drunk, blinking uncertainly after the pounding stallion as he pulled away towards the last flag.

Zouga pulled Tom to his feet, and checked swiftly for strained sinew or broken bone, then threw himself back into the saddle.

'We're not beat yet,' he told Tom. 'There are still the thorns.'

Far ahead Shooting Star was making the turn around the last flag. From there Louise was free to make her way back to the finish line any way she wanted, but there were still the thorns.

Tom was winded, his chest shuddering with the effort of each laboured breath, and they reached the flag in an awkward jarring trot and made the turn. Ahead of them the thorns stretched in a solid green barrier. This was the last obstacle – and beyond it was a clear run to the finish.

A rider had a choice: go through the thorn, or ride wide.

'Which way did she go?' Zouga shouted at the stewards below the flag as he went past.

'She's gone for the gap,' one of them yelled back, and then Zouga saw the little feather of dust a mile or more out on the right subsiding only slowly as the stallion sped away.

The thorn barrier petered out on the rocky slopes of the Magersfontein hills, and there was an open gap below the steep ironstone cliffs – that was where the stallion was aimed.

Grimly Zouga swung Tom around the flag and pointed him directly at the thorns. This route was almost two miles shorter, but he would need every inch of it. Yet he stopped Tom when they reached the edge of the thorns and let him breathe as he untied the heavy greatcoat from the pommel of his saddle and shrugged into it. He buttoned it high at the throat and felt the sweat burst out on his forehead as he pulled on the leather gauntlets to protect his hands.

'Let's go,' he whispered, and lay flat on Tom's neck, as they crashed into the thorn.

The red-tipped hooked points of the thorns skidded over

Zouga's thick felt hat with a rasping tearing sound, and tugged at the shoulders and skirts of the greatcoat.

The brush grew as high as a mounted man's head, the sturdy trunks just far enough apart to let a horse pass, but the barbed branches intertwined and exacted a cruel toll. However, Tom kept going, swinging and chopping from side to side; he dodged between the white barked trunks, ducking his head under the branches, his ears flat against his skull and his eyes closed to slits, maintaining just the right amount of momentum to snap the thorns off their triangular bases and showering both himself and Zouga with a confetti of feathery green leaves. Every few seconds he snorted at the sting of thorn that had penetrated his tough shaggy hide.

Shooting Star's burnished skin was so thin and finely bred that the network of veins and arteries showed through it. The thorns would have ripped it to bloody tatters.

Zouga felt blood trickling down his own neck from where a thorn had nicked his ear, but he crouched lower and let Tom pick his own way through. 'Poor Tom,' he encouraged him. 'Poor brave Tom.' The horse whickered with the pain of the stinging red needles, but did not check his stride. Yet his breathing was easier now, the slower gait had helped him; and the sweat was drying in salty white crystals on his shoulders.

Then abruptly they burst out of the thorn onto the open plain. Zouga tore off the leather gauntlets and threw them away. He ripped at the buttons of the greatcoat and let it fly away, flapping like a great black crow in the wind of Tom's gallop – and then he stood high in the stirrups and shaded his eyes with the brim of his hat.

Swiftly he searched the open ground, but it was empty as far as the tiny specks of colour in the distance: women's dresses and the gay bunting that marked the finish. His heart bounded with relief, and under him Tom lunged into a clumsy gallop.

Still standing in the stirrups, Zouga looked towards the line of hills out on his right hand, and he saw them.

The stallion had turned the far end of the thorn barrier where it ran into the hills and was coming down the rocky slope towards the level ground in a dangerous scramble.

The tiny figure on his back was being thrown about brutally. One instant she seemed to be on his neck, the next she was flung back onto his haunches, as Shooting Star plunged and heaved to keep his balance.

'We have them now, Tom. There it is. There is the line, right under your nose.' Zouga pointed his head. 'They cannot catch us now. Go, old man, go!'

Tom's hooves cracked on the hard earth like the beat of a joyous drummer. The crossing of the thorns had been cruel work, but it had rested him and he was pushing hard now.

' 'Ware hole!' Zouga called to him, and Tom flicked his ears reproachfully. He had seen it before Zouga had, and he jinked around the burrow neatly, while the heads of the curious little ground squirrels bobbed out of the earth as they passed.

The ground was rotten with their warrens, but Tom barely checked his gallop, swinging to avoid the mounds of freshly-turned earth, or occasionally stretching out to step over an entrance hole.

The ground squirrels were almost indistinguishable from their northern cousins, except for the stripe down their furry backs and their terrestrial habit. They stood on their hind legs, like small groups of spectators at the entrance of each warren, their expressions comically astonished and their long bushy tails curled over their backs as Tom pounded past them.

Zouga looked over his shoulder. Shooting Star was off the steep slope of the hills, down onto the open plain, and it was apparent that he was burning the last reserves of his great strength, coming on in a blazing run, driving out with his fore-legs, and then bunching up his sweat-drenched hindquarters to hurl himself into the next stride. Louise was pushing him with her arms, like a washerwoman working over the scrubbing board, but she was too far behind for Zouga to see the expression on her face.

Much too far behind, half a mile behind – and there was less than a mile to run to the line of gaily coloured bunting that marked the finish.

Zouga could clearly see the crowds on each side of the posts, thick as bees at the entrance to the hive, and others were running for the wagons to join them.

He could hear the faint pop of gunfire, see the little spurts of gunsmoke jumping up above the heads of the crowd as his supporters fired into the air in jubilation.

Soon he would hear their voices, catch the sound of their cheers, even above the beat of Tom's hooves.

It was all over. He had won. He had won back his claims, the cherished image of the falcon god – and the five thousand pounds with which he could take his family away to a new life. He had taken on the gods of chance and won.

He had only one regret – that the courage of the horse and rider behind him had been in vain. Careful not to unbalance Tom's heavy unlovely gallop, he looked back under his own arm.

By God, she had not yet accepted defeat. She was driving with all her strength and all her heart, pushing the great horse as hard as she pushed herself, coming on so swiftly that Zouga glanced uneasily over Tom's pricked ears to reassure himself as to the proximity of the finish line. No, there was no chance – even at that tremendous speed – Shooting Star could never catch them.

Already he could hear the voices of the crowd, make out their individual faces, even recognize Pickering, the chief steward, on his seat on the wagon, and beside him Rhodes' unmistakable bulk and the mop of unruly hair. With him to witness it, Zouga's triumph was complete.

He turned for the last time to look back at Shooting Star – just in time to see him fall. It had been much too fast, too uncontrolled, that wild gallop across ground rotten with squirrel warrens. Shooting Star's front legs went from under him. Zouga imagined he could hear the bone break, like the crack of a pistol shot, and the huge horse went down from full gallop, shoulder first, neck twisted around in an agonized contortion like that of a dying flamingo; dust flew up in a cloud, blanketing them, and above it the stallion's hooves kicked spasmodically, convulsively, and then sagged.

The pale beige dust cloud drifted aside, revealing the tragic tangle of horse and rider. Shooting Star lay on his side and, as Zouga reined in and swung Tom's nose back the way he had come, the great stallion made a feeble effort to lift his head off the ground and then let it fall back weakly.

Louise's body had been flung clear. She lay curled like a sleeping child on the bare earth, very still, very small.

'Ha, Tom, ha!' Zouga urged him to greater speed. He was shocked at the sense of utter desolation that assailed him as he galloped back to where she lay. There was something so final, so terribly chilling in her stillness, in the complete relaxation, the lifelessness of that tiny crumpled body.

'Please God,' Zouga spoke aloud, his throat seared by dust and thirst and dread. 'Please don't let it be.'

He imagined the lovely delicate neck twisted at an impossible angle against the shattered vertebrae. He imagined the awful bloodless depression in the delicate dome of her skull; he imagined those huge dark eyes, open and staring, the inner glow fading – he imagined, oh God, he imagined – Then he was kicking his feet clear of the stirrups and jumping down even while Tom was at full gallop, stumbling to keep his balance and then running to where she lay.

Louise uncurled her body and rolled lightly to her feet.

'Come, darling, up darling,' she called to Shooting Star, as she ran to him. The stallion lunged once, twice and then he was standing, head up.

'What a clever darling,' Louise laughed, but with the huskiness of excitement and the tremor of heart-breaking exertion in the sound of it.

She did not have the strength left to vault for the saddle, and for a moment she hopped with one foot in the stirrup before she could find the energy to swing her other leg up over Shooting Star's back, while Zouga stood and gaped at her.

From the saddle she looked down at Zouga. 'Playing dead is an old Blackfoot Indian's trick, Major.'

Louise swung the stallion's head towards the finish line.

'Let's see you run the last lap on equal terms,' she challenged, and Shooting Star jumped away at full gallop.

For a moment Zouga could not bring himself to believe that she had taught the stallion to fall so convincingly, and to lie so still. Then suddenly his concern for her safety, the desolate feeling of believing her dead or maimed turned to fury and outrage.

As he ran back to where Tom stood, he yelled after her.

'Madam, you are a cheat – may God forgive you for that.'

She turned in the saddle and waved gaily. 'Sir, you are gullible, but I will forgive you for that.'

And Shooting Star bore her away towards the finish at a pace that poor Tom could never match.

Zouga Ballantyne was drunk. It was the first time in the twenty-two years they had been together that Jan Cheroot had seen him so.

He sat very erect on the high-backed deal chair, and his face above the beard had a strange waxen look to it. His eyes were glazed over with the same soapy sheen of uncut diamonds. The third bottle of Cape Brandy stood on the green baize of the table between them, and as Zouga fumbled for it, he knocked it over. The spirit glugged loudly from the mouth, and soaked into the cloth.

Jan Cheroot snatched it upright, with a shocked oath.

'Man, if you want to lose the Devil's Own, I don't mind – but, when you spill the brandy – that's another thing.'

Jan Cheroot stumbled a little over the words; they had been drinking since an hour before sundown.

'What am I going to tell the boys?' mumbled Zouga.

'Tell them that they are on holiday – for the first time in ten years. We are all on holiday.'

Jan Cheroot poured brandy into Zouga's mug, and pushed it closer to his hand. Then he poured a good dram into his own, thought about it for a moment, and added as much again.

'I have lost everything, Old Jan.'

'Ja,' Jan Cheroot said cheerfully. 'And that was not very much, was it.'

'I have lost the claims.'

'Good.' Jan Cheroot nodded. 'For ten years those double-damned squares of dirt ate our souls away – and starved us while they were doing it.'

'I have lost the bird.'

'Good again!' Jan Cheroot swigged his brandy, and smacked his lips with appreciation. 'Let Mr Rhodes have his share of bad luck now. That bird will finish him, as it nearly finished us. Send it to him as soon as you can, and thank God to be rid of it.'

Slowly Zouga lowered his face into his hands, covering his eyes and his mouth – so that his voice was muffled.

'Jan Cheroot. It's all over. For me the road to the north is closed. My dream is finished. It's all been for nothing.'

The bibulous grin faded slowly and Jan Cheroot's yellow face puckered with deep compassion.

'It is not finished – you are still young and strong – with two strong sons.'

'We shall lose them too – soon, very soon.'

'Then you will have me, old friend, like it has always been.'

Zouga lifted his head out of his hands and stared at the little Hottentot.

'What are we going to do, Jan Cheroot?'

'We are going to finish this bottle and then open another,' Jan Cheroot told him firmly.

In the morning they loaded the soapstone idol into the gravel cart, and laid it on a bed of straw; then Zouga spread a stained and tattered tarpaulin over it and Jordan helped him rope it down.

Neither of them spoke – until they were finished, and then Jordan whispered so softly that Zouga barely caught the words.

'You can't let it go, Papa.' And Zouga turned to look at his younger son, truly seeing him for the first time in many years.

With a small shock he realized that Jordan was a man. In imitation of Ralph perhaps, he also had grown a moustache. It was a dense coppery gold, and accentuated the gentle line of his mouth – yet, if anything, the man was more beautiful than the child had been.

'Is there no way we can keep it?' Jordan persisted, with a thin edge of desperation in his voice, and Zouga went on staring at him. How old was he now? Over nineteen years, and yesterday he had been a baby – little Jordie. Everything was changed.

Zouga turned away from him, and placed his hand on the tarpaulin-wrapped burden in the bottom of the cart.

'No, Jordan. It was a wager – a matter of honour.'

'But, Mama –' Jordan started and then broke off abruptly as Zouga looked back at him sharply.

'What about Aletta?' he demanded, and Jordan looked away and flushed, bringing up the colour under the velvety skin of his cheeks.

'Nothing,' he said quickly, and went to the head of the lead mule. 'I will take the bird to Mr Rhodes,' he volunteered, and Zouga nodded immediately, relieved that he would be spared this painful duty.

'Ask him when he will be free to sign the transfer of the claims.'

Zouga touched the wrapped statue again as though in farewell and then he pulled his hand away, went up the steps onto the verandah and into the bungalow without looking back.

Jordan led the mules out into the rutted road and swung them towards the settlement. He walked bareheaded in the sunlight. He was tall and slim and he moved with a peculiar grace, stepping lightly and lithely in the soft red dust. His chin was up, his eyes focused far ahead, with the dreaming, yet all-seeing, gaze of a poet.

Men and women, especially women, looked after him as he passed and their expressions softened, but Jordan walked on as though he were alone on a deserted street.

Though his lips never moved, the words of the invocation to the goddess Panes kept running through his mind.

'– Why did you run away? You would have been better with us –' So many times he had called to the goddess, the words were part of his very existence. 'Will you not come back to us, great Panes?'

The goddess was going – and Jordan did not believe he could support the agony of it. Statue, goddess and mother were all one in his mind, his last link with Aletta. Aletta who had become Panes.

He felt desolate, bereaved as though of his dearest love, and when he reached the milkwood fence of Rhodes' camp, he stopped and wild fancies seized him. He would take the goddess, run with her into the wilderness, hide her in some distant cave. His heart bounded. No, he would take her back to the ancient ruined city from which she had come, that far place in the north from which his father had stolen her, where she would be safe.

Then with a plunge of his spirits and a slide of despair in his guts he knew that these were childish dreamings and that he was no longer a child.

With a light touch on the lead mule's bridle, he guided her into the camp, and Rhodes was standing at the front door of his bungalow, bareheaded and in shirtsleeves. He was talking quietly, urgently to a man below the stoep. Jordan recognized him as one of the Central Diamond Company overseers.

When Rhodes looked up and saw Jordan, he dismissed the overseer with a curt word and a nod.

'Jordan,' Rhodes' greeting was grave, perhaps he sensed the mood of the young man before him, 'you have brought it?'

When Jordan nodded, he turned back to the waiting overseer.

'Bring four of your best men,' he ordered. 'I want this cart unloaded – and carefully. It's a valuable work of art.'

He watched keenly as they untied the ropes that held the tarpaulin in place, but cocked the large curly head when Jordan spoke.

'If we have to lose it, then I'm glad it's you that it goes to, Mr Rhodes.'

'The bird means something to you also, Jordan?'

'Everything,' Jordan said simply, and then caught himself; that sounded ridiculous. Mr Rhodes would think him strange. 'I mean, it has been in my family since before I was born. I don't really know what it will be like without that goddess. I don't really want to think about losing it.'

'You don't have to lose it, Jordan.'

Jordan looked at him, unable to bring himself to ask the meaning.

'You can follow the goddess, Jordan.'

'Please don't tease me, Mr Rhodes.'

'You are bright and willing, you have studied Pitman's shorthand, and you have an excellent pen,' Rhodes said. 'I need a secretary – somebody who knows and loves diamonds as I do. Somebody whom I feel easy with. Somebody I know and whom I like. Somebody I can trust.'

Jordan felt a vast soaring rush of joy, something sharper, brighter and more poignant than he had ever known before. He could not speak; he stood rooted and stared into the pale blue and beautiful eyes of the man whom he had worshipped for so many years.

'Well, Jordan, I am offering you the position. Do you want it?'

'Yes,' Jordan said softly. 'More than anything on earth, Mr Rhodes.'

'Good, then your first task is to find a place to set up the bird.'

The white overseer had pulled the tarpaulin aside to expose the statue, and the sheet hung down over the side of the cart.

'Easy now,' he shouted at the gang of black labourers. 'Get a rope on it. Don't drop it. Watch that end, damn you.'

They swarmed over the statue, too many of them for the job, getting in one another's way – and Jordan's heady joy at Rhodes' offer was submerged in a quick stab of concern for the safety of the bird.

He started forward to set the ropes himself, but at that moment there was the clatter of hooves and Neville Pickering rode into the yard. He was astride his mare, a highly bred and finely mettled bay, and he reined her down to a walk.

He shot a glance at Jordan, and his face clouded for an instant – a quick show of irritation, or of something else. With a sudden intuitive flash Jordan realized that Pickering resented his presence here.

Then as quickly as it had come the shadow passed from Pickering's handsome features and he smiled that sunny charming smile of his and looked down at the statue in the cart.

'What have we here?' His tone was gay, his manner carefree and relaxed. As always he was elegantly dressed, the drape of broadcloth showing off his broad shoulders, the tooled leather belt emphasizing his narrow waist, as the polished half boots did the length and shape of his legs. The low-crowned, broad-brimmed hat was cocked forward over one eye, and he was smiling.

'Oh, the bird.' He looked up at Rhodes on the stoep of the bungalow. 'So you have it at last, as you said you would. I should congratulate you.'

The day had been still and too hot, it would change soon. The wind would come out of the south and the temperature would plunge, but until then the only movements of air were the sudden little dust devils that sprang out of nowhere, small but violent whirlwinds that lifted a high churning vortex of dust and dry grass and dead leaves a hundred or more feet into the still sky as they sped in a wildly erratic course across the plain, and then just as suddenly collapsed and disintegrated into nothingness again.

One of these dust devils rose now, on the open ground beyond the milkwood hedge. It tore a dense red cloud of spinning dust off the surface of the road, then swerved abruptly and raced into the yard of Rhodes' camp. Jordan felt his heart gripped in a cold vice of superstitious dread.

'Panes!' The cry was silent in his head. 'Great Panes!'

He knew what that wind was, he knew the presence of the goddess – for how many times had she come to his invocation? Suddenly the whole yard was filled with the swirling torrents of dust, and the wind battered them. It flew into Jordan's face, so that he must slit his eyes against it. It flung his soft shiny curls into his face, and it flattened his shirt against his chest and his lean flat belly.

The broad-brimmed hat sailed from Pickering's head, the tails of his coat flogged into the small of his back and he lifted one hand to protect his face from the stinging sand and sharp pieces of twig and grass.

Then the wind got under the ragged old tarpaulin, and filled it with a crack like a ship's mainsail gybing onto the opposite tack.

The harsh canvas lashed the bay mare's head, and she reared up on her back legs, whinnying shrilly with panic.

So high she went that Jordan thought she would go over on her back, and through the red raging curtain of dust, he jumped to catch her head; but he was an instant too late. Pickering had one hand to his face, and the mare's leap took him off balance; he went over backwards out of the saddle, and he hit hard earth with the back of his neck and one shoulder.

The rushing sound of the whirlwind, the grunt of air driven from Pickering's lungs and the meaty thump of his fall almost covered the tiny snapping sound of bone breaking somewhere deep in his body.

Then the mare came down from her high prancing dance, and she flattened immediately into full gallop. She flew at the gateway in the milkwood hedge, and Pickering was dragged after her, his ankle trapped in the steel of the stirrup, his body slithering and bouncing loosely across the earth.

As the mare swerved to take the gap in the hedge, Pickering was flung into the hedge, and the white thorns, each as long as a man's forefinger, were driven into his flesh like needles.

Then he was plucked away, out into the open ground, sledging over rocky earth, striking and flattening the small wiry bushes as the mare jumped them, his body totally relaxed and his arms flung out behind him.

One moment the back of his head was slapping against the earth, and the next his ankle had twisted in the stirrup and he was face down, the skin being smeared from his cheeks and forehead by the harsh abrasive earth.

Jordan found himself racing after him, his breath sobbing with horror – calling to the mare.

'Whoa, girl! Steady, girl!'

But she was maddened, firstly terrified by the wind and the flirt of canvas into her face, and now by the unfamiliar weight that dragged and slithered at her heels. She reached the slope of the trailing dumps and swerved again, and this time, mercifully, the stirrup leather parted with a twang. Freed of her burden, the mare galloped away down the pathway between the dumps.

Jordan dropped on his knees beside Pickering's inert crumpled body. He lay face down; the expensive broadcloth was ripped and dusty, the boots scuffed through to white leather beneath.

Gently, supporting his head in cupped hands, Jordan rolled him onto his back, turning his face out of the dust so that he could breathe. Pickering's face was a bloodied mask, caked with dust, a flap of white skin hanging off his cheek – but his eyes were wide open.

Despite the complete deathlike relaxation of his arms and body, Pickering was fully conscious. His eyes swivelled to Jordan's face, and his lips moved.

'Jordie,' he whispered. 'I can't feel anything, nothing at all. Numb – my hands, my feet, my whole body numb.'

They carried him back in a blanket, a man at each corner, and laid him gently on the narrow iron-framed cot in the bedroom next door to Rhodes' own room.

Dr Jameson came within the hour, and he nodded when he saw how Jordan had bathed and dressed his injuries and the arrangements he had made for his comfort.

'Good. Who taught you?' But he did not wait for an answer. 'Here!' he said. 'I'll need your help.' And he handed Jordan his bag, shrugged out of his jacket and rolled his sleeves.

'Get out,' he said to Rhodes. 'You'll be in the way here.'

It took Jameson only minutes to make certain that the paralysis below the neck was complete, and then he looked up at Jordan, making sure that he was out of sight of Pickering's alert, fever-bright eyes, and he shook his head curtly.

'I'll be a minute,' he said. 'I must speak with Mr Rhodes.'

'Jordie,' Pickering whispered painfully, the moment Jameson left the room, and Jordan stooped to his lips. 'It's my neck – it's broken.'

'No.'

'Be quiet. Listen.' Pickering frowned at the interruption. 'I think I always knew – that it would be you. One way or the other, it would be you –'

He broke off, fresh sweat blistered on his forehead, but he made another terrible effort to speak. 'I thought I hated you. But not any more – not now. There is not enough time left for hate.'

He did not speak again, not that night, nor the following day. But at dusk when the heat in the tiny iron-walled room abated a little, he opened his eyes again and looked up at Rhodes. It was frightening to see how low he had sunk. The fine bones of forehead and cheeks seemed to gleam through the translucent skin, and his eyes had receded into dark bruised cavities.

Rhodes leaned his great shaggy head over him until his ear touched Pickering's dry white lips. The whisper was so light, like a dead leaf blown softly across a roof at midnight, and Jordan could not hear the words, but Rhodes clenched his lids closed over his pale blue eyes as though in mortal anguish.

'Yes,' he answered, almost as softly as the dying man. 'Yes, I know, Pickling.'

When Rhodes opened his eyes again they were flooded with bright tears, and his colour was a frightening mottled purple.

'He's dead, Jordan,' he choked, and put one hand on his own chest, pressing hard as though to calm the beat of his swollen heart.

Then quite slowly, deliberately, he lowered his head again, and kissed the broken, torn lips of the man on the iron-framed cot.

Zouga thought the voice was part of his dream – so sweet, so low, and yet tremulous and filled with some dreadful appeal. Then he was awake, and the voice was still calling, and now there was a light tap on the window above the head of his bed.

'I'm coming,' Zouga answered, as low as he was called. He did not have to ask who it was.

He dressed swiftly, in total darkness, instinct warning him not to light a candle, and he carried his boots in his hand as he stepped out onto the stoep of the cottage.

The height of the moon told him that it was after midnight, but he barely glanced at it before turning to the figure that leaned against the wall beside the door.

'Are you alone?' he demanded softly. There was something in the way the figure slumped that frightened him.

'Yes.' The distress, the pain, were clear in her voice now that they were so close.

'You should not have come here – not alone, Mrs St John.'

'There was nobody else to turn to.'

'Where is Mungo. Where is your husband?'

'He is in trouble – terrible, terrible, trouble.'

'Where is he?'

'I left him out beyond the Cape crossroad.'

For a moment her voice choked on her, and then it came out with a forceful rush.

'He's hurt. Wounded, badly wounded.'

Her voice had risen, so that she might rouse Jan Cheroot and the boys. Zouga took her arm to calm and quieten her, and immediately she fell against him. The feel of her body shocked him, but he could not pull away.

'I'm afraid, Zouga. I'm afraid he might die.' It was the first time she had used his given name.

'What happened?'

'Oh God!' She was weeping now, clinging to him, and he realized how hard-pressed she was. He slipped his arm around her waist and led her down the verandah.

In the kitchen he seated her on one of the hard deal chairs, and then lit the candle. He was shocked again when he saw her face. She was pale and shaking, her hair in wild disorder, a smear of dirt on one cheek and her eyes red-rimmed and bloodshot.

He poured coffee from the blue enamel pot at the back of the stove. It was thick as molasses. He added a dram of brandy to it.

'Drink it.'

She shuddered and gasped at the potent black brew, but it seemed to steady her a little.

'I didn't want him to go. I tried to stop him. I was sick of it. I told him I couldn't take it any more, the cheating and lying. The shame and the running –'

'You aren't making sense,' he told her brusquely, and she took a deep breath and started again.

'Mungo went to meet a man tonight. The man was going to bring him a parcel of diamonds, a parcel of diamonds worth one hundred thousand pounds. And Mungo was going to buy them for two thousand.'

Zouga's face set grimly, and he sat down opposite her and stared at her. His expression intimidated her.

'Oh God, Zouga. I know. I hated it too. I have lived with it so long, but he promised me that this would be the last time.'

'Go on,' Zouga commanded.

'But he didn't have two thousand, Zouga. We are almost broke – a few pounds is all that we have left.'

This time Zouga could not contain himself and he broke in.

'The letter of credit, half a million pounds –'

'Forged,' she said quietly.

'Go on.'

'He didn't have the money to pay for the diamonds – and I knew what he was going to do. I tried to stop him, I swear it to you.'

'I believe you.'

'He arranged to meet this man tonight – at a place out on the Cape road.'

'Do you know the man's name?'

'I'm not sure. I think so.' She passed her hand over her eyes. 'He is a coloured man, a Griqua, Henry – no, Hendrick Somebody –'

'Hendrick Naaiman?'

'Yes. Naaiman, that's it.'

'He's an I.D.B. trap.'

'Police?'

'Yes, police.'

'Oh sweet God, it's even worse than I thought.'

'What happened?' Zouga insisted.

'Mungo made me wait for him at the crossroads and he went to the rendezvous alone. He said he needed to protect himself – he took his pistol. He went on my horse – on Shooting Star, and then I heard the gunfire.'

She took another gulp of the coffee and coughed at the burn of it.

'He came back. He had been shot, and so had Shooting Star. They couldn't go any further, neither of them. They were both hard hit, Zouga. I hid them near the road and I came to you.'

Zouga's voice was harsh. 'Did Mungo kill him?'

'I don't know, Zouga. Mungo says the other man fired first and he only tried to protect himself.'

'Mungo tried to hold him up and take the diamonds, without paying for them,' Zouga guessed. 'But Naaiman is a dangerous man.'

'There were four empty cartridges in Mungo's pistol, but I don't know what happened to the policeman. I only know that Mungo escaped, but he is hurt very badly.'

'Now keep quiet and rest for a while.' He stood up and paced up and down the kitchen, his bare feet making no sound, his hands clasped at the small of the back.

Louise St John watched him anxiously, almost fearfully, until he stopped abruptly and turned to her.

'We both know what I should do. Your husband is I.D.B.; he is a thief and by now he is probably a murderer.'

'He is also your friend,' she said simply. 'And he is very badly wounded.'

He resumed his pacing, but now he was muttering to himself, troubled and scowling, and Louise twisted her fingers in her lap.

'Very well,' he said at last. 'I'll help you to get him away.'

'Oh, Major Ballantyne – Zouga –'

He silenced her with a frown. 'Don't waste time talking. We'll need bandages, laudanum, food –' He was ticking off a list on his fingers. 'You can't go like that. They'll be watching for a woman. Jordan's cast-off clothes will fit you well enough – breeches, cap and coat –'

Zouga walked at the flank of the mule, and the gravel cart was loaded with bales of thatching grass.

Louise lay silently in the hollow between two bales, with another ready to pull over herself if the cart was stopped.

The iron-shod wheels crunched in the sand, but the night dew had damped down the dust. The lantern on the tailboard of the cart swung and jiggled to the motion.

They had just passed the last house on the Cape road, and were drawing level with the cemetery when there was the dust-muffled beat of hooves from behind them and Louise only just had time to drop down and cover herself before a small group of riders swept out of the darkness and overtook them.

As they galloped through the arc of lantern light, Zouga saw they were all armed. He stooped and lowered his chin into the collar of his greatcoat and the woollen cap was pulled low over his eyes. One of the riders pulled up his horse and shouted to Zouga.

'Hey, you! Have you seen anybody on this road tonight?'

'*Niemand nie*! Nobody!' Zouga answered in the taal, and the sound of the guttural dialect reassured the man.

He wheeled his horse and galloped on after his companions.

When the sound of hooves had died away Zouga spoke quietly.

'That means that Naaiman got away to spread the word. Unless he dies of his wounds later, it's not murder.'

'Please God,' Louise whispered.

'It also means that you cannot try to get out on either the Cape road or the road to the Transvaal. They will be watched.'

'Which way can we go?'

'If I were you I would take the track north, it goes to Kuruman. There is a mission station there – it's run by my grandfather. His name is Doctor Moffat. He will give you shelter, and Mungo will need a doctor. Then when Mungo is strong enough, you can try to reach German or Portuguese territory and get out through Lüderitz Bay or Lourenço Marques.'

Neither of them spoke for a long time as Zouga trudged on beside the mule, and Louise crawled out to sit on the bench of the cart. It was she who broke the silence.

'I am so tired of running. We seem to have run out of lands, America, Canada, Australia, we cannot go back to any of them.'

'You could go home to France,' Zouga said, 'to your sons.'

Louise's head jerked up. 'Why do you say that?'

'When Mungo and I first met he told me about you, his wife – that you were of a noble French family. He told me that you and he had three sons.'

Louise's chin sank onto her chest and Jordan's cloth cap covered her eyes.

'I have no sons,' she said. 'But oh how I pray that one day I may have. I belong to a noble family, yes – but not French. My grandmother was the daughter of Hawk Flies Lightly, the Blackfoot War Chief.'

'I don't understand, Mungo told me –'

'He told you about the woman who is his wife, Madame Solange de Montijo St John.'

Louise was silent again, and Zouga had to ask:

'She is dead?'

'Their marriage was unhappy. No, she is not dead. She

returned with their three sons to France at the beginning of the Civil War. He has not seen her since.'

'Then she and Mungo are,' Zouga hesitated over the unsavoury word, 'divorced?'

'She is a Catholic,' Louise replied simply; and it was fully five minutes before either of them spoke again.

'Yes,' Louise said. 'What you are thinking is correct. Mungo and I are not married; we could not be.'

'It's not my business,' Zouga murmured, and yet what she had said did not shock him. He felt instead a strange lightness of spirit, a kind of glowing joy.

'It's a relief to speak completely honestly,' she explained. 'After all the lies. Somehow it had to be you, Zouga. I could never have admitted all this to anybody else.'

'Do you love him?' Zouga's voice was rough-edged, brusque.

'Once I loved him completely, without restraint, wildly – madly.'

'And now?'

'I do not know – there have been so many lies, so much shame, so much to hide.'

'Why do you stay with him, Louise?'

'Because now he needs me.'

'I understand that.' His voice was gentler. He did understand, he truly did. 'Duty is a harsh and unforgiving master. And yet you have a duty to yourself also.'

The mules plodded on in the darkness, and the swinging lantern did not light the face of the woman on the bench, but once she sighed, and it was a sound to twist Zouga's heart.

'Louise,' he spoke at last. 'I am not doing this for Mungo, even a friendship cannot condone deliberate robbery and premeditated murder.'

She did not reply.

'Many times you must have seen the way I have looked at you – for, God knows, I could not help myself.'

Still she was silent.

'You did know,' he insisted. 'You, as a woman, must know how I feel.'

'Yes,' she said at last.

'When I thought you were married to a friend, it was hopeless. Now, at least, I can tell you how I feel.'

'Zouga, please don't.'

'I would do anything you asked me to – even protect a murderer, that is how I feel for you.'

'Zouga –'

'I have never known anybody so beautiful and bright and brave –'

'I am not any of those things –'

'I could put you and Mungo on the road to Kuruman and then go back to Kimberley and tell the diamond police where to find you. They would take Mungo, and then you would be free.'

'You could,' she agreed. 'But you never would. Both of us are tied, Zouga, by our own peculiar sense of duty and of honour.'

'Louise –'

'We have arrived,' she said, with patent relief. 'The crossroads. Turn off the road here.'

From the bench she guided him as he threaded the cart through the scattered bush and the high wheels bumped over rock and rough ground. A quarter of a mile from the road there stood a massive camel-thorn tree, silver and high as a hill in the moonlight. Beneath its spread branches the moon shadow was black and impenetrable.

From the darkness a hoarse voice challenged.

'Stand where you are! Don't come any closer.'

'Mungo, it's me and Zouga is with me.'

Louise jumped down from the cart, lifted the lantern off its bracket and went forward, stooping under the branches. Zouga tethered the mules and then followed her. Louise was kneeling beside Mungo St John. He lay on a saddle blanket, propped on the silver ornamented Mexican saddle.

'Thank you for coming,' he greeted Zouga, and his voice was ragged with pain.

'How badly are you hit?'

'Badly enough,' he admitted. 'Do you have a cheroot?'

Zouga lit one from the lantern and handed it to him. Louise was unwrapping the torn strips of shirt and petticoat that were bound about his chest.

'Shotgun?' Zouga asked tersely.

'No, thank God,' Mungo said. 'Pistol.'

'You are lucky,' Zouga grunted. 'Naaiman's usual style is a sawed-off shotgun. He would have blown you in half.'

'You know him – Naaiman?'

'He's a police trap.'

'Police,' Mungo whispered. 'Oh God.'

'Yes,' Zouga nodded. 'You are in trouble.'

'I didn't know.'

'Does it really matter?' Zouga asked. 'You planned an I.D.B. switch, and you knew you might have to kill a man.'

'Don't preach to me, Zouga.'

'All right.' Zouga squatted next to Louise as she exposed the wound in Mungo's back. 'And it looks as though it missed the bloody lymph, set in a livid spread of bruise.'

Between them they lifted Mungo into a sitting position.

'Through and through,' Zouga murmured, as he saw the exit wound in Mungo's back. 'And it looks as though it missed the lung. You are luckier than you'll ever know.'

'One stayed in,' Mungo St John contradicted him, and reached down to his own leg. His breeches had been split down the leg, and now he pulled the bloodstained cloth aside to reveal a strip of pale thigh in the centre of which was another vicious little round opening from which fluid wept like blackcurrant juice.

'The bullet is still in,' Mungo repeated.

'Bone?' Zouga asked.

'No.' St John shook his head. 'I don't think so. I was still able to walk on it.'

'There is no chance of trying to cut the bullet out. Louise knows where she can find a doctor, and I have told her how to get there.'

'Louise?' Mungo asked with a sardonic twist of his lips.

She did not look up, concentrating on the task of painting the skin around the wounds with iodine.

Mungo was staring at Zouga, his single eye gleaming, and Zouga felt the scar on his cheek throb and he did not trouble to hide his anger.

'You don't think I am doing this for you,' he demanded. 'I hate I.D.B. as much as any digger on the workings, and I'm not that complacent about deliberate robbery and murder.' And he took the pistol from the blanket where it lay at Mungo's side.

He checked the load as he walked to where Shooting Star stood, head down in the moonlight beyond the camel-thorn tree.

The stallion lifted his head, and blew a fluttery breath through his nostrils as Zouga approached; then he shifted his weight awkwardly and painfully on three legs.

'There, boy. Easy, boy.' Zouga ran his hands down the animal's flank. It was sticky with drying blood, and Shooting Star whickered as he touched the wound.

Behind the ribs, bullet hole, and Zouga sniffed at it quickly. The bullet had pierced the bowel or the intestines – he could smell it.

Zouga went down on one knee and gently felt the foreleg that the stallion was favouring. He found the damage, another bullet wound. It had struck a few inches above the fetlock and the bone was shattered. Yet the horse had carried Mungo, a big heavy man, and it had brought him many miles. The agony must have been dreadful, but the stallion's great heart had carried them through.

Zouga shrugged off his greatcoat and wrapped it around the pistol in his right hand. A shot could alert the searching bands on the not too distant road.

'There, boy,' Zouga whispered, and touched the muzzle to the forehead between the horse's eyes.

The cloth muffled the shot. It was a dull blurt of sound, and the stallion dropped heavily on his side and never even kicked.

Louise was still bowed over Mungo, tying the knots in the bandage, but Zouga saw that her eyes were bright with tears in the moonlight.

'Thank you,' she whispered. 'I couldn't have done it myself.'

Zouga helped her lift Mungo to the cart. Mungo's breath whistled in his chest and the sweat of agony drenched his shirt and smelled rancid and gamey.

They settled him into the nest of thatching grass and spread a screen of it over him. Then Zouga led the mules on over the veld until they struck the track that led northwards towards the Vaal river, and beyond it Kuruman and the vast Kalahari Desert.

'Travel at night, and hobble the mules to graze during the day,' Zouga told her. 'There is more than enough meal and biltong; but you will have to spare the coffee and sugar.'

'Words cannot thank you enough,' she whispered.

'Don't attempt the main drift of the Vaal.'

'Somehow I know that this is not goodbye.' She seemed not to have heard the advice. 'And when we meet again,' she broke off.

'Go on,' he said, but she shook her head and took the reins from his hand and led the mules onto the track.

The cart seemed to merge into the night, and the wheels made no sound in the thick pale sand. Zouga stood staring after them, long after they had disappeared – and then Louise came back.

She came silent as a wraith, running with a kind of terrible desperation, the long tresses of hair had fallen out from under the cap and were streaming down her back. Her face was pale and stricken in the moonlight.

The grip of her arms about his neck was fierce, almost painful, and her mouth was shockingly hot and wet as it spread over his. But the taste of it he would never forget, and her sharp white teeth crushed his lips.

For seconds only they clung to each other, while Zouga thought his heart would burst; then she tore herself from his arms, and with neither a word nor a backward glance, she flew into the night – and was gone.

Ten days after Neville Pickering's funeral, Zouga signed the transfer deeds to the Devil's Own claims, and watched while one of Rhodes' secretaries registered them in favour of the Central Diamond Company. Then he walked out into the cold.

For the first time in living memory it was snowing over the diamond fields. Big soft flakes came twisting down like feathers from a shimmering white egret struck by birdshot.

The snowflakes vanished as they touched the earth, but the cold was a vindictive presence and Zouga's breath steamed in the air and condensed on his beard as he trudged up to the workings to watch the shift come off the Devil's Own claims for the last time. As he walked he tried to compose the words to tell Ralph that this was the last shift.

They were coming up in the skip. Zouga could make out Ralph, for he was the only man who wore a coat. The other men with him were almost naked.

Once again Zouga wondered idly that the men had not rebelled against the harsh measures of the new Diamond Trade Act, enforced by Colonel John Fry of the recently recruited Diamond Police, and aimed at stamping out I.D.B. on the fields.

Nowadays the black workers were compounded behind barbed wire; there were new curfew regulations to keep them in the compounds after nightfall; and there were spot searches and checks of the compounds, of men on the streets even during daylight, and body searches of each shift coming out of the pit.

Even the diggers, or at least a few of them, had protested at the most draconian of John Fry's new regulations. All black workers had been forced to go into the pit stark naked, so that they would not be able to hide stones in their clothing.

John Fry had been amazed when Zouga and a dozen other diggers had demanded to see him.

'Good Lord, Ballantyne, but they are a bunch of naked savages anyway. Modesty, forsooth!'

In the end, with the co-operation of Rhodes, they had forced him to compromise.

Grudgingly Fry had allowed every worker a strip of seamless cotton 'limbo' to cover himself.

Thus Bazo and his Matabele wore only a strip of loin-cloth each as they rode up beside Ralph in the skip. The wind threw an icy noose about them, and Bazo shivered as goose-bumps rose upon the smooth dark skin of his chest and upper arms.

Above him stood Ralph Ballantyne, balancing easily on the rim of the steel skip, ignoring the wind and the deadly drop below him.

Ralph glanced down at Bazo crouching below the side of the steel bucket, and on impulse slipped the scrap of stained canvas off his own shoulders. Under it Ralph wore an old tweed jacket and dusty cardigan. He dropped the canvas over Bazo's neck.

'It's against the white man's law,' Bazo demurred, and made as if to shrug it off.

'There are no police in this skip,' Ralph grunted, and Bazo hesitated a moment and then crouched lower and gratefully pulled the canvas over his head and shoulders.

Ralph took the butt of a half-smoked cheroot from his breast pocket, and carefully reshaped it between his fingers; the dead ash flaked away on the wind and wafted down into the yawning depths below. He lit the butt and drew the smoke down deeply, exhaled and drew again, held the smoke and passed the butt to Bazo.

'You are not only cold, but you are unhappy,' Ralph said, and Bazo did not answer. He cupped the stubby cheroot in both hands and drew carefully upon it.

'Is it Donsela?' Ralph asked. 'He knew the law, Bazo. He knows what the law says of those who steal the stones.'

'It was a small stone,' murmured Bazo, the words and blue smoke mingled on his lips. 'And fifteen years is a long time.'

'He is alive,' Ralph pointed out and took the cheroot that Bazo passed back to him. 'In the old days before the Diamond Trade Act, he would be dead by now.'

'He might as well be dead,' Bazo whispered bitterly. 'They say that men work like animals, chained like monkeys, on the breakwater wall at Cape Town harbour.'

He drew again on the cheroot and it burned down with a fierce little glow that scorched his fingers. He crushed it out on the workhardened calluses of his palm and let the shreds of tobacco blow away.

'And you, Henshaw – are you then so happy?' he asked quietly, and Ralph shrugged.

'Happy? Who is happy?'

'Is not this pit' – with a gesture Bazo took in the mighty excavation over which they dangled – 'is not this your prison, does it not hold you as surely as the chains that hold Donsela as he places the rocks on the breakwater over the sea?'

They had almost reached the high stagings and Bazo slipped off his canvas covering before he could be spotted by one of the black constables who patrolled the area inside the new security fences.

'You ask me if I am unhappy.' Bazo stood up, and did not look at Ralph's face. 'I was thinking of the land in which I am a prince of the House of Kumalo. In that land the calves I tended as a boy have grown into bulls and have bred calves which I have never seen. Once I knew every beast in my father's herds, fifteen thousand head of prime cattle, and I knew each of them, the season of its birth, the twist of its horns and the markings of its hide.'

Bazo sighed and came to stand beside Ralph on the rim of the skip. They were of a height, two tall young men, well formed, and each, in the manner of his race, comely.

'Ten times I have not been with my impi when it danced the Festival of Fresh Fruits, ten times I did not witness my king throw the war-spear and send us out on the red road.'

Bazo's sombre mood deepened, and his voice sank lower.

'Boys have grown to men since I left, and some of them wear the cowtails of valour on their legs and arms.' Bazo glanced down at his own naked body with its single dirty rag at the waist. 'Little girls have grown into maidens, with ripe bellies, ready to be claimed by the warriors who have won the honour on the red road of war.' And both of them thought of the lonely nights when the phantoms came to haunt them. Then Bazo folded his arms across his wide chest and went on.

'I think of my father, and I wonder if the snows of age have yet settled upon his head. Every man of my tribe that comes down the road from the north brings me the words of Juba, the Dove, who is my mother. She has twelve sons, but I am the first and the eldest of them.'

'Why have you stayed so long?' Ralph asked harshly.

'Why have you stayed so long, Henshaw?' The young Matabele challenged him quietly, and Ralph had no answer.

'Have you found fame and riches in this hole?' Again they both glanced down into the pit, and from this height the off-shift waiting to come up in the skips were like columns of safari ants.

'Do you have a woman with hair as long and pale as the winter grass to give you comfort in the night, Henshaw? Do you have the music of your sons' laughter to cheer you, Henshaw? What keeps you here?'

Ralph lifted his eyes and stared at Bazo, but before he could find an answer the skip came level with the platform on the first ramp of the stagings. The jerk brought Ralph back to reality and he waved to his father on the platform above them.

The roar of the steam winch subsided. The skip slowed and Bazo led the party of Matabele workers onto the ramp. Ralph saw them all clear before he jumped across the narrow gap to the wooden platform and felt it tremble under the combined weight of twenty men.

Ralph signalled again. Then the winch growled, and the steel cable squealed in its sheaves. The heavy-laden skip ran on until it hit the striker blocks. Ralph and Bazo drove the jumper bars under it, and threw their full weight on them. The skip tipped over, and the load of gravel went roaring down the chute into the waiting cart.

Ralph looked up to see his father's encouraging smile and to hear his shouted congratulations.

'Well done, boy! Two hundred tons today!'

But the staging was deserted. Zouga had gone.

Zouga had packed a single chest, the chest that had belonged to Aletta and which had come up with her from the Cape. Now it was going back, and it was almost all that was going back.

Zouga put Aletta's Bible in the bottom of the chest, and with it her diary and the trinket box which contained the remaining pieces of her jewellery. The more valuable pieces had long ago been sold, to support the dying dream.

Over these few mementoes he packed his own diaries and maps, and his books. When he came to the bundled pile of his unfinished manuscript, he paused to weigh it in his hand.

'Perhaps I shall find time to finish it now,' he murmured, and laid it gently in the chest.

On top of that went his clothing, and there was so little of that – four shirts, a spare pair of boots – barely an armful.

The chest was only half-full, and he carried it easily down the steps into the yard. That was all that he was taking – the rest of it, the meagre furnishings of the bungalow he had sold to one of the auctioneers in Market Square. Ten pounds the lot. As Rhodes had predicted, he was leaving as he had come.

'Where is Ralph?' he demanded of Jan Cheroot, and the little Hottentot paused in chaining the cooking-pot and black iron kettle onto the tailboard of the cart.

'Perhaps he stopped at Diamond Lil's. The boy has got a right to his thirst – he worked hard enough for it.'

Zouga let it pass, and instead ran an appraising eye over the cart. It was the newest and strongest of the three vehicles he owned. One cart had gone with Louise St John, and she had taken the best mules – but this rig would get them back to Cape Town, even under the additional burden that he was planning to put into it.

Jan Cheroot ambled across to Zouga and took the other handle of the chest, ready to boost it up into the body of the cart.

'Wait,' Zouga told him. 'That first.' And he pointed to the roughly-hewn block of blue mottled rock that lay below the camel-thorn tree.

'My mother –' Jan Cheroot gaped. 'This I don't believe. In twenty-two years I've seen you do some stupid crazy things –'

Zouga strode across to the block of blue ground that Ralph had brought up from the Devil's Own and put his foot on it. 'We'll hoist it up with the block and tackle.' He glanced at the sturdy branch above his head from which the sheave block and manila rope hung. 'And we'll back the cart up under it.'

'That's it!' Jan Cheroot sat down on the chest and folded his arms. 'This time I refuse. Once before I broke my back for you, but that was when I was young and stupid.'

'Come on, Jan Cheroot, you are wasting time.'

'What do you want with that – piece of ugly bloody stone? With another piece of thundering nonsense.'

'I have lost the bird – I need a household god.'

'I have heard of someone putting up a monument to a brave man, or a great battle – but to put up a stone to stupidity,' Jan Cheroot mourned.

'Back the cart up.'

'I refuse – this time I refuse. I won't do it. Not for anything. Not for any price.'

'When we get it loaded – you can have a bottle of smoke all to yourself to celebrate.'

Jan Cheroot sighed, and stood up. 'That's my price.' He shook his head and came across to stand beside Zouga. He glared at the block of blue stone venomously. 'But don't expect me to like it.'

Zouga chuckled, for the first time in weeks, and in an unusual display of affection he put one arm around Jan Cheroot's shoulders.

'Now that you have something to hate again – just think how happy it will make you,' he said.

'You have been drinking,' Zouga said, and Ralph tossed his hat into the corner and agreed.

'Yes, I have had a beer or two.' He went to the black iron stove and warmed his hands. 'I would have had more – if I had had the money.'

'I have been waiting for you,' Zouga went on, and Ralph turned back to him truculently.

'I give you every hour of my day, Papa – let me have a little time at the end of it.'

'I have something of great importance to tell you,' Zouga nodded to the deal chair facing him. 'Sit down, Ralph.'

Zouga rubbed his eyes with forefinger and thumb as he

collected his words. He had tried so often in the last days to find an easy way to tell Ralph that it was over, that they were destitute, that all that toil and heartbreak had been in vain – but there was no easy way. There were only the stark hard words of reality.

He dropped his hand, and looked at his son, and then slowly and carefully he told him, and when he had finished he waited for Ralph to speak. Ralph had not moved during the long recital, and now he stared at Zouga stonily.

Zouga was forced to speak again. 'We shall leave in the morning. Jan Cheroot and I have loaded the No. 2 wagon and we shall need all the mules, double team – it's a long haul.'

Again he waited, but there was still no reaction.

'You will be wondering where we are going and what we shall do. Well, once we get back to the Cape we still have the Harkness cottage.'

'You gambled it all.' Ralph spoke at last. 'Without telling me. You – you, who are always preaching to me about gambling, and honesty.'

'Ralph!'

'It wasn't yours, it belonged to all of us.'

'You are drunk,' Zouga said flatly.

'All these years I have listened to your promises. We shall go north, Ralph.' He mimicked Zouga with a sudden savagery in his tone. 'It's for all of us, Ralph. It's yours to share. There is a land waiting for us, Ralph. It will be yours as well as mine, Ralph.'

'It's not over – I still have the concession. When we get back to Cape Town–'

'You, not me.' Ralph's voice was flat, angry. 'You go back to Cape Town. Go dream your old man's dreams. I am sick of them.'

'You dare to use that tone to me?'

'Yes, I dare. And by God, I'll dare more than that. I'll dare what you are too weak or afraid to dare–'

'You insolent and stupid puppy!'

'You toothless old dog!'

Zouga threw himself half across the table, and his right arm lashed out. He caught Ralph open-handed across the face, and the crack of palm on flesh was stunning as a pistol shot.

Ralph's head snapped back, and then slowly he brought it

upright again. 'That,' he said, 'is the last time you will strike me, ever.' He stood up and strode towards the door, and there he turned. 'Go dream your dreams – I will go live mine out.'

'Go then,' said Zouga, and the scar on his cheek was glassy and white as ice. 'Go and be damned to you.'

'Remember I took nothing with me, Papa, not even your blessing,' said Ralph, and stepped out into the night.

Bazo woke instantly at the touch on his cheek, and reached for the assegai at his side, his eyes wide in the faint glow of the ashes. A hand closed on his wrist, holding his spear hand from the weapon, and a voice spoke softly above him.

'Do you remember the road to Matabeleland, O Prince of Kumalo?'

It took Bazo a moment to gather his wits from where sleep had scattered them.

'I remember every running ford and every green hill, every sweet watering place along the way,' he whispered back, 'as clearly as I remember my father's voice and my mother's laughter.'

'Roll up your sleeping-mat, Bazo, the Axe, and show me the road,' said Ralph.

Diamond Lil did not smile so readily these days, not since the tooth that held the diamond had turned a dingy grey as the root died, and began to ache until Lil wept with the little explosion of agony against the top of her skull. The travelling dentist from the Cape had pulled the tooth and drained the virulent abscess beneath it.

Relief had been immediate, but it left a black gap in her smile.

She had put on flesh also, the consequence of good food and those little nips of gin which bolstered her day. Her breasts, always generous, had lost their individual definition and the cleavage that showed above the richly embroidered bodice was no longer a deeply sculptured crevasse but a thin line where abundant flesh packed against flesh.

The hand that held the bone china teacup was pudgy and

dimpled over the knuckles, the rings that adorned each plump little finger had sunk into the flesh, but the diamonds and rubies and emeralds sparkled in a royal show of Lil's wealth.

Her hair was still lustrous gold, and crimped into long dangling ringlets with the hot-iron. Her skin was still smooth and rich as Devon cream, except around the eyes where it was just beginning to crack into little spider webs of lines.

She sat at the corner of the verandah, on the second floor above the street, where the eaves of the roof were of intricate white wrought-iron mouldings, pretty as Madeira lace. Although there were other double-storeyed buildings in Kimberley these days, not even the offices of the Central Diamond Company across the wide unpaved street boasted such affluent adornment.

Lil's chair was high-backed, and magnificently carved in dark red teak by oriental craftsmen, inlaid with mother-of-pearl and ivory and carried across the eastern oceans by the tall ships of the now long departed Dutch East India Company. It had cost her two hundred pounds, but from this throne she could watch every movement on the main thoroughfares that fed into Market Square, could sense the pulse of the diamond city, could check each coming and going, the scurry of a buyer with a good scent in his nostrils, the swagger of a digger who had turned up a bright one. She could watch the front of the four canteens around the square, all of which she now owned, and judge the volume of trade going through their doors.

Similarly, she could glance to her left, down De Beers Road to the red-brick cottage behind its white picket fence and discreet sign, 'French Dressmakers. Haute Couture. Six Continental Seamstresses. Specialities for individual tastes.' Business was always brisk there – from noon to midnight. Her girls seldom lasted the pace for more than six months or so – before taking the coach southward again, exhausted but considerably richer.

Lil herself worked her old trade only occasionally, perhaps once or twice a week with a favoured 'regular', just for old times' sake, and because it got her blood going and made her sleep better at night. There was too much else that required her constant attention.

Now she poured fresh tea from the rococo silver pot into the pretty bone china cups, hand-painted with pink roses and golden butterflies.

'How many spoons?' she asked.

Ralph sat on the cane-back chair opposite her. He smelled of shaving soap and cheap eau-de-Cologne. His chin shone with a burnish given it by the cut-throat razor, and his shirt was so crisply ironed and starched that it crackled at each movement.

Lil studied him speculatively over the rim of her tea cup.

'Does the good major know your plans?' she asked quietly, and Ralph shook his head. Lil thought on that a while and it gave her a ripple of pleasure to have the son of a foundation member of the Kimberley Club sitting on her verandah. Son of one of the Kimberley gentlemen who would not greet her on the street, who had returned her donation towards the new hospital, who had not even replied to her invitation to attend the stone-laying ceremony of her new building – oh, the list of humiliations was too long to recite now.

'Why did you not go to your father?' she asked instead.

'My father is not a rich man.' Ralph would not say any more, too loyal to explain that Zouga was destitute, that he would soon leave Kimberley with a cartload of his meagre possessions. He did not want Lil to know that he and his father had turned from each other with harsh words.

Lil studied his face for a moment, then picked up the hand-written sheet of cheap notepaper from the tea tray and glanced down the list and the figures.

'Nine hundred pounds for oxen?'

'A full span of the biggest and best animals,' Ralph explained. 'The road to the Shashi river is sand veld, heavy going. I want to be able to haul a full load, eight thousand pounds weight.'

'Trade goods – fifteen thousand.' She looked up at him again.

'Guns, powder, brandy, beads and limbo cloth.'

'What type of guns?'

'Tower muskets. Five pounds ten shillings each.'

Lil shook her head. 'They have seen the breech-loaders. Your muskets won't have much pull.'

'I can't afford breech-loaders, and I wouldn't know where to find a load.'

'Ralph dearie, I could hire a bunch of Whitechapel hags to run my dressmakers' shop and I could get them cheap. But I don't. I pick them young and fresh and pretty. If you think small, your profits are small. Don't be cheap, Ralph darling, never be cheap.' She poured a little gin from the silver flask into the empty teacup before she went on. 'I can get Martini-Henry rifles but they will cost us fifteen hundred more.' Lil reached across and dipped her pen in the ink-well, then scratched out and re-wrote the figure.

'Brandy?'

'Cape Smoke in twenty-gallon casks.'

'I have heard that Lobengula likes Courvoisier cognac, and his sister Ningi drinks only Piper-Heidsieck champagne.'

'Another five hundred pounds – at least,' Ralph mourned.

'Three hundred,' Lil corrected the list. 'I can get it at wholesale prices. Now, ammunition – ten thousand rounds?'

'I'll need at least a thousand for my own account, and the rest to trade with the rifles.'

'If Lobengula gives you permission to hunt elephant,' Lil corrected.

'My grandfather is one of his oldest friends; my Aunty Robyn and her husband have been at Khami River Mission for almost twenty years.'

'Yes, I know that you have friends at court.' Lil pursed her lips approvingly. 'But I have heard that the elephant have been shot out across the whole of Matabeleland.'

'The herds have been driven into the fly belt on the Zambezi.'

'You cannot take horses into the fly and hunting elephant on foot in the fly is not work for a white man.'

'My father hunted on foot, and anyway I cannot afford a horse.'

'All right,' she agreed reluctantly, and made a tick on the sheet.

They worked on for an hour longer, going down the list item by item – and then starting again at the head and going over it all once more, Lil ticking and scratching with the pen – fining it down by ten pounds here and a hundred there, until at last she tossed the pen onto the tea tray, and then poured a little more gin into her tea cup and sipped it with a genteel flourish, her little finger raised, the spirit slurping softly through the gap in the front of her teeth.

'All right,' she said again.

'Does that mean you will lend me the money?'

'Yes.'

'I don't know what to say.' He leaned towards her, young and glowing and eager. 'Lil, I just don't–'

'Then don't say anything until you have heard my terms.' She smiled thinly, without lifting her upper lip.

'Twenty per cent per annum interest on the loan.'

'Twenty per cent!' he gasped. 'In God's name – that's usury, Lily!'

'Exactly,' she told him primly. 'But let me finish. Twenty per cent interest and half the profits.'

'And half, Lil – that's not usury, that's highway robbery.'

'Right again,' she agreed. 'At least you are bright enough to recognize it.'

'Can't we just –' he started desperately.

'No, we cannot. Those are my terms.' And Ralph remembered Scipio, his falcon, with her beautiful pouting breast and fierce cold eyes.

'I accept,' he said, and though she did not smile with her lips, her eyes were suddenly soft and merry.

'Partners,' she murmured, and placed her plump white hand on his forearm. His muscles were lean and sinewy, the skin brick-coloured from the sun. She stroked it slowly, sensually.

'It only remains to seal our bargain,' she told Ralph. 'Come!' She slid her hand down his arm and twined her fingers into his.

She led him through the stained-glass doors, and when she drew the velvet corded curtains it was cool and dark in the room. She turned back to him and reached up to unbutton his shirt at the throat. He stood still while she worked her way down slowly to his belt buckle, and then she placed one hand, palm down, upon his naked right breast.

'Ralph,' her voice was a husky tremor. 'I want you to do something for me.'

'What is it?' he asked, and she stood on her tiptoes, placed her lips against his ear and told him in a whisper. She felt him begin to pull back from under her hand.

'Partners?' she asked, and he hesitated a moment longer and then stooped and picked her up, one arm behind her knees, and carried her to the wide brass bed with the patchwork quilt.

'You will find it less arduous than hunting elephant on foot in the fly,' she told him, and it was dark enough in the room for her not to worry about the missing tooth.

She lifted her arms above her head, opened her mouth and chuckled in delicious anticipation.

'The good thing about life, dearie, is that you can have whatever you want, just as long as you are willing to pay the price,' she told him, still chuckling.

'These are not bullocks,' Bazo told Ralph. 'Each one is the son of a snake mated with the ghost of a Mashona dog.'

They were all strong oxen, big-boned, heavy in the shoulder, with wide straight horns for strength and even yellow teeth – hand-picked by Bazo, who was a Matabele and loved cattle, had lived with the great herds since he was old enough to toddle after the calves.

However, Bazo was not a trek man. He had never worked an eighteen-foot wagon, with an eight-thousand-pound load aboard. He had never tried to put twenty-four trek oxen into the traces.

The entire Matabele nation owned only a pair of wheeled vehicles, and those belonged to King Lobengula. To Bazo cattle were a store of wealth, a source of meat and milk – they were not draught animals. The closest that either he or Ralph had ever come to putting a team into the traces was working the little two-wheel gravel carts.

Ralph had assumed that the oxen he had purchased were trained and amiable, but within minutes of his and Bazo's first attempt to get them into span, the animals sensed their incompetence and became as spooky and wild as hunted buffalo.

It took two hours of wild chasing across the bleak grasslands beyond the town limits, two hours of running and cursing and whip-cracking to bring the bullocks together and get the yokes upon their necks. Half of them were badly winded by then and promptly lay down, and the others backed out and turned their great horned heads towards the load, tangling the trek chain and plunging the entire span into chaos.

The excitement had brought out most of the loafers and idlers from the canteens on Market Square, though they had enough forethought to bring their bottles with them. They formed an appreciative and jovial audience, greeting each new effort by Bazo and Ralph with delighted guffaws and facetious advice.

Bazo wiped the sweat from his face and chest, and looked broodingly down the dusty road to town.

'Soon Bakela will hear of this and come to see our disgrace,' he said.

Ralph had not seen his father since that stormy night, but he had visited Jordan in his tiny office next door to Mr Rhodes in the magnificent new Central Diamond Company building on De Beers Street.

Perhaps Zouga Ballantyne had not yet recovered from the

shock of being deserted by both his sons, but Jordan said that he had not yet left for Cape Town.

The thought of his father witnessing this humiliating scene brought dark blood to Ralph's face, and he fired the long trek whip, at least that was one trick he had learned, and bellowed at the span.

'Nkosana!' There was a salutation at the level of Ralph's elbow, the mild tone belied by the mocking title.

'Nkosi' was a chief, and *'Nkosana'* was the condescending diminutive – usually reserved for a little white boy, an untried child.

Ralph turned and glared at the speaker, who went on to explain in the same condescending tone. 'Only one beast in ten will pull in front.' He pointed out one of the oxen. 'That one there is a lead ox. Any man who knows oxen can see that with both his eyes closed.'

He was a little black gnome, not as tall as Ralph's shoulder. His face was wrinkled and lined like that of a very old man, his eyes were mere slits in the merry smiling folds – but his cap of woolly hair and his little goatee beard were unmarred by a single strand of grey, and his teeth were even and white, the teeth of a man in his full flowering.

On his head was the polished black ring of the induna, and about his waist was a kilt of wild cat tails. Over that he wore a threadbare military-type tunic from which all insignia and buttons had been stripped, leaving small punctures in the fabric, some of which had enlarged into rents from which the lining peaked coyly. In the pierced lobe of one ear, he carried an ivory snuff-box, and in the other lobe a snuff spoon of the same material and a toothpick of porcupine quill. The language he used was very close to Matabele, but it preserved the ancient intonation and classic word structures of Zululand.

So when Ralph asked 'Zulu?' the question was redundant, and the little man shot a contemptuous glance at Bazo.

'Pure Zulu, not the treacherous house of Kumalo, of the traitor Mzilikazi who denied a king and whose blood is now so watered by Venda and Tswana and Mashona that they can no longer tell you if an ox grows horns on its head or on its testicles.'

Bazo bridled instantly. 'Hark!' He cocked his head. 'Do I hear a small baboon barking his boasts from the top of the kopjes?'

The little Zulu grinned at him mirthlessly, and took the stock whip from Ralph's sweaty hands. Then he walked to the tangled span with a jaunty step.

He touched the big black ox on the neck. 'Hau, Sathan!' he greeted him, and at the same time baptized him 'Devil'.

The great ox rolled one eye at him, seemed to recognize his assurance and immediately quietened. The little Zulu loosed him and took him forward, talking to him easily in a bizarre mixture of Zulu, English and the Cape Dutch taal, and chained him into the lead position.

He went back quickly and pulled the red ox out of the tangle by the rein about his horns.

'Dutchman – ' he named him, for no good reason. 'Come, you red thunder!'

And he put him into the lead file beside Sathan and called to them quietly.

'Donsa, Sathan, pull. *Pakamisa,* Dutchman, pick up the chain!' Obediently the pair of bullocks straightened their fore-legs and leaned forward against the yoke – and a miracle happened. The long heavy silver chain from the disselboom came up straight and hard as an iron bar, and those animals on the ground were forced to lunge up onto their feet, those that had backed out were pulled into the span, horns and heads pointing forward. In that moment Ralph learned the single most important rule of the open road, keep the chain straight and true, and all else is possible.

Now the little Zulu moved with a deceptively casual air along the double rank of bullocks, touching and talking and wheedling.

'Hey! Fransman, I can see by your wise and beautiful eyes that you were born to the wheel!' And the sturdy black and white beast was led back to his position at the off-wheel.

It took ten minutes, and then the Zulu put the long lash into the air. It hissed like a black mamba and then snaked forward over the ears of the team, not touching a single hair as it fired explosively. The heavy wagon jolted, the white canvas tent that covered the rear half of the long body shook like the unfurling mainsail of a tall ship and then it was rolling away smoothly.

The Zulu crinkled his eyes at Ralph and called a question. *'Yapi?* Where? Which way?'

'Yakato!' North!' Ralph shouted back joyously, and despite himself Bazo snatched up his war shield and assegai and whirled into a frenzied challenge dance, leaping and stabbing at a host

of imaginary enemies, shouting defiance and ecstasy to all the world.

The road to the Vaal river was the first leg of the journey, and the ruts were axle deep, and red soil raw as a fresh wound, the dust a fog in the windless air through which it was just possible to make out the horns of the two wheeler bullocks. The dust hid from Ralph his parting view of the sprawling town, and its high stagings above the gaping hole which had been his home and his prison for so many years, and by the time that the other traffic on the road had thinned sufficiently for the dust cloud to settle, they had made five miles and the stagings might have been merely a distant line of dead thorn trees silhouetted against the sunset.

The little Zulu called to his boy who led the front oxen, and the child swung them off the road, and the high rear wheels bumped out of the ruts and then crunched through crisp winter grass as the wagon rolled towards a spreading umbrella-shaped acacia which would give them shelter and firewood for the night.

Walking at the front wheel Ralph pondered the two unexpected additions to his company.

The child had come out of the curtain of red dust, naked except for the little flap of his *mutsha* in front, and with the roll of sleeping-mat and the cooking-pot balanced upon his head.

He had placed these meagre possessions on the tailboard of the wagon and then, at a nod and a word from the Zulu, had taken the lead rein and plodded solemnly ahead of the span, his bare feet sinking ankle-deep in the powder dust.

Ralph wondered how old he was, and decided he could not be more than ten years of age.

'What is his name?' he asked the Zulu.

'A name?' The little man shrugged. 'It is not important. Call him Umfaan – the Boy.'

'And what is your name?' Ralph went on, but the little driver suddenly had urgent business at the head of the span and perhaps the dust had clogged his ears for he did not seem to hear the question.

Ralph had to ask the question again, after the outspan, when the Zulu was squatting beside the cooking fire watching Umfaan stir the maize-meal in the black pot.

'What is your name?' And the Zulu smiled as though at a secret thought, and then he said:

'A name can be dangerous, it can hover over a man like a vulture and mark him for death. Before the soldiers came to the royal kraal at Ulundi, I was called one thing –

Ralph stirred uncomfortably at the reference to the battle that had ended the Zulu War. The tattered tunic that the Zulu wore had once been the same dark blue as that of the Natal police uniform and one of those rents in the faded cloth might have been made by the stabbing blade. Lord Chelmsford had sent the Zulu king and most of his indunas in chains to the island of St Helena, where another emperor had died in captivity. However, some of his fighting chiefs had escaped from Zululand and now wandered homeless exiles across the vast continent. The driver wore the head-ring of an induna.

'– It was a name which men once spoke carefully, but I have not heard it for so long now that I have forgotten it,' the Zulu went on, and again Ralph wondered if there was a legend still alive amongst the defeated Zulu of a little induna, smaller than the tall warriors he commanded and wizened far beyond his years, who had led them in that terrible charge into the English camp below the Hill of the Little Hand.

In the firelight Ralph studied the Zulu's tunic again, and he told himself that it was unlikely that it had been taken from the corpse of an Englishman on that grisly field; yet he shivered briefly although the night was warm.

'Now you have forgotten that name?' he encouraged, and the Zulu crinkled his eyes again.

'Now I am called Isazi, the Wise One, for reasons that should be clear even to a Matabele.'

Across the fire Bazo snorted disdainfully, then stood and walked out of the firelight, into the darkness where the jackals piped plaintively.

'My name is Henshaw,' Ralph told him. 'Will you stay with me and drive my wagon all the way?'

'Why not, Little Hawk?'

'You do not ask where I am going.'

'I need a road.' Isazi shrugged. 'The one to the north is no longer or harder than the road to the south.'

The jackal yipped again, but much closer this time, and Bazo paused, changed the assegai to his right hand, and answered the cry, cupping his palm over his mouth to give resonance to the sound; and then he moved on to where a small stone kopje shone in the moonlight like a pile of silver bullion.

'Bazo.' The greeting was a whisper, soft as the night wind in the pale grass, and a shadow stepped from amongst the moon shadows at the base of the kopje.

'Kamuza, my brother.' Bazo went to him and embraced him, open hands upon his shoulders.

'I have a stone in my belly, heavy with sorrow at this parting.'

'We will share the road again – one day, we will drink from the beer pot and fight with our shoulders touching–' Kamuza answered him quietly. 'But now we are both upon the king's business.'

Kamuza slipped the thongs that held his kilt in place, and it sagged heavily to his knees, leaving him naked.

'Hurry,' he said. 'I must return before the curfew bell.' Since the Diamond Trade Act, blacks were not allowed on the streets of Kimberley once the curfew bell had rung.

'You were not marked by the police?' Bazo asked, as he removed his own kilt and changed it with Kamuza.

'They are everywhere, like pepper ticks in the new spring grass,' Kamuza grunted. 'But I was not followed.'

Bazo weighed the fur kilt in both hands while Kamuza swiftly belted the replacement about his own waist.

'Show me,' Bazo said, and Kamuza took the kilt back from his hands and spread it on one of the flat moon-washed boulders.

He picked at the knotted thong that doubled the waistband, and as it came undone he opened the secret pouch of soft tanned leather, crusted with ceramic trade beads. The pouch ran the full length of the wide waistband, the opening concealed by the decorative beadwork, and the interior of the long pouch was divided into cells, like a wasp's nest.

In each stitched leather cell nestled a large pebble that glistened with a slick soapy sheen in the moonlight.

'Count them,' Kamuza instructed. 'Let us agree on the number – and let Lobengula, the great Black Elephant, count the same number into his mighty hands when you lay the belt before him at the kraal of GuBulawayo, the place of killing.'

Bazo touched each diamond with his fingertip, his lips moving silently. '*Amashumi amatatu*!'

'Thirty,' Kamuza repeated. 'It is agreed.'

And they were all large clean stones, the smallest the size of the first joint of a man's little finger.

Bazo tied the kilt about his waist, the fleecy tails of the bat-eared fox dangling to his knees.

'It looks well upon you,' Kamuza nodded, and then went on. 'Tell Lobengula, the Great Elephant, that I am his dog and I grovel in the dirt at his feet. Tell him that there will be more of the yellow coins and the bright stones. Tell him that his children labour each day in the pit – and there will be more, many more. Every man who takes the road north will bring him riches.' Kamuza stepped forward and laid his right hand on Bazo's shoulder.

'Go in peace, Bazo the Axe.'

'Stay in peace, my brother, and may the days disappear like raindrops into the desert sand until we smile upon each other once more.'

Isazi put the span to its first real test in the drift of the Vaal river.

The grey waters were barely flowing, but they covered the hubs of the tall iron-shod rear wheels, and the bottom was broken waterworn rock that clanked and rolled under pressure, threatening to jam the wheels and denying purchase to the driving hooves of the span.

Yet they ran the wagon through under load, leaning into the yokes, noses down almost touching the surface of the river, and the wagon tent jolting and rocking behind them.

Until, under the steep cut up the far bank, the rear wheels stuck and the wagon bed tilted alarmingly. Then Isazi showed his expertise. He swung the team wide, giving them a run at it, and when he called to his leaders and burst the air asunder with the thirty-foot lash that tapered to the thickness of twine they went in stiff-legged, jerked her clear, and took the load out of the river bed at a canter, while Isazi pranced and sang their praises and even Umfaan smiled.

Ralph ordered an early outspan under the tall trees on the far bank, for there was good grass and unlimited water, and the next leg of the road to his grandfather Moffat's mission station was a hundred and twenty miles, hard and dry going all the way.

'See, Little Hawk,' Isazi was still rapturous over the performance of his span. '- See how clever they are. They pick a good patch of grass and eat it up; they do not wander from patch to patch, wasting their time and strength, as lesser beasts might do. Soon they will settle with the cud, and in the morning they will be strong and rested. Each of them is a prince among cattle!'

'From tomorrow we begin night marches,' Ralph ordered, and Isazi's smile faded and he looked severe.

'I had already made that decision,' he said sternly, 'but where did you ever hear of night marching, Little Hawk? It is a trick of the wise ones.'

'Count me amongst them then, Isazi,' Ralph told him solemnly, and walked out of camp to find a place upon the riverbank from which to enjoy the sunset.

Here the banks of the Vaal were churned into mounds and irregular hollows, the old river workings, picked over by the first diggers and now abandoned and overgrown. It was a mass burial ground of men's dreams, and looking upon it Ralph's high spirits that had buoyed this first day's trek upon the open road began to evaporate.

It was the first day in his life that Ralph had been free and completely his own man. Walking at the wheel of his own wagon, he had woven dreams of fortune. He had imagined his wagons – fifty, a hundred – carrying his cargoes across the continent. He had seen them coming south again, loaded with ivory and bars of yellow gold. He had seen in his mind's eye the wide lands, the herds of elephant, the masses of native cattle, the riches that lay out there in the north beckoning to him, warbling the siren call in his ears.

He had been carried so high that now as his spirits turned they fell as low. He looked at the deserted diggings on the banks across the river, the vain scratchings where other men had attempted to turn this great brown slumbering giant of a continent to their own account.

Then suddenly he felt very small and lonely, and afraid. His thoughts turned to his father, and his spirits plunged lower still as he recalled the last words he had spoken.

'Go then! Go and be damned to you.'

That was not the way he had wanted it. Zouga Ballantyne had been the central figure in his life until that day. A colossus who overshadowed each of his actions, each of his thoughts.

Much as he had chafed under the shackles that his duty to his father had placed upon him, much as he had resented every one of his decisions being made for him, each of his actions ordered, yet now he felt as though the greater part of himself had been removed by some drastic surgery of the soul.

Until this moment he had not really thought of losing his father, he had not let the memory of their brutal parting cut him too deeply. Now suddenly this dirty slow river was the barrier between him and the life he had known. There was no going back – now or ever. He had lost his father and his brother and Jan Cheroot and he was alone and lonely. He felt the acid tears scald his eyelids.

His vision wavered, played him tricks, for across the wide river course, on the far bank was the figure of a horseman.

The horseman slouched easily in the saddle, one hand on his hip, the elbow cocked; and the set of the head upon the broad shoulders was unmistakable.

Slowly Ralph came to his feet, staring in disbelief, and then suddenly he was running and sliding down the sheer bank and splashing waist deep through the grey waters of the ford. Zouga swung down from Tom's back and ran forward to meet Ralph as he came up the bank.

Then both of them stopped and stared at each other. They had not embraced since the night of Aletta's funeral, and they could not bring themselves to do so now, though longing was naked in the eyes of both of them.

'I could not let you go, not like that,' said Zouga, but Ralph had no reply, for his throat had closed.

'It is time for you to go out on your own,' Zouga nodded his golden beard. 'Past time. You are like an eaglet that has outgrown the nest. I realized that before you did, Ralph, but I did not want it to be. That is why I spoke so cruelly.'

Zouga picked up Tom's reins and the pony nudged him affectionately. Zouga stroked his velvety muzzle.

'There are two parting gifts that I have for you.' He placed the reins in Ralph's hand. 'That is one,' he said evenly, but the green shadows in his eyes betrayed how dearly that gesture had cost him. 'The other is in Tom's saddle-bag. It's a book of notes.

Read them at your leisure. You may find them of interest – even of value.'

Still Ralph could not speak. He held the reins awkwardly, and blinked back the stinging under his eyelids.

'There is one other small gift, but it has no real value. It is only my blessing.'

'That is all that I really wanted,' whispered Ralph.

It was six hundred miles to the Shashi river, to the border of Matabeleland.

Isazi inspanned at dusk each evening and they trekked through the cool of the night. When the moon went down and it was utterly dark, then Umfaan threw the lead rein over Dutchman's head, and the big black ox put his nose down and stayed on the track, like a hunting dog on the spoor, until the first glimmering of dawn signalled the outspan.

During a good night's trek they made fifteen miles – but when the going was heavy with sand they might make only five miles.

During the days, while the cattle grazed or chewed the cud in the shade, Ralph saddled up Tom and, with Bazo running beside his stirrup, they hunted.

They found herds of buffalo along the banks of the Zouga river, the river on whose bank Ralph's father had been born, big herds, two hundred beasts together.

The herd bulls were huge, bovine and bald with age, their backs crusted with the mud from the wallow, the spread of their armoured heads wider than the stretch of a man's arms, the tips of the polished black horns rising into symmetrical crescents like the points of the sickle moon, while the bosses above their broad foreheads were massively crenellated.

They ran them down, and Tom loved those wild flying chases every bit as much as his rider.

They chased the ghostly grey gemsbuck over the smoking red dunes, and in the thorn country they hunted the stilt-legged giraffe and sent their grotesque but stately bodies plunging and sliding to earth with the crack of rifle fire, the long graceful necks twisting in the agony of death like that of a swan.

They baited with the carcasses of zebra, and the coppery red Kalahari lions came to the taint of blood, and Tom stood down their charge. Though he trembled and snorted and rolled his eyes at the shockingly offensive cat smell, he stood for the shot which Ralph took from the saddle, aiming between the fierce yellow eyes or into the gape of rose-pink jaws starred with white fangs.

Thus, fifty days out from Kimberley they came at last to the Shashi river, and when they had made the crossing Bazo was on his native soil. He put on his war plumes and carrying his shield on his shoulder he walked with a new spring and joy in his stride as he led Ralph to a hilltop from which to survey the way ahead.

'See how the hills shine,' Bazo whispered with an almost religious fervour. And it was true. In the early sunlight the granite tops gleamed like precious jewels. Soft, dreaming, ruby, delicate sapphires and glossy pearl shaded like a peacock tail into a fanfare of colour.

The hills rolled away, rising gradually towards the high central plateau ahead of them, and the valleys were clad with virgin forest.

'You never saw such trees on the plains around Kimberley,' Bazo challenged him, and Ralph nodded. They stood on soaring trunks, some scaled like the crocodile, others white and smooth as though moulded from potter's clay, their tops sailing in traceries of green high above the open glades of yellow grass.

'See, the buffalo herds – thick as cattle.'

There was other game. There were small family groups of grey kudo, pale as ghosts, trumpet-eared, the bulls carrying the burden of their long black cork-screw horns with studied grace.

There were clouds of red impala antelope upon the woven silk carpet of golden grasses. There were the darkly massive statues of the rhinoceros seemingly graven from the solid granite of the hills, and there were the noblest antelope of all, the sable antelope, black and imperial as the name implied, the long horns curved and cruel as Saladin's scimitar, the belly blazing white, the neck of the herd bull arched haughtily as he led his lighter coloured females out of the open glade into the cool green sanctuary of the forest.

'Is it not beautiful, Henshaw?' Bazo asked.

'It is beautiful.'

There was the same awe in Ralph's voice, and a strange unformed longing in his throat, a wanting that he knew could never be satisfied – and suddenly he understood his own father's obsession with this fair land: 'My north,' as Zouga called it.

'My north,' Ralph whispered, and then, thinking of his father, the next question came immediately to mind.

'Elephant – *Indhlovu*? There are no elephant, Bazo. Where are the herds?'

'Ask Bakela – your own father,' Bazo grunted. 'He was the first to come for them with the gun, but others followed him, many others. When Gandang, my father, son of Mzilikazi the Destroyer, half brother of the great black bull Lobengula, when he crossed the Shashi as a child on his mother's hip, the elephant herds were black as midnight upon the land and their teeth shone like the stars. Now we will find their bones growing like white lilies in the forest.'

In the last hours of daylight, when Bazo and Isazi and Umfaan still slept to fortify themselves for the long night's trek, Ralph took the leather-bound notebook out of Tom's saddle-bag.

By now the pages were dog-eared and grubby from the constant perusal to which Ralph had subjected it. It was the gift that Zouga Ballantyne had given him on the bank of the Vaal river, and the inside cover was inscribed:

To my son Ralph.
May these few notes guide your feet
northwards, and may they inspire you to dare what I have not
dared

Zouga Ballantyne

The first twenty pages were filled with hand-drawn sketch maps of those areas of the land between the Zambezi and the Limpopo and the Shashi rivers over which Zouga, and before him the old hunter Tom Harkness, had travelled.

Often the map was headed by the notation:

Copied from the original map drawn by Tom Harkness in 1851.

Ralph recognized the unique value of this information, but there was more. Page 21 of the notebook bore a terse explanation in Zouga's precise spiky hand:

In the winter of 1860 while on trek from Tete on the Zambezi River, to King Mzilikazi's town at Thabas Indunas I slew 216 elephant. Lacking porters or wagons I had perforce to cache the ivory along my route.

During my later expeditions to Zambezia, I was able to recover the bulk of this treasure.

There remain fifteen separate caches, containing eighty-four good tusks, which I was for various reasons unable to reach.

Here follows a list of these caches with directions and navigational notes to reach them:

And on page 22 the list began:

Cache made 16 September 1860.

Position by sun sight and dead reckoning:

30° 55′ E.   17° 45′ S.

A granite kopje which I named Mount Hampden. The largest for many miles in any direction. Distinct peak with three turrets. On the northern face between two large *ficus natalensis* trees there is a rock fissure. 18 large tusks total weight 426 pounds placed in fissure and covered with small boulders.

The current price of ivory was twenty-two shillings and sixpence the pound, and Ralph had added the total weights of the ivory still lying out in the veld. It exceeded three thousand pounds: a great fortune waiting merely to be picked up and loaded on his wagon.

Still that was not all. The final entry in the notebook read:

In my book *A Hunter's Odyssey* I described my discovery of the deserted city which the tribes call 'ZIMBABWE', a name which can be translated as 'The Graveyard of the Kings'.

I described how I was able to glean fragments of gold from the inner courtyards of the walled ruins, a little over 50 lbs weight of the metal in all. I also carried away with me one of the ancient bird-like statues. A souvenir which has been with me from that time until very recently.

It is possible that there is precious metal which I overlooked, and certainly there remain within the walled enclosures six more bird carvings which I was unable to bring away.

In *Hunter's Odyssey* I deliberately refrained from giving the location of the ancient ruin. As far as I know, it has not been rediscovered by any other white man – while a superstitious taboo forbids any African to venture into the area.

Thus there is every reason to believe the statues lie where last I laid eyes upon them.

Bearing in mind that my chronometer had not been checked for many months when these observations were made, I now give you the position of the city as calculated by myself at that time.

The ruins lie on the same longitude as the kopje which I named Mount Hampden on 30° 55′ E. – but 175 miles farther south at 20° 0′ S.

There followed a detailed description of the route that Zouga had taken to reach Zimbabwe, and then the notes ended with this statement:

Mr Rhodes offered the sum of £1,000 for the statue which I rescued.

The following noon Ralph took the brass sextant from its travel-battered wooden case. He had bid ten shillings for it at one of the Saturday auctions in the Market Square of Kimberley – and Zouga had checked its accuracy against his own instrument and showed Ralph how to shoot an 'apparent local noon' to establish his latitude. Ralph had no chronometer to fix a longitude, but he could guess at it from his proximity to the confluence of the Shashi and Macloutsi rivers.

Half an hour's work with *Brown's Nautical Almanac* gave him an approximate position to compare with the one that his father had given in the notes for Zimbabwe.

'Less than one hundred and fifty miles,' he muttered to himself, still squatting over his father's map, but staring eastwards.

'Six thousand pounds just lying there,' Ralph said quietly, and shook his head in wonder. It was a sum difficult to imagine.

He packed away the sextant, rolled the map and went to join the slumbering trio beneath the wagon for what remained of the drowsy afternoon.

Ralph woke to a stentorian challenge that seemed to echo off the granite cliffs above the camp.

'Who dares take the king's road? Who chances the wrath of Lobengula?'

Ralph scrambled out from under the wagon. The day was almost gone, the sun flamed in the top branches of the forest, and the chill of evening prickled his bare chest. He stared about him wildly, but some instinct warned him not to reach for the loaded rifle propped against the rear wheel of the wagon. Below the trees the shadows were alive, blackness moved on blackness, dusky rank on rank.

'Stand forth, white man,' the voice commanded. 'Speak your business – lest the white spears of Lobengula turn to red.'

The speaker stepped forward, out of the forest to the edge of the camp. Behind him the ring of dappled black and white war-shields overlapped, edge to edge in an unbroken circle surrounding the entire outspan, the 'bull's horns' of the Matabele fighting formations.

There were many hundreds of warriors in that deadly circle, and the broad stabbing spears were held in an underhand grip so that the silver blades pointed forward at belly height between the shields.

Above each shield the frothy white ostrich-feather headdress trembled and swayed in the small evening breeze, the only movement in that silent multitude.

The man who had broken the ranks was one of the most impressive figures that Ralph had ever seen. The high crown of ostrich feathers turned him into a towering giant. The breadth of his chest was enhanced by the flowering bunches of white cowtails that he wore on his upper arms. Each separate tail had been awarded him by his king for an act of valour – and he wore them not only on his arms but around his knees also.

His broad intelligent face was lightly seamed by the passage of the years, as though by the chisel of a skilled carpenter, forming a frame for the dark penetrating sparkle of his eyes; yet his chest was covered with the elastic muscle of a man only just reaching his prime and his lean belly rippled with the same muscle as he moved forward.

His legs were long and straight under the kilt of black spotted civet tails, and the war-rattles bound about his ankles rustled softly at each pace.

'I come in peace,' Ralph called, hearing the catch in his own voice.

'Peace is a word that sits as lightly on the tongue as the sunbird sits upon the open flower, and as lightly does it fly.'

There was movement beside Ralph, and Bazo came from his bed under the wagon.

'Baba!' Bazo said reverently, and clapped his hands softly at the level of his face. 'I see you Baba! The sun has been dark all these years, but now it shines again, my father.'

The tall warrior started, took a swift pace forward, and for an instant a wonderful smile bloomed upon the sculptured ebony of his face; then he checked himself, and drew himself up to his full height again, his expression grave – but the feathers of his headdress trembled and there was a light in his tar-bright eyes that he could not extinguish. Still clapping his hands, stooping with respect, Bazo went forward and knelt on one knee.

'Gandang, son of Mzilikazi – your eldest son – Bazo the Axe, brings you the greetings and the duty of his heart.'

Gandang looked down at his son, and at that moment nothing else existed for him in all the world.

'Baba, I ask your blessing.'

Gandang placed his open hand on the short cropped fleecy cap of the young man's head.

'You have my blessing,' he said quietly, but the hand lingered, the gesture of blessing became a caress, and then slowly and reluctantly Gandang withdrew the hand.

'Rise up, my son.'

Bazo was as tall as his father, and for a quiet moment they looked steadily into each other's eyes. Then Gandang turned, and flirted his war-shield, a gesture of dismissal, and instantly the still and silent ring of warriors turned their own shields edge on, so that they seemed to fold like a woman's fan, and with miraculous swiftness they split into small platoons and disappeared into the forest.

Within seconds it seemed as though they had never been. Only Gandang and his son still remained at the edge of the camp, and then they too turned and slipped away like two shadows thrown by the moving branches of the mopani trees.

Isazi came out from under the wagon, naked except for the sheath of hollowed gourd covering the head of his penis, and he spat in the fire with a thoughtful and philosophical air.

'Chaka was too soft,' he said. 'He should have followed the traitor Mzilikazi, and taught him good manners. The Matabele are upstart bastards, with no breeding and less respect.'

'Would a Zulu induna have acted that way?' Ralph asked him, as he reached for his shirt.

'No,' Isazi admitted. 'He would certainly have stabbed us all to death. But he would have done so with greater respect and better manners.'

'What do we do now?' Ralph asked.

'Wc wait,' said Isazi. 'While that vaunting dandy, who should wear the induna headring not on his forehead but around his neck like the collar of a dog, decides what should become of us.' Isazi spat in the fire again, this time with contempt. 'We may have long to wait – a Matabele thinks at the same speed as a chameleon runs.' And he crawled back under the wagon and pulled the kaross over his head.

In the night the cooking fires from the camp of the Matabele impi down the valley glowed amber and russet on the tops of the mopani, and every time the fickle night wind shifted, the deep melodious sound of their singing carried down to Ralph's outspan.

In the grey dawn Bazo appeared again, as silently as he had disappeared.

'My father, Gandang, induna of the Inyati Regiment, summons you to *indaba*, Henshaw.'

Ralph bridled immediately. He could almost hear his father's voice. 'Remember always that you are an Englishman, my boy, and as such you are a direct representative of your Queen in this land.'

The reply rose swiftly to Ralph's lips: 'If he wants to see me, tell him to come to me.' But he held the words back.

Gandang was an induna of two thousand, the equivalent of a general. He was a son of an emperor and half brother of a king, the equivalent of an English duke, and this was the soil of Matabeleland on which Ralph was an intruder.

'Tell your father I will come directly.' And he went to fetch a fresh shirt and the spare pair of boots, which he had taught Umfaan to polish.

'You are Henshaw, the son of Bakela,' Gandang sat on a low stool, intricately carved from a single piece of ebony. Ralph had been offered no seat, and he squatted down on his heels. 'And Bakela is a man.' And there was a murmur of assent and a rustle of plumes as the massed ranks of warriors about them stirred.

'Tshedi is your great-grandfather, and in the king's name has given you the road to GuBulawayo. Tshedi has the right to do so – for he is Lobengula's friend and he was Mzilikazi's friend before that.'

Ralph made no reply. He realized that these statements about his great-grandfather, old Dr Moffat, whose Matabele name was Tshedi, were for the waiting warriors rather than for himself. Gandang was explaining his decision to his impi.

'But for what reason do you take the road to the king's kraal?'

'I come to see this fair land of which my father has told me.'

'Is that all?' Gandang asked.

'No, I come also to trade – and if the king is kind enough to give me his word, then I wish to hunt the elephant.'

Gandang did not smile, but there was a sparkle in his dark eyes. 'It is not for me to ask which you desire most, Henshaw. The view from a hilltop – or a wagonload of ivory.'

Ralph suppressed his own smile, and remained silent.

'Tell me, son of Bakela, what goods do you bring with you to trade?'

'I have twenty bales of the finest beads and cloth.'

Gandang made a gesture of disinterest. 'Women's fripperies,' he said.

'I have fifty cases of liquor – of the kind preferred by King Lobengula and his royal sister Ningi.'

This time the line of Gandang's mouth thinned and hardened. 'If it were my word on it, I would force those fifty cases of poison down your own throat.' His voice was almost a whisper, but then he spoke again in a natural tone. 'Yet Lobengula, the Great Elephant, will welcome your load.' And then he was silent and yet expectant. Ralph realized that Bazo would have reported to his father every detail of his little caravan.

'I have guns,' he said simply, and suddenly there was an intense hunger in Gandang's expression. His eyes narrowed slightly and his lips parted.

'Sting the mamba with his own venom,' he whispered, and beside him Bazo started. It was the Umlimo's prophecy that his father had repeated, and he wondered that Gandang could have uttered it in the presence of one who was not Matabele.

'I do not understand,' Ralph said.

'No matter.' Gandang waved it away with a graceful pink-palmed hand. 'Tell me, Henshaw. Are these guns of yours of the kind that swallow a round ball through the mouth and place the life of the man that fires them in more danger than the man who stands in front?'

Ralph smiled at the description of the ancient trade muskets, many of which had survived Wellington's Iberian campaign and some of which had seen action at Bull Run and Gettysburg before being shipped out to Africa in trade; the barrel worn paper thin, the priming pan and hammer mechanism so badly abused that each shot fired threatened to tear the head off any marksman bold enough to press the trigger.

'These guns are the finest,' he replied.

'With twisting snakes in the barrel?' Gandang asked, and it took Ralph a moment to recognize the allusion to the rifling in the barrel.

He nodded. 'And the barrel opens to take the bullet.'

'Bring me one of these guns,' Gandang ordered.

'The price of each is one large tusk of ivory,' Ralph told him, and Gandang stared at him impassively for a moment longer. Then he smiled for the first time – but the smile was sharp as the edge of his stabbing spear.

'Now,' he said. 'I truly believe that you have come to Matabeleland to see how tall stand the trees.'

'I am leaving you now, Henshaw,' Bazo said, without lifting his eyes from the thick yellow tusk that he had brought from his father in payment for the rifle.

'We knew it was not for ever,' Ralph answered him.

'The bond between us is for ever,' Bazo replied, 'but now I must go to join my regiment. My father will leave ten of his men to escort and guide you to GuBulawayo – where King Lobengula awaits you.'

'Is Lobengula not at Thabas Indunas, the Hills of the Chiefs?' Ralph asked.

'It is the same kraal, in the days of Mzilikazi it was Thabas Indunas, but now Lobengula has changed the name to GuBulawayo, the Place of Killing.'

'I see,' Ralph nodded, and then waited for it was clear that Bazo had more to say.

'Henshaw. You did not hear me say this – but the ten warriors who will go with you to the king's kraal are not only for your protection. Do not look too closely at the stones and rocks along the road, and do not dig a hole, even to bury your own excrement, else Lobengula will hear of it and believe that you are searching for the shiny pebbles and yellow metal. That is death.'

'I understand.'

'Henshaw, while you are in Matabeleland, give up your habit of travelling at night. Only magicians and sorcerers go abroad in the darkness, mounted on the backs of the hyena. The king will hear of it – and that is death.'

'Yes.'

'Do not hunt the hippopotamus. They are the king's beasts. To kill one – is death.'

'I understand.'

'When you enter the presence of the king, be sure that your head is always below that of the Great Elephant, even if you must crawl on your belly.'

'You have told me this already.'

'I will tell you again,' Bazo nodded. 'And I will tell you once more that the maidens of Matabeleland are the most beautiful in all the world. They light a raging fire in a man's loins, but to take one of them without the king's word is death for both man and maiden.'

*

For an hour they squatted opposite each other, occasionally taking a little snuff or passing one of Ralph's cheap black cheroots back and forth, but always with Bazo talking and Ralph listening.

Bazo spoke quietly, insistently, reciting the names of the most powerful indunas, the governors of each of Matabeleland's military provinces, listing those who had the king's ear and should be treated with care, explaining how a man should conduct himself so as not to give offence, advising how much tribute each would ask and finally accept, trying to give it all to Ralph in these last minutes, and then finally glancing up at the sky.

'It is time.' He stood. 'Go in peace, Henshaw.' And he walked out of Ralph's camp without looking back.

*

As Ralph's wagon, with its escort of warriors, climbed out of the low veld, so the heat abated. The air was so sweet and clean that it made Ralph feel as though the blood sparkled and fizzed in his veins.

Isazi was infected by the same elation. He composed new verses to sing to his bullocks, lauding their strength and beauty, and occasionally he slipped in a reference to a 'feathered baboon' or some other fanciful and unlovely creature, while rolling his eyes significantly in the direction of the bodyguard of Matabele warriors that preceded the wagon.

The forests thinned as they climbed, becoming open woodlands of shapely mimosa trees, the paper-thin bark peeling away to reveal the clear smooth underbark, and the branches loaded with the fluffy yellow flower heads. The grass cloaked the undulating earth, thick and sweet, so that the bullocks fleshed out after the enervating heat of the lowlands, and they stepped out with a new will against the yoke.

This was cattle country, the heartland of the Matabele, and they began to encounter the herds. Huge assemblies of multicoloured animals, red and white and black and all the combinations of those colours. Smaller than the big Cape bullocks, but sturdy and agile as wild game, the bulls with the hump and heavy dewlap of their Egyptian forebears.

Isazi looked at them covetously, and came back to Ralph at the forewheel of the wagon to say:

'Such were the herds of Zululand, before the soldiers came.'

'There must be hundreds of thousands, and they would be worth twenty pounds a head.'

'Will you never learn, Little Hawk.' Isazi still returned to the diminutive when one of Ralph's stupidities exasperated him. 'A man cannot place a value on a fine breeding cow or a beautiful woman in little round coins.'

'Yet, as a Zulu you pay for a wife.'

'Yes, Little Hawk.' Isazi's voice was weary with Ralph's obtuse arguments. 'A Zulu pays for a wife; but he pays in cattle, not in coin, which is what I have been telling you all along.' And he ended the discussion with a thunderous clap of his long trek whip.

Small family kraals dotted the wide savannahs, each built around its own cattle stockade and fortified against predators – or against marauders. As they passed the settlements of thatched beehive-shaped huts, the little naked herd boys scampered to alert the kraals, and then the women came out, bare-legged and naked-breasted, balancing the clay pots and hollowed gourds upon their heads, an exercise that gave them a stately dignity of movement.

Then Ralph's bodyguard of warriors from Gandang's regiment paused to refresh themselves on the tart and bubbling millet beer or on the delicious soured milk, thick as yoghurt. The young women examined Ralph with bold and curious eyes. Totally unaware that he spoke the language, they speculated about him in such intimate terms that his ears turned bright red, and he challenged them:

'It is easy to speak the lion's name and question his size and his strength when he is hidden in the long grass, but will you be so brave when he raises himself in his rage to confront you face to face?'

The silence, stunned and incredulous, lasted only a second, then they covered their mouths and shrieked with delighted laughter, before the bravest came to wheedle coquettishly for a strip of ribbon or a handful of pretty beads.

As they drew closer to the stronghold of Lobengula, so they passed the great regimental kraals. Each of them was fifty miles from its neighbours, a day's travel at the rate of a marching impi, the ground-devouring trot that they could maintain for hour after hour.

Here there was no exchange of greeting and banter. The warriors came swarming from the kraal like bees from a disturbed hive, and they lined each side of the track and settled into a deathly stillness, watching Ralph's wagon pass in total silence. There was a blankness in their eyes, the inscrutable gaze with which the lion watches his prey before he begins the stalk.

Ralph passed between the massed ranks at a measured walk, sitting very upright on Tom's back, without deigning to glance left or right at the silent menacing ranks; but when they had passed out into the open grasslands again, his shirt was wet under the arms and between his shoulder blades, and there was a catch in his breathing and a chill in the pit of his belly.

The Khami was one of the last wide rivers to cross before reaching the king's kraal at GuBulawayo.

As soon as Ralph saw the denser and greener growth of mimosa trees that marked the river course, he threw the saddle on Tom's back and trotted ahead to survey the drift.

Ports had been cut into the steep sides of the river banks to enable a wagon to enter the watercourse, and the sandbank between two tranquil green pools had been corduroyed with carefully selected branches, cut to length and laid side by side across the softer going to prevent the narrow ironshod wheels from sinking.

Whoever had travelled this road ahead of Ralph had saved him a great deal of trouble. Ralph knee-haltered Tom on a patch of good grass and went down into the riverbed to check the crossing. It was obviously many months since the last wagon had crossed, and Ralph worked his way slowly over the corduroyed pathway, repairing the damage that time had wrought, kicking the dried branches back into place and refilling the hollows scooped by water and wind beneath them.

It was furnace-hot in the riverbed and the white sand bounced the sun's rays back at him so that by the time he reached the far bank he was sweating heavily, and he threw himself down in the shade of one of the trees and wiped his face and arms with his scarf moistened in the waters of the river pool.

Quite suddenly he was aware of being watched, and he scrambled quickly to his feet. There was someone standing on the bank above him at the head of the roadway.

With a shock of disbelief, he realized that it was a girl – a white girl, and she was dressed all in white: a loose cotton shift that reached to her ankle just above her bare feet. It was caught in at the waist with a ribbon of blue, and she was so slim that Ralph felt he could lift her with one hand.

The dress was buttoned with mother of pearl to the throat and the sleeves reached to her elbows; but the cotton had been washed, ironed and bleached so often that it seemed to have less substance than gossamer, and the light was behind her.

Ralph could clearly see the outline of her legs under the skirt, and it shocked him again so his breathing tripped. Her legs were long and so delicately shaped that he had to exercise his will to tear his eyes from them. With his heart still pounding he looked at her face.

It was pale as bone china, and seemed almost translucent, so that he thought he could see the sheen of fragile bone beneath the skin.

Her hair was pale shining silver blond, brushed into a fine cascade that flowed over her shoulders, and shimmered and shook with each breath that lifted the tiny girlish breasts under the thin cotton.

There were flowers on her brow, and a garland of them over her shoulders, and about the brim of the wide straw hat that she held in her hands at the level of her narrow hips – and Ralph felt a sense of unreality. The flowers were roses. The girl and the flowers seemed not to belong in this wilderness but in some gentle and cultivated English garden.

She came down the cutting; her bare feet were silent and seemed to glide over the sandy earth. Her eyes were huge and luminous blue in her pale face, and she was smiling. It was the sweetest smile that Ralph had ever seen, and yet it was neither shy nor simpering.

While Ralph still stood, self-conscious and gawking, the girl lifted her slim smooth arms and stood on tiptoe to kiss him full upon the mouth. Her lips were cool and soft, delicate as the roses petals at her brow.

'Oh Ralph, we are so glad to see you. Nobody has talked of anything else since first we heard that you were upon the road.'

'Who – who are you?' Ralph blurted, his surprise and embarrassment making him boorish; but she seemed unaffected by the gauche question.

'Salina,' she said, and slipped her hand into the crook of his elbow to lead him up the bank. 'Salina Codrington.'

'I don't understand.' He pulled against the hand so that she had to turn to face him again.

'Salina –' she repeated, laughing now, and her laughter was warm and sweet as her smile. 'I'm Salina Codrington.' And then when it was apparent that the name meant nothing, 'I'm your cousin, Ralph. My mother is your father's sister – Robyn Codrington – but she was Robyn Ballantyne.'

'Good God!' Ralph stared at her. 'I didn't know Aunt Robyn had a daughter.'

'I suppose not. Uncle Zouga never was a good correspondent.' But suddenly the smile was no longer on Salina's lips, and Ralph remembered abruptly that he had never taken the trouble to unravel the tangled skein of family history, except to comprehend vaguely that there was ill-feeling and unsettled scores between Zouga and his Aunt Robyn. Then it came back to him, he had overheard his father recalling bitterly how Robyn had taken unfair advantage by publishing her own version of their joint expedition to the Zambezi months before Zouga's *Hunter's Odyssey* - thereby robbing Zouga of his fair share of critical acclaim, and royalties.

Ralph's touching on the family enmities must account for Salina's quick change of mood, but it was fleeting. She took his arm again, and was smiling as they came up the bank.

'Not one daughter, Ralph. We Codringtons will not let you off so lightly. There are a whole tribe of us, four of us, all girls.' And she stopped, lifted the straw hat to shade her eyes and looked down the winding overgrown track that meandered away across the grassy savannah. 'Oh dear!' she exclaimed. 'I came ahead to warn you – and I was only just in time!'

Down the track towards them pelted three small figures, jostling one another for advantage, their faint squeaks of excitement gaining rapidly in volume, long hair flying wildly, fluttering skirts of faded and patched cloth lifted high above the knees so that bare legs flashed, faces freckled and flushed, contorted with exertion and excitement and recrimination.

'Salina! You promised to wait!'

They bore down on where Ralph stood with the lovely blond girl on his arm.

'Good God!' Ralph whispered again, and Salina squeezed his elbow.

'That's the second time that you have used the Lord's name, Cousin Ralph. Please don't.' So that was the reason for her faint displeasure.

'Oh – I'm terribly sorry.' And he remembered too late that Salina's parents were pious missionaries. 'I didn't mean –' Again he was thick-tongued, for suddenly this girl's good opinion was the most important thing in all the world. 'I won't do it again. I promise.'

'Thank you,' she said softly, and before either of them could speak again they were surrounded by what appeared to be an ocean of small females, every one of which was bobbing up and down with remarkable rapidity, competing vocally for Ralph's attention and at the same time shrieking accusations at their eldest sister.

'You cheated, Salina. You told us –'

'Ralph, Cousin Ralph, I'm Victoria, the eldest twin.'

'Cousin Ralph, we prayed God to speed you to us.'

Salina clapped her hands, and there was a barely noticeable reduction in the volume of sound.

'In order of age!' she said calmly.

'You *always* say that because you are the eldest!'

Salina ignored the protest and picked out a dark-haired child with a hand on her shoulder.

'This is Catherine.' She drew her forward to face Ralph. 'Cathy is fourteen.'

'And a half, almost fifteen,' said Cathy, and her manner changed with this declaration, becoming ladylike and controlled.

She was thin, and as flat-chested as a boy, but the young body gave the immediate impression of strength and suppleness. Her nose and cheeks were peppered with freckles, but the mouth was full and frank, her eyes the same Ballantyne green as Ralph's own, and her thick dark brows were a frame for their bright intelligent gleam. Her chin was a little too large, as was her nose, but they had a determined set and thrust. Her thick dark hair was plaited and piled on top of her head, leaving her ears exposed, small and pointed and lying flat against her head.

'Welcome to Khami, Ralph,' she said evenly, and bobbed a small curtsey, holding her skirts up as she had obviously been coached; and Ralph realized that the skirt was made of old flour bags that had been stitched together and dyed a muddy green. The lettering still showed through: 'Cape Flour Mills'.

Then Cathy reached up and kissed him quickly, and it left a little wet spot on Ralph's lips. Kissing was obviously the accepted family salutation, and Ralph glanced with trepidation at the eager but grubby faces of the twins.

'I'm Victoria, the eldest.'

'And I'm Elizabeth, but if you call me "baby", I shall hate you, Cousin Ralph.'

'You won't hate anybody,' Salina said, and Elizabeth hurled herself at Ralph's neck, got a fair grip and hung on as she plastered her mouth to Ralph's.

'I was teasing, Ralph. I shall love you,' she whispered fiercely. 'Always! Always!'

'Me!' howled Victoria indignantly. 'I'm older than Lizzie. Me first.'

Salina led them with that gliding walk which did not move her shoulders and barely ruffled the white-gold curtain of her hair, and every once in a while she turned to smile at Ralph, and he thought he had never seen anything so lovely.

The twins each had hold of one of Ralph's hands, and they gabbled out all the things they had saved up for weeks to tell him, and skipped to keep pace with his stride. Cathy came up behind them all, leading Tom. She and the pony had formed an immediate accord.

'Oh, he's beautiful, Ralph,' she had said and kissed Tom's velvety muzzle.

'We don't have a horse,' Victoria explained. 'Daddy is a man of God, and men of God are too poor to have horses.'

The small party straggled over the first low rise beyond the river, and Salina stopped and pointed down into the shallow basin ahead of them.

'Khami!' she said simply, and all of them looked to Ralph for approbation.

There was a notch in the next line of granite hills, a natural divide and shed for underground water, which accounted for the spread of lush grass that carpeted the valley.

Like chickens under the hen, the small huddle of buildings crouched beneath the hills. They were neatly laid out, thatched with yellow grass and painted dazzlingly white with burnt lime-wash. The largest building had a wooden cross set proudly on the ridge of the roof.

'Daddy and Mummy built the church with their own hands. King Silly Cat would not allow any of his people to help them,' Victoria explained.

'Silly Cat?' Ralph asked, puzzled.

'King Mzilikazi,' Salina translated. 'You know Mama does not like you using fun names for the kings, Vicky,' she rebuked the child mildly; but Victoria was shaking Ralph's hand excitedly and pointing to a distant figure in the valley below them.

'Daddy!' shrieked the twins in unison. 'There's Daddy!'

He was working in the precise geometrically laid out gardens below the church, a lanky figure whose shoulders remained stooped even when he stood upright and looked towards them, stabbed his spade into the earth and came striding up the hill.

'Ralph!' He swept off the sweatstained hat, and he was bald – like a monk, with just a fringe of silky hair forming a halo around his pate at the level of his ears. It was immediately apparent from whom Salina had inherited her glorious white-gold tresses.

'Ralph,' the man repeated, and he wiped his right hand on the seat of his pants and then held it out. Despite the stoop, he was as tall as Ralph, his face deeply tanned, his bald dome as shiny as if it had been waxed and polished, his eyes pale blue as a summer sky, washed out by heat haze; but his smile was like Salina's – calm and tranquil, so that as he took the hand Ralph realized that this was the most contented and deeply happy man he had ever met in his life.

'I'm Clinton Codrington,' he said. 'And I suppose I must count as your uncle, though goodness knows I do not feel that old.'

'I would have known you anywhere, sir,' said Ralph.

'Would you indeed?'

'I have read Aunt Robyn's books, and I have always admired your exploits as a Royal Naval officer.'

'Oh dear.' Clinton shook his head in mock dismay. 'I thought to have left that all far behind me.'

'You were one of the most illustrious and courageous officers in the African anti-slavery squadron, sir.' Ralph's eyes shone with a still boyish hero worship.

'Your Aunt Robyn's account suffered a dreadful list to port, I'm afraid.'

'Daddy is the bravest man in the world,' Victoria declared stoutly, and she released Ralph's hand and ran to her father.

Clinton Codrington gathered her up and held her on his hip.

'And yours, young lady, is probably the most unbiased opinion in Matabeleland,' he chuckled, and Ralph was suddenly sharply jealous of this palpable aura of deep affection and love which welded the little group, from which he felt himself excluded. It was something beyond his experience, something he had never missed until that moment. Somehow Salina seemed to sense his pang of melancholy, and she took the hand that Victoria had relinquished.

'Come,' she said. 'Mama will be waiting. And there is one

thing you will soon learn, Ralph. In this family, nobody keeps Mama waiting.'

They went down towards the church, passing between the beds of growing vegetables.

'You didn't bring any seed?' Clinton asked, and when Ralph shook his head, 'Well, how were you to know?' and he went on to point out with pride his flourishing crops. 'Maize, potatoes, beans, tomatoes do particularly well here.'

'We divide it this way,' Cathy told Ralph, teasing her father. 'One for the bugs, two for the baboons, three for the bushbuck – and one for Daddy.'

'Be good to all God's creatures.' Clinton reached out to ruffle her dark hair, and Ralph realized that these gentle people were always touching and kissing one another. He had never experienced anything like it.

Squatting patiently on the shady side against the wall of the church were twenty or more Matabele of all ages and sexes, from a skeleton-thin ancient with a completely white cap of wool on his bowed head and both his eyes turned to blind orbs of milky jelly by tropical ophthalmia to a new-born infant held against its mother's milk-swollen breasts with its tiny dark face screwed up with the terrible colic of infant dysentery.

Catherine tethered Tom beside the church door, and they all trooped into the cool interior, insulated by thatch and thick walls of unbaked brick from the outside heat. The church smelled of homemade soap, and of iodine. The pews of rough-hewn timber had been pushed aside to make way for an operating table of the same material.

There was a girl at work over the table, but as they came in she tied the last knot in a bandage and dismissed her semi-naked black patient with a word and a pat – then, wiping her hands on a clean but threadbare cloth, she came down the aisle of the church towards them.

Ralph was certain that she was Cathy's twin, for though she was a little taller, she was as slim and as flat-chested; her hair had the same dark brown colouring, though shot through with tones of russet and chestnut, her skin the same youthful lustre, and her nose and chin the same forceful size and thrust.

Then as she came closer, Ralph realized that he had been mistaken and that she was older than Cathy, perhaps even older than Salina, but not much.

'Hello, Ralph,' the girl said. 'I'm your Aunt Robyn.' Ralph felt the blasphemy of surprise leap to his lips again, but conscious of Salina's hand in his he suppressed it.

'You are so young,' he said instead.

'Bless you for that,' she laughed. 'You turn a prettier compliment than your daddy ever did.' She was the only one who made no effort to kiss him; instead she turned to the twins.

'Right!' she said. 'I want ten pages of copperplate written out before Evensong – and I don't want to see a single blot.'

'Oh Mama! Ralph –'

'Ralph has been your excuse for two weeks. Go – or you will eat in the kitchen hut tonight.'

Then, to Cathy: 'Have you finished the ironing, young lady?'

'Not yet, Mama.' Cathy followed the twins.

'Salina, your baking.'

'Yes, Mama.'

Then there were three of them alone in the little church, and Robyn ran a professional eye over her nephew.

'Well, Zouga has bred a likely boy,' she gave her opinion. 'But I never expected anything else.'

'How did you all know I was coming?' Ralph voiced his bewilderment at last.

'Grandpa Moffat sent a runner when you left Kuruman, and Induna Gandang passed here two weeks ago on his way to King Lobengula's kraal. His eldest son was with him, and Bazo's mother is an old friend of mine.'

'I see.'

'Nothing moves in Matabeleland but the whole nation knows of it immediately,' Clinton explained.

'Now, Ralph, how is your father? I was terribly distressed to hear of the death of Aletta, your mother. She was a lovely person, so good and gentle. I wrote to Zouga, but he never replied.'

Robyn seemed determined to catch up on the doings of a decade in the first ten minutes, and her questions were quick and incisive; but Clinton soon excused himself and left the two of them alone in the little church to return to his gardens.

Ralph replied dutifully to all her questions, while he reassessed his first impression of his aunt. Youthful she looked, but childlike she was not. Now at last he could understand the remarkable achievements of this forceful woman. How she had enrolled at a famous London hospital, one which would never accept a female on its student body, by impersonating a man. Dressed in breeches, she had kept her terms and been granted her doctorate when she was twenty-one years of age. The scandal which attended the discovery that a female had invaded an exclusive male preserve had rocked all England.

Then she had accompanied Zouga to Africa, equal partners in the expedition to find their father Fuller Ballantyne, who had been missing in the unexplored interior for eight years. When she and Zouga had fallen out over the conduct of the expedition, she had pushed on, a white woman alone with only primitive black tribesmen as companions, and achieved the main object of the expedition on her own.

Her book describing the expedition, entitled *Africa in My Blood,* had been a publishing phenomenon and had sold almost a quarter of a million copies – three times as many as Zouga Ballantyne's *A Hunter's Odyssey* published six months later.

Robyn had signed over all her royalties from the book to The London Missionary Society, and that august body had been so delighted by the donation that they had reinstated her as a society officer, had ordained her husband as her assistant, and had approved her heading a mission to Matabeleland.

Her two subsequent publications had not enjoyed the same success as the first. *The Sick African,* a practical study of tropical medicine, had contained ludicrous theories that had earned her the derision of her medical peers – she had even dared to suggest that malarial fever was not caused by breathing the foul night airs of tropical swamps, when this fact had been known since the time of Hippocrates.

Then her further account of her life as a medical missionary, *Blind Faith,* had been too homely in style and too prejudiced in championing the indigenous tribes. She had firmly embraced the beliefs of Jean-Jacques Rousseau and had added her own refinements to them. Her round condemnation of all settlers, hunters, prospectors and traders, and of their treatment of the noble savages, had been too salty for her European readers.

Indeed, scandal and contention seemed to follow Robyn Codrington as vultures and jackals follow the lion, and at each new provocation all her previous adventures would be recalled:

What decent female missionary would provoke men sufficiently to make them fight a bloody duel over her? Robyn Ballantyne had.

What God-fearing lady would sail aboard a notorious slaver, unchaperoned and with only slavers for company? Robyn Ballantyne had.

What lady would choose for husband a man who had been court-martialled, stripped of his naval rank and imprisoned for piracy and dereliction of duty? Robyn Codrington had.

What loyal subject of the Queen would hail the terrible reversal of British arms at Isandhlwana, the bloody death of hundreds of Englishmen at the hands of the savage Zulus, as a judgement of God – Robyn Codrington had, in a letter to the *Evening Standard*.

Who, other than Robyn Codrington, would write to Lord Kimberley demanding that half the profits of the diamond fields that bore his name should go to the Griqua captain, Nicholaas Waterboer?

Only Robyn Codrington would demand of Paulus Kruger, the newly-elected President of the little Transvaal Republic, that he return to Lobengula, King of the Matabele, the land below the Cashan mountains from which the Boer commandos had driven Mzilikazi, his father.

She spared no one. Nothing was sacred to her except her God, whom she treated rather like a senior partner in the business of running Africa.

Her enemies, and they were legion, hated her fiercely, and her friends loved her with equal passion. It was impossible to be unmoved by her, and Ralph found himself fascinated as she sat beside him on the church pew and subjected him to an exhaustive catechism that covered every aspect of his life and that of the family.

'You have a brother,' she seemed to know it all. 'Jordan? That is his name, isn't it? Tell me about him.' It was a command.

'Oh, Jordie is everybody's favourite; everybody loves him.'

Ralph had never met anybody like her. He doubted he could ever bring himself to like her, she was far too prickly. That was the exact word to describe her, but he would never doubt her strength and her determination.

Clinton Codrington came back into the church as the light outside was mellowing into late afternoon.

'My dear, you really must let the poor fellow go now.' He turned to Ralph. 'Your wagon has come up. I showed your driver where to outspan. He seems a first-rate chap, I must say.'

'You will sleep in the guest house,' Robyn announced as she stood.

'Cathy has taken your soiled clothes from the wagon, and she has washed and ironed them,' Clinton went on.

'You will want to put on a fresh shirt before Evensong,' Robyn told him. 'We shall not begin the service until you return.'

He had liked it better on the open road, Ralph thought sourly; then he had made his own decisions as to when he made his ablutions, as to how he dressed and where he spent his evenings – but he went to change his shirt as he was bidden.

The distaff side of the Codrington family filled the front pew. Clinton Codrington faced them from the pulpit. Ralph was between the twins; there had been a brief but ferocious competition between Victoria and Elizabeth to decide who should sit closest to him.

Apart from the family, there was nobody else in the church, and Victoria saw his glance and explained to Ralph in a penetrating whisper, 'King Ben won't let any of his people come to our church.'

'King Lobengula,' Salina corrected her sweetly, 'not King Ben.'

Despite the full attendance, Clinton delayed the commencement of the evening service, finding and losing his place in the Book of Common Prayer half a dozen times – and glancing repeatedly towards the rear of the tiny church.

From this quarter there was a sudden commotion. A small retinue of Matabele women had arrived outside the church. Clearly they were servants, house slaves and ladies-in-waiting to the imposing female figure in their midst. She dismissed them with a royal gesture and came in through the doors of the church. Every one of the Codringtons turned their heads and their faces lit with pleasure.

The way in which this matron paced majestically down the aisle left not a doubt as to her high breeding and her place in the aristocracy of Matabeleland. She wore bangles and bracelets of beaten red copper, strings of highly prized sam-sam beads that only a chief would afford. Her cloak was of beautifully tanned leather, ornamented with feathers of the blue jay and worked with designs of chipped ostrich shell.

'I see you, Nomusa,' she declared.

Her huge naked breasts shone with an ointment of fat and red clay; they pushed out ponderously from under her tanned cloak and dangled weightily to the level of her navel.

Her arms were thick as a grown man's thigh, her thighs as thick as his waist. There were rolls of fat around her belly, and her face was a black full moon, the glossy skin stretched tightly over her abundant flesh. Her merry eyes sparkled from between creases of fat, and her teeth flashed like the sunlit surface of a lake as she smiled. All this size was evidence to the world of her station, of her amazing beauty, of her fecundity. It was also unassailable proof of the high regard of her husband, of his prosperity and importance in the councils of Matabeleland.

'I see you, Girlchild of Mercy,' she smiled at Robyn.

'I see you, Juba, the little dove.' Robyn answered her.

'I am not a Christian,' Juba intoned. 'Let no evil one bear false tidings to Lobengula, the Black and Mighty Elephant.'

'If you say so, Juba,' Robyn answered primly, and Juba pinioned her in a vast embrace while at the same time she called to Clinton in the pulpit.

'I see you also, Hlopi. I see you, White Head! But do not be deceived by my presence here, I am not a Christian.' She drew an elephantine breath and went on, 'I come merely to greet old friends – not to sing hymns and worship your God. Also I warn you, Hlopi, that if you read the story tonight of a man called the Rock who denied his God three times before the call of the cock, I shall be displeased.'

'I shall not read that story,' Clinton answered. 'For by now you should know it by heart.'

'Very well, Hlopi, then let the singing begin.' And led by Juba in a startlingly clear and beautiful soprano, the entire Codrington family rollicked into the first verse of 'Onward Christian Soldiers' – which Robyn had translated into the Matabele vernacular.

After the service Juba bore down on Ralph.

'You are Henshaw?' she demanded.

'*Nkosikazi*!' Ralph agreed, and Juba inclined her head to acknowledge the correct style of address to the senior wife of a great chief that Ralph had employed.

'Then you are the one whom Bazo, my first-born son, calls

brother,' Juba said. 'You are very skinny and very white, Little Hawk – but if you are Bazo's brother, then you are my son.'

'You do me great honour, *Umame*!' Ralph said, and Juba took him in those mammoth arms. She smelled of clarified fat, and ochre and wood-smoke, but the embrace was strangely comforting, not at all unlike the feeling, only half remembered, that he had once experienced in Alctta's arms.

The twins knelt side-by-side at the low truckle cot, both in long nightdresses, their hands clasped before their eyes which were so tightly closed that they seemed to be in pain.

Salina, also in her nightdress, stood over them to supervise the last prayer of the day.

'Gentle Jesus meek and mild –'

Cathy was already in her own bed, hair ribboned for the night, writing the day's entry in her diary by the light of the guttering candle made from buffalo fat and cloth wick.

'Pity my simplicity –' gabbled the twins, at such a speed that it came out as, 'Pretty mice, and pretty me!'

Arriving at the 'Amen' in a dead heat, the twins leaped into the bed that they shared, pulled the blanket to their chins and watched with fascination as Salina began to brush her hair, one hundred strokes with each hand, so that it rippled and flamed with white fire in the candlelight. Then she came to kiss them, blew out the candle, and the thongs of her bed squeaked from across the small thatched hut as she climbed into it.

'Lina?' whispered Victoria.

'Vicky, go to sleep.'

'Just one question, please.'

'All right then, just one.'

'Does God allow a girl to marry her own cousin?'

The silence that followed the question seemed to hum in the darkened bedroom like a copper telegraph wire struck by a sword.

Cathy broke the silence.

'Yes, Vicky,' she answered quietly. 'God does allow it. Read the Table of Kindred and Affinity on the last page of your prayer book.'

The silence was contemplative now.

'Lina?'

'Lizzie, go to sleep.'

'You allowed Vicky to ask a question.'

'All right then, just one.'

'Does God get cross if you pray for something just for yourself – not for Daddy or Mama or your sisters, but just for you alone?'

'I don't think so,' Salina's voice was becoming drowsy. 'He might not give it to you but I don't think He will be cross. *Now* go to sleep, both of you.'

Cathy lay very still, on her back with her hands clenched at her sides, staring at the lighter oblong across the hut where the moon defined the single window.

'Please God,' she prayed. 'Let him look at me the way he looks at Salina, just once. Please.'

'What do you think of Zouga's boy?' Robyn took Clinton's arm as they stood together on the darkened stoep and looked out at the star-pricked black velvet curtain of the African night.

'He's a powerful lad – and I don't mean merely muscle.' Clinton took his pipe from between his teeth and peered into the bowl. 'His wagon is loaded with cases, long wooden cases from which the markings have been burned with a hot iron.'

'Guns?' Robyn asked.

'I think so.'

'There is no law against trading guns north of the Limpopo,' Robyn reminded him. 'And Lobengula needs all the power he can get to defend himself.'

'Still, guns! I mean, it does go against the grain.' Clinton sucked at his pipe, and each puff of smoke he exhaled was denser and ranker. They were both silent for a while.

'He has a hard and ruthless streak, like his father,' Robyn judged at last.

'A man needs that to survive in this land.'

Robyn shivered suddenly, and hugged her own arms.

'Are you cold?' Clinton was immediately solicitous.

'No. A grey goose walked over my grave.'

'Let's go off to bed.'

'A moment longer, Clinton. The night is so beautiful.'

Clinton put his arm about her shoulders.

'Sometimes I am so happy that it frightens me,' he said. 'So much happiness cannot go on for ever.'

His words seemed to precipitate the thick but formless dread that had hung over Robyn all this day like the pall of smoke above the winter bush fires. It weighed her down with the premonition that something had changed in all their lives.

'May God save us all,' she whispered.

'Amen to that,' said Clinton as softly, and took her in out of the night.

The interior of the thatched hall was domed and darkened, so that the patterns of latticed branches and lovingly knotted bark rope disappeared into the gloom above their heads like the arches of a medieval cathedral.

The only light was from the small fire on the clay hearth in the centre of the floor. One of the king's wives threw another handful of dried herbs upon it and oily blue tendrils of smoke twisted upwards towards the unseen roof.

Across the fire, on a low platform of dried clay covered with a thick mattress of furs, silver-backed jackal and blue monkey, bat-eared fox and spotted civet, sat the king.

He was a mountainous figure, stark naked, and his skin polished with fat so that he gleamed like an enormous Buddha carved from a solid block of washed anthracite. His head was round as a cannon ball, surmounted by the induna's ring. His arms were massive, bulging with muscle and fat, but the hands in his lap were strangely dainty, narrow across the pink palms, with long tapered fingers.

His trunk was thickened, his breasts pendulous. All this was flesh which he had carefully cultivated. The beer pots and beef dishes stood close at hand. The thick millet beer bubbled softly and the cuts of beef each had a thick rind of yellow fat. Every few minutes one of his wives responded to a nod or a small movement of one graceful hand by proffering a dish. Weight and size were the mark of a king. Not for nothing was Lobengula called the Great Black Elephant of Matabeleland.

His manner was slow, imbued with the vast dignity of his size and rank. Yet his eyes were thoughtful and deeply intelligent, his features despite the burden of fat which blurred them were handsome, lacking outward traits of the hideous cruelties which any Matabele king had to make part of his life.

'My people expect me to be strong and harsh. There are always those who look for the smallest weakness in me – as the young lions watch the black-maned leader of the pride,' Mzilikazi had explained to his son. 'See how my chickens follow me to be fed.' He had pointed with the toy spear of kingship at the high wheel of tiny specks turning slowly in the sky above the hills of Thabas Indunas. 'When my vultures desert me, I will be as dust.'

Lobengula, his son, had learned the lesson well – but it had not brutalized him. Indeed, there was a line to his mouth that was almost diffident, and a shadow behind the light of intelligence in his eyes that was hesitant, the confusion of a man tugged at by too many currents and winds – a man caught up by his destiny, and uncertain as to how he could break away from its remorseless toils.

Lobengula had never expected to take up his father's spear of kingship. He was never the heir apparent, there had been older brothers from mothers of higher rank and nobler blood.

He stared now across the fire at the man that squatted there. A magnificent warrior, his body tempered to black steel by long marches and savage warfare, his understanding and compassion expanded by close and intimate daily contact with common men, his courage and loyalty proven to all the world ten thousand times so there could be no doubts, not even in his own midnight watches, which is the time of doubts – and Lobengula found himself longing to rid himself of this fearsome burden of kingship and place it on the other man's shoulders. He found himself wishing for that quiet and secret cave in the Matopos hills where he had known the only happy days of his life.

The man opposite him was a half-brother; his blood line, like that of Lobengula himself, reaching back unsullied to the Zanzi of Zululand. He was a prince of the House of Kumalo, wise and brave and untroubled by doubts.

'Such a one should have been king,' Lobengula thought, and his love for his half-brother choked his throat so that he coughed. He moved one little finger, and a wife held the beer pot to his lips and he swallowed once and then signed for it to be taken away.

'I see you, Gandang.' His voice was throaty and low, the sadness still in it for he knew that he could not escape that way.

He felt like a man on a solitary journey through the forest where the lions are hunting. His recognition released Gandang from his respectful silence. The induna clapped his hands softly and began to recite his half-brother's ritual praises, and Lobengula's mind wandered back across the years.

His earliest memory was of the road, the hard road up from the south – driven by the mounted men dressed all in brown, riding brown ponies. He remembered the popping sound of the guns, which he learned only later to fear, and the smell of gunsmoke, spicy and sour as the wind brought it down to where he clung to his mother, and he remembered the wailing of the women as they mourned the dead.

He remembered the heat and the dust, trotting naked as a puppy at his mother's heels. How tall she had seemed, the muscles of her back gleaming with sweat, and Ningi, his sister, in the sling upon her hip, clinging to one of his mother's fat jostling breasts with mouth and tiny determined fists.

He remembered toiling up the stony hills with his father's single wagon rolling and pitching along ahead of them. On it rode Mzilikazi's senior wife, and her son Nkulumane, three years older than Lobengula and heir apparent to the kingship of the Matabele. They were the only ones who did not walk.

He remembered how his mother's back had withered, the beautiful gleaming skin becoming loose and baggy, the ribcage beginning to show through as the famine wasted her substance, and Ningi screaming with hunger as the rich creamy flow from her teats dried up.

This was where the memory of 'Saala' began; it was mixed up at first with the shouting and singing as a band of raiding Matabele returned to the fleeing column. He had first seen Saala in the firelight, as the warriors slaughtered the captured cattle, and Lobengula could almost still feel the hot grease and the bloody juices of the beef running down his chin and dripping onto his naked chest as they feasted, breaking the long days and months of starvation on cattle taken from the white men, the *buni*.

Once his belly was bulging tightly with meat, Lobengula had joined the circle of curious Matabele princelings and princesses who surrounded the captives; but he had stood back from the teasing and jeering and prodding of the other children.

Saala was the eldest of the two little girls. It was only long afterwards that Lobengula learned that her name was Sarah, but even now he could not pronounce that sound. The Matabele raiding party had surprised a small caravan of Boer wagons, and had killed everybody except these two small white children.

Her whiteness was the first thing that had struck Lobengula. How white her face was in the firelight, as white as an egret's wing, and she had not wept as her younger sister wept.

After that the memories grew stronger, Saala walking ahead of him as the slow column wound through thick thorn forest. Saala taking the infant Ningi from his mother when she slipped and fell with weakness in the black mud of the swamps while the mosquitoes formed a dark whining cloud over them.

Exactly where Saala's little sister died, Lobengula could not recall. It might have been in the swamps. They left her small naked white body unburied, and the column marched on.

At last Lobengula's own mother fell and could not rise again, and with her last strength handed little Ningi to Saala; then she curled up quietly and died. All the weak ones died like that, and their infants died with them, for no other women would take the orphans, for each of them had her own infants to care for.

However, Saala strapped little Ningi on her own thin white back in the way that the Matabele carry their babies, then she took Lobengula's hand in hers and they toiled on after the fleeing nation.

By now Saala's clothing had long ago fallen off her thin white body, and she was as the other Matabele girls who had not yet reached puberty, completely naked. She had half forgotten her own language, and spoke only the language of the tribe. The sun had darkened her skin, and the soles of her bare feet had grown a thick covering, hard as rhinoceros skin, so she could march over razor flint and needle thorns.

Lobengula came to love Saala, transferring everything he had ever felt for his mother to her, and she stole extra food for him and protected him from the bullying of his older brothers – from Nkulumane the cruel one, and from Nkulumane's mother, who hated all that might one day stand in the way of her son's claim to the kingship of the Matabele.

Then the Matabele crossed the Limpopo, the River of Crocodiles, and the land beyond was fair, thick with game and running with sweet rivers. The wandering nation followed Mzilikazi into the magical hills of the Matopos. There on a lonely hilltop the king met the wizard of the Matopos, face to face.

Mzilikazi saw fire spring up at the Umlimo's bidding, and he heard the spirits speak from the very air about the Umlimo, a hundred different voices – voice of infant and crone, of man and of beast, the cry of the fish eagle, the snarl of the leopard – and from that day the Umlimo had the reverence and superstitious awe of the king and all his people.

The Umlimo pointed the way north again, and as the Matabele emerged from the broken hills of the Matopos, they saw spread before them a beautiful land, rich with grass and tall trees.

'This is my land,' said Mzilikazi, and built his kraal under the Hills of the Indunas.

However, the Matabele had lost nearly all their cattle and many of the women and children had died on that cruel journey northwards.

At Thabas Indunas Mzilikazi left his senior wife, mother of Nkulumane, as his regent, and he took five thousand of his finest warriors and went out against the tribes – for women and for cattle.

He went westwards into the land ruled by great Khama, and there was no word from him. The seasons came and changed, the rains followed the long dryness, the heat followed the frosts, and still there was no word of Mzilikazi.

Slowly the strict order of Matabele society began to break up, for the regent, Mzilikazi's senior wife, was unrestrained in her intercourses, and she rutted shamelessly with her lovers.

Some of the lesser wives followed her example, and then the common people took sexual licence, the youths, unblooded and without the royal permission to go into the women, lay in wait for the young girls on the path to the water-hole, and dragged them giggling into the bushes.

With the code of morality broken, other vices followed. The remaining cattle, the breeding herds – were slaughtered, and the feasting went on for months. Looseness and drunkenness swept through the nation like a plague, and in the midst of this debauchery, one of the Matabele patrols captured a little yellow Bushman who had wandered in out of the west, and the Bushman had momentous tidings.

'Mzilikazi is dead,' he told his captors. 'I have thrust my own fingers into the stab wound in his heart, and watched the hyena wolfing down his flesh and cracking his bones.'

The senior wife had her guards boil clay pots of water, and

pour them over the Bushman until his flesh fell off his bones and he died, which is fitting treatment for one who brings news of the death of a king. Then she called the indunas into council, and urged them to proclaim Nkulumane king in place of his dead father. However, none of the indunas were fools. One whispered to the other, 'It would take more than a Tswana dog to kill Mzilikazi.'

While they procrastinated and talked, the senior wife grew wild with impatience and sent for the executioners, determined now that there would be no rival for her son. Saala was playing outside the queen's hut, moulding little clay oxen and figures of men and women for Ningi. Through the thatched wall she heard the queen giving her orders to the Black Ones. Frantic with terror for the safety of Lobengula, Saala ran to the other royal mothers.

'The Black Ones are coming for the royal sons. You must hide them.'

Then Saala left little Ningi, now weaned and strong, with one of the royal women who was barren and childless.

'Look after her,' she whispered, and ran out into the grasslands.

Lobengula was by now ten years of age, and was tending what remained of the royal herds: the duty of every Matabele boy, the essential service through which he learned the secrets of the veld and the ways of cattle, the nation's treasure.

Saala found him bringing in the herd to water. He was naked except for the little flap of leather over his loins, and armed only with two short fighting sticks with which he was expected to drive off any predator and to hold his own in competition with the other herd boys.

Holding hands again, the Matabele princeling and the little white girl fled, and instinctively they turned southwards, back the way they had come.

They lived on roots and berries, on the eggs of wild birds and the flesh of the iguana lizards. They competed with the jackals and vultures for the remains of the lion kill – and sometimes they went hungry, but at last they found themselves in the maze of the Matopos Hills where the Black Ones would not follow them. They slept under the single kaross that Saala had brought with her, and the nights crackled with frost so they slept in each other's arms, clinging together for warmth.

Early one morning the old man found them thus. He was thin

and mad-looking, with strange charms and magical objects about his neck, and the children were terrified of him.

Saala pushed Lobengula behind her, and with a show of false courage faced the wizard.

'This is Lobengula. Favourite son of Mzilikazi,' she declared stoutly. 'Who harms him, harms the king.'

The old man rolled his mad eyes, and drooled horribly as he grinned with toothless gums. Then suddenly the air was full of the sound of ghost voices – and Saala screamed and Lobengula wailed with terror, and they clung to each other pitifully.

The wizard led the children, chastened, shivering and weeping, through secret passages and over precipitous trails, deeper and deeper into the hills, until at last they came to the caves which honeycombed the rock.

Here the old man began the instruction of the boy who would be king. He taught him many of the mysteries, but not how to control the ghost voices, nor how to throw fire by pointing his finger, nor how to see the future in a calabash of mountain water.

Here in the caves of the Matopos, Lobengula learned the scope and power of the magical order. He learned how the little wizards, the witchdoctors, were spread across the land, performing the small rites, making rain and giving charms for fertility and childbirth, smelling out the evil-doers, and sending back their reports to the cave in the Matopos.

Here the grand wizards, of which the old man was one, worked the great magics, called up the spirits of their ancestors, and looked into the mists of time to see what the future would bring. Above them all was the Umlimo. It was a name only for Lobengula, Umlimo, a name that even after he had lived five years in the cave could still make him shiver and sweat.

Then when he was sixteen, the mad old wizard took him to the cave of the Umlimo. And the Umlimo was a woman, a beautiful woman.

What Lobengula saw in the cave of the Umlimo he would never speak about, not even to Saala, but when he came back from the cave there was a sadness in his eyes, and the weight of knowledge seemed to bow his young shoulders.

There was a furious thunderstorm the night of Lobengula's return, and the blue lightning clanged upon the anvil of the hills with strokes that tortured their eardrums as they lay together under the kaross. Then it was that the little orphan white girl made the boy into a man, the princeling into a king; and when her term was run she gave him a son who was the colour of the early morning sunlight on the yellow winter grass, and Lobengula knew happiness for the only time in his life.

In their joy they paid little attention to tidings which the mad old wizard brought to their cave.

He told them how Mzilikazi, great with plunder, fat with cattle, had come back to Thabas Indunas, arriving suddenly with the blood barely dried on the spears of his impi, and red rage in his heart.

At Mzilikazi's nod the Black Ones gathered all those who had acted as if the king were dead. Some they hurled from the cliff of execution, some they pegged down upon the sandbanks of the river where the crocodiles sunned themselves, others they skewered with bamboo spikes through the secret openings of their bodies.

But when the mother of Nkulumane was led before the king, she wept so and tore her own flesh with her nails while she called on all the spirits of the dead to witness how faithful she had been to Mzilikazi in his absence, how constant had been her belief in his eventual safe return and how during his absence she had guarded the other royal sons from the Black Ones and had even sent Lobengula into the wilderness to save him that Mzilikazi, who at the bottom was only a man, believed her. However, the others died in their hundreds, victims of the king's wrath, and the nation rejoiced for the king had returned and the good old days were back.

Through all this Lobengula and Saala and their little yellow son stayed on in the cave of the Matopos and knew happiness.

Far away in the south below the Limpopo river, a Hottentot elephant hunter stopped to water his horse at the well beside a Boer homestead that stood not far from the battlefield where the Boer horsemen had long ago first defeated Mzilikazi before driving him out of this country.

'I saw a curious thing,' said the Hottentot to the big, solemn, bearded man who was his host. 'In the southern hills of Matabeleland, I saw a white woman, full grown and naked. She was shy as a wild buck and ran into the rocky ground where I could not follow her.'

Two months later, when the Boer farmer took his family into

the service of Nachtmaal in the new church at Rustenberg, he repeated the strange story which the Hottentot hunter had brought from the north. Someone recalled the story of the massacre of the Van Heerden family, and the two little girls, Sarah and Hannah, taken by the murderous plundering savages.

Then Hendrik Potgieter, that doughty trekker and kaffir-fighter, stood up in the pulpit, and thundered:

'The heathen have a Christian woman as captive!' And the words offended much that the congregation held dear: God and their womankind.

'Commando!' roared Hendrik Potgieter. 'I call commando!'

The women filled the powder-horns and poured the lead into the bullet moulds, and the men picked out their best horses and elected Potgieter as their leader.

Not all of it was for God and womankind; for one whispered to another, 'Even if there is no white woman, I have heard that there are fine new herds in Matabeleland.'

Then the old wizard came to Lobengula's cave and rolled his eyes and cackled.

'The *buni* have crossed the river of crocodiles, riding on the backs of strange beasts. Many men, many men!'

Instinctively Lobengula knew why the Boer commando was coming, and he knew also what to do about it.

'Stay here, with the child,' he ordered Saala. 'I am going to my father's kraal, and I will lead his impis back here.'

But Saala was a woman, with a woman's curiosity, and blood called to blood. Vaguely she remembered that these strange white men had once been her kin.

When Lobengula had gone north to Thabas Indunas, she slung the baby on her back and crept out of the cave. At first the distant sound of gunfire guided her, for the Boer commando was living off the abundant herds of wild game. Then later she heard the shout of voices, and the whicker of horses, sounds that awakened a terrible nostalgia in her breast.

She crept closer and closer to the bivouac, with all the stealth of a wild animal, closer still until she could clearly see the tall sun-bronzed men, dressed to throat and wrists in brown homespun, the white-brimmed felt hats on their heads – closer still until she could hear their voices lifted in praise of their God as they sang their hymns around the camp fire.

She recognized the words, and memories flooded back to her.

She was no longer Saala but Sarah, and she rose from her place of hiding to go down to her people. Then she looked down at her body – and she saw that she was naked. She looked at the child on her hip – and saw that it was yellow, and its features were neither hers nor yet those of its Matabele father.

The awareness of sin came upon her, as it had done to Eve in another Paradise, and Sarah was ashamed.

She crept away, and in the dawn she stood on the top of one of those soaring granite precipices that rend the Matopos hills.

She kissed her baby and then holding the little mite to her breast she stepped out into the void.

Lobengula found them at the bottom of the cliff. He found them before the vultures did, and they were still together, Sarah's grasp on the infant had not faltered during the long plunge from the top of the precipice.

Strangely, both she and the child seemed to be merely sleeping – quiet and at peace.

At the memory Lobengula sighed now, and returned his gaze to his half-brother, the Induna Gandang who still sat across him from the fire.

If only he had been able to escape the prophecy of the Umlimo – for she had foreseen this destiny for him:

> Your name is Lobengula, the one who drives like the wind. Yet the winds will drive you, high as an eagle. Lobengula will hold the spear of Mzilikazi. Yet again the winds will drive you, down, down, down, and your nation with you.

Those were the words of that strange and beautiful woman of the cave, and already the first part of the prophecy had held true.

Mzilikazi, the mighty warrior, had died like an old woman – riddled with arthritis and dropsy and gout and liquor – in his royal hut.

His widows had wrapped him in the skin of a freshly-killed bull, and sat mourning over him for twelve days: until his remains were almost liquid with putrefaction in the summer heat.

After the mourning the regiments had carried his corpse into the Matopos Hills, the Sacred Hills, and they had seated Mzilikazi in the cave of the king. They placed all his possessions about him: his assegais, his guns, his ivory; even his wagon was taken down and the pieces piled in the crevices of the cave.

Then masons closed the opening with blocks of granite, and after the feasting and dancing the indunas of Matabele met to decide who would succeed Mzilikazi as king.

The argument and counter-argument lasted many weeks, until the indunas led by the princes of Kumalo returned into the Matopos bearing rich gifts to the cave of the Umlimo.

'Give us a king!' they pleaded.

'The one who drives like the wind!' replied the Umlimo, but Lobengula had fled, trying even at the last moment to escape his destiny.

The border impis captured him, and led him back to Thabas Indunas like a criminal to judgement. The indunas came to him one by one, and swore their allegiance and loyalty unto death.

'Black Bull of Matabele, The Thunderer! The Great Elephant. The one whose tread shakes the earth.'

Nkulumane was the first of his brothers to crawl before him, and Nkulumane's mother, the senior wife of Mzilikazi, followed her son on her knees.

Lobengula turned to the Black Ones who stood behind him, like hounds on the leash.

'I do not wish to look upon their faces again.'

It was Lobengula's first command, spoken like a true king, and the Black Ones took mother and son into the cattle stockade and twisted their necks, quickly and mercifully.

'He will be a great king,' the people told one another delightedly. 'Like his father.'

But Lobengula had never known happiness again. Now with a shudder he threw off the terrible burden of the past, and his voice was a deep but melodious bass.

'Rise up, Gandang my brother. Your countenance warms me like a watch-fire in the frosty night.'

They spoke then, easily and intimately, trusted companions of a lifetime, until at last Gandang passed the Martini-Henry rifle to his king and Lobengula held it in his lap and rubbed the cold blued metal of the block with one forefinger and then held the finger to his nose to smell the fresh grease.

'Sting the mamba with his own venom,' he murmured. 'This is the fang of the mamba.'

'The lad, Henshaw, son of Bakela, has a wagon filled with these.'

'Then he will be welcome,' Lobengula nodded. 'But now let

me hear all this from the mouth of your own son. Bring him to me.'

Bazo lay face down on the hard clay floor of the king's hut, and he chanted the ritual praises with a catch in his throat, and brave as he was, he sweated with fear in the king's presence.

'Rise up, Bazo the Axe,' Lobengula broke in impatiently. 'Come closer.'

Bazo crept forward on all fours, and he offered the beaded kilt. Lobengula spilled the diamonds from it into a glowing puddle and he stirred them with his finger.

'There are prettier stones than these in every river bed of my land,' he said. 'These are ugly.'

'The *buni* are mad for them. No other stone will satisfy them, but for these their hunger is so great that they will kill any who stand in their way.'

'Tear the lion with his own claws.' Lobengula repeated the prophecy of the Umlimo and then went on, 'Are these ugly little stones the claws of the lion? Then, if they are, let all men see how Lobengula is ready with claws.'

And he clapped his hands for his wives to come to him.

The royal hut was crowded now, rank upon rank of squatting men faced the low platform on which Lobengula lay. Every man of them except Bazo wore the headring of the induna, and their names were the rolls of glory of the Matabele nation.

There was Somabula, the lion-hearted old warrior, and beside him Babiaan, royal prince of Kumalo, and all the others. Their ranks were silent and attentive, their faces grave in the light of the fire which had been built up and whose flames leapt almost to the high-domed roof of the king's hut.

They were watching the king.

Lobengula lay on his back on the built-up platform beyond the fire. There was a low carved headrest under the nape of his neck. Only the tip of his penis was covered by the dried and hollowed-out gourd, otherwise he was stark naked. His great belly was mountainous and his limbs were like tree trunks.

Four of his wives squatted about him in a circle, each of them with a calabash of rendered white beef fat beside her. They anointed the king, smearing the fat thickly over his body from his throat to his ankles. Then when it was done they rose silently, and stooped out through the opening in the back of the hut which led to the women's quarters.

Singing softly, shuffling and swaying to the song, another file of younger wives began to wind into the hut; each of them carried upon her head a beer pot of fired clay; but these pots were not filled with the bubbling millet beer.

The wives knelt on each side of the king, and at a word from the senior wife they dipped into the clay pots and each of them came out with a large uncut diamond in her fingers. They began sticking the stones on the king's skin, and the thick coating of grease held them in the patterns that they built up to ornament Lobengula's gleaming limbs. They worked swiftly, for they had done this before, and under their fingers Lobengula was transformed. He became a creature of mythology: half man, half glittering scaled fish.

The diamonds caught the beam of the fire, and sent it spinning against the thatched walls and high roof, darting insects of golden light that flashed in the eyes of the watchers and dazzled them so that they grunted with amazement, and their voices went up like a choir in praise of their king.

At last the work was done and the wives crept away and left Lobengula lying on the thick soft furs, covered from throat to wrist to ankle in a silver burning coat of mail, each link of which was a priceless diamond; and as the king's chest and belly rose and subsided to the tide of his breathing, so this immense treasure burned and flamed.

'Indunas of Matabele, Princes of Kumalo, hail your King.'

'Bayete! Bayete!' The royal salute burst from their throats. *'Bayete!'*

Then the silence was complete but expectant, for it had become the king's custom that after this ritual display of the contents of the nation's treasury, he would dispense honours and rewards.

'Bazo,' Lobengula's voice was sonorous. 'Stand forward!'

The young man rose from his lowly position in the rearmost rank.

'Bayete, Nkosi.'

'Bazo, you have pleased me. I grant you a boon. What shall it be. Speak!'

'I crave only that the king should know the depth of my duty and love for him. Set me a task, I pray you, and if it should be fierce and hard and bloody, my heart and my mouth will sing the king's praises for ever.'

'On Chaka's royal buttocks, your pup is hungry for glory.' Lobengula looked to Gandang in the front rank of indunas. 'And he shames all those who ask for trinkets and cattle and women.'

He thought a moment, and then chuckled.

'In the direction of the sunrise, two days' march beyond the forests of Somabula, on a high hilltop lives a Mashona dog who deems himself such a great magician and rainmaker that he is beyond the king's arm. His name is Pemba.' And there was a hiss of indrawn breath from the squatting ranks of elders. Three times in the past season the king had sent impis to Pemba's hilltop, and three times they had returned empty-handed. The name Pemba mocked them all. 'Take fifty men from your old regiment, Little Axe, and fetch Pemba's head so that I can see his insolent smile with my own eyes.'

'*Bayete!*' Bazo's joy carried him in a single bound over the grey heads of the indunas. He landed lightly in the space before the fire and he whirled into the *giya*, the challenge dance:

'Thus will I stab the traitor dog –
and thus will I rip out the bellies of his sons –'

The indunas grinned and nodded indulgently, but their smiles were tinged with regret for the fury and passion of their youth which had long ago cooled in their own breasts.

Lobengula sat on the bench of his wagon. It was a big twentyfour-foot four-wheeler built in Cape Town from good English oak, but it still showed all the marks of punishment from its long trek up from the south.

It had not moved in many years, so the grass had grown up through the wheel spokes and around the axle shafts. The canvas of the tent was bleached bone white and crusted with the dung of the hens which roosted on the hoops of the tent framework, but the canvas protected Lobengula from the sun and the seat on the box elevated his head above the level of his courtiers and guards and children and wives and supplicants who crowded the enclosed stockade.

The wagon was Lobengula's throne, and the open stockade his audience chamber. Because there would be white men and women in his audience, he had donned his European finery for this occasion. The long coat encrusted with gold lace had once belonged to a Portuguese diplomat. The lace was tarnished and one epaulette was missing, and the front could not be buttoned over the king's noble belly, not by twelve inches, and the cuffs reached only halfway down his forearms.

The toy spear of kingship, the haft of red wild mahogany and the blade of brightest silver, was in his right hand, and he used it to summon a young boy from out of the crush.

The child was shaking with terror, and his voice so tremulous that Lobengula had to lean forward to hear him.

'I waited until the leopard entered the goat house; then I crept up and closed the door and I barricaded it with stones.'

'How did you kill the beast?' Lobengula demanded.

'I stabbed him through the chinks in the wall with my father's assegai.'

The boy crept forward and laid the lustrous gold and black dappled skin at Lobengula's feet.

'Take your choice of three cows from my royal herds, little one, and drive them to your father's kraal and tell him that the king has given you a praise name. From this day you will be known as "The one who stares into the eyes of the leopard".'

The boy's voice cracked in an adolescent squeak as he backed away gabbling the praises.

Next was a Hollander, a big arrogant white man with a querulous voice.

'I have waited three weeks for the king to decide –'

This was translated for Lobengula, and he mused aloud.

'See how red the man's face becomes when he is angry, like the wattles on the head of the black vulture. Tell him that the king does not count days, perhaps he will have to wait as long again, who knows?' And he dismissed him with a flirt of the spear.

Lobengula took a pull from the bottle of champagne that stood on the wagon seat beside him. The wine fizzed and spilled onto the front of his gold-frogged jacket. Then suddenly his face lit into a beatific smile, but his voice was carping and querulous.

'I sent for you yesterday, Nomusa, Girlchild of Mercy. I am in great pain; why did you not come sooner?'

'An eagle flies, a cheetah runs, but I am limited to the pace of a mule, oh King,' said Robyn Codrington, as she picked her way through the offal that littered the earthen floor of the stockade, and with the fly switch in her hand cleared a path through the crowd towards the wagon, even dealing a stinging cut to one of the king's black-cloaked executioners.

'Out of my way, eater of human flesh,' she told him primly. 'Be gone, child stabber.' And the man leaped aside nimbly and scowled after her.

'What is it, Lobengula?' she asked as she reached the wagon. 'What ails you this time?'

'My feet are filled with burning coals.'

'Gout,' Robyn said as she touched the grotesquely swollen appendages. 'You drink too much beer, oh King, you drink too much brandy and champagne.' She opened her bag.

'You would have me die of thirst. You are not well named, Nomusa; there is no pity in your heart.'

'Nor yours, Lobengula,' Robyn snapped. 'They tell me you have sent another impi to murder the people of Pemba.'

'He is only a Mashona,' Lobengula chuckled. 'Save your sympathy for a king whose stomach feels as though it is filled with sharp stones.'

'Indigestion,' Robyn scolded. 'Gluttony killed your father, and it is killing you.'

'Now you would starve me also. You want me to be a skinny little man of no consequence.'

'A thin live one or a fat dead one,' Robyn told him. 'Open your mouth.'

Lobengula choked on the draught, and rolled his eyes theatrically.

'The pain is better than the taste of your medicine.'

'I will leave you five of these pills. Eat one when your feet swell and the pain becomes fierce.'

'Twenty,' said Lobengula. 'A box full. I, Lobengula, King of Matabele, command it. Leave me a box of these little white pills.'

'Five,' said Robyn firmly. 'Or you will eat them all at one time, as you did before.'

The king rocked with gargantuan laughter, and almost fell from the wagon seat.

'I think I will command you to leave those little white huts of yours at Khami, and come to live closer to me.'

'I should not obey.'

'That's why I do not command it,' Lobengula agreed, with another shout of laughter.

'This kraal is a disgrace, the dirt, the flies–'

'A few old bones and a little dog shit never killed a Matabele,' the king told her, and then was serious and motioned her closer, dropping his voice so that only she could hear.

'The Dutchman with the red face, you know he wishes to build a trade post at the ford of the Hunyani river –'

'The man is a cheat. The goods he brings are shoddy, and he will deceive your people.'

'A runner has brought this book.' He handed the folded and wafered sheet to Robyn. 'Read it for me.'

'It is from Sir Francis Good. He wishes –' For almost an hour, whispering hoarsely so that no other could hear, Lobengula consulted Robyn on fifty different matters ranging from the British Commissioner's letter to the menstrual problems of his youngest wife. Then at last he said, 'Your coming is like the first sweet rain at the end of the long dry. Is there aught I can do for your happiness?'

'You can let your people come to worship in my church.'

This time the king's chuckle was rueful. 'Nomusa, you are as persistent as the termites that gnaw away the poles of my hut.' He frowned with thought and then smiled again. 'Very well, I will let you take one of my people – as long as it is a woman, the wife of an induna of royal blood, and the mother of twelve sons. If you can find one of my people who meets all those conditions, you may take her and splash water on her and make your sign on her forehead; and she may sing songs to your three white gods if she so wishes.'

This time Robyn had to answer his sly and mischievous grin. 'You are a cruel man, Lobengula, and you eat and drink too much. But I love you.'

'And I love you also, Nomusa.'

'Then I will ask one more favour.'

'Ask it,' he commanded.

'There is a lad, son of my brother –'

'Henshaw.'

'The king knows all.'

'What of this boy?'

'Will the king listen to his petition?'

'Send him to me.'

Even from where he stood Bazo could see that the grain bins were overflowing with corn that had been sun-dried still on the cob. There was enough to feed an army, he decided bitterly. There was no chance of starving them out.

The grain bins were cylindrical in shape, their walls of plaited green saplings plastered with clay and cow dung. They stood on stilts of mopani poles to allow the air to circulate below them, and to keep out bush rats and other vermin.

They were perched on the very edge of the precipice.

'The dog has brought good rains to his own fields,' murmured Zama, Bazo's lieutenant. 'He is fat with corn. Perhaps he is a rain-doctor as he claims.'

'Water,' Bazo mused, staring up the sheer cliff. Beyond the grain bins he could make out the thatched roofs of the tribal huts. 'Can we drive them out with thirst?' he asked advice, for Zama had been a member of one of the previous abortive raids upon the stronghold.

'The three other indunas tried that at first,' Zama pointed out. 'But then one of the Mashona that they captured told them that there is a running spring from which they draw all the water they wish.'

The sun was beyond the summit of the hill, so Bazo squinted his eyes against it. 'There is lush green growth there –' He pointed to a narrow gulley that cleft the top of the cliff like an axe stroke but was choked with growth. 'That would be it.'

As if to confirm his words the tiny distant figure of a girl appeared suddenly out of the gulley. She was foreshortened by her height above them, and the ledge along which she climbed was not apparent from where they stood.

She had a calabash gourd balanced on her head, with green leaves stuffed into its mouth to stop the water splashing out of it as she moved.

She disappeared over the top of the cliff.

'So,' grunted Bazo. 'We must climb up to them.'

'It would be easier to fly,' Zama grunted. 'That rock would daunt a baboon – or a klipspringer.'

The rock was pearly grey and marble smooth. There were streaks of lichen dashed across it, green and blue and red, like dry paint on an artist's palette.

'Come,' Bazo ordered, and they began a slow measured circuit of the hill – and as they went so the armed guards on the clifftop above kept pace with them, watching every move they made, and if they approached too close to the foot of the cliff, a hail of rocks fell upon them, striking sparks from the scree slope and caroming viciously past their heads, forcing them to shelve their dignity as they retired in haste.

'It is always the Mashona way,' Zama grumbled. 'Stones instead of spears.'

In places the cliff was riven by vertical cracks, yet none of these reached from base to crest, none of them offered a route to the summit. Bazo looked for a place that had been polished by the paws of wild baboon or marked by the hooves of the tiny little chamois-like klipspringer which might reveal a way up the rock face, but there was none. The cliff girded the entire hill, and transformed it into a fortress.

'There!' Zama pointed to a tiny irregularity in the face. 'That is where two warriors of the swimmers' impi tried to force a road to the top. They climbed as far as that little bush.' It grew in a crack in the face a hundred feet from the base of the cliff. 'And there the ledge narrowed and gave out. They could not go on, nor could they return. They hung there two days and three nights until their strength failed and they fell, one after the other, to be crushed like beetles on the rocks here where we stand.'

They went on, and as the sun was setting they came back to where they had started – the bivouac below the ladderway. Pemba's people had built a ladder of long straight mopani poles, bound together with bark rope, and they had used it to span the lowest point in the cliff – a place where a deep gully descended from the summit to within fifty feet of the surrounding plain. Like a drawbridge, the massive ladder was cunningly counter-weighted with round ironstone boulders, so that it had only to be drawn up on its ropes – as it was now – and the mountain stronghold was impregnable.

When the sun set, Bazo was still leaning on his long shield staring up the cliff, seemingly oblivious to the faint shouted insults of the Mashona that just reached him in the evening silence.

'Pustules on Lobengula's fat buttocks.'

'Puppies of the rabid dog Lobengula.'

'Dried turds of the spavined Matabele elephant.'

Only when it was too dark to make out the top of the cliff

did Bazo turn away – but even then he sat late beside the watch-fire, and rolled into his kaross only after the rise of the big white star over the top of the kopje.

Even then his sleep was troubled with dreams. He dreamed of water, of streams and lakes and waterfalls.

He woke again before light and checked that his sentries were alert before he slipped from the camp and under cover of the darkness crept up to the base of the cliff – at the point directly below the gulley choked with green growth where they had seen the girl carry water the day before.

Bazo heard the liquid chuckling, and his spirits soared. Guided by the sound he groped through the darkness, and found the spring in the base of the cliff. It filled a small natural basin of grey rock and then overflowed to waste itself again in the dry earth of the plain. Bazo scooped a handful and it was icy cold and sweet on his tongue. The fountain came splashing out of a dark rent in the rock face. Bazo explored it in the short time that was left before the strengthening light threatened to expose him to the sentries on the cliff above.

'Up,' Bazo shouted as he strode into the bivouac. 'All of you, up!' And his men came off their sleeping-mats, leopard swift and with the stabbing spears in their fists.

'What is it?' Zama hissed.

'We are going to dance,' Bazo told them, and they looked from one to the other in amazed disbelief.

On the north side of the kopje, farthest from the spring in the rock cliff and from the long ladder drawbridge, they danced. While they danced, all Pemba's people lined the clifftop to watch them, first in puzzled silence and then yelling with ribald laughter, hurling down taunts and stones.

'I count four hundred – without the children,' Zama panted, as he stamped and leaped and stabbed at the air.

'There will be enough for each of us,' Bazo agreed, and pirouetted with his shield high over his head.

They danced until the sun was high and then Bazo led them back to the camp, and when he stretched out on his mat and fell instantly asleep, his warriors looked at Zama with exasperation, but Zama could only shrug and turn his eyes to the sky.

An hour before sunset Bazo woke. He ate a little maize cake and drank a small gourd of sour milk, then he called for Zama and spoke quietly with him until it was almost dark.

Zama listened and nodded and his eyes shone, and while he talked, Bazo was honing the silver blade of his assegai until the light twinkled like tiny stars along its cutting edge.

At dark Bazo rose to his feet, handed his long dappled war shield to Zama and, armed only with his assegai, strode out of the bivouac. At the spring in the base of the cliff, Bazo shed his kilt and cloak and headdress. He rolled them into a bundle and hid them in a rock crevice. Then stark naked with only his assegai tied to his back by a leather thong, he waded across the pool. The reflection of the stars on its surface exploded into chips of light.

The water cascaded over him from the fountain in the cliff and he shuddered and gasped with the cold and then reached up into the dark rocky opening, found a fingerhold, drew a deep breath, and then pulled himself upwards.

With a solid black jet of water racing over his head, he held his breath and wriggled frantically up into the hole in the cliff. The force of water opposed him, and it required all his strength to go against it. Inch by inch, his chest throbbing for air, he fought his way upwards – and then just when he knew he would have to let himself be washed back into the pool, his head broke out – and he could breathe.

He sucked air desperately, wedging shoulders and knees against the smooth water-polished rock to hold himself in the torrent. It was utterly dark, not the faintest glimmering of starlight, and the darkness seemed to have physical weight that threatened to crush him.

He reached as high as he could and found another smooth fingerhold, and with all the strength of his arms gained another few feet, rested a moment, and then reached up again. The rock was like glass, and in places coated with a thick beard of algae, slippery as an eel's skin. The cold was a terrible living thing that invaded his body. His bones ached and his fingers were so numbed that he could barely take his holds.

The water tore at him, battering his shoulders, forcing its way into his nose and mouth and ears, filling his head with its angry animal roaring. Still he went up in the irregular twisting tunnel, sometimes horizontal, wriggling forward on his belly, the roof cracking his skull if he lifted his head too quickly to find the few precious inches of air trapped beneath it. Mostly the tunnel climbed vertically, and he wedged with knees and elbows to hold himself against the cascade, while his skin, softened with water, was smeared and torn away in slabs against the stone; but the inches became yards, and the minutes became hours, and still he went up.

Then the tunnel narrowed so sharply that he was trapped, cold slippery rock at each shoulder and hard heavy rock cramming down between his shoulderblades. He could not go on, nor could he go back. He was trapped in the rocky maw of the mountain, and he screamed with terror, but his voice was lost in the thunder of water and the water gushed into his throat.

He fought with the last of his drowning, desperate strength, and suddenly he kicked himself forward into a narrow cavern where he could breathe again, and where the water swirled into little back-eddies so that he could rest a few moments from its drag.

Even while he coughed and choked on his flooded lungs, he realized that he had lost his assegai, and he groped for it until he felt the tug of the thong on his shoulder; there was still something tied to the other end. Hand over hand he drew in the thong and then his fingers closed on the familiar shaft and he sobbed with relief and pressed his lips to the beloved steel.

It took time for him to realize that the air in the tiny cavern was sweet, and he felt it moving like a lover's fingers on his skin, warm and soft – warmth, that was what made his heart soar. Warmth from the outside world, beyond this icy roaring tomb of water. He found the shaft down which the torrent was sucking air from the surface, and from somewhere came the strength to attempt it. He climbed slowly, agonizingly, and suddenly there was a white prick of light ahead of him, distorted by racing black water.

He thrust his head forward, and the night wind struck his cheek, and he smelled woodsmoke and grass and earth redolent of the lingering warmth of the sun, and the great white star stood in the night sky high above his head. That dreadful passage had connected the fountain at the base of the cliff to the one high above.

He did not have the strength to drag himself more than a few feet from the fountainhead, and there under a bush on the soft bed of leaf mould he lay and panted like a dog.

He must have drifted into an exhausted and cold-drugged sleep, for he woke with a start. The sky had paled. He could just see the branches of the bush above his head outlined against it. He dragged himself out, and he found that he ached down to the bones of his spine and his skinned elbows and knees burned even at the touch of the dawn wind.

There was a narrow path, well marked by many feet from the fountainhead up the last few feet of the cliff, and as he stepped out onto it he looked down and saw far below him the moonsilver forest and the tiny sparks that were the watch-fires of his own bivouac. As he moved, he felt his muscles easing and unknotting, felt the blood recharging his limbs.

Although he was ready for one, there was no sentry at the top of the path, and he peered out cautiously from behind the stone portals of the gulley onto the tranquil village.

'By Chaka's teeth, they sleep like fat and lazy dogs,' Bazo thought grimly. The doors were all tightly closed, and smoke oozed from every chink in the walls. They were half suffocating themselves to keep out the mosquitoes. He could hear a man coughing hoarsely in the nearest hut.

He was about to slip out from behind his rocky screen when faint movement in the gloom between the huts made him sink gently down again. A dark figure scurried directly towards where he hid. He shifted his grip on the assegai, but only a few paces from him the figure stopped.

It was swathed in a skin cloak against the pre-dawn chill, hunched up like an old woman, until it straightened and threw off the cloak. Bazo felt his breath hiss up his throat and he bit down to stop it reaching his lips.

The naked girl was in that lovely tender stage just past puberty, on the very brink of full womanhood. There were the last vulnerable vestiges of childhood in the plump little buttocks and in the kitten awkward way she stood with toes turned slightly inwards. She was naked and the first light touched her sable skin with a lemon glow. Then she turned her head.

She had a long slender neck and the neat little head balanced perfectly upon it. The dome of her skull was covered with an intricate pattern of closely woven plaits. Her forehead was high and smooth, her cheekbones vaulted in the Egyptian way, her lips chiselled into perfect sweeps, symmetrical as the wings of a beautiful butterfly, and the light glinted briefly in her huge slanted eyes as she looked about her.

Then she squatted briefly and her water tinkled against the

earth. It was a sound that unaccountably filled Bazo's chest with a swollen tender feeling, for the act was so innocent and so natural.

She stood, and in the instant before she covered her head once more with the cloak, he had one more glimpse of her face. He knew then that he had never seen anything so beautiful in all his life – and he stared after her as she hurried back between the huts with a peculiar aching hunger consuming his very being.

It took him many minutes to rouse himself, and then as he crept forward he found that, hard as he tried, he could not drive the girl's image from his mind. The pathway that led from the village to the ladder drawbridge was unmistakable. It was broad and its surface beaten smooth. There were walls of worked stone on each side of it behind which the defenders could meet any thrust up the path. There were piles of stones at intervals along its course, placed ready to be hurled down at anybody attempting to force the ladder or fight their way up the path.

The pathway dropped steeply into the gulley, and then ended on a wide level stone platform. The light was stronger now and Bazo could see that there were sentries here; two of them stood on the lip watching the plain fifty feet below the platform, guarding the massive counterbalanced ladder. Farther back four other guards squatted around a small smoky fire, and Bazo's saliva flooded as he smelled the roasting maize cakes. The men were talking in the low sleepy tones of men who had stood a long watch, and their backs were turned to the gulley, for they would never expect an enemy to come from that direction.

Bazo crept closer. There was another pile of rocks at the comer of the platform, ready for the guards to hurl down the cliff. Bazo crawled into the shadows behind it.

He did not have long to wait. Very faintly on the morning wind he heard the singing. Zama had begun the dance below the cliff. The song was the fighting hymn of his regiment, and Bazo's blood thrilled in his veins. He felt the divine madness begin. It was a feeling that other lesser men got only from the hemp pipe.

He felt the sweat break on his skin, and the madness mount from his belly to his heart – felt the blood swell in his throat, felt his eyes burn and bulge.

The guards had left the fire now and crowded the edge of the cliff, peering downwards, laughing and pointing.

'Hear Lobengula's puppies yap!'

'Look at them dance like virgins at the Festival of First Fruits!'

The signal Bazo had agreed with Zama was the moment the battle song ended, but he could barely contain himself that long.

He rose from his crouch, and his muscles twitched, his head jerked like that of a maniac, and in the dawn light his eyes were glazed like shards of ceramic pottery, the red rage of the berserker. At that instant the distant song ended.

Bazo's cry froze the men on the edge of the cliff, it was the bellow of a heart-struck buffalo bull, the screech of the stooping eagle.

In the paralysed moment before they could turn, Bazo struck them. He charged with outstretched arms and swept four of them away into the void. They twisted and turned in the air as they fell, and they screamed the whole way down on a high receding note that was cut off abruptly at the end.

Bazo's charge had been so headlong that he almost followed them over the brink; for a giddy moment he tottered there, and then he caught his balance and spun to strike underhand at one of the survivors. The blade went into the man's belly and out the other side, cleaving his bowels and his kidneys, and crunching through his backbone; and when Bazo jerked the steel clear, the life blood sprayed hotly onto his forearm and his chest. The last sentry ran, silently and desperately, for the pathway, and Bazo let him go.

Bazo bounded along the edge of the cliff and reached the point where the top of the ladder was secured. The ropes that held it were of twisted and plaited bark, reinforced with liana and leather thongs. They were thick as Bazo's arm, and he changed his grip on the assegai to a chopping stroke.

The ropes popped and crackled as he hacked through them. He grunted at each stroke, slitting his eyes against the flying chips of wood and bark.

Behind him he heard the babble of many voices on the pathway. The sentry would call them down like hunting dogs – but Bazo scorned to turn until the work was done. One rope gave, and the massive unwieldy ladder sagged and twisted. He cut again, reversing his grip to swing back-handed, and the other ropes went.

The ladder swung outwards and downwards, gathering momentum, and the timbers crackled and squealed, drowning out the voices of the men coming down behind him. The bottom of the ladder struck the scree below the cliff with a shattering crash, and some of the uprights snapped under the impact. The head of the ladder was still secured at Bazo's feet, and the whole twisted mess hung down like the rigging of a dismasted ship.

Bazo stood long enough to watch Zama lead his warriors swarming up the dangling tangle of rope and timber. Then he turned.

They were coming down the pathway, a solid phalanx of black bodies and sparkling weapons; but their advance was hesitant enough for Bazo to race forward and reach the narrow gap in the wall before the leaders did. With solid rock to guard his flanks, he laughed at them, and it was a sound to stop them dead, those in front pushing back and those behind struggling forward.

One of them threw a long spear and it clashed sparks from the wall at the level of Bazo's head. He drove forward and stabbed into the press of bodies caught in the narrow gut between the stone walls. The screams and moans goaded him – and the blood from the gaping wounds splattered his face and sprayed into his open mouth, a ghastly draught that maddened him further. They broke and fled, leaving four of their number writhing and twisting on the pathway.

Bazo glanced behind him. None of his Matabele had reached the head of the ladder yet. He looked back up the pathway and saw that the real men were coming.

These would be the picked warriors, the best spearmen – there was no mistaking their superiority over the rabble that Bazo had just scattered; they were bigger and more powerful in body, their expressions grim and determined, and their formation ordered and controlled.

They came down in massed ranks to where Bazo stood, their shields raised, their spears poised, and at their head danced a skinny wizened old man with a face ravaged by some terrible disease, his nose and ears rotted away and his cheeks and forehead covered with silver white blotches.

He was hung about the waist and neck with the accoutrements of his magical trade, and he shrieked and gibbered like an enraged ape.

'Kill the Matabele dog.'

Bazo was naked, without a shield, but he hefted the assegai and stood to meet them and their horrid master and he laughed again, the wild joyous laughter of a man who was living a lifetime in his last few seconds.

'Bazo!' The cry reached him, even through his rage, and he turned.

Zama had crawled onto the platform, blown from that long scrambling climb up the swinging twisted ladder. He rose on his knees and sent the great dappled shield skimming across the platform. Like a falcon coming to bate it settled on Bazo's shoulder, and Bazo laughed and went springing forward.

His assegai drove through the wizard's rotting flesh as though it were soft as a boiled yam, and Pemba screeched one last time.

'Bazo, wait! Leave some of them for us!' The shouts of his fifty Matabele behind him, as they scrambled onto the platform, and then Zama's muscled shoulder was touching his as they locked shields and swept the pathway, the way the flash floods of summer scour the dry riverbeds.

It was a beautiful stabbing, a glory which men would sing about. The assegais seemed to hold their keen edge no matter how often they were buried and the spear arms never tired despite the heavy work. The line of Matabele swept the hilltop from end to end, roaring their frustration when the last of Pemba's men threw down their spears and leapt out over the cliff, grudging them that easy death for the assegais were still thirsty and the madness was still on them.

Then they turned and went back through the village, ransacking the huts, throwing a toddling infant high and catching it on the point as it fell, or sending the steel full length out between the withered dugs of some scurrying crone, for the divine madness does not pass swiftly.

With his shoulder, Bazo smashed open another hut, and Zama leaped in at his side, both of them were painted from throat to knee with red running crimson, their contorted faces hideous, blood-glutted masks. Someone tried to escape from the dark interior of the hut.

'Mine!' roared Zama and sped his long steel, and the low early sun struck a ray through the open doorway, sparkling on Zama's assegai and falling in the same instant on the huge slanted terrified eyes and high Egyptian cheekbones of the girl he was killing.

Zama's steel clashed against Bazo's great shield and was deflected past the girl's cheek by the width of a finger, so that the stroke died in the air. Before Zama could strike again Bazo stood over the girl, spreading the shield over her the way a heron covers its chick with a wing, and he snarled at Zama like a leopard whose cub is menaced.

After the first weary day of the return march, while the long file of roped captives was settling exhausted and miserable beneath the grove of msasa trees, Bazo strode down the line and stopped beside the girl.

'You!' he said, and with a careless stroke of his assegai severed the thong at her neck. 'Cook my meal!'

While she worked over the fire, Bazo joked loudly with Zama and his men, trying to prevent his eyes from straying from their faces. He ate what she cooked without showing either pleasure or displeasure, while she knelt at a respectful distance and watched every mouthful he took.

Then suddenly when he had finished eating, she came gliding to his side with that disconcerting silent grace, and she lifted the bunch of wilted leaves from the swollen and crusted spear wound in Bazo's flank. It was an impertinence, and he lifted his hand to strike her – and then let the hand fall. She had not flinched and her manner was assured and competent.

She cleaned the wound with deft fingers and then she unstoppered two of the little buck-horn containers that she wore on her belt and with the powder they contained made a poultice. It burned like fire for a few seconds, but then felt much easier.

Bazo made no acknowledgement, but when one of his Matabele came to rope her back with the other captives, Bazo frowned, and the man passed her by.

When Bazo lay on his sleeping-mat, she curled like a puppy at his feet. He was ready for her to try to escape once the camp settled, but after midnight she had not stirred and he fell asleep.

In the hour before dawn when he rose to check the sentries, there was frost on the grass, and he heard the girl's teeth chattering softly. He dropped his fur regimental cloak over her as he passed and she cuddled down into it quickly.

When he called for the day's march to begin, she had his

bedding roll and cooking-pot balanced on her head, and a dozen times during the march, Bazo had to go back along the winding column for no reason that he could explain to Zama, and each time his steps slowed as he came up behind the girl, and he watched the play of muscle down her back, the roll of her plump black buttocks and the joggle of her glossy sable breasts. But when she turned her head and smiled shyly at him, his hauteur was frosty and he stalked back to the head of the column.

That night he permitted himself a nod of approval at the first taste of her cooking, and when she dressed the wound, he said, 'The heat has gone from it.'

She did not lift her eyes.

'Who taught you this skill?' he insisted.

'Pemba, the wizard,' she whispered.

'Why?'

'I was his apprentice.'

'Why you?'

'I have the gift.'

'So then, little witch, make me an oracle,' Bazo laughed, and she lifted her head and he looked into those disconcerting slanted tar-bright eyes.

'Do not scoff, lord.'

'*Nkosi* – lord,' she called him, but Bazo stopped laughing, and felt the spirits tickle the hair at the nape of his neck. That night, when he heard her shiver, he opened a fold of his kaross and she crept into it.

Bazo feigned sleep, but his body was tense and he was aware of each tiny movement that the girl made as she settled to sleep. It would have been so easy to reach out and hold her down with his arm across her chest while he forced his knee between hers. The thought made him twitch and grunt.

'Lord?' she whispered. 'Something troubles you.'

'What is your name?' he asked, for want of a reply, and found that he was whispering also.

'Tanase.'

'Tanase.' He measured it on his tongue, and it fitted well enough, although he recognized it was a Rozwi name, one of the splinter tribes of the Mashona, and he did not know the meaning.

'I know your name – everyone speaks it with respect,' she said. 'Bazo, the Axe.'

'I killed your master, Pemba. I struck him down with my own hand.' He did not know what compelled him to say that.

'I know,' she whispered.

'Do you hate me for that, little witch?'

'I praise you for that!' Her voice shook with quiet vehemence, and her hip touched his under the kaross.

'Praise? Did you not love Pemba as a dog loves its master?'

'I hated him, and when I foresaw his death in the magic calabash, I was filled with joy.'

'You saw his death?'

'I saw his death – as I saw your face, long before you came to take me.'

Bazo shuddered involuntarily, and she felt it.

'You are cold, lord.' She pressed a little closer to him. Her flesh was hot and soft, he felt his own flesh respond to its touch.

'Why did you hate Pemba?'

'He was evil beyond the telling. The things he forced me to do I will never forget.'

'He used your body?' There was a rough edge to Bazo's question.

'Not even Pemba would dare tamper with the body of one of the chosen ones, for to tear the veil of maidenhood is to destroy the gift.'

'The gift?'

'The gift of foresight which the likes of Pemba value so highly.'

'What then did he force upon you?'

'Dark things, midnight things, torture not of the body but of the spirit.'

Now it was her turn to shudder, and she turned towards him and clung to his broad smooth chest, hiding her face against it so that her voice was muffled and he could hardly catch her next words.

'I did not wish to be chosen, I hate and fear what still lies ahead of me if I follow that road.'

'Pemba is dead.'

'You do not understand. Pemba was but a little wizard, already he had taught me almost all he knew. Then I would have been called by the one whose name I dare not speak aloud. That call will still come – and I shall not be able to deny it.'

'You are under my protection.'

'There is only one way you can protect me, Bazo Lord.'

'How?'

'Make me worthless to them. Destroy this gift which is such a terrible burden.'

'How?'

'As you destroyed Pemba with the stabbing spear of steel, destroy it with your great spear of flesh, tear my veil and let this thing pass from me.'

She felt him, hot and fierce, pressing against her, and her body seemed to melt and become pliant and yielding.

'Ah yes, Lord. Make me as other women, so that I may feel your noble belly on mine in the nights, that I may feel your son kick in my womb and tug at my breast when I give him suck.'

'All these things you will have, Tanase.' Bazo's voice was hoarse with his wanting. 'When we reach GuBulawayo the king will reward me, and give me leave to go in to the women, and take a wife.'

'Lord, it is dangerous to wait.'

'I will not rut on you like a slave girl. You will be the first and senior of all my wives.'

'Lord –'

'Enough, Tanase, tempt me no further, for what you feel, hard though it may be, is not stone but flesh only.'

'*Nkosi*, you do not know the power of the wizards. Save me from them.'

'I know the law and custom of Matabele, and that is all a man should know and heed.'

Bazo's scout came in at a dead run, the sweat snaking down his back and chest, and he shouted his report the moment he came up to the head of the column.

Bazo whirled and barked three sharp orders. Immediately the column closed up, and the captives were forced to squat with a dozen warriors standing guard over them. The rest of the Matabele formed up behind Bazo and he led them away at that gait between a trot and a run which lifted the dust to their knees.

Bazo picked his ambush with an unerring eye. He chose a place where broken ground and thick bush allowed only one passage through, and the single horseman rode into it. The long shields were suddenly all around him, fencing him in as his dun-coloured pony snorted and skittered.

The rifle was half-way drawn from the leather boot at the horseman's knee when Bazo stopped him with a shout.

'Too late for that. You were dead, and the jackals feasting already. You grow careless, despite all that I taught you, Henshaw.'

Ralph let the rifle slide back into its scabbard, and he threw up his hands, pleasure and chagrin warring on his face.

'Shake any tree and a Matabele falls out of it.' His voice was mock-mournful, and he swung down off Tom's sturdy back and strode to meet Bazo.

'I expected to see the induna's ring on your forehead already, oh mighty slayer of Mashona,' he laughed as they embraced.

'Soon, Little Hawk, very soon. But you, I thought your wagon would be heavy with ivory – '

'Done, Little Axe, already done.' Ralph stepped back and looked at him. In the months since they had parted, both men had changed.

In Bazo there remained no trace of the young mine labourer who had worked his shifts in the pit and eaten Zouga Ballantyne's rations. Here was a warrior and a prince, tall and plumed and proud.

Ralph was no longer the callow lad, his every action ordered by his father. Instead he was a grown man, with a jaunty lift to his chin and a self-assured set to his shoulder. Yet though his clothes were travel-worn and stained the training of Zouga Ballantyne still showed, for they were recently washed and his jaws had been clean shaven that very morning. They looked at each other and the affection between them was tempered and hardened with respect.

'I shot a young buffalo cow, not two hours ago.'

'Yes,' Bazo nodded. 'It was the shot which brought us.'

'Then I am glad of it. The buffalo meat is fat, and there is enough even for a hungry Matabele.'

Bazo glanced at the sun. 'Though I am in haste, on the king's business, my prisoners are in need of rest. We will help you eat your buffalo, Henshaw, but in the dawn we will go on.'

'Then there is much to talk about – and little time to do so.'

There was the pop of a trek-whip, and Bazo glanced beyond

Ralph's shoulder to see the oxen come plodding between the trees and the wagon lurching and wallowing behind them.

'You still keep bad company,' Bazo scolded with a grin as he recognized Umfaan at the head of the span and Isazi, the little Zulu, on the flank, 'but the load you carry is welcome.'

From the wagon box hung the raw quarters and shoulders of the freshly-butchered buffalo carcass.

'We have not tasted fresh meat since we left the king's kraal.'

Ralph and Bazo sat at a separate fire apart from their retinues, where they could talk freely.

'The king agreed to buy the guns and bottles that I carried up from Kimberley,' Ralph told Bazo, 'and he paid me generously.'

He did not go on to describe to Bazo the currency in which be had been paid. He did not describe his own astonishment when Lobengula had offered him an uncut diamond, a big bright first-water stone.

His surprise had immediately been tempered by conscience; he had no doubts about where that stone had come from. His conscience lasted about as long as his surprise, and he haggled with gusto, forcing up the price to six stones, which he had picked with an eye trained by many years on the diggings. He knew they would be worth £10,000 when he got them back to civilization.

Thus in a single stroke he had paid for the wagon and team, his entire debt to Diamond Lil – interest and all – and was already many thousands of pounds in profit.

'Then I asked Lobengula to let me hunt elephant, and he laughed and said I was too young and that the elephant would eat me up. He kept me waiting outside his kraal for ten days.'

'If he kept you such a short time, then you have found favour with the king,' Bazo interrupted. 'Some white men have waited from the beginning of the dry season to the middle of the wet, merely for permission to take the road out of Matabeleland.'

'Ten days was long enough for me,' Ralph grunted. 'But when I asked him in which part of his lands I was allowed to hunt, he laughed again and said, 'The elephant will be in so little danger from you, Little Hawk, that you may go where you wish, and kill as many as are stupid or lame enough to let you.'

Bazo chuckled delightedly. 'And how many lame stupid elephant have you found so far, Henshaw?'

'I have fifty good tusks in the wagon already.'

'Fifty!' Bazo's chuckles died and he stared at Ralph in amazement; then he stood up and crossed to the wagon. He untied one of the straps and lifted the canvas cover to peer in at the load, while Isazi looked up from his cooking fire, frowned and called to Ralph.

'This boy's great-grandfather, Mashobane, was a thief, his grandfather, Mzilikazi was a traitor – you have every reason to trust him with our ivory, Henshaw.'

Bazo did not look at him, but glanced up into the trees. 'The monkeys hereabout make a frightful chatter,' he murmured, and then came back to Ralph.

'Fine tusks!' he admitted. 'Like the ones the hunters took when I was still a child.'

Ralph did not tell him that most of those in the wagon were taken even before that time. He had discovered all but two of the caches that his father had bequeathed to him.

The ivory had dried out – lost almost a quarter of its green weight; but most of it was still in good condition, and would fetch the market price once he got it to the railhead.

Though Ralph had hunted diligently for his own elephant whilst he sought out Zouga's ancient dumps, he had had little success. He had killed five, only one of which was a bull and whose green tusks had weighed just over sixty pounds. The others had been small female ivory, barely worth taking.

The great herds that Zouga had described in *A Hunter's Odyssey* no longer existed. Since those days there had been many hunters, some of them inspired by Zouga's own writing. Boer and Briton, Hottentot and German, they had hunted and harried the huge grey beasts and left their white bones piled on the veld and in the forest.

'Yes, they are good tusks,' Ralph nodded. 'And my wagon is heavy laden now. I am on the road back to the king's kraal to ask him for permission to leave Matabeleland and go back to Kimberley.'

'Then when you have gone, we will see you no more,' Bazo said quietly. 'You will be like the other white men who come to Matabeleland. You will take what you want, and never come back.'

Ralph laughed. 'No, old friend, I will be back. I do not have everything I wish, not yet. I will come back with more wagons, perhaps six wagons, all loaded with trade goods. I will set up trading posts from the Shashi river to the Zambezi.'

'You will be a rich man, Henshaw. I am sure of it,' Bazo agreed. 'But rich men are not always happy men. This I have remarked often. Is there nothing else in Matabeleland for you but ivory and gold and diamonds?'

Ralph's expression changed. 'How did you know that?' he demanded.

'I asked, I did not know,' Bazo denied, still smiling. 'Though I do not have to throw the bones or look in the magic calabash to know it is a woman – you have suddenly the look of a dog that smells the bitch. Tell me, Henshaw, who is she and when will you take her to wife?' Then he laughed aloud. 'You have not yet asked her father? Or you have asked and he has refused?'

'It is not a matter for laughter,' Ralph said stiffly, and with an effort Bazo wiped the mirth from his face, though it twinkled still in his eyes.

'Forgive one who loves you as a brother, I did not know it was such a heavy matter.' And at last he managed to match Ralph's portentous expression, while he waited for him to speak again.

'Once, long ago, while we rode up in the skip, you spoke of a woman with hair as white and fine as the winter grass,' Ralph said at last, and Bazo nodded.

'It is she, Bazo. I have found her.'

'She wants you as much as you want her?' Bazo said firmly. 'If she does not, then she is so stupid that she does not deserve you.'

'I haven't asked her yet,' Ralph admitted.

'Do not ask her, tell her, and then ask her father. Show the father your tusks of ivory; that will settle the matter.'

'You are right, Bazo,' Ralph looked dubious. 'It will be that simple.' And then softly in English, so that Bazo could not understand. 'God knows what I shall do if it is not. I don't think I can live without her.'

If he did not follow the words, Bazo understood the sense and the mood. He sighed, and his eyes strayed to Tanase at the cooking fire.

'They are so soft and weak, but they wound more deeply than the sharpest steel.'

Ralph followed his eyes, and then suddenly his own expression cleared and it was his turn to guffaw and reach across to slap Bazo's shoulder.

'Now I recognize the look you spoke of earlier, the dog with the smell of the bitch in his nostrils.'

'It is not a matter for laughter,' said Bazo, haughtily.

Long after the last gnawed buffalo bone was thrown upon the fire and the last beer pot emptied; long after the Matabele warriors had tired of singing the song of Pemba, the ode to their own prowess and courage on the hill of the wizard, and rolled into their sleeping karosses; long after the last captive girl had ceased wailing, Bazo and Ralph sat on beside their own fire – and the drone of their voices and the munch of the oxen chewing the cud were the only sounds in the camp.

It was as though every last moment was precious to them for both sensed that when they met again they would be changed, and perhaps the world with them.

They relived their youth, remembering Scipio, the falcon, and Inkosikazi, the great spider; they smiled at the stinging memory of the fighting sticks, and Bakela's wrath when Bazo gave him the shattered diamond; they talked of Jordan and Jan Cheroot and Kamuza and all the others – until at last reluctantly Bazo rose.

'I will be gone before the sun, Henshaw,' he said.

'Go in peace, Bazo – and enjoy the honours that await you and the woman you have won.'

When Bazo reached his sleeping-mat, the girl was already wrapped in his kaross.

As soon as Bazo lay down beside her, she reached for him. She was as hot as though she was in high fever – her body burning and her skin dry. Silent sobs racked her and her grip was fierce.

'What is it, Tanase?' He was shocked and alarmed.

'A vision. A terrible vision.'

'A dream.' He was relieved. 'It was only a dream.'

'It was a vision,' she denied. 'Oh, Bazo, will you not take this terrible gift from me, before it destroys us both.'

He held her and could not answer her; her distress moved him deeply, but he was helpless to alleviate it.

After a while she was quiet, and he thought that she slept, but then she suddenly whispered.

'It was a terrible vision, Bazo Lord – and it will haunt me unto my grave.'

He did not answer, but he felt the superstitious chill in his guts.

'I saw you high upon a tree –' She broke off, and another single sob hit her like a blow. 'The white man, the one you call Henshaw, the Hawk – do not trust him.'

'He is as my brother, and like a brother I love him.'

'Then why did he not weep, Bazo, why did he not weep when he looked up at you upon the tree?'

Salina Codrington rolled out her pastry with long and expert strokes of the pin. The sleeves of her blouse were rolled high and she was floury to the elbows. Little blobs of pastry stuck to her hands and fingers.

The thatched ceiling of the kitchen at Khami Mission Station was sooty from the open iron stove, and the smell of the dough was yeasty and warm.

A single skein of white-gold hair had escaped the ribbon and now tickled her nose and chin. Salina pursed her lips and blew it away; it floated like gossamer and then gently settled across her face again, but she did not change the rhythm of the rolling-pin.

Ralph thought that little gesture the most poignant he had ever witnessed, but then everything she did fascinated him – even the way she cocked her head and smiled at him as he slouched against the jamb of the kitchen door.

Her smile was so gentle, so unaffected, that his chest squeezed again, and his voice sounded choked in his own ears.

'I am leaving tomorrow.'

'Yes,' Salina nodded. 'We shall all miss you dreadfully.'

'This is the first chance I have had to speak to you alone, without the monsters –'

'Oh Ralph, that's an unkind, if totally accurate, description of my darling sisters.' Her laughter had a surprising timbre and depth to it. 'If you wanted to speak to me, you should have asked.'

'I'm asking now, Salina.'

'And we are alone.'

'Will you not stop still for a moment.'

'The baking will spoil, but I can listen well enough while I work.'

Ralph shifted his feet, and hunched his shoulders uncertainly. It was not as he had planned it. It was going to be a feat of timing and dexterity to sweep her up in arms all covered with flour and dough and with a heavy rolling-pin clutched in her hands.

'Salina, you are the most beautiful girl – woman – I mean, lady, that I have ever seen.'

'That's kind, but untrue, Ralph. I do have a mirror, you know.'

'It's true, I swear –'

'Please don't swear, Ralph. In any event, there are much more important things in life than physical beauty – kindness, and goodness and understanding, for instance.'

'Oh yes, and you have all those.'

Suddenly Salina stopped in mid stroke, and she stared at him with an expression of dawning consternation.

'Ralph,' she whispered. 'Cousin Ralph –'

'Cousin I may be,' he was stammering slightly in his rush to have it all said, 'but I love you, Salina, I loved you from the first moment I saw you at the river.'

'Oh Ralph, my poor dear Ralph.' Consternation was mingled now with compassion.

'I would never have spoken, not before – but now, after this expedition I have some substance. I will be able to pay off my debts, and when I come back I will have my own wagons. I am not yet rich, but I will be.'

'If only I had known. Oh Ralph, if only I had suspected, I would have been able to –'

But he was gabbling it out now.

'I love you, Salina, oh how dearly I love you, and I want you to marry me.'

She came to him then, and her eyes filled with blue tears that trembled on her lower lids.

'Oh dear Ralph. I am so sorry. I would have given anything to save you from hurt. If only I had known.'

He stopped then, bewildered. 'You will not – does that mean you will not marry me?' The bewilderment faded, and his jaw thrust out and his mouth hardened. 'But why not, I will give you everything, I will cherish and –'

'Ralph.' She touched his lips, and left a little dab of flour upon them. 'Hush, Ralph, hush.'

'But, Salina, I love you! Don't you understand?'

'Yes, I do. But, dear Ralph, I don't love you!'

Cathy and the twins went as far as the river with Ralph. Vicky and Lizzie rode, two up, on Tom's back. They rode astride, with their skirts up around their thighs, and squealed with delight every few seconds, until Ralph thought his eardrums would split, and he scowled moodily ahead – not replying to Cathy's questions and comments as she skipped along beside him, until the spring went out of her step and she, too, fell silent.

The bank of the Khami river was where they would part. All of them knew that, without speaking about it. And when they reached it Isazi had already taken the wagon through the drift. The ironshod wheels had left deep scars in the far bank. He would be an hour or so ahead. They stopped on the near bank and now even the twins were silent. Ralph looked back along the track, lifting his hat and shading his eyes with the brim against the early sunlight.

'Salina isn't coming then?' he said flatly.

'She's got a belly ache,' said Vicky. 'She told me so.'

'If you ask me, it's more like the curse of Eve,' said Lizzie airily.

'That's rude,' Cathy said. 'And only silly little girls talk about things they don't understand.'

Lizzie looked chastened, and Vicky assumed a virtuous air of innocence.

'Now both of you say goodbye to Cousin Ralph.'

'I love you, Cousin Ralph,' said Vicky, and had to be prised off him like a leach.

'I love you, Cousin Ralph.'

Lizzie had counted the kisses that Vicky had bestowed on him, and she went for a new world record, a noble attempt, but frustrated by Cathy.

'Now, scat,' Cathy told them. 'Go, both of you.'

'Cathy is crying,' said Lizzie, and both twins were immediately entranced.

'I am not,' said Cathy furiously.

'Oh yes, you are,' said Vicky.

'I have something in my eye.'

'Both eyes?' asked Lizzie sceptically.

'I warn you,' Cathy told them. They knew that expression of old, and reluctantly they retired just out of range. Cathy turned her back to them so they missed half of what followed.

'They are right.' Her whisper was as blurred as her eyes. 'I am crying, Ralph. I hate so to see you go.'

Ralph had not truly looked at her, not ever, his eyes had been for Salina alone, but now her frank admission touched him and he saw her for the first time.

He had thought her a child, but he had been wrong, he realized suddenly. It was the thick dark eyebrows and the firm chin that gave strength to her face, so that he sensed that anything that made her cry was deeply felt. Surely she had not been so tall when first he met her almost a year before. Now the top of her head reached his chin.

The freckles on her cheeks kept her young, but her nose was set in the shape of maturity and the gaze of her green eyes below the arched brows, though flooded now with tears, was too wise and steady for childhood.

She still wore the muddy green dress of sewn flour sacks, but its fit had altered. Now it was baggy at the waist, while at the same time it was too tight across her chest. Yet it could not suppress the thrust of young firm breasts, and the seams strained across hips that he remembered being as narrow and bony as a boy's.

'You will come back, Ralph? Unless you promise, I cannot let you go.'

'I promise,' he said, and suddenly the pain of rejection by Salina, which he had thought might destroy him, was just supportable.

'I will pray for you each day until you do,' Cathy said, and came to kiss him. She no longer felt skinny and awkward in his arms, and Ralph was suddenly very aware of the softness of her against his chest – and lower.

Her mouth had a taste like chewing a stalk of green spring grass. Her lips formed a pillow for his. He had no burning desire to break the embrace, and Cathy also seemed content to let it persist. The pain of unrequited love ebbed a little more to be replaced by a warm and comforting sensation, a most pleasant glow, until with a shock Ralph realized two things.

Firstly, the twins were an avid audience, their eyes enormous and their grins impudent. Secondly, that the pleasant glow which had suffused him had its source considerably lower than his broken heart, and was accompanied by more tangible changes that must soon become apparent to the fresh young innocent in his arms.

He almost shoved her away, and vaulted up onto Tom's back with unnecessary violence. However, when he looked down at Cathy again, the tide of green tears in her eyes had receded and been replaced by a look of satisfaction, a knowingness that proved beyond doubt what he had just come to realize, that she was no longer a child.

'How long?' she asked.

'Not before the end of the rains,' he told her. 'Six or seven months from now.' And suddenly that seemed to Ralph to be a very long time indeed.

'Anyway,' she said. 'I have your promise.'

On the far bank of the river he looked back. The twins had lost interest and started home. They were racing each other down the track, skirts and plaits flying – but Cathy still stood staring after him. Now she lifted her hand and waved. She kept waving until horse and rider disappeared amongst the trees.

Then she sat down on a log beside the track. The sun made its noon and then sank into the misty smoke of the bush fires that blued the horizon and turned to a soft red orb that she could look at directly without paining her eyes.

In the gloaming a leopard sawed and hacked harshly from the dense dark riverine forest nearby. Cathy shivered and stood up. She cast one last lingering glance across the wide river bed and then at last she turned for home.

Bazo could not sleep; hours ago he had left his sleeping-mat and come to squat by the fire in the centre of the hut. The others had not even stirred when he moved, Zama and Kamuza and Mondane, those who would accompany him tomorrow.

Their finery was piled beside their recumbent figures. The cloaks of feathers and furs and beads, the headdresses and kilts – the regalia reserved for only the most grave and momentous occasions – like the Festival of the First Fruits, or a personal report to the king, or, again, the ceremony for which they had gathered and which would start at the dawn of the morrow.

Bazo looked at them now, and his chest felt congested with his joy, joy so intense that it sang in his ears and fizzed in his blood. Joy even more intense in that these his companions of the years, with whom he had shared boyhood and youth and now manhood, would be there again at one of the most important days of his life.

Now Bazo sat alone at the fire while his companions snored and muttered in sleep, and he took each coin of his good fortune and, like a miser counting his treasure, fondled it with his mind, turning each memory over and gloating upon it.

He lived again every moment of his triumph when the lines of captive women had filed before Lobengula and piled the spoils in front of his wagon, the bars and coils of red copper, the axe heads, the leather bags of salt, the clay pots full of beads, for Pemba had been a famous wizard and had gathered his tribute from a host of fearful clients.

Lobengula had smiled when he saw his treasure, for that was what had been at the root of his feud with Pemba. The king was not above the jealousies of common men. When Lobengula smiled, all his indunas smiled in sympathy and made those little clucking sounds of approval.

Bazo remembered how the king had called him forward, and smiled again when Bazo emptied the bag he carried over his shoulder, and the wizard's head, which by then was in an advanced state of decomposition, had rolled to the forewheel of the wagon and grinned up at Lobengula with ruined lips drawn back from uneven teeth stained by the hemp pipe.

A troop of the gaunt, mange-ridden pariah dogs that skulked about the king's kraal had come to snarl and squabble over the morsel, and when one of the black-cloaked executioners would have scattered them with blows of his knobkerrie, the king restrained him.

'The poor beasts are hungry, let them be.' And he turned back to Bazo. 'Tell me how it was done.'

Bazo relived in his mind every word with which he had

described the expedition, and while he told it he had begun to *giya*, to dance and sing the ode to Pemba which he had composed:

'Like a mole in the earth's gut
Bazo found the secret way –'

He sang, and in the front row of the senior indunas, Gandang, his father, sat grave and proud.

'Like the blind catfish
that live in the caves of Sinoia
Bazo swam through darkness –'

Then as the verses of the song mentioned them, Zama and his warriors sprang forward to whirl and dance at his side.

'Like the black mamba from under a stone
Zama milked death from his silver fang –'

When the triumph dance was over, they threw themselves face down on the earth in front of the wagon.

'Bazo, son of Gandang, go out and choose two hundred head from the royal herds,' said Lobengula.

'*Bayete*!' shouted Bazo, still panting from the dance.

'Bazo, son of Gandang – you who commanded fifty so skilfully – now I give you one thousand to command.'

'*Nkosi*! Lord!'

'You will command the levy of young men waiting now at the royal kraal on the Shangani river. I give you the insignia for your new regiment. Your shields will be red, your kilts the tails of the genet cat, your plumes the wing feathers of the marabou stork, and your headband the fur of the burrowing mole,' Lobengula intoned, and then paused. 'The name of your regiment will be Izimvukuzane Ezembintaba – the moles that burrow under a mountain.'

'*Nkosi kakhula*! Great King!' Bazo roared.

'Now Bazo, rise up and go into the women to choose yourself a wife. Be sure that she is virtuous and fruitful, and let her first duty be to set the headring of the induna on your brow.'

'*Indhlovu! Ngi ya bonga*! Great Elephant, I praise you!'

Sitting his solitary watch by the fire, Bazo remembered every word, every change of tone, every pause and emphasis that the king had used to heap his honours upon him. He sighed with contentment and placed another log upon the fire, carefully so as not to wake his companions, and the sparks floated up through the opening in the highest point of the domed roof.

Then a distant sound interrupted his reverie; it was the single whoop of a hyena, not an unusual sound except that it was the first time that he had heard it since nightfall. On every other night the hideous cries of these loathsome animals began when they crept from their burrows at dusk and continued until sunrise.

They haunted the small woody copse beyond the cattle enclosure that all the inhabitants of Gandang's kraal used as a communal open-air latrine. The hyena cleansed the area of excrement during the hours of darkness. For this reason, Gandang's people tolerated the presence of an animal that they usually abhorred with a superstitious dread.

So tonight the single whooping cry at midnight drew attention to the silence that had preceded it. Bazo listened a few seconds longer and then let his thoughts stray to the morrow.

After the king, Gandang was one of the three most important personages in Matabeleland – only Somabula and Babiaan were his peers, so that a marriage at his kraal would have been a momentous event even if it were not his eldest son – himself a newly appointed induna of one thousand – who was to be the bridegroom.

Juba, senior wife of Gandang, and mother of Bazo the bridegroom, had supervised the brew of beer, watching with an expert eye for the bloom of yeast on the germinating sorghum, testing with her own plump finger the temperature of the ground meal gruel as it was malted, judging the addition of the final booster of yeast and then standing over the matrons as they strained the brewing through woven bamboo sieves into the huge black clay beer-pots. Now there were a thousand pots each holding half a gallon of her famous brew, ready to greet the guests as they arrived at Gandang's kraal. There would be a thousand invited guests.

Lobengula and his retinue were already on the road; they were sleeping tonight at the regimental kraal of the Intemba regiment, only five miles distant, and they would arrive before noon.

Somabula was with the king, while Babiaan was coming in from his kraal in the east with a hundred warriors in his bodyguard. Nomusa and Hlopi were coming from the mission station at Khami as Juba's special guests, and they were bringing all their daughters with them.

Gandang had picked fifty fat bullocks from his herds, and the bridegroom and his young companions would begin to slaughter and butcher them in the dawn – while the unmarried girls took the bride down to the river pool, bathed her and then anointed her with fat and clay until she glistened in the early sunlight. Then they would deck her with wild flowers.

The hyena called again much closer this time, sounding as if it were right outside the stockade – and then a strange thing happened. The single cry was answered by a chorus, as though a great multitude of the huge shaggy spotted dog-like beasts had surrounded Gandang's kraal.

Bazo started up from the fire in astonishment. He had never heard anything to equal this – there must be a hundred or more of the ungainly animals out there. He could imagine them, their high shoulders sloping down to meagre hindquarters, the flat snake-like heads held low as though the weight of massive underslung jaw and yellow carnassial teeth was too heavy for the neck.

One hundred at least, he could almost smell their breath as they opened those iron jaws, capable of crunching the thigh bone of a bull buffalo to splinters. They would reek of long-dead carrion and excrement and other filth, but it was the sound of their voices that chilled Bazo's guts and started the march of ghost feet along his spine.

It was as though all the souls of the dead had risen from their graves to clamour outside Gandang's stockade. They whooped and howled, beginning in a low moan and rising sharply in key.

'Oooh – wee!'

They shrieked like the ghost of a Mashona feeling again the steel cleave his breast, and the terrible cries woke the echoes amongst the kopjes along the river.

Almost humanly, they giggled, and they laughed – that maniacal and mirthless laughter. The peals of fiendish laughter mingled with the tormented shrieks, and then with them were the cries of the kraal's watchmen, the screeches of the waking women in their huts, the shouts of the men, still half-asleep, as they scrambled for their weapons.

'Do not go out,' Kamuza shouted across the hut as Bazo sprang to the door with his shield on his shoulder and his assegai in his right hand. 'Do not go into the dark, this is a witchcraft. Those are not animals out there.'

His words stopped Bazo at the threshold. There was nothing of flesh and blood he would not face, but this –

The fiendish chorus reached a climax, and then abruptly ceased. The silence that followed was even more chilling, and Bazo shrank away from the door. His companions crouched on their sleeping-mats, weapons in their hands, their eyes wide and white in the firelight – but not one of them moved towards the door.

All of Gandang's kraal was awake now, but silent, waiting, the women creeping away into the farthest recesses of their huts and covering their heads with their fur karosses, the men frozen with superstitious terror.

The silence lasted the time it would take for a man to run the full circle of the stockade, and then was broken by the call of a single hyena, the same whooping cry, starting low and rising to a shriek. The head of every one of the warriors in Bazo's hut lifted, and they all stared upwards to the roof and the star-pricked sky above it – for that was from where the ghostly cry emanated – from the very air high above Gandang's kraal.

'Sorcery.' Kamuza's voice shook, and Bazo choked down on the wail of terror that rose in his own throat.

As the animal cry died in the night, there was only one other sound. The voice of a young girl, raised in terrible distress.

'Bazo! Help me, Bazo!'

It was the only thing that could have roused him. Bazo shook himself like a dog that leaps from water to land, throwing off the terror that paralysed him.

'Do not go!' Kamuza yelled, after him. 'It is not the girl, it is a witch voice.'

But Bazo tore the locking bar from the door.

He saw her immediately. Tanase raced towards him from the women's quarters, from Juba's own great hut where she had been passing the last night before her nuptials.

Her dark naked body was without substance, like a moon shadow as she sped to him. Bazo leaped towards her, and they met in front of the main gate of the stockade, and Tanase clung to him.

No other person had left the huts; the kraal was deserted, the fearful silence oppressive. Bazo lifted his shield to cover both himself and the girl – and instinctively he turned to face the gateway. It was only then that he realized that the gate was open.

He tried to retreat towards the hut, taking the girl with him, but she was rigid in his arms, rooted to the earth like the stump of a wild ebony tree – and his own strength was sapped by terror.

'Bazo,' Tanase whispered. 'It is them, they have come.'

As she spoke the watch-fire beside the gate, which had long ago burned down to ash and charred logs, suddenly burst into flame once again. The flames sprang higher than a man's head, roaring like a waterfall, and the stockade and gateway were lit brightly by the yellow dancing light. Beyond the open gateway, at the very edge of the firelight stood a human figure. It was the figure of a very old man, with stick-like limbs and bowed back; his cap of hair was white as the salt from the Makarikari pan; his skin was grey and dusty with age. The whites of his eyes flashed as they squinted and rolled upwards into his skull, and glassy strings of spittle dribbled from his toothless mouth onto his chest, wetting the dry parchment skin through which each skeletal rib stood out clearly.

His voice was a quavering ancient squeal.

'Tanase!' he called. 'Tanase, daughter of the spirits.'

In the firelight all life went out of Tanase's eyes; they became blank.

'Do not heed –' Bazo croaked, but a bluish sheen appeared over Tanase's eyeballs like the nictitating membrane that covers the eye of a shark or the cataract of tropical ophthalmia, and blindly her head turned towards the spectral figure beyond the gates.

'Tanase, your destiny calls you!'

She broke out of Bazo's arms. It seemed to require no effort. He could not hold her. Her strength was superhuman.

She began to walk towards the gateway, and when Bazo tried to follow her, he found he could not lift a foot. He dropped his shield, and it clattered on the hard earth, but Tanase did not look back. She walked with a floating grace, light as river mist towards the ancient stooped figure.

'Tanase!' Bazo's voice was a despairing cry, and he fell upon his knees, yearning after her.

The old man held out one hand, and Tanase took it, and as she did so, the watch-fire died down as abruptly as it had flared, and the darkness beyond the gateway was instantly impenetrable.

'Tanase!' whispered Bazo, his arms outstretched – and far away, down by the river the hyena called one last time.

The twins came pelting into the church, tumbling over each other with eagerness to be the first to tell.

'Mama! Mama! –'

'Vicky, I saw first, let me!'

Robyn Codrington looked up from the black body stretched on the table and quelled them with a frown.

'Ladies don't push.'

They came up in a parody of demureness, but hopping with impatience.

'Very well, Vicky. What is it?'

They began together, and Robyn stopped them again.

'I said Vicky.'

And Victoria puffed up importantly.

'There is someone coming.'

'From Thabas Indunas?' Robyn asked.

'No, Mama, from the south.'

'It's probably one of the king's messengers.'

'No, Mama, it's a white man on a horse.'

Robyn's interest quickened; she would never have admitted even to herself how often the isolation palled. A white traveller would mean news, perhaps letters, stores and supplies, or even the most precious of all, books. Failing those treasures there would be the mere mental stimulation of a strange face and of conversation and ideas.

She was tempted to leave the patient on the table, it was not a serious burn, but she checked herself.

'Tell Papa I shall come directly,' she said, and the twins fled, jammed in the doorway for a moment, and then popped through like a cork from a champagne bottle.

By the time Robyn had finished dressing the burn, dismissed the patient, washed her hands and hurried out onto the porch of the church – the stranger was coming up the hill.

Clinton was leading the mule on which he was mounted. It was a big strong-looking grey animal, so the rider looked small and slim upon the broad back. He was a lad, dressed in an old tweed jacket and a boy's cloth cap. The twins danced on each side of the mule, and Clinton at its head was looking back over his shoulder, listening to something that the stranger was saying.

'Who is it, Mama?' Salina came out of the kitchen and called across the yard.

'We shall find out in a moment.'

Clinton led the mule to the porch, and the rider's head was on a level with Robyn's.

'Dr Ballantyne, your grandfather, Dr Moffat, sent me to you, I have letters and gifts from him for you.'

With a start Robyn realized that under the patched tweed coat and cap was a woman – and even in that moment of surprise she was aware that it was an extraordinarily handsome woman, younger than Robyn herself, not much over thirty years of age, with steady, dark eyes and almost Mongolian cheekbones.

She jumped down from the mule with the agility of an expert horsewoman, and came up the steps of the porch to seize Robyn's hands. Her grip was firm as a man's, and her expression was intense.

'My husband is ill and suffering. Dr Moffat says you are the only one who can help him. Will you do it? Oh please, will you?'

'I am a doctor.' Robyn gently twisted her fingers out of the other woman's painful grip – but it was not that which troubled her – there was something too intense, too passionate about her. 'I am a doctor, and I could never refuse to help anyone who is suffering. Of course, I shall do whatever I can.'

'Do you promise that?' the woman insisted, and Robyn bridled slightly.

'I have said I will help, there is no need to promise.'

'Oh, thank you.' The woman smiled with relief.

'Where is your husband?'

'Not far behind. I rode ahead to warn you – and to make sure that you would help us.'

'What is it that ails your husband?'

'Dr Moffat has explained it all in a letter. He sent gifts for you also.' The woman was evasive, turning away from Robyn's scrutiny and running back to the mule.

From the saddle-bags she lifted down two packages, wrapped in oilskin to protect them against the elements and bound up with rawhide thongs. They were so heavy and bulky that Clinton took them from her and carried them into the church.

'You are tired,' Robyn said. 'I am sorry I cannot offer you coffee, we used the last a month ago – but a glass of lemonade?'

'No.' The woman shook her head decidedly. 'I shall go back immediately, to be with my husband – but we shall arrive before nightfall.'

She ran back, and vaulted lightly to the mule's back. None of them had ever seen a woman do that.

'Thank you,' she repeated, and then trotted out of the yard, back down the hill.

Clinton came out of the church and put one arm around Robyn's shoulders.

'What a very beautiful and unusual woman,' he said, and Robyn nodded. That was one of the things that had troubled her. Robyn mistrusted beautiful women.

'What is her name?' she asked.

'I didn't have a chance to ask.'

'You were too busy looking, perhaps,' Robyn suggested tartly, and wriggled out from under his arm and went back into the church, while Clinton stared after her with a rueful expression.

After a moment he made a move as if to follow her – but then sighed and shook his head. It was always as well to let Robyn come round on her own, coaxing only angered her even more unreasonably.

In the quiet of the church Robyn untied the first package, and unpacked the contents onto the table.

There were five heavy bottles with glass stoppers, and she read the labels as she lifted out each one.

'Carbolic Acid.'

'Alum.'

'Quicksilver.'

'Iodine.'

And then the fifth bottle was labelled:

'Trichloromethane.'

'Bless you, Grandfather.' She smiled delightedly – but still she unstoppered the last bottle and sniffed cautiously at the mouth to confirm her good fortune.

The pungent sweet odour was unmistakable. Chloroform was to her more precious than her own life's blood; she would gladly have exchanged drop for drop.

Her own last supply had been exhausted months before and the London Missionary Society was as parsimonious as ever with its stores. She wished she had retained just a few hundred guineas of her enormous book royalties to enable her to purchase her own medicines rather than having to plead for them with the secretary in London by a correspondence which often took twelve months each way.

Sometimes, in a flagrantly unchristian manner, she wished she could have that bloodless myopic little man at her side when she removed an eye damaged by a blow with a knobkerrie and hanging out of its socket onto a black cheek, or when she went for a Caesarian section – all without anaesthetic.

She hugged the bottle to her chest for a moment.

'Darling Grandfather,' she repeated, then as reverently as if it were the fabulous Kohinoor diamond, she set the bottle of colourless but precious fluid aside, and turned to the second package.

A roll of newspapers – *The Cape Times* and *The Diamond Fields Advertiser.* In the weeks ahead every column would be read and re-read, down to the announcements of auction sales and the legal notices; then the newsprint itself would be used for a dozen domestic chores. Under the newspaper – books, wonderful fat leather-bound books.

'Bless you, Robert Moffat.'

She lifted out a translation of Ibsen's *An Enemy of the People.* She admired the Norwegian for his insight into the human mind, and the muted poetry of his prose. Robert Louis Stevenson's *Virginibus Puerisque'*; the title made her pause. She had four virgins in her household, and she intended maintaining that happy condition without allowing any inflammatory literature to thwart her. She flipped through the book. Despite the dubious title, it was merely a collection of essays – and the man was a good Calvinistic Scot. It might just do to let the girls read it, but she would vet it first.

Then there was Mark Twain's *Tom Sawyer.* Here she was less sanguine. She had heard of this American's frivolous and irreverent attitude towards adolescence, industry and filial duty. She would read it carefully before letting it anywhere near Salina or Catherine. Reluctantly she left the other books for future study and turned to her grandfather's letter.

There were many pages, written with sooty home-made ink, and the script was shaky and wavering. She skimmed swiftly through the salutations and the personal news until she reached the middle of the second page:

> Robyn, they say a doctor buries his mistakes: blatantly untrue. I send mine to you. The patient who delivers this letter should long ago have sought the sanctuary of a modern hospital, such as that at Kimberley.
>
> This he has steadfastly refused to do. His reasons are his own, and I have not pried. However, the fact that for over a year now he has had a pistol ball lodged in his body may point to his motives.
>
> Twice I have cut for this foreign body, but at 87 years of age my eyes are not as bright nor my hand as steady as yours. Each time I have failed and I fear that I have done more harm than good.
>
> I know that you have interest and skill in treatment of this type of injury, as so you should, for you have been provided by young Lobengula's warriors with endless opportunity to practise your technique. I recall with admiration your inspired reintroduction of the spoon of Diokles, after nearly 2,000 years, which you designed from the contemporary description by Celsus – and your successful removal of barbed arrowheads with it.
>
> Thus I send you one more subject on which to demonstrate your art – and with him my last bottle of Chloroform; for the poor fellow – whatever his sins – has suffered enough under my knife.

The letter left her with a sense of foreboding – as did the woman who had delivered it. She folded the letter and thrust it into the pocket of her skirt as she left the church and hurried across the yard.

'Cathy,' she called. 'Where is that girl! She must set the guest-house to rights.'

'She's gone to it already, Mama.' Salina looked up as she stormed into the kitchen.

'Then where is your father?'

Within an hour the mission station was prepared to receive

guests, and buzzing with anticipation; but they had to wait until mid-afternoon before a two-wheeled cart of unusually high and heavy construction appeared over the rise before the river. It was drawn by a pair of mules.

The entire family assembled on the front porch of the main building, and all of them had changed their clothing, while the girls had also brushed and dressed their hair with ribbons. A dozen times the twins had to be cautioned for improper comments and unrestrained behaviour, but finally the cart wheeled into the yard.

The woman had put her mule into the traces and now she walked beside the wheel of the cart, which reached almost as high as her head. There was a coloured servant in ragged cast-off clothes leading the mules, and over the body of the cart was rigged a makeshift sunshade of saplings and stained canvas.

Below the porch the cart stopped, and all of them craned forward as a man's head and upper body appeared above its side. He was laid on a straw mattress on the floor of the cart, and now he lifted himself on one elbow.

He was a gaunt wasted figure; the flesh seemed to have melted from the big bones of his shoulders. His cheeks had fallen in and turned a muddy yellow, the hand on the side of the cart was bony, and the veins were roped under the skin like blue serpents. His hair bushed wildly about his head, coarse dark hair that was shot through with strands of dead white. He had not shaved in days; thick stubble covered his jaws and was salted with the same white as his hair. One eye was sunk into a bruised cavity, and it had that feverish glitter that Robyn recognized instantly. It was the look of mortal illness.

The other eye was covered by a black piratical patch. There was something dreadfully familiar about the big aquiline nose and the wide mouth – yet it was only when he smiled that old mocking yet somehow tender smile that she had never forgotten that Robyn reeled backwards, one hand flying to her mouth too late to stop her cry.

She caught for support at one of the mopani poles that held the roof.

'Mama, are you all right?' But Robyn pushed Salina's hands away and went on staring at the man in the cart.

Only one memory out of so many rose up like a freak wave out of a storm-swept sea to overwhelm her. She saw again that dark bush of curls, devoid only of its silver lacing, bowing to her naked bosom. She saw above her the beamed roof of the great cabin in the sternquarters of the slave ship *Huron*, and she remembered as she had a thousand times in the twenty years since then – that pain. The deep splitting incursion that rocked her. Four childbirths since then had not eradicated the memory of it, the agony of passing from maiden to woman.

Her senses wavered, there was a rushing in her ears, she was going to fall, but then Clinton's voice steadied her. The hard fierce tone of it which she had not heard in years.

'You!' he said.

As Clinton drew himself erect, the years seemed to fall away from him. He was once again tall and lithe, stiff with anger as the young Royal Naval officer who had come up onto the slaver's quarter-deck with pistols and a naval cutlass on his hip to confront this same man.

Still clinging to the verandah pole, Robyn remembered the words he had spoken then in that same fierce tone:

'Captain Mungo St John, your reputation precedes you, sir. The first trader ever to transport more than three thousand souls across the middle passage in a single twelve-month period – I'd give five years' pay to have the hatches off your holds, sir.'

Robyn remembered then how it had taken another year for Clinton to get his wish, when off Good Hope he had come back onto *Huron*'s decks, boarding her over the stern in the cannon smoke with his fighting seamen at his back, and how this action had cost him more than a mere five years' pay. He had been court-martialled and cashiered from the Royal Navy and imprisoned for it.

'You dare to come here, to us.' Clinton was pale with rage; his blue eyes, so gentle for so long, were bleak and hating. 'You, you cruel and bloody slaver, you dare to come here.'

Mungo St John was still smiling, taunting him with that smile and the glitter in his single eye, but his voice was low and rough with his suffering.

'And you, you kind and sainted Christian gentleman, do you dare to turn me away?'

Clinton flinched as though he had been struck across the face, and he took a step backwards. Slowly the litheness and youth went out of his stance, his shoulders slumped into their habitual stoop. He shook his bald head uncertainly, and then instinctively he turned towards Robyn.

With a huge effort Robyn gathered herself, pushed away from the supporting pole. Despite the turmoil of her emotions she managed to keep her expression neutral.

'Dr Ballantyne,' Louise St John came to the steps of the verandah. She took the cap from her head, and the thick black plait tumbled out from under it.

'I find it difficult to beg,' she said. 'But I am begging now.'

'That is not necessary, madam. I gave you my word.' Robyn turned away. 'Clinton, please help Mrs St John to put this patient into the bed in the guest-house.'

'Yes, dear.'

'I shall be there directly to make an examination.'

'Thank you, Doctor, oh thank you.' Robyn ignored Louise, but when she had followed the mule cart across the yard to the guest-hut, she turned to face her daughters.

'None of you – not even you, Salina – will go near the guest-house while that man is here. You will not speak to him or the woman, you will not answer if they speak to you. You will do your best to avoid seeing either of them, and if you do by error find yourself in their presence, you will leave immediately.'

The twins were quivering with excitement, their eyes shone, and even their ears seemed to be pink and pricked like those of a pair of young bunny rabbits. They could not remember a day so wildly exciting.

'Why?' gasped Vicky, forgetting herself sufficiently in this incredible series of events to question her mother's order. For a moment it seemed that she would have to pay for the impertinence with a box on one pink ear, but Robyn's hand dropped back to her side.

'Because–' Robyn said softly, '–because he is the devil – the very devil.'

He was propped on the iron cot, with a bolster under his shoulders, and Louise rose from the other cot as Robyn entered the guest-hut carrying her bag.

'Madam, will you kindly wait outside,' Robyn ordered brusquely and, not deigning to see if she would obey, Robyn placed her bag on the chair beside his cot. Behind her the latch on the door clicked.

Mungo St John wore only a pair of baggy white trousers from which one leg had been hacked off high in the thigh. Like his face, his body was wasted by sickness, but there was still the width of shoulder and the solidness of bone that she remembered so well. His belly had sunk in like that of a greyhound, and his ribs stood out in a rack above it, but his skin retained the texture and silkiness of a far younger man, while the body hair that was crimped into curls upon his chest was not marred with silver as was his beard and the hair upon his head.

'Hello, Robyn,' he said.

'I will speak to you only when it is absolutely necessary for your treatment, and you will do the same,' she said, without looking at his face.

She started with the wounds in his flank and back – bullet wounds, she realized, but through and through – and completely healed. Then with a little start she noticed the other old, long-healed scar just below the bullet wound.

She recognized the little white pricks of the suture which had closed the knife-cut. Her own work was distinctive, there was nobody who could throw down those even and precise knotted sutures as she could, and before she realized what she was doing she touched the old hardened cicatrice.

'Yes,' Mungo nodded. 'Camacho made that.'

She jerked her hand away. Mungo had taken that knife-cut when he had intervened to protect her from the Portuguese slaver. He had saved her life that night.

'Do you remember this also?' Mungo asked, and showed her the pock mark on his forearm. That was where she had inoculated him when smallpox had swept through *Huron*.

'Do you remember?' Mungo insisted softly, but she kept her face averted and her lips compressed in a thin hard line as she lifted the dressing from his upper leg.

Then the horror showed on her face. Her grandfather's uneven knife strokes had lacerated the leg from knee to groin, where he had probed and searched for the ball, and his crude stitches had cobbled it all back together like a man repacking a valise in haste.

'Bad?' Mungo asked.

'It's a mess,' she said, and then hated herself for unbending that far, and by inference criticizing her grandfather's work.

The flesh of the leg had that unhealthy putty colour, and there was ulceration in the wounds, that awful sloughing of tissue that hinted at the corruption beneath.

Her grandfather had left drains in the wounds, thick black horse hairs that stuck stiffly out between the stitches. She drew one now, and Mungo gasped but did not flinch. A weak little trickle of watery pus followed the hair out. She stooped and sniffed it and grimaced. This was not the rich creamy pus that the ancients had called '*pus bonum et laudabile*'. From the stink of it, gangrene was not far off. She felt a little icy splinter of dread, and immediately wondered at it; surely there were no feelings left in her for this man.

'Tell me how it happened?'

'That, doctor, is my business.'

'Dirty business, I have no doubt,' she snapped. 'And I want no lurid account of it, but if I am to locate the ball I must know where you were in relationship to the weapon that was fired at you, the type of weapon, the weight and charge –'

'Of course,' he said quickly. 'Your grandfather did not bother to enquire.'

'Leave my grandfather out of it.'

'The man used a pistol; it looked like a single-action Remington army model, in which case the ball would be .44, of lead, cone-shaped, weight one fifty grains, and driven by black powder.'

'Low penetration, break up of the ball if it hit bone,' she muttered.

'The man was lying on the ground, about twenty-five paces distant, and I was in the act of dismounting from my horse, this leg raised –'

'He was ahead of you.'

'Slightly ahead and on my right hand.'

Robyn nodded. 'This will hurt.' And ten minutes later she stood back and called, 'Mrs St John.'

As soon as Louise entered, she said, 'I shall operate as soon as the light is good enough tomorrow morning. I shall need your assistance. I warn you now that even if I am successful, your husband will not recover full use of the leg. He will always have a pronounced limp.'

'And if you are unsuccessful?'

'The degeneration will accelerate, mortification and gangrene–'

'You are frank, doctor,' Louise whispered.

'Yes,' Robyn agreed. 'I always am.'

Robyn could not sleep, but she reminded herself that she seldom could on the eve of an operation under anaesthetic. Chloroform was such an unpredictable substance, the margins of safety were frighteningly narrow, overdosage, too high a concentration or inadequate oxygenation, would lead to primary collapse with fatal depression of the heart, lungs, liver and kidneys.

She lay beside Clinton in the darkness and ran through a mental list of her preparations for the morrow, and set her mind on the procedures she must adopt. Firstly she must re-open and find the source of the mortification. She moved and Clinton stirred beside her and muttered in his sleep. She froze and waited for him to settle.

The distraction altered the direction of her thoughts, and she found she was thinking about the man and not the patient. For a while she tried to prevent it, and then gave in.

She remembered him on his quarter-deck, the white linen shirt open to the throat and his chest hair curling out of the V, his head thrown back to hail the masthead, the thick dark mane of his hair rippling in the wind.

Then suddenly she remembered that morning when she slipped out of her cabin and stepped out onto *Huron*'s main-deck. He had been under the deck pump, while two seamen worked the handles, and clear sea water hissed over him as he stood naked under the jet. She remembered his body and the way he smiled at her without attempting to cover it from her gaze. Then abruptly she remembered his eyes, those flecked yellow eyes above her in the gloom of the cabin, eyes like those of a leopard.

She moved again, and this time Clinton came half awake. He said her name and threw one arm across her at the level of her waist. For a while she lay quiescent under his arm and then slowly she reached down and drew up the hem of her nightdress. She took Clinton's wrist lightly and guided his hand downwards.

She felt him come fully awake, heard his breathing change and his hand went on without her insistence.

Long ago she had learned, painfully, that there were limits to the restraint that she could exercise over her unruly sensuality. So now she closed her eyes, relaxed her limbs and let her imagination run unchecked.

She drank only a cup of the hot coffee substitute that she had concocted of roasted sorghum and wild honey – and while she did so she composed her mind by glancing through her notes.

She always found comfort in Celsus' injunctions, somehow the fact that they were written around the time of Christ made them more poignant.

> Now a surgeon, the chirugus, should be youthful or at any rate closer to youth than age, with a strong and steady hand that never trembles, ready to use left hand as well as right, with vision sharp and clear and spirit undaunted. . . .

Then there was Galen, the surgeon of the gladiators, the Roman who had stored all his experience in twenty-two volumes. Robyn had read them in the original Greek, and extracted the pearls of his genius, which she had used with great success in treating the gladiatorial-type wounds of Lobengula's young men. Though she had substituted alum for corn, iodine for pigeon dung, and carbolic acid for lamp black and oil in the fight against inflammation and mortification.

The kind of trauma that faced her now as she bowed over the long table in the church was much like those described by Galen, though caused by a different projectile. Mungo St John's hoarse, muffled breathing was the only sound in the quiet church. Robyn tested the depth of his coma by pricking his finger with a probe, and then immediately lifted the mask of plaited bamboo and lint from his nose and mouth.

Then she listened to his breathing as it eased, and found herself examining his face as she had not been able to while he was conscious. He was still a handsome man, despite the missing eye and marks of pain and of advancing age etched into his face. Louise St John had borrowed Clinton's straight razor the previous day. Mungo St John was clean-shaven now, and suddenly she realized that the new lines in his face and the silver wings above his temples accentuated the power of the man, while at the same time the relaxation of his mouth gave him a childlike innocence which made the breath catch in her throat.

Clinton looked across at her, and she turned her face away quickly before he could see her expression.

'Are you ready, madam?' Robyn made her voice cold and businesslike, and Louise nodded. She was very pale, the fine freckles standing out in sharp contrast on her cheeks and the bridge of her nose.

Still Robyn hesitated. She knew that she was squandering the moments during which the chloroform was having its blessed effect, but she was seized by a terrible dread. For the first time in her life she was afraid to wield the knife, and a thought transfixed her.

'If you once love a man, can you ever cease entirely to do so?'

She dared not look again at Mungo St John's sleeping face; she felt she must turn and run from the church.

'Are you unwell, doctor?' Louise St John's concern steeled her. She would not let this woman suspect weakness in her.

The leg was painted dark yellow brown with tincture of iodine. It looked like a rotten banana. She snipped her grandfather's stitches and the wound fell open. She saw the depth of the ulceration, and knew from dreadful experience that a wound like this would never heal, even by second intention. Her main task was not to find the pistol ball but to repair this damage.

She went in deeper, down past the thick pulsing snake of the femoral artery, down to the bone, the bared femur, and again she felt her spirits quail. The bone was malformed, yellow and cheesy.

She guessed at the cause, this was where the pistol ball had struck and been deflected away. It had struck a long splinter of bone off the femur, and she picked something out of the dead stinking tissue with the forceps and held it up to the light from the window.

It was a flake of black lead. She dropped it into the bucket under the table and bent once more over the open chasm in Mungo's flesh. There was hardly any blood, a few drops only from the stitches, and the rest of it was slimy yellow matter smelling like a corpse.

She knew the risks of attempting to remove this decomposing

tissue surgically; she had tried it before – and killed in the process. It was drastic treatment which only a very strong man could survive, yet if she closed up, the macabre spectre of gangrene lurked close at hand.

She took up the scraper and it rasped over the exposed bone of the femur. Stinking pus welled up from out of the bone itself. Osteomyelitis, thc mortification of the bony tissue. She worked at it grimly, the scraper was the only sound in the room until Louise St John choked.

'Madam, if you are going to throw up – please leave,' Robyn told her, without looking up.

'I shall be all right,' Louise whispered.

'Then use the swab as I instructed you,' Robyn snapped.

The rotten bone came away, curling off the blade in little yellow whorls like wood shavings from the carpenter's plane, until Robyn reached the porous core – and at last clean bright blood came up through it like wine from a sea sponge that had been squeezed, and the bone around the hole was hard and white as china.

Robyn sighed with relief, and at the same moment Mungo groaned and would have twitched the leg if Clinton had not been holding it at the ankle. Swiftly Robyn replaced the little bamboo basket over his nose and mouth then let a few drops of chloroform fall on the lint covering.

She cut away the rotten ulcerations, working perilously close to the artery and the white cord of the femoral nerve. She found more pockets of sepsis around the sutures with which her grandfather had closed the blood vessels. She cleaned these out and carefully cut away dead tissue.

There was blood now, plenty of it, but clean bright blood. Robyn had reached the most critical stage of the reparative surgery. She knew that there was still infection amongst the healthy tissue and as soon as she closed the wound it would blossom again.

She had mixed the antiseptic the night before, one part of carbolic acid to one hundred parts of rainwater. With this she washed out the open pit in Mungo's leg, and the astringent action of the mixture dried up the weeping blood from the vessels too small to tie off.

She could come out now, and sew up. She had left foreign bodies in before, and often they stabilized and became encysted, causing the patient little further discomfort, but instinct warned her not to do so this time.

She glanced at Clinton's big silver hunter watch, which he had placed beside her instrument case where she could see it readily. She had been in for twenty-five minutes, and experience had taught her that the longer she stayed in the greater the danger of primary or secondary collapse.

She looked up at Louise St John. She was still very pale, but the sweat of nausea had dried on her forehead. She had grit, Robyn conceded grudgingly, and that was one thing she could admire – much more than her exotic beauty.

'Madam, I am about to go after the ball now,' she said. 'I shall only have time for one attempt.'

She knew from Lister's writing and her own observation how risky it was to use her bare hands in a wound – but that risk was preferable to leading with a sharp instrument into the nest of veins, arteries and nerves in the groin.

She had guessed the location of the ball by the restricted movement of the femur within its pelvic socket, and by the focus of intense pain when she had palpated the area while Mungo was conscious. She probed with her forefinger, boldly up into the tissue above the raw scraped area of the bone. The direction of the shot, from ahead and upwards, must be on this line.

She met resistance and tried again, and then again. Suddenly her finger slid into a narrow canal in the hot meat of his thigh, right in to its full length, and then at the very limit of her reach she touched something hard. It could have been the head of the femur or the lower ridge of pelvic bone – but she took up the scalpel.

A fine needle jet of blood from a severed blood vessel sprayed her cheek and forehead before she could twist it closed, and she could hear Louise gagging again, but her hands with the swab barely shook as she wiped away the blood so that Robyn could cut again – and there was a rush of thick creamy yellow matter out of the cut like a dam burst by muddy flood waters. In the flood were little chips and fragments of shattered metal, rotting threads of woollen cloth and other detritus.

'Praise God!' whispered Robyn, and brought her hand out, dripping with the reeking yellow discharge, but with the distorted, misshapen lump of bluish lead held firmly between thumb and forefinger.

The twins had long ago discovered the literary treasure trove that Robyn kept in the locked cupboard against the far wall of her bedroom. Of course, they could only visit it when their parents and elder sisters were fully occupied elsewhere – for instance when King Ben had summoned them to GuBulawayo and Salina was cooking and Cathy was painting or reading.

Then they could sneak into the bedroom and push the chair against the wall so that Vicky standing on Lizzie's shoulders could reach the key.

There were more than fifty books in the cupboard. The great majority unfortunately contained no illustrations. These had proved unrewarding, as the twins' efforts at deciphering the text had been shipwrecked on too many rock-hard words; at other times, just when it was becoming intensely interesting, they would encounter a solid slab of foreign language which they suspected was either Latin or Greek.

The twins avoided these tomes, but the ones with pictures were a forbidden delight, greatly enhanced by danger and guilt. There was even one that had drawings of the inside of women, with and without a baby *in situ*, and another of the baby in the process of emerging.

However, their perennial favourite was the one they called 'The Devil Book' – for there was an illustration on each facing page vivid, lifelike and explicit, of souls in torment and the devils who attended them. The artist who had interpreted this edition of Dante's *Inferno* had dwelt ghoulishly on decapitation and disembowelment, on red-hot irons and hooks, lolling tongues and bulging eyes. Even the briefest stolen perusal of this masterpiece was enough to ensure that the twins would spend most of the following night clinging together in their bed, shivering with delicious terror.

However, this particular visit to the forbidden cupboard was in the interest of scientific research, otherwise they would never have taken the risk while Robyn Ballantyne was actually at Khami Mission.

They chose the time of morning clinic when Mama would

certainly be in the church attending her patients, when Daddy would be mucking out the sties, and Salina and Cathy at their chores.

The raid went with the precision of repeated rehearsal. They left their open readers on the dining-room table, and were down the verandah and had the key within the time it takes to draw a long breath.

Lizzie took guard at the window from where she could cover kitchen, the church and the pigsties – while Vicky got the cupboard open and the 'Devil Book' out and open at the correct page.

'See!' she whispered. 'I told you so.'

There he was – Satan, Lucifer, King of the Underworld – and Vicky had been right. He did not have horns. All the lesser demons had horns, but not the Devil, not the very Devil himself. What he did have was a tail, a magnificent tail with a point like the blade of a Matabele assegai upon the end of it.

'He's got a beard in this picture,' Lizzie pointed out, reluctant to abandon her position.

'He probably shaved it off – to fool us,' Vicky told her. 'Now look!' She took a pin out of her hair and used the black round tip to cover one of Lucifer's eyes. Immediately the resemblance was undeniable, the thick dark curls, the broad forehead, the beaked nose and the piercing eye under arched brow, and the smile, the same satanically mocking smile.

Lizzie shuddered luxuriously. Vicky was right, it was him all right.

'Kitty Cat!' Vicky hissed a warning. Salina was coming out of the kitchen, and they had the book back on its shelf, the cupboard locked, the key back in its hiding-place, and were once more seated at the table poring over their readers by the time that Salina had crossed the yard and looked in upon them.

'Good.' She smiled at them tenderly, they were such an angelic pair – sometimes. 'Good girls,' she said, and went back towards the kitchen.

'Where does he put it?' Lizzie asked softly, without looking up from her reader.

'What?'

'His tail.'

'Watch!' Vicky ordered. 'And I'll show you.'

Napoleon, the aged yellow mongrel, was sleeping in the patch of sunlight on the verandah. He had a ridge down his back, and grey hair around his muzzle. Every few minutes a dream of rabbits and guineafowl made his back legs gallop spasmodically and he would puff off an evil-smelling fart of excitement.

'Bad dog!' Vicky said loudly. 'Napoleon, you are a bad, bad dog!'

Napoleon sprang to his feet, appalled by this unjust accusation, and wriggled his entire body ingratiatingly, while his upper lip lifted in a simpering sycophantic grin. At the same time his long whippy tail disappeared between his legs and curled up under his belly.

'That's how he tucks it away. Just like Napoleon,' Vicky announced.

'How do you know?'

'If you look carefully, you can see the bulge where it comes out in front of him.'

They worked on distractedly for a few seconds, then Lizzie could not restrain herself further.

'Do you think we could see his tail?'

'How?'

'What if we –' Halfway through propounding her scheme, Lizzie faltered. Even she realized that it would be impossible to modify the latrine, drilling a peephole through the back wall, without being apprehended; and their motives could never be convincingly explained, especially not to Mama.

'Anyway,' Vicky quashed the plan effectively, 'Devils are probably like fairies, they just don't go.'

Silence fell again. Obviously relieved that nobody had followed up the original accusation, Napoleon re-composed himself to his dreams, and it seemed the project was abandoned – until Vicky looked up with a determined gleam in her eyes.

'We are going to ask him.'

'But,' stammered Lizzie, 'but Mama forbade us to talk to him –' She knew her protest to be unavailing; that gleam in Vicky's eye was familiar.

Ten days after she had removed the pistol ball, Robyn came down to the guest-house with a crutch carved from mopani wood.

'My husband made it for you,' she told Mungo St John. 'And you are going to use it every day from now on.'

The first day Mungo managed one halting circuit of the yard, and at the end of it he was pale and sweating. Robyn checked the leg and the stitches had all held, but the muscles of the thigh had withered and contracted, pulling the leg an inch shorter than the other. The next morning she was there to watch him at exercise. He moved more easily.

After fifteen days she removed the last catgut stitches, and though the scar was raised and thickened, a livid purplish red, yet there was no indication of mortification. It looked as though it had healed by first intention – the drastic use of strong antiseptic on living tissue seemed to have been justified.

After five weeks, Mungo abandoned the crutch in favour of a stout stick, and took the footpath that girded the kopje behind the Khami Mission.

Each day he walked farther and stayed out longer. It was a relief to be away from the bitter arguments with Louise which punctuated the long periods of her icy withdrawal.

He had found a viewpoint beyond the sharp northern ridge of the kopje, a natural platform and bench of dark serpentine rock under the spreading branches of a lovely old leadwood tree, where he could sit and brood out over the gently undulating grassland to the far blue silhouette of hills that marked the site of Lobengula's kraal.

His instinct warned him that there was an opportunity there. It was the instinct and the awareness of the cruising shark which could detect the presence of prey at distances and depths beyond the range of other senses. His instinct had seldom failed him, and there had been a time when he had seized every opportunity with boldness, with the ruthless application of all his skills and all his strength.

Sitting under the leadwood, his hands upon the head of the cane and his chin upon his hands, he cast his mind back to his triumphs: to the great ships that he had won and sailed to the ends of the oceans and brought back laden with treasures, with tea and coffee and spices or holds filled with black slaves. He remembered the rich fertile lands to which he had held title, and the sweet smell of sugar-cane fields when the harvest was being cut. He remembered piles of gold coins, carriages and beautiful horses – and women.

So many women, too many women perhaps; for they were the cause of his present low condition.

He let himself think of Louise at last. She had been a fire in his blood, which grew fiercer the more often he tried to slake it, and she had weakened him, distracted him, diverted him from his ruthless purpose of old.

She had been thc daughter of one of his overseers on Fairfields, his vast Louisiana estate. When she was sixteen years of age he had allowed her to exercise his wife's Palamino horses; when she was seventeen he arranged for her to move into the big house as companion and maid to his wife and when she was eighteen he had raped her.

His wife was in the next-door bedroom, suffering from one of her black headaches, and he had torn Louise's clothes off her body, possessed by a madness that he had never known before. She had fought him with the savagery of one of her Blackfoot Indian ancestors, but in some perverse fashion her resistance maddened him as much as the glimpses of her hard young flesh, as it was revealed a gleaming flash at a time.

She had clawed red lines down his chest, and bitten him until he bled, but through it all she had not uttered a word or a sound, although a single scream would have brought her mistress or the house servants running.

In the end, he had borne her down onto the thick white pelt of a polar bear in the middle of the floor, naked except for the tatters of her petticoats hanging from her long fine legs, and with his full weight he had spread her and entered her.

Only then had she made any sound, she had gripped him with the same atavistic savagery, legs and arms encircling him, and she had whispered hoarsely, brokenly. 'I love you, I have always loved you, I shall always love you.'

When the armies of the North had marched against them, and his wife had fled with the children to her native France, Louise had stayed with him. When she could she had been in the field with him, and when she could not she had waited for him, filling in the days and most of the nights nursing the wounded at the Confederate Hospital in Galveston, and there she had nursed him when he was brought in half blinded and terribly hurt from the battlefield.

She had been with him when he went back to Fairfields for the last time, and shared his desolation at the burnt fields and ruined buildings, and she had been at his side ever since. Perhaps if she had not, things would have been different now, for she had weakened him; she had dulled the edge of his resolve.

So many times he had smelled out the opportunities – the chances for the coup which would restore it all, and each time she had caused him to waver.

'I could never respect you again,' she had said once. 'Not if you did that.'

'I never suspected you were capable of that, Mungo. It's wrong, morally wrong.'

Gradually it had changed, until sometimes, after another abortive attempt to restore his fortunes, she would look at him with a coldness – a kind of icy contempt.

'Why do you not leave me?' he had challenged her then.

'Because I love you,' she had replied. 'And, oh, sometimes how I wish I did not.'

In Perth, when he had forced her to bait the trap for him, luring in the intended victim – she had for the first time rebelled. She herself had ridden to warn the man, and they had been forced to run again, shipping out on a little trading schooner only an hour or so ahead of the constables with the warrant for Mungo's arrest.

He had never trusted her again, although he had never been able to make the decision to desert her. He found that he needed her still. At Cape Town a letter had finally caught up with Mungo. It was one of five copies sent out by his brother-in-law, the Duc de Montijo, a copy to each of the addresses that Mungo had occupied in the years since his wife had left him. Solange, his wife, had taken a chill while out riding and had died five days later of pneumonia. Her children were in the care of the Duc, being educated with his own, and the Duc hinted that he would resist any attempt by Mungo St John to assume custody.

At last Mungo was free to make good his promise to Louise, the solemn promise he had made to her as they knelt hand in hand before the altar in London's church of St Martin-in-the-Fields. He had sworn in the sight of God that just as soon as he was able to do so, he would marry Louise.

Mungo had read through his brother-in-law's letter three times, and then held it in the flame of the candle. He had crushed the ashes to powder, and never mentioned the letter or its news to Louise. She had gone on believing that he was married, and their relationship had limped on, sickening and staling.

Yet still she could influence him even when she was not physically present. At the dark crossroads south of Kimberley, even when he had seen the diamonds gleam in Hendrick Naaiman's hands, he had not been able to banish Louise's image from his mind: Louise with contempt in her eyes and cold accusation on her lovely lips.

Expert marksman that he was, the shade of Louise had spoiled his aim. He had fired a wink too late, and a touch too wide. He had not killed the Bastaard, but if he had done so, Louise's reaction could have been no more severe.

When he rode back to where she waited, reeling in the saddle, the wounded stallion dragging under him, he had seen her face in the moonlight. Even though she caught him when he might have fallen, and though she had tended his wounds and gone for succour, he had realized that they had crossed a dividing line over which there was no return.

As if to confirm it, he had seen Zouga Ballantyne staring at her in the lantern light with that unmistakable look in his eyes. Many men had looked at her like that over the years, but this time she had returned Zouga's scrutiny openly, making no attempt to hide it from either man.

On the long road northwards, as she walked beside the cart in which he lay wounded, he had challenged her again and she had not denied it.

' – At least Zouga Ballantyne is a man of honour.'

'Then why do you not leave me?'

'You know I cannot leave you now, not as you are –' She left it unfinished, and they had not spoken of it again, though in her icy silences he had sensed the presence in her mind of the other man, and he knew that no matter how desperately unhappy a woman might be she will seldom leave a relationship until she has the prospect of something better to replace it. Louise had that prospect now, and they were both aware of it.

He wondered if he would let Louise go if she finally made the decision. There had been a time not long ago when he would have killed her first; but since they had reached Khami, everything had begun altering even more swiftly. They were rushing towards some climax, and Mungo had sensed that it would be explosive.

For Mungo had forgotten the magnetism that Robyn Ballantyne had once exerted upon him, but now he had been vividly reminded by the mature woman, Robyn Codrington. She was even more attractive to him now than she had been as a girl. He sensed that her strength and assurance would provide a secure port for a man tired to his guts and the marrow of his bones by the storms of life.

He knew that she was the trusted confidante of the Matabele king, and that if his fortune awaited him here in the north, as he had come to suspect, then her intercession with the Matabele would be invaluable.

There was something else, some other darker need within him. Mungo St John never forgave or forgot an injury. Clinton Codrington had commanded the Royal Naval cruiser which had seized *Huron* off the Cape of Good Hope, an action which seemed to Mungo to mark the beginning of his long decline, and herald his dogged misfortune. Codrington was vulnerable. Through this woman Mungo could be avenged, and the prospect was strangely compelling.

He sighed and shook his head, roused himself and used the stick to push himself erect. He found himself confronted by the two small figures. Mungo St John liked all women of whatever age, and though he had not seen his own children in many years, the youngest would be about the same age as these two.

They were pretty little things. Though he had seen them only fleetingly or at a distance, he had felt the stirring of his paternal instincts; and now their presence was a welcome relief from his dark thoughts, and from the loneliness of the past weeks.

'Good afternoon, ladies.' He smiled, and bowed as low as his leg would allow. His smile was irresistible, and some of the rigidity went out of the two small bodies, but their expressions remained pale and fixed; their eyes, huge with trepidation, were fastened upon the fly of his breeches, so that after a few seconds silence even Mungo St John felt disconcerted, and he shifted uncomfortably.

'What service can I be to you?' he asked.

'We would like to see your tail, sir.'

'Ah!' Mungo knew never to show himself at a loss in front of a female, of no matter what age. 'You aren't supposed to know about that,' he said. 'Are you, now?'

They shook their heads in unison, but their eyes remained

fixed with fascination below his waist. Vicky was right, there was definitely something there.

'Who told you about it?' Mungo sat down again, bringing his eyes to the level of theirs, and their disappointment was evident.

'Mama said you were the Devil – and we know the Devil has a tail.'

'I see.' Mungo nodded. With a huge effort, he fought back his laughter, and kept his expression serious, his tone conspiratorial. 'You are the only ones that know,' he told them. 'You won't tell anybody, will you?' Quite suddenly Mungo realized the value of having allies at Khami, two pairs of sharp bright eyes that saw everything and long ears that heard all.

'We won't tell anybody,' promised Vicky. 'If you show us.'

'I can't do that.' And there was an immediate wail of disappointment.

'Why not?'

'Didn't your mother teach you that it's a sin to show anybody under your clothes?'

They glanced at each other, and then Vicky admitted reluctantly. 'Yes, we aren't even really allowed to look at ourselves there. Lizzie got whacked for it.'

'There.' Mungo nodded. 'But I'll tell you what I will do – I'll tell you the story of how I got my tail.'

'Story!' Vicky clapped her hands, and they spread their skirts and squatted cross-legged at Mungo's feet. If there was one thing better than a secret, it was a story, and Mungo St John had stories, wonderful scary, blood-thirsty stories – the kind that guaranteed nightmares.

Each afternoon when he reached the lookout under the leadwood tree, they were waiting for him – captives of his charisma, addicted to those amazing stories of ghosts and dragons, of evil witches and beautiful princesses who always had Vicky's hair or Lizzie's eyes when Mungo St John described them.

Then after each of Mungo's stories, he would tactfully initiate a lively discussion of the affairs of Khami Mission. On a typical day he would learn that Cathy had begun painting a portrait of Cousin Ralph from memory, and that it was the considered and unanimous verdict of the twins that Cathy was not only 'soft' but, much worse, 'sloppy' about Cousin Ralph.

He learned that King Ben had commanded the entire family to attend the Chawala ceremony at the new moon, and the twins were ghoulishly anticipating the slaughter of the sacrificial black bull. 'They do it with their bare hands,' Vicky gloated. 'And this year we are going to be allowed to watch, now that we are eleven.'

He was told in detail how Papa had demanded from Mama at the dinner table how much longer 'that infamous pirate' was to remain at Khami, and Mungo had to explain to the twins what 'infamous' meant – 'famous, but only more so'.

Then on one such afternoon, Mungo learned from Lizzie that King Ben had once again '*khombisile*' with his indunas. Gandang, one of the king's brothers, had told Juba, who was his wife, and Juba had told Mama.

'*Khombisile?*' Mungo asked dutifully. 'What does that mean?'

'It means that he *showed* them.'

'Showed them what?'

'The treasure,' Vicky cut in, and Lizzie rounded on her.

'I'm telling him!'

'All right, Lizzie.' Mungo was leaning forward, interest tempering the indulgent smile. 'You tell me.'

'It's a secret. Mama says that if other people, bad people, heard about it, it would be terrible for King Ben. Robbers might come.'

'It's a secret then,' Mungo agreed.

'Cross your heart.'

And Lizzie was telling it before he had made the sign of good faith. Lizzie was determined that Vicky would not get in ahead of her, this time.

'He shows them the diamonds. His wives rub fat all over him, and then they stick the diamonds onto the fat.'

'Where did King Ben get all these diamonds?' Scepticism warred with the need to believe.

'His people bring them from Kimberley. Juba says it isn't really stealing. King Ben says it is only the tribute that a king should have.'

'Did Juba say how many diamonds?'

'Pots full, pots and pots of them.'

Mungo St John turned his single eye from her flushed and shining face and looked across the grassy golden plains to the Hills of the Indunas, and his eye was flecked golden yellow like one of the big predatory cats of Africa.

Jordan looked forward to this early hour of day. It was one of his duties to check each evening in the nautical almanac the time of sunrise, and to waken Mr Rhodes an hour beforehand.

Rhodes liked to see the sun come up, whether it was from the balcony of his magnificent private railway coach or drinking coffee in the dusty yard of the corrugated iron cottage that he still maintained behind Market Square in Kimberley, from the upper deck of an ocean-going liner or from the back of a horse as they rode the quiet pathways of his estate on the slopes of Table Mountain.

It was the time when Jordan was alone with his master, the time when ideas which Mr Rhodes called his 'thoughts' would come spilling out of him. Incredible ideas, sweeping and grand or wild and fanciful, but all fascinating.

It was the time when Jordan could feel that he was part of the vast genius of the man, as he scribbled down Mr Rhodes' draft speeches in his shorthand pad, speeches that would be made in the lofty halls of the Cape Parliament to which Mr Rhodes had been elected by the constituents of what had once been Griqualand, or at the board table of the governors of De Beers, of which he was chairman. De Beers was the mammoth diamond company which Mr Rhodes had welded together out of all the little diggers' claims and lesser competing companies. Like some mythical boa constrictor, he had swallowed them all – even Barney Barnato, the other giant of the fields. Mr Rhodes owned it all now.

On other mornings they would ride in silence, until Mr Rhodes would lift his chin from his chest and stare at Jordan with those stark blue eyes. Every time he had something startling to say. Once it was, 'You should thank God every day, Jordan, that you were born an Englishman.'

Another time it was, 'There is only one real purpose behind it all, Jordan. It is not the accumulation of wealth. I was fortunate to recognize it so early. The real purpose is to bring the whole civilized world under British rule, to recover North America to the crown, to make all the Anglo-Saxon race into one great empire.'

It was thrilling and intoxicating to be part of all this, especially as so often the big burly figure would rein his horse and turn his head and look to the north, towards a land that neither he nor Jordan had ever seen, but which, during the years that Jordan had been with him, had become a part of both their existences.

'My thought,' he called it. 'My north – my idea.'

'That's where it will really begin, Jordan. And when the time comes, I shall send you. The person I can trust beyond any other.'

It had never seemed strange to Jordan that those blue eyes had looked in that direction, that the open land to the north had come to loom so large in Mr Rhodes' imagination, that it had taken on the aura of a sacred quest.

Jordan could mark the day that it had begun, not only the day but the hour. For weeks after Pickering had been buried in the sprawling cemetery on the Cape Road, Jordan had respected Mr Rhodes' mourning. Then, one afternoon, he had left his office early. He had returned to the camp.

He retrieved the bird image from where it had been abandoned in the yard, and with the help of three black workmen, he moved it into the cottage. The living-room had been too small to hold it; it hindered access to both the dining-table and the front door.

In the small cottage, there was only one free wall, and that was in Mr Rhodes' bedroom, at the head of his narrow cot. The statue fitted perfectly into the space beyond the window. The next morning, when Jordan went to call him, Mr Rhodes had already left his cot and, wearing a dressing-gown, was standing before the statue.

In the fresh pink light of sunrise, as they rode down to the De Beers offices, Mr Rhodes had said, suddenly: 'I have had a thought, Jordan, one which I'd like to share with you. While I was studying that statue, it came to me that the north is the gateway, the north is the hinterland of this continent of ours.' That is how it had begun, in the shadow of the bird.

When the architect, Herbert Baker, had consulted Mr Rhodes on the decoration and furnishings of the mansion that they were building on his Cape Estate, 'Groote Schuur' – 'The Great Barn', Jordan had sat aside from the two men. As always in the presence of others he was unobtrusive and self-effacing, taking the notes that Mr Rhodes dictated, supplying a figure or a fact only when it was demanded, and then with his voice kept low, the natural lilt and music of his rich tenor subdued.

Mr Rhodes had jumped up from his seat on the box against

the wall of the cottage and begun to pace, with that sudden excitable and voluble mood upon him.

'I have had a thought, Baker. I want there to be a theme for the place, something which is essentially me, which will be my motif long after I am gone, something that when men look at it, even in a thousand years' time, they will immediately recall the name Cecil John Rhodes.'

'A diamond, perhaps?' Baker had hazarded, sketching a stylized stone on his pad.

'No, no, Baker. Do be original, man! First I have to scold you for being stingy, for trying to build me a mean little hovel and now that I have prevailed on you for magnificently barbaric size and space, you want to spoil it.'

'The bird,' said Jordan. He had spoken despite himself, and both men looked at him with surprise.

'What did you say, Jordan?'

'The bird, Mr Rhodes. The stone bird. I think that should be your motif.'

Rhodes stared at him for a moment, and then punched his big fist into the palm of his left hand.

'That's it, Baker. The bird, sketch it for me. Sketch it now.'

So the bird had become the spirit of Groote Schuur. There was barely one of the huge cavernous rooms without its frieze or carved door jambs depicting it, even the bath, eleven tons of chiselled and polished granite was adorned at its four corners with the image of the falcon.

The original statue had been shipped down from Kimberley, and a special niche prepared for it high above the baronial entrance hall, from where it stared down blindly upon everyone who came through the massive teak front doors of the mansion.

On this morning they had ridden out even earlier than usual, for Mr Rhodes had slept badly and had summoned Jordan from his small bedroom down the corridor.

It was cold. A vindictive wind came down off the mountains of the Hottentots Holland and as they took the path up towards the private zoo, Jordan looked back. Across the wide Cape flats he saw the snow on the distant peaks turning pink and gold in the early light.

Mr Rhodes was in a morose mood, silent and heavy in the saddle, his collar pulled up over his ears, and the broad hat jammed down to meet it. Jordan surreptitiously pushed his own mount level and studied his face.

Rhodes was still in his thirties, and yet this morning he looked fifteen years older. He took no notice of the first unseasonal flush of blue plumbago blooms beside the path, though on another morning he would have exclaimed with delight, for they were his favourite flowers. He did not stop at the zoo to watch the lions fed, but turned up into the forest; and on the prow of land that led to the steeper cliffs of the flat-topped massif they dismounted.

At this distance the thatched roof of Groote Schuur with its twirling barley-corn turrets looked like a fairy castle – but Rhodes looked beyond it.

'I feel like a racehorse,' he said suddenly. 'Like a thoroughbred Arab with the heart and the will and the need to run, but there is a dark horseman upon my back that checks me with a harsh curb of iron or pricks me with a cruel spur.' He rubbed his closed eyes with thumb and forefinger, and then massaged his cheeks as though to set the blood coursing in them again. 'He was with me again last night, Jordan. Long ago I fled from England to this land and I thought I had eluded him, but he is back in the saddle. His name is Death, Jordan, and he will give me so little time.' He pressed his hand to his chest, fingers spread as though to slow the racing of his damaged heart. 'There is so little time, Jordan. I must hurry.' He turned and took the hand from his heart and placed it on Jordan's shoulder. His expression became tender, a small sad smile touched his white lips. 'How I envy you, my boy – for you will see it all and I shall not.'

At that moment Jordan thought his own heart might break and, seeing his expression, Rhodes lifted his hand and touched his cheek.

'It's all too short, Jordan, life and glory – even love – it's all too short.'He turned back to his horse. 'Come, there is work to do.'

As they rode out of the forest, the course of that mercurial mind had changed again. Death had been pushed aside and he said suddenly:

'We shall have to square him, Jordan. I know he is your father – but we shall have to square him. Think about it and let me have your thoughts, but remember time is running short and we cannot move without him.'

The road over the neck between the main massif of Table Mountain and Signal Hill was well travelled and Jordan passed twenty coaches or more before he reached the top, but it was another two hours' ride beyond that and the road became steadily less populous, until at last it was a lonely deserted track which led into one of the ravines in the mountainside.

In this winter season the protea bushes on the slopes beyond the sprawling thatched building were drab and their blooms had withered and browned on the branches. The waterfall that smoked down off the mountain polished the rocks black and cold, and the spray dripped from the clustering trees about the pool.

However, the cottage had a neat cared-for look. The thatch had recently been renewed. It was still bright gold, and the thick walls had been whitewashed. With relief Jordan saw smoke curling from the chimney stack. His father was at home.

He knew that the property had once belonged to the old hunter and explorer Tom Harkness, and that his father had purchased it with £150 of his royalties from *A Hunter's Odyssey*. A sentimental gesture perhaps – for old Tom had been the one who had encouraged and counselled Zouga Ballantyne on his first expedition to Zambezia.

Jordan dismounted and hitched the big glossy hunter from the stables of Groote Schuur to the rail below the verandah, and he walked to the front steps.

He glanced at the pillar of blue marbled stone that stood at the head of the steps like a sentinel, and a little shadow flitted over his face as he remembered the fateful day that Ralph had hacked it out of the Devil's Own claims and brought it to the surface.

It was the only thing that remained to any of them from all those years of labour and travail. He wondered not only that his father had transported it so far with so much effort, but that he had placed it so prominently to rebuke him.

For a moment he laid his hand upon the stone, and he felt the faint satiny bloom that other hands had made on the same spot on the surface, like the marks of worshippers' hands on a holy relic. Perhaps Zouga also touched it every time he passed. Jordan dropped his hand and called towards the shuttered cottage.

'Is anybody there?'

There was a commotion in the front room, and the front door burst open.

'Jordan, my Jordie!' howled Jan Cheroot, and came bounding down the steps. His cap of peppercorn hair was pure white at last, but his eyes were bright and the web of wrinkles around them had not deepened.

He embraced Jordan with the wiry strength of brown arms; but even from the advantage of the verandah step he did not reach to Jordan's chin.

'So tall, Jordie,' he chuckled. 'Whoever thought you'd grow so tall, my little Jordie.'

He hopped back and stared up into Jordan's face. 'Look at you, I bet a guinea to a baboon turd that you've broken a few hearts already.'

'Not as many as you have.' Jordan pulled him close again, and hugged him.

'I had a start,' Jan Cheroot admitted, and then grinned wickedly. 'And I've still got the wind left for a sprint or two.'

'I was afraid that you and Papa might still be away.'

'We got home three days ago.'

'Where is Papa?'

'Jordan!'

The familiar, beloved voice made him start and he broke from Jan Cheroot's embrace and looked beyond him to Zouga Ballantyne standing in the doorway of the cottage.

He had never seen his father looking so well. It was not merely that he was lean and hard and sun-browned. He seemed to stand taller and straighter with an easy set to his shoulders, so different from the defeated slump with which he had left the diamond fields.

'Jordan!' he said again, and they came together and shook hands, and Jordan studied his father's face at closer range.

The pride and the purpose that had been burnt away in the diamond pit had returned, but with their quality subtly changed. Now he had the look of a man who had worked out the terms on which he was prepared to live. There were the shadows of a new thoughtfulness in his green eyes, the weight of understanding and compassion in his gaze. Here was a man who had tested himself almost to the point of destruction, had explored the frontiers of his soul and found them secure.

'Jordan,' he said again quietly for the third time, and then he did something that demonstrated the profound change he had undergone. He leaned forward and briefly he pressed the soft golden curls of his beard to Jordan's cheek.

'I have thought of you often,' he said without embarrassment. 'Thank you for coming.' Then with his arm about his shoulders he ushered Jordan into the front room.

This room always pleased Jordan, and he moved across to the log fire in the walk-in hearth and held out his hands to the blaze while he looked about him. It was a man's room – shelves filled with men's books, encyclopaedias and almanacs and thick leatherbound volumes of travel and exploration.

Weapons hung upon the walls, bows and quivers of poisoned Bushman arrows, shields and assegais of Matabele and Zulu, and, of course, the tools of the trade to which Zouga had reverted, firearms, heavy calibre sporting rifles by famous gunsmiths, Gibbs, Holland and Holland, Westley Richards. They were racked on the wall facing the fireplace, blued steel and lovingly carved wood.

With them were the souvenirs and trophies of Zouga's work, horns of antelope and buffalo, twisting or curved or straight as a lance, the zig-zag stripes of a zebra hide, the tawny gold bushed mane of the Kalahari lion, and ivory, great yellow arcs reaching higher than a man's head, yellow as fresh butter and translucent as candlewax in the cold winter light from the doorway.

'You had a good trip?' Jordan asked, and Zouga shrugged.

'It gets more difficult each season to find good specimens for my clients.'

His clients were rich and aristocratic sportsmen, come out to Africa for the chase.

'But at least the Americans seem to have discovered Africa at last. I have a good party booked for next season – young fellow called Roosevelt, Secretary of the Navy.' He broke off. 'Yes, we are managing to keep body and soul together, old Jan Cheroot and I – but I don't have to ask about you.'

He glanced down at the expensive English cloth of Jordan's suit, the soft leather of his riding boots which creased perfectly around his ankles like the bellows of a concertina, the solid silver spurs and the gold watch chain in his fob pocket – and then his eye paused on the white sparkle of the diamond in his cravat.

'You made the right choice when you decided to go with

Rhodes. My God, how that man's star rises higher and brighter with each passing day.'

'He is a great man, Papa.'

'Or a great rogue.' Then Zouga smiled apologetically. 'I am sorry, I know how highly you think of him. Let's have a glass of sherry, Jordie, while Jan Cheroot makes lunch for us.' He smiled again. 'We miss your cooking. You will find it poor fare, I'm afraid.'

While he poured sweet Cape sherry into long glasses, he asked over his shoulder:

'And Ralph, what do you hear of Ralph?'

'We meet often in Kimberley or at the railhead. He always asks after you.'

'How is he?'

'He will be a big man, Papa. Already his wagons run to Pilgrims' Rest and those new goldfields on the Witwatersrand. He has just won the fast coach contract from Algoa Bay. He has trading posts at Tati and on the Shashi river.'

They ate in front of the fire, sour bread and cheese, a cold joint of mutton and a black bottle of Constantia wine, and Jan Cheroot hovered over Jordan, scolding him fondly for his appetite and recharging his glass when it was barely a quarter empty.

At last they finished and stretched out their legs towards the fire, while Jan Cheroot brought a burning taper to light the cigars which Jordan produced from a gold pocket case.

Jordan spoke through the perfumed wreaths of smoke.

'Papa, the concession –' And for the first time an angry arrowhead creased the skin between Zouga's eyes.

'I had hoped that you came to see us,' he said coldly. 'I keep forgetting that you are Rhodes' man, ahead of being my son.'

'I am both,' Jordan contradicted him evenly. 'That's why I can talk to you like this.'

'What message has the famous Mr Rhodes for me this time?' Zouga demanded.

'Maund and Selous have both accepted his offers. They have sold their concessions to Mr Rhodes, and both are ten thousand pounds richer.'

Maund was a soldier and an adventurer. Fred Selous, like Zouga, a hunter and explorer. Also, like Zouga, Selous had written a well-received book on the African chase *A Hunter's Wanderings in Africa*. Both of these men had at different times prevailed on Lobengula to grant them concessions to ivory and minerals in his eastern dominions.

'Mr Rhodes wants me to point out to you that both the Maund and Selous concessions are over the same territory as the concession that Mzilikazi granted to you. He owns both of them now – the validity of all the treaties is hopelessly confused and hazy.'

'The Ballantyne concession was granted first – by Mzilikazi; the ones that followed have no force,' snapped Zouga.

'Mr Rhodes' lawyers have advised –'

'Damn Mr Rhodes and his lawyers. Damn them all to hell.'

Jordan dropped his eyes and was silent, and after a long pause Zouga sighed and stood up. He went to the yellow wood cupboard and took out a stained and dog-eared document, so ragged that it had been pasted onto a backing to prevent it falling to pieces.

The ink had faded to brown, but the script was bold and spiky, the hand of an arrogant and cocksure young man.

The document was headed:

EXCLUSIVE CONCESSION TO MINE GOLD AND HUNT IVORY
IN THE
SOVEREIGN TERRITORY OF MATABELELAND

And at its foot was a crude wax seal with the image of a bull elephant, and the words:

NKOSI NKHULU – GREAT KING

Below it a shaky cross in the same faded ink:

MZILIKAZI – *his mark*

Zouga laid the document on the table between them, and they both stared at it.

'All right,' Zouga capitulated. 'What do Mr Rhodes' lawyers advise?'

'That this concession could be set aside on five separate points of law.'

'I would fight him.'

'Papa. He is a determined man. His influence is enormous. He will be Prime Minister of the Cape Parliament at the next session, there is little doubt of that.' Jordan touched the red wax seal. 'His fortune is vast, perhaps ten million pounds –'

'Still I will fight him,' Zouga said, and then stopped Jordan speaking with a hand on his arm. 'Jordan, don't you understand. A man must have something, a dream, a light to follow in the darkness. I can never sell this, it has been all of my life for too long. Without it I shall have nothing.'

'Papa –'

'I know what you will say, that I can never make this into reality. I do not have the money it would need. You might even say that I no longer even have the strength of purpose. But, Jordan, while I have this piece of paper I can still hope, I still have my dream to follow. I can never sell it.'

'I told him that, and he understood immediately. He wants you to be a part of it.'

Zouga lifted his head and stared at his son.

'A seat on the Board of Governors of the company for which Mr Rhodes will petition a Royal Charter from Her Majesty. Then you will have grants of farm land, gold claims, and an active command in the field. Don't you see, Papa, he is not taking your dream away from you, he is making it come true at last.'

The silence drew out, a log crumbled and crashed softly in the hearth; sparks shot up and the flare lit Zouga's face.

'When will he see me?' he asked.

'We can be at Groote Schuur in four hours' ride.'

'It will be dark by then.'

'There are fifteen bedrooms for you to choose from,' Jordan smiled, and Zouga laughed like a man who has been given back all the excitement and eagerness of youth.

'Then why are we sitting here?' he asked. 'Jan Cheroot, bring my heavy coat.'

Zouga strode out onto the verandah of the cottage, and on the top step he checked and reached out with his right hand to the pillar of blue stone. He touched it with a strangely formal caress, and with the same hand touched his own lips and forehead, the gesture with which an Arab greets an old friend.

Then Zouga glanced at Jordan, and smiled.

'Superstition,' he explained. 'Good luck.'

'Good luck?' Jan Cheroot snorted from below the steps where

he held Zouga's horse. 'Damn stone – all the way from Kimberley, trip over the thundering rubbish.' He went on muttering to himself as Zouga mounted.

'Jan Cheroot would pine away if he didn't have something to complain about.' Zouga winked at Jordan, and they trotted out from under the milkwood trees onto the track.

'I often think back to that day when we hit the blue,' Jordan said. 'If we had only known!'

'How could we know?'

'It was I – I feel sure of that. It was I who convinced you that the blue ground was barren.'

'Jordan, you were only a boy.'

'But I was supposed to be the diviner of diamonds. If I had not been so certain that it was dead ground, you would never have sold the Devil's Own.'

'I never sold it. I gambled it away.'

'Only because you thought it was worthless. You would never have accepted Mr Rhodes' bet if you had known that the blue was not the end – but only the beginning.'

'Nobody knew that, not then.'

'Mr Rhodes sensed it. He never lost faith. He knew what the blue was. He knew it with a certain instinct that nobody else had.'

'I have never been back to Kimberley, Jordie.' Zouga settled down in the saddle, riding with long stirrups like a Boer hunter. 'I never wanted to go back, but of course the news filters down the line of rail. I heard that when Rhodes and Barnato made their deal, they valued the Devil's Own claims at half a million pounds.'

'They were the keys to the field,' Jordie explained. 'It just happened that they were the central claims in the main enrichment. But you could never have guessed that, Papa.'

'Strange how right one man's instincts can be,' Zouga brooded. 'And how wrong another man's. I always *knew*, or thought I knew, that my road to the north began in that hole, that terrible hole.'

'Perhaps it still does. The money to take us all to the north will still come from it. Mr Rhodes' millions.'

'Tell me about the blue. You have been with Rhodes through it all. Tell me about it.'

'It changes,' Jordan said. 'It's as simple as that, it alters.'

Zouga shook his head. 'It's like some sort of miracle.'

'Yes,' Jordan nodded. 'Diamonds are nature's beautiful miracles. I'll never forget my own astonishment when Mr Rhodes showed it to me. That hard blue rock is unyielding as any granite when it comes out of the earth, and yet after it has been laid out in the stacking fields for a year or two it starts to crumble. It's the sunlight, we think, that does it. It crumbles up like a loaf of stale bread – and the diamonds, oh Papa, the diamonds. Incredible stones, eleven thousand carats of diamonds each day. The blue is the mother lode, the blue is the heart.' He broke off in embarrassment. 'Sometimes I run away with myself,' he confessed, and Zouga smiled with him. Who could resist this beautiful young man, that was the word to describe him – not handsome, not good-looking, but beautiful, with a quality of gentleness and goodness that seemed to form an aura about him.

'Papa.' Jordan sobered. 'Oh Papa, you will never know how happy I am that you are to be part of it, after all. You and Mr Rhodes.'

'Mr Rhodes,' Zouga thought indulgently. 'Always Mr Rhodes. And yet it's a good thing for a young man to have a hero. Pity this poor world of ours when the last hero passes.'

Can you judge a man by his books? Zouga wondered.

The library was choked with them. One complete wall packed to the ceiling with the sources and references which Gibbon had consulted for his *Decline and Fall*. So impressed had Rhodes been with this work that he had ordered Hatchards of London to collect and, if necessary, translate and bind the complete authorities. Jordan said it had cost him £8,000 thus far, and was not yet complete.

Ranked beside this formidable array were all the published lives of Alexander, of Julius Caesar and of Napoleon. What dreams of empire they must sustain. Zouga smiled inwardly as he listened to the high hypnotic voice of the burly figure with the flushed swollen face as he sat behind the vast desk into whose panels were chiselled the stylized figures of the bird, the falcon of Zimbabwe.

'You are an Englishman, Ballantyne, a man of honour and

dedication; these things have always attracted me to you.' He was irresistible, able to conjure up a gamut of emotions with a few words, and Zouga smiled at himself again. He was in danger of the same hero worship as his own son.

'I want you even more than this concession of yours. You understand, you know what it is we seek, not merely wealth and personal aggrandizement. No, no, it is something beyond that, something sacred.'

Then he came to it abruptly, without flourish.

'There,' Rhodes said. 'You know what I need – you and your concession. What do you want from me in return?'

'What task will I perform?' Zouga asked.

'Good.' Rhodes nodded the untidy leonine head. 'Glory before gold. You please me, Ballantyne – but to business. I had thought to ask you to lead the occupying expedition, to guide it over the ground you know so well – but other men can do something as simple as that. I shall let Selous do it. I have something more important for you. You will be my alter-ego at the kraal of the Matabele king. The savages know and respect you, you speak their language, know their customs, you are a soldier, I have read your military paper on the tribe – and we must not deceive ourselves, Ballantyne, it may come to a military option. Few other men can do all these things, have all these qualities.'

They stared at each other across the desk, both men leaning forward, and then Rhodes spoke again.

'I am not a mean man, Ballantyne. Do the job for me and you can name your rewards. Money, ten thousand pounds – land, each land grant will be four thousand acres – gold claims, each will be five hundred yards square. How many shall we say – five of each – ten thousand pounds in cash, twenty thousand acres of prime land of your choice, five claims on the rich gold reef over which you shot the great elephant that you described in *Hunter's Odyssey*. What do you say, Ballantyne?'

'Ten of each,' said Zouga. 'Ten thousand pounds, ten land grants, ten gold claims.'

'Done!' Rhodes slapped the desk. 'Write it down, Jordan, write it down. But what of your salary while you are agent at Lobengula's kraal? Two thousand, four thousand per annum? I am not a mean man, Ballantyne.'

'And I am not a greedy one.'

'Four thousand, then – and we are all agreed, so we can go to lunch.'

Zouga stayed five days at Groote Schuur, days of talking and planning and listening.

It amused him to see the legend dispelled. The idea of Rhodes as a solitary and brooding man – withdrawn to some high Olympus where other men could not follow, was proved to be a myth.

For Rhodes surrounded himself with men; there was not a meal at which less than fifteen sat to his generous board. What men they were, clever or rich or both, belted earls or farm-born Boers, politicians and financiers, judges and soldiers. And if they were not wealthy, they were powerful or useful or merely amusing. At one dinner there was even a poet, a bespectacled little shrimp of a man on passage from Indian Service back to England. Jordan had read his *Plain Tales from the Hills* and secured an invitation for him, and despite his appearance, the company was quite taken with him. Rhodes invited him to return and write about Africa: 'The future is here, young Kipling, and we shall need a poet to sing it for us.'

Men by the dozen, and never a woman. Rhodes refused to have a woman servant in the house. There was not even a painting of a woman on the walls.

And the taciturn, brooding figure of legend never stopped talking. From the back of a horse as they rode through the estate, striding over the lawns with his clumsy unco-ordinated gait, seated behind the teak desk or at the head of the long, laden dining-table, he talked. Figures and facts and estimates poured from him without reference to notes, other than an occasional glance at Jordan for confirmation. Then came the ideas, fateful, ludicrous, prophetic, fascinating or fantastic – but never-ending.

To a visiting member of the British Parliament: 'We have to make a practical tie with the old country, for future generations will be born beyond its shores; it must be useful, physical and rewarding for both, or we shall drift apart.'

To an American senator: 'We could hold Parliament for five years in Westminster and for the next five in Washington.'

To a rival financier who enviously sniped at his monopoly of the diamond industry: 'Without me, the price of diamonds would not make it worthwhile turning over a stone to pick one up. Kimberley would revert to desert and thirty thousand would starve.'

When they began to plan the grand expedition to the north, Zouga had imagined that Rhodes would concern himself with each detail. He was wrong.

He defined the objective: 'We need a document from Lobengula, ratifying and consolidating all these grants into a single concession, that I can take to London.' Then he picked the man. 'Rudd, you have the legal mind.' And gave him *carte blanche*. 'Go and do it. Take Jordan with you. He speaks the language. Take anyone else you need.'

Then to Zouga: 'We need an occupying force, small enough to move fast, large enough to protect itself against Matabele treachery. Ballantyne, that will be your first concern. Let me know what you decide, but remember there is little time.'

What might have taken another man six months, was accomplished in five days, and when Zouga left Groote Schuur, Jordan rode with him as far as the neck of the mountain. The wind had gone up into the north-west, and then came down like a ravenous beast, roaring dully against the crags of the mountain and bringing in cold, steely-grey rain squalls off the Atlantic.

It could not blunt their spirits, and although their wind-driven oilskins flogged their bodies and the horses shivered and drooped their ears, they shouted above the wind.

'Isn't he a great man? Every minute spent in his company is like a draught of fine wine, intoxicating with excitement. He is so generous.'

'Though he is the one who profits most from his generosity,' Zouga laughed.

'That's mean, Papa.'

'A saint does not make such a fortune in so short a time. But if anybody can do this thing, then it is Rhodes, and for that I will follow him into hell itself.'

'Let's pray that won't be necessary.'

At the top of the pass the wind was stronger still, and Jordan had to turn his horse in until their knees touched.

'Papa, the column – the occupying column. There is one person who has the wagons, who knows the route, can requisition the supplies and recruit the men.'

'Who is that, Jordie?'

'Ralph.'

Zouga watched Jordan ride back down the pass, towards the wind-darkened waters of Table Bay and the sprawling white buildings that clung to the lower slopes of the mountain under the dingy scudding sky. Then he turned his own mount into the wind and went down the other side.

The excitement stayed with him. He realized that it was Rhodes' particular genius to awaken this feeling in men around him. Even though there were quicksands ahead in which he knew he might soon be engulfed, the enthusiasm and quickness of spirit persisted.

Ten land grants meant forty thousand acres of land, but it would take more than £10,000 to hold it. Homestead and wells and fences to build, cattle to stock it, men to work it – all that would cost money, a great deal of money.

The gold claims – he could not even begin to imagine how much it might cost to transport stamp mills and sluice boxes from the railhead. Of course, for lack of money to exploit them, he would have to pass by a hundred opportunities that the new land would offer. In the beginning the land grants of other men would be for sale at bargain prices, hundreds of thousands of acres of the land that he had always thought of as his own, and because he did not have the money, it would go to others.

None of this could break the mood, not the cold rain in his face that numbed his cheeks, not the realization that his dream was still merely a dream. For now at last they were on the move at the breakneck pace set by an impatient man – towards the realization of that dream. So Zouga could lift his chin and sit up straight in the saddle, ignoring the icy snakes of rainwater that wriggled down inside his collar, buoyed high above mundane doubts by the gambler's certainty that at last his luck had changed, the dice were hot for him and every time he rolled the aces would flash like spearheads.

The sheets of rain hid the cottage from Zouga until he turned in under the milkwood grove; then a fluke of the wind opened the slanting silver sheets of water, and his mood popped like a bubble.

He had been mistaken, his luck had not changed, it had all been words and illusion, the caravan of his misfortunes rolled on unchecked – for before him his home was partially destroyed.

One of the ancient milkwoods, weary of resisting the gales of a hundred winters, had succumbed at last; it had come crashing down across the front of the cottage. The roof had given under the blow, and sagged in. The supports of the verandah had shattered and a tangle of fallen roof beams and milkwood branches blocked the front entrance. The living-room would be swamped with rain – his books, his papers.

Appalled at the havoc, he dismounted and stood before it, and his spirits slid further. He felt his ribs constricting his breathing and dread uncoiled in his guts like an awakening serpent. It was the superstitious terror of one who has offended the gods.

The pillar of blue marbled rock that he had set to guard his threshold had been thrown down. It lay half under the tumbled thatch with the shattered verandah support beside it. Once it had been hard and smooth as granite, but the sunlight and the air had rotted it and the fall had shattered it like chalk.

Zouga went down on one knee and touched a rough, irregular lump of the smashed blue ground. The destruction of his home was as nothing. This was the only one of his possessions that was irreplaceable, and the omen of its destruction struck frost into the secret places of his soul.

Almost as a chorus to his dread, a fresh rain squall came booming down the valley, thrashing the trees and ripping at the scattered thatch. Rain beat down onto the broken surface of the rock he was touching, and at Zouga's fingertips there was a tiny burst of white lightning, so dazzling, so searing, that it seemed it could flay the skin from his finger as he touched it. But it was cold, cold as a crystal of Arctic ice.

It had never been exposed to the light of day, not once in the two hundred million years since it had assumed its present form, and yet it seemed in itself to be a drop of distilled sunlight.

Zouga had never seen anything so beautiful, nor touched anything so sensual – for it was the beacon and the lodestone of his life. It made all the striving and the heartbreak seem worthwhile, it was justification for the years he had believed squandered, it exonerated his once firmly held belief that his road to the north began in the gaping chasm of De Beers New Rush.

With hands that shook like those of a very old man, he fumbled open the blade of his clasp knife and gently prised that rainbow of light from its niche in the shattered blue rock, and held it up before his own eyes.

'The Ballantyne diamond,' he whispered, and staring into its limpid liquid depths like a sorcerer into his divining ball of crystal, he saw light and shadow ripple and change and in his imagination become vistas of enchanted pastures rich with sweet grass; he saw slow herds of cattle and the headgear of winding wheels of fabulous gold mines spinning against a high blue sky.

They didn't expect him. He came so swiftly that no runner brought word ahead of him. He had left Rudd and the rest of the party to follow from the Shashi and ridden on ahead, leading two spare horses and changing as soon as the mount beneath him tired. The horses were the pick of De Beers' stables, and it took him five days from the frontier of Matabeleland to Khami Mission.

'I'm Jordan Ballantyne,' he said, and looked down on the family that had hastily assembled on the front verandah of the Mission. The siege was over without a shot fired; he walked in with his curls shining and that warm, almost shy, smile on his lips, and took their hearts, every one of them, by storm.

The gifts he brought had been chosen with obvious care, and spoke of a knowledge of each of them and their individual needs.

There were two dozen packets of seeds for Clinton – unusual vegetables and rare herbs – comfrey and okra, horseradish and turmeric, shallot and sou-sou. For Robyn a box of medicines, which included a bottle of chloroform, and a folding wallet of shiny, sharp surgical instruments.

The latest volume of Tennyson's poetry for Salina, a pair of marvellous lifelike china dogs with moving eyes for the twins, and for Cathy the best of all, a box of oil paints, a bundle of brushes, and a letter from Ralph.

In the first week, while he waited for Rudd and the rest of the party to come up from the Shashi, Jordan used a green twig to divine water, an art that Clinton had never acquired, and helped him dig the new well. They hit clear, sweet water ten feet down. He recited to Cathy a biography of Ralph from the day and hour of his birth, which was so minutely detailed that it took instalments over the entire week to complete, while she listened with a fixed avidity.

He rolled up his sleeves and from the black wood-burning stove produced a flow of culinary phenomena – quenelles and soufflés, croques-en-bouche and meringues, sauces both Hollandaise and Béarnaise – and while Salina hovered near him, eager to learn and help, he quoted to her the entire 'In Memoriam' of Alfred Lord Tennyson, from memory:

'So fret not, like an idle girl,
That life is dash'd with flecks of sin.
Abide: thy wealth is gathered in,
When Time hath sunder'd shell from pearl.'

And she was utterly enchanted by his golden spell.

He showed the twins how to cut and fold from a piece of newspaper all manner of fantastic bird and animal shapes, and he told stories that were the best they had heard since Mungo St John had left Khami.

For Robyn he had the latest news from the Cape. He was able to describe for her the rising stars on the political horizon, and categorize their strengths and weaknesses. He had the latest assessments of the political scene at home. Members of both Houses of Parliament, Cape and home, were constant guests at Groote Schuur, so he could repeat the gossip of that 'wild and incomprehensible old man', as the Queen had called Gladstone. He could explain the Home Rule issue and tell her what the odds were for a Liberal victory at the next election, even after Gladstone's failure to rescue Gordon from Khartoum and his consequential loss of popularity.

'At the Queen's Jubilee the common people on the pavements cheered him, but the aristocracy hissed him from the balconies,' he told her.

For Robyn, this was nectar to a woman lost over twenty years in the wilderness.

Dinners at Khami usually finished by the fall of dark, and the family was abed an hour later, but after Jordan's arrival, the talk and laughter sometimes lasted until midnight.

'Jordan, there is no doubt that if we want Mashonaland, we shall have to square your aunt. I hear that Lobengula will not make a major decision without Dr Codrington. I want you to go on ahead of Rudd and the others. Go to Khami and talk to your aunt.' That had been Mr Rhodes' parting injunction to him, and Jordan's conscience found no conflict between this duty and his family loyalties.

Again and again in that week Jordan returned to extol Mr Rhodes to Robyn, his integrity and sincerity, his vision of a world at peace and united under one sovereign power.

Instinctively he knew which areas of Rhodes' character to emphasize to Robyn, patriotism, charity, his sympathetic treatment of his black workers, his opposition to the Stropping Act in the Cape Parliament which, if passed, would have given employers the right to lash their black servants, and only when he judged that she was swayed to his views, did Jordan mention the concession to her. Yet, despite his preparations, her opposition was immediate and ferocious.

'Not another tribe robbed of its lands,' she cried.

'We do not want Matabeleland, Aunty. Mr Rhodes would guarantee Lobengula's sovereignty and protect him –'

'I read the letter you wrote to the *Cape Times*, Aunty, expressing your concern over the Matabele raids into Mashonaland. With the British flag flying over the Shona tribes, they would be protected by British justice.'

'The Germans and Portuguese and Belgians are gathering like vultures – you know, Aunty, that there is only one nation fit to take on the sacred trust.'

Jordan's arguments were calculated and persuasive, his manner without guile and his trust in Cecil John Rhodes touching and infectious, and he kept returning to his most poignant argument.

'Aunty, you have seen the Matabele bucks returning from Mashonaland with the blood caked on their blades and the captured Shona girls roped together. Think of the havoc that they have left behind them, the burned villages, the murdered infants and grey heads, the slaughtered Shona warriors. You cannot deny the Shona people the protection that we will offer.'

That night she spoke to Clinton, lying beside him in the darkness in the narrow cot on the hard straw-filled mattress; and his reply was immediate and simple:

'My dear, it has always been clear to me as the African sun that God has prepared this continent for the protection of the only nation on earth that has the public virtue sufficient to govern it for the benefit of its native peoples.'

'Clinton, Mr Rhodes is not the British nation.'

'He is an Englishman.'

'So was Edward Teach, *alias* Blackbeard the pirate.'

They were silent for many minutes and then Robyn said suddenly:

'Clinton, have you noticed anything wrong with Salina?'

His concern was immediate. 'Is she sickening?'

'I'm afraid so, incurably. I think she is in love.'

'Good gracious.' He sat abruptly upright in the bed. 'Who on earth is she in love with?'

'How many young men are there at Khami at the present time?'

In the morning, on the way to her clinic in the church, she stopped at the kitchen. The previous evening Clinton had slaughtered a pig, and now Salina and Jordan were making sausages. He was turning the handle of the mincing machine while she forced lumps of pork into the funnel. They were so absorbed, chatting so gaily together, that while Robyn stood in the doorway watching them they were unaware of her presence.

They made a beautiful couple, so beautiful indeed, that Robyn felt a sense of unreality as she watched them, and it was followed immediately by uneasiness, nothing in life was that perfect.

Salina saw her, and started – and then unaccountably blushed so that her pixie pointed ears glowed.

'Oh Mama, you startled me.'

Robyn felt a rush of empathy, and, strangely, of envy for her eldest daughter. She wished that she were still capable of that pure and innocent emotion, and suddenly she had the contrasting image of Mungo St John, lean and scarred and unscrupulous, and what she felt shocked her so her voice was brusque.

'Jordan, I have made up my mind. When Mr Rudd arrives, I will go with you to Lobengula's kraal, and I will speak for your case.'

After a prolonged and unprofitable trading expedition as far as the Zambezi, Mungo had returned with Louise to the kraal at

GuBulawayo, where they were kept almost seven months. But Lobengula's procrastinations worked in Mungo St John's favour.

Robyn Codrington had refused to speak to the king on Mungo's behalf, and consequently he was only one among dozens of white concession-seekers camped around Lobengula's royal kraal.

The king would not have let Mungo leave, even if he had wanted to. He seemed to enjoy talking to him, and listened eagerly to Mungo's accounts of the American War and of Mungo's sea voyages. Every week or so he would summon Mungo to an audience and question him through his interpreter, for hours at a time.

The destructive power of cannon fascinated him, and he demanded detailed descriptions of sundered walls and human bodies blown to nothingness. The sea was another source of intense interest, and he tried to grasp the immensity of waters and the blast of storm and gale across it. However, when Mungo delicately hinted at a land grant and trading concession, Lobengula smiled and sent him away.

'I will call for you again, One Bright Eye, when I have thought on it more heavily. Now is there aught you lack in food or drink? I will send my women to your camp with it.'

Once he gave Mungo permission to go out into the hunting veld so long as he stayed south of the Shangani river and killed neither elephant nor hippopotamus. On this expedition Mungo shot a huge cock ostrich and salted and dried the skin with its magnificent plumage intact.

On three other occasions the king allowed him to return to Khami Mission Station when Mungo complained that his leg was paining him. Mungo's predatory instinct was that Robyn Codrington was disturbed and excited by these returns, and each time he was able to draw out the visit for days, gradually consolidating his position with her so that when he again asked her to intercede with Lobengula on his behalf, she actually thought about it for a full day before refusing once more.

'I cannot set a cat upon a mouse, General St John.'

'Madam, I freed my own slaves many years ago.'

'When you were forced to,' she agreed. 'But who will control you here in Matabeleland?'

'You, Robyn, and gladly would I submit to that.'

She had flushed and turned her face away from him to hide the colour.

'Your familiarity is presumptuous, sir.' And she had left him so that he could keep his revived assignations under the lead-wood tree with the twins. His absence since those first encounters in his convalescence had not dimmed their fascination for him. They had become invaluable allies. Nobody else could have extracted from Juba the vital information he needed for his planning. Mungo had expressed doubts as to the existence of the diamonds, and declared that he would only be convinced if the twins could tell him where Lobengula kept the treasure.

Juba never suspected danger from such an innocent pair, and in the late afternoon, when she had drunk a gallon pot of her own famous brew, she was always genial and garrulous.

'Ningi keeps the diamonds under her sleeping place,' Vicky informed Mungo.

'Who is Ningi?'

'The king's sister, and she is almost as fat as King Ben is.'

Ningi would be the most trusted of all Lobengula's people – and her hut in the sanctuary of the forbidden women's quarters was the most secure in all Matabeleland.

'I believe you now. You are clever girls, both of you,' Mungo told them, and they glowed with pleasure. There was nothing he could not ask of them.

'Vicky, I need some paint. It's for a secret thing, I will tell you about it later, if you can get the paint for me.'

'What colour?' Lizzie cut in. 'I'll get it for you.'

'Red, white and yellow.'

In the end Lizzie stood guard while Vicky raided Cathy's paintbox, and they delivered their offering to Mungo and basked in his extravagant praise.

In his planning, it was not enough merely to get the diamonds into his hands; even more vital was to escape the consequences. No man or woman could hope to reach the frontier without the king's permission; it was hundreds of miles of wild country patrolled by the border impis. He could not grab and run. He had to use guile and perhaps turn the Matabele dread of darkness and witchcraft to his own advantage.

So he planned with meticulous concentration, and waited for the right moment with the patience of the stalking leopard, for he knew that this was his last attempt. If he failed this time, then not even his white skin nor his status as a guest of the king could save him.

If he failed, the Black Ones would wield their knobkerries, crushing in his skull – and his corpse would be flung from the cliffs to the waiting vultures or into the flooded river pools where the crocodiles would rip it into chunks with their spiky yellow saurian teeth. Louise would suffer the same fate, he knew, but it was a chance he was prepared to take.

He was careful to conceal his preparations from her – and this was made easier by the distance that she had for long now been maintaining between them. Though they shared the thatched hut that Lobengula's men had built for them in the grove beyond the royal kraal, and though they ate the same meals of beef and sour milk and stone-ground maize cakes that the king sent down to them each evening, Louise spent her days alone, riding out on one of the mules in the early morning and not returning until dusk. Her mattress of straw in the farthest recesses of the hut she had screened with the tattered canvas sunshade from the cart, and he only once tried to pass the screen.

'Not again,' she hissed at him. 'Never again!' And she showed him the knife that she kept under her skirts.

So he was able to work uninterrupted, during the day, and to hide his equipment under his own mattress each evening. He carved the mask from the naturally curved portion of a hollow tree trunk, a hideous grimacing ape-like visage with staring eyes and a gaping mouth full of white fangs – and he painted it with the colours from Cathy's paintbox.

From the plumed ostrich skin he tailored a cloak that reached from neck to ankles, and for his feet and hands he made grotesque mittens of black goatskin. In full costume he was enough to paralyse even the bravest warrior with supernatural terror. He was the very embodiment of the *Tokoloshe* of Matabele mythology.

Robyn Codrington had given him repeated doses of laudanum for the persisting pain in his leg, but he had saved these for the occasion. He had decided on one of the Matabele festivals, and he waited until the third night when every man and woman of the entire nation, surfeited with beer and three days and nights of wild dancing, had fallen asleep where they fell.

At nightfall he gave the laudanum to Louise in a cup of soured milk, and the tart flavour concealed the musky taste of the drug.

An hour after dark he crept across the hut, drew aside the screen and listened to her even breathing for a minute before leaning over her and slapping her cheeks lightly. She did not move nor murmur, and the rhythm of her breathing did not alter.

He dressed swiftly in the feather cloak, not yet donning the mask and mittens – but blackening his face and limbs with a mixture of crushed charcoal and fat. Then with the mask and a length of rope under one arm and a heavy assegai in the other hand, he crept out of the hut.

The grove was deserted, no Matabele would venture here when the spirits were abroad, so he hurried through it – and from the treeline surveyed the stockade of the royal kraal.

There was a sliver of the old moon rising, and it gave just enough light for him to pick his way, but not enough to betray him to watchful eyes. There would be few eyes open on this night. Even so he crouched low as he crossed the open ground; the cloak made a shaggy hyena shape that would excite no real interest.

At the outer stockade he paused to look and listen, then flicked the length of manila rope over the barrier of sharpened poles.

He climbed up carefully, favouring his bad leg, and peered into the kraal.

It was deserted, but a low watch-fire burned in front of the barred gateway.

Mungo slid down the rope and he crossed quickly to the shadows of the nearest hut, and there paused to pull on his mittens and settle the cumbersome mask over his head before creeping on again towards the inner stockade that guarded the women's quarters.

In the preceding weeks, using his brass telescope from the vantage point of the nearest hilltop, he had been able to see over the walls and to study the layout of the wives' quarters.

There was a double circle of huts, like the concentric rings of a target, but at the centre, the bull's-eye, was a larger hut with intricate patterns of thatch and lacing proclaiming its greater importance. His guess that this was the king's sister's residence had been confirmed when he had seen, through the telescope, Ningi's elephantine gleaming naked body, escorted by a dozen hand-maidens, emerging into the early sunlight from the low doorway.

Now he reached the gateway in the inner stockade, and studied it from around the sheltering wall of the nearest hut. Again his luck held. He had been prepared to use the assegai here, but both the guards were stretched out, wrapped in their furs, and neither of them moved as Mungo stepped over their prostrate bodies.

From inside one hut he heard the low regular snores of one fat wife, and in another a woman coughed and muttered in her sleep, but though his nerves jumped, he went on swiftly.

The door to Ningi's hut was closed. Mungo had honed the edge of the assegai to a razor edge, and with it he sawed through the fastenings of bark rope that secured the opening. The rasp and rustle of the blade sounded thunderous in his ears, and his skin prickled as he waited for a shouted challenge from within. It did not come, but he found that he was sweating as he stepped back and brought out the bladders of goats' blood from under the cloak.

He slit the bladders and splashed the stinking, congealing blood over the portals of the doorway. He had learned from the twins, who were authorities on the supernatural, that a *Tokoloshe* always spurted blood on any doorway through which it passed. It was one of the creature's more endearing characteristics.

Now with the assegai gripped in his right hand, Mungo stooped into the hut and, crouched in the doorway, he waited for his eyes to adjust to the gloom.

The fire in the centre of the large hut had burned low. There was just enough light to make out two figures curled like dogs on the sleeping-mats on each side of it – and beyond it the ponderous bulk of the princess under her furs.

Her snores started as a low grumbling like a volcano, and rose to a whistling crescendo that covered any sound Mungo might make as he slipped across to the first of the sleeping hand-maids.

Before she could stir he had slipped a gag of goat's skin into her mouth and trussed her at the ankles and wrists with a leather thong. She did not struggle, but stared up at his horrific mask with huge white eyes in the firelight. He tied and gagged the second woman before crossing to Ningi's sleeping platform.

That afternoon, as one of the king's guests, Mungo had watched Ningi sitting beside her brother and swilling pot after pot of French champagne. She went on snoring and grunting as he bound her arms and legs. Only when he thrust the gag into her gaping mouth did she snuffle and moan and come out of her alcoholic slumbers.

He rolled her off the platform and she fell with a thump to the clay floor. He dragged her across to where her bound servants lay. It was heavy work, for she weighed 300 pounds or more.

He threw a log on the fire, and when it flared he pranced and capered around his captives, thrusting his hideous mask into their faces and gibbeting at them in fiendish menace. In the firelight their sweat of fear burst out and ran in little rivulets down their bodies as they writhed and wriggled against their bonds.

Suddenly there was a spluttering explosive rush as Ningi voided her bowels with sheer terror, and the hot stink of faeces filled the hut. Mungo threw a fur kaross over them and immediately they were still, their grunts and muffled groans ceased.

He moved quickly then. Returning to the sleeping platform he threw the furs aside, and found a pallet of woven bamboo. It lifted like a trap door, and in the low recess below it were a dozen small clay pots.

His hands began to shake as he reached for one and lifted it out of the recess. His own sweat half blinded him – but through his blurred vision he saw the soapy gleam of reflected firelight in the mouth of the pot.

He could not take it all, there was too much for him to carry and too much for him later to conceal. Moreover, his survivor's instinct warned him that the more he took the more remorseless would be the search and pursuit.

He spilled the contents of all twelve pots into a glittering heap beside the fire, and in its uncertain light made his choice of the biggest and brightest stones from the hundreds that teased him with their twinkling smiles. Thirty of them filled the leather drawstring bag he had brought with him. He tied it back at his waist, snatched up the assegai and slipped out of the hut.

The guards at the inner stockade still slept, and he passed them silently. Below the wall of the outer stockade he stripped off his cloak, mittens and mask and dropped them on the untended watch-fire. Then he heaped branches over them – there would be only ash by morning.

He went up the rope swiftly, hand over hand, and pulled it up after him. The royal kraal behind him was silent in heavy midnight stupor, and he climbed lightly down the outer wall of the stockade.

He bathed in the pool below the camp, washing off the charcoal and fat, and then found his shirt and breeches where he had left them in the hollow of a tree trunk beside the pool.

In the hut he knelt beside Louise and placed one hand, still icy cold from the pool, upon her cheek. She sighed and rolled over onto her side. He felt like laughing and shouting his triumph out loud. Instead, he hid the bag of precious stones under his mattress and rolled into his blanket. He did not sleep for the rest of the night, and in the dawn he heard the hubbub of superstitious fear from the king's kraal, the screams of women and the shouts of men, loudly bolstering their courage against the spirits and the demons.

'This is a cruel thing for a good king to do,' Robyn told Lobengula bitterly.

'Nomusa, you are a wise woman, the wisest that I have ever known – but you do not understand the spirits and demons of Matabeleland.'

'I understand that the world is full of evil men, but that there are very few evil spirits.'

'The thing that entered my sister's hut came from the air. All the gates to the kraal were guarded by men unsleeping; they have sworn to me that they stood at their posts from dusk to dawn, with eyes wide and spears in their hands. Nothing passed them.'

'Even your best men can doze, and then lie to protect themselves.'

'Nobody dare lie to the king. It came from air, and it sprayed rotten stinking blood upon the portals of Ningi's hut.' Lobengula shuddered despite himself. 'On Chaka's scrawny buttocks, that is a *Tokoloshe* trick. No man can do that.'

'Except if he carry blood in a pot to hurl on the doorway.'

'Nomusa –' Lobengula shook his head sorrowfully. 'My sister and her servants saw this great hairy thing, black as midnight and stinking of the grave, with blood and not sweat oozing from its skin. Its eyes were like the full moon, and its voice that of lion and eagle, it had no hands and no feet, just hairy pads.' Lobengula shuddered again.

'And it stole diamonds,' Robyn told him. 'What does a demon want with diamonds?'

'Who knows what a demon needs for his spells or his magic, or to please his dark master?'

'Men lust after diamonds.'

'Nomusa, to black men diamonds have no value, so it could not have been a black man. On the other hand, if a white man had entered my sister's hut he would not have been satisfied with a few stones. A white man would have taken them all, for that is their way. So it could not have been either a white man or a black man – what is left but a demon?'

'Lobengula, Great King, you cannot allow this thing to happen.'

'Nomusa, there has been a terrible witchcraft perpetrated within the royal kraal. An evil person or many evil persons have conjured up a black demon, and I would be no king at all if I allowed them to live. The evil ones must be smelled out, and my birds must feast before we are cleansed of this filthy thing.'

'Lobengula –'

'Say no more, Girlchild of Mercy, words cannot divert my purpose, for you and your family and all the guests at my kraal are summoned to see justice done.'

It took ten days for the Matabele people to come in to GuBulawayo; they came in their regiments, warriors and maidens, ringed indunas and fruitful matrons – the toddlers and the grey-headed toothless old droolers – in their thousands and tens of thousands; and on the morning that Lobengula had appointed, the nation assembled, rank upon rank, regiment upon regiment, a black ocean of humanity that overflowed the great cattle stockade.

There was a peculiar stillness over such an immense gathering, only the plumed headdresses moved softly in the small restless breeze, and a pall of fear hung over them, so palpable that it seemed to take the heat from the sun and dim its very rays.

The silence was oppressive; it seemed to crush the breath

from their lungs. Only once when a black crow flew low over the serried ranks and screeched its raucous cry into the silence, all their heads lifted and a soft sigh shook them, like the wind through the top branches of the forest.

Before the gates of the royal kraal, facing this huge concourse, were drawn up the senior indunas of the Matabele, Somabula and Babiaan and Gandang and the lesser princes of Kumalo, while behind them again, their backs to the poles of the stockade, were Lobengula's white guests, almost one hundred of them, Germans and Frenchmen, Dutchmen and Englishmen, hunters and scholars and businessmen and adventurers, petitioners and missionaries and traders. Soberly clad in broadcloth, wearing hunting leathers and bandoliers or dressed in spangled and gaudy uniform, they waited in the sweltering silence.

There were only two white women present, for Robyn had flatly refused to bring her daughters from Khami for the smelling-out ceremony, and Lobengula had relented and made an exception for them.

The king had given permission for the two women to be seated. Robyn sat beside the entrance to the stockade, and Clinton stood over her protectively while the members of Mr Rhodes' deputation flanked her. Mr Rudd, red-faced and whiskered, with his Derby hat set four square on his head, and Jordan Ballantyne, bare-headed and golden-haired at Robyn's other hand.

Further down the line of guests, Louise St John sat on a stool of leather thongs. Her thick sable plaits hung to the waist of her simple white dress, and the eyes of the men around her kept returning surreptitiously to her exotic high-cheeked beauty. Behind her stood Mungo St John, one eye hidden by the black patch, leaning easily on his cane and smiling to himself as he saw the direction of the eyes of the men about him.

The nation surged like a slumbering black sea struck by a sudden gale of wind, and the plumes tossed like spume. There was a single clap of sound like the volley of massed cannon as every right leg was lifted shoulder high and brought down to stamp the hard earth, and every throat corded and strained to the royal salute.

'Bayete!'

The Great Black Elephant of Matabele came through the gateway, and behind him his wives led by Ningi swayed and shuffled and sang his praises.

With the toy spear of kingship in his hand, Lobengula paced towards the mound of packed clay on which the bath chair, which had been his father's throne, was set, and Gandang and Babiaan, his brothers, came forward to help him ascend the steps.

From his platform, Lobengula looked upon his people, and those closest to him saw the terrible sorrow in his eyes.

'Let it begin,' he said, and slumped into his chair.

There was a ragged chorus of shrieks and whines and maniacal laughter from beyond the stockade walls, and through the gateway came a horrid procession of beldams and crones, of prancing hell-hags and gibbeting necromancers.

At their throats and waists were hung the trappings of their wizardry, skull of baboon and infant, skin of reptile, of python and iguana, carapace of tortoise, and stoppered horns, rattles of lucky bean pods and bones, and other grisly relics of man and animal and bird.

Wailing and hooting they assembled before Lobengula's throne.

'Dark sisters, can you smell the evil ones?'

'We smell their breaths – they are here! They are here!'

One of the witches collapsed in the dust, with froth bubbling over her toothless gums; her eyes rolled back into her skull and her limbs twitched spasmodically. One of her sisters dashed the red powder from a snuff-horn in her face, and she shrieked and leaped into the air.

'Dark sisters, will you bring forth the evil-doers?' Lobengula asked.

'We will bring them to you, Great Bull of Kumalo. We will deliver them up, son of Mzilikazi.'

'Go!' ordered Lobengula. 'Do what must be done!'

Some of them went whirling and cavorting, brandishing their divining rods, one the tail of a giraffe, another the inflated bladder of a jackal on a staff of red tambooti wood, still another the stretched and sun-dried penis of a black-maned lion, the rods with which they would point out the evil ones.

Others crept away, slinking and sly as the night-prowling hyena. Others again crawled on all fours, snuffling the earth like hunting hounds quartering for the scent as they spread out amongst the rows of waiting people.

One of the witches came down the line of white guests, hopping like an ancient baboon, her empty teats flapping against her withered belly, her skin crusty grey with filth and her charms clattering and jangling; and she stopped in front of Mungo St John and lifted her nose to sniff the air, then she howled like a bitch in season.

Mungo St John took the long black hand-rolled cheroot of native tobacco from between his lips and inspected the ash on its tip. The crone hopped closer and looked up into his face, and he returned the cheroot to his lips and returned her stare without interest.

She leapt up to thrust her face inches from his and noisily sniff the breath of his nostrils, and then she danced away – until she faced him again, lifted the long giraffe tail above her head, shrieked like a stooping owl and rushed at Mungo, the tail raised to strike into his face.

In front of him she froze in the act of striking, and Mungo St John took the cheroot from his mouth and he blew a perfect smoke ring, that spun upon itself until it broke in the witch's face and blew away in soft wisps.

She cackled, wildly, madly, and passed on down the line to pause in front of Robyn Codrington.

'You stink like the hyena that spawned you,' Robyn told her evenly in perfect Matabele, and the witch whirled and raced away to where Juba stood in the front line of noble matrons; she raised the switch to strike and looked back at Robyn, gloating loathsomely.

Robyn had gone white as bone, and came to her feet clutching her own bosom.

'No,' she whispered. 'Please, fair sister, let her be.'

The witch dropped her arm and came back to strut and preen in front of Robyn; then again she shrieked, whirled and rushed at Juba, this time she struck, and the tail hissed and snapped on black flesh – but at the very last second the witch had diverted her aim, and the blow flew into the startled face of the young woman who stood beside Juba.

'I smell evil,' shrieked the witch, and the woman fell to her knees. 'I smell blood.'

The witch struck again and again, the tail cutting stingingly into the woman's unprotected face until the tears started and ran down her cheeks.

The executioners came forward and pulled her to her feet. The woman's legs were paralysed, so they dragged her unprotesting before Lobengula, and he looked down on her, saddened and helplessly compassionate, before he lifted the forefinger of his right hand.

One of the executioners swung his war club, a full blow that stove in the back of the woman's skull. The bone crunched like a footstep in loose gravel, and the woman's eyes were driven from their sockets like over-ripe grapes by the force of it. When she fell face forward in the dust there was a bloodless depression in the back of her head into which a man could have placed his fist. The witch scurried away to continue the hunt, and Juba looked across at Robyn. Robyn had fallen back on her chair, trembling and pale, while Clinton put an arm around her shoulders to steady her.

In the packed ranks there was another triumphant shriek, and the executioners dragged a fine-looking young warrior from his place. He threw off their hands and strode to drop on one knee before Lobengula's throne.

'Father of the nation, hear my praises. Great Thunderer, Black Bull, let me die with your name on my lips. Oh Lobengula who drives like the wind –'

The king lifted his finger and the club fell with the flute of a goose's wing.

The chorus of howls and shrieks was unending now as the sisters warmed to their work, and the victims were dragged out and slaughtered – until their corpses were a high mound before the king's throne, a tangle of black limbs and shattered heads, that grew and grew.

A hundred, two hundred, were added to the pile, while the sun reached its zenith and the dust and heat and terror formed a suffocating miasma, and the blue metallic flies swarmed in the staring eyes and open mouths of the dead, and the witches cavorted and giggled and struck with their rods.

Here and there a maiden, overcome with the fear and the blazing heat, fell swooning from her place and the witches pounced upon this irrefutable evidence of guilt and rained blows upon her bare back or glossy breasts, and the executioners hurried to keep pace with their dreadful task.

The sun began its slow descent towards the western horizon, and at last one at a time the witches crept back to the mountain of death they had created. They staggered with exhaustion – the dust had caked on their running sweat, but they bayed and whined like dogs as they pored over the corpses, selecting those they would take with them – back to their caves and secret places – a sliver of the womb of a virgin was a powerful fertility charm, a slice of the heart of a blooded warrior was a wonderful talisman in battle.

'Is the work done?' Lobengula asked.

'It is done, oh king.'

'Are all the evil ones dead?'

'They are all dead, son of Mzilikazi.'

'Go then – and go in peace,' Lobengula said wearily.

'Stay in peace, Great King.' They chuckled and hooted and, bearing their gruesome plunder with them, they shuffled away through the gateway of the stockade.

Three times in as many weeks Mungo St John petitioned the king – asking him to 'give the road' to the south – but each time the king chatted affably for an hour and then waved him away. 'I will think on it, One Bright Eye, but are you unhappy here? Does the beef and beer I send you not fill your belly? Perhaps you would like to go once again on the hunt?'

'I want to go south, oh King.'

'Perhaps in the next full moon, One Bright Eye, and then again perhaps after the rain has passed, or after the Chawala Ceremony, who knows? We will see in good season.'

Then one morning Louise rode out early, as had become her custom – but after she had been gone some hours Mungo realized that this time she had the rifle and bandolier of ammunition, her blanket roll and the gallon water bottle with her.

He puzzled over her behaviour for the rest of that day, but he was not alarmed until night fell and she had not returned. He sat up beside the fire all that night, and at first light he took the second mule and crossed the river to where Rudd's party was camped in grand style in a pleasant glade of the forest. They had six wagons and as many tents made of best quality waterproof canvas, each with sun flysheets.

The horses on the picket line were all blood Arabs, one of which would carry Mungo and his small bag of precious stones to the Shashi river in six days or less. He was eyeing them hungrily, when Robyn Codrington stooped out of one of the tents. She saw him and would have gone in again, but he called to her and jumped down from the mule.

'Dr Codrington, please, it is a matter of extreme urgency.'

Reluctantly she turned back.

'My wife is missing, she did not come in last night.'

Immediately her distant expression changed to one of concern.

'Did she say where she was going?'

He shook his head. 'I can only think that she might have ridden back to Khami – you know she was becoming friendly with your elder daughter –'

'I shall send a servant to the mission.'

'Can you not ask the king to let me go?'

'The king has gone in to his wives – nobody, not even I, dare disturb him until he comes out from the women's quarters.'

'How long will that be?'

'A day, a week – there is no way of telling. I shall send word to you as soon as I have news.'

That night Mungo waited again, and then in the dawn as he crouched, haggard and bleary-eyed, over the smoky fire, listening for the hoof beats of the mule or the sound of Louise's voice out of the darkness – he was struck instead by a thought that chilled his blood and made his guts slide with dread.

He leapt up from the fire, ran into the hut and scrabbled frantically under the mattress. With a blessed soaring relief his fingers closed on the bag, and he pulled it out and fumbled the drawstring open. He poured the bright stones into the palm of his hand. They were all there, but with them was something that had not been there before. It was a folded sheet of paper – and he took it to the fire and held it to catch the light.

'When you find this you will know why I have gone. Even as I write this the memory of those poor wretches who died in their hundreds to pay for your greed rises before me to torment me. With them died the last of my love for you.

'I leave you those blood-spattered stones in the certain knowledge that they are accursed.

'Do not follow me. Do not send after me. Do not think of me again.'

She had not signed it.

Rudd's party was at breakfast under the open-sided dining-tent.

It was a fresh and cool morning. The conversation around the table was intelligent, informed and yet quick and witty, Robyn revelled in it.

She sat at the head of the trestle table and the gentlemen deferred to her. Mr Rudd had been very obviously taken with her from their first meeting, and addressed all his remarks to her directly.

Jordan had supervised the preparation of a gargantuan English breakfast, fresh eggs and grilled gammon, salted kippers and tinned pork sausage, potted shrimps and bloater paste, with freshly-churned yellow butter and hot scones.

Mr Rudd, quite carried away with the spontaneous festive mood, called for a bottle of champagne that had been hung overnight in a wet sack to cool.

'Well,' he lifted his glass to Robyn, 'I am sure we shall be able to survive this rough life and rude fare until the good king makes up his mind.'

Despite Robyn's intercession, Lobengula had not yet ratified the concession that they sought. His senior indunas had been in secret conclave for weeks, but could not reach a consensus of agreement – while Lobengula vacillated and reacted to Mr Rudd's insistence by retiring to his women's quarters where nobody could reach him.

'It may take months yet.' Robyn lifted her own glass and returned Rudd's salute. 'I would not expect Lobengula to make a decision on such an important matter without going into the Matopos Hills to consult the oracle, the Umlimo.'

Suddenly Clinton looked down towards the river, frowned and whispered to Robyn. 'It's that scoundrel St John, what does he want coming here?'

Mungo St John had dismounted at the periphery of the camp, but he did not approach the company under the open-sided marquee.

Robyn stood up quickly. 'Please excuse me, gentlemen. General St John's wife is missing, and he is naturally worried.'

'Thank you for coming,' Mungo said, as she hurried to him. 'I have nobody else to turn to, Robyn.'

She tried to ignore the intimacy of his appeal, and the little jolt that his use of her given name always gave her.

'Do you have news?' she asked.

'I have discovered a note that Louise left for me.'

'Let me see it.' Robyn held out her hand.

'I am sorry. It contains most personal and, I fear, embarrassing, references,' Mungo told her. 'But what is important is that Louise is trying to leave Matabeleland by the southern road.'

'That is madness,' Robyn whispered. 'Without the king's permission, without an escort. The road is obscure, the country wild and infested with lions, she cannot hope to pass the border impis – and they have orders to kill all who do not have the road from Lobengula.'

'She knows all this,' Mungo said.

'Then what possessed her to make the attempt?'

'We argued. She resented the feeling which she knows that I still have – for you.'

Robyn fell back a pace, her cheeks paling and her breath catching in her throat.

'General St John, I forbid you to talk in that fashion.'

'You asked me, Robyn, and once, long ago, I told you that I would never forget that night aboard *Huron* –'

'Stop it! Stop it, this instant! How can you speak like this when your wife is in dire danger?'

'Louise was never my wife,' he said quietly, staring into her green eyes with that single penetrating gaze. 'She was my travelling companion, never my wife.'

Robyn faltered, colour rushed back into her cheeks, and with it came a strange unaccountable pagan joy.

'You told me – once – that you were married.'

'I was, Robyn. Not to Louise. That other lady died many years ago in Navarre in France.'

Robyn confounded herself. She was married to a brave, kind man – in his own way a saintly man – while before her stood the embodiment of evil, the veritable serpent of Eden; and yet she could not suppress this wicked unconscionable elation at the knowledge that he was free – free for she knew not what, or could not bring herself to think on it.

'I shall go to the king,' she said, painfully aware of the quaver in her voice. 'I shall ask him to send men after your – after the lady. I shall ask him also to give you the road, General, and I would consider it full repayment if you would take it immediately, and never return to Matabeleland.'

'What is between us can never be denied, Robyn, as long as we both live.'

'I do not wish to see you again.' With an effort of all her will she steadied her voice and met his eye.

'Robyn –'

'I shall send a messenger to you with the king's reply.'

'Robyn –'

'Please.' Her voice cracked again. 'In God's holy name, please leave me alone.'

However, it was two more days before Robyn sent Jordan Ballantyne to Mungo's camp.

'Dr Codrington bids me tell you, sir, that the king has already sent one of his trusted indunas with a picked body of warriors after your wife. They have orders to protect her from the border guards and to escort her to the Shashi river.'

'Thank you, young man.'

'Furthermore, she asked me to tell you that the king has given you the road. You may follow your wife immediately.'

'Again my thanks to Dr Codrington.'

'General St John, you do not remember me –'

'I am afraid –' Mungo frowned up at Jordan on the back of the dancing Arab mare.

'Jordan – Zouga Ballantyne's son. We met in Kimberley some years ago.'

'Ah! Of course, forgive me. You have changed.'

'General, I know that it is none of my business, but as you are a trusted friend of my father's, it is my duty to warn you that there were unpleasant rumours after your departure from Kimberley.'

'I did not know,' Mungo told him indifferently. 'Still, it is one of life's unpleasant truths that the more prominent a man becomes, the more determined are the mean little men to tear him down.'

'I know that, General. I am associated with a great man –' Jordan checked himself. 'However, a police agent, a Griqua named Hendrick Naaiman claimed that you attended an I.D.B. rendezvous and that when you realized it was a trap you attempted to kill him.'

Mungo made an impatient gesture. 'Why should somebody of my standing, my estate, take such a ridiculous risk as to indulge in I.D.B?'

'That was what Mr Rhodes said, sir. He has repeatedly expressed certainty of your innocence.'

'After I have found my wife I shall return immediately to Kimberley to confront this Naaiman person.'

'General St John, that will be neither necessary nor possible. Naaiman was killed some months ago in a knife fight in one of the drinking canteens. He cannot give evidence for or against you. Without either witness or accuser, your innocence is presumed.'

'Damn it –' Mungo frowned to cover his immense relief. 'I should have welcomed the chance to force his words down his lying throat, now there will always be doubts in some men's minds.'

'Only in the minds of the mean little men.' Jordan touched the brim of his cap. 'I shall not detain you further; you must be anxious to follow and find your wife. Good luck and God speed. I am sure we shall meet again, General.'

Mungo St John stared after Jordan as he rode away. It was hard to grasp the extent of his good fortune – the spectre of unrelenting justice that had pursued him from the south had vanished; he had the road to leave Matabeleland, and an immense fortune in diamonds to carry with him.

An hour later he had visited one of the traders and exchanged the cart and the other meagre possessions he no longer needed for a good rifle and one hundred rounds of ammunition, and he sat the broad comfortable back of the mule, its head pointed southwards, as it skirted the granite hills of the indunas.

Mungo looked neither left nor right: his eye was fixed ahead, towards the south, so that he did not see the slim almost boyish figure on the slopes high above him. Robyn shaded her eyes with the brim of her bonnet and peered after him until the little feather of dust raised by the mule's big heavy hooves subsided into the mimosa forests.

Louise St John was driven on by her need to keep ahead of any pursuit, obsessed with the knowledge that she must avoid the kraals along the road, ridden by the guilt she knew she must share with Mungo, her senses and emotions in terrible turmoil – so that she did not have a chance to regret her hasty action, taken in the shock of discovering the diamonds, nor did she realize the depths of her loneliness – until she had successfully skirted the last of the great kraals and left the pleasant grasslands of the plateau.

Now ahead of her the escarpment fell into the wild land, hot and heavily forested, which she knew was teeming with wild animals and guarded by the merciless border impis.

It was a measure of her desperate need to be free of Mungo St John and all he stood for that she never once considered turning back – though she knew there was sanctuary for her at Khami Mission, though she knew that Robyn Codrington would go to the king on her behalf and he would give her an escort of warriors to the border.

She could not go back, she could not bear the prospect of being close to Mungo St John ever again. The love she had once borne him had sickened into a total revulsion. No risk was too high to escape him and she had to do it now. There was no going back.

She lay the last night beside the wagon ruts that were her tenuous link with civilization and life itself, her own thread through the maze of the Matabele Minotaur, and she listened to the mule cropping grass close at hand and, far away down the escarpment, the faint roar of a hunting lion, while she tried to reconstruct in her mind the map that had formed the frontispiece to Zouga Ballantyne's book *A Hunter's Odyssey*. The account of Zouga's journeys had fascinated her, even before she had met him, and she had studied the map with minute attention.

She judged that from where she now lay the Tati river was not more than one hundred miles due west. No pursuer would expect her to take that direction. No impi would guard that desolate untravelled quarter, and the Tati river was the border between Matabeleland and Khama's country. By all accounts King Khama was a gentle and honourable man; his country was under suzerainty of the British crown, and British justice was ensured by the presence of Sir Sidney Shippard at Khama's kraal.

If she could reach the Tati river and follow it south until she met some of Khama's people who could take her to Sir Sidney

– then he would see to it that she was sent on southwards to Kimberley.

The thought of that town made her realize the true reason for her desperate haste. For the first time she became aware of the terrible hunger within her to be with a man whom she could trust, whose strength would shield her and make her strong again. The man to whom she could at last acknowledge she had transferred the love which Mungo St John had long ago forfeited. She must reach Zouga, and reach him soon – that was the only thing certain in her confusion, and her despair, but first there were a hundred miles of wilderness to cross.

She rose in the first pale light of day, kicked sand over the fire, saddled the mule, and slid the rifle into its scabbard, she buckled the water-bottle and blanket to the pommel and swung up onto his back. With the unearthy red glow of the sunrise at her back, she urged the mule forward, and after fifty paces, when she glanced back, the faint double track of wagon wheels was no longer discernible.

The land through which she rode had a harsh and forbidding grandeur; the horizons were infinite and the sky was tall and milky blue. It was empty of all life, she saw no bird nor animal, and the sunlight was white and fierce. In the nights the stars filled the heavens with whorls and eddies of cold bright light and she felt herself shrinking under the immensity and loneliness of it all.

On the third evening, she knew that she was lost, hopelessly and irretrievably lost. She was barely certain of the direction of the sunset, but she had no idea of distances and her memories of the sketch map which she had thought vivid and clear, had become fuddled and confused.

The gallon water-bottle was empty. She had drunk the last bloodwarm mouthful a little before noon. She had seen no game to provide meat, and she had eaten the last stale maize cake the previous evening. The mule was too exhausted and thirsty to graze. He stood miserably under the wild sycamore tree that she had chosen for her night's camp; but though she put the knee halter on him, she knew that he would not wander. His head hung to his knees. An arrowhead of flint had lacerated the frog of his left fore. He was dead lame, and she had no idea how much farther it was to the Tati, nor in which direction the river lay.

She put a little round white pebble under her tongue to draw her saliva and lay down next to the fire. Exhausted sleep came like sudden black death – and she woke as though she were struggling up from the depths of hell itself.

The moon was up, full and yellow, but it was the mule's fearful snorts and the stamp of his hooves on the stony earth that had roused her. She dragged herself up with the help of the sycamore trunk and peered about her. Something moved at the edge of her vision, something big and ghostly pale, and as she stared at it she caught the acrid ammoniacal whiff of cat. The mule whinnied with terror and broke into a maimed lunging gallop, the halters holding his forelegs so that he was awkward and slow, and the big pale thing came flashing lightly upon him, rising like a huge white bat against the moonlit sky, and settled upon the mule's back.

The mule screamed once and clearly Louise heard his spinal column break as the lioness on his back bit into his neck and in the same movement reached forward to sink her claws into his cheek and twist his head backwards against the hold of her jaws.

The mule went down with a thumping impact on the hard earth, and the lioness immediately flattened herself behind the shuddering and spasmodically kicking carcass and began ripping into the soft skin around the anus – making an opening into the belly cavity through which to reach the titbits of kidney and spleen and liver and guts.

Behind her Louise saw other pale cat shapes coming out of the shadows, and she had just presence of mind enough to snatch up the rifle before she scrambled up into the fork of the sycamore and climbed upwards, driven by a suffocating terror.

She clung to an upper branch and listened to the grisly feast below her, the growling and squabbling of a dozen lions over the carcass, the lapping sounds as they licked the meat off the bones with tongues like wood rasps, and the awful guttural purring and slurping.

As the light of day slowly strengthened, so the noises subsided. The big cats had eaten their fill and slunk away into the bush. Then Louise looked down the trunk of the sycamore into two implacable yellow orbs that seemed to search out new depths in her terror.

A full-maned lion stood at the base of the tree. He seemed as broad across the back as a carthorse, and his colour was a dark bluish-grey in the bad light. He was looking up at her, and as she stared in horror, the great black ruff of his mane came erect in excitation, so that he seemed to swell in size to fill the whole field of vision.

Suddenly he reared up on his hindlegs and reached up towards her, the long, curved, yellow claws unsheathing from their massive pads, and he ripped long parallel wounds down the bark of the sycamore from which the sap swelled in white milky beads.

Then the lion opened his jaws, and she stared into the deep pink cave of his throat. The long velvety tongue curled like the fleshy petal of some weird orchid, and each gleaming ivory fang was long as a man's forefinger and sharp as the point of a guardsman's pike.

The lion roared up at her. It was a gale of sound that struck her like a blow from a mailed fist. It drove in her eardrums and it jellied every muscle in her body. Then the huge beast came up the tree. It climbed in a series of lunges, the yellow claws raking slabs of wet bark off the trunk as it bunched its quarters and drove upwards, those painful gusts of sound still bursting from its throat, the enormous yellow eyes fastened upon her coldly and remorselessly.

Louise began to scream and the tree rocked, the branches tossed and crackled as the great tawny body forced its way through them with a speed and power she would never have believed possible. Still screaming, she pushed the long barrel of the rifle downwards, without aiming she jerked at the trigger and nothing happened except that the lion was closer still.

In her panic she had forgotten the safety catch of the rifle. It was almost too late; the lion reached up and struck the barrel with one enormous paw. The blow jarred her wrists and numbed her arms, but she kept her grip and slid the catch forward with her thumb and thrust the muzzle into the animal's jaws as she pulled the trigger again. The shot was almost drowned in the lion's roars.

The recoil broke her grip on the weapon and it went spinning away, clattered against the branches, leaving her utterly defenceless. Just below her perch the lion still clung to the tree trunk, but the huge shaggy head was thrown back on the arch of the thick neck, and a bright fountain of blood spurted up out of the open jaws, and the gleaming fangs turned rosy red as it washed over them.

Slowly the hooked claws released their deep grip on the bark of the tree trunk, and the cat fell, twisting and convulsing in mid-air until it struck the ground at the foot of the tree. Lying on its side, it stretched out its limbs and arched its back, one last breath choked with blood rattled up its throat – and then it slumped and softened into the total relaxation of death.

Timidly Louise clambered down from the sycamore and, keeping well clear of the carcass, she retrieved the rifle. The butt was cracked through and the breech block jammed solid. She struggled with it futilely for a few minutes, and then dropped it.

Terror still stifled her breathing, and congested her bladder – but she did not pause to relieve it. Frantically she snatched up the small canvas bag that contained her tinder-box and steel, a clasp knife and a few items of jewellery and other personal oddments. She left the bandolier and blanket and the empty water-bottle, for she was desperately driven by the need to leave this place, and she stumbled away from the sycamore.

Once only she looked back. A pair of jackals were already at the lion's carcass, and out of the lemon-pale morning sky the first vulture came planing down on wide elegant wings to roost, hump-backed, in the top branches of the sycamore. It bobbed its foul boiled-looking naked head in gluttonous anticipation.

Louise began to run. She ran with a panicky desperation, looking over her shoulder, so that the thorn bushes ripped at her and her high-heeled riding boots tottered over the broken ground. She almost exhausted herself in that wild run, and when she fell at last she lay face down, racked by the sob of each breath, and with the tears of fear and despair mingling with the sweat of her cheeks.

It took her until almost noon to recover her strength, and gather her determination and get her racing terror under control.

Then she went on.

In the mid-afternoon one heel broke off her boot, and she twisted her ankle painfully. She hobbled on until darkness gathered around her and with it all her fears returned.

She climbed to the high fork of a mopani tree. The cramped position on the hard trunk, the cold and her own fears prevented her from sleeping. In the dawn she climbed down. Her ankle had swollen and turned a deep purple-rose colour. She knew that if she removed her boot once more she would never get it on again. She pulled up the straps as hard as she could and cut a branch of mopani to use as a crutch.

The noon was windless and fiercely hot. The mucous membrane of her nostrils had dried out and swollen so that she was forced to breath through her mouth. Her lips cracked and began to bleed. The metallic salt of her own blood seemed to scald her tongue. The crutch of raw rough mopani rubbed the skin from her armpit and flank, and by mid-afternoon her tongue had swollen into a choking gag like a ball of oakum jammed into her mouth.

That night she did not have the strength to climb to a tree fork. She crouched at its base, and when at last exhausted sleep assailed her, she was tormented by dreams of running mountain streams – from which she woke mumbling and coughing to the worse torment of reality.

Somehow she dragged herself up again when the light woke her. Each step now was an effort to which she had to steel herself. She leaned on the staff, staring through bloodshot eyes and swollen lids at the spot where she would place her foot, then she lunged forward and swayed to catch her balance before she drew her injured foot up beside the other.

'Five hundred and four –' She counted each step, and then steeled herself for the next pace. At every count of 'one thousand' she rested and peered around her at the wavering heat mirage.

In mid-afternoon she lifted her head during one of the rest pauses and saw ahead of her a file of human figures. Her joy was so intense that for a moment her vision darkened, then she roused herself and tried to shout. No sound came out of her dry, cracked, swollen mouth.

She lifted the crutch and waved it at the oncoming figures – and realized at that moment that the mirage and her own hallucinations had tricked her. In her wavering, uncertain vision the line of human figures resolved into a troop of wild ostrich, and they scattered away across the plain.

There were no tears to tell the depths of her disappointment.

Her tears had dried long ago. At dusk she fell face down, and her last conscious thought was, 'It's over. I cannot go on.'

But the dawn chill roused her and she lifted her head painfully and in front of her face she saw a stalk of grass curved under the weight of the drops of dew that hung from it, trembling precariously and sparkling like precious jewels. She reached out her hand and touched it, and instantly the lovely drops fell into the dry baked earth and left no trace of their going.

She crawled to the next stalk and this time let the liquid diamonds fall into her black swollen mouth. The pleasure was so intense as to change its shape to pain. The sun came up swiftly to dry the dew, but she had taken enough strength at least to push herself upright and go on.

The following night there was a small warm breeze that nagged at her while she slept, and because of it there was no dew, and she knew that this was the day she would die. It would be easier to do it here where she lay, and she closed her eyes – then opened them again and struggled into a sitting position.

Each thousand paces seemed to take an infinity, and she was hallucinating again. Once her grandfather walked beside her for a while. He wore his war bonnet of eagle feathers, and his beaded and tasselled buckskins. When she tried to talk to him he smiled sadly at her and his face folded into ancient leathery brown seams, and he disappeared.

At another time Mungo St John galloped past on Shooting Star. He did not look in her direction and the great golden stallion's hooves made no sound. They whirled way into the dusty distances. Then suddenly the earth opened under her and she fell, lightly as a feather from the breast of a goose, lightly as a snowflake, twisting and turning, down and down, then a jarring impact shocked her back to reality.

She lay face down in a bed of sugary white sand. For a moment she thought it was water, and she scooped a double handful and lifted it to her lips, but the dry sharp grains were like salt on her tongue. She looked about her and realized with a sort of bitter triumph that she had at last reached the Tati river and that she lay now in the parched river bed. The fine sand, white as salt, reached from bank to bank – she was about to die of thirst in a river.

'A pool – ' she thought. 'There must be a pool.' She began to crawl through the sand, down towards the first bend in the course.

It opened to another long vista of tall banks, and overhanging trees – but the white glittering unbroken sand taunted her. She knew she did not have the strength to crawl as far as the next bend. Her vision was starring and breaking up again; but she frowned with concentration at the piles of brown ball-shaped lumps in the centre of the river bed, and vaguely realized that they were heaps of elephant dung, and that near them were mounds of sand, like children's sandcastles on the beach.

She remembered suddenly a description of the elephant digs from Zouga Ballantyne's book – and it gave her the final burst of strength to pull herself onto her feet and stagger to the nearest sandcastle. The elephants had kicked aside the sand, and made an excavation in the bottom of the river bed as deep as a man's waist. She slid down into it and began frantically to dig with her bare hands. Within minutes her nails were broken and her fingertips bleeding, and the sand kept collapsing back into her hole, but she dug on doggedly.

Then the white sand changed colour, became damp and firm, and at last there was a glint in the very bottom. She tore a strip of cloth from the hem of her ragged skirt and pressed it down into the hole, then after a moment lifted it to her mouth, and with bleeding fingers squeezed out a drop of water onto her cracked and blackened tongue.

It was as Zouga had always imagined that it would be.

He crossed the Shashi river an hour before high noon on a hot windless day, with the silver and blue thunderheads piled on the far horizons and the teeming forests and hunting veld of Matabeleland ahead.

He sat astride a fine salted horse, and at his right hand rode his eldest son, a man full grown, straight and strong, a man to delight his father's heart.

'There she is, Papa.' Ralph swept his hat from his head and gestured with it to include the horizon of smoky-blue hills and green forests. 'There is your north at last. We are coming to take her now.'

Zouga laughed with him, his golden beard glowing in the sunlight and his teeth as white and even as his son's.

'Not quite yet, my boy. This time we have come to woo her – and the next time to take her as a bride.'

Zouga had broken his journey three months at Kimberley, and with the full resources of De Beers Diamond Mines at his disposal had done the planning that Rhodes had ordered.

He had decided on a band of two hundred men to take and hold Mashonaland, to ride the boundaries of the farms and peg the gold reefs. They were to be supported by a detachment of Sir Sidney Shippard's Bechuanaland Police from Khama's kraal – and another detachment of Rhodes' own police which he would raise. Zouga detailed the arms and equipment that they would need – one hundred and sixteen pages of schedules and lists – and Rhodes approved it with that bold sweeping signature and a curt injunction. 'Do it!'

Four days later Ralph had come into Kimberley with two dozen wagons from the Witwatersrand goldfields, and Zouga sat with him all night in his suite in Lil's new hotel.

In the morning Ralph had whistled with excitement.

'It's so big, so many men, so much equipment—'

'Can you do it, Ralph?'

'You want me to tender for a price to recruit the men, buy the equipment and assemble it here at Kimberley, provide the wagons and oxen to carry it all, horses for the men, rifles and ammunition, machine-guns, a steam engine to power a searchlight; then you want me to tender to build a road to get it all to a map reference, a place which you call Mount Hampden, somewhere in the wilderness, and you want it all to be ready to leave in nine months?'

'You have grasped it fairly,' Zouga smiled. 'Can you do it?'

'Give me a week,' Ralph said, and five days later he was back.

'It's too big for me, I'm afraid, Papa,' he said, and then grinned mischievously at Zouga's expression of disappointment. 'I had to take in a partner – Frank Johnson.'

Johnson was another young man in a hurry, and, like Ralph, had already acquired a reputation for being able to get things done.

'Have you and young Johnson worked out a price?'

'We'll do it for eighty-eight thousand two hundred and eighty-five pounds and ten shillings.' Ralph handed him the signed tender and Zouga studied it in silence. When at last he looked up he asked:

'Tell me, Ralph, what is that ten shillings on the end for?'

'Why, Papa –' Ralph widened his eyes disarmingly. 'That is our profit on the deal.'

Zouga had cabled the tender price to Rhodes at Claridge's Hotel in London, and the following day Rhodes had cabled back his acceptance in principle.

All that was still needed was Lobengula's ratification of the consolidated concessions – and Zouga was under Rhodes' orders to go immediately to GuBulawayo and find out from Rudd the reasons for the delay.

Ralph had immediately elected to ride with Zouga.

'Once Mr Rhodes gives us the word to go – there will be no time for anything else. I have some unfinished business in Matabeleland, at Khami Mission and beyond –' And an uncharacteristic dreamy look had come into Ralph's eyes. 'This is the time to do it. While I still have the chance.'

So now, side by side, Zouga and Ralph spurred their mounts up the bank of the Shashi river and rode into Matabeleland.

'We will outspan here for a few days, Papa,' Ralph said; it was still strange for Zouga to have his son make decisions without deferring to him. 'The grazing is good and sweet, and we will rest the oxen and do a little hunting; there is still plenty of game up near the confluence of the Tati river.'

At the beginning of this long journey together, Zouga had been disconcerted by his son's competitive spirit that turned even the most mundane task into a contest. He had forgotten this trait of Ralph's in the time they had been separated but found now that it had grown stronger and fiercer during that period.

His energy daunted Zouga, who found that on this journey – for lack of other opposition – he was a foil for his son's need to compete.

They shot bird, on foot in heavy cover – guinea-fowl and francolin, Ralph counted the bag and scowled when Zouga outgunned him. They sat late at each outspan over the ivory dice, or the greasy dog-eared pack of cards, and Ralph glowed when he won a shilling, and growled when he lost one.

So now, when he said, 'We'll hunt together tomorrow, Papa,' Zouga knew he was in for an early start, and a long hard day.

They rode out from the wagons an hour before the first glimmer of dawn.

'Old Tom is getting *madala* – he's getting old – but I have a sovereign that says he'll run rings around that fancy beast of yours,' Ralph offered.

'I cannot afford that sort of money,' Zouga told him. He was hard and fit, his long professional hunting expeditions had kept him that way but the pace that Ralph set once he was aroused would be punishing. There was something else that troubled Zouga. When Ralph hunted competitively, he could be murderous. If he were challenged, there was only one consideration for him, the size of the bag.

Zouga had been a hunter for the greater part of his life. He had hunted for ivory, and for the peculiar fascination of the beautiful and noble animals he pursued. It was almost a form of love, that made a man want to study and understand and finally take the quarry irrevocably for his own.

These last seasons he had hunted, of necessity, with many men, but he had never yet met a man who hunted like his own son when his blood was up. It seemed as if the game were merely counters in another of Ralph's contests, the score all that counted. 'I don't want to be a sportsman, Papa. I leave that to you. I just want to be a winner.'

'I cannot afford that sort of money,' Zouga repeated, trying lightly to defuse Ralph's escalating tension.

'You can't afford a sovereign?' Ralph threw back his darkly handsome head, and his green eyes flashed as he laughed delighted. 'Papa, you have just sold that fat diamond of yours for thirty thousand pounds.'

'Ralph, let's make an easy day of it. If we get one giraffe, or a buffalo, that's all we need.'

'Papa, you are getting old. A sovereign. If you can't pay immediately, why then, your credit is always good!'

In mid-morning they cut the spoor of a troop of giraffe, feeding slowly eastward along the river bank.

'I make out sixteen of them.' Ralph leaned from the saddle to examine the huge double bean-shaped spoor in the sandy earth. 'They'll not be an hour ahead of us.' And he put his heels into old Tom's flanks.

The forest alternated with open glades through which meandered little streams, draining the escarpment down to the Shashi river. They were dry at this season of the year, but that did not account for the paucity of game.

When Zouga had first travelled this road, going south from old King Mzilikazi's kraal, the herds had darkened every one of these open glades. In one day's ride he had counted over a hundred monstrous grey rhinoceros, but there had been no counting the silvery herds of fat zebra and clowning purple wildebeest.

In those days, after a man had fired a shot, the dust rising from the galloping herds had looked like the smoke from a bush fire – and yet this day they had ridden since dawn without seeing a single wild animal.

Zouga brooded on it as he rode stirrup for stirrup with his son. Of course, this area was on the direct road to Lobengula's kraal, over which steadily more and more wagons and travellers passed. There were still vast areas beyond where the herds were thick as the grass on which they grazed. But after the road they would cut into Mashonaland – and the railway line that would follow – he wondered what would remain.

Perhaps one day his grandchildren would live in a land of which every corner was as barren as this. He did not envy them the prospect; and even as he thought that, his trained hunter's eye picked up the tiny speck just above the forest line, far ahead.

For a moment he was reluctant to call Ralph's attention to it. It was the head of a giraffe, raised inquisitively high above the mimosa tree on which it was feeding.

For the first time in the hunting veld Zouga felt sick to the gut at the slaughter he knew was about to follow – and he thought to distract Ralph's attention from the herd of huge spotted animals in the mimosa forest ahead. But at that moment Ralph shouted gaily:

'There they are, I'll be damned! They are shy as blushing virgins, they are off already.'

There had been a time when Zouga had been able to ride up to within two hundred yards of a herd before they took alarm. These were still a mile away and already galloping from the two horsemen.

'Come on, Papa. We'll catch them when they try to cross the Shashi,' and they tore into the stand of flowering mimosa.

'Tally-ho!' yelled Ralph. His hat came off and, hanging on its thong, it slapped against his back; while his long dark hair fluttered in the wind of their gallop. 'By God, Papa – you'll have to work to win your sovereign today,' he warned laughingly.

They crashed out of the forest onto another level open plain. The entire herd of huge vulnerable animals were spread before them: bulls and cows and calves, but that was not what caught Zouga's attention.

He pulled his horse down out of its gallop and swung his head away to the west.

'Ralph,' he shouted, 'let them go!'

Ralph looked back at him through the flying dust. His face was flushed with the hunter's fever.

'Warriors,' Zouga shouted. 'War party, Ralph. Close up!'

For a moment it seemed that Ralph would not obey, but then his good sense prevailed. It would be reckless to separate when there was a war party out, and he broke back to Zouga's side and let the panic-driven giraffe tear away towards the river.

He reined Tom to a halt. 'What do you make of them?' he asked, shading his eyes and peering through the heat-distorted air at the squiggly black line, like a shoal of tadpoles in the bottom of a rippling pool, which moved across the far side of the open plain. 'Khama's men? Bamangweto raiders? We are only a few miles from the frontier.'

'We won't take any chances until we know,' Zouga told him grimly. 'Let the horses blow. We may have to make a run –'

But Ralph interrupted him. 'Long shields! And they are red, those are the Moles, Bazo's fellows,' Ralph urged Tom towards the approaching impi. 'And I'll be damned if that isn't Bazo himself out front.'

By the time Zouga came up, Ralph had dismounted and, leaving Tom to stand, had run to embrace his old comrade – and he was already joshing Bazo cruelly.

'Lo, the Moles-that-burrow-under-a-mountain are returning from a raid without women or cattle. Did Khama's people give you the steel farewell?'

Bazo's delighted smile slid off his face at such levity, and he shook his plumes sternly.

'Not even in jest, Henshaw – do not talk like a giggling girl. If the king had sent us to Khama,' and he stabbed the air with his assegai, 'there would have been a beautiful killing.' He broke off as he recognized Zouga.

'Baba!' he said. 'Bakela – I see you, and my eyes are white with joy.'

'It has been too long, Bazo – but now you have the headring on your brow and an impi at your back – we shall shoot a beast and feast together this night.'

'Ah Bakela, it grieves me – but I am on the king's business. I return to GuBulawayo in haste to report the woman's death to the king.'

'Woman?' Zouga asked without real interest.

'A white woman. She ran from GuBulawayo without the king's word, and the king sent me after her –' Bazo broke off with an exclamation. 'Hau! But you know this woman, Bakela.'

'It is not Nomusa, my sister?' Zouga asked with quick concern. 'Not one of her daughters?'

'No, not them.'

'There are no other white women in Matabeleland.'

'She is the woman of One-Bright-Eye. The same woman who raced her horse against yours at Kimberley – and won. But now she is dead.'

'Dead?' All the blood had drained from Zouga's face, leaving his tan muddy and yellow. 'Dead?' he whispered, and swayed in the saddle so that, had he not grabbed at the pommel, he would have fallen.

'Louise – dead.'

Zouga found the sycamore that Bazo described to him, merely by back-tracking the impi.

They had left a good wide spoor, and Zouga reached the tree in the middle of the afternoon.

He did not know why he tortured himself so. There could be no reasonable doubt that she was dead. Bazo had showed him the pathetic relics he had retrieved. The damaged rifle and bandolier, the empty water bottle, and the tatters of cloth and saddlery ripped and chewed by the omnivorous jaws of the hyena.

The ground under the sycamore was beaten and swept of all traces of Louise by the pads of jackal and hyena, by the fluttering wings and the talons of hundreds of feeding, squabbling vultures. It smelled like a chicken coop, smeared with vulture dung, and loose feathers blew aimlessly hither and thither on the soft dry breeze.

Except for a few splinters of bone and tufts of hair, every trace of animal carcasses and the human body had been devoured. The hyena would have gobbled up even the leather of Louise's boots and belt, and the few remaining shreds of blanket and cloth were bloodstained.

It was quite easy to reconstruct what had happened. Louise had been set upon by a pride of lion. She had managed a single shot, there was an empty shell in the breech of the damaged rifle, and had killed one of the cats before being pulled off the mule.

Zouga could imagine every moment of her agony, almost hear her screams as the great jaws crunched through her bone and the yellow claws hooked into her flesh. It left him physically nauseated and weakened. He wanted to pray on the spot where she had died, but he did not seem to have the energy for even such small effort. It was as though the very force of life had gone out of him. Until that moment he had not realized what Louise's memory had meant to him, how the certainty that their lives were intertwined had sustained him while they were apart, how his belief in their eventual reunion had given his life purpose and direction. She had become part of his dream, and now it had been snuffed out on this wild and bloody patch of earth.

Twice he turned back to his horse to mount and leave, but each time he hesitated and then wandered back to sift through the reeking dust with his fingers for some last trace of her.

At last he looked at the sun. He could not reach the wagons before nightfall. He had told Ralph to leave Jan Cheroot and the spare horses at the drift of the Shashi when he went on with the wagons, so there was no urgency. There was no hurry. Without Louise there was no flavour in his life. Nothing really mattered any more, but he crossed to his horse, clinched the girth and mounted. He took one more lingering look at the trampled earth and then turned his horse's head back towards the Shashi and the wagons. He had not gone fifty yards when he found himself circling. It was not a conscious decision to begin casting for outgoing spoor. He knew it was futile, but his reluctance to leave the place dictated his actions.

Once he circled the sycamore, leaning out of the saddle and examining the broken and stony earth, then he moved farther out and circled again, then again, each time opening the radius of the circle. Suddenly his heart leaped against his ribs, and new hope flooded his devastated soul, but he had to steel himself to lean from the saddle and examine the thorn twig, in case he was to be disappointed once again.

The white tear had caught his eye, the twig had been broken half-through and now hung from the main branch at the level of a man's waist. The soft green leaves had wilted, the break was two or three days' old, but that was not what made Zouga's fingers shake.

From one of the curved red-tipped thorns hung a fine red thread of spun cotton. Zouga lifted it reverently and then touched it to his lips as though it were a sacred relic.

He was to the west of the sycamore; he could just make out the top branches above the surrounding bush, which meant that Louise had left that thread on the grasping thorn after she had run from the tree. The height above ground showed she had been on foot, and the broken twig and shredded cloth were evidence of her haste.

She had run from the sycamore and kept going in the direction which she had been stubbornly following, westwards, towards the Tati and Khama's country.

Zouga thumped his heels into the horse's flanks and galloped in the same direction. It was useless to look for spoor three days' old on this rocky ground. The wind had blown steadily for most of that time, and it would have scoured the last traces.

He must rely on luck and speed. He had seen the empty water-bottle and he knew what were the chances of survival on foot, without water, in this country between the rivers. He galloped on the line of her flight, quartering from side to side, searching grimly – not allowing himself to doubt again, concentrating all his mind on the search for another tiny sign. In the last minutes of dusk he found it. It was the heel of a brown riding boot torn from the sole. The gleam of the steel nails had caught his eye. He drew the rifle from its holder and fired three spaced shots into the darkening sky.

He knew she had no rifle to reply – but if somewhere out ahead she heard his signal, it might give her hope and strength. He waited beside a small fire until the moon came up – and then by its light he went on, and every hour he stopped and fired signal shots into the great starry silence, and afterwards he listened intently, but there was only the shriek of a hunting owl overhead and the yipping of a jackal far out across the silvery plain.

In the dawn he reached the wide white course of the Tati river. It was dry as the dunes of the Kalahari Desert, and the hopes which he had kept alive all night began to wane.

He searched the morning sky for the high spiral of turning vultures which would show a kill, but all he saw was a brace of sand grouse slanting down on quick stabbing wings. Their presence proved that there was surface water – somewhere. She might have found it – that was the only chance. Unless she had found water she would be dead by now. He took a cautious mouthful from his own bottle, and his horse whickered when he smelt the precious liquid. Soon the thirst would begin wearing him down as well.

He had to believe that if Louise had reached the river, she would follow it downstream. She was part Indian, and she would surely be able to get her direction from the sun and to know that her only chance was southwards towards the confluence with the Shashi. He turned in that direction, staying up on the bank, watching the river bed and the far bank and the sky.

Elephant had been digging in the bed, but their holes were dry now. He trotted on along the edge of the high bank. Ahead of him there was a rush of big purple-beige bodies as a herd of gemsbuck burst through the rank undergrowth on the far bank. Their long straight horns were like lances against the pale horizon sky, and the diamond-patterned face masks that gave their name seemed theatrical and frivolous. They galloped away into the deserts of Khama's country.

They could live without water for months at a time, and their presence gave Zouga no hope, but as he watched them go, his attention shifted to another distant movement much farther out on the flat open ground beyond the river.

There was a chacma baboon foraging there – the humanoid shape was quite distinctive. He looked for the rest of the troop – perhaps they were in the treeline beyond the plain. Chacma baboon would drink daily, and he shaded his eyes against the glare to watch the distant moving dark blob. It seemed to be feeding on the green fruit of the vine of the wild desert melons, but at this range it was difficult to be certain.

Then abruptly he realized that he had never before encountered baboon this far to the west, and at the same moment he was convinced that there was no troop. It was a solitary animal, unheard of with such a gregarious species, and immediately after that he saw that this animal was too big to be a baboon, and that its movements were uncharacteristic of an ape.

With a singing, soaring joy he launched into a full gallop, and the hooves beat an urgent staccato rhythm on the iron-hard earth, but as he dragged his horse down to a plunging halt and swung down out of the saddle, his joy shrivelled.

She was on her knees, and they were scratched bloody by the stony ground. Her clothing was mostly gone, and her tender flesh was exposed in the rents. The sun had burned her arms and legs into red raw blisters. Her feet were bound up in the remains of her skirt, but blood had soaked through the rags.

Her hair was a dry tangled bush about her head, powdered with dust and with the ends split and bleached. Her lips were black scabs, burned and cracked down into the living meat. Her eyelids were swollen as though stung by bees and she peered up at him like a blind old crone through slits that were caked with dried yellow mucus. The flesh had fallen off her body and her face. Her arms were skeletal and her cheekbones seemed to push through the skin. Her hands were blackened claws – the nails torn down into the quick.

She crouched like an animal over the flat leaves of the vine, and she had broken open one of the wild green melons with her fingers and stuffed pulp into her ruined mouth. The juice ran down her chin, cutting a runnel through the dirt that plastered her skin.

'Louise.' He went down on one knee, facing her. 'Louise –' His voice choked.

She made a little mewling sound in her throat and then touched her hair in a heart-breakingly feminine gesture, trying to smooth the stiff dust-caked tresses.

'Is it?' she croaked, peering at him with bloodshot eyes from slits of sun-swollen red lids. 'It isn't –'

Fumbling, she tried to cover one soft white breast with the rags of her blouse. She started to shake, wildly and uncontrollably, and then she closed her eyes tightly.

He reached out gently and at his touch she collapsed against his chest, still shaking, and he held her. She felt light and frail as a child.

'I knew –' she mumbled. 'It didn't make sense, but I knew somehow that you would come.'

'Will you not dowse the lantern, Ralph?' Cathy whispered, and her eyes were huge and dark and piteous as she crept in under the canvas of his wagon.

'Why?' he asked, smiling, propping himself on one elbow on the wagon cot.

'Somebody may come.'

'Your father and mother are still at Lobengula's kraal. There is nobody –'

'My sister – Salina –'

'Salina is long ago asleep, dreaming of brother Jordan, no doubt. We are alone, Cathy, all alone. So why should we put out the lantern?'

'Because I am shy, then,' she said, and blushed a new shade of scarlet. 'All you ever do is tease me. I wish I had never come.'

'Oh Cathy.' His chuckle was fond and indulgent, and he sat up on his cot, and the blanket slid to his waist. Quickly she averted her eyes from his naked chest and muscled upper arms. The skin was so white and marble-smooth in comparison to his brown forearms and face. It set strange unfamiliar emotions loose within her.

'Come!' He caught her wrist and drew her towards the cot, but she hung back until he jerked her forward and, taken off balance, she fell across his legs.

Before she could break free, he had taken a handful of the thick dark hair at the back of her head and turned her pale face up to his mouth. For a while she continued to struggle unconvincingly, and then her whole body softened, like wax in the candle flame, and seemed to melt over him.

'Do you still wish you had not come, Cathy?' he asked, but she could not reply; instead she tightened her arms around his neck convulsively. Once more she searched for his mouth with hers, and made a little moaning sound.

He goaded her with his mouth and tongue, the way Lil had first taught him so long ago, and she was defenceless as a beautiful soft-bodied insect in the spider's gossamer toils. It excited him as none of the practised and calculating women on whom he had spent his gold sovereigns ever had.

His own breathing started to hunt roughly, and his fingers shook at the lacings of her bodice. The skin of her shoulder was without blemish, silky and warm. He touched it with the tip of his tongue, and she shuddered and gasped, but when he pulled down the light cotton, she shrugged her shoulders to let the cloth come free. It caught for a moment and then slid to the level of her lowest rib.

He was unprepared for those tender and terribly vulnerable young breasts, so pale and rosy-tipped and yet at the same time hard and jubilant in their marvellous symmetry.

He stared at her body, and she watched him through half-closed lids, but made no effort to cover herself, though her cheeks were wildly flushed and her lips trembled as she whispered.

'No, Ralph, I don't want to go – not now, or ever.'

'The lantern –' He reached for it, but now she caught his hand.

'No, Ralph, I'm not ashamed of you and me. I don't want darkness, I want to see your dear face.'

She jerked the ribbon loose from her waist and then lifted her dress over her head and let it flutter to the wagon floor. Her limbs were long and coltish, her hips still bony as a boy's, and her belly concave as a greyhound's above the dark triangular bush of her womanhood. Her skin shone in the lanternlight with that peculiar lustre of healthy, vibrant youth. He stared at it for only an instant and then she had lifted the corner of the rough woollen blanket and slid in under it. The long slim arms and legs wrapped around him.

'There is nothing I would not do for you. I would steal and lie and cheat – and even kill for you, my wonderful, beautiful Ralph,' she whispered. 'I'm not sure what a man and woman do, but if you show me I will be the happiest girl on this earth to do it with you.'

'Cathy, I didn't mean this to happen –' He tried with a last sudden lash of his conscience to push her away.

'I did,' she said, clinging stubbornly to him. 'Why else do you think I came here?'

'Cathy –'

'I love you, Ralph, I loved you from the very first moment I ever saw you.'

'I love you, Cathy.' And he was amazed to find that what be said was the truth. 'I really and truly love you,' he said again, and then later, much later: 'I didn't realize how much until now.'

'I didn't know that it would be like this,' she whispered. 'I have thought about it often, every day since you first came to Khami. I even read about it in the Bible – it says that David *knew* her. Do we know each other now, Ralph?'

'I want to know you better – and more often,' he grinned at her, his tousled hair still damp with sweat.

'I felt as though I had fallen through a dark hole in my soul into another beautiful world, and I didn't want to come back again.' Cathy's voice was awed and marvelling, as though she were the first in all the infinite lists of creation to experience it. 'Didn't you feel that, Ralph?'

They held each other close under the blanket, and they talked softly, examining each other's faces in the yellow lantern light, breaking off every few minutes to kiss the other's throat and eyelids and lips.

It was Cathy who pulled away at last. 'I don't want to know the time, but listen to the birds, it will be light too soon.' Then, with a rush of words, 'Oh Ralph, I don't want you to go.'

'It will not be for long, I promise you. Then I will be back.'

'Take me with you.'

'You know I can't.'

'Why not – because it's dangerous, isn't it?'

But he avoided the question by trying to kiss her again. She put her hand over his mouth.

'I'll die a little every moment of the time you are gone, but I'll pray for you. I'll pray that Lobengula's warriors do not find you.'

'Don't worry about me,' he chuckled fondly. 'We'll fall through that dark hole in your soul again soon.'

'Promise,' she whispered, and brushed the damp curls off his forehead with her lips. 'Promise me you will come back, my beautiful, darling Ralph.'

Ralph started his wagon train south again on the road to the Shashi, and for the first morning he rode at the head of the unusually lightly loaded vehicles. At noon he gave the order to outspan. He and Isazi slept away the hot afternoon, while the bullocks and horses grazed and rested.

Then at dusk they cut the five chosen bullocks out of the herd and tied them to the wagon wheels by leather reins around the boss of their horns while they fitted the back packs. Ralph and Isazi had selected these beasts for their strength and willingness, and during the long trek up from Kimberley he had trained them to accept these unusual burdens with resigned docility.

Jordan had provided Ralph with the precise measurements and weight of the bird statue that now graced the entrance to Mr Rhodes' new mansion, Groote Schuur, and Ralph had used these figures to design the back packs and constructed them with his own hands, not trusting anyone else with his secret intentions.

Each pack could carry two statues like the one at Groote Schuur. They would be slung in woven nets of good mania rope on each side of the bullock, and Ralph had worked meticulously to ensure a perfect fit of the saddle to protect the beasts' back from galling, and prevent the load from shifting even over the roughest ground or on the steepest inclines.

Now, when Isazi, the little Zulu driver, led the file of three bullocks quietly out of the camp and disappeared into the darkening forest, they followed meekly. Ralph stayed behind just long enough to repeat his orders to the other drivers.

'You will double-march to the Shashi river. If the border impis question where I am, you will tell them I am hunting to the east with the king's permission, and that you expect me to rejoin the wagons at any time. Do you understand?'

'I understand, Nkosi,' said Umfaan, who, although now promoted from *voorlooper* to driver, still answered to the name of 'Boy'.

'Once you cross the Shashi, you will trek on as far as the Bushman wells, five days' march beyond the frontier. Lobengula's impis will not follow you that far. Wait there until I come, do you understand, Umfaan?'

'I understand, Nkosi.'

'Then repeat it to me.'

Satisfied at last, Ralph stepped up into Tom's stirrup and looked down at them from his back.

'Go swiftly,' he said.

'Go in peace, Nkosi.'

He trotted out of camp, following Isazi's bullock train and dragging behind him a bulky branch of thorn mimosa to sweep their spoor clean. By mid-morning the following day they were well clear of the wagon road and had entered the mystical Matopos Hills. While the oxen grazed and rested, Ralph rode ahead to mark a trail between the soaring granite kopjes, and through the deep and sullen gorges. At dark they resaddled the bullocks with their packs and went on.

The next day Ralph made a noon observation of the sun with the old brass sextant. From experience he made allowance for the cumulative error in his boxed chronometer, and worked out a position which he knew was accurate to within ten miles. Also from experience, he knew that his father's observations, made before he was born, were usually as accurate. Without them he would never have found the caches of ivory which had been the start of his growing fortune.

His calculations compared to his father's showed that he was one hundred and sixty miles west of the ancient ruined city that the Matabele called Zimbabwe, the burial place of the old kings.

Then, while he waited for darkness to resume the march, he took from his saddle-bags the sheaf of notes which Zouga had given him as a parting gift when he first left Kimberley. He read the description of the route to Zimbabwe, and of the city itself, for possibly the hundredth time.

'How much longer must we march through these hills?' Isazi broke his concentration. He was cooking maize cakes on a small smokeless fire of dry wood. 'My beasts suffer on these rocks and steep places,' he grumbled. 'We should have gone farther south and passed below the hills on the open ground.'

'Where Lobengula's bucks wait and pray every day for the chance to stick an assegai through a skinny little Zulu,' Ralph smiled.

'There is the same danger here.'

'No,' Ralph shook his head. 'No Matabele comes into these sacred hills without good reason. We will find no impi here, and once we come out on the far side, we will be beyond the farthest regimental kraals.'

'And this place of stone to which we go? There will be no impi waiting for us there?'

'Lobengula forbids any man even to look into the valley in

which the stones stand. It is a death-marked place, cursed by Lobengula and his priests.'

Isazi shifted uncomfortably. 'Who sets store by the curse of a fat Matabele dog?' he demanded, and touched the charm on his belt which warded off devils and hobgoblins and other dark secret things.

Despite his assurances to Isazi, Ralph moved with utmost caution in threading the maze of the Matopos. During daylight he hid the bullocks in some thick patch of bush in a rock gorge, and he went ahead to reconnoitre every yard of the way and to mark it for Isazi to follow with a discreetly blazed tree trunk or a broken twig of green leaves at every turning or difficult place.

These precautions saved him from disaster. On the third day he had tied Tom in good cover and gone forward on foot to the ridge from where he could look into the next valley.

Just below the brow he was alerted by the raucous alarm call of a grey lourie, the 'Go-Away' bird of the African bush. The cry came from just beyond the ridge, and as he froze to listen he heard a gentle susurration like the wind in tall grass; he ducked and jumped off the path, sprawling on his belly with his rifle tucked into the crook of his elbows, and rolled under the spreading branches of a low red berry bush – just as the first rank of Matabele warriors came sweeping over the rise ahead of him, with their cloaks and kilts and headdresses rustling – the sound which had warned him.

From where he lay under the bush beside the path, Ralph could see only as high as their knees as they passed, but their gait was that determined businesslike trot which the Matabele call '*minza hlabathi*', to eat the earth greedily.

He counted them. Two hundred warriors in all went past, and the soft rustle of their feet dwindled – but Ralph lay frozen beneath his bush, not daring even to creep deeper into the undergrowth. Minutes later, he heard the soft chant of bearers coming up from the next valley, and then they were trotting past his hiding-place, singing the praise song to the king in their deep melodious voices.

Ralph could tell by the spacing and weight of their gait that they were carrying a heavy litter.

He had guessed that the leading band was merely a vanguard. This was the main party, while the person on the litter was without any doubt Lobengula himself, and following him were his attendants, his high indunas and other important personages. After them again, more bearers carrying sleeping-mats and karosses of fur, beer pots and leather sacks of maize meal and other burdens. They filed past and disappeared, but still Ralph did not rise from hiding.

Another long silence, and then, with only a soft warning rustle, came the rear guard, two hundred more picked warriors trotting past. After five minutes Ralph felt it was safe to crawl out onto the path and dust the damp leaf mould from his knees and elbows.

From the top of the ridge he stared back in the direction which Lobengula's party had taken, puzzled as to where they were all headed and why. He knew from Cathy that Rudd and his party were still at GuBulawayo and that Clinton Codrington and Robyn were with them, negotiating the concession that Mr Rhodes so desperately needed.

Why would Lobengula leave such important guests at his kraal and come up here into these sacred and deserted hills?

There was no answer, and Ralph had to be content with having so narrowly escaped discovery, and to be now alerted to the presence of large parties of warriors in the area.

He moved forward with even more caution than before so that it took three more nights of travel at the pace of the bullocks before they came out of another pass between bald granite cliffs and saw the open forests of tall and lovely trees rolling away below them, silver and charcoal in the moonlight.

In the dawn Ralph climbed the cliff to the peak of the last of the Matopos Hills, and on the eastern horizon – almost exactly where he had hoped to find it – he picked out the far blue silhouette of a solitary kopje standing above the forested plain. It was still thirty miles distant, but the shape of a crouching lion was unmistakable, and it fitted exactly the description in Zouga Ballantyne's notes:

'The hill which I have named "Lion's Head" stands high above the surrounding terrain, and points the traveller unerringly towards great Zimbabwe –'

A man might have walked in the shadow of the massive stone

walls and never known they were there, so dense was the growth that covered them. It was a jungle of liana and flowering creepers, while from the very walls themselves grew the twisting serpentine roots of the strangler figs, wedging open the mortarless joints of the stonework and bringing it down in screes of fallen blocks.

Above the level of the high walls soared the heads of other tall trees, grown to giants in the time since the last inhabitant had fled this place or died within its labyrinth of passages and courtyards. When Zouga Ballantyne had discovered this massive keep before Ralph's birth, it had taken him almost two days to find the narrow gateway under this mass of tangled vegetation, but now his directions and descriptions led Ralph immediately to it.

Ralph stood before the ancient portals and looked up at the pattern of chevron stone blocks which decorated the top of the wall thirty feet above his head, and was seized with a primeval superstitious awe.

Though he could see the marks of his father's axe, and the old stumps cut away on each side of the opening, a veil of trailing plants had regrown to screen the gateway – proof that no human being had entered it since Zouga's visit more than twenty-five years before.

The steps that led up to the gateway had been dished by the passage of the feet of the ancient inhabitants over the centuries. Ralph drew a deep breath, and silently reminded himself that he was a civilized Christian; but his superstitious fears lingered as he climbed the stairs, ducked under the trailing creepers and stepped through the gateway.

He found himself in a narrow twisted stone gut between high walls open to the sky. He followed the passage, clambering over fallen stonework blocks and forcing his way through brush and undergrowth that choked it, until abruptly he came out into a wide courtyard, dominated by an immense cylindrical tower of lichen-coated grey granite.

It was exactly as his father had described it, even to the damaged parapet of the tower where Zouga had broken in to discover whether the interior of the towering structure contained a secret treasure chamber. He knew that his father had ransacked the ruins for treasure, he had even torn up and sieved the earth of this temple enclosure for gold. He had retrieved almost a thousand ounces of the yellow metal, small beads and flakes of foil, finely woven gold wire and tiny ingots the size of an infant's finger, and Ralph knew that the only treasure left for him were the idols of green soapstone.

With a stoop of his spirits, Ralph thought for a moment that someone else had forestalled him. According to Zouga, the stone falcons should have been here in this courtyard, and he started forward, his superstitious chills forgotten in the bleaker fear of having been deprived of his booty.

He plunged into the waist-high undergrowth and waded through it towards the tower – and he tripped over the first of the statues, and almost fell. He crouched over it and with his hands tore away the tangle that covered it, and then he looked into the blank cruel eyes above the curved beak that he remembered so well from his childhood. It was the identical twin of the statue that had stood on the verandah of Zouga's cottage at Kimberley, but this falcon had been cast down and lay half buried by roots and brush.

He ran his hands over the satiny green soapstone, then with one finger traced the well-remembered shark's-tooth pattern around the plinth.

'I've come for you at last,' he whispered aloud, and then looked around him quickly. His voice had echoed eerily against the surrounding walls, and he shivered though the sun was still high. Then he stood up and went on searching.

There were six statues, as Zouga had counted them. One was shattered as though by the blows from a sledgehammer, the battered head lay beside it. Three others were damaged to a lesser extent, but the remaining two statues were perfect.

'This is an evil place,' a sepulchral voice intoned unexpectedly, and Ralph started and spun to face it.

Isazi had followed and stood close behind him, preferring the terrors of the narrow passages and ominous walls to the greater terror of remaining alone at the gateway to the city.

'When can we leave here, Nkosi?' Isazi shot restless little glances into the dismal corners of tumbled passageways. 'It is not a place where a man should stay overlong.'

'How soon can we load these onto the oxen?' Ralph squatted and patted one of the fallen images. 'Can we do it before nightfall?'

'*Yebho*, Nkosi.' Isazi promised fervently. 'By nightfall we will be a good march away from here. You have my word upon it.'

The king had once again chosen Bazo for a special task – and Bazo's heart was big with pride as he led the vanguard of his impi along the secret road that took them deeper and deeper into the dreaming Hills of the Matopos.

The road was well beaten, wide enough for two warriors to run abreast with their shields just touching, for it had been used since the time when Mzilikazi, the old king, had first brought the nation up from the south.

Mzilikazi himself had blazed the trail to the secret cavern of the Umlimo. At every crisis in the nation's history, the old king had followed this road – in drought or pestilence or plague, he had come to hear the words of the chosen one. Every season he had come for advice on the herds and the crops, or to help him decide in which direction to send his raiding impis.

Lobengula, himself an initiate of the lesser mysteries, had first entered the cavern of the Umlimo as a youth – led by the crazed old magician who had been his mentor and his tutor. It had been the Umlimo's word which had placed the toy spear of kingship in Lobengula's hand when Mzilikazi had let it fall from his grasp. It was the Umlimo who had chosen Lobengula in preference to Nkulumane or the other older brothers of nobler birth – and it was the Umlimo who had made him the favourite of the ancestral spirits and had sustained him in the darkest hours of his reign.

Thus it was that Lobengula, plagued by the importunate demands of the emissaries of a white man whom he had never seen, confused by scraps of paper whose signs he could not read, troubled by doubts and tormented by fears, badgered and pulled by the conflicting advice of his senior indunas – was at last returning to the secret cavern.

He lay on his litter, on a mattress of the soft yellow and black spotted furs of the leopard, rocked by the motion of the trotting bearers, so that the naked folds and bulges of his gross black body shook and rippled, and he looked ahead with dark and haunted eyes.

Lodzi – that was the name on every white man's lips. Everywhere he turned, Lobengula heard the name Lodzi.

'Is this Lodzi a king, as I am a king?' he had asked the white man with the red face; for Lobengula, as a Matabele, could not pronounce the 'R' of the name.

'Mr Rhodes is not a king, yet he is greater than a king,' Rudd had replied.

'Why does not Lodzi come to me himself?'

'Mr Rhodes has gone across the sea, he sends us lesser men to do this business.'

'If I could look upon the face of Lodzi, then I would know if his heart was great.'

But Rhodes would not come, and day after day Lobengula had listened to the insistence of Lodzi's minions, and in the nights his indunas cautioned and questioned him, and argued amongst themselves.

'If you give the white men a finger, they want the hand,' Gandang told him, 'and having the hand, they desire the arm and then the chest and the heart and the head.'

'Oh King, Lodzi is a man of pride and honour. His word is like Lobengula's own. He is a good man,' said Nomusa, whom he trusted as he trusted few others.

'Give each of the white men a little – and give the same thing to each of them,' counselled Kamuza, one of his youngest but most cunning indunas, a man who had lived with the white men and knew their ways. 'Thus every white man becomes the enemy of the other. Set one dog on the other, lest the pack set upon you.'

'Choose the strongest of the white men and make him our ally,' said Somabula. 'This Lodzi is the herd bull. Choose him.'

And Lobengula had cocked his ear to each of them in turn, and become more desperate and more confused with every conflicting view, until now there was only one path open to him, the path into the Matopos.

Behind his litter came the bearers with the gifts for the oracle, rolls of copper wire, leather bags of coarse salt, pots of trade beads, six great tusks of yellow ivory, bolts of bright cloth, knives made by his master smith with handles of rhinoceros horn, a considerable treasure to pay for the words which he hoped would give him solace.

The path twisted down like a maimed serpent into the gut of the hills, so that the sun was lost and there was only a narrow strip of blue sky showing between the tops of the granite cliffs.

The rank and thorny vegetation crowded the pathway and at last met overhead, forming a dreary tunnel, and the silence was a heavy oppressive presence, for no bird sang and no animal squeaked or scurried in the undergrowth.

But Bazo led on at the same pace, his head swinging from side to side, scanning for danger or menace, and his grip on the shaft of his stabbing spear was firm, his sweat-oiled muscles tense as the springs of a mantrap, ready to hurl his body forward to meet an enemy at any twist in the path.

There was a stream of slow green water and algae-slick boulders across the track, and Bazo leapt it easily with barely a break in his stride; and fifty paces farther on the bush thinned and the cliffs pinched in to form a natural gateway of stone that led into the looming precipice.

Here a determined spearman could hold a thousand and Bazo surveyed it with the swift appraisal of a soldier; and then he raised his gaze to the ledge high above on which was perched a small thatched watch-hut.

Bazo grounded the butt of his long red shield – and called up the cliff. 'I, Bazo, induna of one thousand, demand passage.' His voice boomed and broke into a myriad echoes against the stone walls.

'In whose name do you come to trouble the spirits of the air and earth?' a querulous old man's voice replied, and a sticklike figure, foreshortened by the height of the cliff, appeared upon the lip.

'I come in the king's name, Lobengula the Black Bull of Matabele.' Bazo scorned to wait on permission or favour and, sweeping his shield up onto his shoulder, he sprang forward through the ominous portals.

The passageway beyond was so narrow that his warriors could follow only in single file, and the grey sand that covered the floor sparkled with starry chips of mica and crunched under their bare feet. The passageway curved upon itself and then opened again without warning over a hidden valley.

The valley was completely enclosed by sheer cliffs, and this narrow passage was its only entrance. The bowl of the floor was lush with green grass, and watered by a clear fountain that sprang from the cliff face beside the gateway and meandered down into the valley bottom.

In the centre of the valley, a thousand paces ahead, was a tiny village, twenty or so thatched huts laid out in a neat circle. Bazo led his warriors down and, with a gesture of his assegai, formed them into a double rank on each side of the pathway that led to the huts.

They waited in stillness and silence until the distant chant of the litter-bearers grew louder, and at last the king's party emerged into the hidden valley – and Bazo led his men in a deep chorus of praise and salutation.

The royal party camped two days beside the tiny stream, waiting on the Umlimo's pleasure.

Each day her attendants came to Lobengula to receive gifts and tribute on the oracle's behalf. They were a strange and macabre motley of lesser wizards and witches; some of them, touched by the spirits they served, were crazed and wild-eyed, others were young nubile girls, their bodies painted and their eyes blank and empty like the smokers of the hemp pipe. There were children with wise old eyes who did not laugh or play like other children, and ancients with withered bodies and sly eyes who spoke with the king in low, wheedling tones and took his gifts and promised: 'Perhaps tomorrow; who knows when the power of divination will descend upon the Umlimo.'

Then on the dawn of the third day Lobengula sent for Bazo, and when he came to the king's camp fire, his father Gandang was already with the king, dressed in full regimentals, plume and fur and tassels of valour at elbow and knee, and with him were six of the other senior indunas.

'Bazo, my fine axe with a sharp edge, I have chosen you to stand by my shoulder when I face the Umlimo – to guard my back against treachery,' ordered Lobengula, and Bazo felt his chest swell with pride at such a mark of the king's trust.

A witch led them, prancing and mumbling and mouthing, through the village and up the far side of the valley. Burdened by his great bulk, Lobengula paused often on the climb, his breathing sobbing in his throat, and he rested on Gandang's arm before going on again, until at last they reached the foot of the sheer high cliff. Here there was a cave in the rock. Its entrance was a hundred paces wide, but its roof low enough for a man to reach up and touch. Some time long ago the entrance had been walled up with square blocks of dressed stone, but the wall had tumbled down, leaving dark gaps like the missing teeth in an old man's mouth.

At a nod from his father, Bazo placed the king's carved stool facing the cave and Lobengula lowered his great black haunches upon it gratefully. Bazo stood at the king's back, his assegai gripped underhand, and pointed forward towards the dark entrance in the rock.

Suddenly there came the terrible spitting, tearing snarl of an angry leopard from the cave mouth, so loud and close and real that the band of hardened old warriors started and swayed, and stood their ground only with an obvious effort of will. The old witch giggled and spittle ran down her chin.

The silence fell again, but charged with promise and the threat of an unseen presence watching them from the utter darkness of the cave's recesses.

Then there was a voice, the voice of a child, sweet and piping clear. It issued not from the cave but from the air above the king's head, so that all of them raised their eyes. There was nothing there except the voice.

'The stars will shine upon the hills, and the Black Bull will not quench them.'

The little group of indunas drew closer together as though to take comfort from one another, and the silence fell again. Bazo felt himself shivering, although his sweat tickled like an insect as it ran down between his shoulder blades. Then he jerked his head as another voice spoke. It came from the ground at the king's feet, and it used the liquid purring tones of a beautiful and seductive woman.

'The sun will shine at midnight, and the Great Elephant will not dim it.'

Again that fraught and frightening silence, before something croaked from the cliff high above them, a hoarse inhuman sound, like the croak of a carrion crow.

'Heed the wisdom of the vixen before that of the dogfox, Lobengula, King of – ' The voice broke off abruptly, and there was a scuffling sound deep in the black maw of the cave, and the old crone who had been nodding and grinning at Lobengula's feet scrambled up and shouted an order in an unknown tongue.

Now there was a flash of movement within the cave, and it caused consternation to Lobengula and his indunas, for they had visited the cave a hundred times and more but they had never seen the Umlimo nor had any glimpse of her presence in the depths of the cave.

This was something beyond ritual and custom, and the crone hopped forward, shouting angrily; and now they could make out what was happening in the gloom. It seemed that two of the macabre attendants of the Umlimo were trying to restrain a smaller and more agile figure. They were unsuccessful, for the person threw off their clutching, claw-like hands and ran forward to the threshold of the cave, where the early sunlight revealed the Umlimo at last.

She was so beautiful that all of them, even the king, gasped and stared. Her skin was oiled and polished to the colour of dark amber.

Her limbs were long and supple as a heron's neck, her feet and hands finely shaped. She was in the prime of her womanhood, her body not yet distorted by child-bearing; although her belly was luscious as a ripening fruit her waist was narrow as a lad's. All she wore was a single string of crimson beads about her waist, knotted at the level of the deeply sculptured pit of her navel. Her hips flared with a delicate line, forming a broad basin to contain the spade-shaped wedge of her sex. It nestled there like a dark furry little animal possessed of separate life and existence.

Her head was perfectly balanced on the long stem of her neck; the neat cap of her hair set off the marvellous domed contours of her skull and exposed the small neat shape of her ears. Her features were oriental, the huge eyes slanted, her cheekbones high and her nose delicate and straight – but her mouth was twisted with anguish and her eyes blinded with tears as she stared at the young induna who stood at the king's back.

Slowly she lifted one hand and reached out towards him; the long, delicate palm was pink and soft, the gesture infinitely sad.

'Tanase!' whispered Bazo, staring at her, and his hands shook so that the blade of his assegai clattered against the rim of his shield.

This was the woman he had chosen and who had been so

cruelly taken from him. Since her going Bazo had sought no other to wife, though the king had chided him, and others whispered that it was unnatural, yet Bazo had held to the memory of this bright, sweet maid. He wanted to rush to her and seize her, to swing her high upon his shoulder and bear her away, but he stood rooted, her anguish reflected in his own eyes.

For though she stood before him, she was as remote as the full moon. She was a child of the spirits and protected by their horrid servants, far beyond the reach of his loving hands and constant heart.

Her attendants came now from the cave behind her, to scold and whine. Slowly Tanase lowered her arm, though for a moment longer her whole body yearned towards Bazo, and then her lovely head wilted like a flower upon the long, graceful stalk of her neck and she allowed them to take her arms.

'Tanase!' Bazo said her name for the last time, and her shoulders jerked at the sound of his voice.

Then a terrible thing happened. A shuddering convulsion ran up Tanase's back, from the perfect globes of her tight, hard buttocks to the nape of her neck, so that the nerves and muscles twitched and contracted on each side of her spine. Then her spine began to bend backwards like a hunter's bow.

'The spirit is upon her,' shrieked the old witch. 'Let the spirit take her!'

They let her be, drawing back from her wracked body.

Every muscle in her body was under such strain that it stood out in clear and separate definition under her glossy skin – and her spine arched to an impossible angle, the base of her skull almost touching the soft flesh at the back of her knees.

Her face was contorted with the unbearable agony of divination; her eyes rolled back into her head so that only the whites showed. Her lips were drawn back so that the small perfect white teeth were exposed in a frozen rictus and creamy froth bubbled from the corners of her mouth.

Though her lips did not move, a voice boomed from her tortured throat. It was the deep bass of a man, the stentorian voice of a warrior, and it bore no trace of the terrible travail of the young woman from whom it issued.

'The falcons! The white hawk has torn open the nest of stone. The falcons are flying. Save the falcons! The falcons!'

The voice rose abruptly into a wild shriek, and Tanase collapsed and writhed like a squashed insect upon the earth.

'No black man, neither Matabele nor Rozwi nor Karanga, none of them would dare desecrate the nest of the falcons,' said Lobengula, and the circle of indunas nodded. 'Only a white man would have the effrontery to defy the word of the king and chance the wrath of the spirits.'

He paused and took snuff, drawing out the little ritual to put off the moment of decision.

'If I send an impi to Zimbabwe and we take a white man in the red act of plundering the ancient place, dare I send steel through his heart?' Lobengula turned to Somabula, and the old man lifted his grey head and looked sadly at his king.

'Kill one of them, and the others will come swarming like ants,' he said. 'Set not a feast for the birds, when it will bring a pride of lions instead.'

Lobengula sighed and looked to Gandang:

'Speak, my father's son.'

'Oh King, Somabula is wise and his words have the same weight as boulders of black ironstone. Yet the king's words are heavier still, and the king's words have been given – *the despoilers of the ancient places must die.* Those are the words of Lobengula.'

The king nodded slowly.

'Bazo!' he said softly, and the young induna dropped on one knee before the king's stool.

'Take one of the wizards to guide your impi to the nest of the falcons. If the stone birds are gone, follow them. Find the despoiler. If it is a white man, take him where no other eyes can see you, not even those of your most trusted warriors. Kill the man and bury him in a secret place, and speak of it to no man but your king. Do you hear the words of Lobengula?'

'I hear, oh Great King, and to hear is to obey.'

Dutchman, the bullock with the narrowest spread of horns, was the only one which Isazi could coax down the narrow passageways and over the tumbled stonework into the temple enclosure of the ruins. In the baskets on his sturdy, dappled back, they ferried out the bird images, even the damaged ones, and repacked them onto the backs of the other oxen which waited outside the massive walls.

With Isazi's skilful handling of the bullocks and their burdens, the work was finished by mid-afternoon, and they roped the oxen in single file. With patent relief, Isazi led them away through the forest towards the south.

Ralph's relief was every bit as intense. He had been uneasy ever since that chance encounter with the Matabele impi in the hills. Now he let Isazi go on with the oxen, while he circled back across their incoming tracks to the north-west of the ruined city, examining the ground with the hunter's eye for any sign that they had been followed, or that there were any other human beings in the area. It need not be a war party – even a band of honey-gatherers or a hunter could carry word back to Lobengula's kraal or alert the border impis.

He knew what he would have to do if he found a wanderer or solitary hunter, and he eased the rifle in the leather boot at his knee. These forests were populous. He saw troops of big-eared striped kudu, sable antelope with snowy bellies and sweeping scimitar horns, big black bovine buffalo and spreading herds of plump zebra with alert pricked ears and stiff, black manes, but there was no sign of human presence.

He was only slightly mollified when he turned back and picked up the spoor of the bullock file five miles on the other side of the ruins. He trotted along the widely beaten sign, and his misgivings returned at full strength. This was too easy to follow.

He caught up with Isazi and his bullock train as the dusk was falling, and he helped him lift the heavy packs down from the backs of the oxen and examine them for galling or saddle sores, before hobbling them and letting them graze. More than once during the night he started awake, and listened for the sound of men's voices – but heard only the yipping of jackal.

In the early light they entered a wide grassy plain; the trees on the far side were a dark line on the horizon, and there were huge troops of zebra grazing out in the open. They lifted their heads to watch the strange little caravan go past, and sounded their curiosity and concern with their sharp, almost dog-like, barks.

Halfway across the plain Ralph turned the bullock train at a right angle to their track, and they marched due east until noon, when they re-entered the forest. Still Ralph headed on east until darkness fell and they camped.

Isazi muttered and complained about the wasted day, and the detour of so many miles out of their direct route towards the Limpopo river and the Bushman wells beyond, where Umfaan waited for them with the wagons.

'Why do we do this?'

'For the benefit of anyone who follows us.'

'They will still be able to follow the spoor we have laid,' Isazi protested.

'I will change that, in the morning,' Ralph assured him, and in the dawn he allowed Isazi to resume the southerly direction again.

'If I do not rejoin you, do not wait for me. Keep on until you reach the wagons, well beyond the frontier of the Matabele. Wait for me there,' he ordered, and he left Isazi and rode back on their spoor of the previous day.

He reached the open grassland where they had made such a dramatic change of direction the preceding morning, and the zebra barked at him. Their stripes were indistinguishable at this distance, and the herds were moving silver-grey masses on the yellow grassland.

'You are going to enjoy this, old Tom.' Ralph patted the horse's neck and then trotted out onto the plain towards the nearest herd of zebra. There were more than a hundred animals in the group, and they let horse and rider approach to within a few hundred paces before bunching up and galloping away.

'After them, Tom!' Ralph whooped, and they tore into the bellowing dust cloud, gaining swiftly on the chubby, striped ranks of bobbing hindquarters. Ralph quartered and turned them, and they gathered up another herd, and then another, until there were two or three thousand zebra in stampede ahead of them.

He rode out onto one flank and pushed the herd over the ground which his bullock train had crossed the previous day. Thousands of broad hooves churned the earth into soft explosions of dust. When they reached the far side of the plain, Ralph forced Tom ahead of the leading zebras and rode across their front, yelling and waving his hat about his head. The dense mass of animals turned like a living whirlpool, and the dust boiled up into the sky.

Back they went across the open ground with Tom delighting in the chase, and Ralph worked them northward until the zebra herds reached the forest line and swung parallel with the trees, and they scoured the earth with driving hooves in a swathe five hundred yards wide.

Back and forth again Ralph drove them, sheep-dogging them deliberately over the bullock tracks on each pass, until at last even Tom's pace was short and knocked up, and he was sweating in black streaks down his shoulders and flanks and blowing like a south-easterly gale over False Bay.

Ralph off-saddled in the shade of the treeline, while out on the plain the zebra herds, skittish and nervous at the harassment – still galloped in aimless circles, or snorted and pawed the torn earth.

'Nobody, not even a Bushman, will be able to pick the spoor through that,' Ralph told Tom, and stooped to lift each of his hooves in turn.

With his clasp knife Ralph prised off Tom's iron horseshoes and bundled them into the saddle-bag.

Without shoes, Tom's tracks were almost identical to those of a zebra stallion. He might go lame before they reached the wagons at Bushman wells, but they could limp in at their own speed, sure at last that there would be no pursuit. Once they reached the wagon, there was forge and anvil to re-shoe him, and Tom would suffer no lasting injury.

Ralph wiped Tom down with the saddle blanket and let him rest for another hour before re-saddling. Then he rode back amongst the scattered zebra herds to mingle and lose Tom's hoof prints amongst theirs before deliberately turning westwards, the opposite direction to Isazi's bullocks. He settled down in the saddle to lay a false trail into the forest before circling back southwards to find Isazi.

Ralph slept until sunrise the following morning, secure at last, and the temptation to drink coffee was too much for him. He chanced a small fire and delighted in the strong hot brew.

When they rode on, the sun was well up, and clear of the forest tops. Ralph let old Tom amble along at his own pace to save his unshod hooves, and he pushed his hat onto the back of his head and repeated the opening bars of Yankee Doodle over and over in a flat tuneless whistle.

The morning was cool and fresh. He felt elated at the success of his coup; already he was planning the sale of the statues. He would send letters to the British Museum and the Smithsonian Institution in Washington, D.C.

Out on his right a red-breasted cuckoo uttered its staccato call that sounded like a greeting 'Pete-my-friend!'.

Tom flicked his ears but Ralph went on whistling happily, slouched down in the saddle.

Old J. B. Robinson, one of the Kimberley millionaires who had made millions more on the new Witwatersrand goldfield, would buy at least one of the birds simply because Rhodes had one. He could not bear –

In the grassy glade ahead of Ralph a francolin called harshly, 'Kwali! Kwali!' only twice, and it rang falsely to Ralph's ear. These brown partridges usually called five or six times, not twice.

Ralph checked Tom and stood up in the stirrups. Carefully he surveyed the narrow open strip of head-high elephant grass. Suddenly a covey of brown partridge burst out of the grass and whirled away on noisy wings.

Ralph grinned and slouched down again in the saddle, and Tom trotted into the waving stand of coarse grass – and instantly it was full of dark figures of dancing plumes and red shields. They swarmed around Tom and the sunlight sparkled on the long silver blades.

'Go, Tom!' Ralph urged, and kicked his heels into his flank, while he jerked the rifle from its bucket and held it against his hip.

As Tom lunged forward, one of the plumed warriors leapt to catch his bridle, and Ralph fired. The heavy lead bullet hit the Matabele in the jaw and blew half of it away; for a moment teeth and white bone flashed in the shattered face, and then were smothered in an eruption of bright blood.

Tom bounded into the gap in their line that the man had left, but as he went through, one of them darted in from the side and grunted with the strength of his stroke.

With a thrill of horror Ralph saw the long steel blade go into Tom's ribs, an inch in front of his toe cap. He swung the empty rifle at the warrior's head, but the man ducked under it, and while Ralph twisted in the saddle, a second Matabele darted in, and Tom's whole body shuddered and convulsed between Ralph's knees as the man stabbed deep and hard into Tom's neck, an inch in front of his plunging shoulder.

Then they were through the line of Matabele, but the assegai had been plucked from the warrior's hand and the shaft stuck out of Tom's neck at a brutal angle that showed the point must be buried in his lungs. Still the gallant old pony carried his master on across the glade and into the first trees of the forest.

Then abruptly a double stream of frothy bright lung-blood burst from Tom's nostrils, and splattered back against Ralph's boots. Tom died in full run. His nose dropped to the earth and he went over in a somersault that pitched Ralph high over his head.

Ralph smashed into the earth, and he felt as though his ribs were stoved in and his teeth cracked from his jaws, but he crawled desperately to his fallen rifle and jammed a fresh cartridge into the breech.

When he looked up, they were almost upon him, a line of racing red shields and pounding bare feet below; the war rattles on their ankles clashed and the hunting chorus was like the deep baying of hounds.

One tall *indoda* lifted his shield high to clear his spear arm for the killing stroke, and the blade flashed as it started down, and then the movement froze.

'Henshaw!' The name exploded out of the warrior's straining throat, and then Bazo continued the stroke, but at the last instant rolled his wrist and the flat of the heavy blade smashed against Ralph's skull above his temple; and he pitched forwards, face down against the sandy earth, and lay still as death.

'You took the irons from the horse's hooves.' Bazo nodded approval. 'That was a good trick. If you had not slept so long this morning, we might never have caught up with you.'

'Tom is dead now,' replied Ralph.

He was propped against the trunk of a mopani tree. There was a bright scarlet smear of gravel rash on one cheek where he had hit the ground when he was thrown from the saddle. The hair above his temple was caked with black dried blood where the flat of Bazo's blade had knocked him senseless, and he was bound at ankles and wrists with thongs of rawhide. Already his hands were puffy and blue from the constriction of his bonds.

'Yes!' Bazo nodded again gravely, and looked at the carcass of the horse where it lay fifty paces away. 'He was a good horse, and now he is dead.' He looked back at Ralph. 'The *indoda* whom we will bury today was a good man – and now he is dead also.'

All about them squatted ranks of Matabele warriors, all Bazo's men drawn up in a dense black circle, sitting on their shields and listening intently to every word spoken.

'Your men fell upon me without warning, as though I were a thief or a murderer. I defended myself as any man would do.'

'And are you not a thief then, Henshaw?' Bazo interrupted.

'What question is that?' Ralph demanded.

'The birds, Henshaw. The stone birds.'

'I do not know what you speak of,' Ralph challenged angrily, pushing himself away from the tree trunk and staring arrogantly at Bazo.

'You know, Henshaw. You know about the birds, for we have spoken about them many times. You know also the king's warning that to despoil the ancient places is death to any man, for I myself have told you of it.'

Still Ralph glared his defiance.

'Your spoor led straight to the burial place of the kings and straight away from it – and the birds are gone. Where are they, Henshaw?'

A moment longer Ralph continued his show, and then he shrugged and smiled and sank back against the tree.

'They are gone, Bazo, flown afar where you cannot follow them. It was the prophecy of the Umlimo, beyond the powers of mortal men to prevent.'

At the mention of the prophetess, a shadow of sorrow passed over Bazo's face.

'Yes, it was part of the prophecy,' he agreed. 'And now it is time to carry out the orders of the king.' He stood up and addressed the squatting ranks of Matabele.

'All of you heard the king's word,' he said. 'What must be

done, must be done in secret; it must be done by me alone, and no other may witness it, nor speak of it after, even in a whisper, on pain of slow and lingering death. You have heard the king's word.'

'We have heard the king's word,' they agreed in deep sonorous chorus.

'Go!' Bazo commanded. 'Wait for me at great Zimbabwe, and wipe from your eyes the things you have seen this day.'

His warriors sprang up and saluted him. They shouldered the body of the man that Ralph had slain, using their shields as a litter, and they bore him away. The double column of running warriors snaked away across the glade and into the forest.

Bazo watched them go, leaning on his own shield, and then he turned back to Ralph, heavily and unwillingly.

'I am the king's man,' he said softly. 'Strictly charged with your death. What I have to do today will leave a deep scar in my heart for all my life, though I live to be an old greyhead. The memory of this thing will keep me from sleep, and turn the food sour and heavy in my belly.' Slowly he paced to where Ralph lay and stood over him. 'I will never forget this deed, Henshaw, though I will never be able to speak of it, not to my father or my favourite wife. I must lock it in the darkness of my soul.'

'If you must do it, then do it swiftly,' Ralph challenged him, trying to show no fear, trying to keep his gaze steady.

'Yes,' Bazo nodded, and shifted his grip on the haft of the spear. 'Intercede for me with your God, Henshaw,' he said, and struck.

Ralph cried out at the stinging burn of razor steel, and his blood burst from the wound and spilled into the dry earth.

Bazo dropped to his knee beside him and scooped up the blood in his cupped hands. He splashed it on his arms and chest. He smeared it on the haft and blade of his spear, until the bright steel was dulled.

Then Bazo leapt up and ripped a strip of bark from the mopani tree. He plucked a bunch of green leaves and came back to Ralph's side. He held together the lips of the deep wound in Ralph's forearm, then he placed the bunch of leaves over it and bound it up with the strip of bark.

The bleeding slowed and stopped, and Bazo hacked the raw-hide bonds from Ralph's ankles and wrists and stood back.

He gestured at his own blood-sullied arms and weapon.

'Who, seeing me thus, would believe that I am a traitor to my king?' he asked softly. 'Yet the love of a brother is stronger than the duty to a king.'

Ralph dragged himself upright against the mopani trunk, holding his wounded arm against his chest and staring at the young induna.

'Go in peace, Henshaw,' whispered Bazo. 'But pray to your God for me, for I have betrayed my king and forfeited my honour.'

Then Bazo whirled and ran back across the glade of yellow grass. When he reached the trees on the far side he neither paused nor looked back, but plunged into them with a kind of reckless despair.

Ten days later, with his boots scuffed through the uppers and the legs of his breeches ripped to tatters by arrow grass and thorn, with his inflamed and infected left arm strapped to his chest by a sling of bark, his face gaunt with starvation and his body bony and wasted, Ralph staggered into the circle of wagons that were outspanned beside the Bushman wells – and Isazi shouted for Umfaan and ran to catch Ralph before he fell.

'Isazi,' Ralph croaked, 'the birds, the stone birds?'

'I have them safe, Nkosi.'

Ralph grinned wickedly, so that his dried lips cracked and his bloodshot eyes slitted.

'By your own boast, Isazi, you are a wise man. Now I tell you also, that you are beautiful to behold, as beautiful as a falcon in flight,' Ralph told him, and then reeled so that he had to catch his balance with an arm around the little Zulu's shoulders.

Lobengula sat cross-legged on his sleeping-mat, alone in his great hut. Before him was a gourd of clear spring water. He stared into it fixedly.

Long ago, when he had lived in the cave of the Matopos with Saala, the white girl, the mad old witchdoctor had instructed him in the art of the gourd. Very occasionally, after many hours' staring into the limpid water, and after the utmost exercise of his concentration and will, he had been able to see snatches of the future, faces and events, but even then they had been murky and unclear, and soon after he left the Matopos this small gift had gone from him. Sometimes still, in desperation, he resorted to the gourd – although, as it was this night, nothing moved or roiled darkly beneath the still surface of the spring water, and his concentration kept slipping away. Tonight he kept toying with the words of the Umlimo.

Always the oracle spoke obliquely, always her counsel was shrouded in imagery and riddles. Often it was repetitive, on at least five previous visits to the cavern the witch had spoken of 'the stars shining on the hills' and 'the sun that burns at midnight'. No matter how doggedly Lobengula and his senior indunas had picked at the words, and tried to unravel the meaning that was tied up in them, they had found no answer.

Now Lobengula set aside the fruitless gourd, and lay back upon his kaross to consider the third prophecy, made in the croaking raven's voice from the cliff above the cavern.

'Heed the wisdom of the vixen before that of the dogfox.'

He took each word and weighed it separately, then he considered the whole, and twisted it and studied it from every angle.

In the dawn there remained only one possible solution that had survived the night. For once the oracle seemed to have given advice that was unequivocal. It was only for him to decide which female was the 'vixen' of the oracle.

He considered each of his senior wives – and there was not one of them that had any interest in anything beyond the begetting and suckling of infants, or the baubles and ribbons that the traders brought to GuBulawayo.

Ningi, his full-blooded sister, he loved still as his one link with the mother he barely remembered. Yet now when Ningi was sober she was elephantine and slow-witted, bad-tempered and cruel. When she was filled with the traders' champagne and cognac, she was giggling and silly to begin with, and then incontinent and comatose at the end. He had spoken with her for an hour and more the previous day. Little that she had said was sensible, and nothing she had said could possibly bear on the terrible pressures of Lodzi and his emissaries.

So at last Lobengula returned to what he had known all along must be the key to the riddle of the Umlimo.

'Guards!' he shouted suddenly, and there were quick and

urgent footfalls, and one of his cloaked executioners stooped through the doorway and prostrated himself on the threshold.

'Go to Nomusa, the Girlchild of Mercy, bid her come to me with all speed,' said Lobengula.

Whereas I have been much molested of late by divers persons seeking and desiring to obtain grants and concessions of land and mining rights in my territories –

Now, therefore, for the following considerations:

Item One, payment by the grantee to the grantor of £100 per month in perpetuity.

Item Two, the provision by the grantee to the grantor of One Thousand Martini-Henry rifles, together with One Hundred Thousand rounds of ammunition for the same.

Item Three, the provision by the grantee to the grantor of an armed steamboat to patrol the navigable reaches of the Zambezi river.

Now, therefore, I, Lobengula – King of the Matabele people, and Paramount Chief of Mashonaland, Monarch of all territories South of the Zambezi River and Northwards of the Shashi and Limpopo Rivers, do hereby grant –

Complete and exclusive charge over all metals and minerals in my Kingdom, Principalities and Dominions, together with full power to do all things that they may deem necessary to win and procure the same and to enjoy the profits and revenues, if any, derivable from the said metals and minerals.

In his fair hand, Jordan Ballantyne wrote out the document from Mr Rudd's dictation.

Robyn Codrington read the text to Lobengula, and explained it to him, then she helped him attach the Great Elephant seal. Finally, she witnessed the mark that Lobengula made beside it.

'Damn me, Jordan, there's none of us here that can ride the way you can.' Rudd made no effort to conceal his jubilation when they were alone. 'It's speed now that counts. If you leave immediately, you can reach Khami Mission by nightfall. Pick the three best horses from those that we left there, and go like the wind, my boy. Take the concession to Mr Rhodes – and tell him I will follow directly.'

The twins ran down the front steps of Khami Mission and surrounded Jordan as he stepped down from the stirrup.

At the head of the steps, Cathy held a lantern high, and Salina stood beside her with her hands clasped demurely in front of her, and her eyes shining with joy in the lantern light.

'Welcome, Jordan,' she called. 'We have all missed you so.'

Jordan came up the steps. 'I can rest one night only,' he told her, and a little of her delight died and her smile with it. 'I ride south tomorrow at first light.'

He was so beautiful, tall and straight, and fair, and though his shoulders were wide and his limbs finely muscled, yet he was lithe and light as a dancer and his expression gentle as a poet's as he looked down into Salina's face.

'Only one night,' she murmured. 'Then we must make the most of it.'

They ate a dinner of smoked ham and roasted sweet yams, and afterwards they sat on the verandah and Salina sang for them while Jordan smoked a cigar and listened with obvious pleasure, tapping the time on his knee and joining with the others in the chorus.

The moment Salina had finished, Vacua leapt to her feet.

'My turn,' she announced. 'Lizzie and I have written a poem.'

'Not tonight,' said Cathy.

'Why?' demanded Vicky.

'Cathy,' wailed the twins in unison. 'It's Jordan's last night.'

'That is precisely why.' Cathy stood up. 'Come on, both of you.'

Still they cajoled and procrastinated, until suddenly Cathy's eyes slitted viciously, and she hissed at them with a vehemence that startled them to their feet, to bestow hasty pecks on Jordan's face and then hurry off down the verandah, with Cathy close behind.

Jordan chuckled fondly and flicked the cigar over the verandah rail. 'Cathy is right, of course,' he said. 'I'll be in the saddle for twelve hours tomorrow – it's time we were all abed.'

Salina did not reply but moved to the end of the verandah farthest from the bedrooms and leaned on the rail, staring down across the starlit valley.

After a moment, Jordan followed her, and asked softly:

'Have I offended you?'

'No,' she answered quickly. 'It's just that I am a little sad. We all have such fun when you are here.'

Jordan did not reply, and after a minute she asked:

'What will you do now, Jordan?'

'I shall not know until I reach Kimberley. If Mr Rhodes is at Groote Schuur already, then I shall go there – but if he is still in London, then he will want me to join him.'

'How long will it take?'

'From Kimberley to London and back? Four months, if the sailings coincide.'

'Tell me about London, Jordan. I have read about it and dreamed about it.'

He talked quietly, but lucidly and fluently, so that she laughed and exclaimed at his descriptions and anecdotes, and the minutes turned to hours, until suddenly Jordan interrupted himself.

'What am I thinking of; it's almost midnight.'

She grasped at anything to keep him from going.

'You promised to tell me about Mr Rhodes' house at Groote Schuur.'

'It will have to wait for another time, Salina.'

'Will there be another time?' she asked.

'Oh, I am sure there will,' he answered lightly.

'You will go to England, and Cape Town, it could be years before you come back to Khami.'

'Even years will not dim our friendship, Salina.' And she stared at him as though he had struck her.

'Is that it – Jordan – are we friends, just friends?'

He took both her hands in his. 'The dearest, most precious friends,' he confirmed.

She was pale as ivory in the dim light, and her grip on his hands was like that of a drowning woman as she steeled herself to speak – but her voice, when at last she summoned it, was so strained that she was not sure he had understood her.

'Take me with you, Jordan.'

'Salina, I don't know what you mean.'

'I cannot bear to lose you – take me. Please take me.'

'But –' he was confused and shaken, 'but what would you do?'

'Whatever you tell me. I should be your slave, your loving slave, Jordan – for ever.'

He tried to free his hands from hers, but he did it gently.

'You cannot just go away and leave me, Jordan. When you came to Khami, it was like the sun rising into my life; and if you go you will take the light with you. I love you, Jordan, oh sweet Jesus, forgive me, but I love you more than life itself.'

'Salina, stop! Please stop now.' He pleaded with her, but she clung to his hands.

'I cannot let you go without telling you – I love you, Jordan, I shall always love you.'

'Salina.' His voice was stricken. 'Oh Salina, I love somebody else,' he said.

'It's not true,' she whispered. 'Oh, please say it's not true.'

'I am sorry, Salina. Terribly sorry.'

'Nobody else can love you as much as I do, nobody would sacrifice what I would.'

'Please stop, Salina. I don't want you to humiliate yourself.'

'Humiliate myself?' she asked. 'Oh, Jordan, that would be so small a price – you don't understand.'

'Salina, please.'

'Let me prove to you, Jordan, let me prove how joyfully I will make any sacrifice.' And when he tried to speak, she put her hand lightly over his mouth. 'We need not even have to wait for marriage. I will give myself to you this very night.'

When he shook his head, she tightened her grip to gag his words of denial.

'So fret not, like an idle girl,
That life is dash'd with flecks of sin.'

She whispered the quotation, with quivering voice. 'Give me the chance, dear Jordan, please give me the chance to prove that I can love and cherish you more than any other woman in all the world. You will see how this other woman's love pales to nothing beside the flame of mine.'

He took her wrist and lifted her hand from his mouth, and his head bowed over hers with a terrible regret.

'Salina,' he said, 'it is not another woman.'

She stared up at him, both of them rooted and stricken, while the enormity of his words slowly spread across her soul like hoar frost.

'Not another woman?' she asked at last, and when he shook his head, 'Then I can never even hope – never?'

He did not reply, and at last she shook herself like a sleeper wakening from a dream to deathly reality.

'Will you kiss me goodbye, Jordan, just one last time?'

'It need not be the last –' But she reached up and crushed the words on his lips so fiercely that her teeth left a taste of blood on his tongue.

'Goodbye, Jordan,' she said, and turning from him she walked down the length of the verandah as infirmly as an invalid arising from a long sick-bed. At the door of her bedroom, she staggered and put out a hand to save herself, and then looked back at him.

Her lips moved, but no sound came from them. 'Goodbye, Jordan. Goodbye, my love.'

Ralph Ballantyne carried up the rifles, one thousand of them, brand new and still in their yellow grease, five in a wooden case, and twenty cases to a wagonload. There were another ten wagonloads of ammunition – all for the account of De Beers diamond mines – another three wagonloads of liquor for his own account, and a single wagon of furniture and household effects for the bungalow that Zouga was building for himself at GuBulawayo.

Ralph crossed the Shashi river with a certain thousand-pound profit from the convoy already safely deposited in the Standard Bank at Kimberley, but with a nagging hollow feeling in the pit of his stomach.

He had no way of knowing whether Bazo had reported him to Lobengula as the abductor of the stone falcons, or whether one of Bazo's warriors had recognized him and, despite the king's warning, had told a wife, who had told her mother, who had told her husband. 'Nothing moves in Matabeleland but the whole nation knows of it,' Clinton Codrington had warned him once. However, the profits on this run, and the prospect of visiting Khami Mission again, were worth the risk.

On the first day's march beyond the Shashi, that risk was vindicated, for it was Bazo himself at the head of his red shields who intercepted the convoy, and greeted Ralph inscrutably.

'Who dares the road? Who risks the wrath of Lobengula?' And after he had inspected the loaded wagons, as he and Ralph sat alone by the camp fire, Ralph asked him quietly:

'I heard that a white man died in the bush between great Zimbabwe and the Limpopo. What was that man's name?'

'Nobody knows of this matter, except Lobengula and one of his indunas,' Bazo replied, without lifting his gaze from the flames. 'And even the king does not know who the stranger was or where he came from, nor does he know the site of the grave of the nameless stranger.' Bazo took a little snuff and went on. 'Nor will we ever speak of this matter again, you and me.'

And now he lifted his eyes at last, and there was something in their dark depths that had never been there before, and Ralph thought that it was the look of a man destroyed, a man who would never trust a brother again.

In the morning, Bazo was gone, and Ralph faced northwards, with the doubts dispelled and his spirits soaring like the silver and mauve thunderheads that piled the horizon ahead of him. Zouga was waiting for him at the drift of the Khami river.

'You've made good time, my boy.'

'Nobody ever made better,' Ralph agreed, and twirled his thick dark moustache, 'and nobody is likely to, not until Mr Rhodes builds his railroad.'

'Did Mr Rhodes send the money?'

'In good gold sovereigns,' Ralph told him. 'I have carried them in my own saddle-bags.'

'All we have to do is get Lobengula to accept them.'

'That, Papa, is your job. You are Mr Rhodes' agent.'

Yet three weeks later the wagons still stood outside Lobengula's kraal, their loads roped down under the tarpaulins while Zouga waited each day from early morning until dusk in front of the king's great hut.

'The king is sick,' they said.

'The king is with his wives.'

'Perhaps the king will come tomorrow.'

'Who knows when the king will tire of his wives,' they said, and at last even Zouga, who knew and understood the ways of Africa, became angry.

'Tell the king that Bakela, the Fist, rides now to Lodzi to tell him that the king spurns his gifts,' he ordered Gandang, who had come to make the day's excuses, and Zouga called to Jan Cheroot to saddle the horses.

'The king has not given you the road.' Gandang was shocked and perturbed.

'Then tell Lobengula that his impis can kill the emissary of Lodzi on the road, but it will not take long for the word to be carried to Lodzi. Lodzi sits even now at the great kraal of the queen across the water, basking in her favour.'

The king's messengers caught up with Zouga before he reached Khami Mission, for his pace was deliberately leisurely.

'The king bids Bakela return at once, he will speak with him at the moment of his return.'

'Tell Lobengula that Bakela sleeps tonight at Khami Mission and perhaps the night after – for who knows when he will see fit to talk with the king again.'

Somebody at Khami must have put a spy-glass on the dust raised by Zouga's horses, for when they were still a mile from the hills, a rider came out to meet them at full gallop, a slim figure with long dark plaits streaming behind her lovely head.

When they met, Zouga jumped down from his saddle and lifted her from hers.

'Louise,' he whispered into her smiling mouth. 'You will never know how slowly the days pass when I am away from you.'

'It's a cross you make us both carry,' she told him. 'I am fully recovered now – thanks to Robyn – and still you make me loiter and pine at Khami. Oh, Zouga, will you not let me join you at GuBulawayo?'

'That I will, my dear, just as soon as we have a roof on the cottage, and a ring on your finger.'

'You are always so proper.' She pulled a face at him. 'Who would ever know?'

'I would,' he said, and kissed her again, before he lifted her back into the saddle of the bay Arab mare which had been his betrothal gift to her.

They rode with their knees touching and their fingers linked, while Jan Cheroot trailed them discreetly out of earshot.

'We shall have only days longer to wait,' Zouga assured her. 'I have forced Lobengula's hand. This matter of the rifles will be settled soon and then you can choose where you will make me the happiest man on earth, the cathedral at Cape Town perhaps?'

'Darling Zouga, your family at Khami has been so kind to me. The girls have become like my own sisters, and Robyn lavished care upon me when I was so ill, so burned and desiccated by the sun.'

'Why not?' Zouga agreed. 'I'm sure that Clinton will agree to say the words.'

'He has already, but there is more to it. The wedding is all planned, and it is to be a double wedding.'

'A double wedding – who are the others?'

'You would never guess, not in a thousand years.'

They looked more like brothers than father and son, as they stood before the carved altar in the little whitewashed church at Khami.

Zouga wore his full dress uniform, and the scarlet jacket, tailored twenty years before, still fitted him to perfection. The gold lace had been renewed to impress Lobengula and his indunas, and now it sparkled bright and untarnished, even in the cool gloom of the church.

Ralph was dressed in expensive broadcloth with a high stock and cravat of watered grey silk that on this hot June day brought beads of sweat to his forehead. His thick dark hair was dressed with pomade to a glossy shine, and his magnificent moustache, twirled with beeswax, pricked out in two stiff points.

Both of them were rigid with expectation, staring fixedly at the altar candles which Clinton had hoarded for such an occasion, and lit only minutes before.

Behind them one of the twins fidgeted with excited anticipation, and Salina pumped up the little organ and launched into 'Here comes the Bride', while Ralph grinned with bravado and, out of the side of his mouth, muttered to his father, 'Well, here we go then, Papa. Fix bayonets and prepare to receive cavalry!'

They turned with parade ground precision to face the church door, just as the brides stepped through it.

Cathy wore the mail-order dress which Ralph had brought up from Kimberley, while Robyn had lifted her own wedding dress from its resting place in the leatherbound trunk and they had taken in the waist and let down the hem to fit Louise. The delicate lace had turned to the colour of old ivory, and she carried a bouquet of Clinton's yellow roses.

Afterwards they all straggled across the yard. The brides tottered on their high heels and tripped on their trains, clinging to the arms of their new husbands; and the twins pelted them with handfuls of rice, before running ahead to the verandah where the wedding board was piled with mountains of food and lined with regiments of bottles, the finest champagne from Ralph's wagons.

At one end of the table Ralph loosened his stock and held Cathy in the circle of his arm and a glass in his other hand as he made his speech:

'My wife –' he referred to her, and the company hooted with laughter and clapped with delight, while Cathy clung to him and looked up at his face in transparent adoration.

Then when the speeches were ended, Clinton looked across the table at his eldest daughter. His bald head shone with the heat and excitement and the good champagne.

'Will you not sing to us, my darling Salina?' he asked. 'Something happy and joyous?'

Salina nodded and smiled, and lifted her chin to sing in her gentle voice:

'However far you go, my love,
I will follow too.
The highest mountain top, my love,
Across deepest ocean blue.'

Louise turned her face towards Zouga, and when she smiled the corners of her dark blue eyes slanted upwards and her lips parted and glistened. Below the tabletop Clinton reached for Robyn's hand, but his gaze stayed upon his daughter's face.

Even Ralph sobered, and sat attentively while Cathy laid her cheek upon his shoulder.

'No arctic night too cold, my love,
No tropic noon too fierce.
For I will cleave to you, my love,
'Til death my heart do pierce.'

Salina sat very straight on the wooden bench with her hands in her lap. She was smiling as she sang, a sweet serene smile, but a single tear broke from her lower lid and descended, with tortuous slowness, the velvet curve of her cheek, until it reached the corner of her mouth.

The song ended, and they were silent for a long moment, and then Ralph pounded on the table with the flat of his hand.

'Oh bravo, Salina, that was superb.'

Then they were all applauding, and Salina smiled at them and the single tear broke and fell to her breast, to leave a dark star upon the satin of her bodice.

'Excuse me,' she said. 'Please excuse me.'

And she stood up and, still smiling, glided down the verandah. Cathy sprang to her feet, her face twisted with concern, but Robyn caught her wrist before she could follow.

'Leave her be,' she whispered. 'The child needs to be alone a while. You will only upset her further.' And Cathy sank back beside Ralph.

'Shame on you, Louise,' with forced jocularity, Clinton called down the table. 'Your husband's glass is empty, are you neglecting him so soon?'

An hour later Salina had not returned, and Ralph's voice had become louder and even more assertive. 'Now that Mr Rhodes has got his charter, we can begin to assemble the column. Cathy and I will start back tomorrow with the empty wagons. Heaven knows we will need every pair of wheels, and I thought old King Ben would never take those rifles off my hands.'

But Cathy was for once not drinking in every one of his words; she kept looking down the verandah, and again she whispered to Robyn, who frowned and shook her head.

'You talk as though the whole affair was arranged for your personal profit, Ralph.' Robyn turned from Cathy to challenge her new son-in-law.

'Perish the thought, Aunty.' Ralph laughed, and winked at his father down the length of the table. 'It's all for the good of Empire and the glory of God.'

Cathy waited until they were once more embroiled in amiable argument, and then she slipped away so quietly that Robyn did not notice until Cathy reached the end of the verandah. For a moment she looked set to call her back, but instead she made a move of annoyance and addressed herself to Zouga.

'How long will you and Louise remain at GuBulawayo?'

'Until the column reaches Mount Hampden. Mr Rhodes doesn't want any misunderstanding between the volunteers and Lobengula's young bucks.'

'I will be able to send up fresh vegetables and even a few flowers while you are at the king's kraal, Louise,' Clinton offered.

'You've been too kind already,' Louise thanked him, and then broke off, and an expression of deep concern crossed her face.

They all turned hurriedly in the direction she was staring.

Cathy had returned and climbed the verandah steps. She leaned against one of the whitewashed columns. Her face was the muddy yellow of a malaria sufferer, and her brow and chin were blistered with droplets of sweat. Her eyes were tortured, and her mouth twisted with horror.

'In the church,' she said. 'She's in the church.' And then she doubled over, and retched with a terrible tearing sound, and it came up her throat in a solid yellow eruption that soaked the virginal white skirts of her wedding gown.

Robyn was the first to reach the church door. She stared for only a moment and then she whirled and hid her face against Clinton's chest.

'Take her away,' Zouga ordered Clinton brusquely, and then to Ralph. 'Help me!'

The garland of pink roses had fallen from Salina's head, and lay below her on the floor of the nave. She had thrown a halter rope over one of the roof beams, and she must have climbed up on the table that Robyn used for her surgery.

Her hands hung open at her sides. The toes of her slippers were turned in towards each other in a touchingly innocent stance, like those of a little girl standing on tiptoe; but they were suspended at the height of a man's waist above the flagged floor.

Zouga had to look up at her face. The rope had caught her under one ear and her head was twisted at an impossible angle to one side. To Zouga her face seemed swollen to twice its normal size, and it was mottled a dark mulberry hue.

At that moment a merciful little breeze came in through the doorway and turned her slowly on the rope to face the altar, so that Zouga could see only her lustrous golden hair which had come down and now hung to her waist. That was still beautiful.

Cathy Ballantyne had never known such happiness as the months spent in the British South Africa Company camp on the Macloutsi river.

She was the only woman among nearly seven hundred men,

and a favourite of all of them. They called her 'Missus', and her presence was eagerly sought at every social activity with which officers and men diverted themselves during the long term of waiting.

The harsh conditions of camp life might have daunted another newly married girl of her age, but Cathy had known no others, and she turned the hut of daub and thatch that Ralph built for her into a cosy retreat with calico curtains in the glassless windows and woven grass native mats on the earth floor. She planted petunias on each side of the doorway, and the troopers of the column vied for the honour of watering them. She cooked over an open fire in the lean-to kitchen, and her invitations to dine were eagerly sought after by men who subsisted on canned bully beef and stamped maize meal.

She glowed with all the attention and excitement, so that from being merely pretty, she seemed to become beautiful – which made the men cherish her the more. Then, of course, she had Ralph, and she wondered some nights as she lay awake and listened to his breathing, how she had ever lived without him.

Ralph had the rank of major now, and he told her with a wink and an irreverent chuckle, 'We are all colonels and majors, my girl. I'm even thinking of making old Isazi a captain.' But he looked so handsome in his uniform with frogged coat and slouch hat and Sam Browne belt, that she wished he would wear it more often.

With each day Ralph seemed to her to become taller, his body more powerful and his energy more abundant. Even when he was away down the line hustling up the wagons, setting up the heliograph stations, or meeting with the other directors of the British South Africa Company in Kimberley, she was not lonely. Somehow his presence seemed always with her, and his absence made anticipation of his return a sort of secret joy.

Then suddenly he would be back, galloping into camp to sweep her up and toss her as high as if she were a child, before kissing her on the mouth.

'Not in public,' she would gasp and blush. 'People are watching, Ralph.'

'And turning green with envy,' he agreed, and carried her into the hut.

When he was there, everything was a breathless whirl. He was everywhere with his long assured stride and merry infectious laugh, driving his men along with a word of encouragement or of banter, and occasionally with sudden murderous black rages.

His rages terrified her, although they were never directed at her; and yet at the same time they excited her strangely. She would watch him with fearful fascination as his face swelled and darkened with passion, and his voice rose into a roar like a wounded bull. Then his fists and boots would fly and somebody would roll in the dust.

Afterwards she felt weak and trembly, and she would hurry away to the hut and draw the curtains and wait. When he came in, he would have that savage look on his face that made something flutter in the pit of her stomach, and it took all her will not to run to him – but to wait for him to come to her.

'By God, Katie my girl,' he said to her once as he leaned on his elbow over her, the sweat still glistening on his naked chest, and his breathing as rough as though he had run a race, 'you may look like an angel, but you could teach the devil himself a trick or two.'

Though she prayed afterwards for strength to control the wanton sensations and cravings of her body, the prayers were perfunctory and lacked real conviction, and that lovely smug and contented feeling just would not go away.

With Ralph it was excitement all the time, day and night, when they were alone and when they were in company. She loved to watch the deference with which other men treated him, rich and famous men older than he was like Colonel Pennefather and Dr Leander Starr Jameson, who were the leaders of the column. But then, she told herself, so they should. Ralph was already a director of the Chartered Company, Mr Rhodes' British South Africa Company, and when he sat down at the boardroom table in the De Beers building, it was in the company of lords and generals and of Mr Rhodes himself, though Ralph grinned and told her wickedly, 'Great men, Katie, but not one of them whose feet don't stink in hot weather – same as mine.'

'You are awful, Ralph Ballantyne,' she scolded, but she felt all puffed up with pride when she overheard two troopers talking of him and one said: 'Ralph Ballantyne, there's a man for you, and no mistake.'

Then at night, after they had made boisterous unashamed love, they would talk in the darkness, sometimes through most of the night, and his dreams and plans were the more enchanting for she knew that he would make them come true.

Her personal rapture was heightened by the mood of the seven hundred men around her, and each day's restraint as they waited for the word to move off increased the tension which gripped them all. Ralph's oxen brought up the guns, two seven-pounders, and the artillery fired shrapnel over the deserted veld beyond the camp, while the watchers cheered them as the fleecy cotton pods of smoking death opened prettily in the clear dry air.

The four Maxim machine-guns were unpacked from their cases and de-greased – and then, on a memorable day, the monstrous steam engine came chugging into the encampment, dragging behind it the electric generator and the naval searchlight which would be just another precaution against night attack by the Matabele hordes.

That night as she lay in his arms, Cathy asked Ralph the question they were all asking one another.

'What will Lobengula do?'

'What can he do?' Ralph stroked her hair, the way he might caress a favourite puppy. 'He has signed the concession, taken his gold and guns, and promised Papa the road to Mashonaland.'

'They say he has eighteen thousand men waiting across the Shashi.'

'Then let them come, Katie, my lass. There are not a few amongst us who would welcome the chance to teach King Ben's buckeroos a sharp lesson.'

'That's a terrible thing to say,' she said without conviction.

'But it's the truth, by God.'

She no longer chided him when he blasphemed so lightly, for the days and ways of Khami Mission seemed to be part of a fading dream.

Then one day, early in July of 1890, the mirror of a heliograph winked its eye across the dusty, sun-washed distances. It was the word for which they had waited all these months. The British Foreign Secretary had at last approved the occupation of Mashonaland by the representatives of the British South Africa Company.

The long ponderous column uncoiled like a serpent. At its

head rode Colonel Pennefather in company uniform, and at his right hand the guide Frederick Selous, whose duty it would be to take the column wide of any Matabele settlements, to cross the low malarial lands before the rains broke and to lead them up the escarpment to the sweet and healthy airs of the high plateau.

The Union Jack unfurled above their heads and a bugler sounded the advance.

'Heroes every one of them,' Ralph grinned at Cathy. 'But it's up to the likes of me to see our heroes through.'

His shirtsleeves were rolled high on his muscled arms and a disgracefully stained hat was cocked over one eye.

'When I come back, we'll be richer by eighty thousand pounds,' he told her, and lifted her off the ground with his embrace.

'Oh Ralph, how I wish I were coming with you.'

'You know Mr Rhodes has forbidden any women to cross the frontier – and you'll be a damned sight safer and more comfortable at Lily's Hotel in Kimberley with Jordan to keep an eye on you.'

'Then be careful, my darling,' she cautioned him, breathless from his hug.

'No need for that, Katie, my sweet. The devil looks after his own.'

'These are not men coming to dig holes.' Gandang stood forth from the circle of indunas. 'They are dressed as soldiers; they bring guns that can break down the granite hills with their smoke.'

'What did the king promise Lodzi?' demanded Babiaan. 'That he may come in peace to look for gold. Why does he march against us like an army?'

Bazo spoke for the young men. 'Oh great King, the spears are bright and our eyes are red. We are fifteen thousand men; can the king's enemies stand against us?'

Lobengula looked at his handsome eager young face. 'Sometimes the most dangerous enemy is a hasty heart,' he said, softly.

'And at other times, Bull Elephant of Kumalo, it might be a tardy spear arm.'

A shadow of irritation at importunate youth passed behind the king's eyes; then he sighed. 'Who knows?' he agreed. 'Who knows where the enemy lies?'

'The enemy lies before you, great King; he has crossed the Shashi river and he has come to take your land from you,' Somabula told him. And then Gandang stood again:

'Let the spears go, Lobengula, Son of Mzilikazi, let your young men run – or as the sun will rise tomorrow, that surely will you live to regret it.'

'That I cannot do,' Lobengula said softly. 'Not yet. I cannot use the assegai when words may still suffice.' He roused himself and his voice firmed.

'Go, Gandang, my brother, take your hot-hearted son with you. Go to the leader of these soldiers and ask him why he comes into my lands in battle array, and bring his answer to me here.'

Frederick Selous rode ahead, a trooper with an axe following him, and he pointed out the trees to be cut.

The trooper blazed them with a slash of the axe, and followed Selous on. The axemen came up behind them, fifty of them, riding in pairs. One man dismounted, handed his reins to his partner, spat on his already callused hands and, hefting the axe, addressed himself to the trunk of the doomed tree.

While his axe thudded and the wood chips flew white as bone in the sunlight, the second man sat in the saddle, his rifle in his hands, and he watched the forest around him for the first plumed head and long tasselled shield to appear. When the tree crackled and toppled, the axeman mounted and they rode on to the next, where he took his turn on guard while his mate swung the axe. Behind them the bullock spans came plodding to chain the fallen trunks and drag them out of the road, and then the whole ponderous caravan rumbled forward.

It was slow work, and on the third day Ralph rode to the head of the column to discuss with Selous the possibility of using the steam engine to haul the smaller trees, roots and all, from the sandy earth. They had left their horses with a trooper and walked forward for a better view of the way ahead when Ralph said quietly: 'Stand your ground, Mr Selous. Do not draw your pistol, and, in God's name, do not show any agitation.'

There were dark and moving shadows in the forest all around them, and then suddenly the dreaded long shields were there, forming a wall across their front.

'Has the king killed any white men?' a deep voice challenged. 'If he has not, then why has this impi of warriors crossed his border?'

'Lobengula has killed nobody,' Ralph called back.

'Then have the white men mislaid something of value – that they come to seek it here?'

Ralph said quietly to Selous. 'I know this man. He is one of the king's senior indunas. The one with the red shield behind him is his son; between them they disposed of eight thousand men. It would be as well to tread warily, Mr Selous. We are surrounded by an army.'

Then he addressed himself to the watching and waiting warriors: 'The king has given us the road.'

'The king denies that he called an army to enter his domain.'

'We are not an army,' Ralph denied, and Gandang threw back his head and laughed briefly and bitterly. Then he spoke again: 'Hear me, Henshaw, no white man steps beyond this place without the word of Lobengula. Tell that to your masters.'

Ralph whispered briefly with Selous, and then faced Gandang again.

'We will wait,' he agreed, 'for the king's word.'

'And we will watch while you wait,' Gandang promised ominously, and at a gesture the warriors melted away into the forest again and it seemed they had never been.

'Pull in the pickets,' Colonel Pennefather ordered. 'Put the wagons into laager. Ballantyne, can you get a message back to Tuli on the heliograph and have someone post up to GuBulawayo to find what are Lobengula's real intentions.' And, as Ralph turned to hurry away, 'Oh, one other thing, Ballantyne, can you start the generator and have the searchlight ready to sweep the area around the camp tonight. We don't want those fellows creeping up on us in the dark.'

Gandang and his son stood together on the crest of one of the little rocky kopjes that dotted the wide hot plain between the rivers.

They were alone, although when Bazo turned his head and looked down the steep back-slope of the hill, he could see the bivouac of their combined impis. There were no cooking fires to disclose their presence to the white men; they would eat cold rations and sleep in darkness this night. The long, black ranks squatted with enforced patience, dense as hiving bees beneath the shading branches of the mopani.

Bazo knew that he had only to lift his right arm above his shield to bring them to their feet and send them racing away, silent and ferocious as hunting leopards, and the thought gave him a savage joy. Reluctantly he turned back, and stood quietly with his shield not quite touching his father's.

The little afternoon breeze coming up from the river stirred their war plumes, and they gazed down upon the laager of the white men.

The bullocks had been penned within the circle of the wagons, and they could see the field guns and the Maxim machine-guns posted at the points of the barricade, their positions fortified with biscuit boxes and ammunition cases from the wagonloads. The gun crews lounged near their weapons, yet somehow the whole scene appeared tranquil and unwarlike.

'In the dark hour before the dawn, we could take them before they could stand to their guns,' murmured Bazo. 'It would be so quick, so easy.'

'We will wait on the king's word,' his father replied, and then started and exclaimed.

'What is it, my father?'

Gandang lifted his assegai and pointed with it southwards, to the pale blue horizon, far beyond the Shashi river, to the faint line of hills, shaped as fantastically as the turreted towers of a fairy castle.

On those far pale hills, something flickered and sparkled, a tiny speck of brightest white light, like a fire-fly in flight, or like the twinkle of the morning star.

'The stars,' Gandang whispered with superstitious awe, 'the stars are shining on the hills.'

*

The little group of officers stood behind the tripod of the instrument and focused their telescopes on the distant twinkle of light.

The heliograph operator called the message aloud, at the same time scribbling it on his signal pad. 'Jove advises hold your position pending clarification Lobengula's intention.' Jove was the code for Mr Rhodes.

'Very well.' Pennefather closed his telescope with a snap. 'Acknowledge message received and understood.'

The operator bent to the prism of the instrument and made a minute adjustment in its focus, turning one mirror to catch the sunlight and the second to reflect it directly towards the line of distant hills; then he seized the handle and the shutter clattered as it blinked the beam of sunlight, speeding the dots and dashes of the Morse code instantaneously across fifty miles of wilderness.

Pennefather turned away and crossed briskly to the massive steam engine on its tall steel wheels. He looked up at Ralph on the footplate.

'Are you ready to light up, Ballantyne?'

Ralph removed the long black cheroot from between his teeth, and gave a parody of a military salute.

'We've got sixty pounds of pressure on the boiler. Another half hour and she'll be whistling out of the valve.'

'Very well.' Pennefather hid his mystification. He neither understood nor admired these demoniacal contraptions. 'Just as long as we have light by nightfall.'

Gandang sat on his shield with his fur kaross of monkey skins over his shoulders. The winter evenings were cold, even here in the lowlands. There were no fires in the bivouac – and he could barely make out the faces of his junior commanders who sat opposite him, for the last flush of the sunset was fading from the western sky.

'It was something that all of us saw, and something that we have never seen before.'

They murmured agreement.

'It was a star, fallen from the heavens, and it lay upon the hills. We all saw it.'

'In the morning I will send two of our swiftest runners to the king. He must know of this terrible witchcraft.' He stood up and let his kaross fall. 'Now I am going –' He did not finish the sentence.

Instead he dropped into a defensive crouch and flung up his shield to cover his head, and around him his warriors wailed like frightened children, their eyes wide and white, glinting in the flood of light that burst down upon them from the sky.

The evening stars were washed out by the brilliance of the great white beam that reached from earth to heaven, and threw the hills into crisp black silhouette.

'The sun has returned,' Gandang croaked in religious terror. 'It is the prophecy, the whole prophecy. The stone falcons have flown, the stars shine on the hills, and now the sun burns at midnight.'

Fort Salisbury
20th Sept. 1890

My darling Kate,

Over two months since last I kissed you – and I am missing your cooking, amongst other things!

You will see by the address that we have reached our destination – although we lost a man drowned, another to drink, a third bitten by a mamba and a fourth eaten by a lion – the Matabele touched not one of us.

So Lobengula kept his word – to the surprise of all, and the disappointment of not a few. After one exchange of insults with old Gandang at the head of 8,000 of his bully boys, they let us pass – and the rest of it was rather tedious – just sweat and blisters!

The great Selous almost lost us once – but then I showed him the pass through the hills which Isazi and I found when we made our little foray to Great Zimbabwe. Selous called it Providential Pass (providential that I was with him, I'd say), and be took the kudos (to which he is welcome). He will probably write another book about his feat!

We reached Mount Hampden on the 6th instant, and it gave me a turn to think that Papa had been the first man here all those years ago.

However, Pennefather, in his great wisdom, decided there was insufficient water there and moved us all twelve miles across here. Of course the man is a new chum, fresh out from home, so how is he to know that this place will turn into a swamp with the first rains. (I intend to be well away by then!)

I have visited some God-forsaken places on my travels – but this one gets the coconut! It's infested with lions – and I've lost 15 oxen to them already. The grazing is sour-veld – the remaining beasts are losing condition – oh, how I long for the sweet-veld of Matabeleland. Trust the Matabele to pick the best stock country, so I'll not be too surprised when others start thinking about Lobengula's herds and pastures. If only the cunning old blighter had thrown his war spear and given us the excuse, we might be hoisting the flag over GuBulawayo now – rather than over this dreary spot.

Oh well! At least I am the only one here with whisky – two wagonloads of it – and doing a roaring trade at £10 the bottle. You shall have the prettiest bonnet in Kimberley when I return, Katie my heart.

The day Pennefather hoisted the flag the boys were free to go their own way – and what a stampede there was! Everyone intent to be the first to peg the gold reef we've heard so much about. Some of them are crawling back already, tail between their legs. This is no Eldorado – if there is gold, they'll have to work for it – and then, of course, Mr Rhodes and his British South Africa Company will take half of it. Of course, they all were happy enough about the Company's cut when they signed on – but they are starting to belly-ache about it now.

We had a message on the 'Helio' this morning that the British South Africa Company shares are selling for £3–15*s*-0*d*. each in London, and 5,000 new shareholders on the books in the first week. Well, all I can say is that whoever is paying that price has never seen Fort Salisbury!

'Young Ballantyne,' says Leander Starr Jameson to me, 'you were damnably lucky to take half your fees payable in B.S.A. shares valued at £1 each.'

'Jameson,' says I, 'it's strange how the harder I work and the harder I think, the luckier I get.'

So I have 40,000 B.S.A. shares, Katie my love, and you will find here attached a letter addressed to Aaron Fagan, my solicitor in Kimberley, instructing him to sell every last one of them.

Take it around to him post-haste, that's a good girl. We'll be well rid of them at a profit of £2–15s-*od.* each, and that's God's truth! Perhaps I'll buy you two bonnets when I come back!

Oh, if only we had Matabeleland – no wonder Lobengula left Mashonaland to the Mashonas! Though they don't call it that any more. The new name that is all the rage is Rhodesia – no less!

What an ungainly name it is, but no doubt Mr Rhodes will be flattered and my brother Jordan will be delighted. They are welcome to my share of Rhodesia – Don't forget to take the letter to Fagan, mind!

Nonetheless, there is still a penny to be made here. I have taken a partner, and we are building a General Store and Bar-room. He will run both businesses, as well as the Salisbury Depot for my wagons. He seems an honest lad, our Tom Meikle, and hard-working, so I have given him a wage of £5 a month and ten per cent of the profits – no point in spoiling him! Just as soon as we get the building up and the stocks on the shelves, I will leave him to it and be on my way back to you.

Mr Rhodes wants me to contract to erect the telegraph line from Kimberley to Fort Salisbury for him at a price of £25,000. I reckon there will be £10,000 profit in it. You shall have three bonnets, Katie, I swear it to you!

I must leave here by the 10th of next month if I am to beat the rains. Once they start the mosquitoes are going to take over Fort Salisbury, and every river between here and the Shashi will be a flood that would break even Noah's heart.

Thus I expect to reach Kimberley by the end of October, so take a good look at the floor, Katie my sweet, for when I get there you will be looking at nought but the ceiling for a week – and my word on it!

Your loving husband,
Ralph Ballantyne
(Ex Major B.S.A. Police Retired!)

'We must have Matabeleland. It is as simple as that,' said Zouga Ballantyne, and Jordan looked up sharply from his pad of Pitman's shorthand.

His father sat in one of the deep buttoned leather chairs facing

Mr Rhodes' desk. Beyond him the green velvet curtains were open and held with yellow tasselled ropes of silk. The view from this top floor of the De Beers Company buildings took in a wide sweep of the dry Griqualand plain dotted with camel-thorn trees, and closer to hand the stacking ground where the blue earth from the Kimberley mine was left to deteriorate in the brilliant sunshine before being made to yield up its precious diamonds.

Jordan had no eyes for the view now; his father's words had shocked him. But Mr Rhodes merely hooded his eyes and slumped massively at his desk, gesturing for Zouga to continue.

'The Company shares are six shillings in London, against three pounds fifteen on the day we raised the flag at Fort Salisbury three years ago –'

'I know, I know,' Rhodes nodded.

'I have spoken with the men that remain; I have spent the last three months travelling from Fort Victoria to Salisbury as you bid me. They won't stay, Mr Rhodes. They won't stay unless you let them go in and finish it.'

'Matabeleland.' Rhodes lifted his great shaggy head, and Jordan thought how terribly he had aged in these last three years. 'Matabeleland,' he repeated softly.

'They are sick of the constant menace of Lobengula's hordes upon their borders; they have convinced themselves that the gold they did not find in Mashonaland lies under Lobengula's earth; they have seen Lobengula's fat herds of choice cattle and compared them to their own lean beasts that starve on the thin sour veld to which they are restricted–'

'Go on,' Rhodes nodded.

'They know that to reach them the telegraph and the railroad must come through Matabeleland. They are sick to the guts with malaria and the constant fear of the Matabele. If you want to keep Rhodesia, you must give them Matabeleland.'

'I have known this all along. I think we all have. Yet we must move carefully. We must be careful of the Imperial Factor, of Gladstone and of Whitehall.' Rhodes stood up and began to pace back and forth before the shelves laden with leather-bound books titled in gold leaf.

'We need to prepare ourselves. You must remember, Ballantyne, that we have technically only the right to dig for gold. As long as Lobengula does not molest us, we cannot declare war upon him.'

'But if Lobengula were to interfere in any way with our people and their rights?'

'That would be another matter.' Rhodes stopped in front of Zouga's chair. 'Then I should certainly end his game for him.'

'In the meantime the company's shares are six shillings each,' Zouga reminded him.

'We need an incident,' said Rhodes. 'But in the meantime we have to prepare and I dare not put it on the wires. I want you to leave immediately for Fort Victoria to speak to Jameson.' Rhodes swung his big head towards Jordan. 'Do not make notes of this, Jordan,' he ordered, and Jordan dutifully lifted his pencil from the pad. 'Instruct Jameson to send me a series of telegrams on the new wires. Telegrams advising against war, that we can show the British Government and people when it is all over – but in the meantime tell him to prepare for war.'

Rhodes turned back to Jordan. 'Take an instruction, Jordan. Sell fifty thousand B.S.A. Company shares for what they will fetch. Jameson must have what he needs to do the business. Tell him that, Ballantyne. I shall be behind him all the way – but we need an incident.'

Ralph Ballantyne sat his horse on the heights of the escarpment which fell away before him, in a tumbled splendour of rocky hills and forests. The spring foliage turned the groves of msasa trees into clouds of pink and swelling scarlets, and the air was so clear and bright that he could pick out the telegraph line all the way to the horizon.

The wires were a gossamer thread that glistened red gold in the sunlight, so fragile, so insubstantial, that it seemed impossible that they ran, arrow straight, six hundred miles and more to meet the railhead at Kimberley.

Ralph's men had laid this line. The surveyors riding ahead to set up the beacons, the axemen following to clear the line, then the wagons bringing up the poles and finally the enormous spools of gleaming copper wire uncoiling endlessly.

Ralph had hired good men, paid them well, and visited them less than once a month. Yet he was proud as he saw the wires sparkle and thought of the importance and significance of this achievement.

Beside him his foreman cursed suddenly. 'There it is! The thieving bastards!' And he pointed to where the line of telegraph poles marched up the side of one forested hill. Ralph had thought that cloud shadow had dimmed the sparkle of the copper wire up this slope, but now when he focused his binoculars upon them he saw that the poles had been stripped bare.

'Come on,' he said grimly, and rode forward. When they reached the bottom of the slope they found that one of the telegraph poles had been chopped through at the base, and felled like timber. The wires had been hacked through, and the scuff marks in the earth where it had been rolled into bundles had not yet been erased by the wind.

Slowly they rode on up the slope, and Ralph did not have to dismount to read the sign of bare feet.

'There were at least twenty of them,' he said. 'Women and children with them – a family outing, damn them to hell.'

'It's the women that put them up to it,' the foreman agreed. 'That wire makes beautiful bracelets and bangles. The black girls just love it.'

At the top of the slope another telegraph pole had been felled and the wire snipped through.

'They have got away with five hundred yards of wire,' Ralph scowled. 'But next time it could be five thousand. Do you know who they are?'

The foreman shrugged. 'The local Mashona chief is Matanka. His village is just the other side of the valley. You can see the smoke from here.'

Ralph slipped his rifle out of its boot under his knee. It was a magnificent new Winchester Repeater Model 1890 with his name engraved and chased with gold into the metal of the block. He levered a round into the breech.

'Let's go to see brother Matanka.'

He was an old man, with legs like a stork and a cap of pure white wool covering his head. He trembled with fear and fell on his knees before this furious young white man with a rifle in his hand.

'Fifty head,' Ralph told him. 'And next time your people touch the wires it will be a hundred.'

Ralph and his foreman cut the fattest cattle out of Matanka's herds and drove them ahead of them, up the escarpment and into the little white settlement of Fort Victoria which had grown up mid-way between the Shashi river and Fort Salisbury.

'All right,' Ralph told his foreman. 'You can take them from here. Turn them over to the auctioneer, we should get ten pounds a head for them.'

'That will cover the cost of replacing the wires fifty times over,' the foreman grinned.

'I don't believe in taking a loss when I don't have to,' Ralph laughed. 'Get on with you, I'll have to go down and square it with the good doctor.'

Doctor Jameson's office, as administrator of the Charterlands of the British South Africa Company, was a wood and iron building with an untidily thatched roof directly opposite the only canteen in Fort Victoria.

'Ah, young Ballantyne,' Jameson greeted Ralph, and secretly enjoyed Ralph's frown of annoyance. He did not share the general high opinion of this youngster. He was too bumptious and too successful by a half, while physically he was all that Jameson was not; tall and broad-shouldered, with a striking appearance and forceful presence.

The wags were saying that one day Ralph Ballantyne would own the half of the Charterland that Rhodes did not already have his brand on. However, even Jameson had to grant that if you wanted something done, no matter how difficult, and if you wanted it done swiftly and thoroughly, and if you were prepared to pay top dollar, then Ralph Ballantyne was your man.

'Ah, Jameson.' Ralph retaliated by dropping the mousy little doctor's title from the greeting, and by turning immediately to the other man in the room.

'General St John.' Ralph flashed that compelling smile. 'How good to see you, sir! When did you get into Fort Victoria?'

Mungo St John limped across the room to take Ralph's hand, and his single eye gleamed.

'Got in this very morning.'

'Congratulations on your appointment, sir. We need a good soldier up here, the way things are going.' Ralph's compliment was an oblique jibe at Dr Jameson's own military aspirations. Rhodes had very recently appointed Mungo St John as the Company's Chief of Staff. He would be under Jameson's administration, naturally, but would be directly responsible for police and military affairs in the Charterlands of Rhodesia.

'Did your men find the break in the wires?' Jameson interrupted them.

'Bangles and bracelets,' Ralph nodded. 'That's what happened to the wires. I have given the local chief a lesson that I hope will teach him to behave himself. I fined him fifty head of cattle.'

Jameson frowned quickly.

'Lobengula considers Matanka to be his vassal. He owns those cattle, the Mashona merely tend the herds on the king's behalf.'

Ralph shrugged. 'Then Matanka will have some explaining to do, and rather him than me, and that's the truth.'

'Lobengula won't let this pass –' Jameson broke off, and the frown cleared. He began to pace up and down behind his desk with excited, hopping, bird-like steps. 'Perhaps,' he twitched at his scraggly little moustache, 'perhaps this is what we have been waiting for. Lobengula will not let it pass – nor, by God, will we.' He paused and looked at Ralph. 'How soon will you have the wires restored?'

'By noon tomorrow,' Ralph told him promptly.

'Good! Good! We must get a message through to your father at GuBulawayo. If he protests to Lobengula that his vassals are stealing Company property, and informs him that we have fined him in cattle, what will Lobengula do?'

'He will send an impi to punish Matanka.'

'Punish him?'

'Cut his head off, kill his men, rape his women and burn his village.'

'Exactly.' Jameson punched his fist into his palm. 'And Matanka is on Company ground and under protection of the British flag. It will be our duty, our bounden duty, to drive off Lobengula's men.'

'War!' said Ralph.

'War,' agreed St John softly. 'Well done, young fellow. This is what we have been waiting for.'

'Ballantyne, can you give me a tender to provide wagons and supplies for an expeditionary force, say five hundred men; we'll need twenty-five wagons, six hundred horses, when we drive for GuBulawayo.'

'When do you expect to march?'

'Before the rains.' Jameson was decisive. 'If we go, then we'll have to finish it before the rains break.'

'I will have a tender for you by the time the telegraph is reopened tomorrow.'

Ralph jumped down from the saddle and tossed his reins to the groom who came running.

Although it was only a temporary lodging which Ralph used on his infrequent visits to check the progress of his construction gangs, his transport stages and his trading posts – yet it was the grandest house in Fort Victoria, with glass in the windows and insect mesh screening the doors.

His spurs clattered on the steps as he stormed up onto the verandah, and Cathy heard him and came running with the baby on her hip.

'You are home so soon,' she cried delightedly, rebuttoning her bodice from the feeding.

'Couldn't stay away from you two.' He laughed and smacked a kiss on her mouth, then snatched the baby from her and tossed him high.

'Do be careful.' Cathy hopped anxiously to try and take him back, but Jonathan gurgled joyously and kicked with excitement, and a trickle of milk reappeared and ran down his chin.

'Mucky little devil.' Ralph held him high and sniffed at his son. 'Both ends at once, by God. Here, Katie.' He handed the infant to her and held her around the waist.

'We are going to GuBulawayo,' he said.

'Who?' She looked up at him in confusion.

'St John and the good doctor and I, and when we get there B.S.A. shares will go to five pounds. Last price I heard before the wires were cut was five shillings. The first message that goes out tomorrow is my buying order to Aaron Fagan – for fifty thousand British South Africans!'

Bazo's impi came sweeping down out of the western forests, silent as shadows and murderous as wild hunting dogs.

'Kill that dog Matanka,' the king had ordered. 'Kill him and all his men.' And Bazo caught them in the dawn, as the first of them came out of their huts yawning and rubbing the sleep from their eyes, and then they chased the young girls cackling and shrieking like hens amongst the huts, and roped them in bunches.

'And all his men,' had been the king's order, and some of Matanka's men were working for the white men, at the Prince Mine, one of the very few paying gold reefs in Mashonaland. They were breaking and carrying the rock.

'Do not interfere,' Bazo told the mine overseer. 'This is the king's business. No white man will be hurt, that is the king's order.' And they chased the Mashona labourers into the crushing plant and stabbed them as they hid under the sorting-tables.

They came racing down the telegraph line, five hundred red shields. The Mashona wiremen were unwinding the huge drums and stringing the shining strands.

'No white men will be hurt,' Bazo shouted as he let his young men run. 'Stand aside, white men.' But now Bazo was mad with blood and boastful with the killing fever. 'This is not for you, white men. Not yet, white men, but your day will come.'

They dragged the Mashona down from the telegraph poles, and bayed about them like hounds tearing a fox to pieces, while the Mashona screamed to their white masters for protection.

'Bring in the cattle, all Matanka's cattle,' the king had ordered, and Bazo's men swept the Mashona pastures, and drove the sprawling multi-coloured herds back into the west in the clouds of their own dust; and with the herds were mingled some of the white men's cattle – for one beast looks like another, and the marks burned by hot iron into the hide meant nothing to the Matabele warriors.

It was all done so swiftly that Jameson had to ride hard with his band of hastily assembled volunteers to catch them before they reached the frontier of the Charterland.

He had thirty-eight men with him, and when he saw the horsemen, Bazo turned back and with the massed warriors at his back he greeted Jameson.

'*Sakubona, Daketela!* I see you, Doctor! Fear not, by the king's orders no white man will be molested.'

But the volunteers bunched their horses, and there was the snick of breech blocks and the rattle of bolts as they loaded. Thirty-eight against five hundred, and they were jumpy and white-faced.

The little doctor spurred forward, and Ralph murmured to St

John: 'By God, the man is a bantam cock, and he'll get us all into it yet.'

But Jameson showed no agitation as he stood in the stirrups and called: 'Men of Matabele, why have you crossed the border?'

'*Hau, Daketela!*' Bazo answered him with mock astonishment. 'What border is this you speak of? Surely this land, all of it, belongs to Lobengula. There are no borders.'

'The men you have slaughtered are under my protection.'

'The men we killed were Mashona,' Bazo replied scornfully. 'And the Mashona are Lobengula's dogs – to kill or keep as he wishes.'

'The cattle you have stolen belong to my people.'

'All the Mashona cattle belong to the king.'

Then St John shouted over him, 'Careful, Jameson, there is treachery here, watch those men on your left.'

Some of Bazo's men had pressed forward, the better to see and to hear. A few of them were armed with ancient Martini-Henry rifles, probably those with which Rhodes had paid the king for his concession.

Jameson swung his horse to face them.

'Back!' he shouted. 'Back, I say.' He lifted his rifle to enforce his order, and one of the Matabele instinctively copied the gesture, half threatening the little group of mounted white men with his rifle.

Mungo St John flung up his rifle, and as it touched his shoulder he fired. The shot was a thunderous burst of sound in the heated dusty air, and the heavy bullet smashed into the Matabele's naked chest. His rifle clattered on the ground, and a little feather of bright crimson sprayed from his chest. The warrior pirouetted slowly, almost gracefully, until they looked into the shocking gape of the exit wound between his shoulder blades. Then the warrior collapsed, and his legs kicked convulsively.

'Do not touch a white man!' Bazo bellowed into the terrible silence, but not more than half a dozen of the horsemen understood the language. To the others it sounded like a killing order. The crash of volleyed rifle fire mingled with the trample of hooves and whinny of panicky horses. The banks of blue gunsmoke blended with the billowing pale dust and the rippling plumes of running warriors.

Bazo's impi was streaming away into the forest, carrying their wounded with them, and slowly the rifle fire stuttered and faded, and the horses quietened. The little group sat, silent and appalled, and stared at the Matabele dead strewn across the open ground ahead of them. They looked like the abandoned toys of a petulant child.

Ralph Ballantyne had not drawn the gold-engraved Winchester from its boot, and there was a long unlit cheroot between his white teeth. He spoke around it, smiling ironically, but his eyes were cold and green and hard.

'I count thirty-three of 'em down, Doctor Jim,' he said loudly. 'Not a bad bag really, even though they were sitting birds.' And he struck a Vesta against the thigh of his riding breeches and lit the cheroot; then he gathered the reins and turned his horses's head back towards the fort.

Lobengula turned the small canvas bag of sovereigns in his narrow graceful hands. He stood in the centre of the goat kraal, and there were only three Matabele with him, Gandang and Somabula and Bahiaan. The others he had sent away.

Before him stood a little white group. Zouga had brought Louise with him to the meeting. He had not dared leave her alone in the cottage beyond the stockade of the royal kraal, not with the mood of the Matabele as it had been ever since Jameson's massacre at Fort Victoria.

Facing the king also, but a little separated from the other couple, stood Robyn and Clinton Codrington.

Still fingering the bag of gold, Lobengula turned his face to Robyn.

'See, Nomusa, these are the gold queens that you advised me to accept from Lodzi.'

'I am deeply ashamed, oh King,' Robyn whispered.

'Tell me faithfully, did I give away my land when I signed the paper?'

'No, King, you gave away only the gold beneath it.'

'But how can men dig for gold without the land over it?' Lobengula asked, and Robyn was silent and miserable.

'Nomusa, you said that Lodzi was a man of honour. So why does he do these things to me? His young men swagger across my land and call it their own. They shoot down my warriors, and now they gather a great army against me, with wagons and guns and thousands of soldiers. How can Lodzi do this to me, Nomusa?'

'I cannot answer you, oh King. I deceived you as I was myself deceived.'

Lobengula sighed. 'I believe you, Nomusa. There is still no quarrel between us. Bring your family, all your people here to my kraal that I may protect you through the dark times that lie ahead.'

'I do not deserve the king's consideration.' She choked on the words.

'No harm will come to you, Nomusa. You have Lobengula's word upon it.' He turned slowly back to Zouga.

'This gold, Bakela. Does it pay me for the blood of my young men?' And he threw the bag at Zouga's feet. 'Pick up your gold, Bakela, and take it back to Lodzi.'

'Lobengula, I am your friend – and I tell you this as a friend. If you refuse the monthly payment, then Lodzi will look upon it as a breaking of faith.'

'Was not the killing of my young men a breaking of faith, Bakela?' Lobengula asked sadly. 'If it was not, then my people believe it to be so. The regiments are gathered, so that they darken the Hills of the Indunas; they wear their plumes and carry their assegais and their guns, and their eyes are red. The blood of Matabele has been spilled, Bakela, and the enemies of the king gather against him.'

'Hear me, oh King, think a while before you let your young men run. What do they know of fighting Englishmen?' Zouga was angry now, and the scar on his cheek burned red as a welt raised by the lash of a whip.

'My young men will eat them up,' said Lobengula simply. 'As did the Zulu at the Hill of the Little Hand.'

'After the Little Hand came Ulundi,' Zouga reminded him. 'The earth was black with the Zulu dead, and they put chains on the legs of the Zulu King and sent him to an island far across the sea.'

'Bakela, it is too late. I cannot hold my young men, I have held them too long. They must run now.'

'Your young men are brave when there are old Mashona women to stab, and young babies to disembowel, but they have never met real men.'

Gandang hissed with anger behind the king's shoulder, but Zouga went on firmly.

'Send them home to dally with their women and preen their feathers, for if you let them run, then you will be lucky if you live to see your kraal burning and your herds being driven off.'

This time all three of the senior indunas hissed, and Gandang started forward impulsively, but Lobengula spread his hand to restrain him.

'Bakela is a guest of the king,' Lobengula said. 'While he stands in my kraal, every hair of his head is sacred.' But the king's eyes had never left Zouga's face. 'Go, Bakela, leave this day and take your woman with you. Go to Daketela and tell him that my impis are ready. If he crosses the Gwelo river, I will let my young men go.'

'Lobengula, if I leave then the last link between black men and white men is broken. There will be no more talking. It will be war.'

'Then let it be so, Bakela.'

It was hard riding. They took the road that Ralph Ballantyne's wagons had recently pioneered from Fort Salisbury to GuBulawayo. They left all their furniture and possessions in the cottage outside the stockade of the king's kraal – and they rode light, with a blanket roll on the pommel of the saddle and a food bag on one of the spare horses that Jan Cheroot brought up behind on a lead rein.

Louise rode like a man, astride and uncomplaining, and on the fifth day, unexpectedly, they came up with Jameson's column in camp around the skeletal headgear of Iron Mine Hill, where the volunteers from Salisbury and Fort Victoria had joined up.

'Zouga, is that how Jameson is going to challenge Lobengula's impi?'

The little encampment looked pathetically inadequate. There were two dozen wagons, and on the canvas tents of most of them Zouga could make out the insignia of Ralph's transport company. But he pointed to the corners of the laager.

'Machine-guns,' he said. 'Six of them, and they are worth five hundred men each. They have field guns also, look at their emplacements.'

'Oh Zouga, do you have to go with them?'

'You know that I do.'

They rode down into the camp, and as they passed the pickets there was a hail that startled the sentries and made Louise's horse shy and skitter.

'Papa!' Ralph came hurrying from the nearest wagon.

'My boy.' Zouga jumped down from the saddle, and they embraced happily. 'I should have known you would be wherever there was something doing.'

Louise bent from the saddle and Ralph brushed her cheek with his fine moustache.

'I still find it difficult to believe that I have a stepmother so young and beautiful.'

'You are my favourite son,' she laughed. 'But I'd love you more if you could arrange a hot bath–'

From behind the canvas screen Louise kept calling for more buckets of hot water, and Zouga had to carry them from the fire and top-up the galvanized hip-bath in which she sat with her thick, dark braids piled on top of her head, glowing pinkly from the almost boiling water and taking full part in the conversation beyond the screen.

Ralph and Zouga sat at a camp table with a blue enamel pot of coffee and a bottle of whisky between them.

'We have six hundred and eighty-five men all in.'

'I warned Rhodes that he would need fifteen hundred,' Zouga frowned.

'Well, there are another five hundred volunteers under Major Goold-Adams ready to move off from Macloutsi.'

'They would never get here in time to take a part in the fighting.' Zouga shook his head. 'What about lines of supply and reinforcements? What happens if we get into trouble with the Matabele? What chance of a relieving force?'

Ralph grinned devilishly. 'I am the whole commissariat – you don't think I would split the profits with anyone else, do you?'

'Re-supply? Relieving force?'

Ralph spread his hands in negation. 'The doctor informs me that we don't need them. God and Mr Rhodes are on our side.'

'If it goes against us, it will be death and mutilation for every man, woman and child this side of the Shashi river. Lobengula's impis are mad for war now. Neither the king nor his indunas will be able to control them once they begin.'

'That thought had occurred to me,' Ralph admitted. 'I have Cathy and Jonathan at Fort Victoria, packed and ready, old Isazi is with them and one of my best young men. I have fresh relays of mules posted all the way from Fort Vicky to the Shashi. The hour Jameson gives the word for the column to march, my family will be on their way south.'

'Ralph, I am taking Louise to Fort Victoria. Can she stay with Cathy and leave with her?'

'Nobody asked me,' Louise called from behind the screen, and there was an angry splash of water. 'I took a vow, until death us do part – Zouga Ballantyne.'

'You also vowed to love, honour and obey,' Zouga reminded her, and winked at Ralph. 'I hope you don't suffer the same insubordination from your wife.'

'Beat them regularly and give them plenty of babies,' Ralph advised. 'Of course, Louise must go with Katie, but you had better leave for Fort Vicky right away – the Doctor is champing at the bit to settle Lobengula's hash.' He broke off, and gestured at a trooper who was hurrying towards their wagon across the laager. 'And it looks as though he has heard of your arrival at last.'

The trooper saluted Zouga breathlessly. 'Are you Major Zouga Ballantyne, sir? Dr Jameson asks you please to come to his tent at your earliest convenience.'

Dr Jameson jumped up from the travelling-desk and bustled across the tent to meet Zouga.

'Ballantyne, I was worried about you. Have you come directly from Lobengula? What are the chances? What force do you reckon he disposes?' He broke off and scolded himself with a deprecatory chuckle. 'What am I thinking of. Let me get you a drink, man!'

He led Zouga into the tent. 'You know General St John, of course –' And Zouga stiffened, his face expressionless.

'Zouga.' Mungo St John lounged in a canvas camp chair – but he made no effort to rise or offer his hand. 'How long it is. But you are looking well. Marriage agrees with you – I have not had the opportunity to congratulate you.'

'Thank you.' Zouga nodded. Naturally he had known that

Mungo was the Doctor's Chief of Staff – but still he was not ready for his anger and bitterness at the confrontation. This was the man who had kept Louise as a mistress, had held her tender precious body. He found that he was trembling, and he thrust the picture from his mind, but it was replaced instantly by the image of Louise as he had found her in the desert, her skin burned off her in slabs by the sun – and it was Mungo St John who had let her go and made no effort to follow her.

'I have heard that your wife is in camp with you –' St John's single eye glowed maliciously. 'You must dine with me tonight; it will be gratifying to discuss old times.'

'My wife has had a long, hard journey.' Zouga kept his voice level; he did not want to give Mungo the satisfaction of knowing how angry he was. 'And in the morning I am taking her into Fort Victoria.'

'Good!' Jameson cut in briskly. 'That suits my own plans – I need a trustworthy man to put a message on the telegraph line for Mr Rhodes. But now, Ballantyne, what is the news from GuBulawayo, and how do you rate our chances?'

'Well, Doctor Jim, Lobengula's ready for you – his young men are spoiling for a fight – and you have a scanty enough force here. In the ordinary way I would say that to take it into Matabeleland without reinforcements or a relieving force in the offing would be suicide. However –'

'However?' Jameson demanded eagerly.

'Four of Lobengula's regiments, those he sent against Lewanika, the king of the Barotse, are still on the Zambezi, and Lobengula will not be able to use them.'

'Why not?'

'Smallpox,' Zouga said. 'It's broken out in those regiments, and he dare not recall them to the south. They can take no part in the fighting.'

'Half the Matabele army out of it,' Jameson exulted. 'That's a nudge from on high, St John – what do you think?'

'I would say it's still a risk, a damnable risk. But think of the stake. A whole country to be won with all its lands and herds and gold. I'd say if we are ever to march, we must march now.'

'Ballantyne, your sister – the missionary woman, what's her name – Codrington, is she still at Khami? Is her family there with her?'

Zouga nodded, mystified, and Jameson snatched up a pencil

and scribbled a message on his pad. Then he tore off the sheet and handed it to Mungo St John. Mungo read it and smiled. He looked like a bird of prey, beak-nosed and fierce.

'Yes,' he said. 'Perfect.' He passed the sheet to Zouga. Jameson had written in block capitals.

URGENT FOR JOVE MATABELE REGIMENTS MASSED TO ATTACK STOP ENGLISH WOMEN AND CHILDREN IN THE POWER OF THE MATABELE TYRANT STOP IMPERATIVE WE MARCH AT ONCE TO SAVE THEM REPLY SOONEST

'Even Labouchère couldn't quibble with that,' Zouga remarked wryly. Labouchère was the London editor of *Truth* magazine, a champion of the oppressed and one of Rhodes' most eloquent and persistent adversaries. Zouga proffered the sheet, but Jameson waved it back.

'Keep it. Send it. I don't suppose you could leave this evening?' Jameson asked wistfully.

'It will be dark in an hour, and my wife is exhausted.'

'Very well,' Jameson agreed. 'But you will return here as soon as you can with Mr Rhodes' reply?'

'Of course.'

'And there will be something else I want you to do on your return, a most important assignment.'

'What is it?'

'General St John will explain.' And Zouga turned suspiciously to Mungo.

Mungo's manner was suddenly placatory. 'Zouga, there's not one of us who hasn't read your book *Hunter's Odyssey*. I would say that it's the bible of anybody wanting to know about this country and its people.'

'Thank you.' Zouga was unbending still.

'And one of the most interesting sections is the description of your visit to the oracle of the Umlimo in the hills south of GuBulawayo.'

'The Matopos,' Zouga told him.

'Yes, of course, the Matopos. Could you find your way back to the witch's cavern? After all, it has been over twenty-five years?'

'Yes, I could find it again.' Zouga did not hesitate.

'Excellent,' Jameson interrupted. 'Come along, St John, do tell him why.' But Mungo seemed to digress.

'You know the old Zulu who works for your son –'

'Isazi, Ralph's head driver?' Zouga asked.

'That's the one. Well, we captured four Matabele scouts and we put Isazi in the stockade with them. He can pass for a Matabele, so the prisoners spoke freely in front of him. One of the things we learnt is that the Umlimo has called all the witch doctors of the nation to a ritual in the hills.'

'Yes,' Zouga agreed. 'I heard of it before I left GuBulawayo. The Umlimo is preaching war, and promises a charm to the impis that will turn our bullets to water.'

'Ah, so it's true then.' Mungo nodded – and then, thoughtfully: 'Just what influence does this prophetess have?'

'The Umlimo is a hereditary figure, a sort of virgin demi-deity that has her origins long before the arrival of the Matabele in this land, perhaps a thousand years or more ago. First Mzilikazi and then Lobengula have fallen under her spell. I have even heard it whispered that Lobengula served an apprenticeship in sorcery under the Umlimo's guidance, in the Matopos.'

'Then she does wield power over the Matabele?'

'Immense power. Lobengula makes no important decision without her oracle. No impi would march without her charms to protect them.'

'If she were to die on the day we march into Matabeleland?'

'It would throw the king and his warriors into consternation. They would probably act recklessly. The Umlimo's charms would perish with her; her advice might turn like a serpent and strike the receiver. They would be demoralized – and it would take at least three months to choose a prophetess to replace her. During that time the nation would be vulnerable.'

'Zouga, I want you to take a party of mounted men – the toughest and the best we have. I want you to ride to the witch's cave and destroy her and all her witch doctors.'

Will Daniel was Zouga's sergeant. He was a Canadian who had been twenty years in Africa without losing his accent. He had fought the tribes on the Fish river and in Zululand. He boasted that he had killed three of Cetewayo's men with a single shot at Ulundi and made his tobacco pouch from the scalp of one of them. He had been in the Gazaland rebellion and fought at the

Hill of the Doves against the free burghers of the Transvaal Republic. Wherever there had been trouble and shooting, Will Daniel had forged his bloody reputation. He was a big man, heavy in the gut, prematurely bald with large round ears that stood out from his polished scalp like those of a wild dog. His fists were gnarled, his legs bowed from the saddle, and he wore a perpetual wide white grin which never touched his cold little eyes.

'You don't have to like or trust him,' Mungo St John had advised Zouga. 'But he is the man for the job.'

With Will Daniel went his henchman, Jim Thorn, half Will's size but every bit as vicious. A skinny little Cockney with the grey tones of the slum-dweller so deeply etched into his gaunt melancholy face that five thousand African suns had been unable to erase them. Dr Jameson had released him from the Fort Victoria gaol, where he was waiting trial for beating a Mashona servant to death with a rhinoceros-hide *sjambok*. His pardon depended on his conduct during the campaign. 'So you can rely on him to do whatever needs doing,' Mungo had pointed out to Zouga.

The other thirteen troopers were men of a similar type. They had all volunteered under Doctor Jim's Victoria Agreement and signed the enlistment document, a document which Jameson made sure remained secret. No copy of it went to the High Commissioner in Cape Town nor to Gladstone's Government in Whitehall, for it promised the volunteers a share of Lobengula's land and cattle and treasures; the word 'loot' was specifically mentioned in the text.

On the first night out Will Daniel had come silently to where Zouga slept a little apart and, as he stooped over Zouga's recumbent form, a wiry arm had whipped suddenly around his neck and the muzzle of a Webley revolver was thrust under his ribs with sufficient force to drive the air from his lungs.

'Next time you creep up on me, I'll kill you,' Zouga hissed into his face; and Will's teeth flashed in the moonlight as he grinned appreciatively.

'They told me you were a sharp one.'

'What do you want?'

'Me and the boys want to sell our land rights – three thousand *morgen* each, that's ninety thousand acres. You can have them for a hundred each.'

'You haven't earned them yet.'

'That's a chance you gotta take, skipper.'

'I thought you were on guard duty, sergeant.'

'Well, it was just for a moment, sir.'

'Next time you leave your post, I'll shoot you myself, without bothering about a court martial.'

Daniel stared into his face for a moment.

'Yep, I reckon you would too,' Will grinned mirthlessly.

Zouga led the patrol south and westwards through the forests where once long ago he had hunted the wandering herds of elephant. Now the tuskers were all gone, and even the herds of lesser game were wild from the unrestrained hunting of the new settlers and they scattered at the first approach of the small party of horsemen.

Zouga avoided the established roads between the Matabele regimental towns, and when they had to pass close to a settlement or the cultivated lands surrounding it, they did so at night. Though he knew that the impis had all answered Lobengula's call and were already assembled at Thabas Indunas, still he felt a vast relief when the granite domes of the Matopos rose above the treetops ahead of them and in single file his horsemen followed him into one of the steep-sided valleys.

That night there was a deputation of four troopers led by Will Daniel and Jim Thorn.

'The boys have all voted, skipper. We will take a hundred for the lot.' Will grinned ingratiatingly. 'There's not one of us have the price of a drink to celebrate when we get home – and you have that money belt around your belly. It must be damned heavy by now, and no good it will do you if a Matabele sniper puts a bullet in your back.'

The smile was still on Will's face, but the threat was naked in his eyes. If Zouga did not buy their land grants, it might be a bullet in the back. They would divide up the contents of his money belt anyway.

Zouga considered defying the big ugly sergeant, but there were fifteen of them. The gold in his belt could be his death warrant. He was in enough danger from the Matabele.

'I have seventy-five sovereigns in my belt,' he said grimly.

'Fine,' Will agreed. 'You've got yourself a bargain, Major.'

Zouga wrote out a contract of land grant sale on the back page of his message pad, and twelve of them signed it. Will Daniel and two other illiterates made their marks, and then they squabbled over the division of the gold sovereigns from Zouga's belt. Zouga was relieved to be rid of them, and as he returned the pad to his saddlebag, he realized abruptly that, if those grants were valid, then Will Daniel was right. He had got a bargain. He decided that when he rejoined Jameson's column, he would buy up all the other grants that were on offer from any of the rootless drifters who wanted to sell for the price of a bottle of whisky.

Zouga had forgotten just how intense were the peculiar brooding silences of the magical Matopos hills. The silence was a thing of weight and substance that made their spirits quail. No bird twittered or danced upon a twig in the dense undergrowth that pressed in upon the narrow path, and no breeze reached into the depths of the granite-sided valleys.

The silence and the heat weighed even upon the hard and unsusceptible men who followed Zouga in single file. They rode with their rifles held across their laps, their eyes narrowed against the glare from the sparkling chips of mica in the granite walls, watchful and anxious, the dense dark green bush about them charged with a nameless menace.

At times the narrow game trails they were following pinched out or ended abruptly in the gut of a valley, and they were forced to retrace their route and try another; but always Zouga kept working south and west. Then, on the third day, he was rewarded.

He cut the broad beaten road that led from GuBulawayo to the hidden valley of the Umlimo. It was wide and smooth enough for Zouga to spur his horse into a canter. At Zouga's orders, his troopers had muffled their equipment, and put leathers over the hooves of their mounts, so the only sound was the creak of saddlery and the occasional brush and whip of an overhanging branch.

The earlier uneasiness was gone now, and they leaned forward in their saddles, eager as hunting dogs on the leash with a hot scent in their nostrils. Jameson had promised them a bonus of twenty guineas each and all the loot that they could carry away from the valley of the Umlimo.

Zouga began to recognize landmarks that he passed. There was a pile of rocks, the largest of them the size of St Paul's dome, and three others, graded down in size, all of them weathered to almost perfect spheres and balanced one upon the other, and he knew they would reach the entrance to the valley before noon. He halted the patrol and let them snatch a quick meal standing at their horses' heads as he went down the line checking their equipment and assigning each of them a separate task.

'Sergeant, you and trooper Thorn are to stay close behind me. We will be the first through the pass and into the valley. There is a small village in the centre of it, and there may be Matabele amongst the huts. Don't stop for them – even if there are warriors with them, leave them for the others. Ride straight on to the cave at the end of the valley; we must find the witch before she can escape.'

'This witch, what does she look like, skipper?'

'I am not sure, she may be quite young, probably naked.'

'You leave 'er to me, mate.' Jim Thorn grinned lasciviously and nudged Will, but Zouga ignored him.

'Any woman you find in the cave will be the witch. Now don't be put off by the sound of wild animals, or strange voices – she is a skilled ventriloquist.' He went on, giving precise details, and ended grimly: 'Our orders are harsh, but they may eventually save the lives of many of our comrades by breaking the morale of the Matabele fighting impis.'

They mounted again, and almost immediately the road began to narrow so that the branches brushed their stirrups as they passed, and Zouga's horse stumbled in a narrow stream, clumsy with the leathers over its hooves. Then he was through and he looked up the sheer granite cliff that blocked their way. The entrance to the passage through the rock was a dark vertical cleft and high above it a thatched watch-hut was perched in a niche of the granite.

As he stared up at it, Zouga saw an indistinct movement on the ledge.

'Look out above!' Even as he yelled, a dozen black men appeared on the lip of the cliff, and each of them hurled a bundle of what looked like staves out over the edge. They scattered as they fell, and the steel sparkled as the weighted heads dropped, points first, towards them. There was a fluting sound in the air all around them, soft as swallows' wings, then the rattle of steel against rock and the thud of the points into the earth beneath the hooves of the horses.

One of the steel-headed javelins caught a trooper in the side of his neck, driving down behind the collar bone, deep into one lung so that when he tried to scream the blood gagged him and bubbled out over his chin. His horse reared and whinnied wildly, and he fell backwards out of the saddle; and then all was milling, shouting confusion on the narrow track.

Through it Zouga craned to watch the ledge, and saw the defenders lining the lip again, each with another bundle of javelins on his shoulder. Zouga dropped his reins and used both hands to aim his rifle vertically upwards.

He emptied the magazine, firing as rapidly as he could pump cartridges into the breech, and though his aim was spoiled by the dancing horse under him, one of the men on the ledge arched over backwards with his arms windmilling wildly and then fell free, writhing and twisting and shrieking in the air until he hit the rock in front of Zouga's horse, and his screams and struggles ceased abruptly.

The rest of the men on the ledge scattered away, and Zouga waved the empty rifle over his head.

'Forward!' he yelled. 'Follow me!' And he plunged into the forbidding crevice that split the cliff vertically from base to crest.

The passage was so narrow that his stirrup irons struck sparks from the rock walls on each side of him, but he looked back and saw Will Daniel pounding along behind. He had lost his slouch hat. His bald head was washed with sweat, and he was grinning like a hungry hyena as he reloaded his rifle from the bandolier across his chest.

The passage turned sharply, and the white sand that floored it splashed up under the hooves, and the mica chips sparkled even in the gloom. Ahead of Zouga a tiny freshet of clear water fountained from the rock, and his horse gathered its front feet under its chest and jumped the stream easily; then suddenly they burst out from the narrow passage, back into the sunlight again.

The hidden valley of the Umlimo lay in a green basin below them, the little village of huts at its centre; and in the base of the cliff beyond it, a mile or so away, Zouga could make out the low entrance of the cavern, dark as the eye cavity in a bleached skull. It was all exactly as he remembered it.

'Troop, into line wheel!' he shouted as his horsemen galloped out into the open behind him; and they swung into extended formation, facing the valley, the rifles unsheathed and cocked, impatient and fierce as they saw before them the prize they had come so far to find.

'*Amadoda!*' shouted Will Daniel, pointing at the band of warriors that were trotting out of the village to face the line of horsemen.

'Twenty of them,' Zouga counted swiftly. 'They'll give us no trouble.' And then he stood in his stirrups. 'Walk march, forward!'

The horsemen moved down the slope, keeping their line – while the warriors lifted their shields high and raced to meet them.

'Troop, halt.' Zouga ordered when the nearest Matabele was a hundred paces ahead. 'Pick your targets.'

The first volley, carefully aimed by hard and experienced soldiers, scythed the line of charging warriors like the reaper's steel; and they went down, falling over their shields, plumes tumbling from their heads, assegais pinning harmlessly into the earth, and yet a handful of them came on without checking.

'Fire at will!' Zouga called, and looked over the sights of his rifle at a bounding Matabele, watching him grow in size with every pace, seized by a strange reluctance to kill a brave man such as this one.

'Jee! Jee!' the Matabele yelled defiantly, and raised his shield to clear his spear arm. Zouga shot him in the notch of bone at the base of his throat and the Matabele spun sharply round, hit the ground with one shoulder and rolled against the legs of Zouga's horse.

Half a dozen of the Matabele had broken in the face of those deadly volleys, and were running back towards the village. The others were strewn about in front of the line of horsemen.

'After them.' Zouga hardly raised his voice above a conversational tone. 'Forward! Charge!'

'Sergeant Daniel. Trooper Thorn, to the cave.' He swung his horse's head to gallop clear of the cluster of huts, and there was the body of one of the fallen Matabele directly in his path. He altered course again to miss it, and both Thorn and Daniel pulled a length ahead of him.

Then the Matabele rolled lithely to his feet, and dodged in front of Zouga. Playing dead was an old Zulu trick, and Zouga should have been ready for it. But his rifle was in his left hand, and he tried to get it across, at the same time trying to turn his horse and shouting an impotent challenge at the warrior.

The Matabele extended his spear arm stiffly and let the running horse impale itself upon the broad silver blade. It went deeply into the heaving chest between the front legs, and the horse reeled from the blow and then went over on its side.

Zouga barely had time to kick his feet out of the irons and jump clear before the carcass hit the earth with all four legs kicking briefly at the sky.

Zouga landed badly, but gathered himself and whirled to face the warrior. He was only just in time to deflect the blood-smeared assegai as the Matabele struck at his belly. The steel rang against the barrel of his rifle and then they were straining chest to chest.

The man smelled of woodsmoke and ochre and fat, and his body was hard as carved ebony and slippery as a freshly caught catfish. Zouga knew he could not hold him for more than a few seconds, and with one hand on the muzzle and the other on the breech, Zouga rammed the barrel of the rifle up under the man's chin into his bulging corded throat, and hooked desperately with the rowel of his spur for the ankle.

They went over backwards, Zouga on top, and he threw all his weight onto the rifle at the moment they hit the hard earth, savagely driving it into the Matabele's throat, and the neck broke with a crunch like a walnut in a silver nutcracker. The warrior's lids fluttered down over the smoky bloodshot eyes and the body went limp under Zouga's chest.

Zouga pushed himself to his feet and looked around him quickly. His troopers were amongst the huts, and there was the thudding of scattered rifle fire as they finished off the survivors of that gallant but futile charge. He saw one of his men chase a scampering old naked crone, her empty dugs swinging and her thin legs almost giving under her with terror. He rode her down, and then backed his horse up to trample her – shouting and swearing with excitement and firing down into the frail, withered body that lay crushed against the earth.

Beyond the village, Zouga saw two horses going up the slope towards the base of the cliff at full gallop, and even as he started forward, they reached it and Daniel and Thorn jumped from the saddles and disappeared into the mouth of the cavern.

It was half a mile from where Zouga had fallen to the base of the cliff. He reloaded his rifle as he ran. The fight with the Matabele had shaken him, and his riding boots hampered each step. It took him many long minutes to toil up the slope to where Daniel and Thorn had left their horses, and by then he was badly winded.

He leaned against the stone portal of the cavern, peering into the black and threatening depths, while each breath he drew jarred his whole body. Tumultuous echoes boomed out of the blackness of the cavern, the shouts of men and the bellowing and snarling of wild animals, the screams of a woman in terrible anguish and the crash of rifle fire.

Zouga pushed himself away from the cliff and stooped through the entrance. Almost immediately he stumbled over a body. It was that of an old man, his hair pure white and his skin wrinkled like a dried prune. Zouga stepped over him, into a puddle of his dark, sticky blood.

As he moved forward, Zouga's eyes accustomed to the gloom, and he peered about him at the mummified bodies of ancient dead piled haphazard against the walls of the cavern. Here and there white bone gleamed through the parchment of leathery dried flesh, and an arm was raised in a macabre salutation or a gesture of supplication.

Zouga moved on through this grisly catacomb, and ahead of him there was a diffused source of light. He quickened his pace as another gale of wild screams was this time mingled with booming inhuman laughter that bounced from the rocky walls and roof.

He turned a corner of jagged rock and looked down into a natural amphitheatre in the floor of the cavern. It was lit by the flames of a flickering orange fire, and from above by a single beam of sunlight that came in through a narrow crack in the high arched roof. The sunbeam was dimmed to an unearthly blue by the tendrils of curling smoke from the fire, and like the limelights of a theatre stage it dramatized the group of struggling figures on the floor of the amphitheatre beyond the fire.

Zouga ran down the natural steps, and had almost reached them before he realized what they were doing.

Between them Daniel and Thorn had the body of a young black girl stretched out on the rocky floor, the girl was naked, on her back with her limbs spreadeagled. Her oiled body was as glossy as the pelt of a panther, her limbs were long and shapely. She was struggling with the desperation of a wild animal in a trap. But her screams were muted by the fur kaross wrapped about her head, and Jim Thorn knelt upon her shoulders, pinning her helplessly while he twisted her arms back against the joint of the elbows and roared with cruel laughter that was too loud for his skinny body.

Will Daniel was over the girl, his face swollen and dark with congested blood. His belt and breeches were down across the back of his knees. He was grunting and snuffling like a boar at the trough. His pale buttocks were covered with a fuzz of sparse curly black hair. He drove against the girl with a wet slapping sound like a washerwoman pounding laundry on a slab.

Before Zouga could reach him, Will Daniel's whole body stiffened and jerked spasmodically and then he rolled off the tender young body, and he was bloodied from the knees to the navel of his sagging, hairy paunch.

'By God, Jim my lad,' he panted at the little trooper, 'that was better than a belly ache. Get up on the bitch for your turn–' Then he saw Zouga coming out of the shadows, and he grinned at him. 'First come, first served, Major–'

Zouga took two strides to reach him, and then he kicked him in his smiling mouth with the heel of his riding boot. Will Daniel's bottom lip split open like the petals of a rose, and be scrambled to his feet, spitting out white chips of tooth, and hauling up his breeches over his monstrous nakedness.

'I'll kill you for that.' He tugged at the knife on his dangling unclinched belt, but Zouga thrust the muzzle of his rifle into his belly, doubling him over at the waist, and then whirled to slam the butt against Jim Thorn's temple, as Thorn was reaching for his abandoned rifle.

'Get on your feet,' Zouga told him coldly, and, swaying and clutching the swelling above his ear, Jim Thorn backed off against the wall of the cave.

'I'll get you for this,' Will Daniel wheezed painfully, still holding his belly, and Zouga turned the rifle back onto him.

'Get out,' he said softly. 'Get out of here you filthy bloody animals.'

They shuffled up the steps of the amphitheatre; and from the shadows of the cavern entrance, Will Daniel yelled again, his voice blustering and angry.

'I'll not forget this, Major bloody Ballantyne. I'll get you yet!'

Zouga turned back to the girl. She had pulled the kaross off her head, and she crouched on the stone floor with her legs curled up under her. She was trying to staunch the flow of her virgin blood with her hands, but she stared at Zouga with the tortured ferocity of a leopard held by the serrated jaws of a spring trap.

Zouga felt an overwhelming compassion sweep over him – yet he knew there was no succour he could give her.

'You, who were Umlimo, are Umlimo no longer,' he said at last, and she drew back her head and spat at him. The frothy spittle splattered against his boots, but the effort made her whimper with pain and press her hands against her lower belly. A fresh trickle of bright arterial blood snaked down her thigh.

'I came to destroy the Umlimo,' he said. 'But she is destroyed not by a bullet from a gun. Go, child. The gift of the spirits has been taken from you. Go swiftly, but go in peace.'

Like a wounded animal she crept on her hands and knees into the dark maze of tunnels beyond the amphitheatre, leaving a speckle of bloody drops upon the stone floor.

She looked back at him once. 'Peace, you say, white man. There will be no peace, ever!'

And then she was gone into the shadows.

The rains had not yet come – but their heralds soared up to the heavens, great ranges of cumulus cloud, their heads shaped like mushrooms. Silver and blue and imperial purple, they stood above the Hills of the Indunas.

The heat seemed trapped beneath them. It clanged down upon the iron hills like a blacksmith's hammer on the anvil. The impis were thick as safari ants upon the slopes; they squatted in dense ranks their shields under them, their assegais and guns laid on the rocky earth before them – thousands upon thousands they waited, every plumed head craning down towards the royal kraal at the foot of the hills.

There was the beat of a single drum. Tap – tap! Tap – tap! – And the great black mass of warriors stirred like an amorphous sea monster rising from the depths.

'The Elephant comes! He comes! He comes!' It was a soft growl in all their throats.

Through the gates of the stockade filed a small procession, twenty men wearing the tassels of valour, twenty men walking proud, the blood royal of Kumalo, and at their head the huge heavy figure of the king.

Lobengula had thrown off all the European gee-gaws, the brass buttons and mirrors, the gold brocaded coat – and he was dressed in the regalia of a Matabele king.

The headring was on his brow, and heron feathers in his hair. His cloak was royal leopardskin, spotted gold, and his kilt was of leopard tails. His swollen ankles, crippled with gout, were covered by the war rattles, but he mastered the agony of the disease, striding out with ponderous dignity, so the waiting impis gasped with the splendour of his presence.

'See the Great Bull whose tread shakes the earth.'

In his right hand he carried the toy spear of polished redwood, the spear of kingship. Now he raised the puny weapon high, and the nation came bounding upright; and the shields, the long shields that gave them their name, bloomed upon the slope of the hill, covering it like a garden of exotic deadly flowers.

'*Bayete!*' The royal salute roared like the surf of a winter sea breaking on a rocky headland.

'*Bayete!* Lobengula, son of Mzilikazi.'

After that great burst of sound, the silence was daunting, but Lobengula paced slowly along the ranks, and in his eyes was the terrible sorrow of a father for the sons who must die. This was the hour which he had dreaded from the first day he took the little redwood spear in his right hand. This was the destiny which he had tried to avoid – and now it had overtaken him.

His voice boomed, and he lifted the spear and pointed to the east. 'The enemy that comes upon us now is like –' the spear shook in his hand, 'like the leopard in the goat kraal, like the white termites in the kingpost of a hut. They will not stop until all is destroyed.'

The massed regiments of Matabele growled, straining like

hunting dogs against the leash, and Lobengula stopped in the centre of their lines and threw the leopardskin cloak back from his right arm.

He turned slowly until he faced into the east, where Jameson's columns were massing far over the horizon, and his spear arm went back to its full stretch. He stood poised in the classic stance of thc javelin-thrower, and there was a soft susurration in the air as ten thousand lungs filled with breath and held it.

Then, with a heart-stopping shout, the cry of a man crushed under the iron wheel of his own destiny, Lobengula hurled the war spear into the east, and his shout was echoed by ten thousand throats.

'Jee! Jee!' They roared, and stabbed at the air with the broad silver blades, stabbing at the still invisible enemy.

Then the impis formed, one behind the other. Led by their indunas, their matched shields overlapping, they swept past the king, fierce in their pride, leaping high and flashing their assegais, and Lobengula saluted them: the Imbezu and the Inyati, the Ingubu and the Izimvukuzane, the 'Moles-that-burrow-under-a-mountain', with their matt red shields held high and Bazo, the Axe, prancing at their head. They wound away into the eastern grasslands, and Lobengula could still hear their singing, faintly on the heated air, long after the last of them had disappeared from view.

A little group of indunas and guards still attended the king, but they waited below at the gate of the stockade.

Lobengula was alone upon the deserted hillside; all the dignity and regal pride had gone out of his bearing. His grossly swollen body slumped like that of a very old and sick man. His eyes were rheumy with unshed tears, and he stared out into the east without moving, listening to the fading war chants.

At last he sighed, shook himself, and hobbled forward on his crippled distorted feet.

Painfully he stooped to retrieve the little redwood spear, but he paused before his fingers touched it.

The blade of the spear of kingship had snapped through. He picked up the broken pieces and held them in his hands, and then he turned and shuffled slowly down from the Hills of the Indunas.

The Company flag stood high above the laager on a slightly crooked pole of mopani.

It had hung limply in the stupefying heat all that morning, but now as the patrol rode in across the open ground above the river bank, it unfurled briefly on a random current of air, snapped as though to draw attention to itself, and then extended its full glory for a moment, before sagging wearily once again.

At the head of the patrol, Ralph Ballantyne turned to his father who rode at his side. 'That flag makes no bones about it, Papa.'

The pretty crosses of St George, St Andrew and St Patrick that made up the Union Jack, had the Company insignia superimposed upon them, the lion gardant with a tusk of ivory held in its claw and the letters under it 'B.S.A.C.' – British South Africa Company.

'Servants of the Company first, and of the queen a good deal later.'

'You're a cynical rascal, Ralph.' Zouga could hardly suppress his smile. 'Are you suggesting that there is a man in all our Company here for personal gain rather than glory of Empire?'

'Perish the thought.' This time Ralph chuckled. 'By the way, Papa, how many land grants have you bought up so far? I am losing count – is it thirty or thirty-five?'

'This is a dream I worked for all my life, Ralph. It's coming true before our eyes – and when it does, I'll have my fair reward, and nothing more.'

The laager was drawn up in its rigid square three hundred yards from the steep banks of the Shangani river, in the centre of a dried-out clay pan. The surface was as flat and bare as a tennis court. The clay had cracked into irregular briquettes that curled up at the edges. They crunched under the horses' hooves as Zouga led the patrol in.

They had been out for two days, scouting the road beyond the river, and Zouga was pleased to see that during his absence St John had taken Zouga's advice and had his axemen hack down the brush around the edges of the pan to open the field of fire. Now any attacker would have to cross three hundred yards of bare clay to reach the square of wagons, all of it under the evil little Cyclopean scrutiny of the Maxims.

As they cantered up, a party unchained the wheels of one of the wagons and dragged it aside to allow them to enter, and a sergeant in Company uniform saluted Zouga as he passed and called after him.

'General St John's compliments, sir, and will you report to him directly.'

'My bet is that you need a drink.' Mungo St John took one look at the dust that clung like flour in Zouga's beard and the dark patches of sweat that had soaked through his shirt. Coldly Zouga nodded his thanks and poured from the bottle that held down one corner of the map.

'The impis are out in full array,' he said, and let the whisky soak the cloying dust from the back of his throat before going on. 'I have identified most of them. There's Gandang's Inyati, and Manonda's Insukamini –' He reeled off the names of the indunas and their impis, glancing at the notes he had made on his pad. 'We had a brush with the 'Moles' and had to shoot our way out and ride for it, but still we reached the Bembesi river before turning back.'

'Where are the impis, Ballantyne? Damn it, man, we have advanced seventy miles from Iron Mine Hill and seen neither hide nor hair of them,' Jameson demanded almost petulantly.

'They are all around us, Doctor. A thousand or more in the trees just across the river, and I cut tracks that showed that two more impis have circled out behind us. They are probably lying across the Longiwe Hills watching every move we make.'

'We must bring them to battle,' Jameson fretted. 'Every day the campaign lasts is costing the shareholders money.'

'They won't attack us here, not while we are in laager, not across open ground.'

'Where then?'

'They will attack in the Zulu way, in broken ground, or thick bush. I have marked four likely defiles ahead of us, places where they will be able to creep up close on either side or lay to ambush the wagons as we pass.'

'You want us to walk into their trap – rather than draw them out?' Mungo asked.

'You'll not draw them out. I think their commander here is Gandang, the king's half-brother. He is far too cunning to come at us in the open. If you want to fight them, it must be in the bad ground.'

'When the serpent is coiled, with his head drawn back and his mouth agape to show the venom hanging like drops of dew upon his fangs – then the wise man does not stretch out his hands towards him.' Gandang spoke softly, and the other indunas cocked their heads to listen to his words. 'The wise man waits until the serpent uncoils and begins to creep away, then he steps upon the head and crushes it. We must wait. We must wait to take them in the forests, when the wagons are strung out, and the outriders cannot see one another. Then we cut the column into pieces and swallow each one, a mouthful at a time.'

'Yet my young men are tired of waiting,' said Manonda, facing Gandang across the fire. Manonda was the commander of the elite Insukamini impi, and though there was silver on his head, there was still fire in his heart. They all knew him to be brave to the edge of folly, quick to take an insult, and quicker still to revenge it. 'These white barbarians have marched unopposed across our lands, while we trail around them like timid girls guarding our maidenheads and giggling behind our hands. My young men grow weary of waiting, Gandang, and I with them.'

'There is a time for timidity, Manonda, my cousin, and there is a time to be brave.'

'The time to be brave is when your enemy stands brazenly before you. They are six hundred, you have counted them yourself, Gandang, and we are six thousand.' Manonda grinned mockingly around the circle of listening men. On the brow of each was the headring of high office, and on their arms and legs the tassels of courage. 'Shame on those that hesitate,' said Manonda, the Bold. 'Shame on you, Bazo. Shame on you, Ntabene. Shame on you, Gambo.' His voice was filled with scorn, and as he said each of their names they hissed with angry denial.

Then suddenly here was a sound from beyond the circle of squatting indunas, a sound in the night that chilled and silenced them all. It was the eerie wail of mourning for the dead, and as they listened it came closer, and with it were many other voices.

Gandang sprang to his feet and challenged loudly. 'Who comes?'

And out of the darkness a dozen guards, half dragged and half carried an old woman. She wore only a skirt of untanned hyena skin, and around her neck the grisly accoutrements and trappings of the witch's trade. Her eyes were rolled up into her head so that the whites flashed in the firelight, and her spittle foamed on her slack lips. From her throat issued the wails of mourning for the dead.

'What is it, witch?' Gandang demanded, his superstitious fears twisting his mouth and darkening his eyes. 'What tidings do you bring?'

'The white men have desecrated the holy places. They have destroyed the chosen one of the spirits. They have slaughtered the priests of the nation. They have entered the cave of the Umlimo in the sacred hills – and her blood is splashed upon the ancient rocks. Woe unto all of us. Woe unto those who do not seek revenge. Kill the white men. Kill them all!'

The witch threw off the restraining hands of the guard and, with a wild shriek, hurled herself into the midst of the leaping flames of the watch-fire.

Her skirt burst into flames. Her wild bush of hair burned like a torch. They drew back in horror.

'Kill the white men,' screamed the witch from out of the flames, and they stared as her skin blackened and her flesh peeled from off her bones. She collapsed and a torrent of sparks flew up into the overhanging branches of the forest, and then there was only the crackle and drum of the fire.

Bazo stood in the stunned silence, and he felt the rage rising from deep within his soul. Staring into the flames at the black and twisted remains of the witch, he felt the same need of sacrifice – an atonement and a surcease from the rage and the grief.

He saw in the yellow flames an image of Tanase's beloved face, and something seemed to tear in his chest.

'Jee!' he said, drawing out the war cry, giving expression to his rage. 'Jee!' He lifted the assegai and pointed the blade in the direction of the river and the white men's laager which lay not more than a mile beyond the dark silhouette of the hills. 'Jee!' and the night breeze turned the tears cold as the snow-melt from the Drakensberg mountains upon his cheeks.

'Jee.' Manonda took up the chant, and stabbed towards the enemy, and the divine madness descended upon them. Gandang was the only one who had reason and fear of consequence left to him.

'Wait!' he cried. 'Wait, my children and my brothers.' But they were gone already, racing away into the darkness to rouse their sleeping impis.

Zouga Ballantyne could not sleep, though his back and thighs still ached for rest from hard riding, and the earth under his blanket was no harder than that on which he had passed a thousand other nights. He lay and listened to the snores and occasional dreamers' gabble from the men around him, while vague forebodings and dark thoughts kept him from joining them in slumber.

Once again vivid memories of the little tragedy in the cave of the Umlimo returned to plague him – and he wondered how long it would be before the news of the atrocity reached the king and his indunas. It might take weeks for a witness to come down from the cave of the Matopos, but when that happened, he would know it by the actions of the Matabele indunas.

From the opposite side of the laager a sky-rocket went hissing up into the night sky, and popped into little red stars high in the heavens. The pickets had been firing a rocket every hour, to guide a missing patrol into the laager.

Now Zouga reached under the saddle that was his pillow and brought out the gold hunter watch. In the light of the sky rocket he checked the time. It was three o'clock in the morning. He threw off his blanket, and groped for his boots. While he pulled them on, his premonition of lurking evil grew stronger.

He strapped on his bandolier and checked the Webley service revolver hanging on the webbing. Then he stepped over the sleeping blanket-wrapped forms around him and went down to the horse lines. The bay gelding whickered as it recognized him, and Jan Cheroot woke.

'It is all right,' Zouga told him quietly, but the little Hottentot yawned and, with the blanket over his shoulders like a shawl, hobbled across to stir the ashes of his cooking-fire. He set the blue enamel coffee pot on the coals and, while it was heating, they sat side by side and talked quietly like the old friends that they were.

'Less than sixty miles to GuBulawayo,' Jan Cheroot murmured. 'It's taken us more than thirty years – but now at last I feel we are coming home.'

'I have bought up almost forty land grants,' Zouga agreed. 'That is nearly a quarter of a million acres. Yes, Jan Cheroot, we are coming home at last. By God, it's been a long, hard road, though, from the pit of Kimberley mine to the Zambezi –' Zouga broke off and listened. There had been a faint cry, almost like a night bird, from beyond the laager.

'The Mashona,' Jan Cheroot grunted. 'The general should have let them stay in the laager.'

During the slow trek up from Iron Mine Hill, many small groups of Mashona had come to the wagons, begging protection from thc assembling Matabele. They knew from bitter experience what to expect when the impis swept across the land in battle array.

'The general could not take that chance.' Zouga shook his head. 'There may be Matabele spies amongst them, he has to guard against treachery.'

Mungo St John had ordered the refugees to keep clear of the laager, and now there were three or four hundred, mostly black women and children, camped amongst the thorn trees on the river bank, five hundred yards from the nearest wagon.

Zouga lifted the coffee pot from the coals and poured the steaming black brew into his mug, then he cocked his head again to listen. There was a faint hubbub, a distant chorus of shrieks and shouts from the direction of the river. With the mug in his hand Zouga strolled across to the nearest wagon in the square, and climbed up onto the disselboom. He peered out of the laager, towards the river.

The open expanse of flat clay was ghostly pale in the starlight, and the treeline beyond it was solid blackness. There was nothing to be seen – except – he blinked his eyes rapidly, for they were playing him false. Nothing, except the blackness of the treeline seemed to be closer, the blackness was spreading towards the laager across the pale clay, like spilled oil or a pool of blood.

Now there was a sound, a rustle like locust wings when the swarms pass overhead, and the engulfing blackness was coming closer, with eerie swiftness.

At that moment another sky-rocket went swooshing up into the night sky, and when it burst, it flooded the pan with a soft, pink light and Zouga dropped the mug of steaming coffee.

The earth was black with the Matabele horde. It swept like a black tide towards the wagons, rank upon rank of great oval shields, and the assegais twinkled in the reflection of the rocket flare.

Zouga pulled the pistol from its holster, and fired towards the racing black wall of shields.

'Stand to your guns,' he bellowed, the heavy revolver bouncing and crashing in his fist. 'The Matabele are coming! Stand to your guns.' And from the black tide swelled a sound like a swarm of bees when the hive is overturned.

The hammer of Zouga's revolver clicked on a spent cartridge, and he jumped down from the disselboom and raced down the line of wagons to where the nearest Maxim was emplaced.

Throughout the laager there was a rush of bodies and the shouts of frightened men running to their posts, and as Zouga reached the corner of the square, the machine-gunner came stumbling out from his bed under a wagon body. His face was a pale blob, and his hair was hanging into his eyes. He was in stockinged feet and his braces dangled down his legs as he hitched his breeches and plumped himself down on the little seat that was built onto the rear leg of the Maxim tripod.

His number two loader was nowhere to be seen, perhaps lost in the milling confusion of newly-awakened bodies, so Zouga stuffed the revolver into his belt and dropped upon his knees beside the ungainly weapon. He yanked the top off the ammunition box and lifted out the first length of the canvas belt.

'Good-oh, mate!' muttered the gunner, as Zouga lifted the shutter in the side of the breech and passed the brass tag loader of the belt through the block.

'Ready! Load one!' he snapped, and the gunner jerked back the crank handle on the opposite side of the block and let it fly home, and the gib at the top of the extractor gripped the first round.

The spears were drumming on the rawhide shields now, and the deep humming chorus of the running warriors was almost deafening. They could only be yards from the barricade of wagons, but Zouga did not look up. He concentrated all his attention on the intricate task of loading the Maxim.

'Load two!' The gunner cranked again, and the feed block clattered. Zouga jerked the brass tag leader and the gunner let the handle fly back the second time. The first round shot smoothly into the breech.

'Loaded and cocked!' Zouga said, and tapped the gunner on the shoulder. Now they both looked up. The front rank of shields and war plumes seemed to curl over where they squatted beside the weapon, like a wave breaking on a beach.

It was the moment of the 'closing in' that the *amadoda* loved and lived for, already the shields were going up on high to free the spear arms and the steel rasped as the blades were cleared for the stabbing.

The joyous roar of the killing chant sundered the night; they were at the wagons, breaking into the laager, and the gunner sat stiffly upright with the gun between his knees and both hands on the traversing handles. He hooked his fingers through the rings of the safety guard, and as it lifted, he pressed his thumbs down on the chequered firing button.

The muzzle was almost touching the belly of a tall plumed warrior coming in between the wagons when the thick barrel shuddered, and a bright bar of flickering light sprang from the muzzle and the hammering clatter dinned upon Zouga's ear-drums. It sounded as though a giant was drawing a steel bar horizontally across a sheet of corrugated iron, and miraculously the warrior was blown away.

The gunner traversed the Maxim back and forth, like a meticulous housewife sweeping a dusty floor, and the continuous muzzle flashes lit the open clay pan with a dancing unearthly light.

The black tide of Matabele was no longer advancing; it stood static in front of the wagons; and though its crest foamed with dancing plumes and the shields that formed the body of the wave heaved and clattered and tumbled, they came no closer. They were dammed by the stroking, flickering bar of light that sprang from the Maxim gun. The solid stream of bullets played like a jet of water from a firehose upon them, and as each of the chanting warriors came racing up, he died on the same spot as the man in front of him had died, and he fell upon his corpse, while another warrior appeared in the space he had left, and the gun swung back, hammering and jerking, and that man went down, his shield clattering on the baked clay of the pan and the flash of the gun reflected from the burnished steel of his assegai as it went spinning from his nerveless hand.

All around the square the Maxims ripped and roared, and six hundred repeating rifles underscored that hellish chorus. The air was blue with gunsmoke, and the reek of cordite burned the throats of the troopers and made their eyes run, so that they seemed to be weeping for the terrible butchery in which they were engaged.

Still the Matabele came on, though now they had to clamber over a shapeless barricade of their own dead, and the gunner beside Zouga lifted his thumbs from the button trigger and twirled the elevation wheel of the Maxim, lifting the muzzle an inch so as to keep the fire on the belly line of the warriors as they climbed over the mounds of corpses.

Then once again the gun fluttered and roared, the glossy black bodies jerked and twitched and bucked as the stream of bullets tore into them.

Still the Matabele came on.

'By God, will they never stop!' yelled the gunner. The muzzle of the gun glowed cherry red, like a horseshoe fresh from the forge, and the steam from the water jacket whistled shrilly as the coolant boiled. The bright brass cases spewed from the extractor; they pinged and pattered against the iron-shod wheel of the wagon and formed a glittering mound beneath it.

'Empty gun!' Zouga yelled, as the end of the belt whipped into the clattering breech. They had been firing for less than sixty seconds, and the case of five hundred belted cartridges was empty.

Zouga kicked it aside and dragged up a fresh case, and the Matabele surged towards the silent gun.

'Ready, load one!' Zouga yelled.

'Load two!' They were swarming into the gap between the wagons.

'Loaded and cocked!' And once again that fluttering beat like the wings of a dark angel dulled their senses, and the barrel swung back and forth, back and forth, washing them away into the darkness.

'They're running,' shouted the gunner. 'Look at them run!'

In front of the wagons lay nothing but the piles of bodies. Here and there a dying man made feeble little movements, groping for a lost assegai or trying to staunch one of the awful holes in his flesh with fumbling fingers.

Beyond the massed corpses, the wounded and maimed were dragging themselves back towards the treeline, leaving dark wet smears on the clay. One of them was on his feet, staggering in aimless circles, using both hands to hold his bulging entrails from falling out of the open pouch of his belly. The Maxim had gutted him like a fish.

Beyond the trees the sky was a marvellous shade of ashes of roses, and the clouds were picked out in smoking scarlets and pipings of pale gold as the dawn came up in silent fury over the reeking field.

'Them black bastards have had enough.' The Maxim gunner giggled with mirthless, nervous reaction to that glimpse that he had just had into hell itself.

'They'll be back,' said Zouga quietly, as he dragged up another case of belted ammunition and knocked off the lid.

'You did all right, mate,' the gunner giggled again, staring with wide horrified eyes at the piles of dead.

'Refill the water in your condenser, soldier,' Zouga ordered him. 'The gun's over-heating, you'll have a jam when the next wave hits.'

'Sir!' The gunner realized suddenly who Zouga was. 'Sorry, sir.'

'Here is your loader.' The number two came up breathlessly. He was a fresh-faced lad, curly-headed and pink-cheeked. He looked more like a choirboy than a machine-gunner.

'Where were you, trooper?' Zouga demanded.

'Checking the horses, sir. It was all over so quickly.'

'Listen!' Zouga ordered, as the boy took his place at the gun.

From the treeline, across the bloodied clay pan, came the sound of singing – deep and sonorous in the dawn. It was the praise song of the 'Moles-who-burrow-under-a-mountain'.

'Stand to your gun, trooper,' Zouga ordered. 'It's not over yet.' And he turned on his heel and went striding down the line of wagons, reloading the revolver from his belt as he went.

Singing, Bazo strode down the squatting lines of his impi, and they sang with him.

He had held their shattered ranks just beyond the edge of the treeline as they came streaming back from the square of wagons. They were re-grouped now, singing as they screwed their courage for the next assault. What remained of Manonda's impi was mingled with his. They had been in the first wave of the attack, and very few of them were left.

Suddenly there was a great rushing sound in the air above the tree tops, like the onrush of the first wild storm of summer. Then in the midst of the squatting ranks a tall column of smoke and dust and flame sprang into the air, and the bodies of men were flung high with it.

'Kill the smoke devil,' somebody screamed, and another shell burst amongst them, and another, leaping fountains of smoke and flame; and the maddened warriors fired their ancient Martini-Henry rifles at these smoke devils, killing and wounding their comrades on the far side.

'They are not devils,' shouted Bazo, but his voice was lost in the barrage of artillery fire, and the pandemonium of warriors trying to defend themselves against something they did not understand.

'Come!' Bazo bellowed. There was only one way to bring them under control again.

'To the wagons. Forward to the wagons.' And those close enough to hear him followed, and the others, seeing them go, went bounding after them. They came out of the treeline in a swarm, and the other shattered impis heard the war chant go up, and turned again back onto the open pan of pale grey clay – and immediately that terrible clattering din, like the laughter of maniacs, began again and the air was filled with the flute and crack of a thousand whiplashes.

'They are coming again,' Zouga said quietly, almost to himself. 'This is the fifth time.'

'It's madness.' Mungo St John murmured, as the racing ranks came out of the trees and over the lip of the river bank, their plumes seething like the surface of boiling milk as they came onto the guns.

The field guns were depressed to the limit of their travel, the fuses screwed down to their shortest range, and the shrapnel bursts were strangely beautiful in the morning sky, popping open like pods of new cotton, shot through with pretty red fire.

The storm of small-arms fire was like the monsoon rains beating on an iron roof, and as the impis came into the drifting banks of gunsmoke, the dense ranks thinned out, and lost momentum, like a wave sliding up a steep beach.

Once again the wave faltered, and just short of the wagons it stopped, hesitated and then was going back, and the storm of gunfire continued long after the last of them had disappeared amongst the trees. In a kind of insensate fury the Maxim bullets tore wet white slabs of bark off the tree trunks, and then one after the other fell silent.

Standing beside Zouga, Dr Jameson scrubbed his hands together gleefully. 'It's all over. Their impis are destroyed, shattered, blown away. It's better than we could ever have hoped for. Tell me, St John, as a military man, what do you estimate their losses to be so far?'

Mungo St John considered the question seriously, climbing up onto one of the wagons the better to survey the field, ignoring the spattering of Martini-Henry rifle fire from the edge of the treeline where a few Matabele snipers were making very poor practice; convinced that raising their sights to the maximum made the bullets more powerful, most of their fire crackled high over the heads of the men manning the wagons.

Standing on the wagon Mungo St John lit a cheroot without transferring his attention from the carnage which surrounded them. At last he said gravely, 'Not less than two thousand casualties – perhaps as many as three.'

'Why don't you send a party out to count the bag, Doctor?' Zouga suggested, and Jameson did not recognize the sarcasm.

'We cannot spare the delay – more is the pity. We can still get in a full day's trek. That will look good in the Company report.' He pulled the gold chain from his fob pocket and sprang the lid of his watch with his thumbnail. 'Eight o'clock,' he marvelled. 'It's only eight o'clock in the morning. Do you realize that we have won a decisive battle before breakfast, gentlemen, and that by ten o'clock we can be on our way to Lobengula's royal kraal? I think we have done our shareholders rather proud.'

'I think,' Zouga cut in gently. 'That we still have a little more work to do. They are coming again.'

'I don't believe this,' Mungo St John marvelled.

Bazo paced slowly down the sparse ranks. This was no longer an impi. It was a pathetic little band of desperate survivors. Most of them had bound up their wounds with bloody bunches of green leaves, and their eyes had that strange fixed stare of men who had just looked into eternity. They were no longer singing, they squatted in silence – but they were still facing towards the white men's laager.

Bazo passed beyond the shortened line and paused under the spreading branches of a wild teak tree. He looked up.

Manonda, the commander of what had once been the glorious Insukamini impi, hung by his neck from one of the main branches. There was a thong of rawhide around his throat, and his eyes were still open, bulging in a defiant glare towards his enemies. His right leg, shattered above the knee by machine-gun fire, was twisted at an ugly angle and hung lower than his other leg.

Bazo lifted his assegai in a salute to the dead induna.

'I greet you, Manonda, who chose death rather than to drink the bitter draught of defeat,' he shouted.

The Insukamini impi was no more. Its warriors lay in deep windrows in front of the wagons.

'I praise you, Manonda, who chose death rather than to live a cripple and a slave. Go in peace, Manonda – and speak sweetly to the spirits on our behalf.'

Bazo turned back and stood before the waiting, silent ranks. The early morning sun, just clearing the tree tops, threw long black shadows in front of them.

'Are the eyes still red, my children?' Bazo sang out in a high clear voice.

'They are still red, Baba!' they answered him in bass chorus.

'Then let us go to do the work which still waits to be done.'

Where ten *amadoda* had raced in that first wave, now two made the last charge across the blood-soaked clay. Only one of that pitiful band went more than halfway between the treelines and the wagons. The rest of them turned back and left Bazo to run on alone. He was sobbing with each stride, his mouth open, the sweat running in oily snakes down his naked chest. He did not feel the first bullet that struck him. It was just a sudden numbness as though part of his body was missing, and he ran on, jumping over a pile of twisted corpses, and now the sound of the guns seemed muted and far-off, and there was another greater dinning in his ears that boomed and echoed strangely like the thunder of a mighty waterfall.

He felt another sharp tug, like the curved red-tipped thorn of the 'wait-a-bit' tree hooking into his flesh, but there was no pain. The roaring in his head was louder, and his vision narrowed so that he seemed to be looking down a long tunnel in the darkness.

Again he felt that irritating but painless jerk and tug in his flesh, and he was suddenly weary. He just wanted to lie down and rest, but he kept on towards the flashing white canvas of the wagon tents. Yet again that sharp insistent pull as though he was held on a leash, and his legs buckled under him. Quite gently he toppled forward and lay with his face against the hard sun-baked clay.

The sound of the guns had ceased, but in its place was another sound, it was the sound of cheering; behind the wall of wagons the white men were cheering themselves.

Bazo was tired, so utterly deathly tired. He closed his eyes and let the darkness come.

The wind had swung suddenly and unseasonably into the east, and there was a cold dank mist lying on the hills. the fine *guti* which made the trees drip dismally and chilled every bone in Tanase's body as she trudged up a narrow path that led to a saddle between two pearly grey granite peaks. Over her shoulders was a leather cloak and on her head she balanced a bundle of possessions which she had salvaged from the cave of the Umlimo.

She reached the saddle and looked down into yet another valley choked with dense, dark green undergrowth. She searched it eagerly, but then her spirits slowly fell again. Like all the others, it was devoid of any human presence.

Since she had left the secret valley, the moon had reached its full, and waned to nothingness, and was once again a curved yellow sliver in the night sky. All that time she had searched for the women and children of the Matabele nation. She knew they were here, hiding somewhere in the Matopos, for it was always the way. When a powerful enemy threatened the nation, the women and children were sent into the hills – but it was such a vast area, so many valleys and deep labyrinthine caves that she might search a lifetime without finding them.

Tanase started slowly down into the deserted valley. Her legs felt leaden, and another spasm of nausea brought saliva flooding from under her tongue. She swallowed it down, but when she reached the floor of the valley, she sank down onto a moss-covered rock beside the little stream.

She knew what was the cause of her malady; though she had missed her courses by only a few days, she knew that the loathsome seed that her pale, hairy, balloon-bellied ravisher had pumped into her had struck and taken hold, and she knew what she must do.

She laid aside her load and searched for dry kindling under the trees where the *guti* had not yet dampened it. She piled it in the protected lee of a sheltering rock, and crouched over it.

For many long minutes she concentrated all her will upon it. Then at last she sighed, and her shoulders slumped. Even this minor power, this small magic of fire-making, had gone from her. As the white man with the golden beard had warned her, she was Umlimo no longer. She was just a young woman, without strange gifts or terrible duties, and she was free. The spirits could make no demands upon her, she was free at last to seek out the man she loved.

As she prepared to make fire in the conventional manner, with the tiny bow for twirling the dry twig, two passions gave her strength to face the ordeal ahead of her – her love and her equally fierce hatred.

When the contents of the little clay pot boiled, she added the shreds of dried bark of the tambooti to it, and immediately the sweet odour of the poisonous steam cloyed upon the back of her throat.

The straight sharp black horn of the gemsbuck had been clipped off at the tip so that it could be used for cupping blood, or as a funnel for introducing fluids into the body.

Tanase spread the leather cloak below the rock shelter and lay on it, flat upon her back, with her feet braced high against rough granite. She had lubricated the horn with fat, and she took a deep breath, clenched her jaw upon it, and then slid the horn into herself. When it met resistance, she manipulated it carefully, but firmly, and then her breath burst from her in a gasp of agony as the point found the opening and forced its way still farther into her secret depths.

The pain gave her a strange unholy joy, as though she were inflicting it upon the hated thing that had taken root within her. She lifted herself on one elbow, and tested the contents of the little clay pot. It was just cool enough for her to be able to bear the heat when she plunged her forefinger into it.

She took up the pot and poured it into the mouth of the long black funnel, and this time she moaned, and her back arched involuntarily, but she poured until the pot was empty. There was the coppery salt taste of blood in her mouth, and she realized that she had bitten through her own lip. She seized the horn and plucked it out of herself, and then she curled up on the leather cloak and hugged her knees to her bosom, shuddering and moaning at the fire in her womb.

In the night the first terrible cramps seized her, and she felt her belly muscles spasm up hard as a cannon ball under her clutching hands.

She wished there had been something formed, a tiny replica of that white animal that had rutted upon her, so that she could have wreaked a form of vengeance upon it. She would have delighted in mutilating and burning it, but there was nothing substantial on which to expend her hatred. So despite the purging of her body, she carried her hatred with her still, fierce and unabated, as she toiled on deeper and deeper into the Matopos.

The joyful cries and sweet laughter of children at play guided her, and Tanase crept along the river verge, using the tall cotton-tipped reeds as a screen until she overlooked the green pool between its sugary sandbanks. They were girls sent to fetch water. The big, black clay pots stood in a row on the white sand with green leaves stuffed in the mouths to stop them slopping over when carried balanced on the girls' heads.

However, once the pots were filled, they had not been able to resist the temptation of the cool, green waters, and they had thrown off their skirts and were shrieking and sporting in the pool. The eldest girls were pubescent with swelling breast buds, and one of them spotted Tanase in the reeds and screamed a warning.

Tanase was just able to catch the youngest and slowest child as she was disappearing over the far bank, and she held the wriggling little body, glossy black and wet from the river, against her bosom while the child wailed and struggled with terror.

Tanase cooed reassurances and stroked the little girl with gentling hands until she quietened.

'I am of the people,' she whispered. 'Don't be afraid, little one.'

Half an hour later the child was chattering gaily and leading Tanase by the hand.

The mothers came swarming out of the caves at the head of the valley to greet Tanase, and they crowded about her.

'Is it true that there have been two great battles?' they begged her.

'We have heard that the impis were broken at Shangani and again those that remained were butchered like cattle on the banks of the Bembesi?'

'Our husbands and our sons are dead – please tell us it is not so,' they pleaded.

'They say the king has fled from his royal kraal, and that we are children without a father. Is it true, can you tell us if it is true?'

'I know nothing,' Tanase told them. 'I come to hear news, not to bear it. Is there not one amongst you who can tell me where I may find Juba, senior wife of Gandang, brother of the king?'

They pointed over the hills, and Tanase went on, and found another group of women hiding in the thick bush. These children did not laugh and play, their limbs were thin as sticks, but their bellies were swollen little pots.

'There is no food,' the women told Tanase. 'Soon we will starve.' And they sent her stumbling back northwards, seeking and questioning, trying to blind herself to the agonies of a defeated nation, until one day she stooped in through the entrance of a dim and smoky cave, and a vaguely familiar figure rose to greet her.

'Tanase, my child, my daughter.'

Only then did Tanase recognize her, for the abundant flesh had melted off the woman's frame and her once bounteous breasts hung slack as empty pouches against her belly.

'Juba, my mother,' Tanase cried, and ran into her embrace. It was a long time after that before she could speak through her sobs.

'Oh my mother, do you know what has become of Bazo?'

Juba pushed her gently to arm's length and looked into her face. When Tanase saw the devastating sorrow in Juba's eyes, she cried out with dread.

'He is not dead!'

'Come, my daughter,' Juba whispered, and led her deeper into the cave, along a natural passageway through the living rock – and there was a graveyard smell on the cool dark air, the odour of corruption and rotting flesh.

The second cavern was lit only by a burning wick floating in a bowl of oil. There was a litter against the far wall. On it lay a wasted skeletal body, and the smell of death was overpowering.

Fearfully Tanase knelt beside the litter and lifted a bunch of leaves off one of the stinking wounds.

'He is not dead,' Tanase repeated. 'Bazo is not dead.'

'Not yet,' agreed Juba. 'His father and those of his men who survived the white men's bullets, carried my son to me on his shield. They bid me save him – but nobody can save him.'

'He will not die,' said Tanase fiercely. 'I will not let him die.' And she leaned over his wasted body and pressed her lips to the fever-hot flesh. 'I will not let you die,' she whispered.

The Hills of the Indunas were deserted; no beast grazed upon them for the herds had long ago been driven afar to try to save them from the invaders. There were no vultures or crows sailing high above the hills, for the Maxim guns had laid a richer feast for them barely twenty-five miles eastwards at the Bembesi crossing.

The royal kraal of GuBulawayo was almost deserted. The women's quarters were silent. No child cried, no young girl sang, no crone scolded. They were all hiding in the magical Matopos hills.

The barracks of the fighting regiments were deserted. Two thousand dead on the Shangani, three thousand more at Bembesi – and nobody would ever count those who had crawled away to die like animals in the caves and thickets.

The survivors had scattered, some to join the women in the

hills, the others to cower, bewildered and demoralized, wherever they could find shelter.

Of all the fighting impis of Matabele, only one remained intact, the Inyati regiment of Induna Gandang, the king's half-brother. Gandang alone had been able to resist the madness of hurling his men over open ground at the waiting Maxim guns, and now he waited for his king's orders in the hills just north of the royal kraal with his impi gathered about him.

In all of GuBulawayo, there was one small group remaining. Twenty-six of these were white men and women. They were the traders and concession-hunters who had been at the kraal when Jameson had marched from Iron Mine Hill. With them, were the Codrington family, Clinton and Robyn and the twins. Lobengula had ordered them all to remain under his protection, while the impis were out in battle array, and now he had called them to the goat kraal for his last audience.

Drawn up before the two new brick-built houses which had replaced the great thatched hut, were Lobengula's four Cape wagons with the teams already in the traces.

About the wagons were a small party of the royal retainers: two of the king's senior wives, four elderly indunas, and a dozen or so slaves and servants.

The king himself sat on the box of the leading wagon. In that wagon were all Lobengula's treasures, a hundred big tusks of ivory, the little sealed pots of uncut diamonds, and the canvas bags stencilled with the name 'The Standard Bank Ltd' containing the sovereigns paid to him during the four years since he had granted the concession to the British South Africa Company, four thousand sovereigns, less than a sovereign for every one of his dead warriors.

Around the wagon were gathered the white men, and Lobengula looked down upon them. The king had become an old man in the few short weeks since he had thrown the war spear on the Hills of the Indunas. There were deep lines of sorrow and despair carved around his mouth and eyes. His eyes were rheumy and shortsighted, his hair bleached silver-grey, his body bloated and misshapen, and his breathing was racked and irregular like that of a dying animal.

'Tell your queen, white men, that Lobengula kept his word. Not one of you has been harmed,' he wheezed. 'Daketela and his soldiers will be here tomorrow. If you go out upon the eastern road, you will even meet them before nightfall.' Lobengula paused to catch his breath, and then went on. 'Go now. There is nothing more I have to say to you.'

They were silent, subdued, and strangely chastened, as they trooped out of the goat kraal. Only Robyn and her family remained.

The twins stood on each side of Robyn. At twenty-one years of age, they were as tall as she. It seemed that the three of them were sisters – for they all had the clear eyes and glossy hair of healthy young women.

Clinton Codrington, standing behind them, stooped and bald, dressed in sober broadcloth that was mossy green with age and shiny at the cuffs and elbows, seemed father to Robyn as well as to the twins.

The king looked down upon them with a terrible regret.

'It is the last time that you will make my eyes glad, Nomusa,' he said.

'Oh King, my heart is on fire for you. I think of what has happened and how I advised you.'

Lobengula held up his hand to silence her. 'Do not torture yourself, Nomusa. You have been a true friend of many years, and what you did was done in friendship. Nothing you or I could have done would have changed the manner of it. It was the prophecy; it was as certain as the fall of the leaves from the msasa trees when the frosts are on the hills.'

Robyn ran forward to the wagon, and Lobengula stooped to take her hand.

'Pray to your three gods that are one god for me, Nomusa.'

'He will hear you, Lobengula, you are a good man.'

'No man is all goodness or all evil,' the king sighed. 'Now, Nomusa, soon Daketela and his soldiers will be here. Tell him that Lobengula says thus. "I am beaten, white men, my impis are eaten up. Let me go now, do not hunt me further, for I am an old sick man. I wish only to find a place where I may mourn my people – and at last die in peace." '

'I will tell them, Lobengula.'

'And will they listen, Nomusa?'

She could not face him, and she dropped her eyes. 'You know they will not listen.'

'My poor people,' whispered Lobengula. 'Will you look after my poor people when I am gone, Nomusa?'

'I swear it to you, oh King,' Robyn said fiercely. 'I will stay at Khami Mission until the day that I die, and I will devote my life to your people.'

Then Lobengula smiled, and once again there was a flash of the old mischievous twinkle in his eye.

'I give you the royal permission which I denied you all these years, Nomusa. From this day forward any of my people – man or woman or child of Matabele who wish it of you – you may pour water on their heads and make the cross of your three gods over them.'

Robyn could not reply.

'Stay in peace, Nomusa,' said Lobengula, and his wagon rumbled slowly out through the gates of the stockade.

Clinton Codrington reined in the mule on the crest of the rise above the royal kraal, and he groped for Robyn's hand. They sat silently on the seat of the little Scotch cart, watching the last pale shreds of dust thrown up by the king's wagons disappearing away in the north across the grassy plain.

'They will never leave him in peace,'Robyn said softly.

'Lobengula is the prize,' Clinton agreed. 'Without him, Jameson and Rhodes will have no victory.'

'What will they do with him?' she asked sadly 'If they catch him.'

'Exile, certainly,' Clinton said. 'St Helena Island, probably. It's where they sent Cetewayo.'

'Poor tragic man,' Robyn whispered. 'Caught between two ages, half savage and half civilized man, half cruel despot and half a shy and sensitive dreamer. Poor Lobengula.'

'Do look, Papa!' Vicky called suddenly, pointing down the rude track towards the east. There was a thick column of dust rising above the tops of the thorn trees, and even as they watched, a distant troop of mounted men rode out onto the grassy plain with badges and weapons twinkling in the sunlight.

'Soldiers,' whispered Lizzie.

'Soldiers,' repeated Vicky gleefully. 'Hundreds of them.' And the twins exchanged a bright ecstatic glance of complete understanding and accord.

Clinton picked up the reins – but Robyn tightened her grip on his hand to restrain him.

'Wait,' she said. 'I want to watch it happen. Somehow it will be the end of an age, the end of a cruel but innocent age.'

Lobengula had left one of his trusted indunas in the royal kraal, with instructions to lay fire to the train as soon as the last wagons were clear. In the mud-brick building behind the king's new residence were the remains of the hundred thousand rounds of Martini-Henry ammunition for which he had sold his land and his people. There were also twenty barrels of black powder.

'There!' said Robyn, as the pillar of black smoke and flame shot hundreds of feet straight up into the still air.

Only many seconds later did the shock wave and the great clap of sound pass over where they watched from the ridge, and the smoke, still spinning upon itself, blossomed into an anvil head high above the shattered kraal.

Lobengula's house that had given him such pleasure and pride was only a shell, the roof blown away and the walls fallen in.

The beehive huts of the women's quarters were ablaze, and even as they watched, the flames jumped the stockade and caught in the roofs beyond. Within minutes the whole of GuBulawayo was in leaping, swirling flames.

'Now we can go on,' Robyn said quietly, and Clinton shook up the mule.

There were thirty horsemen in the advance scouting party – and as they galloped up, the tall straight figure leading them was unmistakable.

'Thank God that you are safe!' Zouga called to them. He was handsome and heroic in the frogged uniform with his brass badges of rank ablaze in the sunlight, and the slouch hat cocked forward over his handsome, gravely concerned features.

'We were never in any danger,' Robyn told him. 'And well you knew that.'

'Where is Lobengula?' Zouga sought to divert her scorn, but she shook her head.

'I am guilty of one act of treachery against Lobengula –'

'You are an Englishwoman,' Zouga reminded her. 'You should know where your loyalties lie.'

'Yes, I am an Englishwoman,' she agreed icily, 'but I am ashamed of that today. I will not tell you where the king is.'

'As you wish.' Zouga looked at Clinton. 'You know that it is for the good of every one in this land. Until we have Lobengula, there will be no peace.'

Clinton bowed his bald head. 'The king has gone to the north with his wagons and wives and the Inyati regiment.'

'Thank you,' Zouga nodded. 'I will send an escort with you to the main column. They are not far behind us. Sergeant!'

A young trooper with triple chevrons on his sleeve spurred forward. He was a fine-looking lad, with high English colour in his cheeks and broad shoulders.

'Sergeant Acutt. Take the six men from the rear three files and see this party to safety.'

Zouga saluted his sister and brother-in-law curtly and then ordered. 'Troop, at the gallop. Forward!'

The first two dozen troopers went clattering away towards GuBulawayo, while the sergeant and his six men wheeled in alongside the cart.

Vicky turned her head and looked directly into the young sergeant's eyes. She took a long slow breath that pushed her bosom out under the faded cotton of her blouse. The sergeant stared, and the flush of dark blood rose from the high stock of his tunic and suffused his cheeks.

Vicky wetted her pouting lips with the tip of a pink tongue, and slanted her eyes at him – and Sergeant Acutt seemed about to fall out of the saddle, for Vicky's gaze had struck him from a range of less than six feet.

'Victoria!' Robyn snapped sharply, without looking back over her shoulder.

'Yes, Mama.' Hurriedly, Vicky slumped her shoulders forward to alter the cheeky thrust of her bosom to a more demure angle, and composed her expression into dutiful gravity.

TELEGRAM MESSAGE RECEIVED FORT VICTORIA 10TH NOVEMBER 1893 RELAYED BY HELIOGRAPH TO GUBULAWAYO:

FOR JAMESON STOP HER MAJESTY'S GOVERNMENT DECLINES TO DECLARE MATABELE A CROWN COLONY OR PLACE IT UNDER THE JURISDICTION OF THE HIGH COMMISSIONER STOP HER MAJESTY'S FOREIGN SECRETARY AGREES THAT THE CHARTER COMPANY IS TO PROVIDE THE MACHINERY OF GOVERNMENT FOR THE NEW TERRITORY STOP BOTH MASHONALAND AND MATABELELAND NOW FALL WITHIN THE ADMINISTRATIVE AREA OF THE COMPANY STOP COMPANY SHARES QUOTED AT £8 LONDON CLOSE STOP HEARTIEST CONGRATULATIONS TO YOU YOUR OFFICERS AND MEN FROM JOVE

FOR JAMESON URGENT AND CONFIDENTIAL DESTROY ALL COPIES STOP WE MUST HAVE LOBENGULA STOP NO RISK TOO GREAT NO PRICE TOO HIGH FROM JOVE

'Reverend Codrington, I am sending out a considerable force to escort Lobengula in.' Jameson stood at the fly of his tent, looking out beyond the laager to the blackened ruins of the royal kraal. 'I have already sent this message after the king.' Jameson came back to his desk and read from his pad:

> 'Now, to stop this useless killing, you must at once come back to me at GuBulawayo. I guarantee that your life will be safe and that you will be kindly treated.'

'Has the king sent you a reply?' Clinton asked. He had declined a seat and stood stiffly in front of the camp table that served Jameson as a desk.

'Here.' The doctor handed Clinton a grubby, folded scrap of paper. Clinton scanned it swiftly:

> I have the honour to inform you that I have received your letter and have heard all what you have said, so I will come. . . .

'This is written by a half-caste rogue, named Jacobs, who has joined up with Lobengula,' Clinton muttered, as he glanced through the rest of the wandering, misspelt and barely literate note. 'I know his handwriting.'

'Do you think the king means it?' Mungo St John asked. 'Do you think he means to come in?'

Clinton did not turn his head towards where Mungo lolled in a canvas camp chair across the tent.

'Dr Jameson, I do not condone your actions or those of your infamous Chartered Company, but I came here at your bidding in order to do what little I can to redress the terrible wrongs that have been perpetrated on the Matabele people. However, I draw the line at having to speak or in any way communicate with this henchman of yours.'

Jameson frowned irritably. 'Reverend, I would like you to bear in mind that I have appointed General St John as Administrator and Chief Magistrate of Matabeleland –'

Clinton cut in brusquely. 'You are, of course, aware that your Chief Magistrate was once a notorious slave-trader, buying and selling the black people over whom you now give him supreme powers?'

'Yes, thank you, Reverend, I am aware that General St John was once a legitimate trader, and I am also fully aware that while a serving officer of Her Majesty's navy, you led an attack on his ship – an action which led to your being courtmartialled, imprisoned and cashiered from the service. Now let us continue, Reverend. If you do not wish to talk directly to General St John, you may address me instead.'

In the camp chair Mungo St John crossed his beautifully polished riding boots and smiled lazily, but his eye was bright and sharp as a bared blade. 'Doctor Jameson, would you ask the good priest if he is of the opinion that Lobengula will give himself up?'

'Would you?' Clinton asked, still without a glance in St John's direction.

'No,' Mungo replied, and nodded his head significantly at Jameson.

'Reverend, General St John is taking out a flying column to bring Lobengula in. I want you to go with him, please,' Jameson said.

'Why me, Doctor?'

'You speak the language fluently.'

'So do many others – Zouga Ballantyne is one of them. He is also a soldier.'

'Your brother-in-law has other important work to do –'

'Stealing the king's cattle,' Clinton cut in acidly.

It was already common knowledge that Zouga Ballantyne had been given the task of rounding up the vast Matabele herds and bringing them in to GuBulawayo for distribution.

However, Jameson might not have heard the remark, and he went on smoothly. 'Besides, Reverend, you and your wife have been close friends of Lobengula for many years, he trusts and likes you. But, since it was Major Ballantyne who delivered our ultimatum, Lobengula looks upon him as an enemy.'

'Not without reason,' Clinton murmured dryly. 'However, Doctor, I refuse to be your Judas goat.'

'Your presence with the column may help to avert another bloody conflict, with the inevitable result of hundreds if not thousands more Matabele slaughtered. I would think it your Christian duty to try to prevent that.'

Clinton hesitated, and Mungo murmured. 'Do point out, Doctor Jim, that after Lobengula surrenders, Reverend Codrington will be in a position to comfort and protect him, to ensure that the king is kindly treated and that no harm befalls him. I give him my word on that.'

'Very well,' Clinton capitulated sadly. 'On the understanding that I am to be the king's protector and advisor, I will go with your column.'

'They follow,' Gandang said softly. 'They still follow.' And Lobengula lifted his face and looked at the sky. The rain drops, heavy and hard as newly minted silver shillings, struck his cheeks and forehead.

'The rain,' said Lobengula. 'Who said they could not follow us in the rain?'

'It was me, my King, but I was wrong,' Gandang admitted. 'When he marched from GuBulawayo, One-Bright-Eye had three hundred men and four of the little guns with three legs which chatter like old women. He also had wagons and one big cannon.'

'I know this,' said the king.

'When the rains came, I thought that they had turned back, but now my scouts have come in with heavy news to tell. One-Bright-Eye has sent back half of his men and the wagons, the cannon and two of the little three-legged guns. They could not ride over the mud – but–' Gandang paused.

'Do not try to spare me, my brother, tell me it all.'

'He comes on with half his men, and two little machine-guns drawn by horses. They are travelling fast, even in the mud.'

'How fast?' the king asked quietly.

'They are a day's march behind us, tomorrow evening they will camp here on this very river.'

The king pulled the tattered old coat around his shoulders. It was cold in the rain, but he did not have the energy to crawl under the canvas of his wagon tent. He looked out across the watercourse. They were camped on the Shangani river, but almost a hundred and fifty miles higher than where the first battle of the war had been fought upon the headwaters of this same river.

They were in thick mopani forest, so thick that a road had to be chopped through it to allow the king's wagons to pass. The terrain was flat and relieved only by the clay hills of the termite nests that dotted the forest, some of them as large as houses, others the size of a beer keg, just big enough to smash the axle of a wagon.

The sky, grey and heavy as the belly of a pregnant sow, pressed down upon the tops of the mopani. Soon it would rain heavily again, these fat drops were merely a warning of the next deluge to come, and that trickle of muddy water, the colour of a drunkard's bile, down the middle of the watercourse would be a roaring torrent again within minutes of the onslaught.

'One hundred and fifty men, Gandang,' the king sighed. 'How many have we?'

'Two thousand,' said Gandang. 'And perhaps tomorrow or the next day Gambo may come to join us with a thousand more.'

'Yet we cannot stand against them?'

'The men we would eat. It is those little guns with three legs, oh King, not even ten thousand warriors, each with the liver of a lion, could prevail when they begin to laugh. But if the king commands, we will run –'

'No! It is the gold,' Lobengula said suddenly. 'The white men will never let me be until they have the gold. I will send it to them. Perhaps then they will leave me in peace. Where is Kamuza, my young induna? He speaks the language of the white men. I will send him to them.'

Kamuza came swiftly to the king's bidding. He stood attentively in the spattering rain beside the front wheel of the wagon.

'Place the little bags of gold in the hands of the white men, Kamuza, my trusted induna, and say to them thus, "You have eaten up my regiments and killed my young men, you have burned my kraals and scattered the women and children of Matabeleland into the hills where they burrow for roots like wild animals, you have seized my royal herds, and now you have my gold. White men, you have it all, will you now leave me in peace to mourn my lost people?" '

There were ten bags of white canvas, stamped with black lettering. They made a heavy burden for one man to carry. Kamuza knelt and tied them together in bunches, and then packed each bunch into a leather grain bag.

'To hear is to obey, Great Elephant,' Kamuza saluted his king.

'Go swiftly, Kamuza,' Lobengula ordered softly. 'For they are close upon us.'

Will Daniel sat his own horse, with the brim of his hat pulled down to protect the bowl of his clay pipe from the drizzling rain, and over his shoulders he wore a rubber groundsheet which glistened with moisture and gave him a pregnant, clumsy look as he slumped barrel-bellied in the saddle.

On lead reins he held two other horses, one was a pack animal whose burden was covered by a white canvas sheet. Daniel no longer bore the lofty rank of sergeant. After his conduct at the secret valley of the Umlimo, Zouga Ballantyne had seen him reduced to trooper, and as an additional mortification, he was now acting as batman to one of the officers of the flying column. The packhorse carried Captain Coventry's traps.

The other horse belonged to Will's old comrade in arms, Jim Thorn. That worthy was crouched behind a thorny shrub a short way off, with his belt hanging around his neck and cursing bitterly in a low monotone.

'Filthy bleeding water, stinking bloody rain – God-forsaken country –'

'Hey, Jimmo, your backside must be on fire by now. That's the twelfth time today.'

'Shut your ugly face, Will Daniel,' Jim shouted back, and then dropped back into his dismal monotone. 'Bloody gut-breaking trots –'

'Come on, Jim my lad.' Will lifted the brim of his hat to peer about him. 'We can't fall too far behind the rest, not with the bush crawling with bloody black savages.'

Jim Thorn came out from behind the bush re-buckling his belt, but wincing with another bout of stomach cramps. He climbed gingerly up into the saddle, and the three horses plodded along in the deep yellow muddy ruts of the horse-drawn carts which carried the two Maxim machine-guns.

The rear of the column was out of sight ahead of them amongst the dripping mopani trees. The two of them had soon learned to loiter at the back away from the scrutiny of the officers, so that they would not be ordered into the thigh-deep mud when the Maxim carts bogged down and had to be man-handled through one of the glutinous 'mopani holes'.

'Look out, Will!' Jim Thorn yelled suddenly, and his oilskins flapped like the wings of a startled rooster as he tried to draw his rifle from its scabbard. 'Look out, bloody savages!'

A Matabele had stepped silently out of the thick bush alongside the cart tracks, and now he stood directly in front of the horses and held up his empty hands to show the white men that he was unarmed.

'Wait, Jimmo!' Will Daniel called. 'Let's see what the bastard wants.'

'I don't like it, man. It's a trap.' Jim searched the bush around them nervously. 'Let's shoot the black bugger and get out of it.'

'I come in peace!' the Matabele called in English. He wore only a fur kilt, without armlets and leg tassels, and the rain shone on his smoothly muscled torso. On his head was the headring of an induna.

The two mounted men both had their rifles out now, and were aiming from the hip, covering Kamuza at point-blank range.

'I have a message from the king.'

'Well, spit it out then,' Will snapped.

'Lobengula says take my gold, and go back to GuBulawayo.'

'Gold?' demanded Jim Thorn. 'What gold?'

Kamuza stepped back into the scrub, picked up the leather grain bag, and carried it to them.

Will Daniel was laughing excitedly as he pulled out the little canvas bags. They jingled softly in his hands.

'By God, that's the sweetest music I ever heard!'

'What will you do, white men?' Kamuza demanded. 'Will you take the gold to your chief?'

'Don't fret yourself, my friend.' Will Daniel clapped him delightedly on the shoulder. 'It will go to the right person, you have the word of William Daniel hisself on it.'

Jim Thorn was unbuckling his saddle-bags and stuffing the canvas sacks into it.

'Christmas and my birthday all in one,' he winked at Will.

'White men, will you turn and go back to GuBulawayo now?' Kamuza called anxiously.

'Don't worry about it another minute,' Will assured him, and ferreted a loaf of hard bread out of his own saddle-bag. 'Here's a present for you, *bonsela*, present, you understand?' Then to Jim. 'Come on, Mr Thorn, it's Mister I'll be calling you now that you are rich.'

'Lead on, Mr Daniel,' Jim grinned at him, and they spurred past Kamuza, leaving him standing in the muddy pathway with the mouldy loaf of bread in his hands.

Clinton Codrington came slipping and sloshing along the bank of the Shangani river. The lowering clouds were bringing on the night prematurely, and the forests on the far bank were dank and gloomy.

The thunder rumbled sullenly, as though boulders were being rolled across the roof of the sky, and for a few seconds the rain spurted down thickly and then sank once more to a fine drizzle. Clinton shivered and pulled up the collar of his sheepskin coat as he hurried on to where the Maxim carts stood at the head of the column.

There was a tarpaulin draped between the two carts and beneath it squatted a small group of officers. Mungo St John looked up as Clinton approached.

'Ah, parson!' he greeted him. Mungo had learned that this address irritated Clinton inordinately. 'You took your time.' Clinton did not reply; he stood hunched in the rain and none of the officers made room for him beneath the canvas.

'Major Wilson is going to make a reconnaissance across the

river with a dozen men. I want you to go with him to translate, if he meets any of the enemy.'

'It will be dark in less than two hours,' Clinton pointed out stolidly.

'Then you had best hurry.'

'The rains will break at any minute,' Clinton persisted. 'Your forces could be split –'

'Parson, you bother about brimstone and salvation – let us do the soldiering.' Mungo turned back to his officers. 'Are you ready to go, Wilson?'

Allan Wilson was a bluff Scot, with long, dark moustaches and an accent that burred with the tang of heather and highlands.

'You'll be giving me detailed orders then, sir?' he demanded stiffly. There had been ill-feeling between him and St John ever since they had left GuBulawayo.

'I want you to use your common sense, man,' St John snapped. 'If you can catch Lobengula, then grab him, put him on a horse, and get back here. If you are attacked, fall back immediately. If you let yourself be cut off, I will not be able to cross the river to support you with the Maxims until first light, do you understand that?'

'I do, General.' Wilson touched the brim of his slouch hat. 'Come on, Reverend,' he said to Clinton. 'We do not have much time.'

Burnham and Ingram, the two American scouts, led the patrol down the steep bank of the Shangani; Wilson and Clinton followed immediately behind.

Clinton's lanky, stooped frame, in the scuffed sheepskin jacket and with a shapeless stained hat pulled down over his ears, looked oddly out of place in the middle of the uniformed patrol of armed men. As he came level with Mungo St John, standing on the top of the bank with his hands clasped behind his back, Clinton bent low from the saddle of his borrowed horse and said, so quietly that only Mungo heard him, 'Read II Samuel, chapter eleven, verse fifteen.' Then Clinton straightened, gathered the old grey gelding with which he had been provided by the Company, and the two of them went sliding untidily down the cutting in the steep bank which the Matabele had dug to take Lobengula's wagons across.

At this point, the Shangani river was two hundred yards across, and as the little patrol waded the deepest part of the channel, the muddy waters reached to their stirrup irons. They climbed the far bank and almost immediately were lost from view in the dripping woods and poor light.

Mungo St John stood for many minutes, staring across the river, ignoring the fine, drizzling rain. He was wondering at himself, wondering why he had sent such a puny force across the river, with only hours of daylight left. The priest was right, of course, it would rain again soon. The heavens were leaden and charged with it. The Matabele were in force. The priest had seen the Inyati impi under its old and crafty commander, Gandang, escorting the wagons away from GuBulawayo.

If he were going to reconnoitre the lie of the land beyond the river, then he knew that he should have used the last of the daylight to ford his entire force. It was the correct tactical disposition. That way the patrol could fall back under the protection of the Maxims at any time during the night, or he could go forward to relieve them if they ran into trouble.

Some demon had possessed him when he gave the orders. Perhaps Wilson had finally irritated him beyond all restraint. The man had argued with him at every opportunity, and had done his best to subvert Mungo's authority amongst the other officers, who resented the fact that he was an American over British officers. It was mostly Wilson's fault that this was such an unhappy and divided little expedition. He was well rid of the overbearing and blunt Scotsman, he decided. Perhaps a night spent in company with the Inyati regiment would take some of the pepper out of him; and he would be a little more tractable in the future – if there was a future for him. Mungo turned back to the sheltering tarpaulin strung between the gun carriages.

Suddenly a thought struck him, and he called down the line. 'Captain Borrow.'

'Sir?

'You have a Bible, don't you? Let me have it, will you?'

Mungo's batman had a fire going, and coffee brewing in the shelter, and he took Mungo's coat to dry and spread a grey woollen blanket over his shoulders as Mungo squatted beside the fire and paged slowly through the little leather-bound, travel-battered Bible.

He found the reference and stared at it thoughtfully:

> And he wrote in the letter, saying, Set ye Uriah in the forefront of the hottest battle, and retire ye from him, that he may be smitten, and die.

Mungo wondered that he was still capable of surprising himself. There were still strange places in his soul that he had never explored.

He took a burning stick from the fire and lit his cigar, then plunged the glowing red of the brand into the black coffee to enhance the taste of the brew.

'Well, well, Parson!' he murmured aloud. 'You have a sharper instinct than I ever gave you credit for.'

Then he thought of Robyn Codrington, trying to consider his feelings objectively, and without passion.

'Do I love her?' he asked, and the answer was immediate.

'I have never loved a woman, and by God's grace, I never will.'

'Do I want her, then?' And again there was no hesitation. 'Yes, I want her. I want her badly enough to send anybody who stands in my way to his death.'

'Why do I want her?' he pondered. 'When I have never loved a woman – why do I want this one? She is no longer young, and God knows, I have had my pick of a hundred more beautiful. Why do I want her?' and he grinned at his own perception. 'I want her because she is the only one whom I have never had, and whom I will never have completely.'

He closed the Bible with a snap, and grinned wickedly across the wide river at the dark and silent mopani forest.

'Well done, Parson. You saw it long before I did.'

The tracks of Lobengula's wagons were clear to follow, even in the worsening light, and Wilson pushed the pace to a canter.

Clinton's aged grey was exhausted by two weeks of hard trekking. He fell back little by little, until after five miles they were loping along with Captain Napier's rear file. The mud thrown up by the hooves ahead speckled Clinton's face as though he was suffering from some strange disease.

The mopani thinned out dramatically ahead of the tiny patrol, and there were low bare hills on either hand.

'Look at them, Padre,' Wilson called to Clinton, and gestured at the hills. 'There must be hundreds of them.'

'Women and old men,' Clinton grunted. The slopes were scattered with silent watching figures. 'The fighting men will be with the king.'

The twelve riders cantered on without a check, and the thunder muttered and shook the sky above the low, swirling clouds.

Suddenly Wilson raised his right hand high.

'Troop, halt!'

Clinton's grey stood, head hanging and chest heaving between his knees – and Clinton was as grateful. At his best he was no horseman, and he was unaccustomed to such hard riding.

'Reverend Codrington to the front!' The order was passed back, and Clinton kicked the grey into a plodding walk.

At that moment a squall of rain stung his face like a handful of thrown rock-salt, and he wiped it off with the palm of his right hand.

'There they are!' said Wilson tersely, and through the drizzle Clinton could make out the stained and ragged canvas tent of a wagon rising above the scrub, not more than two hundred paces ahead.

'You know what to say, Padre.' Wilson's Scots accent seemed even stronger and was incongruous at this place and in these circumstances.

Clinton walked the grey forward another few paces, and then drew a deep breath.

'Lobengula, King of the Matabele, it is me – Hlopi. These men wish you to come to GuBulawayo to parley with Dakatela and Lodzi. Do you hear me, oh King?'

The silence was broken only by the scraping of a windblown branch and the rustle of the rain on the brim of Clinton's old hat.

Then quite clearly, he heard the snick of a Martini-Henry rifle being loaded; and a young voice asked in whispered Matabele from the scrub near the wagon:

'Must we shoot, Baba?'

A deeper, firmer voice replied in the same language. 'Not yet. Let them come closer so there can be no mistake.'

And then the voices were blotted out by a grumbling roll of thunder overhead, and Clinton backed the grey up.

'It is a trap, Major. There are armed Matabele in ambush about the wagons. I heard them talking.'

'Do you think the king is there?'

'I would not think so, but what I am sure of is that even now the main impi is circling back between us and the river.'

'What makes you think that?'

'It is always the Zulu way, the encirclement and then the closing in.'

'What do you advise, Padre?'

Clinton shrugged and smiled. 'I gave my advice on the bank of the river –' He was interrupted by a shouted warning from the rear of the column. It was one of the Americans, his accent unmistakable.

'There is a force moving in behind us.'

'How many?' Wilson shouted back.

'Plenty, I can see their plumes.'

'Troop, about wheel!' Wilson ordered. 'At the gallop, forward!'

As the horses plunged back down the rough trail, the rain that had been threatening so long burst upon them in an icy silver cascade. It slashed at their faces, and stung their eyes, and drummed on their oilskins.

'This will cover our retreat,' Wilson grunted, and Clinton flogged the grey's neck with the loose end of the reins, for the old horse was falling back again.

Through the thick silver lances of falling rain, he caught a glimpse of waving war-plumes above the scrub; they were racing in to head off the patrol. At that moment the grey stumbled and Clinton was thrown onto his neck.

'Jee!' He heard the war chant go up, and he clung desperately to the grey's neck as it plunged to regain its balance.

'Come on, Padre!' somebody yelled, as the other troopers went pounding past him in the mud and the rain.

Then his horse was running again. Clinton had lost a stirrup, and he bumped painfully on the wet saddle, clinging to the pommel for a grip, but they were through. There were no shields or plumes in the bush around them, only the twisting streamers of rain and the gloom of gathering night.

'Are you telling me, Napier, that Major Wilson has deliberately chosen to spend the night on the far bank, despite my direct orders to return before nightfall?' Mungo St John asked. The only light was that of a storm lantern. The rain had washed out the fires.

The tarpaulin over the heads of the two officers flogged in the wind, spilling gouts of rainwater over them, and the lantern flame fluttered uncertainly in its glass chimney, lighting Captain Napier's face from below so that he looked like a skull.

'We got so close to Lobengula, General, within hail of the wagons. Major Wilson considered a retreat would not be justified. In any event, sir, the bush is swarming with the enemy. The patrol has a better chance of surviving the night by stopping in thick bush and waiting for daylight.'

'That is Wilson's estimate, is it?' Mungo demanded, putting on a grim expression. Yet inwardly, he congratulated himself on such an accurate assessment of the Scotsman's impetuous character.

'You must reinforce the patrol, sir. You must send at least one of the Maxims across – now, this very hour.'

'Listen carefully, Captain,' Mungo ordered him. 'What do you hear?'

Even over the rain and the wind there was an echo like the sound in a seashell held to the ear.

'The river, Captain,' Mungo told him. 'The river is spating!'

'I have just forded it. You can still get across, sir. If you give the order now! If you wait until dawn, it may well be in full flood.'

'Thank you for your advice, Napier. I will not risk the Maxims.'

'Sir, sir – you can take at least one Maxim off its carriage. We can carry it in a blanket and swim across.'

'Thank you, Captain. I will send Borrow across with twenty men to reinforce Wilson until morning – and this force will follow, with both Maxims, only when it is light enough to see the ford and make the crossing in safety.'

'General St John, you are signing the death warrant of those men.'

'Captain Napier, you are overwrought. I shall expect an apology from you when you have recovered yourself.'

Clinton sat with his back against the bole of a mopani tree. He had one hand thrust into the front of his sheepskin jacket, to hold his travelling Bible out of the rain. He wished above any other creature needs that he had light enough to read it.

All around him the rest of the tiny patrol lay stretched out on the muddy earth, bundled up in their rubber groundsheets and oilskins, though Clinton was certain that, like himself, none of them was asleep – nor would any of them sleep that night.

Clutching the Bible above his heart, he had the certain prescience of his own death, and he made the astonishing discovery that it had no terrors for him. Once, long ago, before he had discovered how close at hand was God's comfort, he had been afraid, and now the release from fear was a blessed gift.

Sitting in darkness, he thought of love, the love of his God and his woman and his daughters – and that was all that he would regret leaving behind him.

He thought of Robyn as he had first seen her, standing on the deck of the American slaver *Huron* with her dark hair aflutter on the wind and her green eyes flashing.

He remembered her upon the rumpled sweat-soaked childbed as she struggled to give birth, and he remembered the hot slippery and totally enchanting feeling of his first infant daughter's body as it slithered from Robyn's body into his waiting hands.

He remembered the first petulant birth wail, and how beautiful Robyn had been as she smiled at him, exhausted and racked and proud.

There were other small regrets – one that he would never dandle a grandchild, another that Robyn had never come to love him the same way he loved her. Suddenly Clinton sat up straighter against the mopani, and inclined his head to listen, peering out into the utter blackness from whence the sound had come.

No, it was not really a sound – the only true sound was the rain. It was more like a vibration in the air. Carefully, he returned the precious book to his inside pocket, then he made a trumpet of his bare hands and pressed them to the wet earth, listening intently with his ear to the funnel.

The vibration coming up from the ground was that of running feet, horny bare feet, thousands of feet, trotting to the rhythm of an impi on the march. It sounded like the very pulse of the earth.

Clinton crawled and groped his way across to where he had last seen Major Wilson lie down under his plaid. There was no glimmering of light under the midnight clouds, and when his fingers touched coarse woven cloth, Clinton asked softly:

'Is that you, Major?'

'What is it, Padre?'

'They are here, all around us, moving back to get between us and the river.'

They stood-to while the dawn tried vainly to penetrate the low roof of cloud above them. The saddled horses were merely humped shapes just a little darker than the night around them. They were drawn up in a circle, with the men standing on the inside, rifles resting on the saddles as they peered out into the thick bush that surrounded them, straining for the first glimpse as the grey light settled gently, like a sprinkling of pearl dust upon their dark, wet world.

In the centre of the circle of horses, Clinton knelt in the mud. With one hand he held the reins of the grey horse, and with the other he held the Bible to his chest. His calm voice carried clearly to every man in the dark waiting circle.

'Our Father which art in heaven,
Hallowed be thy name –'

The light grew stronger; they could make out the shape of the nearest bushes. One of the horses, perhaps infected by the tension of the waiting men, whickered and scissored its ears.

'Thy will be done
in earth, as it is in heaven –'

Now they all heard what had alarmed the horse. The faint drumming approached from the direction of the river, growing stronger with the dawn light.

' – for thine is the Kingdom,
the Power and the glory –'

There was the metallic clash of a rifle breech from the silent waiting circle of dismounted men, and half a dozen gruff voices echoed Clinton's quiet 'Amen!'

Then suddenly someone shouted. 'Horses! Those are horses out there!'

And a ragged little cheer went up as they recognized the shape of slouch hats bobbing against the sullen grey sky.

'Who is it?' Wilson challenged.

'Borrow, Sir, Captain Borrow!'

'By God, you're welcome.' Wilson laughed as the column of horsemen rode out of the forest into their defensive circle. 'Where is General St John; where are the Maxims?'

The two officers shook hands as Borrow dismounted, but he did not return Wilson's smile.

'The general is still on the south bank.'

Wilson stared at him incredulous, the smile sliding off his face.

'I have twenty men, rifles only, no Maxims,' Borrow went on.

'When will the column cross?'

'We had to swim our horses across. By now the river is ten feet deep.' Borrow lowered his voice so as not to alarm the men. 'They won't be coming.'

'Did you make contact with the enemy?' Wilson demanded.

'We heard them all around us. They called to each other as we passed, and we heard them keeping pace with us in the forest on either hand.'

'So they are massed between us and the river, and even if we cut our way through to the river, the ford is impassable. Is that it?'

'I am afraid so, sir.'

Wilson took his hat from his head and against his thigh he beat the raindrops from its brim. Then he settled it again carefully on his head at a jaunty angle.

'Then it seems there is only one direction that we can take, one direction in which the Matabele will not expect us to move.' He turned back to Borrow. 'Our orders were to seize the king, and now our very lives depend on it. We must have Lobengula as a hostage. We have to go forward – and that right smartly.' He raised his voice. 'Troop, mount! Walk march, Trot!'

They rode closed up, tense and silent. Clinton's old grey had benefited from the night's rest, and kept his place in the third file.

A young trooper rode at Clinton's right hand.

'What is your name, son?' he asked quietly.

'Dillon, sir – I mean, Reverend.' He was smooth-cheeked, and fresh-faced.

'How old are you, Dillon?'

'Eighteen, Reverend.'

They are all so young, Clinton thought. Even Major Allan Wilson himself is barely thirty years of age. If only, he thought, if only –

'Padre!'

Clinton looked up sharply, his attention had been wandering. They had long ago emerged from the thick bush, and were now coming up to the same spot from which they had retreated the previous evening.

The wagons were still standing abandoned beside the rude track; the tents made pale geometrical oblongs of solid canvas against the dark wet scrub.

Once again, Wilson halted the patrol, and Clinton walked the grey forward.

'Tell them we do not wish to fight,' Wilson ordered.

'There is nobody here.'

'Try anyway,' Wilson urged. 'If the wagons are deserted, then we will ride on until we catch up with the king.'

Clinton rode forward, shouting as he went:

'Lobengula, do not be afraid. It is me. Hlopi.'

There was no reply, only the flutter of the wind in the torn wagon canvas.

'Warriors of Matabele – children of Mashobane, we do not wish to fight – ' Clinton called again; and this time he was answered by a bellowing bull voice, haughty and angry and proud. It came out of the gloom and rain, seeming to emanate from the very air, for there was no man to be seen.

'Hau, white men! You do not wish to fight – but we do, for our eyes are red and our steel is thirsty.'

The last word was blown away on a great gust of sound, and the shrub about them misted over with blue gunsmoke and the air about their heads was torn by a gale of shot.

It was twenty-five years and more since Clinton had stood to receive volleyed gunfire; yet he could still clearly differentiate between the crack of high-powered rifles and the whistle of ball thrown from ancient muzzle loaders, and in the storm the 'whirr-whirr' of beaten pot-legs tumbling as they flew; so that, glancing up, Clinton expected to actually see one come over like a rising pheasant.

'Back! Fall back!' Wilson was shouting, and the horses were all rearing and plunging. The fire was, most of it, flying overhead. As always, the Matabele had raised their sights to the maximum; but there must have been a hundred or more of them hidden in the shrub and random bullets were scoring.

One of the troopers was hit in both eyes, the bridge of his nose shot away. He was reeling in the saddle, clutching his face with blood spurting out between his fingers. His number two spurred in to catch him before he fell, and with an arm around his shoulder led him at a gallop back along the trail.

Young Dillon's horse was hit in the neck, and he was thrown in the mud, but he came up with his rifle in his hands, and Clinton yelled at him as he galloped back.

'Cut off your saddle-bags. You'll need every round in them, lad.'

Clinton came in for the pick-up, but Wilson rode him off like a polo player.

'Your moke's half done, Padre. He'll not carry two. Get on with you!'

They tried to make a stand in the thicket where they had spent the night, but the hidden Matabele riflemen crept in so close that four of the horses went down, kicking and struggling, exposing the men who had been standing behind them, firing over their backs, and three of the men were hit. One of them, a young Afrikander from the Cape, had a pot-leg slug shatter the bone above his right elbow. The arm was hanging on a tattered ribbon of flesh, and Clinton used the sleeves of his shirt to make a sling for it.

'Well, Padre, we are for it now – and that's no mistake.' The trooper grinned at him, white face speckled with his own blood, like a thrush's egg.

'We can't stand here,' Wilson called. 'Two wounded to a horse and a man to lead them. They'll go in the centre with those who have lost their own horses. The rest of us will ride in a box around them.'

Clinton helped the young Afrikander up onto the grey's back, and one of the lads from Borrow's volunteers up behind him. The sharp slivers of his shin bone were sticking out of the meat of his leg.

They started back slowly, at the pace of the walkers, and from the thickets beside the track the muskets banged and smoked; but the Matabele were all of them well hidden. Clearly, they were taking no chances, even with this tiny band of thirty-odd men.

Clinton walked beside the grey, holding the good leg of the wounded man to prevent him slipping from the saddle. He carried the two rifles belonging to the wounded men slung over his shoulder.

'Padre!' Clinton looked up to find Wilson above him. 'We have three horses that are fresh enough to try a run for the river. I have ordered Burnham and Ingram to try and get back to the main camp and warn St John of our predicament. There is one horse for you. They will take you with them.'

'Thank you, Major,' Clinton answered without a moment's hesitation. 'I am a sailor and a priest, not a horseman; besides, I rather think I have work to do here. Let somebody else go.'

Wilson nodded. 'I expected you to say that.' He pushed his horse to a trot and went up to the head of the dismal little column. Minutes later, Clinton heard the quick beat of flying hooves and he looked up to see three horsemen wheel out of the straggling line and plunge into the brush that surrounded them.

There was a chorus of angry yells and the low humming 'Jee!' as the Matabele tried to head them, but Clinton saw their hats bobbing away above the low bush, and he called after them.

'God speed you, boys!'

Then, as he trudged on in the mud that was balling to the soles of his riding boots – he began silently to pray.

On the outside of the column, another horse fell, throwing its rider over its head, and then lunged up again to stand on three legs, shivering miserably in the rain, its off-fore hanging limply as a sock on a laundry line. The trooper limped back, drawing his revolver from its webbing holster, and shot the animal between the eyes.

'That's a wasted bullet,' Wilson called clearly. 'Don't waste any more.'

They went on slowly, and after a while Clinton became aware that they were no longer following the wagon tracks. Wilson seemed to be leading them gradually more towards the east, but it was hard to tell, for the sun was still hidden by low, grey cloud.

Then abruptly the column stopped again, and now for the first time the insistent banging of muskets from hidden skirmishers in the mopani scrub was silenced.

Wilson had led them into a lovely parklike forest, with short, green grass below the stately mopani trees. Some of these trees stood sixty feet high and their trunks were fluted and twisted as though moulded from potter's clay.

They could see deep into the forest, between the widely spaced trunks. There, directly ahead of the patrol, stretched across their front, waited the army of Lobengula. How many thousands, it was impossible to tell, for their rearguard was hidden in the forest; and even as the little band of white men stared at their host, the *Jikela* began, the 'surrounding' which had been the Zulu way ever since great Chaka's time.

The 'horns' were being spread, the youngest and swiftest warriors running out on the flanks, their naked skins burning like black fire through the forest. A net around a shoal of sardines, they were thrown out until the tips of the horns met to the rear of the band of white men – and again all movement ceased.

Facing the patrol was the 'chest of the bull', the hard and seasoned veterans; when the 'horns' tightened, it was the 'chest' that would close and crush, but now they waited, massed rank upon rank, silent and watchful. Their shields were of dappled black and white, their plumes were of the ostrich, jet black and frothing white, and their kilts of spotted civet tails. In their silence and stillness, it was not necessary for Wilson to raise his voice above conversational tones.

'Well, gentlemen. We will not be going any farther – not for a while anyway. Kindly dismount and form the circle.'

Quietly the horses were led into a ring, so that they stood with their noses touching the rump of the one ahead. Behind each horse, his rider crouched with the stock of his rifle resting on the saddle, aiming across at the surrounding wall of silent, waiting black and white dappled shields.

'Padre!' Wilson called softly, and Clinton left the wounded whom he was tending in the centre and crossed quickly to his side.

'I want you here to translate, if they want to parley.'

'There will be no more talking,' Clinton assured him, and as he said it the massed ranks of the 'chest' parted and a tall induna came through. Even at a distance of two hundred paces, he was an imposing figure in his plumes and tassels of valour.

'Gandang,' said Clinton quietly. 'The king's half-brother.'

For long seconds Gandang stared across at the circle of rain-streaked horses and the grim, white faces that peered over them, and then he lifted his broad assegai above his head. It was almost a gladiatorial salute, and he held it for a dozen beats of Clinton's heart. Then his voice carried clearly to where they waited.

'Let it begin!' he called, and his spear arm dropped.

Instantly, the horns came racing in, tightening like a strangler's grip on the throat.

'Steady!' Wilson called. 'Hold your fire! No bullets to waste, lads! Hold your fire, wait to make sure.'

The blades came out of the thongs that held them to the grip of the shields with a rasping growl, and the war chant rose, deep and resonant:

'Jee! Jee!' And now the silver blades drummed on the dappled rawhide, so that the horses stamped and threw their heads.

'Wait lads.' The front rank was fifty yards away, sweeping in out of the gentle silky grey rain mist.

'Pick your man! Pick your man!' Twenty yards, chanting and drumming to the rhythm of their pounding bare feet.

'Fire!' Gunfire rippled around the tight little circle, not a single blast but with the spacing that told that every shot had been aimed, and the front rank of attackers melted into the soggy earth.

The breech blocks clashed, and the gunfire was continuous, like strings of Chinese crackers, and an echo came back, the slapping sound of lead bullets striking naked black flesh.

At two places the warriors burst into the ring, and for desperate seconds there were knots of milling men, and the banging of revolvers held point blank to chest and belly. Then the black wave lost its impetus, hesitated and finally drew back, the surviving warriors slipping back into the forest, leaving their dead scattered in the wet grass.

'We did it, we sent them off!' someone yelled, and then they were all cheering.

'A little early to celebrate,' Clinton murmured drily.

'Let them shout,' Wilson was reloading his pistol. 'Let them keep their courage up.' He looked up from the weapon at Clinton. 'You'll not be joining us then?' he asked. 'You were a fighting man once.'

Clinton shook his head. 'I killed my last man over twenty-five years ago, but I will look to the wounded and do anything else you want of me.'

'Go around to each man. Collect all the spare ammunition. Fill the bandoliers and dole 'em out as they are needed.'

Clinton turned back to the centre of the circle, and there were three new men there – one was dead, shot in the head – another with a broken hip – and the third with the shaft of an assegai protruding from his chest.

'Take it out!' his voice rose as he tugged ineffectually at the handle. 'Take it out! I can't stand it.'

Clinton knelt in front of him and judged the angle of the blade. The point must lie near the heart. 'It's better to leave it,' he advised gently.

'No! No!' The man's voice rose, and the men in the outer circle looked back, their faces stricken by that hysterical shriek. 'Take it out!'

Perhaps it was best after all – better than lingering, shrieking death to unnerve the men around him.

'Hold his shoulders,' Clinton ordered quietly, and a trooper knelt behind the dying man. Clinton gripped the shaft. It was a beautiful weapon, bound in decorative patterns with hair from an elephant's tail and bright copper wire.

He pulled and the wide blade sucked with the sound of a boot in thick mud, and it came free. The trooper shrieked only once more, as his heart's blood followed the steel out in a bright torrent.

The waves of warriors came again four times before noon. Each time it seemed impossible that they could fail to overwhelm the waiting circle, but each time they swirled and broke upon it like a tide upon a rock, and then were sucked back into the forest.

After each assault the circle had to be drawn a little smaller, to take up the gaps left by fallen horses and dead and wounded men, and then the Matabele musketeers would creep in again, moving like quick and silent shadows from mopani to mopani, offering meagre targets, the bulge of a shoulder around the stem of a mopani trunk, little cotton pods of gunsmoke in the patches of green grass, the black bead of a head bobbing above the summit of one of the scattered termite nests as a warrior rose to fire.

Wilson walked quietly around the circle, talking calmly to each man in turn, stroking the muzzle of a restless horse, and then coming back into the centre.

'Are you coping, Padre?'

'We are doing fine, Major.'

The dead were laid out with what little dignity was left to them, and Clinton had covered their faces with saddle blankets. There were twelve of them now – and it was only a little past noon, another seven hours of daylight.

The lad who had lost his eyes in the first volley was talking to somebody from long ago in his delirium, but the words were jumbled and made little sense. Clinton had bound his head in a clean white bandage from the saddle-bag of the grey – but the bandage was now muddied, and the blood had seeped through.

Two others lay still, one breathing noisily through the hole in his throat from which the air bubbled and whistled, the other silent and pale, except for a little dry cough at intervals. He had been hit low in the back, and there was no use nor feeling in his lower body. The others, too gravely wounded to stand in the circle, were breaking open the waxed paper packages of cartridges and refilling the bandoliers.

Wilson squatted on his haunches beside Clinton. 'Ammunition?' he asked softly.

'Four hundred rounds,' Clinton replied as softly.

'Less than thirty rounds a man,' Wilson calculated swiftly. 'Not counting the wounded, of course.'

'Well, look at it this way, Major, at least it is no longer raining.'

'Do you know, Padre, I hadn't even noticed.' Wilson smiled faintly, and looked up at the sky. The cloud belly had risen and at that moment a pale ghostly silhouette of the sun appeared through it; but it was without warmth and so mild that they stared at it without paining their eyes.

'You are hit, Major,' Clinton exclaimed suddenly. He had not realized it until that moment. 'Let me look at it.'

'It's almost stopped bleeding. Let it be.' Wilson shook his head 'Keep your bandages for those others.'

He was interrupted by a shout from one of the troopers in the outer circle.

'There he is again!' And immediately firing rifles whipcracked, and the same voice swore angrily.

'The bastard, the bloody bastard –'

'What is it, soldier?'

'That big induna – he's moving about again out there; but he's got the devil's luck, sir. We just wasted a packet of bullets on him.'

As he spoke, Clinton's old grey horse threw up his head and fell on his knees, hit in the neck. He struggled to rise again, then rolled over on his side.

'Poor old fellow!' Clinton murmured, and immediately another horse reared up, thrashed frantically at the air with his fore hooves and then crashed over on his back.

'They're shooting better now,' Wilson said quietly.

'I would guess that is Gandang's work,' Clinton agreed. 'He's moving from sniper to sniper, setting their sights for them and coaching their fire.'

'Well, it's time to close the circle again.'

There were only ten horses still standing; the others lay where they had fallen, and their troopers lay belly down behind them, waiting patiently for a certain shot at one of the hundreds of elusive figures amongst the trees.

'Close up.' Wilson stood and gestured to the ring of troopers. 'Come in on the centre –'

He broke off abruptly, spun in a half circle and clutched his shoulder, but still he kept his feet.

'You're hit again!' Clinton jumped up to help him and immediately both his legs were struck out from under him, and he dropped back onto the muddy earth and stared at his smashed knee caps.

It must have been one of the ancient elephant guns, the four-to-the-pounders that some of the Matabele were using. It was a weapon that threw a ball of soft lead weighing a quarter of a pound. It had hit him in one knee and torn through into the other.

Both his legs were gone; one was twisted up under his buttocks, and he was sitting on his own muddy riding boot. The other leg was reversed, the toe-cap of his boot was dug into the mud and the silver spur stuck up towards the swirling cloud belly of the sky.

Gandang knelt behind the trunk of the mopani tree and snatched the Martini-Henry riflc out of the hands of a young brave.

'Even a baboon remembers a lesson he is taught,' Gandang fumed. 'How often have you been told not to do this.'

The long leaf sight on top of the blued barrel was at maximum extension, set for one thousand yards.

Under Gandang's quiet instructions, the young Matabele rested the rifle in a crotch of the mopani, and fired.

The rifle kicked back viciously, and he shouted joyously. In the little circle a big sway-backed grey horse dropped to its knees, fought briefly to rise and then flopped over on its side.

'Did you see me, my brothers?' howled the warrior. 'Did you see me kill the grey horse?'

Vamba's hands were shaking with excitement as he reloaded and rested the rifle again.

He fired, and this time a bay gelding reared up and then crashed over on its back.

'Jee!' sang Vamba, and brandished the smoking rifle over his head, and the war chant was taken up by a hundred other hidden riflemen, and the volley of their fire flared up.

'They are almost ready,' Gandang thought, as he glimpsed another of the defenders struck down in the renewed gale of gunfire. 'There can be few of them who still can shoot. Soon now it will be time to send the spears for the closing-in, and tonight I will have a victory to take to my brother the king. One little victory in all the terrible defeats – and so hard bought.'

He slipped away from the shelter of the mopani trunk, and loped swiftly across towards where another of his riflemen was firing away as fast as he could re-load. Half-way there Gandang felt the jarring impact in his upper arm, but he covered the open ground to shelter without a check in his stride, and then leaned against the bole of the mopani, and examined the wound. The bullet had gone in the side of his biceps and out the back of his arm. The blood was dripping from his elbow, like thick black treacle. Gandang scooped a handful of mud and slapped it over the wounds, plugging and masking them.

Then he said scornfully to the kneeling warrior at his side. 'You shoot like an old woman husking maize.' And he took the rifle out of his hands.

Clinton dragged himself backwards on his elbows, and his legs slithered loosely after him through the mud. He had used the webbing belt from one of the dead men as a tourniquet, and there was very little bleeding. The numbness of the shock still persisted, so the pain was just bearable, though the sound of the shattered ends of bone grating together as he moved brought up the nausea in a bitter-acid flood in the back of his throat.

He reached the blind boy, and paused for his breathing to settle before he spoke. 'The others are writing letters, afterwards somebody may find them. Is there anybody at home? I'll write for you.'

The boy was silent, did not seem to have heard. An hour earlier Clinton had given him one of the precious laudanum pills from the kit which Robyn had prepared for him before he left GuBulawayo.

'Did you hear, lad?'

'I heard, Padre. I was thinking. Yes, there is a girl.'

Clinton turned a fresh page of his notebook and licked the point of his pencil, and the boy thought again and mumbled shyly:

> 'Well then, Mary. You'll have read in the papers, we had quite a scrap here today. It's nearly over now, and I was thinking about that day on the river –'

Clinton wrote quickly, to keep up.

> 'I'll be saying cheerio, then Mary. Isn't one of us afraid. I reckon as how we just want to do it right – when the time comes –'

Quite suddenly, Clinton found his vision blurring as he wrote the final salutation, and he glanced up at the pale beardless face. The eyes were swathed in bloody bandages, but his lips were quivering and the boy gulped hard as he finished.

'What is her name, lad? I have to address it.'

'Mary Swayne. The Red Boar at Falmouth.'

She was a barmaid then, Clinton thought, as he buttoned the folded page into the boy's breast pocket. She would probably laugh at the note if she ever got it, and pass it around the regulars in the saloon bar.

'Padre, I was lying,' the boy whispered. 'I am afraid.'

'We all are.' Clinton squeezed his hand. 'I tell you what, lad. If you like, you can load for Dillon here. He's got eyes to shoot, but only one arm – you're got two good arms.'

'Bully on you, Padre,' Dillon grinned. 'Why didn't we think of that.'

Clinton draped a bandolier across the blind boy's legs. There were only fifteen cartridges in the loops – and at that moment, out in the mopani, the singing started.

It was slow and deep and very beautiful, echoing and ringing through the forest. The praise song of the Inyati. And Clinton turned his head and looked slowly around the circle.

All the horses were dead; they lay in a litter of saddlery and broken equipment, of crumpled yellow scraps of waxed paper from the ammunition packets, of empty brass cartridge cases and discarded rifles. In the confusion, only the row of dead men was orderly. How long was that row, Clinton thought, oh God, what a waste this is, what a cruel waste.

He raised his eyes, and the clouds were at last breaking up. There were valleys of sweet blue sky between the soaring ranges of cumulus. Already the sunset was licking the cloud mountains with soft, fleshy tones of pink and rose, while the depths of the billowing masses were the colour of burnt antimony and tarnished silver.

They had fought all day on this bloody patch of mud. In another hour it would be dark, but even now there were dark specks moving like dust motes against the high singing blue of the evening sky. The tiny specks turned in slow eddies, like a lazy whirlpool, for the vultures were still very high, waiting and watching with the infinite patience of Africa.

Clinton lowered his eyes, and across the circle Wilson was watching him.

He sat with his back against the belly of one of the dead horses. His right arm hung uselessly at his side, and the wadding over the wound in his stomach was crimson with seeping blood, but he held his revolver in his lap.

The two men held each other's gaze while the singing soared and fell and soared again.

'They'll be coming now – for the last time,' Wilson said.

Clinton nodded, and then he lifted his chin, and he, too, began to sing:

'Nearer my God to Thee,
Nearer to Thee – '

His voice was surprisingly clear and true, and Wilson was singing with him, holding the wadding to his stomach wound.

' – Darkness comes over me,
My rest a stone – '

The blind boy's voice cracked and quavered. Dillon was beside him; though his ankle and elbow were shot through, he lay upon his back with a rifle propped on his crossed knees, ready to fire one-handed when they came. His voice was flat and tuneless, but he winked cheekily at Clinton and grinned:

' – Angels to beckon me – '

Eight of them, all that were left, every one of them wounded more than once, but all of them singing in the wilderness of the mopani forests – their voices tinny and thin, almost lost in the great crashing chords of the praise song of the Inyati regiment.

Then there was thunder in the air, the drumming of two thousand assegais on black and white dappled shields, and the thunder came rolling down upon their little circle.

Allan Wilson dragged himself to his feet to face them. Because of his stomach wound, he could not stand erect, and the one arm dangled at his side. His service revolver made a strangely unwarlike popping sound in the roar of the war chant and the drumming blades.

Dillon was still singing, snatching the loaded rifles and firing, and singing, and grabbing the next rifle. The blind boy felt the last cartridge into a rifle breech, and passed the hot rifle back to Dillon, and then he groped for another round, his fingers becoming frantic as he realized the bandolier was empty.

'They're finished,' he cried. 'They are all finished!'

Dillon pushed himself erect on his one good leg, and hopped forward, holding the empty rifle by the muzzle, and he swung the butt at the wave of shields and plumes that reared over him, but the blow lacked power and was deflected harmlessly aside by one of the tall oval shields; and then quite miraculously a long, broad blade sprang from between his shoulder blades, driven through from breast bone to spine, and the silver steel was misted pink.

'I don't want to die,' screamed the blind boy. 'Please hold me, Padre.'

And Clinton put his arm around his shoulders and squeezed with all his strength.

'It's all right, lad,' he said. 'It's going to be all right.'

The bodies were stripped naked. Their skin, never touched by the sun, was snowy white and strangely delicate-looking, like the smooth petals of the arum lily. Upon this whiteness, the wounds were the shocking colour of crushed mulberries.

Around the killing ground was gathered a vast concourse of warriors, some of them already wearing items of the looted uniforms, all of them still panting with the exhilaration of that last wild charge and the stabbing with which it had ended.

From the dense ranks, an old grizzle-headed warrior stepped forward with his assegai held under-handed, like a butcher's knife. He stooped over the naked corpse of Clinton Codrington. It was the time to let the spirits of the white men free, to let them escape from their bodies and fly, lest they remain on earth to trouble the living. It was time for the ritual disembowelment. The old warrior placed the point of his blade on the skin of Clinton's stomach, just above the pathetic shrivelled cluster of his genitals, and gathered himself to make the deep upward stroke.

'Hold!' A clear voice stopped him, and the warrior stood back and saluted respectfully as Gandang came striding through the parting ranks of his warriors.

In the centre of that awful field, Gandang stopped, and looked down at the naked bodies of his enemies. His face was impassive, but his eyes were terrible, as though he mourned for all the earth.

'Let them lie,' he said quietly. 'These were men of men, for their fathers were men before them.'

Then he turned and strode back the way he had come, and his men formed up behind him and trotted away into the north.

Lobengula had come to the end of his domains. Below him the earth opened into the steep escarpment of the Zambezi valley, wild infernal place of broken rocky gorges and impenetrable thickets, of savage animals and a smouldering crushing heat.

At the limit of the eye the dark serpentine growth of riverine bush outlined the course of the father of all waters, and in the west a tall silver cloud of spray stood against the sky: it marked the place where the Zambezi river went crashing over a sheer ledge of rock in an awesome, creaming torrent, falling over three hundred feet into the narrow gorge below.

Lobengula sat upon the box of the leading wagon and looked upon all this savage grandeur with listless eyes. The wagon was drawn by two hundred of his warriors. The oxen were all dead, the ground had been too rugged and rocky for most of them and they had broken down and died in the traces.

Then the migration had run into the first belt of the tsetse fly, and the dreaded little insects had come to swarm on the dappled hides of the remaining bullocks and plague the men and women in Lobengula's sprawling caravan. Within weeks, the last of the fly-struck beasts was dead, and men, more resistant to the sting of the tsetse, had taken their places in the span and drawn their king onwards in his hopeless, aimless flight.

Now even they were daunted by what lay ahead, and they rested on the yokes and looked back at Lobengula.

'We will sleep here this night,' said the king, and immediately the weary, starving host that followed the wagons spread out to begin the chores of making camp, the young girls to carry water in the clay pots, the men to build the temporary lean-to shelters and cut the wood for the fires, and the women to eke out the contents of the almost empty grain bags and the few shreds of dried meat that remained. The fly had killed the last of the slaughter beasts with the draught bullocks, and game was scarce and shy.

Gandang went forward to the lead wagon and saluted his half-brother.

'Your bed will be ready soon, Nkosi Nkulu.'

But Lobengula was staring dreamily up at the steep rocky kopje that towered above their bivouac. The great bloated trunks of the cream-of-tartar trees had forced the black boulders apart. The little twisted branches, loaded with smooth furry pods, reached towards the uncaring sky like the maimed arms of a cripple.

'Is that a cave up there, my brother?' Lobengula asked softly. A dark cleft was riven into the rock face that girdled the crest of the hill. 'I wish to go up to that cave.'

Twenty men carried Lobengula on a litter of poles and furs, and he winced at each jolt, his great swollen body riddled with gout and arthritis, but his eyes were fastened on the crest high above him.

Just below the rock face Gandang made a sign to the bearers and they lay the litter gently upon the rocky slope while Gandang shifted his shield onto his shoulder and freed his broad blade from its thong as he went ahead.

The cave was narrow but deep and dark. The small ledge at its mouth was littered with the furry remains and chewed bones of small animals, the hydrax and baboon, gazelle and klipspringer. The cave itself gave out the fetid odour of the cage of a carnivorous animal, and when Gandang squatted at the entrance and peered into the sombre depths, there was the sudden vicious spitting snarl of a leopard, and dimly he saw the beast move in the shadows and caught the glint of its fierce golden eyes.

Gandang moved slowly out of the sunlight, and paused to let his eyes adjust to the gloom. The leopard warned him again with a terrifying crackle of anger in the confined spaces of the cavern. It had crept closer and was lying flat upon a narrow ledge above the level of Gandang's head. He could just make out the shape of its broad adder-like brow; the ears were laid back flat and the eyes slitted with rage.

Carefully, Gandang moved into position below the ledge, for he did not want to trigger the charge until he was ready to receive it. Balanced lightly in a half crouch, with the assegai's point lifted and lined up on the enraged animal's throat, Gandang flirted his shield and called to it.

'Come, evil one! Come, devil spawn.' And with another stunning burst of rage, the leopard launched itself, a blurr of gold, upon the tall dappled shield. But as it dropped, so Gandang lifted the point and took the leopard upon it, letting its own weight drive the steel through its heart; and then he rolled backwards under the shield and the cruel hooked talons raked the cured iron-hard hide unavailingly.

The blade was still buried in the leopard's chest. It coughed once, choking on its own blood, and then it wrenched itself free of the steel and bounded out through the mouth of the cavern. When Gandang followed it cautiously into the sunlight, the beautiful beast was stretched out on the rocky ledge in a spreading puddle of its own blood. It was a magnificent old male, the pelt unscarred. The sable rosettes upon its back were not much darker than the dark amber ground, that shaded down to a pure buttery cream on the underbelly. A noble animal, and only a king might wear its fur.

'The way is safe, oh King,' Gandang called down the slope, and the litter-bearers carried Lobengula up and set him gently upon the ledge.

The king dismissed the bearers, and he and his half-brother were alone on the hillside, high above this harsh and barbaric land. Lobengula looked at the dead leopard and then at the dark mouth of the cavern.

'This would be a fitting tomb for a king,' said Lobengula reflectively, and Gandang could not answer him. They were silent for a long while.

'I am a dead man,' said Lobengula at last, and raised a graceful hand to still Gandang's protest. 'I walk, I speak still, but my heart is dead within me.'

Gandang was silent, and he could not look upon the king's face.

'Gandang, my brother. I want only peace. Will you grant me that? When I order it, will you bring your spear to me and by piercing my dead heart let my spirit free to find that peace?'

'My King, my brother, never once have I disobeyed your order. Ever your word was the centre of my existence. Ask anything of me, my brother, anything but this. Never can I lift my hand towards you, son of Mzilikazi, my father, grandson of Mashobane, my grandfather.'

Lobengula sighed. 'Oh Gandang, I am so weary and sick with grief. If you will not give me surcease, then will you send for my senior witchdoctor?'

The witchdoctor came and listened gravely to the king's command; then he rose and went to the carcass of the leopard.

He clipped off the long, stiff, white whiskers and burned them to powder in a tiny clay pot over a small fire. To make the potion stronger still, he pounded a dozen seeds of the poison rope shrub to a paste and mixed it with the lethal ashes. Then from a stoppered buck-horn on his belt, he poured and stirred an acrid green liquid.

On his knees, with face to the ground, he wriggled towards the king like an obsequious cur-dog and placed the pot on the rocky ledge before him. As his withered claw-like fingers released the deadly vessel, Gandang rose silently behind him and drove his assegai between the witchdoctor's bony shoulder blades and out of his pigeon chest.

Then he picked up the wizened skeletal body and carried it into the recesses of the cavern. When he came back he knelt again before Lobengula.

'You are right,' Lobengula nodded. 'No man but you should know the manner of the king's going.'

He picked up the pot and held it between his cupped pink palms.

'Now you will be the father of my poor people. Stay in peace, my brother,' said Lobengula, and lifted the pot to his lips and drained it at a single draught.

Then he lay back on the litter and pulled a fur kaross over his head.

'Go sweetly, my beloved brother,' said Gandang. His noble features were set like weathered granite, but as he sat beside the king's bier the tears coursed down his cheeks and wet the great battle-scarred muscles of his chest.

They buried Lobengula in the cavern, sitting upright on the stone floor and wrapped in the wet green skin of the leopard. They dismantled his wagons and carried them up the hill and stacked the parts at the back of the cave.

They piled Lobengula's tusks of yellow ivory at each hand, and at his feet Gandang placed his toy spear of kingship and his beer pots and eating plates, his knives and mirrors and snuff-horn, his beads and ornaments, a bag of salt and another of grain for the journey – and finally the little sealed clay pots of uncut diamonds to pay his way into the spirit world of his forefathers.

Under Gandang's supervision, they sealed the mouth of the cavern with heavy slabs of black ironstone, then, dolefully singing the king's praises, they went back down the hill.

There were no cattle to slaughter for the funeral feast, nor grain for the beer pots. Gandang called the leaders of the mourning people to him.

'A mountain has fallen,' he said simply. 'And an age is past. I have left behind me my wife and my son and the land that I loved. Without those things a man is nothing. I am going back. No man need follow me. Each must choose his own path, but mine is south again to GuBulawayo and the magical hills of the Matopos – to meet and talk with this man Lodzi.'

In the morning, when Gandang started southwards again, he looked back and saw what was left of the Matabele nation straggling along behind him, no longer a great and warlike people, but a bewildered and broken rabble.

Robyn Codrington stood on the cool shaded verandah of Khami Mission. It had rained that morning, and the air was washed sparkling clean and the wet earth smelled like newly baked bread as the bright sunshine warmed it.

Robyn wore the black ribbons of mourning sewn on her sleeves.

'Why do you come here?' she demanded quietly, but unsmilingly, of the man who mounted the front steps of the verandah.

'I had no choice,' Mungo St John answered her. He stopped on the top step, and studied her for a moment without any trace of mockery on his face.

Her skin was scrubbed and fresh, devoid of either rouge or powder. It was smooth and fine-textured. There was no pouching below her clear green eyes, no blurring of her jawline, and her hair drawn back from her temples and forehead was innocent of silver lacing. Her body was small-breasted and narrow-hipped, tall and supple, but when she saw the direction of his gaze, the line of Robyn's lips hardened and set.

'I should be grateful, sir, if you would state your business and leave.'

'Robyn, I am sorry, but perhaps it is best that the uncertainty is over.'

In the four months since the return of the flying column from the Shangani, a dozen rumours had come out of the bush.

That fateful morning, Mungo St John's column, cut off by the flooded river, had heard heavy firing on the opposite bank. Then almost immediately they had themselves come under fierce attack by elements of the Matabele army. They had been forced to retire, a long weary fighting retreat in the rain that had taken weeks of starvation and privation, until at last the harrying impis had let them go, but not before the gun carriages had been abandoned and half the horses lost.

Nobody had known what had happened to Allan Wilson's patrol on the north bank of the Shangani, but then the word had reached GuBulawayo that the little band had cut their way through the impis, gained the Zambezi, and rafted down it to the Portuguese settlement of Tete, three hundred miles downstream. Later that was denied by the Portuguese and hopes plunged, to be revived again when a Matabele induna coming in to surrender suggested that the white men had been taken prisoner by the Inyati regiment – rumour, denial and counter-rumour for four harrowing months, and now Mungo St John was standing before Robyn.

'It's certain,' he said. 'I did not want a stranger to bring the news to you.'

'They are dead,' she said flatly.

'All of them. Dawson reached the battlefield and found them.'

'He would not have been able to recognize them or be certain of how many bodies. Not after all these months, not after the hyena and vultures –'

'Robyn, please.' Mungo held out a hand to her, but she recoiled from him.

'I won't believe it, Clinton could have escaped.'

'In the bush Dawson met the senior induna of the Matabele. He is coming in with all his people to surrender. He described to Dawson the patrol's last stand, and how in the end they all died.'

'Clinton could have – ' She was very pale, shaking her head firmly.

'Robyn, it was Gandang. He knew your husband well. "Hlopi"

he called him, the man with white hair. He saw him lying with the other dead. It is certain. There can be no more hope.'

'You can go now,' she said, and then quite suddenly she was weeping. Standing very erect and chewing her lower lip to try and stop herself, but her face had crumpled and the rims of her eyelids turned rosy-pink with grief.

'I cannot leave you like this,' he said and limped down the stoep towards her.

'Don't come near me,' she husked through her tears, and she retreated before him. 'Please don't touch me.'

He came on, lean and rangy as an old tom-leopard; but the cruel and swarthy planes of his face had softened with an expression she had never seen upon them before, and his one good eye held her swimming green ones with a deep and tender concern.

'Don't, oh please don't –' Now she held up both hands as if to ward him off, and she turned her face away. She had reached the end of the verandah; her back was pressed to the door of the bedroom which Cathy and Salina had once shared, and she began to pray, her voice muffled by her own tears.

'Oh Gentle Jesus, help me to be strong –' His hands fell upon her shoulders; they were hard as bone and cool through the thin cotton of her blouse. She shuddered, and gasped.

' – Have pity. I beg you. Let me be.'

He took her chin in the cup of his hand and forced her face up to his.

'Will you give me no peace, ever?' she mumbled brokenly, and then his mouth covered hers and she could not speak again. Slowly the rigidity went out of her body, and she swayed against him. She sobbed once, and began to slump into the embrace of his hard muscled arms. He caught her behind the knees, and around the shoulders, and lifted her like a sleeping child against his chest.

He kicked open the door to the bedroom, stepped through and pushed it closed with his heel.

There was a dustsheet on the bed, but no pillow or eiderdown. He laid her upon it, and knelt beside her, still holding her to his chest.

'He was a saint,' she choked. 'And you sent him to his death. You are the very devil.'

Then with the shaking, frantic fingers of a drowning woman,

she unfastened the mother-of-pearl buttons down the front of his linen shirt.

His chest was hard and smooth, the olive skin covered with crisp, dark curls. She pressed her open lips to it, breathing deeply the man-smell of him.

'Forgive me,' she sobbed. 'Oh God, forgive me.'

From his cubbyhole beside the pantries, Jordan Ballantyne could overlook the cavernous kitchens of Groote Schuur.

There were three chefs at work over the gleaming, anthracite-burning Aga ranges, and one of them hurried across to Jordan with the enamelled double-boiler and a silver spoon. With it Jordan tasted the Béarnaise sauce that would go with the galjoen. The galjoen was a fish of the stormy Cape waters; fancifully its shape could be likened to that of a Spanish galleon, and its delicate greenish flesh was one of the great African delicacies.

'Perfect,' Jordan nodded. *'Parfait, Monsieur Galliard, comme toujours.'* The little Frenchman scurried away beaming, and Jordan turned to the heavy teak door leading to the wine cellars below the kitchens.

Jordan had personally decanted the port that afternoon, ten bottles of the forty-year-old Vilanova de Gaia of the 1853 vintage; it had faded to the beautiful tawny colour of wild honey. Now a Malay waiter in long white Kanzu robes, with crimson sash and pillbox fez, came up the stone steps, reverently carrying the first Waterford glass decanter on a Georgian silver tray.

Jordan poured a thimbleful into the chased silver *tastevin* which he wore on the chain about his neck. He sipped, rolled it on his tongue and then drew breath sharply through pursed lips to let the wine declare itself.

'I was right,' he murmured. 'What a fortunate purchase.'

Jordan opened the heavy leatherbound wine register, and noted with pleasure that they still had twelve dozen bottles of the Vilanova, after he had deducted today's decanting. In the 'remarks' column he wrote. 'Extraordinary. Keep for best,' and then turned back to the Malay steward.

'So then, Ramallah, we will offer a choice of Sherry Finos Palma or Madeira with the soup, with the fish the Chablis or the 1889 Krug –' Quickly Jordan ran down the menu, and then dismissed him. 'The company will be coming through presently, kindly see that everyone takes their places now.'

The twelve waiters stood with their backs to the oak panelling of the dining-hall, their white-gloved hands clasped in front of them, expressionless as guardsmen, and Jordan gave each one a quick appraisal as he passed, looking for a stain on the brilliant white robes or a sloppily knotted sash.

At the head of the long table, he paused. The service was the silver gilt queen's pattern presented to Mr Rhodes by the directors of the Chartered Company, the glass was long, finely stemmed Venetian, lipped with twenty-two carat gold to complement the gilt. There were twenty-two settings this evening, and Jordan had agonized over the seating arrangements. Finally he had decided to place Dr Jameson at the bottom of the table and put Sir Henry Loch, the High Commissioner, on Mr Rhodes' right. He nodded his satisfaction at that arrangement, and took one of the Alphonso Havanas from the silver humidor and sniffed it before crackling it against his ear – that too was perfect; he replaced it and took one last lingering look around the hall.

The flowers had been arranged by Jordan's own hands, great banks of protea blooms from the slopes of Table Mountain. In the centrepiece, yellow English roses from the gardens of Groote Schuur, and of course Mr Rhodes' favourite flowers, the lovely blue plumbago blossom.

From beyond the double doors came the clatter of many feet on the marble floor of the hall and the high, almost querulous, voice which Jordan knew and loved so well carried to him.

'And we shall just have to square the old man.' Jordan smiled fondly at the words, the old man was certainly Kruger, the President of the Boer Republic, and 'square' was still one of the central words in Mr Rhodes' vocabulary. Just before the doors swung open to admit the company of brilliant and famous men clad in sombre dinner jackets, Jordan slipped out of the hall, back to his little cubbyhole – but he raised the hatch beside his desk an inch, so that he could hear the conversation at the long, glittering table in the hall beyond.

It gave him a glorious feeling of power, to be sitting so close to the centre of all this and to listen to the pulse of history beating, to know that it was within him subtly to alter and direct, and to do so in secrecy. A word here, a hint there, even something so trivial as the placing of two powerful men side by side at the long dinner table. On occasions, in privacy, Mr Rhodes would actually ask, 'What do you think, Jordan?' and would listen attentively to his reply.

The tumultuous excitement of this life had become a drug to Jordan, and barely a day passed that he did not drink the heady draught to the fill. There were special moments that he treasured and whose memory he stored. When the meal ended, and the company settled down to the port and cigars, Jordan could sit alone and gloat over these special memories of his.

He remembered that it had been he who had written out that legendary cheque in his own fair hand for Mr Rhodes to sign the day that they had bought out the Kimberley Central Company. The amount had been £5,338,650, the largest cheque ever drawn anywhere in the world.

He remembered sitting in the visitor's gallery of Parliament as Mr Rhodes rose to make his acceptance speech as Prime Minister of Cape Colony, how Mr Rhodes had looked up and caught his eye and smiled before he began speaking.

He remembered after that wild ride down from Matabeleland when he had handed the Rudd Concession with Lobengula's seal upon it to Mr Rhodes, how he had clasped Jordan's shoulder and with those pale blue eyes conveyed in an instant more than a thousand carefully chosen words ever could.

He remembered riding beside Mr Rhodes' carriage down the Mall to Buckingham Palace and dinner with the queen, while the Union Castle mailship delayed its sacred sailing by twenty-four hours to wait for them.

This very morning had added another memory to Jordan's store, for he had read aloud the cable from Queen Victoria to 'Our well-beloved Cecil John Rhodes', appointing him one of Her Majesty's Privy Councillors.

Jordan started back to the present.

It was after midnight, and in the dining-hall Mr Rhodes was abruptly breaking up the dinner in his characteristic fashion.

'Well, gentlemen, I'll bid you all a good night's rest.'

Quickly Jordan rose from his desk and slipped down the servants' passageway.

At the end he opened the door a crack and anxiously watched the burly, appealingly awkward figure mount the stairs. The company had done justice to Jordan's choice of wine, but still Mr Rhodes' tread was steady enough. Though he stumbled once at the top of the sweeping marble staircase, he caught his balance, and Jordan shook his head with relief.

When the last servant left, Jordan locked the wine cellar and the pantry. There was a silver tray left upon his desk, and on it a glass of the Vilanova and two water biscuits spread thickly with salted Beluga caviar. Jordan carried the tray through the silent mansion. A single candle burned in the lofty entrance hall. It stood upon the massive carved teak table in the centre of the floor.

Jordan paced slowly across the chequer board of black and white marble paving, like a priest approaching the altar, and reverently he laid the silver tray upon the table. Then he looked up at the carved image high in its shadowy niche, and his lips moved as he silently began the invocation to the bird goddess, Panes.

When he had finished, he stood silent and expectant in the fluttering light of the candle, and the great house slept around him. The falcon-headed goddess stared with cruel blind eyes into the north, a thousand miles and more towards an ancient land, now blessed, or cursed, with a new name, Rhodesia.

Jordan waited quietly, staring up at the bird like a worshipper before a statue of the Virgin, and then suddenly in the silence, from the bottom of the gardens, where grew the tall dark oak trees that Governor van der Stel had planted almost two hundred years before, came the sad and eerie cry of an eagle owl. Jordan relaxed and backed away from the offering that he left upon the table. Then he turned and went bounding up the marble staircase.

In his own small room he quickly stripped off his clothing that was impregnated with the odours of the kitchen. Naked, he sponged down his body with cold water, admiring his own lithe form in the full-length mirror on the far wall. He scrubbed himself dry with a rough towel, and then rinsed his hands in eau-de-Cologne.

With a pair of silver-backed brushes he burnished his hair until his curls shone like whorls of pure gold wire in the lamplight; then he slipped his arms into the brocaded gown of midnight blue satin, belted it around his waist, picked up the lamp to light his way and stepped out into the passage.

He closed the door to his bedroom quietly and listened for a few seconds. The house was still silent, their guests slept. On silent, bare feet, Jordan glided down the thick carpet to the double doors at the end of the passage to tap lightly on one of the panels, twice then twice again, and a voice called to him softly,

'Enter!'

'These are a pastoral people. You cannot take their herds away from them.' Robyn Ballantyne spoke with a low controlled intensity, but her face was pale and her eyes sparkled with furious green lights.

'Please, won't you be seated, Robyn.'

Mungo St John indicated the chair of rough raw lumber, one of the few furnishings in this adobe mud hut that was the office of the Administrator of Matabeleland. 'You will be more comfortable, and I will feel more at ease.'

Nothing could make him appear more at ease, she thought wryly. He lolled back in his swivel chair, and his booted ankles were crossed on the desk in front of him. He was in shirtsleeves, without a tie or cravat, and his waistcoat was unbuttoned.

'Thank you, General. I shall continue to stand until I receive your answer.'

'The costs of the relief of Matabeleland and the conduct of the war were born entirely by the Chartered Company. Even you must see that there must be reparation.'

'You have taken everything. My brother, Zouga Ballantyne, has rounded up over a hundred and twenty-five thousand head of Matabele cattle –'

'The war cost us a hundred thousand pounds.'

'All right.' Robyn nodded. 'If you will not listen to the voice of humanity, then perhaps hard cash will convince you. The Matabele people are scattered and bewildered; their tribal organizations have broken down; the smallpox is rife amongst them –'

'A conquered nation always suffers privation, Robyn. Oh, do sit down, you are giving me a crick in the neck.'

'Unless you return part of their herds to them, at least enough for milk and slaughter, you are going to be faced with a famine that will cost you more than your neat little war ever did.'

The smile slipped from Mungo St John's face, and he inclined his head slightly and studied the ash of his cigar.

'Think about this, General. When the Imperial Government realizes the extent of the famine, it will force your famous Chartered Company to feed the Matabele. What is the cost of transporting grain from the Cape? A hundred pounds a load. Or is it more now? If the famine approaches the proportions of genocide, then I will see to it that Her Majesty's Government is faced with such a public outcry, led by humanitarians like Labouchère and Blunt, that they may be obliged to revoke the charter and make Matabeleland a crown colony after all.'

Mungo St John took his bottle off the desk and sat upright in his chair.

'Who appointed you champion of these savages, anyway?' he asked. But she ignored his question.

'I suggest, General, that you relay these thoughts to Mr Rhodes before the famine takes a hold.'

She gloried in the visible effort it took him to regain his equanimity.

'You may well be right, Robyn.' His smile was light and mocking again. 'I will point this out to the directors of the Company.'

'Immediately,' she insisted.

'Immediately,' he capitulated, and spread his hands in a parody of helplessness. 'Now is there anything else you want of me?'

'Yes,' she said. 'I want you to marry me.'

He stood up slowly and stared at her.

'You may not believe this, my dear, but nothing would give me greater pleasure. Yet, I am confused. I asked you that day at Khami Mission. Why now have you changed your mind?'

'I need a father for the bastard you have got on me. It was conceived four months after Clinton's death.'

'A son,' he said. 'It will be a son.' He came around the desk towards her.

'You must know that I hate you,' she said.

His single eye crinkled as he smiled at her.

'Yes, and that is probably the reason that I love you.'

'Never say that again,' she hissed at him.

'Oh, but I must. You see I did not even realize it myself. I always believed that I was proof from such a mundane emotion as love. I was deceiving myself. You and I must now bravely face up to that fact. I love you.'

'I want nothing from you but your name, and you shall have nothing from me but hatred and contempt.'

'Marry me first, my love, and later we will decide who gets what from whom.'

'Do not touch me,' she said, and Mungo St John kissed her full on the mouth.

It had taken almost ten full days of leisurely riding to make a circuit of the boundaries of the ranch lands that Zouga had claimed with his land grants.

It stretched eastwards from the Khami river, almost as far as the Bembesi crossing and southwards to the outskirts of GuBulawayo, an area the size of the county of Surrey, rich grasslands with stretches of parklike forests and low golden hills. Through it meandered a dozen lesser rivers and streams, which watered the herds that Zouga was already grazing.

Mr Rhodes had appointed Zouga the custodian of enemy property – with powers to take possession of the royal herds of Lobengula. The hundred troopers who volunteered for the duty rounded up almost 130,000 head of prime cattle.

Half of these belonged to the Chartered Company, but that left 65,000 to be distributed as loot to the men who had ridden in to GuBulawayo with Jameson and St John. However, at the very last minute, Mr Rhodes had changed his mind, and telegraphed St John with instructions to redistribute 40,000 head to the Matabele tribe.

The volunteers were incensed at having lost more than a third of their rightful loot, and word was soon spreading through the improvised bars and canteens of GuBulawayo that the cattle had been given back to the tribe after threats and representations by the woman doctor of Khami Mission. Credence was given to the rumour by the fact that the same telegraph message authorized the grant of six thousand acres of land to Khami Mission. Mr Rhodes was squaring the God-botherers, and the volunteers were not going to stand for it.

Fifty troopers, all full of whisky, rode out to burn down the mission and string up the hag responsible for their loss. Zouga Ballantyne and Mungo St John met them at the foot of the hills. With a few salty sallies, they had them laughing; then they took it in turn to curse them fluently and roundly, and finally they drove them back to town, where they stood them a dozen rounds of drinks.

Despite the redistribution to the tribe, still the flood of cattle upon the market brought the price down to two pounds a head, and Zouga used half the proceeds of the Ballantyne diamond to buy up ten thousand of them to stock his new estates.

Now as Zouga and Louise rode together, with Jan Cheroot following them in the Scotch cart with the tent and camping equipment, they passed small herds of the cattle tended by Matabele herders that Zouga had hired.

Zouga had been able to select only the best animals, and he had graded them by colour, so that one herd might consist of all red beasts while the next of only black ones.

Ralph had contracted to bring up all the materials for the new homestead from the railhead at Kimberley – and with the same convoy would be twenty thoroughbred bulls of Hereford stock that Zouga intended running with his cows.

'This is the place,' Louise exclaimed with delight.

'How can you be so certain – so soon?' Zouga laughed.

'Oh, darling, it's perfect. I can spend the rest of my life looking at that view.'

Below them the land fell away steeply to deep green pools of the river.

'At least there will be good water – and that bottom land will grow excellent vegetables – '

'Don't be so unromantic,' she chided him. 'Look at the trees.'

They soared above their heads like the arched and vaulted spans of a great cathedral, and the autumn foliage was a thousand shades of reds and golds, murmurous with bees and merry with bird song.

'They will give good shade in the hot season,' Zouga agreed.

'Shame on you,' she laughed. 'If you cannot see their beauty, then look at the Thabas Indunas.'

The Hills of the Indunas were whalebacked and dreaming blue beneath the tall silver clouds. The grassy plains between were scattered with small groups of Zouga's cattle, and of wild game – zebra and blue wildebeest.

'They are close enough,' Zouga nodded. 'When Ralph's construction company finally reaches GuBulawayo with the railway line, then we shall be a few hours' ride from the railhead and all the amenities of civilization.'

'So you will build me a home here – on this very spot?'

'Not until you give it a name.'

'What would you like to call it, my darling husband?'

'I'd like to have a touch of the old country – King's Lynn was where I spent my childhood.'

'That's it then.'

'King's Lynn.' Zouga tested the name. 'Yes, that will do very nicely. Now you shall have the home you want.'

Louise took his hand, and they walked down under the trees towards the river.

A man and a woman came down the narrow winding pathway through the thick riverine bush.

The man carried his shield on his left shoulder, with the broad-bladed assegai secured to it by the rawhide thongs; but his right arm was shortened and deformed, twisted out from his shoulder as though the bone had been broken and badly set.

There was no superfluous flesh upon his powerfully boned frame; the rack of his ribs showed through, and his skin lacked the lustre of health. It was the dull lifeless colour of lamp-black – as though he had just risen from a long sickbed. On his trunk and back gleamed the satiny rosettes of freshly healed gunshot wounds, like newly-minted coins of pure blue cobalt.

The woman who followed him was young and straight. Her eyes were slanted and her features those of an Egyptian princess. Her breasts were fat and full with milk, and her infant son was strapped tightly to her back so that his head would not jerk or wobble to her long, swinging gait.

Bazo reached the bank of the river and turned to his wife.

'We will rest here, Tanase.'

She loosened the knot and swung the child onto her hip. She took one of her swollen nipples between thumb and forefinger until milk spurted from it, and then she touched it to the boy's lips. Immediately he began to feed with little pig-like snuffles and grunts.

'When will we reach the next village?' she asked.

'When the sun is there.' Bazo pointed halfway down the sky. 'Are you not weary of the road, we have travelled so far, so long.'

'I will never weary, not until we have delivered the word to every man and woman and child in Matabeleland,' she replied, and she began to joggle the baby and croon to it:

'Tungata is your name, for you will be a seeker.

'Zebiwe is your name, for what you will seek is that which has been stolen from you and your people.

'Drink my words Tungata Zebiwe, even as you drink my milk. Remember them all your days, Tungata, and teach them to your own children. Remember the wounds on your father's breast, and the wounds in your mother's heart – and teach your children to hate.'

She changed the infant to her other hip, and her other breast, and she went on crooning until he had drunk his fill and his little head drooped sleepily. Then she slung him upon her back once more, and they crossed the river and went on.

They reached the village an hour before the setting of the sun. There were less than a hundred people living in the scattered huts. They saw the young couple from afar and a dozen of the men came out to greet them with respect and lead them in.

The women brought them grilled maize cakes and thick soured milk in calabash gourds, and the children came to stare at the strangers and to whisper to one another. 'These are the wanderers – these are the people from the Hills of the Matopos.'

When they had eaten, and the sun had set, the villagers built up the fire. Tanase stood in the firelight, and they squatted in a circle about her, silent and intent.

'I am called Tanase,' she said. 'And once I was the Umlimo.'

There was a low gasp of shock at her mention of that name.

'I was the Umlimo,' Tanase repeated. 'But then the powers of the spirits were taken from me.'

They sighed softly and stirred like dead leaves when a random breeze passes.

'There is another who is now the Umlimo and lives in the secret place in the hills, for the Umlimo never dies.'

There was a little hum of assent.

'Now I am the voice of the Umlimo only. I am the messenger who brings you the word of the Umlimo. Listen well, my children, for the Umlimo prophesies thus.' She paused and now the silence was charged with religious terror.

'When the noon sun goes dark with wings, and the trees are

bare of leaves in the springtime – then warriors of Matabele put an edge to your steel.'

Tanase paused and the firelight gleamed on the hundreds of eyes that watched her.

'When the cattle lie with their heads twisted to touch their flank and cannot rise – then will be the time to rise up and to strike with the steel.'

She spread her arms like a crucifix and cried out:

'That is the prophecy. Harken to it, children of Mashobane; Harken to the voice of the Umlimo. For the Matabele will be great once again.'

In the dawn the two wanderers, carrying the infant who was named the 'Seeker after what has been stolen', went on towards the next village, where the elders came out to greet them.

In the southern springtime of 1896 on the shores of a lake near the southern extremity of the Rift Valley, that mighty geological fault which splits the African Continental Shield like an axe stroke, a bizarre hatching occurred.

The huge egg masses of *schistocerca gregaria*, the desert locust, that were buried in the loose earth along the border of the lake, released countless multitudes of flightless nymphs. The eggs had been laid by females in the solitary phase of the locust's life cycle; but so vast was the hatching of their progeny that the earth could not contain them, and though they spread out over an area of almost fifty square miles, they were forced to crawl upon one another's backs.

The constant agitation and stimulation of contact with other nymphs wrought a miraculous change in this teeming tide of insects. Their colour turned to a vivid orange and midnight black, unlike their parents' drab brown. Their metabolic rate surged and they became hyperactive and nervous. Their legs grew longer and stronger, their gregarious instincts more powerful, so that they flowed in a compact body that seemed to be a single monstrous organism. They had entered the gregarious phase of the life cycle, and when at last they moulted for the last time and their newly-fledged wings had dried, the entire swarm took spontaneously to the air.

In that first baptism of flight, they were spurred by their high body temperature, which was raised further by their muscular activity. They could not stop until the cool of evening, and then they settled in such dense swarms that the branches of the forest snapped under their weight. They fed voraciously all night, and in the morning the rising heat spurred them into flight once more.

They rose in a cloud so dense that the sound of their wings was the drumming roar of hurricane winds. The trees they left behind were stripped completely of their tender springtime foliage. As they passed overhead, their wings eclipsed the noonday sun, and a deep shadow fell over the land.

They were headed south towards the Zambezi river.

From the Great Sud where the infant Nile river weaves its way through fathomless swamps of floating papyrus, southwards over the wide savannahs of eastern and central Africa, down to the Zambezi and beyond, roamed vast herds of buffalo.

They had never been hunted by the primitive tribes, who preferred easier game; only a few Europeans with sophisticated weapons had ventured into these remote lands, and even the lions which followed the herds could not check their natural multiplication.

The grasslands were black with the huge bovine black beasts. Twenty or thirty thousand strong, the herds were so dense that the animals in the rear literally starved, for the pasture was destroyed before they could reach it. Weakened by their own vast multitudes, they were ripe for the pestilence that came out of the north.

It was the same plague that Moses' God had inflicted on the Pharaoh of Egypt, the rinderpest, the *peste bovine,* a virus disease which attacks cattle and all other ruminants. The stricken animals were blinded by the discharge of thick mucus from their eyes. It poured in ropes from their gaping jaws and nostrils to contaminate the pastures and infect any other animal that passed over them.

Their emaciated bodies were wracked by spasms of profuse

diarrhoea and dysentery. When at last they dropped, the convulsions twisted their heads back upon their tortured necks, so that their noses touched one of their flanks – and they could never rise again.

So swift was the passage of the disease that a herd of ten thousand great horned black beasts was wiped out between dawn and sunset. Their carcasses lay so thickly that they touched each other, and the characteristic fetid odour of the disease mingled with the stench of rotting flesh; for although the vultures gorged, they could not devour one thousandth part of this dreadful harvest of death.

Swiftly, carried by the vultures and the blundering, bellowing herds, the plague swept southwards towards the Zambezi river.

On the banks of that mighty river Tanase stood beside another watch-fire and repeated the prophecy of the Umlimo:

'When the noon sun goes dark with wings,
and the trees are bare of leaves in the
springtime –
'When the cattle lie with their heads
twisted to touch their flank, and cannot
rise –'

Thus she cried, and the people of the Matabele listened and took new heart and looked to their steel.